PRAISE FOR TIME'S BETRAYAL

"With this monumental work David Cleveland has achieved nothing less than the disinterment of the various skeletons of the American psyche from the Civil War to Vietnam and beyond, and the painting of a multi-generational portrait of a pedigreed American family whose own skeletons not only refuse to stay buried, but actively haunt its progeny. There will be those who, captivated by the author's brilliant insights into the inner workings of the CIA, KGB and M16, and by a canvas that stretches from New England to Prague and Greece to Southeast Asia, will describe *Time's Betrayal* as an international spy novel, which it is, if only in the sense that *Moby-Dick* is a yarn about a big fish and *Huckleberry Finn* a tale of a boy on a raft. But this is not Ludlum, folks, nor is it LeCarré. It is in a league of its own and a class by itself. *Time's Betrayal* is a large-hearted American epic that deserves the widest possible, most discriminating of readerships."

—BRUCE OLDS, Pulitzer Prize–nominated author
for *Raising Holy Hell* and *The Moments Lost*

"*Time's Betrayal* is a vast, rich, endlessly absorbing novel engaging with the great and enduring theme of literary art, the quest for an identity. Moreover, it seamlessly expands that quest beyond the individual to the family, to the nation. *Time's Betrayal* achieves a rare state for massively ambitious novels: it is both complex and compelling. David Adams Cleveland has instantly taken a prominent place on my personal list of must-read authors."

—ROBERT OLEN BUTLER, Pulitzer Prize–winning
author of *A Good Scent from a Strange Mountain*

ALSO BY DAVID ADAMS CLEVELAND

NOVELS

Love's Attraction

With a Gemlike Flame

ART HISTORY

A History of American Tonalism: 1880–1920
Crucible of American Modernism

Intimate Landscapes: Charles Warren Eaton
and the Tonalism Movement

Ross Braught: A Visual Diary

Ralph L. Wickiser: The Reflected Stream
The Abstract Years 1985–1998

Paul Balmer: Cityscapes

TIME'S BETRAYAL

DAVID ADAMS CLEVELAND

For Patricia, Carter, and Christopher,
and for Charles Sheerin

To every man upon this earth,
Death cometh soon or late,
And how can man die better
Than facing fearful odds,
For the ashes of his fathers,
And the temples of his gods?
—Thomas Babington Macaulay

PROLOGUE

FINALLY SPRING HAS COME. IT WAS A LONG WINTER climbing the narrow steps—all fifty-three—to my father's boyhood room each morning, sitting at his desk while staring out the window at the pines over the lake, sifting, sifting . . . endlessly sifting the clues to his disappearance. Lonely, too, without a word from Laura these many months. But now I have almost everything: the family archive assembled by my grandmother, my father's schoolboy letters to her, and his love letters to Suzanne Williams (hers too, sizzling my delicate fingertips), his books and articles from the thirties, his Pankrác Prison diary, the CIA investigation of his defection, and, thanks to Brandt & Harrison's exorbitant bribes and the fall of the Berlin Wall last October, John Alden's Stasi files. Not to mention the foxed manila envelope he left on his desk some thirty-five years ago containing clippings from the 1877 *Natchez Weekly Democrat* and thirty-odd Pinkerton reports. The newspaper clippings I saved from crumbled oblivion by Xerox. I have tracked down most who knew him, and loved him: the man who walked through Checkpoint Charlie in 1953, never to return. No doubt more questions than answers: how my father got entangled in the greatest spy scandal of the twentieth century . . . only to pull off the scholarly coup of his generation, a story to equal Schliemann's.

This morning there is a milky gray light over the lake. Still a hint of winter chill, where the towering white pines reign like gods of first creation. My father's room, tucked in under the eaves, is cramped, and the one window of leaded glass contains eighteen lozenge-shaped panes, so transforming the view of the lake into vertical prisms of swimming light. Not unlike the puzzle of a missing life glimpsed through time. Such a vantage point is a good place to watch for a change in the weather; a place to write and remember and breathe the smells of stored time in cracked bindings and mildewed pages . . . and wonder. From such a height, the landscape of our lives gives the pleasing illusion of intelligibility, the kind of neat continuity we archaeologists love to plot with a well-plumbed trench, strata upon strata layering out our story. As my father and Karel Hollar picked over the bones of Homer for clues to the mysterious sources of his tales. For when I look at the dissolving mist above the lake, one veil lifting to reveal another, I feel the presence of the white pine most insistently—time's sentinels, keeping their watch along the shore as they did when my father was a boy . . . and his father and grandfather. Their cradling upper branches reaching skyward, dusted with first light, look much the same as when he sat here the morning of his leaving.

I often wonder if he felt safe here, as I feel safe . . . as did his heroes from their wall-girt palaces in Mycenae, Sparta, Pylos, and Ithaca— muted one by one as the Dark Ages descended.

I know he spent much of his last night typing—an inconstant Morse code in my youthful dreams—before stealing away at two in the morning to rendezvous with his lover. When I was first allowed to venture up those narrow stairs as a ten-year-old—or had I just turned eleven?—his room was exactly as he'd left it, except for the dusting of yellow pollen imprinted with tiny paw prints. The housekeeper had been instructed to leave it be. Next to the green Underwood on his desk was a cigar box and underneath it the envelope containing the 1877 cuttings from the *Natchez Weekly Democrat* and Pinkerton reports on the fate of Pearce Breckenridge. In the cigar box on a yellowed bed of cotton was the rolled-up skin of a seven-foot eastern diamondback: a freak of nature in the Berkshires. I was so awed by that snakeskin that I neglected the manila envelope, which I stuck away in the bookshelf and promptly forgot, finding myself drawn instead to the pile of well-thumbed volumes on Bronze Age Greece and Crete stacked three feet high on the floor by his desk. Except for the dust and mouse droppings, it was as if abandoned minutes before. I was convinced as a child that my father wasn't really dead, that he might return home at any moment, or that when we were back on Park Avenue after summer vacation, something of him might reinhabit Elsinore to make sure his stuff was exactly where he'd left it. And so I dutifully preserved that mildewed, note-encrusted votive stele of early scholarship on Linear B by Arthur

Evans, Bartlett and Bennett, somewhat perplexed that at least seven pages of illustrations on the script had been hastily ripped from two volumes. For a worshipful bibliophile, an abomination!

Sometimes, deep in a warm August night, I would wake to the sound of tapping, listening intently in my bed as I stared out at the pine-silhouetted sky. I often found myself tiptoeing up the long flight of stairs, convinced it was not a flying squirrel under the eaves, and so might find him seated at his typewriter, fingers poised, gazing over the moonlit lake. For he, too, was a man haunted by the specter of lost stories. Over summer vacations, I taught myself to type on the Underwood—even its name transfixed me. The patter of the keys soothed me. I have always typed to remember. There were moments when I felt that if I could only concentrate hard enough, his voice, *his* story would appear on the page before my fingers. The feeling never left me that on his last day at Elysium he must have been weighing it all in his mind, the lake and the white pines and the possibility of a gamble with the destiny he'd been pursuing since childhood.

His best friend and CIA colleague, Elliot Goddard, author of the investigation on his possible defection, often speculated about his romantic temperament, as if he were a character like King Lear, disposed to shake loose all the cares and business of life in some quixotic quest for redemption. Maybe so. As did Max, our nemesis, who transformed him into a tarnished symbol of imperialist overreach in his first novel, *Like a Forgotten Angel,* to the tune of a million copies sold worldwide . . . and still selling.

As a historian and archaeologist, with serious skin in the game, I'm going to try to avoid playing literary games and stick with the carefully exhumed artifacts of a scholarly life, and a life in secrets, and so let them lead where they may.

Home . . . as they always do.

It was late September—the twenty-seventh, to be precise—1953, and he left about nine in the morning. I know this because my grandmother must have told me about it, though I don't remember her exact words. Actually, a lot I simply overheard. My mother complained bitterly to my grandmother some years later :"I was alone—*alone,* on our last night together." I know that he'd arranged and squared away all the things in his boyhood room, the collections of flora and fauna, the labeled arrowheads, clearing his desk except for the typewriter, cigar box, and the contents of that manila envelope, evidence of an obscure crime involving his grandfather, the Civil War general: a bombshell of assiduous sleuthing by his mother that she'd dumped in his lap only days before. His bookshelves retained the disquieting gaps of the stacked volumes on the floor. He'd fixed himself an early breakfast and then taken the path down to the boathouse and stood alone on the dock, taking in the lake. He was a tall, athletic man with wavy brown hair, large expressive eyes—everyone I've talked to has commented on his intelligent eyes—and quick smile. He walked with a slight limp from the wound he'd received in Greece in late 1943 as an OSS officer working with the Resistance in Pylos. Women still found him attractive—"wildly attractive" was the phrase I've heard from more than a few matronly lips, though never from my mother. His CIA sidekick, Elliot Goddard, liked to tell me he was the most unself-consciously attractive man he'd ever known—"turning the heads of every disgruntled wife in our Georgetown parlors"—and Elliot, being a ladies' man himself, had more than a little experience in such matters. Or as Elliot put it with just a hint of exasperated chagrin: That's what women were drawn to, his sexual innocence, "that naïve obliviousness to his own attraction." Among his colleagues in the Princeton Archaeology Department, I'd detected a grudging reverence for his pioneering work in the thirties, an esteem tinged with unease about a man with money, fueling his ambition and precocious fame . . . "always cutting corners on finds," the retiring head of the American School of Classical Studies in Athens told me, and, unable to resist a rueful shrug, added, "but the only one of us of dirt archaeologists in the OSS who actually set foot in mainland Greece before late 1944. Somehow sweet-talked the Brits, don't you know, who figured it was *their* bailiwick."

That spring of 1953—with the Cold War at fever pitch—a great blue heron had taken up residence on our Berkshire lake and was still feeding in the marsh grass along the far shore in September. As my father smoked a last cigarette, it suddenly took flight and glided over the stump-patterned face of Eden Lake, its reflection trailing behind like a drogue chute the instant before deployment. I have an image of my father intently watching that graceful creature take wing, seeing it circle and finally soar over the pine-serried horizon, even though I have no idea if he ever saw it. All I know is that my mother in her dressing gown saw the heron from where she stood (a glass of scotch probably cradled in her fingers) by the Tiffany window in the living room, knowing that my father had been suddenly called back to Washington.

"When I saw our heron leave, I knew he was gone for good—the Agency bullshit be damned." Perhaps her disgruntled comment to my grandmother had more to do with contemplating his infidelities, real and imagined, than with the call from Allen Dulles.

Standing on the boathouse dock, he might barely have noticed the heron as he stared at the Williamses' place across the lake, McKim, Mead & White's glorious Hermitage, where, I suspect, his frantic lover and nemesis, Suzanne, fretted and schemed.

Whatever the case, my father was passing silently through a checkpoint on the path to one of the greatest fiascos of the Cold War.

As I tell my students, avoid speculation until the facts wring you dry. I know he lighted up at least four Lucky Strikes. At some point, my mother picked up the flattened butts from the boathouse dock and put them in an envelope, which I found in her top dresser drawer many years after her death. I have to believe he was trying to get it all fixed in his head before he left: all the years from his earliest childhood memories of coming up to Elysium; the fieldstone cottage his paternal grandfather, General Alden, hero of Antietam, had built in 1880; and, of course, the Winsted School, an Episcopal bastion of good breeding and stoic character, which the general had founded with the Reverend Samuel Williams in the same year. And there was his own missing father, a thoracic surgeon killed in the First World War. That much we have in common: missing fathers—the Telemachus thing, as Max disparagingly liked to put it: those empty gaps of clean earth that maddeningly refuse our entreaties.

I like to think he was inventorying all the conflicting memories, the better to pack his gear, figuring just which parts of his story he might need to draw on where he was headed.

Picturing him standing on the boathouse dock smoking Lucky Strikes, I find myself haunted by yet another tale compressed genie-like in the manila envelope, the circumstantial evidence of a forgotten crime of revenge that—and I cannot believe otherwise—confirmed my father in his own plan of similar ilk.

And so the river of Time bends us all to its current.

At some point, my father had seen what he wanted to see, took a last drag on his Lucky, and turned his back on his family and the place that might have kept him safe and rooted in the world of his people. My mother told me he hugged me for almost a minute and kissed me good-bye. I was at the kitchen table, having her specialty, blueberry pancakes with Vermont maple syrup and crushed walnuts in whipped cream. She even smiled when she told me this: I left purple slobber on his cheek. I ache to remember. I do remember his smoky breath, the scent of Vitalis in his hair, the crispness of a New England fall in his voice, merged forever with the minuet of nocturnal typing. I remember that after a long hike carried on his shoulders, he would swim me out to the float at the swimming hole in the first blush of evening, kicking on his back, lifting me to the glimmering stars—deceitful authors of our destiny. But that final hug . . . no.

Whenever my mother made me her specialty, I would first stab the blueberries with my fork to make them bleed, as I still tend to do.

And so I have patiently sifted the physical evidence. Many of the answers now lie at my fingertips, organized in scores of neatly color-coded file folders. And I have my own run of catastrophes to offer perspective. But I can't escape the feeling that this place of refuge, the high fieldstone walls of our cottage by the lake and the sentinel pines, holds his secrets fast, as it does his memory. So, too, the high ivy walls and even higher aspirations of the Winsted School. Such places, like the strong points of old, replete with failed dreams and foundering reputations, form the bedrock upon which I plan to build my case.

For these voices, so long becalmed, have again led me back to our woods, where changeless yet ever-changing nature holds a mirror to my eyes, where I hope to catch a following breeze—a glint of sunlight, a shivering leaf, a telltale streak of ripples—of what made him. And what killed him.

Such answers that have come my way are alloyed with time and require the patience of the gods and a gull-eyed beachcomber. But where to insert the first shovel blade, when memory had not, as yet, taken its full toll? A baseline of clean earth, as we dirt archaeologists like to call it, before the famished hopes of mankind gave rise to such infinitely sad yet inspiring tales. As they did for Homer . . .

Before the river within was in full flow.

PART ONE
WINSTED

Mother had always told me I'm his son, it's true, but I am not so certain. Who, on his own, has ever really known who gave him life?

Where shall a man find sweetness to surpass his own home and his parents? In far lands he shall not, though he find a house of gold.

—Odyssey

As is the generation of leaves, so is that of humanity.
The wind scatters the leaves on the ground, but the live timber burgeons with leaves again in the season of spring returning.
So one generation of men will grow while another dies.

—Iliad

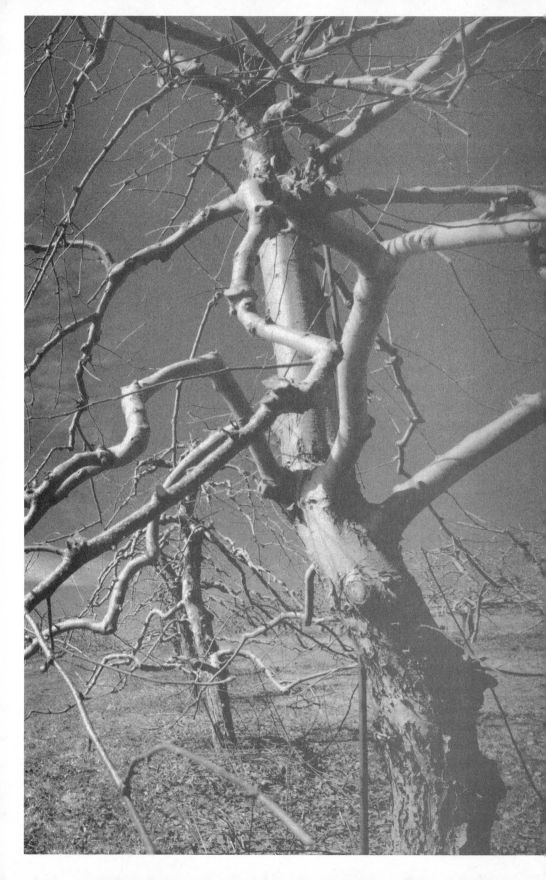

1 PAUL OAKES WAVED ME TO A NARROW STRAIGHT-backed chair—"the nutcracker" we called it—in his spare but bookish study at Winsted, where at fourteen I was in my first year. The sultry October afternoon infiltrated in stealthy low-angled oblongs of sunlight through the six-over-six white-sashed windows. We chatted for few minutes, until he abruptly paused in mid-thought, lumbered up from his desk, and went to a window and squinted toward the football fields. Freshly minted hash marks shimmered on the tarnished green of late-summer grass like ghostly tethers. Something had caught his eye—football practice? Still too early in the afternoon. Perhaps it was the lovely bands of cigar-shaped clouds—lenticular, if I recall correctly, a moody mauve-cream against the clear blue. Then, pushing at his upper lip with the eraser end of his pencil, as if annoyed at the distraction, he swiveled, winked at me, and returned to his desk.

"As I was saying, a man like your father leaves many rumors behind him. . . ." He seemed to catch himself for a moment, as if he'd let slip an indiscretion. "But of course, it's only natural you revere his memory. A son—law of nature and all that—must revere his father."

It was such a weird expression that I couldn't think of what to say.

"I guess so, sir."

I glanced over his shoulder to his trophy wall, where a photo of my father's 1932 championship football team hung with many others. But pride of place belonged to two framed godlike figures hung at eye level: a signed sketch by John Singer Sargent for the oil painting of General Alden hanging in the library, and an inscribed sepia-toned studio portrait of General Patton in full martial regalia, with a long dedication beginning with "To my spiritual adviser, Paul Oakes . . ." As I looked at the faces of these two generals separated in time by a little more than eighty years, an uneasy feeling percolated in my mind: It had to be my grandmother, dead less than a year, Winsted's grand dame and a woman who never left anything to chance, who was—somehow—behind this bizarre interrogation.

As if my interlocutor, too, recognized the awkwardness of the situation, a twinkle flashed in his blue eyes, jarringly magnified as he slipped on his bifocals and glanced down at a sheet on his desk. "Old Ironsides," as many alumni affectionately referred to Mr. Oakes, was a legendary figure by my day. He packed a lineman's shoulders and a bulky neck that threatened to burst asunder his clerical collar at the slightest hint of agitation. With a guttural growl to get my full attention, he began again with his odd questions, probing me, as if convinced of the thing to be ferreted out, yet unsure how to best throttle the nasty little bugger. He droned on about my father, what a great football player he'd been, such a brilliant classicist, a light to his generation. All to the good: Mr. Oakes had presided at my parents' wedding in Washington.

I just wanted to hide.

He sighed and segued into reflections on the hateful years of the early thirties: "Bolsheviks in high places, Klan a plague, Jew-haters . . . uncertain times for a young man coming of age." Again, he suddenly changed tack at my perplexed expression.

"Any of the older boys mention your father to you?"

"Sir?"

He tapped his pencil thoughtfully and turned his head, the inflamed capillaries in his cheeks flashing like diodes.

"So none of the older boys have been . . . well, overly familiar, offered anything surprising in the way of friendship?"

"Friendship—sir?"

I think my scowl at what I'd misconstrued as a question about homosexual overtures from older boys threw him, and he shoved the tiller another ninety degrees.

"Alden, do you consider yourself a good Christian gentleman?" He fixed me with blue bullet eyes.

"Yes, sir; I guess so."

"Guess so, guess so—mean you're not sure?"

"I . . . I never thought about it much one way or another."

In fact, neither my mother nor my grandmother had taken me to an Episcopal service in my life, the only exception being the annual Founder's Day services in the Winsted chapel, which my grandmother—head of the board of trustees for over thirty years—had required me to attend. A matter of family duty.

Paul Oakes grimaced and slid a nicotine-stained finger inside his frayed clerical collar.

Prominently displayed on the desk at his elbow was a well-thumbed 1885 copy of the Reverend Samuel Williams's *Essays and Prayers on Christian Manhood*. Samuel was my great-grandfather's first cousin and cofounder of the Winsted School, a personage my grandmother rarely referred to, and when she did, only in terms of his ne'er-do-well grandson, Bobby Williams, who always elicited a mild snort of derision. Paul Oakes grunted again and returned his gaze to the sheet in front of him; I distracted myself with an assemblage on a nearby wall of wooden organ pipes scavenged from a medieval monastery. Captain Oakes had bought the worm-eaten things in Paris in the closing months of World War II—a carton of Camels for a thousand years of history, he always bragged. He'd been division chaplain in Patton's Third Army. The organ pipes were flanked by examples of illuminated manuscripts going back to the twelfth century and some rather maudlin Rouault lithographs of hangdog martyrs he'd picked up from the print sellers on the Left Bank. Prominent on his bookshelf was his pride and joy, the complete works of Saints Augustine and Jerome, all in leather-bound editions, many in the original Latin. A framed bit of incunabulum in the Winsted colors of crimson and black leaned against the back of the shelf.

Non enim oportet fallaces commemorare fabulae neque philosophorum iminicam Deo sapientiam sequi, ne in judicium aeternae mortis, Domino discernente cadamus.

I began working out a rough translation of this passage from Gregory of Tours: *We should neither commemorate the false fables nor follow a philosophy hostile to God, lest we fall into eternal damnation by his judgment.*

"Alden." I started in my seat. "You are no doubt aware of the recent problems we have been having concerning the sudden increase of scribbling on the toilet stalls in Osborn House basement. I have certainly warned against this kind of despicable behavior. So far, the culprit or culprits have gone undetected. But now I fear the problem has gone beyond one of simple defacement of school property. It has now become a more grievous matter, affecting the moral well-being of the entire school community. There is a cancer growing in our bowels, Mr.

Alden, and if it is not discovered soon and excised from the living flesh of the school, the malignancy will spread and infect the spirit, corrupt the soul. I fear it is the thirties all over again."

His face had become livid and trembling, his voice like a broken steam pipe.

"Mr. Alden, I have had one of my prefects perform the odious task of transcribing some of the tasteless commentary that has recently appeared in the toilet stalls. The list is of remarkable loathsomeness. I would like you to look at this list; no doubt you will be familiar with some of its contents. And then, if you will, I would like you to read it—out loud." He handed me the list he'd been contemplating from the start of our meeting. "This is but the song of fools, but crushed it must be."

I looked at the list of aphorisms. Some were indeed familiar and most showed the sure hand of the master—the true Maxim.

"Read it to me, my boy, in as strong and steady a voice as you can muster. I want to see if the voice matches the thoughts expressed."

Mr. Oakes grabbed for his Camels and quickly lighted up. I blushed deeply and began. I stumbled badly on the German in the first line.

(I quote this list in full for historical accuracy; it represents, I believe, the first recorded writings of Max Roberts and exemplifies the aphoristic style that has made his novels so popular.)

"*Die Lust der Zerstörung ist eine schaffende Lust.*"
"Do pederastic priests lust only in their hearts?"
"Without suffering there can be no God."
"Job knew God was neither merciful nor just."
"Jesus is all prudence and concern for personal salvation."
"It is easier to believe than question."
"They dare to make the divine incarnate, to flatter with dogma, ritual, and sacrament—yet, they know not her face."
"They are procrustean even in their illusions."
"Beware the admonitions of priests, for they know their own temptations only too well."
"Inter urinas et faeces nascimur—and that includes snotty Winstedians, too."
"Christ is the son of Woman."
"If God had wanted us in Vietnam, he would have given us slanty eyes and chopsticks for fingers."

I kept my eyes fixed downward, repressing a grin.

"Well," he intoned loudly through a cloud of smoke, "does any of this calumny ring a bell with you, Mr. Alden?"

"N-n-no; I mean, I've seen that stuff down there, but I didn't write any of it."

"Know who did?"

"No, sir."

"No idea at all?"

"No, sir."

"You're a bright boy, Alden. Tell me, what does this little wager with the dark powers suggest to you—a common theme perhaps? What is the intention of our little crappy-assed scribbler?"

"I'm not sure I know, sir; some of the references seem pretty obscure."

"'Obscure'?" His left hand pawed at the space between us, and I handed back the list. "Why, right at the top here, the words of the hateful Bakunin: 'The passion for destruction is a creative passion.' Could you believe such a thing, Alden?"

"I don't think so, sir."

"Yes . . . yes . . ." He nodded his head, and his blue eyes seemed to expand beyond the frames of his glasses. "There is a worm in our midst, Alden; a demonic and loathsome entity that must be cut loose before it does more damage." For emphasis, a perfect smoke ring fluttered from his lips. "He that diggeth a pit shall fall into it." He raised his forefinger and shook it at me, reaching to impale the faltering smoke ring, a parlor trick he indulged by habit. "'And the seed of the wicked shall be cut off.'" With this, he sprang from his chair and went again to the window. His face, flushed a moment before, seemed suddenly very pale in the sunlight, almost diaphanous, as if something of him were fading away before my eyes. When he began again, he avoided looking at me, but stared out the window and spoke in a softer voice, as if drawn to some ecstatic vision.

"I can feel it in my bones: the 1930s redux. In your father's time here, such radical sloganeering was rampant, though of a more venomous Bolshevist sort." He made a dismissive wave with his hands. "A community, Alden, even the Winsted community, is a precarious organism, a living, breathing thing balanced in the equilibrium of faith and the total commitment of its members. When even a single member of that community fails to share his burden with the others, shirks his commitment or demeans the faith that binds us together, then the whole shebang is placed in peril . . . for the slippage may pull others under, too. We are all part of a greater community . . . for a man must choose the city of God, or the city of Man. We are all ordained to one or the other; it is the choice we all must make."

He placed a palm against the windowpane, as if longing to press through an invisible barrier. "A man's faith is forever tested by the darkness." And then, possibly touched by a change of heart, he turned a more kindly face on where I sat.

"When we are young, Peter, we think the world is the way it is, for better or worse, because it *is*. But it is fragile." He waved a ringless hand through a dust-fevered beam to direct my gaze toward the pair of warriors on his wall. "So very fragile—the light and dark mixed. That is why we are forced to choose." He fixed me with pained eyes. "When I was with Georgie Patton in the late summer of '44, I was tending boys only a few years older than you, who'd faced down German 88's; some survived . . . some not. I held their hands when they died; I listened to their last words and wrote their parents and wives. Life is full of hard choices. In the end, it comes down to a love of the spirit or love of the flesh that sets itself up as rival to God."

I was mesmerized by this sudden intimacy of recollection, how such a wrenching experience might be framed in theological terms, esoteric yet oddly touching. Then, as if embarrassed by his candor, he seemed to catch himself and turned his face again to the window and the spaces of undulating green, white goal posts presiding.

"There have been many esteemed graduates of this school—your father and grandfather, of course, and General Alden, who turned down the governorship twice—dare I say, all haunted by the darkness. Many of our boys have gone on to positions of great power and responsibility; and yes, even now, two of my boys are advisers to the president. Their wills are not their own, but are subject to God and the faith nurtured in their school days. Upon their choices depend the safety and well-being of this country, if not the world. They fight God's crusade in Vi-et-na-a-m"—he winced at his improbable imitation of LBJ—"now that the Communists are entrenched in Cuba, in our goddamn backyard, no less. Let their example be a guide to you, Alden." He snapped his well-worn Zippo bearing the bayonet knife chevron of the Third Army (*We will not falter; we will not fail*), letting the large sinuous flame rear high as he slowly bent forward, a filterless Camel crammed between his lips. And then, through the pall of smoke, his resonant voice like the holy of holies: "It is only natural for each generation to want to remove the ancient landmarks, which our fathers have set, until, that is, you discover the terrible responsibilities bequeathed to you. We . . . well, we were cold and unshaven and unwashed; our own mothers wouldn't have recognized us: But when we entered those camps—oh, Lord, the hideous smells. Your father was with us then. When we saw what was left of those human beings, looked into their sunken jaundiced eyes . . ." He bowed his head. "They saw us as angels who had flung open the doors of hell."

He raised a finger, turning once again on a dime.

"Listen, just be careful whom you fraternize with, son. A man's friends make all the difference."

I sat spellbound: Had he just said my father was with him at the liberation of Buchenwald? Full details would have to wait until years later.

Mr. Oakes's bull terrier came scurrying in, wagging its tail. "Ah, Stokes, so you want a walk, is that it, boy? Want to go watch the boys practice—do you?" He got up and came over to me and put his massive hand on my shoulder. "Okay, Alden, that will be all for now. Can I depend on you to let me know if you find out anything more on this grievous matter?"

"Yes, sir."

"Good boy. I'll be seeing you in confirmation class this spring, won't I?" His grip on my shoulder went right to the bone.

"Yes, sir."

He went to his desk and got his copy of the Reverend Williams's *Essays and Prayers on Christian Manhood* and handed it to me.

"I'm sure your dear grandmother had you peruse the pages, but you might want to nose around in the relevant sections on Communion and tithing before confirmation class." He tapped the embossed crimson-and-gold cover. "A little old-fashioned, I know, but surprising things if you keep your eyes peeled."

My grandmother would never have dreamt of such a thing.

"Yes, sir."

"She was a great lady, Peter. I miss her counsel every day. She did so much for the school; we wouldn't have all the Negro boys we have if it hadn't been for her, and the foreign exchange students. And on that score, would you make an effort to befriend the blacks in your class, especially those from the South? Tough for them to fit in, unlike their more streetwise kind from Boston or New York."

"Yes, sir."

"Oh, Alden, by the way, I know you're a bit new to football, but when you take the snap, don't anticipate—it shows in your eyes. Wait till the ole pigskin smacks your palm. Less fumbles that way, and the defense is more likely to be drawn offside."

"Yes, sir. Thank you, sir."

"And Alden, one more thing. Nothing wrong with being a classics man like John, but keep to the style; do not put too much store in the substance. In this life, there is really only *One* author who matters."

"Yes, sir."

He smiled. "You're—amazing, you know, the spitting image of your father."

I was halfway out the door when I heard my name called a final time. I turned back. He was kneeling by the window, petting Stokes, cigarette at a dangle, his eyes abstracted with the oddest expression.

"You should've seen it, son. When your father—when John threw a long pass . . . it was like time stood still."

"You're amazing," I muttered to myself, hugely relieved as I headed out. It was quite a shock to realize that my mother's lovelorn ambivalence about her hero husband and my grandmother's steely-eyed adulation of her brilliant son were writ large in the world beyond my immediate family. As if my father's memory had suddenly taken on a life of its own.

And to think that Max's jejune scribblings were the instrument of my awakening.

Even worse: that my physical makeup contained some transformative essence, that when brought in contact with those who had known my father, it had the effect of insinuating his ghost into our colloquy. The dark pool of family expectations in which we sink or swim is one thing, but Paul Oakes had so neatly grafted me into my father's public persona—along with the founders of Winsted—that walking on water seemed the only prospect open to me.

As I stood in the October heat outside Osborn House, this dilemma weighing on my mind, I realized I had lied outright, not once, but twice. Due in no small part to Paul Oakes's summoning of my father's shade, which had triggered some latent code of honor, some vague loyalty—but to what and to whom?

I stared across the green sward of the Circle and wondered if maybe my mother's dread-filled reservations about Winsted had been right after all.

"There *are* other schools, Peter. You can stay right here in New York—Collegiate will keep you—a lot of boys do, you know. You go up there, and the winters are long and cold, and they'll all suck up to you and pretend you're something special. Do you really want that? Now that your grandmother's gone, well, we can go to the lawyers and tell them what you'd *really* rather do."

On the day we were supposed to drive to Winsted, she went on strike and refused to order the car from the garage. She was more spacey and hostile than usual that September morning. The night before, she'd stayed late at the Colony Club playing bridge and had blown out her usual quota of vodka tonics. I told her I would take the train up to Winsted from Grand Central and get a taxi from the Route 128 station stop. At which point, she cursed the lawyers, as was her wont, and agreed to drive and play the part of the dutiful parent. It was such a final defeat for her, the last triumph of my grandmother, who had died eight months before. Grandmother, in her role as matriarch, had treated my matriculation at Winsted as a settled duty of family honor.

And with crushing finality, a feeble finger raised, she pronounced from her hospital bed the last time she saw my mother, "It *is* the family school and what John would have wanted. *You*, of all people, owe him that much."

Leaving nothing to chance, my attendance had been stipulated in all the financial agreements at my grandmother's death.

Mother was weepy and morose all the way north on Interstate 95, haranguing me in hopes of changing my mind while flicking away tears of frustration.

As soon as we passed the ivy-encrusted gates, three hours late, I was eager for her to be off. She was snippy and impatient and clearly in need of a drink. She eyed the other mothers in their casual summer wear and decided she was overdressed. Then she embarrassed the hell out of me as she let out a war whoop of a sailor's curse at a recalcitrant bag in the trunk or a spilled carton of books. Not for nothing was she the daughter of an admiral. The other boys' fathers, many of them esteemed alumni, took delight in showing their sons around, relishing the act of continuity as they passed on to their heirs the recollections and admonitions attached to their boyhood memories of Winsted. I was terrified of what the other guys would think—raised by two women! That was the last thing I needed while confronting my peers in those first days and weeks. Then, after I got my stuff stowed away in my cubicle, Mother suddenly made a mad dash for the car without so much as a word about the parents' tea for new boys, much less a kiss good-bye—and off she went. Free at last, I thought with a touch of adolescent irony as I eyed some of the new black kids looking not a little uncomfortable in their khaki slacks and Brooks Brothers button-downs provided as part of their scholarship package.

My mother certainly made a spirited show of avoiding getting sucked into the machinery of institutional memory surrounding our family, not that she hadn't enjoyed the entrée and social connections the family name—thanks to Grandmother—allowed her in New York society once we left Washington after my father's body was returned by the Soviets. She hadn't even bothered to visit the chapel, where there was a carved inscription in the nave to her husband's memory; or the memorial room, where his name and that of his surgeon father (blown to smithereens by a direct hit on his field surgery in the Argonne in early 1918) were recorded on plaques of remembrance; or the new Alden gym commemorating his exploits in Greece—the last of many gifts from my grandmother; much less his class photos in the corridors of Osborn House. There was, too, the splendid library built and endowed by my great-grandfather, the Civil War general, railroad builder, and New York real estate baron. The stalwart portrait of General Alden by John Singer Sargent in his blue-and-gold Union uniform presiding in the reading room provided much comfort in my early years.

My family may have gone back to the *Mayflower*, and our early Puritan divines were by any measure a pretty ruthless and intolerant lot—two returning to England to aid Cromwell's execution of Charles I, but even their Revolutionary War heirs (on my grandmother's side), who fought at Concord and Bunker Hill, paled, at least in my young mind, in comparison to the Civil War exploits of General Alden. The minutemen fought for their freedom from a loose British tyranny in faraway London, but General Alden and his men of the Fifteenth Regiment Massachusetts Volunteers—abolitionists all—fought to remake their country in light of a universal ideal of democratic freedom and fundamental rights, for justice, equality, and human dignity. They had been willing to endure fratricidal war on home ground, and a hideous slaughter on a scale Homer could never have imagined. All for a cause, so I would one day learn, upon which Winsted had been founded, or, more the shame, the disillusionment with that cause by the 1880s.

In the coming years, I, like a Buddhist monk spinning his prayer wheel, would make my silent obeisances with near-unconscious regularity before these family shrines to our better angels. For my mother, the sacrifice of one husband had been enough. She and my grandmother barely spoke, due to—according to grandmother's cryptic accusation—"her criminal and selfish act of disrespect."

On the way home after dropping me off, she was pulled over for a broken taillight and then arrested for drunken driving when she threw up over the officer's ticket book as she tried to slip a hundred-dollar bill into the pages.

Actually, my mother had quickly learned a lot of my grandmother's tricks about how to wield money and charm to worthy ends. Maybe not quite Penelope to my grandmother's Hera, and certainly not in the same intrigue league as Suzanne Williams—my father's Calypso—but no slouch in feminine wiles. That previous spring vacation, she'd shipped me down to Princeton for three weeks to work with a wunderkind classics professor she'd heard was shaking things up in the department. He would go on to write hugely successful novels and movies; his first film, set at Harvard no less, made him a rich celebrity. Mother knew my grandmother wanted me to go to Harvard, so she set about derailing that eventuality by getting me involved with all the brilliant classicists at Princeton: "Why don't you go to the Hun School or Lawrenceville?" she suggested. "You'll be cheek by jowl with your new Princeton buddies." Her plan half worked.

And I correct myself: Paul Oakes was not my first institutional encounter with my father's controversial reputation. My classics tutor had taken me to lunch at the faculty club with members of the Princeton Archaeology Department: I was treated like a spectacular new find just unearthed. Seated at the table overlooking Prospect Garden were legendary men in the field, who spent long summers on digs in Greece, one the head of the American School of Classical Studies in Athens, and at least two others had been in the OSS with my father: "Stuck in Cairo and Izmir, Ayvalik, Candarli, and Kuşadasi, worst luck, with the Brits and Turks breathing down our necks . . . while our Lawrence of the Hellenes sweet-talked SOE to drop him by submarine in Pylos . . . of all godforsaken corners of nowhere."They were all kindly and helpful to a fourteen-year-old, scrutinizing my features like near-sided numismatists, and I may have even impressed them with my knowledge of their work, but behind the sun-weathered smiles and nostalgia and self-disparaging quips about blown OSS operations, the insider asides between sips of Chardonnay, I had detected an uneasy equivocation about their erstwhile colleague. Of course, he had outpublished them all before the war; he'd been on the cover of *Collier's*, "Our American Schliemann," who was racing at breakneck speed to shed light on the lost world of Homer. I heard nothing of this, only sharded insinuations about how he'd maintained his honorary membership in the DAI (the German Archaeological Institute) a little too long for the comfort of his American and British colleagues. How against all warnings and common sense he'd actually made his way back to Greece in the summer of 1940, after most Americans in Athens had hightailed it out in the fall of 1939 with the outbreak of hostilities in Poland. "Damn fool business, and then driving an ambulance for the Greek army up north in Epirus when the Italians invaded, lucky to get out alive. Last Athens train to Geneva and Lisbon . . . before the Germans blew into town."

And yet around that table I detected a certain sneaking admiration curdling their amour propre, that one of their breed had had the gumption to risk it all for the Greece they loved.

I chalked up the professional sniping to the fact that my father had gone into Bronze Age archaeology, a field the classical archaeologists of that generation had always sneered at because they saw it as a black hole, empty of recorded history and bereft of the mighty ideals of Periclean Athens. "Homer! Who the hell was Homer anyway, just some compiler of twisted genealogical trivia and half-baked myths." The finds of Carl Andersen—abetted by Karel Hollar—of Linear B tablets at Pylos in that fateful summer of 1939 changed a few minds, but not entirely. And then my father had foregone his chair at Princeton in 1948, the youngest full professor in department history, to take up the post of CIA station chief in Athens during the Greek Civil War. That, too, I suppose, rankled.

As I pondered my lies to Paul Oakes, not a little perplexed at my vague sense of loyalty and instinct to hold my cards close, I carelessly leafed through the copy of *Essays and Prayers* he had given me. My eye was caught by an underlined passage: *and so let your soul float free on the river of life, the river of Time.*

Well, I thought, I'm all for that, being of independent spirit and released from maternal coddling. In middle school, I'd been a star history student, a budding archaeologist, and habitué of the Metropolitan Museum's Greek and Roman collections. Even at fourteen, I knew my history from the dirt up. But as I glanced from the pages of *Essays and Prayers* and took in the prospect of the Circle arrayed with its handsome Anglican Gothic chapel and sprawling neo-Georgian school buildings, I felt some inexplicable twinge of anxiety bubbling up. Perhaps it was the midafternoon hour in early October, the summer lingering on the cusp of fall, the air a muggy dullness, through which the ancient apple trees on a corner of the Circle sweltered in their garb of ruddy green. Little could I imagine the horrific story behind those bent and tattered veterans of how many winter campaigns, resigned as they seemed to Indian summer's end and the sharp frosts of New England that would strip them bare of fruit and leaves in a matter of weeks. That moment of anticipation and awakening to time's moving shadow still lingers in my mind, and with it the perfume of freshly mown grass and bruised apples, and the hum and beat of cicadas . . . summer's faltering heartbeat. I was on my own. I took a couple of deep breaths and closed the book in my hand and turned impetuously, as if to the hailing of a welcoming voice, to the playing fields beyond, where the blue countenance of Mount Monadnock presided above the distant wooded hills. I was aware of a whistle and shouts and the slap of football pads as practice began for the varsity. Like a familiar tune . . . the rituals of fall training, the discipline and speed and agility . . . as they would have sounded when my father played on the same field thirty years before.

All that, by rights, should have provided a sense of comforting safety to a boy coming of age, from a family like ours, and yet a moment later a panic attack overwhelmed me with an awful vision: a wall of fire sweeping in from the east, incinerating everything in its path. I saw the trees bend and flame, annihilated in puffs of black smoke, the schoolhouse and chapel implode and shatter, our world turned to a charred cinder. I stood trembling. Had it something to do with Paul Oakes's allusion to Buchenwald, German 88's, his face turned to the window and the impending darkness . . . *So very fragile—the light and dark mixed.*

Of course, this was just the nightmare we lived with in those years in the aftermath of the Cuban Missile Crisis, our youthful imaginations inundated with scenes of Hiroshima and the effects of atomic blasts on test sites, the duck-and-cover drills we practiced in our classrooms. As with my tragedy-hardened grandmother, perhaps my apocalyptic daydreaming was a gut corrective to "resting on your laurels," which she always beat into my brain. But I'd like to think it was the budding historian in me, certainly the archaeologist, who soon discovers that nothing is untouched by violence. I knew as much from the Greek and Roman galleries at the Met: the bronze swords, helmets, and chest armor in the display cabinets retrieved from the burnt cities of Homer's lost world. In my first weeks at Winsted, I'd discovered cellar holes near the Naushon River with the fire-blackened remnants of clay jars from the era of King William's War. The nearby mill town of Winsted had been burned to the ground in an Indian raid in 1692 and its first inhabitants butchered or led off into captivity.

War had made our world. And quaint New England had hardly escaped. I didn't need the nearby sprawling military base at Fort Devens to remind me: My father, grandfather, and great-grandfather had all gone to war—and none had been professional military men.

I couldn't help fantasizing about what an archaeologist a thousand years hence would find after a nuclear blast, sifting down through the layers of ash . . . what would survive? Such preoccupations had stirred my father about the mystery of the Greek Dark Ages from the fall of Mycenaean civilization around 1100 B.C. to 800 B.C., when artifacts and written documents begin to appear again, and Homer composed the *Iliad* and the *Odyssey* from bardic tales and rumors of a golden age of gods and heroes. Four hundred years of total collapse, a near blotting out of a brilliant civilization: The recovery of its history and literature obsessed my father. Who, inventorying the bombed-out cities of Germany in late 1945 for the OSS, with reports of Hiroshima still fresh, feared a repeat, which that wall of flame would certainly have accomplished big-time.

Little could I imagine that my great-grandfather, General Alden, had been touched by similar apocalyptic visions, and so had spared nothing for Winsted, hiring Frederick Law Olmstead to lay out his school in a sweeping circular design, so as to embrace a view of quartz-shouldered Mount Monadnock, the nearby Naushon River, and an array of grand elms and oaks and onetime pastures, lovingly preserving the battered

apple orchard as a memorial centerpiece . . . of which only he and
Samuel Williams knew the full import. As Max wrote in his first novel,
"a landscape and architecture replete with symbols both blatant and
refined, coarse and mesmerizing, to foster the confidence of a ruling
class that its sublime sense of noblesse oblige fitted it alone to govern."

How many dozen times on the back porch of Elsinore had my
grandmother recited the tale, how on a summer day in 1878, tramping
the banks of the Naushon River, General Alden had discovered the
orchard. "That fateful day," she called it, when he'd spied an old dilapidated farm on a rising hill above the river with a splendid grove of
apple trees. "Something about the apple trees—you remember now . . .
something about those dear old gentlemen drew his eye. He made an
offer for the whole kit and caboodle on the spot and two years later the
place was up and running."

I tried to picture it, the ghost of that Revolutionary-era farm and
tiny orchard, the haggard trees now the axial point of an expanse of
manicured turf around which the constellation of the school buildings,
redbrick Georgian classicism draped with foursquare Doric colon-
nades, was set with the precision of a timepiece. Across the Circle, as
it was fondly known, the Williams Chapel and the schoolhouse with
its classically proportioned gold dome vied for our allegiance, while
presiding over the nearby playing fields, the new glass-curtained Alden
gym proclaimed the competitive ideals that exalted physical prowess so
dear to the Greek mind.

That fall of 1965, we were still safe—barely—our faltering youth
regulated like a monkish order by the sounds of bells that echoed in
endless profusion across the Circle, summoning us to wake, to worship,
to study and athletic endeavors, and finally to blissful sleep; so cradled
within the regularity of that charming benignity of cascading tones that
none of us could have imagined the kind of human tragedies for which
Winsted had been antidote. The sluggish waters of timeless childhood
still transfixing our gaze, so steeped in the gentle aura of tradition and
reminders of our righteous calling in the world—privileged sons of the
New World that we were—that we could never have guessed how little
time we had.

America was at the apogee of its postwar confidence, that broad
meridian before the calamitous years to follow. Our fathers had saved
the world from the Nazis and Japanese barbarity and were now saving
it from communism. We lived in the shadow of heroes and crusaders,

who in turn had come to believe in ways very different from those of their progenitors, a new faith begot from the horrific conflagrations that had begun in 1914, for which my grandfather and father had paid the ultimate price. These men of my father's generation, then at the peak of their power and prestige, having put their own lives on the line as young men, were now preparing the battlefield for their sons in the far-off jungles of Vietnam.

It turned out I was far from alone in my apocalyptic vision. A dozen Winsted "boys" had played a role in the Cuban Missile Crisis from the CIA to the National Security Council. They knew it had been a near thing. It was they who had convinced my unflappable grandmother to increase her donation for the new Alden gym by a million dollars for the addition of a fallout shelter to accommodate the entire school: a blast bunker that would have done Omaha Beach proud, with eight-foot-thick reinforced-concrete walls. As one wag put it, who had presided at the dedication ceremony for the new gym: "For a month the cement-mixer trucks were lined up at the gate as if it were rush hour at the Lincoln Tunnel."

That summer of 1965, Lyndon Johnson had sent in regular army troops to reinforce the marines around the U.S. airbases in Hué and Cam Ranh Bay. At night in my dorm, as I drifted off to sleep, I could hear the sound of Huey gunships and C-47 transports from the nearby Green Beret training base at Fort Devens. From TV sets in the masters' studies, one might detect the muffled crackle of automatic weapons through jungle undergrowth, recorded on grainy newsreel film flown in to CBS less than twenty-four hours after it had been shot.

Harbinger of my fate alone in my class.

But for a few weeks and months more, we remained safe, and my vision of Armageddon dispersed as quickly as it had come.

I turned at a shout and saw the launch of a football from a moving figure, its grand trajectory rising, rising, rising—spiraling across the dull blue sky, the arc decaying, only to drop safely into the arms of another fleeing figure: two figures in motion connected by the flight of an aerodynamic object across space and time. As good a metaphor for the fleeting affections that bind the generations.

Time stood still, son; it just stood still.

And there it was: my first lie.

Shortly after my arrival at school, I had found myself drawn to varsity football practice. I had been a city kid, born and raised on the pavements of the Upper East Side of New York, and so had little exposure to serious football, only the occasional game of touch in Central Park. But I was impressed by what I saw. And as I watched, one of the players resting on the sidelines (I would later find out he was the captain of the team) looked up and seemed instantly to know me. He tapped a fellow seated at his side and motioned in my direction. Then both seniors came over to where I stood and introduced themselves. They knew my name. They knew about my father's passing records. He'd led two undefeated teams in the early thirties, and his passing and rushing records had withstood the test of time. He'd gone on to play at Princeton. They asked me how I was doing, as if they knew all about me—even mentioning some East Side bars they frequented, of which, of course, I was oblivious. They patted my shoulder and offered to help if I needed their assistance in negotiating the "fucking ropes," as one of them put it. Was I going to try out for JV football?

"Why not—why, sure."

With that, they led me over to the coach and introduced me. Unheard-of courtesy from sixth formers to peon new kids. Preamble to a sacred duty entrusted to them from my father's day.

This encounter had not gone unnoticed. At the far end of the field, a chain-smoking Paul Oakes had taken up his lonely vigil with a leashed Stokes at his side. Ten years before, a boy had died of a heart attack during one of Oakes's vicious practices, bringing his stellar career as varsity football coach to an abrupt end.

My second lie was the real thing. Only a week before, I'd been a couple of stalls down from Max in the so-called Great White Way, a long line of toilet stalls in the Osborn House basement. There were no doors on the cans, presumably to discourage furtive onanism, or worse, homosexual experimentation.

I was startled by his impetuous voice.

"Hey, that your father's name plastered on every wall in this place, John Alden the Third, the one they named the new gym after?"

"Yeah, I guess so."

"Must have been quite a guy."

"I guess."

"Is it true he was the greatest athlete in school history?"

"Is that what they say?"

"I guess you play football."

"I'm giving it a try."

The rustle of turning pages, a *Time* magazine he'd been reading.

"How better"—an audible snort—"to instill leadership and team-work, the competitive drive."

"Do you play?"

"Not this Jew boy. I'm positively allergic to pigskin. So tell me, what's the story with your dad—what happened to him?"

I sat there a little shaken, my pants down around my ankles, as I was asked the crucial question in my life—for which I never had a convincing answer. So disarmed, I fumbled out the one thing I shouldn't have said. It was not the answer my mother or grandmother would have given, but under the circumstances it seemed to have an internal logic all its own.

"He was in the CIA."

I had spilled the beans, just like my mother when she got drunk. We were supposed to say he was in the State Department and had been killed in a tragic accident on the autobahn outside Frankfurt.

"Ah-a, the plot thickens. A spy, a spook, a capitalist running dog."

"Fuck you."

"Did he get shot?"

"It was an accident. A car crash."

"Tough on you." I noted the hint of sympathy in his tone. "It must be something, trying to live up to a guy like your dad—a real hero—a hero's son, huh?"

That shocked me: *a hero's son*. Max had that devastating ability to nail your innermost vulnerabilities, often with a seemingly careless aside. Less intuition, I think, than the ingenious modus of a world-class snoop. Already he'd struck me as a canny outsider trying to insinuate his way into our midst, always hanging around, prying and plotting. Once I'd even caught him in the reading room of the library, staring up at the portrait of my great-grandfather, playing air scales on an open copy of the school history. And charming, too, how his already-long locks of curly dark hair nodded above his inquisitive, strangely mournful eyes. He was handsome as the devil, even as a young teenager, with an unkempt natural elegance that fitted his rapier wit. Whenever he opened his big mouth, every face in the room turned to him. He had a photographic memory, which enabled him to recite entire poems after only minutes of study, or play a Mozart sonata after a couple of run-throughs. And he played the piano . . . like an angel. Guaranteed to keep the girls swooning. His favorite pose, and he was a poser, an actor at heart, was to pretend to be the victim: a Jew set adrift in a sea of goyim. That was how he kept his edge. Was the school rife with anti-Semitism, as he claimed in his first novel? Perhaps the country club sort. But it was the civil rights movement that mattered in 1965, a subject strangely absent from *Like a Forgotten Angel*. Max was always resentful of my black friends because they had real injustices to protest about, while he had to make do with Vietnam and anything else he could dream up. So he kept the pot stirred with his antics, providing juicy material for the short stories and novels to come: the poor Jewish kid taking on the prejudices and foibles of the WASP establishment.

"I was only two," I said; "I barely remember him."

"Hey, so what's with your bureau piled high with all those books on Greece and Rome, the archaeology magazines?"

"I don't remember inviting you into my cubicle."

"Your business is my business; that's how we Jews have made it in the land of the free, home of the brave. That's how come kikes like me have survived and prospered and infiltrated ourselves into your comfortable parlors." The *Time* magazine hurtled into the white-brick wall across from where we sat on our respective crappers. "I mean, your dad really *is* a fucking hero—right; there are all those medals in the display case in the gym from the Greek government."

"He was an archaeologist before the war. He worked with the Greek Resistance against the Nazis."

There was silence for a few moments, as if maybe, just maybe, I had managed to insinuate a serious note: my dad the Nazi killer.

"That's what I mean, pretty tough having a hero for a father, especially a dead hero," Max commented.

Ever flippant, Max had nevertheless hit upon an iron law of civilization. Since Homer and the Greeks, the heroic code regarded fathers of old as paragons to be respected by the present generation. This belief in an age of heroes is the moral cement that holds society together, which my generation, with the help of the Vietnam War, was hell-bent on rendering null and void. A demolition job Max and his kind ultimately failed to complete as "the Greatest Generation" rallied to claim its rightful place in the pantheon of freedom's demigods.

"So what's so great about your father?" I asked.

"That's my point, kemosabe," Max said. "He bigum humbug and me little humbug—plan: We pretend we just like you. Savvy." Max burped for effect. "You see, Winsted is key to the master plan: first your businesses—Hollywood and publishing, then your banks, then your schools and universities—then the world. No heroes here, pal: just fifth column fellow travelers and the like." The creak of a toilet paper dispenser. "But tell me something, Peter Alden, how come you got kicked off the gravy train? Shouldn't you be John Alden the Fourth—like Shakespeare's Henry?"

"Lay off, will you."

"Just wondering, get the lay of the land, so to speak. I mean, your family owns this bit of prime real estate, you and the Williamses."

"It's controlled by the board of trustees."

"Got anything good on the walls of your stall?" he asked. "Just imagine all the immortal words that have been composed while taking a dump. The paint is so thick here, it must go back at least fifty years. Just think what you might find if you could peel back the layers, get down to some bedrock graffiti by the great FDR himself, now lost to posterity. Someone better inform the National Archives. Hell, who knows, maybe these walls will be our last chance at immortality. Let's see, how might I memorialize our little chat?"

"You know Mr. Oakes warned us that writing on the can walls was against the rules, one of his ten commandments: Thou shalt not deface school property."

"That faggot priest, what does he know?"

"He's an Episcopal minister; it's only priests in the Catholic Church."

"Check out your facts, boy; they *are* Episcopal priests. Think Spanish Inquisition . . . the Judas cradle. You're not one of his little informers, are you?"

"Mr. Oakes doesn't seem such a bad guy."

"Listen, pal, learn fast and survive. Know fanaticism when you see it. Any guy who gives up females, fucking, and family for faith is either faggot or fanatic—or child molester. And Oakey-Dokey, with all his windy blather on Christian manhood, scores on all fronts. See the way he delights in chasing us out of bed in the morning, when you've got a hard-on in your cute little pj's. He loves that. And what about that extensive pornography collection of his?"

"You're kidding."

"He keeps it in a box in his closet, for the supposed purpose of dealing with the lewd interests of his boys. If he catches a kid with a

Playboy, he forces him to spend a few hours with his collection of dirty pictures so that the budding pervert can get it out of his system. They are grossly explicit, intensely gynecological. He believes in glutting lustful appetites, not denying them. Destroy them with surfeit, that's his policy. I suppose it explains his drinking and obesity."

"Where do you get all this crap from anyway?"

"A good writer never reveals his sources."

"He'll have your balls for breakfast."

"Old moloch breath will never get his paws on me. Thumbscrew or rack, I won't be sacrificed for his sins—not this Jew boy."

And so in time, the Great White Way became the wondrous palimpsest for Max's early diatribes—his Maxims: our underground press, our rumor mill, the samizdat of revolt, and no amount of Clorox or fresh paint seemed capable of stemming the runic tide that spent itself on that white shore.

Max, taking a page from memory-besotted Proust, claimed he was only interested in the manifestations of a deeper law of continuity: the outsider's belief that the insiders embody some remnant of their forebearers, a fragment of personality enduring through time and space, what we might see today as a straightforward genetic transfer. But Max had no interest in science; it was the translation of ideas and feelings across the boundaries of the past that fascinated him: the emotional underpinnings of our existence, "things of the wind and stars," as he put it in *Like a Forgotten Angel*, that make their way to us and through us in the contending currents on the river of Time.

Whether he first found this metaphor in the *Essays and Prayers*, as I did, I haven't been able to confirm. But if anything, recent advances in the science of genetics have made the metaphor inescapable.

The ingrained habit of who we are.

All the pain Max would cause us, the love and hate inextricably mixed, the careless manipulation of facts, and the many masks he employed were means to elucidating the past within. I do not doubt his sincerity, or that he loved Laura Williams and retained some affection for me, but in the end he used us up and left us orphaned from our true selves in his pages. Excuses for his art. Nor would he deny it. For Max, everything was fair game, including the complications in his own family, which fill the opening pages of *Like a Forgotten Angel*.

When Saul was deposited amidst the splendors of this pastoral paradise of New England rectitude, he felt as if he'd been spirited back in time to some exclusive family reunion to which his Jew ass was not welcome. His chances of survival were not helped by his incredulous father, who cruised in and out of the dormitory whistling a Perry Como number as he unloaded Saul's trunk, his books, sheet music, and two cartons of Twinkies. Jocko Friedman couldn't believe he'd managed the scam, that they'd actually let his son into this elite club of the establishment. Jocko had the open-faced gaze of a dream walker as he read the famous names inscribed in gold lettering on aged oak panels, or chiseled with cold perfection into the granite wall of the Gothic chapel. His son, Saul—little Saul, a part of all this robber baron past, these book-choked temples of learning built on the backs of how many thousands of mill workers and tens of thousands of Chinese coolies? Old money—older than God and squeaky-clean. And to think, only a generation before, his own father, a Jewish blacksmith, had been run out of a decrepit shtetl of seven buildings along a muddy road in the Ukraine by crazed Cossacks . . . TOWDAH! Jocko finally made his exit, still blabbing out wily advice to his son about how to get along with the Big Boys—take it from Jocko, who'd clawed his way up in the Gentile strongholds of white-shoe investment firms. Saul's relief was inexpressible as he saw that Cadillac de Ville, that monstrosity of salmon pink and glinting chrome fins, cruise off past the wrought-iron gates. An eyesore all day parked amidst the polite, unassuming station wagons of the denizens of the Somerset and Knickerbocker clubs. Only then could Saul settle in and reconnoiter to get his bearings: How to infiltrate the sanctum sanctorum? He needed to be a presence and a nonpresence, participant and observer, at once a mover and passive reflector if he was to properly practice his art. He saw himself as a lovely new moon orbiting a dying and alien planet, and this elliptical orbit, if judged just right, would give a gravitational shove that might well alter many things. A delicate act of sabotage requiring pseudonyms and patsies, confederates and confidants. The secret life of such an Underground Man might allow him to tap into the bad conscience of a privileged yet doomed class of parasites. Not that he was immune to friendship. He required a friend, an exemplar of the society into which he'd been thrown and a model for his protagonist's Sancho Panza. This was the delicious task of literary deceit to which he immediately set himself.

As with one of Max's many literary heroes, James Joyce, no great critique of a milieu comes without a certain love for—or sympathy with—the target, much less the feeling of loss and even guilt from the resulting demolition job. I actually kind of liked his dad, Jack—Jocko of his novel—who always kept Max in *Playboy* subscriptions and hard cash. Jack would rocket up to Winsted in his convertible salmon pink Caddy and take us out for a knockout dinner at Durgin Park in Boston and deposit us back at school with shopping bags full of Skippy peanut butter and fruit toasties. In four years, my mother came to visit exactly once. I actually envied Max his living, breathing father, for all his faux pas and social-climbing ways. He wanted only the best for Max. But whenever I told Max as much, he'd wave me off and scowl with some smart-alecky retort.

"Pete, let's face it, you and I—we're fucked. You have a dead hero for a father and I have a living schmuck."

As Max went about setting the stage for his fictional universe, I was grappling with yet more bits of information about my father, this from an unimpeachable source. A month after I arrived, a blue binder appeared from the family law firm of Brandt & Harrison; it contained all my father's letters to his mother from Winsted, annotated and cross-referenced by my cool, calculating, ruthless—and sometimes compassionate-to-a-fault—grandmother before she died. They revealed a lonely, intelligent young man about to face the darkening and uncertain world of the Depression.

October 15, 1928

Dearest Mother,

Can you believe how the weather has changed this October from such terrible heat to the present coolness? Already the leaves are beginning to turn. It reminds me of Elysium in the fall, except, of course, the woods here are less dense, with more deciduous trees. I miss the white pines. There is a wonderful line of sweet gum trees outside my dorm window with enormous boughs like something out of a fairy tale. I have seen some examples of this tree in Central Park but nowhere else around here. I gather they grow in abundance in the South and are cut for lumber. The resinous sap is extracted for chewing gum. At night, bathed in moonlight, the leaves are like pointed stars and are so mysterious and very beautiful. Sometimes I wake myself in the early morning just to stare at them for a few minutes and then go back to sleep. I find them a comfort.

On the following binder page, my grandmother had inserted a photocopy of a page of General Alden's diary for August 12, 1863, annotated in her crisp hand: *The general was in a field hospital near Silver Spring, Maryland.*

> I lay awake most of the night due to the pain of my wounded leg and cursing under my breath at the imbecility of my commander and all the lives lost. It was hot as Hades and I spent the hours staring at the most beautiful sweet gum beyond the tent flaps, its leaves like black stars on gray broadcloth, its scent mingling with that of gangrene and human spoliation, praying that a breeze might stir that firmament and bring some comfort to the interminable hours.

Following this was a photocopy of a letter from Frederick Olmsted, dated October 9, 1879, from the personal papers of General Alden.

> I have noted your request for the planting of four sweet gum trees outside the dormitories on the north wing. I can, of course, do this, but please be advised that the sweet gum is a southern variety and not conditioned for harsh northern winters. I can give no assurances that the trees will prosper over time.

Those tall, sinewy sweet gum trees still grow outside the dorm, and I, too, relished their pointy leaves against the sky, and how they fell away that first fall like yellow paper stars floating down to pattern the grass. These are glorious facts—the real stuff of history, as it should be told—from which a man can then draw his own conclusions.

Max purloined these letters, as he did the headmaster's files and documents from the school archives, and my father's boyhood letters find dull reflection in his first novel, much adumbrated and altered to fit the author's fictional ends—sans citations or acknowledgments of any kind.

2

IT IS NOT A LITTLE UNNERVING HOW EASILY MEM-
ory steals away, and I often wonder how much more would
have vanished without a trace if not for Max's antics. A case
in point, that awful rainy spring of third-form year, blustery
and chilly—bone-cracking, just as my mother had warned. Afternoons
of curtailed and miserable crew practices livened only by evening confirmation classes, where Max and Paul Oakes dueled without quarter.

A miasma of musty leather hung heavy in the damp confines of
the memorial room, a looming Victorian cabinet taking up an entire
side wall crammed from floor to ceiling with rare moldering volumes untouched by human hands for generations. Above the simple
Chippendale mantelpiece: the gold-inscribed lists of the glorious
dead. The names glittered with a dull iridescence, illuminated by a
pair of matching blue-and-white ginger jar table lamps; the entwined
cherry blossom patterns provided the only touches of vivid color in an
otherwise-drab setting of lank chintz curtains and brooding ebony furnishings. My grandfather was included with those who had died in the
First World War, an impressively long list for a relatively small school,
which included the name of a president's son. The list of those killed
in World War II was not as long, a fact I pondered mightily during
those interminable classes, figuring that by 1941 those smart Winsted
boys, noting the odds, had wisely enlisted as officers in the intelligence
services or the navy, avoiding the infantry and the fate of their fathers'
generation in the trenches. My father had a solo plaque of his own,
cheek by jowl with those from the Korean War. A stray addendum, it
always struck me, a death marked in limbo.

The Reverend Oakes sat quietly at a corner table, waiting for the class to settle down and the last stragglers to arrive from study hall. He slowly turned the pages of his Book of Common Prayer in a desultory manner, as if seeking inspiration for his melancholy task or reminders of better days within. At his elbow, ever at the ready, was Samuel Williams's *Essays and Prayers*. My initial fear of him had turned to grudging respect and even fondness as he took me under his wing that first year, working on my passing game and coaching me on the river. He was still an enormously powerful man, every inch the Harvard running back who had rushed for five touchdowns against Yale in 1926, while anchoring the crew team on the Charles for three years. As a young master and crew coach—he took over the varsity football coaching position in 1931—he became renowned for his prowess at single-handedly lifting the eight-man shells from their racks in the boathouse and getting them in the water, where the crew team would find them ready and waiting. Alas, for our generation, those glory days of Henley wins and championship seasons on the gridiron were, like the war, only a windy rumor; his abysmally long and boring sermons were what he was best known for. And the boy who had died of a heart attack in the early fifties, who collapsed in the heat of a sultry September day, desperate to prove himself by making it through his coach's punishing drills during varsity football tryouts.

Looking back, I flinch at those interminable Camels that he smoked, like a bloody-minded suicide, and the growing doubt and regret I detected in his world-weary eyes as Vietnam engulfed his progeny. Like a warrior saint in an incense-shrouded Byzantine icon, he eyed the motley crew before him: what a coddled generation compared to those tough sons of bitches he'd taught and coached in the thirties, who'd endured the Depression and gone on to whip Hitler and Hirohito, only to be humiliated by Stalin in Eastern Europe and then Castro at the Bay of Pigs . . . and were now hell-bent on evening the score by going after Ho Chi Minh.

That evening, Max, instead of hiding himself away in the rear seats, had decided to take his stand. He sat on an exposed flank in the front row, next to a seedy asthmatic boy with large hazel eyes and heavily Brylcreemed hair, who gave off that chemically astringent smell that one, oddly, associated with Dick Clark and Kookie on *77 Sunset Strip*. Nothing of that had rubbed off on Squirrel, as we'd nicknamed him; the poor kid was neurotic and highly strung, with a reedy unbroken voice that elicited snickers (rumor was that his testicles had failed to descend and probably never would). Squirrel was the son of a prominent minister in Dedham and took inordinate delight, much to Max's irritation, in answering theological esoterica with total textual and doctrinal accuracy. Max had Squirrel—and Mr. Oakes—firmly between the crosshairs.

"Everyone here?" asked Mr. Oakes with a final drag on his cigarette. He slipped his reading glasses onto the table before him. "Okay, men: This is the last class before the big day, your confirmation and First Communion. I hope you are ready to face your Maker with respect and gusto. Mr. Roberts, I trust you have gotten those questions about the Trinity out of your craw by this time, because I would very much like to go on to the business of the sacraments this evening. Did you study the Nicene Creed as I suggested?"

Max shifted his weight.

"Yes, sir, I did."

"And did that settle your problem?"

"No, sir, it did not. I still don't see how God can be split up into three parts, for it is written, 'Hear, O Israel: The Lord our God *is* one Lord.'"

Mr. Oakes pulled a weary hand across his broad brow.

"He is not split up, as you put it, Roberts; the Son and the Father and Holy Ghost are consubstantial, of the same substance, one and the same."

Beyond the window, rain began spitting again, dripping from the eaves and overflowing the gutters.

"But if Christ is also God"—Max's hands reached to an invisible keyboard and did a little shuttle service up and back—"or at least a part of God, dwelling separate and apart—part man, part God—then God is a plural deity."

"Roberts, Roberts"—Mr. Oakes palmed his reddened nose, pinching his nostrils between thumb and forefinger as he reached for his reading glasses—"how many times do I have to tell you? It is the Logos you must look to for your answer, the Word, the idea—spirit made flesh in the body of man, in the mask of humankind. Christ is a kind of emanation of God, begotten not created—the Word made flesh—consubstantial—sharing two natures but remaining a single identity. Can't you get that, Roberts? Is it so difficult for a subtle scribbler like you?"

Mr. Oakes bent forward as if to better locate his antagonist, his reading glasses slipping down his nose. We all suspected that Mr. Oakes knew who was responsible for the graffiti in the Great White

Way. Max had been interrogated any number of times, at least twice by the headmaster, and denied everything. Fingerprint experts had been brought in, and they still failed to produce conclusive proof. And the prefects, who could have collared Max, did nothing; they enjoyed the insanity of it too much to see it end.

"I don't get it, sir."

Sarcastic yawns from the others, eyes rolling as if in disbelief that anyone with half a brain could care about the neglected boilerplate of our spiritual inheritance.

"Think of it this way, Roberts. You are the son of your father—right?—physically separate and unique, and yet there will always be a large part of your father in you . . . his spirit a part of your soul; in the same way, God gave life to a human body by endowing it with his Logos—that is, his Holy Spirit—in the same way sunlight fills an empty room but takes nothing away from the source of light. Christ is a reflection of that light but is Himself separate from the source."

He glowered at Max, as if slightly bemused by his own display of verbal dexterity, the lovely, abstruse theology of seminary days still holding water after all the years, after the German 88's, and Buchenwald . . . and now the invasion of the Beatles! Sensing that he hadn't quite made his case, Paul Oakes opened his copy of *Essays and Prayers* and leafed to a passage, holding a finger aloft as he quoted.

"'As the rain is to the earth, the river to the abiding sea, the heart to the body, so the Father is to the Son.'"

Max slowly pulled himself up to his full height in his chair—as if aware for the first time of his impatient audience—and threw off a fantastic run of trills.

"Then why did His mother have to be a virgin? Only gods are born of virgins."

"Stop that idiot business with your hands," Mr. Oakes shouted above a roll of thunder that rattled the glass cabinets containing some of the library's most precious volumes. Then he sat back a moment, pondering. The rain outside continued in earnest, a dull patter through the leaves of the overhanging elms. The windows fogged.

"The Church does not deny that Christ was born into the world; there was indeed a human nature to Him that was willing to make the sacrifice and suffer and die for our sins. That is why we celebrate His sacrifice in Communion"—a staccato wave of his hand chopping air—"which brings us to this evening's subject, the sacraments."

"But how could she have been a virgin?"

Mr. Oakes's hand froze where it had been turning a page in the Book of Common Prayer. The shouted outburst had all heads turned to Max.

"Mr. Roberts"—a pause, a sigh, a large tongue lubricating a pensive lower lip—"you should not travail yourself over such . . . ah, carnal details. Virginity is simply a sign of holiness, a symbol of Mary's worthiness to receive the Holy Spirit."

"But she'd been married to Joseph for years; they had been trying to have children. Surely something must have happened."

"Roberts, you would indeed try the patience of Job. And like your pharisaical forebears, you haggle over unpleasant details and insignificant facts to the neglect of the spirit."

Mr. Oakes removed his glasses, which had fogged up, too, and wearily wiped them with his handkerchief.

Max, ferreting for the jugular, sat higher and stuck his hands under his armpits, like a maniac in a straitjacket. Then he turned to me, with a querulous nod and jut of his eyebrows, as if egging me into the fray.

"Maybe Jesus was more like Achilles, born of the goddess Thetis and the mortal Peleus, a near-divine killing machine, yet crying out against senseless slaughter, a social revolutionary, yet vulnerable to human desires, trading glory for death."

Max blew my mind with this, flinging wide an unexpected door, but I dared not enter.

"Mary was not a goddess, but a humble virgin," came the weary reply from on high.

"Catholics believe," said Max, noting my cowardice with a thrust of his lower lip, "she remained a virgin postpartum and was assumed bodily—goddesslike—into heaven." An ecstatic cadence came into his voice as he jerked from side to side as if fighting his imprisoned hands.

"Nor are we Catholics here—thank God!" Mr. Oakes bellowed. "Let us leave their messy can of theological worms to them. Now back to the subject of this evening's class. Can anyone tell me why we celebrate Holy Communion?"

Squirrel, who had been enduring Max's digressions with growing agitation, shot his hand up in triumph, eyes spinning like marbles.

"To celebrate the death and sacrifice of Jesus Christ, our Savior."

Max grimaced.

"Very good, Mathews." Mr. Oakes smiled with relief. "And why is Christ's death and sacrifice so important?"

"Because He died for our sins," said Squirrel breathlessly, "to save us from eternal damnation—because man is born into wickedness and eternally tainted by original sin and is in a fallen state, a creature condemned to eternal—"

"Thank you, Mathews, you've certainly got the gist."

"Original sin?" Max shrieked, glaring at Squirrel. "Oh right, just like Augustine believed that even the youngest baby was full of sin, and so original sin was passed on from one generation to the next by sexual intercourse, and so it was necessary for Jesus to be born of a virgin"— Max slid a lubricious tongue Squirrel's way—"to avoid contamination."

"That's enough out of you tonight, Roberts." Mr. Oakes stood suddenly, all six foot six of him, hands on the table to steady himself, hunched forward like a right tackle staring at Max across the line of scrimmage—just daring him. "Don't you think it is about time you get your mind out of the gutter? Where the hell do you get this stuff anyway? You don't have to be confirmed, Roberts. Shall I just write to your father and tell him that you do not wish to be confirmed? It's your choice, Roberts."

Max bowed his head in mock contrition. In the silence that followed, I could again hear the rain against the windows, while over the hulking grizzly bear figure, fixed in penumbral space, were the gold letters of my father's memorial plaque like a silent plea from the grave.

How strange, how wonderful, that in retrospect Max's antics around the tortured abstractions of the Trinity should not only preserve that fleeting hour for me but help guide me through the treacherous shoals of father-son relationships. Not to be confused in the literary realm with the anxiety of influence, about which Max was unduly perturbed. Nor the etiolated delectations of the Trinity for which multitudes of martyrs departed this earth, much less the seemingly benign symbol embodied in the name of Trinity College, Cambridge: a doleful way station in the subversion of one generation by the next, and breeding ground for the nest of vipers who murdered my father.

For a week, speculation was rampant. Were they going to let Max be confirmed? Would he even go through with it? How could a righteous Lord—Father, Son, *and* Holy Ghost—not strike the blasphemer dead?

When confirmation Sunday and Founder's Day dawned, it was the loveliest day of that spring, a day of sparking sunshine that lifted the gloom of a rainy May. My mother failed to show, claiming an attack of migraines had laid her low. When I checked with our doorman, Patrick, he told me my mother had returned so drunk from the Colony Club the previous afternoon that he'd had to seat her in the lobby while he found the super's wife to get her into the apartment, undressed, and into bed. Patrick also noted that deliveries of her antidepressants were on the increase.

But the apple trees on the Circle bloomed exuberantly, white and pastel pink cupped in leaves of silvery green. And with the grass freshly mown for the first time and the ambrosial aroma of the clover rising at my footsteps, it was as if a pall of uncertainty had been removed, and I felt safe—very alone, but safe. How could anything be amiss with the world on such a splendid morning? I luxuriated for an hour before chapel in the shade of an apple tree on the Circle, reading the *Odyssey*. It was the Richard Lattimore translation in bound galleys, which my friend and tutor at Princeton had sent me almost six months before it was published. I was honored to have it and spellbound by its pages. A little over a year before her death, my grandmother had taken me on a final summer trip; we flew to Venice, where we spent a few days at her beloved Gritti on the Grand Canal, and then took a cruise ship, which sailed down the Adriatic and toured many of the most famous and beautiful of the Cycladic islands—Delos, where my father had dug in 1939, his last year as a dirt archaeologist, and on to Santorini and Tinos—then made its way to Crete and north again into the Ionian Sea, with stops at Pylos and Corfu and a return to Venice along the Dalmatian coast. My grandmother's heart was already weak, and she never left the ship with the tour groups. She told me once, if not a dozen times, holding fast to the ship's railing like a worshipper at the altar rail, mythic isles breezing by on the blue, "He loved the Greek islands—how he loved them, almost as much as Elysium."

When I entered the chapel, there was Max's name along with mine as bold as you please on the Founder's Day program. All those tedious confirmation classes and wintry black moods had been reduced to a few clean letters on cream-toned thick rag paper emblazoned with the crimson-and-black school crest—an official imprimatur of our entry into the ranks of the elect. Seeing our names brought a tentative smile to my face. Who cared if any of it made sense? This was simply the world as we found it. My growing confidence got another boost: Confirmation Sunday had fallen on Founder's Day. Founder's Day was a tradition going back to the time of my great-grandfather, Gen. John Alden, who had set aside one Sunday in spring to remember those in his Fifteenth Regiment Massachusetts Volunteers who had fallen at Antietam (330 felled in the first twenty minutes, 75 killed, 255 wounded, and 43 dying of wounds), and those on the faculty who had lost comrades and relations in the Civil War. The occasion now included remembrances for all who had fallen in foreign wars. And no less than the bishop of Massachusetts was to preach the sermon and officiate at our First Communion. I turned to the congregation and discovered many faces I knew from the newspapers and my grandmother's circle. Among the esteemed alumni was a cohort of the president's men; they had come because this was to be the final Founder's Day for "old man" Jack Crocket, the retiring headmaster after forty years' service. They were all Jack's boys, though Paul Oakes and our legendary teacher of classics, Virgil Dabney, each had his own following. It couldn't get any better than that for our intrepid band of confirmees seated near the front of the chapel. My grandmother, except during the war years, when she was involved in nonstop charity work, hadn't missed this service for fifty years. My mother had absented herself from Founder's Day since my father died, a track record my confirmation did nothing to alter. And I hate to say, I was just as glad.

Sitting near the front of the nave with Max, those Homeric hexameters still dancing through my brain along with scenes of bone-bright temples against the wine-dark sea—my grandmother's life exordiums a constant refrain—I geared myself up so as not to let down the family. I blinked and raised my gaze, transfixed by the sparkling sunlight in the La Farge stained-glass windows. The Old Testament scenes—such a wicked golden glint on the blade of Goliath's scimitar—vibrated in subtle tones of opalescent color, spilling prismatic rivulets of Delft blue, olive green, milky mauve, and saffron over the nave, a crazy-quilt display, as if animated by the organ's jaunty rendition of Bach's Toccata and Fugue in D Minor. On the high altar, crowned with an austere cross of gold, constellations of tastefully arranged tulips and daffodils simmered gloriously, their perfume released to give cheer to the gray verticality of the Gothic stonework. Even the dull mahogany of the choir stalls exuded orgiastic spates of orange and honey amber, as if about to combust in exultant flame. In those precious moments, as the Bach Toccata breasted the tape, I found my spirit soaring: not a little proud that my family had been instrumental in this celebratory pageantry.

I turned in my seat to fully fathom the distinguished faces in attendance; I noted the quick, stalwart smile of Paul Oakes, and the ironic pout of the saturnine Virgil Dabney—classics teacher to the mighty (later to become my adviser), and others among the faculty as they nodded at their former students: at least three members of the president's inner circle—national security adviser, assistant secretary of state for Southeast Asia, and secretary of the army; not to mention a lean and wintry onetime governor of New York and Roosevelt's ambassador to Moscow, and a former secretary of state under Truman in his pinstripe Savile Row suit, formidable mustache bristling beneath dour gray-green eyes, and a bright-eyed bunch of myrmidons whose lives were dedicated to the country's clandestine services—something of a specialty among the Winsted crowd of my father's generation. I caught the eye of the dashing Elliot Goddard, a classmate and colleague of my father's, who had run the failed Bay of Pigs invasion; and sitting next to Elliot, his ultrabrilliant classmate, who had designed and run the convoy system during the war and later developed the U-2 spy plane in no time flat. A little morose and sunken-cheeked, he had taken the fall for the Cuban fiasco: Medal of Honor from Kennedy and out on his ass the next day. There, too, a row behind, were the Alsop brothers, Joe and Stewart, insider journalists of a decidedly apocalyptic bent when it came to American foreign policy, anti-Communist to the core and pals of the slain president. My father had been a habitué of Joe's Georgetown soirees in the early fifties. What a splendid crew of movers and shakers! Witnessing this pantheon of eastern establishment gods— most had attended my grandmother's funeral service at the Church of the Heavenly Rest on Fifth Avenue—I suddenly became viscerally aware of her absence.

A sigh escaped my lips, and I felt Max's eyes swivel in my direction. She had been the rock of my childhood. I'd never attended a Founder's Day without her at my side! I tried to conjure her flinty-eyed yet kind and stoic demeanor—hazel eyes unblinking as the names of her husband and son were read out from the pulpit, when she'd take my hand and give it a squeeze of assurance.

I loosened my tie and tried to breathe deeply, the mantle of sole representative of my family a sudden and suffocating weight on my chest.

In that moment of terror, I became aware of the presence of my father's classmate and third cousin, Bobby Williams, wheelchair-bound and seated in front of his wife, Suzanne, and their daughter, Laura. As a founding family, the Williamses were placed near the front, across the aisle from me, next to the huge Augustus Saint-Gaudens's bronze intaglio relief embedded in the nave's wall. The Williams Memorial was famous in art history circles and a regular stop on admissions tours.

Why were they there? I'd never seen them there before. I was still unaware that my grandmother had vetoed Bobby Williams's participation on the board since his return as a wounded veteran in 1945. Over twenty years in exile, and now, the moment she was gone, he'd been taken back into the fold. Something in me detected a presence that was sinister, and not a little scary. Not just his burn-disfigured hands and face from the war but an exotic, sallow pallor that in certain lights gave him a distinctly bronze coloring. I knew enough about the bad blood between the families to find myself sweating like a pig: Grandmother had invariably dismissed the subject of Bobby and Suzanne, while my mother had deployed her most poisonous barbs whenever their paths crossed at Elysium.

My spring gladness sprang a leak: I felt exposed, like a hoplite conscript hung out on the right flank of the formation. Max was there, of course, but he only made things worse as I tried to regain my composure.

Art historians consider the Williams Memorial to be Saint-Gaudens's masterpiece. It commemorates the life and tragic death of Samuel Williams II, the eldest son of the Reverend Samuel Williams. (The fictionalized account of this golden boy's sad drowning suicide in the Charles River, is, of course, a famous set piece in Max's *Like a Forgotten Angel,* the title, too, was inspired by the memorial). The angle of sunlight from the stained-glass windows produced a radiant Tyrian purple glow in the bronze patina, so that the phalanx of ascending angels with their offerings of ivy garlands and long-stemmed lilies seemed like a magical portal into a timeless empyrean. Mother and daughter, seated just to the right of the memorial, as if oblivious of their proximity to such a quantum transformation, were, in turn, bathed in a rosette veil of otherworldly light, like a protean echo of those angelic faces in three-quarter relief. I stared like a besotted idiot. A kind of daydream—"skylarking," as grandmother accused me—in which my romantic naïveté struggled to fathom the meaning of this transmigration of artistic inspiration into erotic fixation . . . much less their sudden reappearance at Winsted.

And then I recognized, seated right behind Laura, my godfather, Charles Fairburn, famed archaeologist, classics professor, squadron leader, and survivor of fifty bomber raids over Nazi Germany (MI5 operative, of which I was then clueless), and impeccably turned out in his Gieves & Hawkes tweed suit and Trinity College tie, thinning red hair plastered back off the craquelure of a fine sun-wrinkled brow. I could tell his exacting eyes were fully absorbed in taking the measure of the spectacle on offer, the best his pedigreed American cousins could manage in terms of ceremonial hoo-ha. I noticed, too, how occasionally he would reach to Laura and pat her shoulder; he was Suzanne's first cousin and godfather to her daughter. For Charles, Founder's Day was a rather awkward twofer: two godchildren from two families not on the best of terms, and just to add to the delicious mess, he was fucking Suzanne on the side. Pardon my French, but it was just as well I was as naïve as I was; if I'd know the half of it, I'd have been utterly unmanned.

I can just hear Max at my shoulder, telling me get on with it, enough exposition already—get to the fucking story. But just a little more background is in order.

Laura was about my age; I'd known her from childhood over the summers at our family place, Elysium, a nature preserve in the Berkshires, where the Williamses had their own cottage, Hermitage. But instead of the child of memory, she looked like a younger version of her stunningly beautiful mother ("that nymphomaniac bitch" was the phrase I'd heard more than once behind closed doors from my mother, followed by a "shush now" from my grandmother). I'd seen Suzanne Williams only in passing, and even less of her disabled and reclusive husband, the rector's grandson, Bobby ("that conniving liar of a sorry excuse for a human being"—a Homeric descriptive phrase favored by Grandmother whenever the subject of Bobby came up). I pondered the figure of Bobby for a moment where he sat with head bowed, seeming to scrutinize the names of the recently deceased on the chapel program in his lap, perhaps in search of the classmates he'd survived. On summer vacations, my grandmother always discouraged me from going near the Williamses' "palatial extravagance," Hermitage, as it was known throughout the Berkshires, a McKim, Mead & White Shingle Style mansion—an "artistic treasure chest," according to art history buffs—across the lake from our more pedestrian fieldstone cottage. Worse, if the nude, sunbathing Suzanne Williams should be encamped at the lakeside beach, all plans for swimming had to be postponed until the coast was clear. Now, here they were encamped at Winsted in all their debauched rectitude.

My perplexed stupor was broken when Laura turned in my direction—I feared she had detected my rude stare. But seeing me, she only smiled and then made a dismissive rolling of her inquisitive eyes: *Can you believe this tedious bullshit?* Noticing her daughter's distracted attention as the service was about to get under way, Suzanne also turned my way, her curious gaze segueing to shocked disbelief, then into an expression of what looked like fear mixed with physical longing in the electric blue of her eyes. Those deeply lashed eyes fixed themselves on me with a ferocity I'd never seen—never imagined—in a woman! In the soft refracted light, I saw a long vertical vein of purple straining out in her forehead. I thought she was having a seizure of some kind, but she instantly recovered her aplomb, turned away, and elbowed her daughter to do the same. I'd had intimations of that look—something of the dismay part—occasionally in my mother as I got older, when I might suddenly burst in unexpectedly and catch her unawares, but never this, never the frisson of sexual arousal and repression. I realized, as if the family lawyers had set the brief of charges before me, that she either hated or loved my father, not realizing at my age that her capacity for both was infinite.

I panicked at the thought of inheriting such . . . an enemy?

The feeling of anxious exile conceived in Suzanne's icy stare—one moment king of the mountain, the next a scared little boy—has never left me.

As the organ voluntary rose in crescendo and the choir proceeded down the ambulatory and the congregation stood, I kept glancing across the nave in hopes of recapturing the equanimity that had been mine only minutes before. I boldly examined my foe. Suzanne Williams, nearing fifty and still gorgeous, stood plumb-line straight, head upright, blond hair in a tight chignon, displaying to good effect the long sinewy lines in her jaw and neck and upper shoulders: ever the prima ballerina at the studio mirror. The Saint-Gaudens angel lookalike had been replaced by the sculptor's Diana, now housed in the American Wing of the Metropolitan Museum: the huntress with bow string drawn to cheek to sight the arrow. Even the clean lines of her taffeta dress of silky apricot—probably, I realize now, by Jackie Kennedy's favorite designer, Oleg Cassini—seemed only another assertive accoutrement in her armory. Laura, looking more put out and bored than ever, had returned to being the sulky girl I remembered from childhood summers. She fidgeted with the program, resting her weight on one leg and then the other; her long blond hair, neatly combed out so that it fell in seamless tresses, undulated against her freshly pressed blouse. One hand fingered a silver pin on her blue tartan wool skirt, as if tempted to pull a rip cord. Her breasts rose and fell with what seemed like seething irritation. She had definitely caught up with her mother in the curves department.

Max, ever alert to the "scent of a story," jabbed me with his elbow and bent to whisper in my ear. "What's with the Spearmint twins, Hawkman? You don't look so good." He had missed nothing: the glances, the light on the memorial, the "love-wounded" expression on Suzanne's face, as he would one day write. With his photographic memory, he translated a mere passing moment into a pivotal scene in his first novel: where his protagonist, Saul, first lays eyes on the great-granddaughter of the rector and is immediately smitten, seeing in her the projection through time of the faltering and decayed idealism of her ancestors.

Max had been unusually silent; under his mother's adoring gaze, he was girding himself for his big moment—a moment he'd been dreading for months. He had been shadowing me like a lost dog ever since that last confirmation class—moon-howling across the Circle or curled into a fetal stupor beside my desk; he was either totally switched on or near comatose, a bipolar disposition that would haunt his short life. By Founder's Day, he'd gunned himself to fever pitch: "Hey, dude, if you can't find good material, make it up; failing that, pull down the fucking temple and trip the light fantastic." He'd spent the week before torturing Squirrel. "Bl-oo—od, bl—oo—oo—d of Christ!" At Saturday dinner, he'd performed a mock Last Supper for his growing band of disciples.

Max's parents sat proudly in the first row. His dad looked pretty damn pleased with himself. His mother, Hannah, didn't seem exactly thrilled; she sat nervously fingering the organ music note for note. Her Viennese dirndl, green loden jacket, and Hermès head scarf decorated with Baroque musical instruments added an exotic touch to the Winsted hothouse. "Oh my God," Max had moaned, hand over his eyes, "not her fucking *Sweet Heidi* peasant's getup!" This trotting out of her patriotic Austrian regalia drove Max to distraction: His mother not only denied she was Jewish but refused to admit "at least her Jewish ancestry." Hannah considered herself blue-blood Catholic Viennese. A discreet ivory and pearl cross hung from a gold necklace. Her lovely delicately boned face was very pale as she intently watched the proceedings, perhaps remembering—as I had learned from Max—her own First Communion at St. Stephen's Cathedral in Vienna (not enough to inoculate her against the Nazis). I could see a lot of her artistic features in Max, especially the dark, brimming eyes and quivering lower lip. She was a world-class pianist and teacher at Juilliard and had escaped to England from Austria in 1939 as a teenage prodigy. The rest of her family—"every brother and sister, cousin, uncle and aunt, and her musician parents," in Max's rendition, had perished at Mauthausen, "hauling granite for the streets of Vienna until they dropped." (Actually, granite mined by the inmates during the war went to various German building projects.) Whereas Hannah was completely erased from Max's novels—and her stand-in is one of the flattest of all of Max's characters—Jack was mercilessly caricatured.

Beaming Jack was at Hannah's side. Nothing fazed Jack: he glided cheerily on, relishing the role of proud dad in his Brooks Brothers worsted-wool pinstripe three-piece suit, sartorially holding his own with the Winsted grandees. Behind his easy smiles was a rugged and determined face, decent toupee, and button bright dark eyes. Max liked to say that his dad was tougher than a month-old bagel. A Brooklyn scamp who made it through Bronx High School of Science with straight A's, Jack snagged a full scholarship to Harvard—where he'd gotten an earful about Winsted—and decided to drop Rabinowitz for Roberts. At Morgan Stanley, he'd managed to impress the partners with his tenacity and genius for numbers, going on to be one of the biggest earners in the place, peddling utility bonds. Some years later, Jack confided to me on the way back from our monthly Durgin Park dinner in Boston and three bottles of Grand Cru Pomerol '59—Max dead asleep in the shotgun seat—that he always felt his life was like Joe DiMaggio's fifty-six-game hitting streak. "Boy, every day, what a nail-biter as you wait for the inevitable." But Jack was just where he'd always wanted to be, where he wanted his son to be. How many of us can say that about our lives?

A very different Jack, Jack Crocket, the ancient silver-haired head-master and Boston Brahmin, rose from the choir stalls, moved to the center of the apse, and raised his burly arms as if in benediction to the flock he'd shepherded since the early twenties. In the echoing silence, he nodded to us with a steady metallic stare. These were his boys, with whom he was well pleased, who had won the Second World War, held the line in Korea, and were fast preparing the beachhead in Vietnam. Old Jack was getting out while the going was good.

When the bishop of Massachusetts went to lay his hands on Max to receive him into the Episcopal Church in the name of the Father, Son, and Holy Ghost, we half-expected a bolt of lightning to come down and vaporize Max's diseased gray matter. But everything went smoothly until we all knelt at the altar rail to take Communion. Max maneuvered himself next to Squirrel, who had been exulting all week while enduring Max's assaults: *Bl–oo–oo–d of Christ.* The bishop of Massachusetts, aged and doddering and rheumy-eyed, dressed in an ivory-colored chasuble, made his way down the line of new supplicants, his silver chalice brimming with red wine as he murmured in a soft, holy voice, "This is the blood of Christ, which is given for you . . ." I took my sip of wine— my front teeth clicking on the cold, hard edge of the silver chalice, prompted by Max's warning to avoid cootie slobber. As if solicitous of such hygiene issues, the bishop expertly wiped the rim with a linen cloth and moved on.

Max proceeded to tip the cup forward and gulp down all he could— in for a dime, in for a dollar. Smacking his lips audibly for effect, Max looked up with a wink at the bishop's numinous countenance. The old boy must've been half-blind, for his face remained composed and focused on the celestial light from above. And then Max began hissing at Squirrel, to his left, who was already seething with the onset of an epileptic fit. As Squirrel took the lowered cup to his lips, Max whispered in his ear, "Just think of it as the Virgin Mary's menstrual bl–oo–oo–d." Squirrel jerked upward, as if taking an M16 slug in the spine, fountaining a ribbon of red that splashed murderously all over the white vestments of the bishop of Massachusetts. Got to hand it to the old sport, he just plodded on—seen it all before—as if nothing unusual had happened.

Strangely, for me, that farcical moment figures less vividly in memory than it might because it seemed only an extension of the forebodings of exile I'd already glimpsed in the agitated wildfire eyes of Suzanne

Williams only minutes before. An exile that would include my growing disenchantment with our generation—Max the avatar—for failing to take up our fathers' banner. The bishop's wine-sodden vestments, a gory simulacrum of the assassination scene in *Julius Caesar*, proved as apt a symbol as any of the breached decorum soon to be a universal complaint among our elders, when tradition is trashed and old truths revealed—less as lies than as irrelevancies of a dated antiquarian.

Max's role in this travesty, like so much else in his fabled life, has never been documented by the scholars who have meticulously picked over his early history for clues to his beguiling themes. Like Dylan, he was self-invented. Oddly, Max used nothing of his dramatic confrontations in confirmation class nor the incident at the altar rail, so ripe for low comedy, in his first novel. This was often the case when his mother, Hannah, was a witness and so might upbraid him for exaggeration, as she disciplined his musicianship: "Keep to the notes, Maxy; that is why the composer wrote sforzando, not mezzo forte." And that is why I find myself not a little chagrined that he chose, instead, to write about my ephemeral moment of youthful insecurity—my exchanged glances with Suzanne and Laura—and transposed it into a celebrated three-page scene when his protagonist first falls in love, a set piece that more than one critic has favorably compared with Proust's adolescent vision of the duchesse de Guermantes during Sunday Mass in the church at Combray.

When, as he admitted many years later, Max first fell in love with Laura Williams.

On the chapel steps, I dutifully shook hands in the receiving line for the new initiates. Headmaster Jack Crocket gave me the once-over and muttered gruffly something about my stellar grades—never a word to me about my father, whom he would have kicked out of Winsted but for my grandmother. But as I was about to move down the receiving line, he pulled me back, squeezing my elbow, and brought his huge face close to mine. "Your grandmother was simply the most beautiful woman I have ever known, a star in the firmament of my affection that I will hold dear to my dying day." You could have blown me over with a feather, hearing such sentiments from the lips of Zeus, a hint of tears in his red-rimmed eyes. I had heard many wonderful things about my grandmother, but not that—that men *and* women considered her the great beauty of her generation, especially in upper-crust Boston and among her Northeast Harbor set.

Seconds later, I was moved down the line of Washington luminaries and members of the board of trustees, who shook my hand with a forensic examination of my Clearasil-blotted zits, a moist nostalgia brewing in their eyes as they wished me Godspeed, reciting fond anecdotes, *dans le temp*, when they and my father roamed the carefree woods and fields of Winsted. Even Bobby Williams, slouched in his parked wheelchair, reached up a welcoming, if badly scarred, hand, his burnt and disfigured face in shadow beneath a Panama hat.

"Where'd you come from, stranger? Come see us at Hermitage; why not—don't need to be shy." His reddened eyes, sunk in puffy toffee-colored folds, sought out my face with a kind of rapt fascination. "We won't bite."

"Yes," echoed Suzanne, her gilded Sloane Street tones chiming as the chapel bells began a soft peal. "You simply must come by when you're back again at Elysium." Her hand gripped mine, squeezing harder. "So sorry about your dear grandmama, a loss to us all." And there was not a disingenuous flicker in her predatory stare: this star of the Royal Ballet, this extraordinary beauty of *her* generation of Trinity College traitors.

Although I was unaware of Suzanne's malevolent reputation in espionage circles, I did have a vague sense that the CIA men and their confreres in the receiving line were riveted by my brief conversation with her: God knows how many among them considered my father a traitor and Suzanne his KGB enabler! Perhaps galvanizing Elliot Goddard to my rescue; sizing up the potentially compromising position, he intervened swiftly, taking my arm in a firm grip—"Suzanne, luv, you must release this fledgling youth to his betters . . . he's still underage"— and spirited me away to a quiet spot under a leafy white oak.

Elliot's deployment of a biting cockney accent was typical of certain expatriate circles; he'd also married Suzanne's maid of honor and, as I would find out, to my dismay, was a fanatical advocate of the Oxfordian camp on the authorship question.

"Rumor has it you've taken up football."

"Last fall, I thought I'd give it a try."

Elliot was clearly in political mode, what with his many peers milling around the chapel entrance, and his recent posting to Saigon, where he ran the Phoenix Program to destroy the Vietcong infrastructure in the south.

"That's great. Say, I've got a book for you to read; keep your eyes peeled at mail call."

"Okay."

"We need to stay in touch, young man." His well-tanned and powerful face beneath a crease of silver-blond hair moved within inches of mine.

"Yes, sir."

"You know about the new headmaster?"

"I guess so." He continued gripping my arm, squeezing.

"A disaster . . ." And with a jut of his shoulder in the direction of Bobby and Suzanne, he indicated the source of the disaster. "You'll keep me up to speed about how it goes?"

"Yes, sir."

"My address will be written on page—what year will you be?"

"Sixty-nine."

"Page sixty-nine, then, Vince Lombardi on coaching: 'Winning is not a sometime thing; it's an all the time thing'—something I need to knock into the heads of a few around here."

And with that he was off, collaring the president's national security adviser, whose son was in my class.

The book arrived the following week with a numbered APO address in Saigon penciled between the lines on page sixty-nine: my first taste of tradecraft.

Elliot played football with my father, who had captained two championship teams at Winsted; they played each other at Yale and Princeton. An OSS veteran, Elliot had recruited my father from Princeton for the CIA in 1948. He had been his best man and given the eulogy at his funeral, as he did at my grandmother's service—glowingly; our two families went way back. Although the subject was never broached between us, I always suspected that he was deeply aggrieved at not having been named my godfather. As with everything else in his life, he had taken matters into his own hands.

When I returned to the receiving line, Joe Alsop, the nationally syndicated columnist and a huge supporter of the American effort to hold the line in Vietnam, awaited me. He scrutinized me from behind his round spectacles, inky black ovals magnifying his penetrating and erudite eyes beneath a scanty widow's peak.

"Your pa was a fixture at my Dumbarton Street table, you know." His clipped Yankee cadences rattled forth. ". . . scintillating insights, steely resolve in a crisis, the most serene judgment when many were wetting their pants at Stalin's machinations. You do him proud."

"Thanks. I read all your columns in the *Tribune*."

"I must tell you something, ahum, ahum, ahum . . ." He eyed me like a bird dog on point, aquiver for the dash of wings and jarring shotgun blast. Then, as if mortified at the prospect of confessing to a fourteen-year-old, he nodded with a wince at a book clutched against his chest, just below a perfectly tied bow tie. "A puzzlement to my scholarly soul, ahum, ahum, ahum—you see, the odd thing is, it was the very last dinner I had with your dad on Dumbarton Street—what, spring of '53, with the Kim Philby spy scandal the buzz of Washington; but he only wanted to talk my ear off about the recent translation of Linear B by Michael Ventris. I've never seen a man more animated, more in a frenzy of raw excitement about the implication for Bronze Age scholarship—for Western civilization! He was positively beside himself. And the crazy thing is, he lit a spark in my muckraker soul, and lo and behold, ten years later my first scholarly tome—for you."

"Wow, well thank you."

He proudly thrust the volume into my hands, saluted like a martinet, and returned to his brother, Stewart, whose war-bride English wife was taking family photos with their son.

Duty done, I made a beeline for the shelter of the apple trees, where I'd left my precious galley proofs of the *Odyssey* on a bench. I stripped off my blazer and luxuriated again in the smell of warm sunlit grass and apple blossoms.

A moment later, slipping away from her father, Laura came over to where I sat, her long, lithe, and muscled legs seeming to exult in their quick strides beneath her short tartan blue skirt. At every step, sunlight glinted off the silver pin in the pleats.

"I don't suppose you have a book for me, as well," I said, not a little desperate to be engaging.

"Who, me? Coals to Newcastle," she said as she sat beside me on the rustic wooden bench that circled the trunk of one of the better-preserved trees.

"What kind of crazy shit was going on up there at the altar rail?" she asked.

"Oh, it was nothing." I glanced at her inquisitive face stitched with leaf patterns. "One of the guys—a little highly strung."

"One of those, huh." She sighed and nervously fingered a blossom.

"You're lucky. Mother won't let me go away to school, not since the Boston Ballet apprentice program—and she still insists on coaching me."

I had always found that she and her mother walked a little weirdly—not that I mentioned it—with their high-hipped exaggerated turnout and straight-backed torsos, riding their long legs like the figurehead of a ship. In the translucent shadows across her winsome face, I detected hints of pensive anxieties not unlike mine. She'd slipped off her flats and arched her feet into the grass. Her toes were strangely calloused, almost deformed, and her feet flexible to the point of being prehensile. And it was a little hard to talk over the bell ringers who were cutting loose with a terrific peal that echoed like toy thunder across the Circle.

"Well," she offered, "*here we are.*" I knew she was looking at me for help in keeping the conversation going, but I was still reeling from that jolt of her mother's hauteur in the chapel. My grandmother would have upbraided me for such an impolite, imbecilic silence. After all, we were fourth cousins, or, as my grandmother used to say when she discovered something slightly off-putting in her ancestry, "Well . . . cousins are cousins."

Laura looked at her feet and then back to me. "Mother said getting on the board of trustees has given Daddy a new lease on life."

"I'll bet."

As if irritated, she roughly tore a pink blossom off a branch and began what I could only describe as a forensic dissection of its five petals, pressing them apart to examine the pollen-brimming stamen, bringing the splayed petals to her nose to breathe of their fragrance, only to detach a petal and savagely crush it to a waxy pulp between her fingertips.

"So pink, so unusual, must be an old variety of Bramley's Seedling to keep its pink color so late past budding. Suppose it could be a Winesap, probably tart and juicy, good for cider." She flashed a look of sensual recognition, as if about to lick her smeared fingers or impart a deeply held secret. "Like the old trees at Elysium in the orchard above the lake . . . old, so very old . . ." Her voice dropped to a near whisper, perhaps in awe of some connection forming in her mind.

Something in her instinctual curiosity struck me as attractive yet also off-putting. And as if sensing this, she grabbed my hand and placed the torn blossom in my palm while taking the book Joe Alsop had presented to me.

"I'll trade you."

By the chapel entrance, Bobby Williams was gesturing broadly from his wheelchair like an arthritic Howdy Doody, yakking with the retiring headmaster as if he now owned the place.

"Well, like Mom says, Thank God—*something for him to do at last.*" She said this last bit with an English accent, in unconscious imitation of her mother. Her toes, covered in bits of mown grass, seemed to be busy digging furrows.

"Are you going to be at Elysium this summer?" she asked.

"Not if my mother can help it—maybe solo if I can swing it."

"I haven't seen her in years."

"She hates the place. Almost as much as she hates this place."

She touched my knee for a moment, as if genuinely intrigued.

"At least she doesn't try to control every moment of your life. Try having a mother who's also your ballet coach."

With this, she began fanning the pages of the book in her hand and examining the illustrations. "*From the Silent Earth: A Report on the Greek Bronze Age.*" She cocked her head. "Strange, I thought he was a political columnist." She opened the front cover and read the inscription. "To Peter Alden, in memory of your father: a great man—the greatest scholar and archaeologist of his day. Fair winds as you make good on all your family's promise: Freedom, justice, love, and honor. Joseph Alsop."

I peered at the flowery inscription with its flourishes and curlicues, not a little touched by his inclusion of the Winsted motto.

"Is that how you think of your father," she asked, "a scholar?"

"Why not . . ."

"My mother's got his *Collier's* articles from before the war."

She closed the book as if to emphasize that factoid, and placed it between us, then laid her hand on my knee again, some generous spirit directing her to the reassuring gesture. "Did you ever get the feeling . . . we're not supposed to like each other?"

What to make of that! Fortunately, her mother's call rang out, Suzanne's animated white arms motioning from a gaggle of trustees hanging around the chapel entrance. Lunch was being served in the dining hall. Laura fumbled to get her shoes on.

"I've got to push Daddy," she said. "So . . ." She stood and I stood. "I guess it's kind of weird, you and me, not being in Elysium and everything."

I squinted in the bright sunlight in the direction of the chapel steps, where Elliot Goddard was flirting with her mother, and shrugged.

"*Here* and not *there*." She made a face and then gestured theatrically to the ground and the sky, like I was too obtuse for words. I shrugged again. "Well, congratulations"—she laughed self-consciously and bent and kissed me gently on the cheek—"guess you got to join the club, too." She waved her hand in a lyrical gesture, as if to encompass the Circle and its myriad associations, which presumably included her father, who'd clawed his way back onto the Winsted board. Then she turned to rejoin her parents, only to spin on her heels and fix me with her pale blue eyes, flicking back a strand of blond hair in frustration. "Join us for lunch—I almost forgot: That's the message from her royal highness."

"Maybe, I'll see."

Then yet another Hermes, in the guise of my godfather, Charles Fairburn, the colonel, as he was affectionately known in British circles, came hurrying to my side, as if he'd been wantonly neglectful of his godfatherly duties.

"Well, you don't look changed, much less worse for wear. Never hurt a fellow, if the hymns are good and the padre makes a good show."

When we shook hands, he spotted Joseph Alsop's new book and with a grunt of dismissal popped his lips: a scholar taking it amiss when an amateur dares to poach hallowed territory.

"Pity, such a pity that all they came up with was bookkeeping at Pylos, the maid's shopping lists and the like. Poor Michael Ventris, I think the disappointment killed him. Should have stuck to his architecture."

Another dismissal from a man of many disappointments, or perhaps a brilliant subterfuge on his part, knowing all he knew about my father's quest for that lost horde of Linear B tablets from Pylos. To assuage the melancholy tenor of our one-sided conversation, I handed him the galley proofs of Lattimore's *Odyssey*. For a moment, it was as if he'd been struck deaf and mute. He floated down to the seat circling the trunk of the apple tree and poured through the pages, checking favorite passages, nodding, grimacing, grudging admiration, as if I'd been swept off the face of the earth. Only the sudden tolling of the hour from the schoolhouse checked his reverie, and, looking up from the pages, he realized all had disappeared into the dining hall.

"You lucky beggar—that Princeton confraternity is good to have at your back." He handed me the volume. "I'd stick with the *Odyssey*: The butchery of the *Iliad* is just too damned depressing." Straightening his Corpus Christi College tie, he threw back his shoulders. "Lunch, and I've been instructed to bring the young Alden, scion and heir, along to the Williamses' table and make peace. Coming?"

"We have crew practice. I'm already late."

"A shame. Suzanne will be disappointed." We shook hands, and I smiled at his greasy fingernails. The colonel collected and restored old motorcars; in fact, I could see his splendid silver '38 Bentley Vanden Plus Open Tourer parked in front of the schoolhouse. "And I promised your mother I'd keep a lookout. So, a rain check, next Sunday for lunch on me. You pick the restaurant."

"Sounds good."

"I'll call you." And he strode off at a fast clip to join his mistress and the young girl he thought his own.

That lunch wouldn't happen for another two years.

As I rowed a one-man shell that afternoon, the events of the day spinning through my mind, I wondered as to the curious, if not frustrated, promptings of Laura in our brief conversation. I still marvel at how blithely oblivious I was to all the bad blood between our families, and the odd mixture of lies and self-serving selective memory that had been showered gratis upon me. As if I needed protecting from my own father.

In my school days, my escape was the river.

Rowing was how I first discovered the nature of time, the way a child does, by doing. It is the joy of total exertion, of the rushing wake, the growing momentum at each stroke, moving with liquid heat, as your trailing aqueous footprint evaporates behind, merging into the indifferent past. In the glide between strokes, I felt immortal, racing heart and aching muscles be damned. It is not time that passes, but we who pass. That is the great dream and lie of youth. We think we are moving forward, that we know where we are headed, but all we will ever know already lies in our wake. The experienced rower learns to keep his eye on the fixed point of the past. As a historian, this was a lesson I learned well.

The thing on which Max and I parted ways.

Respect for the past, for the facts, is why I feel bound to mention a few anecdotes about Jack Crocket, even if he played such a minor role in our story. Though he retired after our first year, Jack Crocket serves as the presiding headmaster throughout the pages of *Like a Forgotten Angel*. Max clung to the Reverend Jack Crocket, "old man Crocket," or "old Jack," as he was affectionately called for "artistic" reasons (*Atlantic* interview with Max, September 12, 1981). Crocket went back over forty years, when he was picked by my grandmother to save the school from the scandals surrounding Amory Williams in the twenties. He was cold-cold-roast-beef Boston and then some, a Brahmin intellectual in the mold of Harvard's Charles W. Eliot, and a tradition-loving reformer. Pink-cheeked, tall, and sinewy, with a withering gaze, Crocket had shepherded the school through the decades of the Depression, the Second World War and Korea, and on to our looming involvement in Vietnam. He had known my father as a student and man, and appointed him to the board of trustees after the war; he had spoken movingly about him at a Founder's Day service in 1955, when my father was officially numbered with the dead, the last time my mother attended a Winsted function. Crocket was Winsted incarnate—he knew the names and faces of almost all living alumni; his youthful memories included General Alden, whom he'd heard lecture as a young student at Harvard. He was a conduit of values, steadfast and strong, the vision of the founders and the Winsted motto ever bright in his eyes: freedom, justice, love, and honor. Old man Crocket and my grandmother had brought the first black students to Winsted in the thirties; and in 1963, old Jack took twelve Winsted boys with him to Washington to march with Martin Luther King, Jr.

Max's fictional headmaster, a dyed-in-the-wool reactionary, is pure caricature—something Max's biographers fail to note, much less Jack's disastrous successor. Nor have I found anywhere mention that Max played a piano recital during the closing celebrations for Jack Crocket's retirement. Old Jack sat in the audience with his usual wintry stare. At the end of the performance, as Max closed his program with a Chopin nocturne, the headmaster's face had dissolved into tears.

Said a flummoxed faculty member a row in front of me, "Why bless my soul, I didn't think old Jack had the hydraulics in him."

When I saw those tears, I was instantly reminded: *a star in the firmament of my affection . . .*

The critics—the academic biographers are the worst—extol Max Roberts as the great literary rebel of our generation. When not comparing him to Joyce, Salinger's Holden Caulfied was often enlisted (*Time*): "Saul, the quintessential Jewish outsider, is a Jewish Holden Caulfield, whose revolt makes manifest the hollowness of the WASP establishment and the burning dissatisfaction of the sixties." Max was a great talent, no doubt, but a great literary artist must deal with some semblance of reality, not a self-serving parody of that reality. The word *genius* has been bandied around by the adoring critics: a status granted to those who require immunity from the standards applied to every other human being on the planet.

Hemingway was a foul-mouthed, depressive, wife-abusing alcoholic. Picasso a cruel egomaniac and serially abusive misogynist whose sexual appetites energized his art. And I'm not even going to dignify Jim Morrison with a comment—Max's hero in our school days, who abused his family, his band members, the woman who stuck by him to his drunken, debauched end.

Leave great art behind and all is forgiven.

But the damage lingers with the art.

For me, Max's mind—that crapshoot of genes and memory, that self-absorbed republic of vice and virtue—seemed to spawn the maelstrom of careless irresponsibility that engulfed us. He was my boon companion on a wild ride to nowhere. He invented himself by reinventing us. Perhaps it is worth remembering in this regard that our brains were evolved, not for introspection, but for survival in changing times, and if survival of memory may be regarded as the highest good, and symbolic language and metamorphic imagery our greatest achievement, then Max was certainly a triumph of Darwinism—but not of the truth! When you were with him, you felt as if time stopped, that you had privileged access to an eternal present, that his gig was the only game in town.

Which is why, for four long years, I resisted dropping the dime on the son of a bitch.

May 3, 1929
Winsted School

Dear Mother,

Sorry to disappoint you, but I'm not going to be playing baseball this spring. I've opted for rowing, even if the Naushon does smell a bit ripe on warm days. The mills, especially the paper mills in Winsted, discharge the most horrible things into the river. I know your great admirer and our intrepid headmaster, Jack C. (and baseball coach!) thought I'd make a marvelous pitcher, but I find a certain serenity pulling an oar with my pals. Yes, Elliot talked me into it; he occupies the seat behind me and now grumbles, since the Reverend Oakes made me stroke. There is some indefinable joy in the rhythm and lovely geometries of sweating bodies moving as one. Reminds me of the lyrical patterns found on the best Corinthian pottery. Perhaps I fantasize a bit about Greek triremes scudding the Cycladic blue. Besides, all one hears around the diamond is talk of the Boston Red Sox, something a Yankees fan cannot abide.

And yet another disappointment, I fear: I'm not going to try to get the typescript of my "Alexander the Great" published. I know that project is near and dear to your heart, but it would take too much time, what with my studies—and, at the prompting of a new master of Latin and Greek, Virgil Dabney, I have quite suddenly become engaged with Homer as never before. Virgil Dabney—I'll save a description of this engaging fellow for another letter—suggested I think about translating the *Iliad* into English as a way of bettering my Greek and improving my English prose, which, as you always remind me, *is* my native tongue! I was skeptical at first but then found myself drawn to Homer's subtle artistry and the telling details of a distant world. Of course, there is Homer's scrumptious metaphors of battle and the skullduggery of the gods as they vie to help their favorites among the mortal Achaeans and Trojans, but what surprises me is how Achilles has more dimension as a character than I ever realized: The godlike hero regards the whole thing as a cock-up! But for Patroclus's Zeus-engineered death— slain by Apollo no less—the son of Peleus would have packed up and sailed home. Better a long life tending his vines in bucolic Thrace than immortal glory as a shade in Hades. And then there is all the squabbles over abducted women—Helen, Briseis, and Chryseis—aren't men ridiculous! The frustrating thing is that there is so much more to the story of Achilles than Homer gives us, almost nothing about his father, Peleus, or Thetis, his goddess mother—that had to be an interesting upbringing, being raised by a hero and goddess! Nor does it help starting the epic near the end of the Trojan War, with barely anything about Helen's abduction by Paris, or the early fighting when Achilles, once gallant and chivalrous—and not a little cynical—seemed to be rather ambivalent about the whole bloody mess. His wrathful bloodlust to slaughter Hector is really an aberration brought about by grief and despair, or at least it's nice to think so.

Truth is, I'm getting a little obsessive about all this. Even at night with the general's sweet gum trees rustling the stars beyond my window, I find myself dreaming about obscure passages I can't translate, waking only to sniff around Homer's lines once more for clues to the language eluding me. And not just lost stories, but the unsettling strangeness of the thing—a mystery, like the identity of Homer himself, as if very different times and places are all jostled together—time out of mind and vague echoes of a golden age before even Mycenae came into being. And no, it's not "my overwrought imagination," as you like to call it: We do have snippets from other sources—at least six other epics from the lost Trojan War poems of the Epic Cycle. But the real story remains tantalizingly just over the horizon. Perhaps more will turn up. Perhaps the Linear B tablets that Evans discovered at Knossos will offer clues, if only we could decipher the damn things. I may save my translation for the *Odyssey*; I find Odysseus's quest for hearth and home somewhat more appealing for all his unscrupulous wiles (even if he cheats on Penelope), while Achilles—ever standing on honor—is a bloodthirsty butcher. All those brutal and graphic descriptions of wounds along the banks of the Scamandros remind me not a little of father's medical notebooks from his Argonne field surgery, the ones you showed me last summer at Elysium. I'm glad you got Harvard Medical School to publish them, but I find illustrations of battle wounds a disturbing reminder of yet another pointless war, in which father, as you always tell me, found, like Achilles, little meaning and only cruel suffering— deadly sport for the booty lusts of Agamemnon and the entertainment of the uncaring gods. In some ways, Priam and Hector and the cultivated tastes of Troy are a cut above the barbarous Achaeans.

Off to the river and our long, curved-bottom ships—and yes, the apple trees on the Circle are in full glorious bloom.

> Your loving and not so obedient son,
> John

3 THE MAX I REMEMBER WAS, IF ANYTHING, A LOT crazier than his bookish alter ego in his coming-of-age novel, *Like a Forgotten Angel,* or the conniving, drug-addled lover of his second ballet-world novel, *Gardens of Saturn,* in which Laura and the Williamses get the treatment.

For me, emblazoned in memory, are his endless afternoons seated in detention, raven-haired ringlets bowed, chewed pen a miniature metronome below his right ear: supplicant to the texts he worshipped.

And one day in particular, a day of golden spring green that endures in my mind like an urtext of a Winsted spring, or, as Max would have it, a memory point endowed by his facetious whimsy before Vietnam ended our careless days.

The sun was streaming through the immense fantail windows of the schoolhouse study hall, sprinkling the long rows of desks with a tranquil leafy light—a glorious light I cannot remember having seen anywhere else: first sifted through pink dogwoods, then refracted in the antique glass panes, and finally held in a kind of amber-roseate suspension on the two hundred varnished and ink-incised desktops. Riding high in the oak-paneled study hall, where they gazed blankly from their somber niches, were marble busts of classical philosophers and statesmen and generals (faithful copies of ancient originals—with the exception of Lincoln, Grant, and Washington—made to my great-grandfather's specifications between 1895 and 1908 by an American sculptor working in Rome). These noble paragons stared down from their Olympian perches like slightly jaundiced gods, set in judgment over the living and the ranks of the dead. Reminders of the classical virtues General Alden held dear: freedom, justice, love and honor, as emblazoned in the

Winsted motto. Below, carved into the paneled walls were the names of all the graduating classes going back to 1884.

Max mouthed his leitmotif as he caught sight of me, sticking out his tongue at a contemplative Virgil, while waving off a smelly fart, then the finger directed at the chapel beyond the study hall windows: "Chapel of Love . . . Hades' House." He was copying out lines from Nabokov's *Lolita*. Detention required transcribing lines from a textbook, but he'd quickly realized that no one actually checked the subject matter after the lines were turned in. And nymphets were very much on his agenda. Every now and then, when the duty master wasn't looking, he would furtively open the top of his desk and read the front page of his *Herald Tribune*. When the bell ending detention rang, he flung the newspaper at me, as if I were to blame for the headlines, which noted the escalating fighting in Vietnam and introduction of ever-larger numbers of American troops. Max was horrified at a graphic photo of villagers fleeing from a napalm strike that had overshot its target, leaving charred bodies in its wake of jellied petroleum. Of course, he blamed Winsted, Harvard, and DuPont—not necessarily in that order: all breeding grounds of imperialist flunkies. We were all only too well aware that a handful of Winsted's most esteemed graduates were in top foreign-policy positions, first under Kennedy and then in the Johnson administration. A near score populated the upper ranks of the CIA.

I tossed back the *Tribune* and tried to change the subject as we exited the schoolhouse. Outside, the warm afternoon air and redolent dogwoods and the rhythmic cracks of batting practice quickly banished the stark black-and-white images of a far-off war. How could any mind, especially a young mind, encompass such a spring and such a scene of horror? Max walked slowly, sometimes taking my arm to bring me to a halt as the report of a distant bat sent a ball soaring into the blue. He sighed. "Know what my father told me after our First Communion: 'Well, Maxie, this is the happiest day of my life since the Dodgers beat the Yanks in the '55 World Series.'" Max doubled over with hysterical laughter and, with a tattoo of punches to my shoulder, ambled on. I was yearning to get to crew practice; he to mull over the contradictions of our privileged lives. The ancient stand of bowed and gnarled apple trees glittered a dull scarlet-gray against the two-tone strips of green left by a tractor mower. The halo of dark grass beneath the trees, where the groundskeeper couldn't duck under the lowest branches, was littered with the shriveled blossoms of Founder's Day.

As we drew near the varsity diamond, the sharp pops became more insistent, delightful staccato notes that powered those white specks skyward, their graceful dying arcs ending in the upheld mitts of perfectly positioned outfielders. Forever in my mind, the whispered slap of leather on leather belying time's moving shadow. Max slipped on a pair of mirrored aviator sunglasses, as if to disguise the inquisitive sparkle dancing in his eyes—lest the fervent Boston Red Sox fans who plagued Winsted might take him amiss: a Yankees scout on the sneak, caught between a rock and the oedipal contempt of his Brooklyn-born father. Already, he had a gorgeous full-body tan, concealing the few acne blemishes that marred his Sal Mineo jaw where it merged in a graceful half dimple. He had taken to sunbathing in the nude in his secret forest hermitage near the Naushon River. Somehow he'd managed to weasel out of mandatory afternoon sports—lest he injure his hands, maybe claiming the need for practice time on the Steinway grand in the lecture hall. Since the days of the rector, Samuel Williams, and his son and second headmaster, Amory, Winsted held a special regard for the musically gifted, especially pianists. For this alone, Max got cut big-time slack: tender appreciations that went unmentioned in his novel of renegade adolescence.

"Trying to remain incognito?" I asked, watching the panorama of the school glide by across his face.

"Every little bit helps. They can't accuse this Jew boy of deicide."

"Max, give it a fucking rest."

"Okay—okay, I know: I *know* I'm paranoid."

"Who's the letter from?" I grabbed an envelope from his shirt pocket.

"Beth-an-ey." He snatched it back. "Her second this week."

"You got one from Sally yesterday—such a horndog. How do you do it?"

"Just gotta love 'em, Pete, just got to give 'em some of that ole-time lovin'." He made a little jerking motion with his arm, a leering smile and lascivious bit of tongue work. "Your Dr. Zeus was quite the charmer in that department."

"Hey, broad brows and lightning strikes—knock 'em dead."

"Listen, I only get to write to my girlfriends, see them over vacations, when I am permitted to give up my monastic vows."

"A long, hard summer, no doubt."

"Ah . . . I shall estivate in the horizontal up the Canale Grande," Again with prancing fingers, head thrown back, humming a Vivaldi harpsichord sonata, only to segue into a current hit. "Hey, where did we go/ Days when the rain came?/ Down in the hollow/ Playin' a new game/ Laughing and a-running, hey, hey . . ."

"Behind the stadium/ With you, my brown-eyed girl," I sang out.

"Hey, hey . . . except she had blue eyes. Don't think I didn't see you under the apple trees."

"Is that all you ever think about?"

Max stopped and stared at me, clucking like a mother hen, then spitting it out.

"You do like girls, don't you?"

"Of course I do."

"So tell me about your little Lo-li-ta, your lo-lo, your la-la—your divine lo."

"Drop it, Max. I've told you; I've known Laura Williams since I was a kid."

"That disqualifies?"

He gave me an exasperated look and pushed his glasses down his nose in imitation of the Reverend Paul Oakes.

"You know, you don't have to lust *only* in your heart." He threw his arm around me and humped my thigh. "Ah, my tender virginal friend, if you only understood the goddess of my idolatry, all that you are missing. Ah . . . La Serenissima . . ." Max brought his fingers to his lips and let fly with a heavenward kiss. "They never burned a heretic there."

"Where?"

"Venice. Meine mutter is teaching a master class at the music academy in Venice this summer—on the Canale Grande, no less. I've been enlisted."

"My grandmother took me to Venice on our last trip together. There was this general skinned alive by the Turks, and they sent his flayed skin back to Venice as a warning; they stuck it in an urn in one of the churches."

Max gave me a queasy squint and then made a motion, as if dispersing a bad smell.

"Did I ever relate to you Saint Jerome's views on virginity?" Max composed himself with palms down, hands outstretched, in imitation of Paul Oakes readying himself in the chapel pulpit. "'I praise wedlock, I praise marriage, but it is because they give me virgins. . . . Though God can do all things, he cannot raise a virgin up after she has fallen. He is able to free one who has been corrupted from the penalty of her sin, but he refuses her the crown.'"

"Where do you pick up this crap?"

"Where else, Oak-man's study, his little lending library—better to know thine enemy. How 'bout this: Saint Augustine beat off in church as a kid." Max made a face and pumped his fist crotch-high. "Not that I can blame him. I get the urge, too, during a long, boring sermon."

"Max," I yelled. He had veered off the path to take a shortcut across the Circle. Walking on the Circle, except on Sunday, was strictly verboten.

I began to follow him, but stopped when I caught sight of two prefects in the distance.

"Max," I called again, and pointed to the two figures loitering in front of the dining hall. Catching sight of them, he retreated back to the path.

"Damn," he mumbled, "the Spanish Inquisition has got their spies everywhere."

"Shortcut not worth three black marks, huh, Max?"

"Long cut, you mean—uncircumcised Philistines." He spat, eyeing the prefects. "Only this place could make even the grass sacrosanct— create another icon of inviolability." He grimaced and brought a choking hand to his throat. "What've you got in there?" He made a grab for my bulging pants pocket.

"It's nothing."

He collared my neck in a half-Nelson and began riffling my pockets.

"What is this shit . . . piece of brick?" He tossed the brick fragment in the air, where I caught it. "More arrowheads, and hey, Mouseketeers, a rusty nail?"

"It's an iron nail," I protested, pointing out the squared-off edges, "and over two hundred years old."

He wrinkled his nose at the rusty residue on his fingers.

"You sure are an oddball scavenger." He handed back my finds and glanced across the Circle to see if the prefects were gone.

"It's called archaeology."

"Chip off the old blockhead—huh. When will you learn you can't dig up the past; it's all . . . in *you*." He daggered my chest and sidestepped back onto the grass, holding out his arms as if walking a tightrope.

What Max never understood, even as he disparaged my scavenger instincts, is that archaeology is more about creating the past than discovering it. The stuff we dig up remains mute unless we give it a story. And the more distant, the more obscure the past, the more it becomes our creation. Even the most splendid artifacts beg us to breathe life into them and tell their tale; it is all about fiction, peer-reviewed and scholarly fiction, perhaps, but fiction nevertheless. In this, Max and I were more on the same page than he ever suspected.

"Come on, featherbrain, tell me something I don't know, give me some more lowdown on your dad's sleuthing; surely you know more about his cloak-and-dagger stuff than you're divulging to your best pal."

We'd agreed this was off-limits. My mother and grandmother had told me exactly zero about my father's days in the OSS and, later, the CIA. It was only his years as a world-famous archaeologist before the war that had registered in my youthful imagination (I had read all his books and articles many times over), and a deep-rooted sense that the only real truth was something you turned up, that you could touch. I saw his life, the one glimpsed in the archaeological journals and his magazine articles, his letters to his mother, as one dedicated to historical inquiry backed up by facts, artifacts, a life of integrity and academic probity. His boyhood room at our home in Elysium was my shrine to that probity.

"I told you; I barely remember him, and the CIA stuff is all classified."

He gave me a shove. "You're so fucking brain-dead. You're so weirdly incurious. Almost as weird as your chapel."

"Hardly. It's the Williams Chapel."

"How are you ever gonna get laid, Hawkman? You think the chicks want to talk about football, you think she's going wet her panties over some cruddy arrowhead—hey, babe, I've been out cruisin' for arrowheads all day."

"It's Algonquin and it's over three hundred years old. And you can hold it in your hand—it's *real*, Max, a real piece of the world and a human story."

"Shit, you're such a lost cause."

We stopped and eyed the proud Gothic facade of the chapel, contentedly bathed in afternoon sunlight. Max wagged his finger.

"And speaking of lost causes . . . how do you people manage to reproduce anyway?"

"Chapel sex," I said, desperate as always to keep the ball in play.

I saw a wicked smile crease his lips as he jittered his flattened palm in front of my face like Moe in the Three Stooges, bonking me on the head as I ducked away.

"You're as blinkered as the rest." He grabbed my arm and started hustling me toward the entrance. "C'mon, maybe what you need is a personally guided tour of your precious"—in perfect Boris Karloff—"Chapel of L-o-v-e . . . Hades' House."

"And *bl-o-o-d* of Christ."

We screamed with laughter.

Max held the heavy oak door open for me, bowing as I passed. Inside, it was strangely cool, the crickets silenced, echoing shadows redolent of marble polish, Clorox, and beeswax-infused mahogany. A shaft of light struck the wall of carved limestone across from the door, where the large dedicatory inscription to General Alden took pride of place. The exquisitely chiseled inscription describing his exploits and wounding at Antietam was surrounded by a decorative border of broken shackles. Memorials on either side commemorated early masters and school staff who had fought in the Civil War: "Heroes of the Great Rebellion."

As we walked the side aisle, our footsteps echoing off the checkerboard of black-and-white Carrara marble, Max took my arm as Virgil had Dante's. Above us in the high vaulting of the nave, a saffron-blue iridescence filtered downward from the La Farge windows. Max stopped and pointed out the smaller memorials carved into individual blocks of limestone.

"Spirits of fathers past, huh?" said Max, nudging me. I shrugged. He ran his fingers over some particularly beautiful lettering. "Ah, the Libro d'Oro." A queer rapture came into his dark eyes. "What secrets of their prison house could they tell?"

"They'll outlast your insipid scribbling in the Great White Way."

He looked at me, intrigued.

"Ah, remember, my dear boy, that only the ephemeral has life, only in the passage does our soul have motion; walled monuments are only the silent boundary markers of death, from which there is no return."

I recited from memory: "'Even in the House of Hades there is left something, a soul and an image, but there is no real heart of life in it.'"

This was Achilles mourning the spirit of Patroclus from Lattimore's *Iliad*, which I had just devoured.

How smart we thought our ideas, that our verbal dexterity alone might weave a cloak to keep us safe.

But there is bullshit . . . *and there is bullshit*. Max's was a kind of rehearsal, a playing with disguises, a few of which—his *and* mine—filtered into the pages of his novels. I must have heard the kind of claptrap that flowed that day in a hundred variations. And yet . . . I have to admit, his beguiling words, unlike my more pedantic reflections—how can I put it?—had something of the effect of a pebble dropped into a deep well: the wait, the silence, the tiny distant splash . . . and later, sometimes years later, the outward-bound ripples catch you unawares. As they do on the pages of his novels . . . as they do here.

He raised his eyebrows at the hint of emotion in my voice at Achilles' sentiments and released his grip on my arm, reaching his long, tapering fingers to the inscription on my father's memorial.

JOHN DAVENPORT ALDEN III
1914 – 1954
WHEREFORE BY THEIR FRUITS
YE SHALL KNOW THEM.

"Strange words for such a man?" he said.

"Yeah, any better suggestions?"

"Hmm, what do you think, one of his CIA buddies?"

Silently, I squeezed the arrowhead in my pocket.

As if considerate of my sensibilities—I never knew him to be unkind to my face—he turned and beckoned me toward the nave. Cool pastel light played across the choir stalls and glittered in paisley shadows on the white marble altar, where a plain gold cross shimmered. Max looked around as though slightly lost and loosened his tie à la Rodney Dangerfield doing stand-up. He shook his head and seemed to bite his lip. All I could think was, Dear Brutus drawn back to the scene of assassination.

"I mean . . . it's so . . . squeaky—clean. It's like some kind of Brooks Brothers religion, so well tailored and fully cut that you don't even realize there's a body beneath. I mean, this is supposed to be Christianity—right? So where's Christ?" He gestured upward and turned where he stood, his brown eyes staring blankly like those in the marble face of Virgil in the study hall. "Nowhere to be found: out of office—out to lunch. The cross on the altar is empty—no crucified body rent with wounds, no stigmata streaming blood, no crown of thorns, no agony or passion, no sorrow or weeping. Where the hell is this godhead we're supposed to worship?"

Max stared up at the color-swarming windows of stained glass, those justly famous windows by John La Farge executed in 1890 at a price of $18,000 a pop, or nearly $400,000 in today's money. (These figures are detailed in Max's novel, precisely as he copied them from the artist's invoices in the school archives. Just another example of how fastidious Max could be with facts when they interested him.) Max stood there, entranced, his face luminous as he projected his voice like an actor to the upper balcony.

"And what's all this, pray tell?" He gestured to the sunlit windows above. "Abraham and Isaac, David and Goliath, Samson destroying the temple, Moses and the Ten Commandments?" He shrugged and shook his head. "Those are my people—goddamn it." And then he eyed me as if somehow I were to blame. "You've fucking enlisted *my* people in your little charade. No, no—worse: You've fucking stolen our material! And then messed with it. And what about Jesus' mother? At least the Catholics admit that Jesus had a mother. But you'd never know it from the Winsted chapel—no Virgin Mary need apply here. They prefer women to be as inessential as possible, not even created from dust like Adam—the good earth—but born from his side, from a fucking rib no less. And God knows my people probably started it with all their fastidious taboos about menstruation and impurity. But this is raised to another level of obscenity. To drink the Savior's blood—imagine! It's a fucking pagan ritual: eating the dead god's body and blood. And this blood thing—huh? What's all this fear of defilement, this sin and guilt business? Who's kidding whom? Why is it that they always want to set things apart: men and women, life and death, body and soul, heaven and earth, good and evil, God and man?" His lips trailed spittle as he raged on like the poor spirit of Achilles among the shades. "To justify their power, that's what; to hold sway with another ideology, to break the seamless unity of life on their misbegotten cross of power . . . or drop napalm on innocent peasants. The evil is in us; it's not some theological abstraction."

"Tell it to Hitler or Stalin, or Mao—you're a perfect candidate for rehabilitation in the Cultural Revolution."

I have this lingering image of Max turning and turning there before me in the nave, a slow-motion whirling dervish, light shining within his puzzled eyes as he raved on, seemingly desperate to draw down the plague gods that haunted him. I was mystified yet strangely touched, as if he had removed some blindfold from my eyes and the chapel stood barren around me. First the rituals, then the very stones—Attila could have done no more. I can't properly explain the distancing from life such moments with Max produced—the furious ferment in our adolescent brains that made light of the world as we found it. For things like the chapel (temples and sanctuaries and holy places: and I've excavated more than a few) have always been with us and, I suppose, always will be, even when the faith inspiring their creation is moribund. And yet these places, like memories of home ground, retain a hold in our hearts—a kind of innocent awe at the faith that once inspired them. To entirely disregard such things is to impoverish ourselves.

What Max could never grasp, at least not then, not in the beginning, is that certain places, like the greatest novels, take us over because of their affecting associations of voice and tone, a grace and intimacy of spirit . . . for the music does matter.

In his first novel, this scene in the chapel ends with the following: "'My people got it in the neck—hecatombs for your fucking sins? Like your Christ, your Jew sacrifice, they got crucified by the millions.' Saul shrugged his shoulders, tears streaming down his cheeks, and walked away from his erstwhile friend, knowing that on this and other things they would never be of one mind."

No, Max did not leave his erstwhile friend, nor did he argue when I told him he'd be the first in line for reeducation in Mao's Utopia. He smiled gently, that knowing smile of his, and took my arm and, like the poet had with another wanderer into the realms of the dead, led me down the nave to the enormous Saint-Gaudens bronze memorial dedicated to the rector's first son.

SAMUEL WILLIAMS II—A JOY TO HIS FAMILY,
LIGHT TO THE AGES.

Max reached to the bronze angels, to the young women's faces in three-quarter profile, at once remotely aristocratic but with the barest hint of sensual release in their full parted lips and compressed eyebrows. These were the celebrated models of Saint-Gaudens, and the architect Stanford White, and his painter colleague Thomas Dewing (who painted the murals at Hermitage). Many were the young daughters of poor Irish immigrants recruited off the streets of New York, seduced in a hidden studio and bachelor pad set high above Madison Square Garden, custom-made by White for secret trysts. That exquisite irony did not make it into Max's novel. I watched his delicate yet incredibly strong fingers try to read the rapture on those longing faces (trembling under the lustful gaze of the artist-seducer?), as if the lucent turquoise patina might yield to his entreaties.

Then he was on to the lettering embellished in the Winsted colors of gold and crimson and black.

The inscription celebrates the short life of the rector's eldest son, Samuel Williams II, a Harvard graduate barely twenty-six, who had died tragically and scandalously in 1891.

Like a reader of braille, Max closed his eyes and let his fingers play over the relief lettering as if searching for the notes to a lost melody.

He whispered, "Do you have any idea what this is all about?"

I shrugged. "I suppose . . . just what it says . . . 'let your soul float free on the river of life, the river of Time.'"

"Yes, yes—the boilerplate, but don't you see. That's the point . . . the deceit . . . all of it hushed up and then forgotten. Nobody remembers— or cares."

"Enough, I'm out of here—already late for crew practice."

He whispered, "The prodigal son, Sam—a golden-haired athlete and classics scholar. Three years out of Harvard, he committed suicide. He was part of a crowd of known homosexuals, artists, composers, and poets. Jumped into the Charles dead drunk out of shame and unhappiness and anxiety that he'd be revealed and bring disgrace to his family—especially his father, Samuel, the rector, who had cofounded Winsted with your great-grandfather. Sam's younger brother, Amory Williams, second headmaster, knew all about it—and worse. Amory had been taken on to teach classics—here, at Winsted; he was part of the same homosexual underground, that Harvard circle of aesthetes. Amory taught classics for almost thirty years at Winsted before he became headmaster. All the nude classical statues of male heroes and gods in the classics classrooms belonged to him. This man—think of it—the man your grandmother fired, taught here for *decades*, taught beautiful young boys their Latin and Greek, their Ovid and Homer, watched them grow, watched them swim nude in the pool he had specially built for his lovelies, watched them go off to the First World War and never return . . . and as far as anyone knows, never laid a hand on any of them. And he loved this chapel, this place above all things. The rector, his son Amory, and his daughter, Isabella, built the chapel to Sam's memory, son and brother—that golden boy—who embodied, in

the eyes of his demimonde, the highest Platonic ideals of boy love, the
ennoblement of patriarchic values . . . the light, the color, the music, the
poetry and incense of the Mass, the mystic unity in the risen body of
Christ. Think of it: Amory's headmaster, teacher of classics, a homosexual—who married late and to a fabulous, wildly talented artist—forever
filled with unrequited love for his young students *and* the Episcopal
Church." Max took my arm and brought his face close to mine. "I mean,
doesn't it just slay you? The ambiguities and unrealized feelings—the
delicious contradictions that haunt this place—everywhere you look. I
mean, zap, wham, powee-e-e."

I was dumbfounded. I couldn't tell if he was kidding, if he was making it up as he went along—but what a compelling tale. (And accurate
in many but not all details!) What wonderful grist for the future novelist. No wonder he became so obsessed with this story once it began to
materialize in his mind. I felt stupid, incurious, if not simply benighted.
Within weeks of Founder's Day, galvanized by my exchanged glances
across the nave with Suzanne and Laura Williams, when, for a few
magical moments on a certain Sunday—two at most—in spring, the
Saint-Gaudens memorial becomes magically illuminated by the angled
sunshine through stained glass, he'd already managed to plow through
the two published volumes of school history, purloined school records
from the library archives (as he later purloined my father's letters), and
was slowly, very carefully and systematically stealing files from the headmaster's office. He'd even gone into the archives of *The Boston Globe* and
Boston Herald. All this and more would notoriously find its way into
Like a Forgotten Angel. (*The New York Times Book Review* heralded its
publication like a nonfiction exposé of the eastern establishment.)

And yet for all his digging and intuitive genius, he missed the back
story, and with it, my father's story. He came tantalizingly close, getting
most of the sad scandals surrounding the suicide of the rector's son
and Amory Williams's disastrous run as headmaster and dismissal by
my grandmother (casus belli of the families' split), but missed the most
extraordinary tales of all. I hasten to add, this is always the fatal flaw of
careless historians: They become enchanted only by the details that fit
the story they've already fallen in love with.

"The thing I don't get," he went on, fingering the intaglio inscription
from the *Essays and Letters,* "is the uneven pattern of the wording, the
letters highlighted in gold. You see the pattern they make, like a mushroom or a tree; but if you justify the left margin and read the letters

in vertical rows top to bottom and bottom to top, it spells out: "Eternal love and peace—Pearce Breckenridge." I can't figure it out. Who is Pearce Breckenridge?

That's how close he got, literally at his fingertips.

Perhaps I am being unfair, for it took me half a lifetime and the fall of the Berlin Wall to be able to answer his question. Part of the answer was contained in the envelope my grandmother handed to my father just days before he left, the one containing the 1877 clippings from the *Natchez Weekly Democrat* and the thirty-odd Pinkerton reports, and part lay in the correspondence between General Alden (who had been well acquainted with ciphers in his army days) and the rector, Samuel Williams, from 1863 to 1890 that my grandmother had selectively dug out of the family archives. Max had easily deciphered the memorial inscription, a feat—unlike the staggering complexity of deciphering Linear B, which obsessed my father and his colleagues—not to be sneezed at.

I could not then, even as a budding historian, conceive such a tangled coil of causation—even now it boggles the mind—around my own family. But one thing certainly was dawning on me: Something very dear and near to me was under threat . . . and my best friend could not be trusted.

Like Odysseus pouring his blood libations in Hades, Max had stirred up our underworld spirits.

It happens when you break the cocoon of childhood, when the past is no longer the past. When you turn your head to the flash of movement in your peripheral vision: the thing glimpsed in the mirror behind you, between lines on a page that seem strangely familiar . . . in a woman's sigh of release when she looks right through you, and you realize you are alone . . . and never alone.

Never . . .

And so I find myself returning to the image that endures—not the comic stand-up, the persecuted outsider and addicted balletomane of his novels, but my Max, like an ecstatic shaman, slowly turning in that prismatic glow from the La Farge windows, traveler in the fourth dimension, as he embarked on his journey into our hearts and lives, as he began to deconstruct the world as we found it, and so confound us with his.

Where he remains. We his subjects and abettors. His prisoners in time.

4 WHEN I ARRIVED BACK AT WINSTED IN THE FALL
of my fourth-form year, the older boys were wearing their hair
longer, frayed jeans instead of khakis, and dismissive smirks
became de rigueur. Once cigarette smoking in the woods and
stashed pints of Jim Beam had constituted reckless behavior. Now LSD
and even heroin were found in the possession of sixth formers. Not
to mention older brothers and sisters, and recent graduates on campuses across the country, who were definitely up to no good. And even
though a continent separated us from the Dionysian frenzy of Haight-
Ashbury, Jim Morrison's orgiastic pleas throbbed down darkened hall-
ways in the wee hours. But the Doors were the least of it.

No one could figure what funky weed the trustees had been smoking to produce the likes of the Reverend Byron Bertram Folley. Was it
a joke, a deception, a freak blunder on the part of those oh so wise men,
many who ran large Wall Street firms that specialized in mastering
risk-reward ratios or, worse, CIA division chiefs who were tasked to
know the critical importance of leadership and character in maintaining the integrity of institutions, much less faltering regimes that needed
bucking up? Some said they made their decision on the assumption
that a little change of style would be beneficial for a tradition-bound
school like Winsted, where the growing unrest over Vietnam was lapping the ramparts. The self-critical New England mind understood the
need for adaptation—hadn't the Boston Brahmins and their die-hard
Red Sox fan progeny been trying to catch up with their oh so suave
and savvy New York cousins for a century? And so, just perhaps, a more
sensitive and understanding shepherd, and, yes, a non-New Englander,
might better fill the bill for headmaster. New blood, never a bad thing.

Perhaps, too, a little old-time religion to spike the tea and crumpets variety of fossilized Episcopalian preserved under glass at Winsted.

The real blame, as Elliot Goddard had warned me, belonged to Bobby Williams. Only a failed musician, a failed KGB agent, a failed B-17 navigator, and failed husband and father—and traitorous childhood friend of my father—could have come up with such an absurd and inappropriate candidate for headmaster. But Bobby was the grandson of the rector and the son of Amory Williams and so—perversely having come to Jesus at the last—stood foursquare for preserving the vital role of religion in the life of the school: he who in 1930s Party meetings at Cambridge with Anthony Blunt and Guy Burgess had sneered at religion as the opiate of the masses. Bobby had insisted on heading the search committee and then pruned out the opposition by scheduling the crucial vote when his adversaries—who had real jobs— were indisposed. He'd ended his harangue to the Winsted board with a dire warning: "Give up on mandatory chapel attendance and sacred studies and there will be nothing left but . . . 'bare ruined choirs, where late the sweet birds sang.'"

Elliot Goddard, who had been on the search committee with Bobby Williams, told me years later that he almost lost his lunch when he heard reports of Bobby's spouting that bit of Shakespeare. And Elliot was an expert on Shakespeare—and the earl of Oxford. But without my grandmother on the board, and with Elliot stuck in Saigon during the crucial vote, Bobby had managed to sneak his candidate across the finish line.

When Byron B. Folley walked into opening assembly that September with his oversize pearl white Stetson and alligator-skin cowboy boots—a cross between Elmer Fudd and Elmer Gantry—and stared at us with his tiny nearsighted eyes, screwed like too-tight bolts into his face, and cried out with a pinched and stuttering southern drawl "Hy-y-ya, boys," 250 teenage hearts missed a beat or two. "Boys, what a joy of joys it is for me to come among you in this venerable citadel of learning on such a gorgeous September morning. Oh, do I have good news for you, boys—the gladdest of glad tidings, the joy of joys. Jesus is with me, boys. He is my strong right arm. Hallelujah, He is risen and back among us. Rejoice, boys, your ever-lovin' Savior has come." In the ensuing silence, as Byron Folley raised his eyes to the ranks of pagan virtues on their high pedestals, we realized something alien had been insinuated into our midst. Some in the sixth form panicked that their

LSD trip of the night before had taken a dark turn. Faculty members pondered early retirement. Byron, belying the romantic associations of his first name, hailed from Waco, Texas, and had made his way to us by way of Yale and New York's General Theological Seminary, and a handful of New England prep schools where he had—astonishingly—been a big hit with the boys. The trustees—even with Bobby Williams leading the charge—weren't complete idiots. And huddled with the black scholarship kids, Byron could be a sympathetic soul. But at Winsted, he was an immediate and unrelenting flop. He simply was unable to bear the mantle of authority so ably and fiercely worn by his predecessor, Jack Crocket, who had commanded respect by the sheer weight of his prophetlike physiognomy and thunderous voice. Byron Folley came off as a pygmy compared to the "old man." Perhaps the trustees had underestimated the Waco gene, much less the closeted evangelical streak, which, like the Grand Canyon, was a good eighteen miles wide and more than a mile deep—once you eased your toes over the ridgeline. It wasn't that he was a nut case or not well intentioned, but something in the air of those disturbed times took him over, resulting in the most unseemly enthusiasms in an educated man.

Winsted thrived only on respect—heroic respect for patriarchal tradition and the will to govern by it, as Paul Oakes's Augustinian God ruled, a hidden ineffable hand that moves souls by unquestioned fiat. A similar failure had marked the disaster of Amory Williams's headmastership forty years before, until my grandmother weighed in and eased him out. Byron Folley's crackpot demons were different from Amory's, but the disasters were much the same: He could never conjure the necessary patriarchal abstractions, the unseen mover of the spirit—leadership values as they are quaintly called today—and worse, he was intimate with God—on a first-name basis!—*and* His living breathing son, Jesus Christ. It was as if Max's vacant appeals in the chapel on that long-ago spring afternoon had actually shaken the vault of heaven and brought down a shower of shit.

Be careful what you ask for.

Great leaders inspire loyalty and fear of failure. Byron Folley fooled nobody, inspired no one, and seemed more intimidated by the job than able to intimidate by it.

Where once a hoary-browed prophet had presided, there now sat a slightly plump and balding ersatz idol. The rector and Jack Crocket had been thoroughly Old Testament in their ways; Byron Folley was wimpishly New Testament, all agape, Holy Spirit, and kingdom of God. Or as Max put it in the Great White Way: "seething with beady apocalyptic visions." There was something almost common about the man, almost too American. The faculty took an instant dislike to him because he was such a letdown from the ageless authoritarian figure who had kept their demesne in good order; the boys, like a pack of hounds smelling blood, sneered at him for his primness and lack of physical or athletic stature.

To be fair, Byron Folley was facing tough times, times that would severely challenge even the finest headmasters and college presidents of the day. Whether an oak or a reed, all would bend and adapt. Byron Folley picked his moment on stage poorly, as the growing antiwar fervor was morphing into a radical antiestablishment counterculture. Nor was this quite the cosmic revolution Byron had in mind: the drawing near of the end-time. Raising his pug nose to the whiff of joss sticks, he quivered with intimations of the Second Coming.

But we don't get to pick our revolutions; they pick us. And like poor Byron Folley, we easily mistake one for the other.

Byron might just have squeaked through except for another big problem: his persona—or lack thereof—fit not at all with Max's literary ambition, much less the plot for the bildungsroman he was brewing up, in which a Jack Crocket stick figure was resurrected as the protagonist's nemesis. That is why Byron is absent from *Like a Forgotten Angel*—as if he never existed. A true nowhere man. Erased like a suspected Trotskyite from a Stalin-era politburo photo.

Max was first fascinated and then totally confounded by the appearance of Byron Folley. It wasn't just that Byron Folley didn't fit his idée fixe of Winsted; he didn't fit his evolving story line: the ossified institution that discriminated against Jews, in which Saul would play the role of outlaw misfit. Byron Folley would rise in the pulpit and raise his hands to heaven and proclaim, "Yes, Jesus was a Jew, is a Jew, and a Jew He shall remain to the end of time—a light unto the Gentiles." That blew Max away—burn the first draft. The Winsted in his novel remained a static, unredeemed caricature (thus the odd undercurrent of nostalgia and reverence for authority that pervades *Like a Forgotten Angel*, as if our first year were preserved in amber).

Even Max had to give Byron Folley his due; under his tenure, Winsted greatly increased the number of blacks, especially southern blacks, and other minority students, following a policy that my grandmother had instituted as far back as the thirties. Evening after evening, Byron and his southern-belle wife would invite the black kids over to the headmaster's house for cookies and milk. They would congregate in the parlor and discuss race relations and civil rights legislation and later shed tears at the assassinations of Martin Luther King, Jr., and Bobby Kennedy, and get along like a house afire. Often they would stand by the fire in Byron's study and sing gospel hymns while his wife played the piano. I never heard any of my black friends ever say an unkind word about Byron.

And yet the road to hell . . .

The dress code was relaxed, long hair was discouraged but permitted within limits; weekends in Boston and Cambridge to attend antiwar rallies were encouraged as a way of letting the boys blow off steam. All this produced an incendiary rage in Max, as if Byron Folley were out to personally thwart his literary enterprise.

"He's an imbecilic straw man, a feeble usurper, worse than Kerensky." I put my hand over Max's mouth as his voice echoed like an M16 on full automatic down the moonlit halls of Winsted. "He's got to go—what's the matter with the school board, have they lost their marbles? Do something, Hawkman; this moron is fucking with your heritage."

We assumed Max was intent on getting himself kicked out—and sooner rather than later. But that was not his plan—no, not at all. He wanted the return of some mythic Winsted that would mercilessly persecute him for being a Jew.

First intimations of Max's calibrated strategy of regime change became apparent to many of us on a warm morning in early October. We were waiting for Paul Oakes's sacred studies class to begin; cancer surgery the previous summer had left him with one lung, and his days were a struggle. Construction workers on a rotted-out portico of the schoolhouse were banging away; their hammers echoed like a distant claxon, or so it seems through the haze of recollection. Near midday, the leafy shadows beneath the apple trees on the Circle formed eerily perfect circles with an obsidian patina to them, and glints here and there of free falls. Last class of the morning and everyone was yawning and hungry for lunch and for release into the green outdoors of football and soccer practice, the purple blue of Monadnock presiding against a fall sky. The repair work caused our sacred studies class to be shunted to one of the large classics classrooms, where Amory Williams's infamous nude gods roosted on the corner pilasters—one of an insouciant winged Hermes with a skinny pecker, looking quite erect wagging in the breeze—while across the room a magnificently muscled Apollo displayed an appendage that—though uncircumcised—any self-respecting American male would be only too delighted to sport. These had always been cause for embarrassment during tours for prospective students and their parents, and the source of much ribald humor down the generations (in some Washington circles, they were referred to as "Amory's pecker gods"), but because they were of ancient lineage and had been there since anyone could remember, the pecker gods remained permanent fixtures in the Winsted landscape. (Ten years later, when Winsted went coed, the girls adopted them as mascots and gave them pet names—these employed as fond shorthand for their boyfriends' endowments. And in the case of speedy Hermes, a premature ejaculator.)

Poor Amory: Time's betrayal of his immodest desires only buried his reputation deeper.

The class before us had been a sixth-form AP section in ancient history, a course I had been desperate to take because I knew I could ace it, as my father had. I was turned down because of my age. A large wall map displaying Alexander's empire hung on one side of the blackboard. On tables at the rear of the classroom were scale models of catapults and ballistae, Roman siege engines, and assorted mock battle scenes set amidst papier-mâché fortifications; these, too, were turn-of-the-century vintage. Tattered and dusty, they had been fixtures forever: How many Winsted doughboys had entered the trenches beguiled by those toy warriors? What instantly drew my eye was a map of the Euphrates River that had been drawn in blue chalk on the center blackboard; and next to it, in yellow chalk, a plan of the Battle of Gaugamela, pitting Alexander and Darius, with little arrows describing a flanking movement. Off to the side a cryptic sentence: *The swelling of the Nile is produced by summer rains in the Abyssinian mountains.* Below this was an equally arcane quotation: *And I too, if I were Parmenio.*

I found myself bewitched by these textual fragments on the blackboard, and pondered the common thread.

Waiting and waiting for Paul Oakes to show, I kept turning from the inviting landscape beyond the open windows to the words on the blackboard, the tantalizing sinuous blue and the echoing phrases, these, for some reason, wafting me back a couple of months to the previous August, when I'd begun to go through the cardboard boxes of my father's writings. They had been stored under the eaves in his boyhood room at our cottage in the Berkshires. I'd discovered the prodigious typescript of his "Life of Alexander the Great," written when he was thirteen, a year before he started at Winsted. Reading though the dense text, which described an Alexander driven to conquest by the humanitarian ideals of his teacher, Aristotle, I had marked various revealing passages with postcards Max had sent me from Venice over that summer. He'd been helping out with his mother's master classes at Palazzo Pisani on the Grand Canal. Every lunch, or so it seemed by the two-inch deck, he wrote me a postcard emblazoned with a nude by Titian or Veronese or Tintoretto, each with an erotic limerick of his composing, signed "Chef Boyardee." It was strange when reviewing the yellowed and brittle typescript of my father's "Life of Alexander" to absorb the youthful ardor of his scholarship interspersed with dark-toned womanly flesh smeared in Bolognese sauce—almost as strange as that sensual curve of the Euphrates juxtaposed with the words on the blackboard. Then it came to me: "And I too, if I were Parmenio" was the reply made by Alexander to his general, Parmenio, who had advised against what he considered a foolhardy attack on the Persians. My father had noted with gleeful irony in his biography how Alexander had later murdered the loyal and wise Parmenio because of an assassination plot by the general's son, Philotas: "Here a case of the father paying for the sins of the son. And so the inseparable nature of love and treachery—an idea so central to the Greek mind: the essential passions that stir us into and out of being."

With such thoughts simmering in my daydreaming brain, I gazed upon the crystalline sunlight drifting across the room, which also had the disconcerting effect of blotting out the words on the blackboard in reflected glare. The smoky opacity gradually transformed the blackboard into a translucent window hovering in space, which in later years I might associate with a canvas by Mark Rothko. And the hypnotic rhythm of the workmen's hammers further set my mood adrift. First it was thoughts of a gorgeous Adonis-like Alexander, another of Amory's pecker gods across the room—this reminding me of one of Titian's nude Venuses bathing in a forest pool, until I found myself again indulging memories of the previous summer rowing on our lake, when I had discovered Laura Williams swimming her laps between the float and beach. As I shipped the oars, struck by the beauty of her rhythmic strokes, she grabbed hold of the side of the float and climbed out, long rope of sun-bleached blond hair to the waist of her red racing suit, water sluicing down the new curves of her ballet-trained body, her slightly upturned nose flecked with peeling sunburned skin like a naiad of perpetual summer. The sun was behind me and the reflection off the water was intense, cloaking me in glare, as it had Odysseus when he first set eyes on white-armed Nausicaa. I watched silently as she adjusted the straps of her suit, pulled at the bunched elastic over her rear end, and then dived, clean as a whistle, and disappeared toward the beach in widening rhythmic ripples that echoed in iambic pentameter over the lake.

I adjusted my crotch and turned to Max beside me, his head intently bowed as he feverishly underlined pages in his Old Testament. That was not good . . . that was not good at all.

For a brief moment more, I luxuriated again in the feeling of invisibility, and how time, for the scholarly mind, becomes a luminous ever-welcoming continuum, merging sensation and memory, as was often the case when I was rowing alone, in the pause between strokes, or when I rested oars to better feel the glide as the earth slowed beneath my suspended body.

"Well hi-y-a-a, boy-a-s. How you all doin' on this wonderful God-ever-lovin'-you day?" Bryon Folley proceeded to the lectern with crablike steps, two Bibles clutched close to his chest (he was convinced that our benighted lack of familiarity with the Bible was due to over-reliance on the King James Version, the archaic language of which obscured God's moving message to His creation). "Sorry I'm a bit late. Had some last-minute business to attend to with some of our esteemed graduates in the nation's capital." Placing his two Bibles on the lectern, he went to the windows, scowled at the hammering outside, and pulled down the blinds, then took a deep breath and turned back to the class with an ecstatic smile.

"Now, as you all know, I like to take over some of the sacred studies classes every so often just so that I can acquaint myself better with you boys and see what kind of spiritual progress you are making with your teachers." His insect eyes squinted at us. Max looked at me and groaned under his breath. "The Reverend Oakes, who has been indisposed of late, has been kind enough to let me take your class today. Now I realize that you as fourth formers are learnin' the Old Testament this term—but why should you poor boys have to wait so long for the good news?" He threw up his hands and inclined his chin toward heaven. "Why wait . . ." he squeaked in a smooth liquid drawl as he caught sight of the well-endowed Apollo. Stepping back, eyebrows popped, as if from a Texas sidewinder, he scuttled over to the blackboard, where he picked up the eraser. With determined strokes, the Euphrates disappeared in a long smudge of blue. In huge red letters he wrote *The Kingdom of God* across the blackboard and turned to us. "Behold, the good news." Fingering the lapels of his green madras jacket, he began to pace up and down in front of the class on an axis that placed Amory's amorous Apollo just beyond his peripheral view.

"Today, I want to tell you boys about the Kingdom of God. Now can anyone here enlighten me about the Kingdom of God?" He continued to pace, absorbed in some inner rapture as he steeled himself from the marvelous appendage ranging nearby while he waited for a reply. Nobody answered. He stopped and looked around as if for a show of hands. Blank faces met him everywhere. Tiny beads of sweat tobogganed his furrowed brow. "Now come on," he complained, "surely someone here must have some notion. . . . I mean, what are we here for, what are we all waiting for, what is the g-o-o-d news?"

One small voice in the back hesitantly piped up.

"Is it . . . is it heaven, sir—is it heaven?"

Max snickered and repressed a laugh.

"Heaven, you say," replied Byron Folley coaxingly. "Well, not exactly; heaven comes before the Kingdom of God and may be thought of as something of a forerunner or precursor—a spiritual model of the holy kingdom, if you like." He looked around like a man discovering he has been talking to a crowd who turn out to be foreigners and so have understood exactly nothing of what he's been saying. "Now think, boys, think what is it that comes at the end-time, when Christ shall come again. What is it that Christ shall do?" No answer. Every face avoided his incandescent stare, as if a fat booger jittered on his flared nostrils. "Come on, boy-a-s. Why, you say it every morning in chapel when you repeat the Apostles' Creed. Now just think. What is it that Christ does when He shall come again?" Byron Folley watched as a few pairs of lips began to murmur the Apostles' Creed. A hand shot up.

"'From thence He shall come to judge the quick and the dead.'"

"Right, good work, boy," he said. Max clapped his hands to his throat and pretended to quietly choke. "And what happens then? What does that mean?" With the sudden grunt of the runner out of the blocks, Byron Folley launched into his harangue. "What do we wait for, what do we pray for and ache for and call out to God on our knees for?" Silence. "Why, for God's rule," he pleaded, "for His reign on earth when the time is fulfilled. For after the cosmic catastrophe and the new dawn of terror and tribulation, the dead will arise again—yes, they will, and the Son of Man will be our judge and Savior." He looked wildly around the room. The boys in the first row cowered back in face of the verbal onslaught. "Don't you see, that *is* the Kingdom of God. Can't you feel it in your bones, boys, smell it in the light of the day—how close it is— oh, joy of joys?" A spasm of ecstatic pleasure seemed to ripple through him and his breathing slackened.

"But, sir," asked one boy, his voice quivering, "what happens in the Kingdom of God, sir?"

"We are all resurrected bodily from the dead and live forever in God's eternal kingdom."

"Even if we have turned to dust, sir?"

"My young friend, anything is possible for God."

"Bullshit!"

Every head spun in Max's direction. The echo of his outcry rang out like a ricocheting bullet.

"If," said Max with a belligerent jut of his jaw, "we are to be bodily resurrected"—his hands ran a cantering arpeggio across the desk- top—"both men and women, then . . . is there really sex after death?"

The classroom tittered. Byron Folley fixed Max with fear and loath- ing: the real sidewinder.

"You will control your foul tongue, boy." The headmaster took a step forward and tried to stare down his spiritual foe. "'For when they rise from the dead, they neither marry nor are given in marriage, but are like angels in heaven'—Mark twelve:twenty-five."

Hammer blows from the workmen on the roof began again.

Max sighed as his jaw seemed to take a slow-motion punch.

"Too bad; at least there'd be something to look forward to."

"You must think of it in terms of Paradise," said Byron Folley, "the Garden of Eden. As it was in the beginning, so it will be in the end." His imploring hands were shadowed on the floor in front of him.

"Then why the hell bother with all the stuff in the middle?" Max glared defiantly in his seat. "Why does God make man go through all the suffering and turmoil if He can end it anytime He pleases and turn the world into paradise?"

Mr. Folley seemed stunned for a moment by the outburst.

"It is all part of God's divine plan."

Max's fingers clenched into fists.

"Just like the six million gassed and tortured to death by the Nazis—that was part of God's perfection of a divine plan?" His voice grew louder, and Byron Folley backed up a step or two, as if to take him fully into range. "Or is that just another appropriate sacrifice, another quota of sin and guilt to be plowed back into the ash heap of humanity, another cry for bloody redemption?"

We watched tensely, drawn to the ache of emotion in our classmate's voice. Byron Folley became very rigid and thoughtful. He eyed the heretic carefully and began to stalk up and down with quick little gyrating motions.

"There is, Mr. Roberts, such a thing as evil in this world." He stopped pacing; a low simmering heat filled his words, as if something inside were being slowly strangled. A jutted upward glance at the huge uncircumcised schlong mocking him and a wave of disgust. "Oh . . . I know that such things are discounted today in our modern enlightened so-ci-ety. The devil is a myth, they say, merely a figment of our imagination, our collective unconscious—gone the way of belief in witches and goblins. But"—and he raised his finger and slowly pointed it at Max—"Satan is still among us, where he fell from heaven like lightning, where he pursues his ends with the most subtle craft, the most terrible guile. 'For we wrestle not against flesh and blood, but against principalities, against powers, against the rulers of the darkness of this world, against spiritual wickedness in high places.' Yes, even now our boys are fighting and dying in battle against his evil powers in Vietnam, sacrificing themselves as Christ sacrificed Himself for us to end the evil one's reign on earth. There is the source of pain, the root of suffering; it is he who has corrupted the spirit and blackened the soul."

Max raised himself, his lovely chin line clenched in agitation.

"Then God is no longer omnipotent and almighty," shouted Max, "or is it just that He allows evil to exist for his own amusement?"

Headmaster Folley brought up a hand as if to swat an annoying fly.

"Satan has no part of Him, no hold over Him."

"'I form the light, and create darkness,'" declaimed Max. "'I make peace, and create evil: I the Lord do all these things.' Isaiah forty-five: seven." He slapped the open Bible on the desk.

"That's right. God allows the existence of evil. He deigns to keep

Satan around at his bidding and mercy." Byron Folley pulled a hand-kerchief from his jacket pocket and wiped his brow.

"Then God is cruel and unloving and kills us like flies for sport."

"God is righteous and just," came the sputtered reply. "He punishes the evildoers, punishes them in limitless and eternal fire to repay them for all the pain they have caused on earth. He protects his children with His righteous fury."

"So," snarled Max, "because Hitler and his torturers might fry for all eternity, that somehow repays the suffering of the innocent six million who died, heals the terrifying memories of horror and loss of those who remain behind, somehow makes up for all the lives that never ran their course—entire generations snuffed out? Is that God's balance of justice; does He really so carefully balance the suffering of so many against the pain of eternal damnation for so few?"

I watched entranced as tears formed in Max's eyes. Byron Folley began clawing at his face, hooking a finger into his white liturgical collar.

"G-G-God," he stammered, "God moves in mysterious ways." He turned to the window, blinking into the concentrated light as he tried to collect himself.

Max pounced.

"Job knew that God was neither merciful nor just."

Byron Folley, hearing this echo of an aphorism in the Great White Way, wheeled on his heels, his face flushed with blind fury, and walked over to Max. "You, Roberts, and your sort, are a dangerous influence in this school." He poked a finger in Max's chest. "You may be a precocious young man and a very talented musician, but your smarts run shallow like a swamp. Suffering has its logic in God's plan for us, like everything else. God gives man free will; He offers us the choice of good or evil, right and wrong. And, as with any choice, there must be consequences. If man chooses to misuse his freedom, to disobey God, then he must suffer the inevitable consequences of his actions. There can be no other way but obedience to God's will."

He stood breathing in clenching bursts like some victorious gladiator, foot pressed on the neck of his victim.

Then Max stood and thrust his face into the headmaster's.

"Let me get this straight. You're saying that God's cruelty is okay because it is a kind of punishment, a divine retribution—necessary, of course, for man's ultimate salvation? And, of course, morality requires punishment, so therefore suffering is necessary—God is cruel for our own good . . . save the rod, spoil the child." Max paused and licked his lips obscenely. "Well, let me tell you something—sir. If God uses suffering as a means to achieve His ends, then life is only a means, man is only a means . . . existence is meaningless; and God is only a cruel, morally perverse, and uncaring puppeteer." Max dropped into his seat. The class gasped with anticipation. Byron Folley stood rigidly red-faced. "Better the Old Testament," said Max in a lowered voice. "God kicks the shit out of you whenever He damn well pleases and says, 'Too bad—whatcha gonna do about it?'"

Byron Folley continued to stand rooted. We could almost hear his mind grinding shut and collapsing in upon itself. Abruptly, he turned and walked over to the blackboard, erased his first message, and began to write. At that moment, his secretary came to the door and called to him.

"Headmaster, your call from Washington has come through."

"Thank you, Miss Bishop." He continued staring at the blackboard for a second; then his shoulders sagged and he turned and marched quickly to the door. "You boys may be excused; period's almost over anyway."

Everyone turned to look at Max where he sat, head bowed, strangely quiescent as he madly scribbled notes—the chutzpah! Then a tremendous cheer went up.

I gave a last look at the blackboard, where in huge red letters *God Is* . . . hovered expectantly upon that chalky blue eternity.

Love and treachery.

New York, October 13, 1899

Dear Cousin Samuel,

I had a chance to visit Winsted on Thursday and spend some time with John, who is all set for Harvard next year and medical school—so he insists, down the road. I can't think of a better career for a young man today with all the advancements in science to relieve human suffering—when I think back in horror on how primitive the field hospitals were back in my days of soldiering. I am even more delighted that he need never fight in another war; the recent dustup with Spain should satisfy delusions of glory for this generation and some.

But my reason for writing: I was not a little disappointed not to find you in residence—another crisis, I gather, back in Cambridge that had resulted in your absence for the better part of a week? Dare I ask for more explanation from you? I know Sam has been a great worry to you with his drinking and the company of aesthetes he keeps at Harvard. I've heard reports of behavior in his set that will surely besmirch the name of Harvard and, dare I say it, Winsted, and you. Has your dear Eliza been filling his mind with grief for PB again? Are your sure you've recovered all the correspondence in her possession? Find something for her to do, to occupy herself. Another lover, if must be, to settle her mind and heart, or the whole sorry business will surely out someday.

Look how well your Isabella has done, finding her way in that brilliant marriage and her eternal honeymoon in Venice. Her purchase of Palazzo Barberini has made all the New York papers, along with stories of how she keeps the most brilliant soirees in Venice. I am tempted to visit, as rumor has it she has become quite the voracious collector of old master pictures—and a museum in the Back Bay! I prefer my Innesses, but a tour of Venetian architecture tempts the engineer in me.

But you simply cannot leave the school unattended for weeks on end. Amory, of all people, is simply not up to taking over in emergencies—he is an emergency! My John tells me things—the embarrassed looks—about what goes on during swimming classes. It is one thing at the swimming hole at Elysium, discreetly concealed in our woods, but at Winsted the boys—and they are mostly city boys—should be wearing bathing costumes. If you don't stop Amory, I will. Winsted is not Periclean Athens, not a Greek gymnasium. And there were half a dozen similar issues hanging fire: Your faculty is in near revolt. The trustees are not happy. If bad reports from the boys get back to their parents, we will have a damnable time recruiting a full class for next year. New York society considers Winsted a bastion of traditional New England probity and Christian manliness. Do not even consider putting it about that Amory might succeed you as headmaster; he will never be ready. We must be prepared to hand over our work to a successor outside the family; it is in the nature of things. We are too close to Winsted and should, in time, step aside for new blood.

And for Christ's sake, get Amory married, find him a dependable woman who can toe the line, a good faculty wife who doesn't require the full trappings of the matrimonial state. A keeper and amanuensis who will put an end to talk and innuendo. Surely daughter and sister Isabella must have such an artistic female in her coterie—a musician would be just the trick for Amory. Duets—perfect.

While on the subject of Amory, I had the shock of my life reviewing the new classics classrooms in the west wing of the schoolhouse. Amory's decorative scheme is simply not acceptable. I know—Amory has bent my ear on his connoisseurship—the sculptures cost a king's ransom and are faithful reproductions of the original Greek and Roman models. But not everything from the Greeks is appropriate for our boys, even if Amory, with all his degrees from Harvard and Heidelberg, delights in them. I know quite a bit about classical statuary from my collection of busts in the school hall, and many of Amory's "models" are from second-rate, degraded Hellenistic examples—entirely suspect. Some verge on the obscene. I am no prude in such matters, but there are limits—no, good taste and common sense. And, as you are well aware, our agreement is that the schoolhouse is my province in terms of design, furnishings, and curriculum. The chapel and the moral development of our charges is your domain. I told Amory the statues must go or at least be replaced with more discreet versions. A few female goddesses, it seems to me, would add a little balance to Amory's *excessively* masculine pantheon!

I will be back at Winsted Tuesday of next week for the board meeting—we meet then in earnest.

Yours,
John Alden

5 THAT WINTER, MAX TEAMED UP WITH THE ELEC-
tronics whiz of the class, and the two of them painstakingly
fed wires through the system of pipes connecting the Osborn
House basement with the headmaster's residence. Drilling a
hole in the floor of Folley's study, they planted a microphone inside a
terra-cotta statue of Saint John the Baptist, a tacky Mexican antique
that Folley had bought in a Guadalajara flea market. I didn't learn the
details until years later; it was the best-kept secret in our class. In his
novel, Max referred to the operation as "Ultra." Over the following
years Max recorded all faculty meetings and so had access to a rich
flow of intelligence, which allowed him to run rings around Byron Folley—keeping one step ahead of the posse, while providing the novelist
manqué with a rich supply of material, insider poop that would rock
the establishment when it was published in *Like a Forgotten Angel*, not
to mention disinformation to be disseminated in the Great White Way.
It is no small irony that an institution that had produced more than
its fair share of CIA operatives should have itself been so thoroughly
penetrated, its dirty laundry and faltering confidence rumored and gos-
siped to doped audiences at summer parties on Martha's Vineyard and
Fishers Island and in Northeast Harbor.

Bobby Williams would later pull at this oar with his leaks to the
press.

Max's insurgency proceeded with more run-of-the-mill gambits to
draw out and test the Folley regime. There was the skunk—an unfortunate case of roadkill—which had, though severely mangled, managed
to drag itself into the ventilating system of the chapel before dying,
producing a stink so bad that services had to be canceled for a week

94

as the place was fumigated. There was the infamous cold morning in January when, staggering bleary-eyed into the schoolhouse study hall after chapel, we found the ranks of marble busts utterly transformed: stony lips of luscious ruby red, cheeks of rouge and scarlet, and those heavy-lidded opaque eyes alive with mascara in brilliant blues and purples—and hair varying from jet black to auburn to deepest cherry-orange and shocking pink. You could have heard a spider fart. (Only Washington, Lincoln, and Grant were spared.) It was as if the vice squad had crashed some wild party in the reign of Caligula, every cross-dresser, transvestite, and drag queen in town dressed to the nines. Amory Williams, and his tragic golden-boy brother, Samuel II, would have thought they'd died and gone to heaven. Max never missed a chance to doff his hat in tribute to those who languished in that sorriest circle of hell, the netherworld of forbidden desire and fear of society scandal. Such delicious moments provide much of the low comedy in *Like a Forgotten Angel*.

But in Byron Folley, Max had met an opponent who, too, knew a thing or two about strategic retreats and timely dissembling. Max, our self-proclaimed princely playwright (stay tuned for more on Hamlet), had underestimated Byron's stage management: All were messing with the chairs on the *Titanic*.

As the months of his first year crept past, Folley, whom Max had taken to calling "Joy-Joy," began diligently ferreting out the arcane marginalia of the Winsted ethos—bowing to tradition where necessary, tweaking around the edges when he thought no one was looking, and slipping in the sucker punch on the sly. He proceeded apace to redecorate the chapel with the trappings of the vital religion he preached, including garish evangelical slogans and patriotic prayers for our boys in Vietnam, while eschewing the exquisite archaisms of the King James Version for the pedestrian Revised Standard Version. *Essays and Prayers* vanished from the chapel program except when Paul Oakes, his powerful voice reduced to a whispered croak by cancer surgery, preached on Sunday. As the chaotic assault of war protest, drugs, sex, and rock and roll filtered into our midst, Byron Folley sought to inoculate us. He saw himself as ministering to the old dying patient, the dried-up and fossilized faith of New England, cold and sterile, like its long winters, which even the veneer of high-Episcopalian manliness dating from the 1880s, once championed by Samuel Williams to scions of Beacon Hill and

Washington Square, could not save. "Give yourself to the good news, boys. Trust in Jesus your Savior—oh joy, raise your eyes to the blessed skies—hallelujah, Lord!" And like medicine men of old, he hawked his potions among us, bringing in a motley collection of characters: the crippled and sick, the recovered drug addicts and twelve-step crusaders, who claimed to have been miraculously healed by the Holy Spirit and set on the road of deliverance, now proclaiming the glory of God and Jesus Christ to all who were willing to pay the standard lecture fee. Winsted was scandalized.

My enfeebled adviser, Paul Oakes . . . it seemed like his massive heart was shriveling before my eyes as, day by day, his beloved chapel began to be transformed with *spiritual renovations*. He winced with disgust each time he took his accustomed seat in the ambulatory, withdrawing from the life of the school, as he withdrew from me, a living ghost investing his few remaining haunts. Before Christmas, a five-foot-tall jet blue terra-cotta figure of the Virgin Mary with baby Jesus—bought from the same tourist dive in Guadalajara as the Saint John the Baptist—took up vigil by the side of the altar to mark the holiday season . . . and then stayed, and stayed—a fixture by Easter. For years to come, Joy-Joy's "Blue-Eyed Babe" to the boys, "That thing" to the older faculty, presided at chapel services, her wide Bambi eyes a pitiful reminder of our kitschy fall. Needless to say, this affront to Max's narrative veneer never made it into the pages of *Like a Forgotten Angel,* which contained one famously parsed passage noted by every critic: "Hung on the chapel door in large letters was an invisible sign for all those who cared to see: *No Virgin Mary Need Apply.*"

It was about this time, as my football career began to take flight, that I first learned of my father's friendship with the legendary and slightly suspect Karel Hollar, who would vie with my father in the late thirties for the accolades of greatest archaeologist of his generation. This was delivered promptly by hand the first week of term in a blue binder, fastidiously organized by my grandmother, from Harrison & Brandt containing my more of my father's Winsted letters.

November 15, 1929
Winsted School

Dear Mother,

Another long and fascinating letter from Karel Hollar on the latest finds made by the Germans during last summer's digging season. As ever, new discoveries spark more theories on Homer and the Greek Bronze Age. Karel sends his regards to you; he says his father often mentions you and Aunt Isabella's Palazzo Barberini. Our weeks in Venice swim in my head like a dream. How I miss Karel's tour of the *spolia* as we floated down the Grand Canal, and your inept chaperoning at a distance! Karel urges me to consider studying at Leipzig next summer, where he is headed—the greatest minds in the field of Bronze Age scholarship are there, he writes. Cambridge might disagree. Karel's mind is such a sardine can of ideas that they can't tumble out fast enough in conversation, much less on his scribbled pages. And yet I await his letters like messages from the gods. He has convinced me to forgo classical Greece and concentrate on Homer and the Bronze Age. He writes that he is certain that more Linear B will turn up somewhere in Greece or the Ionian Islands and that we must dedicate our lives to deciphering it. We ponder the characters in correspondence: Is it related to Etruscan or Phoenician? Karel is sure it is an early form of Greek. And so frustrating because Evans has released few illustrations of his tablets from Knossos; there just isn't much script to work with. But I am smitten and my translation of the *Odyssey* only tantalizes more.

What I find fascinating is how the Greece of the *Odyssey* is like glimpsing the infancy of our world—already ancient in Alexander's day. Reading the original Greek, one feels as if one is searching back in time for answers to questions about our basic nature—simple things: honor, loyalty, courage—destiny and fate. And a golden age to rival the Minoans. Homer's text is clearly layered with a flotsam and jetsam of telling details, Bronze Age anachronisms preserving the various stages of the poem's composition like the layers in an excavation trench. What puzzles me is how before about 700 B.C. the written window closes on what went before. Almost five hundred years of darkness from the fall of Mycenaean civilization circa 1100 B.C. to the first glimmerings of Greek civilization as we know it. Imagine, a dark ages lasting for five hundred years! What terrible thing could have happened to so thoroughly destroy such a brilliant civilization?

Of course, my adviser, Virgil Dabney, tends to play down the coherence of Homer. Being a Latinist, he would. Virgil agrees with Milman Parry that the *Odyssey* is just a compilation of oral epic poetry.

Am I boring you?

Well, I believe there was a real live Homer. One really needs a single author—don't you agree?—a towering genius to anchor our humanity. Without inimitable heroic voices like Homer's or Shakespeare's—a single mind to encompass the moral contradictions of an uncaring

universe—where would we be? That, of course, is the problem with the
Bible—such a mishmash of authors, of Paul's incoherent Platonism
and hodgepodge of myths around sacrificed and risen gods. One shud-
ders. What I love about the *Odyssey* is that it is a recognizable world
that is as present as the rising sun, a vibrant shining light, a golden age
as distant from Periclean Athens as we are from the Crusades. Karel
goes on about Homeric Greece as if it was some kind of primitive
Rousseauian community of equals. Ridiculous, of course—it was an
aristocratic, if not feudal, world—but being a socialist, he would. And
since the market crash, there seems to be more and more spouting of
socialist ideas, even in the halls of Winsted!

Do you hear any more about the financial crisis? Has it hit us hard?
You never tell me anything about the family finances. One hears rumors
among my pals of fortunes lost. Even the town of Winsted, already
down on its heels, has been hit with more mills closings. The country
roads around these parts are filled with laid-off men asking for work
at the farms and orchards. The collection plate on Sunday was quite
full when Mr. Crocket announced that the money would go to a soup
kitchen in the town. Elliot Goddard and Joe Alsop say—presumably
from their fathers—that the worst is over and things are on an upswing.
Let's hope so, but I sometimes wonder if the last war, where we lost
Father, might end up being our Trojan War. And another dark ages just
around the corner? I hear your voice: "Don't be such a pessimist; your
father wouldn't stand for it." I do miss Father, as you do, of course—it
takes something out of one. His name comes up among the older masters: what a great scholar he was—and yes, a great pitcher for the eleven.
People tell me he was such a raging optimist, up on the latest medical science, just as you always said. A commonsense progressive like
Teddy Roosevelt, according to Mr. Crocket. Well, we could certainly
use some of his optimism right now. The world seems vulnerable and
cruel, and, yes, dark, without him: Let's hope not five hundred years
worth.

All I have is you—perhaps you are my Nestor! Shall I call you
Mother Nestor? I do love your stories about Father, your "soaring idealist." I guess I do think a lot about the unfairness of how Father died
saving lives: that no matter how hard we try to do the right thing, our
fate rests with the gods. I am not a fatalist—how can I be with your
voice always ringing in my ears: "You'll just have to pick yourself up by
your own bootstraps, since your father isn't here to do it."

Perhaps it is just the November chill in the air that gets me blue,
intimations of the long, cold winter ahead at Winsted—and so thinking of summers past at Elysium, when you or nanny tied my laces, as it

once was when I was younger and the afternoons echoed with Bobby's piano practice over the lake, and the nights were full of jazz bands and bright Japanese lanterns floating across the water, and the gay life that even you—why is it you will never admit it now?—took such delight in. I remember your stories about Hermitage when waking me the next morning, of great singers and actresses, dancers and musicians—and the painters, too, or was it just one special painter?

After Amory, and now the crash, I guess those days are gone for good.

And speaking of the devil, Bobby Williams, yet another budding socialist, continues to be a royal headache, still complaining to those who will hear him out—almost no one—about how badly you and the board treated his father. I hear Amory rarely leaves his house in Cambridge, that his wife has run off to Paris with a fellow painter, and he is threatening to sell Hermitage. Bobby struggles to hold his head up and pretend it is nothing, but I know it bothers him. We all know you did what you had to do. Everybody loves Jack Crocket—well, respects him, and of course he is always going on about you with a soft twinkle in his eye!

Do you suppose if we actually believed the chapel poppycock that life might be easier?

When I pass by the chapel, or the hall, and hear Bobby practicing, I remember the good old days at Elysium, the sweet summers full of Chopin and sweet ferns and high-bush blueberries and your sweet smiles gliding in to wake me with tales of your Arabian nights.

We won't have to sell Elysium, will we? I don't think I could bear that.

Everyone says Bobby is headed for Carnegie Hall.

Will you be up for the big game next week against St. Mark's? Two more wins and we are New England champions!

> Your loving son,
> John

Seated at my father's desk in his boyhood room, staring out at the lake and the towering white pines and what is left of Hermitage, I struggle to remember exactly what I thought coming upon the name of Karel Hollar for the first time in my father's letters. When they, too, had been young men on the verge of remarkable careers, until war intervened. I knew that Karel Hollar had been a famous Czech archaeologist, something of a renegade and iconoclast with crazy ideas, an upstart in the ranks of the rather stodgy German archaeology establishment between the wars. Like my father, he saw himself in the mold of Heinrich Schliemann, the discoverer of Troy and Mycenae, and the golden treasure hordes that had first hinted at the true splendors of Homer's Bronze Age. As young men, Karel and my father had spent many summers working together, but in the late thirties they had gone separate ways, disagreeing about the search for the fabled site of Nestor's Palace at Pylos. It was said my father was convinced that the palace would have to be like Mycenae and Tiryns, with massive high stone walls, and so clearly visible. Karel had taken a different tack, joining forces with Carl Andersen, an American archaeologist at the University of Cincinnati, and together they settled on a nondescript site on a hill overlooking Navarino Bay with no visible walls. They chose the hill of Epano Englianos by triangulating from the positions of large Bronze Age tholos tombs in the vicinity, tombs that looked to be those of important aristocrats. It was an inspired surmise, and in the summer of 1939, on the very first day of digging, they discovered a treasure trove of Linear B tablets, the first outside of Crete, from what turned out to be the storerooms of Nestor's Palace. This extraordinary find would revolutionize the field of Bronze Age archaeology, making headlines around the world before being quickly forgotten in the rush to war.

That much I knew: a lot of the story was in Joseph Alsop's book about Pylos and the Bronze Age, the one he'd put into my hands the previous spring. But nothing about the hint of scandal connected with the name Karel Hollar, something of which I later heard from my Princeton colleagues—perhaps because of his eccentric early career and associations with Nazi sympathizers in German archaeology circles, and later rumored irregularities about missing finds at Pylos in the late summer of '39 in the haste to close the site, or because he'd ended up in the Wehrmacht and died ingloriously in a Russian POW camp. By my day, Hollar's name had a vague aura of tragedy: a brilliant, hard-driving young Turk snuffed out by war. In my father's adolescent letters—and I had no inkling—I was reading the opening chapters of *his* harrowing odyssey, for the protean Karel Hollar, classicist, archaeologist, Wehrmacht captain, Soviet spy, British MI6 operative, and GDR minister of mines, was the reason for my father's disappearance behind the Iron Curtain in 1953.

And yes, this was the true story Max never discovered—even as he read every word of those letters. Nor could he have made this one up in a thousand and one nights of prying into my family's affairs . . . as good a story, dare I say, as any tale out of the pages of Homer.

And a story that would take a devastating turn, and with it my life, just weeks later.

That fall of 1966, the senior quarterback had been injured in preseason tryouts and I'd replaced him on a temporary basis. The game was like second nature to me, as if I'd been born to play. I won the starting role. I found myself enthralled with the strategy of the game, the exhilaration of the moment, the speed, and the indescribable joy of connecting with a receiver far downfield. I felt very much in control of things. We had an exceptional running back, a black kid from Jackson, Mississippi, with massive thighs and viselike arms—one fumble in two years—and the ability to change direction on a dime. And speed to burn, the only guy faster than I. A big-play artist who could make it happen. His name was Jerry Gadsden, a year older and a class above me. Jerry could've been the next Gale Sayres; Yale certainly thought so. Next to Max, he became my best friend. Jerry was the most real and honest human being I'd ever met: What you saw was what you got with Jerry, no bull-shit, no pretense, although, he certainly kept his home life under wraps. Coming from the South, "from redneck land," as Jerry called it, where the Klan still flourished, he was in awe of the fact that my great-grand-father had been a general in the Union army. "That great-grandfather of yours, the one in the library, just how many Klan sons of bitches did he kill? Not enough, clearly, since they still all over my neighborhood."

My arm and Jerry's running and sure hands got us six wins in a row, with only two games left in the season. By our next-to-last game, against Rivers High School, the word had gotten out in alumni circles that the football team was having a great season. The downside for me: Alumni of my father's generation were returning in droves to watch games. I'd see them lined up on the sidelines in their tweed jackets, slouch hats, athletic ties, Harvard scarves—intent on my every move. Then after the game, they'd come up to me on the field and grasp my hand and hold on as if for dear life. If I heard it once, I heard it fifty times that fall: "A dead ringer for your dad, right down to the passing motion, the head fake, the quarterback sneak." Some had tears in their eyes about high times in the early thirties. How could the thirties bring back tears for anyone? All my father's letters were filled with references to the long shadow of the Depression, even if his mother had gotten out of the market in 1928. The family fortune had been in New York City real estate, and her advisers knew a bubble when they saw one.

People forget the bad stuff.

The Rivers game always proved controversial, mostly because we always got our asses kicked. Rivers had been included in our schedule for decades, going back to some distant relationship between old man Crocket and a Harvard roommate, a Rivers principal in the thirties. Rivers wasn't in our prep school league; it was a public school on the south side of Boston. It was five times the size of Winsted, and the players were big and mean, streetwise and talented, and they always ate us alive, and delighted in rubbing our snotty noses in the mud. But we thought we had a chance that year, or at least Jerry Gadsden thought we had a chance; he'd taken the measure of those Southie kids—racial slurs and all—in games from previous seasons, and knew he could run rings around the best of them. And we almost pulled it off. It was parents weekend and the board of trustees was meeting and having its annual dinner in the headmaster's house. The sidelines were packed. We were up by three points late in the fourth quarter. Jerry had scored three touchdowns, two running, one on a forty-five-yard reception. We were driving for the end zone. There was a Rivers linebacker I really didn't like, a compact red-haired meatball, quick as the devil, who'd been taunting Jerry—nigger this and nigger that—all game long. Every time I threatened to complain to the ref, Jerry told me to just shut the fuck up. I was stepping back to pass, totally in control of the situation, ignoring the verbal abuse and threats from across the line, when, an instant after the hike, something hit me . . . something in the mid-section and then as I hit the dirt a crack to my jaw like someone had swung a baseball bat. That's all I remembered. I woke up on the side-lines on a stretcher with a headache and blurred vision and a jaw that didn't feel all there. I'd fumbled and the ball had been returned eighty yards for a score. We lost the game.

An hour later I was still lying in the training room in the gym, less woozy, still disoriented, but with the exception of black-and-blue bruises along my swollen jawline (the doctor said my mouth guard saved the teeth), no worse for wear. But I felt awful; I felt like I'd let the team—everybody—down. I'd never been in a situation of responsibility like that before, when so much had been riding on my performance. I thought I'd been up to it; I thought I was untouchable. Jerry had tried to cheer me up, coming into the training room, taking my hand, smiling and laughing and telling me not to worry: "You did your best, man. . . . I was with you; I know about these things. And I took care of it. And—you wait, we'll get 'em next year." What things? I wondered. Then the coach and the other guys all came by and put in a good word, but I still felt rotten. I was nonplussed, too, that all that good feeling of being in control of a situation could have been obliterated so fast. It was a good lesson: the fickle gods of the blind side. The doctor checked me out. The trainer wanted me to keep quiet for a few minutes more before I showered and changed. He left me and went to tidy up elsewhere. On the other side of a partition were the men's room and the urinals. I heard two men come in and continue a conversation they'd been having. I knew they were trustees, because they were talking about the new gym and overruns in the budget.

"Unbelievable the money we sunk into this place—but a damn sight better than the old gym."

"Alden money, you mean, including those eight-foot-thick concrete walls."

"Wasn't she something, though—the old lady . . . one tough broad."

"Last of the wine, last of the Puritan conscience . . . what she'd had to endure . . . her husband, then John."

"Her face, her eyes . . . when we told her: eight-foot concrete reinforced with steel."

A laugh. "I remember her words: 'My Lord, are you gentlemen crazy—what do we have to be so frightened of?'"

"How do you explain the end of the world to a woman of a certain age—doyen of New York society?"

"Well, now we've got a little reminder of Omaha Beach on the Circle."

"Might save the boys from the blast, but fallout, radiation . . . I wonder."

"Tell me about it. . . . I had Constance and Joey head down to Maine during the Cuban Missile Crisis."

"Did you really?"

"I feel bad. Breach of security. Cowardly, I suppose."

"God's sake . . . yes, you should have been shot."

"Wife and child . . . but you're right."

"Could you believe John's boy out there today. I felt like I was in a dream. As if all the years—know what I mean?"

"Did you notice the head fake, the misdirection, just like John . . . as if nothing could touch him."

"And not a wobble on the pass."

"It made me sad, actually—whole business ripped me apart."

"You don't really think . . ."

"That they turned him?"

"Betrayed his country—John?"

"Another of Philby's recruits—Stalin's whoremaster."

"You and Angleton."

"No, Angleton's crazy as a coot; he sees traitors at every watercooler in the firm. And don't be fooled by his lies: Angleton was taken in by Philby hook, line, and sinker."

"Elliot—loyal Elliot—still defends John."

"Elliot needs friends; in fact, he needs the living *and* the dead to defend him—two or three hundred by my count."

"I'll defend him—Elliot, I mean. In his telling of it, Kennedy just lost his nerve with the air cover. And Ike would have sent in the marines and saved us the whole missile fiasco—stitch in time."

"I asked Elliot at the game about the latest mess, since he's just back from Saigon. Didn't seem too happy about it—*politics, always politics*—not happy at all."

"He's gonna become the world's expert on fucked-up operations."

"Hundred thousand, two hundred thousand troops . . . now we're up to our necks."

"It's going to be a bigger fuckup than Korea. And to think a brigade of marines would have deep-sixed Castro."

"Got to hand it to Elliot, like you said, a loyal motherfucker, still carrying the flame for John."

"You say a word against John and he'll plant you six feet under."

"Maybe that's why Elliot's the ultimate survivor."

"That's why they gave him the Vietnam mess. Our intrepid Cold War warrior—it will finish even him."

"I wouldn't count him out; he's got connections to trump the devil. Allen loves him—they talk Shakespeare and Chinese Export porcelain."

"Listen, once the press gets ahold of it. . . . that kind of loyalty only paves the highway to hell."

"Are you going to the headmaster's dinner tonight?"

"No, I've already said good-bye to my son. And I can't stand that pusillanimous pipsqueak anyway. And Bobby Williams—Suzanne . . .

Christ's sake—don't get me going on those two: Philby's creatures all. I've got a late flight back to D.C. I'm doing *Face the Nation* at nine in the morning."

I lay there listening and not listening, as if from another dimension of time, my mind struggling to make sense of those searing sentences spilled into memory between flushing urinals and running faucets. Betrayed? Traitor? Like short-fused limpet mines, those words attached themselves to everything that kept my life afloat. As I showered and dressed, I kept dismissing the thing like a bad dream: if I could only wake up a little more, clear my head, get some fresh air. As I made my way out of the gym, I stopped at the display case containing my father's medals and citations from the Greek government, and from William Donovan on OSS letterhead, extolling his work with the Resistance during the war. I gazed upon the black-and-white photo, yellowed and creased, which shows him standing in a columned portico in the agora with a motley band of Greek military and Resistance fighters. The photograph was annotated in my grandmother's hand: *Medals Ceremony, Athens, Agora, 1949.* At the feet of the man with his arm around my father, again in my grandmother's elegant cursive script: *Nestor.* The name swam in my disoriented brain: another Nestor, like a family joke, a sardonic refrain? This Nestor hardly conjured visions of Bronze Age palaces and warriors huddled around flame pits listening to tales of heroic battles. The Nestor in the photo had a rough beard and deep-fissured eyes, a flat, hard face and gnarled forehead; dark hair cascaded in oily ringlets; he wore what looked like an old suit jacket over khaki fatigues, concealing anything in the way of insignia or rank. There was something of the bandit or peasant irregular in his stocky carriage. He barely came up to my father's shoulder. My father was smiling, but it was a forced smile above a dark business suit. His face seemed anxious, his cheekbones stood out, a smudge of black hair lay pasted on a sweaty brow, and his eyes were shadowed in the noonday sun and seemed distracted by something beyond the frame of the photo. Casually held against the side of his trousers was a cane—you had to look very closely to notice it. He had the look of a man (he was then Athens CIA station chief) who was uneasy, if not unhappy, to be where he was.

Perhaps this is a retrospective reading, for my grandmother was an excellent editor and this was precisely the image she wanted to remain . . . OSS, not CIA.

And who, I wondered again, the whisper of flushing urinals behind those eight-foot blast walls like a ringing in my ears, was Philby . . . and Angleton?

Just hours before, I had passed the display case with my usual nonchalance: just one more memento of my father's esteemed life. Suddenly these things—"relics of obscure glory," so described by Max—took on added weight: They mattered a great deal to me. These tangible proofs of a hero's life became my gold standard. Surely, such artifacts—much less the name emblazoned on the new gym—put the lie to those obscene speculations in the urinals, which threatened the meticulous ingenuity of my grandmother's grip on the family legacy. In the following years, as I bailed frantically, her handiwork of incised lettering kept me afloat. But the damage had been done, as is often the case with loose talk.

Outside, it was dark and chilly—a first hint of frost. I breathed deeply, shaking my head. I was shocked that the daylight was gone, the hard pinpricks of silver stars already over the Circle. I was an hour off schedule, out of sync with my habitual postgame routine—and winter looming. I walked slowly toward the dining hall, wanting things to comfortably settle back to how they'd been before the fourth quarter. I wanted company and I didn't want company. Jerry, I knew, was off working on his history paper for Monday. And Max—where the hell was Max? Who ever knew where Max was? He never came to football games. Never a pat on the back—You did great, Hawkman. (He once told an interviewer that all the school football scenes in his first novel were constructed on a single Sunday afternoon in 1975 as he watched NFL games on TV.) Most of the guys were off at local restaurants with their parents, discussing grades and teacher conferences held that morning. My mother could never be bothered and I never gave her reason, at least not on the grades front.

As I was walking around the Circle, alive to the aroma of woodsmoke, my head began to clear. I found relief in the dark's anonymity and the comforting thought of a retreat to the library, where I, too, had begun a deep dive into the *Odyssey* (checking Lattimore to see if I might do better).

Then I was aware of a presence behind me—an unsettling thing, because in the ambient light I'd seen nobody. I kept walking, holding on to my aloneness, as if by ignoring the footsteps they were bound to fade. My name was authoritatively called. I turned to a man in a suit and overcoat. He halted half a moment to light a cigarette, snap the lighter shut and exhale, inhale again and fix me with an unnervingly knowing smile.

A messenger from the gods holding my fate close to his.

"Hello, Peter." He moved to quickly take my hand, shaking it vigorously, lingering to keep me close as he examined my face. "Survived, I see?"

Elliot Goddard, his blond hair slicked back in a perfect crease, expertly reached to my jaw, as had the doctor who examined me in the training room, to appraise the damage.

"I'm okay, sir . . . and thanks for the Vince Lombardi book." It had been less than six months since I'd seen Elliot Goddard in the Founder's Day reception line. He'd served under my grandmother on the Winsted board since 1962. (*The New York Times* had even noted the fact, calling it a "closing of the ranks" after the Cuban Missile Crisis.) Elliot had often visited at Elysium in summer when I was a kid, invited by my grandmother. And he'd been best friends with my father at Winsted and later in the OSS and CIA. My father's letters are filled with anecdotes about Elliot, which my grandmother seemed to have relished. She'd dated his widowed father briefly after her husband had been killed in the First World War; they'd danced at the Vanderbilts' in Newport, sailed together on Buzzards Bay, and on some counterfactual level she must have wondered how drowning her grief in a second marriage might have provided her with the husband and companion of a lifetime she'd never had. Her one comment about his old seafaring Rhode Island family stuck with me: *They made their fortune as slavers.*

"The kid who threw the punch—he slipped a lace key into his jersey and palmed it before he hit you. The little shit should have been thrown out of the game; and the coach who put him up to it should be suspended, if not fired."

"The coach?"

"I knew they'd try something like this—they did it in my day, too. I was over on the Rivers sideline. I saw the coach order the hit. I've put it to Coach Alexander and Mr. Folley; they will file a protest with the league on Monday. Such unsportsmanlike behavior is unacceptable in this league. Rivers has always been a breeder of bullies—not that we didn't give them a pasting three years in a row when John and I played." He shrugged. "But *we* took the game seriously." With that backhand dismissal, he took another drag on his cigarette, his rugged good looks illuminated by the burning ash. "Here, walk with me to the headmaster's house; I'm already late for dinner." He put an arm around my shoulder. "Nice game, Peter. I always liked quarterbacks who knew how to use their running backs and not just their receivers." He snorted in acknowledgment of his little joke. "Paul Oakes says you've progressed much faster than he expected—poor guy, a shadow of himself with one lung missing. I've tried to convince him to try an experimental program at Walter Reed, but no go." With this, he examined his cigarette and then tossed it. "I swore to my wife I'd quit—only my second today."

Elliot Goddard squeezed my arm. "And the Gadsden boy—you should've seen him rip into the son of a bitch who hit you. The next offensive play, Jerry blocked the left tackle fifteen yards in reverse, halfway to his own bench, before dropping him. It took three guys to haul him off the field, nasty little bugger."

That was the first I'd heard of it, and I suddenly wanted to throw my arms around Jerry.

"Isn't Jerry incredible? It's . . . well, it's like handing the ball to a gale-force wind."

"Gale-force wind, huh, I like that. Took some doing to get Jerry. Went down to Jackson, Mississippi, myself. Can't get much deeper in the Old South than that. Dirt-poor, two brothers—one in jail, one in the army—five sisters, dad abandoned the family, mother drinking. I got a tutor working with him for two years until we got his grades up, until he was ready for Winsted. Had to pry him away from his besotted mother: her eldest, her pride and joy. Now he's got a chance to make something of himself. I've got the Yale coach down next week to check him out, so be sure to give him the ball."

No wonder Jerry never wanted to talk about his family.

"He's smart," I said. "Jerry is in the library all the time. Latin kind of throws him, but I've been able to help him with that, and history."

Elliot gave my shoulder another squeeze.

"That's the ticket. We need black kids like Jerry. The world's got to know that we mean what's written in the Declaration of Independence. That we stand for something more than just making money and kicking Commie ass." Elliot paused for a reaction, reviewing the silhouetted apple trees on the Circle as if they were on parade. "So, what do you and Jerry think of the new headmaster?"

Even then, even with a pro like Elliot guiding the conversation, I think I probably realized this was the essential point—that and making sure Jerry looked good the following Saturday. I was pleased to be consulted by a man who was already a legend in his own time. Not that I really knew as much then, but I had an inkling from the stray remarks in the urinals. Gathering accurate intelligence from sources on the ground—tradecraft—was Elliot's specialty when he wasn't upending tiny countries like Guatemala.

"I think there are some style issues, but maybe . . . we'll just get used to him—or he us."

Elliot laughed and I winced and my jaw throbbed.

"'Sith nor th'exterior nor the inward man/Resembles that it was.'"

Elliot barked another laugh at this quote from his favorite author, and as we neared the lighted windows of the headmaster's house, I turned and saw every muscle in his powerful face flex as it went through a repertoire of expressions from amusement to knowingness. His blond hair, in the diffuse lamplight from the doorway, reminded me of the color of tarnished bronze in a Mycenaean breastplate at the Met, the way it sparked with highlights along the edges of his clean part. "I hate to let you in on a dirty secret—what are you now, fifteen, right?" I nodded. "But style, more often than not, ends up being the crucial factor. The perception of an event is often more telling than the event itself." This bit of professional wisdom, with a grin attached, came out as an inside joke. Only a few years before, his pals had bowed to White House pressure and set in motion a coup to overthrow the South Vietnamese president, Diem, because it was felt his aristocratic hauteur and persecution of Buddhists, among other foibles, had lost him the necessary popular support in the face of the growing Communist insurgency. Perception had triumphed over the reality: Diem was *all* they had. No bench strength whatsoever.

"Perhaps . . . he's trying a little too hard," he said.

"The seniors, the prefects can't stand him. They mock him to his face."

"Well, seniors, like the faculty—if all you've ever known was old man Crocket . . ." He shrugged. "Tough act to follow. Even in our day, the old man—and let me tell you, he was old—Harvard does that to you—when he was young—was like George Washington on Mount Rushmore: boring, humorless, immovable on most subjects, but at least you knew who stood by you at the Battle of Trenton. Your dad was the only boy I ever knew to stand up to old man Crocket and get away with it."

This tidbit only got my head spinning again: Jack Crocket's silence all the more ominous.

"John and I used to laugh about it, but at the time it was pretty damn scary."

Elliot, as if sensing my rising consternation, dialed it down a notch.

"I mean, John was such a classics man; he wore it on his sleeve, so to speak. Pop off in sacred studies class about Homer's take on divinity and such like—over my pay grade, of course. Chip off General Alden's block, if you know what I mean: seeing what he'd seen at Antietam . . . well, the received claptrap no longer held water. We had to find our own way . . . ."

That went right over my head. I could sense Elliot stiffen a little, his powerful bandy legs gaining a half step as we continued, as if to change the subject: the secret society he'd concocted with my father their senior year.

All that mattered, from what I'd overheard: Elliot was a loyal ally. I never forgot it.

"My father was a great scholar," I said, as if needing to anchor our bond of loyalty in a safe harbor. "His papers on Homer, his excavation reports in Crete and the Peloponnese are still quoted in scholarly texts today."

This seemed to bring Elliot to an abrupt stop, just short of the arc of flickering lamplight from the white-columned portico of the head-master's house. He must have detected the needy note in my voice. He nodded benignly, respectfully, as he adjusted his blue-and-white Yale letter tie.

"Ah," he said, as if discovering a more convenient truth to impart. "Maybe that's a good way of . . . well, of looking at things. And of course you're right. Your dad *was* a serious scholar—sometimes one forgets how the war changed things." His eyes turned to the darkness at our backs and his face went into eclipse. "Such a serious guy, the way he used to scold me in the huddle: 'No more brooding in your tent, Elliot.' I had quite the temper back then; you see, I couldn't bear to lose. And fear of losing—he liked to tell me—is what causes mistakes." A self-deprecating smile bloomed on his lips, and his shoulders under the camel-hair overcoat went slack. "That's why he was so popular. He was a congenital optimist, always looking for the best in people." He raised his eyes to the expanse of the Circle, a hint of light in the rose window of the chapel, and sighed with something touching a faint nostalgia.

"That was quite a trick in the Depression, and if the Depression didn't knock the optimism out of you—killed my favorite uncle, the war sure did. People stopped believing in the fundamentals; they lost perspective . . . and worse: Bad ideas get a purchase in this world. That's what makes it so hard—optimism, I mean. But when you're stuck dealing with the criminal mind, you're a lot safer believing the worst. Believe me, better to be wrong and pleasantly surprised. Otherwise, you get eaten alive."

This passed for sage advice from someone who'd overthrown governments and infamously failed to overthrow the one that really mattered. A man haunted by screams for help from the Cubanistas he'd trained, who were abandoned and killed and captured on the swampy beaches of the Bay of Pigs. These sad details were, of course, unknown to me then. What had riveted my attention was his description of my father's optimism, when his letters were filled with a pessimism touching on an inner darkness that I knew only too well. I wanted to shake my head, tempted to ask about his friend and teammate who brooded to his mother about a looming dark age, who pined for the return of a golden age, for the Elysium summers of his youth, the thing glimpsed in his glowing descriptions of the island of the Phaeacians in his translation of the *Odyssey*.

And yet Elliot saw nothing of this.

"You could feel it in the quickening rhythm of his stroke as we neared the finish . . . we were inspired to keep up."

Had my father disguised it all so well? Did it have something to do with his equivocation about Elliot's unpleasant behavior: his merciless bullying of Bobby Williams, his tantrums and selfishness on the field? Like Jerry Gadsden, Elliot had protected my father, laying out more than a few opponents who had made illegal hits on his quarterback. It was Elliot who got kicked out of games, got a reputation as a brawler, and so was scolded by old man Crocket for unsportsmanlike behavior. While my father, smelling like roses, got all the glory—and three championship seasons.

I suppose I was crazy and naïve to trust Elliot, because the moment he sniffed out the compromising affair between my father and Suzanne (a Philby go-between), he'd used it to get him to give up Princeton and return to Athens in 1948 as CIA station chief.

But on that cool October evening, with American boys beginning to die by the hundreds in Vietnam, I was drawn to Elliot's loyalty to my family, to the fragile code of honor that Max so trashed and yet failed to decipher. For Elliot Goddard's fate and that of my father—at least in the eyes of history—still hung in the balance, and they hung in tandem. With Cuba a still-festering fiasco, Vietnam was to be a make-or-break attempt to hold the line for his generation: The whole policy of containment was at risk. Elliot's crowd knew their reputations for good or ill were up for grabs, dependent on another insecure Texan's last throw of the dice as half a million troops went in.

And Elliot's Phoenix Program was just beginning its deadly harvest.

Of course, in the gaslit lamps of the white Doric-columned portico, this unfortunate history to come was but a phantom on the wind. The Circle was our refuge, our brass bottom self-respect, the cocoon of our identity, from which we drew strength . . . and safety. We talked urgently about headmaster Folley. Here, too, Elliot tried to be loyal and circumspect about a man he detested: They—the board—would all look stupid ditching the little turd after only a year. Maybe he could be brought along: somehow learn to talk the talk, walk the walk. Damage control was on Elliot's mind.

"You know what bothered me at your age?" Elliot asked, moving us to a convivial parting, eager now to go on into the brilliantly lit interior of the headmaster's cozy residence, where his fans and detractors were waiting for updates of far greater import than Byron Folley's failure of leadership. He paused for effect. "How Shakespeare could exist without there being a Shakespeare to write those extraordinary plays. It really bothered me: no manuscripts, no autograph copies of the plays, no history for the playwright, as if this huge lie was being perpetuated generation after generation."

I stood there wide-eyed, wondering if I was hearing right: How had we stumbled onto this subject?

He began to gather steam on his pet theory but then waved it off as he realized he really did have better things to do.

A little over a year later, a book arrived all the way from the American embassy in Saigon by an Englishman named Looney (which can't have helped his cause), "*Shakespeare" Identified*, written in 1920, which makes the case that Shakespeare was in reality Edward de Vere, the seventeenth earl of Oxford. From my father's letters, I knew that Elliot had been passionately carrying the flame for the seventeenth earl of Oxford since Winsted days, since his favorite uncle gave him Looney's book during his fourth-form year. As far back as Yale Law School, he'd neglected his studies to read the plays again and again, detecting the exquisitely subtle legalisms strewn throughout. Only someone trained in the law could even begin to grasp such subtleties, he always told me. He became obsessed by the detailed references to Venice and Italy, the insider knowledge of court politics. During his Wall Street lawyer days before the war, he took any firm business in London, haunting the Bodleian in search of clues for the greatest fraud in literary history. In London during the war, head of an OSS Jedburgh team waiting to be dropped into occupied France after the D-day landings, he sometimes found himself in a near panic with the thought that a bomb-damaged block, a burned library, might have forever destroyed the evidence for de Vere's authorship. As he told me years later, "Even after I got back from Brittany, every time I heard a buzz bomb overhead, I wondered if that might be the one to do it." By 1975 and the Church hearings into the CIA, with his career in shambles, Elliot retreated to his Buzzards Bay home to lick his wounds and write his unfinished magnum opus, proving that the Bard was in fact Edward de Vere.

But on that night, Elliot was a lifesaver and a steadfast tie to my father, a Cold Warrior still trying to keep our country safe and the CIA's reputation alive after the near death of the Bay of Pigs. He was still a magnetic presence then, his strong nose, which always struck me like the nose of the Indian on the buffalo-head nickel, lifted with an aggressive flexing of the nostrils toward the firelit parlor. The trustees were all gathered in the foyer before dinner, the headmaster's mousy wife passing around Texas hors d'oeuvres (pulled pork on potato rolls, Elliot complained), and there was Suzanne Williams standing tall and resplendent behind her husband's wheelchair—the sullen, skulking, disfigured Bobby. She drew every male eye in the room, including that of Elliot Goddard, who watched her covertly through the glass door from the gaslit shadows of the portico. He'd had a thing for her—who hadn't; he'd met his English wife at Suzanne's wedding. She'd been maid of honor at the ceremony in the back garden of Colonel Fairburn's country house in Sussex, just weeks before Elliot parachuted into Brittany. Elliot had talked Shakespeare to his bride-to-be and gallantly promised her, half in jest, that if he survived the war, he'd marry her. And he did, with three daughters—Goneril, Regan, Cordelia—to prove it.

I've often asked myself why I didn't just ask Elliot about the overheard conversation in the urinals. I was in awe of this man and I hoped I'd heard wrong. Besides, Elliot would have had to lie to me, because

Kim Philby had defected to the Soviets only three years before and the fallout was still rippling through the intelligence services of the free world. Elliot and my father had first met Philby at Bobby and Suzanne's Sussex wedding in June 1944. Philby, the most icily smooth and debonair of the Cambridge Five traitors; Philby, who deceived and besmirched everyone he touched; the man who murdered my father.

I can just see Max's horrified face. "Don't give your ending away, Hawkman. Keep the reader in suspense."

But this is not fiction. I'm just trying to set down the facts.

And James Jesus Angleton, head of CIA counterintelligence, who knew Kim Philby's diabolical machinations only too well, became convinced my father had tried to defect to Moscow, where he'd been quietly disposed of; and that Elliot, if not complicit or simply careless, was fatally compromised.

"How's your American history?" Elliot asked as we shook hands. His eyes, now glittering with interior light, turned again to the happy gathering and, as I followed his longing gaze, I too, recognized Suzanne wearing a sequined evening dress that showed off the tensile bone work of her shoulders and upward curve of her breasts.

"We don't really take American history until sixth-form year."

In the fantail window above the door, a huge luna moth had settled, a transfixing aquamarine-and-turquoise flame for wings. I was struck by its beauty and wondered if I might reach up and grab it, if I'd make a fool of myself by doing so.

"Yes, yes." He pondered this impatiently. "That's what I remember, too." Elliot rejiggered his crotch. A glow came into his eager face, as it must have on the playing field decades before when a play to his liking had been called, and his chieftain's nose lifted to the warming smell of the crackling fireplace. "Tell me about the Monroe Doctrine."

"The Monroe Doctrine?"

"What it is, what it means, what it implies."

Pathetically, I had no idea, and my gaze kept straying to the luna moth—emblem of summer's fading—just out of reach.

"Tell me the names of Henry the Eighth's wives."

I rattled them off.

"Well"—and he placed his hand on my shoulder in a parting gesture—"maybe I need to have a little conversation with the headmaster."

More than twenty years later in cold, rainy Prague, with the Berlin Wall pulled down just days before, and Elliot on his last legs, he'd bemoan again about the big *if* of his career—the counterfactuals we historians so love to contemplate—if that little shit Jack Kennedy had only had the balls to invoke the goddamn Monroe Doctrine and defend our backyard from Soviet aggression—hadn't Teddy R. stolen Cuba fair and square in the first place?—if that womanizer had sent in the marines to run Fidel out of fucking Cuba from the get-go—and fuck plausible deniability—then all the other catastrophes from the Bay of Pigs, the Cuban Missile Crisis, and even Vietnam could have been avoided. If *his* boys hadn't been left to die on that godforsaken beach without the promised air cover, it all might have been different. . . .

And so it might.

But he couldn't tell a fifteen-year-old kid that kind of thing. And Vietnam hadn't even become Vietnam—or not quite. And Philby was spilling the beans in Moscow and planning his autobiography, and Suzanne was waiting.

And that's when I remembered where I'd heard the name before; Joe Alsop had mentioned it: . . . *spring of '53 with the Kim Philby scandal the buzz of Washington* . . .

Not much to go on, but enough.

December 2, 1929
Winsted School

Dear Mother,

Here is the gist of my essay on Homer and the tangled morality tale of the *Odyssey* for sacred studies class—your thoughts, please?

I expect your protégé Mr. Crocket is going to put me through the ringer.

Odysseus is a great warrior and force for moral rectitude, but also a famous schemer and liar. He often turns out to be a pirate and despoiler and proud of it. Not quite on the up-and-up. He loves his wife and son, longs to return to his island kingdom and be reunited with them—all the while lying in the arms of another woman, Calypso. But a hero gets to have it both ways. Then when he finally returns home, he exacts the most terrible revenge on his wife's suitors, piteously slaughtering well over a hundred. How does that sit with the Ten Commandments, or, dare I say, King David's thousands slain?

Well, the mortals in the *Odyssey* are forever prostrating themselves and making sacrifices to the jealous gods, who decide their fate on the basis of whimsy and injured pride. Destiny, they call it when things turn out badly. Or Zeus blames Poseidon for Odysseus's trials. Or condemns humans for blaming their troubles on the gods, instead of looking to their own reckless ways—as he puts it, compounding their pains beyond their proper share. Telemachus, in turn, blames Zeus for dealing to each and every laborer on this earth whatever doom he pleases.

So, Zeus *is* wicked and vindictive, punishing entire cities for the merest slight. His treatment of the Phaeacians at the end of the epic, setting a mountain around their city, merely for transporting Odysseus home, is a travesty of justice. And yet—this will be my thesis: There is a certain moral grandeur as the poet has his characters seek to make sense of a cruel world and find a way to take control of their fate. They may beseech their gods, but in the end these mortals are left to their own devices. They succeed or fail according to their choices, good or bad.

Dare I ask Mr. Crocket if his God is responsible for our Hoovervilles and breadlines? If it is the wise all-knowing God of *Essays and Prayers,* who directed a five-hundred-pound shell onto father's operating theater, then I wash my hands of Him.

I think my central point is that in Homer's universe men attempt to placate the gods (fate) as best they can, while in the Old Testament, a jealous God (with absolute power and no competitors) does exactly what He pleases and mankind can do nothing but grin and bear it.

So which book do you chose, Mother Nestor, or, as you like to say, which better accommodates our free will?

Write me as soon as you can with your comments. My essay is due next week and the wrath of the temple looms.

Karel Hollar and I are in furious correspondence over the location of the land of the Phaeacians. He says it must be Corfu, but I feel by internal evidence that it may well be Minoan Crete—and poor Nausicaa forever immured by wicked Zeus!

The situation with Bobby is still no better: The more he complains, the more he is picked upon by all and sundry. Elliot's cruelty to Bobby is awful, but Bobby's "radical airs," as Elliot describes them, just make him wild. I try to keep an eye on Bobby at your insistence, but he rejects everything; he is really his own worst enemy: extolling Stalin as the savior of the Western world! His mother's debauchery in Paris is the source of endless crude gossip. If only he'd stick to his music; I still love to hear him practice the piano or organ in the chapel and dream of better days.

Elliot got thrown out of the football match on Saturday for using obscenities. He has not learned to control his temper even after his last visit to Mr. Crocket's study. Nevertheless, I'm glad to have him on my side of the line of scrimmage, my valiant Diomides. By the way, when Elliot comes to visit in the city over Christmas vacation, don't bring up Shakespeare. You will never hear the end of it.

It was a terrible thing about Elliot's uncle.

Love, John

PS: Please send me my large volume of Evans's Linear B tablets.

6 THE SUMMER BETWEEN FOURTH AND FIFTH FORM, our "Summer of Love," I got my driver's license, I got my own car, and I drove out west by my lonesome to an archaeological dig in Arizona, site of a lost Hopi village. I wanted to put miles between myself and my family's roots, which seemed less roots and more like snares. Go where nobody knew me. I wanted to get my hands dirty like my father and like General Alden when he went west to build the railways. I fell in love with the anonymity, the wide-open spaces beyond the Mississippi. And I did exactly what my mother had warned me against—sworn me against. I picked up hitchhikers everywhere: ripe-smelling hippies headed to the Haight or a rumored commune somewhere near Takilma, Oregon; runny-nosed addicts snorting cocaine in the backseat; soldiers on the way back from leave and headed for Vietnam—changing (after a fight at home) the names of beneficiaries in their wills; bandannaed Indians, near comatose and smelling of whiskey, returning penniless to their reservation—silent as a tombstone for a hundred miles; an obese tuba player on his way to a band competition in Salt Lake City who passed gas for 210 straight miles; a leggy showgirl returning to Vegas (she had a Henckels kitchen knife strapped to her calf, which she made sure I noticed as she climbed in) after burying her father somewhere in Iowa; the unemployed moving from one town to the next with expectations of a new job, a new life, which they described in telling detail; an abandoned wife with black stitches and a yellow bruise over her right eye, which she kept resolutely turned away from me, but which I could clearly see in my right-side mirror; and a talkative wife, frail as a windblown juniper, visiting her jailed husband three states over, dressed in a miniskirt and stiletto-healed white go-go

boots (he was in for life for murdering their son in a poker game, and when I dropped her off at the penitentiary in Dearborn, she had tears in her eyes and asked if I'd like to meet her husband: "You'd so remind him of Billy—make his day"). I listened to their stories and lied about mine; I learned their lingo and I learned to disguise my New England accent. The freer I felt, the less apprehension—that something might be expected of me, that I owed anything to anyone.

How I yearned to lose myself in those vast spaces, the russet-and-orange rock formations framing the milky blue skies of the Southwest, the stubborn green and purple of the sagebrush, the vast night skies alive with shooting stars silhouetting Yosemite's El Capitan, the hush of dusk settling over a desert fragrant with dust, creosote and the scent of rain, and the sweaty exhaustion of a day's digging in the red dirt, when every shard of bone and pottery cried out to be heard. The only thing I missed was rowing and maybe our white pines, and, at least by summer's end, Max (impressed as a monitor in his mother's master class at Tanglewood) . . . the cuttlefish bone in my cage, as he put it: "the better to sharpen your beak, Hawkman."

I fell in love with my country and all its odd and troubled, lonely and loyal people, many of whom seemed to be wandering that summer, escaping troubles known for troubles unknown, some piece of turf beyond the setting sun to keep them safe. So many drifting west, especially pimply young soldiers from the South and Midwest headed to Korea, Guam, Subic Bay, and Saigon, farm boys, black and white, who'd never seen a big city, whose openness and honest nature reminded me of Jerry Gadsden, whom I missed terribly.

Only years later did I recognize something of myself in my great-grandfather's travels, General Alden's years out west, "his wilderness years," as my grandmother described them, after his wounding at Antietam in 1862 and dismissal by General McClellan, when he spent a decade away from the East, building railroads through the Rockies and the Sierras, making his fortune as he remade himself and tried to forget parts of himself . . . and the agonized cries of his men in the Cornfield at Antietam, ripping open their tunics to see if they were gut-shot. He, too, had found safety in the vastness of the country and had returned to invest something of that exultant freedom in Elysium, and even Winsted, which the years had polished to a dull mediocrity.

Something lost . . . which I longed to rediscover and Max to appropriate for his own uses.

Before school and early football camp, I drove up to Elysium for a break and to see if I could locate something of the yearning that nagged my footsteps. I drove in from Pittsburgh in my by then not so new Chevy Impala (11,284 miles), the safest car on the road, according to the dealership that had sold it to my mother. It was the first time driving myself through the Berkshires, returning home from across the country, and it gave a certain poignancy to the high summer and the tall sinewy white pines, which seemed to be exuberantly flagging me on. But when I reached our cottage, I was crestfallen to find it in disarray, shutters still closed from winter—except for one that had rotted off its hinges—grass uncut, fallen tree branches everywhere, matted leaves in damp clumps on the veranda, and, inside, a year's worth of dust and mouse droppings. Plaster was down, windows broken, spiderwebs on every surface. Since my grandmother's death, my mother had taken a perverse revenge by refusing to return; she summered with her Colony Club bridge pals in Southampton or Martha's Vineyard; she preferred being near the sea, she told me—"always have, always will." Spoken like a true admiral's daughter. She hadn't even bothered to have the custodial staff keep up the basics, as if by letting the place go to hell I might be dissuaded from "holing up in the Alden mausoleum." I didn't bother to call her or complain. I spent the first week cleaning, fixing up stuff, picking up the fallen branches, and mowing the grass. Following the precise instructions passed on to me by my grandmother—"the rituals of the manse," she called them—I wound the three clocks in the living room, polished the brass pots over the fieldstone fireplace, carefully cleaned the Tiffany windows overlooking the lake, and very, very carefully dusted the frames of the Innesses, Wyants, and Homer Dodge Martins—my great-grandfather's favorite painters—in the Inness gallery.

Flying squirrels had gotten into my father's boyhood room in the attic, chewing on his books and manuscripts and collections of flora and fauna. Fortunately, they'd overlooked the typescript of his "Life of Alexander," which I'd left on his desk, next to his green Underwood typewriter. I leafed through the pages, more amazed than ever at his scholarship, and smiled in recognition when I found interleafed among them Max's postcards from the previous summer, his old master nudes and dirty limericks from Venice. How comforting to find everything pretty much as I'd left it, as my father had left it, including the cigar box with that impossibly huge eastern diamondback skin, the framed prints and memorabilia on the walls, and, at my feet, the pile of books on the floor—maybe it was time to return those volumes on the Greek Bronze Age to their slots on the shelf?

Once I had the house back to some semblance of normality, I began jogging the woodland paths first blazed by General Alden for his wife, children, and the families of railway financiers and conservationists who stayed for weeks at a time in the summers. I began rowing laps in our lake to get back in shape for football in September. I also unlocked the gun locker in the basement and got out a .22 and went to the shooting range to practice my marksmanship. This, too, I did more by rote than because of any real enthusiasm, a ritual I'd known from early childhood, when my grandmother had arranged for the caretaker to take me to the range for target practice over summer vacation. Tom Malloy was an old Irishman with pale, red-veined cheeks, a veteran of the First World War, who had first been hired by my grandmother (he'd been a stretcher-bearer in my grandfather's regiment in the Argonne, so she told me) and had taught my father to shoot as a boy. Tom's father, Sean Malloy, a Civil War veteran, had later joined the Pinkertons, when he'd been hired by General Alden as a bodyguard for Pearce Breckenridge. Following that debacle, Sean had been taken on as the first caretaker at Elysium. A bit of family history—the tragic tale of Pearce Breckenridge—as invisible to me as it had been to Sean's son, Tom. I didn't really care for messing around with firearms, and I had zero taste for hunting, and yet I was a pretty good shot, and every time I hit a bull's-eye I felt Tom's squeeze on my shoulder as he said, "Another good hit, lad." And being pretty good seemed reason enough for keeping my eye in, for staying in touch with long tradition.

On one of my jogs, near the end of my stay, a day near ninety and humid, I headed for the beach at the head of our lake for a swim to cool off. Here, by the fifty-foot bluestone dam, the water was deep and cool. I was running full tilt, with every intention of stripping off my shorts and T-shirt—I had my T-shirt in my hand—and diving straight in. I was startled to find Bobby and Suzanne Williams sunning themselves in the last of the afternoon light. Bobby was in a white Adirondack chair, his wheelchair stowed nearby, with his head thrown back under a broad cream-colored Panama hat—his burn-scarred face had to be kept out of the sun. Suzanne was stretched out on a huge striped beach towel, stark naked except for a pair of fashionable sunglasses, a paperback in her hand. I was dumbfounded. Not that they didn't have a perfect right to be there. The whole property, the nature preserve of twenty thousand acres, was held in common by our two families and had been for over eighty years and four generations. Our two cottages shared the lake but occupied opposite shores, so that except for boating activities, the hiking trails, and use of the beach, there was little reason to ever run into anyone from the other clan. And after the Amory Williams scandals of the twenties, fraternization pretty much ceased. The beach and swimming area, with its cedar dock and float, had once provided neutral ground, and in the 1880s through the turn of the century the men traditionally swam "buck naked" at the "swimming hole." Suzanne had always proved a problematic presence at the beach for her various states of undress, and a source of irritation for my mother and grandmother. And the phrase, delivered in a rising dismissive hiss—"She's at the beach"—echoes as a desultory disappointment out of my earliest childhood memories.

I had never seen Bobby Williams out of his wheelchair, nor had I seen a nude woman before, and certainly not one so handsome and incredibly fit for her late forties. My first reaction, besides embarrassment, was shock at the honey-blond growth of pubic hair where Suzanne's long, muscled legs merged into the sharp angle of her hips. None of Max's Venetian nudes, nor his *Playboy* magazines, had quite prepared me. And there was no retreat. I'd dashed though the concealing trees and burst onto the sand to within five feet of the water before realizing they were there. I stood panting like a big stupid dog with my shirt in hand, afraid to go in, afraid to go back.

Bobby looked up from under his Panama hat while Suzanne, with icy aplomb, simply flipped a part of the beach towel over her waist and stared at me though her dark glasses, her small but bobbing breasts an insinuating presence. The sun was in their faces, and Suzanne first held up her hand to her eyes to reduce the glare. I began to back away with rapid apologies, fearing a repetition of Suzanne's look of horror in the chapel the year before, much less that bulging purple vein.

"Ha," snorted Bobby, "last of the Mohicans."

He held out his hand for me to shake, motioning me over with the agile fingertips that had once dazzled the ivories in concert halls on two continents, including the cities of Moscow and Leningrad.

His slick-skinned hand was clammy and unpleasant. But he smiled serenely, his face mostly in shadow beneath the brim of his hat. In turn, Suzanne propped herself on an elbow and reached for my hand, which she gripped and held for long seconds as I sought to decipher the expression behind the lake glare in her dark glasses. It took some doing not to look at her breasts.

"I was wondering," Bobby sang out with the sudden animation of a lounge singer behind a piano, "if we were to have Elysium all to ourselves this summer. 'Where be the Aldens?' I was just saying—right, Suzanne dear?—just minutes ago, 'Where have they all fled?'"

I fully registered this insouciant opening gambit of Bobby Williams, entirely typical of him in that it implied both delight at our demise and sadness that he'd have no one left to mess with. His intimate conviviality, a thing his naked wife seemed to playfully echo in her dark, bemused gaze, implied the rarified sanctum sanctorum of our proud, if sad, history. John Alden and Samuel Williams had built this woodland preserve as an escape from pestilence and trouble, where the pious could share nature raw and in the buff, in all its innocent splendor. For a brief moment, like some trick of the mind, harking back to those alpha males of generations past who skinny-dipped apart from their corseted females, Suzanne's charming and blithely careless display seemed less about sex and more a symbol of high-minded hauteur, a kind of sylvan tableau, something of a Williams specialty, in my grandmother's memory, right up to the early twenties. About the time this Emersonian vision of nature's unencumbered spirit succumbed to the Jazz Age. Something Max picked up on as he dissected the rarified Transcendentalism of the Williamses in his second novel, *Gardens of Saturn.*

Making perception the reality, as Elliot Goddard liked to say, is the one great trick of the twentieth century. And Suzanne, with her Party cohorts, was a master at such legerdemain. But in this case, I think not. If I have learned anything, it *is* about sex; it's always about sex.

My father in his love letters and Pankrác diary had called her his Calypso: goddess, sorceress, and so much more.

"Yes, the younger generation has fled the nest," said Suzanne, breaking her amused silence. "Laura has gone, as well. The Boston Ballet is touring in Australia this summer, and they decided to take her along to the antipodes as a reserve member in the corps de ballet."

She was both bragging as a mother and letting me know not to bother looking for Laura or asking about her—she hadn't missed our little colloquy at Winsted under the apple trees—which I'd had no intention of doing anyway. It was also her way of letting a new male on the estate know the coast was clear and she was the only game in town: a thing dully registered in some obscure corner of my being.

"How's your dear mother doing?" asked Bobby.

My standing shadow was flickering across their upturned faces as I awkwardly wiped at my dripping chest with the T-shirt.

"She's—last I heard—at the Edgartown yacht club, playing bridge."

"Ah yes, played a few hands myself in the war, forever waiting between ops."

What are ops? I wondered. Bobby hadn't even bothered to attend my grandmother's funeral; it might have provided him with a onetime chance to spit on her grave.

"By all accounts, I hear you've become the great white hope of the football team."

What to make of that? But I tried to be polite, as my grandmother would have insisted, even to a sworn enemy, a cousin yet. What I knew from my father's letters was that Bobby had been excused from football his second-form year—his hands were too fragile to put at risk. Thus the nickname "Fragile Fingers" that pursued him through Winsted and beyond in certain circles. I also had a pretty good idea from my father's letters how much Elliot Goddard had hated Bobby—and still did. To the world at large, Bobby was a wounded war hero, a navigator on a B-17 shot down over Germany. His classmates, especially those in the CIA, knew otherwise. To me, the slick pinkish scars on the lower portion of his face, neck and hands, and lifeless legs were a piteous testimony to some hellish experience. Surely he deserved sympathy.

"It was a pretty good season. We lost only one game."

"Yes, the Rivers game. I was there. I gather a rotten bunch of misfits."

"No, you weren't." Suzanne's expectant smile turned to an irritated frown. She slid her dark glasses down her nose and her enormous blue eyes just sliced though me, seeing me and not, carefully examining my sweaty body from head to toe. Her knuckles rose white where they clutched her knee and the bit of modest towel. "You insisted on attending that tedious meeting of the now-defunct Missionary Society."

"Well," he sputtered. "Business before pleasure . . . I was there in spirit."

She shook her head, and there was a flush now in her cheeks as she pushed the sunglasses back into place, as if preferring to examine me with more anonymity. "You detest football," she said, as if determined to stir things up. "You always have and you always will—just quoting you, darling." Her English accent was rapier sharp and her magnificent breasts expanded with each breath, nipples bristling in a jittery dance of divine power over the fallen lump seated next to her.

"Now that we've got you cornered," he went on, as if oblivious to his wife's displeasure, "tell me what you think of the new headmaster, Mr. Folley?"

"He's certainly . . . different," I offered.

"Yes, a change—that's the point I keep making. A change, some fresh air. We need to shake the old place, juice it up, inject some heart-felt spirituality—not empty ritual and dusty claptrap. I've suggested my grandfather's *Essays and Prayers* be included in the sacred studies curriculum again. A best-seller in its day, you know."

I nodded, thinking about the copy given me by Paul Oakes almost two years before, which I hadn't returned and had barely glanced at. "Well, I guess Mr. Folley has managed a few good changes. Although some aren't especially thrilled with the stuff in the chapel."

Suzanne allowed a repressed snicker and a nod, as if to urge me on. Bobby kept prompting with a thin smile, wetting his lips. "I hear the younger boys love him, his conviviality and approachability. He's assured us that we'll up the ante of scholarship boys. He's offered to go directly to the NAACP to help them recruit more blacks for Winsted."

This was true, and he dangled this bait because he knew the initiative had originally come from my grandmother.

"That sounds like a fine idea."

As if fiendishly reading my mind, he said, "I do miss your grand-mother's wise counsel, you know; things just aren't the same without her stalwart presence."

"Folley is a dimwit, a half-sunk ship," said Suzanne. "Suck us all down, too."

He ignored this.

"I've got him on board to allow the boys to attend Symphony Hall on Thursday afternoons, and visit museums in Boston—protest Vietnam on the Common, if they like. And his speakers program is certainly adding to the mix of viewpoints . . ."

That really set Suzanne off. "Oh, do shut up, Bobby. You know the man's a bloody disaster, and you're the only one defending him on the board."

My ears were flapping.

"That's because they're all Goldwater Red-baiters who wouldn't know a progressive nationalist cause if it bit them."

"Don't make yourself ridiculous. You know they're true-blue Democrats just serving time until Bobby throws his hat in the ring—Johnson's the only game in town."

"One Kennedy getting us blown up over Cuba was enough."

"Nothing to fear, now that you've got your own bloody fallout shelter." She looked at me with plucked eyebrows raised in amazement. "Have you seen our concrete bunker, our hideous underground mausoleum tucked in at Hermitage?"

"Bunker?"

"Surely you must've at least heard them building the damnable thing. Christ, what a racket. Dug up half of my rose garden. Who'd want to survive anyway?"

"Enough, Suzanne. Besides, Gene McCarthy's the one to oust that idiot redneck cowboy from the White House. Texans have been dyed-in-the-wool imperialists since Sam Houston screwed Mexico."

"Then why the hell did you foist Folley on the board, *your* Texas idiot."

"Well, you just wait. I've almost got Folley talked around on Vietnam, and then we'll get the faculty on board—wait till *The New York Times* gets wind of that!"

She threw back her head, her shoulder-length hair a golden freshet in the waning sunlight; she smiled at me, her brows flexing with something between a knowing look and murderous pleasure, as if to say, *See, I've drawn out the pathetic creature from its lair for you. Step on it for me, will you . . . please.*

"Ah yes, you'll do Kim"—she threw her paperback at him and the towel slipped off her knee—"and *dear* Anthony proud yet."

"Suzanne!"

"Just look what we've come to."

Bobby dropped the hand protecting his face. "Why don't you come by for dinner? There's something I've been meaning to show you."

"Not tonight, dear."

"Oh, but you must. After all, your grandmother was such a fervent supporter of the arts."

"We have guests, dear . . . remember, *your* headmaster."

"But couldn't we fit the boy right in?"

"Another fucking night. . . ."

ANTHONY BLUNT TO MOSCOW CENTER, 1937.
KGB FILE 58380

Bobby Williams, whom I have known for several years now, has performed his duties well. He is one of the leaders (as a person, he is not an organizer) among the Americans in the Communist Club in Cambridge. He has a keen mind and his talent in the music world draws in many admirers. He is extremely devoted to the Party and completely dependable, although he has not quite let go of certain romantic notions. Considering his family connections (his grandfather founded one of America's most prestigious schools; President Roosevelt is a graduate), impending fortune (his ravenous aunt amassed one of the greatest old master collections in America), and his ability to circulate in the world of art and politics, it stands to reason that he has a bright future ahead of him . . . He strikes one as being very young and full of enthusiasm, and he can be considered capable of secret work; he is devoted enough for it.

As I ran back to the house, my panic only grew, as if in my absence a break-in had happened and the place lay ransacked. I looked around, checked my grandmother's locked archive room under the stairs, and then dashed up to my father's room. Everything looked okay. I breathed deeply of the healing aroma of mildewed books in the close air under the eaves. It was steamy hot and I stripped off my clothes and shoes, as if they, too, were contaminated. A bunker, a mausoleum, a fallout shelter at Elysium? I went to the Underwood and tapped at the keys, turning to the glimmering sunset over the lake, which appeared like wildfire in the uppermost branches of the attendant pines.

As I look back on that sixteen-year-old tapping distractedly at the springy keys, perhaps a Morse code plea for help, I better recognize the threat he'd only just glimpsed. I try to cut him slack for his failures, his naïveté, and yet urge him to keep his wits about him, as I do my students.

That previous spring, there had been a vicious editorial in *The New York Times* about how the president's top foreign policy advisers, many Winsted boys, shared the same self-serving values of a privileged elite nurtured on shabby excuses about noblesse oblige, "beyond archaic and not a little self-satisfied, attitudes utterly out of sync with the modern world . . . and the quagmire in Vietnam."

Bobby had been leaking to the press.

I squinted across the lake to where the Williamses' glittering

Hermitage, white clapboard feathered in green and red-mauve, began to fade along the far shore. And as I did, I became aware of my aroused state, painfully so. And though I suspected nothing then of her affair with my father, or my godfather, Colonel Fairburn, I realized that Suzanne Williams was either my sworn enemy or my only ally. That she'd vetoed Bobby's dinner invitation to save me . . . from herself.

I glanced down at the pages of my father's typescript, where one of Max's postcards greeted me, a Titian nude staring up at me from a Renaissance divan, a discreet hand in her crotch, "pleasuring herself with the light fantastic," in Max's limerick. I sat down, exhausted, but even more annoyed at my aroused state, and began to go though the dusty pile of books by the desk, which I'd reverently kept in place since the first day I'd been allowed up those fifty-three steps, just as my father had abandoned them. Two or three volumes had charts of Linear B characters hastily torn out. I began going through them again, pausing at the ripped borders of the missing pages from works by Sir Arthur Evans and Nigel Bennett on the clay tablets excavated from Knossos. What could have possessed my father to indulge this sacrilege as he hurried back to Washington, and then Berlin, as worker uprisings convulsed East Germany that summer and fall of 1953? Had it something to do with the decipherment of Linear B the year before by Michael Ventris? As I pondered these imponderables, figuring I might as well return the volumes to their empty places in the shelves, I flipped the pages of a dog-eared German text on Minoan pottery and found slipped into the pages a group of five black-and-white Kodak snapshots of a plumpish man and two striking women.

The photos were stuck together, faded, with deckle edges, and each with tiny black smudges at the four corners on the back, as if pulled loose from a photo album. One of the women I recognized as my grandmother, the younger version I'd never known, in a tight flapper-era dress just above the knee, with a long strand of pearls to the waist. Her auburn hair was bobbed and set off an expressive face of large twinkling eyes and lush full lips, the very attractive woman, it occurred to me, that Jack Crocket might well have fallen in love with. She was posed beside an older paunchy man with thinning hair and squinty eyes, whom I recognized as Amory Williams, Winsted headmaster from 1914 to 1926. His eyes were baggy and dark-circled, his complexion a sallow gray—thus the moniker "the Moor" from the boys. The other woman I didn't recognize. She was about my grandmother's age and wore, if anything, an even skimpier bead-encrusted dress with a straight front that at once compressed and showed off a bulging bosom; she had long dark hair flung across her shoulders in theatrical disarray, a large Latin nose, and a wicked, fun-loving smile that showed off her perfect white teeth. The three were posed with arms around one another, standing on the wide veranda of Hermitage, overlooking the lake, where the white pines—maybe fifty years before?—had not grown to full height. Two photos showed the same group in evening dress with their backs to a stone railing on a narrow balcony, where carved griffins with spread wings presided like mascots. The bulbous dome of the Salute beyond gave away the location: Isabella Williams's Palazzo Barberini on the Grand Canal. Holding the photo up to the light, I could better see the exotic Latin-featured woman next to my grandmother, who struck a pose like a Spanish dancer, with a hand held high over her thrown-back head, waist bent like a spring and her hip thrust alluringly toward my laughing grandmother. Two women enjoying each other's company. While Amory was just his usual dour self.

Only then did it hit me: Amory's wife—the notorious artist, according to my father's letters, who, after demolishing her husband's reputation, had fled to Paris with her lover to live a life of debauchery. Picasso, it was rumored, just one of her many conquests.

I didn't even know her name.

On the back of one snapshot I found scrawled in my father's adult hand *Halcyon days saved from the fire!*

It was in that moment that I realized my grandmother had a life carefully kept from me, a beautiful young war widow, heiress rich as Croesus, who, less than a decade later, would dismiss Amory as head-master, hire Jack Crocket, appoint herself head of the board, and get rid of the dead wood, until she had her own band of loyalists in place, ready to navigate Winsted through the Depression and the war, bring-ing in scholarship kids and black students years ahead of Winsted's New England peers.

It turned out my father (my mother, too, for that matter) had a habit of sticking correspondence into the pages of books he was read-ing, and there marooned. When I later went through his books from the P Street house in Washington, removed to my mother's apartment in New York, I found early letters from Karel Hollar and others, though none of Suzanne's letters, which he carefully concealed before return-ing them to her before he disappeared.

Searching the remaining books in the pile for more flotsam that might have escaped the editor's red pencil, I found none and so decided to return them to the shelves. And as I did so, one by one, methodically, so that I'd remember where each title was placed, I came upon the manila envelope containing the Pinkerton reports and newspaper clippings from the 1877 *Natchez Weekly Democrat*, the envelope that I had found on my father's work desk some six years before, when I had first climbed the stairs to explore. I had casually disposed of the envelope, shelving it because its contents seemed too dated to be of interest. Again, as I had once or twice before, I slid out the newspaper clippings—more fragile than ever; the headlines were about a bizarre shooting and a murdered family in Natchez; the Pinkerton reports described some kind of investigation into the burning of a school . . . but all of it so long ago—the twenties seemed ancient enough!—to my then fretful mind that I couldn't possibly fathom the relevance. The newspaper clippings were crumbling at my touch and so I carefully slid everything back and replaced the envelope as before.

A perfect example of the unprepared mind's inability to recognize critical facts; and so the story of Pearce Breckenridge would have to wait another twenty years.

And a moment later, I repeated the same mistake.

Hanging on the wall by the door was a framed postcard addressed to me and my grandmother at Elysium. The black-and-white photo was of the Museum of Antiquities in Leipzig, a nineteenth-century image of row upon row of glass vitrines displaying a famous collection of Greek pottery and artifacts. Taking the frame off the wall and turning it around, it was possible to read the back of the card through a glass panel, a professional framing job done by a shop in nearby Pittsfield. In my father's exacting hand was a fragment from a longer poem or narrative, presumably a translation from the Greek—the archaic phrasing struck me as awkward—about a merchant prince's voyage from Pylos to the island of the Phaeacians. It began abruptly, in medias res, and ended just as abruptly, as if missing a beginning and end. I'd never been able to track down the source. It was dated January 7, 1954, and had been postmarked two days later from a tiny town in East Germany; a smudged ring canceled the dunish orange stamp emblazoned with the faces of Stalin and Wilhelm Pieck: *Monat der Deutsch-sowjetischen Freundshaft.*

How perspicacious of my grandmother to have had that postcard framed for me as a memento, while, I would learn years later, absolutely denying its existence, even to Elliot Goddard, who, heading the CIA investigation, was near desperate for clues to my father's disappearance.

If I'd had one ounce of real intelligence, I'd have realized that the date on the card was nearly four months after my father had walked through Checkpoint Charlie and dropped off the face of the earth. At least four months on the loose before his capture! But because my grandmother had put it there in plain sight, hanging glumly by the door, I hadn't thought much about it. Her opaque MO and feminine wiles had been refined in her years running the all-male Winsted board.

So I replaced the postcard where it had hung—dumb creature of habit that I was—and began going through my father's photo albums from the twenties and his Winsted and Princeton years, something I had done many times before. But now it was different: I'd read his letters, I'd met people who knew him, and after two years at Winsted and a summer out west, something of the tone of his voice filtered back to me in the clear, the thrum of his heartstrings, the ambition in his soul, so that the young man playing football, rowing on the Naushon River, standing with Elliot Goddard at a victory bonfire was no longer a complete stranger.

When I came to photos of his student years in Europe, in Leipzig and Prague, in Venice and digs in Crete, I also recognized the blond boy often pictured at his side: older by about two years, the one colleague in his generation as smart as he, if not smarter, and possibly even more ambitious—a smooth-talking risk taker of Czech and Austrian parentage negotiating the treacherous politics of prewar German archaeology, who looked not a little like a young Oskar Werner—all the rage back then for the likes of Max, who thought *Jules and Jim* the greatest antiwar movie ever made: Karel Hollar. I understood my father's bond with Karel; I could sense it in that broad face and high Slavic cheekbones and ruffled blond hair. He was not as tall nor as athletic as my father— more a scholar's scholar, keenly bookish; he wore glinting steel-rimmed glasses and a dreamy smile to disguise the ambitious heart of an ideologue . . . a heart of stone.

My father's nemesis, or maybe his second nemesis if Suzanne isn't discounted as a force of lustful nature.

Then and even more so now, those albums encompass for me his halcyon days, his golden age: a place where he and Bobby Williams still cavort on that lakeside beach from which I'd just escaped. And in canoes

with paddles poised, fishing off the float, arms thrown around each
other where they sat silhouetted before a campfire. And, too, pictured
together at Hermitage on that same veranda where my grandmother
had posed with Amory and his wife, that storied McKim, Mead &
White cottage over the lake, masterpiece of Arts and Crafts vernacular
design, decorated with superb examples by Sargent and Whistler, Zorn
and Dewing. Where Bobby practiced three and a half hours—no more,
no less—every summer afternoon while my father waited. I had been
over to Hermitage just once as a child, when Laura had invited me on
the sly while her parents were away and a mopey teenager with stringy
hair was in charge. Laura played the same Steinway grand that Bobby
had played for my father, beneath the once-famous murals by Thomas
Dewing, where—though plaster flaked from a leak in the ceiling and
the furnishing seemed threadbare—those same begowned forest naiads
(twins of the angels in the Saint-Gaudens memorial) stand in a twilit
meadow, their plunging décolletage designed to display their long aristocratic necks and flinty aloofness, blissfully listening for the elusive
song of the hermit thrush.

As I turned the pages to the studio portraits of Bobby—presumably
given to my father by the young prodigy—where his large hands caress
the keys, his intent face bent so that a shock of blond hair dangled
above the delicate upswept nose, lips pursed as if in imitation of a humming Glenn Gould, I felt as if I might have liked that superbly talented
musician, reminding me not a little of Max. How I envied their artistry,
that connection to life's lingering graces, from which I felt excluded.

I swallowed back a pang of regret, whether for myself or that
pathetic figure, time's casualty, in the Adirondack chair on the beach, I
couldn't say. And in that state of banishment, as I put the albums away
and turned again to the fading light off the lake, where it passed though
the lozenges of leaded glass and filled that treasure room of scholarly
remove like a retreating tide, I found my eager thoughts returning to
Suzanne's lush breasts and wispy honeyed mons. Once more engorged
like some yelping Pan and yearning more than ever to see behind those
liquid green Foster Grants: that dreamer of a Calypso woken to find
the dead come back to life—the ghost she and her fellow conspirator
had loved and lusted after and hated in equal measure.

Nemesis one, two, *and* three.

Or was it four?

I rack my brain to remember when exactly it dawned on me, when

I became obsessed with the name Philby. Was it Joe Alsop's passing reference, that dismissive, if awed, snort from the urinals, or even the nude Suzanne's "Kim," spat out like a piece of gristle, or later from the lips of Virgil and Elliot? It seems to have always had a demonic association, like a malignant putrefying force of nature forever upwind, if out of sight, a slightly inebriated figure in a Savile Row pinstripe suit leaning across a cocktail shaker with a charming, insidious smile; the sibilant syllables like a beckoning siren song: fill-be, fill-me, fill-me.... Soon enough the name tiptoed through my waking hours and entered my anxious dreams in hobnail boots.

"What are you doing here!" I exclaimed, loaded down with bags and my Johnny Unitas posters.

"Escaping, old sport—what about you?" He turned to me with a dreamy crinkle of his thick eyebrows, as if a little chagrined by his Gatsby imitation. The smell of dope was overpowering.

"Only varsity players are allowed back early."

Max leaned back from his desk in a gray smoking jacket and ascot, all the while admiring a blue-and-white Chinese ginger jar.

"I'm *playing* an organ recital," and he demonstrated a few airy notes on the ginger jar in his outstretched hand, "for the parents of the new boys. Practice, practice, practice . . ."

I stared in disbelief at the museum posters, art books, and Chinese Export porcelain inundating our study.

Note: our hippie pad in *Like a Forgotten Angel* decorated with psychedelic posters of the Jefferson Airplane, Janis Joplin, and the Doors, Indian batik throws, North Vietnamese flag flanked by Black Panther banners and a blowup of an intently staring Malcolm X: "impeccably dressed, mesmerizingly handsome, the baddest blackest dude on the block, who presided over Saul's revolutionary coven."

What I found was the lair of an aesthetic dandy: a Walter Pater wannabe, an Oscar Wilde imposter.

"What the fuck is going on here?"

"Fucking is the least of it, old sport."

That's when I first got clued in about Max's summer of love. Fed up with his mother's master class at Tanglewood, he hitchhiked one night down the Mass Pike to Boston and into the arms of his paramour, a middle-aged restorer at the Isabella Williams Museum, better known as Palazzo Fenway. They'd first met the year before, when Max became obsessed with the Saint-Gaudens memorial in the chapel, funded by Isabella; he was doing research in the Palazzo Fenway library when this forty-year-old divorced mother of two, whose specialty was paper conservation, offered her services, and one thing had led to another. Max, standing and bending over his desk, graphically illustrated the stand-up sex he'd engaged in with his lover before the famous Sargent painting of Spanish dancers in the palm court of Palazzo Fenway. A feat of daring gymnastics that I found quite breathtaking in its mechanics.

"Two children, you see, as wide open and welcoming as the Lincoln Tunnel."

Max's sudden espousal of this infamous Gilded Age maven of sweetness and light, coming just days after my run-in with Bobby and Suzanne, bowled me over—literally. I remember sinking into our couch in a near faint, exhausted and confused by Max's verbal assault, closing my eyes to the joss sticks burning in the corner as I asked myself how I'd been so stupid as to agree to his pleas that we share a study.

It was uncanny, how, in our different ways, we were both in pursuit of the same fugitive truth that had upended so many lives . . . time's betrayal.

In his manic moments, Max couldn't stop talking about *his* Isabella. How she had been the grande dame of Boston society, teaming up with Berenson to collect old master paintings, as well as artists and writers and musicians . . . and men, lots of men. "A lover's lover, even James was smitten." Isabella summered in Venice at her Palazzo Barberini with the likes of Sargent and Henry James, a brilliant raconteur and charismatic patron, who seduced with style and intellectual verve rather than looks—a face that, like her brother, Amory's, had an olive hue, setting off her handsome but decidedly masculine features. She laughed off her Boston Brahmin father, "that paragon of Winsted snobbery," and preferred to portray herself as a woman of deep spiritual reserve and mysterious depths, taking to exotic dress, which her coterie of artists translated to fabulous canvases of swirling silk and brocade, and so preserved her haunting dark-eyed sexual allure for posterity. At her brother Amory's sexual peccadilloes she laughed hysterically, offering to buy up all his penis gods for her boudoir. The great and near great flocked to her fashionable Venetian soirees. Money, charm, and biting wit got her through a troubled marriage to a rich New York financier, along with personal tragedy and a tortured spiritual life that led to her conversion to Catholicism late in life. Some wrote of her fanciful art patronage as a reaction to her beloved brother's suicide, or perhaps her husband's depression—he, too eventually killed himself—and her young son's death from scarlet fever, age six. Wrote James in a letter from Palazzo Barberini in 1892: "She is often melancholy and remote, keeping the pianist at his keys long after midnight, as she pines away on the divan for some joy out of her childhood that has irrecoverably fled." Amory's disgraceful exit from Winsted in 1926 only added to the troubles of her declining years. In the early thirties, Isabella gave up Palazzo Barberini and retreated to Hermitage in the summers, and chilly, damp Palazzo Fenway for the remainder of the year, living out her life as a recluse, as Boston society, which had once struggled mightily to embrace her largesse and rebellious ways, now turned up its collective nose at the Catholic convert . . . as the world passed her by.

Max was enthralled by this feminist avatar fallen from grace, and Isabella's story finds plentiful echoes throughout *Like a Forgotten Angel* and in his second novel, *Gardens of Saturn,* where the Williamses are treated as paragons of a lost American spiritual paradise, and Laura Williams the disinherited heir.

This was the world Max was really drawn to, not the countercultural shibboleths his adoring critics and readers ascribe to him and his protagonist.

A brilliant con job.

And looking back, I realize how Max's first sojourn in Venice and his old master nudes had all been preparation for his latest role—his essential self—and the novels to come. Chinese blue-and-white ginger jars filled mantels and shelves, and more would arrive every week from antiques shops in Cambridge and on Lexington Avenue. The pea green walls of our study were plastered with museum posters of Whistler, Sargent, Vermeer, and Titian's famous *Danaë and the Shower of Gold,* which Isabella, with the help of Bernard Berenson, had managed to snatch from the grasp of Henry Clay Frick.

"What about my signed Johnny Unitas poster and my posters of Knossos and Mycenae?" I protested.

"What I'd like to know is why more of the glorious Palazzo Fenway, or that dreamy Hermitage, didn't rub off on your stultifying Winsted? You will take me there, won't you—Elysium, where you summer? Don't you see, we need more great art; we need to dedicate ourselves to art— give ourselves to art. What say you, Hawkman?"

"My grandmother"—I waved away the toke he offered me—"saw

them as degenerates. And she saved Winsted by getting rid of Isabella's brother Amory Williams in 1926."

"But you won't give me the juice on the Aldens, much less your father. Where is your magic, my brother, your hold on the world that keeps us all in thrall? Or have I been barking up the wrong tree? Perhaps I need to switch horses, a different narrative perhaps, since you're such a dead-ender, my king, my prince, my mighty Fortinbras, my young Hal—what say you: I need material."

"Fuck you, Max."

"No, no, no . . . temper, temper. Feed me, sport; I'm just an open book."

"With all your snooping—a duster, huh?"

"Have you ever seen Palazzo Barberini, sport?"

"Yes, yes, I have, with my grandmother, the year before she died. It was a crumbling disaster; she could've bought it for a song."

His eyes lit up. "Ah, sad . . . and so romantic, a ruin of memory." He let loose with a lungful of smoke in my face. "Just think of all who paid court to the grand lady. I've seen a letter from Sargent in the archives; he writes that she could bring herself to climax as she posed, simply by force of her imagination."

"Wet dreams, Venice—why not."

"But she lives on in art, Hawkman, in Palazzo Fenway, in her collections . . . and will they be able to say the same of us?"

"We"—and I thought of all the hours dusting gilded frames the previous week—"General Alden collected real Americans, like George Inness and Homer Dodge Martin."

At this, he frowned, with a gesture of sheer incomprehension.

"And I'm informed [this from the paper conservator] on good authority that there is much more at Hermitage . . . and Elysium." I waved him away as he hovered in my face. "Please, please, please . . ." He knelt and began kissing my fingers. "You'll take your best pal, your old buddy there."

And so it began. In the year and a half remaining to us, I had to listen to his endless theories about the glories gone with the wind: that extinguished vein of Transcendentalist spirituality and belief in art for art's sake that had so animated the best in America's past, the neglected path of truth and beauty, which might have made the world a better place and saved the country from pointless wars.

"Why can't Winsted embrace that wonderful part of its heritage instead of the militaristic, imperialist past of *your* great-grandfather?"

And so it went.

Max never failed to dress the part—hardly the hippie attire his protagonist Saul adopts in the novel—wearing old threadbare smoking jackets, a maroon silk scarf indoors and out, and adding a repertoire of effeminate hand gestures and intonations of speech that became fixtures of campus hilarity and high jinks during those somber years. And that is how I remember him attired in our study, leafing through a book in his lap, spellbound before his reproduction of Titian's *Danaë and the Shower of Gold*—"the money shot," as he described it, or scribbling away on a short story, making it up as he went along . . . taking what he pleased.

I wouldn't even mention his subterfuge, his misdirection—what writers do—if it weren't for his most beloved chapter of *Like a Forgotten Angel*, as his protagonist indulges his own summer of love: where Saul hitches out to the Bay Area and plays a gig with Janis Joplin, shares a joint with a pimply-faced Jimi Hendrix, and fills in keyboard backup for Gracie Slick. These portraits and anecdotes are so convincing and delightful that even I would prefer to believe them. What critics call his "insouciant panache" and "larger-than-life escapades," especially Saul's drug-addled days and raucous nights in the Sausalito hippie commune. Readers have utterly failed to realize the superabundance of check marks on an era's to-do list. Max mixes in just enough truth and fetching details to make it all seem plausible. Except, he was never there. For much of it, he picked my brain: The knife-packing Vegas showgirl and the farting tuba player are verbatim.

As the Summer of Love faded in the smoke of burning Watts, and 1968 brought us the assassination of Bobby Kennedy and Martin Luther King, Jr., and millions marched in the streets and on college campuses, Max—"our most intimate chronicler of late sixties malaise" (*Time* magazine)—was, in fact, holed up in our study and the carrels of the library, embracing his new calling: the writing life. Academics still come to me and try to fit Max and his "texts" into the protest movement of the late sixties, as if his writing evokes some inner voice of the antiestablishment pieties of that era. Even when I patiently tell them the truth, they don't get it.

We, his fictional victims, fit none of their theories, or, more precisely, no theory fits us, except the lives we tried and failed to live.

In my own way, I tried to indulge Max and see if a little Williams nostalgia might put my growing preoccupation with my father in some kind of perspective.

One could hardly avoid the great Sargent portrait of the rector, Samuel Williams, in the dining hall. Presiding like an Old Testament patriarch over his creation, he stands in the chapel pulpit, one hand on the carved pelican, the other resting on a morocco-bound copy of *Essays and Prayers*, what our generation considered Victorian poppycock but which had sealed the reputation of Samuel Williams in the 1880s as a longtime abolitionist and radical Republican unionist. Spending time with the portrait of Winsted's cofounder and first headmaster, I couldn't fail to be impressed with his tall and well-built figure, his linebacker shoulders filling out his white vestments. His hands were huge, and I wondered if they'd managed to translate to his grandson Bobby's early prodigies as a concert pianist. In Samuel's staring face, energized by a few flamboyant strokes of impasto, especially his full head of blond hair and glittering blue eyes, I thought I detected something of the moral integrity and bristling energy I'd felt in his great-granddaughter, Laura. Although, to give the devil her due, Suzanne contributed her own witch's brew in that department.

And so I found myself prompted to begin a dutiful reading of *Essays and Prayers*—something Max never bothered to do. I wanted the man behind the Sargent portrait, to see if the voice on the page fit the righteous pose, the deep-set eyes pinched as if in rapt examination of his inner soul. His pale brow, wrinkle-free, seemed immune to doubt, what his contemporaries described as the hauteur of a Roman aristocrat combined with the cool detachment of an ascetic monk. A physiognomy that for over thirty years kept boys trembling, so awed by his unimpeachable rectitude that they found it hard even to speak in his presence. Hardly the melancholic depressive I sometimes detected in the lines of General Alden's letters to his first cousin, and the rolling eyes of my grandmother in her last years as she edited their letters over summers on the back porch at Elysium.

Even to my less than discerning mind, something was amiss. The words in *Essays and Prayers* found ill lodging with the image before me, or rather, some did, but a lot didn't. Uncannily scattered amidst the entirely pedestrian theology and hearty exordiums were seams of mellifluous and soaring romanticism of a distinctly Emersonian cast. And I was not the only one who noticed the discrepancy. Paul Oakes, I realized, had, on my first visit to his study two years before, bestowed on me his own annotated copy of *Essay and Prayers*. He had marked many of those passages of fiery abolitionist sentiment and Transcendentalist fancy, like nuggets of gold in otherwise-prosaic slurry: . . . *and so let your soul float free on the river of life, the river of Time. . . . Give yourself to the trumpet call and burn with the undying spirit of golden youth aborning in every man and every age.* "Wow," he'd penciled in more than a few times in his exacting hand—a thing pretty shocking in itself. It was as if some willful and wild spirit played through those pages, appearing here and there in an underlined paragraph, only to fade out completely, the heady politics of abolitionism and Reconstruction replaced by a dark, brooding inner life carapaced with a thunderous, if conventional, morality. Christ was often referred to as "the Master," an exemplar of the spiritual life devoted to the service of humanity. It was as if the author had slowly given up on some firebrand earlier self for the platitudes of received doctrine, while the ethics of a life dedicated to good works elided into an abstract remove and etiolated higher calling.

This didactic, pedagogical verbiage grew edition by edition, choking off all but the most diligent reader from detecting the ecstatic heart within.

By the third edition (which Paul Oakes had put into my hands), when Samuel Williams was headmaster, Winsted boys were admonished to be clean-living, truthful, unselfish, and deeply Christian in spirit. The author warned against overindulgences of every kind: overeating, overdrinking, smoking, and the resulting immorality—read sex. This veritable horror of unclean thoughts and actions runs like a turbid stream through the pages of *Essays and Prayers*. (The doorless toilet stalls—unheard of today—and cold showers in the morning to quash waking erections were geared to discourage sexual vice. "Sentimentalism," the euphemism for masturbation, was an expellable offense.) Behind this fastidious Victorian bunkum, one detects a near horror of sexual urges, except as a necessity within the bonds of marriage to produce offspring.

When I inspected the Sargent portrait of my great-grandfather in the library, the wiry, dark-haired General Alden seemed to smile at my consternation with his cofounder, the Reverend Samuel Williams. The general never abandoned his abolitionist fervor, or rather, it found outlets in his building projects as New York moved uptown from Washington Square, his charities for medical research and educational foundations, and his support for the progressive politics of his close friend and fellow outdoor enthusiast, Theodore Roosevelt. As his admiring contemporaries in the Knickerbocker Club wrote in memoriam, "A man who has seen a company of his comrades mown down like tenpins is not likely to look favorably upon the Lord. . . . And so John, our dear general, took it upon himself to leave this world a better place than he found it: His hand can be found on any of twenty blocks from the Forties to the Seventies, in the new wing of Memorial Hospital and the American Cancer Society, and, of course, in his beloved Winsted School."

But the most delicious irony, the thing I liked to dwell on in my student days jousting with Max, was Samuel Williams's visceral dislike of artists. This, I never stopped pointing out to Max. Samuel distrusted artists as a class of people, people whom he suspected of having unreliable relationships, who sheared close to the adulation of the flesh and the devil. In *Essay and Prayers,* artists tend to be written off as mere spectators of life and not active, dutiful participants. This from a man who had fathered artists: his son and heir, Winsted's second headmaster, Amory: Amory, the Moor (Moor-or-less in his last years as headmaster), he of the penis gods, the sensitive poet, pianist, and organist, who married belatedly to a wildly talented painter who then abandoned him; Amory, who almost single-handedly destroyed his father's work. And the rector's eldest son, Sam, Harvard's golden boy classicist, whose tragic early death to alcohol forever hung over the Williams clan. And daughter, Isabella, the Medici princess of Boston, who patronized artists of every stripe for decades, only to drown her sorrows in obscurantist popery . . . languishing in obscure memories, as Sargent put it in a letter to his sister, "of some exotic larger-than-life personage out of her childhood: 'my father,' was how she put it to me more than once, with a magical voice and fiery piano technique, who seems to have disappeared as if he'd never been. Perhaps it is delirium tremens—terribly sad, really."

What Max did not know (I believe he never cracked the cover of *Essays and Prayers*), what I did not know, was that Pearce Breckenridge had a big piece of *Essays and Prayers*—and much else besides: an authorship, like the man himself, like Elliot Goddard's Edward de Vere, erased from living memory.

As Max did to my father in *Like a Forgotten Angel.*

But I get way ahead of myself. The more I confronted Max with what I thought the fatuous failures of Samuel Williams, the more he concentrated on the rebel Isabella, and so lost the thread, the truth about Samuel, and ultimately, Pearce Breckenridge: the central truth that might have anchored his novels in the world as it is.

Not a little ironically, looking back, I do find Samuel was spot-on about one thing: his horror of sex. It was about sex; it always is.

7 ELLIOT GODDARD HAD HIS WORK CUT OUT FOR him in 1967–1968, our annus horribilis—what with the Tet Offensive and the subsequent expansion of the Phoenix Program—although he'd be the first to say that the Tet Offensive broke the back of the Vietcong and allowed for their near eradication by 1970. He had little time to counter Bobby Williams's insidious machinations in league with his creature, headmaster Folley. Bobby, just as his father, Amory, had embraced the whirlwind in the twenties, encouraged Folley to champion the antiwar movement and curry favor with the increasingly radicalized students and faculty, thus trumping the growing alarm of the trustees by making himself so popular with the masters and boys as to be unassailable. Whether Folley saw this embrace of the Left as his best bet to retain his job or as yet another harbinger of the coming apocalypse is difficult to judge; like most officeholders, he was probably happy to hedge his bets. But Elliot did manage one small coup on the home front; he got the ailing Paul Oakes to step down as my adviser, turning "my delicate case" over to one of the most extraordinary men I've had the pleasure to know.

Virgil—even when I was sixteen, he always insisted that I call him by his first name—was late for our first scheduled meeting. Fall that year came early and the air was crisp with promise of another long pre-global-warming winter. Virgil Dabney's study was a daunting mess, stuffed and stacked with heaps of worn books, miscellaneous papers, and decades-old academic journals. Volumes of Roman history and philosophy were scattered over almost every inch of the floor, with hundreds of raggedy index cards sticking out of the closed pages like

some invasive species of exotic vine. On his desk, the latest archaeological journals lay open and heavily underlined in red pencil. The
place smelled of moldy bindings and stale cigarette smoke and, it must
be admitted, unwashed clothes. Over the course of a year, his study
became increasingly difficult to maneuver in as the clutter piled up, not
unlike an archaeological site at the end of the season, before the excavated debris has been carted away. The cleaning ladies were forbidden
entrance, lest they disturb some configuration of open volumes and the
painstakingly located references that would provide a new insight into
the thoughts of the Epicureans under Marcus Aurelius, stoic emperor
and Virgil's hero. A thick layer of dust soon settled over everything—
everything, that is, except his most prized possessions, his original red
morocco-bound first edition of Gibbon's *Decline and Fall,* which was
housed along with other antiquarian treasures he'd excavated from
Herculaneum, where he spent his summers, in a glass and mahogany
reliquary of fusty Victorian vintage: The hulking thing filled a sunless
back corner of his study. Upon entering, he always gave the glass a
quick swipe with his oversize handkerchief.

Over his desk hung a perfect reproduction of a Roman standard
made to his specifications by a leather craftsman in Florence, where
he'd been stationed after the war. Virgil was then a young first lieutenant, one of the Monuments Men, as they were known, art historians
and classical scholars assigned to protect artistic treasures during the
Allied slog up the boot of Italy. When I first knew Virgil, who was by
then overweight and seemingly blind as a bat, it was hard to believe
he'd once been in the front lines, crawling through the cold mud in
hopes of making contact with his counterparts in the Wehrmacht to
arrange a cease-fire and save an ancient landmark from destruction.
Imprinted in gold letters on the burgundy-colored standard was his
favorite quote from Gibbon: *But the practice of superstition is so congenial
to the multitude that, if they are forcibly awakened, they still regret the loss
of their pleasing vision.*

Nearby, hung cheek by jowl, were two tenebrous etchings by Piranesi, one of the Porta Maggiore and the other of the Temple of the
Camenae. These views of ancient Rome always fascinated me, for they
seemed to sum up Virgil Dabney better than any words ever could.
Over my last year and a half at Winsted, on many a dreary evening
deep in rapt discussion, my eyes would drift to those tiny figures lurking in the shadows of the Porta Maggiore, poised in dwarfed silence,

gesturing extravagantly to one another as they pondered the passing of all things—the glory of an enlightened empire that had once straddled the known world: Pax Romana. It was that romance of a golden age, of a philosopher king like Aurelius—the republican virtues that connect us most unequivocally with the grandeur of our Founding Fathers (Washington, Jefferson, Adams, Hamilton, and Franklin, as well as the beloved Lincoln, were uppermost in Virgil's pantheon)—that he championed to his boys. A quest echoed in my father's ardent biography of Alexander the Great, as it was in his translation of the *Odyssey* ("tucked around the edges, just out of sight, one detects rumors of a better, more enlightened age of trade and prosperity," he wrote to his mother); it explains, at least partly, his catastrophic gamble to be the first to translate the purloined Linear B tablets from Pylos.

This, a scholarly obsession to recover voices lost to time, he shared with both Karel Hollar and Virgil, who, nevertheless, liked to remind me how he differed with my father on many things; he, Virgil, was a Latinist, while my father was a Hellenist.

"And Homer no less—what, I ask you, may be discovered about the Bronze Age before the invention of writing?" A subtle jab at what Virgil considered my father's sometimes fanciful "grasping at invisible straws . . . and, ah-da-dum, no straws—no bricks."

"But," I protested, "we now have the translations from Pylos and Crete of all those Linear B tablets."

"Oh yes, I know—the flame ever before your father's eyes, but so sad it all came up a duster, laundry lists of Nestor's undies and such like."

This was unfair, because the inventories from the palace storerooms give terrific insights into the daily life of the Mycenaeans; and as if to make quick amends, Virgil grinned with a self-deprecating wave at his Piranesi etchings: a scholar who viewed the despoiled ruins of Rome through the secret longings of the imagination, those seven hills that sheltered the once and future hope of mankind. And a passion he instilled in his beginning Latin classes. On the opening day of term, the boys found the names of the seven hills written in huge yellow letters on the blackboard; beginning with Palantinus and then Aventinus and so on, each hill served as an organizing category for the study of Roman life and culture, with its peculiar associations of character traits, laws, and Roman notions of civic duty. It was a fascinating and systematic pedagogical tool—strangely echoing the call to duty in *Essays and Prayers*—and geared to young imaginations. In my father's day, the names became shorthand expressions for the bullshit of official life. Among Virgil's crew in Washington, "*Capitolinus ferunt*" meant being called to the White House for consultations.

But Virgil's influence went far beyond that of beloved teacher, as Elliot Goddard, with a shocking lack of discretion, let on to me that following spring on a whirlwind trip from Saigon for a trustees meeting.

"Looks can be deceiving. Virgil's the guy, our Signore Moneybags, who saved Italy from the Communists in '48. More to the point, his brother is right hand to J. Edgar at FBI, a resource nonpareil."

Virgil was the cutout between the virulently anti-Communist Hoover and his like-minded patriots in the CIA: Virgil's Winsted boys.

"Now, hold on a minute, I'm supposed to review your file." He picked up the manila file from his desk. "What's this eighty-five in Latin, ninety in Greek? Your father never got lower than ninety-five, one hundreds."

"Careless. My mind wanders these days."

He snorted at my confession of weakness and the very real distractions that were beginning to plague me. His belly protruded over his belt; gray pants cuffs bunched on his shoe tops. Pausing to light up a cigarette, he began again to scan the contents of the manila folder. His graying hair was swept back in unkempt disarray, chunky runnels like shagbark hickory crowding a huge cranium until falling away in greasy tangles to his frayed shirt collar, stained a Brylcreemy off-yellow. Even when alert, his fleshy features had a peculiarly downward slant, like a Daumier caricature, his owlish eyes so heavy-lidded that he seemed the very embodiment of the world-weary. As I watched expectantly, he lowered himself into his chair and remained absorbed, cigarette hand balanced on elbow, his lengthening ash splashing unnoticed onto his dark lapels and cascading into his lap. Then he looked up, seemingly surprised that I was still there, and began speaking in that haunting, rhythmic basso continuo that I would come to know and love.

"Ah-da-dum . . . I have only excellent reports of your work from my esteemed colleague Mr. Oakes. Honor role for three terms, not a single black mark for two years. Varsity quarterback—superlative record. An exemplary citizen in every way." He thumbed the pages in my file. "Much like your father . . ." He fixed me with a soulful look, realizing that for any boy such a remark might cut in unintended directions, and shifted his weight as if to accommodate the release of a silent fart. Then he sighed again and launched into his introductory leitmotif, which

prefaced most matters of a personal or delicate nature. "Ah-da-dum
. . . there is one thing that puzzles me, though." He bent his head to
glance at a handwritten note in my file. "This business of your roommate, Maxwell Roberts, how in blazes did that little arrangement come
about? Surely you could have found someone of a more congenial
frame of mind."

"He's just a friend; actually, he makes me laugh."

"Yes, so I gathered from the thunder-voiced Reverend Oakes,
who—the poor fellow—was greatly concerned that he's having a del-
eterious influence on you." Oakey, as Paul was fondly known to *his*
"Washington" boys, and Virgil had been pals and gentle rivals for over
thirty years.

"Sir?"

"Ah-da-dum . . . nothing indecent, you understand." At this he
almost cracked a smile. "But the wily Roberts has—and his most recent
adoption of a Wildean homosexual persona [nothing escaped Virgil] is
most regrettable—has been skating on rather thin ice since the first day
of his arrival at Winsted. Cynicism and irony can be tolerated only if
they are put to positive ends, to positive critiques that lead to reform or
the illumination of a subject. The golden-voiced Cicero was a master of
subtle irony, but cynicism as an end in itself—futile. Don't you agree?"

"Yes, yes . . . in fact, I do."

"The cynics were a messy lot, all tearing down and never building up—typically Greek in that way—little loyalty to an institution.
But I digress. The critical point is this: One bad apple can fuck up the
whole barrel. [Virgil was the only faculty member I ever heard use the
f word with a student—that and his tortured metaphors and epigraphs
were how he made sure he had your attention.] Now the wise man
picks his friends carefully. He chooses those who will uplift and
challenge him to be more than he is—confirm him in the pursuit of
excellence, of honor and virtue—stand by him to the end. This is the
mark of true friendship; this is noble comradeship. Do I make myself
understood?"

"Couldn't agree with you more, sir." I struggled to peer through the
pall of smoke over his desktop.

"Now that we have that bullshit out of the way"—he tossed the
file—"you can call me Virgil."

"Yes, sir."

"I gather you lent your hand to a dig out west this summer."

Virgil drew in a long breath and pulled himself slightly forward, blinking, as if to get me better into view.

"A lost Hopi village discovered last year," I told him. "But they rarely let us kids do the important work; mostly we just get to clean up and haul dirt. We were allowed to keep a few pottery shards."

Virgil smiled knowingly at this and leaned in closer, his eyes deepening, as if aware of a thought that nagged, slowly beginning to clarify in his mind.

"You must get farther afield, back to the source—the source, Peter, like your father."

My head was spinning, trying to gage the drift.

"Your father spent an entire summer in Germany after fourth-form year, studying at Leipzig, I believe, top experts in the field of Greek studies. In his last years, he was always running off to Germany and Crete—Knossos was his Emerald City."

"Yeah, that's right. He was already teaming up with Karel Hollar."

The moment the name left my lips, I sensed I'd hit a nerve. The merest flutter of those embedded eyes, the merest flinch.

"Ah, Hollar, yes, I'd almost forgotten about him."

"Did you know him?"

"I worked mostly in Italy before the war. But I remember your father's . . . enthusiasm, shall we say. And yes, once or twice at symposiums in Cambridge, with Nigel Bennett and his crew."

"What was he like?"

"Bit of a duck out of water, a pusher, a striver with no fixed address, no loyalties. Hard to know if he was Austrian or Czech—where his allegiances lay."

"But so brilliant."

"And then there was some trouble with Carl Andersen's excavations in Pylos in 1939, some irregularities—but tell me, how do you know about Karel Hollar?"

"They wrote journal articles together."

"Of course."

"And I've been reading about him in my father's letters to my grandmother from when he was here at Winsted."

His eyes fixed me like a bird of prey.

"She kept everything, then?"

"Yes, over her last years she was endlessly organizing things in the family archives."

Those jet black eyes deepened as if I had vanished from view.

"One of the truly great ladies of her generation; how many times I was favored to sit at her splendid table."

"She would have let me spend the summer in Greece. My mother absolutely refuses."

"Perhaps I should have a word with the fair lady. I know good people who could take you on—and goodness knows you don't have to go to Germany anymore. You would learn a great deal. And given the unfortunate mood of the country, a rural dig on Crete—plenty of Bronze Age finds for you to plunder and ponder [Virgil loved alliteration]—wouldn't be the worst way to spend one's summer before sixth-form year."

"If you could talk to her, that would be great."

There were shouts outside the window, and tree shadows were already lengthening across the playing fields, as if urging on the fall and the dreaded winter to come. If our interview went on much longer, I was going to be late for practice, something I suspected Virgil could not appreciate. And yet he immediately picked up on my longing gaze and nodded sympathetically.

"What a wonderful athlete, your dad. Did you know he sat in that very chair? He was my dorm prefect and I advised him on his senior work." He spread his arms as if to embrace his cluttered study. "Ah-da-dum . . . the years, so hard to believe the years have passed so quickly." He held up his cramped hand, stubby fingers stained with ink and nicotine, and turned his palm to his round, incredulous eyes. "I was a young man just out of Yale graduate school and he, like a prized gladiator, was about to face those uncertain years of the early thirties—not unlike these times of upheaval and attack on our most basic values. Don't you find it appalling?"

I nodded in knowing agreement, even though I didn't have the foggiest. His eyelids compressed to a concerted squint, as if reading a sad future in the lines of his meaty palm.

"In the face of everything, your father possessed a certain confidence, self-contained and concerted—concrete in his allusions, a thing splendid to behold. I was pleased to offer him my best thoughts as I offer them now to you."

"I've heard it said he was quite an optimist?"

He canted his head as if to a distant sound. He must have known I'd gotten this from Elliot Goddard.

"An optimist? Well, perhaps to his peers. He felt heavy responsibilities."

"And his translation of the *Odyssey*—did he ever finish it? His letters are full of the difficulties."

Virgil's eyes rose to mine, light sparking in the olive green irises at the thought of such a scholarly argosy, or perhaps at mention again of an epistolary resource of which he'd been unaware.

"Yes, yes . . . a translation; I'd almost forgotten. I must go back to my files and seek it out."

I wanted to ask if he'd read my father's biography of Alexander the Great, but time was pressing and he must have felt the necessity of establishing our bond on a firm footing, as I'm sure Elliot Goddard had urged.

"Peter, how can I put it? Some men, like nations, are endowed with sterling qualities and smiled on by fortune. They have a special calling, a singular responsibility to make the most of their abilities and their opportunities; they lead, while others choose only to follow. Your great-grandfather, the general, with the Civil War of recent memory, founded the school to produce just such leaders of men, to uphold the Winsted motto: Freedom, Justice, Love, and Honor. I like to think your father died defending such ideals. I don't say such things to pump you up, only, a man must know from whence his powers come. I don't need to tell you: Your family has a rich history of service to the nation. Such tradition of service has always been critical to the life of our country and this school. Rome withered when her greatest families failed to serve her. I quote the immortal words of Seneca to you in this regard: 'Man's ideal state is realized when he has fulfilled the purpose for which he was born; such a goal is only earned by keeping one's gaze firmly fixed on the proper stars; a man may be born for leadership, but he must still earn it.'"

He stared into my eyes with a wistful look.

"Money, social rank, connections—yes, they come into play but are themselves of little worth if a man's character has been corrupted by puerile pleasures. And these days . . . ah-da-dum . . . we are sorely in want of good character in high places. I am reminded by nearly every headline of the faltering spirit of the thirties." He ran a thumbnail up and down the underside of his chin, brushing the whiskered patches his razor had missed. "Depression—terrible times. Reds were everywhere, insinuating themselves into the highest reaches of government:

State Department, Treasury—even the White House. Alger Hiss was
the tip of the ice cube. Everything Winsted stood for was being called
into question by men in its very ranks who were suborned and misled.
And now the *Times* again echoes such defeatist sentiments and extols
these young rabble-rousers and their gullible fellow travelers. We as
teachers and scholars are here to direct and train; we are your living
link to the past and to the grand traditions that have served so well,
though"—he wagged his stubby finger like a damaged metronome—"I
fear, constantly pressed by the forces of superstition, anarchy, and hate
that now divide the country. General Alden's Winsted is *your* heritage,
Peter. One need not be a slave to tradition; rather, let it be your guard
and your strength. Do not harbor any distractions lightly; do not lurk
in others' shadows. Be your own creator, lest you be led astray. Do you
get my meaning, young man?"

I wasn't exactly sure where this was all leading, but it sure sounded a
lot more promising than *Essay and Prayers*.

"Superstition and anarchy," I echoed speculatively, ". . . fixed on the
proper stars. . . ." I thrilled at the thought of General Alden being summoned to my corner.

His eyes sparked, as if we had hit upon some synergetic flash point.

"Do not misunderstand. The business with the wily Max Roberts
bothers me little—I, too, can enjoy his antics. But history . . . ah-da-
dum . . . history is replete with examples of false friendships that prey
on the soft belly of our aspirations and lead us to destruction. Maxwell
Roberts is only the fox making a stir in the henhouse. The ecclesiastical authorities [this was a reference to the "rooster in chief," as Virgil
referred to Byron Folley]—you never heard me say this—are idiots;
they are all fluster and bluster and so easily taken in by the pacifists
and their Soviet patsies. They have no idea what they face, for they are
a spent force. Let us hope the trustees can redeem themselves [that is,
fire Joy-Joy]."

Virgil bent far forward over his desk and motioned me toward him
as if to impart a confidence, a sharp glance left and right as his saurian
eyes emphasized the discretion that must be maintained in the matter.
He passed a finger across his throat. "The Catholic Church provided
the armature of superstition and peasantlike hatreds for the butchering Nazis. And today, powerless and worn down to barren symbol, the
Church has nothing to offer but the hope of afterlife, which, to the man

of vigor, would be a living hell. Ah-da-dum . . . your father's Homer, as you just reminded me, most poignantly pointed this out in the descent of Odysseus."

Virgil gestured extravagantly, echoing the exuberance of the pilgrims in his Piranesi prints, turning his face to the banner above his desk and the words of the magisterial Gibbon.

"But Homer—whoever the fuck he was—was an artist, not a moralist, neither a chronicler nor a repository of truth. True character must be drawn from a deeper repository than art and religion can offer. The moral principles we live by must be rooted in the tenets of civilization that have proven their value and virtue over the course of the millennia. These are the things that nurture the solitary and strong. Look at Lincoln, at Grant and Patton, even Eisenhower—individuals of absolute integrity who knew their place in the long line of moral and constitutional competency that has allowed our civilization to endure while others have foundered. They never doubted themselves, though the burden of doubt is essential to the examined life, as much a curse as a blessing. The gods are capricious in these matters and we must beat them at their own game. But remember, when Rome's great families failed to defend her, to trust her legacy, when traitorous Constantine took up the superstitions and intolerant prejudices of the cross, they were a goner. We did nothing about Lenin and Stalin, Manchuria or Munich, and reaped the terrible whirlwind. The fatal flaw of a democracy is its inability to act in time."

Virgil threw himself back bodily into his chair, as if needing to jolt himself free of the terrible vision that rose before him, going on to tell me of a battle during the Italian campaign in that terrible winter of 1944, and an orchard of no more than three acres containing the sprawled bodies of over a hundred American dead.

"Those shattered young boys call out in my dreams."

He bent closer across his termites' nest of a desk, as if to reveal another horror.

"The water, the fluoride . . . you know about the fluoridated water? Never drink from a public fountain. Fortunately for us, the school has its own artesian well. Pretty soon you'll see the citizenry dying like flies."

"Dying?" I asked, watching alarmed as he lighted a match, the reflected flare caught in the picture glass over the Porta Maggiore, as if his beloved Rome were again threatened with conflagration as it had been by Attila. But he was finally on to the raison d'être of our conversation.

"Your father was betrayed by friends, in places high and low." Virgil held up his wide paw once more, as much to silence his indiscretion as to give me warning. "Can't tell you any more than that—and you never heard me say this: But watch yourself; the Communist menace never sleeps." Virgil made a fist. "You and I must hold the bridge—eh, my fine Horatio. Won't be long before they cook my gander, too."

I was not a little pleased to think I was being recruited by Elliot Goddard and Virgil—charter members of the Winsted secret society—in their covert action to topple Bobby Williams and his creature, Byron Folley. But I was being played; the stakes were much much higher. Something my father had faced full on for the first time after he graduated from Winsted.

July 14, 1933, Leipzig

Dear Mother Nestor,

Since you left two weeks ago, Karel Hollar and I have been busy every waking minute with our studies, preparing for a glorious return to Crete! We go out to a lot to restaurants and beer halls, discussing all the latest publications on excavations in Knossos and the Peloponnese. My German has improved. I can actually speak it well enough now that sometimes when I'm with Karel's friends, or we meet strangers, they don't even realize at first that I'm an American. But it's also a little disheartening because I'm hearing things about Herr Hitler that are very distressing. His supporters don't like Britain and America, and even less the Soviet Union and the Communists, and they hate Jews with a passion. Rarely a day goes by when there isn't an incident of some kind in the streets against members of the Communist Party. Just the other morning we were gathered at a street corner as a band of brownshirts marched past singing. Karel grabbed me and pulled us back into a doorway. All the others gave the salute, Heil Hitler. Except for one old man who failed to do so. Two of the brownshirts jumped him and beat him senseless. There was blood streaming from his head. No one intervened; no one protested. Everyone was frozen with fear. Karel has learned to lay low; he says many Jewish students at the university are beaten up. The Nazi brownshirts are threatening Jews and painting anti-Jewish slogans on the windows of their shops. The kind of bullying and intimidation that goes on turns your stomach. This atmosphere of hatred and resentment is poisonous. There is a dark, malevolent mood you can almost touch. I thought Karel was so absorbed in his scholarship that he simply ignored what was going on, but then he confided to me in secrecy that he is a member of the Czech Communist Party: "The revolution is happening everywhere," he assured me. Not that I'm entirely surprised, given his view on things. He says that Stalin and the Communists are the only hope against the likes of Herr Hitler and his band of bullies. He even took me to a secret Party meeting, where I met people dedicated to social justice. They talk excitedly about the wonderful things Stalin has done in Russia, building new cities and industries; their commitment to improve the lot of the workers is quite contagious. Perhaps President Roosevelt might take on an idea or two, since things in American are now such a mess.

Love,
John

I was relieved to have such an ally as Virgil, even with all his dire ruminations and often depressing, if not downright crazy, theories. How to take a man seriously who believed fluoridation was a Communist conspiracy, that Roosevelt's White House was a den of Soviet spies, that John Lennon was bankrolling the antiwar movement, that Jack Kennedy had the Secret Service sneak women into the White House—a man who carried a full catsup bottle in his inside pocket to every meal!

I still kick myself for not having figured out what was what sooner, given how I was providing intelligence on a silver platter: when curiosity trumped my fear and I brought up the name I'd overheard in the urinals. Unlike how I felt about Elliot, I trusted Virgil.

"Philby?" he said. "You heard them mention Philby?"

"So, who is he?"

"Don't you ever read the papers? Or maybe it's just a bit before your time. Kim Philby is a Soviet spy, a kingpin of vipers: slick, debonair, a world-class operator. He'd been under suspicion for years, since the early fifties, but the Brits just couldn't break him and much preferred to believe otherwise rather than deal with the truth. The rotten bastard finally defected out of Beirut some four years ago. Sword of Damocles hanging over half the free world's intelligence services."

"Was my father involved with him?"

"What, a cocktail party, an embassy reception—who in the top echelons in Washington in the early fifties wouldn't have crossed Kim Philby's path: That's what he did."

"Kim, Kim Philby . . ." I suddenly remembered how Suzanne had screamed "Kim" at Bobby on the beach at Elysium, and I mentioned this to Virgil.

Virgil became so still in his chair, I feared his heart had suddenly stopped beating.

"Well, she would; her brother was at Cambridge, same as our esteemed trustee, Mr. Williams." His eyes barely blinked. "What else did she say?"

"That was it . . . Oh, and Anthony."

"Anthony who?"

"Just Anthony."

"Anthony, not Tony?"

"Anthony."

"With the British emphasis on the second syllable, as in *ton* of shit?"

"She certainly has an English accent."

"It's late; you'd better get on your way to practice."

I was being played by some of the very best.

Although my belief in Virgil's and Elliot's loyalty to my father was not misplaced, it didn't mean they harbored no doubts as to his veracity, much less his judgment: a high-ranking CIA officer who sheds his official identity and disappears behind the Iron Curtain without warning, without trace is either defecting or gone plum loco. And they saw in me a possible answer to the heartbreaking mystery that had threatened their careers and caused them no end of distraction, perhaps an antidote to their worst nightmares: that my father might turn out to be an American Kim Philby, a confederate of the same, or even another Alger Hiss . . . the absolutely unthinkable. A traitor, not just to his country, but to their faith in an unimpeachable class of men and their sense of honor.

By the end of fall term, Byron Folley, fearing the night of the long knives was fast approaching, began to waffle. With immediate hopes of a spiritual awakening dashed, greeted by resentment and a passive-aggressive faculty, he made a leftward pivot to placate the forces arrayed against him. It was as if he had sniffed the heady air of revolution, the sweet stink of dope mixing with the miasma of smoldering joss sticks—in his more ecstatic moments interpreted as signs of the beginning of the end—and simply thrown open the floodgates. Bowing to pressure from Bobby Williams, he did away with the King James Version and the Book of Common Prayer for the banalities of the Revised Standard Version, and then, oddly, began quoting from *Essays and Prayers* in chapel, latching onto those very passages that Paul Oakes had underlined about fiery abolitionist sentiment, even assigning sections to be studied in sacred studies classes. But wrapping himself in the Winsted flag only made him look more ridiculous. At Bobby's urging, he began inviting left-wing preachers and activists who took a decidedly skeptical view of the war in Vietnam: It was our Christian duty to do no harm, and to refrain from engaging in an unjust war. With the Blue Madonna now a fixture by the altar, further innovation began apace: Evangelical slogans and bright tapestries with a menagerie of doves, lambs, and fishes dangled from the Gothic stonework, and by spring, blatantly antiwar symbols and peace signs hung there, as well.

Trying to please all, he pleased no one, least of all Max, whose spells of depression became more frequent as his narrative arc began to crumble.

Once the sixth form had blatantly indulged in liquor and cigarettes; now cocaine and psychedelic drugs became the thing, with no retribution in sight. The faculty was scandalized but impotent. Then a sixth former tripping on LSD fell or threw himself off the chapel tower (Max devoted half a chapter to this incident in *Like a Forgotten Angel*). The papers called it a drug-assisted suicide. The school maintained it had been a tragic accident. The boy's parents filed a negligence suit. Rumors flew. *The New York Times* and *The Boston Globe* had a field day as our bastion of the establishment lost air speed. The trustees wrote worried letters to one another. By the late fall of 1967, with the trees bare bones against an iron sky, a bitter lethargy had settled over the school.

As if I didn't have enough on my mind, the mood among my black friends began to sour. I had always taken a degree of pride in my family's championing of civil rights. Not for nothing were those broken shackles carved into the granite of General Alden's memorial in the chapel. At least that part of the Winsted heritage was unassailable, which even Byron Folley had done so much to strengthen with his pastoral counseling of the black kids from the South. Almost to a man, they were teammates on varsity football, many recruited by Elliot God-dard. We were the elite of a proud and winning tradition going back General Alden, who had Frederick Law Olmsted lay out the football field as an integral part of the grounds. My black friends had voted to make me cocaptain with Jerry Gadsden my junior year. An unusual accolade, but I was good: I was the quarterback, and I was making them look good for the college recruiters. The black players stayed away from drugs, while some of my best athletes, white kids from famous families, including my wide receiver, son of the president's top foreign policy adviser, were heavily into cocaine, and worse. The blacks who had come from the streets, under the pastoral aegis of Bryon Folley and the evangelist succor of an ever-loving Jesus, seemed immune and aghast and then incredulous at the drug experimentation of their white team-mates. And as Huey Newton and the Black Panthers became infamous and black pride gained traction, incredulity turned to scorn.

Jerry Gadsden would look at me with his big soulful eyes and shake his head in disgust as our wide receiver dropped another easily catch-able pass.

"How can that stupid motherfucker think he can get away with this shit? We've been working too hard for him to waste all our lives," Jerry said.

Holding that talented team together, with everything else on my mind, was tough. Each game, I had to figure out who could be depended upon and who not. The tension between the black and white players simmered. Nevertheless, we won every game, with only the Riv-ers game standing between us and the New England championships. We hadn't beaten Rivers since my father's team did it twice in 1931 and '32. And after the altercations of the previous year, when I'd been knocked out, we knew there would be trouble.

On the first play, as I prepared to take the snap, I heard the usual round of racial slurs coming from across the line. The Rivers team, mostly big and brash kids from the old Irish neighborhoods of South Boston, were trying to unnerve our black players. I called a time-out. I walked back to the sideline, with Jerry fuming at my side, and told our coach what was going on; I suggested he protest to the referees and the Rivers coach; I told him we should refuse to play if that kind of behavior was tolerated. Jerry slapped my helmet and told me to stop crying like a baby, shut up and play. Our coach got the referees and the opposing coach in a huddle and, with a lot of nodding heads all around, the issue was seemingly settled to everyone's satisfaction. The Rivers coach across the field went through the motions of lecturing his players. But as soon as we returned to the line of scrimmage, the racial slurs began again with renewed ferocity. The defensive tackle who had rung my bell the previous year was the worst: "Watch yourself, you nigger-loving quarterback; you're going down first." I called an audible bootleg, thinking I'd avoid the onslaught, only to take a vicious hit. The big-mouth defensive tackle spit in my face as I lay under the pileup. I was going to complain again to the coach, but Jerry hauled me up out of the pile and scolded me.

"Shit, man, grow up. Your bullshit just gets these cracker assholes more riled up. Let me take care of it; you just concentrate on winning the game."

Three plays later, Jerry and our huge left guard, a black kid from Macon, Georgia, took out my nemesis, the right defensive tackle, with a vicious double hit. The son of a bitch's helmet went flying and he was out of the game with a broken collarbone. A grumbling quiet came over the Rivers line. It was still a grudge match and came down to a final touchdown catch by Jerry, after he had already run for two touchdowns and 322 yards, a school record. When he extracted himself from the pile of tacklers in the end zone, he walked back to me, looked me up and down and with a determined smile, shoved the football into my gut. "It's your ball now, captain Alden [not Peter]. This nigger is done running your football for you—for you and everyone else around these parts."

We kicked the extra point, and thirty seconds later, Jerry left the bench—his last game as a senior—without so much as a slap on the back or a hug in our moment of triumph. I just shrugged it off, overwhelmed with all the commotion on the field as the students and alumni went wild. But something was missing. I stood there, kids slapping my shoulder pads, and there was Jerry, striding off, his compact battering-ram shoulders aswagger against the approaching dusk. On the sidelines, assistant coaches from Yale, Harvard, Princeton, and Dartmouth were waiting to glad-hand him—a shoo-in for a full Ivy scholarship of his choice. Yale had the inside track, since Elliot Goddard had personally paid for the tutoring to get him out of Jackson, Mississippi. Jerry liked Elliot; they were thick as thieves: they saw the world as it was. And Jerry became a star in New Haven the following year.

After that game, Jerry barely spoke to me again. I had thought we were pals, members of a band of brothers, that connecting with him on a forty-yard pass—that thing of speed and grace I had seen in my head, like second sight, moments before it happened, settling into Jerry's outstretched hands at full tilt two steps ahead of any defender in the league—made us special: gods apart.

Not for Jerry.

I blamed the world for fucking with his head, as Max and everything else was fucking with mine. That fall, instead of sitting with his classmates, or at the jock table, he'd begun sitting with the other black brothers in the dining hall. Byron Folley had authorized the establishment of an exclusive black table, where only the black brothers were allowed to sit. An Afro-American society was formed and then a section of chapel was provided so the black kids could sit together during services. I thought it pretty ridiculous how they began to segregate themselves, the very thing the civil rights movement had tried to remedy. They boycotted the school mixers because they didn't like the choice of bands; they boycotted unsympathetic speakers and walked out on chapel talks by esteemed alumni. Anything we tried to do to make amends only seemed like more poor excuses for our latent racism, as if there was no escaping the sins of our fathers.

But with Jerry, it was somehow personal. What had happened to all the talk about my abolitionist great-grandfather, the Civil War general—had that stopped counting for something? Jerry was such a magnetic personality, so open, so gifted, so genuine in his appraisal of life, with such a deep-souled sweetness about him; the thought that he'd become cynical and scornful was devastating to me. It didn't help that he hung out in Byron Folley's special Bible study class, as if Byron were some gentle Moses for the exiled black kids. Byron Folley even dialed down his evangelical fervor and had us all read Claude Brown's *Manchild in the Promised Land*, which we discussed in sacred studies with the rapt fervor of converts to a new religion. Jerry seemed bemused and never opened his mouth, even though I knew he'd read every page— there were underlinings throughout his well-thumbed copy. I assumed it was all too raw, too close to home, that Claude Brown's Harlem was a reminder of Jerry's childhood in Jackson, Mississippi, at least if Elliot was to be believed.

Late that fall in the weight room, I finally confronted Jerry about his cold shoulder to me.

"You wanna know, man, what tees me off. It's just you, the way you like to pretend you're like everybody else—that it doesn't matter."

"What doesn't matter?"

"Don't you know that your family is paying the whole damn freight for my being in this white man's Cadillac of a school?"

"How so, paying?"

His compact body coiled and uncoiled as he lifted the barbell to his chest.

"It's called the Alden Scholarship Fund."

"Well, first I've heard of it."

"You don't know?"

"Not exactly . . . I don't pay much attention to that stuff."

"That's your fucking problem, man; you think everything is just because it is."

"Why should I ask about something I don't even know about?"

"Well, I had to ask; it's something you have to fill out on your college application."

Jerry glanced at me, his handsome dark face streaming sweat, his neatly cropped hair damp and shining as he held the barbell out to take its full weight in his forearms.

"It's not coming out of my pocket."

"Not coming out of your pocket—what kind of bullshit is that, not coming out of your pocket?"

"I don't see it; I don't touch it; I don't have any say what happens to it. It's just money."

"'Just money.' You know what it costs to go here? Jesus, it's enough money that my mother could provide for the whole family for a year. Money is money. In my neighborhood, kids kill each other for nickels and dimes—shit."

"Does it make me, I don't know, different, better or worse?"

"How do you think it makes me feel? Hell, and it's all the same with the other brothers; they all got your name stamped on their file."

"So what do you want me to do about it—change my name, renounce my family?"

"We're not owned; we're not slaves anymore—don't you get it? I don't like the idea of playing football just to make you all look good, like you really give a fuck about my people—make you feel better about yourselves. I play because I want to, not because it's gonna make Yale or Harvard look so damn good, like you're all doing the world a fucking favor."

"So what, exactly, are you blaming me for?"

"Because you really don't care."

"Don't care about what?"

"Like you and Max, with your heads in your books, full of ideas and shit about this, that, and the next thing, when the real world is all about eating shit."

"You know he drives me crazy half the time."

"You dig his shit, man, and you know it."

"Come on, man, you dig his shit, too—admit it. You love it when he criticizes this place. And you've got your nose in a book as much as I do."

"Maybe, but it's *your* world—I'm just along for the ride until I find something better. Then maybe I'll do it my way."

"It's nobody's world—it's everybody's world. It's the same world for everybody. You read the same history I do: Every man is accountable for his own actions; we all have our own choices to make."

"Try that in my old neighborhood and see how far it gets you."

"Hey, I've read *Manchild in the Promised Land*. In the end, it's the same neighborhood: We're born, we live, we choose, we die."

Jerry looked at me with something akin to pleasure, still pumping, the sinews in his neck popping.

"You think you all so damn smart to be reading that Claude Brown shit—get you in touch with *our* pain . . . wash away your white-ass sins."

"Choices are still choices."

"Is that right . . . is that right, my white-boy philosopher. In my neighborhood, we're born and then we die . . . *too damn soon*. What choices?"

"You're like a god out there, Jerry, on the playing field—Jesus, you're a pleasure to watch."

"I'm running for my life—how about you?"

"It's the same neighborhood."

"Listen . . ." He paused, collecting his thoughts. "That man, Claude Brown, he has talent; he writes almost too well. But what's in his head is and isn't what's out there. And it'll never be your neighborhood—understand, and you should be glad—that heroin thing . . . that's just another name for the Grim Reaper."

"Okay, so it's a different neighborhood. And so what am I supposed to do—kick down the doors, set fire to the buildings, drug myself to—hey, come to Jesus?"

At this, Jerry smiled faintly.

"It's hard being beholdin'."

"I don't give a rat's ass; I've got my own problems."

"Trouble with you people, you've had it so easy, so much your way, for so long, you don't know your ass from a gopher hole."

"You don't hear me complaining."

"That's cause you got a college deferment—no Vietnam for you."

"You got it, too."

"That why I came here, why I play ball—not like my brother in Vietnam. Where I come from, it's the army or jail—seems like." Jerry eyed me uneasily. "Maybe you should talk to my brother, see how much he likes the army. He writes me long letters from Saigon; he just made sergeant—proud as can be. Maybe you'd like the army; Willie says it's the one place where the black man and the white man are equal—where a black man can get ahead without getting lynched. Where black and white die just the same. Willie's one tough nigger—you don't wanna know."

"Maybe I should go; maybe you're right . . . maybe just because you have a college deferment—"

"No you don't—don't you believe a word I just told you. I'm looking forward to playing against you—Princeton boy."

"You should be proud of your brother."

He gave me a half smile.

"Why would I want to go kill Vietcong? I don't see them in Jackson hanging with the Klan."

"Now you sound like Max."

"Willie knows how to take care of himself; his best friend over there is a cracker, his commanding officer, no less. Smart. Not like you hanging out with that Max. That boy is up to no good. You can't trust people like him, Jewish people—he gonna eat your lunch someday, and then cut your throat."

"Now listen to you. Was that a racist remark I just heard?"

"You should hear my mother on the subject; she's had to pay rent to Jews all her life."

"Max is just Max. He's harmless."

"You don't get it, do you?" Jerry eyed me up and down, his brown eyes sparking with a hint of alarm. He handed me the barbell, staring straight into my eyes as I took hold—at least seventy pounds more than my usual carry. "He's a godless Judas leading all you rich white boys to hell and damnation."

"You're fucking with me," I gasped, straining.

"I'm not fucking with you; Max is fucking you all. It's not just weed and shit anymore. Serious shit—heroin, man. I pulled our wide receiver out of the toilets last week; he coulda died."

"Jocko?"

Jocko was my wide receiver; his father was adviser to the president.

"He was passed out, hardly breathing. I had to carry him to the infirmary."

"No way."

"They got him to the hospital just in time."

"No way."

"Why do you think he missed all those passes this year?"

"Well, I overthrew him a few times."

"No, you didn't. He slowed down or stumbled; he couldn't see his dick except to pee."

"Christ."

"Don't you ever *see* anything? Did you ever look into his eyes? Always check the eyes—man." His burned into mine. "Would I fuck with your mind? These boys of yours are seriously fucked-up. How bad is that? It's heroin that's killing my people back home. I got one brother's in jail because of heroin and Willie in Vietnam. And you know why your friends are doing it? Max, that's why, and all his bullshit. They got money and nice homes and a school like this with good teachers. Why they messing with this shit? You tell me."

"Folley say something to you about Max?"

"He don't have to—not unless I'm blind, like you."

"I don't understand how you can stand him . . . that evangelical stuff."

"Listen to you, Mr. Lap of Luxury, so above it all. Where I come from, being right with Jesus is a powerfully good thing. For people who don't have nothing, feeling that you got some help from the Almighty matters. God gives you all this beauty and everything you ever need and what do you do: let a Jew like Max make you think it stinks."

"Jerry, he's just . . . Max."

"Try it from my side, brother Alden. Like not having a home to call home, where you'd rather be than this cold corner of hell—and it seems to get colder every year. And then you find this shit happening, like it's all a joke, like they want to play games with their spoilt lives because they got nothing better to do. It's discouraging. It's messing with my mind. Maybe I should go to Ole Miss and really get my head messed with. At least it would be warmer."

"You'll be a star at Yale. You'll have all the white pussy you want. Elliot Goddard will set you up just fine."

I was struggling to curl the weights to my chin.

"You sounding more and more like Max—know it?"

"I'm jealous, that's all."

"That Elliot, got to hand it to him . . . at least the man knows what he's paying for. You know where you stand. I like that."

"You've got it made, Jerry. People like you—you're a good guy. You'll be a fucking rock star in New Haven."

"Where I come from, they don't like me—not anymore they don't. My people think I've done gone north and lily white and sold out. That I'm better than they are because of my education, because of talking 'up-pit-y'—that's what my mother calls it. I'm supposed to hate all this. Complicated, you have no idea how—here, gimme me that before you kill yourself."

"I'm sure your mom is proud of you."

A flicker of incredulity passed over his features as he brought his face close to mine.

"I don't know who my pappy is; my mother don't know, either."

8 THOSE WORDS OF JERRY'S AFFECTED ME MORE than I knew. I felt like embracing him, which I didn't but wish I had; I felt like such a fraud in my comfortable life, bantering around existential ideas with Max, as if they mattered, as if anyone but us really cared.

Max always told me I was a fool and simpleton to think history offered any answers, or, more precisely, to trust in facts alone, things scientific and logical, which only, so he said, asked the how of things, never the why. He came to believe only in stories, only in the artful arrangement of words on a page, as if words had a magical life of their own, divorced from reality, or, worse, could change reality. "Desire," he proclaimed, "the maelstrom of desire, the desire of desire, is what makes us who we are."

By the winter, his desk was a slush pile of library books, books on art and literature, and the novels of Wolfe and Conrad and the "most blessed" Faulkner (favorite of his adviser and English teacher, Charlie Springfield), and, of course, his well-thumbed Riverside edition of *Hamlet*.

"You is so-o-o full of shit," I cried, employing Jerry's exasperated southern intonation to strengthen my resolve.

"Without memory of desire translated to page and canvas, we do not, will not exist, much less endure. Art is how we survive. Art is how we travel in the realms of gold. Time travel, Hawkman, you of all idiots should understand. We must burn, 'burn always with this hard, gem-like flame,'" he said, quoting Walter Pater, Isabella Williams's favorite author.

How many times have I heard that refrain in my head as I have brushed away caked mud to find the painted shard of a leaping dolphin or Achilles in pursuit of Hector, or some tiny clay figurine clutched in a skeletal hand—how many? And like so much of what Max said, it sounded profound and esoteric at seventeen and eighteen, but in the long run I came to believe that the artist's way (and perhaps I share this with Samuel Williams) is perilous with self-deceit and self-justification . . . a kind of truth, but not the truth one can rely on. Even if desire rules our lives, it does not tell us where to take a stand: the responsible choices. For that, we must endure the tedious business of digging deep, uncovering the armatures and support beams, the cracked foundations upon which we overbuild. Stand in the hot sun for weeks and months sifting the dirt in these graveyards of human desire, and even the most dewy-eyed romantic learns that it's tough, exacting work. All these lost souls were filled with desire for life until some other murderous fool's desire laid them low.

And so we argued and fought and bullshitted into that long winter's night . . . until a strange missive from Elliot Goddard sent us reeling to yet another dance.

In *Like a Forgotten Angel*, Max entitled chapter 6 "The Winter of Our Discontent." Critics call it the "Shakespeare chapter," in which the Brooklyn-born Saul first discovers the shattering depths of Shakespeare while performing in a school production of *Hamlet:* All the identity issues of the play, so the academics assure us, foreshadow the author's conflicted relationship with his Jewish father and Catholic mother and the disaster of his parents' divorce. For scholars, Max's fictional construct, his "seething Elsinore," is invariably interpreted through the malaise of America's Vietnam nightmare. In playing the dark prince, Saul is forever changed and so embarks on his literary career. I am told that teachers of ninth-grade English, when Shakespeare is first introduced in most high schools, love this chapter and have their kids read it as an introduction to the powerful, life-changing experience of the Bard. All well and good. But they don't know the half of it.

In January, as tryouts for the Dramatic Society's *Hamlet* began, a book arrived for me from Elliot Goddard, care of the American embassy, Saigon. The Tet Offensive had taken over the news, Vietcong sappers had almost overrun the American embassy . . . and Elliot was sending me a book on the Shakespeare authorship question! I ripped open the package, to find J. Thomas Looney's *"Shakespeare" Identified*, published in 1920. Elliot had inscribed the frontispiece:

> For Peter, with affection, from Elliot Goddard. Let this volume open your eyes to the contradictions that surround the human enterprise. An example of how one man, a schoolteacher no less, asking the right questions, was able to solve the greatest mystery of English literature and put a face—after almost four hundred years!—to the plays. This will change your life: The true wisdom of the plays is now revealed. *Question the common wisdom.* Semper fi, Elliot.

I was not a little leery of Elliot from my father's letters: his bullying of Bobby Williams and his temper tantrums on the football field. And filled with an eerie sense of dread that he and Virgil were in cahoots with me about something that went far beyond the clear and present danger posed by Byron Folley. Something my research in the periodical archives on Kim Philby and the Cambridge spies only heightened: Almost all reports agreed that at least one, if not two, Soviet spies in the ring remained at large. And now, in the middle of the Tet Offensive, Elliot was sending me Looney's book identifying Edward de Vere, seventeenth earl of Oxford, as the author of the Shakespeare canon. I was touched by Elliot's inscription, his loyalty to my father, his love of misdirection, but hardly moved to read the damn thing. Then Max found the book lying on my desk, saw the inscription—I can just see his eyes lighting up—and stayed up all night devouring the text. The next morning, I faced a bleary-eyed convert to de Vere's cause.

"Far-out, Hawkman. I mean, a real CIA spy sends you this from Saigon, revealing the greatest secret in history—this is beyond cool."

Max was beside himself.

"Don't you see, Looney provides a more sympathetic and believable creator for Shakespeare's creations, not a figurehead, an empty stage name, but a living, breathing person subject to all the trials of the human condition, trials that would explain both the extraordinary individuality and universality of the work. You got to read this."

"This is bullshit, Max. Shakespeare is Shakespeare, not some CIA conspiracy."

"You don't get it. Edward de Vere *is* the playwright—he's Hamlet—he's the fucking prince—it all fits."

Max was fascinated with how Looney made his discoveries, starting with surmises about the kind of man the author of the plays would've had to have been: a genius with words, somewhat mysterious in his manner, perhaps eccentric, unconventional, of pronounced literary tastes and with recognized talents among his contemporaries, a man who obviously had dealings with both the court and the theatrical world, a habitué of Elizabeth's inner circle, a man who traveled and knew Italian manners and the geography of Venice like a native, who understood war firsthand and the complexities of the law. Using these criteria, Looney searched the records of Elizabethan England. With no preconceived notion as to a candidate, he stumbled upon his man, Edward de Vere, who filled the role perfectly.

Max, puffy-eyed, brought his face inches from mine. "De Vere was probably a bastard son, an intimate of Elizabeth, and a *bad* boy—always on the outs with the powers that be. He had a tempestuous relationship with his wife, Sir William Cecil's daughter. He was close enough to Elizabeth and the throne to feel it in his bones but unable to grasp the crown for himself. And get this, Hawkman, he probably didn't even know who his father was, maybe not even his mother . . . jumpin' Jiminy Cricket—such material!"

"That's absurd. He was the seventeenth earl; he'd have known damn well who his father was."

"Look at Hamlet; he has no idea who the fuck he is, or what he wants. Look at you. . . ."

Of course, Max felt deep down he was describing himself: the Jewish pariah and outcast, Pater's true prince burning with an even brighter flame, privy to all the foibles of the Winsted court, that crumbling bastion of the eastern establishment.

So like the conspirator he prided himself on being, primed with his loony insights, Max took on the mantle of the dark prince, the tragic Edward de Vere, stirring the pot of intrigue to create the stories that would redound to his everlasting fame.

And, truth in telling, Max's crazed enthusiasm about the unknown author didn't leave me untouched. Something of his shape-shifting quest informed my growing uncertainties as I read through tattered copies of *Time* and *Newsweek* in the cage of the library, inspecting the gray and grainy, if not self-satisfied, face of Kim Philby, and those of his comrades, Guy Burgess and Donald Maclean, all safe in Moscow, thumbing their pitiless British noses at the world: three of the Cambridge Five. I had it down to the number of days that Kim Philby's posting to the British embassy in the early fifties had overlapped with my father's return to Washington from Athens—where he'd been CIA station chief—in February 1950: 433.

As I reread his Winsted letters full of youthful fascination with Homer's authorship, I agonized at the thought that this budding, idealistic academic had gotten caught up like so many others during the Depression and later in Kim Philby's treachery.

Winsted, January 11, 1931

Dear Mother Nestor,

Here's a small sampling of my latest translation of Book 7, about King Alcinous's palace:

> Walls plated in bronze, crowned with a circling frieze glazed as blue as lapis, ran to left and right from outer gates to the deepest court recess . . .

> And dogs of gold and silver were stationed either side, forged by the god of fire with all his cunning craft . . .

> And young boys, molded of gold, set on pedestals standing firm, were lifting torches high in their hands . . .

> Here luxuriant trees are always in their prime, pomegranates and pears, and apples growing red, succulent figs and olives swelling sleek and dark. And the yield of all these trees will never flag or die, neither in winter nor in summer, a harvest all year round. . . .

What do you think? Surely Homer had to have visited such a splendid place, full of such telling detail. No author could have made this up. I opt for a single genius, not a mere compiler of an oral tradition; a writer who knew the world of which he wrote, not a scribbler standing on the shoulders of others.

Tell me what you think.

The beauty fairly takes my breath away.

Your loving Telemachus

Max was devastated when the director gave the role of Hamlet to a sixth former, a tall Nordic blond with watery blue eyes and striking chin. (He subsequently went on to acting school at Yale and became a star of stage and screen and a regular on *Law & Order*.) Not that Max's acting talents went unrecognized. He was offered not one but two roles, the grave digger and the foppish courtier Osric, comic parts that quite suited his antic mind, if not the persona of the aesthetic dandy he'd been cultivating all fall. Max didn't see it that way. He claimed the director was an anti-Semitic bigot—he taught German, didn't he? And Nietzsche, another anti-Semite: "Look how the little fucker goes around humming sicko Wagner—Wagner, no less, Hitler's favorite!"

Max committed the whole play to memory. I witnessed him memorize it in less than two weeks; he knew every line. He became the play; he became its hidden author. Not unlike, as he always reminded me, one of those book people in *Fahrenheit 451,* doing his impersonation of Oskar Werner, my stand-in for Karel Hollar. "If I liked boys, Oskar would be my man." He absorbed the play into his pores and with it all the latent unrest and chaffing against authority of that cold, cold winter. It was as if all the currents of mindless revolt began to infect the play's characters as they were translated through Max's manic moods, where they turn up in the oddest places in *Like a Forgotten Angel.*

These were the good demons in his fight against lurking depression.

Max took it upon himself to subtly recast *Hamlet;* he began coaching other actors, or he'd stand in for missing players down with the flu epidemic that swept the school that winter, not only speaking the role perfectly but imitating the peculiar mannerisms of the missing actor. Then, like a stand-up comedian, he began to interpolate lines, adulterating phrases by making sly allusions to contemporary events. He kept the cast in stitches, his facility for mimicry outlandish. The image lingers, especially on the Circle in winter: Max surrounded by his groupies, a phantom psycho from a B movie dressed in velvet smoking jack and maroon scarf, outstretched arms and head bobbing above the fray like protean beasts on a merry-go-round, while his frozen breath, his schizoid soul fled . . . scattered to the four winds.

When called upon in class, Max responded as a character in the play, confounding teachers in sonnet form. If the unwary tried to have a conversation, we found ourselves facing a Polonius or Claudius or even the fair Ophelia . . . or was it Nixon, or the ghost of Kennedy, or the latter's playmate, Marilyn Monroe? Max's favorite was to play Hamlet or Gertrude in drag as a limp-wristed Oscar Wilde. I'd hear a roar of laughter from across the dining hall and would turn to see an entire table convulsed in hysterics and Max fiddling with someone's trousers. And Byron Folley at the head table turned to the commotion with a fretful ridging of his brow, like a man tiptoeing through a nightmare forest, knowing the enemy's footfall but not the point of attack. The more the rules were relaxed, the more Max took every advantage. Radicalized by his spirit, student unrest boiled over.

Max saved the most brazen of his antics for the director who had slighted his prodigious talents at tryouts. For as long as anyone could remember, this older effeminate gentleman, Herr Moffet, had been referred to as "Biddy Moffet," or "the Bid" for short. He was a teacher of French and German, a seedy pear-shaped creature with a balding oversize head, out of which peered tiny gray eyes enmeshed in heavy steel-rimmed glasses. The poor man was legally blind. He spoke with an affected lisp and moved with miniature windup steps. The Bid was an old-world fairy to his manicured fingertips. And, too, he was prone to the most histrionic fits of pique. Max, with the merest jut of an eyebrow, or the flip of a wrist, could materialize the Bid during rehearsals and reap pandemonium among cast and crew.

Max had a torrid affair going with the girl playing Ophelia, a gorgeous and talented redhead from our sister school. After the paper restorer at Palazzo Fenway finally tired of him, Max remained enamored of Susan, as fun-loving as she was intellectual, for almost a year. (If only Susan had been enough for him, everything might have turned out differently.) They couldn't keep their hands off each other. And one afternoon, right before rehearsal was to begin, she and Max were interrupted by the Bid as they were finishing up a tryst in a backstage changing room—a stand-up quickie. They knew it was the director because he'd always arrive whistling the Prize song from *Die Meistersinger*. Susan grabbed her panties from the floor, giving herself a quick wipe, pulled down her skirt, and, handing the damp panties to Max, sashayed out onstage singing Ophelia's mad song as if nothing were amiss. Max watched while the Bid hung up his tweed jacket and disappeared behind the lighting board to mess with the stage lights for the thousandth time. Then he sidled over to the jacket, removed the extra-large silk handkerchief, a staple of the Bid's sartorial splendor, and replaced it with the stained panties. Some minutes later, rehearsal under way, the Bid was back in full regalia with megaphone at the ready. As the rehearsal continued, the director regularly produced the panties from his jacket pocket to dab his sniveling nose or pat his agitated brow. Word of the cum-soiled panties having spread like wildfire, cast and tech crew maintained an intent vigil on the Bid's pocket, internally hemorrhaging while trying to repress their laughter. Actors went up on lines and missed cues and staggered into the wings as if from a burst appendix. Which only increased the Bid's agitation, panties at the end of his forearm sweeping like a windshield wiper in a downpour across his sweaty brow.

By dinner, word had gotten around. Boys cruised the Bid's table for a glimpse of the dangle at his pocket. Every head in the hall was turned, breathlessly await for panty extraction. Finally, a faculty wife, noticing the sea of canted faces, spotted the offending undergarment daintily aflutter below the Bid's mustache as he dabbed at a drip of consommé. Her eyes widened, and widened farther—unbelieving. Boldly making her way past the ranks of leering grins, she wordlessly snatched the panties from the Bid's pocket and stowed them in her purse, ignoring his protest as she rushed for the ladies' room.

Perhaps Max's most disconcerting stratagem was his inveterate wordplay on everybody's parts, often done with such suggestive guile that it got to the point where the actors were constantly going up on their lines. Actors began to panic when approaching passages that Max had adulterated for comic affect. For this and other crimes, the Bid threatened to throw him out of the production, though by the week before opening it was hard to imagine who could replace him. And his acting—from rehearsal to rehearsal never the same as he varied his accents and pacing—was mesmerizing. The word was out and opening night was packed to the rafters.

Things went well. Only a few hitches where actors blew up on their lines due to the verbal minefields previously laid by Max. Max had actually behaved himself during the last week of rehearsals, as if even he understood the sanctity of the material.

That is until act 5.

It floods back to me, every detail, each time I'm backstage. Max had twisted my arm to take a minor role as the English ambassador, and since I was at something of a loose end in the afternoons until crew practice began in the spring, I became his "wingman," as he liked to put it: "You, me—Horatio, what say you sport, to tell my story, your story—what have you."

I was curious to see if Max could play the role of grave digger straight, let Shakespeare's character come through and not his comic interpretation (at rehearsals he'd channeled both a drunken W. C. Fields and Soupy Sales). In recital, Max might alter tempi in a Mozart sonata, but he'd never vamp it. And there was Yorick to be considered, a poignant tale indeed: the jester and childhood friend to the orphaned de Vere—so Max believed—who had wiped the young earl's tears and brought a smile to his face. Max took Yorick's skull home to our study each night, "just for safekeeping—someone to talk to while you hide yourself away in the library cage." Yorick had become our mascot, a toothless confidant haunting our lives that winter—along with Kim Philby and Jerry's admission about his pappy . . . of fathers known and unknown, and sons in search of an author to give them life.

Standing in the wings as the curtain was about to go up on act 5, I noted a distant look in Max's eyes, an expression of deep concentration—as when his hands hovered above the keyboard at the start of a recital—reminding me of a prewar photograph of my father knee-deep in an excavation trench on the island of Delos, examining a recent find. Concern flooded my brain. I'd also seen that look translate moments later into comatose depression, from which I feared he'd never rise. Then Max looked up from the grave and found his wingman. His face dissolved into a smile and he winked, a finger to his lips, an insouciant grin as he pointed into the grave and gave me a thumbs-up. For a moment I panicked, but then, absorbing this lovable character with powdered hair and a wrinkle-lined face and tattered, mud-stained clothes, I felt at ease once more, allowing his transformation before my eyes into a weary, life-battered grave digger . . . a premonition of what I was to become, what my father never lived to be.

As the curtain went up, I had to resist the impulse to run and embrace him before it was too late. Perhaps a lover's first insight into all the unknown lives we are yet to inhabit, as circumstances distance us from our own, when our youth dims, when our bountiful memories gain ballast and ripen and spoil, and with them the fateful links to our former selves and the world of our fathers.

As a single spotlight illuminated the darkened stage, I thought I saw tears in the grave digger's eyes, but they may have been my own.

There, standing in a grave was a mud-spattered old man, patting himself, blowing dust off his sleeves, his world-weary Cockney accent filling the auditorium. Knee-deep in death, every gesture and pose and lisped couplet eliciting guffaws from his adoring fans. He was Max; he was, always and forever, Max. As Hamlet approached the grave site with anxious trepidation, Max began to produce some unscripted props from the nether regions. It began with a bra or two, and again the infamous panties—already the stuff of campus legend—all produced in character with a comic rolling of the eyes and delighted looks of lovesick ecstasy as he breathed deeply of their scent; he then began flinging the female undergarments about the stage, snapping a garter belt into the howling audience, while Hamlet and Horatio looked on agog. Max never missed a beat, helpfully mouthing Hamlet's lines to the disconcerted prince.

And then he began with the condoms: reaching down into the grave, pulling hard with all his strength, getting his back into it, until the elastic came free with a loud snap that sent him reeling backward. He gamely examined the excavated rubbers with a wondrous grin, hyperventilating as he prepared for refueling. Escaped his grasp, the condoms rocketed outward as hundreds of outstretched hands made their hosannas. Max's reply to that most profound theological conundrum—first posed by him to Byron Folley in sacred studies class—on the possibilities of sex in the afterlife.

At the climatic juncture, Max reached down into the grave one final time to pull out a lighted jack-o'-lantern carved with the face of Alfred E. Newman, affixed with a note: *What, Me Worry?* Presented with this door prize, our Nordic prince stood in catatonic stupor as Max conducted him through his soliloquy on his beloved Yorick and moldy Caesar turned to clay. The body of Ophelia, convulsed with hysterical giggles, toppled off the flower-strewn catafalque.

Max would have been finished right then and there if he hadn't been required for the penultimate scene, in which he made his final appearance as Osric.

Needless to say, the apoplectic Bid flapped around backstage like a headless chicken, screaming out dire warnings, anything to get through to the final curtain. All the while the mighty soldier Fortinbras was pacing nervously backstage, preparing to mount the parapet, from which he was fated to deliver the closing lines of the play. Fortinbras, a sixth former and football captain, had been picked for the role because of his martial stature but was hardly the sharpest tool in the shed. What's more, he and Max had a running feud going back years. The previous spring, Max, sneaking around after lights-out, had awakened him at three in the morning before an important crew race; the next day, the race was lost by a bow length, and the oarsman, blaming Max, saw to it that he got six black marks in retribution.

And so, harboring his revenge, Max had weeks before devised a twist on Fortinbras's closing words, "Go, bid the soldiers shoot," changing it

to: "Go, soldiers, shoot the Bid." It became the catchphrase on everyone's lips. Fortinbras smiled gamely, figuring he was immune.

Now, as the fatal moment approached, Max confronted the pacing Fortinbras backstage and kept repeating the adulterated line to
his quaking face. Moments later, the armored, sword-carrying, clanking Fortinbras mounted the parapet, visibly shaking as he desperately
stared out over the corpse-strewn stage. And right below, there was
Max, confronting him again with the sardonic grin of the pumpkin
head. All backstage were riveted. The Bid glared from the wings. The
football captain summoned his last lines but halted in sheer terror and
consternation before the fatal phrase. Frantically, he looked around for
help, where, on the stage below, Osric was mooning him. The audience
tittered. In a final agonizing burst, Fortinbras blurted it out: "Go, shoot
the soldiers—No, I mean . . . the Bid—No—Yes, shoot the Bid, goddamn it," bellowing, ". . . shoot all the goddamn motherfuckers." With
that bloodcurdling shriek, he hurled himself to the stage and dashed
off after Max, who was already halfway to the stage door. As the curtain
mercifully descended, the litter of bodies onstage heaved with deathless
laughter.

When I remember back to that play within a play, I am still haunted by
the prince's expiring words and Max's to me: "Tell my story." Whether
it was Hamlet's or Edward de Vere's, or my father's story, or even that
of Pearce Breckenridge or Karel Hollar, or perhaps Max's or my own,
nothing of the truth found its way into *Like a Forgotten Angel.*

They were going to kick Max out. No if, ands, or buts. He was history.
They threw the book at him. To make sure the charges would stick,
he was accused of exposing himself to the audience when he turned
to moon Fortinbras. Byron Folley wanted him so badly, he could taste
it. But they didn't reckon with Max's latest ally and new adviser, the
Reverend Charlie Springfield, who threatened to resign if the decision
wasn't reversed. Max was Charlie's prize student. The faculty meeting
went on until three in the morning, at least that's when the tape ran out
on Max's recording system. He was saved by the miracle of a friendship.
Charlie Springfield was the most beloved teacher and minister of his
generation: "the conscience of the school," some called him. He said
Max's performance was a glorious bit of impromptu acting—the most
inspired and hilarious thing he'd ever witnessed. A compromise was

reached. Max was suspended for two weeks with the admonition: One more strike and he was out for good.

The Reverend Charlie Springfield taught the advanced literature courses, mostly for fifth formers studying for their English AP exams. On the face of it, Max and Charlie had a most unusual relationship: a charismatic minister—a wounded and decorated World War II veteran from North Carolina; and a highly strung Jewish kid from the Upper West Side by way of Brooklyn, a confirmed atheist and hell-raiser.

Besides detestation of Byron Folley, Charlie and Max were united in two burning passions: literature and opposition to the Vietnam War.

Perhaps no teacher in our day inspired more respect for his fiery preaching than Charlie Springfield. We actually looked forward to hearing his sermons on issues of the moment, a relief from the theological abstractions preached by his mentor, Paul Oakes. Charlie was a pacer in his classroom, goading his rapt students to dig into the guts of their assigned novels, challenging us to wrestle with the texts as if they were bearers of our adolescent souls' affliction. Part of his allure had to do with the brooding darkness of his southern drawl—how we imagined Faulkner or Thomas Wolfe would sound—and the heat lightning that flashed in his milky gray eyes. He was a figure of many rumors: of the terrible fighting he'd barely survived in Normandy; of a preacher father's suicide; of an identical twin who had died of sudden crib death, for whom he'd been renamed; and an early first marriage, to a poetess who'd died of cancer. He drank too much, he smoked too much, he punctuated his conversation with deep belly laughs, and he liked nothing better than to regale us with the outrageous stories of his small-town youth and run-ins with local crackers from the backwoods of North Carolina.

Max was convinced he was the reincarnation of Thomas Wolfe.

Charlie Springfield, of course, figures large in Max's novel; his murder on Memorial Day is the tragedy that changes everything for Saul. For this reason, I'm reluctant to include him in my narrative: He lives too magnificently in *Like a Forgotten Angel* for me to tamper with. But he was also the first to give me a glimpse of my father during the war, an honorable glimpse that sustained me for many years. So Charlie enters my story as a friend and truth teller and so much more.

Charlie had been a year behind my father at Winsted, and I got the feeling during our AP classes that Charlie didn't like me much, the reason being, so I assumed, because he hadn't liked my father much— or worse, he held some grudge or had been privy to rumors along the lines of what I'd overhead in the gym urinals. There wasn't a person I ran into during my Winsted years—if the person had been a friend or acquaintance of my father—about whom I didn't wonder, Are you holding back some terrible secret?

I figured, too, that there was no competing with Max, who had gotten his marching orders from Charlie: the operative license quoted from Faulkner prominently displayed above the blackboard in his classroom:

> An artist is a creature driven by demons. . . . He is completely amoral in that he will rob, beg, borrow or steal from anybody and everybody to get the work done. . . . He has no peace until then. Everything goes by the board: honor, pride, decency, security, happiness, all, to get the book written.

Every time I saw those words, I smiled: Samuel Williams nodding in his grave.

The very demons that drove Max to his early death decades later.

With Max banished to his mother's apartment in New York, I found myself, on a late-winter morning, summoned by Charlie to stay after class. He beckoned me over to a chair by his desk with a forthright smile and proceeded to apologize.

"Peter, I have been thinking ill of you and I realize I do you a great disservice. Will you forgive me, sir?"

Charlie exuded the charm of a Dutch uncle and the self-deprecation of a humble minister of God, hardly the highfalutin mantle of the Episcopal Church. I was instantly disarmed.

"I'm sorry, sir, I've actually been trying very hard to keep up with the reading assignments."

"No, no, your work's just fine." He paused, distracted, and waved his broad hand with a look of annoyance as he glanced over my shoulder at a scuffle in the hall beyond his half-closed door. His face was a little puffy, and there were broken capillaries in his acne-scarred cheeks and dark circles under his eyes. I could smell a medicinal odor on his breath. Dull winter light from the windows was reflected in his eyes: the dreary prospect of the Circle in three feet of snow. "I realize"—and he turned back to me with a searching smile—"with Max at home, how much of the show—haw-haw—he is apt to steal. But the fault is within me, sir, for I've made the cardinal error of judging someone by the conduct of a relation; and in this case, I fear I am doubly wrong."

"You knew my father?"

"He was a year ahead of me."

"You were friends?"

"No . . . but enough to know we all have to live with the father the Lord has given us—believe me, a tricky business under the best of circumstances, and your circumstances, like your father's, cannot have been easy." He loomed over his desk toward me, as if the resemblance could go without mention. "I was a scholarship boy, you understand, from small-town North Carolina, alone among a bunch of Yankee blue-blood assholes. And in those days, the boys here were genuine a-holes, right out of the playbook of Fitzgerald's Tom Buchanan. And I fear I judged him by the yardstick of schoolboy intemperance. That and a rusty memory."

"You mean you didn't like him?"

I grew a little feisty, after his mellifluous drawling around the bush. He laughed heartily, and I smiled as we took each other's measure, my eyes straying to the quotes from Conrad's *Heart of Darkness* on the blackboard, and the wonderful Rockwell Kent illustrations from *Moby-Dick* framed on his classroom walls.

"It didn't help that I was here on the forbearance of an Alden scholarship. And your father was a paragon: captain of varsity football, senior prefect, handsome like Douglas Fairbanks, popular and *rich*." He laughed. "Haw-haw: What's not to hate?"

"And I'll bet he didn't give a damn about Faulkner."

He grinned at my stab at levity and tapped the bust of the blind Milton that adorned his desk. The splayed backs of the paperback novels from which he'd been quoting in class were lined up on the desk like miniature roofs scattered by a twister.

"Faulkner! My goodness, I didn't even know of the man's existence. And just for the record, I nearly failed all my sacred studies classes—I hated anything to do with religion. Fathers!" Again he laughed that deep belly laugh of his. "I had to work hard to survive—everyone was so damned smart, so well prepared before they even showed up at Winsted. Socially, I dwelt in the stink of my backwoods ghetto. I guess I resented how easy it seemed for the Yankee gentry. Even the Depression didn't seem to slow them down. And frankly, that portrait of John's grandfather, Winsted founder and hero of Sharpsburg, in the library didn't help any. My mother's side of the family had been impoverished by Sherman's murderous rampage."

"You're saying my father was a snob?"

"His beauty, I think, was that he swam easily in the adulation that came his way." His large shoulders rose and fell for emphasis. "It was his hangers-on like Elliot Goddard and our boy in the White House, the president's national security adviser and their ilk who made sure I knew my place. I've never known *such* people born into *such* certainty."

Not a little embarrassed by this confessional tone in a man I admired so deeply, I had let my stare wander to one of the Rockwell Kent woodblock prints, this showing the huge tail of Moby Dick thrust above the waves, having just flipped a pursuing whaleboat. The boat was suspended upside down in midair, its crew of four tumbling like puppets into the dark sea: a near-perfect illustration of blind fate. Seeing those falling figures, all to be drowned except one, and trying to keep my wits about me, I was tempted to ask, "Sir, then why the hell have you been teaching and ministering at this crappy school for over twenty years?" But I chose a more circumspect approach.

"One thing I believe I can say about my father"—I was thinking of his letters to his mother—"what certainties he had, he didn't come by them easily."

"A scholar and a gentleman"—his eyes sparkled—"and good that you should have such a high opinion of him . . . given everything." Here he seemed a little hesitant, and my heart felt like it had missed a beat. "I can never forget him arriving on the Circle with his mother in a huge Cadillac Sport Phaeton, a deep, somber gray with whitewall tires, like New York royalty, and a gray uniformed driver unloading his fine leather suitcases. She was something, your grandmother; they don't make women like that anymore. Many on the faculty still revere her influence on the board, getting colored"—he winced and caught himself—"black boys into Winsted. She was very kind to me after the war, as was your father."

I stared into his brooding eyes, flecked with pale winter sunlight, above which a forelock of dark hair bobbed. I wanted to ask, "So, why did you hate him so?" But before the thought had fully formed—or a more diplomatic way of putting it—he had moved on to his own complicated explanation.

"Even after getting my Ph.D. at Yale, I enlisted in the infantry; I didn't want to have anything to do with being an officer. In graduate school and later teaching public school in Asheville, I had dabbled in union politics; I'd been a member of the Communist Party. The Hitler-Stalin pact cured me of that. I was a romantic; I wanted to show my childhood companions back in the foothills of North Carolina that I was still one of them; I wanted to be just one of the boys who hit the Normandy beaches." He shook his head, as if the stark wintry landscape beyond the window had caused an involuntary shudder. "Most of the young men I landed with, and most were teenagers, lie under white crosses above Omaha Beach." He took a deep breath, as if he'd been trying to quash the craving, then fumbled out a Camel from the soft pack at his elbow, letting the flame from his Zippo dance at the end of his cigarette, a point of fire we could share to ward off the chill. With a sigh of relief, he let loose an upward geyser of smoke.

"Your father came to visit me in a medical clearing station in Avranches; how he knew I was there, I have no idea. Perhaps the omniscience of the intelligence boys in OSS. But I was surprised that he'd do that, since he didn't really know me except as a socially graceless brat at Winsted. I was in horrible pain; even the morphine didn't help much. He read to me from the *Odyssey*—he apologized, said it was all that he had with him except for a Baedeker guide to Normandy and Brittany—and he smiled that enchanting smile of his. He told me, and I believe he was in earnest, that it was the greatest story ever told about men finding their way home from a pointless war. *Pointless* was the word he used, and that was what I remembered again the other day scanning the latest headlines in the *Times*." He gestured to where I sat, as if in explanation. "Strangely, it felt good coming from his lips. He provided me with something in very short supply at that particular moment: hope. The surgeons weren't sure they could save my leg. As he ended his visit, he put his book aside, stood, unbuckled his belt, and pulled down his trousers to display the nastiest scar on his thigh, long and ugly and red as a devil's lopsided sneer. He explained it all to me, told me about his months of therapy and what I could expect. I recognized in that moment the healing properties of time and memory. He was—none of us was—no longer the dashing schoolboy hero I remembered from a decade before. His face was hardened, his eyes ringed from loss of sleep and haunted—a bad time in Greece, he told me; he used a silver-handled cane to get around. Yes, his visit gave me hope and it was the elixir I required at that time: to remember the generous boy he'd probably been and the blindness of my young prejudice, and how much of all that—even the chapel I had once hated—might survive the horror of the moment to welcome back the future."

Charlie Springfield took a couple of deep drags and I could see his shoulders slump as he picked up his book bag in preparation for departure.

"So there it is, my boy. My apologies for jumping to all the wrong conclusions, for remembering the wrong things. . . . It's just this damned Vietnam mess has got everything so confused."

Those words of remembrance from Charlie got me through that winter and the difficult years that followed.

France, July 27, 1944

Dear Mother Nestor:

I still struggle to come to terms with this Normandy abattoir, since it seems only days ago I was at Bobby's wedding, as improbable as it was splendid. You would have loved it—how Charles Fairburn's Sussex Shangri-la on the cusp of the South Downs danced with lavender fox-gloves and riotous rainbow-hued rhododendrons. And such a backdrop to the women's spring finery under close escort by the khaki-clad and beribboned British high command and smart pinstripes of the intelligence services. Of course, the Brits look down on us OSS types as neophytes in their imperial game, to be endured but rarely taken seriously, not that it ever stopped them from trying to extract every bit of information on our operations when not offering deprecating advice regarding our ineptitude. One Kim Philby talked my ear off for over an hour, consuming champagne like cheap beer, while probing for details on Greece—surprising, since the Brits run that show like Capone's Chicago. Impressive experience in Spain and Portugal, worldly erudition, full of practical wisdom and charming in that disingenuous British way, which always leaves one slightly suspect as to ulterior motives. A close pal of the bride's brother (casualty of Tobruk) at Cambridge and named—can you believe it—after Kipling's Kim by a famous father he seems to respect and detest in equal measure, a legendary colonial type gone native along the line of Lawrence of Arabia.

But all that secretive intelligence chatter and nuptial cheer seems unreal a few miles behind the front lines: The grim reaping of high-explosive shells puts paid to our grand strategies in the stink of burning and decayed bullet-ridden bodies that are men no more. What I saw in Greece, or even in bombed-out London, pales in comparison, and every impulse yearns for return to my office at Princeton, or a dusty excavation in the Peloponnese—and yes, a woman's embrace—you may rest easy on that score, though complicated beyond even your wildest dreams! Things of simple virtue and decency have orphaned us, abandoning us to a wildfire of hatred and intolerance, never, I fear, to be put right in our lifetimes.

Just this afternoon I spent some time with Charles Springfield at a medical clearing station in Avranches. His leg was torn apart by German 88 fire—an antiaircraft weapon that the Germans have employed to terrible effect on advancing infantry and tanks. I stumbled on Charlie by pure happenstance; it was the sound of his Carolina drawl that alerted me to his presence in the ward. You see, I find myself drawn to the evacuation hospitals we chance upon, as if some nostalgic curiosity compels me to witness the kind of work that Father did before he was killed. The doctors and nurses I encountered here are doing such splendid duty, often under horrific conditions. And so my admiration grows by the minute for Father and the lifesaving surgery he performed in similar circumstances only twenty-six years ago.

I wanted you to know that his good deeds will be remembered, as will all your good work.

And I like to think it was memories of Father that led me to "pudgy" Springfield, as we once called him as new boy, lying on a litter set on sawhorses under a canvas tent in the postoperative ward of the field hospital. He was no longer the chubby kid I fear I once teased as a thoughtless youth, but a rail-thin soldier, dirty, unshaven, with a bandaged leg recently out of surgery. I pulled up a crate and sat with him to comfort him as best I could. His best friends were killed at his side. I shared many of my own experiences in rehabilitation and read to him from my copy of the *Odyssey*. He asked me why the *Odyssey* and I told him it was my way of getting outside of time. Homer's voice shatters time, I told him, and births stories of men and women in all their essential humanity and flaws, as vivid as the wounded soldier in the next cot. I told him it was a story about surviving hardship—with all its terrible violence—and returning home to our common humanity. I think that helped Charlie.

It was an odd thing: As I read to him, I kept seeing him as a scared little boy, as the little boy he once was and is no more, yet could no longer see myself in similar guise, as if I had never been young, as if those days are now utterly lost to me. It did us both good, I hope, to be companions once again, at least in spirit—old boys. You remember, Charlie was one of your scholarship boys from the South, when you insisted Winsted expand its scholarships to include southerners and Negroes.

Something I was put in mind of when one of the orderlies in the ward, a tall, intelligent Negro, was cursed at by a southerner, who cruelly disparaged the good man who was trying to dress his wound, demanding that a white orderly change his bandages. I saw Charlie wince at the incident, and he shook his head at me and repeated the word, "shameful—shameful." And Charlie is right. The way the Negro troops are treated is shameful and a blot on all we supposedly stand for. Back in London, there are racial incidents when black and white American soldiers rub shoulders. It disgusts me. When this damn war is over, let us do what we can at Winsted to set our own house in order, to set our country on a better path. And you, dear Mother Nestor, must look into the life of General Alden, as you have so long threatened to do, and so to let his career as an abolitionist rededicate our lives to his vision.

I am on the road again with my OSS unit, sorting out the devils from the deviled, prisoners and liberated alike. Patton is a killer, an enraged Achilles—and just what these times require.

Put your mind at rest, dear mother, I am safe and in no danger.

John

Charlie Springfield helped me realize just how much the Vietnam War was poisoning everything. When I glanced up at John Singer Sargent's imposing portrait of my great-grandfather over the mantelpiece in the reading room, I noticed his troubled eyes, gray with vertiginous black irises (two mere flourishes of Sargent's brush) under florid brows, a distant stare hinting at the terrible losses of Antietam. In those days of Vietnam protest and the country's self-hatred, I felt the general's stock falling daily. Military leaders of every stripe were disparaged, as were notions of honor and duty and commitment to the freedom of all peoples. That winter, the school's annual participation in the town of Winsted's Memorial Day parade was under review by the faculty, even though a near company of General Alden's men lay in the town cemetery. Without them, there would have been no Winsted School; without men like them, a truncated and benighted nation.

That is how I differ with Max: We may step into the same stream as our forebearers, but the stream is always different. What remains the same for all is the search for the true author . . . and the desire to return home.

Barring the possibilities, as Odysseus did, of bringing cheering reports of sons' deeds to the land of the dead, the only hope that remains is to pass on faithfully the deeds of those who have gone before us and make good on their sacrifices.

Our elders are memory's guardians. When their good offices are impeached, so, too the joys and hopes that sustained them. If we turn our backs on them from bitterness or pique, or unjustly neglect them as shadowy and insipid figures of low comedy, or scorn them for the flawed human beings they certainly were—that we all are—we find the hope that once glittered in their eyes—as it does for us—has turned to fool's gold long before we reach the end of our journey.

That, at least, is what I try to teach my students. As Jerry Gadsden said, it *is* complicated . . . for the author of our lives remains ever elusive.

9 AS I OPENED THE SCHOOLHOUSE DOOR IN SEARCH of Max, my wayward grave digger, I glanced back at the moon-lit snowdrifts lapping the plowed paths, as if a grudging March still insisted on choking the lovely green of the playing fields that would come with the spring. Max had been my February thaw, my March madness, and now, just days after his return from suspension, had gone missing on my watch. It was past one o'clock in the morning and he had failed to turn up in our room, and, given his precarious status, this was an expellable offense. Charlie Springfield had told me he could do just so much for Max and, as I left his classroom after our little talk, asked me to "batten down the hatches on our literary lion until I can properly instruct our brother in his calling."

My teeth began to chatter as the vague heat of the interior engulfed me. I listened for the shambling footsteps of the night watchman but heard only that steady Canadian wind gnawing at the eaves. As I searched the dark study hall, the marble busts that my great-grandfather had commissioned in Rome stood out like a ghostly jury in their oak-paneled niches, while in the moon-shadowed rear of the hall, imprisoned behind a grid of sashes, Lincoln, Grant, and Sherman, triumvirate captains of the slaves' liberation, presided over the mess we'd made of things. What would they think, I wondered, of how my contemporaries celebrated hopes of a North Vietnamese Communist liberation of the South?

Then I wandered into the central passageway of the schoolhouse, which was lined with framed letters from U.S. presidents. The letters on White House stationery, beginning with Grant and ending with Wilson, were addressed to my great-grandfather: "My Dear General Alden . . ." "Well now, General . . ." "Dear John, what a pleasure it is for me to write to your boys at Winsted. . . ."The letters praised the general's good work in education, especially his championing of character, leadership, and service to one's fellow men; the letters were handwritten and contained touching personal asides. As if I hadn't quite realized it before: what a famous man and what a formidable reputation. Now his school was derided in the press, as were many of its graduates, for leading the nation into a terrible war: blamed on an elitist tradition of noblesse oblige out of touch with the new realities. Who defended him now except the crepuscular Virgil Dabney and the ailing Paul Oakes and the likes of Elliot Goddard, controversial even among his colleagues.

"Oh the benighted multitude!" Virgil moaned at our late-night huddles for jelly doughnuts and coffee. "Don't they understand that Ho is just a proxy for Brezhnev and Mao, just another murdering criminal ruling by terror: what will the butcher bill look like? . . . Ah-da-dum . . . what horrors when the long-whiskered Ho gets his bloody hands on the rest of Southeast Asia?"

And so I took something of a perverse consolation in Charlie Springfield's kind words about my father, even if it was only Max he really cared about.

With these glum thoughts, I made my way slowly up the stairs to the second floor, where the music practice rooms occupied the far wing. A huge central corridor stretched from one end of the building to the other, part of which was devoted to the trophy heads of an intrepid president's African safari; all his sons and grandsons had attended Winsted. It was eerie as could be, what with these wild beasts on the prowl in the intense moonlight pouring from overhead skylights, their glass eyes dreamily aglow like creatures in some anesthetized limbo. Further on was a huge mural salvaged from a WPA project (run by a Winsted graduate) of the nine Muses and three Graces as they danced in a pastoral garden surrounded by ivy-clad walls. Their Art Deco somewhat streamlined eyes of blue outlined in gold seemed to follow me as passed to and fro. Then I detected the telltale notes of a distant piano and, my heart jolted to life, I departed the precincts of these fair maidens and hurried on my way.

When I opened the door of the dark practice room, Max did not even look up, but continued to play, silhouetted by the moonlight from a side window. Pungent smoke further obscured his figure.

I went to him, and he looked up at me with a slow, graceful turn of the head, his eyes a remote glassy white. Jerry Gadsden's admonition sprang to mind: *Look at the eyes, man; friend or foe, always look in the eyes.*

The lilting Chopin nocturne lingered beneath his left hand as he held out a glowing joint. I shook my head. "Take it, you silly bastard," he hissed. I was hurt by his tone. He tried to smile. "Take it, Hawkman . . . it'll do you some good."

"What do I do?"

"Just inhale deeply and hold the smoke in your lungs."

He turned back to the keys, digging into the bass line.

"Jesus, Max, you just got back from suspension; you're on probation. If the night watchman catches you, you're a goner."

"Charlie will take care of it; I'm untouchable, man."

"Nobody is—"

"Just do it—time you began to live a bit dangerously . . . walk on the wild side."

"You know this shit gets you depressed."

"Do it," he shouted, as if to bring down the roof.

I took a drag and coughed. A hint of a grin replaced his frown. I tried again, this time keeping the smoke taut inside my lungs. Max picked up the tempo of the music and modulated into a rock-and-roll riff, a hint of the Jefferson Airplane and Haight-Ashbury as if to spur me on. I took another drag and held it deep. The joint had burned nearly to my fingertips and I handed it back to Max, who deftly finished it off. The music shifted again to a haunting rhythmic melody. My chest seemed to expand with painful emotion, my breath tight, as a sublime beauty flowed from the moonlight.

"What is it?" I whispered, less afraid of being heard than of breaking the mood.

"My own transcription," he said, "the adagio from Rachmaninoff's Second Symphony."

I went over to the window, feeling tears coming to my eyes, and a transforming faintness as the moonlight began to intensify, as if my brain were emptying outward to embrace the infinity of white gathering on the snowbound horizon. Out there, somewhere in the music, I thought I detected snatches of my father's voice from his letters: singing the praises of white-capped seas and the white geometries of Santorini and the prospect of a golden age. The next moment, as if a switch had been thrown on my impending clairvoyant madness, I was convulsed by claustrophobia, as if trapped in Max's nightmare. Terrified, I turned from the window and practically jumped out of my skin at the sight of my own distorted shadow bent over Max's bowed figure. He was a phantom, shrouded in a hazy corona, the ivories of the piano a prancing iridescence beneath his fingers.

And then, as if he knew, he turned to me and smiled.

"You're all right, just relax."

"I feel a little weird."

"Not to worry. I'm your wingman—remember?"

I shook my head, trying to free myself from a cacophony of voices. I walked over to him and reached a hand to his shoulder, where his dark curls brushed my fingers. It felt good to make sure of him that way, that he was okay, that we would be okay. I began massaging his neck muscles. I could feel a release of pressure and his skin warming and the radiating sense of safety embodied in my touch.

Something of this careless caress made its way into *Like a Forgotten Angel* and, with it, intimations that the infatuation of the protagonist's best friend went beyond mere friendship. On this, the record speaks for itself.

"Can you hear it"—he hummed—"winter, like the dull . . . slap of an oar along the gray canals of Venice—eh, rowman?" His fingers deftly rippled over the keys. "You and I and Palazzo Barberini and the spirit of Henry James." He bowed his head and then turned to the pale moonlit night beyond our window. "When the spirits of the great masters arise, the choiring angels will usher them onward with this music."

My massaging fingers came to a halt. His words, the tone, sent a shiver down my spine: images of those orgiastic angels in the Williams Memorial bronze mixing with that of Max curled into a fetal position on our couch, immovable.

"Angels," I murmured, my head spinning. "A world . . . fanned awake by angels' wings."

"Yes . . . angels."

"Must be cold in a grave," I offered with a shiver, "especially this time of year."

I squeezed his shoulders—where the wings grow, as if feeling for the source of his strength, his genius, something of the untrammeled desire that might yet set me free.

"I'm glad you're still playing," I told him. Max had sworn off practicing during the rehearsal for *Hamlet*. "I'd really miss hearing you play."

"Mom's pretty upset right now. She wasn't thrilled when I was sent home. So, I promised I'd continue practicing—but *just* two hours a day."

His parents had divorced that summer and he told me only late in the fall, when his father stopped showing up in his pink Caddy to take us out to dinner at Durgin Park. The music slowed, then grew quieter, as if moving into the distance to give us some breathing space in that tiny room.

"It's one of Mom's favorites. Her father, Oscar, knew Rachmaninoff; he played violin in the first performance of the symphony in Vienna. Oscar thought he was exempt by being"—he segued into his mother's Viennese accent—"a beloved first violinist in the Vienna Philharmonic." Max hit a discordant phrase. "But he wasn't—they murdered him anyway. My mother still pretends that dying of starvation and overwork in a concentration camp is the same as dying of natural causes."

"Stick with the music Max, even if it's just to get laid."

"No, I'm done. I've talked to Charlie about it—it's all or nothing. There's no halfway in this life, none at all."

"Well, I like to hear you play."

"What had lived up to hope?" he sang out. "What had withstood the scourge of growth and memory? Why had the gold become so dim? O death in life that turns our men to stone! Lost, oh lost." He seemed to pause, as if to await my rejoinder; I returned to massaging his neck in hopes he'd keep playing.

"So that's it—you were at Charlie Springfield's tonight." I tried to cover the hurt in my voice. "Reading his notebooks on Thomas Wolfe . . . *again*."

"Yeah, baby-sitting. Actually, I was reading though Charlie's war diaries."

"No way. How come you didn't ask me to come?"

"I stuffed myself with Joshua's Twinkies."

"Why didn't you tell me?"

"He's my mentor, sport. You've got that fascist Virgil Dabney on your team and you can keep him."

"He's not so bad; actually, he's pretty damn funny."

"Charlie doesn't like him for beans, thinks he's a bad influence on the boys, worse than Goldwater, which is about as bad as it gets in Charlie's book."

"Shit, Charlie fought in France."

"So tell me, what's the deal with you, hanging out in the library cage with all the periodicals? What's up, Hawkman? I thought we were best buddies. Why are you holding something back?"

"Who, me? I'm a fucking cipher, like you always say: dependable and trustworthy and so completely boring."

"Hey, the flip side is not a bed of roses. Just look at Charlie." He lit up another joint and let his head roll backward as he stared into my eyes. "There's something wrong there, a little scary. . . . I just—can't put my finger on it."

"Mr. Springfield, Charlie?"

"It's in the faces of his kids; they adore him, but some part of them is terrified of him, of losing him."

"Do you have to dramatize *everything*? He's just"—and I thought back to our conversation in his classroom of just a week before—"intense . . . like you."

"Wasn't he great in class this morning?"

Charlie had put on quite the performance, pacing the classroom, with that unruly lick of dark hair teasing an eyebrow, voice thundering, as if forever on the trail of the fleeting specter—the ineffable burning vitals of life, as he liked to put it, "that ride herd on our lives."

Max stopped playing. "He frightens me sometimes—really. You see it when he's with his kids, that look in his eyes, like the kids are all there is in the world, all that is good and sane, and he is so desperately trying to hold on to it—to them."

"Max." I could see it in his eyes, the creeping darkness. I shook him. "Don't make such a big fucking deal out of it, okay?"

"You have no idea."

"Okay, so I'm not his big buddy, like you."

"Listen, I'm not being paranoid—I swear. I love the guy. It's just he's so incredible, so passionate. He's taught me so much about literature and writing already. It's like I can't imagine what I'd do without him." He paused. "But his war diaries . . . Terrible things. He'd try to describe the scene of battle, and then there'd be a dash of pencil point: 'The English language gives up on me.' That's what he wrote, '*My beloved* English language gives up on me.' Can you believe it? Is such a thing possible?"

"Did you ask his permission to read that stuff?"

"He didn't say I couldn't."

"Jesus, Max, you can't just keep poking into everybody's shit like that."

I retreated to the window, as if something inside me knew to leave that particular subject well enough alone. I gazed out over the snowbound sweep of the Circle. Staring intently at the blur of apple trees against the white, I fought back tears, concentrating on their pulsing shapes, like albino amoeba under a microscope. I was shivering, eager to change the subject.

"You know," I said, "you could give your dad a call, just talk about stuff."

My heart leapt at the sound of my own voice, as if some part of me—how crazy—longed—how it longed—to do just that.

He turned from me with a snort of disgust and resumed his playing, his forehead brushing the keyboard, as if listening for the faintest pianissimo. Then, reaching into his jacket pocket, he pulled out a postcard and handed it to me. I went to examine it in the moonlight by the window. The photo was of a phalanx of cliff divers in Acapulco riding the air halfway to the water. A few words were scribbled on the back that I couldn't read. I handed the card back.

"My father, the fucking hypocrite," he spat. "There he is in Acapulco with some friggin' whore he's now planning to marry, and he has the moxie to send me this fuckin' postcard after kicking my mother out of our apartment—schlemiel." He slammed down the piano cover and joined me by the window, his face undergoing a transformation in the pale light. "O lost," he moaned.

I felt like letting him have it: like father like son—huh? A real ladies' man.

"I hate to say it, but I kinda like your dad, and Durgin Park."

He slugged me in the arm.

"You have done it—right? You're not *still* a virgin?"

Again I rolled my eyes. "C'mon."

"Seriously, it's not enough just to hang out with jocks, with Virgil cooking up conspiracies and bemoaning the past. You've got to live, man. I fuck, therefore I am—don't you get it? This is all we've got, time to spend your seed."

"C'mon, it's time you took a cold shower and went to bed. Besides, 'tis death and dishonor should they catch us in here at this time of night."

Max smiled and sauntered past me with a new swagger to his step.

"Hah—'tis you they're really out to get. Beware the council of ten, Hawkman. They'll pluck you to the last feather."

Max scowled. "So tell me, is the lugubrious Virgil behaving himself, keeping his hands off his . . . ah-da-dum . . . his young and handsome protégé—that is, when conspiracies against man and nature are not afoot."

"Fuck off."

"Listen," he grabbed my arm in mid-stride, "speaking of lechery, have I got a girl for you. Susan wrote me and said she has this friend— Barbara something or other, intellectual WASP—blue-eyed Athena, just your type. A guaranteed score—dig it—ready to go down on her knees before your lordly member."

"Know what your problem is: You don't ever know when to stop."

"No, really. Susan says she's gorgeous, looks like Julie Christie. . . . Besides, we gave her the clippings in the paper about your heroics in the Rivers game—all those touchdown passes and shit. Word is, she fantasizes about going out with a Winsted football captain."

"Jerry ran in three of those touchdowns—get your facts right."

"Football captain," he sneered, "just like your father."

"When was the last time you even bothered to come to a game— great wingman you are."

I shook loose from his grasp and walked away down the corridor. He ran after me and tackled me from behind, rolling on top, holding my arms down.

"Whaddya say?" He stuck out his tongue lasciviously. "Will you, at least, go out with her? Doesn't mean you have to go muff diving or anything."

I pushed up with both arms, lifting him bodily, demonstrating my added strength since working out with Jerry all winter.

"You know what happened the last time." I lowered my arms, bringing him closer. "My blind date almost died of terminal boredom."

"Are you kidding? She expired of terminal horniness—you never laid a hand on her." He flicked his tongue again. "Got to get in there boy, to the wetness, all the way to the creamy wetness."

"Since when are you recommending prospective football captains?" I suddenly flipped him over, pinning him, glaring at him in triumph.

"I might make exceptions," he huffed, the wind knocked out. "Still haunted by that fair and warlike form . . ."

"Okay, okay, I'm sufficiently impressed with your ability at instant replay."

"I'm much better at foreplay."

He reared his head up and tried to kiss me. I dodged his lips.

"No doubt."

He rolled over on one elbow and brought his face close to mine.

"You do like girls, don't you?"

"You know, I *do* have a life outside of this place."

"Really, so, whaddya do when you're not here?" He blew into my hair. "I have the hardest time imagining you anywhere else—haunting this mausoleum of your ancestors. Except there's Elysium—right, Berkshires somewhere? Hermitage? So how come you never invite me, your buddy, your best pal? You've become so secretive these days; you're even hiding your notes from the periodical cage, aren't you?"

"That's what I mean—it's private, okay?"

"So what's with that Laura Williams—your apple blossom queen? How does she fit into this picture?"

"Ah, maybe that's just going to remain my little secret."

"I mean, that blind date wasn't so bad-looking. Didn't you even kiss her?"

"She . . . I dunno . . . when we said good-bye she kinda did this thing with her tongue."

"Yes, yes . . ."

"Like down my throat, and I think her braces chipped a tooth."

Max rolled away, hysterically pounding the floor.

"What makes you so goddamn fucking smart—huh? Just because you memorized all of fucking Shakespeare."

"Please, de Vere to you, seventeenth earl . . . Edward de Vere."

"Stick with fucking Chopin, Max."

He looked at me a little oddly, as if momentarily confounded, and then waved me off and turned his attention elsewhere.

"O Muses, O lofty genius, now assist me."

His laughter echoed down the length of the great moonlit corridor. And somehow, I no longer cared. Above, the huge WPA mural of the three Graces and nine Muses glittered with a spectral radiance: gold-and-lapis-lazuli eyes watching us.

He burped.

"Ah . . . so I tempt you, do I? Will you choose . . . the nether path of laughter and forgetting? Free of your father's example and Virgil's poisonous ministrations. I give you the path of art . . . of life." Max spread his arms wide, as if to receive an invisible lover, pumping his pelvis. I lay beside him, two swimmers afloat. Above us, the three Graces gazed benevolently from their garden; transformed by celestial light, their streamlined presence was a comfort. "They try to conquer time with his meaningless death," he whispered to me. "She gives her body in all-bounding love."

"'All-bounding love?'" I echoed in a hushed voice, hoping to lower the volume.

To no avail. With a series of howls and catcalls, Max, on his haunches, began braying at the moon. But instead of terror, I found myself convulsed in fits of laughter. A moment later, in yet another protean display, he turned onto all fours and began crawling toward me in his favorite imitation of Bert Lahr as the Cowardly Lion.

"Courage, Hawkman," he snarled. "Ya-a-a . . . got to have courage." With this, he roared in my face and licked my ear.

I was so weak from laughing that I could barely fend him off. Then he rose and stood like a maestro calling for silence. He walked down the hallway to where the ranks of mounted trophy heads gazed like a menagerie at feeding time.

"Hear the words of Ecclesiastes: 'Wherefore I perceive that there is nothing better, than that a man should rejoice in his works; for that is his portion: for who shall bring him back to see what shall be after him?'"

"Just think, Pete, how quickly it rushes away from us, and still we fear to choose."

"Choose?"

"'Behold!' he wailed. "'The jaws of darkness do devour it up. So quick bright things come to confusion.'"

And, proud to be his wingman, I hit my mark: "'Lovers and mad-men have such seething brains . . .'" For an instant I was stymied, until he mouthed the next phrase from *A Midsummer Night's Dream*, "Such shaping fantasies, that apprehend more than cool reason ever comprehends. The lunatic, the lover, and the poet are of imagination all compact.'"

He bowed to me.

"Well done," he bellowed, patting me on the rear. "Hawkman, there's hope for you yet."

"*Doceri ac docere.*"

He smiled wickedly.

"Right on, brother." He led me to the wall of trophy heads. "And that is why we must hold the mirror up to nature, Pete; that is the divine task of the poet, the writer—to be the author of our own lives."

"'To show virtue her own feature,'" I proudly declaimed, "'scorn her own image, and the very age and body of the time his form and pressure. . . .'"

Max put his arm around my neck and planted a wet kiss on my cheek. "And to think when I first knew you, your nose was firmly buried in Thucydides. You've come a long way, Hawkman. Don't slip back now—for Virgil's pit still looms. 'For some must watch, while some must sleep.'"

"'Thus runs the world away.'"

"And how will you remember me, Hawkman, when I'm gone?"

"You're not going anywhere—without me."

"In ten, fifteen years, what will you-we remember? Maybe you'll remember a moment or two, but all the time we spend together will fog over to an indistinct cloud of recollection, unless, that is, we take time in our own hands and re-create it, reshape life out of life—make of it something memorable, animate it with genius, give meaning where there is only emptiness. That is the role of the true artist—the writer— our only hope."

"Max . . ." I sighed, beginning to run out of steam as I slipped back from my high.

He looked at me with ecstatic eyes.

"What must I do to convince you? What must I do to save this night for you—transform and give it special place in the pantheon of our—yours and mine—divine memory?"

With that, he reached to a huge lion head, grasped it in his arms, and, with a horrible creak, wrenched it free from the wall.

"Courage . . . Hawkman," he cried out. He raised the lion's head to rub noses, as he had so often done with Yorick's skull. "This prize trophy shall await our next contestant, Joy-Joy, on his desk come the morning." I hung my head, knowing I'd failed. Max, after dancing a little jig, turned on his heels and marched down the corridor toward the headmaster's office, the lion's head tucked securely under his arm. Then, seeming to forget something, he stopped, turned, and bowed in my direction, his moon-shadowed thespian halving itself, then vanished into the stairwell as brave Achilles had vanished into the kingdom of the shades.

The next morning, I couldn't get Max out of bed; his depression lasted almost two days, what he called his "gloomy-doomy Viennese melancholia."

I have gone over it a million times in my mind: where Max's magic ends and the conniving begins. Because everything he said was true: I remember that night as if it were yesterday; his antics made the moment live. Of course, the lion's head caper is a set piece in *Like a Forgotten Angel*. And yet, here he was just back from suspension, Byron Folley and the senior master just the day before had warned him that the slightest infraction would result in instant dismissal, and a day later that lion's head greeted headmaster Folley on his desk. But not a word—nothing came of it.

I believe Max was already in cahoots. That, or he had so much dirt from his bugging of the headmaster's study (a page out of J. Edgar's playbook) that Byron Folley dared not move against him.

Nor did Max's pleas to the Muses go unanswered.

Out of the blue, early that spring of 1968, Laura Williams began writing me. While helping her father open their cottage, Hermitage (where they lived seven months out of the year when not on Boston's Beacon Hill), she stumbled on a cache of love letters from my father to her mother. Suzanne Williams had hidden the letters on a high shelf in the back of her closet, where she knew her wheelchair-bound husband could never get at them. The letters changed Laura's life—both our lives—all our lives. The world she had known, as she put it to me many years later, "evaporated before my eyes in the hand of a man I never knew." That's when she began writing me for the first time—not a word about what she had found, but around the edges, her hurt and curiosity began to make their way into my consciousness. I found her oblique asides and inquiries strangely appealing, echoing a yearning in myself. "Yesterday," she wrote in one of her first letters, "I walked to that lonesome white pine in the old pasture by the lake. Maybe it was just the smell of pine and sweet fern, but I found that the wind over the lake spoke to me as never before—oh, of many things, but not in a language I've yet learned." She knew from the letters that the abandoned pasture—"Pine Meadow" we called it—a twenty-minute walk from Hermitage and Elsinore was where Suzanne and my father rendezvoused for their assignations, where her mother had always walked with her as a young child.

Discovery of those letters further strained her already-difficult relationship with her mother. Where once Laura had only suspected deceit, now she saw it everywhere. As Max wrote of his heroine in his second novel, *Gardens of Saturn,* "Her youth evaporated in a sun-filled room above the lake while sitting on her mother's bed reading those erotic letters. The voices translated her out of time . . . and into a world of illicit desire, the like of which, even for a dancer, she never imagined the human body so designed." Max described the tensile, tough ballet dancer at seventeen: "a woman with a deep intuitive need to foster equilibrium in her surroundings, driven to find a male both steadfast and free of taint, and so provide the launching pad to her own stardom, outside her mother's sordid orbit."

So Laura and I began to write to each other. Her letters were chatty, gossipy, flirtatious and daring, and always humorous—probing ever so lightly for insights into the man her ballerina mother had first met in early 1944 in a rehabilitation hospital in Guilford, south of London, where Suzanne, shamed into nursing by her military father, worked as a physical therapist. By that spring of 1968, Laura was an apprentice with the Boston Ballet, and her budding career was chock-full of odd characters and dramatic moments onstage—something she liked to write to me about. We were able to open up in those letters in ways we had been incapable of doing in person.

That cruel spring of 1968, bracketed by the bloody violence of the Tet Offensive and then the assassination of Martin Luther King, Jr., in April, was a time of bitter wind and icy rain that refused to give up its grip. There was still ice on the river by the start of crew practice. After King's assassination, Jerry Gadsden just stopped talking to me, as if I had lost all moral standing in his eyes. The black guys huddled at their table in the dining room, displaying a contempt that made us all feel complicit in King's murder in Memphis. Soon a disparaging cynicism crept into all conversations. The worst for me was Paul Oakes's personal struggle through that winter, after his return from a second round of cancer surgery and chemo: an unsettling symbol of the frailty of the old order.

He would stagger around the Circle through ice and drifting snow, bulging canvas book bag thrown over his shoulder, his once-huge frame bent like those ancient apple trees on the Circle. His gaunt face had a jaundiced pallor, the fierce twinkle in his eyes extinguished. He always refused my help with his book bag, refused to admit anything was amiss, but seemed glad of my company. By spring crew practice, he could no longer make the walk to the river, but drove himself down in his wine red Ford Thunderbird and parked where he had a view of the boat landing and the comings and goings along the river. Often he waylaid me as I was jogging to the river, warning me of icy patches ahead as he rolled down his window and suggested I hop in. And there he'd be upon my return, sitting in the Thunderbird, gazing over the river, lighting up the occasional Camel, even after his oath of abstinence to his doctor "on a stack of the King James Version."

Those first days on the river that spring were strangely ominous, and not just because of all the floating ice: Cobra gunships and C-130's from nearby Fort Devens constantly roared overhead. To read the newspapers, you'd have thought the U.S. Army had been crushed by the Tet Offensive, and yet there seemed to be more activity at Fort Devens than ever. Seeing those mighty machines churn through the chilly spring skies, I found myself curious, emboldened, until I was regularly rowing past the barbed-wire fences and the huge signs posted on the riverbank that warned rowers and canoeists from trespassing on U.S. government property. It was no joke: The Green Berets were said to be conducting live-fire exercises over the sprawling marshes and woodlands of Fort Devens. But I enjoyed tempting fate, slipping from one world into another—from the cocoon of school life, where Max spent every moment huddled in the library writing short stories for Charlie Springfield and Jerry gave me the cold shoulder, into a world of powerful machines and purposeful activity. Feeling somewhat forlorn, one day I just kept going, past the barbed wire and warning signs, full steam ahead. On and on . . . and then, maybe a mile father, there it was—a bizarre Potemkin village of straw and bamboo huts, a perfect mock-up of Vietnamese hooches translated to a barren New England riverbank. The first time I saw it, I just stared, oar blades poised, until the current returned me upstream. This bizarre disjunction of time and space—the thrilling, exotic risk inflamed my imagination from the moment I woke each morning till I hit the sack: that bamboo village along the river a staple, too, of my dreams.

It was on my return from one of these missions that Paul Oakes confided in me the thing that had clearly been on his mind for some time. Sadly, it couldn't wait.

He put his hand on my shoulder, switched off the purring V-8, and gazed at me through sunken eyes, their blue centers gone a dull gunmetal gray.

"How are you and Virgil getting on?"

"Great, I guess."

"Virgil's a good man. Just don't believe everything he tells you."

I had to smile. "Well, that's a great deal—a lot to take in."

"Listen, I know damn well he and your dad . . . well, your dad was something of a protégé."

A helicopter gunship roared overhead and we both watched through the windshield as it faded off down the river, where the tallest trees patterned the sky with eyelets of green.

"But neglecting the spiritual life . . ." He nodded to himself and stroked the loose folds at his jaw. "Things like that, you see: Sometimes it takes more than *just* character. It can get pretty lonely without something more to hold on to, something larger than yourself."

He gestured to the river, where the first buds of spring were creeping forth in the beeches and oaks; and I was almost ready to reply along the lines of how I found rowing offered solace of a kind. But he had something else in mind.

It was the cold spring, he went on, that so reminded him of another April, in 1945, when he'd been division chaplain in Patton's Third Army. By pure happenstance, he'd crossed paths with my father. "What, nearly a year since I'd seen him when I presided at Bobby Williams's wedding on a lovely June day in Sussex. Your dad had been best man." My father was traveling in a jeep with a joint OSS-army intelligence unit, gathering information from prisoners and going through captured documents. I was all ears, figuring that this must have taken place about nine months after he'd seen Charlie Springfield in the field hospital outside Avranches. Paul Oakes joined my father's jeep brigade so they'd have time to catch up; Charlie Springfield, later to become a protégé of Paul in the Episcopal ministry, was a subject, as was Bobby Williams, who'd been shot down in July of '44, and Elliot Goddard, who was back in England after being parachuted into Brittany two months after D-day.

Paul Oakes lighted up a Camel and thoughtfully exhaled out his side window.

Their jeep was traveling just behind the tank unit that liberated Buchenwald. They had no idea what they had stumbled upon. The lead tanks had smashed through three barbed-wire fences enclosing the camp; the accompanying infantry had been fully prepared for a fight, carbines and bazookas at the ready. Except the Germans were gone. Slowly, the disoriented and terrified inmates crept out of the cell blocks in their striped uniforms: "walking cadavers, hardly believing we were

Americans, hardly believing the Krauts had fled in the night and they were still alive." The terrible smells of the place forced them to hold cloth over their noses; the crematorium still belched black smoke from tall brick chimneys. The camp guards had abandoned the hellhole only hours before. It was behind the crematorium that they found the perfectly stacked bodies lying crisscrossed at ninety-degree angles; it was the "neatness and thoroughness that had gone into the ghoulish task" that most disturbed Paul. "Son, the black-and-white photographs you see in books never account for the color, the gray-green of the bodies, and the smell . . . and the precision of the stacking, like goods at the end of a production line."

But that wasn't what Paul Oakes wanted to talk about. It was something that happened days later, after the *Look* photographers had covered the horror, after Patton saw to it that the German townsfolk were paraded through the camp as witnesses to the "abomination on their doorstep," after my father and Paul had had a few days to absorb what Paul called "the hypertrophic fanaticism" behind the genocide. "It's the enormity of the evil that resists human analysis. It was enough to make me seriously give up my faith; not until I was back home could I begin to find a way to deal with it. It surprised me how much tougher—if that's the right word—your father turned out to be—coming from such a cushy New York background." (Paul was born in Portland, Maine, from an old seafaring New England family.) "It troubled me that it didn't seem to affect him as it did me. I began to wonder if my faith was a weakness, not a strength. I chalked it up to what he'd been through in Greece. I remember how he shook his head. 'My Greece is gone,' he said—that's how he put it. He let on that he'd killed Germans in Greece, and worse: He'd witnessed the indiscriminate murder of civilians. I'd seen a lot of bad things that year, God knows the Falaise Pocket was no picnic for the soul, but I'd never had to pull a trigger. I felt lucky I'd never been put to the test."

I was struck by his confessional tone: how a man of his power and certainty and toughness of character had no disposition for the dirty work, for the duty his faith might abhor, something, I discovered years later, he shared with Samuel Williams. And to have this perceived "failure of character" highlighted by the conduct of a former student can't have been easy. But something in his narrative still didn't fully register with me: What exactly had he expected my father to do in terms of the harm to his spiritual life?

Then Paul got to the heart of the matter. Just hours before they were scheduled to move on, a young overwrought army private ran up to Paul with distressing news. Some of the camp survivors, a few of the stronger ones, had managed to get past the army guards stationed around the gaps the tanks had made in the barbed wire; they had made their way to the nearby village, where they found one of the camp guards in hiding. They had forced the guard to return with them and were questioning him in the crematorium. The PFC wanted Paul Oakes to tell him what he should do. "Of course, he should've gone to his sergeant, but instead he came to me—and my curiosity got the better of my common sense." Paul Oakes and my father followed the private into the crematorium, which by then had been largely cleared of bodies. Even so, the smell was "ungodly." The camp inmates were standing around a small man in trim civilian clothes, well fed, his frightened eyes streaming tears. They were questioning him, angrily accusing him in a Babel of tongues. Even my father, who spoke perfect German, could barely understand them. Soon it became clear what "mischief" they had in mind. "I should've had the PFC go get the sergeant, but I was afraid that once I sent him off, he might never come back, and we could hear the tanks moving off."

Someone among the camp survivors produced a thick rope and handed it to the cowering German guard. He dropped it. They told him to pick it up. They told him what he had to do. His resignation growing, he began to follow their instructions, tying a noose, thirteen loops; he fumbled it more than once and had to start over. "They had lived with death and knew its procedures in detail. And on his third or fourth try, he got the noose perfect and they made him put it around his own neck." By then he'd been so browbeaten, he didn't need to be told twice. They had him climb up on a table and flip the end of the rope over a steel beam, breaking a light fixture in the process, the broken glass sprinkling his hair like a fall of snow. Someone tightened the end of the rope by fastening it to the steel door handle on one of the ovens—"done so quickly, so deftly that it seemed to have happened all by itself." Then his hands were tied behind his back. At this point, the American PFC, who carried a Thompson sub-machine gun, turned to Paul Oakes and asked him what to do—shouldn't they stop this thing? "I was riveted by the scene before me, but it was as if I were a million miles away; I was in a cold sweat in that foul-smelling place and the hounds of hell were yapping in my guts. 'Where's your sergeant?'

I asked. The man told me his sergeant was off on the other side of the camp with the departing tank crews. So I turned to John beside me, to my quarterback, a leader among men, an example of the best we produce. He just shook his head. 'I have no authority here,' was what he told me, 'I'm not even attached to your unit.'"

The pressure of Paul Oakes's hand on my shoulder tightened as he told me this doleful tale, and I had little doubt he was looking to me as he had looked to my father at that moment, waiting for a reaction, but I was speechless.

Standing at the edge of the table, the German guard had tears streaming down his face. "Poor fellow was shivering, pissing his pants." The camp survivors continued their vituperative chorus of orders, "bobbing their heads and spitting. The poor beggar caught sight of me, I suppose the crosses on my collar, that I wore an American uniform. He said something to me in German. John touched my arm. 'He's asking for absolution,' he said. I could only shake my head; I really didn't do that kind of thing. The voices of the survivors rose against him. First he tried to leap off the table, but the men surrounding him grabbed him and planted him back on the table and made it clear what they expected. Then without another word or even a whimper, the German guard gingerly stepped off the table into space and the survivors pulled the table away." Paul's hand loosened on my arm. "You see, that way he slowly . . . slowly strangled, his face turning one terrible purple-red color after another as his body shook and his legs swam in the air, like a swimmer trying to break the surface."

Paul took the steering wheel in his hands and leaned his head forward toward the chrome dash. "My stomach couldn't take it and I walked away before the man's soul had quite fled his body. Outside in the fresh air, I began vomiting, as did the private; between us, we made quite a mess. Your father patted me on the back and handed me a cigarette, lit from the one he was smoking, as if the whole thing had been . . . *all* in a day's work."

I was listening raptly, trying to decipher the tone: all in a day's work. Paul bent back from the steering wheel with a confused expression on his ravished face. Was he aghast, admiring . . . or just terribly, terribly sad for my father?

Paul Oakes had no more to say on the subject; he grunted and kept his face averted from mine, as if suddenly regretful of an indiscretion. He switched on the ignition, gunning the motor and twirling the radio dial until he'd tuned in some favorite Sinatra. He put the car in drive, "And so, tell me . . . you've never said a word about *Essays and Prayers*." But here I think I surprised him, for I had dipped into it in my attempt to fathom something of the character of Samuel Williams. And so I mentioned the odd discrepancies in the text, the moving abolitionist passages and soaring bits of Emersonian idealism that he had underlined. For the first and last time, we found a subject on which we could freely engage, that and our days on the river. I hope it made him happy.

I have often wondered if he felt guilty for burdening me with that macabre story about Buchenwald, released from his conscience after more than twenty years. Did the thing disturb his sleep, creep up on him as he surveyed the action on the gridiron or watched his boys row on the river? Had it threatened either his faith or his faith in my father, which I had a sneaking suspicion had come close to being the same thing. Did the story's telling ease his passing a few months later? Otherwise, he surely would have waited until my graduation or even college. I had a feeling, even then, that his reluctance to tell me had less to do with his own role in such a painful incident than his concern about damaging my feelings about my father. Facing his own end, I think he accepted the moral obligation to articulate the circumstances—that was the New England conscience in him. Perhaps he felt he had failed me in some way. It had not been easy for him to turn me over to his rival, Virgil. Perhaps he felt he owed the telling to my father. Whatever the case, he unburdened his conscience and reballasted mine.

The image of a hanging man, kicking for the surface, remains embedded in my memories of an icy riverbank in April. When people come to me at reunions and tell how terrified they were of Paul Oakes, all I can think of is a man who went to his grave wondering if he had the fortitude to take a life and glad, that in this, he had been spared . . . perhaps a sin of omission and no more.

He was one of the lucky ones.

It turned out, Paul had dropped an unintended clue to the circumstances that had led my father to Checkpoint Charlie. He had mentioned that my father had volunteered for the OSS intelligence unit following the American advance through France and into Germany; that his wounding in Greece and disability had qualified him for duty stateside. "But he wasn't having any of it; he was like a man still in the hunt."

As indeed he was, for Karel Hollar.

10

ONLY WEEKS LATER, MY MOTHER MADE A quixotic foray to Winsted—the first and only time she showed in my four years there. Her presence on Winsted soil brought to bear the full impact of Paul's recollections; every time I so much as looked at her, I couldn't help thinking, She loved and slept with and made a baby with the man who calmly stood there smoking a Lucky Strike while a man danced in space, slowly strangling. Did she know? Would it have been something he'd have told her late at night as they lay in bed together? Was it the kind of thing that might have soured their marriage? Or was he already a very different man by the time of their marriage in 1950? Like so many of his generation, had he simply dispatched such horrors to a dark space labeled "the war" and gotten on with his life?

And then there were the rumors and speculation around his death, the third rail of our relationship.

And now, Kim Philby.

"You've put on weight." She grabbed hold of my upper arm as we walked the Circle. "And muscle, too—egad! Well, at least they feed you."

"I spent the winter in the weight room. Rowing, too."

"Would you like me to come to a race? Your father always talked about rowing on the river."

"Of course."

"You're so handsome. . . . Any girlfriends on the horizon?"

"Mom . . . really."

My mother's visit was prompted by my plans to spend that summer on Crete, working at an excavation near Phaistos. Virgil had managed to wrangle a spot for me on a Princeton-organized dig—no small thing, since the places were reserved for grad students. In this, I was following in my father's footsteps; he had worked on digs in Greece and Crete with Karel Hollar since he was sixteen. Mother was well aware of this and was not pleased: New Mexico was one thing, but Greece, where my father had come to grief in '43–'44, where he'd been CIA station chief in Athens in '48 and '49, was another matter. For my mother, Greece was less a place than a black hole that had swallowed some irrecoverable part of her husband before they'd even met. She and Virgil had a long conversation, from which I was excluded. To make matters worse, the school really laid it on thick for her visit. After the death of my grandmother, my mother had some discretionary say in the charitable donations of the family trusts, and gifts to Winsted. Funding that had come fast and furious in previous decades had slowed to a trickle, mostly providing scholarships, the very thing that had so pissed off Jerry Gadsden. At the head table over lunch, Byron Folley fawned all over my mother, while Max, seated on her other side, engaged her with a charm offensive the like of which I'd never seen. That in itself should have been a tip-off, *and* the fact that he'd been invited to join us at the head table.

But I must admit to taking a certain smug pride in showing her around the school, rubbing her nose in the memorials to her husband, the splendid new gym named in his honor, and that grand temple of learning, the Alden library, given by General Alden. Some part of me still wanted to win her over; after all, her own father had been a decorated naval officer in the Battle of the Coral Sea. I figured she'd be impressed by the Sargent portrait in the main reading room. The distinguished portrait of her father "the admiral" hung over the fireplace in our living room in New York. A man I barely remember, since he died at Walter Reed Hospital in 1955, and his wife a year later. That was when my mother cleared out all my father's things from the house on P Street and had them shipped to Elysium. Our apartment in New York, my grandmother's old apartment, was then filled with the admiral's books and navy mementos.

In my callow adolescent mind, I saw her as a usurper. Critical of Winsted, critical of Elysium . . . much less the sacrifices of her own husband. It didn't help that she was such a lightweight compared to my grandmother, who had her own distinguished Boston roots; nevertheless, when she married into our family she took up her new responsibilities with a loyal vengeance. Grandmother had not only been the first woman on the Winsted board; she had managed the family foundations and charities "like John D. Rockefeller," according to the obituary in the *Herald Tribune*, which called her "the doyen of New York society philanthropy." My mother had zero interest in such things, only the quiet comforts of the Colony Club's bridge room. I was young and unfeeling and I guess she frustrated me. There were moments when I actually thought, How could my father have married such a lush?

I got that from my grandmother, whom my mother feared and resented. When we moved from Washington in 1955, Grandmother tried as best she could to ease my mother into her Upper East Side women's social and charity circuit, but it was a poor match. Mother could never quite talk the talk or walk the walk, and insisted on buying her clothes secondhand, like her Presbyterian navy-wife mother, and was always a few years out of fashion. She did take to my grandmother's bridge circle; she'd grown up with the game on military bases and was a superb player. And once had been a championship tennis star at the Chevy Chase Club, where she'd met my father. No one ever accused her of being stupid. But she seemed incapable of moving on after my father's death. She never showed any interest in remarrying. Not that she carried my father's flame. What do you say about a man whose career is in secrets: "Well, I guess I'm supposed to be happy with that one lousy star at the entrance to Langley"? Eventually, a psychiatrist got his fangs into her and she built her life around those twice-a-week therapy sessions. God knows what they talked about. By my Winsted years, her drinking began to take a toll (she'd lost her license for DUI and so took the train from New York), mostly because of her interminable bridge games at the Colony Club, when she liked to keep company with a vodka tonic at her elbow. She was a big reader of naval histories and adventure novels set on the high seas, but it was a means of escape and not engagement. All I ever heard in her voice were hints of betrayal and how life had cheated her.

After lunch, as I finished up our tour of Winsted on one of the first warm and springlike days of late April, we settled into a momentary truce. Perhaps because she was already a few sheets to the wind by the time we made it to the library, presumably from the Bloody Marys on the train from New York, or a glass of sherry with the headmaster, or maybe she had a pint stashed in her purse. She was almost chatty. She kept touching me, running a hand through my hair. Standing before the Sargent portrait in the reading room, she reminded me that my father had regularly shown it to her on Founder's Days after they were married. "You were along once or twice, but too young to remember." Standing corrected, I got my father's class yearbook and we sat together and began flipping the pages, as if testing each other. Then she said something very strange, pointing to my father's handsome face, the shock of dark hair, the thrust of his dimpled chin, the heavy eyebrows that merged at the apex of his narrow nose. Even in a studio photograph, his eyes had a striking brilliance and intensity of focus that jumped off the well-thumbed pages.

"Next year when you graduate, it will be almost the same length of time from the year of our marriage as it was from when he graduated in 1932 to the year we were married."

What was I to make of that bit of esoteric triangulation; did it have something to do with bridge strategy? She continued to leaf through the pages as if genuinely interested—hadn't she looked though the copy at home?—as if recognizing the young faces of my father's classmates for the first time, that extraordinary pantheon that was quite literally running the country at that very moment: the president's national security adviser, five ambassadors, an undersecretary of state, secretary of the Army, not to mention a bunch of assistant secretaries of state, two nationally syndicated columnists, and a phalanx of top guns at the CIA, including Elliot Goddard, who was masterfully trying to turn the failure of the Tet Offensive to the advantage of the South. Three were on the Winsted board of directors with Bobby Williams. She pointed them out, smiling to herself, bemused. Of course, she'd known them all from the early years of their careers and marriages, when she had gone with my father to their Georgetown homes, when they had plotted to save the world into the wee hours of the morning in a haze of bourbon and the finest Medoc. When it must have seemed the fate of the West had been handed to them on a silver platter. She paused at the photo of a dashing and handsome Elliot Goddard; she'd liked Elliot and his English wife; Elliot had always been good for a laugh, even in the darkest of times. She had cried on Elliot's shoulder at the memorial service for my father. Then she turned the page and tapped the photo of the president's adviser, pressing at the large round head and prepossessing brow, which contained one of the great brains of his generation.

"We used to meet him all the time at Joe Alsop's house for dinner."

She said this with what felt like a shiver of fear or an attack of nerves; she placed the yearbook in her lap to keep it from shaking.

I sat back a moment, pondering that young and eager face. (I was immediately reminded of his son, once my favorite receiver, who had come to grief that fall on the field and off; the boy Jerry Gadsden had found unconscious from an overdose in the toilets, who had only recently returned from a rehab clinic.) I could feel the memories flooding her eyes. She smiled again and told me a little story about one of those Georgetown soirees at "Joe's," a humorous thing from her standpoint. How it had been two o'clock in the morning and the men were still vigorously arguing around the dinner table, everybody more than a little tight. And suddenly John (my mother at that moment for the first time began using his Christian name with me, not "your father," as she had before) got up from the table and announced they were going home; he grabbed my mother's hand and headed for the door. My mother was "a little tipsy," and she had a hard time walking. As they went down the front walk to the street, she caught her heel in a gap in the brickwork; "those treacherous Georgetown brick sidewalks were just minefields for high heels." She'd broken her heel and was stumbling. John, who rarely drank to excess, was perturbed, and demanded she just take off the damn shoes, helping her out of both. Then, my father, clutching one of her shoes in each hand, and she prepared to make the short walk to their own town house two blocks distant. Something made my father stop. "It was an impulse thing." He made a face and let fly with one of her shoes at the bay window of Joe Alsop's house, where the national security adviser stood watching them go (he was then a lowly undersecretary of state). The first shoe bounced off the window harmlessly. But the second, minus a heel, and with the added shout of "egotistical myopic know-it-all" to speed the shoe on its way, shattered a pane of glass. For a moment, my father stood stunned, and then he laughed as those inside, mostly old Winsted chums, who came to the bay window and stared out. "He stuck out his tongue and made a face at them—first and only time I ever knew him to do something like that." Then he gave them the finger and began walking away with my mother trailing in her stocking feet. He muttered under his breath, "The closest he's ever gotten to the carnage was cruising a mile offshore of Omaha Beach."

"Carnage," she repeated. "Isn't that an interesting word? He was always good with words; he always made you sit up and take notice."

The next morning, as my father rushed off to work, he had her write out a check to Joe Alsop for the damage, and walk it over to Joe's home with his apologies.

My mother sat there in the library with me, blinking in the backwash of this story, perhaps because she hadn't thought of it in years, or perhaps given the high profile of the president's adviser—he was on the front page nearly every other day, it seemed—the incident gained an added relevance, lost upon her until that moment. For me, it was the first clue that my father's relationships with these "wise men," these masters of the universe—decades before their financial brethren would take over the title—had not always been the best: an echo of which I had overheard lying on my back in the gym training room. An egotistical myopic know-it-all—imagine!

But then she said something that opened a window into my parents' lives as never before.

"We were happy back then, those years in Washington."

She had never talked to me about Washington, about his time in the CIA: I had been given to understand that it was something that couldn't be discussed because of its sensitive nature. Like the cover story about the accident on the Autobahn outside Frankfurt.

"When he came back from Athens?"

"Oh, he was such the golden boy. The Greek Civil War was one of the very few successes they had after the war. John told me that holding the line in Greece meant a great deal. They thought he could do anything after that; everybody wanted a piece of him, from the Alsops to Allen Dulles."

"So he really was a hero?"

She smiled tentatively. "He never saw himself that way; it was an unpleasant job that had to be done. We had a whirlwind romance and all he could ever talk about was getting back to Princeton and his archaeological work. 'Mary,' he used to say, 'with the civil war in Greece over, soon the American Archaeological Institute in Athens will reopen and we can get back to digging.' We already had a house picked out in Princeton."

"So, what happened?"

She looked up from the pages of the yearbook with a look of mild surprise that it wasn't obvious; then her eyebrows tightened and she nervously swiped back strands of hair.

"Washington happened; I guess the world happened, one crisis after the next. Just when one thing seemed under control and we might be able to slip away from the craziness, something else came along—just one more crisis—that the Winsted crew wanted John to handle. For a while, it was the Albanians; then it was the Soviet atom bomb and China and then Korea . . . and Stalin dying—East Germany, always East Germany."

"What about Kim Philby?"

I saw her chest collapse with the intake of a sharp breath as I got out the name that had been on my mind all day—for months since Virgil had clued me in the previous fall.

"What makes you say that?"

I pointed to the page open on her lap with a debonair studio portrait of Elliot Goddard and lied as if it had become second nature.

"Elliot mentioned his name to me, something about how Philby complicated all their lives."

She winced and I saw her knuckles whiten.

"Why is Elliot hanging around you?"

"He isn't. He's in Saigon. He's on the board of trustees. He's in and out of Winsted maybe twice a year."

"I know he's in Saigon, fucking up that country, as well."

That was her father, the admiral, talking, the man who to the day he died had recommended against a ground war in Asia, especially in the jungles of Southeast Asia. He had a heart attack at his desk in the Pentagon. "Korea killed him: thank God he never lived to see the morass of Vietnam," she said once.

"What about Kim Philby?"

She turned the page from Elliot Goddard and closed her eyes for what must have been a minute.

"Our marriage at Chevy Chase Club was the toast of the town. My father had made it to the Pentagon, a decorated admiral who'd saved his ship and the lives of his men at the Battle of the Coral Sea. And John was a wounded veteran of OSS—Oh So Social—bet you never knew people called them that—decorated by the Greek government and surrounded by his loyal Winsted mutual-admiration society."

"Until Kim Philby came along."

"What ho, our British cousin, dear Kim. My father couldn't stand him, picked him out as a British spy at the first cocktail party he attended. Which he *was*, of course, chief of MI6 Washington."

I had never heard this kind of mocking sarcasm from her before.

"So you knew him? Dad knew him?"

"Knew him—*of course not*—of course we did. We were in the same line of snake oil. I knew Aileen, his wife, as well, and their three—no, four kids. Poor woman seemed on the edge of a nervous breakdown half the time, smoking like a chimney and washing down her anxiety with gin. That's where I learned to drink, you know, at those endless Georgetown cocktail parties and diplomatic receptions. My mother was a teetotaler, and Father had the discipline of a saint."

"So, did Philby get secrets out of Dad?"

"He got them out of everybody. Jesus, he was the liaison between MI6 and the CIA; he was privy to every goddamn operation they had going. Oh Lord"—a hand flew to her brow, cradling it for a moment— "how many times waking up in the dead of night—oh, long after Philby had been recalled to London and his bastard pals Burgess and Maclean had defected—did I find John awake and staring out the window at headlights on P Street. He couldn't tell me anything—never, not a word; none of them told their wives anything—but around the edges I got the picture: the Balts and Ukranians and Albanians who had died in operations given away by Philby to the Soviets. Tip of the iceberg, for all I knew."

"Was Dad blamed?"

"He blamed himself for being a damn fool. All the brilliant Winsted boys got outsmarted by that supercilious, charming con man with his smooth British conviviality and hauteur. 'Teaching us our business' was how one of John colleagues put it—maybe it was Elliot when he was drunk enough at one of Joe Alsop's dinners—all such a blur now. They looked up to Philby—Angleton licked his boots—as a man of infinite savoir faire out of centuries-long experience in the secrets of running an empire. How those old Etonians, denizens of White's Club, claimed Olympian status above anything Winsted or Skull and Bones had to offer. What stupid little boys to think they had something to learn from their British cousins. My father, Scots-Irish to his core, instantly saw through all the stink of Philby's pretense . . . what fools they'd made of themselves in Singapore in 1942."

"Would Dad have come under suspicion because of Philby?"

I'm not sure she even registered my question. As she talked, she'd been turning the pages in the Winsted yearbook, perhaps impressed by just how many idealistic young faces she recognized from Washington days, habitués of Joe Alsop's soirees, denizens of Langley and the eighth floor of the State Department and the White House Situation Room. But then she grunted at the slight anomaly resting under her chewed nails, black sheep of the fold: a photo from *The Boston Globe* of Bobby Williams seated at the piano in Symphony Hall for a Young People's concert. Again she grunted, running a fingertip over the clear-eyed face and ardent features touched with the merest hint of a Latin complexion bent to the keyboard, the face she'd known only as that of a burned and scarred wreck of a man in a wheelchair.

"Of course, his real pals were Bobby and Suzanne, his fellow Trinity College aesthetes and Red admirers—thick as thieves."

I remember looking up from her trembling hand on the page to the portrait of General Alden, mesmerized by her changed tone and acuteness of vision, like a shift in the wind, of something she hadn't thought about in years, reremembering it just as she was describing it to me, if not reediting the scene in light of our recent conversation, and possibly Philby's defection to Moscow five years before.

She and my father had been married a little over a year and I was barely three months old, and it was August at Elysium, a respite from Washington, and the happy couple had been invited over to Hermitage for cocktails and dinner. It turned out that Bobby and Suzanne had a little surprise waiting. Coming out onto the wide veranda overlooking the lake, they discovered that Kim and Aileen Philby and the four children were up from Washington for a week's vacation. My mother remembered the scene vividly, walking through the French doors and seeing Kim and Suzanne standing by the railing, drinks in hand, nosing at each other's necks, "as if they were in heat." The russet-orange sunset was showing in the upper branches of the white pines across the lake, illuminating the fieldstone walls of our cottage, a blush of purple dusk on the smooth water dotted by stumps and lily pads. Bobby was in his wheelchair over by the drinks table, oblivious of the cooing couple, staring fixedly out at the lake. One of the Philby's older children, "a girl with stringy hair," was playing the piano in the living room, not very well, according to my mother, since Bobby quickly absented himself to go inside and coach her on the right notes and tempi. My father was clearly upset, said my mother with a certain retrospective irony in her voice. "He'd been given two weeks free and clear and there, unannounced, was the chief of MI6 Washington, invited up to Elysium, John's home turf, bringing in his baggage all the cruel worries of a cruel world, while Suzanne, being Suzanne—Christ, she'd just given birth to her own daughter a month before—was flirting with Kim like an old college sweetheart in front of *his* wife and *her* husband, as if they simply didn't matter."

My mother paused at this point because she must have realized that Suzanne was also flirting in front of her husband, although I don't think she knew they'd been lovers then, and was not going to disillusion me now.

"Everyone knew Kim was a ladies' man—the ladies in particular; they loved his toothy smile—good teeth, too, everyone said, for a Brit—the aura of danger, man of the world, the cute nervous stutter and ability to talk about anything with expertise, that British upper-crust savoir faire. Always impeccably tailored, well, a little dowdy, but he tied his bow ties like a midshipman. And when he discovered my father was an admiral in the Pentagon, he took an extra interest in me, as well—a twofer, I suppose."

Suzanne and Bobby had been well-behaved hosts, according to my mother, announcing right from the start that there was to be no talk of politics or Washington. "Yes," said Suzanne, "the world be damned for one night, a night just for us refugees."

My father had apologized that his mother couldn't make it; a little under the weather had been the excuse, but everyone knew she was on the outs with the Williamses going way back.

"If Bobby Williams thinks we're going to put him on the Winsted board, he's got another think coming" was what my grandmother had told my parents as they left for Hermitage.

"Not that our arrival didn't prevent Suzanne from still monopolizing Kim; she hung all over him—showing off her 'darling' little girl—dumping her baby in his arms—as first the champagne flowed and then the wine, what with all the conversation about Cambridge *dans le temps,* when she'd been taking the British ballet world by storm. To hear Bobby talk, politics was the last thing on their minds at Cambridge. He spent his days drinking, studying the Romantic repertoire, and playing concerts, as if the thirties had been a barrel of laughs. All Suzanne wanted to talk about was her brother, who'd been in Kim's class at Trinity—that's how they'd met. Francis, *dear* Francis, killed at Tobruk—*frightful business.*"

My mother snorted as if in disgust at her aptitude for cruel mimicry and closed the yearbook over her hand, still marking Bobby's page, as if trying to keep something caged within.

"It was poor Aileen, Kim's wife, I was worried about that night. Hardly blame her for being out of sorts in her mousy way, always flicking glances at Suzanne, who was queening it over all the males. Aileen was concerned about the children, who were out playing in unfamiliar surroundings. When she drank, she'd get all wound up. She kept flying from the dinner table to check on them. I told her we could call our baby-sitter at Elsinore and have her come over to help out—your grandmother could watch you. Then, poor thing, she either stumbled or fell off the veranda, went right over the railing, maybe six feet to the ground. Kim rushed out and found her in a heap in the garden, no worse for wear except for a cut on her arm. Strangely, she'd taken a steak knife from the table and had it concealed in her sleeve. Suzanne and I and Kim got her into the house and fixed up and put her to bed, then got the children to their rooms."

Here my mother paused and withdrew her hand from the yearbook and made a kind of pantomime of closing it, handing it to me to be replaced on the shelf.

"Your father got left for some time with Bobby downstairs. I gather that didn't go over so well, either. He was fuming and sullen all the way back to Elsinore, probably the subject of the board came up and something about a bunch of paintings Bobby's mother had done."

I was transfixed by my mother's recollections and not a little troubled, although I didn't let on. The thought of Kim Philby, whom in the previous months I'd built into a *bête noire*, at Elysium made me almost physically sick. I comforted myself with the thought that he had only been at Hermitage, but the image lingered: Philby and Suzanne at the railing of the veranda, staring out at our cottage, cooing and plotting. And I was thinking, too, of the secreted photos I'd found tucked into one of my father's books, of my grandmother pictured with Amory and his wild artist wife on that same veranda some thirty years before—the thing conflating in my mind's eye: a sense of an illicit and lurking menace to everything I held dear.

I remember a shiver going through me, and a vow never to return to Hermitage, notwithstanding the sometimes sweet, even touching words in Laura's recent letters to me, which now took an ominous cast.

As we made our way to the memorial room to wait for my mother's taxi, I pressed her as much as I dared on Philby and his impact on my father's reputation.

Exasperated with my persistence when she had other things she wanted to discuss, she tried to draw a line under the subject. "Let me put it this way: When he disappeared without a word, without a trace . . . and in the years after the Soviets returned his body, Washington clammed up on me. Nobody, with the possible exception of Elliot Goddard, came to me, and his visit was mostly in an official capacity. None of the wives came to visit. I was never invited over for dinner or drinks. I was a pariah; they were afraid of me. Once my father died from the strain of overwork—sometimes I think it was shame over his son-in-law—I took your grandmother's offer to move into her apartment in New York. It was the kindest thing she ever did. And just in case you're wondering, the last time I saw your father, the last morning, before he drove back to Washington from Elysium, he told me he'd made up his mind—he'd had enough. He was going to buy the house in Princeton, resign, and take up his professorship after the New Year."

She raised a flattened palm and leaned forward in her armchair as if to steady herself, staring out the window at the large elms that had just come fully into leaf. Perhaps because of her use of my father's first name for the first time in our conversations, or mention of Suzanne's flirting, I noticed her as a woman, that even at fifty—and despite the drinking—she was still nice-looking, her auburn hair cut to just below her shoulders, touched with gray here and there, her cinnamon eyes flecked with the sunlight through the green canopy of the elms. She wore a white blouse and gray cardigan and green plaid wool skirt. Very practical, very Filene's Basement. The rain showers of the morning had cleared to leave a bright afternoon. The apple trees in the middle of the Circle showed a thin, blurry green.

Outside, cries of my form mates echoed as they played stepball. I could tell there was something she still wanted to say to me before she left—a resolution on the summer had yet to be reached—but she seemed distracted by the constant slap of the tennis ball against the dormitory steps. She glanced at me obliquely, never quite looking into my eyes.

"What are they playing?" she asked finally in a wavering voice, "those boys out there with the old tennis ball?"

"Stepball," I replied.

"What is the point of the game? What are they trying to do, exactly?"

"Each guy has a number. Whoever has the ball calls out one of the other numbers and then throws the ball against the steps, and the boy whose number has been called must grab the rebounding ball cleanly, without bobbling it, before it reaches the grass on the Circle; otherwise, it is a strike against him. The guy who grabs the ball then calls a number in turn and throws the ball—from the point where he has grabbed it—against the steps, trying to get an angle and speed that will make it difficult for the next boy whose number is called . . . and so on. If you miss the steps with your throw, it's also a strike."

"And what happens when you get a strike against you?" My mother turned slightly in her seat to get a better view of the game.

"Three strikes and its buns-up. You have to kneel down on the steps and bend over and the other guys each get to throw at your ass."

"That sounds rather cruel," she said, grimacing.

"Oh, no, it's only a tennis ball. It can't really hurt—the humiliation is the point."

"Oh, I see." She sighed and glanced out the window again, possibly avoiding the line of sight that put her in view of my father's plaque on the wall next to those who had died in the Second World War. "And of course the stronger boys will be able get out the weaker in pretty short order, or the ones they don't like: Washington—huh."

For someone who spent her afternoons at the bridge table with elderly matrons, she didn't miss much.

"You know," she went on, "your father wasn't exactly thrilled with this place—with everything. I remember an aside to one of his colleagues at our wedding about a blowup in the office: 'Same old snake pit—just like Winsted.'" The way she said it, the precise intonation, I knew she had heard it in her mind, his voice, something of him translated through time and space to me in the beat of an eyelash. She seemed a little stunned by how it came out, that sudden transmission through the years of static. Then she brightened, as if to pull herself back from a precipice. "I liked your friend Max, such a delightful boy, so full of humor and intelligence. Why don't we ever see him in New York? Now that you've got your driver's license, why don't you take him up to Elysium?"

That was curious. I assumed that Byron Folley had taken the opportunity to warn her about Max's bad influence on me.

"All right, I will."

"Good," she said. She turned to me straight on where I sat near the fireplace. "I know I haven't been the greatest mother, but I am proud of you, Peter. Maybe I've taken your schoolwork for granted—God knows your father was so brilliant. And Mr. Dabney only had the nicest things to say about you. It's just . . ."

She got up and came over to me, bending to kiss my forehead and then staring up at those memorial lists above the mantelpiece with a look of disdainful pride.

"You think I didn't love him, Peter? You think I don't care?"

Her eyes began filling with tears, and I wanted to go hide.

"It's okay, Mom . . . really."

"Don't let them make you think"—and she waved at the gold lettering—"that this is really what it's all about. It's not. This is crap. This is about boys who never grew up."

I was aghast.

"How can you say that? These men *died* for their country!"

"Your father," she shrieked, "didn't *die* for his country."

The silence was something terrible.

"You mean because he was killed in a crash on the Autobahn?"

"Do you believe that?"

"That's what you told me to believe. Do you know something different?"

"They're all professional liars. They twist everything that was ever any good into fucking granny knots."

"Did they lie about Dad?"

"I don't know"—she wiped at her tears—"but it wasn't the truth."

"Does Elliot Goddard know?"

"Listen, I only want *one* thing out of you. I want you to promise me that you will never do *this*. . . ." She gestured wildly toward the wall of memorials. "I don't want you to end up in Vietnam."

"Vietnam!"

I was incredulous.

"You heard me."

"For Christ's sake, haven't you heard about college deferments?"

"Just promise me."

"Look around you. Do you see anybody supporting the war in Vietnam? Everybody hates it—they put goddamn North Vietnamese flags on their walls."

This note of outrage in my voice only added fuel to the flame.

"For once in your life, young man, just promise me something. No if, ands, or buts."

"Promise what?"

"You heard me. I'll let you go to Crete this summer, if that's what you really want. But you promise to stay out of this stupid war, even if it takes going to Canada."

"And if I get drafted?"

"You can live anywhere for as long as it takes."

A honk outside signaled the arrival of her taxi. I was almost giddy with relief. But I promised—whatever it took to get on that Princeton dig in Crete.

Only now do I begin to understand how personality comes most alive through the pained eyes of those we have loved (or even loathed); that the cumulative force of these expressions of pain or loss when reflected in our own longings reanimates the cold facts and breathes new life into the subjects of our loss. The cardboard caricature falls flat; the spirit gains substance and takes wing. The scholar, the historian, certainly the archaeologist is constantly faced with the cruel proof of this: the pitiful artifacts of past lives that refuse the breath of life. Because only through the physical proximity of another human, who shares with you an emotional bond with the person in question, do the years truly fall away and the soul stands revealed. But these chances are as fleeting as the dimpled swirls in our wake. We see only as far as we can invoke our quarry with the passion of autobiography. We *are* the authors. We are the underworld, the Elysian Fields, the far bank of the river Styx, where the breathless dead await our call. The dead pass through us just as surely as we will one day pass through the living. Just read your Homer . . . and hold close those you love most dearly . . . and listen.

Not a week after my mother had extorted her pledge, my godfather, Col. Charles Fairburn, came to visit me at Winsted. I assumed this had been at the prompting of my mother. But in fact, it was Suzanne Williams who had called up her first cousin and, by then, full-time lover, demanding he check things out: "Why in God's name is my daughter writing to John's boy?" Suzanne had no idea her daughter had discovered her cache of love letters. Laura told me later that Suzanne had found an unmailed letter addressed to me in her purse. "She steamed it open—really; I thought people only did stuff like than in the movies." The colonel, as everyone in my family called him, was clearly flummoxed by the whole business. To the very end, I doubt he fully understood the role he'd been assigned by Suzanne in her great charade. MI5 may have recruited him to keep an eye on Suzanne, "Firebird" in the Venona decrypts, but he ended up just another one of her willing enablers— besotted, probably from childhood, when they'd grown up near each other, first cousins and playmates on Cadogan Square in London and at his country estate in Sussex. There, at Hillders, the Fairburns' grand faux-Tudor country house, Suzanne and Bobby had been married in June of 1944, my father serving as best man, with Charles giving away the bride. All Suzanne's previous lovers and Cambridge comrades had been in attendance, including Kim Philby and Anthony Blunt, whose name and significance I did not know then, the Anthony who'd gotten Virgil all in a tizzy, who wouldn't be exposed as a spy until 1979, when Margaret Thatcher famously outed him in the House of Commons.

Anthony Blunt, the great art historian, keeper of the queen's pictures, had recruited Kim Philby, Donald Maclean, Guy Burgess, and others, including Bobby Williams, at Trinity College, Cambridge in the thirties.

Seeing the colonel's gleaming silver '38 Bentley cruise past the school's stately wrought-iron gates and parade around the Circle brought back the exotic, if distant and dutiful, godfather he had been to me in early childhood. He never missed my birthday, always sending a card and a book on archaeology, often signed and inscribed works by the famous Bronze Age, Cambridge University archaeologist, Nigel Bennett, with whom my father and Charles had worked in Crete in the thirties. The cards and presents had kept coming, but the visits were fewer and farther between.

"Has it really been two years?" He shook my hand and looked me over, not without a painful hint of recognition in his nut brown eyes. "Just look at you. . . . Your father would be proud, yes indeed."

"There's a crew race this afternoon; you should stick around."

"Don't mind if I do. Will you be rowing?"

"If you can get me back from lunch on time."

He turned to take in the view, where warm sunshine bathed the apple trees on the Circle, fountaining flecks of joyous green skyward. As always, I was taken with his antique cars, in this case a Bentley, a four-and-a-quarter-liter MX Vanden Plus Open Tourer, with worn red leather seats and rosewood paneling. It smelled of pipe smoke and embodied something of a bygone era of gentility, tea, and oak-smoked-salmon sandwiches, when the classics reigned supreme at schools like Winsted, when boys were warned not to ride on the running boards of automobiles. I was reminded, too, of Charlie Spring-field's description of my father arriving at Winsted in the late twenties in the family Cadillac. The colonel was dressed to perfection in a tweed jacket and gray flannels, his red hair combed back from a widow's peak, his nasal upper-class accent like a slightly tarnished trophy of Edwardian vintage. We took a quick tour of the grounds and he nodded approvingly, as well he might: The place had been modeled on English public schools of the 1880s and the chapel might well have gotten him all choked up if he cared much for its Anglican counterparts. I detected a certain nervous preoccupation, if not a wistfulness, in his sharp pilot's eyes, as if the vista of school buildings and the undulating spring green of the playing fields reminded him of his own school days at Rugby.

"Of course, I heard many good things about this place from your father, summer of '39, I believe. Recommended it highly."

The note of regret in his voice was quickly superseded by his perplexing fascination with the gym, less for the display case of my father's medals from Greece, or its marvelous sprung basketball floor and generous windows to optimize sunlight, than for the eight-foot-thick reinforced-concrete bunker that made up the foundation of the building, the infamous bomb shelter—for which my grandmother had anted up a cool extra million. The colonel was gob-smacked, as he put it; he paced the entire circumference of the concrete blast walls, his shiny black leather wingtips smeared in mud and mown grass as he let his fingertips brush the rough-edged reinforced concrete.

"Extraordinary. Did they really think it would do any good?"

He was inspecting the air intakes, his large hands busy fingering the metal housings, intrigued the way an archaeologist might be intrigued with the unearthed remains of ancient battlements—analyzing the threat they were designed to counter and whether they had survived assaults, been pulled down by invaders, or plundered for stone by later inhabitants. I kept quiet about my grandmother's extra million.

"There is water and rations stored for a couple of months," I offered with no great enthusiasm. None of us had ever taken the possibility seriously.

"What madness . . ." Colonel Fairburn shook his head. "With the world blown to bits, much less the radiation—well, it might as well be a mausoleum, a fancy charnel house."

With that comforting thought, we walked back to take in the chapel, where, after a cursory glance at my father's memorial stone, he crossed the nave to spend some minutes gazing upon the Williams Memorial bronze and Saint-Gaudens's line of sorrowing angels. His fingers lingered upon the angelic faces in relief, the half-parted lips and tightened arc of the eyebrows in the moment of sexual release. He wasn't the first to notice the resemblance to Suzanne, and now to her seventeen-year-old daughter, his goddaughter, Laura, in whom, I was soon informed, he had more than a passing interest.

"Where to, Peter? Where does one chow down in these parts?"

We walked back to the Bentley and I glanced over at my godfather's sunlit profile as I inspected its splendid interior, every bit of chrome, wood, and leather simmering with soft flame-textured light. I loved the way such archaic machines still showed the distinct functions of their parts, especially the round headlamps standing up from the streamlined wheel guards, even as I despaired of my technical competence around machinery of any kind.

"The Bull Run," I announced. "Best roast beef for miles."

He took a last lingering look around and cocked his head, his eyes alighting on mine and lingering. "By Jove . . . you've grown."

At least he didn't say "spitting image."

Ten minutes later, we were in the parking lot of the Bull Run, cheek by jowl with Fort Devens, the gleaming Bentley like a royal personage at Ascot slumming amidst the riffraff of late-model Chevys and pick-ups. As we got out, the air was seared by a terrific roar of screaming engines. A huge propeller aircraft skimmed overhead and disappeared behind a row of tall trees. I checked an instinct to duck, but the colonel's face only brightened, his thick eyebrows pinched expectantly forward, waiting. I followed his stare, scanning past the ten-foot-high mock-up of a longhorn steer at the entrance to the parking area, and then to that line of concealing maples, from which, an instant later, another enormous four-prop aircraft loomed, rising sharply into the sky, only to bank in a tight 360-degree arc and dip back down again for landing. The look of profound pleasure on Colonel Fairburn's face has never left me: a man thrilled and mesmerized by the sound of engines and fine machinery put through its paces.

A faint but inescapable hunger seemed to course through me—for what, I couldn't say. At best, I could change a flat tire on my Chevy Impala.

Then, with the stink of aviation fuel sifting down, the colonel turned to me and put an avuncular hand on my shoulder and told me in the most matter-of-fact way that they were Lockheed C-130B's practicing short-run drop-offs. That explained the air traffic I so often heard on the river while rowing.

"In the mid-fifties, I tested the C-130A for the RAF. Best damn aircraft I ever flew, a most superior warhorse."

"How do you know these are C-130*B's*?"

"The A's had Aero Product three-bladed propellers; these are four-bladed Hamilton Standards—more power, more lift."

Inside, ahead of us, we found four Green Berets from Fort Devens waiting in line to be seated. They looked as if they'd just come from field exercises. Their camouflage fatigues were sweat-soaked and streaked with dirt and grass stains, their faces hastily washed but still showing remnants of black grease stick and a three-day growth of beard. The cigarettes they smoked barely disguised the odor of long hours of exertion in the outdoors. My heart was pounding as if I'd developed some fantastic crush. Seeing these soldiers conjured again those uninhabited thatched huts by the river. A year before, Barry Sadler's song "The Ballad of the Green Berets" had been a huge Top Ten hit. Something in my wannabe Homeric soul yearned to draw near them, hear their banter, to warm myself in their nuts-and-bolts front-line existence. They were huge men, khaki-and-green shirtsleeves barely containing their bulging biceps. I thrilled at the look of absolute purpose in their eyes, the confidence in themselves and their brothers in arms, and their mission in life. I could feel my chest actually swell with admiration. Trying not to stare at their faces, I strained to make out their chatter: shoptalk about the limitations of some APC's they'd been testing. But it was the demeanor of the hostess who came to seat them that really did it for me. She was short and stocky, with big breasts and a bouffant hairdo; she wore a miniskirt and white go-go boots. A flinty respect for the soldiers glittered in her heavily mascared eyes. She couldn't resist touching them on an elbow or shoulder, joking with them—flirting. She'd been round the block with their breed and only wanted more. As they left to go to their table, one of them turned to put out his cigarette in an ashtray near the door. Our eyes met. It couldn't have been for more than a second or two, but there was a certain look of inner peace in the compressed redness of his sleepless eyes, a fierce nonchalance and fortitude, or perhaps scorn at the sight of the sniveling preppy kid standing in the doorway. I pulled myself to full height, silently defending myself: *Yeah, but I can throw a fifty-yard pass and place it on a dime, and Princeton is recruiting my ass. And this distinguished gentleman flew bombers over Germany in World War Two.* But I felt a complete fraud. And then as the Green Beret turned for his table, I recognized his face . . . or thought I did.

The previous Sunday on our day off from practice, I'd again rowed myself upriver past the No Trespassing sign. The soldier had been standing in the Vietnamese village along the riverbank, almost like he'd been waiting for me to show. He was a Green Beret in full combat gear, M16 cradled on his arm, eyes watching me out of black-and-green camouflage makeup as I glided into view, my oars poised, my momentum giving way to the current. Maybe he was as incredulous as I. He let his M16 slide off his arm and dangle in one hand. He held my stare for the longest time, as if about to shout at me, tell me to turn the fuck around and get the hell out of there. Instead, he just smiled, his proud gaze still holding mine; slowly, he came to attention and saluted. Through the heat of my aching breath and sweat-blurred eyes, I felt humiliated. The current was beginning to return me downriver. In a kind of panic at my imbecilic situation, I dropped my right oar and returned the salute. Then he turned away as I drifted out of sight.

The sense of humiliation stuck in my craw. Was he joshing me, or did I represent something to him, a world where a young man can row on the river for the simple pleasure of being alive? A salute for his comrades who never returned for the chance?

Now I know the answer.

I took a seat across from my godfather by a bay window overlooking the tree line that obscured the busy landing field at Fort Devens. Observing the colonel's distracted gaze, I took comfort in the thought that he might be able to shed some light on my father's life, adding something to the stray fragments that had been coming fast and furious over the last months. And best of all, I saw him as someone outside Winsted or CIA circles, an academic and archaeologist, a longtime colleague and intimate of my father with no hidden agendas . . . my godfather.

I couldn't have been more wrong.

"So," I continued probing, "you didn't see that much of my father during the War?"

He stirred his G and T with a pinkie, as if a little miffed that I had taken up this line of inquiry, or maybe the gin was not up to his expectations.

"Flying bombers?" He cupped his palm in front of his chest. "Well, there was Bobby Williams's wedding, of course, and a few times for drinks in London. It was the years before the war, you see—halcyon days, long summers on digs in Crete and elsewhere, Cambridge, of course. When we tried to pretend the world wasn't going to hell in a handbasket; when your father and I had German colleagues who actually weren't Nazis."

"Like Karel Hollar?"

Charles Fairburn looked at me with mild shock.

"You know about Hollar, then?"

"What's not to know?" I realized I'd imitated Max's Jewish phrasing, how he talked about his father's Brooklyn family. "My father mentions Hollar in his student letters to his mother. They were in Leipzig and Crete together. Hollar was on the University of Cincinnati dig when they discovered Nestor's Palace and the mother lode of Linear B tablets. That must have been a big deal in 1939."

He smiled gamely at my enthusiasm and slid two fingers to the side of his temple, as if pondering where to take the conversation.

"Your dad never got over it; those two had been such competitors in the early years, worthy competitors, if you take my meaning; they simply lived and breathed Homer. Never seen anything quite like it. John was on a Delos dig when he got the word. He was—what do you Yanks call it?—sucker punched."

"He was sure there would have to be walls, fortifications still showing."

"Going by the tholos tombs to locate the site was a stroke of genius. Hollar was a slippery one; he'd switch horses at full gallop. That and a tireless appetite for risk. Of course, once the thing is found, it always seems so obvious. The rest of us felt like fools, but then the war came and we had more important things to feel foolish about."

"Sounds like you didn't like him much."

"Hard to trust someone who first thumbed his nose at the German Academy in Athens to team up with John and Princeton, and then drops John to go with Carl Andersen's Cincinnati boys, even if he picked the winner. Absolutely driven, you know, more so than your father. One always wondered where his true loyalties lay. He seemed to dance around the edges, his mind elsewhere. Protean, the way he switched languages in a blink of the eye. Viennese accent always put me on edge. And he had some kind of brouhaha with Carl at Pylos, some irregularity with the Linear B tablets. If the war hadn't happened, Carl and Cincinnati would have banned him from further digging in Pylos. Nigel Bennett didn't like him much, either."

Nigel Bennett was another legendary figure who played a crucial role in my father's career; a Cambridge don who worked with Sir Arthur Evans at Knossos, helping publish the Linear B tablets from Crete while trying and failing to decipher the script. During the war, Bennett famously headed up British intelligence at Bletchley Park and was instrumental in breaking the German Enigma code. My father's library included all of Nigel Bennett's books on Crete, every one inscribed and signed.

"What did Bennett have against him?"

"Hollar and your father believed that the Mycenaeans held the key to Homer, that mainland Greece, not Crete, would ultimately prove more fertile ground. Hollar was convinced that more Linear B would turn up in Greece."

"And he was right, and the Minoans weren't the British Empire of the Bronze Age. It's beginning to look quite the opposite."

"I think"—a flicker of irritation snapped in his eyes and he turned to the window as another C-130 lifted above the trees—"Hollar drove us all a little batty with his Germanic abruptness—his mother was Viennese, Czech father, half Jewish, I believe . . . a tenacious bugger. Thought he was going to be the next Heinrich Schliemann, until the war ended his career—all our careers, worst luck."

The pause for the snide afterthought, "tenacious bugger," seemed to signal a shift to a darker mood.

"What a tragedy it must have been—I mean, a famous archaeologist like that, dying in a Soviet POW camp."

The colonel settled back in his Windsor chair and watched the smoke from his pipe evaporate against the window as he kept tabs on those flights out of Devens. It occurred to me I was interrogating Charles Fairburn the way Max pursued me, right down to his intonations and syntax.

"Yes . . . the waste multiplied by millions."

I found it hard not to be distracted by the constant uproar at the table of Green Berets as the beers began to arrive en masse.

"Was my father a good soldier—I mean, good at what he did . . . with OSS in Greece?"

He looked at me with barely concealed irritation.

"Well, you've got his bloody medals out there like a Harrods window, don't you?" He waved this off and drained his glass. "As your generation is apt to put it, was he *into* what he did? And the answer is, I have no idea. Most of us were just making do. I certainly got my comeuppance. I'd been flying since I was fifteen. My father raced some of the first motorcars and flew in the First World War, but then an ice storm in '33 killed him. Once the war put the kibosh on my work in Greece, I was thrilled at the chance of flying. Actually, I wanted to fly the new Spitfires, but I was deemed *too* old at thirty. So I ended up flattening cities at night while running from ack-ack and 109's . . . until they chained me to a desk for the rest of the war."

His cheeks developed a ruddy flush, his once-serene eyes flashing above the neatly tied ascot and upright posture. The Green Berets at the nearby table didn't help—chugging beers, laughing, and, it seemed to me, facing life full bore. The colonel flicked glances their way and shouted for the waitress, ordering another gin and tonic—"if you can't find any Gordon's, top up the other, will you, dear"—and a Coke for me. Then he leaned meaningfully across our table, as if to discharge an unpleasant duty.

"Don't get me wrong. It was dangerous work your father did. Those medals weren't given to slackers. Behind enemy lines—no walk in the park."

I was hanging on his every word, every confirmation that my father was truly the hero I knew him to be, echoing the ambivalent awe I'd detected when his name was broached in the Princeton Archaeology Department.

"They speak well of him at Princeton."

"Well they might—frustrated, his American colleagues who went into OSS, thinking they'd get in the thick of it, get back to Greece to fight the Nazis. Trouble was, we had that theater on a short string, only allowing our SOE chaps to actually operate on the mainland. Most American OSS languished in Turkey and the Ionian Islands, baying at the moon. You see, John was the only American we actually let in on the game."

"With all his experience, he'd have been perfect."

I saw him flinch at my enthusiasm.

"Greece was a British theater run out of Cairo. The Americans in OSS wanted in on the spoils but were never given the resources or access. I only have this secondhand; John never really talked about it, but I noted his irritation. Clearly, he was the most qualified of the Americans. But that still doesn't mean he was meant for such duty, even if he may have loved the Greeks, with all their penchant for petty quarrels. Physically, morally—yes, of course. But you see"—and the colonel tapped his burnished temple—"he lived in his mind—another place and time, like Karel Hollar. A scholar at heart with an academic's tendency always to be weighing the issue, when all that was required was to act. And for an American, he was quite an old-fashioned chap. Hated machinery, while most Americans make a fetish out of the latest model. Like my father, who was married to his damn cars and aeroplanes. Most Americans love machines, or they love what machines of war can do. A democratic nation is like that, you see: save lives, kill the enemy on the cheap. If it hadn't been for air superiority, naval gunfire, I doubt the Normandy breakout would have succeeded. The German is a tenacious fighter, a highly trained and competent killer. And you see, special forces—OSS or SOE type of thing, partisan work behind the lines—were only effective when the Hun was on his heels, or the teams were out of reach in the mountains. Otherwise, they'd hunt you down like an animal and take revenge on every living soul in the vicinity."

I was hanging on his every word. "Well, he must have done something right if they made him CIA chief in Athens after the war."

He grabbed the gin and tonic from the waitress and downed half of it.

"What so often amused me . . . John would often call me up on Saturday mornings in Washington, one of his Georgetown pals—you see, their Jaguar wouldn't start, or the MG had popped a gasket. Badly designed, shoddy workmanship, and they couldn't even get spare parts in the years right after the war. But I'd come over and give them a hand, jerry-rig it until the garage could get the part from England."

This was the first I'd ever heard that their paths had crossed in Washington; as long as I could remember, the colonel had been teaching at small New England colleges.

"Did you know Kim Philby?"

That was a conversation stopper. His eyes met mine, compressed beneath reddish blond brows, as if I'd kicked his shins under the table and he pretending it was nothing.

"Why, in God's name, would you ask such a question?"

"Philby was in Washington when my father returned from Athens in 1950."

His veined cheeks twitched as he took another swallow of his drink.

"You've been busy, I see." He gave me a cold smile. "Always the stickler for facts, like your father. Well, here're two happy facts that have given me some consolation in my life: I was at Christ College in Cambridge with Nigel Bennett; and in the early fifties, when I wasn't teaching, the embassy in Washington often called me in on military procurements, testing aircraft for the RAF—that sort of thing. So, to answer your question: Philby was at Trinity with his band of buggers, and with the exception of a couple of cocktail parties at the embassy in Washington, I never laid eyes on him."

These were half-truths at best: Kim Philby was a guest at Suzanne and Bobby's Sussex wedding in June of 1944; and even besotted with Suzanne, Charles Fairburn, as an MI5 agent, surely got something out of her about Philby, most likely about his early Cambridge days with her beloved brother, Francis, martyred in the antifascist cause. Nothing of this was on offer.

The stocky waitress with the terrific breasts came to take our orders. Printed on the inside of the menu was the story of how the Bull Run had gotten its name. The first owner, a tavern keeper back in 1861, had been sitting on the stoop peeling potatoes when a rider clattered up on horseback and shouted out the great news: a sweeping Union victory at Bull Run. The owner was so inspired by this erroneous news, he decided to rename his place in celebration of the victory. My great-grandfather had been in the Second Battle of Bull Run, and that hadn't worked out any better.

"Did he ever tell you much about his work with the CIA?"

This was only fuel to the flames.

"Christ, boy . . . they can't even whisper in bed to their wives at four in the morning. And to tell you the truth, I was amazed they managed to recruit him back into the game after the war. He'd been beaten up, a bad leg wound. He had a cushy spot at Princeton. That's all he ever wanted to do—that's all he ever wanted to talk about. With Karel Hollar out of the game, he thought he had the decipherment of Linear B to himself, with the exception of this American girl in Brooklyn who'd spent the war working the subject like a hedgehog. He went bonkers when Ventris deciphered Linear B in '52—we all did. A second-rate architect, no less. Why John threw it all away, I'll never understand."

His face flushed in agitation, and those two fingers again slid to his temple. Clinking glasses from the table of Green Berets drew his gaze as the soldiers were taking turns patting the rump of our waitress.

"Do you have any idea what really happened to him?"

"Good Lord," he shot back, "you're his son—what did they tell you?"

He bent toward me over the noise, bringing his expectant face closer to mine.

"They didn't tell me, nor did they tell my mother. . . . That's why I'm asking."

"Hah, they like to believe loyalty in keeping secrets is the great treasure, you see. They don't tell tales on one another. They want to believe the best about one another, as they do about themselves. They live by their own rules and consider themselves a breed apart. Part of the romance of the business, I suppose . . . obscure deaths in faraway places and all that. Tough on the women—your mother, of course. You seem to have come through it quite nicely—I'm sure it can't have been easy."

That, the cynical tone, I think, was MI5 counterintelligence grumbling: ex-policemen and colonial officials who took a sour view of the aristocratic airs and clubby exclusivity of Etonians like Philby in MI6.

He continued to stare at me full bore, possibly aghast at his own carelessness, or perturbed by some residual loyalty still outstanding.

"Here's what I want you to understand, young man: There is no romance in the damn business. I loved flying but hated what I had to do. The only thing"—and he wagged his finger at me—"the only thing your father really gave a damn about was deciphering Linear B, and when Ventris pulled it out of thin air in 1952, I think it hit him hard."

"That he'd missed his chance?"

"That he'd missed his chance—we all had. . . . There's only *one* first." This time, he actually daggered my chest with his grease-stained index finger. "Keep to your knitting while you can, Peter. There's nothing there"—and he waved dismissively at the table of Green Berets—"for you."

This was probably the one truth he uttered, the one piece of good advice, whether dismissing the Vietnam War or damning my father's romantic indulgence, or both. After the war, Charles Fairburn had been recruited by MI5 to ferret out Philby and his fellow traitor Guy Burgess, who arrived in Washington as second secretary in the British embassy in 1950, rooming with Philby and his family. Suzanne Williams was also to be watched, for both the FBI and MI5 suspected her of being the courier for Philby, and, before that, for Donald Maclean, who had passed on U.S. atomic secrets in the late forties while first secretary at the British embassy in Washington. The colonel's role, all legit, testing aircraft for the RAF, was the perfect cover.

A sudden silence across the room. The biggest of the four Green Berets, whose eye I had caught in the waiting area, bowed his head, crossed himself, and took the hands of his comrades around the table as he said grace.

Seeing that, I felt a lump in my throat: Max had killed the possibility in me.

The Colonel saw it, too, and gave a dismissive snort. "The finest men are wasted on something that shouldn't have been started in the first place and can't be won."

Our meal arrived, great bloody slabs of beef—not as good as Durgin Park—dangling over the sides of the plates. It gave the colonel the chance to divert the conversation to the real subject of our lunch: his goddaughter.

"Have you seen much of Laura recently?"

"Laura? No, I mean, I think it's been at least a year since the last Founder's Day, when she was at Winsted with her parents."

"The reason I even bring it up is that Laura asked her mother if she could come to a crew meet next week; and . . . well, when pressed, I gather, she offered that you had invited her."

"I did nothing of the sort. It was her idea."

"So, you *are* writing?"

"For the last month or so . . . I don't know, she just started writing."

"It seems her ballet classes and schoolwork keep her pretty busy. They have rehearsals on the weekends. It might be hard for her to get away."

Laura wrote me a few days later to let me know that her mother had nixed the plan.

"Watch out," she warned, and underlined the rest: "She's on the warpath."

My lunch with Colonel Fairburn ended a bit abruptly since I had to get back for a crew race. Our lunch had run long and he claimed another pressing appointment and did not stay as he had said he would. He had lied about virtually everything. He knew that Karel Hollar had been a KGB agent and had not died in a Soviet POW camp. As a friend and colleague of my father, a MI5 agent, the colonel knew of the many lunches my father had with Kim Philby at the Metropolitan Club in Washington, conversations, no doubt, passed on to Moscow Central. In fact, Charles Fairburn knew more of the details around what happened to my father than Elliot Goddard, who had written the CIA report on his disappearance. Twenty-one years later, in the weeks after the fall of the Berlin Wall, I would discover that it was Colonel Fairburn who had presented my father with a dangerous, if not foolhardy, plan in September of 1953 to ferret out Philby's perfidity once and for all: a glittering opportunity that caused him to hurry back to Washington from Elysium, and on to Berlin with a discreet stopover in Cambridge along the way.

My father always had his own way of doing things.

The colonel, too, probably suspected that my father had been Suzanne's lover, so his motives, to say the least, were never unmixed.

And that I, if not quite the reincarnation of that lover, threatened the one thing he cared most about in his sad life.

Letter discovered between the pages of Sir Arthur Evans' *The Palace of Minos*, volume 3.

April 17, 1932
Universität Leipzig

Dear Friend John,

Yes, you have the news, soon to be published: A German team found a large fragment of a Linear B tablet in the Argolis late last summer. I believe that is now the third confirmed find outside Crete. Your Evans—yes, I know he's British, but his thinking infects the Americans—will dismiss this as another import from Crete to mainland Greece. You and I know it isn't so. I am convinced there will be more Linear B uncovered in Greece, and you and I will be the ones to do it.

How goes your work on the decipherment? Again, your Evans holds all scholarship back by not publishing the Knossos tablets, only a handful out of his two thousand—a scandal, I say, a scandal. No drawings, no photographs—nothing more while we suffer. Ah, but I have a bit of good news for you, I heard it from my professor: There is a Finnish scholar, Johnannes Sundwall, who went to Crete and recorded thirty-eight tablets examined in a museum. Evans will not be pleased. But something that will add to the two hundred we now have.

Where is our Champollion, where is our methodological demon to map our way through the labyrinth? Evans and Bennett are too fanciful, I think; the Cambridge boys have too many preconceived ideas that inhibit all their minions. We must be like scientists; we must have a method. I fear this is not my strength; I, too, much want to be out under the sun, digging in the earth. You have a better mind, yes, for such a system? Three things I am almost sure of: First, Linear B is a syllabary; second, I will bet everyone in Evans's circle at Cambridge that it is not a Minoan language (Linear A—yes), but was developed on the mainland, maybe an early type of Greek; and third, we must be careful not to assign a single sound value, because if it is an inflected language, we must leave the door open for the language to find us without distractions.

So, when you translate your Homer, look for ghosts, seek out traces of an earlier language or anachronisms of place or material objects. List your ghosts for me in your next letter—ah, the lovely ancient words— there is the key to open for us the door to Homer's treasure.

On the trees in Neumarktstrasse the buds are coming. But Germany only darkens, and so sunny Greece beckons all the more for June.

Your friend and colleague,
Karel Hollar

11 THIS SEEPAGE OF IMPRESSIONS ABOUT MY father's life over that desultory spring of assassination, riot, and protest, as I neared draft age, only heightened my sense of anxiety that everything I knew and loved was under threat. I found myself drawn to things past, to old certainties, to the fading values that had come out of the abolitionist movement and the Civil War, upon which my people had founded Winsted.

I can remember walking into the library and instinctively looking up for assurance at the Sargent portrait of General Alden, and feeling only a terrible sadness at his once-sterling reputation. If such a thing was so fragile, so fleeting, what hope was there left for any of us? Even with all the histories of Antietam, his memoirs and letters, his sacrifice and that of his men in the Fifteenth Regiment Massachusetts Volunteers, their legacy seemed under threat. Even the likes of Jerry Gadsden could be dismissive of that once-honored generation of abolitionists. "Truth be told, your people, your general beat the pants off those southern slaveholders, and then retreated to their safe homes up north and let those crackers butcher and degrade black folks for another hundred years. Like amnesia, man, a hundred years of forgetting, like people just forgot what that Civil War was all about."

All too true.

What had happened to our faith in the struggle for human dignity and freedom, and Lincoln's "better angels of our nature"? In 1968, American exceptionalism was in bad odor.

I found myself looking into the troubled eyes of the general's portrait, as I'd looked into the hard eyes of that Green Beret captain, and wondering what I missed, what I lacked as a human being . . . bred out of me. Even Max, more and more preoccupied with his short story writing, neglected me as a lost cause.

John Alden, an engineer by training, had learned his trade the hard way, at Bull Run, and Ball's Bluff and during the Peninsula Campaign when he became a favorite of George McClellan, a professional soldier and organizational genius. Alden's efficiency and bravery prompted his speedy rise to general. By Antietam, Alden had been through enough galling retreats; his Massachusetts men had marched from Washington though the lush landscapes of western Maryland, singing abolitionist hymns, anticipating a fight on home ground after the malarial marshes and fetid water of the Peninsula Campaign. He pushed himself and his men to break the Confederate line at all costs. It was a horrendous gamble but a victory there and then might bring a quick end to the war. Brigade after brigade was fed into the slaughter pen and massacred. Finally, the rebel line broke and began falling back. That was when General Alden was shot off his horse. A bullet shattered his right ankle. He tried to get back on his mount, but he was bleeding profusely and began to faint. His aides carried him back to a dressing station. By the afternoon, he was in excruciating pain and woozy from loss of blood and unable to vigorously participate in the planning to follow up the limited successes of the morning with further attacks. "I failed to put steel in George McClellan's spine: a man I admired but a man afraid of losing and so unable to win." By all accounts, a quick response that afternoon and in the days following would have pinned the Confederate army against the Potomac and ended the war in a matter of weeks, saving the nation another two and a half agonizing years.

That deadly wager on high body counts for a decisive victory weighed on Alden all his life, as regrets tend to do. "The thing was graspable; Johnny Reb was reeling, and we had Lee with his backside in the Potomac." So much staked for so little gain. It marked him—marked him as a gambler in human souls. He'd gambled with his men's lives and lost the wager. That's how he saw it, even though Antietam was a victory that saved the Union and prompted the Emancipation Proclamation, when Lincoln finally realized the North had to take off the gloves and get freemen into the fight. A week after the battle, as Alden was still recovering in an army hospital in Silver Spring, Maryland, McClellan dismissed him for his complaints to the papers about his commander's indecisiveness and incompetence. Alden had been an early admirer of McClellan, but he knew a missed opportunity when he saw one, and he never forgave McClellan. "McClellan cared only about the Union, but union without the destruction of slavery was union with the devil and his filthy spawn."

It was the dismissal that set him on the path to his fortune.

"He lit out for the West," as my grandmother put it, where he surveyed for the railroad and designed their bridges, and made "handfuls" of money, and finally came home, not to Boston and Cambridge, where he and Samuel Williams had gone to Harvard and become fervent abolitionists, but to New York, where he invested in real estate and made another, even larger fortune. President Grant was a personal friend and urged him to run for governor of New York. The great preacher and abolitionist Henry Ward Beecher, who introduced him to the work of the artist George Inness, also urged him to run, to get back in the fray before it was too late, "get some teeth into the reconstruction of the South before all our gains are lost." Alden refused the call. (The manila envelope with the newspaper cuttings from the 1877 *Natchez Weekly Democrat* and the Pinkerton reports spelled out his final heart-wrenching failures in the abolitionist cause.) And he did so again when the Republicans asked him to run for the Senate. He wanted nothing more to do with public life. "The South and the southerner be damned, the bondsmen and their dastardly supporters in the Democratic Party can go to hell." Alden retreated into making money, engaging in philanthropy that set the mold for Carnegie and Rockefeller, collecting classical statuary and George Inness paintings, and building Elysium and the Winsted School with his cousin Samuel Williams.

Having now encountered Bobby Williams in the flesh, I couldn't help but wonder why a fighting general, a superb businessman, and an organizational genius felt the need to team up with the likes of Samuel Williams—*Essays and Prayers* just didn't cut it—to found and run a school for boys.

A fascinating tale that even a Kim Philby might have failed to unearth.

At his funeral in the Winsted chapel, General Alden was remembered as the best of his generation, and a man shadowed by loss. He was haunted by the failure of Reconstruction, by the lynching of blacks in the Jim Crow South that occurred with sickening frequency in the decades before his death in late 1918, which his friend Theodore Roosevelt was been helpless to stop, and by the graves of a near company of his men in the Winsted cemetery, where he, too, was buried: a commander still. He died in the terrible outbreak of Spanish influenza in the fall of 1918. A month before, he'd received word of his doctor son's atomization when a five-hundred-pound German shell made a direct hit on his surgical field station in the Argonne.

And so I found myself latching onto the last echoes of that great man's hopes for his nation, as my father had in his letters to his mother from France and Germany in the waning months of the war, as their country went to war with itself once again. I found myself craving the voices of those who remembered him as he once was, as the dead in Hades craved Odysseus's blood libations, and news of their sons, their glorious sons.

Doc Steele was an institution. He'd been head of the history department for forty-odd years and took personal pride in fine-tuning some of the best and brightest minds of my father's generation. Educated in Germany and at Oxford, Doc believed in the tutorial method for developing critical thinking in his young charges. For Doc, the classics and sacred studies, even math and science, were mere window dressing for a man's liberal education. He taught us the nuts and bolts of statecraft and the legacy that informed political purpose. A pragmatist to the core, he equipped his boys to deal with the hard world as it really was. Through his steady eyes we might see our way past the complexity and deceit of human affairs to the vital truth . . . the vital center.

Doc wanted to believe in the worst way that we *were* the vital center.

"A balanced and pragmatic mind, boys—that's the ticket."

Old Doc was about to have a grand chance to put some of his handiwork on display. It was the school's eighty-eighth birthday and many of the top guns in Washington would be on hand to celebrate, including the president's national security adviser who had decided, on very short notice, to give a speech about our involvement in Vietnam. The president's adviser was one of Doc's boys.

In morning class, with his protégé's address scheduled for that evening, Doc fairly jitterbugged before his lectern. His patrician voice boomed, with its hints of British inflection from his days as a Rhodes scholar. Still tall and slender at almost seventy, he retained the dashing good looks of the scholar athlete, a sterling mechanism crowned with a shock of snow-white hair tamed back with a discreet dose of Vitalis, while his wide-apart, sea green eyes glittered with agitation as he preached the still-pressing drama of history's close calls. He paced before us with the gravitas of the worldly sage who has touched all the bases and then some.

Doc launched into his classic lecture on the meaning of history. He'd been delivering this now-famous lecture, with pithy updates, to the advanced sections—including my father's class—as long as anyone could remember, which he illustrated at crucial points with close-arm drills from the time of Frederick the Great. Doc was a great fan of the Prussian king who—after two world wars fighting the Germans, one would have thought his subject slightly tarnished—represented, in his well-traveled mind, an obscure, if vivid, baseline in the scheme of human affairs.

History, he never ceased reminding us, was not about blind economic forces, but about man qua man—the unique figures who have shaped the world by force of character. "No man or nation can escape the burden of history," he repeated, for our individual lives are connected in an unbroken line of cause and effect stretching backward and forward in time.

"That is the heritage that binds us." He charged across the room as if to viciously thrust an eighteen-inch bayonet into the stomach of a Saxon grenadier. "No generation"—he pressed a foot on the skewered foe and pulled out his blade with a guttural grunt—"can escape this responsibility."

He spoke to us of the great men who had changed the course of history. "If it had not been for Luther and the Protestant triumph in Germany and England—thank God for Thomas and Oliver Cromwell, who set the seal of English liberty on the land—we might all be speaking Spanish and going to confession on Sunday." He eyed us with a woeful stare that spoke of the benighted plague of the Inquisition.

History was the tug of the old and new, the revolt of the sons against the fathers—witness the irony of Frederick the Great, who as a youth reviled his cold Prussian father, only to end up much like his old man, even surpassing his pedantic father in the meticulous requirements to patiently build little Prussia into a European power.

Doc stood to attention, shouldering his invisible but weighty musket, moving it from shoulder to shoulder with quick, precise movements, then bending to one knee to demonstrate the firing position, and counting off the seconds it took a first-rate rifleman to reload and fire again. His body took the impact of the recoil and he staggered up, wiping sweat from his domed brow. "The Prussian marksman could get off six shots in a minute, twice the speed of the best infantry in Europe of the day. A withering fire, an oblique and mobile formation—a formidable killing force."

How Doc loved to go on about poor Frederick, portraying the fate of the fallen idealist who spent his declining years plagued by the memories of the death and destruction that had filled his reign. But what a soldier, what a determined general . . . that poor little Prussia should survive! (Survive to fire a five-hundred-pound shell at a surgical station, killing my grandfather and dozens of the wounded and nurses!) Somehow these thoughts on things Teutonic inevitably led to his most dire warnings against Hegelian idealism and economic materialism. Somehow, that dirty little bearded Jew, Karl Marx, a man with no practical experience of the world, a library-sated intellectual, had inserted himself into the historical process, preaching his blather of class struggle and historical necessity.

"Marx was a fake, a charlatan; even his research was a fraud."

"Never!" he admonished, circling the room like a master sergeant inspecting the latest timorous offering to the war gods, "use the word *inevitable* in a paper you write for this course, or I guarantee you an automatic F. Got it?" He inspected the attentive faces, a few trying to blink back stubborn morning hangovers. "Man must be free to create his own destiny." Doc pointed out a few in the pantheon, the framed photos of Lincoln, Grant, Teddy Roosevelt, Churchill, Eisenhower, and George C. Marshall that hung above his desk. "Be forever vigilant of those who manipulate with half-baked ideas, who use ideas to gain their odious ends and crush freedom from the earth, who prey on the natural resentments and jealousies of the downtrodden. We are a practical race, gentlemen; we are doers and pragmatists first, thinkers second. Believe only in what you can touch, what you can ascertain with your own eyes, what can be proved to the judge and jury of a well-tempered mind. Experience the world, boys. Touch its face. But keep your wits about you. Remember, sometimes it is necessary to make your own facts and prove what is true by its accomplishment."

He turned like a weary general from the appalling wastage of the battlefield and retreated to the front of his classroom, where he began methodically to raise the maps of Europe—1500 the Reformation, 1648 Treaty of Westphalia, 1815 Treaty of Vienna, 1914 on the eve of the Great War—century after century, snapping them upward into neat rolls until the blackboard appeared with the word FREEDOM scrawled in blue chalk. He patted his forehead with a handkerchief and waved at the board.

"That is what America must stand for in the eyes of the world. It is what we have always fought for, from Bunker Hill and Gettysburg to the Battle of the Bulge and Inchon. It is the cross we bear." I wondered if that cross included the Battle of the Ia Drang Valley or the recent repulse of the Vietcong during the Tet Offensive. He nodded gravely as he prepared to dismiss us with a reminder about the president's adviser's lecture in the hall that evening. "Remember, boys, some men take instinctively to their calling, while others will never hear the call. But we are all called to serve in our own way."

How simple, how commonsense seemed Doc's vision of history. Surely, here was a fine echo of General Alden's creed. No complex dialectic of economic forces, just the interplay of great men and experienced judgment, the champions of progress and justice against those of dark reaction, our fate decided by the passionate will of a chosen few, the great-souled statesmen who, by force of will, might yet redeem the world. Churchill was Doc's great hero. "And don't forget, boys, his mother was an American beauty, as fierce in intellect as she was stunning to behold." Doc had married an Englishwoman after the war, a fourth cousin of Winston Churchill, so he had some skin in the Winnie game.

Perhaps he never heard the snickers or saw the yawns in the back of the classroom, or didn't care. He believed that in times of crisis there would be enough good men—just enough—to step forward, to hold his shining standard high.

As we left his class, he called me over to his desk and motioned me to sit. He picked up a handwritten note on his desk and reviewed it one more time. Then he bounced his shaggy eyebrows at me and smiled, still breathing hard from his exertions. He indicated the note with a White House letterhead on his desk. "Mac wants to meet with you after his address to the school *privately*, at the headmaster's house." A look of fondness and surprise mixed in his green eyes, catching the sunlight from the window. I nodded my compliance, still a little churned up in the backwash of his oratory.

"He knew your father, of course," he continued. "They were friends and colleagues."

I had an inkling from my mother's little story about the shoe with the broken heel and the shattered windowpane on a street in Georgetown, which, at the very least, hinted at a more problematic friendship. Of course I said nothing, just nodded and prepared to go. Then he said my name as if he needed to add something, maybe give me a little briefing about the man, a little historical perspective. Something seemed to be bothering him. A moment of doubt perhaps? I waited. The sunlight shone in his white hair, again bringing out the turbid green of his fervent eyes. After having delivered his stirring lecture forty times, sending boys from forty sixth forms off into the world, he was on the cusp of his proudest moment . . . or so one would have thought. His boys were coming back to pat him on the back, to see if old "Steeljaws" was still on the march, to thank him for all he'd done for them. He shook his head. And it hit me: My father was one of the few who wouldn't be coming back. Many had died in World War II as young men, but only one, a marine colonel, had died in Korea, and so far no one from the school was serving in Vietnam, unless you counted Elliot Goddard and some of his more intrepid CIA colleagues.

Doc's smile expressed gentle feeling, a deep affection, and he reached with a half shrug across his desk and patted my hand. And then he just shook his head again and said I could go.

I got up.

"No, wait." He waved me back to the seat. "The way things are going around here . . . I'd just like to tell you how much I miss your father."

"Thank you, sir."

"He was a terrific student, of course, but I never knew him as a coach or even a dorm master. He was rowing in the spring, when I was on the tennis court. But you know what really impressed me: He spoke perfect German, I guess from that summer he spent in Germany studying at Leipzig. I knew nothing about his scholarship, but I was touched by his profound respect for German culture—a dicey thing, even then, with the memory of the First World War still fresh, with Hitler coming to power. There's no one left today who even remembers how German scholarship was once esteemed." He paused while passing his heavily calloused hand through his white hair, needing to ease out the significant facts from his encyclopedic brain. "But you see, what I remember . . . how much your father loved music, especially Bach and the piano work of Mozart and Beethoven. His friend the Williams boy, extraordinary talent on the piano, was always playing on the Steinway grand in the hall, or the organ in the chapel. I liked to stop and listen, and I'd often find John there. It seemed odd to me, with all his athletic prowess, that music held such a place in his life. And you know, as a teacher, when your boys come back, as they always do, one can't help comparing the student to the professional man, the life that has evolved from an early aptitude and passion. Time and again, I can spot the match; I think, Yes, I could see the man in that boy. The president's adviser, for example; I knew that Mac was headed to the top job after only a week in class. And I did see something of your father when he returned from the war, when he was on the board of trustees in the late forties and early fifties—not that I was an intimate; and I could never quite place that boy seated with his head bowed pensively listening to a Bach sonata or a Mozart rondo. He was a war hero, by all reports, a man on the way to the top reaches of government, where, God only knows, his talents were sorely needed. One detected the weight of the world on his shoulders."

He smiled gently and raised a long finger. He seemed almost relieved, and then he shook his head. "Yes, the boy, and the man . . ." His eyebrows expanded upward. "Well, I just wanted you to know that I miss him and I often think about him when I hear Mozart."

Doc, too, couldn't help but be rattled by recent events: city streets in flame, protests on campuses and in Washington, and the relentless criticism in the *Times* of his boys and their pedigree. Perhaps he was having second thoughts about what he'd wrought, the way he'd portrayed the historical imperative to his boys who now ran the country. For the most part, things had gone pretty well up to the Vietnam War. Doc's crowd had played an exalted role in the Second World War and had saved the heartland of Europe. But then they'd failed in the roll-back of Communist expansion in Eastern Europe. And then China had gone down to the Reds. Korea had been an expensive and cruel blunder: A Winsted boy, before Doc's time, had failed to draw the line at the Yalu. Senator Joseph McCarthy had given anticommunism a bad name. Then there'd been the hiccup of the Bay of Pigs, in which three of Doc's boys had featured, a botch to end all botches, due to an inexperienced, womanizing president who lost his nerve and failed to commit the military decisively and in a timely fashion. Elliot Goddard had escaped that fiasco by the skin of his teeth. Payback had come with the Cuban Missile Crisis—near Armageddon, and then another humiliation. The president's adviser had a lot to answer for, and now, because of the Cuban fuckup, he was up to his chin in the Vietnam morass, where they'd been compelled to draw the line. And truth be told, Vietnam wasn't even in the neighborhood of those maps of ye olde Europe on Doc's wall—that heartland of Western civilization we were sworn to protect. And well, a land war in Asia . . . Eisenhower had thought a land war in the jungles of Asia was madness. Was it possible that Doc's boys had gotten in a little too deep and maybe hadn't covered all sides of the question? Maybe the Oxford tutorial system didn't work as well in the White House. Maybe the better part of valor was to cut our losses and let Vietnam go Communist. Draw the line in Thailand or India, both of which had viable governments—did they not? Besides, you've got the whole wide Pacific in which to drown those red dominoes.

In the histories that would one day be written about Doc's influence on his best and brightest students, he would grudgingly express these second thoughts. If such reservations disturbed his mind during our conversation after class, he'd changed his tune by dinner, and most assuredly when he introduced the president's adviser in the hall before the speech, which would be quoted in full by *The New York Times* the following morning, and harshly critiqued by *Pravda* that evening.

Or possibly our conversation—and it really wasn't much of a conversation—might have been prompted by Doc's many contacts with the powers that be. Had he heard darker hints about the disastrous calamity of my father's "defection"? Did he know any more about Kim Philby's machinations and his CIA boy's fawning, and that outstanding joker in the deck: Anthony?

Perhaps he just felt sorry for me.

At dinner I sat with Max at Charlie Springfield's table. Up at the head table the president's adviser sat with Byron Folley and Doc and other esteemed members of the board of trustees and their wives, including Elliot Goddard, Bobby and Suzanne Williams, and a number of top-ranking CIA officers. Many were Doc's boys. Precedents were being broken, the press was being allowed to cover the president's adviser's speech. This had been Byron Folley's idea; he was basking in the reflected glow of the publicity. But the trustees, to a man, were annoyed at the headmaster's lack of discretion. They grumbled behind his back, barely able to say a civil word to "that hick of a pipsqueak." Gentlemen, especially those in public life, were expected to keep low profiles and avoid drawing attention to themselves or their backgrounds. Their schools, like their clubs, were sacrosanct, offering a degree of respite from the public eye, where they drew strength among their own kind.

Nevertheless, dinner was a magnificent affair. The school was on its best behavior for its birthday celebration: white shirts and blue blazers to the skies. I kept looking up at the head table, behind which Sargent's towering portrait of the first headmaster, Samuel Williams, claimed pride of place (Sargent, a pal and confidant of Samuel's daughter, Isabella, had painted the general and the rector in consecutive sittings). Bobby Williams glowered uncomfortably in his wheelchair next to the president's adviser, although he must have taken some comfort that the imposing portrait of his grandfather had his back. Suzanne smoldered in icy elegance, attracting every male gaze; a quick glance and I might have taken her for Laura, who had not been included in the occasion, the wheelchair chores falling to her mother.

I wondered if the president's adviser was concerned about his golden-haired son, a phenomenal athlete and wide receiver, only recently back from rehab. I could count on two hands all the touchdown passes he'd dropped the previous fall. Now he'd grown his hair past his shoulders and couldn't concentrate enough to sign his name. Max and I wondered if the Secret Service agents at the doorways carried guns under their coats. We couldn't take our eyes off the famous man. His commitment and brilliance seemed to shine in his round, compact face, only the merest strands of hair disguising the impressive size of his cranium. His movements were quick and decisive, his intelligent eyes darting with impatience. He had a reputation for not suffering fools gladly. Which made it tough on Byron Folley, who tried to act the part but nodded woodenly like a windup marionette at every word uttered by the brilliant alumnus, who was the adviser to another boy from Texas, who'd also made it big in the world of the bold easterners but had now fled the heat of the kitchen and bowed out of the upcoming fall election. For the president's adviser, this, too, would be his last hurrah in government before history shoved him from the world stage, where the critics sharpened their knives. Doc sat up straight as a half-driven nail, beaming and proud; he knew as well as anyone that the affairs of state had been committed to able hands, to one endowed with the wisdom of the ages. He had seen to that.

Only the Reverend Springfield seemed soured by the whole affair. He slumped forward at the head of our table and brooded darkly, hardly touching his food—unusual for a man normally jocular and garrulous.

Charlie Springfield had been a class behind the president's adviser and had known him as man and boy. He remembered the boy as brilliant and utterly self-confident—too brilliant, in his opinion; for having mastered all the facts of history so as to marshal them in the blink of an eye, he suffered no doubt; only now it was lives and not just the debating society's trophy at stake. People were dying; young soldiers were dying in great numbers at obscure jungle coordinates because of advice he was offering to a besieged and lame-duck president. Charlie Springfield did have doubts. He abhorred senseless slaughter and was no stranger to war, having landed on Omaha Beach, where many in his platoon had been killed (while the president's adviser had monitored the landings through binoculars from a navy cruiser three miles offshore).

"Your dad," Charlie Springfield said to me suddenly, "would never have been taken in by the blather justifying this war."

I was startled by this remark so abruptly flung out for all to hear. Had he picked up such a view when my father visited him in the hospital, or had their paths crossed again after the war, when my father had been on the board of trustees?

"What part of the blather wouldn't he have been taken in by?" I asked. Max was shaking his head at me: Don't go there, Hawkman. Charlie Springfield was not just a little drunk; he was smashed. I could smell it on his breath.

"It's not a fucking game; it's not fucking imperial satraps out of Kipling striding the world stage . . . oh, Christ."

Charlie smacked the table with his fist. His acne-scarred cheeks had turned beet red; he could have been choking to death. He glared at the head table, a curl of dark hair falling above his eyebrows. Our table fell silent. Max made another signal in my direction to keep my big mouth shut. Charlie swept the lock off his brow and a moment later shoved his chair back and strode out of the dining room.

Just as well he left before the birthday cake was presented at the head table, before the school stood to sing the traditional "Blue Bottles." Nor did he bother to attend the president's adviser's speech; he'd heard it all before. Charlie Springfield had gone home to finish work on his sermon for next morning's Sunday chapel.

That night, the hall was packed. The newspapermen were there with their notebooks and cameras. The lectern was a tangle of microphones.

The television klieg lights transformed the dowdy hall into an incandescent moment of Cold War history. Byron Folley made a brief introduction, then cannily turned the podium over to Doc, who made a proper introduction, telling his famous story about the president's adviser's class, which was the most brilliant class he'd ever taught. He said that when he'd arrived as a young master after a year of teaching at Dartmouth, he had expected to be disappointed with the quality of students. Was he shocked! By God, if they weren't already superior to the college boys.

Then there was another famous story, about how when it came time for the president's adviser to take his advanced placement exam in history, he hadn't liked the choice of exam questions and so had taken the liberty of rewriting one of the questions and answering it in his own terms. The examiners had to decide whether to flunk him or give him the highest grade possible. Doc smiled, knowing he didn't have to reveal the outcome. The crowd tittered. Even those who were against the war couldn't help but feel a sense of pride. After all, he was one of our own. Come what may, we really *were* a magnificent bunch.

When the president's adviser took the lectern, there was loud clapping and then expectant silence. All the television lights came on, cameramen bent to their eyepieces, and soundmen adjusted their levels. Our boy nodded gravely for ten or fifteen seconds—almost an eternity under that incandescent glare—and looked at us and then spoke in a medium forthright voice. He had been busy and had not had time to prepare his remarks, but he would try to address the issues that might be uppermost in our minds. The newsmen pricked up their ears, because it meant he would be speaking off-the-cuff, and off-the-cuff always meant news. Doc smiled because he knew that extemporaneous speaking was what his boy did best.

And he was right. The president's adviser waxed eloquent, barely pausing, as if he were in a trance, and we could almost hear the fine machinery of his mind whir like those great IBM computers behind closed doors at the Department of Defense. He told us how Americans hated war, how we had been dragged into both the world wars, and Korea too! He hated war because he had seen what had happened at Pleiku; he had seen the wounded. He told us this with a grim face. There were tears in his eyes when he continued. He had talked to many of the badly wounded, talked to our boys who had lost legs and arms and who lay suffering in the field hospitals. He was devastated by their sacrifice and stirred by their heroism. They had done their duty and paid the supreme price. It was not a war we wanted. But the North Vietnamese and their backers in the Soviet Union and China had chosen to test us; they had forced our hand. The United States was thus compelled to retaliate against escalating aggression. No country could be allowed to think that it could get away with uncontested aggression, for it only led to more aggression, until we were in a mess like we were against Hitler and Hirohito. He told us in a hushed voice that the president had resisted the decision to bomb the North as long as he could, but he had been compelled to make the hard choice.

"No one"—and he made a fist and stared at it gravely—"could be allowed to doubt our resolve. If not us, then who?"

He went on in a searching voice. If we backed down, where would we have to back down next? What would become of the others: Cambodia, Laos, Thailand, and then Indonesia . . . and the people, the bloodbath that would be sure to follow? We had given the South our word and we would never desert an ally. What would our faithful European allies think if they saw our resolve falter? "Gentleman," he told us, "it's a rough and dirty world out there. It comes down to one thing: toughness and nerve . . . to stand up for what you believe in. It is America's responsibility as a free people."

He reminded us of the stirring words of our slain president, the man who had brought him to the White House: to pay any price for freedom. At the end, he gazed at us and spoke in an intimate and quiet voice. "Gentlemen, the one lesson our generation has learned the hard way was the lesson of Munich: Appeasement never solves anything, but only begets more aggression and leads to greater and greater danger. Freedom requires toughness and the nerve to stand fast and hold the line. This is the lesson of my generation: the wisdom of our fathers' fathers—it has been our triumph—its neglect our failure."

They gave him a standing ovation. In the end, we stuck by our own.

As instructed, after the illustrious man and the other dignitaries had left the hall, I made my way over to the headmaster's house. It was a warm spring evening, hinting at early summer and freedom from care, and the grass on the Circle had been recently mown and the aroma of the cut grass and the ancient apple trees seemed to rise in delicious updrafts like an ambrosial harvest. I stopped and stared at the smoky leafed-out forms of the apple trees, feeling myself drawn to them as if they were old friends. I was put in mind of something my grandmother had told me in the hospital during her last illness. I went to see her almost every day at Lenox Hill Hospital after school and she'd talk about early times when she was a girl. She thought it important that I should hear it from her, and not from a memoir or letters or a diary, "although," she said, "I've stored up and organized a bushel or two for you to peruse when you're older. The voice carries," she told me, "farther than you dare imagine." I remember her telling me about the apple trees. About how my great-grandfather had been scouting out places for the new school he wanted to build and how he'd come upon the near-abandoned Revolutionary-era farm and the unpruned orchard. How he'd been taken by the "demeanor of these winter-battered trees in the early summer of '78," like old men bent and browbeaten and huddled toward one another as they related tales of famous battles and comrades lost. He'd circled and circled the old trees until he knew in his bones that this was the place where he wanted to build his school, preserving the ancient trees as a reminder, a centerpiece of what once had been and was no more . . . of some enduring truth that must be kept before young men's eyes.

And as I was remembering my grandmother's story, I heard a noise from the branches of one of the trees. There on a sturdy bough about seven feet off the ground was a silhouette of a sitting man. I knew it was a man, as opposed to a boy, by his size and baggy pants and the suit jacket hung over the branch at his side. I realized he'd been watching me for some time, as if he'd been waiting, as if he knew my story.

"Hey," the specter called out. "What'd you think of Mr. Hotshot?"

"What's that?" I asked, taking a few steps closer, peering upward.

A hand reached down, like the hand of God out of a cloud in one of Giotto's early frescoes.

"Get your butt up here."

I was dumbstruck . . . Elliot Goddard, a trustee, CIA station chief in Saigon, sitting on a branch in the dark, swinging his legs like a smart-alecky kid. I took his hand and he pulled me—his strength was impressive—and in seconds I was beside him. All around us indistinct figures passed, retreated, and dispersed to lighted doorways.

"Don't you love it," said Elliot. "I used to hole up in this tree for hours. Watch the moon come up over Mount Monadnock. Lovely to be all alone right at the center of things . . . and nobody the wiser."

I was quite taken by this unaccustomed view, at once familiar and not, and by this man who seemed to appear and disappear in my life like the Cheshire cat.

"So, how'd he do?" he asked.

"Oh, it was a great speech."

"Mac can be damn convincing."

I could barely make out his face, just his blond hair like tarnished silver, his royal nose a convexity of assurance to go with his powerful jaw.

"He told us about Munich and the dangers of appeasement."

"Yup, good ole Munich . . . should've run Chamberlain out of town on a rail."

I detected a world-weariness.

"Did Doc tell his little story about Mac?"

"Oh yeah, about his history AP."

He laughed, and this furthered my sense that these inner-circle anecdotes had begun spreading virally, imagistic stations of the cross upon which the cognoscenti built their arguments and justified their brilliance to one another.

"I'll bet the Monroe Doctrine doesn't get much air play in Steel-jaws's class. Does anybody even teach American history around here?"

Elliot was reprising his bête noire.

"The seniors have it as an elective."

"Lord God—an elective, the Monroe Doctrine is an elective. Tomorrow at the trustees meeting, this is going to be top of the agenda." He reached and shook a branch. "So, what's the White House's latest reading on the Vietnam entrails?"

It took me a few seconds to process this—wouldn't he, of all people, know? "Oh . . . he was explaining why we have to take a stand and what was at stake."

Elliot laughed.

"Stand fast—hold the line." Elliot gave a jaunty salute. "Mac was making the same speech to your dad twenty years ago, back in '48, when we were trying to coax your dad out of the ivied halls of Princeton."

"Why did he—did you have to do that?"

This was followed by silence. Elliot knew that his indiscretions tended to be his undoing.

"Cushy—Princeton—cushy as it gets. Then he'd had a rough war in Greece. Me, I had a couple of weeks of excitement in Brittany dropped behind enemy lines, and the rest was a cakewalk. And that guy in there tonight, he got no closer to Omaha Beach than a little sea spray. But your dad saw the worst of it. He volunteered for an intelligence unit with Patton to go in right behind the point of the spear. He spent a lot of time in those flattened German cities interrogating some of the worst of those sons of bitches. Not to mention, to put it delicately, the not so discret modus of the Soviet security forces in Berlin and Prague and other beauty spots."

How did it follow: my father's reluctance to abandon the cushy confines of Princeton?

"So, he volunteered?"

"Listen, he had a ticket home after he was wounded in Greece. But he wanted to be back in the field . . . a score or two to settle."

"A score?"

"The Germans had killed a lot of his people in Greece."

"Mr. Oakes told me about when he and my father arrived at the liberation of Buchenwald."

"Oakey told you that? . . . Well, that was damn straight of him." Here a note of chagrin that I had a nugget of information that had gotten past him. "Want to tell me, or I suppose I can get it from him?"

"I think he told me in confidence."

"How is the old man? I just got here; haven't had a chance to stop by and see him."

"He doesn't look so good, not after his operation and the chemotherapy; sometimes he can barely make it around the Circle."

"I'm sad to hear that. I'd hoped NIH might lick it for him. He was the fittest man I ever knew. When he was football coach, he'd arm-wrestle the entire team in succession and beat every last one of us. Tougher than any drill sergeant I ever encountered in basic training. He thought your dad walked on water. Well he should; John got him three league championships in a row and an invite to Henley."

Somehow the shared intimacy of the moment, the smells of earth and apple blossoms, the glittering stars allowed an unburdening of frustration on my part. Or maybe it was because I'd stood my ground on the story of the lynched German guard, exclusively mine as things went downhill for Paul Oakes.

"Mr. Goddard, is it really true that he died in an automobile accident on the Autobahn?"

Again silence, and I could just make out Elliot's perplexed face turned to the upper branches and the starlit sky beyond. I knew I'd put him in a tight spot: I was appealing to his honesty at the altar to his gods.

He put a hand on my shoulder. "I know it's not much to go on, but it's the best *we've* got for you right now. If it makes you feel any better, there's not a day in Saigon when I don't wish he were there to bounce things off of, although there are plenty of days when I'm just as glad he doesn't have to face the shit."

His warmth was utterly disarming. "How *bad* a mess is it?"

I saw him lower his eyes to my face and grimace, as if hearing in the cadence of my voice an echo of another time and place. He took a couple of deep breaths.

"No, it's an incredible opportunity. The Vietcong took a terrible beating at Tet. They lost tens of thousands and their terrorist infrastructure has been fatally compromised, if not obliterated. But you'd never know it from CBS or *The New York Times*. Now we have a real chance to win back the provinces in the South. The trouble is, you can't just *hold the line*; you have to play to win. And guys like Mac don't know how to play to win. It's not enough to have the right instincts; you have to find a way to win and minimize your costs." He grabbed my arm and squeezed. "You never heard me say that—never, right?"

In this moment of candor, I thought I detected something of an echo of General Alden's failed gamble and frustration.

"Sure, okay."

"There's a lot we can do, a lot we're doing. We're organizing the South Vietnamese local defense forces. We're training their army; they need better officers and generals. We can buy them time, but unless we cut off the Ho Chi Min Trail it is going to be a war of attrition, and this country doesn't have the patience."

"Does that mean more bombing? Do we invade the North? What do we do?"

I saw a grin come over his face . . . again, the echo.

"Whoa there, I didn't get you up here to discuss Vietnam. I'm just a foot soldier and this is all way above my pay grade. My ulterior motive involves the Yale football coach—good friend of mine—who would like to sign you up for the team."

"Yale? Well, I haven't really thought about it."

"Don't be coy, Mr. Alden. Surely you've been getting recruiting letters?"

I had, over fifty by latest count.

"A few."

"Yale would be a good home for you. I can see to that. Jerry Gadsden will be there; you'll have your favorite running back. You're good enough to win a starting job as quarterback. You know, they come from as far away as Iowa now—where our star quarterback's from, the guy who led Yale to the Ivy League title last fall. But he graduates next year—that's where you come in."

"I can certainly think about it."

"Don't let Princeton turn your head. I'm sure you feel some loyalty there."

"They told me I could have my father's number."

"Shit," and he laughed. "And I thought *I* knew how to recruit. I'd hate to see you play against Jerry Gadsden."

"I don't think he'd mind. In fact, I think he might prefer it."

"I thought you were good pals."

"Not after this year."

"You mean the King assassination?"

"And the riots and everything. The black guys have their own table in the dining hall now. I feel like I have a scarlet letter on my chest, a red *R* for racist."

"Fuck that bullshit, not after all the years we fought these issues on the board to get more blacks into Winsted. And your grandmother— she was a human dynamo on the subject." He sighed. "So what's new—so the world goes to hell and sticks its big finger in your eye. Well, we're just going to have to make this work; we're just going to have to work it harder. If we can't get race relations right in this country, we've got no case to sell to the world. And I'm out in every godforsaken malarial-ridden province and backwater hamlet in Vietnam making the case, goddamn it, and this goddamn school is part of the case. It's who we are."

The tree branch was shaking with the power of his emotion. I felt like saying "tell that to Jerry Gadsden." But Elliot was way ahead of me.

"When you're over there, the war is like a bubble; Vietnam is a bubble—of good men sacrificing themselves for a common cause. What we do there, well, sometimes it's hard to reconcile with the shit going on back here. You'd think it was the same shit, but it isn't. Maybe that's our problem. Maybe people back here need to see the mass graves in Hué, the executed villagers with their genitals stuffed into their mouths. You think I like it; you think any of us like it? When back in Saigon, after a few drinks I can't even stand to read the newspapers or the cable traffic. I curl up with my Shakespeare and read my Thomas Looney and contemplate the slings and arrows of court politics in the sixteenth century."

This cri de coeur almost brought tears to my eyes. It was the first spontaneous and genuinely shared emotion from an older man I'd yet experienced in my life. Paul Oakes's story about the German camp guard had been close, but it felt more like a set piece designed for my moral edification.

"So, you never wrote me: What do you think of Mr. Looney?"

"It got my roommate all hot and bothered. He'd love to talk to you about it."

"And you?"

"Hard to believe such a secret could have lasted four hundred years."

He snapped his fingers. "Like yesterday—the plays. Not a day goes by that I don't have to deal with an Iago, a Prince Hal, a Coriolanus. And the Anthonys—you don't want to know."

"Art holding up the mirror to life."

"Art *is* life. The greatest art is about politics, *and* . . . at the highest level."

"So the biography *is* important?"

"The veil lifts; the characters live and breathe—like the past itself. You, if anyone, should understand."

"About my father?"

"Our prince, who would have been happy to remain a prof in Tiger Town."

"Do you think?"

Elliot sighed and our branch dipped and rose again.

"That Edward de Vere could be lost to history—the unfairness, the injustice. It rankles the soul."

"And none of his admirers, his literary confederates—wouldn't they have revealed the truth?"

"Ah, but Ben Jonson did just that in the preface to the First Folio, as de Vere did in the sonnets: 'That every word doth almost tell my name, showing their birth, and where they did proceed.'"

In that instant, I realized it was Elliot Goddard who had fixed that epitaph in stone for my father in the chapel ambulatory.

By their works ye shall know them.

"And what about Kim Philby? What part does he play in my father's story?"

Elliot didn't miss a beat; Virgil had already filled him in.

"He's our Iago."

"A traitor . . . a false friend."

"Mephistopheles, the cancer burning our guts out."

"Should I know more about him . . . and Anthony—not Mark?"

Again, he put his hand around my shoulder, squeezing hard.

"Ah, I see Virgil has taken you firmly under his wing."

"Not exactly. These names kind of keep popping up."

"Certain stock characters do that—like a law of nature. May I suggest you keep all this to yourself: certain names"—and I saw him jut his jaw toward the lit interior of the headmaster's house—"still hang fire—trust me." Elliot squeezed my shoulder again. "So, you've been keeping Virgil properly apprised of the follies of our favorite headmaster?"

"Yes, sir."

"And others in his camp, a certain couple who summer in your neck of the woods. Discreetly, you understand, very . . . and if the conversation should move to your father or Cambridge days and Cambridge matters, well, Anthony's last name would indeed be a useful tidbit to know, now that Philby has fled our grasp."

I remembered I was supposed to be meeting with the president's adviser. I hurriedly excused myself and hurdled back to earth. As I reached up to shake hands good-bye, he offered me this:

"Listen, young man, I don't really care if it's Princeton or Yale, just as long as I get to a chance to see you play *all* four years. Is that a deal?"

"Sure," I said, not thinking much about it. But there was actually quite a bit to think about; for instance, how the CIA station chief in Saigon could strip off his jungle fatigues, grab a quick shower, catch a flight from Tan Son Nhut for San Francisco, and then Boston—not Washington, where his wife and three daughters eagerly awaited his brief home leave—rent a car and drive to his old school for its eighty-eighth birthday celebration and trustees meeting, park and—not even bothering about the president's adviser's speech—walk over to an old stand of apple trees and climb up into the branches of his favorite and assume a perch he'd first known as a boy, and remain there for hours. Or at least he was still there when I finished with the president's adviser.

And to keep me playing college football—out of harm's way—for four years, which he thought, at the very least, he owed my father.

Perhaps he felt he owed it because he'd been station chief in Berlin in the fall of 1953 when my father arrived from Washington on Allen Dulles's orders to see what might be done to support the worker uprising against the East German regime: when he'd disappeared through Checkpoint Charlie without a word, without a trace. Leaving Elliot almost as much in the dark as I was. A darkness in which debts seem to come due.

Only years later did Elliot fill me in on the details, and only then did I fully grasp why Elliot never showed at the speech or the reception for the president's adviser: He was the man at JFK's elbow who had advised against the use of airpower to save Elliot's Cubanistas fighting for their lives at the Bay of Pigs, who had advised against simply sending in the marines and taking Fidel out once and for all. He was a man who had never learned how to play to win. Not unlike the brilliant George McClellan, whom General Alden had come to despise.

12

WHEN I REACHED THE RECEPTION AT THE headmaster's house, the place was teeming with alumni and trustees—many familiar from newspapers and television—forming a scrum around the beaming face of the president's adviser. He was being showered with congratulations. People were basking in the reflected glory of one of their own kind. Suzanne had parked Bobby by a bay window, where he could overlook the playing fields while she helped the headmaster's wife pour tea and coffee for this gathering of the great and good. Although neglected by everyone, Bobby seemed quietly content to stare out at the stately elms that shadowed the night sky. For a moment, I almost felt sorry for him, remembering Doc Steele's story about how my father liked to discreetly listen to him play, as I often sought out Max, now a rare occurrence indeed. The thought caused me to turn to Suzanne, and as I did, she glanced up from the tea service at her elbow and her intent expression dissolved into one of lost wonder. She smiled, her glittering blue eyes touched with sliver shards, projecting a warmth that was actually inviting. What had happened to "on the warpath"? What names hovered on her supple lips?

Before I could think twice, Byron Folley's wife, following Suzanne's stare, caught sight of me, too, and, hurrying over, quickly ushered me past the two Secret Service officers by the reception area and into the headmaster's study, telling me with the Gentile aplomb of a southern belle out of Macon, Georgia, to sit tight while she got the "man of the hour." She had clearly been given her instructions. I didn't have more than a minute to inspect the bookshelves and the religious knickknacks scattered about the headmaster's study before the president's national security adviser entered with quick, purposeful strides and closed the door behind him. He moved toward me as if he would send his splendid forehead crashing into my chest. He then took my hand and, in the same gesture, motioned to a pair of chairs emblazoned with the school crest.

I was petrified to be sitting across from this brilliant man. He was only inches away and he leaned far forward for intimacy. This was the compact face and tight working jaw I'd glimpsed on the front pages of *The New York Times* and on the cover of *Time* magazine, no less, whispering in the ear of two presidents. Just that morning, he'd chaired a meeting of the Joint Chiefs, with the fate of thousands of young men's lives hanging in the balance.

He smiled while his reddened eyes swept my face like sonar.

"I just wanted to thank you. I wanted to thank you for being a friend to my son. I know how Jack thinks the world of you."

"Oh, Jocko—Jack's such a great receiver," I gushed. "The way he manages to get himself open makes it a cinch for me."

He bent closer over the intervening space, a new eagerness flickering in his nut brown eyes.

"He's that good, is he?"

My effusive lies were effortless. "And hands . . . he makes my worst passes look like I parked it on a dime."

"I gather he had a tough fall season."

"It was tough for all of us; the competition in the league was pretty intense."

"I feel terrible. What with things as they are in Washington, I wasn't able to get to a game last fall."

"My mother hasn't been to a game in three years."

I thought it was a helpful remark, but I wasn't sure how it went over, since he didn't smile or nod.

"How is your mother? I don't think I've seen her since . . . well, it's been a long time."

"She's fine." I knew he meant the memorial service.

"I don't know how Jack ended up such a fine athlete." He pulled at his jaw. His fingers were perfectly manicured. "I dreamed of doing what he does, at his age, at your age. I had poor eyesight. I failed all my eye exams for the army in 1941. I tried to memorize the chart, but they still caught me out. I'm okay for tennis if I don't have to play net."

I thought of Elliot Goddard's dismissive anecdote about the man sitting across from me: peering through binoculars three miles off Omaha Beach. Or was it three hundred yards off the beach in an LCD? This little story and its permutations seemed to take on a life of its own within certain circles.

He put his palms together before him and intertwined his fingers.

"I know Jack had problems in the fall; I know he was ill. And I wanted to thank you for your discretion . . . and for being a friend."

It was Jerry Gadsden who had told me. It was Jerry who had found him overdosed on heroin in the toilets. He'd probably saved his life, because Jerry knew just what a heroin OD looked like. He had dragged Jocko to the infirmary and put him in the ambulance for the hospital. It was Jerry he should be thanking, not me.

"I know what you did and I appreciate your friendship for my son. You understand, if his name ever got in the papers . . . what it would mean."

I nodded, wondering if it was a mistake or if somebody had told him it was me on purpose. What's in a name . . . .

"Tell me, is he so unhappy? I can barely get a word out of him. His mother is beside herself."

That stumped me. Suddenly, I saw in front of me a man with a sick child. And desperate for him to be well again. Jerry had told me about the terrible state in which he'd found his son. And that spring, back from rehab, Jocko had been furtive and glassy-eyed, barely speaking. Jocko had been the golden boy of our class. And Jocko wasn't the only one. There were days when it seemed as if some infectious agent had gotten past our walls and was picking guys off one by one.

But I didn't tell him that.

"I think it's got to be hard . . . with so many protesting the war."

He nodded, his lips pressing tight, as if he were gripped by sudden pain. I could see nothing of the handsome son in the father.

"It's been rough on the family. But I thought Jack understood, what was at stake, what had to be done."

"It's hard," I offered again, realizing that I was being provocative for my own sake. "When the world"—and I made a feeble gesture toward the four walls and the Circle beyond—"thinks it might be a mistake."

"Does he think it's a mistake?"

"I think it would be hard for any of us, with a dad so much in the public eye—and all the controversy. He's got to be feeling the pressure. And, of course, with his loyalty to you . . ."

"Loyalty?" His brow flexed as if his superior brain had stripped gears, or I'd inadvertently tossed in a monkey wrench. "I'd never presume on his loyalties to make up his own mind. In the end, we're all called on to come to terms in our own way, in our own time." A spark of anger flared in his eyes. "Your father certainly had his own take on affairs of state."

At this, I felt a surge of hidden pleasure, as if I'd been looking for the right button and by instinct had actually pushed it. I longed to toss out a name or two.

"I thought your speech was terrific."

He flashed a dismissive frown, his gaze settling fully on my face once more.

"Forgive me for saying it, but you remind me of your father at the same age. I can't tell you how just the sound of your voice brings back a dozen schoolboy conversations. It's one of the great disappointments in my life that he's no longer here to offer me counsel."

I was floored: *offer me counsel.* As if he were reading my mind thought for thought, he continued.

"Not that we always agreed. But his instincts were sound, his judgments well constructed. I respected him enormously." He leaned closer again. "In our senior year, in 1932, he opened my eyes to the pitiless evil we faced. To this day, his prescience in these matters amazes me. His read on events in the early thirties affected me deeply, and time has only vindicated his terrible vision."

He was reeling me in hook, line, and sinker. Was it my father's morbid fascination with the Greek Dark Ages and the collapse of Mycenaean civilization or Virgil's reports from his brother in the FBI?

"A terrible vision?"

"Stalin, the destruction of the Kulaks, the great famine in the Ukraine, the work camps—I heard it first from him. And then later, the monstrous appetites of Hitler. He'd traveled in Germany over summers while we were still at Winsted . . . he was friends with some famous German archaeologist; the details escape me, but his insights were electrifying. He'd smelled the smoldering sulfur fumes."

Virgil, I thought, as a vision swam up before me, not a vision of hell, exactly, but of a man walking in air: slowly strangling. I must have seemed slightly catatonic at that point as my imagination rushed to encompass the new data.

"And John was a real scholar, so unlike most of our classmates, who were headed into law and banking. I appreciated that in him; I was a history and politics man at Harvard. I appreciated his clarity of thought—unlike the lucubrations of so many woolly-headed academics. He appreciated how the light of the past might illuminate the present, even in the darkest days of the Depression, when the country had lost its way." He reached out to my arm. "I never leave here without visiting the portrait of your grandfather in the library."

"Great-grandfather . . . thank you, sir."

"We need to remember where we come from."

He slackened his grip, his head nodding. "You would be just the person to explain it to Jack—I know how much he respects you—if you feel up to it. Explain the spot we're in: If the extreme Right has its way, we'll blow one another to smithereens; if the far Left has its way, they'll let us be steamrolled by the Communists, making excuses at every bad turning, justifying capitulation or putting off hard decisions by resorting to morally ambiguous arguments. We're caught in the middle—you see"—he made a motion with his hands, a little circle between us, including me, and his son . . . our people—"holding the line, balancing the dangers and costs of defending the free world. Perhaps time is on our side, perhaps not, but a collapse in Southeast Asia could be catastrophic. Making Stalin's bloody depredations, even Mao's, look like child's play down the road. If we show weakness, they'll eat us alive."

He stared at me glassy-eyed, like a cornered animal. I was in such a panic of sensory overload, I couldn't get a thing out.

He must have sensed my discomfort, for he stood suddenly. He waved a hand, as if disgusted with himself for letting his exasperation get the better of him in front of the likes of me. Then he smiled stoically and made a cursory survey of the headmaster's study, noting with a scowl the religious trinkets, the plaster-cast statue of Saint John the Baptist by the fireplace, which contained the microphone for Max's secret taping system. (This was the source for the corrupted version of my conversation with the president's adviser that appeared in *Like a Forgotten Angel*. The source, too, of Max's portrayal of my father as a neofascist schoolboy in the early thirties.)

He reached to shake my hand, and with a motion of his head to include the place where we were standing and all that it represented, he said, "Nobody ever said it was going to be a picnic."

I was tempted to ask him about Kim Philby but figured I'd had my shot.

"I thought you were great tonight, sir," I finally managed to say.

He kept the handshake tight. "Would you keep an eye on him? Do keep an eye on Jack for me. Explain it to him, what's at stake. He won't speak to me anymore."

I am still moved by the memory of a man pleading for help for his son . . . a man who had been instrumental in sending tens of thousands of young sons to their deaths in the jungles of Vietnam. Such a burden should be borne by no man. On the other hand, his three sons never served, nor are their names numbered among the glorious dead.

The next morning, the Reverend Springfield was soused. He walked pretty steadily up the aisle considering his normal limp and his shattered right leg—still containing fragments from an 88 shell in an action that had cut in half two of his best friends. But I could see the booze in his eyes—Jerry had taught me that, my mother, too—those soft gray eyes that shone with a dull anger, as if he'd had four or five stiff ones instead of his usual two or three. The others in the chapel procession were looking funny, too, like they knew something was amiss but were trying to pretend that it would be okay.

Byron Folley pulled at his clerical collar as he walked up the aisle and there was sweat on his face and he wasn't even pretending to be singing the hymn. The Reverend Paul Oakes was there, too, dragging himself along, looking pale and withered, and carefully glancing over at Charlie Springfield every now and then as if afraid the younger man might drop in his tracks. Years before, Charlie Springfield had been his protégé; they went back a long way together: the kind of friendship between an older man and a younger with little in common but a rock-bottom faith.

Everything went just fine until the sermon came along, and then things stopped going fine. Everybody knew it the instant the last verse of the sermon hymn was being sung and the Reverend Springfield pulled himself up from his seat in the choir stalls and staggered up the steps of the pulpit. The youngest boys knew because they were in the front and they could see his angry, vacant eyes, which searched the high spaces of the chapel for inspiration. The faculty and trustees and the president's adviser and the CIA boys sitting farther back realized it because they knew from long experience how a man looks and behaves when he has had a few too many.

The Reverend Springfield had the look of a prophet about him and he let 'em have it right between the eyes. As the hymn ground to a halt, he gripped the sides of the pulpit, where two carved pelicans waited in silent vigil, gripped so hard that his knuckles rose like white knobs; then, as if he might be having second thoughts, he began to sway back and forth. His large livid face bunched tightly around the eyes, which glared, yellow-gray and slightly bloodshot, at the congregation, like the eyes of the world-weary hunter who's been on the trail of his quarry for years and, at the very moment the prey's in the crosshairs, realizes the meaning was all in the chase and not the kill.

"Good mornin'. . . ." he bellowed in his best Carolina drawl, which he knew immediately put all the Yankee establishment on edge. He pointed his finger at us as he fumbled with the slips of paper in his copy of *Essays and Prayers,* where he had scribbled a few notes. He roared mightily: "My subject is pride, pride and doubt. I speak of life-destroying pride, death-defying pride, spirit-devouring pride that with ambitious aim sets itself against the love of God."

Then he really let us have it, using the poet Milton as his main text, warning the powerful and influential gathered before him how those who make them idols are like unto them, and so is everyone that trusteth in them. He tore into the presumptions of U.S. foreign policy in Vietnam. Then he began speaking of the rebel angels, measuring our pride against theirs. Who the hell did we think we were, for even the goddamn angels, he shouted, the rebel angels, were kicked out of heaven because of excess pride, yes, even the angels. . . .

I couldn't resist a glance at the Williams Memorial, in front of which Bobby and Suzanne sat and beamed with seraphic smiles.

Charlie turned to the pages of *Essays and Prayers,* letting us know he was dipping into the dark waters of the Winsted pedigree.

"'What is this path of darkness we are treading with such a fixed and obdurate countenance, looking neither forward nor back to ask why, why the path of darkness? For the path, like the river of life, is long; like the river of Time, it floweth we know not where, but on its waters we are bound for eternity . . . black and white, North and South, in destiny shared.'"

His voice echoed down the nave, where the president's adviser and the trustees and the faculty must have been twisting a little in their seats. I noticed Elliot Goddard, too, with a rancid smile on his face.

"Don't you see?" he howled, eyeing no one but eyeing all. The young-est boys right below him looked up with wonder because they'd never heard a grown man go on like this. "Don't you see our presumption in claiming this jus divinum for ourselves, our nation: to reach out our hand and force our will where we have no right to be? Beware the temptation of God-like reason that seeks to expose what is mortal and unsure to all that fortune, death, and danger dare, even for an eggshell . . . yes, gentlemen, even for an eggshell. We forget who we are. We hear only the song of fools; we overstep our bounds and trample indiscrim-inately in places we are not wanted."

Byron Folley sat rigidly in his seat, not moving a muscle, as if he were facing a firing squad. Mr. Oakes sat hunched over, his face obscured by his large hand, which pawed steadily at his ravished brow. While Virgil Dabney, seated in the shadows at the side of the nave, glowered with a sardonic scowl.

"Listen to the sage advice of Seneca, who wrote"—and he fum-bled for a slip of paper, this for Virgil's crew—"on the importance of simplicity, modesty, and restraint in public affairs; frugality and thrift—mercy that is as sparing with another's blood as though it were its own, knowing that it is not for man to make wasteful use of man. One must learn the pleasure, wrote Seneca . . . the small satisfaction of knowing that we know nothing. Yes, gentlemen, my fine esteemed friends, we must learn our limits, for we have fallen on evil days. 'For sweetest things turn sourest by their deeds; Lilies that fester smell far worse than weeds.'"

Max shoved his elbow into my side as he caught his mentor's eye. "De Vere," he said, and sighed, his eyes brimming with tears.

The Reverend Springfield pulled himself up as high as he could in the carved pulpit, where the two stoic pelicans seemed to buoy him on sturdy wings. Then he spread his arms in Miltonic rage.

"'O shame to men!'" He bellowed. "'Devil with devil damned firm concord holds, men only disagree of creatures rational, though under hope of heavenly grace: and God proclaiming peace, yet live in hatred, enmity, and strife among themselves, and levy cruel wars, wasting the earth, each other to destroy.'"

He paused for effect, panting and passionate.

"These, too, are the toils of sin and pride and arrogance."

Byron Folley remained pale and motionless. Mr. Oakes was still bent over, his face hidden from view. Max, beside me, had tears streaming down his cheeks. I could not resist a look over my shoulder to where the president's adviser sat listening intently, and right behind, with their elegant wives, the CIA men faced stoically forward. Elliot sat there beaming—relishing the weave of art and politics—with his stunning wife and his eldest daughter, who had flown up from Washington that morning. Two of his compatriots were in the row behind, two grandsons of a former president: One had orchestrated a coup d'état against Iran's prime minister, Mohammad Mosaddegh in 1953; the other had once headed the CIA technical division that developed biological poisons for use against Castro and enemies in the Congo. Behind them, another classmate of my father's and close colleague of Elliot's; his hobby as a boy had been making train schedules, and he had gone on to develop the North Atlantic convoy system, then the Marshall Plan and the U-2 spy plane, topping his career with the master plan for the Bay of Pigs. He took the fall for that failed operation, or failed execution; he was given the congressional Medal of Honor and dismissed from the CIA. The night before, I had seen him prowling his old haunts in the library, where as a young boy he had composed those railroad timetables to amuse himself. These men knew when their heritage and pedigree were being invoked in a critique of itself. Nor were they immune to self-scrutiny, these honorable men; they had made their moral calculation: for the greater good.

"'What if earth . . .'" boomed Charlie Springfield, tears welling in his unhappy eyes, "'what if earth be but the shadow of heaven, and things therein, each to other like, more than on earth is thought?' And what if we, the outcast of the world, the tired and hungry and persecuted who arrived on these distant shores in search of a new kingdom, a new paradise on earth . . . what if we shall become like those rebel angels, thinking ourselves like them—self-begot, self-raised, and sui generis." He pointed an admonishing finger to dissuade us from such ideas of American exceptionalism. "Our puissance is our own?"

He nodded at us sagely as a longing smile eased across his fleshy face.

"Is that what it has come down to for us? Is that why we have made this long long journey on the river of Time—come all this far to this new land, in search of some prelapsarian innocence, where we might begin again, make a new start? Lost . . . Oh lost."

He bowed his head for a moment.

"Or will we learn like Job, at least to question—even stand up to our God and say, And where is the place of understanding? Man knoweth not the price thereof." He paused and his eyes gravitated downward and he slowly fingered one of the carved pelicans at his side, the way one would the head of a beloved child.

"Will we learn to accept God's great gift to us . . . the gift of doubt? For that is the price of understanding. For God did not deny Adam and Eve knowledge in the Garden, for the knowledge of good and evil exists for all eternity and is for man to know; but only that man should see that it is not gained by deceit, or quickly, or easily—not as a facile thing to be gained by selfish shortcuts, but a truth enshrouded in doubt, enfolded with love, and finally given as grace is given, freely . . . existing always within you."

He raised his eyes heavenward and smiled as if he would laugh down the moon and stars.

"For, my friends, wisdom and truth begin at home: 'by small accomplishing great things, by things deemed weak subverting worldly strong, and worldly wise by simply meek.'"

He lowered his gaze slightly as though suddenly concerned for the younger boys, who were grouped nearest to him below the pulpit. He looked into their small faces and uncertain eyes and gave them a friendly smile, touching his white vestments where his heart would be, and whispered as if to impart a secret only to them.

"It is inside men"—and he winked at the boys below him—"for there is the garden of your heart's desire, which must be carefully tended; that is where true paradise is found."

A strange, tremulous look came into his eyes, as if some invisible hand had suddenly snatched from him the power of speech. And just like that, he shrugged and retreated to the choir stalls. It was the last sermon he ever gave.

I couldn't help turning again to the stoic face of the president's adviser and wondering what was going through his mind: bobbing in high waves, his poor eyes trained through binoculars on a long line of gray beach, rising and falling in the nauseating swells of that overcast June morning. And there, stretched before him an entire continent all the way to Siberia, there on its very edge defended by concrete bunkers and steel obstacles and barbed wire . . . where tiny figures ran and fell and huddled under a hail of machine-gun fire and mortars, the surf running red with their blood and guts.

At the end of the service, as before, I strategically stationed myself in the ambulatory, helping to tidy up and collect chapel programs. I was able to keep an eye on the departing alumni as they passed my father's memorial. I noted how Elliot Goddard and at least four of his colleagues paused before the inscription, two or three reaching to the carved letters as if to impress an invisible fingerprint in tribute or sorrow.

A patriot . . . a traitor? Or just another name, another lost boy on the river of Time?

Most of the Sunday papers carried a front-page article on the president's adviser's speech. The headlines told of a hardening of U.S. policy toward the North.

The following day, we began marching practice for the Memorial Day parade in the town of Winsted. Charlie Springfield was senior drillmaster. It was an old school custom to participate in the town's Memorial Day parade, which concluded at the town cemetery, where the Civil War dead had been laid to rest. The tradition had been instituted by General Alden, who had led a company of men from the town—though almost two decades before he built his school nearby, most of these had died at Antietam. The marching was judged good for community relations and a worthy experience for the boys to join in the honoring of those men who had died for their country, now including men from the town of Winsted who had died in both the world wars and in Korea. Recently, two twin brothers, drafted together, had been killed in the same unit on the same day in Vietnam. The blue-collar citizens of Winsted were fiercely protective of their memory. Over the last few years, the school's lackadaisical marching had met with little enthusiasm, and in the current rebellious antiwar atmosphere . . . well, the older boys and younger faculty wanted no part of it.

The sixth-form prefects had always been responsible for drilling the younger boys and overseeing the practices, but not this year; they resisted nearly to a man. So Charlie Springfield stepped in and person-ally took over the drilling. We were in for a shock. If he was anything, Charlie Springfield was a mass of contradictions. After all, he was a decorated soldier who had served his country honorably and knew all about the nature of sacrifice. As he had told me, many of his comrades lay under white crosses in the American cemetery on the bluff over-looking Omaha Beach.

So on those luminous and warm sunset evenings after dinner, the newly mown grass fragrant with dew, Charlie Springfield would come limping down to the practice fields, slightly tipsy, laughing and mak-ing quips to the boys about their long hair and disheveled looks. Then suddenly it was all business, and he'd be shouting out commands like a master sergeant, his voice echoing across the green playing fields as he strode up and down the platoons, giving corrections and calling out the cadences until the boys got it right. It was a strange metamorphosis that seemed to come over him, as if the military lingo of drill practice caused something to snap in his brain, as if he were transported back to a different place and time—two worlds struggling inside him.

Often, he would turn just plain ornery and tear into boys on the slightest provocation. That shocked the hell out of me. Maybe it was his drinking; maybe it was the humid heat of those late-spring eve-nings when the sappy cut grass coated our shoes as we marched. It was a disconcerting thing to see the brooding, dark anger begin to well up inside Charlie Springfield as he drilled us, as he began cursing and shouting at us, lecturing us about our slovenly behavior and unpatriotic attitudes. It was as if we were guilty of some obscure sin for which our only expiation was a perfect drill formation. The boys became scared and dumbfounded by his behavior. They grew quiet as the onslaught mounted evening after evening, as though one of their own kind had inexplicably turned on them.

He would run up to a boy in the ranks and yell in his ear. "You slovenly unkempt son of a bitch, you think you can act like this all your damn life—time you grew up; now get the cadence right—right, left, right, left, right, left . . . column to the left . . . march. You scoundrels, you scum, so you think that being Americans means you can sit back on your tender lily white butts all your life and smoke dope 'til the second coming? Think you can just waltz through life without paying your dues? Sometimes a man has gotta learn to fight for the country he loves, for the land his fathers sweated to build and died to defend."

And then inexplicably, Charlie Springfield began turning on Max, yelling and cursing at him, singling him out for special abuse when he was no worse than any of the others. It was bizarre the way he worked Max over, because we knew that he loved Max (he'd already submitted two of Max's short stories to *The Atlantic*). And I saw it get to the point where Max had tears in his eyes, and I swear Charlie Springfield did, too—tears of anger or frustration. It didn't make sense. And poor Max, who could take anything, was shaken up for first time I could remember.

But we got it right. By God, we got it right.

Memorial Day turned out to be brilliantly sunny, with barely a whisper of a breeze as we lined up under the great spreading elms by the schoolhouse to begin our march into town. We were all dressed in white ducks and white shirts, dark blazers, and overseas caps that could not hide the long hair of the older boys, which dangled down to their shoulders, not to mention the peace buttons and flowers prominently displayed on their lapels. Charlie Springfield, sporting his campaign ribbons and a Silver and Bronze Star, inspected the ranks, sending many away to polish up their shoes or change a shirt.

On the stroke of eleven from the schoolhouse bell, we set off toward the town of Winsted, a little more than two miles away. Relations between the school and the locals had been rapidly deteriorating over the past year. To the townies, mostly blue-collar workers from the nearby textile mills and paper factories, Winsted was a school for spoiled rich boys, the sons of the owners of the factories where they and their fathers and grandfathers had spent their lives toiling. And what with the slow, ineluctable demise of the textile factories and the increasing reports of drugs and antiwar agitation on campus, the townspeople were definitely not enthusiastic about our participation in their Memorial Day celebrations. Memories of those twins killed in Vietnam were still raw. We, in turn, had been explicitly warned to avoid any kind of confrontation.

The minute we arrived in the town, the catcalls and snickering began, making it hard to keep calm. Charlie Springfield walked up and down the platoons, his medals gleaming on his lapel, trying to keep our guys in line. He seemed like his regular old self, trying to make jokes, as if we'd done our thing, made a decent show, and didn't really have to take it all that seriously anymore. But then I could see him begin to stiffen and get angry as the abuse from the crowd grew in intensity. It seemed to trigger something in him. He told to us quietly, tensely, that we were to keep looking straight ahead and pretend we hadn't heard a thing.

The main street of the town by the drugstore and firehouse was lined five- or six-deep along the sidewalk. People were waving American flags and pulling apart six-packs of Budweiser. It was twelve o'clock and we were marching right down the center of the street, where there was no shade from the lofty oaks that picketed the parade route. Our shoes pulled on the tarry road surface. The worst of it was that we could move only at a snail's pace. There were Boy Scout and Girl Scout troops in front of us and then veterans from the local VFW post, none of them moving very fast. It soon turned into a humiliating experience as we were forced to march in place in the blazing heat, forced to put up with the snickering comments from the crowds on the sidewalk. "Rich-boy snobs," "Faggot hippie Commies," "Rich boys never gonna be in the army—daddy will see to that," "Get haircuts, you rich boy creeps," "Gawd sakes alive, they're like a bunch of women; fighting would be too good for them."

Charlie Springfield was getting more and more flushed, and he finally turned to the crowds and shouted for them to shut up. He tried to increase the pace of the march, but there was no speeding up those Scout troops or the veterans from the VFW post. Behind us was a color guard from the army base at Fort Devens and then a band from the local high school. We were right in the middle, cut off, with no retreat possible. Sunlight glinted menacingly off the instruments of the marching band to our rear; splinters of eye-searing chrome sparked on the parked fire engines. It seemed like every can of beer in the crowd reflected back shards of jagged silver. We were told to halt, to keep marching in place. My face was a blur of sweat and heat. Then the abusive language got heaped in bucketfuls. Some began spitting at us.

Charlie Springfield, red-faced, went up to one of the town cops along the parade route and asked him to do something about the abusive behavior of the crowd. The cop smiled at him icily from behind his dark glasses and shrugged, obviously enjoying the spectacle and the irritation in Charlie's face. The thickest part of the crowd was centered down a bit farther, by the firehouse, where a lot of teenagers and younger children had gathered to sit on the town's spanking new fire engine to watch the parade. The sixth form was becalmed right in front of them. A frenzy of jeering began. I could see that Charlie was fuming as he yelled for the crowd to be quiet; then he turned on the sixth formers and demanded they hold their tongues. But some of the sixth formers couldn't take it any longer and began eyeing the crowd maliciously, responding first under their breath and then louder, until their cries were as loud as their tormentors'—"Fuck you, buddy; fuck you, asshole"—cries that were like sporadic gasps for air after we'd been drowning under the hail of epithets for a good half hour.

And then the parade slowed down even more, grinding to a halt right in front of that damned fire engine, which seemed perversely to take the glare of that swollen sun and stick it smack in our faces. Charlie hobbled as best he could among the sixth formers and pleaded with them to be quiet, but it did no good. The ranks had broken. We stood defiant. Through the glare I could make out the grinning faces of teenagers and some of the old veterans who were enjoying the three-ring circus. And there was a fat policeman who stood by the fire engine with his hands on his black-belted hips. The bastard was sneering with pleasure.

An ice-cream cone was thrown. It smashed against the white ducks of one of the guys in front of me, a chocolate smear down his leg. Then as if a signal had been given, other bits of food were thrown at us. The ranks became scrambled as we tried to duck the missiles. Charlie Springfield yelled at the fat policeman.

"For Christ's sake, do something, will you!"

The policeman only grunted with amusement and tipped his hat. A beer bottle careened into the rank in front of me, striking someone on the back and shattering on the street. Then a can hit somebody in the head. A boy was down.

Then it happened: Something burst inside Charlie. I saw his jacket open and realized there was a drab olive holster on his hip. He reached under his jacket and pulled out his old service .45 semiautomatic and stood there in front of the crowd and began firing it wildly into the air. Those in the crowd, like a huge multicelled organism, shrieked and fell to the ground or began dashing in all directions. We stood frozen in place—catatonic at the impossible sight, blinking at the quick explosive bursts from the pistol, which shattered the air and seemed to put the whole world into centrifugal motion, except for those of us who remained rooted. Charlie got off seven shots, when the noise of his gun was suddenly joined by the noise of another gun, maybe two or three shots that came from the fat policeman by the fire engine, who must have been a great shot, since two of his bullets hit Charlie Springfield right in the chest and the third seemed to take off his right ear. Charlie just stood there, barely moved by the impact, as if surprised by all the commotion, his eyes suddenly very peaceful. He lowered his arm and looked queerly at the pistol in his hand, as if he didn't quite know why it was there, and kept looking as he slumped to the pavement. For a moment, he knelt on the tarmac as if in prayer and then pitched forward onto his face. I think he must have been dead by the time he was down; that policeman had known where to place his shots. Max was the first one to him. He grabbed Charlie up as one would a lover, both arms around him to support his body, as if lifting him from the earth would save him, but he was gone.

The death of Charlie Springfield—Christian Foster in Max's novel—forms the central climax of his narrative. The protagonist's shocking loss of his only friend and mentor on the faculty precipitates his slide into depression, from which he escapes only with the publication of his first short stories. But Max adjusted the facts in a way that proved not only unfair to Charlie but harmful to his family: the cause of the lawsuit a decade later by Charlie's son, Josh, who for years had shared his Twinkies with Max when he baby-sat for the Springfields. In the novel, Max described how Charlie fired two shots in the air and, seemingly stunned and then despairing at the chaos of screaming spectators, turned the gun on himself, firing a single shot to the head. A suicide. Max's lawyer claimed artistic license. Max said, to use a more recent term, that Charlie's action constituted a suicide by cop: Charlie would have known the likely outcome of pulling a gun in a crowd and beginning to shoot with police present. I was there; I saw the look of surprise and bafflement on Charlie's face; something had snapped in his mind and, for a terrible moment, he lost touch with reality. I suspect he may not even have remembered that his gun was loaded, and he abhorred violence. Utter incomprehension filled his eyes as he slumped to the street, and an unwillingness to leave us or his family. At the inquest, an investigator testified that the ammunition had been purchased over ten years before; his wife said the .45 had been kept at the back of a top shelf with all his old army gear and that she'd never known him to take it down except on Memorial Day.

Max and I and others testified at the inquest on the shooting, but it didn't change anything. The cop said that there had been children about and that a man who was blasting away into the air could just as easily have lowered his aim. And I suppose he was right, although I made the point that I thought Charlie had gotten off seven shots, which meant the .45 was empty, unless there had been a round in the chamber. The forensic expert agreed the gun was empty, but the cop only shrugged. "Who's counting?" he said. When the investigating panel was presented with an affidavit from a psychiatrist in Boston who described treatment for manic depression and a family history of schizophrenia, the case was open and shut. I have a distinct aural memory of those shots. I often hear them in my sleep—seven distinct shots, even after all the other shooting I've heard. It was as if the world I had once known, which had been crumbling through my fingertips, was obliterated in a matter of seconds, scattered like that crowd was scattered.

We never reached the cemetery that Memorial Day, the place where the town assembles once a year to pay their respects to the war dead, going back to three minutemen, one who died in skirmishes as the British retreated to Boston in 1775, and two others at Bunker Hill. My great-grandfather is buried there. He could have been buried in Brookline, near the family homestead, where his ancestors are buried, or at Elysium, where he was happiest. But he chose this mill town cemetery, and, as with the location for the school he founded, he chose wisely. Here were buried more soldiers from his regiment, who had died at Antietam, than anywhere else; mill workers and sons of mill workers, they had all enlisted on the same day in June 1861. That was why he chose to become one of them. In the end, he wanted to be near the men he had led into battle. That responsibility never ceased to weigh on him. When I return to school for reunions, I leave time to walk the winding road into town and down Main Street and past the firehouse, where I halt a moment to remember, and up into the low hills above the Naushon River to visit that lovely cemetery with its crowning red oaks and scattershot of white azaleas, where I pay my respects at my great-grandfather's grave, which sits among those of men who died for their country. The stone is a simple granite marker and contains only his name and dates and an inscription: *He ably led his men in the cause of abolition. Let the bell of freedom ring.*

Since my school days, since the loss of those twin brothers, there have been a few added graves of soldiers who died in Vietnam, along with a few more of recent vintage. I visit their graves, too. I never knew them . . . and yet I do.

☿
☓

13 IN THE WEEKS AFTER THE SHOOTING, MAX and I became closer than we'd been before or since, at the very moment we'd grown most apart. Charlie had been the father Max had always longed for. His grief allowed us a short-lived intimacy, whether holding his hand while talking him out of a depressive stupor or rubbing his back while he practiced the Aaron Copeland pieces for Charlie's memorial service. Max shed the dandy persona of just eight months before and became a sober denizen of the library carrels, where he wrote his first short stories, and where I often discovered him staring at Thomas Wolfe's *Of Time and the River*, Charlie's personal copy, given to Max shortly before Memorial Day: a peace offering after the cruel bullying during marching practice. It was a thirties edition, with a tattered olive green Art Deco cover, underlined and annotated throughout. "It's like having something of him alive to me." And Max imitated Charlie's cadence perfectly: "A greatly flawed novel . . . but ah-ha-ha, what magnificent flaws."

Max squeezed my hand. "Charlie wanted me to have it—like he knew, so I wouldn't forget him."

He went on a lot like that.

The trustees, in their infinite wisdom, decided to close Winsted for ten days before final exams to let the boys return to the comforting arms of their parents. The board dealt with the publicity fallout, as if anyone except the school community could care less with America's inner cities on fire, protestors taking over campuses, and Robert Kennedy's assassination only weeks away. That was when I made a fatal error of judgment. Max was just so down, so devastated at the thought

271

of returning to his mother's new studio apartment on the Upper West Side, conveniently near her Julliard students; she'd been ousted from her ex-husband's swanky place on Fifth Avenue, where his twenty-two-year-old playmate ruled the roost.

"Boobs to die for, but the thought of them going at it next to my bedroom makes me want to throw up."

"Well, I guess, we could go up to Elysium. Peace and quiet to study for our AP exams."

"Hermitage! Your Impala or my Mustang, Hawkman?"

I picked him up at his mother's dowdy Riverside Drive apartment.

Max threw his bag into the backseat and wrinkled his nose. "It's like strudel-stinking Vienna in there. She's packed the place with a menagerie of Biedermeier antiques. *And* her Viennese dialect gets more unintelligible each day. Worse, she refuses to speak *your father's language.*"

We headed up the Hudson for the Taconic Parkway. The early June sunshine in the newly leafed trees was glorious, heralding our escape from the teeming mess on every front page in the country. I tried to warn him about some of the idiosyncrasies of our place at Elysium.

He waved it off, "You think *you* have issues? A stinking Shylock for a father [Jack had taken away the Mustang], who glories in his adopted WASPness and now plans to marry one—she's pregnant, I hear. And a mother who pretends Mauthausen was a holiday camp—who identifies with the monsters that destroyed her people. . . . What's not to like about *my* family."

But my reservations blew away in the green miles we put between ourselves and the city, evaporating in the rising pressure in our ears as we sluiced into the foothills of the Berkshires. With the turn onto the winding gravel road that marked the beginning of our property, we became goofy kids again. A look of anticipation flooded Max's eyes as the forest began to embrace us, lacing the strip of blue above with pointy hemlock boughs and tawny oaks and the white pines' soaring urgency. In the overgrown pastures hemmed with toppled fieldstone walls, deer and wild turkeys turned a blithe eye at our passing and held their ground. Max leaned out his window to breathe in the loamy scents of pine, stretching out a hand to ride the inland seas of nodding fern lapping the rotted pilings of jagged stumps.

Back then, his rapture quickly became my own, stirred by his inchoate longings, that the felicities of the woods and a literary life might actually save us from life's disasters. But now I recognize, as I do in myself, the hungry look of the grave robber who has stumbled upon his heart's desire: the undisturbed tomb, the fusty air of the inviolate sanctuary, when the first glitters of released time catch the squinty eye of the nimble thief. Yet I was glad for him to be smiling again—that *my* home made him happy. As we neared our cottage, the fiery dance of leaf-filtered sunlight only intensified our glorious mood as the burning incense rising from the winter-steeped pine needles filled our brimming nostrils. And so we broke into our favorite chorus from those long-ago, careless months at Winsted.

"You-o-u, re my brown-eyed girl . . . Do you remember when we used to sing, Sha la la la la la la la la la la te da . . ."

Emerging from the palisades of pine, the mute glimmer of Eden Lake rose before us, reflecting jade shadows across the sky. Here, my family's last line of defense against the successes and failures of life, public and private—those dual imposters, as Churchill described them. And for Max, a bountiful harvest of tantalizing themes for his novels yet unborn.

I laughed at his antics as our rustic country house hove into view around the corner of the lake. The spring light, with the leafing oaks and maples still three weeks behind their lowland cousins, glittered on the walls of raw fieldstone, here and there splashed with sandy hues of umber and bluish gray, and this transformed into scintillating pebbled planes of sunlight as we pulled into the drive. The deep-set leaded glass windows in the stonework simmered with a dull, forbidding opacity under the severely angled roofline. Max whistled and jumped out of the car, looking up at the exotic Romanesque turrets and dormer windows that shouldered the steep roof: a raggedy mimic of the European prototypes that had first inveigled my great-grandfather in his engineering classes at Harvard before the Civil War. Beneath a cone-shaped central cupola, crowned with an ice-damaged weather vane, sat a welcoming dovecote of vaguely Chinese design, which, for as long as anyone could remember, had been taken over by bats and barn swallows in the spring.

Grabbing my textbooks from the trunk and hurrying in Max's wake, I found myself somehow changed, strangely beguiled by the Tiffany windows, which pulsed with reflected tones of green and turquoise and cerulean blue, lending an airy grace to an otherwise-ponderous exterior by Richard Morris Hunt. Having Max buzzing at my elbow was like acquiring an extra set of eyes, a brain transplant: I was placed in the odd position of both defending my family and parrying his genuine enthusiasm with ironic demurrals. I realized, as if for the first time, that my home was hardly lovable, except by those accustomed to its crazy quilt of rooms, off-kilter diamond-patterned windows, and hidden alcoves and chunky Arts and Crafts furniture, much less the sprawl of heirlooms that spoke to the eclectic taste of General Alden, abetted by his wife and then his daughter-in-law, who, decade by decade, had judiciously culled the more offensive and uncomfortable furniture. My grandmother, true to her New England antiquarian genes, had been careful to preserve the essential character of the 1890s, reupholstering when possible or replacing the broken-down "back-breakers" when necessary with period reproductions and strategically inserted foam padding.

For me, it had never been about tradition or antiquarian fidelity; it was simply the world as I found it: my father's home, a place as integral to the landscape of my youth as the white pines that shadowed the creeping hours, their ambrosial scent on warm dry days when the breeze blew off the lake the very essence of childhood well-being.

Max cased the joint like a second-story man on the prowl. He flattened his nose to the windows and cantered his fingers along the swirls of leaded glass as he hummed Ravel's "Pavanne for a Dead Princess." On the lakeside veranda where my grandmother had spent so many of her summer hours, he blew the pollen dust off the back of a wicker rocker, tested the porch swing on its creaking chains, and dipped a finger in a fifteenth-century baptismal font—a crud-filled birdbath—and pronounced himself satisfied with the view.

I dutifully played the cicerone he demanded of me, trying to distance myself by adopting my grandmother's lecturing tone. I pointed out the family portraits, the shelves of photo albums and scrapbooks, the huge bluestone fireplaces, and mantelpieces festooned with seventeenth-century copperware heirlooms and clunky stopped clocks. With ritual gravitas, I wound the three largest clocks in the cherry-wood-paneled living room, each with its rusty key and distinctive and charming chime—the first job handed down to me as a child by grandmother. But Max couldn't wait, pushing on to the next room, and the next, pausing only a moment lest a first impression escape him, his eyes electric with tinctures of emerald green as he turned guiltily to the sunlight flooding the Tiffany skylights.

"It's so fucking magnificent—if a tad dark and dowdy," he blurted. "It *is* you; it reeks of the dark prince Hal—you, you mossback antediluvian, you history-encrusted barnacle."

I made a point of showing Max the paintings in our small gallery, thinking he'd like that, given his infatuation with Isabella Williams's collection at Palazzo Fenway in Boston. My mother had banished "those gloomy George Innesses" from the apartment in New York, so all thirteen Inness landscapes were now together again in the Inness Gallery, custom-built for the purpose. All were late examples from the 1880s: moody, poetic, contemplative, mostly scenes of abandoned meadows where a few magnificent trees presided at day's end, the pellucid atmosphere of dusk something you could cut with a knife.

As had been the case with Winsted, General Alden and Samuel Williams split the duties of the Elysium syndicate; Samuel took care of the lake and its swimming beach, the general took charge of the reforesting and conservation of the ten thousand acres of land. He drafted armies of laborers from the docks of New York and Boston to dam an old mill stream and build the lake, christened Eden Lake by Samuel Williams. Paths were hacked out through the underbrush and laurel so their wives, both famous society ladies of the day, could pass unencumbered in their wide skirts. Streams were bridged and bluestone slabs laid down where the footing was precarious. And year by year, the woods, cut by the first settlers, began to slowly return, along with the wildlife. Extraordinary berry patches sprang up, to the delight of children, and became the favored destination of family walks. White pine and hemlock began to reclaim the abandoned fieldstone-walled pastures, along with white, red, and chestnut oaks, and the silver birch that took to the old meadows like a lost love. Within decades, white-tailed deer began to filter back, and with them the black bear and bobcat and even a few nesting bald eagles. By the turn of the century, visitors were remarking in the guestbook about how thrilled they were to see game again in the forest, to feel "the wildness of the land as it once was." It was no small achievement, a wilderness preserve only a few hours by train from New York and Boston. Spurred on by the conservation ethic of his friends Theodore Roosevelt and Gifford Pinchot, General Alden had been ahead of his time. The annual summer vacation became a pilgrimage to "our woods," a joyous event dutifully recorded in the guestbook year after year, summer after summer: "We are back! . . . The woods welcome us again! . . . Oh, woods and fields and Eden Lake—our true self!"

"Far-out," purred Max as we finished going through the first of the photo albums. "So this is your domain, Hawkman, your dark, forbidding castle, your nefarious robber-baron past. You don't really call it Elsinore, do you?"

It was, in fact, named after my great-grandmother, Elsie Whitney Davenport.

"And your robber barons, by the way, were considered the nouveau riche opportunists by my great-grandfather; he was *old* Boston."

"No doubt."

Max, with a frenzy that seemed to feed on itself, grabbed for the other albums and scrapbooks, eager to stuff his craw with yet another precious load of primary sources. I guided him through the warren of black-and-white Kodaks, most faded to sepia: the garden parties and boating regattas on the lake, the tall, handsome women in billowing silk and taffeta dresses posed with teacups and parasols and sailor-suited children. Max often stayed my hand as I turned the pages, his quivering fingers resting on a photograph of the soaring cupolas and wide verandas of Stanford White's Hermitage across the lake, where Isabella's and Amory's artists and wannabe artists, musicians and playwrights, set the tone with string quartets and later jazz bands by the lakeshore, creating sylvan tableaux in the sprawling rose gardens, where, at the end of Max's hovering finger, fleets of canoes and rowboats, and a sleek silver-beaked gondola imported from Venice, all hung with Chinese lanterns, drifted like ghostly fireflies over the black water.

"Ah," intoned Max, "'to burn always with this hard, gemlike flame.'"

And in his echoed aphorism of Pater, a realization came to me of how close our family and the Williams family had once been during those endless undisturbed summers of genteel elegance and carefree pursuits, as memories of the Civil War faded and the mechanized slaughter of the First World War was yet to be.

I led Max to the floor-to-ceiling shelves in the library. Books by the yard in finest morocco bindings exactly as those long-dead idlers had left them. The complete works of Shakespeare, Thackeray, Dickens, Cooper, Longfellow, Trollope, Irving, Sand, Tolstoy, along with the great historians Herodotus, Thucydides, Gibbon, Macaulay, Carlyle, Parkman, Motley, Henry Adams, and dozens more. But pride of place went to a long shelf containing signed and inscribed editions of Emerson and Thoreau, along with those of Burroughs, Muir, Theodore Roosevelt, and his circle of naturalists.

"They *read*!" said Max, in a hoarse whisper. Slowly, he ran a finger-tip—oh how lovingly—across the ranks of bindings, drawing a dusty trail of gold-stamped titles.

I took down a particularly precious volume that my grandmother had shown me summer after summer from the time I could read. On the frontispiece in a beautiful blue but faded script was an inscription and signature and date: *To my young friend—and a most gifted scholar and patriot, John Alden. May these words offer you solace and distraction in the face of the vexing duties you have assumed. Ralph W. Emerson, Concord, June 7, 1861.*

"He *knew* Emerson?"

"Yes—well, and they corresponded until Emerson's death." I closed the book of Emerson's essays and carefully replaced it on the shelf and smiled to myself. "A little *too* American—n'est-ce pas?"

"Oh," cried Max as he again reached to those gold-embossed names, "to be numbered with such immortals."

Max chuckled as he lingered over a scrapbook of postcards and correspondence from summer idylls in Venice, the antique time-lapse photographs of canals and piazzas, where fashionable couples sweltered in crinoline stillness. The last page contained snapshots of my grandmother and grandfather on their honeymoon, standing on the balcony of Isabella Williams's Palazzo Barberini.

"My grandfather was a child trying to survive the Tsar's pogroms," said Max, staring at a snapshot of family members in a gondola by the Gritti. "But on my mother's side"—his voice rose with pride—"they lived a grand life in Vienna, going to the opera, hanging out with musicians and composers—and *honeymooning* in Venice." I heard his mother's soft Viennese intonation in those words, as if maybe, just maybe, he yearned—if just for a moment—to believe in her Belvedere and St. Stephen's fantasies.

"Oh, Hawkman, if only you'd been with me that summer in Venice. How we'd have danced the light fantastic till dawn!"

Not a little in love with Max's fantasies, I threw caution to the wind and conducted Max to a small sunless back room, "the archive room," my grandmother had always called it, where she had spent her last years sifting through and organizing all the family's papers and cor-respondence. When I opened the door and flipped on the light, Max became breathlessly silent. On the highest shelves were boxes of letters and documents relating to my great-grandfather's Civil War service, and his years out west, and the many veterans groups of which he was a member (for good reason, she had refused all entreaties by Harvard to take on General Alden's papers). The middle shelves consisted of boxes storing the records of his buildings in New York, the railroad stations he'd designed, and his records and letters detailing the early days of Winsted and Elysium. The lowest shelves contained documents relating to the Great War and my grandfather's "glory days" at Harvard Medical School.

I pulled out some volumes of my grandmother's collection of *The New York Times* war supplements, a weekly magazine section devoted to news and photographs of the Great War in Europe. The supplements consisted mostly of photographs printed, as proudly stated on the masthead, by the new rotogravure process, which graphically detailed the genesis of the horror, beginning with lines of jaunty young soldiers marching off to war, and then, in issue after issue over four long years, the transformation of that quaint postcard Europe into a twentieth-century hell of mud and trenches: blackened muddy seas of shattered trees and breastworks, seeded with the shredded flesh of obliterated lives, flayed bodies enmeshed in the barbed wire like tattered moths in a spider's web: how many hundreds of thousands cut down by interlocking fields of machine-gun fire?

I could feel Max tense up—he had no stomach for such things. I noticed his trembling fingers as he picked through those fragile pages, acidic paper crumbling at our touch: the unimaginable abomination of it all. I directed his attention to one issue in particular, which had riveted me as a kid, a full-page photo of the ruins of Louvain Cathedral. "Just a pile of rubble," I said, and shrugged, remembering my early fascination. "I always wondered how God could exist if he allowed such destruction of his holy places."

Max chuckled nervously.

"Not to mention, *dear God*, the people—huh?"

"I was just a kid."

"Good instincts, though."

But what I wanted to make clear to Max was that my grandfather was not a soldier, but an army surgeon. I showed him the collection of exuberant letters he wrote to my grandmother and General Alden on the way to the front, how he took pride only in saving the lives of the wounded. His horror, if that's what he felt as the wounded and dying arrived at the medical station, was tempered by exhilaration at the technical experience he gained. A lifetime's work compressed into months. "How strange to be up to my elbows in gore, my eyes strained to the limit, my head reeling with the stink, and yet I get better by the hour, by the day, until I almost believe myself capable of raising the dead—if only it were so and not a case of nervous madness." He wrote to his father, General Alden, telling him of the medical advances he was pioneering to handle traumatic wounds, knowing well the stories of the general's agony at Antietam: General Alden had to warn off two surgeons—putting his pistol in the face of one—who were intent on amputating his shattered leg.

General Alden died in the influenza epidemic of 1918, a month after he got the news of his son's death in France. My grandmother, who nursed him in his final weeks, who grieved for her husband as the general grieved for his son, told me, as she lay in her hospital bed at Lenox Hill, of the General's one consolation, "that at least his son, my husband, had died saving lives and not taking them."

None of this found its way into Max's novel, nor mention of my grandfather's grizzly medical notebooks, many pages spotted with blood—and perhaps iodine—where he had diagramed and described surgical procedures for dealing with the most traumatic wounds. Such procedures had been considered impossible before the war. The notebook, with commentary by other military surgeons, was published in a facsimile by Harvard Medical School in 1921: the bible on the subject until the Second World War gave another generation of surgeons an opportunity to further refine his pioneering work. Max finally pushed the pages away before he became physically sick. And as he did, I remembered Colonel Fairburn's words to me, trying to explain my father's inexplicable detestation of machines. In those medical notebooks was the grisly apogee of a century's perfection of killing technology. It had cut the heart out of my family and left an exposed nerve—inexpressible in so many words.

If Max was similarly moved, it is not reflected in *Like a Forgotten Angel*. Not that he was he exempt from ruminations about his own heritage. The First World War had sent his father's family fleeing from a Ukrainian ghetto to New York's Lower East Side, while the males on his mother's side got swept up in the officer ranks of the Austrian army—killing a good number of Italians at Caporetto, ultimately keeping them in Vienna under the illusion of being decorated veterans and patriotic Austrians, thus easy pickings for a later and even more systematic slaughter.

I think we were glad, finally, to get out of that stuffy and depressing little room, my grandmother's prodigy of organizational genius with a time fuse attached. She never believed in making it easy for me, or my father; she rarely gave it to you whole hog, but delivered her clues in discreet packages—verbal, written, or by dropped hints—letting time and circumstances work their will on the recipient's capacity to discern the import.

In the master bedroom, I pointed out a photo in a silver frame on the bedside table. It had belonged to my grandmother, a photo she had often noted to me as a child, and which had been with her at Lenox Hill during her last illness. The photo was of my grandfather in 1917, dressed in a medical officer's khaki uniform on the front lawn of Elsinore the morning he left to go off to France. In the photo, my father, aged three, is standing next to him, a little toddler in a cowboy suit reaching up to the leather holster of his soldier father. The child holds a cricket bat in his other hand. There is a look of rapt fascination in that face, perhaps proud, perhaps attracted to the new uniform, though at three he could scarcely have known what it was all about. His father, for his part, does not seem to acknowledge his son in any way, but stares off with a taciturn smile, his cap placed at a jaunty angle off a widow's peak.

I often wondered if it even crossed my grandfather's mind that he might not come back. Did he go down to the lake, as my father had on his last day, for a final look, to linger in the shade of the pines and breathe in their blissful scent? So safe, so infinitely far from those cruel battle lines of hellish mud and bloated flesh, which he, too, must have glimpsed in *The New York Times*. Maybe like so many in his generation, he was simply thrilled at the chance to serve a noble cause, a war to end all wars, to remake the world in America's image.

My grandfather's death really was a freak, and it happened only two weeks before the armistice. My grandmother was changed by the shock: A curtness and reticence, some called it "a remove," replaced her once-girlish effervescence. She became adept at going through the proper motions of being a war widow. I heard anecdotes around the dinner table from old friends about how she got caught up in the party swirl of the twenties and was considered something of a hard drinker and flirt. But once her grief had subsided and no one else came along "who could hold a candle to your grandfather," she settled down soberly, taking over the Winsted board in 1927 (when she got Amory Williams fired as headmaster and brought in Jack Crocket), throwing herself into charity work in the Depression, endowing hospitals and professorships at medical schools in memory of her husband, and later scholarships for disadvantaged youths and black students from the Deep South—the very thing that had brought Jerry Gadsden my way, only for him to turn his back on me.

Grandmother also made darn sure her darling son got all the best. My father was raised pretty much at arm's length, first by nannies and later by the finest tutors money could buy, and, of course, went off to Winsted as soon as he was old enough. She did not cling to him; she did not inflict her grief on him, because that would have been selfish and harmful. When I was growing up and questioned my grandmother about my father, she would list his accomplishments in a very even tone, as if reading them off a CV. "Not to give you ideas" was a favored expression. Her "remove" lingered, as if, so it seemed to me, her son were never quite real to her, as if once burned, her second love could only be a tepid reminder of the first, and possibly as ephemeral. An attitude that could only have been hardened by circumstances, when her son survived the war "by the skin of his teeth," only to disappear under extremely suspicious circumstances in Berlin, with only a pathetic cover story for explanation. She never displayed grief for her son in my presence and scolded my mother if she did so. "Feeling sorry for yourself," I heard her say more than once to my mother, "is not only a waste of time, but an unkind imposition on John's son. What's past is past; progress in moving forward is the only thing that counts."

And she never forgave my mother for spreading her son's ashes on Lake Carnegie at Princeton.

"Just like you," said Max, replacing the silver-framed photo, "your dad grew up without a father. We are all Prince Hals—huh, Hawkman, Richard the Second and Eddie de Vere—fatherless exiles all."

"Spare me."

"'O cursed spite, that ever I was born to set it right.'"

Max would play on these themes in his novels: that the fatherless child will fill the vacuum in his life with something grander, with an idealized version that will serve as a foundation for an allegiance far stronger than any flesh-and-blood model would have warranted. This bit of pop psychology is, I suppose, why absent fathers suffered such distortion in his pages, as when Max turned his very alive and kicking father—and a doting one at that—into a caricature of a social-climbing Jewish banker, cruelly dispensing with many of Jack Roberts's endearing and generous traits, all to make him a better foil for his bookish, introverted son. If anything, the caricature of his fictional stepmother is even crueler; after *Like a Forgotten Angel*'s publication in 1978, she had to stop going to parties because of the stares and snarky questions invariably put to her.

"So, where's that room of your dad's—the one you used to tell me about, the one at the top of the stairs? Remember, you once told me you had a dream about that room."

Not only had I forgotten the dream; I'd forgotten I'd told Max.

Max had already spotted the spiral staircase with its banister of carved rosewood and twigwork leading to the upper story. He just barged ahead, barely able to conceal his pleasure as he began counting each of the many stairs like a kid with a bad case of OCD.

"Fifty-one," he announced, running his hands admiringly over the rosewood railing, "fifty-two, fifty-three steps to heaven."

My father's childhood room, and his father's before him, was a kind of purpose-built hideaway under the eaves, showing the angles of the roof in the tongue-and-groove paneled walls and ceiling. A dormer window of leaded glass with a small window seat overlooked the lake. From a child's perspective, that westward view seemed to be at one with the topmost branches of the tallest white pines that grew in profusion along the lakeshore. By afternoon, the room was transfigured by the luminous plumage of the pine boughs; every breath of air that stirred the needles sent a thousand shimmering tones of green cascading inward, a light transmuted and diced in the leaded glass and then refracted off the shiny oak flooring, until the whole room throbbed like the inside of an emerald. The catbird seat was the swivel chair at my father's Stickley desk with its inviting pigeonhole compartments. From there, the panorama of the treetop skies unfolded in a never-ending display. Who needed dreams when an endless daydream presented itself each time one glanced up from the Underwood typewriter? This had been my father's retreat from his nannies and tutors and from a very demanding mother, where his boyhood aspirations amidst his father's books on natural history and medicine had taken first flight.

"Oh my God!" Max exclaimed as he turned from the window and

spied the typewriter on the desk. This was the green Underwood on which my father had written all his early journal articles and books. Max bent and tapped the keys and then let himself down in the swivel chair, testing it, tilting forward and back, right and left, moaning as he reached again to the keys, as if to the opening phrases of a Mozart sonata, his words a distorted echo of my own hopes. "It's a writer's dream—my dream, not yours—for a novelist, not a knucklehead scholar of everything dead and dying."

"Well, thanks a fucking lot."

"Adopt me, graft me . . . just exile me to this room—I'll do anything."

He sprang up and kissed me on the forehead before busying himself ransacking the place. Attila would have been impressed with his thoroughness.

I drifted over to the window, as if to allow some alter ego of myself to freely rifle my father's things, some fictitious self that I had sought to embrace for Max's sake, at great risk of everything I wanted to believe in. I thought of the Green Berets holding hands in prayer at the Bull Run, and how uncomfortable the sight had made me. Watching Max on the prowl, I had the oddest sensation, a kind of otherness, as if I'd stepped out of the loyal circle of the people I loved, whose blood I carried, only to find them returned to me changed, at a remove—as I would years later, in a story not my own and forever out of reach.

I had spent years reassembling my own narrative, pulling together the artifacts of my father's life, which my mother had carelessly dispersed to the attic and his hideaway at Elysium, including boxes of his books and memorabilia from the house on P Street, his office at Princeton, and what had originally been my grandmother's apartment on Fifth Avenue, where he grew up. The only way she'd gotten away with this sacrilege was because, in grandmother's last years, she could no longer manage those fifty-three steps to the top floor. "You go up there and take care of it," she'd tell me. "Time is on my side—and yours, too, for the truth will always out. You stick to your guns no matter what anybody tells you." In this, she was a stoic, like Thoreau (she kept a volume of his journal writings on her bedside table), through and through. "Keep your eyes peeled—use your head; don't let anything slip by." And she'd laugh as she'd wave a hand in front of my face, as if wondering if there was anything behind my distracted gaze.

Besides my father's books, the built-in oak shelves contained his collections of flora and fauna pretty much as he'd had them as a boy—I'd

taken care of it—neatly labeled with their Linnaean classifications
(how he'd taught himself Latin), along with the arrowheads, the rock
samples, the albums of coins and stamps. Then there were the athletic
trophies and medals from Winsted and Princeton. Max pounced like
a relic hunter, fingering the cups and ribbons, weighing them in his
hand, as if only by appropriating their concrete reality could he properly describe them in his books yet to be written.

Then he came to the shelf of artifacts from my father's many digs,
most of them shipped from his P Street home in Washington. Max
began fingering the terra-cotta votive figures with their pointy breasts,
the large painted shards of Late Minoan and Late Mycenaean ware,
and a fragment of a fired clay tablet with crudely incised symbols.

"What's this?" he asked, examining the strange curlicues.

I took the fragile object from him. "It's part of a Linear B tablet,
probably from Pylos."

"What does it say?"

"Oh, just inventories mostly: chariot axels, perfumed oil,
sheepskins—"

"Your hand's trembling."

"No it's not."

"Your hand's trembling," he repeated.

"Time, Max. Just imagine . . . how long ago."

And I returned this object of deep time to its place on the shelf.

There is a much-commented-upon passage in Max's novel describing
my father's collection of arrowheads—no mention whatsoever of the
Minoan and Mycenaean artifacts—where the narrator lingers in loving
detail over the shape of the points, the mere touch conjuring in his
mind the excitement of first discovery and the primordial world evoked
for the finder.

> Saul's fingers trembled as he caressed the bluestone points, luxuriat-
> ing in the rich veining and tiny undulations on the chipped surfaces,
> seeing in the same moment not his hands, but those of this Über-
> mensch reaching into the earth to extract the arrowhead, freeing it
> from dirt so that the sunlight caught its prismatic surface for the first
> time in hundreds of years. Saul felt the thrill, the erasure of time, and
> the enchantments of those first forests and that near-impenetrable wil-
> derness, where the Indian stalked his prey, when cougar and gray wolf
> roamed at will, before the European diseases ravished and reduced the

indigenous peoples to a shadow of what had been, when the land, wild
and free, had been their Eden.

Saul quickly dismissed such romantic notions. It was the hunting
and killing that would have filled such a man's imagination. A token of
one warrior passed on to another.

Here, in my father's boyhood room, among his books and collections, Max's misbegotten notions of a "warrior cast" had its origins.
Even then I had heard enough from Elliott Goddard and Charles Fairburn and even the president's adviser to know otherwise. I watched
with a detached fascination as Max began going through my father's
photo albums of Winsted: where a young Elliot Goddard sprinted
downfield; where a conspicuously mufti-attired version of the president's adviser stood with a phalanx of uniformed football players. The
later was the team manager and carried a first-aid kit, his steel-rimmed
glasses opaque circles in his unassuming face: "a minion among warriors," as Max would describe him. Except now he directed the fate of
tens of thousands of warriors, including the likes of the Green Berets
I had ogled at the Bull Run. I couldn't help wondering, even then, at
the cruel ironies of such a happenstance. The back of the album had
been pasted with yellowed newspaper cuttings of stunning upsets and
victory bonfires: the days when Winsted football made it to the second
pages of *The Boston Globe* and *New York Times* sports sections. Max
passed over these with barely a ripple of interest; since he had already
pilfered the school archives, this was old hat.

The album assembled by my grandmother, gold-stamped on the
leather cover *Elysium Summers,* Max found even more compelling.
Here was the private world behind the public facade he yearned to
master: the novelist's stock-in-trade. There were photos of my father
in the early years with Bobby Williams, canoeing, hiking, standing on
the diving board (my father was a superb diver and swimmer—the
thing Laura always found most spellbinding about his childhood). As I
watched Max turn the pages, an act that oddly took me out of myself,
as if viewing things from a distant vantage point, I realized how large of
stature my father really was when posed next to his contemporaries in
their bathing suits on the beach; his corded muscles stood out even in
a relaxed pose, and his ever-present shock of dark hair set off his deep-
set eyes. In another photo, he was rowing a shell on Eden Lake, oars
poised for the next stroke, eyes focused with a kind of nervous pent-up

energy. By the last pages, Bobby Williams seemed to have disappeared from these summer sojourns, as if muscled aside by my father's Winsted teammates. They are all there celebrating their recent graduation in the spring of 1932, including Elliot and the president's adviser and at least three others I recognized from Winsted Founder's Days, important players in the CIA. The absence of Bobby Williams, "scion of truth and beauty and a higher calling," from these photos was duly noted by Max the novelist.

"Ringleader?" Max intoned, pointing to a page of photos so titled by my grandmother. "Of running dog imperialist flunkies, no doubt."

"Tough as they come, Max." I dismissed his insouciance and retreated again to the window, opening it for fresh air, happy to again rejoin my aloof self.

The smell of pine and the view made me giddy, full of certainty and happiness of a kind, the home ground that had kept my grandmother going. A lemony orange sun was easing downward through the treetops in a halation of green. I felt a terrible love, and terrible longing—a pang of loss: How could my father have turned his back on all this, and why? A place my grandmother had treasured because her husband and son had loved this place, and that love had become part of their love for one another and so was passed on to me, not in so many words as in the rhythms and habits of her passing days. Even facing death, she did not waver. She was the most unsentimental person I'd ever known, and yet the life of service she led, the steadfast values she adhered to, emanated a love that I felt in every sinew of my body.

That courageous love so absent in my mother.

"One tough banana," my mother liked to say disparagingly. "Cross your grandmother at my peril, not yours." But that was because grandmother put loyalty to family above all things, and family was place. She came from old New England stock, as old as ours, if not as prosperous. But once married, she nailed her standard to the Alden masthead and took her stand. She outlived most of her generation and relished doing so because she thought she could amend their mistakes. I came to accept and then admire her gallows humor, especially during her last stay at Lenox Hill Hospital. She lay there in the semidarkness with the muted roar of traffic on Lexington Avenue beyond the window, her mind sweeping back to her childhood and her ancestors, where she drew strength, passing on anecdotes whose full meaning came to me only in retrospect, as they did in that moment as I stared out at the lake while Max rummaged through my father's books: the truth hiding in plain sight. She was unflinching at the end.

"You are tough for those you love." It was one of the last things she told me, and she'd gripped my hand. Her blue eyes staring up from the hospital pillow still proclaimed her no-nonsense faith in what can be done. "Let the best of the past live through you," she'd whispered, "so the lives of those who came before you, those you have loved and who loved you in turn—errors and all—will not perish from this earth."

And I knew she was defending my father.

Her stoic plea against the dying of the flame—to leave me with the certainties of her life—further confirmed me in the life of an archaeologist. I was reminded of a Greek funeral stele I'd discovered in the classical collections of the Metropolitan Museum, which I visited every day after school on the way to Lenox Hill. Aristocratic families would commission these carved images of their dead, which included a telling epitaph, and erect them in conspicuous places near the family home. Most were for the young who had died of disease or in battle without leaving heirs. In the Met's classical gallery, I'd stare at the handsome sculpted faces of those young men who had died thousands of years before and wonder about them, as I wondered about my father.

Standing by the window over Eden Lake, carapaced in some vague approximation of my maturing impressionable self, I was stunned by how my grandmother's words gained resonance juxtaposed with the handsome face of a young man on a Met stele, a slender column crowned by a winged sphinx, which figured like a place of quiet pilgrimage for me during those last weeks of my grandmother's life. The youth holds a pomegranate in his hand and an aryballos is strapped to his wrist. He must have been quite the confident athlete with his well-formed torso and runner's legs. But it was the dedication from his mother and father that I found most touching, words that referred to the stele almost as if it were a living thing, as if by erecting such a splendid memorial on home ground, something of the spirit of their lost boy might be forever preserved. I couldn't help wondering how long it had stood before a rival clan tore it down or the Persians toppled it just for the pleasure of its destruction. And in that moment, just as Max began his own demolition job, thoughts of that toppled stele brought on a wave of despair, of the violent precariousness of all things: how being right was never enough if fate and matters of perception, as Elliot and

Virgil put it, could trash your best efforts. Tears welled in my eyes at the vulnerability of our life's enterprise.

Turning from the lake and the light hovering around us like the purest emanation of a watery starburst, I made a preemptive strike to convince Max and, truth be told, myself of my father's bona fides. I began by telling him the stories that had been a fixture of my youth, from the lips of our aged caretaker and forest manager—dead five years, Tom Malloy. Tom, a raggedy-assed marine, as he described himself, had been badly wounded in 1918 at Belleau Wood, and my grandfather—they'd practically grown up together at Elysium—had saved his life, removing a machine-gun bullet that had just missed his heart. Tom was probably one of the cases illustrated in my grandfather's surgical notebook, since Dr. Alden had attended him in the postoperative phase of his recovery, when the drains had to be removed from his chest cavity. Tom had been nearby in a recovery ward when the German shell hit Dr. Alden's surgery. In my grandmother's eyes, this coincidence, Tom's proximity to her son in his last moments, who had stitched him back together—much less the vivid proof of my grandfather's handiwork, a jagged ten-inch scar across his chest—caused her, so she told me, to hire Tom immediately upon his return to the States as the Elysium caretaker, filling the shoes of his late father, Sean Malloy, whom she'd known from the first years of her marriage. In later years, her gaze would often linger on Tom—"the last man to see my son alive"—as she often put it; little suspecting that his father, Sean Malloy, had been the last in General Alden and Samuel Williams's circle of conspiracy to see their beloved Pearce Breckenridge alive.

A fine woodsman and crack shot in the marines, Tom had been born and raised in the Berkshires, and before the First World War had been a lumberjack and fishing and hunting guide. He liked nothing better than to regale me with stories of my father's youth: drawn to the woods "like the Algonquin of yore." Tom described a boy who saw the woods as a testing ground, pushing himself to the limit and beyond. "Find if there was a breaking point to him," as Tom put it in his bark of an Irish brogue, an echo of his father, Sean, which he always used when the subject of firearms came up. "A crack shot, too, the best I'd ever laid eyes on." In the late fall and even in the first days of winter, my father would swim the icy lake, see how long he could endure the cold with furious exercise to maintain body heat—a foolhardy business that had once resulted in a bad case of pneumonia. I caught intimations of a strained relationship with Bobby Williams, how once—they were about twelve at the time—my father harangued Bobby, daring him to dive into the lake after an overnight freeze had left a thin coating of ice on the surface. My father stripped to his shorts and executed a perfect dive off the board with palms flattened against impact, and slipped through. Bobby had been terrified. It was twenty seconds before my father reappeared, surging up through the ice and wading onto the beach, breaking ice all the way. He then gathered up his clothes and made a mad dash for home and a hot tub. "Tried to make a man of the Williams lad, but the material was lacking."

Years later, these tales of bullying would be confirmed to me by Suzanne Williams, as were the circumstances that led to the eastern diamondback skin in the cigar box.

"One summer, the lad had got it in his head to hike the woods at night by moonlight. No food, no water, no compass. See if he could get himself good and lost. When I asked him why he bothered, he told me it was to see if he could get himself frightened." Old Tom laughed at my father's antics but clearly admired his guts and stamina. "He was a hard young'un was Master Johnny. Do whatever it took to steel himself, and then some more for good measure.

"But I'd tell him a little of Belleau Woods and that'd take the steam out of him." When my father first began studying archaeology in Leipzig over summers, Tom Malloy was fit to be tied: "You see, the machine gunners were the worst. We'd knock out one nest in all that underbrush and the next would open up on your flank, but only when you'd silenced the first—sneaky as hell; and they'd keep killing you until the moment you got into them with your bayonet, and then they'd surrender easy as you please." Tom had set out photos of the Kaiser on the rifle range when he took me shooting, and he was quick to let me know where I stood in the pecking order. "Master Johnny was almost as good as his grandfather—General Alden, that is—who, I heard tell, was the best shot in the Berkshires. Doc Alden, your granny said, could take it or leave it."

Relating these tales to Max, hearing Tom Malloy's voice in mine, feeling my grandmother's promptings, I began to better appreciate the story of my father's early adolescence, not just because I'd recently passed through similar way stations but also because the human dimensions of the stories gained a new reality in the very telling—in the resonance of the recurring patterns, which cried out for a narrative structure. I went over to a bookshelf where my father's copies of Homer were arranged, in Greek and in English and German translations. With renewed curiosity, I slipped these time capsules free, feeling the pollen-dusted pages, opening the eighteenth-century morocco-bound editions of Pope and Chapman and the 1932 T. E. Shaw translation of the *Odyssey*, inscribed as gifts from his mother in the mid-twenties. Flipping through the pages, spilling the dried flowers secreted there on his rambles, seeing the annotations in his adolescent scrawl, the underlinings of raw, untrammeled human experience that drew his gaze—of hardships endured on storm-tossed seas, of loss and privation and homesickness—I realized that what Max would interpret as a youth hardening himself for a warrior's life was just the opposite: My father went to the woods, immersed himself in nature, and tested himself as a way of gaining an insight into Homer's exploration of the human condition. He was trying to connect with Homer's heroic world, its nobility of purpose, vitality, honesty, adventurous courage—the honor-bound code of an archaic breed of warriors that valued truth telling among equals. By drawing closer to nature, he was steeping himself in the strange and obscure power of Homer's poetry.

This, too, I had discovered in that moment, because my Greek had improved to the point where I recognized this exotic strangeness, its remoteness and mysterious depths, with hundreds of words that remain untranslatable—even to the ancient Athenians . . . as if ghostly precipitants, echoes of even more ancient stories out of the mists of time. And I couldn't help wondering, as I still wonder, with whom he identified: the proud, fate-bound godlike Achilles rooted in the ways of an archaic past, or the inventive, all-to-human Odysseus, homeward bound and forever in search of a return to a golden age, and willing to employ any stratagem and all his ingenuity to cheat destiny: the warrior who gained eternal glory in Hades, or the mortal who made it back alive to his wife and son.

Max grunted at me wide-eyed. "You guys shoot guns?"

I couldn't help laughing at the look of incredulity on his face, which prompted me to an overstatement I'd pay for in spades.

"Yup, we have an arsenal downstairs in the gun room. And a rifle range. I'll take you shooting tomorrow; it'll be good for you, put some hair on your chest."

In *Like a Forgotten Angel,* our use of firearms and Tom Malloy's stories, with much dramatic embroidering, are deployed to garnish themes of the "ethos of the warrior cult," how my father and his CIA cronies were baleful avatars of an imperialist violence that led to the assassinations of the Kennedys and Martin Luther King, Jr., and even the Diem assassination in Vietnam: the prideful delusions (in Charlie Springfield's eyes) that fucked up everything about America in those years. Well, as I tried to explain to Max, my grandmother had ancestors at Lexington, a grandfather killed while leading black troops in the battle of the crater at Petersburg. You had to learn to respect a weapon, so she insisted; otherwise, your fear of it would leave you vulnerable.

If she told me once, she told me a hundred times: "You must embrace your fears and the things that frighten you. If you don't, they will take on larger or distorted proportions in your mind. And your enemy will take full advantage of the fact."

The reason I even mention these details is that I held none of this back from Max, because I had no idea there was anything to hide. That my father was truly a prepossessing athlete and rugged outdoorsman didn't dispose him to military solutions—far from it. As I would find out, he truly managed heroic feats in Greece during the war, but as I also know from my own experience, feats of physical courage, even what are thought of as acts of bravery, on and off the field, are often acts of happenstance and emotional exhilaration—the instinct, in the moment, to live to the hilt or survive. One is simply lifted by circumstances, by the life force rather than rising to them.

The real irony is that nearly everything, clues big and small, that would ultimately provide answers to my father's fate passed through our hands that afternoon, including the manila envelope containing the newspaper clippings from the *Natchez Weekly Democrat* and the Pinkerton reports. As I had done the previous summer, we glanced through them quickly, then slid the fragile contents back into the envelope without another thought. So did a good part of the tale of Pearce Breckenridge come under Max's scrutiny, only to remain a fugitive myth for another twenty years. Even the framed postcard of the interior of the Museum of Antiquities in Leipzig was examined by Max, and the archaic verses on the back, and rehung on the wall by the door without so much as a shrug.

I am being unfair, of course. How could anyone, then, have put the pieces together? But for the record, Max had his chances.

Laura never let on to Max about her mother's cache of love letters from my father, a trove that included the very same postcard, but with different verses copied out in my father's hand. My mother, too, had been sent one of the three identical postcards, with yet another verse, which she had slipped into one of her favorite Hornblower novels, only to be forgotten.

My grandmother had an innate feel for how the truth will out; her favorite aphorism from Pasteur says it all (the framed quote hung on the wall of her husband's office at Harvard Medical School): "In the fields of observation chance favors only the prepared mind."

Perhaps Max was too inveigled by Hermitage. Among the framed photographs from the twenties was one of Bobby Williams and my father with their arms around each other on the sprawling piazza of Hermitage. Max inspected it minutely, and as he did, I was reminded of the photos of my grandmother and Amory Williams and his artist wife on the same veranda, bringing instantly to mind my mother's description of coming through the French doors and finding Kim Philby and Suzanne flirting by the railing, an image so real, it was as if I'd been there myself.

He tapped the glass. "Wow, look at that place . . . Hermitage. So what's with you and the Williamses?"

"What about them?"

"Founding families and all—once bosom buddies, but I don't exactly see you guys mixing it up at trustees meetings and stuff. Why so standoffish?"

"My grandmother didn't like them. I don't know, goes back to the twenties, when she was put on the Winsted board to get rid of Amory Williams."

Max shot me an intrigued look. "You'll take me over there, right—to Hermitage?"

"We're hardly likely to be invited."

"Hawkman, you must, must, must wrangle us an invite. What a story: the golden boy's suicide in the 1890s, that so, so sexy Saint-Gaudens memorial, and then there's Palazzo Fenway—I mean, what an unbelievably cool place. All those Vermeers and Titians, and that so, so sexy Spanish dancer by Sargent. Kemosabe, you really need to make powwow with such wonderful people. Me like to meet them."

"Cool your jets, Max. My grandmother"—I was going to say my grandmother considered them decadent failures—"felt sorry for them."

Max took my arm and squeezed gently, a peculiar smile on his face.

"Remember, Hawkman, art is long and life is short. And I *saw* you with their daughter. I mean, the *granddaughter* of Isabella Williams— Queen of Boston's Back Bay—that's pretty far-out, man."

"Laura Williams, and she's the great-niece; Isabella was Samuel Williams's daughter, Amory's sister."

I should have wised up to his disingenuous blather: Max knew exactly what the relationship was. How many warning signs did I need? I should have had the good sense to march him down the stairs and out the door and have driven back to New York. Or maybe taken him shooting right then and there, which I did the following day, and scared the shit out of him. But instead, my adopted role as cicerone got the better of me.

"The Williamses were . . ." Max said, sidling up to me, purring like a feline in heat, taking my arm. "My God, they were intimates of John Singer Sargent and Henry James; the Williamses knew everyone who was worth knowing. They collected the greatest artists in the world— Titian's *Danaë and the Shower of Gold*—do Johnny Holmes proud—"

"Hey, you don't think George Inness was a pretty great artist? You think you're so fucking smart, Max, but there's more to it than just art." I pulled my arm free. "Let me show *you* something."

What I wanted him to see, to register, were the precocious scholarly achievements of my father. In this, I sought a margin of safety.

I had found the mother lode of my father's early writings the summer before I started at Winsted. It had been there in the sweltering recesses of the attic, smelling of bat shit and mildew and dusty cobwebs. Cardboard boxes of his exiled books, his juvenile writings. My hands must have been shaking, because that detail, too, made it into Max's novel—when I pulled out things from his adolescence where I had carefully arranged them: histories of Greece and Rome, works of classical literature and philosophy—not in translation, but in the original! And the dates! My grandmother had inscribed them all with the dates when she had bestowed them on her darling prodigy. At seven, he was reading Gibbon; by eight, Homer and Cicero in Greek and Latin. I was intent on laying out the evidence of my father as a world-class scholar. I was in a defensive crouch.

Thumbing through the worn and annotated pages of these old books, Max became very quiet—even he was a little in awe of such scholarly accomplishments, not that it affected his ultimate portrayal of my father in his novel. When I saw him so engaged, my trepidations seemed to float free as minute by minute the sunset glow off the lake began filling the room.

And there was more. I carefully got down the manuscript in the cardboard slipcover I'd made: my father's life of Alexander the Great, neatly typed, six hundred pages with elaborate footnotes and bibliography. He was still working on it during his first year at Winsted. And this was even before the modern biographies of Tarn, Burn, or Wilcken had been published. He had absorbed all the ancient authorities: Diodorus, Curtius, Plutarch, Justin, Arrian. He had exhausted all the scholarly journals and had done independent research in the Columbia library on recent developments in papryology and numismatics.

"You'll find your favorite babes inside—some of the hottest history porn ever."

I watched Max go through the pages until he came upon the first bookmarks in the text, a postcard of Titian's *Venus of Urbino.*

"Oh, my"—he smiled in recognition—"where did . . ." He picked up the postcard and flipped it over. "Chef Boyardee—lives!" He laughed and began turning the pages to find more missives of that summer he spent in Venice.

"My dad was clearly inspired by Zeno, with his emphasis on a world of universal brotherhood and harmony, a world state subject to a common law . . . ruled by a philosopher king. He *was,*" I continued, a little breathless, "the youngest man ever appointed to a full professorship at Princeton. He was a *scholar,* Max—that was his real calling."

"A philosopher king, like Charlie said, can just as easily become a tyrant."

"He was a romantic—maybe we all are, worst luck."

"Listen, Hawkman, I'm not questioning his bravery, that he was a Nazi-killer, as you like to remind me. But like your pal, Winsted's very own national security adviser, they're all spewing self-serving propaganda about Vietnam; they're lying through their teeth—they lie about everything. You heard Charlie—"

"Charlie, Charlie—fuck what Charlie said."

"Well now, aren't we getting a little crotchety."

"Don't you get it? What I'm dealing with here? Don't you think I'm desperate to find out what happened to him—what went wrong? Shit, every day, every goddamn day, that's what I wake up to." I shook my head in exhaustion. "Enough, let's get out of here before I lose my mind, while we've got some daylight left."

Max looked a little shell-shocked.

"Know something, you've changed."

"Pot calling the kettle black—you're fucking protean."

"Ever since you've let Virgil get his claws into you, you've been furtive as hell."

"What's Virgil got to do with anything?"

"You're hiding something. You know stuff you're not letting on about."

"Stuff—stuff? Jesus fucking Christ, I invited you up, didn't I? What do you want me to do, open a vein?"

"Charlie didn't like Virgil for beans; he said he's a McCarthyite, a Red-baiter, told me I should keep you out of his clutches."

"Thanks, I can take care of myself, Max, and it's none of your damn business."

"You and Elliot Goddard—remember: Virgil was a guide to a very unpleasant place."

"And I'm no Dante, and just you remember, Max, what the road to hell is paved with."

Max smiled and put his arm around me.

"I'm . . . sorry, and I'm your honored guest." Max moved to the green Underwood typewriter and ran his fingers sensually over the keys, "I'm just—you know how it is." He glanced up to the window, catching sight across the lake of what he'd really come for. "Lead on, masked man— Hi-ho, Silver, away."

14

834 FIFTH AVENUE

November 12, 1931

Dearest Son,

I have indulged your whims much over the last years, but you have reached the limit with the missive I have from Jack Crocket, now in my hand. According to his queries, not only has Harvard admissions not received a word from you, although all your Winsted records have been forwarded, but he has it from your "new mentor," Mr. Dabney, that you are intent on entering Princeton next year. I will not hear of it; I will not pay for it; I forbid it. It is enough that I have indulged your quixotic enthusiasms for the classics, and your desire to go dig under every rock in Greece and Crete, but the very least you can do is to go on to Harvard, where your father and grandfather and great-grandfather went—and my father and so on and so forth. You may think it is a joke and of small matter, but my grandfather's likeness resides on a pedestal in Memorial Hall for his heroics in the mine at Petersburg. And dare I remind you that a new wing of the medical school is named after your father? Why would you turn your back on everyone and everything dear to our families! I have long since given up the hope that you might go into medicine—God knows, you could never have competed with your father in that arena. So, you have my word: you never need go near the medical school or dirty your hands in advanced chemistry. And the Classics Department at Harvard is certainly as good as that at Princeton, if not better.

More to the point, this country is a mess, and Europe a bigger mess, and I'm not so certain burying your head in the sands of the ancient world is the best way to serve your country or yourself at this difficult time. We are going to the dogs and your generation is going to have to pick up the pieces. You owe the country and your people the very best you can give of yourself: hiding yourself away in the depths of the library and summers in an excavation trench—and I don't much like Karel Hollar or his supercilious father—is not the way I've raised you.

I hear the Harvard football coach is beside himself, according to Jack. And you know what a big supporter of yours Jack is. I will be up for the St. Mark's game on Saturday; then you and I and Jack will have a sit-down and go over your future.

> Until then,
> Mother

We walked the lake shore in silence. The sun was a low bronzy red, illuminating the highest boughs of the white pines like miniature clouds of azure-gray. A sultry iridescence simmered on the water, while a thick carpet of pine needles hushed our footfalls, inundating us with their winter-hoarded scent. Such blissful moments made me want to whoop with sheer joy at the freedom of the woods. We stopped often just to stare out at the lake and wait. As if on cue, a wood thrush would suddenly call out, its eerie, transpiring notes like a forlorn paean cascading from the treetops. Even motormouth Max seemed struck dumb. General Alden had called such moments on the verge of dusk the "Inness hour," and the expression had stuck in family parlance: "Inness time," "Inness light," or, as my grandmother often announced, "I'm off to the back porch for my hour with George."

Years later, Max would write of his main character, Saul, in *Like a Forgotten Angel*, still in mourning as he visited his friend's Berkshire home for the first time, that he'd never known how sadness and joy could be so completely merged as to seem one transcendent emotion, "wafting on the evening breeze . . . how the absolute finality of death and the exuberance of spring could find common ground."

> *For the first time, Saul truly felt as if he'd penetrated to the root stock of these people's lives. All around him, from the bouquets of creamy-pink laurel to the aspiring pines greening the sky, he detected an instinct to retreat from the world of money-getting and easy exploitation, as if some vague ancestral spirit had directed them to upland dreams of their better selves, as yet unspoiled by the nightmares of their careless lives and blind conceits. This was their religion, their hope that their lives could yet be put right by an unconditional love of the land.*

Perhaps if Max had just left it at that.

"I can't believe you denied me this garden of earthly delights until now." He shoved me playfully. "*And* your dark, forbidding castle."

"So, do you still think we're really as terrible as you like to make out?"

"Who needs 'em," he shouted. "You and me, pal, against the world—forever."

With this, he sprang into a thicket and grabbed a broken branch, which he hacked at with his penknife to produce a semblance of a walking staff. He held it up like Charlton Heston parting the waters of the Red Sea.

"Onward." He stepped in front of me and proceeded to lead the way along the woodland trail that hugged the shoreline. "Still planning for early admission to fair Wittenberg, my prince?"

"Princeton—best classics department around."

"A prince for Princeton, following in good old dad's footsteps."

"So what's it going to be with you, Max, Harvard, Yale—perish the thought."

Max took a vicious swing with his staff at a patch of ferns, neatly clipping off their tops.

"Fuck 'em all. And *Juilliard.*"

"Hey," I shouted, "don't do that."

"They're just ferns."

"Well, they're my ferns. And I'm here to protect them from insane writers who prefer to cheer on the world as it goes to hell."

Max sneered. "Know what your problem is? You think this place gives you a right to be above it all, that it will protect you."

"From what?"

"From life—the whole fucked-up country."

"No more fucked-up than what's inside your head, you and your pothead pals."

He turned on me, eyeing me, and spread his arms.

"Even your pal Jerry Gadsden realizes how fucked-up your people are."

"Well, fuck him and fuck you—Jerry doesn't like kikes like you, either."

He smiled.

"Of course, if I could escape to a place like this—if I *had* your room overlooking the lake, if I could *work* there—well, I'd try to keep kikes like me out, too. But then, I'd become just like *you.*"

"An insane recluse poet, that's just what we need around here."

"Better than a lamebrain Neanderthal jock with balls for brains."

"Know what the problem is with writers, Max? They only produce words; they don't *do* anything."

Max raised his staff to those simmering skies of lavender and orange, the lake a plane of striated gold when stray gusts of wind stirred its surface.

"My words will outlast heaven and earth . . . that cuts and divides the nations, fathers and sons. . . ." He inhaled deeply and pointed his staff in my direction. "Guess what, Napalm Breath: One day soon the likes of you and me will have to grow up, face this lousy world we got ourselves into."

"With words or *actions,* do you suppose?"

"We will . . ." He paused, as if the pulsing glare off the lake, the far shoreline throbbing with greens and russet browns, had distracted him. "We will dwell apart in that world beyond words."

"Remember, Max, Occam's razor: *Entia non sunt multiplicanda praeter necessitatem*—just keep it simple."

"Yes, ha-ha, why yes. Let us—between us—re-create the world, in metaphor and symbol, forging the connection—you and I, we'll discover worlds behind worlds."

"You mean worlds built on words."

His eyes widened to the lakeshore awash with the hovering boughs of hemlock. He stabbed at the earth with his rod. "Where everything has its place in the cosmic order, without a niche left unfilled, and all of it connected in a vast, timeless hierarchy."

Max had been indulging himself in things medieval (a concoction of all the Shakespeare and literary criticism he'd been reading), and so was partial to philosophic fancies, to closed systems with marvelous feedback loops that, of course, went nowhere. But that was the point. We were young and free and ripe for building glittering castles in the air.

"You and your great chain of being—writers . . . cursed to draw the connections."

"Know what Charlie told me once? He said that mankind developed language because we refuse to accept the world the way it is."

"*Hunters,* Max"—I knew how to push his buttons—"early hominids probably needed language to communicate, to better locate and hunt down prey, and to stay out of the clutches of saber-toothed tigers. Survival, it's all about survival."

"Ah, of the fittest, no less. Spoken like a true, bloodsucker scion."

"Like I said, keep it simple."

"After Charlie's funeral, Mary Beth gave me some of his notebooks, told me to sort through them and do what I wanted with the material. Some of it was from his sermons, and some were short stories about his childhood in North Carolina, and his father, who preached hellfire and brimstone. I guess it was too private for him even to think about getting it published. Looks like his old man smacked him around for even thinking out of turn. Getting away to Winsted on a scholarship was his lucky escape, where Paul Oakes took him under his wing—can you believe it?"

"That any of them were ever young men," I mused.

"Like us."

"Like us," I echoed. "But we will never grow old, Max. At least you won't—you're impervious to reality, a juvenile delinquent for life."

"It's all too strange—Charlie, I mean. Raised by a Pentecostal firebrand, beaten to a pulp by his father, becomes an atheist at Winsted, sees guys getting killed all around him in Normandy, almost losing his own leg, and yet when he gets back home—what does he do? Goes to New York, General Theological Seminary and becomes an Episcopal minister, teaching literature in a boys prep school. So how do you figure?"

"Maybe war does things to you. Charlie wouldn't be the first."

At this, Max raised his dark eyes skyward and shrugged.

"Once upon a time . . ." Max sighed, and as he turned from the lake to squeeze my shoulder, I saw through the glittering light that there were tears in his eyes. "Charlie wrote in one of his sermons, 'It is sometimes necessary to bend an ear to nature's mirrored stillness in hopes of catching the whispered solicitudes of the angels: there on the wing, where they dream of life before the Fall.'"

That became the opening sentence in *Like a Forgotten Angel*.

We stood for a moment longer on the shore of Eden Lake, listening as the wood thrush began again. I thought of Charlie Springfield's last sermon, his warnings about the temptations of the rebel angels: his barely veiled critique of my father's classmates and colleagues—enshrined as the central leitmotif of *Like a Forgotten Angel*. And yet, how magnificent those rebel angels—flying in the face of a righteous God, needing to shear close to evil to fight evil: fire with fire. For a while yet, we were preserved from such choices, such "terrors of the soul," as my father wrote in a letter to Suzanne Williams. I waved Max out of the way as I again took the lead along the path. We must have walked for a quarter of an hour, keeping an eye on the sun as it began to dip behind the trees, the elongated shadows, like us, mute sojourners along the trail. Then Max tapped my shoulder and pointed toward the lake.

"What's that?"

There was movement on the surface of the lake, quick and regular and smooth. At first, I thought the beavers or otters might be out, and then I recognized the motion of a swimmer. We were near the beach, and the swimmer was returning from the middle of the lake toward the plank float that demarcated the beach area.

I assumed it was Suzanne Williams but said nothing to encourage Max. He pushed in front of me and began to hurry along the path, glancing again and again toward the swimmer and her crimson-pink coruscating wake. As we rounded the path near the head of the lake, where the sandy beach was tucked into an inlet near the dam, Max grabbed my arm.

"Who is she?" he demanded.

I looked out and watched the swimmer approach the planked float at the apex of the log barrier.

"No idea." I turned toward the fork in the path that would lead us back to our house, but Max held his ground.

The swimmer reached the float and grabbed hold and with a single motion lifted herself up and out of the water and stood gazing, as we were, at the burning sky in the west. She was wearing the same red bathing suit I remembered from previous summers. Then she threw back her head to get her long blond hair behind her shoulders, grabbing the wet strands between her hands to wring out the water. She became very still, as if listening, as we were, to the song of the wood thrush. A ripple of breeze spread across the lake and disappeared. More of the womanly contours of her body began to register in the fading light, the suit like a flame rising from her buttocks to her shoulders. I realized it was Laura. Even if there was little of the young girl of memory and a lot more of her mother's assertive breasts—and a lot more of the asser-tive seventeen-year-old who'd been writing me all spring. But for a few moments more, her face still indistinct at a distance, she remained less a woman and not quite a girl: an image of freedom—tall and proud and lovely to behold, more an enchantment of the mind than a real person, a naiad of the lake and woods called into being by the song of the wood thrush. As the sunset grew in intensity, more vesperal flames flickered at her shoulders. I smiled, remembering my father's underlinings in the *Odyssey* of an hour before. Nausicaa, I thought, the beautiful princess, watcher along the shore, who had befriended the shipwrecked Odysseus. And then, as if aware of the idiotic literary allusions or callow adolescent longing directed her way, she suddenly dived into the lake. A near perfect dive, her body knifing into the penumbra of flame and shadow with barely a ripple. It was as if the liquid translucent light into which she'd cast herself had simply claimed its own.

We stood mesmerized as she swam toward the beach.

"Do I hallucinate," said Max, "or is that the gorgeous creature you were with on the Circle at the trustees meeting?"

"C'mon, let's go."

"Oh no you don't. She's the one, isn't she? Laura Williams, your little secret. Your hometown squeeze. The letters from Boston at mail call: light blue envelopes, Chanel No. 5, if memory serves."

Knowing Max, he'd probably rifled my desk and read her letters.

"She's just a kid."

"Hey, man, we're all just kids—remember."

"C'mon."

"Where does she abide?"

"Hermitage, just above the lake over there."

I could hear his breath catch as he turned to my half gesture and spotted a huge while clapboard house peeking through the trees across the lake. I could detect his brain scraping gears as he jumped the clutch from first to fourth. His eyes were riveted on the shoulders and arms and kicking feet moving effortlessly toward us, crossing the boundary of rose-reflected light and into the shadowy olive gray nearer the shore.

"She's our angel," he intoned. "The angel of Hermitage."

"Angel?"

"One of our forgotten angels."

"C'mon, we need to do some studying before dinner—and you need a cold shower."

"You will introduce your best buddy, of course."

"Max, let's just get back, okay?"

"You're not being . . . *ter-ri-tor-ial*, are you?"

The expression, with its unmistakable implications of elitism, was so far from the truth that I found myself bewildered.

He planted his staff in the soft sand and pulled up his sleeves.

"Now watch, my fine-feathered friend; I'm going to show you how it's done."

Max went to the side of the beach and began gathering a handful of purple-and-white violets. He held them up in triumph.

"Always start with flowers—always."

Bouquet in hand, he waltzed over and met Laura at the water's edge as she emerged dripping from the lake. Max bowed and presented her with the flowers, spouting Ophelia's sonnets on Hamlet's inconstant love. Max's antics soon had Laura smiling and laughing and weaving the violets into her dripping hair. She mugged and assumed ballet poses for him, and soon both were in stitches. She kept glancing my way, as if to say, *Where did you find him?* I smiled and shrugged and went to get her towel where she'd left it on a beach chair with her clothes and sandals. As she dried herself, she chatted away with Max, as if they'd known each other forever. Her skin was goose-bumped in the chill of the late afternoon; she was, definitely, no longer the kid I remembered. Her one-piece red burgundy bathing suit left little to the imagination, especially her nipples, an aching presence through the bulging fabric, a lovely counterpoint to her slender torso and tensile legs fluidly arrayed with smooth ridges of muscle from thigh to calf. As we chatted, she kept pulling at the straps across her shoulders as if she, too, were aware of her breasts and was making sure the suit showed them to best advantage. And she was not shy as I had once known to her to be, but playful and giggly, giving as good as she got from Max. She handled him with ease. The sexual energy between them, the banter, their teasing body language, felt as if it might ignite the pine-perfumed dusk. And not a word to us that she'd just signed a contract with the American Ballet Theater (in her world, as big a deal as it gets) and was home to celebrate.

To celebrate her escape—the discovery of my father's love letters in her mother's closet a couple of months before had confounded her and turned her into a wary gambler, hell-bent and all-in—to flee the coop with the first guy she landed.

Yes, I was jealous, as the erotic buzz in the air seemed to close one gate on the past as it opened another onto an even scarier future. Something of my childhood was dissolving before my eyes. Sensing her instincts for freedom, I was filled with the pang of exile. For the first time, I wanted to deck Max. It was as if I finally recognized his true colors. What a complete fool to invite him up. Why had I ever listened to my mother? By introducing his predatory sexuality into my home, my childhood, everything had been put at risk.

He would say, as he told eager interviewers at the height of his fame, that he was only doing what artists do: falling in love and so stirring new life into being. He so reveled in his readers' embrace of his alter ego, the awkward outsider barely surviving the recalcitrant and often hostile goyim, that he rewrote his own past. He'd glibly expound on *The Dick Cavett Show* about his school days and early years as a young writer, as if he were the real embodiment of his character's Jewish insecurities—a Woody Allen to a young Diane Keaton, or maybe Mariel Hemingway; going on and on about his father's gauche brownnosing and his mother's shtetl phobias. Entranced by his hero Thomas Wolfe, he wanted his readers to believe he wrote thinly veiled autobiography. When he was an insider's insider, slicker than slick, and made himself *right* at home.

Perception *is* everything: He literally wrote himself into another life. We should all be so lucky.

As for me, having just turned seventeen—how can I put it: We are all creatures of habit and resistant to change; but habit is also how we come to know the world, the place where we master our sea legs, that point of reference we keep our eye on as we row our heart out. And something of that world as I had found it, as I watched Max and Laura go at it, was slipping away.

"No way—I'm done," she shrieked, and cuffed Max on the shoulder. He'd suggested we all swim out to the float, implying a skinny-dip in the fast-approaching dusk.

"Snapping turtles," I told him, and gave Laura a knowing look.

Max covered his crotch protectively.

"Me, they wouldn't bother with." He gave me a shove. "But him, GI Joe, they'd choke to death."

"Oh, you'll like the water snakes," said Laura.

"No," said Max.

"The great northern water snake—size of anacondas," I added.

"Takes one to know one," said Max, glancing at my crotch. "How about we go get high or something."

"Max," I protested, thinking of Laura's parents nearby and Bobby Williams a trustee. I took his arm, as if he needed to be put on a leash. "Poor guy hasn't been the same since his father died."

I don't know what prompted that inanity—maybe the shooting of Charlie Springfield; it just came out that way.

"I'm sorry," said Laura, seeming caught off balance by the sudden interjection of a sad and sober remark.

"What?" Max looked at me like I'd just shoved a knife in his ribs.

"Did I say something?" I asked.

"What he means," said Max, frowning. "My father just had his divorce finalized."

"You can tell how broken up he is about it," I said.

"Life goes on," said Max, pulling free of my grip.

Laura smiled and moved toward where her clothes lay.

"You guys can't be out of school yet."

"No," I said, "they closed the place down for a week before exams."

"Oh my God!" she exclaimed. "I heard about it from my father, that terrible thing about an English teacher getting shot."

This had the effect of silencing us both for a moment. The way she had put it . . . a *terrible thing,* as if it were only a story, something you read in a newspaper about other people, something possibly made up and never quite real.

"Yeah," said Max, not letting a little tragedy distract from more pressing opportunities.

"I'm sorry," she replied, biting her lip.

"How about you?" Max asked. "Are you out of school already?"

"I've been auditioning in New York."

"Ah . . . you're a *dancer?*" said Max.

Laura raised her leg in a long extension and arched her foot in a beautiful, unbelievable curve of tendons and flesh ending in calloused toes.

"My mother teaches piano at Juilliard."

"Really."

"He's a misbegotten prodigy in real life," I said.

"One of those." She laughed. "So, how's crew?"

"We did okay." I shrugged.

"I *am* planning to get to a football game next fall—no matter what," she said, nodding at me with a knowing beat of her eyelashes and a dismissive glance toward her house.

"Great," I said.

Max flashed a curious little grin in my direction as Laura turned her back for a moment to slip into her sandals.

"Come on people now," he sang, playing a little air piano for our amusement, "everybody get together—let's party ri-i-ght now . . . Hey, let's dance—why not? What do you guys do around here for fun, anyway?"

Laura and I looked at each other and shrugged: the discordant note in a place where our entire childhood had been under the strict control of parents—party? That word, with its evocations of boozing and flirting and riotous release, had played no part in our woods, at least not in our generation.

"Anybody do drugs or alcohol?" Max wagged an invisible cigar and wiggled his eyebrows à la Groucho. "I've got a little stash back at the car."

"What stash?" I said.

"Take it easy," snapped Max. Laura giggled.

"Her dad, Max, *is* on the board of trustees."

Laura raised her hands as if surrendering.

"Don't worry about them. I barely speak to my parents if I can help it."

We both turned to her where she stood with clothes in hand, towel around her waist: auditions in New York . . . a woman on the move and eager for a following wind, any wind, to fill her sails.

"I've got it," said Max. "Let's go back to Pete's place. We'll drive, get some pizza, some beer. We'll have a party down at your boathouse, Peter. We need to go into Pittsfield and get some food anyway—right?" He looked at me imploringly. "We'll dance in the moonlight, invite a few deer or raccoons—whatever you've got around here—to join our gig."

"Black bears," I said.

Laura got her wristwatch out of the pocket of her shorts and glanced at the time.

"Listen, we've got a whole house full of food, and my mother's got a roast in for dinner tonight. It's my father's birthday. Why don't you come right now and have dinner with us. I'm sure he'll be thrilled with you guys: how Winsted and the rest of the country is going to the *dogs.* Believe me, it's his favorite subject."

"Splendid," crowed Max. "A done deal."

Before I could say boo, Max had eagerly accepted for the two of us and we were off to Hermitage.

My life had been hijacked. And Max was a made man.

Faced with this fait accompli, I had a panic attack: I realized how bizarre that in all the years growing up I had darkened the door of Hermitage exactly once (an August day long ago, when Laura's teen-age baby-sitter had unwittingly invited me to tag along for lunch at

Hermitage, Suzanne and Bobby being otherwise disposed), nor, for that matter, had Laura been to our place, at least as far as I knew. It was as if some unspoken but absolutely compelling taboo was about to be broken—and both Laura and I knew it.

Max, clueless to this backstory—as he would have it—had worked his magic and blithely sent us off on the path that would change all our lives. The dinner to come, elaborated on at length in *Like a Forgotten Angel,* forms the transition from the protagonist's early school days and the shooting of Christian Foster [Charlie's name in the novel] to the love story and the events that form him as a writer. It is also where Max hijacks our family story for his own purposes. As he told Dick Cavett, "Well, you see—that's the way it was; I kinda fell in love with the Williamses and their place. First it was my summer with my mom in Venice when I discovered Palazzo Barberini, then Palazzo Fenway, then Hermitage—wow, full of artists from stem to stern—the Sargent watercolors of Venice blew me away, and the letters from Henry James . . . *Wings of the Dove*—what's not to love?"

Translation: I made it up as I went along.

Even as we walked that evening, the full blush of the night beginning to settle over the narrow, winding trail to Hermitage, I felt like an insubstantial presence trailing in Max's and Laura's photogenic wake (the *Us* magazine celebrity couple of the seventies). His eyes—I could tell—savoring the sweet shape of her neck and bony shoulders as he exhausted his repertoire of risqué jokes. And there I was, tamely following along through the thinning shadows, footsteps hushed by the thick pine needles, a life to be eclipsed in the glamour of their celebrated notoriety. Laura was to go on to be one of the greatest ballerinas of her generation (the heroine of novel two, *Gardens of Saturn*) and Max the supreme chronicler of his "age of dissatisfaction" (*Newsweek*). Written out of existence, I would spend half a lifetime clawing my way back into the light . . . when she returned to rescue me. How can I compete with Max's rendition of our entrance into Bobby and Suzanne's Hermitage, which surely demonstrates, if nothing else, how seduced he was by his *own* adolescent longings . . . and how absolutely accurate he could be with details when it suited.

Except, as will be seen, when the backstory changes everything.

15

SAUL FOUND HIMSELF IMMEDIATELY EN-
tranced by this tall, shapely young woman, not so much
by her physical beauty as by her unaffected naturalness. She was so at home in her skin. Well, she owned
the place, didn't she? The woods and lakes were just an outer layer of
epidermis, a raiment casually tossed across her shoulders. He felt in
some way that he had known her already in a thousand guises. Her
face, the straight nose with the barest crinkle at the tip, and soulful sea
blue eyes flecked with green at the irises, the high carriage and aloof
charm: He'd read her story in a novel. She was cast as one of Fitzgerald's ingenue beauties; or James's tragic heroines—a Milly Theale;
perhaps a maiden of unaffected Puritan stock out of Edith Wharton.
Her virgin virtues, deliciously, hanging by a thread. She reminded Saul
of the angelic goddesses in the family's Saint-Gaudens memorial he
had so admired. Surely, she embodied the last best hope of her peoples'
moribund bloodline.

This feeling of Saul's was confirmed the moment her home appeared
ahead of them between tall masts of white pine, like woodland schoo-
ners sailing the hills. It was a summer palace of lightness and grace, of
white-columned porticoes and elegant arched windows that hinted at
Venetian filigree. The long lines of white trim and white sashes against
broad spaces of gray clapboard seemed to happily embrace the sprawling hillside above the lake, snuggling tight into the surrounding lawns
and English gardens overlooked by a wide-decked piazza. Strategic
verandas, jutting from the piazza, corralled with simple white railings,
were placed to indulge views of the lake and the woods beyond, as if
the only purpose of nature was to be savored by human eyes from dawn
until dusk. There was an Emersonian clarity about the place, a Tho-
reau-like simplicity. The moment they broke free of the surrounding

woods and the song of the thrush and the intermezzo of thrumming crickets, the breath of the pines was subsumed by a medley of floral scents. Roses, pink and yellow, elbowed their steps as they passed through a gravel-paved garden and onto a side veranda on the piazza. A glaze of amber light seemed to float outward from every window, as if the place was one great Chinese lantern held up above the lakeshore as a beacon for all who believed in the best life had to offer, and so might commit themselves body and soul to that prospect.

Saul imagined himself an ardent lover merging into the flaming arms of his recumbent love, prey to a spiritual force finer than he had ever known. The twist of nervous energy in his gut was knotted further as they passed through the green Dutch door off the garden side of the piazza and their guide, their intrepid Diana, her girlish breasts girdled in blood-red spandex, raised her contralto cry to the split-beam rafters of the sumptuous interior to let her parents know she had returned with unexpected guests. It was then, in the ensuing embarrassed silence—mother failing to show—that Saul found himself truly bewitched. It was as if he'd awoken into the fluid yet fixed idyll of a Sargent watercolor. The great room was of timeless perfection. A symphony by Samuel Barber played on the stereo. A roaring fire crackled in the open hearth, the fireplace decorated with blue-and-white Delft tiles. On the carved mantelpiece supported by ebony caryatids were the most gorgeous blue-and-white ginger jars—such old friends to welcome him, he was all but weeping for joy! And above this a sprawling mural, actually a canvas triptych of 1890s vintage of pale, long-necked women in pastel gowns set amidst a blur of sunset meadows in various tones of jade and viridian blue. These demure maidens, though staring off into a haze of indeterminate space, dominated the room. Their mixed expressions of sad longing and active perception seemed to give voice to the very atmosphere of the place: of intellectual refinement and tasteful aspirations beyond the common lot. Saul couldn't take his eyes off these transcendental muses. One cradled a lute, another a lyre; the third raised her deep-set eyes from an open text, as if just aware of the viewer's watching presence.

Saul was ready to bow down before them and abase his crepitating Hebrew soul. This, he thought, was the secret heart of the WASP establishment, where their better angels took flight.

Everywhere he looked, there were more paintings in hand-carved gold frames of poetic landscapes, others of fragile still lifes or subtle florals with blurred forms and low-keyed colors of near-hypnotic intensity. A few family portraits were scattered into the mix, and not your typical stultifying poses of puritan probity, but employing dramatic chiaroscuro and odd angles that probed the troubled psyches of these vanished grandees of a bygone age. Nepalese temple bells tinkled out on the veranda. A stone Buddha statue occupied a corner by the French doors. The furniture was the finest Arts and Crafts or Mission style in polished oak and cherrywood. Aubusson rugs covered the antique pine flooring. On the side tables, Tiffany lamps disgorged fluid spates of gemstones upon dog-eared volumes neatly stacked about their tendriled bases.

In the seeming eternity that Saul and his friend had been left to themselves while their young Diana went to find her parents, he felt overcome, as one who has stepped into a Buddhist or Shinto temple, a fallen creature cast down amidst the revered objects of a shaman's trance. Without his notebook, he disciplined himself to remember every detail. A frisson of guilt swept over him as he spotted the Steinway grand and went and touched a key, the tender tone ringing clear in the high wood-beamed space. He turned his gaze once again to those redemptive goddesses presiding above the mantel. Surely, thought Saul, he had finally penetrated to the sanctum sanctorum, to the still-beating heart of a near-extinguished faith. Surely, these people, these all-American aesthetes, these first-team Transcendentalists, had been on the right path.

Where had they fallen short, when had they faltered, what had deep-sixed their spiritual enterprise? The great wound of their relinquished pride?

As Saul stood before the fireplace, feeling the warmth of the flames and deep in contemplation, their host's mother finally arrived, not from the kitchen, but from her bedroom on the floor above, which was connected by a spiral staircase of carved ebony banisters. Like mother, like daughter, she was tall and gracious. Her blond hair was done up in a chignon and she had obviously fled at her daughter's call, changing into a blue satin dress before meeting the unexpected guests. As she approached to greet Saul's friend standing by the piano, Saul could actually see the blood rise to her face, and, for the merest of instants, her whole frame crumpled back on itself like a luffing sail, only to billow forth again, their hands meeting, lingering, steadying each other, while her face dissolved into a beatific—no, joyous smile. A moment later, she turned to Saul where he waited by the fire. She could easily have been the model for the maidens on the wall above. As she moved to greet him, her satin dress swishing about her knees, Saul saw her daughter's high, pale brow and wispy eyebrows and long, angular neck—a ballet dancer's build right down to the slim hips and delicate motions of her hands. She was so well preserved for a woman nearing fifty that even as she halved the distance across that grand living room, she might well have passed as a twin sister. She could not have been more welcoming or more sanguine about "us boys" crashing her husband's birthday party.

Moments later, Saul turned to the squeak of rubber on wood and saw her husband suddenly appear from down a hallway, wheeled into view by his daughter, who was still dressed in her wet bathing suit. Even seated in his wheelchair, he was a formidable figure, not so much in stature, since his body had clearly atrophied from his years as an invalid, as in the intense, restless physiognomy: his fiery red hair and badly scarred face, out of which impassioned eyes blinked rapidly as if to incinerate the strangers who had arrived unbidden to his lair. Saul's first instinct upon being confronted with this wounded veteran of the air war over Germany was to flee, as if the smears of burnt flesh about the cheeks and chin, the shaking hands and lashless, bloodshot eyes were those of some hell fiend come to rage at the world. That and the weirdness of this poor man's being wheeled in front of him like a carcass off a delivery truck. But as Saul was to find out later, they had stumbled into this poor man's clutches on a good day.

Her father reached out a shaky hand to his unexpected guests and was all bonhomie and easy conviviality, directing Saul and his friend to find themselves drinks and raid the pantry for cocktail goodies. It was as if this marvelous room still retained the power to work its magic on the high priest of the cult. Saul's friend came over to shake the trembling hand outstretched from the wheelchair, and the man's forehead, which had seemingly escaped burns, tightened in hard vertical creases, with an expression somewhere between grimace and ecstasy.

Within minutes of sitting down at dinner, Saul found himself madly in love with mother and daughter, their faces hovering just beyond the flaming coronas of the silver candelabra. And there they were fated to remain. For all the genuine conviviality of these people, he knew he would remain an outsider, even with the deployment of his best musical talents and skill as a witty conversationalist. He did not embarrass himself, nor was he in anyway slighted, but he soon realized that on this evening he would be hard-pressed to claim the center of attention. His history was not theirs. For there was another seated with them at that spectacular table, although all the extra chairs had been set aside. A ghost hovered at their elbows, an uncanny presence that would remain all evening and that seemed to charge the gorgeous setting with cold, fluid electricity, a kind of oscillating current of love and hate the likes of which he'd never experienced. It was the great mystery of the unlived life and its undying remnant that haunts the living, the very thing that would prompt him to become a writer in later years. Oddly enough, here, amongst these strangers, was the key to the sealed door and the sad fate of his own lost people.

ISKHAK AKHMEROV TO MOSCOW CENTER, "STEPHEN" ON "AMADEUS," OCTOBER 1939; "AMADEUS" REPORT, KGB FILE 58380

Amadeus [Robert Williams] and I have cemented our friendship. He is now eager to listen and take my advice. I am exerting as much ideological influence as I can on him. We discuss endlessly the Nazi-Soviet Pact. He claims the nonaggression pact was tantamount to collaboration, that instead of fighting against fascism and fascist aggression, the USSR has chosen to collaborate with Germany. I repeat that it is only a tactical move on our part, until the Germans have exhausted themselves. I turn the conversation back to larger issues of social justice and the fraternal movement in his homeland. This emboldens him. He wants to keep giving ever larger sums to the CPUSA but I have warned him that if he really wants to help us, he must cut all ties with the American Communist Party and Helmsman [Earl Browder]; otherwise, he will be in jeopardy and potentially prey to exposure from FBI infiltration. I have suggested he not discuss with anyone his days at Cambridge, nor mention the names of our English friends, especially Stanley and Johnson [Kim Philby and Anthony Blunt].

As a musician, he is prone to romantic flights and is inexperienced in the political arena. Now with the fascist war upon us, he is seeking a position outside artistic circles, where he has many contacts; he has met with Eleanor Roosevelt (the president knew and admired his headmaster grandfather); he sought her advice about a position in the federal government. His preference is the State Department, where he has many classmates and graduates of the Winsted School, which his esteemed grandfather founded. His family connections allow him access to many top New Dealers: "This means I could easily find any position." Amadeus suggested he could meet with Henry Morgenthau and Harry Hopkins. This may be difficult for him to achieve, given his lack of practical experience and school days reputation, and might represent a danger for us, since he knows from CPUSA fraternal circles many of our friends in State and Treasury. He has mentioned to me more than once, Frank [Laurence Duggan], Jurist [Alger Hiss], Ernst [Noel Field], and other friends who share his ideological views. I have warned him never to mention his work for us, or to attempt to recruit anyone without our express permission. I have encouraged him to remain in his artistic circles, or even explore possibilities in Hollywood, where he might find employment as a studio musician or composer of film scores, and so help us find legal jobs for our people. But the outbreak of war in Europe has changed his perspective; he now feels useless as a pianist, especially as he sees more and more of the men in his school and college circles headed for government or the military. His latest thought is that the U.S. Army Air Corps might be a useful posting for him, since he was an excellent student of mathematics; he has asked that this idea be conveyed to Moscow Center and if any guidance might be given about what armament technologies might be useful to us. This seems like an impossible leap from his present circles of politically retrograde aesthetes but might prove useful down the road if he was in a position to gather military information. It might fortify his character, as well. And remove him from the many Trotskyites that swim in the sea of his money and largesse. I have agreed to take the twenty thousand dollars he has offered as Party dues in arrears for his years at Cambridge and touring abroad and give it to the CPUSA under other names. I have also suggested he find a wife and normalize his living situation so as not to draw attention to himself.

Max's "ghost," of course, was my father. In *Like a Forgotten Angel*, Max got many of the nuances of that evening right: Suzanne's angry stupefaction, Bobby's conniving conviviality, and Laura so nonplussed at the bizarre crosscurrents of conversation that she barely knew which way to turn. Confusion abetted by her own secret: She'd read a good portion of my father's and Suzanne's love letters to each other—a bit of sly snooping she held close to her chest with a perfect poker face—not that Suzanne didn't suspect something was amiss: Why else would Laura suddenly be writing to me? And although Laura had only limited knowledge of the historical background to the correspondence beginning in 1944 and continuing for nearly ten years, the last being the third version of the postcard of Leipzig's Museum of Antiquities, she had caught wind of some extremely alarmist language in my father's letters—and her mother's—that suggested Bobby and Suzanne might be Soviet spies. And by implication and association, my father—and that was just the half of it. Letters that accused her mother of an affair with Kim Philby; letters that Elliot Goddard and Virgil Dabney would give their eyeteeth to get hold of.

So, perhaps this is as good a place as any to fill the reader in on a bit of background, or, as Max would call it, the backstory for Bobby Williams's birthday dinner at Hermitage in the spring of 1968.

The tone of near panic that fills my father's and Suzanne's correspondence from 1948 (when Elliot recruited him into the fledgling
CIA from Princeton) to 1953 is due to the FBI closing in on hundreds of KGB agents, brought to light by the confessions of Soviet
operatives Elizabeth Bentley and Whittaker Chambers, and confirmed
in the Venona decrypts of Soviet cable traffic, gathered by U.S. Army
intelligence in the early forties, deciphered in the late forties, but only
released to the public by the U.S. government many decades later. The
decrypts also pointed to a KGB spy in the British embassy in Washington between 1944 and 1948, who, after exhaustive investigation, would
turn out to be Donald Maclean. Bobby Williams's code name in the
Venona decrypts was "Amadeus" and Suzanne's was "Firebird." Venona
confirms Suzanne as a courier for Donald Maclean ("Homer"), one of
the Cambridge Five spies, who was then first secretary in the British
embassy and privy to the most closely guarded British and American secrets, including information on the development and technical
details of the atom bomb. His American wife, Melinda, lived in New
York with her parents. While on visits from Washington, Maclean
would drop off top secret documents and microfilm, which Suzanne
would pick up and deliver to the Soviet consulate in New York. Warned
by Kim Philby, who had access to the Venona material in his role as
MI6 liaison with the FBI and CIA, Maclean and his fellow Cambridge
conspirator Guy Burgess ("Hicks") defected to Moscow in 1951,
before they could be interrogated and confronted with their treachery,
although their whereabouts would remain a mystery until 1956. Kim
Philby ("Stanley"), one of Suzanne's lovers from before the war, posted
to Washington in 1949 as MI6's liaison with U.S. intelligence, would
also come under suspicion at this time with the defection of Maclean
and Burgess. Upon getting wind of the successful American decrypts of
Soviet cable traffic while posted in Washington, Philby had managed
to get word though a KGB courier to Moscow Center that Maclean
was in danger—that they were all in danger of being exposed as KGB
agents. Whether Suzanne also acted as a courier for Philby in the early
1950s as she did for Maclean in the late forties—my mother's story
about finding them cooing to one another on the veranda at Hermitage would certainly imply as much—has never been confirmed, but the
circumstantial evidence is abundant.

The Maclean-Burgess defection immediately put Philby in jeopardy
of exposure, and he, too, was recalled to London. Philby played his

shaky cards brilliantly, confounding his MI6 and MI5 interrogators, and enlisting his friends and old-boy network in British intelligence to stand by him. His fellow Etonians and clubmen in White's simply couldn't fathom that one of their own—a man they'd raised a thousand glasses with—had betrayed their upper-class bloodline: a betrayal that would have made him responsible for the deaths of hundreds, if not thousands, of compromised agents: a catastrophe of incompetence that would have besmirched a generation of British intelligence. There was plenty of circumstantial evidence of his spying, but nothing conclusive. After years in the wilderness, and countless fruitless efforts to break him, Philby—incredibly!—was taken on by MI6 once again and posted to Beirut as an intelligence agent to cover Mideast affairs. Only in 1962, when his fellow Cambridge traitor Anthony Blunt was finally exposed by an American he had recruited almost thirty years before, did a mysterious acquaintance of Philby's come forth to provide the crucial proof of his long-standing perfidy to MI5 (British counterintelligence, comparable to the FBI), precipitating Philby's defection to Moscow from Beirut in January 1963. Most historians now agree that a chagrinned MI6 simply let him escape rather than suffer the reputational embarrassment of a full-blown trial.

But in the early 1950s, Anthony Blunt ("Johnson"), who had recruited Bobby Williams at Cambridge in the late thirties, remained undetected. The frantic atmosphere in intelligence circles after Maclean and Burgess defected, the suspicion that Kim Philby had utterly compromised Western intelligence, and fears of other Cambridge moles like Blunt still at large, not to mention their American counterparts like the Rosenbergs, Alger Hiss, and Harry Dexter White, and scores of others who had infiltrated top posts in the U.S. government and defense industry—and many more lurking in the code names of the Venona cables—set the stage of paranoia and fear that surrounded my father's disappearance into East Germany in October of 1953.

So when Virgil Dabney and later Elliot Goddard pricked up their ears at my mention of "Anthony" from the lips of Suzanne that afternoon on the beach, it was because they knew precisely whom she was referring to: five years before, in 1963, Bobby Williams had betrayed his old Soviet recruiter at Cambridge and traded this information to the CIA and Elliot Goddard to get back on the Winsted board; most likely with Suzanne's connivance, he had ratted on Anthony Blunt, by then the keeper of the queen's pictures, Sir Anthony Blunt. (As I would learn two decades hence: In 1962, Suzanne had flown to London and deftly managed her own hatchet job on her onetime lover.) For over fifteen years, offered immunity from prosecution by MI5, Blunt remained in limbo, fiendishly holding his cards close, as he was relentlessly questioned about the disastrous breaches of intelligence that he and Philby, Maclean and Burgess, and at least one other in their Cambridge circle had perpetrated. Blunt would not be officially exposed until Margaret Thatcher did so in parliament in 1979, finally forcing Blunt's resignation from all official posts. British MI6, like Elliot Goddard and his CIA cohorts, was not eager to have these egregious security lapses known, and on that lovely evening at Hermitage in the spring of 1968, the reputations of these men of secrets and their dashing legacies remained precariously intact. For good reason, Elliot and Virgil had intimated that they would be pleased to know anything more about "Anthony" that I might discover. Suzanne's role in these spy scandals, particularly her association with Donald Maclean and Kim Philby, and her love affair with my father were uppermost on their minds, information, should she talk, that could be used in the ongoing interrogations of Anthony Blunt in London, shedding light into just how much damage the smirking Kim Philby, recently awarded the Order of Lenin in Moscow, had done . . . and if she had compromised my father, as well—willingly or not.

So, even though Max gives a vivid and amusing rendition of our dinner conversation at Hermitage—a conversation that revolves almost exclusively around him—I offer the reader an alternate version, a version that, with the facts provided by the Venona decrypts now firmly in place, cuts closer to the truth of this murky matter.

"Who wants to select a grace to say for us?" Bobby held up his copy of *Essays and Prayers* at the head of the table.

"Grace!" exclaimed Suzanne, staring him down from the opposite end.

"We've *never* said grace at this table—ever," said Laura, sitting across from me on her father's right.

"Don't be stupid. We've always said grace in this family and it's high time—with these two Winsted gentleman as our guests—to revert to tradition."

"Your . . . tradition, since when?" Suzanne gulped her wine.

Laura, wearing a wrinkled pink sports shirt, her hair scraggly and untouched from swimming, rolled her eyes and shot a look at me: *Get me outta here.*

Little did anyone at the table, including Max, know that I'd actually picked my way through *Essays and Prayers*—I felt I owed it to Paul Oakes, and because of a nagging sense that I needed to better know a potential adversary. Something my grandmother always hinted at, though never in so many words: "One should feel sorry for them, you see. Alcoholism is bad enough, but those awful European diseases— those isms: this, that, and the next thing—bad ideas in the hands of weak-minded people *and* artists, always a recipe for disaster."

"Here, I'll read something," I offered.

Bobby handed me the volume with a significant look. "Check the frontispiece."

The copy was a maroon morocco-bound, gold-stamped one, old and well used, annotated throughout. It was signed by the author, Samuel Williams, and dedicated to his son Amory. A rare first edition.

"Samuel's copy given to Amory, my father."

I felt I was being tested in some way, as Bobby gave me a significant look. I found the passage that had previously caught my eye and read it out to those gathered. Max was near incredulous and Laura smirked the moment Bobby bowed his head.

"'Nature wears all the colors of the spirit and so becomes the symbol of spirit, surrounding us with glory if we only learn to see again with innocent eyes and so read her dreaming mind. There is God's design in every wind-bent blade of grass and green brushed leaf. Be like a painter to your soul and so let your soul soar free on the river of life, the river of Time.' Amen."

"Bravo," said Bobby, "very nicely read. Your father would be proud of you, pulling it off like that with such composure. Don't you think, dear? Wouldn't John be proud?"

Suzanne glowered. "Of course he would."

"'Be like a painter to your soul . . . ,'" said Bobby, rolling the cadences in the tone of some Victorian patriarch, and waved at the walls of the dining room, hung with Sargent watercolors of Venice. "Well, I think we could all use a little moral uplift, especially at Winsted these days. One can always teach reading, writing, and arithmetic—but values: Who teaches values anymore? Who stands up for the oppressed and downtrodden? Values were the centerpiece of Samuel's plan for Winsted, what made the school's reputation throughout the country, what poor Charlie Springfield preached to us: humility and understanding the limits of our power."

"Rubbish, dear," said Suzanne, pouring herself another glass of wine. "Children don't want to hear about your stuffy old grandfather. And Amory was worse—you never stop talking about how much you hated your father—'hypocritical ass,' wasn't it, if I remember?"

Bobby, bristling, rolled his wheelchair backward some six inches and shot forward into the huge dining room table with a wrenching crunch of the armrests. The silver candelabra shivered and the wine in our glasses sloshed.

"Samuel, at least, stood up for what was right. He used to lecture his boys, even when they had gone on to Harvard, Yale, and Princeton, about the evils of drinking and sexual debauchery. He wrote thousands of letters to his boys and their parents about the terrible damage of divorce. He upheld the inviolability of family. And Winsted *was* family. At least he tried to give his generation some sense of limits and a grounding in civilized and socially meritorious values."

"Debauchery, my arse," Suzanne shot back, raising her empty glass.

"Dear . . ."

"Then he should have kept a better eye on Amory—and his wife, the great artiste who almost managed to drown herself in the Grand Canal in front of her own son." Suzanne glared down the table in her resplendent red satin evening dress, her décolletage a thing spellbinding, especially when the tendons in her neck tightened as if ready to snap and her bosom seethed. "And can't we change the subject? I suspect the boys have had enough of Winsted blather after last week. And your daughter has some good news on your birthday—of course, she might have had the good grace to at least comb out that rat's nest and wear a dress."

That brought things to a halt for a moment, and I glanced beyond Laura's irritated pout to the wall behind, where the Sargent watercolors hovered in splendor, the candlelight adding to the aqueous feel of the broadly brushed colors, which deftly conjured gondolas under the aquamarine belly of the Rialto bridge, and the sheer white domes of the Salute above curlicues of Istrian marble, and one watercolor in particular, framed in black mahogany, which kept catching my eye, of a veiled woman lying back on cushions in the prow of a gondola, her lips parted in a kind of ecstatic swoon, the glitter of reflected sunlight off the canal alive in her half-lidded eyes.

"Oh, I was worse as a kid: John and I ran wild and free . . . like a heronry around here." Bobby sighed and then offered Laura a sympathetic frown. "Yes, yes, the thing with poor Charlie was frightful. I can't understand it. Surely someone must have known the man was unstable. He was a year behind me and he was struggling like the devil to survive back then. I was a dorm prefect and he was teased unmercifully about his thick Carolina drawl, his hick Christianity, and spotty complexion. At Yale, he became a library mole. Why the hell such a Carolina cracker ever wanted to return to Winsted is beyond me."

I glanced across the table at Max, who was sitting next to Laura. His ears were flapping at mention of Charlie; he'd barely touched his barley and morel (hand-gathered by Suzanne that morning) soup. Laura cringed, glancing at me to gauge the damage of her father's broadsides as she nervously swept strands of hair behind an ear.

Suddenly, the silent Max came to attention, took a gulp of wine, and held up his glass as if in silent salute. "He loved Winsted, he loved the river and the playing fields, and the chapel—yeah, he really loved"—Max nodded appreciatively to Bobby—"the chapel more than anything."

Laura took in Max's obsequious words and smirked at me. She brought a hand to her throat in a choking gesture, as if to say, *Well, at least he didn't call it the Williams Chapel.*

Bobby pondered this for a moment. "The chapel—yes, how strange for a Southern Baptist. But why didn't Folley catch on about the man's schizophrenia, or are all southern Democrats so confounded that they vote for the likes of Kennedy while they shoot down Freedom Riders. Just look at LBJ, another southern yokel so far out of his depth that he lets his Winsted minions get us deeper into this miserable war, for *Je-sus sake!*"

"Oh"—Suzanne's contralto echoed like a bell in the high-beamed ceiling—"but you so enjoyed informing on them, dear, just like you *obviously* did on Anthony."

"Suzanne!" Bobby slammed his wheelchair into the table again.

"Well, soon you'll have Nixon to go after, too, if the country's not burned to the ground by then."

Bobby flinched at the word *burned.* I almost felt sorry for him. The burn scars on his cheeks and chin, reflecting the candlelight like awkward brushstrokes in a Cubist portrait, gave me the creeps. As he careened between subjects, he kept wheeling his chair a perfectly measured six inches back—like cocking the hammer of a gun—and then either snapping forward like a human battering ram or gently—adagio molto—touching the armrests to the mahogany: a stunt that kept all on edge. He rarely made direct eye contact. He kept looking down, as if preoccupied with our wraithlike reflections on the vast mahogany tabletop, his lashless eyes blinking rapidly. Perhaps this was his way of dealing with all the pained looks he'd endured, much less the scorn he'd earned in certain Winsted circles among the agency men privy to the Venona decrypts and his outing of Anthony Blunt.

"Actually, Headmaster Folley," I offered, "has been pretty soft on Vietnam recently. To listen to his chapel talks, you'd think he'd been against the war the whole time."

Bobby smiled icily, casting a significant look at Suzanne. "Well, maybe he's getting some *real* religion—if he knows what's good for him."

She raised her refilled glass. "Now that he's getting a little help from the *Times* editorial page about the fascists on the Winsted board. Unlike our poor Anthony, who suffers in a slough of despondency and disgrace—abandoned by those who supposedly loved him."

To my dismay, Bobby let this go and, draining his wine, pointed at the bottle of '59 Pomerol and then at Laura, who dutifully refilled his glass. "So, what do you boys think about making Sunday chapel voluntary?"

"Is that a serious possibility, sir?" replied Max enthusiastically, eager to mix it up on a subject nearer to his heart.

Bobby nodded in Suzanne's direction. "Not if I . . . *and* the headmaster have anything to do with it." He cantered his fingers on *Essays and Prayers* at his elbow, reminding me not a little of Max's tic in that department.

"Maybe it would be a good idea," I said. "It's a little rough on some of the boys to have dogma forced down their throats, to feel they have to conform, when there are Catholics and Jews in the student body who might find it awkward." I gave a nod to Max across the table, hoping he'd back me up. "Religion, after all, should be voluntary. It should be a free choice to attend chapel, to believe as you see fit."

Bobby cocked a pale reddish orange eyebrow, as if I'd just sprung the trap he had carefully set.

"Spoken like a true Alden—your father, our long lost Alcibiades, would *indeed* be proud."

"*Bobby*," hissed Suzanne, this time in warning.

"Or is it *Kim—Kim-kim-kimmy* we're really missing, dear," Bobby snorted and wiped at his runny nose, "our dear Moscow-departed cousin?"

With this, he sent the cutlery rattling around the table. I started and looked past Suzanne's shoulder to the French doors, which gave out onto the piazza and its view of a moonlit Eden Lake . . . and on the far shore, my home, where I'd definitely rather have been.

"Laura dear"—Suzanne pushed herself unsteadily to her feet—"let's gather up the soup plates and bring in the roast beef. I sense the carnivores are out and require a feeding."

Bobby chuckled and gave me a triumphant sneer full of faux masculine prowess, as if to say, *One must go for the jugular when dealing with the weaker sex.* "The boys, the way I see it, voluntarily chose to go to Winsted in the first place. Nobody made them do it; that's *their* choice. There are close to twenty percent scholarship boys now—what?—twelve percent blacks. You take the king's shilling, you do his bidding. That's the Winsted way. Without boundaries and guidelines for behavior—the chapel as a regular refuge of quiet certainty—the place runs riot; it already runs riot, from what I hear in trustees meetings."

As Laura picked up my soup bowl, she touched a sympathetic hand to my shoulder.

Raising a clenched fist, Bobby turned to Max, as if neglectful of his guest.

"Max, do we run riot under our Mr. Folley? Or do you think our headmaster, our Texas Ranger, begins to understand that religion is a handmaiden to the creation of a more socially just society?" Bobby smiled at his sarcasm and gave me a playful salute. "Winsted offers you a tepid Episcopalian balm that won't stress your brains or your credulity. Think of it like a great big gravy bone given you to gnaw on, and growl at, and fight over—until you find something that suits you better . . . as your father did." With a significant look for my benefit, Bobby rattled on, one insider to another, while the coast was clear and Suzanne had yet to reappear from the kitchen. "In the old days"—and Bobby twined his forefinger and second finger—"the Aldens and Williamses were like that—saving this country from negligent capitalists and their self-serving notions of laissez faire. Once, freedom and social justice *were* the Winsted agenda, not cruel and pointless wars in far-away places."

"Roast *raw* beef, anyone?" announced Suzanne. "Now which one of you boys would like to do the carving? It's nice to have some real men around here for a change."

I was selected to carve and so tried to encourage Max to take over some of the conversational chores, remembering my grandmother's admonition: *A boring guest never sits at the same dinner table twice.*

"What did the headmaster call Vietnam, Max," I said, "in sacred studies class—a crusade against godless communism?"

"Did he really!" exclaimed Bobby.

"More like a sign of the coming apocalypse, if memory serves," said Max graciously.

"Really."

"But that was over a year ago," I added. "He's evolved since."

Suzanne stood beside me as I loaded the plates, her arm laid casually across my shoulder.

A forced smile from Bobby. "Damn well better evolve if he knows what's good for him. Perhaps I'll give him a call and turn the screws on his flaccid pecker, just in case."

"Oh"—Suzanne's hand suddenly gripped my shoulder—"I'm sure there must be somebody else you could sell out, dear, to get your oh so progressive views across. Given how much the Winsted board is *really* worth to you."

This snide comment probably had something to do with her recent conversation with Elliot Goddard at the reception for the president's adviser, when Elliot had continued to ply her with questions about Anthony Blunt, who was then undergoing intense interrogations by MI5 in London.

Laura smiled at her mother's repost and mouthed to me, *Take that.*

Bobby, the wind out of his sails, gave his wine a pondering swirl. "So, tell me, men, tell me about the drug situation. The boy who fell from the chapel tower—what's your take on that?"

"Drugs," said Max, putting in an oar and catching a crab, "they are everywhere today, sir. I suspect what goes on at Winsted is no different from anywhere else."

"In my day, Max, in your father's day, Peter, there were plenty of high jinks about, plenty of drinking and smoking and carrying on with girls from the town, but it was only the stuff of youthful energy and blowing off steam, not a concerted effort at undermining authority for its own sake. And these campus Marxists nowadays are a particularly spineless bunch—your SDS and Black Panthers, carping on and on and only offering pabulum for solutions. Don't you agree, dear?"

"In our day," said Suzanne with a tightening of her jaw, "we were up against the fascists in Germany, Italy, and Spain—and Japan. Our freedoms were under threat from every quarter." She gave me a significant look. "Some of us paid a heavier price than others."

Bobby was clearly not moved. "But what about that sniveling jumper from the bell tower—drugs, too—what's the truth?"

Suzanne Williams, whose unconcealed stares had been making me uncomfortable all evening, pointed her knife at her husband. "I don't think anybody can predict what can happen with these drugs. I'm sure the headmaster was as upset by the accident as anybody."

"It was a suicide, not an accident, and, in this case, no illegal drugs were involved," said Max a touch conspiratorially, as if to merge his opinion with the insider tone of the conversation. "The poor kid had been depressed. His dorm prefects couldn't get him up in the morning. They put him in the infirmary for observation. He walked out of the infirmary at three in the morning in his pajamas and climbed the tower, and that's how they found him."

"Oh, how frightful!" cried Suzanne, glancing at her daughter with a shiver of maternal concern.

Bobby cocked the wheelchair. "And now we have the shooting on Main Street all over the *Times*. Well, Winsted is being pilloried. Perhaps this will finally be enough to get some resignations from the war criminals on the board."

"But then whom will you have left to sell out, dear?"

Staring with bloodshot eyes at his wife, Bobby kept his wheelchair in motion, rocking back and forth, as if to generate enough kinetic energy to ram the table through his wife at the far end.

"And where in hell"—the armrests violently collided with the table, so that everyone jumped—"did he get that stupid gun in the first place?" He waved at his glass, and the moment Laura had it filled, it was drained with a gulp. "Did he have a loaded gun in his house with his children, and his students dropping by—Christ, the man must have been out of his mind. In my day, he just hid himself away in the library."

"The wine, dear," chimed Suzanne in a soothing voice, "and *your* drugs—sorry, medications: doctor's no-no."

324 DAVID ADAMS CLEVELAND
Max's face came alert, as if two little antennas on his brow had sprung to life.

"He loved books . . .," Max murmured, which was Max's way of saying: "I loved him." "He was the finest teacher I've ever known, a great teacher, but I don't think he could resolve the contradictions of the war in Vietnam. It ate at him."

"This stupid Vietnam mess," Bobby snapped, his voice rising to a near scream. "It's just a metastasized cancer from the Red-baiting of the fifties. It will be the ruin of us. Why can't we learn to leave well enough alone? Charlie had that much right. The North Vietnamese simply want to provide a more just society for their people and rid themselves of an oppressive imperialist heritage."

"Ah, do I hear the echo of a certain editorial in the *Times*?" said Suzanne.

"Don't you agree, Peter? Surely you're not taken in by all this blather from the administration about the North Vietnamese only being proxies for the Soviets and the Chinese."

"Somebody seems to be arming them . . . and the Vietcong," I replied.

"They are nationalists, agrarian reformers, and anti-imperialists—anti-fascists, for Christ's sake. They just want their own country back and to be left in peace."

Max and Laura both looked at me like I was out of my mind to engage this drunk at the head of the table.

"It seems the South Vietnamese just want to be left in peace, too."

"There isn't a *South*. It's a false dichotomy. They're all Vietnamese; they want what all people want: social justice. There wouldn't even be a war if we had just stayed out of it and let them solve their own problems. There were so many missed opportunities for rapprochement with Ho Chi Minh—like Mao, he just wants to reform things; he only wants what's best for his people."

"You do sound just like sweet Anthony sometimes, do you not?" said Suzanne. "Pity, too, no more convivial conversations with Kim. I'm sure he'd like to hear your views. Of course, if you shout just a little louder, he just might, all the way to Moscow."

"You're drunk, you fool."

"Give your besotted father some more wine, Laura. He needs some catching up."

"If we'd only engaged with Stalin instead of always threatening the Soviet Union, we could have avoided the whole mess in the first place. The Cold War was simply cooked up by the military-industrial complex. Even Eisenhower figured out that much. It's idiots like Elliot Goddard and *his* Winsted toadies who are to blame for this madness. Five years ago, they almost got us blown to smithereens fucking around like little boys in a sandbox, throwing sand in one another's faces. And now we reap the whirlwind. If we don't nuke ourselves to kingdom come, we'll bleed ourselves dry."

"Boys, I think you should visit my dear husband's fallout shelter. Now there's a happy prospect. More roast beef, Max?"

Bobby stared hard at the play of reflections on the tabletop. "Funny . . . how Moscow got wind of all our nuclear arms technology so quickly."

"You're full of shit, dear; shall I wheel you to the commode?"

Bobby eased his face upward to launch a smirk down the table. "Precisely the kind of indiscretions that got his father killed."

Silence descended for many long seconds, and before I could summon my wits to ask about the "indiscretions," Suzanne sprang up and grabbed Max's plate.

"Laura has some good news for you, dear. Peter, cut some more slabs for Max, if you please—and yourself. You both look as if you haven't properly been fed in a while."

Bobby quivered with a simmering rage as I set to carving.

"How many lost opportunities . . .," he continued. "All the wars in this horrific century have been mistakes. If we'd just left things well enough alone . . ."

Suzanne's eyes narrowed as she now stared at her wineglass. "My father was wounded on the Somme, nearly blinded. My brother was killed in North Africa. Don't tell me they fought for nothing." She rose even higher in her seat, narrow chin thrust forward. Then she reached for the bone-handled carving knife where I'd set it on the table and pointed it directly at her husband. "And you . . . and don't forget Peter's father was badly wounded in the war fighting the Nazis. I . . . should know, confound it: I nursed him though six months of rehabilitation."

At this, Suzanne looked at me and wiped tears from her eyes, then held up her flattened palm.

"Laura, tell your father your good news."

We were all jolted as Bobby again slammed his wheelchair into the table. "And look at us now in Vietnam, napalming civilians and indiscriminately bombing the people of North Vietnam—are we any better? We've become masters at indiscriminate murder from on high; we've outdone the Nazis."

"Well, you should know, even though you always liked to blame the Norden bombsight . . . or was it shaky hands, do you suppose?"

"I—"

"Shut up, dear. Laura—speak, tell your father."

"I auditioned this week with American Ballet Theater . . . and, well, I just heard yesterday: I've got a contract for the coming year."

"That's great," said Max.

"Congratulations," I said.

"It's a triumph," said Suzanne. "I talked to Tudor last night on the phone; he said she was by far and away the best at the audition. ABT and Lucia are very pleased."

"What does it mean, you have a contract?" asked Bobby.

"For a year, I'm guaranteed a place and a salary in the company."

"In New York?"

"Sure, I mean, we'll be touring, but yes, New York."

"That means what?"

Suzanne handed Max another slice of beef. "We'll get her a good apartment in a good neighborhood and I'll be there a lot to make sure all goes well. In fact, after tonight, I may just move in with my talented daughter."

"That's my birthday present: You're going to leave me?"

Suzanne smiled serenely, perhaps triumphantly, and touched Max's elbow.

"Max, I want to hear more about your piano, about your mother and her famous students at Juilliard—do tell."

At this, Max, who had been computing the possibilities of Laura's New York apartment, launched into full sycophancy.

"Oh, she'd be thrilled with your Steinway grand, and I couldn't help noticing you've kept it perfectly tuned. Like everything else around here. Mr. Williams, I can't get over how beautifully preserved everything is, your home and the artwork. Almost as fine as Palazzo Fenway."

Bobby sighed. "God forbid, Max—not Palazzo Fenway, that dusty old shrine to self-absorption."

"Oh, but sir, it's exquisite."

Bobby gave a quirky smile, seemingly distracted and out of sorts with this new line of conversation but willing to give it a chance. "Yes, my aunt's little museum does seem a crowd pleaser. Well, I do my best—God knows—to keep it all going. Notwithstanding lighting problems and endless leaks. Electricians and plumbers—the old pile is a sinecure for their unions. But the world tires one, Max. It's all about raising money these days. Everything takes more and more money. The insurance is something awful."

Max only brightened.

"But I think it's fantastic the way you've kept your home the way it is . . . not just like some museum, but, like you said, keep the *traditions* going."

"Do we make a life here, Suzanne—family traditions?"

"We try, dear, we try."

"Your aunt Isabella must have been a fascinating lady," said Max. "To have met Sargent and James and summered in Venice—wow." Max gestured to the wall behind me, where even more Sargent watercolors of Venice were hanging.

"She hated the woods. Not enough sycophants for her amusement. And Palazzo Fenway always spooked me as a child. Auntie could be charming one second and cut you to the quick the next. Really a mausoleum to a rather eclectic Victorian taste. My father, Amory, couldn't stand visiting the place and her moldy old masters gave him nightmares. He told me he was sure one of the soldiers in the *Judith and Holofernes* would come out at night and cut his throat."

Max bent toward his host like an intimate. "And their summers in Venice . . . Palazzo Barberini and the moonlit gondola rides."

"Ah, so you know something about all that?" Bobby cracked one of his rare smiles of the evening.

"Tell Max about how your mother—the *great* artiste—tried to drown herself by jumping off the balcony of Palazzo Barberini."

The ensuing silence, as if exhaustion had finally set in, was so complete that I took the plunge, figuring it was now or never.

"Mr. Williams, Max is something of a piano prodigy; you should really tell him about your playing days at Cambridge and the teachers you studied with."

"Prodigy, I don't think so," said Max.

"Cambridge must have been exciting in the thirties," I said.

"Oh very," offered Suzanne. "Do tell the boys, dear, about the Music Society. It was Anthony, wasn't it, who procured your first concert at

Wigmore Hall. How he blew the trumpet for you back then, his little American protégé."

"Wigmore Hall." Bobby sighed, a certain calm coming into his eyes as he stared into the night beyond the French doors. "You were there, weren't you, dear?"

"I was there," she admitted.

"I was good, wasn't I? Everybody said so."

She hesitated and then smiled: the first and only kindness to pass between them that evening.

"Good, yes, you were very good; the Chopin was splendid."

"Truth is," said Bobby, "most of the great figures in music were in Germany then, many on their way to exile as the fascists took over. I studied mostly theory and composition." The wistful look on Bobby's face deepened, and with it, the tone of his undamaged skin color—chameleonlike—seemed to deepen as well. Or so it struck me in retrospect. "Trouble was, to be a true artist, you must give up the world; and Cambridge was full of politics—exciting stuff. I found it rather hard to concentrate on my studies. My practicing was affected by the tenor of the moment."

Suzanne pointedly raised her glass and nodded. "And Anthony's wooing, no doubt. How he stuck by you to the end, silly fool. Kim always told him you couldn't be trusted."

Bobby lowered his gaze in a kind of panicked stupor. Max, looking not a little confused by the unreferenced names, made an attempt to right the conversation.

"My mother said the same thing about musicians in the thirties; of course, she thought the best were in Vienna. The only reason she even managed to escape to London in 1939 was because she truly was a prodigy. Her British supporters in London managed to talk the foreign office into giving her an entry visa. Summer before last, when I was helping her run her master class at Palazzo Pisani, she told me all about how she got one of the last trains out of Vienna for London before the invasion of Poland. Venice, you see, well, the city made her very sad because she'd played recitals there as a teenager before the war, at La Fenice. Everyone in her family was a musician—they all died in the camps—and had either played concerts in Venice or gone on holiday. Their apartment in Vienna was filled with mementoes of Venice. Every site we passed that summer, she was reminded of something, of some long-lost print or painting of Venice that had hung on the wall of her childhood room, a glass paperweight on her desk. She was allowed only one suitcase when she left."

This was the first time I'd heard Max speak sympathetically about his mother.

"What an unusual young man you are in this day and age to care about such things," said Bobby, clearly moved. "Most young people think of fascism as a quaint bogeyman. Take Laura, for instance. . . ." He smiled at his daughter as if to make amends for neglecting her accomplishments. "None of your friends could care less about history or politics, much less old Isabella's Venetian nightmare. Most of them can barely speak English and have nothing interesting to say even when they try. It must be all those mirrors, don't you think, looking at their tits all day, wondering if they're thin enough."

Suzanne flung her napkin down the table, where it settled on her husband's untouched plate.

Laura grabbed the napkin, a blood-red stain expanding at a corner. She swiped at her unruly hair, her face blushing. "Daddy, you forget I used to go there a lot with you. People love Palazzo Fenway. Mother and I and Colonel Fairburn were there for the Christmas carol service—it was the most beautiful thing, with all the hundreds of candles. And the brass players from the Boston Symphony. Remember how much you used to like the Vermeer?"

"Christmas . . . where was I?"

"You didn't want to go," said Suzanne, emptying her wineglass and passing the serving dishes of roasted potatoes and string beans. "Not since they kicked you off the board."

Bobby looked across at his wife, his face tensing, as if suddenly aware of some remote but very real menace. He squinted at our gathered reflections on the table as the serving dishes were slid his way, and then made a gesture of dismissal or possibly despair.

"So, where's my fucking birthday cake?"

Max's rendition of that evening in *Like a Forgotten Angel* has remained a crowd pleaser; according to one critic, "the most lusciously romantic scene in either of his novels." Bobby provided the focus for Max's evocative dive into the splendors of the Williamses' idyllic past. For me, knowing what I now know, it is the women's faces that haunt me . . . and the paintings: Laura, whose emerging sense of self, if not her libido, had been abruptly diverted by the raw lust that leapt off the pages of those erotic letters secreted in her mother's closet, that frantic, even tortured love—not so much forbidden, certainly not by shame, but by fear of disloyalty and ruin; and Suzanne, playing for time as the radical loyalties of her youth crumbled, still clutching tight the memory of a man who might as well have been there in my stead, in the very moment she recognized, as if in my face, how all the betrayals and sacrifices she had endured could, at the end, undo everything she held dear—not the least of which, her daughter's career.

Only weeks before at Winsted, Elliot Goddard had intimated to her the extent of Bobby's perfidies over the glittering tea service in the headmaster's house. For more than fifteen years, Elliot had been fishing for her vulnerabilities, for the love letters he suspected could ruin them both, or just possibly bring closure to the nightmare of Kim Philby's exposure as a Soviet mole and his defection in 1963, and my father's unsolved disappearance ten years before that: the sword of Damocles hanging over his legacy.

Little did he know that, in terms of closure, Suzanne had long beaten him to the punch.

And I blame myself for not having had the gumption to confront Bobby and Suzanne on their home turf and at least get some of the truth out of them. Everything conspired to keep me off balance: Max's sycophancy, for one thing, and then there was Laura, seventeen years old and headed for stardom within the year, who seemed to lean on my every word, trying to catch my reaction to every twist in the conversation. She seemed so worldly-wise to me, and so much a rebellious young woman of the sixties that I felt utterly out of my depth and inept. Though resisting the regal polish of her mother, she emanated a frothy beauty as natural as the spring woods: Her scraggly honey-blond hair, still concealing a purple petal or two, cascaded in unkempt ringlets off her brow; her blue, softly lit eyes, flickering behind full lashes, sought mine throughout the evening as if for assurance of a kind I couldn't fathom. She wore a pink sport shirt with frayed collar and no bra, two identical protrusions in the faded cotton heralding a body alert to its needs.

And then there was the ever-imperious Suzanne . . . I was simply petrified. And I guess her mention of having nursed my father during the war only further messed with my mind: I kept wondering if I'd heard right. Suzanne, of course, in her crimson silk evening dress with the deep décolletage—something fashionable out of Paris in the fifties—stole the show, as was her wont. Emotionally ragged and having had too much to drink (fuming inwardly, I wrongly assumed, because of her braless daughter's unkempt hair), she still managed a stunning stage presence for the remainder of the evening. Her hair was more brassy than golden, like her daughter's, and sumptuously set in soft waves that fell to her bare shoulders, her makeup applied with taste and precision to define the high cheekbones and frame the searing blues of her eyes, her pale English skin superbly preserved, with only the merest hint of wrinkles. No one could mistake them for anything but mother and daughter, and yet, poised in flickering chiaroscuro like figures in a Georges de La Tour ensemble as they listened to Max's Chopin after dinner, they were far from identical, as if some baffling genetic struggle hung in the balance. Yet one more mystery to remain unresolved until twenty years later, and something Max would capitalize on in his second novel without knowing the half of it.

But for Suzanne—Bobby, as well—only two things really mattered: that her past as a Soviet agent remained hidden so as not to bring dishonor on her family and derail her daughter's career, that her treacherous disloyalty not be discovered for fear of retribution by a vengeful KGB.

Youth and age . . . past and present leavened by depthless deceit . . . and all that's lost in translation over the fleeting years.

After dinner, at Bobby's urging, Max played the Steinway concert grand in the drawing room—played better than I'd heard him in a year, in spite of, or maybe because of, all the wine he'd drunk. He played Mozart and Chopin. Laura and Suzanne were visibly moved. Their bodies seemed to come alive where they sat listening beneath the Dewing murals. Bobby had tears in his eyes, his fingers covering the notes on the armrests of his wheelchair; between pieces, he could barely contain himself. "Oh yes, wonderful touch, Max, and your lyricism is first-rate. Do you know the Chopin Nocturne in E-flat Major Opus Nine? Whom did you say your mother studied with? . . . Yes, of course, now I remember her name." I suppose Max simply got carried away with his rendition of that evening. It's in the cadences of his prose, in the moonlight flooding that elegant drawing room overlooking the lake, every note at his fingertips evoking the past, when Bobby had been young and had practiced hours every afternoon over the long, careless summers of the twenties, when my father, as a boy, would stop by to listen, reading in the garden or on the piazza as he waited for Bobby to finish. That, in Max's second novel, was the Williamses' golden age, Fitzgerald's Jazz Age, when Amory Williams was headmaster at Winsted and his summer home was filled with visiting musicians and artists of every stripe from Europe, or "up from New York" for a long weekend. Max's playing, and later his prose, immortalized that free-spirited world, glimpsed in the artworks hanging in discreet corners and alcoves—left by visiting painters—especially the Fauvist figurative works of Amory's "crazy" wife, Amaryllis, a fabulously talented painter who ran off to Paris with her teacher from the Art Students League, leaving her son, Bobby, and headmaster husband, and setting in motion the string of scandals that resulted in Amory's forced resignation in 1926.

But those painful events were nowhere in evidence that evening, only the artistic and erotic residue channeled through Max's rendition of Chopin's nocturnes—all of it infused with the smells of the spring woods wafting through the wide-open French doors giving onto the piazza. Or perhaps it had something to do with the many silver-framed photographs carefully displayed on the huge concert grand, which peered over Max's shoulder as he bent to the keyboard—black-and-white shadows of the twenties that merged into more somber images of the thirties. Bobby's short career as a concert pianist was captured in several: a dashing young man in white tie poised at the keyboard in the music hall of Trinity College, Cambridge; a triumph at London's Wigmore Hall (arranged by Anthony Blunt); a single performance at Boston's Symphony Hall at a children's concert; and performances at small recital halls across the country during the Depression. But it was the five or six publicity photos of Suzanne that Max's playing seemed most to animate in the imagination: a white goddess posed in arabesque with the Sadler's Wells Ballet, dancing roles from Aurora and Odette/Odile to Giselle at a gala for King George VI in 1938. Careers and lives cut short by the war (and orders of the KGB or, as it was in those days, the NKGB and GRU) but living on, at least for that evening in Max's playing, and Suzanne's merciless expectations for her daughter . . . and in Max's novels.

Even with all the unpleasantness at the table, I couldn't help feeling sorry for Bobby with his burnt and arthritic hands as he listened intently to Max play, his sad eyes filling with tears, as did Suzanne's. I found myself glancing from the silver-framed publicity photos of the twenty-year-old phenom of the prewar European ballet world to her present incarnation—Suzanne's cool English hauteur softened by the music and flaming candelabra that had been brought in from the dining room. Her arms and legs responded to the music in restrained miniature gestures, like a kind of shorthand, as she wiped the side of her hand along her cheek to catch a stray tear. Many years later, at the Sussex estate of Colonel Fairburn, the last in her string of lovers and conspirators, she told me a version of her first meeting with Bobby in wartime London, when he played the piano in her family home on Cadogan Square, the music punctuated by the terrifying passage of a buzz bomb across the night sky. But I suspect her tears had more to do with the Cambridge Bobby of her youth, the Red Bobby recruited by Anthony Blunt—for that one glorious moment at London's Wigmore Hall, when she, too, had been a star, and recruited, "seduced of my virginity and bourgeois susceptibilities" by Kim Philby, when the cause of antifascism animated their hearts, when an idealized Soviet Union stirred their souls, when the talented Bobby gave it all up for the fraternal cause—as she did the ballet world for nursing—to navigate B17's over Germany and pass on to his handler and then his wife critical data about the far-from-certain accuracy of the Norden bombsight. When they betrayed their countries with icy conviction. Or was it really, as she told me all those years later, about the life and the man that fate had presented her in the Guilford rehabilitation hospital in early 1944, the one true love stolen from her, for which her daughter and her daughter's career would serve as partial recompense, something along the lines of her confession to me at Colonel Fairburn's home in Sussex: "The only times I felt truly alive was onstage and then in the fight against fascism . . . and in your father's arms."

Was I an ally or yet another threat to that legacy of love?

ANATOLY GORSKY TO MOSCOW CENTER, MAY 1946,
KGB FILE 45100, VENONA DECRYPT 1491

We undoubtedly need to find a good courier for Homer [Maclean]. All our people complain of the lowered quality of contacts since the war. Unfortunately, we do not have suitable candidates since the defection of Clever Girl [Elizabeth Bentley] and the freezing of our apparatus. We have few Soviet operatives available, I explain to little avail. The CPUSA people we do have are not adequately developed politically and are unqualified for their tasks and topics. And so I have met again with Firebird [Suzanne Williams] in Boston and she has agreed to serve as courier to Homer's wife, who has now relocated to her family's home in New York City. Homer visits most weekends from Washington. Firebird is delighted at the prospect of trips to New York, and she and Homer's wife were friends in Cambridge and London, so meetings between them should appear to be inconspicuous. Firebird complains bitterly about being "trapped" in Boston's Beacon Hill with her injured husband, Amadeus [Robert Williams]. She suggested relocating to New York and even resuming her dancing career. I have warned her against drawing too much attention to herself; MI5 may still suspect her from her prewar days working with Stanley [Kim Philby]. At least she does not have ties to CPUSA; Amadeus dropped all ties before the war. I assured her that she does well to nurse our fraternal comrade in his time of need; she has money and flexibility to travel at irregular intervals. She even talks about moving to Washington and starting a ballet school, where she will be well placed to help us reestablish our government networks, now mostly run by CPUSA people, who lack discretion and reliability. I have promised to relay her thoughts to Moscow Center. Of her dedication to our cause, there can be no doubt; of her loyalty to her husband, there are many doubts. I do worry about her discretion. She reminds me of Clever Girl: a sophisticated and independent and talented woman of great sexual needs. Even Stanley is not immune to her charms. Her husband clearly is not meeting her requirements in that department.

When Max finished playing, Suzanne stood, a little rocky, as if awakened from a dream, and went over and gave Max a theatrical kiss on the cheek to thank him, and announced that she and Laura were going to do kitchen duty. "Maid's off, the attendant is off—everybody's off—so it's Laura and me for kitchen duty. Come, dear." Max asked if he could help—anything to hang out with Laura—and was recruited to dry dishes. Suzanne nodded to where Bobby sat, head bowed, asleep in his wheelchair.

"Keep an eye on him for a few minutes, Peter, until I'm back, and then Laura and I will get him off to bed."

No sooner had they disappeared than Bobby started awake and looked around as if he didn't recognize where he was. Then he saw me and smiled, and despite his disfigurement, I sensed a real warmth and happiness in his eyes.

"That's all that really matters, you see . . . the art that lives on, that survives our ridiculous preoccupations." And he waved me over. "Come, I'll show you something, you'll understand better."

He released the brakes on his chair, wheeled around and began to propel himself down a long passageway to a far wing of the cottage that adjoined the veranda nearest the lake. The floorboards squeaked and I noticed signs of damp and leaks almost everywhere on the paneled walls and ceiling. Bobby halted before a large oak door with a key in the lock. "If you'll do me the favor or turning the key; the lock needs an oiling." My first sensation upon stepping into the huge darkened space was the musty warmth held inside, released like a long-held breath, redolent of dust, oil paint or turpentine, something vaguely spoiled but immemorial, savory of hard sweat and creative doings. Moonlight streamed in through a northern skylight, casting indistinct shadows across the floor, where they leapt in angled geometries to scramble up the tongue-and-groove paneling. A line of six-over-six sashed windows stretched along the entire length of the studio, the swirls in the antique glass adding to the smoky luster of Eden Lake, a compact plain of pure white behind broad stripes of blackest black.

"The light switch is behind you on the wall," I heard Bobby say.

I didn't want to move; I didn't want to spoil the dreamy feeling of the whiteness, the simple purity of its play across the hand-carved weightless rafters, illuminating a workplace of tireless labor, a thing mute yet fluid with possibilities, reminding me of the old photographs I'd seen of George Inness's Bloomfield studio in a scrapbook General Alden kept on his favorite artist. I could make out easels and worktables and posing platforms, and shelves littered with still-life bric-a-brac: bottles, vases, drop cloths, wax fruit, Kabuki masks, plaster reproductions of classical figures—all female, including a near-life-size Venus de Milo and a stunning Winged Victory—not plaster, I realized, but cold marble, which seemed to absorb the moonlight and so emanate a throbbing lucent whiter-than-white whiteness in the carved feathers, as if the outstretched wings were in actual flight or descending from heaven. In storage bins, hundreds of canvases were lined up like so many books on a shelf. Underfoot, the floorboards were tacky with old paint or spilled thinners.

"All right, leave the light off if you like. I agree, it's quite nice, soothing on the eyes."

Bobby wheeled himself around in a quick tour, as if to make sure everything was just as he'd left it. I went to a worktable where tubes of Windsor & Newton oils were precisely laid out next to a palette encrusted with hardened arabesques of faded color. Campbell soup cans, labels preserved under varnish and devoid of irony, held clumps of brushes adhered as one.

"I loved it in here as a boy, when I was allowed to watch my mother paint, on her good days. Or when she recruited me as a model—a little discomfiting by my teenage years, posing in the buff for one's mother. But nudity was very natural for her; on hot summer days, she painted that way. Only a few art historians remember her now—though that is changing, but in her day, in the early twenties, she was the toast of progressive art circles in Boston and then New York. Later, even Paris got excited over her work, her lovers—a little hard to separate the two. She had the most gorgeous red hair and green eyes and a laugh that echoed like the wind in the eaves. Her banker father staked her to the Beaux-Arts in Paris before the First World War, but she fooled him and studied with Matisse instead. That's where Amory, my father, met her. She got him to buy the Matisse nude of a satyr in the drawing room. All of Isabella's Matisses in Palazzo Fenway came by way of Amaryllis. Amory was a musician and connoisseur, or so he liked to think, of classical sculpture. Not much of an eye for modern art, but he liked my mother's figurative things and doted on her in his way, not that she was cut out to be a headmaster's wife—nor he a headmaster, I suppose. "My wild filly," he called her, "not a harness that can hold her." August 1914 sent them both fleeing back to Boston—she, six months pregnant, so I'm told, where they were married. Convenient for her, the money, the society patronage, as even old Boston tried desperately to keep up with New York. She refused to live at Winsted, spent the winters in New York teaching at the Art Students League—had Chase's old studio on Eightieth and Broadway—and then her summers here at Hermitage. Amory built the studio for her, a new addition custom-made to her specifications. She was the life of the parties here in the twenties; all her artist friends from New York were up every weekend: actors, musicians, playwrights—all in the guestbook. That was my summer world growing up—big names, bigger egos, who drank themselves silly. The stuff that went on would make your hippies of today blush. But at least they had *real* talent. Amaryllis didn't take on phonies."

I tentatively squeezed a zinc tube and turned to where Bobby sat in his wheelchair, half-turned to the windows, his features softly illuminated like one of those publicity photos on the Steinway grand. I could see how once he had been very attractive.

"It must have been fun for you and my father."

"We would sneak around at night, watching the boating parties, the carryings-on of the adults. They hung Chinese lanterns on the canoes and paddled out on the lake, sometimes a dozen or more, and drifted. . . . Someone would start up with his violin or another his trumpet or saxophone, and they'd serenade one another, improvising under the stars. One could watch and listen for hours, until dawn. Father enlisted me to play during cocktails and dinner. John wasn't allowed to come over, of course, but it never stopped him. We were wild little boys back then, wild as Indians, though I could never keep up with him. I was forced to practice for three hours every afternoon; that was my father's doing—Mother couldn't have cared less. John was my escape to the faraway woods and the old pastures and the swimming beach. He knew every corner of the property. Nobody paid any attention to me except for him. I doted on his attention, worse luck. As I did my mother's . . . only when she needed a male model, when the mood struck her, when she wanted to show me off to her pals, when her drinking hadn't completely taken her over. She tried to get her hands on John, too, get him to pose for her, but he was far too shy for that sort of thing."

I stared up into the skylights, where the tallest of the white pines flagged the night sky with their inky blottings.

"I'm sure our place was pretty boring," I said, admiring again the articulated feathers of the Winged Victory of Samothrace, "even for a scholar like my father."

"A scholar, perhaps, but he'd scare me to death the way he tempted fate. He had a streak in him of the daredevil, as if he always had to prove himself to someone—although certainly not to me."

"His mother was pretty tough on him."

He laughed. "Winsted's iron maiden. You have no idea. . . . She might as well have put a bullet through Amory's head."

"She had a tragic life, first losing her husband, and then her son."

At this, he only smiled and pointed over to the bins.

"See those canvases over there? Take them out and prop them against the wall. I've been meaning for you to have a look. Here, I'll turn on the lights for you."

"Oh my, *here* you are!"

Suzanne had discovered us in the studio, her voice flustered, as if we'd been caught in some impropriety. Reclaiming her husband with the efficiency of a baggage handler, she wheeled him off to bed.

"Bedtime, dear. Max and Laura are just finishing up. Do turn the key in the lock, Peter, as you leave."

I drifted out to the veranda, reeling, wanting to escape, waiting for Max so we could beat it. I was gripping the railing when I thought again of my mother's description of walking through the French doors and finding Kim Philby and Suzanne—*canoodling* was the word she used—on the piazza. I put my hands in my pockets, shivering even though it was quite warm. The moon was full, a throbbing white orb gliding over the topmost boughs of the pines. Seeing Elsinore across the lake, the faint glitter of its deep-set windows like glaucous eyes, I felt as I'd been transported through a mirror, watching myself . . . observing an old washed-up world of arcane principles that no one gave a hoot about anymore.

Then Laura found me.

"I left Max drying; he never stops talking. But thank God he saved me from having to play the piano and being *endlessly* criticized."

She seemed edgy, lost, trying to apologize to me for having to put up with "everything" over dinner. She had gleaned just enough from the love letters to have found some of the exchanges between her parents not a little frightening. She was desperate to tell me all, to broach her worst suspicions . . . but was I a potential ally or an even greater menace?

Twice she apologized for something "stupid" in her last letter to me. Then she found the pluck to put it out there.

"I think my mother misses your father," she said.

"Yeah?"

I turned to where she stood by the veranda railing, her face bathed in liquid light, as if she weren't quite there, as if she, too, was only intent on escape. She wouldn't look me in the eye.

"You heard what she said at the table. How she nursed your father in the war."

"Yeah, I hadn't realized that."

"Me, neither," she replied, lying (their correspondence had begun the day after his release from the hospital in late April 1944). "I was wondering if you knew—I sometimes feel that I'm the last to know anything around here. Was he wounded badly?"

"I think he almost lost a leg. . . . He had a long red scar on his thigh. He was fighting with the Greek Resistance."

"So . . . he really was a hero?"

Her uncanny echo of my like-minded questions to others gave me a start.

"Oh, I guess. There's a display case in the gym at school with his medals."

"Yes, I've seen them; my mother showed them to me."

"Okay."

"The family thing is a little weird, huh? My father said they were best friends growing up at Elysium."

"Yeah, he was just telling me."

"Sorry you had to endure that tonight."

"Well . . . they were third cousins."

She tried to laugh, to make light of it: "And you're the only cousin I've got; Mom's brother was killed before he had time to marry."

"Sad, isn't it?"

"How pathetic. A dying breed—well, this place would kill off anybody."

"Your father was just telling me how my father was best man at his wedding at the colonel's home in Sussex."

"Hillders—'Tara,' that's what my mother calls it—her Elysium. Where she spent all her summers growing up."

"Charles Fairburn gave me a lot of shit about your coming to visit Winsted for the crew race."

"Tell me about it. He's weirdly protective for a godfather, but I'm sure she put him up to it. I told you: She opened a letter I wrote you. She's such a royal bitch."

"She seems pretty proud of your getting into that dance company and everything."

"Damn right—and the excuse for moving down to New York." She was fidgeting with a strand of hair, her eyes glancing off mine as these pieces of our intertwined history were inventoried. "She's using me, you see, to get away from my father. She's always threatening to divorce him. I feel like a pawn in an elaborate chess game—a game I was born into . . . but, I'd like to know, *who's* moving the pieces?"

I understood exactly what she meant.

"The unknown author." I smiled to myself.

She placed her hand on mine where it rested on the veranda railing. It was less a gesture of intimacy or fondness and more one of solidarity—that she hoped she could trust me.

"And . . . *Kim*," she said tentatively.

"Kim?"

"My father mentioned the name at the table tonight."

She'd seen the name in the love letters.

"Oh . . . I have no idea," I said, lying.

I heard her sigh into a long, uncomfortable silence.

"Will you be around this summer?"

"I'll be in Crete on a dig."

"Lucky you. Summer, I take the company class in New York. Fall we're in rehearsal and performance at the Met but I'll definitely get to Winsted for a football game."

"You don't—I mean if it causes trouble—have to do that."

"But I want to. I'll be free of all this. I'll be there."

"Thanks."

We stood there, becalmed, drained of conversation. Something in the healing white of Eden Lake allowed us a hope of repose, of standing fast against the tides, as if we'd glimpsed new paths, but without signposts. I felt her sigh and her hand shifted as she tossed back her hair, as if she might lay her head against my shoulder. Dazzled as we were by that moon-haunted world, we failed to hear her mother, who stepped onto the piazza and abruptly began ordering her daughter around. For an instant, startled, Laura's hand had squeezed mine and shot away.

"After you put your rehearsal kit in the dryer, go up and say good night to your father; he's in a state. He wants to know more about New York—just tell him it will be for only a few months a year. And, while you're at it, why don't you comb out that disgusting rat's nest."

Alone again, I found my head spinning, partly from the wine, but mostly because of the paintings Bobby had gotten me to pull from the bins. They were all nudes, some more finished than others, in a wonderful slashing style, a mixture of early Matisse, using bold primary colors, neutral backgrounds, and expressive Fauvist energy in the brushwork. I did not recognize the tall, leggy model until Bobby told me. She was beautiful, stunning, with the lithe, sinewy strength of a long-distance swimmer, small upcurving breasts and fountains of muted color to indicate her mons of pubic hair. Even then, with the overhead lights on, I couldn't believe my eyes. How could I? It was beyond comprehension.

"She used to swim in the nude over from your boathouse late at night and go right to the studio door off the piazza to pose for Amaryllis.

They'd be at it for hours and then she'd swim back early in the morning, with nobody the wiser. Were they lovers, too? you're probably wondering. Most likely. Amaryllis was like that: Art was her means to love."

I heard the piano again in the drawing room, and slowly the white of the lake and the disquieting beauty of those raw nudes—every paint mark lush and still alive, as if set to canvas only yesterday and not fifty years ago—dissolved, to be replaced by images of Max at the piano, as he had been an hour before, as I'd found him at practice over the previous years . . . his presence a comfort in all the confusion, and a vague source of happiness. Something about the music and the moonlight and the milky gray roofline of our cottage across the lake . . . as if I were watching my world from a reverse angle, from a place more joyous than what I had ever known, as if I was poised to escape, if only I had the wits to flee, as Laura was on the verge of doing.

The more I gazed outward, the more that aqueous expanse of the lake, like a glacial abyss, took on a hypnotic intensity. . . . Who were we—really? Who were those people residing across the lake in that fortresslike cottage of raw fieldstone—so unlike the elegant and charming clapboard Hermitage with its French doors and panoramic embrace of creation. From somewhere beneath the eaves, Tibetan temple bells chimed. I realized, that though full of *things*, our house was utterly empty—my grandmother now three years dead and my mother refusing ever again to darken the door of "that Victorian monstrosity." Was it really a mausoleum, like Max said? I found myself almost glad to be where I was on the piazza of Hermitage, hoping Laura might return and Max continue playing into the night. And maybe Bobby's words *were* full of hope.

"You see, young man, as they say, *ars longa, vita brevis*. You're a classicist, what does it mean?"

"Human life is short, but art goes on forever."

"But what does it mean?"

"What it says."

"I fear they don't teach the classics like they used to a Winsted. It comes from Hypocrites and the reference is to the art of healing. Or as Chaucer put it, 'The life is short, the craft so long to learn.' Ask your friend Max, or any musician, or a dancer—enough of them around these parts. Or as Sir John Davies put it, 'Skill comes so slow, and life doth so fast fly; We learn so little and forget so much.'"

He'd swiveled in his wheelchair and faced me straight on for the first time, his bloodshot eyes drifting from my face to my feet and back again.

"Perhaps another way of putting it is that the spirit of the paintings will survive. For you see, Amaryllis's reputation *is* on the rise, along with that of the other Americans who worked in Paris when she did. Collectors and connoisseurs are already beating the bushes for her things. And in time, I will release these to the market, as the Buddhists release caged sparrows . . . so returning their song to the skies: the story of a wonderful artist and her model. So have no fear, she will live—oh, how she will live on."

I found myself struggling with the doubts that seemed only weakness and disloyalty. Doubts in my grandmother's refrain about the cousins across the lake: how Amory steadily drank himself to death after his wife left him, leaving a string of homosexual alliances that the trustees had to hush up. How the board had to deal with the serial lovers of Amaryllis in Paris; how she ended her tragically short life an embittered syphilitic, dying in a Swiss sanatorium in 1936.

But there was no denying the glamour of the Williamses in the twenties. Max saw to that in his second novel, *Gardens of Saturn*. As he put it to me, as if echoing Bobby Williams on the way back to our cottage that night, "Hey, so what if they're royally fucked-up. Their art collection and the sad, glittering stories about their fucked-up lives will last forever. Material like that—it's what makes life interesting . . . makes us alive."

As would Amaryllis's Fauvist figurative paintings, singing their songs for higher and higher prices as collectors of American modernism clamored to score an example of this feminist icon: "A Georgia O'Keeffe on steroids, full of sexual energy and the expressive power that only boys like Gottlieb and Motherwell were once thought to own" (*ARTnews*).

Except for Civil War historians and the loyal alumni of Winsted, General Alden was virtually unknown (American art history specialists extolled his Inness collection); my grandfather's innovative surgical techniques were footnotes in medical history; and my father was increasingly forgotten as his classmates and colleagues dropped by the wayside.

Doing the right thing is never a guarantee.

There were footsteps behind me. But I was so dazzled and transported outside myself, I did not turn from the moon and the lake and the white pines. From behind, I was encircled by hands and arms, which began at my shoulders and slid themselves across my chest to fully embrace me, and tightly, too. It was a woman's body, her soft breasts pressed against my spine, her perfumed face tucked into the crook of my neck. I was so surprised that I couldn't get a word out. Fear and shock gripped my heart. I could smell the wine on her breath as she hummed along with Max's Chopin. A thigh lifted to ride my hip. Then her lips were pressed into the nape of my neck and I could feel her kisses boring into me: a thing so desperate and alive that I thought my very soul was being sucked from my body. And as if to leave no doubt, one of those hands slipped down into my crotch and held me there as she whispered words I have never forgotten.

"Take care of yourself, darling, and don't ever forget—never—that you are loved. Truly, truly—blessedly loved."

With that, she was gone. It was probably only seconds, although in my mind it lingers: the incarnate spirit of that sumptuous infinite whiteness, and of the wide sea of love that might yet buoy us to safety. I finally turned, only to see the retreating figure of Suzanne Williams in her evening dress, hurrying back through the French doors.

In a moment of doubt and despair, a prayer had been answered—whether angel of grace or spirit damned, I had no clue. But for the first time, I had felt the staggering power of a woman's love.

1321 P Street
May 30, 1951

Suzanne,

I just heard from Angleton this morning that Donald Maclean has disappeared in London; they think he and Guy Burgess may have defected to Moscow—both KGB agents! You've known Donald for years. Is it possible? Wasn't it your friend, his wife, Melinda, you told me you were visiting in New York the last three times we met at the Carlyle? You swore you wouldn't lie to me again—but how can I believe anything you say anymore? Angleton is like a fox terrier with his nose in a den of rats; he has access to some source of information about KGB activity that goes all the way back to the war years and before. And now suspicion has fallen on Kim, as well—a nest of Cambridge traitors. Do you understand the implications, the consequences? I just had lunch with Kim at the Metropolitan Club last week; he can charm the rattle off a sidewinder—how he goes on and on about you and your ballet days before the war—and Kim has been privy to our most top secret operations—both he and Maclean since at least the postwar years. They knew everything about our operations in Albania and Greece—and Korea! The very thought sinks me into the lowest circle of hell. What is it about your Trinity College crowd? And now that I think about it, weren't they all at your wedding? I remember Kim, of course. Was Maclean there, too? And some other tall buffoon who hung all over Bobby—his mentor, his Trinity godhead, wasn't it—an art historian? It was Philby who wouldn't let you, the blushing bride, off the dance floor. And Bobby—that pathetic little monster, is that how he got mixed up in this, too, this Cambridge—what to call it? Damn him to hell. There's no end to this horror story.

Even Elliot walks around the office like he's been kicked in the balls. He hates Angleton, who used to fawn all over Philby—his onetime mentor—and now has turned on him. Elliot is terrified that Angleton's suspicions might prove correct, since he's palled around with Kim, as well. Nor is Elliott looking so good with his British wife—*your* maid of honor. Of course, Elliott constantly asks about you—he doesn't trust you an inch, or your "retirement from the stage." Nor should he. Nor should I. Fool that I am.

And your cousin Charles keeps showing up in Washington on RAF business, nosing around, suggesting we have lunch, and Fairburn isn't in town to discuss procurements or archaeology with me—not now, not anymore. What is it with you Brits and your clubby old-boy gang of incurably disloyal and disingenuous gentlemen? Your cynicism will sink us all!

You said it was long over between you and Kim—Cambridge days, right? You haven't been fucking him, as well?

Don't write to me. Don't ever use the phone. The FBI is all over the place. McCarthy is subpoenaing every Communist and suspected Communist in the land. Don't mention anything of this to Bobby. I will be at Elysium this weekend, probably late, very late, what with the long drive. I'll come alone; I'll tell Mary that mother has demanded I go up and fetch the Innesses, as I promised, for cleaning in New York. Mary finds long car trips hard. Meet me at Pine Meadow by the lake—say 3:00 AM. And not a peep—not a fucking peep.

John

B

16 LATER, MAX AND I WENT DOWN TO OUR BOAT-
house, where we sat across from each other in the dark
on the twin docks under the sloping roof. We said little,
each lost in our private thoughts about the evening. He,
falling in love (at least in his novel); I, still a little brain-dead from the
million-volt shock of Suzanne's embrace, and happy to be safely back
home. The stars were coming clearer as the moon settled behind us.
Across the lake, only a single light glowed in the upper story of Hermitage. Laura had not been allowed to come with us—early-morning
pickup for Albany and the train back to New York. Like a time traveler
returned to his own place and time, I was just a little spooked, a little
drunk, but happy to believe that nothing had really changed. There was
the lake as I had known it from earliest childhood, an obsidian smooth-
ness mirroring the comforting stars, the woods a silver-gray palisade,
the night a huge encompassing diamond-studded shield against
encroaching chaos. It was a world of predictable habit and seasonal
cycles upon which I could depend. Except it was empting fast.

"Here," said Max, coming over and handing me his joint.

I finished it off quite expertly, waiting.

"Who were those people they kept mentioning at the dinner table:
Kim and Anthony?"

"No idea."

"You're lying to your best pal, again. I saw your eyes light up like
beacons at the mention of those names."

"You're imagining it."

"Who you gonna trust if not me? You think *Virgil* really gives a
damn?"

I felt the world shifting on its axis, and I closed my eyes, wanting the images on the canvases to fade away, as if I could just wake up, relieved . . . because that corrupt version of my grandmother I'd just glimpsed simply would not fit with the world as I'd found it.

I thought again of her in her last illness, and how alone she had seemed, though I think my presence at her hospital bed helped. My mother was at best useless and, worse, even hostile after getting wind of the restriction in my grandmother's will. I loved the sound of my grandmother's voice, with its high nasal vowels, which was the voice of her people, and all she'd tried to pass on to me. What extraordinary stories she could tell. How much she had lost . . . first a husband and then a son, denied their company in the house by the lake, where she had first come to love them. She could have returned to her own family place in Northeast Harbor, but she didn't. Oddly, after Suzanne's bizarre embrace on the piazza—as the sensation took root—I felt inexplicably empowered, as if her words had only heightened my family's love for Elysium, something of them and their past renewed in me. *You are loved.* The thing burned in my blood, and my heart quickened at the thought of her hand moving to my crotch. My senses sharpened as I opened my eyes. Looking at the lapping water, I detected ripples come from an infinite distance, as if voices from all things and all places were opening themselves to me . . . where the solar winds stirred the stars.

If one could only listen hard enough, what stories—what answers might be voiced? Or was the answer simply a thing of flesh and desire, flesh moving through flesh? The oak-ribbed rowboat, which had been my father's and his father's and his father's before him, stirred in the slip, the rope on the davit creaking as if whispering to me, perhaps of some new departure. In that craft, I had first learned the possibility of escape, of moving through space by my own exertions (at five or six, and I'd given my mother a terrible fright when once I'd gone missing for a whole hour). The boat rocked so gently. I thought about my father standing on the dock on the day he left and never returned. I wondered what had been going through his mind, as I had a thousand times before. Had he not loved my mother enough? Had he not loved me enough? My soul yearned to believe that he was a good man in a good cause doing his duty. And not a traitor. How much of his cold determination to do what he had to do was in me? And again I felt Suzanne's possessive hands slipping over my body as if to know it as her own—to protect me or someone else?—but not enough to keep him here, to keep him safe.

And yet . . . and yet, in Bobby's and Suzanne's eyes I had glimpsed something of his return.

I looked out at the lake-reflected starlight and wondered if there had been a time of joy before such uncertainties and sadness had entered my world. And I imagined how it might have been with those Chinese lanterns drifting over the lake as a violin or saxophone sang out, to be joined by others, and the desires unleashed in their wake. Oh, the aching beauty of such a thing. Or were such times of joy simply the rare exception, surrounded by times of sadness, and there was no such thing: one without the other? Youth wants to believe in a golden age of heroes, of innocent, untrammeled desire; it is an instinct as old as the race. I sensed such preoccupations in my father's scholarship, and couldn't help wondering if such a romantic quest, such a belief, had proved more a hindrance than help to his ultimate fate.

Staring out, I tried to conjure the image of a young woman, a widow with a young child, coming down to the boathouse late on a warm summer night, dropping her bathrobe and slipping into the lake, headed for that distant light, for the welcoming embrace of the artist who might immortalize her. She had been a long-distance swimmer since her childhood in Northeast Harbor. "My God, don't be such a sissy. Eden Lake is like bathwater compared to the sea," she'd say.

The rocking of the boat ceased and the sounds of lapping gave way to a deeper silence, to the myriad woodnotes, the cricketing stitches sewn into night's tapestry. I turned to Max, who was sitting across from me like a silent twin, his back against a wooden support column, lighting up his second joint of the night, his deceptively careless features emergent in the glow of a match. We were both, in our different ways, early veterans of loss. But the full reality of that knowledge, the perspective that only the pastness of one's own past can truly give, was not yet ours to share. Those images—Max's "memory points," brightening and polished by time—the dependable truths of experience, would accompany us on separate journeys. But for those few remaining minutes, we tried to hold on to the tiny paradise before us: between strokes, before the glide fails, before we must again get our backs into the race or yield to the returning current.

"You *will* invite her to the fall dance, I assume." Max said this while watching his match flicker out at his fingertip. A dribble of smoke passed from his lips and drifted off.

"She said something about coming for a football game."

"Well, there you are—she's crazy about you."

"She's nothing of the sort. . . . We've just been around each other since we were kids."

"Believe me, I know the signs. I just wish it were me. Boy, her mom let me know in no uncertain terms—clearing the decks for you—that when I finished the drying, I was to go back to the piano. 'Play a few more pieces, please, Max, for my husband; it will help him get to sleep,'" she said.

"We just talked."

"Did you notice the way her mother looked at you?"

"They're a mess. That place gives me the creeps."

"You lie. I saw you; you were almost as dazzled as I was. Even if they're a dying breed—huh, like you guys. But what a way to go . . . immolated in a gemlike flame."

"Did you notice the rot in the shingles, the broken gutters? And the faucet in the bathroom sink came off in my hand."

"Well, maybe you could give them a hand. I'm sure it's tough taking care of an old place like that—taking care of that poor old guy."

The sympathetic note irritated me.

"Here today, gone tomorrow."

"Just don't let anybody take this away from you." Max gestured toward the lake. "And don't let Byron Folley get his unctuous paws on you, either."

"You keep saying shit like that—so what's the latest on the faculty meetings?" Max had finally taken me into his confidence about his taping system in the headmaster's study.

"Paul Oakes retires after graduation, if he makes it. They'd like to ease out your pal Virgil Dabney, too. Even Doc Steele isn't planning to hang on much longer. And from what Mr. Williams had to offer at dinner, I'd say it looks like he's all that's standing between Folley and a trustees lynching party."

"Good riddance."

"And how, brother."

"They'll be gone." I sighed aloud. "We'll be gone."

I saw Max smirk to himself, as if he knew something I didn't.

"You're such a bullshitter, Max. You and your little mysteries."

"Hang tight, Hawkman, and keep your nose clean of Homer for a while, give the rampaging Achilles—a fucking maniac, man, and sacker of cities—and Odysseus a rest." Max gestured again to the lake and the stars. "Remember, life is mysterious for a reason."

"A reason?"

"Did I ever tell you about Mutianus Rufus?"

"No . . . don't tell me."

"Mutianus Rufus, a friend of Erasmus—Luther, too. You know, that priest with the Oedipus complex."

Max took another long drag on his joint, his head drifting back against the wooden pillar, eyes shining in the ambient light off the lake. Above us in the rafters, there was a slight rustle from the nesting barn swallows, presumably getting high. Beyond, the swooping of bats above the water as they dive-bombed the sleeping stars.

"Listen, tonight was plenty weird enough without your adding to it."

"One fucked-up bitter dude—huh. But he was fucked-up dropping high explosives on the Nazis, so I'll give him a pass. Besides, they were a pretty cool crowd. I looked at the scrapbooks in the library; the old man played a youth concert at Carnegie Hall before the war."

"So he must have been pretty good?"

"I read the *Times* review, polite—but hey, Carnegie Hall. And she— queen bee, she was the real deal, a prima ballerina before the war; she was front-page news in the art press whenever she performed."

"All a little before your time, don't you think?"

"There's no such thing, pal." Max snapped his fingers. "*Time*, it's like that."

"Yeah, well . . . easy for you to say: I'm stuck with *the founding families* thing. And I don't want to have anything to do with *them*." I motioned to the distant light across the lake.

"So you say, but you're in queer city, man, so smoke your joint and cozy up to the distaff side of things. You could use a little love in your life."

I took the joint from where he'd walked it over and left it next to a davit and lighted up.

"His bullshit about Vietnam pissed me off."

"I thought he had it about right."

"You would: comparing the United States to Nazi Germany."

"I wouldn't go that far."

"It's one thing to say we shouldn't fight, another to pretend that the Vietcong are all sweetness and light."

"Look at you, all set to become one of Doc's boys. I guess when you've got this, and money, no one can touch you: You're entitled to be a running dog imperialist."

I held the smoke deep in my lungs as I had been taught, not that I was a big fan. But at least his stash was now out of the car and to be consumed before our return. I coughed.

"I'll register for the draft, just like everyone else—except you, of course," I said.

"If it wasn't for that, I wouldn't even bother about college."

"That's what never ceases to amaze me about you guys: Everybody mopes around, complaining about how bad things are, feeling sorry for themselves. Do you really agree with those people, Max, the SDS guys, Huey Newton's Black Panthers, who want to tear down everything that made our country great?"

"A little housecleaning is always good for the soul."

"Well, Stalin and Mao sure knew a thing or two about house-cleaning. Maybe you can be the Cultural Revolution of the literary world—do a little spring cleaning of your own."

"If I can take down a few imperialist flunkies, that'll be just fine."

"Well, I agree with Doc: I think we do have some moral responsibilities as a country, to try to help people who are being taken over by the Communists. People like you would be first on their hit list if they ever got a toehold here."

"Oh, we're back to dominoes, are we?"

"No, doing something because it's right, that needs doing, like fighting Hitler."

"Spare me your quaint morality tale, featherbrain. Next, you'll be telling me America fought Hitler to save the Jews. Let me tell you something. Hitler declared war on us. And the Jews in Europe were being murdered long before the war started, and nobody did a damn thing about it. Who turned back the refugee ships—huh? And even when the war got started, nobody did anything to try to stop the Nazis from exterminating the Jews. FDR and Churchill knew all about the concentration camps. Did they even try to bomb the railway lines to the camps? And let me tell you something else: If Pearl Harbor hadn't happened and the Nazis had gone quietly about the Holocaust,

I guarantee you, nobody would've gone to war to save them. It would've been business as usual."

"So . . . we were wrong to do nothing then, but right to do nothing now?"

"You can't justify napalming peasants, women and children, as taking the moral high ground. Didn't you listen to anything Charlie had to say? It's none of our business; they don't want us there."

"Sin of hubris—huh." I released the smoke from my lungs. "Well, Charlie fought for his country and was proud of it."

"The Nazis are one thing; women and children are another."

"So you blame Roosevelt for not stepping in and saving the Jews, but what about when the Communists take over and start butchering their class enemies? What then?"

"Who cares if some of the riffraff get knocked off; it's a fucking civil war."

"Easy, as long as you're not the riffraff."

"Who cares—I'm sorry, it's far, far away. And like Charlie said, who are we to butt in? Who are we to demand the world *be* like us? We're totally fucked-up, man. Look what they did to Martin Luther King and President Kennedy—how fucked-up. Half the people in this country carry guns and think evolution is a myth. Your Christian militia and the KKK are still using blacks for target practice—what do you expect the Black Panthers to do? Your problem is, you want the black brothers at school to love you for your good intentions—and your right arm. It's not enough."

"My father cared."

"Yeah, well look where it got him. And by the way, that roomful of guns back there is pretty fucking creepy. You guys could arm a militia."

I tossed what was left of my joint at Max and looked longingly at the rowboat. I was mad. I was hurt. We'd been around the block on these subjects a hundred times. Between the wine and the dope, I felt only a dull, remote pain, a loneliness I couldn't put a name to. I closed my eyes, just wanting silence, everlasting silence, to forget everything. I told myself, keep your head down, go to college, get the work done, play football for Princeton . . . row your heart out on Lake Carnegie, and by the time you open your eyes again, maybe it will have all gone away.

The second toke seemed to do the trick. The lake had grown around us, a great window of silvery blackness through which the silent stars shone like beacons. In the treetops behind us, that still-unblemished moon hovered on the ridgeline, feeling its way into the underworld. More bats began spilling across the darkness, dipping wings to the lake, tapping out Morse code on that stellar membrane. The silence stayed with us for a little while longer, holding us close.

"Sorry," said Max, "that wasn't fair."

"It's okay."

"The truth is, I don't have the guts to go out on the streets and . . . and bomb police precincts. Frankly, those dudes are such fucking bores—they're idiots."

I turned to Max, a little amazed at this near confession. "You'd rather read about it, or write about it—huh?"

"Sometimes, I just can't believe Charlie's dead. I see how beautiful your lake is and I can't believe it . . . how anything bad can happen. Isn't that ridiculous. Park me in that room of your father's with a typewriter, looking out over this lake, and a tag team of Playmates of the Month couldn't drag me away." Max was staring intently, squinting, a tone of frustration as he began again. "And you know, there was so much fire and life and love in Charlie. It's like he battled death for so long, fought it to a standstill . . . and then in an instant, he's lying in the road and it's all over."

Max's pale face was gently illuminated by the silvery iridescence that encompassed us. His curly hair dangled about his shoulders. He was older, but magically young, like an image of Gabriel I had once seen emerging from the gloom of a canvas by Caravaggio.

"You played beautifully tonight, Max. I was really moved. You have a great gift; you should be proud and happy."

"I'll take a good woman like Laura any day."

"Well, now you can go back to Wendy." Wendy was the restorer at Palazzo Fenway with whom Max had an on-again, off-again thing going. She'd been writing him, and Max read me her letters. She wrote the most unbelievable pornographic love letters, leaving nothing to the imagination. My suggestion was also to protect myself, and Laura, some part of me knowing that if it came down to Laura and Max, I'd always play second fiddle. "Or Susan—how is Susan, by the way?"

"Take her—Laura—to the fall dance, or, I swear, I will," he said.

"Gee, Max . . . I guess you really liked her, more than Wendy, huh?"

"I do, it's true, I do, and what a beautiful night for it, too. Outside, under the stars, like animals, when we can be most human."

"You two were sure flirting up a storm at the beach."

I thought I saw that infamous flicker of a smile.

"So, maybe we'll elope and go to Venice and kiss beneath the Bridge of Sighs."

"Ha-ha . . . you and Venice." Suddenly, I was feeling no pain.

"Venice," he said quietly, with an almost sibilant reverence, "is the one place on earth where art and life have come together in timeless consanguinity."

I squinted, the better to see his face, if his expression might betray his mood. The flicker of his eyebrows when he used a word he loved.

"Weren't those Sargent watercolors something?"

"The finest, shit, man."

"Blissing out on truth and beauty—cool," I added.

The ocean of stars stirred before us.

"Art . . ." He wet his finger and held it up, as if testing for those solar winds. "Art, Pete, didn't you feel it there tonight, in that fabulous place?" and he looked out over the lake to those dark French doors. "I mean, yeah, the Sargents, and there were Whistler etchings in the library."

"Maybe you've missed your calling. Maybe you should be a painter."

"Their whole place was like that . . . radioactive."

I sighed. "Sounds about right," I said, and thought again of Suzanne's and Laura's watching eyes across the table in the candlelight, except the eyes seemed to merge as one in my mind, along with that craving embrace on the piazza.

"'There's not the smallest orb,'" he sang out, "'which thou behold'st but in his motion like an angel sings, still quiring to the young-eyed cherubins; such harmony is in immortal souls; but whilst this muddy vesture of decay doth grossly close it in, we cannot hear it.'"

My heart was beating so fast, I felt giddy.

"The golden age . . .," I replied, words failing me.

"Edward de Vere's golden age," he echoed back. "Exiles all . . . you and me and Eddy boy."

"'How sweet the moonlight sleeps upon this bank! Here will we sit and let the sounds of music creep in our ears.'"

I looked serenely across to where Max sat watching me, nodding slowly, playing silent notes on his kneecaps.

"Know what," Max said, "there was another bit in Charlie's note-books, where he wrote, 'The romantic mind is condemned to the misuse of knowledge, not for wisdom but as a resource for power, the dream for the actual, the deathless dogma for unflinching reality.'"

"Well, you should know: the great romantic fallacy—huh."

Somewhere far out on the lake, there was the sound of flapping wings, the honking of a nesting heron disturbed by a fox or snapping turtle. Then silence again. I thought of the flight of that great blue heron that my father had watched from the dock of the boathouse as he smoked his last cigarette, the rhythmic bellow of its wings as it sought altitude. Or that's how I imagined it.

"I believe we were speaking of angels," said Max.

"Yeah, yeah... the golden age, yeah... and the rebel angels—far-out."

Max nodded. "That's it, you see.... That's got to be it: Charlie saved his greatest sermon for last—like he knew."

"Yeah, Max; Charlie was the best."

"Pretty cool customer—you tonight, with that grace . . . you almost got Charlie's rhythms perfect."

"For you, pal . . . friend."

"Angels . . . it's so fucking far-out, man . . ."

"Angels . . ."

"Yes . . . wow, a nunnery of angels, a star nunnery—just think of it, an infinite hierarchy of bitches: angels and archangels, principalities, virtues, powers, dominations, thrones, cherubim, and seraphim . . . and that invisible celestial light beyond imagining . . . a whole fucking universe, man, of celestial pussy."

"A long haul to get laid, Max. Like my grandmother always said, 'A lot of track that needs laying.'"

I laughed. Everything felt hysterical.

"Maybe, like you *always* tell me about keeping it simple, maybe it's just cold and dark and empty out there—like that guy Yuri said—you know, the Soviet cosmonaut: 'I've been to outer space and there's no heaven.' Or maybe the best thing that's ever happened in this fucked-up world . . . is that girl of yours—Laura. Grab her, man, before she slips through your fingers. Because, just maybe—what do you think?—she's as good as it gets." Max lowered his leg over the planking of the dock and tapped the taut surface of the lake with the toe of his sneaker. A ripple of motion spread out before us, a vibrant plea into space for the answers we never found. The reflected stars quaked and then gently returned to their places in the celestial choir.

"Here's to love"—I sighed—"*and* celestial pussy."

"Waters of Helicon," purred Max, as if about to proclaim an invocation. But then his tone completely changed. "Hey, pal, don't listen to me. My family's even more fucked-up than yours. I hate my father's guts, and my mother drives me nuts. And what's more, when I'm here in this beautiful place—even hanging out with a fucking rich goy like you—I feel safe, like I belong. How pathetic is that. Like I could play that wonderful Steinway overlooking the lake—get the girl, and live happily ever after. Not the fucked-up bad dream from before we were born."

"A Hollywood ending . . ."

He took a deep breath, as if he'd finally exhausted himself. I was worried he might be slipping into a downer, which happened a lot when he'd smoked too much. If I'd been sitting next to him, maybe I'd have put an arm around him, maybe I'd have hugged him—maybe not. Maybe he was waiting for me to talk him out of it. Not that he ever really listened to me. Then he went on, his voice very hushed.

"It's nice to think the stars are our destination, but who knows, maybe they're just the forgotten signposts of our failed journey. A bunch of burnt-out suns dead as doornails for a million years already."

"A cosmic bummer," I offered. "But I wouldn't mind being one of those rebel angels and setting the world on fire—at least once."

"Like your old man."

The dope was having its usual effect on me. I felt the energy draining away, like at the end of a race when you're totally done in, beyond exhaustion . . . lungs sucking in the sweetness of the glide, and the spreading wake its own dying reality.

But then Max seemed to get a second wind. I could feel him reaching back with his oars, reaching out with his raised arms as if to embrace that fantastic night sky and the dwelling place of his gods.

"*Lo cielo i vostri movimenti inizia*,' was how Dante put it. Even Aquinas recognized the influence of the stars in our lives. Of course Augustine believed that spirits made use of the heavenly bodies to aid them in their evil sway over us. That is why I prefer Mutianus Rufus. . . . Have I mentioned him to you already? I feel like I'm losing my mind here."

"Yeah, you said something . . . a friend of somebody, you said."

"Erasmus, I think I said. Anyway, Mutianus Rufus wrote this really cool thing: '*Est unus deus et una dea, sed sunt multa uti numina ita et nomina. . . . Sunt enim occulta silentio tamquam Eleusinarum dearum mysteria. Utendum est fabulis atque enigmatum integumentis in re sacra.'*"

I was surprised at how good his pronunciation was, since Latin had always bored him. But he got by on his photographic memory. I asked him to say it again while I attempted to translate.

"There is but one god and one goddess, but many are their powers and names. They should be hidden in silence as are the Eleusinian mysteries. Sacred things must be wrapped in fable and enigma."

"Silent Thalia," he whispered.

"Ah . . . Thalia," I echoed back.

We sat inured to the silence a while longer, with only the creaking davit to remind us otherwise. At some point, Max got up and stood for a long while, leaning on the staff he'd made for himself on our walk, like an Arcadian shepherd in a Poussin painting, contemplating his scattered flock.

Suddenly, his voice came to me harsh and unyielding.

"Maybe you're right, man, it's just bullshit. Maybe without people like you, we'll all get fucked up the ass by the bad guys."

I saw him shrug his shoulders and look up with a lost expression at the dome of stars, his voice mocking—exhausted.

"'Now my charms are all o'erthrown.'"

With that, Max broke his staff across his knee and tossed the pieces far out onto the lake, where they landed with a thin echoing slap, splintering the night and sending the stars careening. He turned and went back toward the house with his stash, where he would stay up half the night poking his nose into things.

The hell with exams.

I took my chance and got into the rowboat and quickly rowed myself out into the middle of the lake, until the boathouse became invisible against the wooded shore. I rowed and I rowed, getting my back into it so that I could fully test my strength and clear my mind, only shipping the oars every so often to feel the stars glide by overhead, and listen, and so lose myself in the spaces of time and memory . . . while along the nearby shore, the sound of Tibetan temple bells echoed like conspiring gods.

We arrived back at school the Sunday before exams, and I immediately went to my favorite carrel in the library and began studying. Max had been such a distraction at Elysium, treating me like his personal docent, that I'd gotten little accomplished. It was a cloudless late-spring day and I found myself frequently looking up from my work and staring out at the comforting expanse of the Circle, where the stand of apple trees, those old bent veterans of centuries past, clothed in somber leaf-age, shimmered like miniature storm clouds against the sun-drenched grass. I saw Paul Oakes walk out of his dorm and go over to his wine red Thunderbird. He was very thin. I could see he was having a hard time walking. Everyone knew Mr. Oakes was dying. We'd seen it there in his weary, sunken eyes during the memorial service for Charlie Springfield. He'd given the eulogy for Charlie, telling us how he'd known him as man and boy, visited him when he'd been wounded at a military hospital in Avranches (two days after my father's visit). And how he'd read to him from First Corinthians about the abiding nature of faith, hope, and love—and how love (the King James Version called it charity, but it was really love, so he assured us) was the most important of all these things. And how faith sustained by the work of charity toward our fellow men engendered love—love that got Charlie through almost a year of painful rehabilitation and then sparked his interest in returning to seminary on the GI Bill. He told us how he'd had a hard time convincing Charlie to return to Winsted after Charlie had spent two years as pastor of a small blue-collar parish in South Carolina. He told Charlie that Winsted needed him, needed him to demonstrate the efficacy of the Gospel in our daily lives, and how a man could fight and kill for his country and not lose his essential humanity . . . and remember, above all things, to love his fellow man. "'The boys,' I kept telling him, 'need to hear this from someone who's been there, who comes from a different world than they're used to . . . and broaden their sympathies for those less fortunate than themselves. You can do it, Charlie; you can help them be better people, better citizens.'"

None of us had even suspected that bond of faith and love that Paul Oakes and Charlie shared. "You see, Charlie was like a son to me. And on Memorial Day last, a day to remember our fight for unity and freedom and justice for all races . . . I lost a son and a friend." Another drop of clarity in that painful sea of youthful insouciance. Paul had tears in his eyes when he made his way down from the pulpit, holding firm to the railing to keep himself from stumbling. In that fifteen-minute eulogy, the formidable Reverend Oakes had revealed more of his underlying humanity than in all his years of sermonizing.

After his story about the prison guard at Buchenwald, I didn't know quite where things stood between us. He had been there in his wine red Thunderbird at every crew race that spring, watching me like a great old shambling horned owl from a distant perch. He'd always nod and smile at me at the beginning of a race, and give me a thumbs-up at the finish. But he offered no more advice, no more insights. I wondered if I was a disappointment. Maybe I should have shown more interest in *Essays and Prayers*. I really wanted to see more of him, to ask him more about my father. But he seemed so fortified by his faith, so intent on holding out over that last spring, for one more race, one more crew season. Virgil had told me, shaking his head sorrowfully, that he'd refused the final rounds of chemo. "Ah-da-dum . . . which might prolong the agony but not Paul's life. They've given him lots of painkillers, but I don't think he takes them, either—wants his mind clear."

As I watched him that afternoon from the library window, he opened the door of his Thunderbird, took a book from the glove compartment, and tossed his keys onto the front seat. There was something decisive in the way he did that, I thought later. Mr. Oakes was that kind of man, the old-school kind of Christian who knows in his heart that in the end it must be his decision, between himself and his God . . . alone. And I was just sitting there in the library, remembering his words from the eulogy for Charlie, watching as he walked slowly to the center of the Circle and sat on a bench that circled the base of one of the apple trees. He sat facing the chapel. I realized how much he loved the chapel and the Circle, which had been his preserve for so long, the garden of faith, hope, and love he had cultivated for most of his adult life, except for the war years, when he had joined on as an army chaplain, to be close to his boys in need. It was such a nice day that I found it hard to concentrate on my studies—what with all the birdsong in the oaks and elms outside the window, and the shouts of boys playing stepball, and the bell ringers were practicing in the bell tower and some of their peals were not the greatest I'd ever heard. But I managed to get a little work done, and the afternoon drifted by like nothing had happened, and before I knew it, it was almost time to get changed for dinner. I gathered up my books and prepared to leave, when I looked out the window and noticed that Mr. Oakes was still there, sitting on that bench under the apple tree; not that it was unusual, because I was so used to him being there by then, and it seemed so appropriate, somehow, that he was still there: Hadn't he'd been there all afternoon, sitting peacefully, reading?

And it occurred to me—*Essays and Prayers* be damned—that now was the perfect time for that little conversation. Just to thank him and wish him well and tell him how much I had enjoyed his eulogy for Charlie.

And with that thought, something inside me sort of burst, like a little bubble floating up from the bottom of a quiet pond, inexplicably, except you figured some complicated chemical reaction, some inexorable process of slow decay and metamorphosis, had occurred out of sight and mind to produce that bursting bubble. That was how I felt, so I went outside, where the newly mown grass smelled sweet and the green of the trees was such a delight because those damned New England winters were always so long. I made my way around the Circle until I was nearly in front of the chapel, and then I slowly turned, a casual turn, as if I had nothing on my mind, and gave a friendly wave over where Mr. Oakes sat under the apple tree. Then I boldly walked right up to him and said hello and stood in front of him and looked into his dull gray eyes, which looked blankly at the chapel. A ringless hand was pressed between the open pages of the worn King James Version in his lap, his head slightly tilted against the gnarled trunk of the ancient tree. Mr. Oakes was dead, possibly for hours. He seemed only dreaming to me . . . perhaps of his days on the Charles, or Henley, or various Olympic courses, dreaming of the glide, or maybe—just maybe—seeing one of my father's fifty-yard passes breeze the air one last time.

He had taken every last one of the painkillers he'd been storing up for weeks.

17

TEN DAYS LATER, EXAMS OVER, I WAS ASLEEP on the last night of the term before Prize Day. It must have been about two in the morning when I felt a tug at my shoulder. A voice called my name, close to my ear. It was a sixth former, my cocaptain of football—Fortinbras in mufti. He told me to get dressed: no questions, no noise, no bullshit. "Just move your ass, Alden." I groggily obeyed and followed him out into the warm summer night. In the center of the Circle, he gripped my arm and made me swear I would never divulge anything that was about to take place. "Swear . . . on what?" I asked. "Swear on your sweet father's ass—that's fucking what." Being Max's roommate put me in bad odor with his hulking presence. "Here, swear on this, asshole." He handed me a pint bottle of Jim Beam and told me to take my fill. I wasn't much of a drinker, but I did as I was told.

I was taken to the fives courts and led down a pitch-black corridor and directed to the last court and then to a chair. I sensed there were others around me but could see almost nothing. I was sufficiently intimidated and mystified—the Jim Beam easing me under—that I didn't make a peep. There was whispering in one corner; then a stark voice issued from the darkness.

"Gentlemen, welcome and congratulations, you have been chosen from your class to replace those of us who will be graduating tomorrow. We are leaving Winsted in your sorry hands. But this is serious business, especially now in this era of upheaval—what with you wimps left running the show. You have been called here to take certain oaths and carry out certain obligations as members of an elite fellowship that was founded over thirty-five years ago to help perpetuate the highest ideals of citizenship. We are a brotherhood: the Black Eagles—at least we were until you lamebrains came along—dedicated to freedom, justice, love, and honor . . . among thieves—heh, heh." Another voice called out: "The fucking American way, or was I misinformed as a kid by Superman?" "Shut the fuck up," the first voice retorted. "Now, where was I? We are your link—nurturing the best instincts of the young and sustaining the commitments of the old—in a broad confraternity across the generations. We believe that as members of this school community and as citizens of this country, we have a special role to play in the battle for a better world. To this end, the society was founded upon the enduring virtues: freedom and justice, love and—" He was interrupted again. "—you fucking already said that."

"Did I . . . I can't fucking see a fucking thing without my glasses."

A derisive cry: "Right on, brother."

"Get the fuck on with it."

Suddenly, a flashlight beam illuminated a small portion of the ceiling, where an archaic image of the sun had been pasted against the yellow plaster. I could just make out the shape of the figure holding the flashlight and the dark forms of a few of my teammates seated in a circle, surrounded by another circle of standing figures, all members of the senior class. The whole thing had the feel of an adolescent prank, not entirely believable, but not easily dismissed, either. The speaker was directly behind me and his voice echoed out again in the small chamber. "The sun, gentlemen, symbol of reason and the balanced mind, those qualities that exalt man above his fellow creatures, the wisdom to create the good and true and beautiful: that which endures."

I thought I heard somebody's drunken guffaw, followed by a chorus of snickers.

The first flashlight clicked off and another came on, illuminating another section of the ceiling, where a black Roman eagle stood proudly perched on a Corinthian column. "The eagle, symbol of strength and watchfulness, a creature with physical courage and wide perspective over the affairs of men, eternally vigilant, ready to take action when duty calls."

"Get on with it, man. I need to take a leak."

Again, another beam flashed onto the ceiling, revealing a spear and shield.

"The spear and shield, symbol of power and authority, the manly art of war, the determination to use force, to fight when necessary, to take a stand against tyranny, to protect and defend freedom and democracy wherever threatened."

Somebody laughed. "Right . . . let's get out there and kick Joy-Joy's ass."

"Hey—far-out."

Another beam of light fell on a pair of clasped hands.

"The handshake, symbol of solidarity and citizenship, of honor and trust between men, that unshakable bond of brotherhood in the face of those forces that would make a mockery of civilization's achievements and seek the enslavement of the spirit, both body and soul."

Noises erupted from the corridor. The flashlight flicked off. A door slammed. Voices. Commotion. Sounds of a scuffle. The person behind my chair hissed, "What the fuck is that?"

The overhead electric lights came on in an eye-numbing flash. I blinked desperately. There were more voices—shouts. I looked around and discovered that we had been surrounded by two of the night watchmen and about five members of the faculty, all with scornful looks of triumph on their faces. From among their ranks, the Reverend Byron Folley came waltzing into the center of the room like a bassett hound who had just cornered a burrow of jackrabbits. The headmaster beamed at our dismayed and drunken faces and let out a little whoop of pleasure.

"Well . . . well," he crowed. "What do we have here?" He spotted each of our faces with his black bullet eyes and grinned. "Now I hope you boys haven't been drinking"—he bent over and picked up a pint of Jim Beam—"or been engagin' in some kind of i-l-legal activities, have you, some sort of secret ca-ba-al maybe? You know that's not how things are supposed to be. . . . Isn't that right, Manning?" He went over to the senior prefect and gently plucked a leather-bound book from his grasp. He leafed through the pages and examined the signatures and nodded knowingly. "And what fine artwork!" He gestured at the ceiling. "Now who in the world do you suppose is responsible for all this?" With that ringing question, he walked over to where I sat and grinned at me.

And that was how the secret society begun by my father and Elliott Goddard, abetted by Virgil Dabney, some thirty-odd years before was finally busted up. It had taken much waiting and watching. And yet, for Byron Folley it proved to be a Pyrrhic victory, for that leather-bound register he had so gleefully snatched up contained not only the name of my father but over two hundred other names, including those of the president's adviser and a bunch of Doc's boys, along with those of Elliot Goddard and at least ten CIA officers, and four members of the board of trustees. Few, if any, of these men still put much store in the secret society (Skull and Bones was a different matter). For most, it represented no more than youthful nostalgia—the elitist thrill of a further winnowing among the already elect, which, with the passage of time, dulls as a blood sport worth the candle. Nevertheless, the Black Eagles ranked high in memories of youthful ardor, of fraternal high jinks and male bonding and the budding awareness of mature passions: a faith in something greater than self. A faith that had been to put to a real test for many in the Second World War and the Cold War to follow.

The secret society's dissolution was the straw that broke the camel's back: Byron Folley's.

Headmaster Folley had taken particular interest in rooting out the secret society, an obsession, no doubt, passed down from the previous headmaster, Jack Crocket, who had caught wind of the Black Eagles at its inception in 1932. Folley assumed he was inheriting a great responsibility. The very idea of a secret cell, especially one with the taint of heresy, was anathema to the "ecclesiastical authorities," as Virgil Dabney always phrased it. Unfortunately for Byron Folley, his triumph was that of an outsider over the quintessential insiders. A slap in the face, an insignificant gaucherie, but enough to leave a most unpleasant taste. At a special summer meeting, the board of trustees, led by Elliot Goddard, quietly and unceremoniously dismissed Folley and replaced him with the senior master as acting head. In the same meeting, Bobby Williams, who was something of an expert on underground conspiracies as a member of the CPUSA and later a KGB agent, who had spurred on Folley to ferret out and destroy the secret society, was himself voted off the board for leaking board minutes to the newspapers.

I wouldn't have given a tinker's damn if it hadn't been Max who had tipped off Byron Folley. Because of his bugging system and pilfering of school files, Max knew that Folley and Paul Oakes had been on the lookout for the Black Eagles, and that I was a prime candidate for recruitment, since my father had been under suspicion at its formation in 1932. This was reason for Paul Oakes's early interest in my friendship with sixth formers (the secret society was made up almost exclusively of sixth-form football players and their legacies). Max was so brazen in his betrayal that he actually gave me the evidence of his perfidy, a copy of a purloined letter of May 14, 1932, from the headmaster to my grandmother. It was waiting on my desk the following morning. Much of this made its way into Max's novel, further substantiating his conspiracy theories about the nefarious inner workings of the eastern establishment. Max thought he was doing me a favor, that I'd thank him. Perhaps he was feeling guilty; he was already writing to Laura Williams, giving her helpful tips on Upper West Side apartments.

But his sneaking and snooping around finally got to me. I told him to go to hell; I told him I was not going to room with him senior year.

It may have been a tiny act of betrayal, but it was still a betrayal.

The May 1932 letter from Jack Crocket, then a young headmaster, was an odd and searching one, especially for a man esteemed, certainly late in his career, for his moral righteousness and absolute purpose. He wrote to my grandmother, whom he'd known as a teenager at summer dances in Northeast Harbor, that he had been worried about her son for some time. Top of his class, splendid athlete, well respected by his peers. "Perhaps too well respected" was how Old Jack put it. "There is something too intense about the boy, too serene and self-assured, as if he must suffer no weakness or doubt. It is not a question of overween-ing pride, for he does not suffer from the sin of hubris, but, rather, a lack of fear, an absence of guilt or sense of sinfulness." The headmaster went on about rumors of a secret society. There was no conclusive proof, but enough circumstantial evidence from an unimpeachable source that "your obstinate boy" might be one of the ringleaders. (I paused when I read this the first time, remembering how my grandmother had written "Ringleader" under the photo of my father's graduation party at Elysium.) A secret society was something Jack Crocket would never tolerate at Winsted. He knew only too well from his own school days what mischief and moral turpitude was bred by such cabals. "It is un-American," he wrote. "It has the stink of Bolshevik conspiracy about it." An ironic term, considering how so many in the secret society, later members in good standing of Yale's Skull and Bones and Har-vard's Porcelain Club, would spend their professional careers battling that very conspiracy.

At some point during the "investigation," which took place in the early spring of my father's senior year, the headmaster had asked my father into his office to confront him with his suspicions. Old Jack described in his letter how my father had steadfastly maintained his silence in the face of all the evidence. The headmaster was not surprised, since such secret societies are "well known to be sworn to secrecy." He decided to test the boy; he asked him to swear on the Bible. The boy refused the oath and informed the headmaster that he put no authority in Scripture. The headmaster was dumbfounded. "Flabbergasted" was the expression he used. Did he believe in God? the headmaster asked. "No sir." Did he believe in anything? "In freedom, justice, love, and honor—sir." This was the school motto, of course, formulated by General Alden and Samuel Williams and emblazoned on the Winsted crest. The headmaster was livid; he sent the boy out of his office with the admonition "You had better remember, my boy, that this is a Christian school in a Christian nation, and you had better turn your thinking around before it is too late and you endanger your immortal soul." The headmaster ended his letter to my grandmother with a recommendation that some male member of the family talk to the boy. He feared some irredeemable character flaw. "The waste of such a lad would be a terrible thing."

Freedom, Justice, Love, and Honor: The words are chiseled into General Alden's chapel memorial, the creed of his abolitionist generation. Maybe it had gone right over Jack Crocket's head. I began to understood his coldness to me, and more so when I got my hands on my father's letters from senior year.

That June of 1932, my father went on to graduate summa cum laude, captain of football and crew, winning all the major academic and athletic prizes. He was senior prefect and valedictorian. I imagine Old Jack was squirming a bit in his seat on Prize Day, as well he might have, I decided, when I discovered the pass he'd given to Bobby Williams.

There was one more thing that Max left on my desk, along with the copy of the headmaster's letter to my grandmother: Xerox copies of notes in the headmaster's hand from a faculty meeting of the same period. It makes clear that the informant—that "unimpeachable source"—who had ratted on my father to the headmaster was none other than our homegrown Bolshevist, Bobby Williams.

Things were never the same between Bobby Williams and my father: Elysium, if not Winsted, tainted.

Byron Folley fired Virgil Dabney on Prize Day—just like that. As it turned out, Virgil was himself a member of the secret society— the only member of the faculty; he'd kept physical possession of the leather-bound registry for all those years (in the vault of a local bank).

He was a man who specialized in loyalty. Virgil took this news with utter equanimity; the school had gone to the dogs anyway. It was time to leave. He'd been greatly saddened by the death of Paul Oakes. Only a week before, he had made a final plodding pilgrimage to his rival's citadel for the memorial service to Paul Oakes in the chapel, climbing uncomfortably into the pulpit to share with us a few choice and fond memories of his honorable opponent. He must have felt a bit like his hero Cicero at the final demise of Catiline, the way a man can love a good competitor, the ideological contest that adds a keen sharpness to the shadow play of life. With their rivalry (a rivalry that, in Virgil's mind, stretched back two thousand years) ended by default, he was only too happy to take early retirement.

"How can they do this to you?"

"What?"

"Just kick you out like this."

Virgil smiled and handed me more books to be packed in cardboard boxes.

"Headmaster's discretion."

"What about the board?"

"They have yet to be alerted or consulted."

"Then go to the board, appeal."

"It's a good time to move on."

His precious morocco-bound volumes of Gibbon had to be individually wrapped and packed in a special crate. I felt the very years of his life stored up in those well-thumbed volumes, his rough yet gentle soul linked through those underlined pages; and it saddened me how they now had to be packed away to be shipped off to some RFD number in rural Nebraska. He was returning to the family farm, which his father had left him many years before. Like a world-weary Roman sage, he was retiring to the provinces from whence his people had come and the land that bred the values he so cherished. He once told me how, as a kid growing up in the Midwest, he thought his home part of the frontier way of life. Like me, he'd begun his career as an archaeologist looking for Arapaho arrowheads. Virgil was convinced that character ultimately came from the land. He was a true Roman in that way, a true stoic, dismissing the prestige and trappings of public life for the simple ways of small-town America. He rarely visited his boys in Washington, except for holidays to visit with his FBI brother, who served as J. Edgar Hoover's right-hand man. Without fail, "my Washington brethren," as he put it, returned to see him in his cluttered study at Winsted, where they got the got the latest dope from J. Edgar.

Virgil knew, from his brother, the substance of the Venona decrypts, the KGB penetration of the highest reaches of the U.S. government, almost forty years before the story was released to the public: the reason his boys hung on his every word.

"I'll write to Elliot Goddard," I suggested. "He damn well owes me."

"It's already done."

"I'll bet that scumbag Bobby Williams had something to do with this, too."

"No doubt."

"You know, he's been leaking stuff to *The New York Times*—about Winsted, about certain trustees."

Virgil looked up from the volume of Gibbon he was placing in a crate.

"Yes?"

I told him about the dinner at Hermitage, about how they'd tossed around the names Kim and Anthony like accusations against one another.

He walked over to the window and stared out over the Circle and took another long drag from his cigarette. I watched the smoke drift across the room, for a moment obscuring the Piranesi prints on the wall, where those tiny pilgrims stood before the vast ruined walls of ancient Rome, their extravagant gestures speaking to the poignant loss of all that had been and was no more.

Then from out of the swirling clouds of smoke, the voice ineffable: "Ah-da-dum . . . they never liked heretics." He began to ramble in his gravelly bass voice, a searching preamble to the subject we both knew was at hand. "Those with whom they disagreed and couldn't immediately quash." Did he mean my father? Then he glanced at me and back to the window and the playing fields and the stern face of Mount Monadnock in the distance. A pensive look came into his eyes beneath the oatmeal-colored eyebrows, scraggly and beetling like those of a Saint Bernard.

"Their God," he went on, and I guess he must have meant the God of Samuel Williams's *Essays and Prayers*, "may presume to call on them individually for humility and charity toward others, but in camera *He* only endows them with the ferocious appetites of *His* maniacal will."

He nodded, perhaps to his reflection in the window.

"The totalitarian mind . . ." He put a finger to his temple and pulled a silent trigger. "Old Jack, a lovely man, but way out of his depth. One cannot fight against these new ersatz pseudo religions with the moribund doctrines of the dead and dying, or turn the cheek to the enemy. The Greek mind, as your father well understood, valued competition and excellence—the Homeric spirit of individual worth and freedom. Your father struggled to uphold this legacy, the vision of his grandfather, the general. It is a fight to the finish, until the slaveholders are finally vanquished."

Virgil did his best to explain, to weave me back into the world as it was in 1932. My father, at the prompting of Elliot Goddard, had gone to Virgil in his senior year; he had been worried about a certain strain of cynicism and deepening lack of confidence in members of his class (Bobby Williams being the most egregious example), which in turn engendered a lack of respect for Winsted's tradition in the younger boys. "The Red menace, you see, was already afoot. His intelligent eyes shone with such perplexity—oh my, how one could lose oneself in his eyes." Virgil's own owlish eyes widened for emphasis as he waved away his smoky outpouring. "Elliot was pretty tough on him, suggesting he wasn't holding up—I think he called it 'my family's end of things.' I'm certain he meant General Alden—Elliot had a thing about the general. On the one hand, John had to deal with the Williams boy, that fallen scion of the once-proud Williamses, and, on top of it, his best friend and rival, Karel Hollar, turned out to be a Communist as well."

"Hollar was a Communist?"

"Robert Williams was a romantic, an artist, a dreamer and a schemer. Hollar was the real thing, son of a Czech politician, if I remember, hardened in the ideological skirmishes of the thirties. And later, it can't have helped that John's Cambridge circles in Greek Bronze Age archaeology, Evans's and Bennett's crowd were infiltrated by radicals of every stripe. How many sensitive souls were poisoned in those days."

"Are you telling me Bobby Williams was more than *just* a Communist?"

"My lips are sealed—you never heard a peep."

"They had Kim Philby up to Hermitage."

"Who told you that?"

"My mother mentioned it."

"I'm so glad I got the fair lady talked around on Crete. You'll have the summer of your life digging in Phaistos."

"Tell me about Anthony—that name was hurled like a javelin across the dinner table by Suzanne."

It was the first time I think I ever saw Virgil visibly flinch.

"Cambridge again, trouble, the worst kind."

"It seems *Anthony* once arranged for Bobby Williams to perform at Wigmore Hall in London."

"To be blunt, my friend, I have already been more than indiscreet. People's lives and careers are still at stake. The world hangs in the balance. If Vietnam goes, hold tight to your rip cord."

Virgil had gotten what he needed out of me. But I hung around, helping with packing his books, in hopes I might still pocket a few crumbs.

"Ah-da-dum . . . what with the Nazis coming to power—a hornet's nest of nefarious competing interests. The Reds were everywhere, nibbling around, insinuating themselves. No wonder the poor boy was confounded: A romantic mind is always susceptible. And there was the Japanese invasion of Manchuria—a nasty bit of business there. Your father and I were together on Memorial Day, right before his graduation, at the town cemetery; we were standing at his grandfather's grave—up there on that little knoll above the Naushon River, there with all the other graves of Massachusetts's fallen in the general's regiment. One couldn't help being moved . . . my, my, all those brave souls who had fought for the abolition of slavery." Virgil nodded as the scene at the grave site came back to him, his hands undulating. "He asked me for advice. It was the darkest night of the thirties. Many were falling prey to the siren song of socialism. Slavery on the rise everywhere— slavery, you see."

I tried to picture it in my mind, as I still do: a young master of Latin and Greek and my father, only ten years younger, standing before General Alden's grave on that knoll above the river as Virgil portrayed the abolitionist struggle as one ongoing and unfinished.

Virgil's midwestern upbringing had made him skeptical of big government and big ideas, and, later, the Roosevelt administration's attempt to manipulate all things public and private. In Virgil's mind, the Black Eagles were a praetorian guard to counter Communist inroads, a way to uphold the great republican virtues of Periclean Athens and Cicero's Republic, the leadership of the enlightened few esteemed by Hamilton and Madison in the Federalist Papers, with just a dash of Gibbon's skepticism of dark religious enthusiasms to leaven freedom's crusade. Together, Virgil and my father wrote the preamble.

"Ah-da-dum, perhaps the indiscretion of my inflamed youth . . . unless one is a Lincoln or Jefferson, how can such sentiments be adequately expressed."

I realized as he finally turned his jowly stare on me, just before I had to go, that he, too, was struggling to come to terms with the fallible scholar my father had been.

"Your father was a first-rate man. But he was not a natural leader—that is to say, he did not live to lead the charge. Not a Douglas MacArthur—or Patton, if you take my meaning. Elliot always had to prompt him to the stage. Perhaps he felt diminished by the example of his grandfather—what man would not. He loved his sports and his books and the outdoors. If not for family obligations . . . ah-da-dum, the weight you see, I doubt he would have felt obliged to take a stand. Otherwise, he would've been content. . . ." He motioned to the nearly empty bookshelves of his study. "He was the finest scholar I ever knew—such a waste."

Then Virgil went to the Piranesi print of Rome's ancient walls, reaching to the glass with his stubby fingers as if to ponder the shadow play of light upon the ruins. "There was something . . ." Again he paused, tapping at the glass before the Porta Maggiore, fingering the dust. "He had a difficult war, no walk in the park—he saw things no man should see. It hardened him, I think, forcing him to go straight to the heart of the matter, discarding what was no longer necessary for the survival of his beliefs. Men—most especially young men—find it hard to abide such candor in others. They may admire the mind, even be seduced by the certainty, but find it difficult to warm to. And for such a romantic soul . . . as a boy, as a youth—the hardest thing to jettison—faith in our better angels, if one is to remain whole. Perhaps that is why he often seemed so lonely to me. Never easy being an Alden . . . heh?"

He shrugged and looked at me and then back to the Porta Maggiore as if a little lost. I was greatly moved by his attempts at candor and wished I could have just gone and hugged him.

"Are you saying, in the end, he wasn't tough enough?"

Virgil looked at me uneasily. "One's heart's desire can be a dangerous thing."

"You said he was the best, a scholar."

"The last time I saw him"—Virgil smiled fondly—"all he wanted to talk about was Linear B."

"It must have been a hot topic—what, in '52 or '53?"

"September of '53. He seemed in a rush to get back to Washington—such a rush. Sad . . . very sad, how it turned out, mostly palace inventories . . . ah-da-dum."

A taxi horn sounded outside. It was my ride to the Route 128 station and my train to New York and a flight to Crete.

We shook hands. Virgil promised to put in a good word for me at the Princeton Art and Archaeology Department for college admissions. He asked me to write to him in Herculaneum, where he spent his summers, to let him know how Phaistos was going. I left him standing on the steps of his dorm, gazing out over the Circle in all its summer splendor. As ever, the tremendous girth of his belly weighed down his trousers, and the cuffs remained perpetually bunched on his scuffed shoes. Sweating in the June heat, he looked as though he was melting before my eyes. That's how I prefer to remember him, there overlooking the Circle, holding the line.

After Vietnam and Princeton, we stayed in touch mostly by letter. Then on a warm November morning in 1979, I was reading the *International Herald Tribune* in a taverna near my apartment in Athens, when I saw a front-page story about how Margaret Thatcher had gotten up in front of parliament and denounced the queen's keeper of pictures, Sir Anthony Blunt, as a confessed KGB spy, who been exposed as the fourth Cambridge spy, after Burgess, Maclean, and Kim Philby, in 1963, but had been granted immunity from prosecution and allowed to retain his position as art adviser to the queen. Thatcher called it a "fifteen-year cover-up." Minutes after her denouncement, the palace fired Blunt and stripped him of his knighthood. The end of the news piece noted that an American source had been responsible for tipping off the British about Blunt in 1963.

The next day, I hopped a flight to Rome and took the train down to Herculaneum, where Virgil spent eight months of the year. He was older and had gained even more weight and moved with some difficulty. He also drank more than he should. We talked about old times and laughed about Byron Folley. Virgil took me on short little forays around the town of Herculaneum. Unlike Pompeii, only a tiny portion of the ancient Roman town had been uncovered after the eruption of

Vesuvius in A.D. 79. Most structures remained buried in mud and ash. When we walked the back streets of the modern town, Virgil's face took on a most peculiar expression: an intent watchfulness mixed with a wistful longing. He poked around in alleys, asked strange questions of total strangers. His Italian was excellent. He seemed haunted. He often told me about his war experiences: how Rome had been narrowly saved by the German withdrawal, how Florence had suffered terribly from the Wehrmacht demolition teams blowing up the approaches to the bridges over the Arno; how he had shed tears at the ruined Columbaria Library. "The torn and burned books and manuscripts in the rubble— oh dear, oh dear."

We would sit in a café or bar and drink a glass of wine and exchange more sad tales. It was then, for the first time, he shared with me his great obsession.

In the eighteen century, there had been a monastery nearby, and the monks, digging a well, had discovered the remains of the ancient city covered by the eruption of Vesuvius. A partial excavation around the well had revealed a first-century Roman villa. Not just a villa, exclaimed Virgil, but a library with thousands of papyrus manuscripts, all burnt to cinders by the heat of the volcanic material that had inundated the town. Many of the papyri were discarded—the monks didn't even know what they were—while others were deposited in a library, where they were stored as oddities. They called the partially excavated villa the Villa of the Papyri. But unbelievably, the villa and tunnel, the old well shaft to the partial excavation, had been abandoned at some point and lost. The monastery closed, torn down and forgotten. New buildings were erected. But somewhere—and Virgil grabbed my hand as he said this, his lips dripping wine—somewhere the opening to the tunnel was hidden and with it access to one of the greatest unexploited treasures of the ancient world. "Ah-da-dum," he moaned as a great shiver went through his heavy limbs, "texts that might utterly change our view of the ancient world—yes, and who we are. Think of it, just imagine, a classical library, still intact, and the vast majority of the volumes still untouched since they were covered over two thousand years ago. Imagine what might still be there, preserved in amber. The lost plays of Aeschylus and Sophocles, Plato in the original—think of all the lost works of the great epicurean philosophers, the histories and literature of the ancients that might yet be brought to light." Virgil trembled as he told me these things, his eyes burning with the waning light of the afternoon. "All their voices—imagine," and he jabbed a stubby wine-stained finger toward the pavement and the underworld below our feet. "Just think of it!"

"Yes," I replied, "but then Linear B never panned out to much, did it?"

"But this is different. We know what is here," and he stamped to illustrate how nearly in reach it was.

I finally admitted to the reason for my visit.

"It was Anthony Blunt, wasn't it?"

"Anthony, who?"

"Come on, old man—it was in the newspapers yesterday. Margaret Thatcher just announced his name in parliament. They're calling him the fourth Cambridge spy. Keeper of the queen's pictures, no less. The *Tribune* and London *Times* this morning reported that he was exposed in 1963 by an American he had recruited at Cambridge in 1937."

"So I've heard."

"So, it *was* Bobby Williams. And 1965 was the year he was taken back on the Winsted board."

"Sounds about right."

"Was it a trade? Anthony Blunt for the Winsted board, which Bobby joined the year my grandmother died? Would Elliot have countenanced such a thing?"

"You're growing reputation as a scholar—and a digger—is, I see, well deserved."

"Did Blunt give up Philby to save his skin?"

"Tell me the latest about doings in Corinth."

"All three, Philby, Burgess, and Maclean safely out of the way in Moscow, where they can keep their secrets."

"Oh, ah-da-dum . . . and tell their inebriated stories over tea and whiskey. Just you wait, the secrets will out; they always do."

"Is Bobby Williams the fifth, the fifth Cambridge spy the papers have been speculating about?"

"What makes you think there's only five?"

"Jesus . . . so how's Elliot doing?"

"We no longer stay in touch."

"Really."

"The Church hearings you know . . . my boys got shafted."

"Maybe he'll have time to finish up his book on Edward de Vere."

"Or sailing on Buzzards Bay, if he's smart."

I didn't get much more out of him. He did regale me about how he and James Jesus Angleton had spread the unvouchered CIA cash around to secure the Christian Democrat victory over the Communists in the Italian elections of 1948. Angleton, head of CIA counterintelligence, had always believed the worst about my father. But even the paranoid Angleton was gone, and, with the housecleaning of the Church Committee, the CIA of my father's day.

"They can't recruit anyone worth a damn now: Who wants to make a career as a doorstop?"

Virgil was a bit fragile and a bit drunk. My back hurt like the very devil. We returned to his pensione exhausted. I left for Athens and Corinth the following day and never saw my friend again.

As we parted for the last time in the front parlor of his pensione, he sighed mightily and examined my face closely, no doubt seeing something of my father, age almost forty when they had last parted on the Circle in 1953.

"I keep searching for the right image of your father to leave you with—a thing fraught with danger for the young. There was something Byronic about him—'a fire and motion of the soul'—know it?—and his preoccupation with the Hellenes—the obsession with Homer, his adventurous soul, his physical prowess—about the women, I have no idea. But . . . ah-da-dum, I think that would be wrong of me, to conjure such a shade. Interestingly—I don't think I've ever mentioned this to you—he liked to memorize long passages from Wordsworth. He once told me he liked to recite Wordsworth as he hiked the woods. Well, for what it's worth, I think he was happiest there."

A few years later, I received a small package from Virgil's executors containing a framed photograph. I had often seen the photo on his desk. It was of a much younger Virgil Dabney and some fellow uniformed Monument Men posed by a jeep in front of the Coliseum just after the liberation of Rome. His paunch is hardly noticeable, and there is a smile on his helmeted face of the most sublime satisfaction—conquering heroes returning in triumph after nearly fifteen centuries: The barbarian Hun had been beaten back from the gates of the Imperial City. It must have been his proudest moment. To hear him talk about Rome, it was as if it hadn't changed for two thousand years. I don't think he had ever entered a church or cloister there—for him, they simply obscured the view. On the back of the frame was an inscription, carefully typed and signed by him. It was a quote from Seneca.

As it is with a play, so it is with life: what matters is not how long the acting lasts, but how good it is. It is not important at what point you stop, stop where ever you will; only make sure that you round it off with a good ending. It was signed "Fondly, Virgil."

This brought tears to my eyes, for by 1982 I prided myself on just how much I'd stopped caring about my father, and so resigned to let history forget him. His name had never come up in the Church hearings, probably just as well. So I lacked an ending, good, bad, or indifferent. I thought I had moved on.

I wrote to the executors of Virgil's estate, inquiring about his Piranesi prints, and found that they had been scattered with all his books and possessions in an estate auction in Lincoln, Nebraska.

And yet I was haunted by something Virgil had told me that day as I left for the train station at the end of my fifth-form year, when I had pressed him one last time on what I sensed were so many conflicting impressions of my father—*dizzying* I think was the word I used—that I found myself a little stupefied.

"Look at it as a sign of greatness," he said as he shook my hand at the open door of the taxi. "Show me a great man whose soul has not been fought over by his supporters and detractors . . ." He gripped my hand tight and nodded to himself. "Perhaps it is better to have died with the game still in doubt than with the final whistle blown."

About ten years after Virgil died at his farm in Nebraska, a housewife in Herculaneum called a repairman to have her washing machine fixed. When the repairman pulled the washing machine back from the wall, he discovered a gaping hole in the floor behind it. Eventually, a team of archaeologists from the Bureau of Antiquities was called in and they lowered themselves into the hole. It turned out to be a tunnel going down over twenty feet into an excavated chamber. At the bottom was a perfectly preserved Roman mosaic floor and upright columns. They had found the eighteenth-century excavations and the Villa of the Papyri. A year later, some of the burnt papyri scrolls were being carefully exhumed. And a few years after this, an American team, using the latest in infrared photography, was able to begin making out the characters on a few of the burnt scrolls. One of them turned out to be the work of a local epicurean philosopher—a very minor figure—complaining about the degradation of the social whirl back in Rome. "Who can be trusted," the author wrote in one fragment, "when these people go around flattering their friends to their faces while fucking their wives behind their backs."

Winsted, June 6, 1931

Dear Mother Nestor,

Well, I just got elected senior prefect. I hope that meets with your approval, even if I'm not going to be a Harvard man. Frankly, it was something I neither sought nor wanted. Just dealing with Bobby Williams over the last year has been quite enough trouble, thank you, without now having responsibility for the whole damn student body. It was Elliot who pushed this, rounded up the votes. Sometimes I wish he would just butt out of my life. Handling Elliot on the gridiron and on the river is another chore. You know me better than I do: I'm really more the retiring sort—rather have my nose in a book or rowing on the river. But if this honor makes you proud and happy—enough to stop with the Harvard brickbats—I will fulfill my duties as best I can. Believe me, with the kind of nonsense that goes on around here these days, it will not be easy.

I am looking forward to summer and joining forces with Karel Hollar in Leipzig and Greece, and Nigel Bennett's dig in Knossos this season looks to be especially promising. Although I must admit to missing Elysium and our long summers together in the woods. And truth be told, I will miss days at Hermitage with Bobby; there is something indescribable about his piano playing in the mountain air, the way the notes shine in the quivering pine shadows and carry over Eden Lake. Something evocative of childhood. Bobby has invited me, as he does every year, to join him and his mother and his aunt Isabella at her palazzo in Venice in August. I know you would never allow it, but perhaps as a graduation treat next year we can find some way to accept Bobby's invitation. I still think about the Sargent watercolors on the walls of Hermitage.

Bobby has developed something of a radical following here amongst those boys with socialist leanings. They read Marx and Lenin and D. H. Lawrence, *Lady Chatterley's Lover*, no less—don't breathe a word to Mr. Crocket. Marx is okay, but *Lady Chatterley* would surely get even Bobby or me expelled! Being around Bobby's crowd of literary and artistic types produces a strange longing in me I cannot quite resolve. I tire easily of their blathering cant, and yet their ideas and antibourgeois posturing, their frisson of rebellion, does stir the soul. (It is all I can do to keep Elliot from throttling Bobby.) One does long for the fraternal ties and passionate attachments—'to burn always with this hard, gemlike flame.' Does that register with you Mother Nestor, such passions—perhaps your Inness hour? Oh, I suppose I feel that way about Homer and the Greeks, but hardly in the league of *Lady Chatterley.*

One moment, Bobby is defending his father and condemning you; the next minute, he is calling him a rich fool and claiming his mother is one of the greatest artists in Paris. He pleads guilty about all their money but is always willing to spend it on a good time. His crowd talks endlessly about equality, social justice, and brotherhood, and then traipses off to the swellest resorts, living the high life. They have no loyalty to anyone or anything—just Lenin and Marx, with Stalin the great star in their firmament. But when Bobby plays the piano, all my doubts go up in smoke and I am glad to be within earshot.

See you in New York in a week, then off to Elysium and Wordsworth for a brief respite, until the boat for Germany and Greece. Europe is such a mess these days, but so is America; sometimes I feel it would be best to retreat to Elysium and my books, dare I admit it, a little Chopin and lots of *Lady Chatterley.*

Love,
John

That summer before my senior year, I went to the islands for the first time. I worked on Crete with the Princeton excavation team at the Minoan palace of Phaistos in the south of the island, overlooking the Messara Plain. Later, I was able to visit Santorini and Delos and other sites where my father had worked in the last summer before the war. Phaistos held me spellbound—just to contemplate the longevity of the civilization that had flourished there and, day after dusty day, inhale the views over the undulating scribble of vineyards, olive and lemon groves dwindling to a hazy crease of distant blue. And presiding in the west, the sun-drenched shoulders of Mount Ida shrugging off the early-morning clouds tinged with saffron. What spectacular finds that summer: a Kamares-style jug of Middle Minoan II vintage with intricate polychrome geometries of red and off-white biomorphic forms that would do an early Rothko proud; and, most spectacular of all, a large clay disk impressed with a zodiac of pictographic signs that still remain undeciphered to this day. How we pondered those tantalizing symbols into the mothy night that summer, as if we held the magical key to unlock a silent world. And the endless arguments about the kouloures—the stone pits in the paved palatial courts: Were they for grain storage, or planters for trees that served in ceremonial harvest rituals, or just convenient places to dispose of trash?

I sometimes felt I'd slipped back into prewar times, when my father had worked in Crete with Karel Hollar, as if the terrible German occupation of Greece and the cruelties of the civil war had never happened. Even working on my Modern Greek with the locals—navigating around the Cretan dialect—the subject never came up, as if the young should be spared the memory of such massacres and reprisals. All I could think about was the grandeur of the past, of how life at Phaistos may have continued uninterrupted, except by earthquake and fire, for six hundred—even a thousand years! How Phaistos had been one of the cities described in Homer's *Iliad* that had sent men and ships to Troy. Each morning I woke ecstatically to the crystalline sunlight playing on the ashlar stone of the palace, to the rhythmic cadences of the cicadas and the scent of dust and tamarisk trees, and those blazing blue skies encompassing the far horizon, where the blue sea, corralled by the rocky shore, stretched to infinity. I still dream of those blue skies and bluer seas of the Greek isles. Just the color blue takes me back. I felt strangely safe there, digging in the dirt and dusty rubble for shards of the Minoan past, for a fragment of Linear A, hoping against hope that another find of Linear B tablets might yet be discovered. The smallest bit of broken pottery—even a painted fragment—and my hands would tremble with wonder at the age of the thing: who had last handled it and what stories it might tell. Here, I thought, truly was a golden age, perhaps the lost Atlantis, poignantly bereft of defensive walls, where artists and poets flourished in peace: taproot of what was best in Western civilization. As never before or since, I felt my father's passion for this work and so, for a while, found myself incredibly happy.

The team lived in a simple camp, professors and grad students working and socializing cheek by jowl. My presence seemed to spark the memories of two Princeton professors, then in their sixties, who, as the weeks went by, began to speak to me in asides about my father's work in the thirties, first spontaneous anecdotes and then considered praise for his scholarship. Perhaps they were just being nice as they got to know me, because I heard no more disgruntled hints about his lavish spending and personal funding of digs (how if an excavation looked promising, he'd hire twenty workers on his own dime to expedite the work)—things I'd heard around the faculty lunch table at Princeton three years before. Instead, over long camp evenings with the hum of the generator in the background and lubricated by liberal glasses of Vilana wine, I sensed from these two veteran diggers a wistfulness for a colleague who had been swept away by events beyond everyone's control. "The war, you know . . . by God, he loved the Greeks for all their filthy political passions and endless squabbles." The director of the program looked at me with a hint of awe. "Somehow he managed to get back to Athens in 1940, raised funds for an ambulance, and helped evacuate the wounded out of Albania. I believe he was the only American in OSS to actually get to the mainland before the last month of '44—the rest of us clodhoppers were stuck in Izmir and the Ionian Islands. For all his derring-do, I was flabbergasted when he left Princeton in 1948 . . . worst luck: I never knew a man so deeply enmeshed in his work—so consumed by the chase to decipher Linear B. If he hadn't gone to the CIA, I'm sure he'd have beaten Ventris to the punch. A waste, when you think about it, a mind like that." He put his arm around me. "So, glad to have you on board; you will do him proud."

I didn't have a radio. I didn't even bother with old issues of the *International Herald Tribune* or *Time* magazine that filtered into our camp. It was weeks before I knew about the assassination of Bobby Kennedy. I didn't know that Soviet forces had invaded Czechoslovakia. And I remained blissfully oblivious of the war in Vietnam, soon to be Nixon's war. Of Max's betrayal and those dazzling, if troubling, nudes of Amaryllis, and the shadow of Kim Philby . . . like so much else that summer, they simply faded into that vaporous oblivion of dusty blue.

Although I wrote to my mother as I'd promised, I never heard from her. From Max, not a word, not that I'd even given him an address. Only Laura wrote me, telling me about her new apartment in New York City and the foibles of her colleagues in the ballet world as she prepared for the American Ballet Theater's fall season. "They have plans for me, so they whisper—well, it doesn't exactly make me popular with the other girls: Life is a snake pit—hiss, hiss." She was always brutally candid and wickedly funny, and I found myself smiling when I read her letters. The only blip on the blue came near the end of the summer, when she wrote that Bobby Williams had been dismissed from the Winsted board, and Byron Folley fired as headmaster. "Daddy is in a tailspin and my mother has left him—she swears for good—and has reinstated herself as my overseer in New York: an apartment one block from mine! Her royal highness, queen bitch is kicking my ass every day. She's constantly talking to my teachers and attending class. There is no escape—yikes!!!"

Reading her words, I detected in myself a tiny pang of guilt . . . or was it triumph?

When I arrived home at the end of the summer, I found a letter from Elliot Goddard elaborating on the decision of the board of trustees and thanking me for all my good work. "Now we want you on the front line, holding the line." He wrote me that the board was intent on turning the page on the unfortunate developments of recent years. Winsted's reputation had been damaged and the board was committed to repairing the school's image: "not unlike the brouhaha of the late twenties, when the board—and your dear grandmother—got rid of Amory Williams." The board even asked Virgil Dabney to return, but he had shrugged them off and was happily ensconced in a pensione in Herculaneum. The trustees were prepared to do "whatever it takes to rebuild Winsted's reputation, and if that means getting rid of trouble-makers—wholesale, among the students—so be it. Our interim head is prepared to do what it takes. Coeducation is also on the docket for discussion—what do you think about that?" (Elliot had three daughters.) He asked for regular reports to be sent to his APO address at the American embassy in Saigon.

Crete seemed like an ancient dream.

The first days of early football practice in the fall were a disaster. There were players who did not return, players who could not or would not play, and those who played but shouldn't have played because they were too besotted or stoned to see their hand in front of their face. The president's adviser's son, once my best receiver, was in a California rehab center. But the absence of Jerry Gadsden was the hardest to bear: He had gladdened my heart in ways I couldn't fathom. He was my Willie Mays until he became a Jackie Robinson—already making waves in New Haven. And Jerry's black brothers arrived back with huge Afros and equally huge chips on their shoulders. As our best fullback put it to me on the second day of preseason, "Hey, man, why should I promote your elitist self-interested bullshit? You think I get off on all those well-dressed white dudes cheering for me on the sidelines—after what they did to Dr. King and Bobby Kennedy, shooting down my people in the streets. You think they care about me: that fast nigger boy who's gonna make their school look good, make them look good and so, so damn liberal because they let blacks into their schools. Enough of that shit. You give me the ball when I tell you to give me the ball—I don't care what coach has to say about it. Only reason I'm doing this—I need the college scholarship, you hear me, man? And if you can't help me look good when I need to look good, then you can run the fucking ball all by yourself."

I was walking on eggshells.

And then a miracle happened. We got a reprieve. But as with any miracle, a price came attached.

I was standing, exhausted, on the field after practice, my ribs sore as hell from unnecessary hits—just in case I wasn't getting the message from certain black defensive linemen—staring at the horizon toward the river, where the sun glittered in the treetops, a tarnished orb of expiring flame. I was feeling sorry for myself. I knew that even my best effort was going to fall short. Senior year, football captain—all the work over all the years and we were headed for disaster: That's what I'd be remembered for. And then the coach was walking toward me with a pensive look directed at the muddy clipboard in his hand. I didn't even want to hear it. He patted me on the back, his marine haircut bristling against his battering ram of a skull. He put an arm around me and walked me over to the sidelines. He told me there was an exchange student from Czechoslovakia, an Alden International Scholar (another of my grandmother's scholarship funds), and a champion soccer player and gymnast, who might be able to kick field goals and extra points.

"You've got to be kidding."

He jutted his jaw in the direction of a blond-haired guy in a wrinkled blue warm-up suit sitting in the grass over by the benches; his legs were splayed wide as he bent his torso so that it was almost flat against the ground. I groaned in amazement, thinking, Shit, how could a guy do that, stretch like that? So the coach introduced me to Vlada Radec, who got up slowly, smiled so that his Slavic cheekbones stood out like the tail fins on Jack's pink Caddy, and shook my hand with the grip of a trapeze artist making a split-second grab. And like that, this thing inside me sort of gave way like a trapdoor opening, and I was in free fall; we kept the handshake going for the longest time while those steely blues divined each and every weakness in my soul, letting me know with wordless certainty that I was, in fact, holding on for dear life even if I didn't quite know it yet. I have only felt that way twice in my life, first with Vlada and later with Lt. Theo Colson.

There was something deeply masculine about Vlada that went beyond his lady-killing good looks, or the burnished lines in his durable face and powerful yet sensitive hands. For a political person—the thing stamped into his soul by the events of 1968 in Prague—he always seemed serenely unself-conscious, projecting a caring, impulsive purity, and, as Virgil had said of my father, a fire and motion of the soul: quenchless, insatiable, the way a pedigreed animal relies on inbred instinct. In the highly charged radical atmosphere of that time, his candor about his cause was both enviable and outsize. There was magic about him, like the glitter of a reflection in a still pool that you ache to reach into, hoping against hope it is the real you. Magic of a healing kind: the priceless power to attract allies and enemies alike. Everyone loved him, and within that field of attraction lay a promise to be better than you were.

The coach said he would like to try a few field goals; he called the center over and quickly explained to Vlada what he must do. Vlada smiled, a tad puzzled, and asked a few questions in his accented but excellent English, then nodded his head like there was no problem, even though he had kicked only soccer balls all his life.

"Ah, a goal kick—yes?"

So we set it up, and I had this feeling inside, this great rush of adrenaline, like when you take the snap and see the configuration unfurl before you, the seams and pockets just like it's marked with the little arrows in your playbook, except now the playbook and the arrows are in your head and you know exactly how you're going to make it happen before it happens, like second sight. I couldn't even feel my ribs anymore as I bent down to take the snap. And then I took the snap cleanly and placed it and felt Vlada's movement toward me, then the ball was gone, not like I had expected, with a hard bump, but with a soft, beautiful slap, as if his whole foot had wrapped around that football and lifted it heavenward. I could feel the power and grace of the impact reverberate through my arm and my whole body like some god had touched me. I didn't even look up right away because of that wonderful feeling, but when I did look up, I saw that ball still sailing, high above the uprights. It would've been good from forty yards or more. I turned around, and there was the coach standing there with a big grin. And then I looked at Vlada and he stood there looking at us with this expression, as if to say, *is that all you guys wanted me to do?* But that was precisely what the coach wanted him to do, and it was going to be good enough to win every game for us that fall.

Vlada was the finest all-around athlete I'd ever worked with—not as fast as Jerry, but a better athlete. And he had the kind of charisma that put the fear of God into opponents. All I had to do was get the ball inside the fifty-yard line and he was good for eight out of ten attempts. But it went beyond skill; his spirit of good-natured camaraderie was infectious. He laughed at our squabbles and made us feel foolish. The growing respect he engendered along with an absolute will to win soothed the black-white divide. He made us whole; he made us players once again. Halfway through the schedule, we'd developed bootlegs and quarterback sneaks and fake field goals that ran rings around our opponents. If I got a pass to him in the open, he was gone. He could outrun anyone on any field that fall. Hard to believe, but sometimes I thought he was actually quicker than Jerry Gadsden—not faster on the dead run, but quicker at slipping tackles. We were a team again. Nothing fazed him. Even when he was beat up, he got the job done. The black players adopted him as one of their own and welcomed him at their table in the dining hall. Unarticulated but very real: Their politics and his were fed by the same sense of historical oppression. By the end of the season, Vlada had letters from twenty-six universities offering him a football scholarship. But he didn't give a damn.

That August, the Soviets had invaded his homeland.

Unlike most of my classmates, who wandered the halls bitching about their miserable life and country, Vlada lived with a real and terrible weight on his shoulders. His life at Winsted was a respite from purgatory. He lived a life in limbo, waiting for word about his father, Janos Radec, the famous dissident, professor of politics and history at Charles University. Janos Radec had been a member of Dubček's government during the Prague Spring; he was one of the first arrested in the Soviet crackdown. Vlada was desperate to return, desperate for news about his father, who was in jail and had a long-standing heart condition. His mother relayed information in smuggled letters. She told him to stay put, avoid making a fuss, especially to the newspapers, which were more than willing to interview him and make a stink about the imprisonment of his prominent father. Not for a moment did his anger and guilt at not sharing in the trials of his family leave him. It glittered in his blue eyes. After he'd made a winning touchdown,

I could detect his frustration, the swagger, the flicker of utter disdain beneath that sweaty wedge of a forehead. There was a kind of mute, reckless anger written into his every gesture: a fearlessness played out on and off the field.

Late at night, I'd find him bent to his shortwave transistor radio, listening to the Czechoslovak service on the Voice of America. I would find him in the dining hall each morning, combing the papers for news about home, about Prague. Many mornings, he would barely touch his food.

He was mystified by how none of the students seemed to care. "Don't they know what has happened to my country? Why they protest all the time? If Vietnam is Communist, everything will be kaput; these are bad people, evil people. What is the matter with their heads?" And he'd point out an especially sullen crew at an adjoining table, our class radicals, who regularly marched a North Vietnamese flag around the Circle to demonstrate their bona fides. "Don't they understand anything?" Vlada would squeeze my arm until it hurt. "Don't they understand that only America can fight the Communists?"

How could I explain it to him?

The thing that really tore me up was how much Vlada loved America. While I'd been in Crete that summer, trying to forget about my country, Vlada had been traveling all over America—an America I had glimpsed only once, on my cross-country drive the summer before, when I'd worked on a dig in Arizona. And his beautiful large hands could do more than just catch passes; Vlada turned out to be, of all things, an accomplished bluegrass guitarist. In June, he'd traveled down to Mississippi and sought out legendary black musicians, some of whom he'd heard on pirated records or recorded off the Voice of America, only to find, to his chagrin, that they'd died years before. So he sought out their colleagues, fellow musicians, who taught him pickings he hadn't been able to learn from records. He'd made friends along the way, strangers who took him in and shared a meal of Cajun chicken and black beans, who talked about themselves in accents he could barely understand, who'd never even heard of Czechoslovakia, much less that the Soviets had invaded his homeland. People just took to him—women especially. Handsome like a young and blond Clint Eastwood, he wore his heart on his sleeve. All that fall, he regaled me with enthralling stories about my own country. In his words, in his eyes, in his bluegrass riffs, I could feel the endless highway receding from the back window of a

Greyhound bus; the great stretches of a furrowed Missouri landscape; the sprawl of the muddy Mississippi and the parade of grain barges heading south; and rural slums in North Dakota where the remnants of Indian tribes played bingo into the night, until they keeled over from alcohol poisoning; and a Kansas farm town with one hardware store and a rat-infested grain silo where he'd taught gymnastics at a 4-H club when his cash ran out. Names and places, familiar and not: places I'd never seen for myself, people I'd never met. I was transfixed and humbled by all he had to tell of the good people of my country, who were not at all like the mophead complainers at Winsted.

When the tanks rolled in to crush the Prague Spring, he'd been at the Grand Canyon. As he told me this, pausing in his playing, he pointed to his head and asked me to try to imagine it, to see that vast earthen landscape of red cathedrals and endless fluvial caverns carved like a banner of freedom under a clear blue sky, and to know—"to see, see such an evil thing"—that those brutal machines were clanking through the cobblestone streets of his neighborhood in Prague. I could only shake my head.

Of course, Max took an immediate dislike to Vlada, describing my friendship with him as an "unchecked" and perverse infatuation. But I made a point to avoid Max and his crowd of protestors and druggies. The interim headmaster was beginning to bestir himself, the school to crack down; it was only a matter of time before Max's crowd stepped over the line. As senior prefect, like my father before me, I was entrusted with the responsibility of enforcing the rules. From my father's letters, the parallels to his day and Bobby Williams's Marxist spawn did not escape me. I figured the less I saw, the better: One headmaster and a member of the board of trustees was plenty. I played football and studied like hell, and tried to ignore Max's pleadings. Off the field, Vlada and I spent most of our time in the stacks of the library, where we had adjoining study carrels. And here Max eyed us and bided his time as he worked on his short stories.

And this, the cruelest irony of all: world-class athlete, gifted musician—and Vlada's greatest aspiration was to be a writer . . . like his famous father.

Another writer!

Looking back on my school days with Vlada, I am still filled with piquant joys at his unyielding, magnificent faith in freedom, which, even with his betrayals of me and others, I must be grateful for—that, and the key, twenty years later, he would put in my hand to my father's fate.

If I have learned anything, it is the strangeness of our chaotic entanglements, far stranger than quantum mechanics, harder to conceptualize than a million buried shards . . . yet uniting us in time and space in ways we can never know until the thing is done.

It was a role not unlike that which Karel Hollar played in my father's life.

Or as Max put it to me in one of his more acid moments, "Admit it, man, you're in love with him; I always suspected as much."

18

THAT FALL, AS SHE'D PROMISED, LAURA IN-
vited herself to the football game with St. Mark's—
our big rival—with the understanding that she would
be my date at the fall dance. In her letters to me that
summer on Crete, there'd been an apologetic undercurrent about her
parents' behavior, as if she was intent on disowning them. When Bobby
got dropped from the Winsted board—so she wrote that fall—he "went
ballistic," threatening legal action against the trustees; he'd gone to the
newspapers with his complaints about the "warmongers corrupting
Winsted's values." Everything she did seemed couched in putting distance between herself and her past. She had fulfilled all her high school
requirements and Barnard had accepted her as a part-time undergrad-
uate while she pursued her ballet career. We were both teenagers, but I
felt she could've been twenty-five, with a job and salary and apartment
of her own. In the ballet world, she was considered a phenom. "Actually,
it's kind of the pits. The company director and Antony Tudor—he's a
choreographer—are always talking about how much I remind them of
my mother. Yuck! Actually, I think I'm better, certainly than the other
bunheads. Sometimes I wonder if they even learned to read: nothing
to talk about!"

Laura arrived late by taxi from the Route 128 station. It was Indian
summer, warmer than anyone could remember for early November.
She had mentioned in a brief phone call problems about getting away
because of rehearsals for an upcoming performance, and avoiding
detection by her ever-vigilant mother. I happened to glance over at
the home crowd on my way back to the bench after Vlada had kicked
a thirty-five-yard field goal in the third quarter, and there she was, just

standing there on the sidelines, intently watching me. She wore a white sports shirt, a short maroon plaid skirt, gray knee-socks, and loafers, as if she were playing the part of a preppy schoolgirl, when, in fact, she belonged to a very different milieu in New York. I found it odd seeing a woman on the sidelines who was actually there to see me play, much less someone from childhood, from Elysium. I raised my hand and almost stumbled. She waved back, with that funny little ironic smile of hers. Her hair was done up tight behind her head; she was elegant, she was beautiful. I thought maybe I should go over and at least say hello, but a shout from the coach ended that idea.

Her presence reminded me again of the strained conversation around the dinner table at Hermitage, and the names over which her parents jousted. I had a sense that Laura knew something I did not, and it was hard to get my mind back on the game.

Football frightened my mother; she sent me clippings from the *Times* about football injuries and brain-damaged kids. She used that as an excuse to avoid coming to games: "The psychiatrist says it will only increase my anxieties." I'd never worried about injuries and never thought much about the crowd. I liked the speed, I liked the physicality, but most of all I liked the thrill of making something happen out there, of coordinated, well-trained bodies pulling off a beautiful play. I loved the feeling of teamwork. It made me feel whole, made me feel part of something good and alive, and never more so than with Jerry Gadsden and, on this warm afternoon, Vlada Radec. But the sense of being watched, of putting on a performance, went against the grain, because it spoke of consciousness, of the need for success because failure might disappoint. It amounted to the difference between throwing the ball and aiming it, between instinct and calculation. Because of that false consciousness, I almost blew the game. I fumbled once and threw two interceptions. It didn't help that one of my own clumsy linemen managed to kick me in the jaw: two stitches and a bruise a mile wide. But with Vlada's four field goals and two touchdown catches, we managed to pull it out.

Laura waited for me while I showered and changed and the doctor put in the stitches. She was standing in the entrance foyer of the gym, looking at the memorial display case to my father containing the grainy black-and-white photograph and his medals arrayed below.

"You okay?" she asked.

I worked my jaw a little self-consciously. "It looks worse than it is."

She reached a hand toward my chin but seemed to stop just short of the stitches, her fingers hovering for an instant, then dropping back to her side. Her blue eyes, flecked with little bits of green around the irises, were very soft and glowing and had none of the brittle hardness I was so used to seeing in Vlada's blue eyes.

She tilted her head. "It was funny seeing you out there with a helmet on and everything."

"Yeah."

"I mean, I kind of knew it was you, by your build and because somebody told me, and you have a number on your back." She had deepened her voice and hunched her shoulders, doing a perfect imitation of a lumbering football player.

I laughed at her antics. "Mud gladiators."

"Oh"—she shook her head and I noticed the self-deprecating twist of her eyebrows—"congratulations."

"It's okay; it wasn't a great game."

"An undefeated season and your last game . . . until Princeton."

"If I get in."

She smiled, as if she knew something I did not, and then indicated the display case.

"Your dad . . ." Her voice almost broke and she took a quick breath. "Tell me about the medals."

"He was with the OSS in occupied Greece during the war. I guess after the war, too—except it was the CIA by then, during the Greek Civil War against the Communists."

"Nestor," she said, pointing at the photo, captioned *Medals Ceremony, Athens, 1949.*

"Nestor?"

"Yeah, see the name written beneath the man standing to the right of your father?"

I blinked and brought my face closer to the glass. I'd almost forgotten. There, printed in my grandmother's hand was the name, *Nestor,* in nearly faded black ink at the feet of a bearded figure, shorter than my father, stocky and powerful, like the tough laborers on Crete I'd gotten to know that summer. I squinted, not a little abashed that it had gone out of my mind. But not hers: Twenty years later it would be she, with Elliot's help, who would track him down.

"So . . ." She paused, as if casting around to get some image in her mind to settle out. "So, he really was *extraordinary*—a war hero?"

It seemed less a question and more like she'd been weighing some less flattering possibilities. I didn't like the tone of her voice.

"I guess so." I shrugged. I couldn't help thinking back to that dinner at Hermitage with a sense of dread . . . and how somehow the spirit of Kim Philby had hovered at her mother's elbow.

I was eager to go, but she lingered, as if reluctant to give up on the display case, as if it held her a little in thrall, like the reliquary of a warrior saint. I realized I hadn't answered her question about what he'd done to receive the medals; I realized I didn't really know. Just like I'd been oblivious of the name Nestor . . . with all its evocations of untold stories, and unknown authors.

Outside, the air smelled good, very warm, very dry, leaves crunching underfoot.

"Almost beach weather," she said. "Almost, summer at Elysium."

I knew exactly what she meant: summers growing up.

"Amazing, the heat."

"Funny," she said, looking over at the now-empty football field and bleachers, "I don't really like football. I mean"—she smacked her forehead in a theatrical gesture—"I don't understand it much."

"It's definitely an acquired taste."

"No, actually, what I was trying to say was . . . I enjoyed it—seeing you play."

"Thanks."

"What I really mean is—you looked like you were enjoying yourself, even if I couldn't see your face."

"Today . . . I was struggling."

"It's in your body, the way you move, the rhythm, the balance when you run, the poise when you turn, holding your direction to the last instant—the joy. . . . You're very physical . . . very sexy, I guess."

She screwed up her mouth and blushed when she said it, as if she knew it sounded a little insane in that context. I glanced at her uneasily, aware of how intent she was to express exactly what she had felt, as if making sense of her feelings, or at least justifying them, was important to her. And sensing this—how she liked to dig for the truth—made me feel a little better about her.

"Today, I was just trying not to screw up. Spring my tight end and get him out in the open and get him the ball."

"Oh yes, that blond kid; he was so fast."

I could hear it her voice: *Talk about a sexy guy.*

"Vlada. He's an exchange student from Czechoslovakia, our kicker. He saved my life; he saved our season. Wait 'til you hear him play guitar at the dance."

She touched my elbow. "But you, you like to . . . *move*." She caressed the word, as if it had some special meaning for her, some deep sensual association.

"Like you said, my last game."

"Is that why they carried you off the field like that?"

"It's just traditional. It's the St. Mark's game. There'll be a bonfire tonight before the dance."

Saying those words suddenly brought the reality of it home. I gazed back at the field: the muddy ground-up strip of turf obliterating the white hash marks, the sod that would freeze with little ice puddles on the first frost, take the first powder of snow like a salt flat, until buried for the winter under deep white swells, to reappear in the spring as a muddy glue, until the first green sprouts began to hide the damage and later the lazy cleated jogging of a few outfielders aired it out further, until the high summer heat brought it around again lush and green and soft, smeared on knee pads with the first tackle of fall. It was as if I saw it all in an instant and knew that for me, in this life, it was done.

I don't know how I knew, but I did.

"It's a big deal—huh?" I heard her ask, like she'd been far away.

"It used to be, in your father's time, my father's time." That was a queer way of putting it—inserting the distant past into our conversation—but it was inevitable. I was wondering if she had any idea what had happened between our fathers: how Bobby had betrayed the secret society . . . and my role in his demise.

She made a dismissive motion, as if I didn't know the half of it.

"He was very musical, you see. . . . Music was his life."

For a moment, she took my arm as if to steady herself after this apology, or like a fellow conspirator confirming her defection.

I was going to say something, but out of the corner of my eye I saw the football coach coming toward us with a stubborn grin. He stopped just short, looked from Laura's face to mine, lowered his head like a friendly dog, and butted me playfully in the chest. It was very endearing, if a little embarrassing. He held out the clipboard that had been under his arm. "You did it—I just finished the math," he croaked out— "with three yards to spare; you broke your father's passing records."

"Yeah?" I said, suddenly feeling a little faint.

He looked at Laura, studying her face, acknowledging her exquisite pedigree—and that she was with me—and directed his next words to her. "I never saw this kid's father play, but I've talked to guys, the most tight-ass—excuse my French—fellows around here, who, when deep in

392   DAVID ADAMS CLEVELAND

their cups, have reached back and related with wide-eyed wonder what it was like to see him play. It's been my privilege to work with this"—he reached up and grabbed my neck—"son of a gun and see for myself into the heart of a great talent." He turned up my chin and examined the stitches. "That's why I do what I do."

"Thanks, Coach." I'd never seen him so happy and I knew he had worked so hard to make it happen for us—Vlada's field goals making the difference—and that this moment of familial camaraderie was to acknowledge making a success out of disaster, which any true coach will tell you is the sign of true character.

He seemed to collect himself and very formally held out his hand to greet Laura.

"Hi, I'm Charlie Alexander."

I snapped to. "Oh, Mr. Alexander, this is Laura, Laura Williams."

He held her hand in a lingering shake and I saw his face relax into a quiet, almost soulful smile at the familiar name—just a hint of an inflected glance toward the chapel, as though some kind of connection was gelling in his mind. He looked from one face to the other—boy—girl—and back again, as if some arrow, some hopeful road sign, had come clear in his mind's eye that led to a future for me after football, and school and college and grad school and first job, to some indeterminate point where some life cycle was to begin again and re-create itself in new guise. I thought I saw relief there in those blooded slate gray eyes, even the hint of tears, as he savored some sense of the continuity of things—or some vague hope in the healing bonds of romantic attachments. He finally backed off, as if to say, *Well, now it's Princeton's turn,* and made his way to the station wagon parked off the Circle, where his gorgeous blond wife and three blond daughters waited to take him home.

If only, I thought, life worked out like the play charts on his clipboard: the arrows, the X's and O's, the names and game stats that might add up to a winning season. (One of his lovely daughters would die at forty of breast cancer, leaving two children and husband and parents to forever mourn her courageous, unfillable absence.)

As we watched the coach walk away, I had an anxiety attack. What was I going to do with Laura Williams for twenty-four hours? I surveyed the Circle and the apple trees heavy with mottled red, and I could already spot members of my class with their dates for the weekend, strolling together, some holding hands, or stealing a kiss. And I knew as sure as the sun would rise the next day that it would go far beyond that by the end of the dance. I'd heard enough in the locker room.

We began to walk a little aimlessly, making conversation. I kept looking at her askance, feeling her bodily presence beside me, her breasts less pronounced in the sports shirt than in the bathing suit of the previous spring. Why had she wanted to come? Why did she want to be with me? I tried to be rational, to reason it out. It wasn't as if she was my girlfriend. And I knew what the other guys had in mind with their dates. Could I have it in mind? Would it just start to happen if we were around each other enough? Did it require booze or dope or something? Clearly, the others already wanted it. What did they want at the end of the day, at the end of the dance? Desire? They desired girls—which meant what? They wanted to touch them, to kiss them. The rest of it was a little too unnerving to contemplate, especially with the daughter of Suzanne and Bobby Williams . . . and thoughts of Amaryllis's erotic nudes, a kind of defilement of propriety, which had merged in my mind with images of Kim Philby and Suzanne on the piazza of Hermitage. We exchanged shy glances, as if she knew exactly what was going through my head. She seemed to be trying hard to move us somewhere where the past couldn't touch us—even if we both knew it did. And I didn't mind, in theory, the idea of being close to her, but I didn't really want to touch her, at least not yet. I wanted to find out more about her, as if she might be witness to something I still needed to understand. Like her mother's embrace on the veranda in the moonlight, a thing that kept flashing in my brain like heat lightning.

"So, how's Max?" she asked.

I wanted to tell her the truth, but I didn't.

"Max is Max." She gave me a funny look. "He's got some big secret up his sleeve, something about one of his stories being published."

"Yeah . . . Did I tell you how much I love being in New York?"

"I guess so."

"It's so different from Boston, Winsted, Elysium. Know what I mean? You're a New Yorker."

It was distinction I hadn't given much thought to.

"The world as it is . . ."

"Rather than the one that can never be."

"Well . . . ." It was a striking thought, but I had no idea where to take it.

"Barnard was really nice about granting me early admission. But

I'm worried about how much time I'll have for my studies when the season gets under way. Everything seems to happen at a hundred miles an hour now."

"Sounds like you must be pretty serious about ballet?"

She shrugged and looked down at her loafers.

"My mother *was* serious." She grimaced. "God, everybody in New York remembers her . . . like it was yesterday."

I understood exactly. "She was that famous?"

"She was incredible. People in the company who knew her then say she was the greatest ballerina of her generation. They say if it hadn't been for the war, and other stuff, she would have been another Margot Fonteyn. And then, of course, they look at me like I'm the Second Coming."

The "other stuff" I assumed was Bobby. In her frustration, I detected an echo of my own and so found myself drawn to try to read more of her driven and restless body language.

"You must be pretty damn good, then."

She waved it off. "Don't you ever worry about getting hurt out there?"

"Not really. Although I did get knocked out last year."

"Yikes." She stopped for a moment and looked me over. "I worry a lot about getting hurt, about injuries."

"Doing ballet?"

She rolled her eyes: *You've no idea.*

"I had tendonitis really bad last year and I couldn't dance for six weeks. I thought I'd go crazy."

I could hear it in her voice, the agony of that enforced layoff—her desire to keep on doing what she was doing, which, in spite of her bullying mother, had become her life. And it finally dawned on me what she had been trying to tell me back at the football field about movement. It was as if I had stepped back a moment, and in the thin sunset light of fall, I could finally see her whole: her beautiful, long, finely muscled legs, the lyrical arms, which often shaped the air as she talked, her back held high and free, head elegant and poised. She was quite thin, not even very womanly, in the sense that there were few obvious curves to her, and she was athletic and strong, her hair tight against her head so that the delicate tendons in her neck stood out when she glanced to the right or left. And there was the lovely ease with which she moved, the way Vlada moved with such grace and poise, like some embodiment of the body's majesty. That feeling relaxed me, and the sense that we had something in common besides our families. And that was when I began to notice the eyes of my classmates turning in our direction. They were surprised, and I think I was secretly pleased.

We'd gotten around the Circle as far as the chapel and we both stopped as if confronted by the implausibility of our situation.

"I told you, didn't I, my mother has left my father?"

"Yes."

"At least she has her own apartment. She doesn't know I'm here."

I looked at her blankly, stuck.

"Okay, I suppose we'd better go in," she said, heading for the chapel. "Don't you think?" And she eyed me with an expression eliding between sarcasm and temptation. "Do our duty—*right?*"

In a very businesslike way, she strode to the Williams Memorial, that lush and sentimental bronze sculpture with its phalanx of garlanded angels, and paid her respects with a matter-of-fact nodding of her head. She touched the dedication to her great-uncle, the golden-haired Harvard teacher of classics, who had died at his own hand out of frustration and guilt and fear for the love he could indulge only at great cost and danger to his family. I thought of Max's perplexity at the oddly colored lettering, and the name *Pearce Breckenridge* bizarrely picked out in maroon at a diagonal from top left to bottom right in the inscription. Her fingers seemed to hover over the lettering as if to detect some faint vibration, or allow her artist's intuition to uncover the truth, which neither she nor Max, nor my father, for that matter, with all his instincts around textural decipherment, managed to uncover. Instead, it was left to my grandmother's sleuthing in the family archives, where it would finally find us in a manila envelope tucked into a shelf of the works of John Burroughs.

As if thwarted, her fingers strayed to the faces of those talismanic angels, where she might have more luck with their disquieting expressions of grief mixed with sexual longing.

Then, as if to disabuse me of any such nonsense, she turned to where I stood and made a devil-may-care face.

"They were," she said, pausing, as if searching for the mundane truth behind the beautiful facade, "such sad and desperate people."

I had to smile at such a concerted act of disloyalty. "Hah, spoken like a true New Yorker."

She gave me a bemused look and walked the twenty paces to my father's memorial stone chiseled into the ambulatory wall. I had the sense her feet knew the way by long habit, as if guided by her mother's steps on Founder's Days past. She reached to the carved letters, as I had seen Suzanne do, words that I was sure Elliot Goddard had commissioned to best express consternation for the man he had loved but never understood. And there her fingers lingered, and I saw her eyes slowly close and open many seconds later, as if some pent-up surfeit of emotion was discharged in the act.

"You know, my mother was madly in love with him . . . and *he* with her."

And without even waiting for a reaction, she took my hand and led me out into the shadowland of that dying day, as if to say, *Enough— enough, we are alive and still kicking. Nothing else matters.*

We walked in silence down to the river and back. I wanted to ask her what she meant, but she held on to my hand as if for dear life, as if she held a phantom finger to her lips, pleading for time: *Please, not yet.* I realized that she had a history in this place, but no real affection for it, nothing she really cared to belabor—not if it was to come between us. Then she just opened up to me, talking about herself as if she were someone else, and I began to realize what a lonely and miserable childhood she'd had.

"Hermitage is like a glorified penal camp: seven months of the year without friends nearby. And then there were the endless commutes to school and ballet class."

"So, now you've escaped to New York."

"Now I have a taskmaster breathing down my neck. And my father accusing me of having abandoned him, too. After being kicked off the board, he has nothing left."

I wondered if I was being enlisted in that escape. She couldn't have put it into so many words; that wasn't her way. She was always guided more by instinct than by calculation, by faith in her talent, her way of moving and feeling her way toward the joy in life she so yearned to discover. As she described it, "Every step has to be like the first time." She was on a crusade, hoping to find in her dancing a path to something better than the rigorous, loveless childhood she had known. Art was her savior. In that, she was very much a Williams. And, too, in the way she held back that trump card of those love letters until the last moment.

All this, in an adulterated version, became the theme of Max's second novel, *Gardens of Saturn*, in which his heroine escapes her family to ally herself with the flamboyant protagonist: two fabulous talents thumbing their noses at the ballet and publishing establishments, rebels and exiles remaking the world as they transform themselves into the celebrity couple of the seventies.

We got through the rest of the afternoon—somehow avoiding the subject of our parents, what with the football reception and showing her my study and hanging out with Vlada and then Max and later dinner and the bonfire and the time set aside for the girls to get changed for the dance. Laura was staying at the house of one of the younger faculty members, the handsome new art teacher, which was a nice touch, and gave us a little time apart to reestablish our equilibrium. But when I went to pick her up, the fall leaves on the road scenting the air, I couldn't help feeling that her provocative remark in the chapel had less to do with her revelation about an affair between Suzanne and my father and more about declaring her independence—and perhaps goading me to assert myself and break free of the closed-off emotional life for which Max always criticized me.

I found myself sweating with apprehension. Even with the stars glittering, it remained strangely hot, as if the lingering summer-like weather was another reminder of what she'd been hinting at: that nothing is ever lost. It didn't help that as senior prefect I'd been instructed to enforce the rules of behavior at the dance: no sex, no booze, no drugs. Fat chance.

I came to the front door of the old Colonial white clapboard house with the brass eagle knocker, feeling a tightness in my chest and the stitches in my chin a little itchy. It was like arriving at a girlfriend's house to pick her up for a date and having to make a good impression on her parents, something, as a New York apartment dweller, I'd never done. Except it wasn't her parents, and it seemed that the new art instructor and his petite wife couldn't care less about the chaperone business or whether Laura got home at a precise hour or not.

"There you are, Peter," the art instructor said. "The other girls have already left. I was just about to take Laura to the dance myself." He winked at his wife. "At the very least, I want to do her portrait tomorrow."

Then she came out of the living room and I realized why he hadn't been kidding. She was wearing a very short blue silk dress and pumps. She was all legs and arms and swanlike neck, like a yearling—ready to bolt. It was a dress for midsummer, everyone agreed, and just like that we were off on the ten-minute walk to the dining hall and the dance.

We walked in silence, as if afraid to break the wonderful spell of the night, perhaps feeling the thermal currents at our backs: still so young, so alive, and so able . . . just to walk away from everything. The smells of the brittle leaves infused our lungs, replaced minutes later as we neared the Circle with its more earthy fragrance of rotting apples and wood smoke seething from the carefully doused logs of the abandoned bonfire, crawling like a milky mist over the fields to lap at the forest edge.

At the dance, my form mates couldn't take their eyes off Laura. Perhaps they detected some distant aura in her name, but probably not, given how most were oblivious of such things. More than one swaggered up to me, already high, and whispered in my ear, "What a beaut. You've obviously been waiting for the right girl to come along." The *right girl*—oh, what an entrancing thought. Even the black guys on the football team with their arms around their dates came up to me and embraced me and asked how my jaw was feeling. "Well, brother Alden, I was a little worried about you, man. I mean, you white boys sure do have your problems, but there are problems . . . and *there are problems*." It seemed that with a little booze, a little dope, and beautiful women in the mix—not to mention full scholarships to the Ivies, a racist world might yet be put right.

By the time the tables had been pushed back and the band set up and the dance was under way, I was feeling quite relaxed, as if, unbeknownst and unbidden, I'd pulled off a coup. With the other guys and their dates chatting with us, Laura and I seemed immune to delicate subjects.

"You really liked *Rosemary's Baby*?"

"It's kind of cool and creepy, and it was filmed a block away at the Dakota."

"Why would anyone drink the awful stuff those people gave her?"

"Oh, doctors can sweet-talk you into anything."

She was not as sophisticated as some of the other girls who had grown up on the Upper East Side, but she was smart. She had been a voracious reader as a girl (Max had this thing about listing her favorite books in his second novel). She was always a step ahead. She worked the edges with sure-footed aplomb. She was someone who had put all her life into one thing, but that one thing was like a lamp illuminating everything else. She was surprising and often funny and very physical.

Her air of intrepid confidence was noted by everyone—a woman with a job and place of her own in New York. The girls, of course, were beside themselves: *a dancer with American Ballet Theater—really!*

Even Max came up to us, friendly and intimate as could be, giving Laura a long hug as he complimented her on "that sassy blue dress," grasping my shoulder, as if to say, *See, see, this is what I've been telling you about all along—lover boy.* He did insist on his right to at least one dance. His main squeeze, Susan, she of the purloined panties, was down with the flu; while Wendy of Palazzo Fenway had dumped Max for her Italian Renaissance professor at Harvard. With Laura at my side, I felt his singleness acutely, his loneliness and loose-endedness. I had a girl! I felt magnanimous. We laughed together, the three of us, as if the awkward conversation around the dinner table at Hermitage had never happened. Little did she suspect, the law of unintended consequences being what it is, that Max had managed the demolition of her father and Byron Folley, with a little help from me around the edges. The band was tuning up and the tech crew was testing the lights and sound system and taping down cables. Even Max's longhaired pals, looking somewhat dapper in their senior blazers with the Winsted seal emblazoned on the pocket, were on their best behavior. They gathered around with their dates and even went out of their way to make small talk with me, as if the hard feelings of the previous year had evaporated like the wood smoke of the bonfire. The girls complimented Laura on her daring dress and exchanged discreet giggles and catty comments. It was as if I'd finally shown my hand and it was a straight flush. Like I'd joined the club, the only club that, in the end, really mattered.

Then the lights were turned down low and the band launched into a scream of acid rock—good covers of Cream, the Doors, and Jimi Hendrix—while the dance floor pulsed with amoebic subaquatic light, turquoise and reds and denim blues, pierced with blinding concussive strobes. The crowd around us melted away and reconstituted itself on the dance floor in a chaotic sea of pumping flesh and sweat-streaked faces. The guys jettisoned jackets and ties; the girls tossed their shoes. Laura and I sat staring at the dancers, and I was suddenly deathly afraid. It was as if I'd managed this new trick just so far but that the next step might spell disaster. Oh my God, I thought, she is a professional dancer! I panicked at the fraudster I clearly was. Laura just sat calmly, a bemused smile on her watching face: firmly on safe ground.

We sat and we sat. Over our shoulders on the dining hall walls, the portraits of the old headmasters and the most venerated trustees were veiled in shadow, as if blessedly relieved of presiding at such orgiastic rites. Her great-grandfather, the rector Samuel Williams in his surplice of purple and white, his huge hand resting on *Essays and Prayers*, stared out from under faded varnish at the head of the hall.

I was amazed at the transformation of my classmates, how the brittle decibels and hallucinogenic light show could provoke such a transformation in the human race. Desire burned in their eyes as they offered themselves to their disaffected gods with grinding pelvises and ecstatic grimaces; and when the music slowed, it was all they could do not to rip off one another's clothes. The country may have been in turmoil, but sex reigned supreme in the hearts and minds of the young, as it always has and always will. And it was hot, hotter than Hades, even with all the windows thrown wide to that lovely fall night.

A couple of glasses of the spiked punch helped me put it all in perspective, and who knows, maybe the ticket of desire, as Max always assured me, was the only ticket that needed punching. I stole looks in Laura's direction to see if she was unhappy with just sitting. Did she have a ticket, too? She sat primly and patiently, as if to give me time. She watched the dancers, nodding to the beat, and then shed her shoes, as if in solidarity with the other girls. She tapped one foot on the parquet floor and then the other. I could see the long muscles in her calf flexing. Then she did something extraordinary; she pointed that tapping foot—not so much pointed, more like her foot had taken on a life of its own, arching magically, as if the line of her leg could mimic a curving arabesque.

It was a little disconcerting, a beautiful prehensile foot like that. Dancer's feet, hardworking and highly trained feet, and they knew exactly where they wanted to go. In fact, they had desire written all over them.

And that's when it happened. I'd managed pretty well all afternoon, but when I hung back and didn't ask her to dance, she simply stood and wordlessly took my hand and led me to the floor. For a while, I managed okay, just the rock and roll and a blur of lights and the feeling of bobbing in her wake. She was into it all right and she was resplendent and graceful, and it turned out okay being along for the ride. I figured the racket of screaming guitars and jittery strobes would hide me from scrutiny. And she was such a natural that I nearly forgot myself. She was enjoying herself, as if she'd shed all self-consciousness. Perhaps she'd smoked a joint with some of her admirers in the ladies' room. I found myself more and more envious of her way of moving. It was not a thing of blatant sensual display—not like some of the other girls, who seemed on the verge of shimmying out of their dresses—but a kind of calm rapture. Much of it was pure ballet, I guess, for I had never seen such things before: her turns and sweeping leg extensions displaying those gorgeously arched feet. The girls certainly noticed her. The other couples gave her room, revealing my clodhopping inadequacies. Thankfully, the band, as if it had exhausted itself—or intuiting I might need a little help—settled into a stretch of melodic slow ballads. Relieved for a moment, I counted myself lucky to have gotten through. And then the specter of desire, which had kept a safe distance all afternoon, was staring me in the face.

The Troggs, "Love Is All Around," was what did it; she was even mouthing the words as she fitted herself into my hands, as if compelled by etiquette, merging her motion with mine. We were quite proper; we were quite reserved. She guided me into a slight variation on the basic two-step, minus the clinches in evidence all around us. We continued to hold each other at arm's length. She held herself high, head erect. I could feel the warmth of her skin under my palm, the subtle rift of her backbone. There was perspiration on her brow, her thin eyebrows damp and expressive as they rose and fell to the words of the song, accenting her distant blue eyes. If this was all there was to desire, I felt happy to be along for the ride.

Then her eyes found mine and she smiled, but with a hint of longing, of an ache that required soothing. I felt a need in her to draw closer, to whisper a question, to say yes to whatever I should ask. It was hard not to respond when all those around us were in full embrace with eyes closed, kissing and fondling and generously yielding to one another. We were like a lightly rigged skiff running a gauntlet of moored trawlers. *Who are you?* I wanted to ask, looking again at her serene face, fearing to catch something of Suzanne there—and not, and then seeing the trembling line of her mother's long nose highlighted for microseconds in the flickering light. *I am here,* I imagined her saying; *I am my mother's daughter. Tell me who you are and if you are your father's son.* Her hand tightened in mine, as if she were begging for an answer. I could smell the scent of her, shampoo or soap or perfume riding the heated sweat on her skin, lovely and damp to my touch, the scent of a life in motion, telling me everything I ever needed to know of a young woman's yearning to yield herself to time and circumstance.

But what chance did we have, two antediluvians struggling for escape velocity? She was holding my hand tightly, her thumb testing the contours of my fingers. I squeezed in return, as if my hand had taken on a life of its own, to assure its mate of its steadfastness. I saw her eyes crinkle in a half smile as she mouthed the words to the song: *I feel it in my fingers, I feel it in my toes/ Love is all around me and so the feeling grows/ It is written on the wind, it's everywhere I go/ So if you really love me, come on and let it show.* There were tears in her eyes as the song was ending, and in what seemed the most forgiving of motions, she simply slipped into my embrace for a moment, holding herself tight against my chest, with my arms around her, then pulling wordlessly back as the music ended. My heart sang out as I breathed once again.

The room seemed to go through a waking, couples separating, blinking, going for drinks, to the ladies' room to smoke some dope, to sit by the windows to cool off. It was nice to be apart, to recoup a little, to look back. The fruit punch had already been thoroughly and surreptitiously spiked. But since I hadn't seen it happen, I didn't need to report it. We went to the large windows and stood sipping our cups of punch, looking out over the Circle as the vodka began its magic. We seemed to have run out of things to say—except the unsaid. Other couples were huddled in the corners, making out or brazenly lighting up joints. As witness to such major infractions of school rules, I should have taken steps. It was the kind of thing, "patterns of abuse of trust and common sense," that Elliot Goddard had asked me to keep an eye on and report to him. The acting headmaster, too, had said he was depending on me.

Fuck 'em.

Then there was the squawk of a microphone and we turned, thinking the band had already returned from its break. But it wasn't the band; it was Vlada taking a seat and adjusting a microphone to his acoustic guitar. I was delighted, because I'd been hoping he wouldn't just stay holed up in the library as usual. I knew how good he was and knew that he had been reluctant even to show up at the dance because he didn't have any decent clothes. I'd lent him a shirt and an old jacket and tie, and he looked great. Laura and I went over and pulled up chairs and listened as he began to play. Pretty soon, most of the other couples were standing around and listening, too.

The band's techie got a side spot on him that slowly changed from deep blue to a damask red, highlighting his down-to-earth persona: those Slavic cheekbones and that glorious shock of blond hair and pale, oh so pale, unblemished face. His voice was mellow, unaccented, capturing the tones of some mythic American heartland. He mixed up his bluegrass with more recent country and western hits of Johnny Cash and Buck Owens—music almost unknown to his audience—then sending his listeners into near ecstasy with some recent hits by Crosby, Stills & Nash. I'd heard him working on the songs over the last few weeks; he'd play the record a few times and within an hour he would have it down. The girls watched, enraptured, their dates holding them tighter. Even the returning band members gave him a long round of applause when he finished his set.

I introduced him to Laura, and she seemed more than a little thrilled; she touched his arm once and then again. He seemed almost happy for the first time I could remember, as if for a brief moment thoughts of those Soviet tanks in Prague and his ill father had slipped his mind. We drank more punch together, and that helped, too. We laughed a lot. Vlada even put his arm around Laura and squeezed her tightly in an affectionate way, like she was one of the good guys, part of America's greatness, someone who cared about the serious issues of life. We sat together as the band began to stoke the decibels again. I suggested that he and Laura dance together. I was feeling good and a little proud and happy to be among friends—like we were all on the same team. Vlada demurred at first, but I insisted, and Laura grabbed his hand and led him to the dance floor. They danced splendidly together. They made a very handsome couple. I found myself envying them: the commitment and faith to their lives that seemed to shine in their faces as they exchanged smiles.

Then Max came along and cut in on them. That was okay, too, since he'd been promised a dance. Vlada came over and drained his punch, made a face, put his arm around me, and murmured into my ear. "Hold on to this one. Hold on hard, my friend, because any man will want to have her." He then began to tell me a little bit about how he'd been betrayed by his girlfriend, who was a gymnast on the Czech Olympic team, and that something had gone wrong that summer in Mexico City, something about a document she had signed. I never got the full story out of him—or maybe I hadn't listened closely enough—until many years later, but clearly he was hurting. Finally, he embraced me and told me that one day I would drink with him in Prague: "The best beer in the world and we, my friend, will drink to a free Czechoslovakia." Again, he put his arm around me and gave me a hug of solidarity. Then he disappeared for the rest of the evening.

I enjoyed watching Laura and Max dance. They were really good. I couldn't believe how well Max danced. I couldn't think where he had learned to dance so well, since he wasn't much of an athlete. He was so animated, so free and sexual with his body. She was laughing and mimicked his goofy dance steps, only to assert herself and run rings around him on the dance floor, flirting freely with her body. I envied the way they laughed with each another. Then there was a round of slow dances. I wondered if I should break in on them and reclaim her. But it wasn't as if he was moving in on her; hell, Susan, his girlfriend, was lying sick in her dorm just twenty miles away. And they were dancing at arm's length, chatting, smiling, enjoying themselves. She was so leggy, almost tomboyish in a charming way, almost androgynous—especially there with Max, about the same height and with the same lean build. I found it kind of appealing. Then I saw her beg off at the end of a song and wave to me, indicating she was going to make a pit stop.

Max came over for a couple of minutes and made small talk, as if we might be able to kid around like we used to. But his heart didn't seem to be in it, and I guess mine wasn't, either. I had a feeling he wanted to tell me something. In days past, he would have rattled off a laundry list of advice and techniques on seduction. But not that night. He seemed kind of sad. I figured he was just missing Susan. Then he shrugged and disappeared in the direction of some of his pals, who were beginning to look a little wasted and furtive as they contemplated opportunities to get away with their dates. I just hoped that whatever they were up to, they'd be discreet. If I didn't see it, I wouldn't feel guilty about doing nothing.

In *Like a Forgotten Angel*, which is always referenced as Max's great autobiographical novel, the senior dance is the pivot point that sets the stage for his second novel, *Gardens of Saturn*. Betraying his classmate and friend and his longtime girlfriend, Saul falls in love with a ballet dancer, at the very moment she has fallen in love with her date: the boy she'd grown up with like a brother. Consumed with guilty passion, Saul nevertheless pursues his new love with relentless deceit, knowing full well he will have to destroy the friendship that had led him to the love of his life.

Convoluted on the page as in life, Max wrote unflinchingly.

When Laura returned, she took my hand, as if it was the most natural thing in the world, and we held hands for the rest of the dance. By the band's third set, there weren't a lot of folks left at the dance; in fact, the dining hall looked positively deserted. The band's best stuff echoed high in the beamed spaces, under the remote stare of Samuel Williams, and seemed to languish without bodies to reanimate. We stood holding hands, danced some more, but the critical mass of energy had evaporated. No one wanted to say the obvious thing. I was feeling a little tightness in the pit of my stomach, which even the spiked punch hadn't affected. Then she just looked around and shrugged and said it: "Want to go out and get some fresh air?"

"Sure," I said. "It's hot in here."

The faculty chaperones, fearing to venture onto the dance floor, were downstairs, yakking it up in the lounge. The rule was simple: You couldn't leave the dance unless you were returning your date to the faculty home where she was staying. As senior prefect, I was theoretically responsible to see that my classmates obeyed the rules. So, officially, we were leaving the dance and heading straight back . . . like everybody else. It was a little charade, but everyone seemed pretty cool about it. We shook hands with the chaperones and tried not to give away the vodka on our breath. As soon as we were outside, Laura again took off her shoes and walked barefoot. She then took my hand and squeezed it tight. And suddenly I had the feeling, a feeling very different from when she had first done it, that maybe she had taken my hand because something had frightened her. We continued around the Circle toward the road that would lead back to the art teacher's house. Just before we reached the fork for the gate, she stopped and raised her face to the warm night and the hazy stars overhead.

"Smell that?" she asked.

"Apples."

"Crab apples."

We looked toward the middle of the Circle, where the little grove of scrawny apple trees was just visible in the ambient light.

"Come on," she said. The grass was thick underfoot with shriveled, worm-eaten, and rotten apples. She breathed deeply again. "Oh my God, what a wonderful smell."

It *was* a wonderful smell. And hearing those ecstatic words from her lips, I felt almost dizzy, as if some essence of our childhood was rushing to overwhelm us, as if we were falling backward, holding hands in a deep dive. I had never been that drunk before. The sudden distancing from myself was exhilarating. I felt scared and confused and happy all in the same instant. My head filled with voices from my father's letters and half-remembered scenes from summers at Elysium: *Like angels stopped upon the wing by sound of harmony.* We sat down on a bench that circled one of the apple trees, leaned back, and stared up at the stars. We were both more than a little wasted.

"I hope you don't mind," she said, "but I smoked some dope in the girls' bathroom—I mean, everyone was smoking and handing around joints."

"You never told me—right?"

"Jesus, all they wanted to talk about was Vlada—like they'd all wet their panties."

It was an interesting, if crude, expression that opened a window and left me a little anxious and confused, as when you recognize a new departure and ask yourself how you got there—what brought you to this precarious moment that might just change your life. My thoughts spiraled into the night. I thought about General Alden, in my grandmother's telling, as he first came upon the old farm where he would build his school, before he knew, or perhaps the moment he knew this was the place he was searching for. Was it a moment like this, I wondered, when something is just revealed to the heart? He would have been in his forties, with a cavalryman's whiskers, and a limp from the minié ball that had shattered his ankle and knocked him off his horse at Antietam. Certainly a more violent and life-changing moment that had, by many twists and turns, led to the day when General Alden discovered that a near company of his men was buried in the Winsted town cemetery. They'd worked in the same mills on the Naushon River and had signed up together after the fall of Fort Sumter. And on an August afternoon, after paying his respects at the cemetery and contemplating the best way to memorialize the sacrifice of his men, he'd abandoned his carriage and decided to exercise his bad leg and to ease his mind. He walked the riverbank until he'd reached a low hill and slight promontory above the Naushon River. Climbing the rise, he came upon the old farm and the abandoned orchard. There had been a dilapidated red barn and stone walls surrounding overgrown pastures. I remembered the old photo my grandmother had shown me of a white clapboard farm building with broken windows. He had been so taken by these evocative ruins of a vanishing past—"You see, it was the unpruned apple orchard that stirred your great-grandfather most deeply"—that the next day he wired his old Harvard classmate and first cousin, the Reverend Samuel Williams, and suggested the abandoned farm as the site of the new school they were thinking of founding. In a following letter, he had written how seeing the graves of his men that morning and then later the abandoned farm and orchard had broken his heart—the headstones and the haggard apple trees coming together in his mind as emblematic of his generation's hopes and failures after the South had "returned to its evil ways." Later, when he signed the contract for the land, his instincts were confirmed. The farm had indeed belonged to an old Yankee farmer—"five generations the family had worked that land"—whose two sons had been in his regiment "shot down and wasted at Antietam." The general had broken down in tears when he learned this.

That was the story as my grandmother had passed it on to me—but not the whole story.

Of course, my sense of my life as part of a causal chain that connected me with Winsted and those apple trees was a romantic illusion, because there had been plenty of turning points before that August afternoon in 1880 that I knew nothing about, like the 1877 crime reported in the faded newspaper cutting from the *Natchez Weekly Democrat* preserved in the manila envelope. And Pearce Breckenridge was one more part of the complex algorithm that had shaped the destinies of General Alden and Samuel Williams, along with yet another handful of life-changing moments in the lives of my grandfather and father, Bobby and Suzanne, and a host of other events—two world wars, for instance—that had led us to a bench beneath the apple trees.

But on that warm fall night the only moment that really mattered was the present . . . the scent of rotting apples and the stars . . . and the unfettered desires of young lovers . . . and wet panties.

Some foolish part of me, inebriated or not, still felt the need to keep faith with the past I thought I knew . . . or forgo it forever.

As if Laura sensed something of this, she spoke first after many minutes of silence.

"We're supposed to cover for one another, you know."

"Oh."

"The other girls. The deal is, the first one back says that the others are still at the dance . . . depending."

She spoke of this calculus matter-of-factly, possibly because it had been mentioned to her casually. Besides, what could be wrong about just sitting there holding hands? Then I had a revelation: This was what it was all about, where it had all been leading since invitations for the dance had been sent and accepted; possibly the way it had been for every male and female since the beginning of time. The real surprise for me was that the girls seemed as hell-bent on the momentous possibility of coupling as the boys. Of course, this was obvious to anyone with half a brain. I was just blind until the vodka opened my eyes. It might as well have been written in banners across the sky, in the air we breathed. Without desire, the world we inhabited would not exist, so who cared how we got here or how we played our hand? The love generation—that was how history might remember us. What could be simpler? Who cared what had happened to our parents.

Her hand tightened on mine. We were sitting close. The smell of the still-warm earth and the apples was like a calming wave lapping around us.

"In case you haven't heard," she said suddenly, as if needing to get it out of the way, "my father's suing the school."

Elliot Goddard had written me as much from Saigon.

She went on in a near frenzy of confession. "He's crazy and he's driving my mother crazy—not that she's not already crazy. She just shows up in New York at rehearsals, like she owns me—and she's not supposed to be there. And no one's looking after him."

I looked up, feeling the bark of the tree at the back of my head, picking out the constellations, as if some part of me preferred the certainty of those patterns to the tortured loyalties she expressed about her father.

Then she asked, "Were you ever scared?"

"Scared?"

"When you were a kid—about getting blown up by a nuclear bomb?"

Staring up at the stars, who could believe such a thing: stardust to stardust? But I went back in my mind: the duck-and-cover drills in school, the *Twilight Zone* episodes about the end of the world . . . cinder cities of smoking ruins. And I remembered how vividly I'd imagined that wall of flame engulfing the Circle three years before. I shivered.

"I suppose during the Cuban Missile Crisis and everything. But I'm not sure I could really believe it somehow, that we'd blow one another to smithereens."

"Except my father is convinced it's going to happen. And worse, he keeps saying how we deserve it, because we've been such jackasses, that we've let ourselves be led by the military-industrial complex down the road to kingdom come. That's why he built the bomb shelter at Hermitage: that's why he insists on staying there most of the year instead of in Boston. He thinks Boston and New York will be the first cities to be incinerated."

Then I remembered the summer some years before, after the Cuban Missile Crisis, when I'd heard the sound of trucks and construction vehicles across the lake at Hermitage and had wondered what was going on, and had never bothered to find out. So that was it, a bomb shelter. The realization was somehow deflating at that moment.

"He's paranoid. He keeps talking about how the Soviets never forgive traitors. He keeps a gun in his desk. Mother makes sure he can't get his hands on bullets."

The panic and frustration in her voice as she told me more about Bobby's apocalyptic visions was just a little sobering. Not to mention her description of the nightmarish German bomb shelter in which he'd been trapped and burned at the end of the war. I stared up through the branches at the comforting presence of those points of light, thinking how pathetic we'd all seem to a man like General Alden—ready to blow ourselves up at the press of a button, even if he'd found it necessary to build retreats like Winsted and Elysium: one to make the world a better place, one to escape to—"a salve for the soul," as my grandmother explained it. Even my no-nonsense grandmother, a little after the Cuban Missile Crisis, had been talked into donating that extra million to build the bomb shelter in the gym. As Colonel Fairburn had pointed out, nothing would survive the hydrogen bomb.

"And then there's Vietnam. He never stops going on about the war. I mean, it's a terrible thing—the war." She squeezed my hand. "You'd never go, would you?"

"I'll have to register for the draft on my eighteenth birthday"—I shrugged—"but I guess Princeton football will trump all."

I felt her shiver. She definitely seemed rattled, because she suddenly squeezed my hand even harder, as if to hold me there beneath the apple trees.

"If my parents knew I was here with you, they'd go ballistic."

She gestured despairingly.

"They barely know me," I protested.

And she shivered again, even though it was still warm. I felt her move closer to me, like a change in atmospheric pressure; the very air had a presence and a weight.

"I really can't stand my parents," she said, as if trying to explain it to herself. "I don't know where I belong."

And there again was her mother's embrace in the moonlight, her kisses on my neck, and her hand reaching to my crotch.

It was uncanny how Laura seemed to sense my thoughts. "She's been having an affair with her first cousin, Colonel Fairburn, for as long as I can remember. She told me last week—we were having lunch after she showed up at rehearsals out of the blue—that she's terrified of being around my father: 'that I'll strangle the bloody monster . . . or he'll shoot me.'"

She got her mother's intonation perfectly.

"Why did you say that in the chapel, about your mother . . . and my father?"

"I'm sorry. I didn't mean for it to come out like that."

"Come out like what?"

Her head drooped, as if she'd had the wind knocked out of her.

"I found their letters. Last spring, I was stuck helping dad get Hermitage set up for the season. My mother was hanging out at the colonel's, as usual. I wanted to find some way—I don't know—of getting back at her. I'm not proud of this, you understand. I went poking around her things, all her memorabilia. In the back of her closet I found some Harrods biscuit tins, full of old letters. Your father's letters to my mother, beginning in 1944 . . . almost ten years' worth. And my mother's letters to him. I don't know if he returned them to her or somebody else did. I spent an afternoon—I couldn't help myself—reading them."

Her head slipped down against my shoulder, as if she'd fainted, as if the admission had unnerved her. I was petrified, but I put my arm around her shoulder, my heart beating so fast, I feared I was going to throw up.

"Oh Peter, the love—you would die."

What to say to that?

"Oh, but there's worse."

"Worse?"

"Much worse."

She was shaking; she was sobbing. What she couldn't tell me and what I'd have to wait over fifteen years to find out from Max's second novel: She had been so enthralled by the searing obsessive physicality of the love expressed in those letters that she had ended up lying on her mother's bed, masturbating as she read. She had never imagined such physical yearning between a man and a woman. She had grown up chilled by the clinical deceit between Bobby and Suzanne, the unending parsing of the truth, and then by the milieu of the ballet world and the gay men she'd danced with, who manipulated her body magnificently but without erotic interest of any kind. Those letters had wakened her to the desires of her own body.

And that wasn't even the *worse* part.

"You know the name they kept saying that night at dinner: Kim?"

"Yeah, I guess."

"Well, that name comes up in the letters. He was a friend or lover or something of both of them. And there was stuff about the FBI and Soviet spies—crazy stuff. I have no idea what it was all about, except it terrifies me."

"Does your mother know you read the letters?"

"I'm sure she suspects something . . . why I started to write you."

So on that night with me beneath the apple trees, she was hardly the intrepid free spirit I took her to be. She was weary and lost and desperate to find something to hang on to.

I remember the softness of her hair against my jaw and the stitches, a slight stinging sensation, but not bad. It was as if she feared to embrace me the way she had on the dance floor . . . as if the truth would utterly estrange us. She was crying, and so I held her tighter, and she drew herself into me and folded her arms around me, and I could feel her wet cheek against my neck. We held each other like that for a while, and then, as if we'd given ourselves over to the urges of gravity, we just slipped off the rough wooden bench and into the grass, where we lay quietly holding each other.

I lay there looking up through the grizzled, threadbare branches to the hazy star patterns, smelling the earthy aroma of the apples and the grass mingled with the scent of her body and the softness of her hair, strangely feeling as though we had been transported to another realm, as if we'd sunk below the sea of stars and were hiding ourselves there, resting on the bottom of an ancient sea and staring upward through the concealing fathoms to the distant lights of the world that had spawned us, glimmering beacons of a past from which we sought escape, if only we were able to kick free and head for the hills.

If only the moment had taken us there.

I wondered if that's what being lovers meant, the secret chrysalis protecting you from past and future: the moment. The idea was a comfort. And, too, it felt okay to be lying in the grass with a girl . . . as close to the earth as one could get this side of the grave. I felt a great peace come over me, that it was okay just to be myself, to be alive and free in the desire of the moment. Perhaps it was the eternal dream of escaping our lives into the lives of others, the thing, as Max insisted, fiction does best: the glorious dream that draws us to the arms of the beloved, to be re-created in the arms of our amorata . . . until we awake and find the glide faltering, when again we must get our back into moving the world on its way.

But then I felt her pull free of my arms, raise herself on an elbow, and look steadily into my eyes. Her face was the barest shadow above me, but I could see that her hair had come loose and was hanging down across her shoulders. The faint sound of music disturbed the silence like the anthem of a distant summer: the leitmotif, the Jimi Hendrix riff of our generation longing for a freedom earned by our fathers that few were willing to earn again. Then her wet lips were against mine, a rippling current moved by the distant music, as if eager for a reply. It was okay. It felt good. And so what if I was senior prefect and a little drunk; we were in the chrysalis of the music and the moment and seemingly free to be whoever we pleased. I was wondering if she would use her tongue, or if I should take the lead, as Max had explained it to me: "Start with the ears, always begin with the ears, licking from the outside in." She was so tender, kissing my eyes, my cheeks, carefully kissing the bruise and stitches on my chin as if to heal me. But I knew suddenly what I felt in her body was not peace, but the unfolding of incandescent desire.

That got me a little panicked.

"Do you like the way I look?" she whispered.

"Yes."

"I know I'm pretty skinny."

"I like skinny," I said, which was true.

"Dancers, you know, are supposed to be skinny."

"Tonight, out there on the dance floor, you were really good."

"Yeah, well, that's about *all* I'm good at." I saw her silhouetted head nodding, as if she were sarcastically agreeing with herself. "But right now, I want to be bad . . . I really do."

It was a plea to the gods of first creation. I was a little stunned, a little anxious, because I saw the glint of desire in her eyes, the edge in her voice . . . like the embodied electric scream of that distant guitar.

She was rubbing the front of my pants.

"I'm a little wasted," she said.

"Me, too."

"But I don't care."

"Me, either."

She took my trembling hands in hers and kissed the palms and put them on her hips. She slid the straps of her dress off her shoulders and let the top of her dress drop to reveal her bra. Then she slipped out of the bra. She pushed my hands up to her breasts. I was surprised because they were bigger than I remembered from seeing her in her red bathing suit, and very soft in contrast to her nipples, which were incredibly hard. It wasn't unpleasant, but I suddenly felt very alone, the peace I had known staring at the stars now gone, wondering desperately how the next steps were supposed to take place. Maybe I needed to do the ear thing. I thought of movies and books, but it all seemed between the lines. I liked the feel of her breasts and the sense of her heart pumping beneath, but she was looking down at me with her hair all rumpled behind, just waiting.

I was all set to try kissing her ears.

"Aren't you supposed to take your clothes off?" she whispered hoarsely.

"Yeah, sure."

I got to my knees and methodically began undressing. I told myself that these things were just supposed to happen. I remembered even being told in some sex-education class that boys had to be careful because they tended to get swept away, ending up doing things they would later regret. But I didn't feel any of that. I even folded my clothes. I was embarrassed. Then she was naked in my arms and we were lying together. We were kissing very softly, but I felt a little mechanical about it, a little distant. I felt a hand on my hip, rubbing up and down very lovingly. Her leg slipped over mine and I felt her soft mons brush my thigh. That was a little unsettling, and there were other smells now, a little different from before. My throat was dry. And then she touched me, very uncertain but hopeful, a sense of gladness and wonder in the squeezing of her fingers. And again, I thought of her mother, her hand.

"Are you ready?" she asked.

"I think I'm a little drunk."

"Me, too."

Ready? It seemed like such an absurd question. And I realized she knew no more about what she was doing than I did. Except there was desire in her voice, all over her body, exuding its own earthy scents . . . whether for me or for the distant rhythm of the band, or the passionate words in those hidden letters, or the escape she so desperately sought. But I was not ready. That much I understood, and it wounded me to the core.

"Look at me," she said with a hint of desperation, inclining my head upward. "Do you think I'm pretty? Do you like me?"

I looked at her where she knelt, my eyes seeing her raw white flesh and bobbing breasts and the triangle of wispy hair below her flat belly, the Circle a great pressing blur around us, the stars a sorry presence.

"Do you want me, Peter?" she pleaded. I could feel her desperate eyes search my desireless flesh.

"Of course."

I saw her smile. "You've got a beautiful body."

She reached out and drew me to her, pulling me down on top of her and putting her arms around my back, as if to crawl beneath me, hide herself there. Her legs were open, her thighs wide and receiving. But nothing happened, just like I knew nothing would happen. Then after a while, she was crying. Then the schoolhouse bell sounded out the chords of midnight as if they were exploding in our ears. I rolled off. She was kneeling in the grass, striking the earth with her fists, pulling out tufts of grass and cursing.

"We're so goddamn proper . . . we'll die first; we'll just die."

It was as though another person was there, wounded to her soul. We got dressed and walked to the gate. She told me good night, saying I didn't need to walk her back to the art instructor's home. I grabbed hold of the open wrought-iron gate to steady myself, and watched her take a few steps down the road, leaves stirring at her bare feet. Then she turned back to me, glancing up and then down to the useless shoes she carried in one hand.

"You're right," she said. "Of course, *you're* right."

She left early the next morning without breakfast. Why would she want to go to the Sunday chapel service? She had an important rehearsal that afternoon in New York.

19

I WALKED FOR HOURS THAT NIGHT, WAITING for the booze to wear off, going down to the river, trying to get things clear in my mind. It was difficult to figure out which was worse, failing to perform or hearing those words about my father from her lips. But where was the evidence? Why should I believe anything she said? Maybe her parents had put her up to it. The only irrefutable evidence was that I had flopped. I tried to think it through—a thought experiment: step back from present emotion and retrofit the possibility of my father's affair with Suzanne. Did it square with memory? Certainly my mother's cold ambivalence and reluctance to talk about her marriage made sense in light of Laura's little bombshell, much less her refrain of delay, echoed by my grandmother at childhood swimming time: "She's *still* at the beach." And that embrace on the moonlit veranda—an ice pick in the belly: Suzanne was all about performance.

And the "worse" part?

It was crushing to think my father betrayed my mother for such a woman, a Soviet spy—was that the implication? KGB—FBI . . . And Bobby, too. It was one thing to be a Communist, another to be a KGB agent. Elliot's and Virgil's interest in Suzanne and Bobby made terrifying sense. Was I staring at a pattern of betrayal in my father's life, as well—a perfidious private life echoing something even worse in his professional life, another nauseating ripple of doubt from that overheard conversation in the gym?

I stood on the bank of the river, staring across the glimmering void at a tall oak that greedily held its cache of shriveled leaves as if never

to let go. A harvest moon nudged the downstream horizon of gesticulating branches.

Loyalty was, above all things, what my grandmother had instilled
in me. I dismissed my father's possible betrayal of his country. Besides,
both Elliot and Virgil had assured me on that score. But Virgil was
gone and Elliot was in faraway Saigon. I picked up a rock and threw it
across the river, and another, and another, aiming at the steadfast oak
as if to loosen a few of those leaves and let them fall to the river below
. . . until I was a little winded. Breathing hard, feeling more myself, I
turned from the breasting moon to a wavering glow in the sky upriver
and listened. Beyond the gauntlet of pine, oak, and bedraggled maple
that fingered the obsidian curve of the river to the west I could just
make out the distinctive chuff-chuff-chuff of helicopters from Fort
Devens. It made me smile to think how even the night provided no
respite for those intrepid warriors. And I thought again of that Green
Beret in the mock Vietnamese village saluting me as the drift recalled
me with oars raised, and his comrades with heads bowed, saying grace
at the Bull Run.

I nodded to myself. Truth be told, some part of me had always
wondered what the hell my father had seen in my besotted mother,
daughter of a decorated admiral who'd saved his ship in the Battle of
the Coral Sea. A jaundiced view I had no doubt absorbed around the
edges from my grandmother.

But he'd betrayed me as well, just walked away.

I picked up another stone, but this time spared the ruddy moon-
tinted oak and tossed it in the slow-flowing river, watching the ripples
spread to the far bank and elongate downstream toward the far encompassing sea as the stars grew pale and faded from sight. *Lo cielo i vostri
movimenti inizia* . . . maybe yes, Max, maybe no. I despaired at the
thought of the long winter only weeks away and the agonizing wait
until spring thaw and crew practice.

I finally walked back, racked by these ill-fitting puzzle pieces and
my inability to assemble a picture in my mind that offered any kind of
certainty. So I forced myself to come to terms with the tangible issue
at hand: On reflection, it was simply ridiculous to feel that we had to
have sex our first time together, much less that I wanted to have sex
with Laura—what, with the daughter of *that* woman! A realization
only confirmed by the evidence of an unfolding Satyricon as I neared

campus: discarded women's shoes, still-warm joints and pint bottles, stockings and a disgusting jockstrap looped on a bare tree branch. "Jesus fucking Christ." I was relieved that I had *not* simply let myself get swept away. And it had nothing to do with Laura or me being too proper. It was just too damned soon, too out of the fucking blue. Just because everybody else was doing it didn't mean we had to. Lucky I'd kept my head.

But the moment I tried to put such thoughts in a letter—we were supposed to write thank-you letters—on the following day, my reasoning sounded absolutely silly, so I wrote something utterly innocuous. And then there were the other guys, who looked at me with new respect, figuring I'd gotten laid—not that I was going to disabuse them of the notion. A knowing smile was all it took. The dance was already the stuff of class legend. Delicious gossip circulated about the fumbling old night watchman who had actually managed to catch two couples *in flagrante delicto* in the equipment room of the gym. Two boys had been forced to write letters of apology to their dates' parents for having taken advantage of their daughters! That really put the cat among the pigeons. I couldn't think of anything more appalling.

In the weeks that followed, I often found myself lying in bed late at night going over it again and again, which got me worrying less about my father's betrayals and more about my lack of performance. I couldn't get the details out of my mind. I liked the way she had kissed me. I decided I liked her—in spite of Suzanne and Bobby—and the more I thought about it, I realized I *really* liked her body. When I awoke at night and remembered the smell of the grass and the apples, and the softness of her breasts, and how the points of her nipples grazed my palm, I felt as if I had been born anew inside, and the warm flush of desire that then came over me was very real—disconcertingly so, especially when I woke to the soaked crotch of my pajamas. That was pretty good evidence of something. I began to dream of Laura and that night under the apple trees and the loveliness of her young body and perky breasts and the smell of her mixed with the earth.

That dream has never left me.

And I understood, in retrospect, that it was not lack of desire—or even the sad history of our families—that had thwarted us, but the lack of memory. We were still babes grasping for desire in a vacuum, without the vital force of memory to guide us. Once that marker had been set, I found my memories were filled with desire, desire that would not have hidden its face one night longer, once memory of the beloved had taken root. Once *our* past had merged with the deeper past.

I did not write her that, because I didn't completely understand my feelings and I wasn't going to make more of a fool of myself trying. But I thought I made it clear that I wanted to see her again, "to talk things over." In fact, my body ached with desire at the prospect . . . almost as much as the itch to see those love letters in the Harrods biscuit tins.

And perhaps that was the real irony of our sorry affair: Fumbling my way to that desire had brought me closer to the truth about my father than anything I was to find out for another two decades.

Laura hadn't been kidding about his near-pornographic love letters, and Suzanne's . . . desire and deceit—and, yes, betrayal—twined so tightly as to be nearly indistinguishable.

The acting headmaster—old-school and some—by demanding that two of my classmates write notes of apology, had brought on yet another disaster.

A week after the dance, he summoned me to his office and told me he was very disappointed in how I'd handled behavior issues at the dance; obviously, I had done nothing to keep things under control. He pointed to a copy of *The New York Times* on his desk. This time, the article was not about the trustees and Vietnam, but about a civil suit against the school from one of the parents who had received the letter of apology. Their daughter insisted it wasn't rape, but the parents and their lawyer claimed otherwise, citing the spiked punch and rampant drug use.

"And from you, of all people, I would have expected better. You're the senior prefect. Your great-grandfather founded this place, for Christ's sake. And now look at this mess."

"Sir, I can't be expected to police the fields and woods—and just so you know: The school chaperones couldn't even be bothered to leave the faculty lounge during the dance."

The headmaster—more out of touch than even old Jack Crocket— went on and on about *The New York Times*, about the falling enrollment, about annual fund-raising, which was going nowhere.

He made me promise to put the fear of God in my classmates. I struggled to keep my mouth shut, because I would have laughed in his face.

He barely lasted the year. The following spring, the trustees announced the appointment of a replacement, a paragon of New England probity who shepherded in coeducation and renewed Winsted's reputation.

Thoughts of my father's letters in the Harrods biscuit tins secreted on a shelf in Suzanne's closet reminded me: The binder of my father's schoolboy letters for his sixth-form year had not arrived that fall, as his other letters had the previous three years.

I phoned the attorney at Brandt & Harrison who handled the family trusts and business affairs. It turned out the firm still had the binder of letters from my father's senior year.

"Why weren't they sent in the fall like before?"

"I have no idea."

"Have you read them?"

"No, they remain in a sealed binder, as your grandmother turned them over to us."

"Why can't I have them?"

There was a long pause as documents were consulted.

"It says here the senior-year letters are to be given you when you inherit."

"Inherit what?"

"The estate, at which point the letters will belong to you."

"When will that be?"

"Ah, you know your mother is contesting that."

"Contesting what?"

"The age you come into your inheritance."

"Can she do that?"

"She can try."

"Why *is* she doing that?"

"Perhaps that is a conversation you need to have with her."

"What is the age that I come into my inheritance?"

"Twenty-one."

"In four years."

"That's correct . . . when you are at Harvard."

"At Harvard?"

"That's what's here."

"But I'm not going to Harvard, goddamn it. I'm going to Princeton, I think."

"Well, that should prove interesting."

"But I'll be twenty-one, right, so maybe it doesn't matter where I go to school."

"Would you like me to put you in touch with a good law firm to contest that point for you?"

"I couldn't pay them anything."

"You wouldn't have to, until settlement."

"But I'd like to see the letters now."

"Our hands are tied."

"What kind of retainer do you guys get handling the family trusts and all that?"

"I have no idea."

"Well, why don't you go to your senior partner and inform him of my request. And if you guys can see your way on the letters, three or four years from now I won't have to bother looking for a new law firm for the Alden family trusts."

"That sounds like a fair request."

"Call me back tomorrow."

I never did have that conversation with my mother. But it was clear why my grandmother had delayed my father's letters from senior year, why she didn't want me to see them until I had assumed wider family responsibilities. My father whined about the onerous duties of being senior prefect in a time of shifting allegiances, when the Depression was inexorably strangling long-held views and values. Even at Winsted, boys were withdrawn because families had lost all their money. Two Wall Street fathers had committed suicide and the ghastly details had been all over the New York papers. And if that wasn't enough, there was the near scandal of the Black Eagles, when Bobby had informed on the secret society, creature of Virgil Dabney and Elliot Goddard, to which my father had been recruited as figurehead. My grandmother had probably realized that revelations about the secret society in the letters could fall into the wrong hands or might even put me into a perilous position—"deniability"—especially if I hadn't been picked.

November 3, 1931
Winsted School

You don't have to believe everything Mr. Crocket tells you; he is far from omnipotent. And contrary to appearances, Mr. Dabney is a damn fine fellow, even if he does dress like a hobo sometimes. He's got the finest mind for the classics I've ever seen, with the possible exception of Karel Hollar. And who cares if his teeth are bad, as you say, and he pours catsup over everything. I find him a splendid Falstaffian character—that's Elliot's take on Virgil. Mr. Dabney is more Roman than the Romans, as if he just arrived by time capsule from the Capitoline Hill—by way of Nebraska, of all places, via Yale—surely you can't hold that against him, as well. I find his judgment on issues of the day, like his hero Seneca's, to be ballasted by a deep commonsense understanding of history and human nature. His brother is a top man in the FBI and so he seems to have access to all the inside Washington gossip. He has developed quite a following among some members of our class— Elliot leans on his every utterance and treats him like a sage. I will see that you have a chance to spend more time with him when you're up for the next board meeting. I know how you love eccentrics—tickle you to the bone.

December 6, 1931

I've had enough—enough. After the incident in the toilets, Mr. Crocket has told me I must take Bobby in hand and keep him out of trouble. I want nothing to do with him anymore—can't you please talk to *your* headmaster? It's difficult enough being senior prefect without being responsible for my cousin, who doesn't want to have anything more to do with me, either!

January 18, 1932

I am sick of this charade. What would you have me do—inform on him? Yesterday, I found political tracts from the Communist Party of America in Bobby's desk drawer. Along with copies of the *People's Daily*. These people always couch their appeals in admirable goals, citing human justice, international solidarity against fascism, the alleviation of poverty, and the rights of Negro citizens to the ballot. But such ideas for social justice are never discussed in terms other than revolution, or the overthrow of the existing order. To listen to them is to believe we are mere pawns in a blind mechanistic class and economic struggle.

I get enough of this from Karel, but at least he has the fascists to contend with.

I repeat: I am not my brother's keeper—I don't care anymore.

February 17, 1932

Bobby continues unabated to couch his overtures to the younger and susceptible boys by an appeal to their vanity and by throwing around the names of family friends, mostly artists and writers of radical repute in his mother's Parisian circle. He promises his recruits an introduction to these famous personages (someday), inveigling with talk of sumptuous parties and mysterious women to further tempt his unsuspecting partners. And yet he openly describes his father as that "drunken and lecherous fool." It is almost as if his hatred and disappointment with his family has become a hatred of Winsted, and our country, and everything we stand for. I have little doubt that Bobby would gladly sacrifice Winsted to his embittered revolutionary aims.

And I must tell you, he has nothing good to say about you; he tells the most abominable lies, which I can't repeat.

Don't ask me for any more reports.

April 18, 1932
Mr. Crocket and I have now had many talks about Bobby. I tell him that Bobby wants to be expelled, to become a hero to his fraternal brothers in revolution. He agrees with me but advises that we must not be too hard on Bobby, given the family troubles, and fears for the school's reputation. I gather his father, Amory, is in a bad way. "Bobby is one of us," so Mr. Crocket advises me. "We need to stick by him as good Christians. We must not make an example of him—the press would have a field day."

Well, Christian duty is not enough. Virgil Dabney has been filling my ears with reports of famine in the Ukraine and wholesale starvation; he gets this from his brother and colleagues in Italy. Have you heard any of these reports?

April 28, 1932
The hypocrisy of Mr. Crocket is simply breathtaking. First he enlists me to try to help our fallen angel of Winsted, and now suddenly he's taking Bobby's word that I am behind the formation of a secret society that goes against the principles of the school.

At least Judas had the decency to hang himself. Cambridge can have him and good riddance.

I can't graduate too soon. This is all a distraction from my work on Linear B and Homer.

May 6, 1932
I didn't mean to upset you. Yes, rest assured, I will be here for graduation—if only to thumb my nose at Mr. Crocket.

And, by the way, you'll be pleased to know for my valedictorian address I will be citing Wordsworth—yes, the Romantic poets class this spring did rub off—and Keats' "Ode on a Grecian Urn" as my text. You know the passage: "And, little town, thy streets for evermore/ Will silent be; and not a soul, to tell/ Why thou art desolate, can e'er return." This just haunts me no end when I look out over the Circle and wonder what the distant future will make of us. As does Wordsworth's "Like angels stopped upon the wing by sound/ Of harmony from Heaven's remotest spheres." Elysium at sunset—your Inness hour? Maybe I can throw in a little Thoreau, if you like. I'm sure you'll let me know how I do.

Oh, did I mention that Karel's father has been elected to the new Czech government as head of the ministry of culture? His parents are spending August in Venice. We have been invited! So after Crete, maybe we can do Venice, sans Williams, before Princeton in the fall. What do you say, Mother Nestor? You and I and La Serenissima! The Gritti as a graduation present?

And Karel, I'm sure, has some big ideas to put to you!

Vlada seemed changed after our senior dance—more distant, more anxious, full of moody introspection. Maybe it was due to the end of football season and the chill of an impending New England winter. He disappeared into the depths of the study carrels in the library stacks, where I regularly sought him out; his pale face and high cheekbones and his dark-ringed depthless blue eyes could be mesmerizing.

Letters from his mother were more infrequent, as if the world of his youth and childhood in Prague was going into slow eclipse. All he knew was that his father was still being held incommunicado in a military hospital in the suburbs of Prague. Gustáv Husák's puppet regime, put in place by Soviet tanks, was slowly turning the screws.

His world had shrunk to books.

Vlada devoured library books until he collapsed with exhaustion in the small hours of the morning. He read books the way a condemned man might pore over Scripture in the hours and days before his execution. His desk carrel was piled with books. Battlements of books rose steadily from the floor around him. He haunted the stacks, drifting up and down the aisles, reading titles, taking out a volume, reading for five or ten minutes, then returning it to its place or adding it to his collection by his desk.

He drove the librarian to distraction.

She was an older spinster from Savannah, Georgia. Her blue-gray hair was exquisitely coifed and she wore a uniform consisting of a starched blouse with a cameo brooch of a young Persephone rising, and a knee-length black skirt, pale stockings, and white Tretorn sneakers. She patrolled the library like a meter maid on speed. The world might be collapsing, but she remained mistress of a scholarly and ordered oasis. Even the school bells rarely penetrated to the sacrosanct stacks of the library. Vlada was at once worshipper in the temple of this high priestess and a barbarian at her gate. He rarely bothered to check out a book, preferring simply to add it to the pile beside his chair or carelessly reshelve it in the wrong place. The librarian was apoplectic. Her patient Georgia accent seemed to harmlessly roll off Vlada, leaving no detectable trace. He would nod at her complaints about his MO and then make the most ridiculous excuses in broken English for his failure to return books. This disingenuousness mystified and intrigued me, since his English was near perfect. I realized that the cold authoritarian mien of the librarian produced a kind of reflex deceit in Vlada: a survival instinct instilled from a young age. She was the keeper of books—and so of ideas—an institutional power, and thus a suspect authority to be sidestepped.

A guerrilla war ensued. The librarian would surreptitiously remove books from his piles during class time and replace them on the shelves; Vlada, on his return, instantly noting the deficit, would go and seek out his missing companions, and again, beaverlike, reconstitute his enclave. The arcane logic behind his organizing principle always eluded me: history, politics, criticism, art history piled one on top of the next with no discernible chronology or theme. He kept it all in his head and in the jottings of his notebooks.

Vlada stayed up half the night. I barely got any sleep because I loathed giving up our vigil for my chilly sheets. I would look up from difficult Greek translations at three in the morning, my vision blurry, and across the aisle in the darkened stacks there he'd be, hunched over in his carrel, furiously taking notes. Endless cups of coffee left constellations of tan rings on his desktop. His pale face got paler, his eyes bleary and red-veined and heavily bagged, like some vampire off his feed. He was determined to devour in his last hours and days all the books he might never find again in Prague, transcribing thousands of passages into notebooks. He was losing weight though gorging his mind, the surfeit of which might have to last a lifetime. Twenty years later in his dingy hovel of an apartment outside Prague, he would show me those well-thumbed notebooks with the Winsted crest on a crimson cover, from which had flowed some of his most important writings. Vlada had decided to be a writer from an early age, like his father: a political calling, a way of navigating the shoals of a "counterfeit life." He once told me he couldn't remember a time when he hadn't thought of himself as a writer: "Oh, for a few minutes a bluegrass artist, or an international football star—but always, I think, a writer . . . if the truth is to be found." He was torn between an instinct to return home to his ailing father and the desire to finish out the academic year.

Max, on the other hand, seemed newly charged up after the senior dance; he became more furtive than ever. He began sniffing around Vlada's piles of books: a fellow traveler in the realm of ideas, a fellow autodidact. Max's initial hostility to Vlada melted away when he discovered Vlada's short stories and realized he was in the presence of a writer as dedicated to his craft—if not more so—as he was. They began spending time together discussing books and writers. Impassioned arguments sprang up from the shadowed stacks like flash floods. I'd watch, not a little miffed, as my erstwhile friend, my Caravaggesque Gabriel, butted in on my blond Knight Templar; their noisy whispering illuminated by a single desk lamp, books opened and texts located and voices down the ages enlisted in their contest: Vlada, that the Soviet onslaught on his homeland was part of the same monstrous totalitarian conspiracy as the North Vietnamese invasion of South Vietnam; Max, that the capitalist ruling classes were rotten to the core and losing their grip on the world anyway, and so what did it matter as long as the rising spirit of liberal humanism triumphed and brought about a fundamental change in human consciousness, a new fraternal order of peaceful coexistence led by artists!

Vlada laughed this off with a dismissive wave and drew a finger across his throat, as if to say, *You're next.*

Max countered by locating a copy of an obscure English translation of a book of essays that Vlada's father had written years before, in which the case is made for socialism with a human face—where intellectuals and artists call the shots.

Max gloated at his discovery.

Vlada conceded his father's stirring words with an ironic twist of the lips. "Yes, sure, but now they are dead or in jail. Without freedom to express ideas, to champion ideas, how will the world change for the better? Ideas alone are worthless . . . without power . . . and then that same power always corrupts even the best ideas." He made a fist and sheathed it in his other palm to suggest the paradox, and then thrust a daggerlike finger into Max's chest. "In my country, you would be the first to disappear, without a word, without a trace. For us, art is not a gentle game of the intellectual, but a matter of who lives and who dies."

Then Vlada squinted in the near darkness, as if to make out something beyond the area of illumination provided by his desk lamp. He mumbled a phrase in Czech, cleared his throat and thought again, and then tried to phrase it for Max in English so that he might understand the conundrum. These words appeared in slightly different form in Vlada's first book, and were later appropriated by Max in the dedication to Vlada in his second novel.

"The Pope had ideas, Robespierre had ideas, Marx and Lenin, Hitler and Stalin had ideas—and the power to make them a cruel reality. Power and ideas are the unstable elements we juggle like nitroglycerin. The writer who seeks the truth can trust nobody—not even himself. The evil ones will steal his fire, as Prometheus stole from the gods, and butcher humankind."

At our age, thoughts like that left us giddy.

Max managed to talk Vlada into translating a few of his stories into English for us, helping him with idioms. I could feel the power of his words and images even in translation, and the metaphors he conjured with a supple sarcastic prose. Sometimes he wrote about his childhood, small tales about the odd comings and goings in his Prague neighborhood, where everybody had a secret to hide and everyone sidestepped the truth—how the actual physical landscape could be warped by the imbecilities of a culture built on lies and half-truths. He wrote fantasy stories and poetry. One of those stories, which he read to us in a first draft, was published years later in his first book of short stories. It begins with a little boy wheeling his toy wagon down cobblestone streets, where he picks up broken toys and bits of furniture from garbage cans; each passerby sees some lost object from his childhood in the boy's wagon, invoking daydreams of carefree youth and the sheer inconsequence of daily life; the lost objects become the only reality that matters. Upon the publication of these stories some years later by a press in Vienna, he was compared with Kafka, Kundera, and Havel.

I weighed in occasionally in these debates, but I dared not say what I really wanted to say: *Stay, Vlada, stay with me until the summer and then see how things are.* I tried to tempt him with descriptions of Elysium and our well-stocked library and about my great-grandfather's paintings, and the tall pines . . . how he could have the place to himself and the peace to write. I even fantasized that maybe we'd go on to college together—why not? The Princeton football coach (Yale, too, prompted by Elliot Goddard) recruited him as field goal kicker and offered him a full academic scholarship and stipend.

"Think about it, playing before thousands of people . . . and think about the library—you'll have a field day. And the girls—you'll be a fucking star!"

He was tempted; I could tell he was tempted. . . .

And then in early December, he received a long letter from his mother. His father had finally been released, but only because he had suffered a second and more serious heart attack in prison. After a week in the hospital, he was allowed to return to their apartment. He was in a weakened condition, with no job, no telephone, no pension, and was warned against communicating with anyone in his former circle around Dubček.

"They take his job . . . his reason for living," Vlada said, tossing the letter onto the desk. "Then his dignity is finished; there is no purpose for anything . . . and no friends and no money."

His face was a jaundiced yellow in the dim lamplight, eyes hollow and tired.

"Isn't there something that can be done?"

I realized the instant I'd spoken how little conception I had of a world where nothing could be done, where there was no redress. His smile showed no bitterness, only a certain incredulity that I could be so naïve. He bent closer, as if make sure I got the message, making a show of chopping with the edge of his flattened palm.

"They kill very, very slowly, by first corrupting our language, and with this they destroy the spirit, then the body. In Prague, even a heart attack is part of the calculation."

I wanted to hug him, how I just wanted to hug him.

On one of our last nights together, I noticed that Vlada seemed more agitated than usual, as if he was having a hard time concentrating. When I walked over to his desk late that evening, I thought I saw him wiping away tears as he quickly folded a letter and replaced it in his pocket. I figured it was from his mother and more bad news about his father. But he seemed to have had enough of that subject and shoved back his chair and walked me over to my study carrel. He picked up the English lit anthology I'd been reading and examined the page of under-lining from Charlie Springfield's AP class of the year before. Vlada ran a hand through his ratty blond hair, by then down to his shoulders (he'd vowed not to have it cut until he returned home), and murmured his approval as he flipped through my underlined pages, stopping to read notes I'd scribbled in the margins from Charlie's lectures. He lingered over the section on John Milton, bending to the page to make out my hurried handwriting.

"Brilliant," he said, stabbing at a passage with his finger, "your most noble poet, the most heroic voice in the English language; it is the voice of freedom, of human dignity in face of oppression—yes?"

I nodded gamely; there was a kind of desperation in his voice.

It seemed a terrible injustice that he had never had a chance to be taught by Charlie Springfield, and I told him so.

"Max has told me everything about this great man."

That took me down a notch.

Ever eager to curry favor, I told Vlada he could have my English lit anthology once the AP exams were over. Where he was going, he needed it more than I did.

"But these are your notes? You had these ideas from your teacher—precious things, yes?"

"You know, he was wounded in France fighting the Nazis."

"Really . . ." Max hadn't mentioned that, nor that Charlie had been against the war in Vietnam. "The same as your father—yes?"

"He was CIA station chief in Athens, fighting the Communists in the Greek Civil War."

"He was a great man. I have seen the medals in the gym."

"Yes, the medals . . . they're quite something, I guess."

He caught my uncertain tone, as if I didn't know my own mind, and he made a fist, touching it to my shoulder as if anointing me.

Then he cocked his head, touched his ear. We were quiet and lis-tened. Very faintly, I thought I could hear the noise of engines and then some distant muffled thuds, nearly inaudible unless you were listening for them. I thought for a second and then told him that the sounds must be coming from Fort Devens, about two miles distant. Night training exercises, I suggested. Special Forces . . . Green Berets.

"The Green Berets!" he exclaimed, slamming a fist into his palm.

"Freedom fighters . . ."

Vlada's face lit up, keen, intense, like a bird dog that had caught the scent. He gave a comical salute and announced that we were going to see those Green Berets. I laughed because I thought he was kidding. But he wasn't. Some point of equilibrium had shifted inside him and the decision had been made. He was going with or without me. I was dumbfounded. I told him we could get kicked out of school just for leaving the grounds at night, especially given the crackdown since the infamous dance—much less illegally entering a U.S. army base! Vlada snorted at my excuses and then looked me hard in the face, his slate blue eyes boring deeply into mine. He gave me a friendly slug in the arm. "A man must be a doer of deeds, not just a speaker of words," he told me in his Slavic-toned English. "Words without action—it is impossible." That was how he put it. The paraphrase was uncanny: ". . . life is nothing and words are empty if a man is not prepared to put his life in danger." It was the ancient Homeric injunction! After our long football season, Vlada knew just the right buttons to push.

And for this little walk on the wild side, he had chosen me and not Max.

Passing the portrait of General Alden as we left the library, he gestured to the dim uniformed figure above the mantelpiece.

"You have his face," said Vlada. "It is, I think, the face of a liberator."

As I said, the right buttons.

The night had a slight chill to it, as that long, warm fall finally gave way to the inevitable. I began to walk the road to Fort Devens. Vlada grabbed my arm. "Are you crazy?" He directed me into a cornfield and a stealthy cross-country slog—a lesson in how differently we saw the world. Vlada led me through harvested pumpkin fields, shallow copses, backyards, and garden plots. I didn't even bother to protest that we were trespassing, it was so beside the point. He was guided by the distant sounds of war games, stopping every now and then to relish the growing whine of rotors and the crackle of automatic weapons. A hazy mottled gray moon, lapped by mauve clouds, lighted our way, but only just, and I was thrilled to have Vlada's powerful shoulders, bent to the near darkness, guiding me, to be on his team. We passed through some fruit orchards and skirted a pheasant farm. Vlada laughed as the caged pheasants dashed to the far corner of their enclosure at our approach. Then he got down on all fours and howled like a wolf as the poor gorgeously attired creatures stumbled over one another in retreat. When we came to a fence, he'd vaunt it with the ease of a champion gymnast, which was exactly what he'd been back in Czechoslovakia as a boy. He'd laugh as I carefully climbed over. Twenty minutes later, we came to Route 211, just down from the Bull Run restaurant, and, with no headlights showing in either direction, we dashed across the road and into the high marshy grass on the far side.

A sturdy chain-link fence, ten feet high, with menacing barbed wire at the top, confronted us about fifty yards farther on. Every ten yards, there were very official U.S. government signs warning about trespass, with graphic skull and crossbones in case the illiterate or foolish didn't get the message. One sign warned of an active firing range. I don't think Vlada even bothered to read the signs, easily visible as the scattered clouds lifted and the moonlight intensified. I was all set to call it a night; we'd had our little adventure. But Vlada just stood there in the knee-high grass as if mesmerized by the sounds of those Hueys, a sound I would come to know like the voice of a first love. The noise was louder now and more distinct, the rhythmic chug of props dicing the air, punctuated by the staccato report of automatic weapons. There were flashes of red and green in the distant treetops and traces of rising smoke.

When I looked at Vlada, I found him staring at me as if amused.

"You okay?" he asked.

I tried to make light of it all.

"It's ridiculous"—I shrugged—"you can't turn a New England landscape into Vietnam."

"So, we find out just how well they do it."

I figured we were done. Maybe grab a pizza in the nearby town and head back. But before I'd even formed the thought, Vlada grabbed onto the chain-link fence and was pulling himself up as if to recklessly skewer himself on the taunt strands of wicked barbed wire at the top. My attempt at protest was drowned out by his sharp commands. He gestured to my right. There were some broken bits of lumber half covered in the grass. He told me to hand him a piece. I pulled out a length of rotted two-by-four and passed it up to him. With what seemed practiced skill, he shoved the length of lumber between the strands of barbed wire and twisted them in such a way as to produce a gap wide enough for an agile person to slip through. In another second, he was under the wire and waiting for me on the far side of the fence.

"Now you," he shouted, an impatient scowl scribbled on his forehead.

It was like a jolt of paternal judgment, the thrust of a white jaw, the gleaming teeth and glittering eyes . . . and the sweater: Vlada was wearing the sweater that my grandmother had knit for my father and then given me when he disappeared. I'd passed it on to Vlada a week before. I was suddenly frightened, as if I'd just awakened from a bad dream.

"What, you have a problem?"

Vlada reached into his crotch and grabbed himself and made a lewd face. The look of sarcastic disdain mortified me. I leaped for the fence in a kind of angry panic. When I got to the two-by-four jammed between the barbed wire and began to squeeze through, I felt a prick and my ankle caught. And with the pain came a flashing image of Vlada at his desk an hour before, quickly folding up a letter and returning it to his pocket . . . as if I'd missed something. Something about his furtiveness . . . I froze. Then Vlada was right there on the opposite side of the fence, pulling my pant leg free, making good my trespass.

As soon as we hit the deck, Vlada was off again, leading the way through the high grass, moist and chilly to the touch. There were no paths or markings, and the place had been left to grow in a wild state. We reached a heavily wooded area, marshy and thick with creepers and rotting trunks. Bereft of most leaves, the remaining scrub oaks and ground cover were thick enough so that the forest floor remained in near darkness and only the briefest glimmerings of moonlight gave us any sense of what the next footstep might bring. Even Vlada managed an undignified pratfall every few minutes, and soon we were both soaked and muddy from head to foot.

As we drew nearer to the whine of choppers, Vlada stopped and pulled me to his side, pointing to his nose and repeating, "Benzene—yes, can you smell the benzene?" I could hear the excitement in his voice, and I nodded my head, thinking he was truly mad, and wondering what the other smell was that was drifting through the woods, blending with the stench of stagnant water and rotting vegetation. It was cordite.

Up ahead, there were flashes of dancing light through the trees. My heart was slamming away in my chest, so hard that I could barely breathe.

Suddenly, the dark wood split wide open with a terrific angry roar of hovering choppers. I saw Vlada sprint forward to a patch of light where the woods gave way to a small thicket and an open space beyond. As I drew near him, crouching and cringing at the terrible noise above me, I saw him motion me to get down and be quiet, as if anybody was likely to hear us above that din. And then I was snug beside him and we were kneeling behind thick undergrowth. Before us spread a kind of grassy plain, silver and misty in the moonlight; and into this clearing, the sleek hornet-faced Hueys were nosing downward to hover above the rotor-flattened grass and disgorge uniformed figures, who spread out, crouching and firing off brief bursts from their weapons toward the woods to our right. Red and yellow flares burning in the grass sent upward-cascading columns of acrid smoke. Splayed, writhing shadows danced in all directions. The shrieking engines and small-arms fire, the smell of exhaust and cordite, made for a hellish, if thrilling, vision.

We watched spellbound from our hiding place as dark jungle-fatigued figures streamed from the choppers with a precision that, even then, my untrained eye could appreciate. The teamwork and supreme sense of willful mastery those men epitomized brought a lump to my throat. I wondered if I was going to run out of air or my heart was going to explode. Vlada knelt there beside me, arm across my shoulder, his jaw shot forward like a rifle bolt, eyes keen and unblinking: a prophet beholding the holy of holies.

And then a new flight of choppers charged over the treetops and into the clearing as the first flight lifted off and away, and the soldiers who jumped from these came right toward us. It was as if we had been watching a movie, in a dream of relative remove and safety—instants later to find ourselves sitting ducks. For the first time in my life, I knew I was going to die and told Vlada as much. He turned to me and his whole face lit up, as if I'd told the greatest joke. A tremendous belly laugh exploded from his lips, loud enough that the sound seemed to clear a space for itself above the terrific blast of the rotors. He pulled my ear close to his mouth and yelled that they were not using real bullets, just blanks. How did he know that?

No tracers—obvious. (He'd done his military training at seventeen: Warsaw Pact–style with live ammunition.)

We curled ourselves down into the bushes and waited for the onslaught.

Bodies hurtled past us, coming within inches of where we lay. I got glimpses of their blackened faces beneath their helmets. Determined and sweating, they cursed and yelled to one another with a show of bravado from long months of training together—perfunctory stuff in the controlled chaos of field exercises . . . when nobody was firing back.

And then they were past us, merging into the thick woods. The choppers spun off with a world-weary whine to vanish into the night sky. An eerie silence descended and we got up and looked carefully around like shipwreck survivors, the mists churning and settling, the dying flares sending ungainly pink shadows scudding over the grass to slink away. I was amazed to still be alive. In the soft light, I could just make out a triumphant gleam in Vlada's eyes. He brought his sweat-slick golliwog face close to mine and yelled with a kind of insane joy, "You are all that stands between us and slavery; you are the last hope of liberation; your country is the last hope for freedom."

20

UNIVERSITÄT LEIPZIG
April 4, 1932

Dear John:

I despair of Germany. The brownshirts are out every morning in the streets like hoplite formations to terrify the city into complete submission. I have never been so happy to have both my Czech and Austrian passports. Don't bother to come this June; we will go direct to Athens and Crete—yes. Or will you go first to visit Nigel Bennett in Cambridge?

I have been dreaming about blue monkeys; obviously, I am going crazy. A professor told me that he had a report from a colleague that a villager on the island of Thera had discovered some buried frescoes of Minoan character with blue monkeys. Blue monkeys! How strange, if true. Where would the monkeys have come from? My mind has been much in a frenzy all winter going over the finds of last summer at Knossos, and the most recent journal papers. Do you notice how many works of pottery of Mycenaean, Late Helladic have been coming to light on Crete? What can explain it? If Minoan culture was the dominant one, how is it that Mycenaean wares, swords, seals, funerary figures are to be found in such number on Crete? Unless we—your mighty Sir Arthur Evans—have it wrong and there is more to mainland Greece than we suppose. Have you noticed that the latest scholarship on Mycenae indicates that the great walls were built only in the last one hundred years before 1200 B.C., and in two or three stages, as if suddenly there was appearing on the scene a threat? This means that for eight hundred years, as with Knossos, there were no walls: They lived in peace with their neighbors. So why did they have to build walls—who were the people and where did they come from who threatened to end such a golden age? Could it be the Sea People, according to Egyptian sources? And then the Dark Ages—your bête noire—an age of iron and illiteracy, so it would seem, until Homer comes on the scene to reveal stories of a lost world.

Unless our Homer was copying from another source—Linear B?

I have been sniffing the wind, my friend, and everything I see and read tells me there is more on the mainland and islands of Greece to be found—much more. What if those Linear B tablets that are driving us both mad have something to do with the Mycenaean artifacts turning up on Crete? What if they are not Minoan, but Greek—you know I have always suspected the language may be a form of archaic Greek. Maybe we are wasting our time on Crete; maybe Evans has got us— what is that American expression of yours?—barking up the wrong tree. Maybe my Schliemann was on the right track in more ways than we yet understand. Where is Pylos? Where is Nestor's Palace? Where is the palace of Menelaus in Sparta? That is what I wish to know. I long to discover more of this invisible world of communal wealth and harmony, where every man and woman—when women were worshipped as gods!—had their say in public affairs and a right to keep the fruits of their sweat and labor. Until some warrior breed, some violent dark uprising—no different, I wonder, from the Nazis—came along to dispossess the people and enslave them. Believe me, in the brownshirts I see the specter of slavery again. They wish to make Europe into a land of helots.

How goes it with your work on Linear B? I have been too busy finishing journal articles. What would you think, my capitalist friend, my rich American, with all your money—from the tyranny of the academic machine can we be released? Why should we have to wait all year for the summer months? Why should we not undertake our own digs, hire our own workers, go where and when we please? Do you think your mother might approve of such a plan? Would she finance it? Let us plan to put it to her in Venice in August: she will make you famous—yes, yes, the same for me. This way you can better justify all your gold—you will sleep better. I can smell the possibilities; I can smell the dust and oleanders, the lemons and olives, and taste the wine. Let us dazzle the world, you and I—what can stop us?

Karel

A few weeks later, Vlada was gone. He had been planning to spend Christmas vacation with me. Two days before Christmas, he called me in New York from Logan Airport to say that his father had died of a final heart attack and that he was hurrying to catch the first flight home. I was devastated. I felt his pain and loss for his beloved and respected father—unequivocally. Thoughts of my fickle loyalty to my own father left me with a hollowness that longed to be filled by his voice.

I tried to keep the conversation going despite the bad connection, with the clamor of a departure lounge in the background. He wanted to tell me something. There was a long pause.

"Peter, Peter . . . just fuck her—go fuck her."

And he hung up.

At first, I thought I'd just heard wrong. I tried to get hold of Max. For three years, I had hung out with Max over the holidays in New York; we'd gone to parties and debutante balls, or to hear his mother's students play Christmas recitals at Julliard. He knew Vlada was supposed to be staying with me, and there had been lots of talk about getting together. Max never phoned. When I called his mother's apartment to let him know about Vlada's father, there was no answer. I called Julliard, but found that Hannah was in Vienna for Christmas and New Year's.

Then I tried Laura, even though she hadn't replied to any of my letters; I figured at least she'd want to know the news about Vlada. I tried to phone her apartment, but directory assistance had no listing. I called the American Ballet Theater and left messages; then I was told the company was performing *The Nutcracker* in Washington over the holiday season. I left more messages for her at the Howard Johnson motel on Virginia Avenue, where the corps de ballet was staying.

Nothing.

When I got back to Winsted after New Year's—after a painful and unhappy Christmas with my mother—I felt like a fraud going through the motions of a pointless existence. With Vlada gone and Max and I washed up, all purpose seemed to have departed my life. I'd been granted early admission to Princeton, so even work didn't matter, and spring on the river seemed infinitely far away as the snowdrifts and brittle cold turned the winter into one icy battlement

And then, as if the horror story of 1968 refused to give up its grip, we learned that Jerry Gadsden had been killed in a hit-and-run incident in his hometown of Jackson, Mississippi, in early January. There were many conflicting reports. Jerry had been a star running back at Yale that fall of his freshman year. NFL teams were eyeing him. A Winsted classmate at Yale told me he had a white girlfriend; they were devoted to each other. Jackson, Mississippi, had been a tinderbox after the riots of the spring and summer. So bad that Jerry left early for Yale and worked in a Head Start program in New Haven. One of the brothers on the team told me that Jerry's childhood friends had abandoned him. He had an older brother in the army, another in jail for drug dealing, and another killed years before in a drug deal gone bad. Some said the hit-and-run hadn't been an accident. Jerry had been on the way to the pharmacy for his mother's blood pressure medication the day before he was to return to Yale, when a car left the road and hit him on the sidewalk. They never identified the car or the driver. The police were overstretched. Those of us who knew Jerry, especially those of us who had played football with him, were crushed with grief. Even with our troubles, I'd loved him. His essential goodness and grace stayed with me. He had stood by me.

The shooting of Martin Luther King, Jr., had been a national tragedy and disgrace; Jerry's death seemed mindless and random. I went to a memorial service at Yale and came back hollowed out. His blond girlfriend was an absolute wreck.

Even with all the racial tensions of those years, our love for Jerry remained a thing apart.

I had never felt so empty. For the first time in my life, I felt the kind of depression I'd so often seen in Max. I just studied and slept and went to class. I couldn't even bring myself to shoot baskets or work out in the gym. The black brothers just made me feel more sad about Jerry, and guilty and helpless to change anything. I was filled with a restless yet dead energy. I dreamed about Laura, about lying in the grass encircled by her tender arms, but it was a desire heaped with an inexpressible sadness and dread, which three feet of snow only made worse.

I barely saw Max that winter. He told me he'd been with his mother in Vienna. If anything, after Vlada and Jerry, he seemed reenergized. It was as if he existed in some parallel universe with his crew of druggies, the rebellious and disaffected and disillusioned who wore their attitudes like a badge of honor. It seemed as if he knew something I didn't.

I figured it mostly had to do with the February issue of *The Atlantic* and his first published short story.

Before he had died, Charlie Springfield had submitted—unbeknownst to Max—some of his short stories to an editor friend at *The Atlantic*. The stories had languished on the editor's desk until late in the year, when the editor had come upon them again quite by chance.

He was much impressed with the work of a student of his dead friend. The story in the February issue was a bittersweet tale about the collective memories of children in a summer camp for Jewish kids in the Catskills. Over the course of a hot August, the children discover in conversations with one another the strange gaps in their past. Some are missing family members, some have no idea where their parents came from, and all have experienced unaccountable losses: parents, grandparents, aunts and uncles and cousins who were destroyed in the concentration camps. Their parents had resorted to white lies to cover up the truth. It was poignant stuff, and made more so for me because it was a part of Max's life he had rarely shared with me. These themes of loss and exile, so wonderfully elucidated in his very first story, remained an undercurrent for the rest of his career; in his last days, they took a terrible toll.

The story in *The Atlantic* was his ticket out, a stepping-stone to his celebrity life.

It confirmed him in his belief that one can't just write stories; one must live them—make them up as one goes along, knowing, if need be, that a little editing can ease you past Go if anything has gone amiss. Or, as he famously put it later in *People* magazine, "One can't just live to write; you must write the stories that have allowed you to live."

And so Max prepared a final act, a final indignity to provide yet more indelible material for his fictional world waiting in the wings.

It happened on a particularly cold night, a night of parched, silent cold, not a hint of wind. I was at my library carrel, studying for the last of my APs, when I happened to look out the window and saw a figure hurrying across the drifts of white on the Circle. The figure staggered and fell and got up again and fell again. Why would anyone in their right mind be trying to cross though almost four feet of snow when the paths were fully plowed? Finally, the figure made it across and disappeared into the chapel. At first, I just let it go. But then the absurdity of the thing began to rankle: Whoever it was had to be stoned out of his mind. And the chapel should have been locked at night. It had always been locked after the suicide jump from the bell tower two years before. I looked at my watch: 2:00 A.M. I was the senior prefect; I was supposed to be responsible; I was supposed to keep an eye on things. Elliot Goddard had been writing me regularly from Saigon with questions about the acting headmaster: Was he up to it? Was he the kind of man who could bring back the respect and civic idealism and commitment to service that had characterized Winsted in the time of Jack Crocket? "Without a renewed patriotism as a shared civic responsibility, Winsted and the country will wither and turn against itself. Tell the kids about Pericles, Aristotle, and Plato—that's where Jefferson got his sense of patriotic duty from, and your father." And what were my views on coeducation? That, too, was an option under serious review by the board of trustees.

As I watched through my window, I saw other figures slip into the chapel.

I could have closed my eyes. I could have gone to bed. I could have dreamed of Laura in her red bathing suit diving off the float, and the blue skies and bluer seas of faraway Crete, and white pine boughs flagging summer sunsets, and dipping oars . . . and that endless glide.

I hated the thought of going out into that freezing night and having to pull rank on somebody, or, worse, bust a whole bunch of assholes who'd gone into the chapel to do drugs or God knew what.

Damn it. Maybe that was my problem: I always kept shirking my duty, refusing to take responsibility for my life.

The path around the Circle crackled with rock salt. I could detect only the vaguest glimmer of light through the chapel windows. I felt like an idiot. Then there was just the barest hint of music, the whisper of the organ. I slipped past the great oak doors, into the warm womblike darkness. Bach was being played, like a vibrant presence in the rising currents of incense from joss sticks and marijuana joints being passed around in the front of the nave. I breathed deeply, gasping as the warm air hit my frozen lungs, as if, at the end of a violent sprint, overcome by a queer otherworldly sensation, of a familiar place transformed by the evocation of nameless spirits. Through the near darkness, a mysterious flickering of candlelight came from the apse. People were gathered there in the front row seats. Max's crowd. My eyes adjusted slowly, and for a moment I had the oddest sensation, as if I'd been transported to a summery night at a pagan festival, with tall, straight trees extending their sheltering boughs, and in the perfumed air wafting over me, fervent hopes that the gods would prove generous and kind.

Then I noticed that a large sheet had been hung in front of the altar. I felt no particular alarm at this odd business and actually found myself drifting pleasantly under the spell of the Bach and the pungent dope, which, too, reminded me of that night in the boathouse with Max when we had sat across from each other looking at the stars reflected in the water. A feeling of peace came over me. I knew it was Max playing the organ, and my mind went back to our early days, when I would visit him in the practice rooms late at night. This was the Max I had loved, the music I had loved.

In the darkness of the ambulatory, I walked the few steps to my father's memorial and unconsciously reached up to the carved letters, as if my touch might yet elicit an answer: *Wherefore by their fruits ye shall know them.* For a moment, in touching the cold stone, I felt the proximity of death, or at least the belief in the surcease of one life so that another might take wing.

I was glad of my anonymity.

I made my way toward the shadowy front of the nave, where the lines of sorrowing angels in the Williams Memorial glimmered in the blush of candlelight. Those robed beings seemed a mere precipitant of the darkness as a lilac patina flickered in their distant faces and trailing robes. I touched the delicate features of the lead angel, as if needing to draw some connection in my mind between her expression of release and the words on my father's memorial, between deceit and desire: the invisible essence of the past that wafts through the air we must breathe or die.

As I did, I registered the maroon letters in the inscription, spelling out the name of one Pearce Breckenridge. I sat and ran my fingers across the letters, as if mere sensation might reveal their secret, only to resign myself to those capricious currents of time that float up the forgotten names of people and places, only to fade again into obscurity.

The music segued into a slow adagio. The draped drop cloth in the front of the apse parted and a figure appeared, a woman with hair held tight against her head to show off her brittle, angular beauty. She wore a cream white leotard and pale pink toe shoes. The Bach adagio swelled from the ranked organ pipes like a mighty breath of air filling the chapel. She began to dance as if swirled in eddies of sound. The dance—her motion, her absolute aliveness—was so lovely to behold and such an evocation of the music that the fact it was a dancer, a familiar face, seemed to first escape my dreaming brain. Her arms and legs edged the phrases like those of some mythic goddess, shaping the very space of her unearthly presence, her limbs arching outward and then inward as if borne on currents of solar wind, lifting to arabesques, flicking into quicksilver turns, one and the same with the fleeting notes. All the while, her ecstatic eyes implored her followers' devotion.

Only when the music ended and she curtsied and ducked behind the drop cloth did the silence lay bare the reality. In the murmur of drunken applause from the front pews, I recalled those silver-framed photographs of Suzanne Williams poised in arabesque, the scrapbooks of Kodaks recording Amory's celebrated summer fetes of the twenties, when Amaryllis and her fellow artists had staged sylvan tableaux, had danced in the moonlight till dawn, while imploring the Muses to smile on their exquisite taste and good breeding and oh so lofty aspirations: the celebrated and gifted souls who were nature's chosen few.

Max strode forward like a master of ceremonies, regaled in full concert attire of white tie and tails. He bowed to his coven of miscreants in the first rows and they gave him another round of besotted hoots and catcalls. I found myself thinking back fondly on his role as the grave digger in *Hamlet* and smiled, in spite of myself, at this most recent transformation. Then he, too, exited behind the draped drop sheet concealing the altar, which, moments later, fell away. A blaze of sparks poured from Roman candles attached with gray duct tape to a tall stepladder to the right of altar. Stretched on the altar, cushioned on pillows of crimson and blue, lay a nude woman wearing dark glasses. Her head was theatrically thrown back, blond hair draped over one shoulder, arms reaching out to the shower of sparks cascading over her white skin. The sight was so fantastic and surreal that my mind seized up.

She was beautiful and young, more beautiful than in my dreams.

In my dreams, she was lying in the grass beneath the apple trees.

Max, of all things, was busy taking photographs.

It was a tableau. Titian's Diana ravished by Zeus in the guise of a shower of gold in Palazzo Fenway.

I might have been drunk or stoned and so laughed it off. In retrospect, I should have been concerned the fireworks didn't burn her, much less burn the place down.

I caught the back of the seat in front of me as if to save myself from falling.

I remember standing in the shadows and screaming at the top of my lungs. I remember my shout echoing in the nave, like furies pursuing my footsteps, as I flung myself out the door and into the cold.

The school wasted no time. I went to the headmaster the next morning with my list of those I'd identified, and some I hadn't. Max had already left with Laura. Eight other members of the sixth form were ultimately expelled. They were gone two days later. The purges had begun.

But I wasn't waiting around. That following night, I made my own escape. I went to my dorm and packed what I needed in a duffel bag. I walked out into the brittle starlit night and breathed deeply of the cold. I took a last look at the glazed mantle of snow covering the Circle, at the palsied shapes of the apple trees socked in tight. A perfection of a kind, for a day, a month, a year, but a perfection more appropriate for the fallen than the living. A perfection in the guise of safety.

I tried to remember everything, as if it might be compassed in one long icy breath: the flight of a high-angled pass, the hard pull of my oar through rushing water, the sun-spangled branches passing overhead—when our bodies were young and strong and we would last forever, until the glide fades to stillness and the current takes you over and the river of Time returns you home.

I slung my bag across my shoulder and proudly walked the road into town, where I would catch the late bus to Boston and the recruiting center off Copley Square. As I walked, I kept turning to those distant unshepherded stars, the words of the psalmist like an angel's whisper in my ear: *For I am a stranger with thee, and a sojourner, as all my fathers were.*

Berlin, March 17, 1946

Dear Mother Nestor,

How that name out of my careless boyhood gives me comfort in this devastated city full of human misery. I thought you should be the first to know that I am coming home. I've resigned. The OSS is finished. I've done everything I can do here in this wasteland of our bombers. I've got my spot back at Princeton and nothing will pry me lose to return to this benighted continent except the renewal of the digging season in Greece and Turkey—no time soon, given the political turmoil. I will stop off a few days in London; I suppose I should visit Bobby Williams in hospital before he and his British wife, Suzanne, return to the States.

I'm afraid all I have is bad news about Wilfred Hollar and his wife. You seemed concerned about them in your last letter. I was able to visit Prague briefly, although the Soviets control it now with an iron hand. Anna died of pneumonia in the months before the end of the war, and Wilfred was hung by Communist partisans in the streets of Prague after the city was liberated. I'm sorry to be the bearer of such news.

Karel Hollar, I have just learned, died in a Soviet POW camp. If you find that surprising, don't. It is how the Soviets do business; friends are often more suspect than foes. I can't say that I'm sorry for the bastard, only that we had some unfinished business, which is now concluded.

A long night has descended across this continent, another Dark Age, which may well outlast our puny lifetimes.

I long for Elysium and my books, and you, Mother Nestor, the only sane thing left in this world. I should arrive in Washington in about a week and will be in touch with you then about my return to New York via the Archaeology Department at Princeton.

Love,
John

PART TWO
GREECE

But quiet to quick bosoms is a hell,
And there has been thy bane; there is a fire
And motion of the soul which will not dwell
In its own narrow being, but aspire
Beyond the fitting medium of desire;
And, but once kindled, quenchless evermore,
Preys upon high adventure, nor can tire
Of aught but rest; a fever at the core,
Fatal to him who bears, to all who ever bore.
                                        —Lord Byron

116. ΔΗΛΟΣ - ΣΤΟΑ ΤΩΝ ΛΕΟΝΤΩΝ - DELOS - THE TERRACE OF THE LIONS

⊕

21 OFTEN WHEN I CLIMB THE STAIRS TO MY father's boyhood room overlooking the lake, sometimes feeling like a child climbing the boughs of a towering pine, I am moved by memories of war. Sometimes my own, but more often stories passed down to me about my father and great-grandfather, along with the deeds of ancient warriors and statesmen—my academic expertise, what with half a lifetime unearthing their shattered bones and iron hoplite swords. Having one's own stories to tell changes the perspective, when your past becomes the past and breathes of time immemorial. War changes us. The horror needs little elaboration. As my father wrote to Suzanne in the first year of their love affair from the ruins of Leipzig in 1945: "If the avoidance of violence is civilized man's greatest triumph, I am witness to our civilization's abject failure." And he was only at the halfway point of a century that saw the violent deaths of 160 million. Sadly, the sacrifice of war also demonstrates the strengths of our beliefs, the price of liberty in terms of loss and pain. But surviving, even with your faith intact, can lead to a more troubling fate than the fruits of victory or ashes of defeat. As General Alden found, as did my father, as did I.

You still have blood on your hands.

And so, to the islands . . . to my father's beloved Delos where he first caught wind of the discovery of Linear B at Pylos.

Dreamscape, memoryscape, mere pebbles flung across the Aegean blue—just check your Google satellite. Rock-strewn coastlines guarding precious plots of stubbled pasturage, groves of dusty-green laurel and age-stooped olive trees. I fell in love with those deep blues on Crete the summer before my senior year. But there is something special

about Delian blues, backdrop to bone white columns against sea and
sky—take your breath away, yielding to the weary time-traveler visions
of hope in loss as pristine as they are ancient. That most lovely of a
digger's illusions, of a golden age ready to yield its secrets in the next
shovelful.

Even the name Delos still enchants: as it did for the ancients, Apollo's sacred isle adrift upon a mythic sea.

As it was for my father, seated on the hood of his jeep in a shattered Leipzig amidst the remains of his student haunts, desperate to
keep warm, when he wrote to Suzanne of his longings: "We'll sail
to Delos—you will love it there, the sunlit temples amidst the sepia-
singed barley grass and purpled thistle blur. Oh the silence, so clean, so
blue, especially when the capricious Meltemi has calmed in the evening
and the chirp of the crickets resonates, toward twilight, when the sun's
lingering heat rises in updrafts and the stillness finds you unaware. Oh
darling, if only we could find our way back there, a refuge in the lee of
time—were it only possible."

They never made it. And how strange that Suzanne's daughter
should be the one to return them there, at least their story . . . in lee
of time.

I, too, had sought refuge on Delos. I had climbed to the highest
point, the summit of Mount Kynthos, thinking, hoping maybe she
wasn't going to show. It would have been a stretch to make it from the
airport to the ferry in time. I'd left word at the museum office, just in
case. After a busy summer, I had escaped for a week to check on some
new finds and would've soon been back in my office in Athens, but I
guess she couldn't wait: History, too, that fall of 1989, with the fall of
the Berlin Wall on the horizon, couldn't wait. Fifty years between the
coming of one war and the end of another.

Below my perch, the bay fanned outward to the glittering arc of
the earth, the sun swelling as if threatening an apocalyptic bursting as
it touched down in the west, shaping the broken vertebrae of nearby
Rhenia and Tinos in luminous veils of lemon-violet. I was sweating like
a pig from my climb, my back aching. The Meltemi, which had blown
fiercely all day, had suddenly died, leaving a supersaturated calm, incandescent and brittle, and everywhere the soundless sizzle of day's end.
I had a sabbatical that fall. No classes at Princeton, no arriving grad
students back at the American School of Classical Studies in Athens
to shepherd toward Ph.D.s. And another book in the works, a new

look at Thucydides in light of events since Vietnam. Perhaps a chance to insert a little autobiography—"the personal touch," as my publisher and agent encouraged—into my history writing. Maybe to demonstrate the relevance of at least one "dead white male" to the issues of today—Thucydides, that is. Little could I imagine that the capstone to my work in progress was simmering on the vast blue horizon unfurling to the northwest.

Movement . . .

A flash of color amongst the temple sanctuaries on the lower slopes of Mount Kynthos. I blinked, squinting, wiping at my forehead, tense like the hunter aware of the prey but unable to distinguish it yet from its cover. And worse, not at all sure if I wasn't the one being stalked. As I watched, the tumbled marbles, the slabs of weather-scoured whiteness returned to their fixed and comforting sameness.

Then again, a winged glint of refracted light . . . blond hair shifted across her mobile shoulders. She was facing out to sea on a small promontory along the path to the processional stairway and the summit. Following her gaze, I could just make out the receding wake of the Piraeus ferry, the ship a vague stain of albumin on the farthest plane of most intense cerulean blue. I knew that as reluctant host I should call out to her, but the thing seemed to stick in my throat, stifled by apprehension: how such a cry—not unlike my anguished scream in the chapel twenty years before—would violate the sanctuary of time itself, those ramparts that had kept her a young girl of seventeen in the grass beneath the apple trees, standing on a float in a red bathing suit. A cry would certainly transform her back into flesh and blood, and adorned in all the regalia of her celebrity life, if not preceded by the trumpet calls of my rival for her love.

I reached into the back pocket of my jeans and pulled out her cryptic letter, a fax that had found me at the museum office on Delos just days before.

September 20, 1989

Dear Peter, you're a hard guy to pin down, much less find. Your secretary in Athens gave me your itinerary and the fax number. I'm flying overnight to Athens on Friday, Sept. 23, and will get the first ferry. I will meet you on Delos. We need to talk. I've got some pretty troubling but very important information about your father, and much else. A lot has happened, as I guess you must know from Colonel Fairburn—or maybe not; he is always a little vague about you and I can't quite tell how much you two have been keeping in touch. This is important. So please don't disappoint me and do another no-show. We need to get our heads around this! I look forward to seeing you—trust me, I really do. Love, Laura.

Get our heads around, how I hated that stoner expression. Twenty years since I watched her walk off toward the art instructor's house, turn, and launch those wretched words my way: "Of course, *you're* right." I remembered her nod, followed by a shrug. Sure, I felt sorry for her. Max's death three years before had made it to the front page of the *Athens Daily News,* bemoaning, along with the *Tribune* and *The New York Times,* his failure to complete his long-anticipated third novel. Colonel Fairburn had indeed written to me about Bobby Williams's suicide and arson, burning down Hermitage. I was saddened but not surprised. The colonel helped Suzanne through her breakdown, hospitalization, and trial for neglectful manslaughter: leaving her husband with an eighteen-year-old attendant and a loaded gun. Acquitted by a grand jury, she'd gone to ground with Charles Fairburn at his country house in Sussex, England.

As for my being a "no-show": Princeton, my junior year; she asked me to meet her in New York, but I just couldn't face it.

At my yell, Laura seemed to start, as if touched by the invisible hand of my panic and confusion. She turned with that easy, generous motion that had become a signature note for her, onstage and off. I stood to show myself. I waved. I shouted that I would come down. She returned my wave and indicated with an impetuous bit of pantomime, running in place and wiping her brow, that she was intent on joining me above. Her body, I soon discovered, had an ingenious language all its own.

There was something particularly unnerving to have her in sight for so long on that winding path to the summit without actually being near enough to touch her hand or see her face up close. Perhaps those twenty years needed the added minutes to unwind themselves before my inquisitive eyes. Her tall, all-too-familiar body glided in and out of glossy patches of bay-tinted sunset, past a scattering of upright and fallen columns: the memory of adolescent legginess shorn up with confident strides, if carefully measured. At a distance, she seemed to have assumed a regal bearing, maybe not so thin, perhaps more of a womanly thinness, a thing of diet and rigorous exercise and conscientious care.

I watched as she glided effortlessly through the silent groves and temple precincts, reminding me of Max's description of her dancing her most famous role in Antony Tudor's ballet *The Leaves Are Fading*: "an embodiment of love's inexorable desire to claim its own before death intervenes."

Well, she'd certainly experienced her fair share of death, and so had I. A faltering step—a stumble? My breath snagged in my chest. She caught herself on an altar stone and pushed on. I bent forward where I sat, squinting, breathing evenly again. Her pace slowed at the point where the path steepened and rose to the summit on a final processional stairway of crude stone steps. She turned once, twice, and again to the encircling sea and that great sputtering ball of flame that threatened to incinerate the retreating ferry. Second thoughts? Was the writer of that impetuous fax losing her nerve? The celebrity ballerina who had danced with an aging Nureyev and had been partnered by Baryshnikov in his prime, her prime. And what about that young Diana in nothing but dark glasses on the chapel altar, whose idea of sport was getting eight guys kicked out in the winter of senior year?

Sweat trickled in torrents down the inside of my sports shirt, and my four-day growth of beard was slick and itchy.

How pale she seemed. But she had found her rhythm on that tricky limestone staircase and was marching upward with renewed determination. And her face, such a striking whiteness in my sun-drenched world, as if maybe she'd only been locked away all those years and everything I'd seen in the papers was pure fantasy, along with Max's second novel, *Gardens of Saturn*. Her hair was a bit shorter—a businesslike cut full of no-nonsense probity. Her blue denim skirt reached barely to her knees. "Jeest . . ." I actually flinched at the sight. A hinged bit of steel and spandex enveloping her right knee, fully visible as she mounted the upper tier of the processional stairs. Oh, the sadness of that . . . the telltale sign of age and vulnerability—not even forty.

I rose in anticipation, giving myself a few moments to get the weight off the small of my back, stretching from side to side to relieve the pressure and pain. Possibly to shuck the chance I might be in love with her knee brace, that it might put us on a more even footing. I was drawn to her sweaty face, the gracious high curve of her brow, the thrust of angled chin and upswept nose, the depth of her eyes still hidden in shadow . . . wanting to catch the first imprint of age on the young girl who'd thrown me over. But her face remained lowered as she concentrated on the rocky and treacherous steps. Her T-shirt, a green ABT logo on a field of interlaced lilac leaves, was soaked; her breasts shifted visibly with her exertions. For an instant, her incipient presence transformed the bubble of space-time around me: the smell of pine and sere grass and rotting apples and wood smoke and sun-drenched lake water and a girlish figure in a red bathing suit diving into green depths. In a heartbeat or two, it was gone, dissolved in the steps it took to meet her at the top of the processional stairway, where I reached through that frail membrane of memory to take her warm hand in mine.

We staggered together like drunken comrades, hugging awkwardly. She laughed, took a step back, and curtsied with a mocking smile, as if to dismiss all the improbabilities that had brought her to this place.

Then I saw her eyes lift to mine, blue as before—now reflecting the glorious blue on every horizon—beneath shaped eyebrows, but nothing much more in the way of makeup to hide the crow's-feet, the merest hint of cupping at the chin, though not a gray hair in sight. A jolt of recognition in my chest: I saw much of her mother's face, or was it the echo of that bear hug and the pressure of those hands reaching under my armpits and moving downward? And, as if possessed with a sixth sense, she came right back to me and kissed me tenderly on the cheek and put her arms around me for a moment more.

"Remember me—it's me." She didn't take her eyes off mine, as if to indelibly imprint herself. Then a playful slug in the arm. "You . . . haven't changed much."

I saw her eyes move down my body, and I instinctively sucked in my gut and pulled myself to full height.

"Long time no see," I managed to say, which was, at least, wholly accurate.

A vaguely amused smile eased up the corners of her lips, and I recalled something in Max's second novel: how she'd refused to have her lips done, augmented with plastic surgery, even though the assistant director of the American Ballet Theater had mercilessly harassed her, calling her "Skinny Lips" in rehearsals, until she poured a cup of scalding coffee in his lap.

The shock of the thought: how I knew every sentence in that novel, how it imprisoned her in my memory as Max's first novel imprisoned me, caused me to slouch, as if I'd strapped on a full field pack.

"Nothing really!" she exclaimed, breathing hard with her exertions.

She snapped her fingers like a .22-caliber shot. "What"—she wiped at her streaming brow—"a mere decade or two?" Her eyes stared sharply into mine. "You okay?"

"Fine . . ." I waved at the guttering horizon. "A blink on the cosmic calendar."

"Enough to blow off a whole fucking career."

This indelicacy broke something in me, the sense of despair in the throaty final syllables, the jitteriness at the corner of her eyes. And I thought of Jerry Gadsden's admonition: *the eyes, man . . . always look in the eyes.* Then, seeming to shy from the unhappy subject, she turned a moment to get a hair clip from her pocket to pin up her shoulder-length hair from a heated neck. She bent way forward to throw her hair in a cascade to be gathered and corralled, the motion so sudden and graceful that I found myself catching my breath, her upper torso moving like a well-oiled hinge over her small waist. Then she bent again as she reached down to adjust the spandex brace on her knee. Perhaps to conceal the pale stitched scar—evil thing—peaking out. I winced, yet so envious of the mobility of her back that I could have cried.

"Sorry I wasn't at the quay to meet you. I wasn't exactly sure when you'd get here," I said.

She worked her bum knee a little. "I got a taxi from the airport to Piraeus, and they'd already pulled up the gangplank of the ferry. But my taxi driver had a pal on deck and he got them to lower it for me. I left my bag at the office in the museum; they said you'd be somewhere around here."

"Not wasting time."

"I never do."

There was defiance in her voice, and I thought again of the dancer in Max's novel hurrying down Broadway to Lincoln Center, late for rehearsals and appointments, viciously banging her toe shoes against the dressing room wall to soften them. Her days were lived from minute to minute, every nerve focused on the moment when the curtain lifts . . . odd, here amidst such a necropolis, that anyone could be in such a rush.

"Greece isn't exactly famous for efficiency of communication," I told her. "A while back, though, around the time of the Battle of Marathon, they had a pretty good messenger service."

"Mind if we sit?" she asked, as if to fend off my facetious tone. "The ole knee ain't what it used to be."

We sat on the worn outcropping of the summit, staring out to sea. The rock face was warm, like a hearthstone at the center of the flaming horizon. Mauve electricity filled the infinite beyond. Updrafts off the bay hinted at a returning breeze. And a lovely floral-scented womanly dampness wafted over me. My panic shifted into high at the memory of that smell, a panic not unlike what I'd once felt surfacing from an easy dive on a Bronze Age shipwreck: for three-quarters of an hour absorbed in a wonderfully preserved site of scattered amphorae and stone anchors, only to surface and find the dive boat gone, a bright sky turned cloudy, and the comforting headland along the shore looking utterly unlike what I'd remembered. Riptides, invisible as they are deadly.

"Amazing . . ." She gestured toward the flickering horizon. "I can't believe I'm actually here." She leaned forward, as if to encompass the coming dusk. "Last night, New York, now this, so beautiful, like another world."

I glanced at her, seeing the flinty sapphire dazzle of her eyes, and then out to where she gazed, as if her words had a transforming effect on the scene below us: the templed slopes beribboned with streamers of amethyst light, the lichen-spangled marble of the ancient sanctuaries showing in silvery blue planes of cubist jottings, while the walls and stony contours of the ancient town began to merge as one moiré stain on the twilight.

"Not to put a too fine point on it," I finally said, "but why are you here?"

She didn't immediately reply to my rude interjection. How could she? She had a boatload of reasons. The delay of her reply might have been due to her going down her checklist, rearranging items in order of importance: Where could she start without scaring me off? She had sweet-talked Elliot Goddard—or worse—to get bits and pieces of classified information, which was more than I'd managed; she had been in correspondence with Vlada Radec: how she kept that little infidelity close to her chest. And, with Elliot's help, she'd actually managed to run down the Greek Resistance leader pictured in the photograph with my father in the Winsted gym. But her real coup was discovering the copies of my father's love letters to her mother, first ferreted out twenty years before, which she was now threatening to turn over to Colonel Fairburn—or Elliot Goddard and the CIA—if her mother didn't tell her "the goddam truth." There was also the little matter that all the

Williams money was gone—finito. She was suing her mother about that, too. Oh, and her career was fucked and her lover dead. No wonder she was a little overwhelmed.

"I think," and she patted my knee, "to bring you home."

"You're kidding."

"You've been missed."

I turned slightly, seeing her eyes askance, a little bloodshot at the corners: overnight flight, probably plenty of smoking Greeks if she'd flown Olympia Airlines.

"I'll bet."

"Okay, *I* missed you."

There was the barest hint of vulnerability as her voice faltered. That broke something in me. I had been living for seven years with all the explicit details of Max's second novel: the full panoply of their on-again, off-again love life. And the heroine's dismissal of her previous boyfriend at the school dance: that naïve crush from childhood. Their crazy, frenetic, upside-down, fast-lane celebrity life. And the pills, the tendonitis, the heroin, the arrests . . . talk about a list. But Max was gone, dead and gone. And as I stared out at the space of glittering sea and sky—blue on fading blue, heartache on heartache—I tried to imagine this perverse gap in the world: Max gone and yet the imprint of his words more indelible than ever.

"I read *Gardens of Saturn*," I said.

"Hah—PEN/Faulkner Award, National Book Award—who hasn't? You know, it's a crock of shit."

The harshness and hurt in her voice was awful to hear.

"I'm sorry, Laura, about Max. I was sad to hear what happened."

She touched her knee, touched mine, then touched hers again.

"Thank you. I knew you would be, even after everything."

"It doesn't mean I forgive him about the novel, the first one."

"*Be-lie-ve* me, I understand."

"Yeah?"

"I should know."

The echoed sentiment first struck me as mocking, but the helpless shrug indicated something closer to contrition, or confession.

I added. "But *now* . . . it's out there."

She followed my disgusted gesture. With her own spread palm directed at the far horizon, she seemed to confirm as much with a knowing nod.

"Yup, doesn't matter how many times you read *Gone with the Wind* . . . Rhett Butler will always be Clark Gable."

It took me a little while to figure. "Because now it's out there, it's the reality."

"It's what everybody's read, and now remembers," she said. "And there's no putting the genie back in the bottle. I tried a lawsuit, and that only got it more attention. And now with the estate contested . . . you know his mother, Hannah, has Alzheimer's. Oh God, what a mess."

"I'm sorry."

She pursed her lips and nodded to herself.

That fatalistic nod sent an icy shiver through my veins, probably not too different from the effect of embalming fluid on mortified flesh, arresting further metamorphosis. We were stuck. How many hundreds of thousands of pairs of eyes had read of my betrayal—the eight innocents I'd handed to the headmaster. How many had read the lies Max invented about my father, his right-wing conspiracies, his McCarthyism, his rabid Red-baiting and ignominious drunken end as a disgraced CIA spy on the German Autobahn? I glanced at Laura. She had turned resolutely away, as if embarrassed at what might be going through my mind. I recalled Max's description of her legs spread to her lover's gaze as only a dancer's body could manage, the tendons splayed in her neck as she cried out "like a fox caught in a leg trap" during her orgasms. Mere words on a page, but at least as permanent as the bay and the islands. And yet, as I stared out, absorbing her presence beside me, I remember seeing a breeze sweep the bay, a line of ripples far off, scudding over the purple dark sea.

"Nothing lasts forever," I offered, as if to give voice to that distant hope.

"Peter, your father didn't die on the Autobahn; he was alive for over a year in a Prague prison. He was alive, and his colleagues, even his friends, his government didn't or couldn't get him out."

It sounded like an emphatic plea, as if that distant breeze were a warning sign come from far upstream . . . of a dam that had given way and the wall of water on the move.

"Where did you get that crazy shit . . . and what the *fuck* are you doing here anyway?"

Perversely, Max had stuck with the accident on the Autobahn cover-up in his novel, using it as an ironic comment on a failed CIA agent, a drunkard killed in a mundane traffic accident. Max described, in graphic detail, a collision with an East German lorry carrying twenty thousand eggs: "The Mercedes lay upside down in the ditch, burned like an overcooked omelet."

I found myself, oddly enough, clinging to Max's version.

"I thought you'd want the truth."

"What's it to you? Why do you care?"

I watched the ripples out on the bay swirl and fold back upon themselves.

"Don't you want to know what happened?"

"From you . . . whom have you been talking to?"

"Elliot Goddard, for one. And Vlada, too; we've been writing since Max died. He wrote me that he thinks he can confirm what Elliot told me about the prison in Prague. I'm going to meet him in Prague; Vlada and Max stayed in touch, you know."

I think I detected a hint of guilt in her voice.

"Prague?"

"Prague."

"Writers—huh."

I hadn't seen Vlada since Winsted, Elliot since he visited me in my San Diego rehab clinic. His career had gone down in flames at the Church Senate committee hearings on CIA assassinations and assorted skullduggery.

"So, you've been talking to Elliot—quite the trick getting Elliot to talk?"

"Yes, he sends his warmest regards; he's a big fan of your books."

She definitely sounded guilty.

"Yes, I remember now, the letters—the love letters in the Harrods biscuit tin in your mother's closet."

"Peter, they're wonderful, *sad* letters. You see, it's not the letters so much—not really. It's what Elliot told me. . . ."

She placed her hand over mine, as if to keep me anchored in harm's way, as if she, too, wanted a good grip in face of that onrushing wall of water.

"Spit it out—you're killing me."

"They were Soviet spies. Bobby Williams was engaged in Soviet espionage since before the war. And my mother in England, and maybe later in New York—it sucks."

This bit of news didn't exactly floor me, since she'd dropped something of that little bombshell on the night of my nonperformance—didn't

help my state of readiness—and I had found out as much from conversations at Winsted with Elliot and Virgil; and Virgil—how much I
missed him—had pretty much confirmed it all to me ten years before,
in 1979, when Anthony Blunt had been denounced in parliament by
Margaret Thatcher, that Bobby had tipped off Elliot and the CIA in
1963 about Blunt's—Sir Anthony's—recruiting him as a Soviet agent
at Cambridge in 1937. All that—and Blunt dead some six years—I'd
simply given up caring about. They were all dead, except Elliot . . .
and Suzanne. How she put it *did* floor me. She didn't say, "my father,"
but "Bobby Williams," as if he were some distant offstage figure, an
inscrutable Iago, whose suicidal arsonist machinations she was intent
on distancing herself from.

"Elliot told you that—was immunity from prosecution part of the
deal?"

"Worse, he admitted that he used it to get your father to join the
CIA in 1948."

"Well . . . you kind of mentioned it that night on the Circle, the love
letters."

"I did, didn't I?"

"You did."

"I brought copies for you to read."

"Forgive me for repeating myself: Why here, why now?"

"I thought you'd like to know."

"Okay—"

"What else could I do?"

I felt her hand shaking.

She added, "Because I *need* your help."

"Sounds like you've been doing just fine without me."

"I told you: I brought your father's letters, Xeroxes; the originals are
with my lawyer in New York."

I looked at her, her head canted upward in a half grimace, as if
these disclosures hadn't been easy to get out, or track down, the tendons
in her neck straining cords of white on white. I had almost managed
to forget about those love letters, along with the associated humilia-
tions, while lying in the grass beneath the apple trees. Like a sick joke.
The lingering shame flooded back. I felt faint, as if I'd been suckered
into seeing the river, while she casually flipped her face cards on the
green felt.

"With your lawyer?"

She grabbed my hand.

"Whatever happened to your father . . . part of it's in those letters, but a lot isn't." The power of those clutching fingers again pumped ice through my veins, even as warm sweat trickled into my mouth. "Elliot told me that your father's association with Bobby and Suzanne, much less Kim Philby, left many in the CIA convinced he'd defected behind the Iron Curtain."

On the horizon, nodes of flame began to wink out, leaving an unbroken line of red, not unlike an infected incision. Kim Philby had died—it was front-page news in all the papers—the year before in Moscow; he'd been buried with highest military honors.

"Fuck, Elliot." Those disembodied voices in the gym urinals from so many years before—dismissed, almost forgotten—whispered again in my ear.

"Listen, Elliot just wanted to be sure; believe me . . . Elliot has his own demons." Right, I thought, like trading a place on the Winsted board for Bobby's betrayal of his Cambridge recruiter, Anthony Blunt. "I mean, the letters alone don't paint a pretty picture: Your father never informed on them; he protected them." She took a deep breath. "And I've got to tell you, there's a postcard to my mother that your father mailed from East Germany, postmarked January 1954, months after he disappeared."

The framed postcard hanging on the wall of my father's boyhood room appeared before me like a prosecutor's indictment shoved into my hand.

"Did you . . . *tell* Elliot about the postcard?"

"Yes; he was a little agitated about it."

"Did you show it to him?"

"No way . . . well, the letters are my ace in the hole—your ace, too."

I had to smile: a woman who kept her wits about her.

"The postcard was from the Museum of Antiquities in Leipzig, a bunch of nineteenth-century vitrines displaying ancient objects," I said.

Her hand tightened.

"How did you know?"

"My grandmother got the same card, with lines of some kind of archaic poetry translated into English."

"About a voyage and a betrothal . . . but it didn't seem to make much sense."

"A voyage and betrothal . . . ." That was the moment I realized that

Suzanne's card contained a different text. "And you're just the messenger . . . of glad tidings." I shifted my weight to see her better, to
find the words that expressed what was coming at me from out of that
aqueous sunset. Her features were lit in soft flame, like the doctor's face
illuminated by the X-ray viewer as he examines the telltale spot for
malignancy. Then, nervously, she was pulling at the spandex above her
knee with her free hand. The hand on mine showed fingernails broken
and chewed, a silver ring with inlay of lapis lazuli and a vaguely Navajo
design.

"I was hoping you could help, that you'd want—to know."

The added pressure of her hand, if translated into a cry for help,
would have shouted down the sky. As it was, the lingering heat of the
day had settled around us like the edge of a tropical depression.

"You say he was held in a Soviet prison?"

"A Czech prison in Prague, for maybe a year in 1954. That's all I
have in the way of details; I'm hoping Vlada can help on that score."

"That's what you got out of Elliot? That must have been a good
trick."

"Elliot didn't exactly offer it on a silver platter. It's been on his conscience all these years: their failure to get him out alive. He swore me to
secrecy, he could—seriously—be put in jail for telling me."

I was just a little in awe of what she'd managed.

"How did you get it out of him?"

She smiled a tad coyly. "I was performing at the Kennedy Center
in Washington. He came backstage after a performance. He knew my
mother in London during the war; he was at her wedding, where he
met his wife, her maid of honor. Believe me, the whole business weighs
on him, after all he's been through."

"And my father . . . was Bobby's best man," I snorted. "A nest of
vipers, no doubt, in the eyes of the FBI."

Her words brought images of Elliot withering under interrogation
by Senator Frank Church's committee in 1975, as he was blamed for
the CIA's culture of domestic spying and the attempted assassination
of Castro, which he'd had nothing to do with. I remember as a sophomore at Princeton watching him sweat it out under the klieg lights
and thinking, It could've been my father. When I'd had dinner with
Elliot at the best French restaurant in Saigon, he offered me a reassign-
ment to army intelligence in Saigon—"Your dad would still be plenty
proud—or even," he'd offered, smiling, "Hâu Nghĩa, where you can
practice your surfing, in safety."

I had turned down the safety option, and nothing had been quite the same between us after that.

"How's Elliot's wife?"

She bristled at my insinuation.

"She died of breast cancer a few years ago. His daughters' marriages are a mess."

Were those the confidences of an ally or a lover?

"Well, I gather Cordelia, Goneril, and Regan were instrumental in his backing for coeducation at Winsted."

"I should hope so, and upping the minority admissions, too. He told me that he always felt he owed as much to your grandmother."

I couldn't help smiling. "She liked Elliot's father."

"I don't think she ever liked me much. As a kid, I was terrified of her."

"She didn't like your parents—her instincts about people were good. I'm sorry about your father, and Hermitage."

"He sent his male attendant off on an errand. Then he set the fires and wheeled himself out on the piazza overlooking the lake and shot himself. My mother, of course, admitted to the police that she knew about the gun in his desk drawer, but she insisted it was unloaded. She played the sorrowing widow to the grand jury, even thought they'd barely lived together anymore. The attendant was supposed to check his study for bullets once a week; he had hiding places all over the place."

"So, it wasn't her fault."

"On the day before the fire and suicide, a Federal Express box had arrived with the .45-caliber rounds from an Ohio gun store. My mother was at Charles Fairburn's place in Brookline. Charles took care of her after her breakdown."

Laura shook her head, more a shiver of despair, it seemed to me, and I realized she was not in great shape. Over the last three months, she'd gone through knee surgery and a long rehabilitation, flat on her back much of the time, mulling it all over, while drying out and trying to get off the painkillers, the antidepressants, with fellow company members dying all over the city.

We grew more silent as the sun set. Laura's fingers twined themselves in mine and I felt something release in her, perhaps just a sigh as her breathing eased from the climb. Out to the northwest, a vagabond chink of cloud-reflected light guttered on a peak of distant Rhenia, while all around the arc of the earth began to burn with a rosy iridescence, the sky softening further to a florid mist, which, in turn, overspread the far islands, cooling us as the seconds passed. The sky and sea merged like a single vibrating plane on an endless Rothko canvas.

"You know," she said finally, as if she'd been girding herself for the admission, "all the way over on the flight, on the ferry, I realized that the one thing I *really* needed to ask you, the question that troubled me most all these years: Did you go to Vietnam—your reason—because of me, because of Max and me?"

Her fingers pulsed, as if echoing her heart's sudden contraction, and that impulse, translated to the barest spasm on my upper thigh, where our hands were interlaced, went straight through me, like a blast of neutrinos from a decaying star: passing without shape or mass or residue.

"I was fed up, I guess. . . . I was hurt."

"Because of us, the stupid juvenile prank in the chapel?"

"Straw that broke the camel's back."

"We thought maybe you'd really gone wacko."

I tried to laugh it off. "I did, I went to wacko land, a place as beautiful as it was wacko."

"And you're . . . okay?"

"*What you see is what you get.*"

She laughed at my Flip Wilson imitation. "Oh"—she sighed deeply—"Max just wanted to fuck with everybody's mind, keep the pot stirred. But you, of all people, should've known that."

"At least you were seduced by a master."

"It was never easy, never, ever."

Her plaintive cry, and it was a cry, seemed to leap bodily from her. I turned from her tears, embarrassed, letting my gaze dwell on that festering rashy red of a horizon, hoping that deliquescent tissue of expiring time might reveal something worth adding.

What I then said to her, feeling very small under that proscenium sky, was about the last and most imbecilic thing I ever expected to admit. "I never forgot that night in the grass . . . and the trees and the stars and you."

She squeezed my hand, lingered and let it go, then spread her arms like a supplicant before an infinite altar.

"Because this is so beautiful, I'd like to believe that you got lost and just stayed lost because it was so beautiful. That would be nice, that you don't hate me."

The words were those of a lost girl.

"*My* father," and I think I said this with some emphasis on the possessive pronoun, "loved it here."

"I know." She pulled a picture from the pocket of her skirt and handed it to me. "He wrote to my mother about Delos a lot."

It was a snapshot from the summer of 1939 of my father dressed in khaki shorts and shirt and safari hat, standing next to one of the famous Delian marble lions. The face was only just visible under the broad brim of the hat, revealing shadowed eyes, bushy dark eyebrows, an impatient chin. In his right hand he held an archaeologist's measuring rod. My grandmother had had the same photo in a silver frame in her room. Her version was dated August 1939, his last summer in Greece before the war. He was at the height of his fame as an archaeologist—"the boy wonder," he'd been called in the American press. It was a publicity shot for his lectures and books. Not a little ironic that it was on Delos that my father had received a hurried letter from his friend and rival Karel Hollar, describing the just-discovered horde of Linear B tablets on a hill near Pylos, a letter I discovered tucked away in the pages of my father's volume on the Delian excavations.

July 14, 1939

Writing in haste. First day, five hours in using a zigzag trench aprox 100 meters long, 2 meters wide, hit stone walls of what was clearly a large building, layer of black in red earth, as if great fire had swept the complex. By late afternoon, the first Linear B tablets were discovered!! No doubts, the script is the same as from Knossos, though size and shape of tablets is different and because of fire these clay tablets are hard as rock. Must be archive room of palace to have so many in one place, must be hundreds. Clear that the Englianos Ridge is the location of Nestor's Palace. The numbers of tablets will certainly make the decipherment feasible without having to rely on Evans's tardy scholarship.

Can you send me funds for hiring extra workers—immediately? I have a sense of where some extra digging might pay off for us. Stay on Delos for time being. We don't want Carl A to get nervous about extra attention.

I handed back the photo, as if it was yet another solvent to the few certainties I'd managed to surround myself with over the previous years. Even the ancient ruins seemed unstable, the scattered remains of chalky white beginning to show in luminous relief against the ash gray earth. I could feel the heat of the day rising and there deploying thermal sails to the night's breeze.

She gripped my arm.

"Peter, they loved . . . they loved like you can't believe. Enough to make you blush, like a kid seeing his first porno tape."

That shocked me, not just the image of my father and her mother making wild and sinful love, but that, after everything, she could still be championing their cause. Or was she doing something else: jumping ship, fleeing the horror of Bobby's arson-suicide, or her misspent youth with Max? That was something to warm to. Again she reached out her arm in supplication, as if to embrace the out-there: that fading stain of red transforming the floating landscape, the last emanation from some immense brazier at world's end. The breath of the sea, the scent of brine, offered its own hope of escape—or was it atonement, the chance to dip our oars one last time, while our failing bodes might just manage it: to feel the glide?

Just enough that we could relax and speak of other things.

"It's hard to believe that people could live here," she said. "It's so dry and desolate."

"It's been a dry summer," I said, remembering the lingering warmth and erotic ache of that long-ago fall at Winsted. "The island is parched, but in the spring with the flowers—you wouldn't believe how beautiful. There's actually a good supply of water on the island. I can show you the cisterns. In the fourth century B.C., there were over twenty-five thousand people living here."

She pointed. "Look."

Over Tinos, a glaucous fragment of the moon issued from the angle of a mountain peak. Nearby, on the dark hillsides of Mykonos, electric lights began to flicker on, forming tendril patterns, as if to mimic the unshed stars above. Below us, the walls and columns of the ancient city, livid and aglow, began to emerge anew from the shadows. And out on the bay, a long white wave—harmless as a child's splash in a wading pool—moved across that vast plane of burnished silver.

"My father loved this place, almost as much as Elysium. You see, Delos was sacred to Apollo, god of light and truth, art and healing—our better nature. Although Achilles would hardly have seen it quite that way. The goddess Leto gave birth to both Phoebus Apollo and Artemis—right around here on the summit of Mount Kynthos, but it's the straight-shooting Apollo who really figures in the island's history. The

Delians built a sanctuary to Apollo to foster peaceful trading ties and, with Athenian backing, created a kind of neutral port and emporium for the exchange of artisanal goods. There was even a Delian festival held every four years to honor the god with dancing, music, drama, and recitation of poetry." I paused. "Sorry, I'm boring you."

"No, no"—she seemed almost excited—"go on."

"The Athenians, who always tended to push their own agenda, went a little overboard in their embrace of Apollo's sacred island; they decided in all their imperial wisdom to purify the place—passing a law that no one could die or be born on the island. The dying and pregnant were shipped over to Rhenia. Then they really got into it and had the graveyards dug up and the bones removed, as well. Then one thing led to another and they got rid of the Delians and replaced them with merchants and temple custodians . . . based their Delian league and treasury for the common defense against the Persians on the island . . . a long, sad tale told by a fool. Nevertheless, Delos remained an oasis of prosperity and trade that lasted well into Roman times, when it became an international emporium for the transshipment of goods from all over the Mediterranean. One of the wonders of the ancient world when you think about it: a sacred isle without fortifications of any kind, where all peoples respected its sanctity and prospered."

"And, like you said, he—your father—was drawn here."

"In a way, it was a great human success: the best in the Greek character."

She smiled at this, as if strangely relieved.

"You know, I've enjoyed your books."

"Can't live by fiction alone."

"Tell me about it."

"I've started a new book on Thucydides. And the Athenians and the tragedy of imperial overreach."

"Gee, that's too bad. I've been boning up on my Homer, hoping to impress you."

And then, giving it a few beats, her voice rose again, tentative, probing like sonar pulses for an echo.

"Maybe I shouldn't tell you this, but I think my mother's unhappiness . . . I think she blames herself—for something she did or didn't do—that he never came back."

She said this with a sad, incantatory throatiness, the first vaguely forgiving thing I'd ever heard her say about her mother. Then I saw her gaze drift downward as if following some skein of light to the moon-lit walls and columns below. A leviathans' graveyard. Bleached bones thrown up by the sea and wasted by time, and so, finally impervious to further metamorphosis. I had always found comfort in such things.

"Is that in the letters?" I asked.

"Oh, much worse. You see, that's how I've grown up . . . like it lives in me."

What the fuck to make of that! I felt her whole body stiffen and then release.

"It's so beautiful," she said hurriedly, as if to let her previous thought pass unnoticed.

"Yes."

"It makes me happy, because I can understand why you'd want to stay. That you'd have good reasons."

She twisted where she sat, tossing her shoulders from side to side as if to relieve chronic tension, then turned her gaze once more to the hovering palace of the moon, stretching her arms, fingertips reaching toward the crown of Ariadne hanging suspended toward the north-west, as if setting a quadrant to mark out our path home.

"It's kind of like a dawn," she whispered. "Pale and dreamy, like a thing asleep, where your dreams come and go, things you've forgotten, from when you were a child, or maybe even from before you were born."

This was the plea of a woman who had nursed Max's mother, Han-nah; who'd nursed her colleagues in the first terrifying wave of the AIDS epidemic; who'd nursed her despair at Max's dissection of her life in his second novel, only to have him die alone of a heroin overdose. I thought I had seen bad things in war, but violence and death on the battlefield have a terrible logic, a territory all its own. What she'd gone through was worse. People she had loved who died with no logic or necessity or blame.

"You have the letters?"

"I brought copies for you."

"How did you get them?"

"After her breakdown, I found them stashed in her closet at the colonel's house." She grimaced to herself. "Well, I was looking for them, actually. I'd read some of the letters years before, when I was snooping around in my mother's things at Hermitage."

"Why did she keep them?"

"I found a copy of Kim Philby's autobiography, *My Silent War*. A signed copy, dated a year or so ago, right before he died in Moscow."

"She's not mentioned, is she?"

"At worst—or is it best?—she was a bit player. But no, not that I can tell, not by name."

That was a lie, or, at best, a half-truth. She said nothing about the inscription, the photograph, the secret documents and other things she'd also uncovered. She didn't yet trust me; she didn't trust anybody, least of all herself.

"You're a regular sleuth."

"You don't want to know. I lived with the expert, for years. He even read my fan mail."

"Max—Jesus."

"The man in the photo, in the gym, I found him for you, too. *Your* Nestor."

"*My* Nestor?"

"But tell me, I've been blabbing on so, what about you—what do you see out there, like Max always said, 'with your head in the sands of time'?"

I gave it a beat or two, trying to keep my scholarly reserve as I processed her echoed sarcasm. How to explain that great inland sea of the past that now included at least half my life?

"A blood-dark sea."

"As in wine-dark sea?"

"No, no, no literary metaphors here. More like the arteries or currents that circulate the things of this world as we know them—the lifeblood of civilization: where trading ships, tiny fragile craft of wood and pitch, sail and oar, plied their trade routes for thousands of years, hugging the shore for safety, carrying both necessities and luxury goods from one land to the next, whether obsidian from Milos, or copper from Ugarit and tin from Sardinia, cedar planks from Lebanon, olive oil and wheat and wine from Pylos, Mycenae, and Tiryns, from Knossos and Phaistos. . . ."

I gave her most of the laundry list of two thousand years of Mediterranean trade.

"Amazing, how the traders endured, the artisans endured in the face of catastrophes natural and man-made, forever reaching out across the seas to trade, to feed and clothe and delight the eye with exotic and beautiful objects—to honor the diffident gods even as the gods began to turn on one another and call for the extermination of their rivals.

. . . The trade goods—lots of pottery—which remain and endure for us to find and remember, so we might make up stories about lives long ago lost to history . . . so, I guess, we might try to do better . . . but I go on . . ."

"No, thank you."

Years later, she told me it was like hearing the voice of a man she'd dreamed about but never known.

Exhausted, we finally stood, a little chilled by the breeze, which began to blow steadily. We were lucky with the moonlight, because the steps down the slope of Mount Kynthos were tricky even in daylight. We touched, held hands, helped guide each other.

And we were far from alone.

As we made our way through the temple sanctuaries toward the museum, my father might as well have been our guide, for he was a palpable presence between us, the dead hand of his yet-vital personality leading us down the byways of the lives he had touched and that, in turn, touched ours. When we got to the museum, headquarters for the French archaeological team, Laura got her small roll-on bag and pulled out a large manila envelope, placed it my hands, and asked to be shown to the women's dormitory.

"I think, if you don't mind, I'll go sleep . . . forever."

She was exhausted from her overnight flight. Exhausted by the completion of the first part of her journey, which was to find me and put those letters in my hands. I introduced her to some of the women archaeologists, and she immediately charmed them with her perfect French. They found her an unoccupied bed for the night. I couldn't even think about dinner and went straight to the small museum library, where there was a desk and a good reading light. I stayed up half the night reading, more than a hundred letters stretching from May of 1944 to the fall of 1953, including many of Suzanne's letters to my father over the same period, which, so she explained to me a few months later, he'd returned to her the night before he'd left Elysium for Washington and a flight to Berlin, when he'd left her and his wife and two-year-old son, forever.

Hard to imagine, in this day of disposable e-mails: the hording of love letters, ten years of heated correspondence punctuated by sex.

Suzanne's lifeline . . . the text that might yet save her—and my father, too.

22 I WAS ENTHRALLED UPON MY FIRST READ-
ing of those love letters, as I tried to get the drift
of the ups and downs of their nearly ten-year-long
affair. It was not so much the tone of my father's
voice or even the discomfiting details of their sex life that I found most
unsettling. Nor even the unnerving intimations of Bobby's spying and
Suzanne's—and my father's involvement with Donald Maclean and
Kim Philby. It was the vast distance I'd put between my father and
myself since Winsted and Vietnam. Although I had, in a sense, followed in his footsteps, I had actually managed to let him go; I had
ceased wondering about him, caring about him, looking to his life for
answers or guidance, much less approval. I had given up on any sense
of loyalty or allegiance to the cause for which he had died. Or so I had
thought. Nor had I paid much attention to his academic passion for
Homer and Bronze Age Greece. I'd become something of a hardened
cynic. Reading the letters at that small desk under a single hanging
bulb, with the Meltemi whistling past the library's high open windows,
I rediscovered my younger self, when my father's fate had loomed large
in my life. Through the voices in the letters, I was confronted not just
with what I had become—a dispassionate and detached academic
archaeologist and historian—but with all I'd given up to get there.

And by doing so, I'd abandoned the field to Max.

June 23, 1944
"How can it be that you married Bobby—that you never told me, that
I knew nothing? Did he give you that engagement ring, the one you
always wore—that you insisted didn't matter? My God, I'm trampled

to bits by all this. Worse, I can't get your body out of my mind, your breasts, your cunt, your hungry lips—the taste of you. I thought I'd get it out of my system forever two nights ago; now it's worse than ever. I'm mad for you. I can't sleep for the desire, even with the perfidy and ugliness of what we've done.... Did you manage to dispose of the sheets?"

Even now, after Suzanne's admissions to me, the lies and manipulations of this disciplined ideologue amaze. Kim Philby had first recruited her in London as a courier between his visits to Spain as *The Times*' correspondent in 1937. Her brother and Philby had been friends at Trinity College, Cambridge. Stalin's purges in Moscow had eliminated the experienced old-guard Soviet handlers in the late thirties, and Philby, Donald Maclean, Guy Burgess, and Anthony Blunt—the core of the Cambridge spy ring—had, for almost a year, been cast adrift and neglected by Moscow Center; the Lubyanka offices of the NKVD had been literally emptied by executions in the basement cells. "The new handlers who arrived in '38 and '39," Suzanne complained to me months later, "were amateurs and paranoid survivors. Often we were on our own."

In the spring of 1944, Suzanne had nursed my father at the rehabilitation center in Guilford, Surrey; for weeks, their clandestine affair went on behind drawn curtains in the wards and storage rooms. She'd dismissed her engagement ring—a boy overseas who didn't really matter to her. Not a word about the upcoming marriage until two days before the event, when he'd received, not just one invitation to the wedding, but two. Suzanne had managed to convince him that it was pure coincidence, fate.

June 23, 1944
Don't you see, I knew I could never give you up—never! Our night together only proves it. I realized I was fool to always think I must do the sensible thing. The sensible thing is a trap. Bobby is back to base in two days. Come to me at Cadogan Gardens. My leave from the hospital is a full week. You must come to me. I will die without you inside me again. Soon, soon, come soon. I can't stand it. I can still taste your semen. I am all hollowed out without you. Yes, I got to the housekeeper in time to dispose of the sheets.

They had slept together on her wedding night—a betrayal as enthralling as it was terrifying—a powerful and fanatic Circe!

And so it went for the first few weeks as the world watched for news of the invasion of France and then the harrowing slog of the Normandy breakout. Bobby was flying over Germany and my father and Suzanne were stealing hours for sex together at her London home—or more precisely—in Cadogan Gardens, the park on the square of huge Dutch revival town houses. They had a thing about sex out-of-doors, dangerous sex, under the buzz bombs, where they might be discovered. It was as if they were addicted to the danger of discovery, as they had been on her wedding night—and before in the hospital in Guilford. For weeks, she'd crept into his curtained bed in the recovery ward, where he lay flat on his back, immobile and in delicate condition. Oral sex was the best they could manage . . . silent hours surrounded by the mutilated and dying. Desire for full-throttle intercourse galvanized my father in his physical therapy. Then sex outdoors would become their modus operandi, as if to banish memories of the burn ward in Guilford, and big-time at Elysium from 1946 on. Their explicit language, the sheer carnality of their exchanges shocked me. I had never used the word *cunt* with a woman in my life. No wonder Laura had handed me the letters and excused herself so abruptly. I grimaced at the realization that she had first read the letters at the age of seventeen, that her mind had been full of their pillow talk as she lay there in my arms under the apple trees on the Circle. I groaned at the memories of my stunted sexuality but found myself inflamed by the references in the letters to their passion's crucible—those weeks together in the Guilford hospital. For I, too, knew something about hospitals and long periods of rehabilitation . . . and a kind pair of hands.

The letters over the remainder of 1944 were filled with remorse and guilt and a growing frenzy as they were separated for longer periods of time, as my father traveled with his OSS intelligence unit in France. "Why do you have to go?" complained Suzanne. "I don't understand. You've done enough; everyone says so. You said yourself they've offered you a cozy office job right here in London, right here where we can be together more often. And your leg is far from fully healed; you shouldn't be out in the field again."

And then as if they weren't guilty enough: "My God, I got the telegram just now; Bobby's been shot down. Their B-17 broke up and only two parachutes sighted out of ten crew. Help me, come back. I can't deny that some part of me wished it to happen—yes, imagined it, contemplated it. Did my longing for you bring it about? Come back. I need you here."

They both seemed to go a little crazy over the fall and winter of 1944–1945. My father persisted in remaining in France, interrogating German prisoners, searching through captured documents as Patton pressed on to the Rhine. "The German prisoners stream past, tens of thousands of faces, shell-shocked, starved, relieved—ten thousand sons of bitches, spared, after all the horror they've perpetuated. The SS are the worst; they still smile when they think we're not watching."

Paul Oakes had gotten it right: my father *was* on the hunt, and, as I would realize a few days later when I finally met "our" Nestor, on the hunt for Karel Hollar.

When the telegraph came that Bobby had survived and was a prisoner of war, both expressed guarded relief that at least they didn't have his blood on their conscience. Suzanne's frustration was heightened; she complained about his dogged pursuit of captured German prisoners: "You could be fucking me instead; you could be cracking me open instead of their malevolent viper brains." They stole two days together in a Paris hotel as Bobby, at least in their minds, safely languished in a POW camp. They begin searching for names to give to the desire that consumed them: "the beast," "this fuck creature," "this bear grip," "this devil's bargain with death" and, after a round of anal sex the Paris hotel, "this shitty, shitty thing called love that shits all over us . . . yes, and makes this shitty war go away."

I realized from these early letters that my father had no idea Suzanne was a Soviet courier, much less that she was probably relaying information she got out of him about OSS operations in Europe to her Soviet handlers in London. And Bobby, it seemed, had convinced him at the wedding that he'd turned against his early Communist leanings in 1939 upon hearing about the Nazi-Soviet nonaggression pact. "Bobby, a true-blue all-American patriot—who would have thought?" A cover-up Bobby's Soviet handler in New York had insisted upon when he returned from Cambridge in 1939, and confirmed in the Venona decrypts of Soviet cable traffic in 1947, which Elliot Goddard hung around my father's neck as he pressed him to join the CIA in the spring of 1948: "among other things, a way to inoculate yourself against infection, Suzanne, too, I hate to tell you."

As I read their epistolary erotica, I felt a shameful tightening in my gut, part sexual, part a realization that I was now a few years older than the man writing those letters. Did my boring life lack such a sexual drive, the frisson of such erotic daring? For sure, I better understood the cold pursuit of his duties, the hardened indifference I detected in Paul Oakes's rendition of his reaction to the Buchenwald prison guard's ghoulish dance at the end of a rope. Glimpsed again when Suzanne wrote in the spring of 1945 as my father's OSS unit was combing the bombed-out German cities: "your lust for revenge, like mother's milk. Why do you persist? Can't you give it up? Can't you put Greece behind you? Fuck my behind if you will—fuck me arse and cunt and mug and put this perverse thing, whatever it is, out of your mind. Lose yourself in me: take me in every damn orifice you can fathom; feed me your goddamn sweet spunk so I don't have to bear the stench of the wards. How I hate the petty valor of this damn country."

From somewhere in Germany, he wrote:

There's the chance I might get back to London next week; the offensive into Germany seems stalled for the winter, but you never know. It's so cold. My leg has stiffened up—as has my third leg as soon as I set pen to paper and think of you. Just writing gets me hard. Even your panties have lost their scent, even when I wrap them around my cup of steaming coffee to warm them. God, how I want you—how I hate myself for wanting you—your brimming, sloppy cunt with my tongue inside, how the cold and the brittle stars and the bombed-out towns seem full of the same lustful hate. How much fucking will be needed to repopulate this world? Can there ever be enough fucking?

And she:

I wait, I wait; the waiting is the worst. I fell asleep with my fingers inside myself last night, wanting it to be you, wanting to find something of you left inside me. But there was only emptiness. I can't get off without you. I dream of your cock or your tongue inside me, one or the other, as if that is the only thing that matters in the universe. I dread the hospital—every bloody day—and all those mangled young men and their desperate faces—as if I'm their bloody miracle worker. It's so dark and so cold; I'm sick of this crappy little island and its foolish and fading glory. Hurry, hurry . . . so I don't have to worry about your safety anymore. Oh my John, you are a born survivor; when I am with you, I feel so alive—is that the American in you, that vital, gorgeous American innocence? Don't lose your innocence; don't lose the hope of something better in this life. I dream of returning to the stage, where

I can dance for you and stop being your nursemaid imposter. Hurry back—warm me, fill me, love me as I love you.

Gone, shattered, obliterated was the young man I'd known from his schoolboy letters, with his romantic infatuation over Homer's princess, Nausicca, the reluctant adolescent who needed Elliot Goddard to set him up with a date for their senior dance, when, as Elliot put it, his unself-conscious physical charm drove girls wild. Gone, too, the tweedy Princeton academic. Replaced by lines on pages dripping with frenzied sadness, that drew them back again and again to their early days together in the Guilford hospital, like the miraculous golden age of first kisses so revered by long-married couples. Suzanne's "whatever it is" haunted their every exchange. "Your miraculous recovery—that you can still walk." "You saved my life" was repeated in many of my father's letters. "You save my life every day. Do you think it's just your hands, your beautiful strong hands—maybe I'm only in love with your hands?" The moment I read those words above the song of the Meltemi, I understood so fully that I felt the blood drain from my head.

"Do you remember the milky light through the ward window?" she wrote. "Even now it fills me with longing. When I walked in there this morning, I wet myself with the memory of that light and those first weeks of unrequited—was it unacknowledged?—longing. Did you know how much I wanted you? You were such a sick whippet; I never knew anyone so sad—why were you sad? You've never told me, you know, what made you so sad. Your sadness is so different from the others', and from mine." After reading my father's painful description of the liberation of Buchenwald (though not a word about the prison guard), she wrote, "Yes, yes, I've seen the reports in the papers. Don't let it get you down. You must let me wring the neck of the sadness in you—this broken thing in you, I can feel it, darling, in your sad eyes, even in the sad bittersweet taste of your semen, which I love when it is mixed with me. I ache for your love—isn't that enough to banish what ails you? Tell me I'm enough."

And a day after this she wrote:

I miscarried at three this morning. A bloody little worm of a boy, I think. Please forgive me. I tried to hold on to him as best I could, but the work in the wards is so exhausting. Oh John, sorry, sorry, sorry— come back soon. I need you ever so much, my love—I need you to fill me up again and take me away from this place. I can't stand tending any more wounded, and they keep coming and coming—Arnhem was a disaster.

I think it was three or four in the morning when my eyes and my back finally gave out, as if I'd humped a million miles from Cadogan Gardens to the battlefields of France to the rubble of Germany to a peaceful interlude that was postwar America, and then back to Greece as CIA station chief during the Greek Civil War, and then the early fraught years of the Cold War. As Laura had warned me, the letters from their last years spoke of evasion and conspiracy and deceit—on both sides, like caged animals circling each other for advantage.

The Meltemi was rattling the high windows of the library, a low fluty kind of insistent whisper, swirling dust balls in the bare corners, as if to remind me of all I'd abandoned. My mind reeled backward and forward in time: a young man defending his father and his school and his country . . . no more. If sex and desire could have saved him, Suzanne would have been the one to do it. Intimated in her embrace on the piazza of Hermitage on that moon-glutted night, and in the arms of her daughter under the apple trees, if only it had been in me.

I was overwhelmed by a sudden anger at what felt like a history of deceit, and Laura's words about how they "didn't or couldn't get him out" of that Prague prison. That took me back to Hâu Nghĩa Province, where I had been stationed with Lt. Theo Colson and Sgt. Willie Gadsden, Jerry's brother, and the sometimes inept but always determined South Vietnamese colonel Minh, and our plucky district militias that feared to fight without American advisers and air support—and who surprised themselves when they did. And the NVA regulars who were indoctrinated to sacrificial slaughter, and the medevacs that refused to land under fire, and the B-52 strikes that could have stopped the NVA's 271 Division on the doorstep of Cambodia had there been better intelligence from our prisoners. And Nixon and Watergate—and all the shithead politicians who had gotten us into the mess and then let us down.

The letters replaced any lingering schoolboy romantic notions with bruised and bloodied flesh, and a carnal craving still virulent across decades. And with it an image of a seventeen-year-old girl staring into a display case of medals and a photograph of my father posed with Greek fighters, and one in particular, labeled in my grandmother's hand, "Nestor."

My Athena was leading me back to the truth . . . to the beginning of our story, a story that began way before we were born, before my father and grandfather were born.

When I woke late the following morning from an uneasy sleep, I felt as if the world I thought I knew had undergone a seismic shift. The morning light was more brilliant than usual, flooding the high windows of the men's dormitory; the Meltemi's low droning was more persistent, the lines of cots with their folded blankets and toilet kits more spare of appearance. It was as if everyone had awakened on tiptoes as they made their noisy morning ablutions, fearing to wake the late sleeper . . . newly estranged from his own life. I thought I smelled coffee from the mess and then I realized I was chilly: The Meltemi was blowing from the north. I sat up abruptly and my back went into a spasm, much worse than its usual morning briar patch of pain and stiffness. It took me a good hour's worth of exercises to get mobile, and I yearned for a hot bath instead of the lukewarm shower available in the crude amenities of the museum washroom. I popped an added dose of Demerol with my coffee and downed some buttered rolls with apricot jam.

According to the black-scarfed crone of a custodian, Laura had left the museum hours before; the ancient woman motioned to her ears, making little circles and funny faces, as if the American woman might be a little crazy. I had no idea what she meant, but the phrase from Max's novel sprang to mind: "a world unto herself."

I found Laura standing off to the side of the main excavation trench. By late September, only a skeleton crew remained to tidy things up after most of the teams and their students had returned to their universities for the fall. She wore a faded blue T-shirt, inscribed *Free the ABT 100*, khaki shorts, Nike running shoes, tortoiseshell dark glasses. A yellow Walkman cassette player was attached to her belt and yellow earphones covered her ears. Her hair was pulled back tight with an elastic band. Her long neck and striking jawline set off her pale features; she looked a lot better after a night's rest. She didn't hear me, intent on the team of archaeologists working in the trench below, intent on her therapy, with one hand resting on a marble slab as she bent and stretched to her soundless music. The steel brace of the evening before had been replaced with a simpler elastic wrap. I watched her for a time, registering her beauty anew amidst the ruins and a deep cerulean sky. How was it I knew her so little and yet felt I knew so much and yet probably knew next to nothing at all? Such was the spell of Max's fictional straitjacket. Her striking image at a fifty-foot remove reminded me of a recently uncovered inscription on Delos that I'd come to see. It commemorated a visit to the temple of Apollo by a party of Ionians some 2,600 years ago: They arrived in their trailing robes to praise Apollo with their boxing and dancing and song. *Anyone who met them, then, when they were gathered together, would say that they were immortal and would never grow old.*

Just another voice from the past inhabiting the living, enough to bring tears to the most veteran of diggers.

I noticed how every now and then she winced, as if the stretching exercises were causing her discomfort. She had always been a hard worker, as Max had found out, to his chagrin: always on tour, always too exhausted from rehearsals and performances for sex, and famously (he'd devoted an entire chapter to this trauma) abandoning his "lazy, ever-prevaricating ass" in Venice, after her abortion, to return to New York and rehearsals and a life without him.

Watching her, examining her face closely, a sensation of fear curdled with hatred rose into my throat, pressing there like a constricting hand. I gasped for breath. Something from the last of the letters, when I could barely keep my eyes open . . . the name: Kim. Kim Philby.

I came up behind her and gently lifted the earphones from her ears—tempted, like Iago, to whisper that name—and placed them over mine, as if to steal her power of motion, as if to escape into her celebrity life by way of that thin umbilical cord and fathom her—like mother, like daughter—perfidious soul. She didn't startle or miss a beat. *La Bayadère,* she told me, something she'd once rehearsed with Natalia Makarova. The repeating motif and slow phrasing were perfect for the light therapy she was doing for her bum knee.

She took the headphones from my ears and stowed them around her neck. "So, what did you think of the letters? I've been dying to know what your reaction would be: whose side you'd take."

"Is it about taking sides?"

"You tell me. If I were you, I'd be defending your mother. Max always said you were such a loyal sort."

"Well, from such an expert on loyalty—"

"I was sorry . . . to hear the news about her."

"Long time ago now."

"The way I figure it, the reason your father tried to make a break with Suzanne in the summer of '48 was because Elliot tipped him off about the fact that Bobby and my mother were Soviet agents."

That much had certainly been broached in the letters.

"To get him to join the CIA and go back to Greece as CIA station chief. But how did Elliot know? That's what I'd like to know."

"Oh, he was cagey as hell. I think it had something to do with army intelligence and decryption of Soviet cable traffic—I'm not supposed to talk about it. [Even in 1989, the Venona decrypts had yet to be released to the public.] Elliot admitted they used the new information to get him to leave Princeton—*back into harness* with the fledgling CIA."

"You've known—about your parents, I mean—for twenty years."

"Well"—she raised her eyebrows at me—"suspected, until I got my hands on everything. Why do you think I stayed away? You don't think that fucks with your mind—much less what it might mean for my career? As if Max wasn't bad enough."

I thrilled at her sentiments.

"I suppose Elliot told you that in 1963 he talked Bobby into turning in his Cambridge recruiter, Anthony Blunt?"

Her body tensed and I felt her eyes burning behind her sunglasses.

"No, you're fucking with me—right?"

"A quid pro quo, for a place on the Winsted board."

"Anthony Blunt . . . keeper of the king's pictures?"

"Queen's pictures, by the time Margaret Thatcher finally accused him publicly in 1979."

"Shit, Bobby used to reminisce about that asshole, Anthony: his days back at Cambridge, when he was nearly famous. He and *dear Anthony* hung out at the Fitzwilliam Museum, and Palazzo Barberini in Venice—I think he even visited Palazzo Fenway one summer to see Isabella Williams's old masters."

Her tone, her syntax of distancing herself from her father seemed positively creepy.

"Don't forget Wigmore Hall."

"Right, Wigmore Hall."

"So, they were Anthony Blunt's lovers? *Both* Bobby *and* Guy—"

"Don't fuck with me. Elliot didn't mention any of that."

"The crown jewels—I don't think so. Only what he needed to give you—that's how it works in the intelligence game."

"And now you're such an expert?"

"I've played a hand or two."

I was enjoying myself talking tradecraft, lapping up her dismay, how I was getting back at her and her damn family, redirecting a precious bit of life-changing news her way for once.

"Elliot"—she raised her dark glasses, her blue eyes blazing as she grabbed my wrist and squeezed—"didn't tell you this, did he?"

I smiled. A woman who thought she had her man dead to rights.

"A source, almost as good."

Tears welled in her dilating eyes as the implications washed over her, and her thousand-yard stare spoke of the embittered disaster of Bobby and Suzanne's split, illuminated by the full glare of their traitorous lives, to their countries, their lovers, and each other. I'm sure it must have occurred to her, as it did to me, that Suzanne had arranged the Federal Express delivery of .45-caliber ammo for Bobby's Colt pistol on the day after Kim Philby died in Moscow. The gun he kept, as he always insisted to Suzanne, in case the KGB came after him, which indeed they might have had word of his betrayal of Anthony Blunt reached Moscow Center. *And* having the perfect executioner—his estranged wife—for the job.

I gave her time; I climbed down the ladder into the excavation area and busied myself with my French colleagues. Half an hour later, tears wiped, composed, she joined me. I looked up from a sorting tray of pottery shards. She gave me a knowing look, an imperious straightening of her back, so that her head rose to my height, as she watched me.

I said as matter-of-factly as I could, "I hope you're wearing sunblock."

"Tons. Can't you smell it?"

"So," I asked, "what were you thinking—that night of the dance, under the apple trees?"

"Confused. Scared to death. At seventeen . . . well, to think people did those things."

"Ah, the letters—you were . . . shocked?"

"And I wanted you in the worst way."

"Oh right, Max's childhood crush—"

"No—don't go there." She waved her hands as if to banish the thought. "From the letters, I realized how much of your father was in her . . . in me . . . in Elysium. He'd been there the whole time, don't you see: mother and me at the lake, on the beach. She taught me to swim before I could walk. We always swam in the nude, always . . . like they did in the letters. And when I was a little girl, we hiked for hours—all over God's creation—until I thought I'd drop. And we'd stop and have picnics or pick blueberries, or nap or collect flowers; I knew my wild-flowers and the trees before I knew my ABC's. Only when I read the letters did I realize that we walked the paths they walked, hung out in the places they went to fuck each other—sorry, but those letters are so fucking graphic."

"And I was such a flop."

"Wrong time, wrong place. We should have been in Elysium; it was so alive when I was a little girl, and it was all about him, don't you see. They were happy there, until Elliot tipped him off about the spying. I was happy there, incredibly so, at least until fucking ballet took over my life."

"Rumor has it you're a star."

"I hated it. I hate it." She shook her head with such vehemence that I found myself perplexed, as if she was trying to convince me of some-thing, some golden age of love before Elliot spoiled it all. A kind of faith in which she needed to make me a believer as well, while treading softly, very softly.

"The stuff about our boathouse, well . . . the splinters in her ass from the dock—quite unforgettable."

"Do you mind?"

"Jesus, no wonder my mother hated the place."

Elysium, my onetime sanctuary . . . where for years they had indulged in ravenous guilty and deceit-fueled sex—if they'd been wild-fires, they'd have obliterated our woods.

"Peter." I started at my name, lost in a stand of three white columns in the near distance, simmering on the blue. "We need to tell the truth about your father; we need to get him back before it's too late."

"I'm afraid Max got to him first."

"You're the historian. We've got a lot of what we need. And I've spoken to this old guy in Pylos, the one named Nestor in the photo-graph—that's only his nickname, by the way; he was head of the Greek Resistance in the Peloponnese. He knew your father, like a brother, he said. They worked together during the Greek Civil War, as well. I heard his voice come alive on the phone when I mentioned your father's name, your name. He's throwing a party for us. We've been invited to spend the weekend with him. A big party, he said, a reunion of the Resistance fighters. That should give us a good start."

Her use of *we* sounded like yet another stratagem.

"How did you find him?"

"Elliot knew all about him; he'd interviewed him back in 1954 or '55, when he wrote the CIA report on your father's disappearance."

"Elliot wrote the report, too?"

She took my arm.

"Tell me about your father, Peter. What he did here—what you do: Get me up to speed. I liked it last night when you talked about all the trading ships and the names of those ancient places."

She shot me a penetrating look, again raising her dark glasses, her blue eyes taking in my leery face. The student from hell: the one's who's read all the texts before the semester has even begun—who keeps you honest.

"I'm a teacher."

I pointed out the grid system of wires placed over the area of excavation that allowed us to map unearthed objects in terms of time and place. From a sorting tray, I selected a large shard, a pottery fragment of Late Helladic II from a strata of Mycenaean settlement on Delos between 1400 and 1200 B.C., at the height of the Mycenaean empire and influence—something my father would have relished.

"Like I said last night," and I took her hand in mine and placed the dirty fragment in her upturned palm. "Spit on it."

"Spit?"

"Or I can spit, if you prefer."

She raised her palm and delicately spit on the shard. I took her hand again and rubbed the wetted area with a finger until the dried mud liquefied and revealed the amber glazing and red floral motif, typical of the period. I bent to a knee and drew in the dirt the shape of a kylix, a stemmed cup with looped handles on either side, and showed her the part of the cup from which the shard in her hand had come. "The patterning is more formalized, stylized compared to earlier Minoan models, which had a greater degree of naturalness and more expressive design." I looked into her eyes. "You're the first to gaze upon this artifact in over three thousand years." With that, I folded her fingers tightly around the fragment, as if it were a creature that might escape. "Think of it as energy: the skill and purpose of the maker of this kylix, his delight at painting the design, the way his lines echo the shape of the cup while abstracting the floral motif . . . the careful transport of this artifact across the seas to find a willing buyer, who, in turn, would find delight in the elegant shape and abstraction of natural forms, perhaps engendering a sense of wonder—you see"—and I squeezed her fist tighter still—"energy translated from the hand of the maker to the covetous eye of the beholder: a feeling of status and belonging that beauty incarnate bestows upon the possessor—that his world might somehow, against all the odds, survive the violence that waits on every horizon. We see only the ruins of worlds, and yet, for the people who lived here, there were interludes of peace and prosperity that lasted, sometimes for hundreds of years. And these"—and I unfolded her fingers so that the rays of sunlight sparked on the red glazing—"are testaments to their lost stories."

She reached a hand to my lips, not to hush me, I sensed, but to better feel the tone of voice.

"And words, too?"

"Oh yes, but alas, so very rare."

"So you're happy—with what you do, I mean?"

"The truth. It ends up being pretty arbitrary, trying to bring order to this chaos—but it's what you find along the way that makes it worthwhile." And I quoted her the inscription that had been discovered that summer at the temple of Apollo.

"So many lives," she said, looking around at the strata layers, each carefully labeled with little green plastic tabs.

"Grave robbers . . . kids digging for buried treasure."

She turned to the shard of the kylix again, an amber glow against the white of her palm.

"Actually, wasn't he—your father—fascinated with the influence of Minoan civilization on early Bronze Age Greece? The possibility of a golden age—right? Mentioned by Hesiod and implied in Homer, something like the way Odysseus thought of the island of the Phaecians, a better place and time."

I took the shard from her palm and carefully placed it back in the sorting tray.

"Sandbagged . . . you've read my father's journal articles."

She indicated her strapped knee. "I've had time on my hands. I've read everything I could lay my hands on, including *your* books and articles."

A guilty smile eased up the corners of her mouth as she caught my expression: as relentless as her mother.

For an hour, I led her among the ruins of the major sanctuaries, as I had done with my Princeton students for nearly two decades, and finally on to the lion's terrace built by the Naxians at the entrance to their sanctuary near the sacred lake.

"Here you are, your lions," I said.

She got out her photo of my father and began inspecting each of the five remaining lions of the original sixteen until she found the one he had posed beside. She fingered the lion's worn marble flanks shorn by centuries of exposure, its mouth agape in a toothless roar.

"August 1939 you said this photo was taken." She seemed to be assessing the figure for damage. "What's that, fifty years, almost to the day, imagine."

"Fifty years"—I snapped my fingers, imitating the way she'd done it the night before—"like nothing." I motioned to the ruins of the town and the blue of sea and sky.

She playfully petted the mane of Naxian marble and spoke to it in perfect imitation of Bert Lahr.

"Courage, you just gotta have courage."

That was their little pick-me-up—Max and Laura's—replayed to each other in moments of crisis and disappointment. And a comic leit-motif in *Gardens of Saturn*.

"Funny, this guy reminds me of something. I can't quite—"

"Venice. The Venetians stole one of the marble lions—their mascot, after all—and put it front of the Arsenal."

I watched carefully as something in her expression fell.

"C'mon, I'll take your picture," she said, pulling from her pocket an expensive compact Nikon. "Stand right here where your father was."

"No, I'm not in this picture, but you are."

I took the camera from her hand and she gleefully assumed a con-sciously touristy pose. Then as I was about to snap the shutter, she threw back her head, rubbing her chest so that her nipples showed beneath the T-shirt.

"A little cheesecake for the fans—as if I have any left."

I handed back the camera.

"There are plans to put this pride of cats in the museum, before they're totally ruined by weather, and replace them with copies."

"No, really, how sad." We resumed the tour. "Hey, how come you're walking so off balance?" She stopped, appraising me with a critical tilt of her head.

"Bad back. Comes from all the years digging ditches."

"You're out of alignment. You need to see my chiro, best in the busi-ness. He's saved my life more times than I care to remember."

I shrugged and we continued.

"So," she said, as if suddenly annoyed at my professorial airs. "Do you ever wonder about those guys you got kicked out of school?"

I stopped short. "Kicked out?"

"Max couldn't have cared less, but the others—I don't know."

"They got themselves kicked out."

"We heard you gave the headmaster a list."

"He had a list with Max's name at the top. I did confirm a few facts."

"But it came from you, don't you see. It fucked people up with their colleges, their student deferments—Vietnam. They still talk about it, about you. . . . We all do."

"Well, I never said anything—not a peep about *you*."

"Loyalty, was it, to the old school? Protecting the families, the founders?"

"I figured you'd have enough on your hands with Max."

"Touché." She waved me off and took the lead on the winding path through the tumbled sanctuaries, striding purposefully on with her bum knee as if to leave me in the dust.

I found myself pissed off: *they still talk about you.* I had a self-image, for better or worse, in terms of the circles in which I'd grown up, of someone who'd pretty much fallen off the face of the earth: a faded bogie on the radar screen. I'd never been back to a Winsted reunion. Occasionally, I had wondered about my classmates at reunions, deep in drink and sentimental blather about their radical school days—especially those now on Wall Street. Did they remember me, and how? Certainly not in terms of my hero father and his generation and their *good* war. Only one other poor son of a bitch in my generation at Winsted had actually ended up in Vietnam. To some, I belonged to a very exclusive club of fools and fascists.

"Yikes . . ."

I heard her startled cry and I rushed ahead, to find her standing at the entrance of a temple enclosure where a large green lizard, maybe three feet from nose to tail tip, eyed her from a mosaic floor.

"They're absolutely harmless," I assured her. "But they do grow incredibly large on the island. They have no natural predators here."

With that assurance, she strode boldly forward, and the lizard cocked its emerald-gray head, blinked a lifeless eye, and scampered across the mosaics to disappear with a furtive swish of its tail into a fissure of the surrounding wall. She began circling the mosaics, staring down at two gold-and-turquoise dolphins rising above a line of blue-crested waves.

"I don't suppose . . . did you find my mother at all sympathetic in the letters?"

She raised her face to me, her eyes neatly hidden behind her dark glasses.

A passage in one of my father's last letters leapt to mind:

"What is this black spell we have cast over each other? The thought of death only saddens me, in that it would be the end of you, too. Do you suppose it is the prospect of nothingness that makes me so hungry for your kisses, that all I can think about is crawling into your body and having you wrapped around me again like a second skin?"

"I only wish she had managed to save him, keep him from going," I replied.

She paused, her shoulders going slack.

"Somebody once told me that you were always *such* a good sport," she said. I rolled my eyes and she looked away. "When your father disappeared, Elliot and a whole team of CIA interrogators questioned Suzanne and Bobby for days. They, of course, denied everything."

I went to a low stone wall and sat to relieve the pressure on my back, covering my face in my hands.

"That's why we can't just leave it," she called after me.

Wiping cold sweat from my eyes, I glanced up with sudden anger: something about how she was painstakingly distancing herself from an inconvenient past.

"Were you really in love with Max?" I blurted out.

She snapped a bemused look at me.

"In love . . . I was crazy about him. You think my mother was a seductress, Max was in a league all his own."

"Well . . . now I feel better."

"Peter, he told me—Max assured me you were gay."

I shouted, "Of course he did. It's in his fucking novel, and we know it's *all* true."

"So, you're really—"

"Like father like son—in the novel, remember?"

She eyed me, intrigued.

"Listen," she said, "if it makes you feel any better, my publicist, his publicist, they used to get together for lunch at Lutèce and plot our bad-boy scenarios . . . feed the piranhas of the press."

"So, where did the fiction stop? Tell me, what's left of the real you?"

She sighed. Her lips quivered as she paused, testing her knee by moving forward and back, as if to summon her resolve to go on.

"Don't hate me, and don't hate Max. I had to watch him, and others, fall apart for years, and worse. Don't make me go there, okay? Consider yourself lucky."

I watched Laura's face lift to the blithe blue of the bay and her jaw tighten.

Listening to her pleading voice, I thought back to that wonderful fall afternoon and her words after the football game, as if she'd made a discovery: "But you like to . . . *move*." And, for a moment in the cooling breeze, I felt again the sense of speed and physically mastery that had been that last football game, lighter than air. Perhaps she caught something of this in my distant stare, for she seemed to blink back tears behind her Foster Grants as she circled the mosaics, inspecting the patterns of waves and leaping dolphins.

"Besides, I really liked your books; they're fascinating—really." She paused, as if surprised by a genuine rush of emotion. "It's just, well, fifth-century Athens wasn't exactly a bed of roses for women. No legal rights, no intellectual life, barely allowed out of the home, dying like flies in childbirth while their men went off to slaughter one another or bugger one another—sex slaves, breeders; I gather the big boys only fucked their women from behind, and up the ass, like one of the guys—huh."

She flung this at me like a prosecutor's battering of the star witness.

Not that I was about to give her the satisfaction of a defense—not of the life of women in fifth-century Athens. In my books, I had assiduously touched all the bases of feminist criticism and then some. I had made my case about how much better off women were in Athens than anywhere else in the ancient world at the time; they were mothers, and daughters, and lovers—the social glue. Athena was the patron goddess of the city. Full and rounded female characters were found in the works of Aeschylus and Euripides; their true voice came through to us, as it did in Homer. And, yes, they did have legal rights and could own property. And, yes, maybe dying in childbirth was an unpleasant prospect, but certainly not as bad as getting chewed up on the left flank of a hoplite phalanx, stomped to death, with your entrails spilling in the dirt.

"But who am I to talk?" she sighed. "I'd have turned out to be a Medea or Clytemnestra, not to be trusted with having children."

I eyed her uneasily, finding myself a little fed up with her fragile emotions. "Perhaps a Sappho, or Cassandra, forever warning us of our sad fate."

"Fate is such a guy thing." She took off her glasses as if to make a show of her sincerity, and as she did, in the bright sunlight, I saw the track marks on the inside of her left forearm, ancient scars whose memories still lingered. "Know what the great thing about you is? You know nothing about me—you see," and she slapped the elastic wrap on her knee. "I'm all washed up, a clean slate. My orthopedic surgeon said it's six months before I'm even supposed to take a light class again— if it heals. He advised retirement, like he did two years ago, like he did the year before that. I was strong, you know, a workhorse. I had the best turnout and extensions and I was quick, smooth and quick, Balanchine quick and *so* on the music. Every goddamn choreographer wanted to see if he could break me—push his latest gig, with my body to experiment on. *Oh Laura,*" she went on with an affected lisp, *"you're the only one who can do my new ballet—one extra performance, we know you can do it.* I lapped it up. I was a fool for punishment and to prove to my mother that Max hadn't fucked up my career. And then, one day, they start replacing you with seventeen-year-old bun heads who can stick their toe in their ear but haven't even located their clitoris." She grimaced and rubbed her knee. "So you try harder and take more risks and do more than your fair share, and you're still the greatest—until you break."

A ship's horn sounded off the bay. The day cruiser from Mykonos was making the turn into the harbor, where it would disgorge hundreds of tourists to inundate the ancient city. I suggested we escape the multitudes and make our way to the far side of the island, which was largely deserted of life, ancient or modern.

There we walked on the empty beaches, barely speaking, as if needful of the silence and the gentle lapping of the waves. She removed her shoes and walked on ahead of me in the shallow surf, as if wanting a certain distance to properly feel the stones against her battle-worn feet. She carried a bouquet of wildflowers she'd picked along the way—ruby red poppies and purple crocuses that still grow in abundance in the fall, like altar flowers among the ruins. And every now and then she'd retreat from the water's edge, kneel and plant a stalk amid the sand and shingle, little flags, as if to mark her journey, bread crumbs to find her way home. As a kid, I'd found similar floral flagpoles crowning miniature battlements in the sand of our swimming beach at Elysium.

I enjoyed seeing her like that, walking slowly, head bowed, her proud, bitchy voice stilled for a time, all the accumulated losses coming to bear upon her still-girlish figure. In truth, I felt a little stranded in her wake. She had come expecting a reckoning of sorts, to confront me with the letters and my past—our past. But standing there in the shallow surf, at a remove, she could have been any beautiful woman; she could have been seventeen again; she could have been the young princess Nausicaa come down to the beach to find the shipwrecked Odysseus.

How strange our idealizations of women and the multitudinous guises in which we cloak them: goddesses, fertility figures, images of chastity and justice, Madonna, muse, and model, icons of motherhood and sirens of libidinous release.

She, in turn, would have laughed off such abstractions: "Oh my God—enough of your scholarly obsessions, Dr. Alden—shall I call you Doc Alden—professor? Your head is not only clouded with the justly obscure but most of the time it's entirely beside the point." The physical world was the only reality that mattered to her, living, as she did, with the effects of gravity and aging muscles, and witness to the grip of an insidious disease on her colleagues, which all the expanse of blue skies and sea could not wash away. At that very hour, another old friend, a danseur noble, a man who had partnered her a hundred times at Lincoln Center—lifting her like a windblown leaf across that enormous stage, lay in his small apartment on West End Avenue, dying, scarred with lesions and ghastly melanoma, wheezing out his last breaths. She had said a final good-bye the morning of her flight to Athens.

How often did she chastise me: "What the fuck do you know, Alden?" She'd had enough of heated ideological cant when Max's radical friends dropped by at all hours, when she was so desperate for sleep. "Hasn't the century had enough of your bullshit that you can't at least save it for lunch and not three in the morning?" She had exhausted her body to dance on the world's gilded stages, cheered by balletomanes and a president whose son had first met her in ballet class. She hated herself for wanting the adulation and hated herself for hating it—what the fame game had cost her and Max.

But there was something else on her mind that I couldn't quite put my finger on. Years before, I had pretty much gotten over my obsession about Kim Philby; hers, recently, had taken on a life of its own.

Laura had stopped again ahead of me, Nikes dangling by the laces in her hand. Above us, drifting like moored kites, seagulls bobbed and dived in the brine-scented air. Then she bent and picked up a stone and began washing it in the water, a look of almost childlike wonder in her eyes as she slipped her dark glasses to her forehead to better inspect the prize. Her hair was loose and blowing, her eyes flashing with reflected light. And I thought, Yes, she's her mother's daughter: proud and brazen and devoted . . . and dangerous.

We were not exactly spring chickens: How much damage could we yet do?

"Of course . . . *if* you've got everything you need *here*." She said this as I drew a few steps closer, within earshot, but the remark was less directed to me than an explanation for herself. Mindful of what she'd only recently faced up to, I felt a wave of inchoate guilt for a world of shirked responsibilities.

It wasn't as if I didn't have a life. There were my books, my classes and students; my lectures got top ratings from the Princeton kids; my course on the Acropolis building programs had five stars in the informal course guide put out by *The Daily Princetonian*. Maybe my office hours were a little spotty, maybe I was a little hard to get in touch with, since I spent half the year in Athens and on digs, but that was what great scholarship required: sacrifice and focus. And yet the kids scurried to get into my classes. For many classics majors, I was even something of a celebrity; for budding archaeologists, a star performer in the field. Those professors who had known my father were dead or retired.

I winced inwardly, turning my eyes to the speeding flight of the white gulls.

She pursed her lips and began again to examine her stone. Her blue T-shirt billowed for moments like a spinnaker, a full-bellied fertility goddess, a momentary image of pregnancy, until luffing a second later to return the outline of her small-breasted figure. Then she came to me, her hands dripping, and handed me the stone she'd washed.

"For you," she said, and was about to move away again when she paused, a question shadowing her face. "Would you call them love letters? Do you think it was love? Or was it just incredible sex? Incredible because it was illegitimate: a nurse and her patient, a wife and her lover, a spy and her target. Fueled by guilt and a bad conscience. Is great sex *love*, or just love's way of giving birth to the future? Or can there be love without great sex?"

"Maybe sex was how they could lose themselves."

"God, I hope so."

She gave me an uneasy look and moved on down the beach.

I stood examining the gift. The smooth white quartz was shot through with tiny black striations, like an arcane script from some unspeakably remote age. I smiled and looked to where she stood on the beach, stopping again as if something out there on the blue sea had caught her eye. And again, her wonderfully innocent yet how canny questions put me in mind of Nausicaa, and of my father's prewar articles speculating on the connection between Minoan civilization and Homer's Bronze Age Greece.

That age of innocence, given up fifty years before on the eve of war . . . when he and Karel Hollar engaged in a conspiracy that would have, if discovered, ended his professional career.

My father had been obsessed with Homer's scene—an image that had haunted him from his school days as he worked on his translation of the *Odyssey*—when the castaway Odysseus, washed up on the shore of the Phaeacians, finds himself entranced with the noble beauty of the princess, she of the white arms, Nausicaa. What had intrigued my father was how this young woman could have so transfixed the world-weary, battle-hardened Odysseus that he'd been taken out of himself, forgone his usual strategy of canny aloofness with a plea from the heart, hoping this fair maiden might assist him in returning to his home and wife. And, too, how the impetuous Nausicaa had gently faced down this stranger, a terrifying brine-covered apparition out of the sea, as he must have seemed, and responded with a brave offer of hospitality, clearly ready to take Odysseus as a husband if he'd have her.

Little could my father have imagined how closely his life would follow art.

He speculated in his article that the literary style and somewhat archaic language, much less the vision of the land of the Phaeacians, untroubled by war and tumult, a culture of civility and generosity toward strangers, might have harked back to memories or stories of the golden age of Minoan Crete, or perhaps the early years of the still-undiscovered Pylos of Nestor, when the Greeks, before they were Greeks, had emigrated from the northern steppes: a Bronze Age warrior culture discovering the marvels of an island civilization in brilliant bloom. Was this the Atlantis of Plato, the true golden age that Homer projected upon the Phaeacians from the dark ages of post-Dorian Greece? So my father had speculated as late as 1939 in his last journal article before the war, on his last visit to Delos, when he and Karel Hollar had split their bets, my father financing a dig on Delos to explore for Mycenaean artifacts, perhaps a cache of Linear B tablets deposited in a sanctuary to Apollo, while Karel teamed up with the American Carl Andersen to find the palace of Nestor.

And I, too, was put in mind of the passage in Homer where Odysseus recalls a trip to Delos, describing a lovely palm tree growing near the altar of Apollo, to which he had compared Nausicaa, a sight that had stopped the grizzled Odysseus in his tracks: that something so beautiful could just appear from the hard earth.

With Laura standing down the beach from me, and my father's anguished letters still fresh in my mind, much less thoughts of him languishing in a Prague prison for over a year, I was overcome with emotion at all that had been lost. That if there was any truth to be found, maybe it might yet allow us to move on, that time's arrow was not just a one-way street to the grave, but a path to forgiveness, or at least forgetting.

Time: in the guise of a lithe not so young woman on the beach with windblown hair, reminding me not a little of Telemachus's lament: "Who, on his own, has ever really known who gave him life?"

And so, like Odysseus remembering his youthful infatuation, perhaps with a younger Penelope, or more likely like a young Telemachus agonizing about the fate of his father, I found myself transfixed by this image of a woman standing in the surf, remembering something of how I'd felt on that warm fall afternoon when I had run with the swiftest, when I had held a winsome girl in my arms under the apple trees and the future had rolled out before us like a silver carpet of moonlight.

When an iota of the desire in those letters might have saved us.

I continued to watch her as she pondered another stone in her fingers, only to realize that her downward gaze was directed to her reflection in the clear water, or perhaps had slipped deeper still, to her shadowed self on the sandy bottom, one image of a crystalline iridescence, the other darkly indistinct, like separate apparitions of a single soul locked in a struggle for her true identity. She dropped her stone, watching as the obliterating ripples did their work, and then, in what seemed an instinct for self-preservation, she reached into the sea, as if into the very heart of her troubled self, and scooped up a handful of sand and pebbles, letting the wet mass ooze between her searching fingers.

The sensation seemed to produce a petulant thrust of her jaw. "Skinny-dip, anyone?"

I had to laugh, because she'd gotten it out in perfect imitation of Max on that late afternoon at Elysium—when we'd still been just innocent enough to scorn our innocence.

She began by pulling off her T-shirt. It wasn't as if she was daring me, or making a display of immodesty; rather, she was reaching across time to something of what we once were and might again be. A kind of paralysis came through my limbs, my abdomen a sharp point of constricted muscle. I felt the panorama of blue sea and sky came to focus in her body, the way her weight rested on her good leg as she pulled the shirt over her head, how the raised hip bone began an upward rhythm through her torso, up and across the indent of her belly to the gentle swaying of her pointed breasts, ribs just visible below, further animated in the sudden inclination of her head and brilliant jet of hair whipped by the breeze as she bent to ease down her shorts. The white of her back glowed in the afternoon sun, every muscle and tendon and dentil molding along her backbone standing out, springing the long arch of her neck. Then she remembered the knee brace, bending again to force the elastic down, a band of redness between calf and thigh, like the mark of a slave's shackle. Her things stowed in a pile, she went dashing into the blue without a backward glance, a sensual line of white flesh, blond hair loose and flowing as she disappeared with a thin splash beneath the Aegean.

I undressed slowly, never taking my eyes off the area of disturbance where she had disappeared. Her head and shoulders rose far out. She had gone an amazing distance underwater. She swam with effortless, crisp strokes and I followed into the water. The sea was cool, thrilling as it reached my crotch. I squinted into the sunlight. She was moving outward, faster than before, ripples in her wake catching points of gold. She switched to the butterfly stroke, shoulders and back rising and plunging, dolphinlike. Such a pleasure to behold that my breath caught in my chest. I made a halfhearted attempt to swim closer, but she was too powerful. Had she drawn me purposely into her element to demonstrate her competitive prowess? That she could always swim circles around me? After treading water a while longer, I swam back into shore and lay down in the sand to dry off. I watched her swimming far out, a little worried, but not much, envying her freedom.

I must have fallen asleep, for I was shocked awake by a handful of cold water poured into my crotch. She was standing there stark naked, laughing at my reaction, then wagging an admonishing finger at me and warning that a sunburned cock would spoil me as a lover. Max redux—how many of his little quirks and mannerisms she had picked up. I was annoyed as she laughed again, my eyes slipping in and out of the shadow of her body where she stood over me. When she turned for her clothes down the beach, I couldn't help noticing the tampon string between her legs.

Of lingering youth and last chances.

$\mathcal{L}$

23 IN THE FOLLOWING DAYS, WHICH THEN stretched unexpectedly into months, we were like trapped spelunkers on a shared lifeline with a single instinct: to move toward light and air. Take it from an expert on the underground, those vast lands of the dead: What is found is often discovered in the most arbitrary way, and the artifacts of past lives find us as much as we find them, unvoiced and unavailing if we are not already halfway to the conversation. It was all about the prepared mind, I told my students, or was it the prepared heart? Artifacts were the easy part; they were what they were, and the truth they told was a fine thing, belied only in the interpretation. But lives are a different matter: tales told around campfires, in the flickering flames of lovers' whispers, in fevered correspondence, recounted in the brimming eyes of friend and foe, in the calibrated squint of the interrogation cell. For the religiously minded, such moments offer windows into the soul, which, like the turbid contents of twin alembics—poured one into the other and back again by the skilled alchemist—transform us, the perceiver and the perceived, as our memories mix and alter in the very act of telling, to become a hybrid . . . as the story of my father became part of our story.

In search of the true author of our lives.

A search that began in earnest on the deck of the Piraeus ferry, as I began seeing that post–World War II interlude of peace transformed into the Cold War, as Elliot got his hooks into my father, just as Elliot had arranged for a huge bouquet of roses to be presented at Laura's curtain call for a Kennedy Center production of Tudor's *Lilac Garden*, prelude to a nostalgic dinner together at the Terrace Restaurant atop the Kennedy Center. Three days later, on Laura's day off, Elliot invited her to dine at his splendid Virginia home overlooking Little Falls along the Potomac, a two-minute drive from CIA headquarters at Langley.

"For Christ's sake!" she exclaimed, fending me off as we walked the deck of the Piraeus ferry. "How else was I supposed to get the truth out of him? You sure didn't manage much."

After his disgraced career, his wife's cancer, his daughter's shaky marriages—"You raise them with all the love and advantages, but judgment in men I must've neglected"—Elliot soldiered on with his biography of Edward de Vere, bridge at the Metropolitan Club, golf at Chevy Chase, weekend luncheons at Paul Nitze's Tidewater farm. On the Winsted board, he had pushed through coeducation and gotten black enrollment up to 12 percent, and promoted the hiring of women and minority teachers. By the late eighties the school's reputation was again flying high and the Vietnam years were a bad memory. "Well, now it's a country club, but that's how the kids like it."

The spring evening was warm and inviting as they had dinner on the brick patio overlooking the river. Laura found herself drifting under the perfume of the frangipani blooms, the undertones of rushing water, the twitter of nesting cliff swallows, not to mention the spectacular view of the palisades on the far shore of the river, hovering in a band of mauve-green against the encroaching dusk, marred only by the constant scream of aircraft following the Potomac to National—later to be Reagan—Airport. She found herself strangely relaxed in Elliot's company, considering he'd slit Bobby's throat on the Winsted board in the summer of 1968 when they jettisoned Byron Folley.

I debated whether to tell her about my bit part in Bobby's firing.

"Positively princely" was how Laura described him to me, with his full head of blond hair slicked back. He wore a beautifully tailored iron gray suit—he still got all his suits from his Savile Row tailor—and a striped Winsted tie. "I thought, for a Williams, at the very least, I should display the colors," he told her.

The Philippine housekeeper "vanished" after preparing the cold salmon and artichoke salad. But Laura was hardly concerned about chaperones; she was intrigued and glad to hear about a fascinating life and disappointments not her own. The iced champagne helped, and later the '63 Vieux Château Certan, "a robust Pomerol with a hint of vanilla," dusty from the basement cave, wafted the past up from the glittering back of the moonlit river—a life of secrets, a life in the shadows, gambling with the fate of the Western world.

"My dear, you remind me of somebody, your gorgeous mother, of course . . . but no, not your mother."

I could just picture Elliot unabashedly staring into her eyes, as I, too, was taught to do in military intelligence.

"I never had the pleasure of seeing her dance but I danced with her at her wedding where I met my own lovely Margaret," Elliot told Laura.

Laura motioned with a spread palm toward the foaming wake of the ferry. "That was a little weird, how he'd married my mother's maid of honor. How he went on and on about what a wonderful spring day it had been at Colonel Fairburn's estate in Sussex—as if it were yesterday, even though he knew it was all a big charade. Of course, he didn't tell me he'd been after my mother—after Bobby shot himself and her breakdown—trying to get the truth out of her."

"And which truth was that, pray tell?"

"About why your father walked through Checkpoint Charlie and disappeared into the arms of the Soviets. And other stuff . . ."

"So, you were both on the same page, so to speak."

Laura was a pro's pro around older sophisticated men. She had dined out with choreographers Ashton and Tudor, enduring their biting British wit and caustic remarks. Balanchine had flirted with her in class and felt her up; he taught her many extraordinary things about wine and food—"four wives, and it's like they didn't exist." Elliot was of a different order: powerful, athletic, magnetic, artistic in his own way, and dedicated to old-time virtues and courtesies. Above all, he was loyal to the truth as he saw it: whether Edward de Vere or my father. And he loved women. He'd loved his wife. He loved his daughters.

"*Of course*, he came on to me—thank God. A real man."

I don't think she cared about being seduced; she cared about finding out about her mother's lover. And she saw in Elliot much of what she suspected Suzanne must have loved in my father—"or choked on."

"There was a primal faith in him, a patriotism, I suppose, which I found riveting—me, who cared squat about all that stuff. I knew I was supposed to hate everything he stood for, but I wanted to understand it, from the *inside*."

By the time the dessert of Devonshire cream and fresh-picked strawberries from an old friend's—and an apex Cold Warrior's—Tidewater farm arrived, their conversation gravitated to politics, to the first economic reforms that Gorbachev had introduced into the Soviet system, which Elliot dismissed as cosmetic and not likely to make an appreciable difference unless the whole house of cards was kicked in. He had been showing her one of his prized blue-and-white ginger jars, Jiajing, from the sixteenth century, displaying the Chinese characters hallmarked on the base—"*Beautiful vessel for the rich and honorable*," in translation.

"Not so rich," he said laughing, "but still honorable."

She began pressing him on what had gotten him into a life of secrets.

Leaning on the railing as the bare-ribbed islands slipped by, I could imagine Elliot's predatory eyes as he told her about Romania in '45. "Did he tell you how he watched in horror as Stalin's henchmen loaded up boxcars of terrified Romanians at the end of the war, shipped off for execution or to disappear into the vast gulag?" I asked Laura.

"How did you know about that?"

"We were at a restaurant in Saigon, over the curried shrimp. Did he tell you how in his official capacity as an OSS officer he'd literally pulled Romanian friends out of the clutches of the NKVD police at the Bucharest train station?"

"Are you making fun of him?"

"I'm marveling."

"When he told me things like that, his eyes blazed. It sent a chill through me—the conviction of the man. Imagine, seeing terrible things like that."

I had to smile: If she only knew the half of it. I pictured Elliot snowing her with tales of derring-do, with just a dash of tradecraft details to leaven the mix, stroking the porcelain in his hand as he scolded himself for bringing up such horrors.

Laura had been used to getting her way with men, exchanging fame and favors, but she wasn't quite sure what she had to offer Elliot. So she snuggled in and began mooning on about her parents' rotten life and her disappointed stage mother, whose star-crossed ballet career had been ended by the war. When she found this going nowhere, she flipped all her cards. She admitted to Elliot her knowledge about Suzanne's affair with my father, and about the letters.

The affair was old hat. "So," he said—his face had hardened, as if he could barely breathe—"you've got their letters, John's letters—and hers? Somewhere safe, I hope?"

"With my lawyers. And I made copies."

"How long were they writing?"

"Almost ten years."

Elliot smiled, but she caught the panic in his voice. "I feel so much better, my dear—that you've finally come clean. Perhaps we can trust each other now."

She realized that he had known all along of her ulterior motive—his ulterior motive, that this sort of thing was his stock-in-trade. He put the ginger jar on the table between them and tapped it with his nail until it produced a sweet, clear ring. He raised a finger and smiled again.

"You see, it was the affair that brought John back into his nation's service after the war."

I felt Laura's hand on my arm and pictured Elliot's judicious nod, his angular nose rising and falling as he worked the conversation to the critical subject. "Bullshit!" I exclaimed. "It's only his career and legacy he's worried about."

"Young lady, you don't happen to know about Edward de Vere, the seventeenth earl of Oxford, do you?" he continued. "He is our unknown author, the man behind the Shakespeare plays. As your mother's lover—or is it lovers?—was behind so much that transpired in those difficult times: a man elusive, troubled by women, a most reluctant suitor of the world's troubles but bound to the essential imperative of his illustrious upbringing, his very nature, what became the driving force behind our policy of containment."

"Unknown author?" she asked, thinking she'd had too much to drink, since she'd heard that name from Max's lips more times than she cared to remember.

"Lost to history and fortune's fickle hand."

Elliot was no fool. He was sharp as ever, but he also understood how the CIA's legacy was under threat. The Church Senate committee hearings had stomped on everything they had stood for. Within years, the Freedom of Information Act would start shedding light on his old CIA files, along with the most closely held secrets, the unending fuckups of Allen Dulles's early years that tumbled out in the decade after the fall of the Berlin Wall.

Two months later, at the American embassy in Prague, my suspicions were confirmed: If my father went down—if Suzanne or Bobby had recruited him—Elliot's legacy got flushed with them. And something else preyed on his mind that night overlooking the Potomac.

"No one in your generation can begin to understand how dark things looked to us," Elliot told Laura, "how near a thing it was in 1947 and 1948. Poland was gone to the Communists, Czechoslovakia was going, and Britain was financially exhausted and in retreat from the Greek Civil War; the Greek Communists were on the verge of triumph. The April 1948 elections in Italy had been a near thing; the U.S. Sixth Fleet had been stationed in Naples in case the Communists won. And this was before China went Red, before Korea, before the Soviets got the bomb—one crippling body blow after another. We were going under, and we needed experienced men, good men, honorable men for dishonorable work. And we needed to buy time for the free-world democracies to get back on their feet."

Elliot took her hand in his.

"And the gist of the letters?" he asked.

"Plenty of sex and even more contempt for each other."

"Lovely . . . and the last postdate?"

"A postcard from East Germany."

Laura stared into his eyes from behind her raised wineglass. She knew she had him.

"Dated when?"

"January 1954. Some kind of museum, I think, glass display cases in a museum."

"A message?"

"Some kind of poetry about a voyage and betrothal."

"Betrothal . . . but no names, for instance, Kim Philby, or perhaps one Anthony Blunt—were they mentioned?"

She'd laughed to cover her fear, because she knew by then who Philby was: Philby had certainly figured in the letters, but Anthony Blunt had not."

"Anthony?"

"Or a Melinda, perhaps? Or a Burgess, Guy Burgess?"

"Wrong millennium, I'm afraid. There was a Lakedanos and a Philo-wona, prince and princess—weird stuff."

"Could it have been some kind of code that your mother might have passed on . . . to others?"

I had to laugh.

"What he wanted to get out of you was whether my father knew about Anthony Blunt from Bobbie or Susan back in 1954, or worse, years before—the key to Philby and the whole Cambridge spy ring."

She looked at me trembling, or maybe it was just the sea breeze in her hair.

"Or"—she nodded to herself—"if he knew Philby was the MI6-CIA mole."

"The secret of the century."

"If he did, if he didn't turn over the names to the CIA—"

"Or, the FBI, he would have been complicit—or worse—in maintaining the cover of a bunch of dangerous traitors."

"And Melinda? She comes up a lot in the letters."

"Donald Maclean's wife, who lived in New York with their children. Maclean visited her on weekends from Washington, to give her top secret materials for her Soviet handlers—including crucial documents on the development of the atomic bomb."

"Shit. She was a friend of my mother's. My mother visited her in New York when she went down from Boston to meet your father at the Carlyle."

I took her arm and steadied her.

"So, tell me you didn't have to sleep with him."

"I traded him information."

"What, the names, Philby and Melinda—Donald Maclean?"

"And the message on the postcard."

"I thought you said he hadn't seen it—that you didn't let him see it?"

"I copied out the inscription and sent it to him."

"Like mother like daughter."

"Fuck you . . ."

"Go on about Elliot. He must have been beside himself."

"For someone out of touch, you seem pretty on top of all this."

"When Philby died in Moscow last year, it was all over the papers again."

"They're all dead—dead and gone."

"Except your mother, the sole survivor of that crew. Was it true, what my father accused her of in the letters: fucking Kim Philby?"

"Let's talk about something else? I'm rather enjoying the view."

"After his first tour of Greece with the OSS," Elliot told Laura, as they picked over the backstory on my father, "after he got fixed up, he was not the same man. He could have honorably returned stateside, but instead he chose to slog it out in France and Germany interrogating those filthy bastards. I figured Suzanne had her claws in him. When he returned to Princeton early in 1946, when I returned to Wall Street, I thought we were done." Elliot sipped his wine and nodded. "Stalin had other plans. . . .

"John was number one on my list, from our first director, Beetle Smith, by way of Bill Donovan. Greece was a critical priority. Greece was tottering under a Communist insurgency in the north. One of the top republican generals, nicknamed 'Nestor,' a guy John had worked with in the Resistance, asked for John personally as part of the American team when we took over from the Brits. Everything hinged on Greece. If Stalin intervened, if Tito acquiesced, it could go against the West along with the whole eastern Mediterranean.

"John point-blank refused. It got to the point where he just hung up on me when I rang his office phone at Princeton."

Elliot finally threw in the towel, tried to put it out of his mind that his reluctant quarterback didn't want to play on the team anymore. Then something caught his eye when he was processing security checks for a bunch of his new recruits. In the secret FBI testimony of Soviet agents Elizabeth Bentley and Whittaker Chambers, Bobby Williams was fingered as a Soviet courier, confirmed by army intelligence intercepts of Soviet cable traffic, Venona. Before the war, after his return from Cambridge and between gigs as a concert pianist, Bobby had been passing U.S. government secrets, much along the lines performed by Whittaker Chambers; he photographed and transmitted official papers from the likes of Alger Hiss and other Washington spies working in State and Treasury. Nevertheless Bobby chaffed at being a mere courier; he desperately wanted to gain access to secrets himself, but all his attempts to get into government failed. In 1942, Bobby joined the U.S. Army Air Corps as a bombardier. Soviet cable intercepts showed he had passed on details of the Norden bombsight from Maxwell Field, near Montgomery, Alabama. When this information was cross-referenced with British counterintelligence, to see if Bobby continued passing information once he was posted to England, Bobby's marriage to Suzanne, née Brierly-Henderson, stage name Suzanne Portman, immediately drew scrutiny. Suzanne was suspected by British M15 of conveying information before the war for her Soviet handlers, although once the Soviets were allies and she was working in a military hospital, she was largely ignored.

"It was like a load of buckshot in the balls," Elliot said.

Getting off at Princeton Junction and taking the jitney to the campus station, Elliot pondered whether he should tell John anything—just let it go, let the chips fall where they may. He wasn't even sure if John was still seeing anything of Suzanne. She'd left England in 1946 and moved to Boston with Bobby. "A decorated and wounded veteran—enough to turn your stomach." The idyllic campus of collegiate Gothic buildings and tall stately elms draped in spring foliage—"so safe, so charmingly safe"—only reinforced Elliot's sense that his best friend from school days, "best quarterback I ever played for, including Yale, who as a kid our senior year got me all steamed up to save the world," was out of the game and out for good.

"John looked like his old self—not the hangdog face I remembered around Suzanne's splendid digs on Cadogan Square. He'd gained weight, his face had filled out, and he was beginning to get around without a cane. Up to his elbows in his office with stacks of journals and bits of broken pots and reams of photos, as if he were planning to entomb himself for the rest of eternity. I picked up a photograph of some kind of clay tablet with crude characters scratched into it and couldn't make head nor tails of it.

"It's a Linear B tablet excavated from the palace at Pylos in 1939, in the National Archaeological Museum in Athens," my father told him. "We've been trying to decipher the language since the early part of the century, when Sir Arthur Evans discovered similar tablets at Knossos. So far, no go—nobody can crack it."

Elliot had smiled when he handed the photograph back; deciphering, breaking codes was very much on his mind. He suggested a walk by Lake Carnegie.

Elliot had appointments with half the crew team later that afternoon; three seniors would join the CIA after graduation. For an hour or so, they waxed nostalgic about football and rowing days at Winsted. Then Elliot slipped in hints about all the bad news from Europe, how Greece was teetering in the civil war, how close it had been with the Italian elections, when their favorite classics teacher, Virgil Dabney, still working with the Monuments Men, had been recruited by the fledgling CIA to carry suitcases of cash to pay off politicians and union leaders, and so save Italy for the West. "Virgil and ninnykins Angleton did a fine job."

My father was polite, attentive, concerned, especially with the bad news out of Greece, but he shook his head at any thoughts of reenlisting in the fight.

"But what pissed me off . . . when he began to complain to me about recruiting the Princeton oarsmen: 'the wonderful kids,' he called them as we stood and watched practice. And they were wonderful, and plenty of wonderful Yale kids had come on board, as well. Then he stopped me right there on the path and looked at me with that glittering intense stare and stabled a finger in my chest. Didn't I have something better to do than put those kids in harm's way? That got my goat. Minutes later, I was spilling top secret beans. I told him about the FBI files on Chambers and Bentley and the interception and decipherment of Soviet cable traffic—could have gone to prison for that. I told him the whole government had been infiltrated with Soviet spies, State, Treasury, the White House—crawling with informants. He didn't believe me; he just downright dismissed it. That's when I just let it out; I told him about Bobby . . . and Suzanne. I told him to come down to my office in Washington and I'd show him the file. 'It will turn your stomach,' I said. You might have thought I'd put a gun to his head and pulled the trigger. It was that kind of reaction. I was picking up the pieces for the next hour.

"John, think about it. You can go back to Greece, sniff around the ruins—they need you."

A week later, my father walked into Elliot's office on the Mall in Washington.

"You could have blown me over with a feather; he didn't even want to see the damn file on the little shit and his bewitching wife. He became the rock, the mainstay as we built the organization during those terrible years of Korea, when Stalin got the bomb, when it was just one horror story after another."

Princeton, April 6, 1948

Dearest Suzanne,

Will you be at Elysium this weekend? It is imperative that I see you.

I just had a very disheartening meeting with Elliot Goddard. He seems to know about us, around the edges in his bluff, hinting way. Did you ever blab anything to Margaret about us? Things his wife might have passed on to Elliot? Elliot got all hot and bothered about Soviet spies in the U.S. government, and he had some pretty shocking things to say about our true-blue Bobby. Not that I would put anything past the little shit, but I did think he'd turned a corner when he joined the Army Air Corps.

Of course, Elliot is back in government—bored by Wall Street—and recruiting young men here and elsewhere for a new intelligence service. I don't know all the details about his allegations but will find out more soon. The atmosphere in Washington is poisonous; desperate accusations fly right and left. We must be very careful. Make sure to burn this letter when you're done—and not a word to anyone.

I'm afraid Mother is already at Elsinore for spring cleaning, which complicates things, as usual. I think she suspects about us; I can hear it in her disapproving voice, her hard scrutiny—ever keeper of the votive flame. Summer will be awkward.

Leave me a message at the white pine in the meadow about when we can meet.

Conspirators in our own lives—that's what we've become! We talk about love; we tell each other how much we love, but is it the act of love that we love? Your body is never out of my mind. I can't handle a piece of sculpture or pottery in the university museum without getting hard for you. Isn't that repugnant? You laugh, you cackle, but I'll have you cunt deep and all.

Friday night, late—such a long drive from Princeton.

I just remembered I promised Mother that I will oversee the cleaning of the Tiffany glass windows in the living room, a delicate, time-consuming job. She always lets me know how my father and grandfather took pride in the job. There is something in that, I suppose: that art survives the disasters of the moment—take it from an aging digger.

I think about you every minute. I count the seconds.

Love, John

Less than two years after his Princeton meeting with Elliot, after over a year in which he'd been Athens station chief, my father was playing golf on weekends at the Chevy Chase Club in Washington with the admiral's daughter who would become my mother. In the early fifties, a drive from Washington to the Berkshires for a weekend was an arduous ordeal, especially for a man in the days before automatic drive with a bad left leg, which still gave him pain. A gentle stroll on the links became his preferred therapy. Shortly thereafter, he was married to my mother in the National Cathedral, with Elliot Goddard serving as best man and Colonel Fairburn an usher.

He, too, had seemingly turned a corner, but there remained Elysium, and Suzanne—and then the bombshell of Kim Philby.

When we spoke at the embassy in Prague two months later, even with the Berlin Wall down, Elliot still had very mixed feelings about that Princeton meeting: spilling the beans about the Soviet cable intercepts to a man in bed with a Soviet spy had been about the stupidest thing he'd ever done. And it didn't help that he had a bad conscience. Three of the seniors in the eight-man shell they watched that day became recruits. One of those seniors would die four years later in the shoot-down of a spy mission over Communist China. Elliot had loved that boy like the son he never had, felt personally responsible, and never got over it. He mentioned this to Laura and later to me. He remembered that afternoon at Princeton in the spring sunshine, the flash of oars on the lake, his boy as handsome as they come, from a fine old Farmington family—it brought tears to his eyes. He never forgot those flashing oars and the handsome sweating face as the boy stood eagerly on the boathouse landing to hear about how he might help his country in the fight against communism.

Elliot was surprised and not a little terrified when my father showed up in Washington a week later. "John was smoking a mile a minute, walking around my office like a caged animal." Elliot figured that my father had broken it off with Suzanne. But he wasn't sure. Nor was he absolutely sure that John hadn't known all along about Bobby and Suzanne . . . or worse. Under normal circumstances, my father would never have been allowed to join the fledgling CIA; his ties, his prox-imity to known Soviet agents would have ruled it out. So Elliot swept it under the rug.

"What are they going to do about Bobby and Suzanne?" my father had asked with some urgency.

"During his training at Maxwell Field, Bobby was passing infor-mation to Soviet handlers, technical specifications, blueprints of the Norden bombsight, assessments of accuracy. Presumably he kept at it in London during '44, still milking us at parties for information. Jesus Christ, John, he was milking us at his wedding and she was passing the stuff on."

Elliot recalled my father's face compacted like a fist at this point in their conversation.

"What's going to happen?"

"Probably nothing. That's the thing: the lack of evidence, Bobby's word against that of others. Without documents in his—or her—pos-session, FBI surveillance of transactions, witnesses, nothing will hold up in court. Unless these bastards get caught red-handed with pilfered documents, or caught lying—then you prosecute for perjury. Otherwise, they deny everything or just plead the Fifth. The problem is, the FBI can't introduce the Soviet cable traffic into evidence; it's too sensitive. And the worst of it is, there are still hundreds of undetected spies out there. It'll take decades to clean them out."

"And Bobby's a hero."

"A wounded hero of the air battle over Germany."

"Maybe better to keep it that way."

Elliot smiled and placed a comradely hand on his old quarterback's shoulder.

"Just make fucking sure those two stay tucked away in the woods: out of sight, out of mind. The Republicans are accusing the Democrats of being lax on security—and worse, and the Democrats are going to have to prove their bona fides by being tougher than the Spanish Inquisition on a bad day. And we'll get caught in the middle. Just you watch: The politics will kill us."

In the ambassador's office in Prague, Elliot leaned into my face.

"I gave John the chance he needed, to get away from Suzanne and temptation. I did him a favor and he jumped at it. And when he came home, he married your mother."

Elliot winced inwardly and sighed.

"I cleaned up John's file. I even expunged things about his dealings with the Communist Resistance in Greece during the war. I gave him a clean bill of health. I got him back on the team, where we needed him, and how. And he was brilliant, the best of the best, until he betrayed us—betrayed me. I don't know if Philby got to him; I don't know if it was loyalty to Suzanne or if she had him by the balls or what, but doing what he did in '53 was a disaster beyond comprehension. If he'd made a clean breast of his love affair with Suzanne to the FBI, an unwitting lover, they might have swept it under the rug. The worse of it was still having Philby in circulation for another ten years, only to have the spineless Brits let him escape to Moscow. And I think they did it on fucking purpose, so they wouldn't have to put him on trial and air their dirty, incompetent laundry in public. Just like they tried to cover up Anthony Blunt's role for over fifteen years. Thank God for Margaret Thatcher—now there's a woman for you."

That's when I confronted Elliot about the trade of Anthony Blunt for Bobby Williams's place on the Winsted board.

But I get ahead of myself. . . .

To his credit, my father was instrumental in one of the few successes of the early Cold War era: the defeat of the Communists in the Greek Civil War. He spent over a year in Athens in 1948 and 1949 and then returned to Washington, where he ran the Southern Europe division of the CIA, focusing on Greece, Albania, Yugoslavia, and the Balkans—when he worked hand in glove with his British counterpart, Kim Philby. Elliot had been posted to Berlin in 1950 as station chief, the front line of the Cold War against the Soviets.

In 1953, there was an outbreak of rioting by East German workers; the riots threatened to become widespread, and there was the possibility the GDR government might be overthrown. Policy makers in Washington were tempted to provide moral and even armed support to the union protestors. Agency hawks led by Allen Dulles and Frank Wisner thought this might be the long-anticipated chance for the CIA to roll back the Iron Curtain. For the recently elected Eisenhower and his administration, the situation in East Germany was a potential opportunity to prove its anti-Communist credentials. Pressure from Secretary of State John Foster Dulles on his brother, Allen, then the new director of the CIA, had prompted the call from Washington that caused my father to leave Elysium on a fall morning in the fall of 1953. Allen Dulles wanted his fellow Princetonian for consultations. My father knew Germany; he spoke the language perfectly, he had interrogated hundreds of German prisoners in the last days of the war, and many of them were Communists. Now many of those same German Communists were in power in East Germany. After a week going over the situation with Dulles and Wisner, and monitoring all the cable traffic from Berlin, my father decided, "suddenly, very suddenly—not a moment's notice," according to Elliot—to fly to Berlin so as to be closer to developments on the ground.

"He arrived at the Berlin office looking like he hadn't slept for days; he was very overwrought. The pressure from the White House for some real results was enormous. John was all business, determined but at wit's end with Allen, 'That preposterous old fart, even if he did go to Princeton,' John muttered. There was something fragile about his face and eyes that I hadn't seen in him since the last year of the war. I'd catch him staring out the window with a glassy-eyed look, as if Berlin was about the last place he wanted to be. The next moment, he was demanding to see everything we had on the rioting, every scrap of intelligence. He wanted to debrief some of our operatives personally, and he spent hours and hours with them."

"'They're licking their chops in Washington,' he told me. 'They want to break it open. All Allen and Frank Wisner talk about is getting arms to the rioters.'

"I told them, as I've told you," Elliot said to John, "we have no way of doing that, certainly no way of delivering weapons without the Soviets knowing the score. Besides, we both know what it would mean . . . in their backyard."

"John looked at me and closed his eyes. 'World War Three.'"

"Anything useful out of the agents? I asked him."

"'I don't believe any of them. They're liars, cheats, opportunists, or double agents—take your pick. I think you have to assume every network you're running has been compromised.'"

"I was incredulous. 'That bad?'"

"'Elliot, what the hell have your boys been doing here all this time?'"

"'Clearly nothing worth squat.'"

"'We're deaf, dumb, and blind—it's worse than Korea. How can the Dulles boys want us to overthrow a government when we don't even know what's coming at us?'"

"I remember your father gesturing to the bomb-damaged blocks outside the window of our offices, toward the bleak urban landscape of the East sector. He was in a black mood, so was I. And he'd spent summers in Germany when we were kids, when I was sailing on Buzzards Bay and Bar Harbor. He *knew* these people. We were all pretty rattled by what we found ourselves up against. We couldn't find a chink in the armor anywhere."

That was the last time Elliot saw my father. He didn't show at the office the next day, nor the next. His telephone in the staff apartment went unanswered. They checked out the apartment and found the bed neatly made, as if it hadn't been slept in for some time. Most of his things were still in the room, including his diplomatic passport. "That set off more alarms, because you couldn't go anywhere in the city in those days without your passport. Unless he'd used his regular passport. We put out an all-points alert. We were concerned about a possible kidnapping, something that happened a lot, on both sides. Then we got a report from Checkpoint Charlie about a man who had passed through alone two days before; he wore a beautifully tailored gray pinstripe suit—impeccably dressed, which was why the guard remembered him so well—and carried a large very expensive black leather attaché case. He handed the guard a brand-new American passport in his own name, not the diplomatic passport one would use on official business. We showed the guard a photograph of John and got a positive identification. He had simply walked across like the hundreds of others who passed through every day to or from work. Oh, and the guard said he was using a silver-handled cane, and limped. That's what really got me worried: John hadn't used a cane in years and he walked just fine, at least for eighteen holes.

"It was your worst nightmare, a security catastrophe on a par with Philby. He was the man who knew everything, soup to nuts. He'd just spent a week with our most sensitive files. With the Dulles brothers— with Ike! It froze every ongoing operation, forget about arms deliveries. We were in a state of complete paralysis. We contacted his family, all his colleagues and acquaintances—nothing. We had to sit on our hands and wait it out. I did not share any doubts I might have had—I figured I owed John that much. Hell, I spent my adolescence passing that portrait of his grandfather in the library every goddamn day—that's what the fight was all about. Winsted and the Aldens were our gold standard. I was never so depressed in my life.

"You have to understand, Maclean and Burgess had disappeared two years before, in 1951. We assumed they had defected to Moscow, but we didn't know for sure; the Soviets weren't tipping their hand yet. And that fucking Philby was still on the loose, playing cat and mouse with the press and MI5 and MI6, who would actually hire him again later and post him to Beirut. We wondered, Have we got a Maclean and Burgess defection on our hands—was he part of it? Angleton knew how much John had worked with Philby, and he knew about Bobby and Suzanne, and he knew I knew something about John's affair with Suzanne. So I was caught in the middle, holding the bag of shit."

In the American ambassador's office in Prague, Elliot looked at our questioning faces and snorted. "That's right, boys and girls, I kept my mouth shut; I risked everything—not the least my reputation and career."

In early 1954, the United States was contacted by the Soviets about the capture of a top CIA agent. The Soviets knew exactly who they had and what he was worth.

"Thank God, I thought. I was never so relieved as at that news. Of course, they were in no hurry to make an exchange or to offer much in the way of details. But at least he wasn't a traitor! Maybe he'd just snapped, who knows. But as long as they had John and potentially

everything he knew, our hands were tied. The negotiations went on forever. They claimed he'd been arrested with a concealed pistol and had
been part of a plot to assassinate a high GDR government official. That
seemed pure poppycock. Then, a year later, right before his scheduled
exchange for three Soviet agents, the Soviets informed us that John had
died of a sudden heart attack. They seemed as baffled and disappointed
as we were. If he'd really been a double agent, as many in the Agency
speculated, it is hard to believe they would have killed him. Like
Maclean and Burgess and Kim Philby, our ever so loyal and infinitely
cynical Cambridge cousins, they'd have given him a medal and a pension and he'd have lived out his days as a Moscow celebrity. But it was
convenient certainly, just returning his body and personal effects. That
way, we never knew how much information they got out of him, or
what he gave them. There were no signs of torture but he'd clearly lost
weight. Solitary confinement, relentless interrogation, threats, constant
anxiety, depression . . . maybe it went too far and his heart just gave
out. Pathology showed nothing in the way of drugs or poison. We were
days away from executing the exchange—three top spies for him—I
just can't understand. Whatever the case, the damage was deep and
widespread. We just never knew, and not knowing is like bluffing with
bad cards, and worse: hole cards your opponents have seen.

"In '57 or '58, after the Hungarian uprising, we got a couple of defectors, a Soviet general and a Czech secret police official. That's when we
heard that John had been held in Pankrác Prison in Prague for most
of 1954. The Soviets told us he'd been captured in East Germany; the
Czech defector told us the American spy had been captured on the
Czechoslovakian border with Hungary. We knew heads had rolled in
the GDR, and as the Soviet general put it, after that close call with
the East Germans, Moscow was taking no chances with the fucking
Hungarians."

So Laura had given Elliot a copy of the inscription on the back of the
postcard, which he spent months mulling over, to no avail. With the
postmark of January 1954, Elliot got one critical clue: My father had
been on the lam in East Germany for almost three months. If the card
wasn't a hoax, that is. Laura promised to hand over the letters once
she'd had a chance to share them with me—if I agreed.

Then history played a trump card. Two months later in Prague, with
the Berlin Wall down and the Velvet Revolution filling the streets of

Prague, Elliot would get his chance to read the letters. By which point, we had the missing piece of Karel Hollar's role in this pitiful charade. With Suzanne and Charles Fairburn and the others to provide supporting roles come Christmas.

All in all, I had to hand it to Laura: I thought she got the better part of the trade with Elliot, but nothing of the answer that really mattered to her.

And like her scheming mother, she'd carefully withheld the critical documents in the horde her mother had hidden in the colonel's home, damning documents, secret documents that would have stood up in court and convicted a coven of KGB spies. From Elliot, from me, until she was sure of what she needed to know.

24

TOPICS IN CLASSICAL ARCHAEOLOGY AND Literature was the course I'd taught at Princeton the previous spring. A bright-eyed student had asked, "But why Telemachus—what does he matter to the story of Odysseus's return? And why should Odysseus's son risk a journey to Pylos and Sparta and abandon his mother, the hard-pressed Penelope, as if information about his father's fate would necessarily await him in those places, much less make a difference to the outcome? What is the plot function?" (Needless to say, the kid was a budding screenwriter.) I explained to my brilliant students that without certainty as to his father's fate, Telemachus was stuck in uncertain limbo and in danger of losing his patrimony. The wise Athena had encouraged his journey to Nestor's Pylos to gather rumors of his father's return from Troy as a way of proving to himself that his father's intrepid spirit coursed through his own veins, a man of *both* words and deeds.

Just as Vlada had said to me on the night we broke into Fort Devens and almost got ourselves arrested and kicked out—or killed! While the subject of Laura's paternity was the third rail we dared not touch: the last trump card Suzanne held defiantly to her steamy breast.

After docking in Piraeus, where my Land Rover was garaged, Laura and I headed south into the Peloponnese, with quick stops at Mycenae and Tiryns, getting as far as the picturesque fishing town of Nafplio on our way to Pylos, where the vivid tales of an old Resistance fighter, Neokosmos Grigoriadis, aka Nestor, awaited us on the following day. For some reason, I had found our short tour of Mycenae oppressing, something about the massive walls, cyclopean, according to ancient

512

sources, which put me unaccountably on edge, even after the many times I'd led my students through the ruins. Once I had looked on Bronze Age Mycenae as a backwater to my more exalted scholarship on classical Athens. Now those massive battlements, from which Agamemnon had sallied forth to a ruinous war against Troy, struck me as depressing evidence of a dynamic martial culture unable, at the end, to withstand the inroads of a relentless enemy, or enemies. If such a citadel with all its natural defenses could be so overwhelmed by the mysterious forces arrayed against it—still a riddle to this day—what hope for any of us? Somehow, Laura's presence at my side, her constant probing, much less my father's letters, only heightened my foreboding, as if those walls heralded yet another invisible nemesis lying in wait—stones best left unturned. Nor did the hubbub of Nafplio exactly soothe my nerves, a tourist trap, just another overnight stop for blue-and-white Argos buses on their way to and from Mycenae and points south. My back was a mess after our crawl through the smog-choked outer suburbs of Athens, and the chance of a decent hotel room, a hot bath, and good mattress was not to be dismissed. I parked the Land Rover and she lingered on the waterfront while I went in search of a room.

"Don't bother with separate rooms—I'm a big girl now—just make sure there's a good-size tub and plenty of hot water."

After registering, I went back to the quay and the Land Rover to get our bags. I spotted her in a phone booth next to a bar. She was talking, listening intently, and when she hung up, it was with a stricken look on her face. She walked slowly out onto a dock off the quay. When I went to her and touched her shoulder, she didn't move a muscle.

"I'll never hear his voice again."

She had checked in with her friend and onetime dance partner long-distance. They'd danced at the Met and Covent Garden together. She told me how sick he'd sounded and how he didn't want to talk about it. Instead, he asked her to tell him about where she was, to describe the picturesque fishing town, the surrounding hills and walls, the blue of the bay and the color of the boats, and the smells. "Calamari—fried in olive oil," she'd told him. She'd heard him sigh. "Not that, dear, I'll be sick to my stomach." And then he'd hung up. She hoped her call had helped.

"He says he likes to travel in his mind."

The embayed blue was broken only by the moored fishing skiffs of beige and green and rusty red, nodding on the crescent of the inner harbor. It was late afternoon, the sun low to the surrounding hills, the remainder of the day held in peaceful suspension before the night-life of the harbor would send it on its way. The many restaurants and tavernas along the waterfront were gearing up for a night of music and dance to entertain the tourists. Creak of a rope on a rusty davit, and nearby, the crank of a blue awning being rolled up outside a quay-side restaurant, a waiter setting the tables, a scent of sea and garlic and roasting lamb.

How to imagine AIDS in such a world?

With all the passionate voices surging in my head, I wondered if it might be time for me to play the second-chance lover. Even with a bum back, I was considerably younger than Elliot Goddard, the great love of Laura's life was dead, and another colleague was dying at that very moment. So maybe I would get my chance simply by outlasting all my rivals.

Then she reached for my hand with the instinct of one just awakened from a dream.

"So, is our room all set?"

"What the doctor ordered."

"A big tub, right? The knee needs lots of soaking."

"Huge tub, and I made sure there was plenty of hot water."

"Thanks. Thanks for everything."

"For what?"

"For putting up with me."

"I never stopped wanting to put up with you."

"You were always so . . . gallant."

Her shoulders sagged as she looked out on the jagged hilltops behind the town of whitewashed buildings, and the jostling waves of red-tiled roofs corralled by the long crenellated walls of the old Venetian fortress. The blushing pink of the cloudless sky silhouetted the walls where they peeked above the hill crest. She took my hand and led me back to the hotel. I noticed that her wrist, where she'd wrapped the strap of her bag, was banded with red welts.

The room was small, sparsely furnished, two beds side by side facing French doors and a balcony overlooking the bay. On a side wall hung a simple cross. We went and lay on our beds, resting, perhaps contemplating the first moments of new intimacy. Actually, my back was hurting so much that I could barely think of anything else. I went into the bathroom and downed a double dose of Demerol, noticing her toilet kit packed with prescription bottles, a small pack of Tampax discreetly tucked behind the toilet. The mattress was firm and I warmed to the chance of a good night's sleep as the medication did its thing. From the restaurant below came the sound of laughter and cutlery being set out; on the bay, the chug of diesel motors, fishing boats returning. Above us, the white stucco ceiling shimmered with reflected light off the water. Pale, pale blue dusted with lilac . . . out of which her voice and other voices floated up to me.

"Does your back bother you a lot?"

"Good days, bad days; damp weather is the worst. That and driving for *more* than an hour."

"Remind me to give you a massage. I'm something of an expert."

"Don't worry about me. A little rest along with some wine and I'll be as good as new."

That was an exaggeration, but compared to the condition of the man at the end of her overseas line, I wasn't going to complain, or mope.

"Why won't you tell me what happened to you in Vietnam?"

"Because I don't want to think about it. . . . I'd rather think about you."

"Well, you'll see how the massage helps. And then I'll show you a whole bunch of exercises for your back and spine I learned in my physical therapy sessions. Pilates, it was developed for dancers, but it will do you a world of good. I do the stretching exercises every morning, without fail."

I was impressed with her businesslike attitude about body pain, for I knew something about injured bodies and physical therapy, as my father had, as Suzanne had. But the oscillating light on the ceiling, like a skylight into a realm of disembodied voices, guided me elsewhere— to Maureen, my physical therapy nurse at the VA hospital in San Diego.

Maureen's voice was throaty and comic. She dealt with the quadriplegics and burn cases, and me. As such, it was an intimate relationship, and the body remembers kindness; it never forgets who's been good to it.

In the ward on the top floor, we could watch the sunset over the Pacific. She always began with a massage of my lower back and so was the first each morning to endure my bitching and complaining. It had taken a battery of small operations to get all the shell splinters out. And she would be there to work the torn-up muscle and return something of the lost flexibility. She had strong and wonderful hands, and a croaking laugh at my groans as she'd chatter on with her stories about her two daughters, who were champion cheerleaders and baton twirlers, and her husband, who was a flight sergeant on an aircraft carrier in the China Sea. And when she got the kinks out and the pain would ease, sometimes I'd get these terrific erections in my shorts. Not a little embarrassing. But Maureen would give a wicked laugh and call me her "lucky boy" and tell me to stop bitching, because I was in a lot better shape than her quads, not to mention the poor bastards who had had their genitals shot off. And once, as if to prove her point, she just yanked down my shorts and started pumping with her latex glove and baby oil, and then, to my astonishment, stuck in a finger and massaged my prostrate. It was like my very life flooded out of me. I never felt anything quite as incredible before or since. Maureen just laughed. "Jesus, worse than my husband on the first day of shore leave," she scolded, efficiently swabbing the decks with Kleenex. She put a raised finger to her lips after stripping off the latex—a vow of silence on my part—and told me to stop feeling sorry for myself.

"Dream, why not, about the wonderful sons you will have with a very lucky girl."

I think she said such things to all the guys who were still functioning—to keep them going.

Such thoughts caused me to adjust my crotch and look over at the other bed, where Laura was lying, staring out the French doors. She might have been napping; I wondered what she was taking. The double dose of Demerol was certainly taking me down. I turned my gaze to the undulating hillsides beyond the doors and the fortress wall, miles and miles of them snaking up and down like sturgeon's fins, like some miniature version of the Great Wall of China transported to charming Nafplio. The crusaders and then the Venetians had built those walls against the depredations of raiders, in hopes of keeping the forces of chaos and ruin at bay. Walls, walls, walls . . . how many wrecked walls had I unearthed? Like the massive walls of Mycenae and Tiryns I'd shown Laura on the way to Nafplio, thrown up in the decades around 1300 B.C. by the Mycenaeans as their world came under threat from the mysterious Sea People. Which should have offered a little perspective on those forty-five-year-old walls of wire and concrete a few hundred miles to the north, portions of which were, at that very moment, lying breached and unattended at points along the Hungarian-Austrian border. The Iron Curtain through which my father had passed, never to return . . . walls perversely designed to protect Europe's heartland from chaos, death, and ruin.

Where Vlada awaited our return.

As I lay on my bed, the gentle light flooding inward prompted another voice, that of my grandmother on the back porch of Elsinore overlooking the lake during her Inness hour, when the lake and shoreline came alive with rich and sensuous greens, when she liked to write letters or read her Thoreau and Emerson—or impart essential truths. I realized, after my father's letters, how much of his identity and mine had been shaped in the gentle admonitions that came our way like clockwork, and the scrutiny of her eagle-eyed glare.

"Oh, I think they're missing someone who didn't come home from the Civil War—don't you think?"

This in reply to a young boy's question about the lonely watchers on the dusk in the Inness landscapes in my great-grandfather's collection.

The "Old General" was her name for my great-grandfather when she nursed him at the end. She told me how he had gone on and on about a friend of his, a southerner from Natchez, Mississippi, Pearce Breckenridge. A story he got out as he lay dying, sprays of pine shadowing his face, wheezing hideously from the Spanish flu.

"Pearce Breckenridge," I whispered to myself, stunned I'd forgotten all about that story—that I'd failed to connect it with the name encoded in the Saint-Gaudens memorial. It was as if Laura's presence and the love letters had the effect of recalibrating my memory for deeper dives.

"Rollicking days at Harvard they had in the 1850s, he and his friend, the handsome, poetry-spouting Pearce. But it wasn't Harvard days, or even the Civil War he talked about at the end, but a trip before the war as a Harvard student to visit his classmate's plantation in Natchez, Mississippi. Pearce Breckenridge, the soul of southern dignity and rare intelligence, but living in a land of 'such degeneracy, injustice, and shame.' He went on so about the appalling misery of Negro enslavement he had witnessed, to which his noble friend seemed blissfully oblivious. He talked about the lines of bowed heads and scarred backs of those chained souls marched along rural roads or transported in filthy carts. 'How could the sensitive mind of dear Breckenridge be so blind to such darkness and depravity?'

"You see, I think that's what put your great-grandfather—that visit to the plantation in Natchez—irrevocably in the abolitionist camp. I'm almost sure of it."

More than sure: she knew for a certainty.

"The Old General talked more and more about the hours he spent in Hannibal on the banks of the Ohio River while he waited for a train east, a train back to Boston and sanity. He told me how he lingered on the boat landing after taking a paddle wheeler up the Mississippi from Natchez, and something about how that river, a geographic body, a line on a map, could divide lands free and unfree, that bothered him greatly. He said he found the abstraction unnerving. Even then, on his death-bed, he wrung his hands. How was it that a few hundred feet of water could demark such 'absurdly noxious notions of human inequality? And this when Ohio was teaming with great things: free men busily building towns and engaging in fevered commerce, and everywhere the most beautiful farms, while just across that slow-moving river lay a land of darkness and diseased souls, broken-down and abandoned farms, unimproved lands and malarial marshes and primeval woods.' He just couldn't believe that such a thing could exist. 'Weren't we a young and enlightened nation? It beggared my youthful mind that a mere watery line could demarcate freedom and abysmal servitude. We Americans, a free people—how was such degradation of the human spirit possible? And to this evil, my dear Pearce Breckenridge was in complete thrall!'"

The sound of my grandmother's voice, as if she'd suddenly come alive in me after more than twenty years, sped me back to a muddy and shallow and malarial river snaking its way along the western border of Hâu Nghĩa Province. The Vam Co Dong River didn't quite border on Cambodia, but seven kilometers was close enough. In the spring of 1972, I was part of an American advisory team to a South Vietnamese regiment of militia that patrolled the Vam Co Dong River and tried to keep the Vietcong and North Vietnamese Army from infiltrating men and supplies from Cambodia. How many days had I spent in obser-vation posts along that godforsaken mosquito-breeding river, peering through binoculars into the impenetrable jungle distance beyond its far banks, knowing full well from the reports of deserters and captured documents what hunkered down there, in deep bunkers and jungle lairs, waiting and probing, subsisting on lies, preying on primal emotions of fear and envy and resentment, and threats of murderous violence and midnight assassinations. Talk about a fragile line between freedom and despotism: Pol Pot's terror and bloodlust breeding a nightmare beyond reckoning.

What would the Old General have made of Pol Pot, after the Cornfield of Antietam, after the trenches of the Western Front, after Buchenwald and the gulag?

"Something is either right or wrong, Peter—which is it?" My grandmother invariably asked me.

Her forebears, like her husband's, came over on the *Arabella* in 1630 with John Winthrop. And like an old spring that still produces a trickle of fine clear water, something of Winthrop's claims for a covenant with God and a faith that the rule of justice and mercy is the great good and end of life flowed within her. It was the same simple vision of good and evil—good men make a good community—that energized the abolitionist faith of General Alden and the founding of Winsted.

To bring her point home for a young boy, she removed a black leather book from a leather carrying case and handed it to me. It was an old traveler's Bible, tattered, worn, and inscribed with the names of the men in General Alden's regiment, whom he'd vowed to keep safe. When I opened the pages, I found a diagonal bloodstain, like the suspended blade of a guillotine. Half the pages were stained, many stuck together. He'd carried the Bible in his uniform pocket while mounted on his horse at the Battle of Antietam. I remembered how my hands shook at the blood-soaked pages as I sat in my wicker chair by the lake with a glass of pink lemonade. Mightily impressed with this heirloom, I remember asking, "Did he die?"

He did and he didn't, or at least Pearce Breckenridge did.

It was a lovely green landscape of hazy light and vaporous heat on that hot morning of September 17, 1862, as my great-grandfather strained to see into the distance, mounted on his nervous mare. Beyond a swath of golden corn, Confederate troops were massing in front of rolling hills. On that day more, Americans would die in battle than on any single day in the nation's history. The early fog had burned off quickly, revealing to the waiting Union troops the green hills and farmers' fields along the meandering Antietam Creek. The first Union troops attacked into Lee's northern flank, right through the rows of corn in front of where General Alden had posted himself on horseback—"a fool thing to do," opined the regimental historian—so offering a clear target for a rebel sharpshooter. For a generation, reference to *the Cornfield* would invoke thoughts of slaughter and a killing ground running with blood. But for a few minutes more, it was just a cornfield and the cornstalks were high and green, flowing with silk tassels like liquid honey in the morning sun. That was how my great-grandfather spoke of the field of battle in his declining years, a glimpse of a lovely world before it was imprinted in the minds of thousands with disaster and heartbreak.

His Massachusetts boys entered the Cornfield itching for a fight, for they were not green troops and had already known their share of humiliation and slaughter in the Seven Days' Battles of the Peninsula, when, just miles from Richmond, incompetent generalship had denied them victory. They were frustrated; they thought they might have had the war won three months before in Virginia. The unit in front of them was hit by a murderous fire from a brigade of Georgians stationed in the grassy pastures just to the south. The Confederates directed their aim to the spaces between the rows of corn. The boys in blue were stopped cold by the concentrated fire, their bodies littering the rows of shattered stalks. General Alden was bringing up his reinforcements of Massachusetts men to be fed into this hellhole of concentrated shot and canister fire; they had already been receiving artillery rounds from Confederate batteries on the small plateau near the Dunker Church to the west. Alden was clearheaded and concise about the terrible business at hand. He was sure he had a preponderance of forces on that field and he was willing to take the risk—and this, he wrote years later, was the worst decision any commander had to face—to take high initial casualties in order to make a breakthrough, roll up the enemy's rear, rout him, and pave the way to victory. With the greater number of troops available to the Union forces, a sharp concerted pressure would break the Confederates and pin them on the Potomac.

Alden was a veteran, an engineer by training, an abolitionist by disposition, and a man of enormous physical vigor. He saw it in his mind and knew exactly what needed doing: bring the entire division in together in a single coordinated attack, not seriatim, as had happened over and over in the Peninsula Campaign. But the smoke was confusing. There was yellow-black smoke cascading like a fiendish exhumation of Hades. And then the terrible screams and shouts. Chaos as shells exploded nearby. Walking wounded filtered back to the dressing stations, getting in the way of troops moving forward. His good friend Brigadier Hartsuff had been wounded by a shell fragment when he went forward to reconnoiter, while Colonel Christian, who had been commanding a brigade of reinforcements going in just ahead of Alden, had lost his nerve under the deadly hail of canister fire and was found wandering aimlessly in the rear. For a while, there'd been a command breakdown. "Fatal delays" was how Alden had described it to one newspaper reporter. He was growing increasingly impatient, intent on getting his Massachusetts veterans into the thick of it before the Confederates could further reinforce their positions. He was more and more convinced of the chances for a breakthrough if pressure could be maintained, and he believed in his men: They had the moral fervor to do the necessary thing.

The Fifteenth Massachusetts was edgy for a fight. Many were veterans of useless marches and frustrated attacks in the Peninsula Campaign. They had scores to settle going back to Ball's Bluff in the first months of the war. They wanted to prove themselves and the rightness of their cause. Among their ranks were staunch abolitionists, men who cared little one way or another for the cause of union, but everything for freeing the slaves. This was their religion, their being, and if an idea was to triumph over evil self-interest, they were the men to do it. There were few like them in the Union army. They were disciples of the slain abolitionist John Brown. They had popularized an old revivalist hymn by setting new words to it, about how John Brown's body might be moldering in the grave, but his soul was marching on. Their commander, the prissy Gen. George McClellan, who had provided them the means but not the moral fervor to win—another Alden contribution to the regimental history—had taken an instant disliking to this marching song, but it stuck. Possibly those lyrics were playing through their minds as they headed into the smoke and din, that and a lot of praying. Alden maneuvered his brigade into the battle for the Cornfield, past scenes of stygian butchery. Men lay in heaps, many torn apart by canister fire, the still-living clutching at their wounds, tearing at their clothing, calling out for water and help. Alden heard those cries to his dying day; he sometimes walked the paths at Elysium alone, he explained, to escape them.

As fate would have it, the Fifteenth Massachusetts ran smack into a charge of Confederate reinforcements, a tough hardscrabble brigade of Louisiana Tigers from the bayous and docks of New Orleans, the men ornery and belligerent as two-hundred-pound catfish—this from one of their Confederate officers. Alden troops were cut to pieces by accurate rifle fire, and he was an obvious target, mounted on his horse. As he moved forward, directing his troops toward the breakthrough he knew could be theirs, a minié-ball tore into his right ankle and knocked him sprawling to the ground. His horse probably took the same bullet, because it was found later wandering the field, whinnying in pitiful terror, with its intestines trailing in the dirt. Two of his officers rushed to Alden's assistance and got him to his feet, at which point he used his sword as a cane to move around on his shattered ankle. He shouted and hobbled, trying to make himself heard above the din of battle and reclaim some order among his ranks. He was desperate for a view of the field through the churning gun smoke, desperate to rally his men and redirect them for the breakthrough. Chaos. Rank upon rank of the most godly souls had gone down as if scythed, falling by the tens and twenties as each rebel volley found its mark. The regiment took unheard-of casualties of something over 60 percent. Where were the other regiments? Where were the reinforcements? When Alden finally gave the order for withdrawal, only about thirty-two men were able to accompany the regimental colors to the rear.

The battle raged on as more Union reinforcements were slowly and haphazardly brought up in uncoordinated assaults, an inauspicious beginning to a numbing host of lost opportunities.

General Alden tried to remain close to the action, to help direct Hooker's First Corps into the next attack on the weakened Confederate northern flank. His boot was dripping blood. He was beginning to pass out. His officers forced him onto a litter, which they carried around as he continued to give orders and prompt his fellow commanders to move with alacrity and spirit, but when he began to lose consciousness, they took him to a dressing station in the rear, where a surgeon immediately attended his ankle.

He described the scene in a letter home to his first wife as a nightmare dreamed in the Inferno. Everywhere, neatly corded stacks of severed limbs in the dirt. Because of his rank, he'd been immediately attended to, his boot sliced off and the shattered ankle washed down and bandaged. The surgeon recommended immediate amputation because a wait would give sepsis a chance to set in, at which point they'd have to take more than just the foot. Alden made it clear he wished to keep the foot and ordered the ankle bandaged and splinted so that he might get back to his command. The doctor obeyed, but when Alden tried to get up, he fainted dead away and found himself minutes later lying on a litter, abandoned by his officers and the shock beginning to wear off, and with it waves of pain running like a torrent up and down his leg. He had lost too much blood to move on his own and so for a time he was forced to lie there with the din of battle in his ears, men rushing every which way, and rumors of victory and defeat flying in snatched yells.

An hour later, two of the general's officers came to find him and give him word of the battle. Victory seemed in sight. His spirits soared and newfound strength surged through his body. He enlisted their help to carry him to command headquarters, where he found McClellan's staff stuck, as my great-grandfather described it in a letter to a fellow officer, "in the business of failure . . . failing to take the initiative, failing to exploit quickly where successes has been gained, failing utterly to turn the bloodied and battered northern flank of Lee's army, which had been our plan from the start." From descriptions of other officers and reports from the field, Alden was convinced the day could yet be won, if only McClellan would commit Porter's two reserve brigades on the right, and bring the Fifth and Sixth Corps into action to roll up the Confederates and pin them on the Potomac, and then destroy the South's army in detail and so end their capacity for war making. His Massachusetts boys had died to provide that opportunity.

Alden's position was awkward. He had been something of a protégé of McClellan and had admired his organizational skills. Trained as an engineer at Harvard, Alden had won his spurs as a logistics expert in the building of the Army of the Potomac and later in expediting the transport of men and material during the Peninsula Campaign. His general's commission had been won in some minor but not unimportant skirmishes along the Rappahannock during the retreat back to Washington. Now he pulled himself up from his litter and hobbled to the table, where his commander was studying the field maps, and offered his opinion in no uncertain terms. As usual, McClellan was convinced of the availability of vast Confederate reinforcements ready to fall on his battered and tired troops at any moment. He was intent on conserving his fresh divisions and holding fast to the few acres of savaged and bloody ground already bought at such prodigal loss. Alden was not the only officer aghast at this lack of killer instinct, especially those officers who understood the full magnitude of the sacrifices already incurred, much less the tenuous position of Lee, who had his back to the Potomac and no reinforcements in easy reach. In another letter to a professor friend at Harvard, Alden wrote, "Most of us felt that the battle was only half fought and half won."

The throbbing pain in his leg, his anger and horror as confirmation of the numbers of men killed and wounded in the Fifteenth

Massachusetts that day were brought to him prompted him to vociferous and pointed complaints within the hearing of his commander, not to mention the liberal amounts of whiskey he'd taken for medicinal purposes. That night and in the days following, he would share his misgivings with a correspondent from the *Washington Herald,* a distant cousin, George Adams: "Questioning the failure to use cavalry for intelligence, the disastrous habit of throwing reinforcements into battle in driblets, without coordination and without mutual support." He was a logistics expert, after all, and he knew whereof he spoke.

Much of Alden's diatribe turned up in the *Herald* the week following the Battle of Antietam, by which time Lee had managed to withdraw his army behind the Potomac to safety. It was patently clear that McClellan, though winning the battle and saving the Union, as the general described it in his dispatches to President Lincoln, had failed to follow through with a concerted punch that might have taken the Army of the Potomac to Richmond that fall, instead of three long years later. Nevertheless, before he himself was relieved of command by Lincoln, "Little Mac" cashiered General Alden a week after the battle (he was lying in the hospital when he got the official letter), and my great-grandfather was out of the war.

But not before he had set in motion a series of events more fantastic than anything conjured in Max's novels, a tale Max had come tantalizingly close to uncovering when he'd deciphered the name of Pearce Breckenridge in the Williams Memorial by Saint-Gaudens.

General Alden lay on a litter in the shade of a shot-up sycamore after refusing the amputation of his foot. He was woozy from loss of blood and frustrated not to be with his men and desperately worried that the battle was not being brought to a victorious conclusion. Then, in the near distance, he noticed a large group of Confederate walking wounded corralled behind a split-rail fence. They were guarded by a couple of Union soldiers, and a single Union doctor was attending to the more badly wounded lying on the ground. "The most ragtag outfit of exhausted and sullen creatures I ever laid eyes on," he wrote to his first wife. Many were barefoot, emaciated, dressed in castoffs. But there was one man in particular upon whom his stare lingered. The face was oddly familiar. He was "coffee-complected, with a long pointy nose and dark eyes close together, as if staring down a barrel." The man, "agitated, frantic," seemed to be in his mid-twenties, a blood-soaked rag

tied around his forehead, and was tending a wounded man on a blanket by the split-rail fence. A gray officer's coat had been hung across
the fence but "offered little shade in that hellish heat." Through the
floating smoke and roar of canister shot and the screams coming from
the dressing station, General Alden watched this man going about his
ministrations. "The face of the Confederate soldier was so familiar that
I thought for certain I was dreaming. It was a face I knew from some
other life but could not fix it in my presently deranged life." Alden
noticed the oddness of the man's dress: "He was one of the best dressed
of the group, wearing a silk shirt and a fine pair of tan breeches, certainly nothing in the way of a uniform." The other Confederate soldiers
turned snarling glances in the man's direction and snapped orders at
him, alternately cursing him and pleading with the two Union guards
for water. But there was little water to spare at that time in the heat
of battle in midafternoon. "The poor soul seemed completely overwrought by the circumstances of his wounded compatriot, the most
piteous wails issuing from his lips."

At some point, Alden's curiosity got the better of him and he
ordered the soldier who attended him to help him up. He staggered
over to the split-rail fence, which he could prop himself against for a
better view. "The fine—no, beautiful—face of the man in his extremity
of grief and consternation had me in its grip." And then it came to
him. "Breckenridge—Pearce—could it be?" Alden called out the name,
and the man kneeling by the side of the wounded soldier looked up
as if terrified. "He looked a fright, trembling; a bullet seemed to have
grazed his forehead, and his white silk shirt was caked with his or his
companion's blood."

"Pearce?" asked General Alden again. "Is it you?"

"Jason, sa."

"Pearce Breckenridge?"

The man, his face streaming with tears, pointed to the ground, where
the soldier lay severely wounded.

"Mista Pearce Breckenridge is terribly hurt, sa."

"And you are . . ."

If this had been the conceit of a novel, Max might have laughed or
rejected a plot that employed such a bizarre coincidence. Jason Breckenridge was Pearce Breckenridge's slave and manservant. His master
lay in the grass, his entrails hanging out and his life slipping away.
Alden had actually met Jason in the Breckenridge household when

he had gone to Natchez, Mississippi, to visit his classmate in 1855. His puritan probity had first been outraged, then aghast at Jason's clear resemblance to Pearce, and worse, that Pearce made no attempt to hide the fact that Jason was, in fact, his half brother, *and* born of his mother's house slave, no less, who was herself a fair-skinned mulatto. They hadn't even bothered to hide the shame of the circumstance, but felt they were doing a great kindness by providing Jason a benevolent arrangement: He had been educated and saved from the fields and slave quarters. As Pearce put it in their college days, "You see, Alden, we are not such fiends as you Yankees like to make us out. Can you say you treat your mill workers any better: that we take our charges into our homes and treat them as near members of the family."

General Alden, with his aide's help, moved closer to the figure lying on the blanket, his face in shade from the coat hung across the fence. "My God," he wrote to Samuel Williams, "it was Pearce, his fair-haired face gazing up at the infernal sky drifting with smoke, his blue eyes wide and unblinking, barely a mark on his skin, though a terrible wound exposed his abdomen. I shouted out his name as I had a hundred times—no, a thousand times—in Harvard days, but I was too late—it was too late, for dear Pearce had given up his soul only minutes before."

For the first time that day, tears came to his eyes, not for all the men of his regiment who had died, but for a Harvard classmate and a Confederate officer he had greatly admired. "For those happier days when our youthful ambitions were all aflame, before I'd made my fateful trip to his home and we had parted ways forever," he wrote.

He described Pearce Breckenridge as having one of the finest minds in their class, a scholar, a poet, a philosopher of "more than passing insights." They had studied together, roomed together, discussed mathematics and Greek architecture. Pearce Breckenridge, scion of a rich and powerful Natchez cotton family, had come north for a Harvard education and to study the classics and English literature. "How many nights full of drink and fellow feeling had we discussed the merits of Plato as against those of Aristotle, or Aeschylus over Euripides." Pearce had teased Alden about his still-unformed abolitionist views, reminding him that Athens, too, was a slave-owning and a slave-making society—though forever touting high-mindedness as its citizens exploited their far-flung empire. "They worked them to death in the silver mines. And don't forget your wage slaves, your factory men—

and women, too, I dare say—who labor for starvation wages," Pearce told him.

For all their spirited talk and disagreements, they had been fast friends—for three of their four years at Harvard, before Alden had taken up Pearce's invitation to visit Mississippi. And friends, too, with Samuel Williams, Alden's cousin at Harvard who was studying in the divinity school. Pearce knew his Bible better than Samuel did and could effortlessly quote Scripture supporting the institution of slavery, if not its benevolent purpose of raising the Negro from perpetual darkness. Pearce and Samuel often argued deep into the Cambridge night, as Pearce noted chapter and verse: The right of holding slaves was clearly substantiated in Scripture, both by precept and example. "In fact, the believers and beloved—(first Timothy, chapter six, one through five)— were to be granted even greater respect by their slaves because of their righteous faith." For both Alden and Williams, their debates with the swashbuckling romantic figure and aristocratic gentleman from Natchez had always ended in a convivial draw, since neither had been south of the Mason-Dixon Line, and "all remained on the level of theory and wine-softened sophistries." Pearce's erudition and bon-vivant anecdotes had charmed the Yankee cousins and their Boston families.

"As fine a man, as brilliant a soul—even if we had finally fallen out—as I had ever known. And now he lay butchered at my feet." So Alden wrote to Samuel Williams, safe back in Cambridge.

Alden had ordered the Union doctor to come over to attend to Pearce Breckenridge, but the doctor only confirmed the obvious: a fatal gut wound, for which the primitive medical know-how of the day had no remedy.

General Alden was in such a weakened condition himself that when the doctor stood back from the dying Pearce Breckenridge with a shake of his head, Alden fainted into the arms of his aide. Only later in the day was he able to regain enough of his faculties to participate in the grand strategy sessions with George McClellan. And throughout those deliberations, which might have changed the course and duration of the war, Alden was plagued by the dead face of his Harvard classmate, and similarly haunted by the face of his slave Jason. "It was as if some part of Pearce was saved from the catastrophe of that day—a mocking salvation, but a Lazarus nevertheless."

As the night's deliberation and prevarications wore on, Alden became more and more frustrated, and also filled with dread that his friend's body would be thrown into a common grave and lost. He knew the parents, after all, as much as he disapproved of everything they stood for. "The thought of annihilation for such a fine name, for Pearce's fiery intelligence, just one amidst the indiscriminate hecatombs of miserable deaths drove me to distraction." Finally, bone-weary and a little intoxicated from the whiskey he'd been taking for the pain, he had his aide help him outside to search for Jason and the corpse of his friend. They were still together. Jason was curled up alongside his master in the dewy grass by the split-rail fence, littered with broken sycamore branches. "The stench of that place, even with the heat of the day dissipated, was like nothing I'd ever known." The dead had been stacked like so much cordwood against the fence to await the morning's burial detail. "Jason had refused to be separated from the body of his master."

As General Alden approached, Jason screamed in terror. He had awakened from a terrible nightmare. He took a swipe at Alden with his fist, but the aide blocked the blow with his boot and was about to deliver a kick, when Alden stopped him. "The poor man was startled out of some terrifying dream—one can only imagine in such stygian surroundings." When Jason calmed down, they began to talk. To Alden's surprise, Jason turned out to be quite well spoken when out of earshot of the other Confederate prisoners. "Pearce's manservant could read and write and was conversant with books—books that he had often read to Pearce when our old friend had a migraine or by the campfire when Pearce's poor eyes had wearied. He even had Pearce's intonation and quick intelligence, something he sought to hide within earshot of the gray-clad rabble round about." From the flames of a nearby campfire, Alden could just make out Jason's features as they continued to talk. "It was the strangest thing, the resemblance to Pearce; if not for the complexion and the dark hair, which was long and fell in lank curls, I would have thought it was the spirit of our Pearce in the underworld preparing to cross the river Styx."

Jason asked Alden if they might say a prayer for the fallen Pearce. It was then that Alden reached into his coat pocket and got out his Bible, and, opening it to a passage from Isaiah, found it stained with blood. "Perhaps with my blood, which had soaked my uniform, or from the operating table soaked with the blood of multitudes. It took me quite aback, since the Bible had come down the generations and was inscribed with the names of the men in my regiment. Jason, seeing my consternation, gently took the Bible from my hands and found the passage from The Psalms: 'Yea, though I walk through the valley of the shadow of death, I will fear no evil.' His voice was clear and stately, poised like the eagle upon the breeze—oh, dear cousin, so like the deceased himself. It was I who shed tears and not he."

General Alden began going over the options with Jason. Perhaps a private burial might be arranged for Pearce and the body reinterred at a later, more propitious date. But then all hell might break loose in the morning and who knew what the battle might bring. And then there was the matter of Jason—what to do with Jason? He refused to leave the body of his master: They had been raised like the brothers they were.

Technically, the slave Jason Breckenridge was not yet free. This was the fall of 1862, before the Emancipation Proclamation. Jason was either a captured rebel soldier and thus liable to be taken to a prison camp or a slave and thus contraband of war. "The brutish rebel prisoners would just as soon have slit his throat if given half a chance." If a slave liberated by the Union army, he might be held by the government as confiscated property and so employed to do war work, and later, as thousands of blacks were to do, he might fight for his freedom. Within months, with the signing of the Emancipation Proclamation, Jason would be free in the liberated South but possibly not in Maryland, still an occupied northern slave state in 1862.

"Was he truly free? I cannot be sure, Samuel." So wrote Alden in the letter of explanation that Jason would carry. "And I am near out of my head with fretting and exhaustion and sorrow for my multitudes of dead. What a piteous hell we have made for ourselves, with the groans and calls of the wounded and dying like the screams of harpies in Dante's Inferno. Do they scream for revenge, do you suppose, or to us to make good on their sacrifice? And this man, Jason, will go nowhere away from the body of his beloved master—our departed friend who held his chains."

In near desperation to save some "iota of humanity," Alden came up with a plan that he later admitted was "ill-conceived and fraught with the desperation of the moment." He forged a legal document of manumission from one Pearce Breckenridge of Natchez, Mississippi, freeing his slave Jason upon his death. He handed this document to Jason along with a hastily composed letter to Samuel Williams, forty dollars, and fresh clothes. Late on the following day, after Lee's withdrawal, when it was clear that McClellan had no intention of vigorously pursuing Lee, Alden instructed one of his officers to wrap up Pearce Breckenridge's body and take it and Jason in an army ambulance to the rear, and from there to Hagerstown to purchase a coffin; at which point, the officer was charged to accompany both coffin, body, and Jason on a train to Philadelphia and thence to Boston and Cambridge. The officer was instructed to deliver Jason and Pearce's body and a hastily scribbled letter to his cousin and Harvard classmate, the Reverend Samuel Williams on Brattle Street. This action was cited, too, when Alden was cashiered: "causing the dereliction of duty of one of his officers and the misuse of government property by commandeering an ambulance." The young officer managed to carry out this difficult, if not awkward, task with some alacrity, arriving in Cambridge in the evening two days later to present Samuel Williams with the shocking evidence of what their abolitionist fervor had brought to pass.

"Teach this man to love freedom and God in equal measure," read Alden's scribbled note to Samuel Williams. "I trust you will find an appropriate resting place for the body of his master, our classmate and dear friend, Pearce Breckenridge. Write me soon, cousin, and tell me what you think, you who loved this man. I bid you adieu from the field of battle. If sepsis does not set in, I will survive, with or without my foot, but if not, I trust you, of all people, to do the necessary and just thing for this ex-slave. The time for debate and exquisite metaphysical flights is over. On this matter, your Bible will no longer save you. Believe me, this bloody war has closed the gate on the past—the stakes now are far too high for return, and we must press forward with alacrity or die in the attempt."

25

"OH, THERE YOU ARE."

I heard her sigh as I opened my eyes. I stared up at that aqueous ceiling and the light all around us, feeling as if we were floating on that great blue bay beyond our balcony.

"So, do you think I was crazy to come, then?" she asked.

She seemed to be prompting me back to earth out of an oceanic vastness.

"As you said," I replied, "you don't seem to have had much of a choice."

"I would have gone crazy—that's what. I've been a little lost recently, a little scared. My doctor said I needed to get away from New York."

"It was a good idea."

"Mother used to tell me when I complained that the choices we make were made for us long before we even knew they were choices."

I looked over to where she lay on her bed, her profile a lovely composition against the sheer white of the wall behind, head propped on a pillow to better see the colors of the bay. Her hands were crossed over her breasts as in one of those Gothic tomb sculptures. Except her feet were bare, her toes rhythmically pointing and unpointing, arching those ugly yet beautiful feet that I recalled so well from the night of our sixth-form dance.

"It's a little strange finding out your father's not your father," she said. "Even if Bobby—do you mind if I call him Bobby?—wasn't quite the monster everyone thought he was."

"Like Max—or was it Telemachus?—always said, We can't pick the guy who knocked up our mother. And as much as he complained about his dad, I actually took quite a shine to Jack. Did you ever meet Jack, the big bad banker?"

On the subject of Max, it was as if she hadn't heard or didn't care.

"Bobby doted on me," she told me. "He loved me. Deep down he yearned for a kind of perfect world, free of injustice, where music and art mattered more than anything because they were an expression of man's highest calling. He just hated a world he couldn't change."

"Well, I guess that explains how he and Max got on so famously," I replied.

"You like rubbing it in, don't you?"

"Sorry—but someone in bed, so to speak, with the likes of Anthony Blunt, Guy Burgess, Donald Maclean, *and* Kim Philby—traitors responsible for the deaths of thousands . . . you're well out of it."

I thought I'd nicely laid to rest any lingering misbegotten loyalties or affections.

"Bobby gave me piano lessons even though he could barely play anymore. Even his voice was musical. He could explain music with a sensitivity that actually brought tears to my mother's eyes. Even now I'll dance a passage and think how he'd work the phrasing. When I was a little girl, he'd have me sit in his lap, and comb my hair, and read to me, and he'd call me 'his little miracle.' For years when I was a kid, he called me that, 'my little miracle.' God knows how Mother managed that neat illusion—but then she *was* the Houdini of sex."

"So he was . . ."

"Capable of producing a child? At least he thought so—she could convince him of anything. But nothing was quite the same again after that night when you and Max visited Hermitage."

"Max and I?"

"He asked you to read a prayer from Samuel Williams's *Essays and Prayers*."

"Yes, just a little awkward."

"We'd never said prayers at a meal, never. And just like that, it began, first with his grandfather and *Essays and Prayers*, and then this religious thing began to take him over. It drove my mother *insane*. First, she came to live with me in New York, until she got her own place— thank God. After he was kicked off the Winsted board, he converted to Catholicism. He became like a monk with his keepers, railing at a fallen world, of which I was one of the truly fallen. I couldn't go back, for years."

"Angels," I murmured to myself a little wistfully. "So, Colonel Fair-burn—he really believes you're his daughter?"

"My mother has her first cousin wrapped in so many knots, he doesn't know which way his dick is pointing."

"Well—"

"They just headed for the hills, you see, back to his Sussex mansion, living in the past like two antiquarians: when they were kids growing up there, when she was a star with Sadler's Wells, when he was a famous archaeologist at Cambridge. My lawyer got me to agree to go to their wedding this November . . . and make peace."

She turned to me to get my reaction. Her pale blue eyes sparked as she tried to smile and make light of her dilemma. That sounding board of a blue bay produced more soft hoots, the cough of an old diesel engine, the splash of a mooring rope: vesperal hymns of a harbor at day's end.

"The old do that, escape into the past."

"Forget it." She turned from my note of vague sympathy, sighting along her upraised right leg to where it ended in a perfect arch. "The past . . . well, did you ever go snorkeling? I did once in Key West. We did two weeks of performances down in Miami and then we had a week off. It's like that, you see, like you're floating on this great inland sea and all that has ever gone before you forms the ocean floor, those deep caverns and ridges, some of them reaching up as reefs and shoals, even islands. And as you float above you can feel the warm currents—sometimes they kinda catch you unaware, so that you are buoyed up, warmed through and through with the hidden life there below, which you can never quite touch. Because even staring down, even when you try to dive down and touch bottom, it's always falling away from you—the past, I mean. It's just what you feel in your bones . . . there in the music, in the steps, where those feelings come from. Sorry, I know you think it's flaky, but that's how it *feels* to me. It's as lost as you and I will be to our great-great-grandchildren."

My heart fell at her elegiac, brave words: a disciple of Max, womanly wisdom from my fair Athena.

Later, after dinner, we strolled the waterfront of Nafplio with the other tourists and a few locals, teenagers wheeling on one another's arms. The stars and a half-moon drifted on the bay amidst the lights of returning fishing boats. Bouzouki music or revolting Euro pop played in the harbor-front tavernas. My back—we had shared three bottles of a superb Allagiannis Savatiano, with hints of mango and lemon around the edges—was behaving itself. We were feeling no pain. She wore a white blouse, barely buttoned, showing her pale, long-tendoned neck merging into the upper curve of her breasts. Her hair was tight in a chignon, so that the handsome oval of her face and the looping ringlets of her hair showed her features to best advantage. We walked in silence along the quay, touching hands, staring out over the water and the star-reflected night. I could not help noticing how she instinctively turned and smiled at the garish strobe lights and disco beat coming from the tourist joints along the harbor. Everything about her body language—the way she swayed her hips or twirled her skirt—yearned for that music, to discard the elastic brace that sheathed her knee, to be healed, to be free again. How many wild New York parties and dance clubs were encompassed in her longing smiles, when she and Max had danced the night away at Studio 54? I tried not to think about it. Especially the famous censored photograph in *People* magazine, when she'd danced topless with a coterie of nude male dancers from the Joffrey Ballet.

We stood gazing out at the fortress of Bourtzi in the middle of the harbor, like a slightly dented hat floating on a glassy sea. Above us, long walls snaked the hillsides, and the Venetian castle of Palamidi loomed on the edge of darkness, plucking out starlight as we continued our stroll.

"Lots of walls," she said.

"The Venetians built them and the castle."

"Venice . . ." There was a kind of ache in her voice. "Venetians seem to be everywhere around these parts."

"Venice," I echoed, wondering if I might elicit something of Max's mocking refrain that often edged her tone of voice.

She took my hand and turned and kissed me, lingering for a moment, and then hugged me. I hugged her back.

"You taste like wine."

"So do you."

"I know I'm a little drunk, but that was nice." She attempted a childish giggle.

"From Patras, a vineyard on the west coast, the Allagiannis Savatiano."

"I meant you. It's nice to know . . . more about *you*."

"Today me, tomorrow my father." I shrugged. "It's strange, you know, twenty years ago—no, twenty-four, when I spent a spring break at Princeton, I thought I detected irritation in his older colleagues in the Archaeology Department, a hint of controversy about his free spending habits and what one guy described as his 'cowboy gallivanting,' whatever that was about. Before my senior year at Winsted, in Crete, I rarely heard anything about it, just reverence for his scholarship, his intrepid work in OSS: first American into occupied Greece. But these days, even his reputation as an archaeologist has evaporated among the younger people in the profession. He's become a vaguely mythic figure, a name attached to a professorship, a gallery in the museum. Nobody in the field even mentions his articles and books. You see, without a major find, a major discovery—nobody, in the end, remembers."

"And Winsted?"

"A name on a wall. Nobody left who knew him."

"Not for Elliot, not for my mother, not for me. This is our chance, before they're all gone."

"Like you said . . . *lost* as you and I will be."

"At least you and Max and Vlada have your books."

I turned on the quay to her down-turned face, highlighted in the play of garish lights from a nearby disco, and touched her quivering chin, until her eyes again found mine.

"Ah, but you *lived*—you *really* did," I told her, and I meant every word. "You brought joy to how many thousands."

She smiled and seemed to breathe deeply of some fragrance; lifting her face to the sky, she pointed.

"Orion."

I followed her gaze to where Orion's belt teetered above the obsidian mirror of the bay, as if yearning to merge with its triplicate echo, blue giants ballasted by the pinkish plume of an expanding nebula.

"Don't tell me you're a stargazer like Max."

"He had a thing about stars—he did, that boy."

It was the first real flicker of affection for Max I'd detected in her voice. And it seemed to produce a response, as if to some veiled desire writ large in the heavens, for she suddenly reached up and began pulling out bobby pins, letting down her hair and shaking it loose.

"Perhaps he should have been a medievalist," I offered, wanting to put the brakes on her transformation. "Funny, how someone who so loved to find order in chaos could have lived such a disorderly life."

She glanced at me in the half-light, her long hair flaring, as if caught by a stray current of solar wind, as if glad she'd succeeded in drawing that bit of bile from my soul: what, I realized the moment I spat it out, could just as easily have been construed as a criticism of her life, as well.

She turned her face again to the night sky. "It was *my* mother who taught me the stars; she liked to say the stars were a kind of first language, like the invisible notes of birdsong, and how the succession of wildflowers is the only measure of time that really matters."

In this, I sensed less a defensive tone than a cry of abandonment . . . or was it a yearning to belong? And I was put in mind of all the books on botany and astronomy on my father's shelves, and how many times, opening the pages of one of his books, a dried flower would slip free.

"You mentioned the Philby autobiography you found with the letters: What did the inscription say?"

Without hesitation she recited: "'For Suzanne, a love never betrayed. And you, my darling, the best of all. Kim.'"

I nodded, not a little bewildered, struggling, and—following her gaze skyward, as I had followed Max's stellar gaze from our boathouse all those years before—tried to put it aside.

"For me, the stars always seemed a little unnerving. I mean, you spend your career puttering in the earth for scraps of lost lives, the glimmering fragment that will add another syllable to a lost history; while out there, murmuring away every night, are billions of notes of data, infinitely old, from various eras separated by millions of years—and all of it flooding away from you, as tempting as they are unintelligible, of worlds that have flickered out a billion years before Paleolithic men painted their bison in the flame-lit caves of Lascaux."

From a disco along the quay, the incongruent strains of a Jerome Kern standard, "I'm Old Fashioned." She laughed incredulously, as if she'd been found out, and turned to me and took my hands in a slow two-step, slipping a hand to my shoulder as she had on the night of the senior dance. Her parted liquid lips seemed poised on a memory as she kept her eyes firmly turned to the heavens.

"Jerry Robbins . . . I did the second performance."

"Who?"

"You don't find it some comfort to be part of them—the stars, I mean, to know their names, to wonder about their journey?"

"With so many lost stories of our own . . . just a drop in the ocean—pretty small potatoes."

"I kinda feel like they're my friends, that I'm at the heart of their journey, the midpoint of all things—but what the fuck: I'm old-fashioned."

She squeezed my hand as if to put a stop to any hint of self-pity and expertly led me in a few turns, then, breaking away a moment to dance a few steps, arms extended to an invisible partner, she closed her eyes as she hummed along with the music.

"Well," I said to her, "I feel a little bit less insignificant here with you and—who did you say—Mr. Robbins?"

"And Mr. Kern—two Jeromes."

She returned to me and nestled her head against my ear as if better to whisper.

"I don't think it's about being bigger or smaller; it's only how alive you are. Even when I'm on the stage at the Met—and it's a huge, scary space, especially in a solo—I feel like I'm just about where I need to be, that I can project enough feeling—when I'm perfectly on the music— to fill the thing, as fully alive as God or nature ever meant us to be. There were moments when I knew I could be anything. . . . Well, maybe not Astaire."

With all the wine and Demerol, I ended up being good for nothing. I fell asleep as soon as I lay down on my bed. Sometime later, I awoke from the most violent nightmare, the kind of nightmare that I had pretty much banished toward the end of my freshman year at Princeton. I'd been proud of how, by forcing myself to focus intensely on my studies, steeping myself in the ancient past, I'd strangled my own past. Keeping my mouth shut and my mind engaged on work seemed to banish bad feelings; as Maureen put it, "Listen, soldier—live in the present and find yourself a sweet girl and the past will take care of itself." The Demerol helped, my students helped, even if they thought anyone who'd served in Vietnam was an idiot or a loser. But there I was on the floor, awash in sweat, the bedclothes kicked the hell all over the place, and Laura beside me, cringing in her T-shirt and panties as she held one of my arms and shied away from the other. I was mortified and shivering with fear because I had been trying to save myself from drowning, from being pulled under, as if the Vam Co Dong River had come alive, as if all the floating bodies had risen up as one.

"Jesus Christ, I'm sorry, I'm sorry."

"Peter, are you okay?"

"Of course I'm okay."

I was indignant, furious at myself. She let go of my arm and reached to rub her shoulder, where I must have hit her pretty hard; she had a big purple bruise there the next morning.

"You scared me to death."

"Scared you—shit."

"Are you sure you're okay?"

"Well . . . I was, I was just fine until you came along."

She reminded me of that all the way to Pylos by giving me the silent treatment.

26

IN HOMER'S *ODYSSEY*, BAD DREAMS WERE always an ominous presentiment, a sign of a god's displeasure, a warning to keep a watchful eye—and keep the sacrifices coming. I couldn't shake the feeling as we drove to Pylos that I was getting myself into something I'd regret. And I realized how completely I'd broken with my father, forgoing his field of Greek Bronze Age archaeology to specialize in the golden age of Periclean Athens—so complete a break that I'd barely set foot in the Peloponnese, much less Pylos. But it was a distance that had served me well. It didn't help my sense of dread and anxiety that Laura kept her nose buried in her heavily underlined copy of the *Odyssey*, a way of avoiding conversation while rubbing the bruise on her arm just in case I'd forgotten. I felt I should warn her not to get her hopes up. Neokosmos Grigoriadis—our Nestor—could just as easily turn out to be a blowhard disappointment with a hidden agenda that had best be left alone. Names can be dangerous. And the Greek Civil War was hardly a dead issue: Scratch any Greek of a certain age and you will hear horror stories as terrible as anything Stalin or Pol Pot had perpetrated, if on a lesser scale. I had long learned not to talk politics—it never ended and never well. The recent socialist prime minister, Andreas Papendreou, whose father had been a right-of-center prime minister after the war, had deep roots in the fratricidal passions of the Greek Civil War, and even though educated in America, he played the anti-American card with the best of them, especially concerning issues of Cypress and Turkey. What I felt like telling her but saved my breath: No mortal can enter the same stream twice, but names—*Philby, for one*—can attach themselves like millstones around your neck, bearing with them the treacherous burdens of a past not your own.

I was skeptical our little jaunt would produce anything good but felt I owed it to her to give it a try. Even if my father hadn't trusted her mother an inch.

Nor did it help that Laura—a voracious reader and long in thrall to Max's theory that we are the stories we tell and so come to believe in them more than reality—saw the world through names, just as she had experienced life onstage, inhabiting various characters through choreography and music until they were second nature.

So, on the winding coastal road all the way to Pylos, troubled by the recurrence of old nightmares and leery of the meeting with this self-proclaimed Nestor and the dredging up of glorious OSS exploits, I sought to distract myself with more practical ambitions. As we reached the west coast, I began relishing the glorious views of Navarino Bay and contemplating the island of Sphaktiria shimmering in the cobalt blue distance. Sphaktiria presented a more productive possibility for our journey, for Sphaktiria was where the Spartans were famously defeated by an Athenian force in the Peloponnesian War. It had been one of the very rare occasions in which the Athenians had actually cut off, isolated, and beaten the Spartans in a land engagement. I realized that my book on Thucydides could certainly benefit from a visit to Pylos and a firsthand survey of the typography of Sphaktiria, the kind of specifics and detail in my writing that I prided myself on, often encouraging my students to get their noses out of their notes: "Get some dirt under your fingernails, people, a feel for the lay of the land." I found myself relishing the opportunity: After enduring the wartime reminiscences of some grizzled veteran, I'd have a chance to take photographs and make notes on the ancient battlefield of Sphaktiria—even visit the excavations of Bronze Age Pylos, which I had sorely neglected, and turn the trip into a windfall. Laura, with her well-thumbed copy of the *Odyssey,* would certainly enjoy a visit to the real Nestor's Palace . . . the wise king of Homer and storyteller of epic battles.

"Left at the white house with green shutters up ahead." She pointed, looking up from her printed instructions. "Well, it certainly feels like the place, sandy Pylos, and the wine-dark sea, and . . . *on the trail of your father's widespread fame.* No horses, though—wasn't Nestor a breaker of horses?"

"Give the Homer a break, okay?"

"Max always said you were obsessed with the *Odyssey.*"

"Yeah, yeah, yeah, just like he wrote in his novels—and you, of all people, know how full of lies they are. So, enough of the bullshit, okay? Let's meet with this guy and hear what he has to say. Then we can look at the Mycenaean excavations of Pylos down the road, and a few other odds and ends I have in mind."

We turned onto a private dirt road that led to a sprawling walled compound overlooking Navarino Bay. It seemed to stretch the length of a broad promontory, surrounded by an imposing sandstone wall painstakingly constructed with interlocking patterns of thin pinkish stone. Concertina wire ran along its entire length, and the razor barbs, glinting menacingly in the waning light of afternoon, didn't offer much comfort. The dirt and gravel road ended at a huge wrought-iron gate with leaping dolphins forming the apex of a series of branching floral patterns. Two security guards stood on either side, one with an M16 slung over his shoulder, the other with a clipboard in hand.

"Oh great." I smacked the steering wheel. "What the fuck have you managed to get me into?"

After a night of bad dreams, that M16 was just about the last thing I needed.

"Hey, relax, will you? Why so jumpy? I'm just following the directions I was sent."

The guard with the clipboard was wearing a blue Yankees baseball cap—that was a relief; it could've been the Mets. He casually came over to my window and checked off our names on his list. Speaking into a walkie-talkie, he alerted someone to our arrival as the guard with the M16 opened the heavy gates onto a gravel drive. My fellow Yankees fan waved us through.

"Hey, they've been worried when you'd get here. Just follow da drive through da gardens and orchards. You'll see Nikos waiting for ya at da big house." He tipped his hat. "Welcome. You guys are da honored guests."

"Say, how's Tommy John holding up?"

"The old guy can still throw a hell of a sinker, but not enough to save the Yanks."

"I hear the Toronto Blue Jays are going to take it."

"Toronto—Toronto, I tought they just played hockey up dere."

The white gravel drive wound past elaborate gardens and nurseries, corralled by immaculate lawns and hedges, while stately poplars lined our way toward the main house. In the distance were fan-shaped palms, wonderfully radiant in the sunset, their fronded undersides bathed in mustard-orange half tones. As we got closer, the green lawn became patterned with spiraling arabesques of neat flower beds, the perfectly trimmed herbaceous borders setting off rows of pansies: blue, bronze, and lavender. Scattered in spiky clumps and clusters were a few ancient olive trees, like lingering personages from an earlier era, relics of what might once have been extensive groves. I was reminded of the haggard apple trees in the Circle at Winsted. We passed a swimming pool and tennis courts and fruit orchards and the air swelled with the fragrance of apricots, oranges, and lemons, the sweet citrus scents giving way to the smoky aroma of a barbecue as we neared the main house.

Try as I might, I could not help conjuring images of the splendid Bronze Age palace of Nestor, which excavations in the decades since the war had revealed on a hilltop just a few miles down the road. The huge building that came into view was hardly a Bronze Age citadel, but impressive enough, a smorgasbord of traditional Greek white geometries with a sprinkling of Spanish Colonial ranch style circa Beverly Hills of the 1920s. Venetian Gothic windows did add a nice touch, along with dutiful postmodern detailing—the functionless columns in a blind portico being the most egregious example. Long balconies dripped with flowering hibiscus and honeysuckle and offered spectacular views of the gardens and Navarino Bay. Off the entrance driveway was a parking lot filled with a small fleet of Volvo trucks and silver Mercedes with prominent CB antennas. Two male peacocks strutted by the front entrance and greeted us with piercing cries. Nestor's elder son, Nikos, waved to us from the massive front door of rusticated oak.

"You won't believe how much I've heard about your dad from the old man," Nikos told me. He shook our hands warmly, lingering with Laura, as so many did because they half-remembered her from the days when the paparazzi filled the pages of the celebrity press with her photos. She had her hair up in a chignon, a blue skirt just covering the knee brace, and she seamlessly segued from Homer to full flirting mode as she stepped out of the Land Rover. Nikos couldn't have been more American: not a trace of an accent, dark hair barbered in compact layers, trim in build, and nicely dressed in a blue blazer and khaki slacks. Bare feet in tattered loafers, he could have been hosting a party in the Hamptons. Two porters quickly got our bags from the back of the Land Rover and took them to our rooms. "Since I was a kid, I've been hearing these stories." Nikos motioned us into the house with a smile and an exaggerated roll of his eyes, as if these endlessly repeated stories of resistance days past and the civil war had become well-worn chestnuts of family lore, which only confirmed my skepticism about our venture. "We're in for it tonight, my friends; he's got the old crowd here, and you guys are the main attraction."

"This is so great," said Laura, taking in the beautifully furnished home.

Nikos was a lawyer in Boston by way of Harvard and had a stunning Italian-American wife, who knew all about Laura's ballet career. Their three children were in high school and all had come to visit granddad for the occasion. "We only come back here for holidays. But since my brother took over the restaurants, my dad spends more time in Pylos— the country-squire, old-country thing. With the socialist government in Athens, he's got to be crazy, but he *hangs in there*."

"I'm looking forward to meeting your dad," I said.

After we got settled in our rooms and washed up, Nikos gave us a quick tour of the house as he conducted us to the office wing. Room after room was filled with very up-to-date Milanese modern furnishings, and many rooms were packed with books: stuffed into shelves, in piles on a coffee table, tumbled stacks by easy chairs. One might have thought it was an academic's summer house.

Nikos smiled. "I should tell you: He's not the same man your father knew during the war and after. My old man, since he retired from the day-to-day running of the restaurant business, has become a *philosopher*—a big reader; he will talk your ear off—so, that's my due diligence: You've been warned."

Nestor's offices were in a complex toward the rear of the house, overlooking the gardens. We found him hunched over his messy desk, intently scribbling notes on a legal pad. I later realized these were notes for his dinner speech. He was a big man, once compact and powerful but now overweight due to age or infirmity. His full head of white hair was immaculately pomaded back from a pinkish brow lined with ragged creases. When Nikos waved us into the office, Nestor glanced up with a start, as if his mind had been elsewhere, as he registered our sudden appearance. It was almost comical how his expression shifted from surprise to incredulity and then finally to a smile of recognition. And then he was up with a grunt, a great bear of a man, papers flying as he lumbered around his desk to engulf me in a hug that elicited an embarrassed laugh from his son.

"My God . . . it can be no one else." He pushed me to arm's length, squinting behind his thick lenses, embraced me again, and again shoved me back for another inspection. I felt like a trapped insect under those magnified lenses, his eyes tearing up. "The last time I saw John was in Athens in 1949—he must have been what, about thirty-five, and you must be . . . ."

"A couple of years older."

"Jesus Christ—I'd have known you anywhere. So the son has finally found his way to old Nestor." Realizing he'd been forgetting himself, he turned to Laura. "And so it is you, beautiful lady, I have to thank for bringing this son of a gun my way."

Nestor took Laura's outstretched hand and brought it to his lips, lingering in his kiss, and his son laughed again.

"Take it easy, Pop, you're going to embarrass these good people."

Nestor swiped at his tears and gave Laura a regal nod, his watery eyes sparking with highlights, as if he were seeing something in her that quite captivated him.

He growled, clearing his throat. "After all the years and lives, something of your father remains to me—good old Johnny A., friend and comrade." He put a hand on my shoulder and cast a nodding glance again at Laura. "Yes, I would have recognized you, Peter. Perhaps not the young OSS officer I first met on the beach in '43, but for sure the not so young CIA man that saved us in the civil war of '48–'49."

It was a refrain I hadn't heard since school days. I had steered clear of my father's circles and had turned down, on more than one occasion, invitations to join the Winsted board of trustees led by Elliot Goddard. And yet I was moved; there was nothing rehearsed about Nestor's enthusiasm. His were the genuine effusions of an old man who, as I would soon find out, was struggling with the truth as much as I. Nikos escorted us down a corridor toward the gardens, with Nestor still wiping copious tears, waving his arms from a barrel chest as we passed offices seemingly papered with photographs of restaurants he owned in the United States, in New York, Boston, Philadelphia, and points west. On the back veranda, overlooking the gardens and a spectacular array of arbors beyond, he stopped short of the steps, struck by a thought.

"Did you know . . ." He raised a hand as if making a pledge to his gods, his open-necked shirt displaying a hairy chest and a glittering gold medallion. "Did you know that it was your father who gave me the name Nestor? On the first night, the first hour when the submarine dropped him on the beach, he gave me the name."

"Come on, Pa," said Nikos, "save it for later, or we'll never get through the dinner on time. I'm worried about the older guys; some of them don't look so good."

Nestor ignored his son and winked at Laura as he attempted a kind of awkward apology, as if concerned we might take amiss the business about his name. "No, no, you must understand. It was a joke; at first it was, I think, a joke. I had no idea back then what it meant to be a *Nestor* in *Pylos*."

"*King* of Pylos," I said, laughing, more and more intrigued as my forebodings seemed to be taking on more of a farcical cast.

"Yes, king," agreed Nestor, echoing my laugh and spreading his arms expansively. "Your dad knew all about kings and heroes. What an educated man."

"He was that, Nestor—shall I call you Nestor, or do you go by Neokosmos?"

I noted a flicker of disdain. "Nestor. My old friends call me Nestor." He made a motion about his face as if to portray a mask. "Now I'm stuck."

"You see, Nestor, my father might have been one of the greatest scholars of his generation if the war hadn't intervened," I said.

The old man grimaced at the protective tone in my voice, which, in turn, prompted a note of regret or self-justification, and a significant look from his son.

"Isn't that the truth." Nestor pawed his hairline in a gesture of despair. "My God, eight years of my life when I returned from America, first the Italians, then the Germans, and then the fucking Communists—eight endless years and how many lives, half a million of our people dead. What a terrible waste to take such things into old age. I hope you are not like Nikos and his brother, who don't give a shit about what happened here."

"We *care*, Pop," said Nikos.

"Not enough to prevent you from spending your years at Harvard protesting the war in Vietnam."

"Pop, that hardly follows."

"Follows, follows what? You don't think killing Communists is an honorable thing for a young man?"

Nikos smiled. "In Greece, maybe. In Southeast fucking Asia—sorry for my French." He nodded apologetically to Laura. "Come on, everybody's waiting for us."

Nestor took my arm. "Did you protest, too? Did you burn flags?"

"No flag burning. I was a bookworm, like my father."

Laura smiled half playfully, half daring to keep the pot stirred.

"Better than that, he fought in Vietnam," she told him.

"Yes, I heard something about all that from Elliot Goddard."

"Not a big deal. I was a language expert, part of an advisory team in 1972 helping the Vietnamese local militias get their shit together."

A look of deep pleasure came into Nestor's face as he eyed me.

"Praise the gods"—he nodded, brushing the underside of his chin with his fingers in the Greek gesture for the workings of fate—"that you are safe and something of John remains. Children are a blessing," Nestor smiled sweetly at us and winked at Nikos. "Some more than others. His brother, too damned busy to come, heh." He put his arms around Laura and me. "You said you two were cousins?"

"Fourth or fifth—isn't that right, Peter?"

"Fourth. Our families go back a long way."

"Yes, yes, there is a resemblance." Nestor scrutinized our faces. "A beautiful and mysterious thing." Nestor reached to his son and pinched the side of his neck. "But my Nikos, the gods be praised, has his mother's beauty—God rest her soul—and his old man's brains—although maybe not his lion's heart."

"Dad, your guests are going to lynch us if you keep them waiting any longer."

A waiter in a white linen coat ran up and handed Nestor his jacket and the notes he'd forgotten in his office. Nestor struggled to get his thick arms into the sleeves and then extracted a set of amber worry beads from the pocket. Our route to the promised "genuine American barbecue" turned out to a circuitous one, as Nestor was intent on our viewing his domain before the daylight was gone. He wanted us to see him for who he was, that he hadn't misappropriated the name Nestor or come by it under false pretenses. He was clearly proud of his gardens, especially of the painstaking labor that had been required to transform the dry, rocky soil of Homer's "sandy Pylos" into something approaching a lush English garden. This had been in the works since the late fifties, he explained, and still required a legion of gardeners to keep up. He told us he had single-handedly revived the citrus-growing business in this part of the Peloponnese. Nestor was very intent that we see the extensive orchards that provided fruit for his table, picking apricots and limes and handing them to us to smell. As we walked, he became more expansive, asking us about the States, complaining of recent emigration laws that made it more difficult for him to get in staff for his restaurants. He had nothing good to say about the present socialist government in Athens.

"They lead the people to ruin again, as before, and spit in the face of Greece's greatest friend, America."

As we neared an enormous arbor thick with hanging vines, the plaintive lament of a bouzouki band could be heard over the murmur of the guests. The cavernous arbor, thick with cooking smoke, gave way to a central space of tables arranged about a barbecue pit, where an entire side of beef was turned on a spit over a roaring coal fire, tended by two sweating youths stripped to the waist. There must have been close to a hundred diners at various tables, already well into the wine and enjoying the bouzouki band. Nestor's tardy appearance brought yells and greetings. White-coated waiters were efficiently shuttling food and drinks among the guests. Then some of the older men at the head table spied Nestor and stood with their raised glasses and sang out more greetings in his direction, which he returned with waves and hugs. A quiet fell over the scene as Nestor made introductions. Children scampered to the sides of parents. The undersides of the leafy arbor were alive with flickering notes of translucent colors—emeralds and copper-orange and burnished gold.

Seated at the head table were the men Nestor and my father had fought with in the Resistance and later against the Communists during the civil war. Their names poured in exclamations from our host's lips: Achilleas, Christos, Dimitrios, Harisis, Alexo, Sotiris—men with the names of heroes, gods, and saints, most old and infirm and many showing the effects of wounds from their days as fighters in the hills around Pylos and the north of Greece. Some used canes, two were in wheelchairs. Laura basked in their stares. I felt devoured, as more than once she nudged me forward to acknowledge a greeting. Every one of them had known my father, and in their glittering fire-softened eyes and wine-smoothed voices I detected a wellspring of memory swirling like sudden rapids. When they found I spoke Greek, many broke into tears, as if they'd seen the Second Coming. They patted my back, gave me rough kisses, praised my father effusively, so much so that I wanted to slink away and withdraw from what suddenly felt like a fraudulent life and mistaken identity. Laura, on the other hand, seemed mesmerized by the reactions of these wizened fighters, savoring the near-ritual fare of tearful accolades that came to so many lips. She took a place to Nestor's left and sat there like his warrior queen, proud and tall, as if drawing strength from the flow of wine and words, more confident than ever in the instincts that had led her to this place.

"New York prime," Nestor crowed to me, pointing out the beef. "Had it specially flown in from the States."

Waiters filled our glasses before they were half-empty, and Nestor was on his feet bellowing out toasts to the faithful. He spoke movingly of dead comrades, saying their names with a dirgelike rhythm, and urged parents to teach their children what had befallen them and all they had sacrificed for the sake of Hellenic freedom. "Remember the cause of freedom and solidarity between Greece and America." The old fighters at our table barked their assent, raised their glasses, and downed their wine. Moments later, our candelabra-lit table with its centerpiece of tiny crossed Greek and American flags was gridlocked with plates of appetizers—tiropitakia, piperies psites, gharithes vrastes—along with salads swimming in fresh tomatoes and hunks of feta cheese, warm bread, and bowls of olives. And when the initial commotion had died down, Nestor turned to me, took Laura's hand in his great bear's paw, and proclaimed in a fervent whisper, "Fate, a lousy business—heh, that a man should not live to know his son, and a son his father. He was one helluva a guy. Let me tell you, I have never met one like him—never."

"Thank you," I said. And as I nodded to the candlelit faces fading into and out of shadow, I noticed a striking woman at the very end of our table: tall, pale-skinned, with long, flowing dark hair and intense deep-set eyes. She was staring at me in a way that recalled the penetrating stare of Suzanne Williams that night at the dinner table at Hermitage. Then she glanced down and away, as if aware she was being impolite. She began speaking to a one-armed veteran at her side. I couldn't recall being introduced to her. Then Nestor touched my arm as if he'd noticed how I had been distracted, and by whom, and wished to reclaim my attention.

"He stirred our soul," said Nestor, "in a very dark time. In him, the best of what we hoped for ourselves and our people had a human face, a heroic face."

The hyperbole was beginning to get to me, and I began downing my wine—and really good wine at that—to soften the cynical spirit I felt coming over me. I couldn't refrain from making a face at Laura, and she instantly shot me a fierce look of intense sobriety, as if to indicate that

I must act the part. What part? I had defended my father's rectitude right to the banks of the Vam Co Dong River, and then some. I was amazed at how much she drank and wondered how much Xanax she had downed. She was leaning on Nestor's shoulder, becoming more animated by the moment, first childlike and then doing more of her flirty courtesan thing, encouraging Nestor to tell us about the war and my father. The bouzouki band had her all loosened up and giddy, and she was playing her character out of Homer for all it was worth—and worse, not even realizing she was doing it.

As if Nestor needed encouragement.

The fire glinted on the great lenses of his thick glasses and he held out a wine-wet hand to the fire and the smoke, as if in oblations to his gods. For a moment, he seemed stuck, but only for a moment, and he was soon off and running, reentering the world of his waning youth, those terrible and disastrous years of invasion, occupation, and civil war that had devastated every person at our table. Fathers had buried sons and daughters; sons and daughters, fathers. Whole families had been exterminated by starvation and execution and butchery.

Nestor relished the description of my father's tiny rubber raft bobbing in the darkness off the beach, taking forever to close the distance between the British submarine out of Bari and the shore. The moon was nearly full, the submarine a sitting duck, but the Germans had only recently taken over from the surrendering Italians, who had occupied the Peloponnese in 1942, only to go over to the Allies in the early fall of 1943. It took the Germans a few months to collect the Italian units and get their claws into the occupation. Nestor remembered a tall, powerful figure, along with his British radio operator, staggering in from the surf, eyes all the more brilliant for the black camouflage grease on his face.

Nestor touched a shaking finger to his temple.

"An American, not British, OSS, not SOE, though the British were providing all the logistics and equipment. Perfect Greek, too, a little educated maybe—like you, but like a native, like the rich guys from Athens, the great shipping magnates. And his handshake, a grip like a vise. Only an idiot would try and put one over on the owner of such a handshake. But it was his name that confused me. I knew that name. The face, too, but where?"

Like the skilled storyteller that he was, Nestor paused, looked around to make sure he had our attention, smiled, and raised his glass for a refill. The glass glinted rubies in the blaze of firelight. With his left hand, he began fingering his worry beads, beginning a soft clicking that continued all evening, like the song of an overnight train in your sleeping ear.

"There was something in his voice, something about his face."

Nestor had left Greece as a boy in 1917, during World War I, to work in his uncle's Newark, New Jersey, restaurant. By the time of the Depression, he owned five restaurants in New York, one a fairly upscale Italian restaurant on Lexington and Seventy-third Street. He had returned to Greece in late 1940 to bury his father and to find a bride, a rich man by Greek standards. Preparations for the wedding took longer than expected and there were complications with the embassy about American immigration papers for his new wife. Most of Europe was under German occupation; the American embassy was short-staffed, communications shaky. Then the Italians invaded from Albania, followed by the Germans in the spring of 1941. "It offended my American sense of what was right and wrong—you might say, idiot that I was. I mean those sneaky Italian bastards pouring across the Albanian border—I knew their kind from Brooklyn." The Germans were another matter. So when my father showed up on that beach, Nestor was a battle-hardened veteran and a resourceful resistance leader who had gone to ground in his hometown of Pylos. And a widower, for his young wife had starved to death in Athens during the first winter of the German occupation.

My father may not have been in combat, but he'd driven an ambulance in northern Greece during the Italian invasion and knew frontline warfare; he had been well trained by the OSS in guerilla tactics—top among his class of recruits, an outstanding marksman, and eager to return to the Peloponnese, where he had worked in the decade before the war. Allied intelligence in Cairo wanted to prevent an incipient civil war between the Greek Resistance groups, the royalists and republicans under the banner of EDES and the Greek Communist Party, KKE, controlling the combined front groups, EAM-ELAS. By the fall of 1943, the opening salvo of the fratricidal Greek Civil War took place as the Communists attempted the destruction of all non-Communist Resistance groups, saving their worst savagery for Marxist splinter groups in their own ranks.

As they made their way inland from the beach, mules loaded down with supplies and radio equipment, climbing the tiny goat trails Nestor had known in his childhood, my father barraged him with questions.

"A thousand questions, and always one more." The quality and quantity of arms, ammunition supplies, numbers of active fighters, local men or ex-Greek army, republican officers or EAM sympathizers; training, security of communications, German troop movements and strength. But the thing that surprised Nestor was that this American, still wet from the surf, seemed to know an awful lot about local geography.

"Hell, he knew the villages, the roads, the trails as if he'd spent years in the country."

As I would soon learn, there was nothing arbitrary about my father's landing on that beach near Pylos in the fall of 1943. He had volunteered himself, cornered OSS chief Bill Donovan and lobbied for an American presence in Greece—insisting that OSS and America couldn't afford to be dependent on the British for intelligence and influence in this crucial southeastern flank of Europe. He was by any measure the best man for the job, given his intimate knowledge of the area and his language skills, but Greece and Yugoslavia were a British area of operations. The British reluctantly agreed to joint operations between OSS and their British counterpart, SOE, focusing most of their resources on northern Greece, especially toward the end of 1944, to harry the retreating Germans. My father was indeed the first American OSS officer in mainland Greece and the only one in the Peloponnese, something of a backwater for Allied subversion, with only a few German naval bases offering substantial targets. Only later would I find out that both my father and the SOE had ulterior motives for the Pylos operation. Of this, Nestor knew only as much as my father let on. By the time they stopped to rest in the relative safety of the high hills overlooking Navarino Bay, John offered one version of his operational orders.

"He had a mind like that." Nestor raised an open hand draped with the amber worry beads and shut it into a clenched fist. "If the Allies were to support the republican Resistance fully, we needed to be an effective fighting force against the Germans, like the Communist ELAS—the British favorites, in the north. We were instructed to put our differences with the Communists aside and find a target of opportunity: A German naval base was high on the list.

"'If you can't unite and put politics away for the duration of the war, postwar Greece will be a mess.'That's what he told me, and he was right about the mess. But he had no idea what monsters we were up against."

They were standing together on a ledge above the sea. The tall American offered Nestor a cigarette, a Lucky Strike—pure heaven for

Nestor, who'd hadn't had an American cigarette in over two years. The flame of the Zippo lighter lit my father's face in the dark, his Hollywood face like that of a saint in an icon, said Nestor—such a handsome American face.

"Like a fucking million dollars, a movie star, I thought. I must've seen this guy in a movie. First, we figured we must've run into each other in the north when he drove his American ambulance—the Italian fighting in Albania. But it was your dad who remembered. He smiled at me and laughed and put his hand on my shoulder. 'Alfredo's,' he told me, 'Lexington, between Seventieth and Seventy-first streets—or is it Seventy-second?"

"Seventy-third, boss."

It was Nestor's flagship restaurant, from which his empire would expand in the fifties and sixties once he returned from the Greek Civil War. My father had gone there for dinner many times with his mother when he was home from Winsted, from Princeton, a six-minute walk from the apartment on Fifth Avenue.

"You had to see it. Me, a kid arrived in America with a dirty shirt and my father's blessing to go to work for my uncle—what?—twenty-five years later, standing in this place where as a child I'd come to watch the goats for my father. And there I was in the middle of a war with this rich American guy, a class act, a family that owned half of New York, to hear what people said—with me, there, in that place, talking about how we were going to kill Germans and make nice with the Communists. Who could have made up such a story?"

Who indeed? In spite of my skepticism, I found myself relishing Nestor's every word—not so much because of the romantic scene of firelight and fine wine, but because it was the countertext to Max's novel—the troubling truth he hadn't bothered about, and a story he could never have dreamed up.

"John put his hand on my shoulder. 'We shall call you Nestor.'"

"'Yes, Nestor, king of Pylos, a wise ruler and intrepid warrior . . . let me tell you something about him.'"

I couldn't help laughing when Nestor said this. It was, of course, the exhilaration of the moment, of surviving the first contact with the enemy with your nerve intact, when joy in life reaches a fever pitch and the mind races to fortify itself with familiar analogues. Yes, my father had reached for the model of Odysseus, his boyhood hero: a giver of names. But it was also his way of boosting morale and building respect and an esprit de corps among the ranks of these devastated men who had known victory over the Italians, only to have it snatched away by the Germans. Now, a year later, the Greek Resistance had been largely taken over by the Communists under the fronts of EAM and ELAS. The Communists had a long history of subversion and clandestine warfare; their propaganda and strong-arm tactics allowed them to destroy the moderate republican Resistance groups either by subterfuge or pitiless elimination. My father's attempt to expound on democratic principles was almost laughable in Nestor's eyes.

"Democracy, free elections, rule of law, individual rights: It's how we Americans think, don't you see—forget the romance business. But the Communists don't care about our American niceties, not when they have a gun to your head. And let me tell you, the Greek Communists—all these smart-ass intellectuals who brought chaos and ruin to my old country—we should've shot them all. I know, I know what you're thinking: I'm just a right-wing businessman without even a high school education."

But Nestor quickly realized something else about my father: something from his youth, a vague romantic yearning for a golden age and an inbred distaste for industrialized killing.

As he and my father rested and smoked after their climb, the vast night distance began to fill with a faint drone. The sound grew louder, and then over the sea tiny wedges of black appeared against the gray night, followed on across the whiter sea by winged shadows racing for the place where they stood. It was an enormous formation of American bombers, moonlight glinting in the pilots' windows, sparking on the front nose-gunner turrets—mechanical insects looming larger as they flew so low to the water that they might have been giant water bugs skating across the white surface. As the bombers drew closer, Nestor, my father, and the others found themselves actually looking down on patterns of silver wings sluicing silver waves until they reached the island of Sphacteria; then, within seconds of disaster, these apparitions of an industrial age leapt skyward, motors screaming for altitude, as if to fly right into the cliff face and annihilate them all with their screaming buzz saws. Some of the men dropped to the ground or dashed for a nearby cave. Nestor said he had never seen anything like it; the sky was packed with a hundred, more. Nestor and my father held their ground, eyes inching up as the bombers shot past barely a hundred feet over their heads, shooting the escarpment above, so close that the night darkened for seconds and their hair blew in the back draft. Then an instant of almost complete silence followed as if it had all been a trick of their minds. What Nestor remembered so well—and why he felt compelled to tell us about it—was how different his reaction was from my father's. He found this display of American might exhilarating— as if a sign from the gods that my father's presence among them was going to change everything. But the tall, keen-eyed American had only shaken his head with weary despondency, explaining to Nestor that they were Mitchell B-49's, probably headed for the Ploiesti oil fields in Romania, perhaps a daring night raid, something exceptional.

"'What a shame, Nestor, what a goddamn shame—don't you think?'" Nestor, perplexed, had turned to my father's distant stare, the smell of exhaust fumes sifting down around them. "'Sad how men have learned to fight with such machines, high explosives delivered from a great distance. Don't you think so? What the German bombers have done to London, sad, so terribly sad, so little nobility of purpose left in the world. The gods have gone mad, Nestor; the gods have turned against their creation—what do you think?'"

Around our dinner table, Nestor looked at us with head high, as if to display something of my father's demeanor, repeating himself to get my father's cadences near perfect. "'So little nobility of purpose . . . the gods have turned against their creation.'" He looked at us with an expression of bafflement. "Those were his exact words to me. I never forgot them. What could an uneducated man say to that? Was I stuck with some American professor who knew nothing about modern warfare, who had never experienced German artillery fire?" Nestor spun the worry beads and snapped his fist shut. "'Sure, boss,' I told him, looking into his intelligent eyes, 'but if those bombers kill lots of Germans, it's okay with me. And, while they're at it, they can kill the Communists, too, those depraved sons of bitches.'"

In that moment, I suddenly understood something—deeply, viscerally: the lonely childhood of my father absent his father, a brilliant surgeon blown to smithereens by a German artillery strike. In that split second of compression, past and present squeezed to nothing, I, too, bridled at the horror of mechanized slaughter . . . I who had blithely called in B-52 strikes on Communist staging areas in Cambodia.

"The truth," said Nestor, "without Captain Alden, nothing would have been possible." As I looked down the table, I saw confirming nods in the flame-fevered faces; all except one, the tall woman at the very end of the table, who took everything in quietly, her eyes barely blinking, watching from some distant place inside herself. "You see, your father taught us to believe in ourselves—not just fighters but warriors. He taught them the American way—out of many, one. Not like the Communists, who always found ways to pit brother against brother, family against family, rich against poor. Even the poorest farmers among our fighters knew about America and rich Americans." And Nestor laughed at those down the table who screamed out in Greek words that meant "Yes, rich American Greeks like you." Nestor stood and bowed, sharing their laughter as he gestured like a royal personage to his court. Then he raised his hand to make a serious point. "John did not come like the Moscow-trained cadres and play on the jealousies and resentments and battered pride of our people—no, he filled them with the pride of their democratic ancestors. He reminded them that they had a grand history of freedom to die for and preserve."

Nestor patted Laura's hand and made eye contact with his former fighters as if to confirm the truth of his words.

"The picture never leaves my mind, when we were huddled around the fire at night. The flames in his eyes as he told these men the history of their race and recited to them from the great poets of their people. We sat for hours sometimes, like children at the knee of a grandfather. John explained how Greece had once been the center of the civilized world, as if he had been there—when Athens was a city of great statesmen and lawgivers, poets and philosophers, a civilization where the arts of sculpture and architecture reached a perfection never to be surpassed. Our men were proud again to be Greeks, a people of such history and tradition. You see, no longer peasants haggling in the marketplace, but fighters for the cause of civilization, for freedom and justice."

By the end of the initial toasts, I was feeling no pain—I was happy to embrace the man portrayed by Nestor. The kernel of my father's biography, contra Max, was taking shape in Nestor's telling. But as the evening settled down and Nestor got drunker, confining his words mostly to me and Laura, he became more introspective and perturbed, his portrait darker. Part of the problem turned out to be that the Resistance fighters "sat around on our asses most of the time. John and the British radio operator, Malcolm, had brought lots of small arms and ammunition, even Bren guns, bazookas, and three Thompson machine guns—boy, like right at home in the Bronx. But not the high explosives we needed if we were going to do something big. Six weeks until the explosives and grenades finally arrived by airdrop."

With the Allied successes in Italy, Greece looked less and less a potential beachhead for an allied thrust north through the Balkans. Not that the British didn't keep the pot stirred in Greece, hoping to hold down German forces that might be transferred to the Italian theater and later to France. And then there was the ongoing battle of the Dodecanese islands of Kos, Samos, and Leros, which had been held by Italian troops and would soon be contested by the British and Germans as the Italian units surrendered. Disruption of German naval assets in Greece and the islands became a high priority for the British.

"I wanted to wait it out, until the Germans withdrew, and then take care of the Communists before they took care of us. And you kill a German, they kill ten of your people—a hundred—worse."

Nestor sighed into his wine.

"As your father always put it to me, between Scylla and Charybdis—how's my pronunciation, professor?"

"Near perfect," I told him.

Nestor smiled. "You see, because of that damned name, I've become the old dog forced to learn new tricks. Do I not live up to the name your father gave me?"

He said this not entirely in jest, and I could detect a bitter irony creeping into his voice as he drank, shaking his mane of white hair, his worry beads atwitter in his massive hand. Nestor was struggling to fit the discordant pieces into a more convincing picture, especially the quixotic, perhaps devious, aspects of my father's nature that would end up changing all our lives.

"He kept telling the guards that he couldn't sleep, that he needed a short walk. Even Malcolm, his British radioman, never seemed to catch on—actually, Malcolm must have known something, but he never made a peep. John would sometimes be gone half the night. But who in their right mind walks in the hills at two in the morning and doesn't return, sometimes until dawn? So I told the guard to alert me the next time your father wanted a midnight stroll. It was a full moon when the guard woke me, maybe a week later, and pointed in the direction John had taken. Where the hell was he going—what was he thinking? You go right off the fucking edge in daylight unless you're a goat. And so I followed him, half-asleep, picking my way along the cliff trail, accompanied by my shadow plastered against the rock face. Every once in a while, I caught sight of him far ahead when the path curved, just a moon glint off his rifle. Where was this crazy guy leading me? We had gone maybe seven or eight kilometers north along Navarino Bay, until the path broadened out when it reached a broad plateau, a place called Epano Englianos. The moonlight was so bright, it almost hurt my eyes. A turkey shoot, I thought, if the Germans have patrols out, but even they wouldn't be so stupid. John was nowhere to be seen. I moved quietly, trying to see but not be seen. There were some old walls. I did not remember those walls and excavations from when I was a boy—it seems people had been digging trenches in the sandy earth. I thought maybe they were defensive positions for soldiers, but they were empty, just rubble and old walls.

"Then I heard voices and I dropped to one knee. Peering into the distance, I saw two men sitting in an area that had been excavated. There were stone walls, what remained of stone walls. And just their shoulders and heads showed above the piles of earth. Each was bending toward the other in deep discussion, and they gestured to something one of them was holding. The other had a stick and seemed to be drawing in the dirt. As I crept closer, I found that I was hearing German spoken. I switched the safety on my Thompson and covered them. They were so intent on their discussion, their drawings in the dirt, that they didn't hear me until I was practically on top of them. I told them—John and the other man—to raise their hands. Your father recognized me immediately and this big smile spread across his face.

"'Nestor, you are just the man. 'Welcome home, *my* king, to your palace.'

"That was exactly what he said, 'to your palace.' And he laughed like a drunkard—drunk on the moonlight, so delighted with himself—even as I kept my barrel pointed at his heart. Then he stood and introduced his friend; he called him a very old friend, a captain in the Wehrmacht no less.

"'Karel, I'd like you to meet Nestor.'

"The man stood, a brick or a stone in one hand, a cigarette in the other. He put the cigarette to his lips and reached out to shake my hand. I leveled my gun at his smiling face and told him not to move a muscle.

"'Take it easy, Nestor, I've know this man since school days. We were at Leipzig together, Cambridge, too. Point that thing away, just in case you shoot the greatest archaeologist of our generation.'

"The German bowed to John and laughed.

"'Perhaps an exaggeration, but coming from you, friend, an honor.'

"They were like that, you see, sucking up to each other, like old pals. This Karel guy, this Wehrmacht captain, had been in Pylos in the summer of 1939 and had dug up the walls where they were sitting on Epano Englianos—I couldn't believe the shit they were telling me. I held my gun on the guy and told John to take the Luger from his holster and give it to me.

"'What have you got in your hand?' I asked John.

"They smiled and John took this mud brick and handed it to me with the Luger. I could just make out some markings on the thing. And in the dirt where they'd been sitting, they had been drawing similar marks with a stick.

"'It's an ancient language, Nestor, what your people spoke over three thousand years ago. What you're holding in your hand is a voice, perhaps a story, a life from three thousand years ago. We have a slight problem, though: We can't read it. The language is lost.'

"This German, Karel, tried to explain it to me, and I could see how stuck they were—words without meaning. He was tall as John, spoke perfect Greek, even English like a Brit. Very elegant, with a long nose, and impatient, darting eyes. He wore his officer's uniform under a sheepskin coat. I didn't like the look of him, and it took a lot of talk from John to change my mind, and even then I didn't like him; I still don't like him."

"Karel Hollar had an actual Linear B tablet with him?" I said, agog at the thought.

"His 'lodestone,' he called the thing."

"They were colleagues," I explained. I looked at Laura, who seemed puzzled at this turn of events. "Rivals in the field of Bronze Age Greece. Karel had signed on to an American team from the University of Cincinnati under Carl Andersen and they dug those first trenches in July and August of '39. They were the discoverers of Nestor's Palace and also, more important, hundreds of Linear B tablets. An astonishing discovery because, up to that time, the tablets had been found only on Crete. Karel Hollar died in a Soviet POW camp at the end of the war. The excavations of Nestor's Palace weren't resumed again until 1955."

Nestor eyed me over his wine. "Another Communist dead—that's good news."

"He was a Communist?" I asked. "And I thought he was Czech."

"Are you kidding—and in a German uniform?" Nestor smiled what for him was an ironic smile. "He was British SIS—military intelligence—but in my book all those guys were Communist sympathizers."

My mind was scrambling for context. I remembered my father's letters to his mother in which he'd mentioned Karel Hollar's Communist sympathies in the early thirties. Many of Hollar's professional journal articles had been couched in Marxist analysis, but by 1936 or thereabouts, it had become more balanced and technical; one assumed, given the rise of the Nazis, he wasn't going to flaunt his ideology in German archaeological circles. But professionally, given his obsession with Greek Bronze Age archaeology, Hollar couldn't avoid involvement with British specialists in the field like Sir Arthur Evans and his protégée Nigel Bennett at Cambridge. What I hadn't realized and would only learn months later was that Nigel Bennett had run British SIS and their code-breaking operation during the war. So, this extraordinary scene that Nestor described on a moonlit night in wartime Greece began to make sense of a sort—but something was fishy.

"Hollar was a secret agent for British intelligence?"

"Like the fucking war was a big joke, something that had spoiled their little game, distracted them from the important things in life!" Nestor looked from Laura to me in a conspiratorial manner. "To be honest, I wasn't sure which one was crazier. They seemed like different people when they were together, or John did. They offered me cigarettes; they wanted to let me in on their little deal, like there was a pot of gold beneath the earth. I had interrupted them, you see—all their drawing in the dirt; they were building palaces out of thin air."

After an hour of their exasperating talk and scratchings in the dirt, Nestor told my father he'd had enough.

"'How can you trust a man wearing that uniform: The Germans murdered my wife; she was only nineteen.'"

At this, Karel Hollar had turned to Nestor, "like some kind of Cambridge gentleman in his London club."

"'Actually,' he said, 'I'm from the Sudetenland. My father is Czech, my mother Viennese . . . Jewish, although she hides it magnificently.'"

Nestor looked at my father and was galled to see a twinkle in his eyes.

"'The only thing that matters is that you're wearing that uniform.' I told Hollar.

"'Karel, I think what Nestor is trying to say is that it's a difference without a distinction.'

"Karel Hollar opened his sheepskin coat and examined his uniform and made a face.

"'The tailoring leaves something to be desired, I fear. Nevertheless, its fits well enough that I am sure it will get me killed sooner or later—what do you think, John?'

"'Nestor, Karel is with us. He's been working for the Brits from at least '37, if I'm not mistaken.' Your dad even winked at the bastard as he produced a piece of paper from his pocket. 'Here's the Wehrmacht's complete order of battle for the Peloponnese and the islands, including the disposition of naval forces and airfields. The battle for Kos is going on as we speak. I just spent the hour before you showed up putting it to memory, and when we get back, I'll get Malcolm to radio the contents to Cairo HQ.'

"'Impressive,' I told them. Your father read off the lists while I checked the sheet. Then he took out his Zippo and set it on fire, dropping it to the ground so as not to give off more light.

"'We both have the same orders, as I've told you a dozen times. The royalist and republican Resistance and the Communist Resistance must join to fight the Germans.'

"'The Communists are not on our side,' I told him; 'they're on *their* side—your pal's side, and waiting to slit our throats.'

"'They've been on our side since Hitler invaded the Soviet Union.'

"'Fine, leave them to kill one another—they do fine at that, too.'

"'Karel is in touch with the Greek Communists, ELAS in the Peloponnese. We must try to bring about reconciliation. As you know, those are my orders: a joint front against the Germans.'

"'Easy for you two to say. When you're back on Fifth Avenue and your pal is back in Berlin or Prague or Vienna or wherever, the Communists here will hunt us down like animals.'

"Karel smiled, Nestor told us, "the smile of a guy who knows he's got everybody at the table beat."

"'Nestor—may I call you Nestor?—the Communist Party and comrade Stalin want a free Europe and a better future, with equality and opportunity for all peoples. The Nazis are finished; they are being bled dry on the Eastern Front by the armies of the Soviet Union. It is only a matter of time.'

"That Karel was such a smooth talker. I waved my gun barrel in his face.

"'Where did you get that scar . . . there *and* there?'

"'Ah, street fighting. I think 1933. I believe I killed at least one Nazi brownshirt.'

"'Karel . . . did you really?'

"'The German smiled and shrugged at John. 'I didn't want to harm your sensibilities,' he said."

Nestor, noting the surprise in my father's voice, decided Karel Hollar was bad news from start to finish. He raised his gun.

"'You killed Nazis and now you are one of them?'

"'I'm first a Sudetenland Czech—possibly Austrian, and then an antifascist freedom fighter.'

"'A fucking mongrel Communist. Show me your identity papers.'

"'I'm afraid I can't do that.'

"'You will unless you want me to blow your fucking head off.'

"'As you wish.'

"Karel Hollar opened his arms as if to welcome my bullet."

"'John, if you ran into a guy like this in New York, who fills your mind with so much fucking bullshit, what would you do, hand him the keys to your apartment?'

"'Nestor, this isn't Seventy-third and Lexington.'

"'Damn right, it's not, and you need to get something straight: I can smell Communists a mile away. If he was killing Nazis before the war, he had to be a Communist. Once a Communist . . . the tiger never loses his stripes, even if he is British SIS, even if he is a Wehrmacht captain, even a pal of yours. Even a rookie cop would be the first to tell you: *a highly suspicious person with no fixed address.*'"

Karel smiled at Nestor's little joke.

"'Even in New York, the times are difficult for good men who defy the forces of tyranny and servitude. Tell me something, Nestor, do you allow Negroes in your restaurants?'

"'What kind of question is that?'

"'Are they still lynching Negroes in America?'

"'Not in my neighborhood, buddy, and we serve all kinds—as long as they can pay.'

"'The Communists and Jews in Germany are all dead, or hiding.' Karel Hollar gestured to his face as if miming a mask. 'So, you see—'

"'So, Karel Hollar is not your official name, your army name?'

"'Nestor, Karel has already put his life in danger coming here to give us this information. I don't need to know what name is on his identity papers—if one of us is captured, we will be tortured for that name, endangering every SIS operative in Greece.'

"'Jesus, you Communists change your names like your underwear. I should just kill you right here and save the three-ring circus.'

"'But my dear Nestor, surely you understand how the Wehrmacht does business these days: You shoot me and they will massacre an entire village. The SS are soulless beasts. That's why I came here, to destroy them, to remember better times, ja, John, when the world was young . . . and Crete and Venice.'

"'Spare me the schmaltz. Are you telling me'—and I looked from one to the other—'you boys didn't just stumble upon each other . . . so SOE and SIS and OSS had this all arranged?'

"Your father smiled like a guilty schoolboy, like he did when he and his mother came by my restaurant for dinner.

"'Talk to Cairo HQ. Although in some ways I prefer to think of it as a peculiar working of fate that two so-called enemies can find each other in such a beautiful place in the middle of all this madness, and remember what is *really* important.'"

This insouciant tip-off from my father's went right over Nestor's head.

"'Spare me. The Germans have been killing my people for two years now. You fucking starved my wife to death in Athens.'

"'I'm sorry—truly.'

"'Nestor, I've known Karel since I was a schoolboy. Over the years, we've spend months together in Leipzig and Cambridge, Crete and Venice. We've authored journal articles together. If you can't trust him, you can't trust me. Besides, the time has come to act. We must put aside our differences for the common good. And Karel can help us—'

"'A freedom-loving German, are you? Is there such a creature?'

"'My father, too, is of Jewish extraction. Perhaps you understand better?'

"'A Jew and a Communist: well, now we're getting somewhere.'"

Nestor bounced a flat palm off his forehead, as if more amazed than ever.

"'John, you should have stayed in New York,' I said. 'Hell, I should have stayed in New York. This whole continent has lost its mind. You can't believe anybody—in *anything*.'

"Karel nodded. 'As you say, I've been conspiring against my own family since I was a child.'

"'So, German, Jew, Communist, SIS. What exactly *do* you do for the Wehrmacht?'

"'As you see, my Greek is perfect and I am a mechanical engineer and demolition expert.'

"'Nestor, Karel's orders are to help us. We've got a plan.'

"'Jesus, John, how can you believe anything this guy tells you? New York is one thing—love, hate, or something in between—but business is business and no one cares as long as you don't welsh on a deal, and you're not fucking his wife. But here—a Communist is a Communist.'

"Karel laughed. 'Ah, John was right about you, to give you such a name. A born philosopher.'

"'Fuck you, buddy. I'm not done with you yet.'"

That was when Nestor first got wind of the attack on the E-boat base in Kalamata—a plan that had Karel Hollar's fingerprints all over it. Karel provided both a sketch of the base's defenses and detailed diagrams for placing the explosives in the ships. My father was enthusiastic because it required a joint operation of Nestor's EDES republican Resistance fighters and the main ELAS Communist units around Kalamata, precisely the kind of thing Cairo was encouraging. Nestor admitted they were all sick of sitting around and watching the war go by. Hollar's schematic plans of the torpedo boats—three Type 37 Flottentorpedoboots—based in the harbor of Kalamata were beautifully detailed, "like an artist's."

"Hollar explained: 'Even limited damage will make them inoperable, and the Kriegsmarine don't have the technicians, parts, or facilities to repair them in Greece. As good as if they were sunk in a thousand meters.'"

Karel Hollar proposed a quick surgical attack at dusk, which would result in limited casualties. The demolition teams could be in and out within twenty minutes. If the teams were thought to be a British or American commando unit, wearing official uniforms, the chances of retribution against the civilian population would be minimized.

Nestor had spun his worry beads: "At least it would be Kalamata that suffered reprisals and not Pylos."

The plan required the Communist Resistance forces around Kalamata to cover the escape route back to Pylos and hold up the arrival of German reinforcements. And Hollar could deliver the Communists.

"You see, your father trusted this guy Hollar, because they spoke the same language, shared the same dreams—like smarty-pants Einsteins without street smarts, heh."

"'Nestor,'" John explained to me, "'it's the best way to show HQ in Cairo what we can do. Now we have the explosives. And if the Greek Resistance fighters can make common cause, who knows, maybe the Allies might opt for a push up the Thessalonica gap. Sounds to me like the Americans and British are bogged down in Italy. The German occupation here could go on for years. And how many more winters of starvation can your people take?'"

Nestor shook his head, even taking Laura's hand for moral support, as if needing more than Dutch courage to spit out the name of his nemesis, then head of the Communist Resistance in Kalamata, later a commander of ELAS in northern Greece.

"Kostas Kelayias, may his soul rot in hell. I told your father he couldn't trust Communists, not Hollar, not Kelayias—give up such thoughts! I told him up north in Epiros the Communists were murdering our people right under the noses of the Germans, their own families, for Christ's sake—for their crackpot ideas. Even in New York, the Communists were the most vicious union organizers. They'd beat up your employees; they despised the business owners."

I saw Nestor squeeze Laura's hand, as if apologizing for his language; he then slipped into what seemed a more confessional mode. He stared down the length of the table to where the tall, longhaired woman sat, her eyes blank flaming shadows in a rigidly set yet lovely face.

"But I was just a restaurant owner, uneducated, and they were scholars, so what the fuck did I know? Up there on Epano Englianos, those two were like gods with their heads in the clouds. One minute we're discussing torpedo boats at Kalamata, the next, stories of palaces rising out of the dust, grand entrance gates, water supplies and cisterns, citadel walls. This Hollar, the talented engineer, had it all set up in his mind. They couldn't stop blabbing, those two. Hey, I admit it: I was impressed, Hollar carrying around this clay tablet like a charm, fingering it, stroking it as he talked, needing to make me understand about a language no one could understand. Maybe the source for Homer? Maybe a lost tale from the *Iliad*? Crazy stuff. Those two began describing it to me, something about polished stones, a white throne shining with oil. What a pair of dreamers."

"They were talking Linear B?" I asked. "In the middle of all that, they were talking shop?"

"Until the morning's first light."

"And Hollar had an actual tablet with him?"

"Two, one in each pocket."

"Two . . ."

But Nestor had turned to Laura, patting her hand while she looked at him with wide, beaming eyes.

"Old Nestor"—she paused and recited the rest—"took his seat on the polished stones, a bench glistening white, rubbed with glossy oil, placed for the king before his looming doors."

Nestor kissed her hand. "What about looming doors?"

"The throne of King Nestor, from the *Odyssey*."

"Not you, my dear—a scholar, too?"

"No, just a dancer, but I once loved a writer of words."

Laura shot me a knowing look. She was playing Nestor for all he was worth.

When he got on the subject of Kostas Kaleyias, Nestor's worry beads went into overdrive as the uncertainties mounted and the shadows in the arbor lengthened and darkened, as the cooking fire died to embers. How well I knew that feeling: when you try to explain to yourself or others the pattern of events that were once fixed in your mind, but that on the telling, and retelling, begin to slip around.

The worry beads clattered on the table as he reached for his refill.

"Who would have thought that Kostas Kaleyias would end up being the worst of them? Eyes like the blackest Kalamata olives, watching you from the cave of his skull. Hey, but wonder of wonders—another scholar, just like Hollar and your dad—as if I needed any more educated God's gifts in my life. Kaleyias was slick, an architect. And get this: His headquarters was under a large British army tent, perfectly camouflaged, in the hills above Kalamata. He had this huge green typewriter on a table. He was typing when John and I entered, and he kept typing, as if we didn't exist, as if the most important thing in the war was to produce more words. But you see, he *was* an educated man and a scholar; he had studied in Bologna—French philosophy and classical architecture. His father was a wealthy olive oil merchant in Kalamata, and it was soon clear how much he thought of his old man and his wealthy friends. They were all dead by 1945—Kaleyias saw to that.

"When he finished, he jumped up and told us to sit—'Any allies of the Soviet Union are our friends'—on British-issue camp stools. Where did he get all the equipment? That's what I asked myself. We had no tents, no camp stools—and no coffee; Kaleyias got us wonderful coffee. Before a minute had passed, he and John were on first-name terms. And their ideas were flying fast and furious. My heart groaned—scholars! That Kaleyias, so serious, never any laughter—not even a little joke now and then. You talk to people who knew him and they'll tell you how calculating he was. I guess it takes a proud man to run the party of the poor and oppressed. How else to triumph over the capitalist 'bloodsuckers' and our cowardly Glücksburger king? How he went on. But without laughter, there is no humanity, nothing of the earth and the Greek soul. Books, books—those Communists learned it all from books and Moscow."

Nestor glared down the table toward the tall woman at the far end, who sat rigid, like a silent goddess, and listened intently.

The negotiations were long and painful, according to Nestor. Kaleyias didn't want to risk any of his forces for an attack that only produced "suffering for the Greek people." He talked my father and Nestor into upping the ante on their side: more men to make sure of success. Then another hour of logistics and exchanging maps. Nestor finally had had enough and brought up the subject of revolutionary justice in the north of Greece.

"'Commissar Kaleyias'—I thought he would enjoy my use of such an esteemed title—'have you ever been to Moscow? I hear everyone in Moscow is very pleased with Stalin's revolutionary justice.'

"I saw the look in his eyes, the hungry wolf watching until your back is turned.

"'Moscow is fighting heroically on a front a thousand kilometers long. As we are fighting the monarchofacists. And, by the way, how are Zervas and his imperialist cronies? Perhaps they will escape to New York, where you can serve them American hamburgers. You would keep them well fed, no doubt, with all your hundreds of restaurants—*Amerikana.*'

"He tried to laugh at his little joke. At that moment, I knew I was personally marked for death; I was one of the bloodsucking exploiters of the people with my hundreds of restaurants."

Once they had a basic agreement, my father shared with Kaleyias the diagrams Hollar had made of the defenses of the E-boat base; Kaleyias was impressed, especially with the sketches of the torpedo boat and instructions for laying the demolition charges in the engine room.

"'What a skillful draftsman!' exclaimed Kaleyias. 'Your man is a brilliant artist.'

"'So,'" I asked our new Communist ally, "'of course you know our German Wehrmacht friend. Ah, what is his name now? The name escapes me.'

"I watched his face carefully, just the beginning of a smile."

"'Did you notice the new Mannlicker and Mauser rifles my men carry? It is good to know who one's friends are.'"

Nestor turned with utter disgust from the table and made a show of spitting behind him. And for a moment, he just stared off into the surrounding darkness, as if something out there were stalking him—after all the years, its tracks still leading in circles. He lowered his voice.

"You understand, I'm not saying John was a pushover. He could be tough with Kaleyias, charming but firm, thoughtful in practical matters. And Kaleyias was far from a fool on military affairs—a fox who survived to the very end. He took us through the nearby village and across to the crest of a hill, where Kalamata was spread out below us. We spent time with binoculars examining the roads and approaches to the base. He advised us on the best path through the mountains, and the best roads into Kalamata, where we wouldn't be noticed by informers. He pointed out where his men would block the approaches from the east to prevent German reinforcements so our men could retreat into the mountains.

"By the end of the day, we were drinking to one another's health and those two were practically dancing the Kalamantianós in celebration of a united front against the fascists. Then they were on to modern architecture and how it relates to the classical orders. It was your father and Hollar all over again. I thought I was losing my mind."

Nestor's voice rose with sudden emotion, as if the elusive thing was again failing his grasp.

"They spoke the same language. . ." Nestor pointed a forefinger at his head and pulled a trigger. "The moment we left that British army tent, the typewriter was going again, spewing poison—good God, like there was no tomorrow."

27 YEARS LATER, WHEN I MANAGED TO GET hold of my father's declassified OSS files, it was clear that most of what he'd told Nestor was accurate: The primary goal of his mission had been to get the Communist forces, ELAS, and the republicans and royalists, EDES, to cease hostilities and work together against the Germans. Unlike the north of Greece, where German rail and road links were vital targets of Allied sabotage, the Peloponnese offered few strategic targets of importance. The attack on the German E-boats was considered a rare coup by OSS, and an even rarer example of cooperation between the Communist and non-Communist Resistance. Much of my father's reputation within OSS and later in CIA circles grew out of that costly success. He was personally praised by OSS head Bill Donovan for his initiative, diplomacy, and personal heroism in the attack. The citation in the file notes that he was wounded in "the attack on the naval base at Kalamata." This was misinformation or a lie. Either documents were misplaced from his file or information had been deliberately destroyed, possibly by Elliot Goddard, who scrubbed his OSS file in 1948 to clear his way into the CIA, or the contents had been doctored by the OSS Southern European and Balkan branch, notoriously filled with Communists and fellow travelers. They might well have expunged anything derogatory about the Communist Resistance in Greece. On the other hand, my father never contradicted those reports, formally or otherwise, even in moments of candor with Elliot or Suzanne. Perhaps he did so with his mother, but if so, she took his failures of judgment and his catastrophic fealty to Karel Hollar to her grave.

Nor was there any mention in the OSS files of a meeting with a

British SIS operative in Pylos, although it was noted that the mission had produced valuable intelligence on German troop dispositions in the Peloponnese. British HQ and SOE-SIS in Cairo obviously kept this card to themselves—and do so to this day—while my father never breathed a word about Hollar to OSS or later the CIA. If knowledge of the Linear B tablets Karel Hollar had stolen and concealed had become known, much less that this sometime Wehrmacht officer was a double agent, my father's reputation and career, already under threat from Suzanne and Philby, would have been finished. In the end, I realized which of Homer's heroes my father set his compass by: the long-suffering Odysseus, the man of many disguises, of infinite guile and stratagems.

Again and again, Nestor apologized to Laura for boring her with war stories—"for which women have no use." But she hung on his every word, as if her life depended on the telling; which, in a sense, it did: It was the ambush north of Kalamata that put my father in the Guilford rehabilitation hospital and into her mother's bed. Reminding me of what a fifth-century B.C. Athenian artist inscribed on a red-figure urn I once turned up in the Agora: *Ask not too much of the gods, for their answers may reveal more than you bargained for.*

Nestor, initially hesitant to get into the regret game over the E-boat base, soon warmed to his subject. The shadowy faces up and down the table grew more intent on his every word, eager to hear of their part in the tale of the attack. Nestor admitted that the raid had been their only snatch at glory, the only thing "worth a hill of smelly beans" in terms of the German occupation of the Peloponnese. The civil war, he was saving for my ears alone the next day. John had led them well, planned every detail, trained individual units for specific tasks. Timing was key. They gained complete tactical surprise. Three groups attacked simultaneously at two in the morning and overwhelmed the guard posts with grenades and quickly penetrated the perimeter before those in the garrison could get out of their protective bunkers. Kaleyias's ELAS units blocked the port road and prevented the Germans from bringing in reinforcements; the escape route to the mountains remained open. Two, maybe three of the large E-boats were disabled. Karel Hollar's diagrams of the Type 37 torpedo boats were accurate in every respect; the ships' engines were never repaired. Two E-boats were scuttled in Kalamata harbor in July 1944, and a third towed out to sea and then cut loose and lost during an Allied air attack. Casualties were light. The

Germans lost more than thirty soldiers. Kaleyias's men had acquitted themselves well. Telephone and telegraph lines were cut; a German tank and troop transport had been left flaming in the central square of Kalamata.

Kaleyias and ELAS would eventually claim exclusive credit for the E-boats, even as Nestor's men left notes behind for the Germans that the attack was a British commando raid.

The worry beads, which had remained mostly silent during Nestor's descriptions of the attack, began to clatter again in earnest as he related the details of their perilous retreat through the mountains to Pylos.

"For five hours, as we made our way into the foothills west of Kalamata, we were heroes—exhausted heroes, but proud and happy men. Only three dead and two wounded. Pride showed in the men's faces. Your father had commanded well; he had shown much courage in battle. We had accomplished our mission. We could still see the smoke rising from the E-boat base in Kalamata. Once high in the mountains, it would be hard for the Germans to follow. We thought we were safe."

I often try to picture it in my mind, that five-hour march up into the mountains in the early dawn hours of late October 1943. My father and Nestor had led a successful attack. My father had proved himself under fire, something every soldier facing combat for the first time worries about obsessively. Against all the odds, they had successfully enlisted the Communist Resistance in the attack. In a tiny way, they had played a part in turning the tide, even as the Germans took over the Dodecanese, even as the Americans and British were engaged in an endless slogging match up the boot of Italy, while the Soviets were pushing back the Wehrmacht on all fronts from the Baltic to the Black Sea: a blood zone of mass butchery and shootings and gassing and starvation of tens of millions—a genocidal evil on an industrial scale, without precedent in human history.

A moment to be savored, perhaps for the last time in my father's life.

Nestor lifted his salt-and-pepper eyebrows and sighed.

"They hit us a little after dawn. Machine-gun and rifle fire from above swept many of our men from the steep mountain trail. We lost eight men in the first seconds of the ambush. There was almost no cover. We couldn't move forward or back; we were pinned down. Kaleyias had positioned his men well. We were dead men—we all knew it. John and I had been at the front of the column and we survived because we had just passed in front of a slight rock overhang when the Communists opened up and so we were spared. Those who had not been shot or who were wounded huddled behind rocks along the path. If you moved out from cover, they shot you from above. I remember John's face as we crouched behind that outcropping of rocks—bullets like hailstones snapping all over that godforsaken path—pale as a ghost, all the life gone out of him. I thought, Where's that movie-star smile now—that brilliant scholar? It was the face of a terrified man." Nestor lowered his voice. "But I am being unfair. Not fear, but a vision of hell: the idiocy of his faith in a world where a man like Kaleyias could hear reason and be content with anything but absolute power over men's souls.

"'Are you sure they're not Germans?' he asked me.

"'Jesus, the Germans don't know the mountains. Those weren't German uniforms. They're *andartes,* Communist forces. So now you have your answer: your pact with that devil Kaleyias—we're dead men. There is no way out of this. They don't take prisoners. Even you, in your American uniform.'

"His face—the horror and disappointment in his eyes—was the saddest thing I ever saw. He had been made a fool and now we were all going to pay for his absurd American hopes. John crouched with his face in the dirt. Already a dead man, I thought, his romantic dreams of some perfect world going with him to his grave—our grave.

"I pointed up the mountain. 'If they have grenades and start rolling them down on us, we're fucked good.'

"I saw John raise his head, his beautiful eyes fixed on me. Did we have any grenades left? he asked me. No, only explosives. Two charges remained after the three ships we had blown up.

"'Maybe if I can get the explosives above them, the blasts and rock slides might dislodge them from their positions.'"

"'And us, too! See how far up the mountain they are.' I lifted my head over the rocks for a moment to check the distance, and the machine gun opened up. The stones above our head disintegrated into dust. "'Fifty-sixty meters, seventy-five-degree angle. Why do you think Kaleyias suggested this trail? They have every inch covered—anything that moves will die.'

"I could see him making up his mind to something—his jaw tight; it was the look of a man with nothing left to lose. He dusted off his rifle and checked his ammunition. He wiped down his rifle with the sleeve of his uniform and test-fired it. Then he crawled to the edge of the overhang to survey the path behind and ahead. Our wounded were screaming with pain, somewhere they had tumbled down the mountain. There was a shallow gully just ahead of us that paralleled the path, maybe a meter deep. He pointed there, grimaced, and shook my hand.

"'I'll try to take a few out—maybe draw their fire, get them to group together on the trail above us. Get the explosives prepared with a short fuse. . . . Fifteen seconds should do it, no more. And when I signal to you, light the first stick and toss it to me, okay?'

"'Sure, boss, but I wish we were back on Seventy-third and Lex. It's been nice knowing you.'

"'Did I ever tell you your pasta Alfredo tasted like shit? Get the explosives ready.'

"When I had the fuses set and ready to be lit, John slapped me on the back and made a dash for that gully, maybe five meters from the protection of the rocky overhang. Immediately, they opened up on him, a storm of bullets whipping the air. But he got into the gully and lay flat. They were shooting high, and the gully gave him just enough protection so that they couldn't quite nail him without standing and exposing themselves. Where he could see better the positions of the *andartes*. Where he could see the placement of the machine-gun. He waited. When one of the Communists stood for a better shot, John popped up on one knee, aimed, shot, and was down again in seconds. It was an amazing thing; he was actually picking them off one at a time. Just the heads and shoulders above the crest of the ridge—only head shots. At least four of their dead came tumbling down to join us. But I think he may have shot more. I could hear shouts from above—'Kill the Amerikana'—as they concentrated more and more rifles on him. They knew it was him—his uniform; they knew it was the American, and they wanted to kill him in the worst way. I yelled to my men to try to cover him with returning fire, but most could not move without being killed on the path, and they couldn't shoot like your father.

"I had the two charges ready with a fifteen-second fuse. John signaled to me to light the first and toss it to him. He caught it, stood, and threw the charge—my God, he had an arm—way up the mountain above us. Then a huge explosion, screams, rocks pouring down like all hell had broken lose. Well, I thought, better to die from the rocks than from a bullet. When the rocks stopped, John raised himself, waited, and then got off another shot. A scream from above and then the machine gun opened up, but the fire was not so accurate. John signaled for the next charge. Again I lit the fuse and tossed it to him, and again he threw the explosives way up the mountain. But this time, the machine gun had him in range and a bullet caught him in the thigh the very moment he had let fly with the last charge. The second explosion seemed even bigger than the first, and this time the machine gun and the crew operating it came tumbling down from above. When the debris and dust cleared, I could see John clutching his leg. I dashed to where he lay on his back in the gully, covered in debris, torn apart by the cactus that grew in that sheltered spot. He had a bad wound in his thigh, blood like crazy. I got a tourniquet around his leg and tightened it. By the time I got that done, I noticed that some of our men were moving on the path. There was no more gunfire from above us. It was all silence. Kalayias's men—what was left of them—had pulled out.

"'You fucking crazy American.' That's what I said to him, because it took a crazy son of a bitch to shoot like that, to throw like that. 'You saved us, you fucking idiot. I think you saved our asses.'"

The old Resistance fighters at the table, and later that night, echoed Nestor's sentiments. *A miracle. A savior.* Some spoke of how the sticks of high explosive seemed to take flight when my father had thrown them, defying gravity to land so far up the mountainside. Forty-six years later, they seemed to have forgiven him for getting them into the mess in the first place. At the time, though, even after Kaleyias's men had broken off the ambush, the company of Resistance fighters was in bad shape. Many had been killed—killed by other Greeks. My father had been hit in the thigh, a gaping wound that had splintered the bone but had missed a major artery, or he would have bled to death in a matter of minutes. Nestor was amazed he survived. He was very weak, passing in and out of consciousness; he'd been caught in the last rock slide, ground up in the scree and scratched all over by the cacti—blood, thorns, and dust. They cleaned him up as best they could with the precious water they carried and made a makeshift litter out of blankets. The survivors took turns carrying him and the other wounded into the high mountains on the journey back to Pylos.

"Three days of hell. The Germans were on our trail. The spotter planes were flying overhead. We were low on water. Even friendly villages had their informers and feared reprisals, should they give us help. And Kaleyias, too, had his big-eyed snitches, everywhere."

At this point in his story, Nestor seemed to go into a trance, losing steam, whether out of weariness or drunkenness, or the sheer exhaustion that memory of such hardships brought on. The nightmare they endured for fleeting success: "The Germans were finished whether we blew up their damned boats or not." He tried to describe the hurt he saw in my father's bruised and swollen face.

"When he gained consciousness, he never complained of the pain. But in his eyes was the knowledge of the devil's price for those three German E-boats."

I could see Laura wince at Nestor's descriptions, pursing her lips as she glanced at the dying fire. And then I realized it wasn't the fire that had caught Laura's attention, but the tall woman at the end of the table, her eyes brimming with tears.

All I could think about was how my father had placed those head shots, and the feel of squeezing a trigger with a man's head in your sites . . . fifty to sixty meters uphill, not an easy shot by any stretch, but maybe far enough that at least individual features were not recognizable.

The words in Suzanne's letters registered again in my mind: *The terrible sadness . . . John, what is this terrible sadness?* Was it his eleven comrades killed on the trail, or the celebrated head shots . . . or what came next?

When I finally got hold of my father's CIA files from the late forties, when he was station chief in Athens, the reverberations of that ambush in the mountains above Kalamata came through loud and clear in his report to his superiors. Nestor was right: He had glimpsed the destruction of my father's youthful idealism.

> In my opinion, unlike the Italian and French Communists, the Greek Communists seem congenitally unable to conceive of sharing power with any other political party. There is a primitive, atavistic streak in their leadership that is utterly dead to their ancient democratic heritage. There is no common ground, no basis for trust. They are suspicious, disdainful, overweening in pride, bloodthirsty, and utterly brutal in their methods; their use of terror against their own people is on a par with the worst of Stalin.

Nestor struggled to finish his tale even as many of the guests at the other tables were interrupting to take their leave. Even at the head table, many of the older guys were nodding off.

They finally made it back to Pylos, Nestor continued. It was too dangerous to take my father into town, so they smuggled out a local doctor to attend the wounded in the foothills. The morphine was exhausted and the doctor had nothing for the pain. My father was weak from loss of blood, exhaustion, dehydration. Both the Germans and the

Communists had informers. Nowhere was safe. The doctor did the best he could to clean and disinfect the wound and sew up the thigh. But he could do nothing with the splintered bone. It was too dangerous to try to evacuate him by sea, so Nestor decided to have my father carried high into the mountains to a sheepherder's summer shelter. There he was hidden over the bitterly cold winter of 1943–1944. "The Germans put out rewards for his capture—Communists, too—the Amerikana. Allied HQ in Cairo was desperate to get my father evacuated. Nestor was able to trade on their desperation and managed to get his resistance forces resupplied with food and medical supplies, guns and ammunition, and tents. Nestor's men waited out the winter and licked their wounds.

"Revenge was in our hearts. . . . We survived on hatred and American K rations. We got him out that March of '44—still cold that spring, like winter would never end. They got their precious cargo back, a little worse for wear." He seemed to check this hint of sarcasm, even as Laura leaned around Nestor to give me a significant look. "We didn't have much time—John and I. There had been problems. The Germans were panicking that spring and more deadly than ever, as they feared an invasion of Europe that might cut them off in Greece. The Communists were gaining strength—eliminating all rivals. John and I had only a few moments to discuss the needs of the republican Resistance—we were fucked. I doubted I'd survive.

"When the signal from the submarine flashed on the dark sea, the men waiting with us—how many at this table?—had tears in their eyes. John went to all of his comrades and embraced each one in turn. He hobbled on a shepherd's staff. His eyes were still bright with the light of one who has cheated death. We joked, we laughed, and we talked about the E-boat base." Nestor turned to those at the table and raised his wineglass. "Without the E-boat base, what did we have to show for ourselves—heh? Even if Pylos had paid a terrible price. When I shook John's hand, I saw that his finger was bandaged. 'You've been wounded again,' I said, trying to make a joke. He did his best to smile, to joke. 'A goat,' he said, 'a goat on the trail down from the mountains bit me.' Our parting was a sad business. He was not the same man who had arrived on that beach six months before—ah, but he was alive, heh? I put my arm around his shoulder and kissed him and promised him revenge for everything we had suffered. We would find Kaleyias and all who had betrayed us. He could only nod his face, wet with wordless tears; brave words would not bring back those we had lost.

"When he walked into the surf, all the men surrounded him to help hold the rubber boat. Four men lifted him from the sea and put him in the arms of the sailors. The navy guys rowed like men possessed to get him back to the sub. There would be no more help for us in the Peloponnese from the British and Americans until the fall of that year. I had tears in my eyes, not for all who had died, but for this rich American—for all of us Americans who are rich to live in such a country without Nazis and Communists—my God, such a curse. And it's not over, even now—still, right here in Greece, as if the past never happened."

Nestor gazed wearily into his glass.

"You know, back in the darkest days, that smile of his, that boyish smile, well, it got us through a lot. How I wanted to believe in him, be an American like him—believe in a world where such insanity wasn't possible . . . and Greece, once the glory of the world. Now we know the cost. You go now to Athens, you go to the cities, and the young remember nothing of the past; they prefer to spit on the Americans—with Reagan's missiles and the neutron bomb. And what, I ask them, what if the Americans stop believing in their dream, stop giving a damn about Europe—tell me, then: What becomes of the world? I know Americans, I am an American. If we don't believe in ourselves, who will believe in anything?"

In the last of the flickering firelight, the candles guttering and dying, Nestor's stalwarts stood as one and refuted their captain's despairing reflections. They cried out, "No!" And then came a chorus of toasts to a free and democratic Greece . . . bring back the generals, bring back the king. Nestor, buoyed by their cries, struggled to his feet and raised his glass in a final toast. Nikos and Laura were at his side, shoring him up.

"Freedom, and prosperous lives for our children."

Then Nikos, the ever-dutiful son, helped his father away from the table and off to his bed and rest.

Immediately, I was surrounded by Nestor's old fighters. They circled me in the fading firelight like spectral figures to take my hand, to embrace me, kiss me, and offer their fond memories of my father in their wine-softened breath. They couldn't get over that I spoke Greek like my father—sounded just like him, they said. They drew tight about me, as they had when they accompanied my father to the waiting rubber dingy, their calloused hands holding on to mine as if for dear life. In the flickering light, their roughly expressed sentiments seemed even more vivid than Nestor's had. Each had a story: "I carried your father back from Kalamata"; "I stayed with him in the mountains"; "I brought him and the woman food and medicine"; "I was just behind him on the trail when we were ambushed by the Communists"; "I saw him shoot those bastards—what, like Davy Crockett!" How they went on and on about the shooting; they all had different body counts for his sharpshooting.

It was as if each and every one had appropriated the singular moments and wanted to imprint his version on me: of heroism, of god-like skill, so as to fortify my mind and encourage the role they wished for me to assume in keeping his memory alive. "Tell your children," the old veterans echoed. "Tell them how it was with your father . . . for your children to know."

Confronted with the very real heroism of my father, I found myself struggling to be the son they expected of such a man. I thanked them; I stood up straight in spite of the growing pain in my back; I nodded graciously, trying to summon tears to match theirs. I tried to give them something of him in return for their kindness. But I quailed at the feeling of how much more alive *in them* he seemed: what men who had been in battle together *and* survived felt for one another. And so I did my best to send them properly on their way. I thanked them for their sacrifice, for the democratic Greece made possible by their bravery and the sacrifices of their dead comrades. I wanted them to find in me some distant reflection of the man who had stood in that gully and picked off their tormentors, not the faithless, disillusioned Vietnam veteran with a bum back.

As the last of the old Resistance fighters limped off into the shadows, I collapsed into a chair, my wretched back aching. I was holding a wooden shepherd's staff of shoulder height. It was of a reddish wood, worn and blackened where it had been gripped for endless miles. One of the last of the veteran fighters had put it in my hand and had told me it was the shepherd's staff my father had used on his return from the high mountains, the one he had given up once safely in the rubber dingy—a gift I had failed to properly acknowledge. I felt the rough knotted surface against my palms and brought my face close to smell the old wood as my eyes ran with tears. For a while, I gazed into the dying flames as white-coated waiters cleared up. Then I pulled myself up with the help of the shepherd's staff and went in search of Laura. I found, to my chagrin, that the staff eased my walking as I began exploring Nestor's nocturnal gardens. A gibbous moon wallowed amidst the stars. The scent of lemon and myrtle put me at ease, belying the dangers invoked by the glinting strands of razor wire on the citadel walls. I wondered what Max would have made of Nestor's account, and some part of me smiled . . . the new evidence that surely would make a mockery of his novel.

Then I heard women's voices speaking English.

I found Laura and another woman sitting in the near dark along one of the gravel paths where grapevines grew in abundance overhead. They had moved a couple of the folding chairs from the dinner table, taken one of the kerosene lamps, and found a more secluded spot. The glow from the lamp barely hinted at their bowed bodies where they leaned into one another as if whispering the most intimate of confidences. As I drew closer, a deep growl rumbled out of the darkness. Something at one woman's feet rose from the gravel and shook itself. I heard a sharp command and then a whimper. The beast sat back on its haunches, wary of my approach. In the feeble light I could just make out a Great Dane with gray-and-white markings. As I reached to Laura's shoulder, it lunged and was instantly brought to bay with another tug on a choke collar and spoken to firmly in French.

"Alors—asseyez-vous, asseyez-vous."

The Great Dane, dripping slobber from its mouth, lowered itself to the ground and looked up at me with gleaming yellow eyes. Its mistress got up and took a step in my direction and told me in French-accented English that there was nothing to fear from the dog. I recognized her immediately as the striking woman who had sat at the far end of our table. She was indeed tall, taller than Laura, with dark hair that fell in thick cascades and framed her milky white brow and wedges of dark eyebrows. As she moved closer, I could see that her face had a more olive-complected tone, with rugged, almost masculine features—very Greek, more handsome than petite—to which her wide almond eyes, Modigliani eyes, added an expressive and haunting quality, as if her full yet compact sibylline lips were eternally poised to whisper a warning. I leaned on my staff, squinting, as she told the dog to wait and took another step. She reached to the smooth reddish crook of the staff and fingered the wood, as if not quite believing what was there. Her eyebrows rose into a down-slanted pinch, making visible two tiny scars that thinned out the tapering hairs. We hovered before each other as if some invisible barrier separated us—neither daring to cross.

Laura rescued the moment, taking my arm and making introductions.

"Peter, this is Joanna." She got the Greek *Yo-anna* just about right.

"She took care of your father over the winter while he was recovering in the mountains. Her father was the doctor who saved his life."

I could tell by the way Laura's eyes burned into mine that she was pretty overwrought. Her voice kept catching. And as I shook hands with Joanna, she, too, began to tremble and her eyes welled with tears. I was so numbed by the emotions of the evening that I found myself easily drawn into her embrace—an embrace as awkward as it was tender—which gave her dog the chance to sniff my leg from foot to thigh. Strangely, her hair smelled of disinfectant and alcohol, a distinct hospital smell, and with it, a world of unpleasant associations.

"This was your father's?" she asked, resting a hand again on the staff.

"One of the old men just left it with me."

Joanna bent and kissed the crook of the staff and wiped at her eyes. "Forgive me," she murmured. "The resemblance to your father is very strong. He was using this when we walked down from the mountains." And she pointed out the carving of a horned ram's head on the underside of the crook.

When I looked up, I found Laura glaring.

"They were . . ." Laura wiped at her eyes. "They were lovers, Peter. Joanna had his child."

The older woman shrank back with a soundless gasp at this indiscretion, her lips forming an oval of distress. Obviously, they had been talking for some time and this had been told in confidence.

Joanna took Laura's hand.

"My friend, please."

"I'm sorry," Laura said. "The whole thing just blows my mind."

"A child?" I asked.

Joanna shook her head, a deep breath released in a pitiful sigh.

"My son, a long time ago, during the Civil War in 1949."

"You've got to tell him, Joanna, how it was. Take my chair, Peter. He's got a bad back," she said to Joanna. "I'll get another."

A moment later, the three us were seated in a tiny circle in the near darkness. I felt as though we were plotters in our host's home, going over Nestor's many outtakes. It soon because obvious why Nestor had skimmed over the business about getting a doctor for my wounded father.

"Nestor was a very hard man in those days, such a hard man."

Joanna was trying to be generous even as she struggled with her words in describing that first encounter. She had been seventeen at the time, working as a nurse in her father's clinic in Pylos. The family was terrified of the Germans because of their Jewish background. The Italians couldn't have cared less, but once the Germans occupied the Peloponnese in 1943, the SS began sniffing around for Greek Jews to deport. And there were plenty of Greeks willing to sell out her family. "And my father the only doctor in the town." Joanna was assisting her father in a high-forceps delivery when Nestor and one of his men burst into the examination room and demanded that the doctor leave with them, instantly. Her father had dismissed the order and suggested the men leave, given the delicate procedure at hand. The laboring mother was groaning in agony. Nestor was oblivious. He put a gun to the doctor's head and cocked it. Joanna had screamed in terror. The doctor brushed the gun away and began with the forceps. "Shoot me," he told Nestor; "then both the woman and the baby can be on your conscience." Another agonized cry from the woman in the stirrups and a fuller appreciation of the moment dissuaded Nestor in his threats. He sank into a chair and waited. He was wild, Joanna told us, his face torn up and bruised, his eyes red and sunken with exhaustion. He fell asleep.

"An animal run to ground."

Joanna's French-accented English was excellent, but I had a sense that she was being more than a little careful in how she put things. It turned out, as Joanna began to tell her story, that Nestor had severely edited his.

Having Laura present made the difference. How many times as a child I'd stumbled on a heated conversation between my mother and grandmother, only to have their voices drop, their words become allusive and cryptic: that secret world of women and their unnerving judgments of mankind.

"When Nestor took my father and me to your father in the hills, we had to wear a disguise." Joanna made a circling motion around her head, as if winding a scarf. "If people see us, they will certainly report this to the Germans. Because everyone in the village knows my father very well; he was the only doctor. We have to make a long walk, in a circle, and return to the far side of Pylos. And then we find John there in the hills—ah, *mon Dieu, c'est terrible* . . . in the beginning, we think he is dead." She made clawing motions at her face. "His face had many cuts. And his leg . . . my father feared gangrene."

"A hospital—Kalamata,' he told Nestor. 'Or Patras, He will die otherwise.'

"'You, Doctor, save his life or you will pay with your daughter's.'"

Her father did the best he could under the circumstances. He swabbed out the wound, trying to remove all the dirt and dead flesh. There was nothing he could do about the splintered bone without major surgery. He poured disinfectant into the wound and sewed him up. There was no morphine. The pain was such that my father passed out. Nestor informed the doctor that his daughter was to stay with them and nurse the American; she would travel with them into the high mountains. As if he needed to emphasize his point, Nestor put his gun to Joanna's head and told her father that if the American died, or they were betrayed, he or the guards would shoot her. Nestor had a reputation for making threats, especially among the Communists in Pylos—and carrying them out. Her father said she was the only trained nurse in Pylos; she was indispensable to his work. But pleas were to no avail. Her father took Joanna aside and explained what she had to do to take care of the wound and, hopefully, keep this American alive until he could be evacuated. He didn't have much hope.

"He has lost too much blood. There is a high risk of infection. She is just a girl—please.'

"Nestor pointed at me. 'Just make sure she knows what to do. We can get you medical supplies. Tell me what you need.'

"'The Germans watch my clinic; they have informers everywhere.'"

The doctor returned to Pylos while the others headed for the highest mountain pastures to the north of Pylos. The tiny, winding sheep tracks were treacherous, especially when carrying a heavy litter. Spotter planes were constantly overhead, forcing them to take shelter and hide. During stops, Joanna checked the bandages, bathed my father's fevered brow. They trudged on. Their destination was a shepherd's summer shelter, "nestling in the clouds," was how Joanna put it. Barely a shelter even in a warm summer, just a hovel of rock-piled walls and branches and a few boards thrown up overhead to keep off the sun and rain. It would soon be winter. The guards did what they could to patch the walls with mud and dried dung. They draped camouflage canvas over the roof and disguised it further with sod and dirt so it wouldn't be spotted from the air. They could light a fire only at night, when the smoke wouldn't be seen.

"In the day, even with the sun, the cold was terrible."

The guards shuttled food, water, and medicine, fuel for the fire, and fresh warm clothing, and occasionally verbal messages from the world beyond. Malcolm, the British radioman, kept Cairo apprised of the precarious situation, and parachute drops brought them more food and medicine. Often Joanna and my father were left alone for days with only the sound of the wind and the freezing drafts that found every crevice in the patched-together stonework. Joanna didn't expect him to live; her father had told her death was the likely outcome. If he should die, she had plotted her escape, which in the winter would have been suicidal along the treacherous trails. She was an educated town girl; she knew little about the countryside, much less the mountains. She tried to remember the route they had taken, reviewing it in her mind, but only got more confused.

"Every time I wake, every time he sleeps, my first fear . . . is he still alive?"

For the first month, late November and early December, the weather held and it got below freezing only at night. My father was racked with fevers and chills, often delirious, and could take food only sparingly. The guards, herders who knew the mountains, showed her how to make a fire and nurse it along. She made soup at night, hot broth, which he could get down. But he lost a lot of weight. And there was always the pain. And then in late December it got bitterly cold and the extreme weather was relentless, one of the worst winters in memory. Fortunately, my father was stronger by then, but it was a near thing.

"The cold . . ." Joanna tilted her head up, closed her large eyes, and seemed to shiver, her head shaking as she reached for the neck of her dog.

I found myself utterly moved by her struggle with these memories, attempting to make sense of the experience of a seventeen-year-old girl under enormous stress . . . and then something else. She was remembering how the cold had nearly killed them, how each morning she pushed the drifted snow away from the entrance, broke off and collected the icicles that had crept downward each night from the wattle and wood roof.

"C'est très important," and she'd seem to catch herself and continue in English with a hint of apology for her awkwardness. "You must understand, it was never the daring of lovers, to sleep together, to keep the cold from our bones. The heat of each other was the same as life itself, so elemental—yes, so true, so close to the heart. Little was ever spoken, not in words, only the necessity. Later there came other things, but as life comes and is natural for a man and woman. Our life in that place was so simple, you cannot imagine. Even now, I can no longer see it—how it was. We had hours and days with nothing. Just the darkness and the wind and the cold and each other, and his life . . . inside mine, like the fire at night from the embers. Later, when he did not die, we had words." She gestured outward toward the faint light, as if we might, too, hear those words if we just kept silent enough, listened hard enough. "John . . . *mon Dieu,* I never knew a man who lived so inside his words. His Greek, so perfect, so refined, the way my father, who came from a very old and educated family in Athens, spoke. He recited the ancient poetry to me in the darkness and, when he explained the words, it was as if those places and times came to life for us. It was like a dream that we woke into every morning. A dream, do you understand?"

I nodded my head, feeling a shiver of recognition pass through me. Joanna's long dark hair flared as a night breeze passed over Nestor's garden, and with it the smell of the sea mixing with the smoke and lemony scent of the garden.

"Do you know what he called me?"

And I knew, the moment she said it, as if I'd always known.

"Nausicaa," I replied.

Laura repeated it. "Nausicaa."

"Yes, Nausicaa." Joanna smiled with relief, if not wonder, that we were all privy to some secret once sacred to her heart alone.

I don't know if it was the wine and Demerol, or the long evening, but hearing the name Nausicaa from the lips of Laura and Joanna transformed the conversation for me. It took me back to those freezing winters at Winsted, when I had first read my father's letters to his mother, when he had written about his infatuation with Homer and the gentle land of the Phaeacians, and the lovely princess Nausicaa, who had saved the shipwrecked traveler. Remembering the cold of those New England winters and the romance of distant islands under blue skies, I absolutely understood how, close to death, miserable and cold, my father might have reached back to his youthful enchantments for succor. Just the name Nausicaa opened a window into his soul for me and into the pristine simplicity of their precarious existence in that shepherd's hovel. I felt how he might have transported himself back to some distant, archaic world to blunt the horror of the moment, to the lives of the humble sheepherders that people the background of the *Odyssey.* Listening to Joanna speak in her mellifluous, if halting, English, their lives flooded up before me as if from the pages of the

Odyssey, a place and time of the most innocent of human pleasures, of food and drink, sheepskin fleece and warming hearth, a society of simple codes, of hospitality to strangers, honoring friends, where men aspired to godlike grace. I could imagine what it must have been like to come back to life in her arms, as the shipwrecked Odysseus had woken on the Phaeacians' shore to be restored to life by those gentle and kind hands, as I had fallen in love with Maureen's hands in the VA hospital with views of the blue Pacific in the distance. Joanna had been a young and frightened and very brave girl, reading herself into the mind of a stranger whose death might have meant her own, an exotic stranger who embraced her with the poetry of his fading youth.

Joanna never mentioned the word *innocence,* but theirs must have been a kind of profound respite, as the earth warmed, and he gained strength and could practice walking by holding on to her arm and the shepherd's staff. They were awkward around each other, as if their winter embraces had been a myth.

"You see, like the smoke in the blue sky, like a dream."

Joanna couldn't resist a smile, as something of that fleeting joy of their last weeks flared in her face, as the flat tip of her nose rose and her nostrils widened as if breathing again that fine spring air.

"He told me many things. He helped me with my English. We recited English poetry. In the spring, when the snow had gone and we walked to exercise his leg, he told me of his home and America, of these magnificent trees [white pine, I told her] standing tall in the sky. I could see in his eyes how much he wished to return to his home. And I wanted to know everything of that place." She made a gesture of enormous breadth that might encompass the four corners of the earth as viewed from a mountain peak. "For me then, with him, we spoke of a better world, of peace . . . and yes, children." She smiled and held up her hand, her long, tapering fingers undulating like waves. "'Like angels stopped upon the wing by sound of harmony from Heaven's remotest spheres.'" She bent to me. "Did I say it correctly?"

"Perfect," I replied, and I believed she had my father's flat New England speech rhythms ringing in her ear as she recalled those lines of Wordsworth that he'd cited in his valediction to his graduating class.

As if now a little annoyed at this rival for her mother's love—so unlike the brazen, erotically charged language in the love letters between my father and Suzanne—Laura injected a more sobering note. She really didn't want to hear any more about innocence and simplicity, not after the heated and hurried assignations that might have called her own life into being.

"And the child, Joanna?"

Joanna seemed to struggle to collect her thoughts.

"For a few weeks, the sun was so near, the sky so blue, and we were finally warm and the war far away." The dog sat up, hackles raised and ears pricked, as if something had disturbed it. It growled, perhaps at an unseen night watchman. We could see no one. "Shh," she scolded, and the Great Dane whimpered and lay down once more. Joanna sighed. "But then the world can wait for him no longer." They had been delayed three days by bad weather and spring snowstorms in the mountains. When my father and Joanna made it to the outskirts of Pylos, Nestor's men, who were to escort John to the rendezvous with the submarine, did not appear. Their two guards were very nervous. They waited on a hillside above Pylos, concealed by scrub grass and bushes. Joanna pointed out her home, her father's clinic. "I could have touched them, the rooftops seemed so near, and Saint Dimitrios, the church in the square, and my street, Maniakiou Street, where I played as a girl." It was almost too beautiful, she told us; it had rained in the morning and the colors, the white stucco of the buildings and reds of the terra-cotta rooftops, the sprays of blue and yellow spring flowers in the window boxes, were dazzling, like a travel poster of better times. Joanna brought her spread palm to her lips as memory of the horror overcame her once more, and again I noticed the tiny scars running through her eyebrow, and larger jagged scars on the backs of her hands. "Too quiet, windows shuttered, streets empty, not a soul in sight. Something was very wrong. The guards were arguing, one wanted to go back to the mountains, the other to wait it out.

"Then I could hear something, motors, trucks coming near—smoke, first the smoke. They came along the coast road from north and south, surrounding the town. Whistles and shouts and more shouts. We saw soldiers jumping out of the trucks. German soldiers in gray uniforms and black helmets, guns in their hands. Orders were shouted. The sound of boots in the streets. There were officers with lists, and they directed the soldiers to doors. They would knock and then break down the door. They were finding people, taking people, pushing the people into the street. There were gunshots and screams, glass breaking and explosions, and then fire. I was amazed at the dark yellow smoke over the orange rooftops. I could not believe what I was seeing. But I knew it was real because of the way John was watching, as if he understood something I could not. I asked him what we should do. But he only shook his head and moved forward to see better. He had binoculars and kept saying something to himself, a name."

"A name?" I asked.

"Yes, a German name. I was terrified. He kept the binoculars to his eyes, watching something."

"Hollar," I said. "The name he said—was it Karel Hollar?"

"Something like that, a German name. I kept asking John if he saw my father, the doctor who had dressed his wounds after Kalamata."

Her eyes seemed to empty of focus, forcing herself to go on.

"The soldiers were moving with much speed, as if they had only minutes to finish—hurry, hurry. They were like little machines, and there was no way to stop them. Shouting, shouting, so much shouting. The women's screams . . . I still hear them—the women, yes. The people they took from the houses were marched through the streets to the town square, very near where we were hiding, where there is a church, where in the morning there is a market, where I went with my mother every day as a child. A priest in black robes came out from the church and ran from one German officer to the next, asking questions, pleading for an answer. But the soldiers pushed him away. One of the soldiers hit him with his gun and the priest fell and did not move. There is a wall by the church, and the soldiers put all the people there. Mostly, they were men, but also some women, women who would not leave the men. Then I saw my father and my mother and my sister. I screamed; John put his hand over my mouth. My father was trying to get my mother and sister to leave, but there was an officer with a list, and he pushed them back into the crowd. I pointed to my family. I told John, 'See, my father, the doctor, who saved your leg. It must be a mistake.' I turned to John, but his face was hard and empty. He was staring, squinting, then using the binoculars. I asked him if he could see my family, but he didn't answer."

"Oh my God," Laura said, reaching to take Joanna's hand.

"Did you hear Nestor tonight talk about Karel Hollar?"

She shook here head. "Why do you think he put me at the end of the table, so far from you?"

"There was a Wehrmacht captain, Karel Hollar—an archaeologist, a friend of my father's from before the war."

"The name began with an K—I think it was so, like the name of

Carole Lombard. There was a German officer with a list of names in the square. They had exactly one hundred names. I could see him counting, checking his list. John tried to get me to close my eyes. He held me hard. 'Close your eyes . . . close your eyes.' When the soldiers began shooting, I thought my head would explode. I tried to reach out to my family, but John held me very hard and put his hand over my mouth because I was trying to scream. I fainted. When I revived, there was only silence."

Mercifully, the Great Dane rose, sniffed the air, and began whining. Joanna put her arms around the beast and whispered to it, steadying herself. Laura held on tight to Joanna's hand, her face streaming with tears.

Joanna had watched as her parents and sister and ninety-seven others were executed in cold blood. My father had witnessed a man, someone he had trusted, organizing and carrying out the shooting of one hundred citizens of Pylos in reprisal for the Resistance forces hiding the man responsible for the attack on the E-boat base in the mountains. The list had been carefully compiled with the help of Communist informers—so Nestor told me the next day. Not a single Communist sympathizer in Pylos was executed. No wonder Nestor and my father could barely speak to each other when they met up after six months on the evacuation beach. The Germans had been planning a trap, and only the delay due to bad weather prevented my father and Joanna and their two guards from walking straight into it. Joanna told us she nearly lost her mind. Later she had vivid memories of Nestor and my father arguing loudly about her fate. Nestor might well have killed her out of fear she'd be captured and tortured and would reveal information. My father finally got Nestor to promise to move her out of the Peloponnese, to Athens, where she had an uncle. She was in shock. Just before my father left for the rendezvous with the British submarine, they had a few moments together. They cried in each other's arms. It was then she discovered the crude bandage around his finger. She insisted on dressing the wound and found a deep laceration that had gone right to the bone. She realized she'd bitten him on the hillside as he tired to prevent her screams. The last thing she did was to properly bandage the finger.

"Then I promised him, when he left for the submarine, that I would never cry again."

"Did you know about the baby—did you know you were pregnant?"

Joanna shook her head and patted Laura's hand.

"Not until later. I never expected to see John again. I thought I had died, that I had cried my last tears."

Joanna's harrowing odyssey of almost five years' duration had only just begun.

As she told us her tale about her escapes and her child, I found myself mesmerized, not only by her harrowing vicissitudes but by how the tattered remnants of my father's youthful imaginings had provided her with a lifeline to survive. How the name Nausicaa, which had sparked his moral and romantic conscience as schoolboy, became her nom de guerre, her disguise. I recalled how he'd complained to his mother in his letters about the wickedness of Zeus: how the king of the gods had spitefully circled the island of the Phaeacians with mountainous walls, cutting them off forever from their trading livelihood—out of pride and pique because of Nausicaa's kindness in speeding Odysseus back to his homeland. My father had complained bitterly to his mother in those letters at the arbitrariness and cruelty and pettiness of such an act of vengeance by Zeus, lord of the gods: "What of poor Nausicaa—what became of her? Homer is silent. And the *Iliad* is only worse, where Hera trades Zeus the destruction of Argos, Sparta, and Mycenae for the raising of Troy."

For such moral obtuseness, Plato wanted to ban Homer—and the obscene behavior of his gods—from his ideal republic. Why Longinus found the ways of the gods, both the generous and selfish, uncanny models of the best and worst in human behavior; how he saw Homer's world, where the gods act like men, and the men like gods, as a metaphor for mankind's inescapable folly. For the young Joanna, who had grown up in a close community of security and respect, there seemed no end to the gods' madness and retribution. And as she told us of her many escapes, I registered viscerally the horrors my father had witnessed, as described in his letters to Suzanne in 1945 and later, the obscenity of a world imprisoned, not in this case by mountains and rivers, but by walls of concrete and barbed wire that within three years would stretch across Europe from the Baltic to the Black Sea.

Nestor had been true to his word. Two days after my father escaped from occupied Greece, into the arms of his Calypso in the Guilford rehabilitation hospital, one of Nestor's men accompanied Joanna on her trip north by way of Patras to Athens and the home of her uncle,

Spiros, her father's brother. She had escaped the massacre of her family for another impending massacre in the making. Her uncle was Jewish, part of an old Athenian Jewish community, the Romaniote, with roots in Greece going back thousands of years. By the spring of 1944, the Jews of Thessalonica had already been deported and gassed at Auschwitz and Treblinka. The SS had turned their attention to the Jews of Athens. When Joanna slipped in through the back door of her uncle's home, she found the family in hiding, terrified, barely able to get enough food. Distraught as they were to learn of the fate of Joanna's parents and sister, they were preoccupied with their own survival. They knew in detail about the fate of Thessalonica's Jews. Joanna was a new face on their street, without a proper identity card, and another mouth to feed. Spiro's devoted wife, Anna, was a tough and resourceful Greek woman of peasant stock; she found a hiding place for Joanna in an upstairs room. Joanna was warned not to put a foot outside the house. Anna's family was from a small village in northern Greece, near the border with Albania. Her father was a miller and prominent landowner, and her marriage to Spiros, an esteemed Athenian doctor—even if a Jew—had been considered a coup among the people in her home village. As the SS circled ever closer to the Jews of Athens, Anna made the decision to try to escape with her daughter and Joanna to her father's village, where they thought they would be safe, where the Communist Resistance was strong. Spiros would stay behind and tend to his many patients, who were suffering horribly from malnutrition and lack of the most basic medicines. Spiros was close to the chief rabbi of Athens, Elias Barzilai, who tipped him off about the closing net: the SS had come to him and demanded the records of Athens's Romaniote community. Instead of turning over the records, Barzilai burned them and escaped Athens to the Communist Resistance. A day later, Spiros arranged for Anna, his daughter, Olga, and Joanna, renamed Nausicaa, to leave the city and make their way to Anna's village.

As Joanna put it to us, "From one burning pot into another fire."

For a time, after months of being hunted by the Wehrmacht near Pylos and hiding from the hungry eyes of the SS in Athens, Joanna found life in the village of Babouri, high in the Mourgana Mountains, to be idyllic. She was reminded of the mountains north of Pylos, but these mountains were more lush and green, and there was food and shelter in the mill of Anna's father, Vasilo. Vasilo was proud to provide sanctuary for his daughter and the two adolescent girls. All the women were experienced nurses and constantly in demand throughout the region to take care of the sick and injured.

Then two events changed everything. Joanna realized she was pregnant (her periods had stopped, but she thought this due to malnourishment), and the Communists took over the village of Babouri. Being pregnant and unwed in a very traditional peasant society was problematic at best. So the resourceful Anna concocted an elaborate cover story. Anna and Vasilo let it be known that Joanna, Nausicaa, was not the daughter of Anna, as originally put out, but her niece—which was true—and that her family had been executed by the Germans in Pylos, along with her husband of six months. Vasilo further let it be known that the husband had been a Communist fighter and so a martyr to the cause of the enslaved working class.

"Vasilo always had his finger to the wind, you see; he thought my Communist husband would help his business once the Germans were gone and the Communists came to power in Athens."

Once it became known that Joanna had a martyr for a husband, and a Communist one at that, the villagers began to dote on her. It helped that she had a stark beauty, with her expressive eyes and long dark hair and soulful, troubled smile. Even her name, Nausicaa, gave her a mythic allure, and she would let on about Homer and the princess on the shore, who saved mighty Odysseus, when people asked about her name. And she was saving lives as a nurse. Olga, her first cousin, was a big-city girl through and through, and she found the peasants in the village stupid and full of nonsensical notions. She missed Athens, even if 300,000 Athenians had starved to death during the occupation, even as liberation from the Germans had resulted in the catastrophic second round of the civil war in December, when the Communist forces under ELAS fought the government and the British for control of Athens and Greece. The mass reprisals, which had included the widespread gouging of victims' eyeballs, then the slow hacking to pieces of the still living by ELAS punishment squads, had sickened even the most battle-hardened British troops. Joanna and Olga and the villagers were spared such details. Joanna was Olga's only real company in the village, the only woman her age she could talk to about men. Olga became fascinated by Joanna's story about the American OSS captain whom she had nursed back to health: the true father of her child. Late at night, when the girls slept in the same tiny bed in the loft of Vasilo's mill, Olga wanted to know everything about the American. Joanna swore her to silence.

"She thought it was the most romantic story she had ever heard. She would reach over and place her hand on my belly and say, 'Tell me about the rich American, such a hero. Tell me.' So I recited the poetry your father had taught me and remembered the cold and our little fire and how the stars at night burned like diamonds."

"'And he gave you the name—Nausicaa—from Homer—the name of an island princess, like something in the cinema.'"

The problem was that Olga was terrible at keeping secrets.

Joanna delivered her son, my father's first son, in late December 1944. He was a huge baby, and only the skilled hands of Anna got Joanna through the difficult birth. The village celebrated. The boy was healthy and vigorous, a miracle under the circumstances, with powerful amber eyes and a full head of dark hair. Joanna named him Giannis, after her martyr husband, and the villagers looked upon the birth as a good omen as they celebrated the end of the German occupation. The Communist leadership in the village, even after the defeat of that December's uprising in Athens, celebrated the coming triumph of the People's Republic.

"I was so thankful he was healthy. After everything, I feared the worst; but the mountain air was good and the food over the summer had helped me gain weight. I had milk, much milk. Giannis was my deliverance, my consolation; he had been with me on that hill when I had watched my family die. Some part of them—and John, the time we were together—survived. Giannis, I believed, would be my family's salvation."

But then village life in Babouri began changing. At first, the Communist forces had been seen as liberators and patriots, but once the Germans were gone and fighting against the democratic and republican forces became widespread, a subtle shift took place. Babouri became a strongpoint and regional command center. Supplies were requisitioned, labor conscripted, and mandatory ideological training for all villagers became a daily grind. Most of the commanders of the ELAS forces were proud, educated men, many lawyers, schoolteachers, or petty government officials who disdained the rich, entrenched, and corrupt oligarchs. They were also paranoid and saw traitors to the cause everywhere. As the fighting heated up in the south, as ELAS came close to capturing Athens, the regimentation of life in Babouri began to grate on many. Joanna was a favorite of the Communist fighters; she helped nurse the wounded—after all, hadn't her husband been a martyr to the cause of the oppressed?

"It was months before we knew what happened in Athens. We heard nothing from my uncle Spiros. Anna worried herself sick because Spiros was a supporter of the royalists. The Communists boasted openly of killing monarchofascist supporters in Athens, then of killing the imperialist British."

It was a near thing. The Communist secret police kicked down doors all over Athens, rounding up suspected traitors and republican and royalist supporters and executing thousands; in the end, they murdered twice as many as the Germans had managed to kill in the last years of the occupation. Only a British-brokered peace got the Communists to agree to disarm and enter the new democratic government with 20 percent of the seats. But the new government in Athens could barely assert itself, and the Communists in Babouri remained a watchful presence, many retreating to Albania and Yugoslavia to bide their time. Uncle Spiros had only just survived in Athens; his home had been broken into by the Communist secret police, but he had been hiding in a friend's apartment. By the spring of 1945, once Athens finally seemed safe, Anna and Olga slipped out of Babouri in the dead of the night and returned to Spiros. It was decided that Joanna and her young baby would stay for the time being with Anna's father in Babouri, where she was liked and respected for her nursing skills, where the handsome Giannis had become something of a village mascot and a hope for renewal.

"In the spring of 1945, there was more food in the village, maybe more than in Athens. Giannis was growing fast and was happy. I had my work with the villagers. There was danger only in Pylos, according to Uncle Spiros; the Peloponnese had been totally overrun by the Communist *andartes*. In Athens, people would talk; I had no identity card."

Although Joanna never admitted it in so many words, her uncle found it convenient to dispense with his niece and her illegitimate child—another two mouths to feed, and a little boy who might well bring dishonor on the family when Joanna's cover story came under scrutiny. She never forgave her uncle for not bringing her back to Athens with Olga, as she never forgave Nestor for precipitating the events that led to the death of her family. For over a year, Joanna lived a quiet and relatively uneventful life with her young son. She longed for Pylos and the sea, but her memories only brought on bouts of anxiety and depression. She wrote to Anna and Olga in Athens and received reports of life returning to normal—and from Olga, reviews of American movies and hints about Joanna's "secret American lover." Olga wrote, "Maybe he's searching for you, Joanna. Maybe he would want to know about his son?" Joanna was tempted by Olga's romantic skylarking: "Maybe you could visit Athens. Maybe you could get a note to the American embassy, maybe your American, at the very least, would want to know about his Giannis?"

"Oh, I was a fool. I couldn't make up my mind. I was confused. Was I in love with your father? I didn't know if we had a love affair, a romance, as Olga liked to tell me, or if we were just strangers thrown together in the storms of those days. When we made love, when we made our child, it was as if John was coming to life again in me—and saving my life, let me tell you. Nestor would have carried out his threat to kill me if John had died in the mountains. John, you must see, had been with me when my family died. . . . Where does it go from such a place? But Giannis, he was real and happy and such a beautiful boy. I thought if he was happy and healthy, all would be well."

But things were far from well. Like a sudden squall, Communist forces out of Albania and Yugoslavia descended on Babouri in the fall of 1947. And they came to stay. No more hit-and-run guerilla tactics: the Greek Communists had committed themselves to taking and holding ground, liberating towns and forming a provisional government.

The Greek Civil War had begun in earnest. The atmosphere in the village changed overnight. Command posts were established, homes taken over, including Vasilo's mill, which was requisitioned for military use and later became a jail and torture center for political prisoners. Vasilo, once the most prominent man in the village, was now scorned as a landowner and exploiter, while his connections with his daughter and her family in Athens put him in double jeopardy. The increasingly rigid Communist Party line was enforced with a vengeance. Anyone suspected of deviating from the latest directive or supporting the government was arrested and tortured and, more often than not, brutally executed. The local church was desecrated and closed, the priest humiliated in front of his flock in the town square. Food was requisitioned and confiscated, villagers threatened and intimidated, made into beasts of burden, forced to carry supplies up and down the mountains or dig endless trenches and networks of fortifications. In a land of plenty, villagers began to starve. The once-close social fabric frayed as poisonous rumors flew and informers seemed everywhere. As the civil war grew increasingly pitiless, the Communist commanders became more strident in their demands for total obedience in pursuit of the great struggle. In the early months of the civil war, with the lethargic, disorganized response of the government forces, the Communists thought they had their monarchofascist enemies on the run, but then the momentum slipped away as the Americans took over from the exhausted British, as modern weapons, new training, better tactics, and logistical help were provided by the American military mission. In the late spring of 1948, when my father returned as CIA station chief in Athens, he played a key advisory role in disciplining and better coordinating the government forces to fight an insurgency, liaising between the Greek and American military to create a more efficient and seamless command structure.

As the tide slowly began to turn in the government's favor, ELAS became desperate and fanatical, more vicious and paranoid than ever. Every villager in Babouri had to play his or her part: Women cooked and baked bread for the troops, both men and women were impressed as *andartes* to fight the government forces, forever marched up and down the rugged mountain trails between fortified redoubts, while the children were enlisted to gather wood to keep the fighters from freezing, or sent into government mine fields to unearth and diffuse mines. Even the three-year-old Giannis had to attend the makeshift school house each morning to participate in Communist Party songs about their brave Russian brothers and how the brave Greek children, too, would soon be taking up arms, to press the struggle onward for "our precious freedom!" Portraits of Stalin presided over all public areas.

By the fall of 1948, the situation had become desperate. Joanna and Giannis, along with Vasilo and his wife, were allowed the use of a single upstairs room in Vasilo's home; all the other rooms were given over to billeting Communist fighters. They were lucky; many of the homes of other prominent citizens who had fled or were under suspicion for reactionary views had been put to the torch. Joanna was still looked on favorably by the Communists, given her martyr husband and nursing skills, now more in demand than ever as the nationalist forces moved closer and wounded *andartes* streamed back to the medical station in the village, then were evacuated to Albania. But suspicion of Vasilo's capitalist sympathies, especially concerning his doctor brother-in-law, "the Jewish bloodsucker capitalist," living the high life back in Athens, put everyone connected with Vasilo under constant scrutiny. Their food rations were reduced and Vasilo and his wife were given the most back-breaking work, carrying mortars and mortar shells up and down the mountain for the *andartes*. All communication with the outside world had ceased.

"If only I had gone back to Athens with Anna and Olga. If only I could have seen the world as it was and not how it existed in my mind. How my new name, Nausicaa, could not protect me or give me strength. I could not understand these people, the Communists. Their presence turned a world of peace and beauty into one of constant fear. They poisoned the soul of everyone they touched. Everyone lied; every-one hated—like beasts, they turned on one another to save themselves. Those who tried to escape through the battle lines were caught and tortured. We could hear their cries in the cellar of Vasilo's mill. Later, we heard the shots when they were executed. We had no contact with the world beyond: our world had descended into madness. All I wanted was to survive and protect Giannis; I worked like a slave in the medical station to make sure I had food for my son. Can you imagine a child growing up in such a world?"

Then Joanna's luck ran out. On a cold, snowy morning in December 1948, while she was working in the medical station, two *andartes* sud-denly arrived and arrested her. Her hands were tied and she was escorted to what had been Vasilo's prosperous mill, where now the commandant awaited her in his office and interrogation center on the first floor. She was terrified, for when she addressed the *andartes* as comrades, pleading to know what was happening, they spat on her and told her to shut up. She was taken to the office of the new commandant for political security, Kostas Kaleyias. She had no idea who he was or where he was from, and fortunately for her, he had only fragmentary informa-tion on her identity. Kaleyias had escaped from the Peloponnese when the Communists had finally been overwhelmed by the government forces in early 1948; the battles had been relentless as the ELAS fight-ers were systematically ferreted out of their mountain lairs and finally exterminated or captured and interned on prison islands. Kaleyias had managed to escape and spent many months in Albania and Yugoslavia, possibly Moscow, and was now back in Greece, seeking vengeance for the defeat in the Peloponnese by a crack division of government troops under his nemesis. Col. Neokosmos Grigoriadis, known to his officers and troops as "Nestor," was a tough soldier who liked to get his hands dirty. Nestor's men had been newly outfitted with modern weapons

and retrained in counterinsurgency warfare by the commander of the
American mission, Gen. James Van Fleet. A battle-hardened veteran
of World War II, Van Fleet, against specific orders, had frequented the
field of battle and come under fire so as to better guage his adversary,
soon instilling vigor, competence, and a new ruthlessness in the Greek
officer corps. In May 1949, Van Fleet was pictured on the cover of *Time*
magazine under a combined banner of a Greek flag and an American
one, heralded by Truman as the man who had won the war in Greece
against the Communists.

Joanna barely noticed Kaleyias, the new commandant for security,
when she first entered the interrogation room, for Giannis was seated
in a chair next to his desk.

She stifled a scream. She was prevented from going to her four-
year-old son by the *andartes,* who held her arms.

"Comrade, sit." Kaleyias held up his gloved hand, motioning for her
to be quiet as she called out to her son. "No harm has come to your boy.
We have just been having an enlightening chat."

"But he has done nothing."

"Of course he has done nothing. He is a wonderful, intelligent child
who has clearly learned much from his mother." Kaleyias, his face
sunken, bearded, rheumy-eyed, turned to the boy. "Giannis, recite for
your mother again the poem you recited for your teacher last week. Tell
us about the angels."

Giannis sang out proudly, "'Like angels stopped upon the wing by
sound of harmony from Heaven's remotest spheres.'"

"Good boy." Kaleyias turned to Nausicaa. "Comrade, how extraordinary. It seems the child can recite the English poet Wordsworth. Do
you speak English with your son? No one remembers you speaking
English in the village."

"No, comrade, only a few words, a little from school, from films."

"Wordsworth is not from films. And the boy's accent is not even
English; it is an American accent. How can that be?"

"There was a book of English poetry in my father's office. I learned
it there. The only pronunciation I knew was from American films, and
Greeks who returned from America."

"So you knew Americans?"

"No, only Greeks who had been there."

"Such a handsome child. So tall, so intelligent—just look at his eyes."

"My husband's eyes."

"Ah yes, your martyred husband—from Pylos?"

"Yes, comrade. He was shot by the Germans."

"Yes, yes, I know"—Kaleyias examined a document on his desk—"and also your father—the doctor—mother, and sister. How was it you managed to escape?"

"I was taking medicine to a patient of my father's, an old woman who lived outside of Pylos."

"Lucky for you. But we have no record of your husband"—Kaleyias looked down again—"Giannis Mitros, being a member of the Communist Party of Greece."

Joanna had chosen Giannis Mitros as the father because he lived two houses down from her family in Pylos, was the right age, had the right name, and she'd witnessed his execution in the square with her parents.

"Comrade, he went to meetings. He spoke highly of the work and aspirations of ELAS."

"I have to tell you, comrade Nausicaa Mitros, no Communists died in the fascist massacre that day in Pylos . . . mostly"—Kaleyias ran his finger down a list—"monarchofascist traitors and Jews."

"My husband died at the hands of the Nazis."

"Your father and your uncle must have been pleased with your marriage."

At this point, Joanna was smart enough not to let herself be caught in a lie that was unnecessary to her survival.

"The truth comrade, Giannis Mitros and I were not married—not yet. I was with child. I left Pylos to live with my uncle in Athens because of the death of my family. . . . I was afraid, too, that the people of Pylos would condemn me for the child."

"Stupid bourgeoisie, so narrow-minded about such things. But still you have your son. A remarkable boy. And a remarkable name, Nausicaa—out of Homer. And even more remarkable: Did you know that your son just recited Homer for me—and in the ancient Greek of Homer!"

"My father was at university in Athens; he taught us lines of ancient Greek."

"You Jews are a remarkable people, how you absorb our culture and make it your own—almost as good as the Americans."

Joanna was near panic: remembering the letters from Olga under her mattress.

"When you escaped Pylos, when you were in Athens," Kaleyias continued, "did you meet any Americans, perhaps downed pilots being smuggled away to Turkey, or OSS agents making contact with the old rightest regime under Papandreou or Zervas, perhaps?"

"I was in hiding; I saw nobody but my uncle and his wife and my cousin."

"Ah, your uncle." Kaleyias tapped the papers on his desk thoughtfully. "A sad thing, now that Roosevelt is gone, the Americans have become the creatures of the British, it seems, the new imperialists, the arsenal of capitalist exploitation. Our enemies. Yes, a sad thing, comrade Nausicaa Mitros"—and he glanced at Giannis, who was folding and unfolding a piece of paper—"the Americans have shown their true colors."

Kaleyias, it seemed, couldn't quite make the leap of imagination to grasp precisely what was staring him in the face, but he had sniffed enough around the edges to have grave doubts about Nausicaa's loyalty. Worse, Giannis intrigued him: a child of such natural intelligence, and such a quick learner, what he described to Joanna as "an intensity of spirit." "He will be a great light to our Communist Party someday: a son of the revolution, the son of a martyr . . . let us hope not *two* martyrs."

Joanna was too valuable as a nurse; she could do most of what a doctor could do in terms of treating the wounded. As a warning, she was given a glimpse of the holding cell in the cellar where the tortured and battered lay in their blood and excrement, awaiting execution—enough to terrify her so that she was near speechless. Then she was returned to the medical station. As a guarantee of her loyalty, Giannis was placed with another family and she was allowed to visit him only once a day after work.

"I feared I would go crazy with worry. But I had to survive for my son. I drowned my fear by treating the wounded; the more I could save, the better chance I would survive."

Kaleyias had her watched. He began visiting Giannis. He provided extra rations for the boy. Joanna would go to her son in the evening and find him singing a Communist song: "Take up your weapons, take up your arms! Onward to the struggle for our precious freedom!"

As the civil war began to go badly for the Communists in late 1948, a terrifying rumor spread like wildfire through the Communist-controlled mountainous regions of northwestern Greece. The Communist Provisional Government announced a new policy, the *pedomasoma*, or "the forcible gathering up of children." The strategy was to take children between the ages of three and fourteen from the Communist-controlled villages and relocate them to friendly socialist countries behind the Iron Curtain. At first, the scheme was justified as a way of protecting the children; then it quickly evolved into a ruse for securing the loyalty of parents left behind, while providing a new cadre of indoctrinated fighters for the future. Even as the Communist revolution in Greece went down to disaster, the ideals of Communist Greece would be preserved abroad. It was an act of suicidal folly and flew in the face of the family bonds so dear to Greek culture. The women of the villages became more desperate than ever. In Babouri, as the Communist forces lost ground to the government, the KKE security apparatus, under the command of political commissar Kaleyias, took over their lives. Informants were encouraged: Nothing in the village moved without being noted. Under unrelenting ideological pressure, a few children were given up voluntarily by desperate mothers, but most were simply abducted, taken from their families and marched across the border to Albania, where they were carried off to various fraternal Communist nations in Eastern Europe.

"It was a nightmare, except there was never a morning. First, Kaleyias limited my visits with my son, and then he had me transferred deeper into the Mourgana Mountains, to a medical station nearer the border with Albania. He laughed at my tears, telling me how fond of Giannis he had become, how he would want only good things for the boy. 'I will make sure that he gets a proper education, Nausicaa, that he is well fed and has proper clothes; he will be trained to be an architect, perhaps, an engineer, an officer or high official in the new Greece that is coming. Comrade Nausicaa, you will be so proud of your son—son of a princess, is that not right? Perhaps Odysseus had his way with the young princess after all.' My only hope was to befriend the Communists, to work hard, to learn all I could about their plans. The last time I saw Giannis was in February 1949. Unlike the other children, he was growing and healthy, no sign of malnutrition, goiter, rickets, or, God forbid, tuberculosis—things widespread at that time. Three weeks they kept me away. I was shocked by how good he looked compared to children in other villages. I was happy; I was terrified. He was smiling and singing their songs. I was given half an hour with my son before I was ordered back to my post, a six-hour walk up the mountain to the medical station. I learned later that Giannis was evacuated that after-noon with the rest of the children from the village. They were marched into Albania and from there to many different places.

"I pretended to be loyal, to accept the fate of my child. I was watched; always I was watched. They had taken Olga's letters. In the last weeks, we were overwhelmed by wounded *andartes*. They brought them day and night, the dead and wounded—the most terrible wounds—and women fighters, too. The nationalists had napalm from the Americans, and the burn wounds were like nothing we had seen before. By then, we didn't have field dressings. My God, the suffering. I never believed such a thing was possible. I asked about the children in Albania. I asked if I might go visit my son. And the commandant would smile at my concern and tell me I was too valuable to leave my post. 'Your son is safe now, comrade, safe with our socialist brothers.'"

Joanna was captured by the government forces when her medical center was overrun by Greek government commandos in the winter of 1949. By many accounts, she had served the Communist cause with a diligent and unwavering spirit; she had saved many lives. Her situation was complicated. She had no idea if Giannis was still in Albania or had been relocated to another country; if she turned on the Commu-nists, denounced the horrors she had experienced, and word got back to Kaleyias or others in the Party hierarchy, her son could be in danger. The civil war would grind on for the remainder of 1949. Who could vouch for her? Anna's father, Vasilo, the miller, had been executed by the Communists for trying to escape with his wife to the government lines. Joanna was interrogated by government army officers, who were much more interested in the fate of the Communist commissars who might have escaped across the Albanian border, or gone into hiding, than in the plight of her son. She gave the name of her doctor uncle back in Athens, but that seemed to get her nowhere. Then she overheard the name of an army colonel, a nickname bandied about among the mili-tary officers in the interrogation center because of some extraordinary operation during the last weeks of mountain fighting.

"Is this *Nestor* from Pylos?"

"What is it to you?"

"He knows me. He knew my family in Pylos. Tell him that I am here, Joanna, the girl who took care of the American in the mountains."

A week later, she was in Athens, reunited with her Uncle Spiros, Anna, and Olga. She had to be discreet, for fear that any disparagement of the Communists might endanger her Giannis. Sunny Athens in the spring of 1949 provided no comfort for the bleak despair she felt at the loss of her son and the anxiety that she might say or do the wrong thing. She was soon suicidal, so utterly depressed that she could barely rise from her bed in her uncle's splendid home, or even take food. Anna and Olga did their best but were unable to revive her spirits. That was when her hatred of Nestor festered and gained weight "in my soul," threatening her sanity—even as he finally put her in touch again with the father of her child.

"Why did you hate Nestor?" asked Laura. "Because he'd forced you to nurse Peter's father in the mountains?"

Joanna looked at us with her empty, dark, helpless eyes, heartbreaking to witness.

"Nestor butchered Kaleyias like a pig; he bragged to me about his revenge."

Laura and I glanced numbly at each other in the faint light from the kerosene lamp; all we could do was wait until Joanna began again.

"You see, the only list of names that we had from the village of Babouri and the other villages in the mountains . . . Giannis's name was not on the list. Kaleyias changed my son's name; that monster gave my son another name, and no one knew which name on the list was Giannis's name. They split the children up; they sent some to Hungary, some to Romania, and others God knows where. It was never possible to be sure of the right name, even if the Communists weren't lying when they told us they had lost track of many of the children."

"Oh my God." Laura bit her knuckle and reached again to Joanna's hand.

"All this time and you haven't been able to locate him?"

Joanna shook her head and gave a bleak sigh.

"It has been over forty years." Joanna turned to me, a dull spark in her dark eyes. "Your father tried to help me. He assured me he would use every resource of the Greek and U.S. governments to find my son . . . his son."

"So you did see him again?"

"This time, it was he who saved my life. He was already at the American embassy in Athens when I returned from the mountains and went to live with my Uncle Spiros—Spiros, who did nothing, who told no one about me—nothing."

Nestor, too, it seemed, had not been eager to say anything about

Joanna. It took over a month, after he'd gone to where Joanna was being confined in a government holding cell in the northern town of Kastoria, identified her, and had her released, before he called the American embassy and the CIA station chief.

"Your father made everything possible." Joanna spread her arms in a gesture of humility and supplication. "I had no idea he had been in Greece for over a year fighting the Communists. He came to me in my uncle's house. I was sick in spirit; I'd had a breakdown. My uncle gave me medications—the wrong medications, I know now. I couldn't even get out of bed. John came to me and sat on the bedside; he called me Nausicaa; again and again he called me by that name. At first, it terrified me to hear it: the hidden woman I had been in Babouri, the name from the lips of Kaleyias, but strangely, in time, in John's American voice, the name Nausicaa—of a loved one—allowed me to wake, like Persephone rising from the underworld. I told him about Giannis. We cried together. He told me how from the very first day in Athens he had asked Nestor about me but had been told I had been kidnapped, or worse, by the Communists, and that making too many inquiries could endanger my life.

"Then every day he made me walk with him in the Agora, in the sunlight, as he taught me about the ancient ruins of Athens. He brought food from the American embassy, chocolates—lots of chocolates—and made sure I began eating again to build up my strength. We had to be careful not to be recognized. . . . If the *wrong* people knew. . . . He assured me that he would do everything possible to find Giannis. I did not even have a photograph to show him—not one, not a single one; I felt I had failed to protect his son." Joanna looked at me and put a palm to my cheek. "He would be older than you now, imagine that, just a few years older."

Over those weeks in Athens as Joanna recovered her strength and fought off depression, my father began the delicate, agonizing business, with Nestor's help, of trying to track down the whereabouts of his son. As Nestor later told me, it was devilishly tricky, because if the Communists had gotten wind of the specifics, much less the paternity of the child, Giannis would have been turned into a hostage, a bargaining chip, or worse. So Communist defectors and prisoners were interrogated carefully and discreetly to try, at least, to learn the name that Kaleyias had given the boy. They eliminated names on the captured lists by matching them with other children whose identities could be confirmed. But there always remained seven or eight names that couldn't be pinned down because the parents had been killed or had disappeared. And they had no photograph.

Just hearing the name Nausicaa whispered by Joanna, and the revelations about their lost son, cast a new light over all the disconnected patterns of my father's past. I felt his early adolescent longings translated into the sudden absences, long silences, and the "terrible sadness" mentioned in Suzanne's letters. And the scraps of reminiscences from my Winsted days, from the lips of Paul Oakes, Virgil Dabney, Charlie Springfield, and my godfather, Colonel Fairburn, began to form into a very different picture: It was not just Karel Hollar he'd been after, but word of his lost son.

It was almost 2:00 A.M. by the time we left our chairs. We spent another hour strolling in the gardens, our steps lighted by the moon. Laura and I each took one of Joanna's arms and walked her to her car, savoring the fragrant night and the cubist jottings of Nestor's vast home aglow under the moon: stucco rectangles and parallelograms of palest yellow, blanched ocher, and simmering cream rising in tiers from the mauve-green of the garden, where the masses of dripping vines off the staggered balconies topped everything off like swirls of icing on a wedding cake. The Great Dane was in near ecstasy, prancing like a small filly, circling around and around, nose to the earth. The gravel crunched beneath our feet as we stopped on our way out before the fountain, where the carp rose like silvery phantoms at our approach.

Joanna laughed as they nibbled at her fingers.

"Do you understand how he saved me? He didn't tell me to forget or be brave. He became my professor, every day when we walked in the Agora. We could not console each other. Instead, he told me my son must admire an educated mother. That I must work hard so that I could teach him well. He gave me books to take home with me. We met by the Stoa of Attalos at five o'clock every day and began our walk. Then we would stop and he would point at this building or that statue and he would begin to explain, rebuilding the ancient city for me out of the air, the columns—Corinthian, Doric, Ionic—until I knew the architecture by heart, until I could see it in my mind. That was his way with me: He made me his student, and if I failed to listen, or remember the lesson from the day before, he scolded me. He made me mad; he shamed me—but he made me talk, made me think, look. Until I could build from nothing, you see . . ." And she tapped a finger to her eye. "From nothing."

It was odd, after that long evening of hearing about my father's disasters, his obfuscations and mistakes of judgment—the troubling appearance of those Linear B tablets in Nestor's telling, and his heroic snatch at redemption on that treacherous hillside trail above Kalamata, to be left with a final image of him strolling in the ancient Agora with Joanna, lecturing away, recalling for me something of those gesticulating figures in Virgil's Piranesi prints. But, as Joanna made clear, by conjuring the past, he was trying to heal her present gripped by depression—and perhaps his own—by goading her to rebuild her life. "The anger, you see, freed my brain; now I do the same with my patients who suffered in the war," she said. He got her thinking about a deeper past, which subsumed the aches of the moment, through which she might glimpse a better future. "He made everything possible—everything." He paid for her to move to Paris, where she was tutored in French and then enrolled in the University of Paris, and then medical school. They stayed in constant touch, though they never saw each other again. Updated reports on the futile search for Giannis were sent to her in Paris on a regular basis. In the early fifties, during the height of the Cold War, information of any kind out of Eastern Europe and the Soviet Union was at a premium. When she finished medical school in the spring of 1954—a full year ahead of others—my father failed to make it to her graduation as he had promised, nor did he send any explanation for his absence.

"He had been captured," Laura said before I could get out a word. "The Soviets had him locked up in a prison in Prague for almost all of 1954, where he died."

At this, Joanna simply went to Laura and hugged her for over a minute, and then did the same with me.

Only when Laura visited Joanna's hospital in Pylos the next day, when I met up with them late that afternoon, did I realize how completely my father had planned for the worst. In 1955, as she was interning at a Paris hospital, Joanna was contacted by Brandt & Harrison and informed of my father's death in the line of duty. An endowment had been set up to fund the building of a hospital for Pylos. Joanna was designated the director and was given carte blanche to design the buildings to her specifications and hire doctors and staff. Out of the blue, she was, in effect, handed some five million dollars to fund the hospital of her dreams . . . to build from nothing.

"No time," she said, breaking into a broad smile as she showed us around the impressive pediatric ward, "to mourn . . . only to build."

Joanna invited a young French architect whom she knew from the university to come to Pylos to help with the design; they would eventually marry. The Alden Hospital in Pylos, completed in 1959, won every architectural award in Greece of the day, and now serves the whole southwestern part of the Peloponnese; it has one of the finest pediatric departments in all of Greece—Joanna's specialty. I had probably reviewed the line item for the endowment and running expenses of the hospital in Pylos a dozen times over the years in my capacity as trustee for the family foundations, and thought nothing of it. My grandmother, the trustee for the family foundations after my father's death, had poured money into the hospital, without question, and, as far as I've been able to tell, without any correspondence or communication with Joanna.

Did my grandmother know about her lost grandson, Giannis? Not a word to anyone—but I realize now that she knew; of course she knew. She and my father were thick as thieves at the end: They more than shared—they intuited each other's secrets. Why else would she have put into his hands in his last days at Elysium the story of the lost Pearce Breckenridge?

In front of the hospital in Pylos is a memorial dedicated to the victims of the Nazi massacre in the spring 1944: 107 names carved in the finest Naxian marble.

And so we said good night to Joanna by the open door of her Mercedes station wagon, with the Great Dane—named Apollo!—whining in the back at having been denied a longer romp in Nestor's garden. We hugged and kissed and lingered and made arrangements for a visit to the hospital on the following day, and then went reeling to our different beds and troubling dreams.

I didn't even make it to bed. My back was so inflamed that I took a triple dose of Demerol and curled into a reclining chair on the balcony off my room; pulling myself into a fetal position while clutching the gift of the shepherd's staff, I waited for the pain to ease. On the horizon, Navarino Bay glittered in broad painterly swaths of nacreous gray. I could still make out a trickle of smoke from the arbor, drifting upward past the walls of Nestor's citadel, dispersing on the night breezes that played across that gleaming bay filled with history's misadventures: those lovely highlights of spun silver incised on pewter, which wavered and dispersed and formed again like some airy script, indecipherable yet begging for decipherment. I was glad to be alone, and yet realized I never would be again. The past from which I'd been gaining escape velocity since my return from Vietnam sixteen years before was overtaking me . . . the glide slowing, the current reasserting itself. Everything I remembered, thought I remembered, or imagined was being reshaped before my eyes, as if the silverpoint jottings upon Navarino Bay were just daring me to try my hand at a new translation.

I was deeply touched by what Joanna had told us, especially about her walks with my father in the ancient Athenian Agora. As a young man at Winsted, I would have been thrilled by Nestor's account of my father's heroics—his sharpshooting, his godlike feats and near-suicidal daring in flinging those sticks of explosives up the mountain. But curled in fetal oblivion with knees to my chin, with moonlit Navarino Bay beckoning, it was his kindness and patience with a young woman suffering a deep trauma that warmed me. Was he just being his scholarly self with her, keeping his distance? Or, as she suspected, was he finding ways to lead her out of her depression? Or was he just yielding to his instincts as a teacher? And what a great teacher he might have been. It was a strange feeling to find myself drawing closer to my father as my admiration grew in the discovery of a very different person from the one of my youthful imaginings. What I had always considered, on some level, his desertion of me, framed by images of him at Elysium on the morning he left, standing on the boathouse for a last smoke, or walking with taciturn determination past Checkpoint Charlie, began to recede as I saw a man in search of a son, another son, to be sure, from yet another woman, a son he had never seen . . . but no longer a man who had abandoned me lightly. In search of the son of a woman he couldn't or wouldn't marry. "How could we?" Joanna told Laura the following day: "We had seen too much. And the danger, until he was safe, *mon Dieu!* . . . yes, even today."

Was it just the danger to their son, or guilt over those 107 victims in Pylos?

When my father agreed to join the CIA and go to Athens in 1948, he broke with Suzanne. From 1948 to 1950, there are very few letters, mostly from Suzanne, who was in agony about his leaving her. He was a free man and yet not.

Because when he married my mother in the spring of 1950, the affair with Suzanne was again under way. Elysium, his beloved home ground, held him still, and proved his downfall.

How the gods weave their subterfuges into our lives, as fateful as they are arbitrary.

With all this new history, I was more mortified than ever by the emptiness of my mother's place in my heart, my mother, who, while doing ninety in a fifty-mile-per-hour speed zone, had run her Mercedes into a bridge abutment on the Taconic Parkway in 1972.

I kept thinking how Joanna had repeatedly used the phrase *savais-tu*—a distinction not always available in English—which speaks of a knowledge inherent in the body, something she as a woman and an obstetrician who had delivered thousands of babies understood better than anyone. It reminded me of what Max always told me, that the most deep-rooted of our instincts shape our perceptions; that by bowing to our bodily desires and reverencing our simple pleasures, our true selves will emerge. What Joanna and my father had found together sheltering in a shepherd's hut against the winter's cold. Was this the lesson offered by the fair Nausicaa, who, surviving her imprisonment, embraced the fate of the gods and lived a life of service to her fellow men?

"He was like a god, you see—a god for a seventeen-year-old girl, an American, an educated man—alive to what makes us truly human."

How I would have liked to leave it at that . . . if not for the damned Linear B tablets and the treachery of Karel Hollar.

A man bewitched by three graces, or was it four: Mother Nestor?

And one, Suzanne, forever hedging her bets, who had betrayed his fate to her wretched gods.

And therein the lesson of how I learned to steal fire from Max as he stole from me, as all artists do.

As the wise king of the Phaeacians, Alcinous, said of Odysseus's prolonged agony of return, "The gods brought this about: For men they wove the web of suffering, that men to come might have a theme to sing."

Look around you, friends. Their sad memorials are writ everywhere.

I drifted off on the balcony, gripping the ram's head crook to my lips, staring out at the setting moon tipped like a broken shackle upon the sea, the lingering scent of wood smoke, lacquered oak, and sweat, like the ebbing heat from some disastrous fire that had consumed a near century, dissolving into the silver distance as the cooling currents moved us on . . . as sleep took me under, and so finally oblivious of those commanding walls where the concertina wire glinted like bladed scimitars on the night translucent.

Just another failed monument to an old man's troubled dreams.

28 I AWOKE TO FLICKERING SUNLIGHT AND the smell of strong coffee, but not just coffee . . . bacon and eggs and burnt toast, the distinct smells of an American diner, something that reminded me of the Lexington Avenue diners of childhood, or, more recently, PJ's Pancake House on Nassau Street in Princeton, places impossibly distant from Navarino Bay.

When I made my way downstairs after my exercises, I realized Laura was already long gone to visit Joanna's hospital in Pylos, and a huge argument had erupted around the breakfast table between Nestor and Nikos and the rest of the family. Nestor wanted to take me for a walk in the foothills but refused to have any security men accompany us.

Shying away from the upraised voices in the dining room—though yearning for some of that wonderful coffee—I began a brief reconnoiter of the house, waiting for things to calm down. I was fascinated to find that there were books lying around all over the place, most on European history, ancient and modern—a lot on World War II—but also including volumes on philosophy, art, mythology, and literature. There were novels and books of poetry, many well thumbed and underlined. And I noticed the latest archaeological journals—and yes, my three most popular books, published by Princeton University Press. Books stacked and abandoned, open pages facedown by half a dozen favored chairs.

My father's Nestor had become something of an autodidact, had become the name my father had bestowed on him, and from what I'd gathered from Joanna, a lot more besides: a man adept at skillfully playing the audience of the moment.

I made a swift foray into Nestor's office, and there in a corner, not entirely overlooked when we first met, was the framed photograph of my father and Nestor amidst a line of military men on the steps of what I now recognized was the Temple of Hephaestus in the Athenian Agora. The photo was a twin of the one in the display case in the entrance area of the Winsted gym. Except here was included a complete catalog of names—signatures, I realized—along the bottom margin, including Nestor's: Col. Neokosmos Grigoriadis, doubtless for official purposes. But he was out of uniform, preferring, in this instance, the role of Resistance leader. I peered into the face of my father as if to detect some change after all I'd found out the night before, but found only the same troubled eyes and distracted off-kilter stare, canted stance and cane pressed against his khaki pant leg. And yet, in his stare—yes . . . something new.

After a huge breakfast, Nikos took me aside.

"Nestor had a triple bypass last year, and half a cancerous lung removed the year before; it's a miracle he's still with us, much less walking. And he still smokes on the sly, the old goat. He's on half a dozen medications and he should be back in the States, where the medical facilities are a *lot* better. He's planning to die here—of course—except I don't want it to be *here*, *today*, on those treacherous trails—not with my wife and kids around. Our flight to Boston is booked tomorrow, and I have a meeting in L.A. on Tuesday."

Father and son reached a compromise: one guard, a slow pace, and the security guard would keep his distance.

The garrulous teller of tales from the previous night was strangely silent for a good half hour as we made our way along the hillsides above Navarino Bay; he gazed out where the hill shadows on the blue retreated slowly shoreward. The paths were narrow, but the earth was well trodden. Nestor carried a staff, a shepherd's crook of some antiquity, which, he told me, had been his father's. Following his lead, I had taken the ram's head walking stick the veteran fighter had given me the night before, the one my father had used on the trek from the mountains to the rendezvous with the submarine. I was surprised to find how much it helped, and chagrinned to think I was putting it to good use.

Nestor, dressed from head to toe in white, would have been a sitting duck for a sniper: a cream-colored Panama hat with a bleached alligator band, a white silk shirt unbuttoned to the waist, displaying a chest of gray hair and a gold medallion or two, baggy white flannel trousers, and tattered white Nike tennis shoes inscribed with the name Ilie Nastase on the heel. The amber worry beads occupied his other hand and flipped in steady counterpoint to his steps.

We reached a small promontory where the trail opened out onto a view of Navarino Bay. The sandstone slopes covered in clumps of stunted cedars reached to within feet of the waterline, leaving a blistered border of rock to outline the crystal blue. Stopping to rest, Nestor got out a monogrammed handkerchief and mopped his brow. Then, with a quick glance to where the guard was nearly out of sight, Nestor produced a silver flask from his back pocket, which he held up to his meaty lips before handing it over to me. One swallow was plenty. Ouzo is an acquired taste; at body temperature, it's a good deal more than an acquired taste.

"Know why I wanted to bring you here?" he asked, craning his neck to make sure the guard was out of earshot.

I handed back the silver flask.

"The excavations of Nestor's Palace, where my father met with Karel Hollar."

"Hey, smart boy, chip off the old block. We'll go a way the tourists never see, the way I went there as a boy—a way I haven't been since that night in the fall of '43." Nestor gave me a significant look and ambled over to the rock face to take a piss.

"A great idea," I said. "Something I should have done long ago."

"Why didn't you—*and* come see me?"

"Once upon a time, when, as they say, I began to follow in my father's footsteps—well, you see, Nestor, it led me to a place along a river in Hâu Nghĩa province, where, in retrospect, I'd rather not have been."

"Then you're a fool, because it's not what your father would have wanted. I never knew a man who so hated his fate. He would have been happy for you to be the great scholar you are—and I've read all your books; he would have been very pleased."

I bowed and thanked him for the kind words.

"I was here as a boy with my father's goats." Nestor gestured to the horizon like some Charlton Heston parting the Red Sea. "I'd throw rocks. I'd dream about being a rich man in America."

"You did it, the American dream and some."

He waved off my comment like a bad smell.

"Not like you rich guys—a godlike Alden. I had to do things that I am not proud of; I will never tell my sons."

"Believe it or not, when I see a stretch of sea and sky like this, Navarino Bay, Sphaktiria, Pylos, the history in these names and places—what we are, or *were*—it's a flash in the pan, our family." I snapped my fingers. "In the stream of time, what we get from our families is like so many names on the wind."

He made a face at what must have struck him as slightly ludicrous posturing on my part. Nestor seemed to angle himself for a better view, as if to find some configuration of fact and fiction that would put it in proper context for me. Then he smiled, as if remembering an off-color joke.

"*You* people . . ." He shook his head and pointed toward the shore below. "There was the beach where he was dropped by the submarine, and right about here was the place where we rested and watched those bombers come flying from the sea."

I could readily see how that climb from the beach would have tired even a fit man like my father, despite the help of mules to carry the supplies and radio equipment from the submarine.

"Funny, you're not the first to tell me that he disliked—how did my godfather put it?—*machines*."

"For a city boy who lived on Fifth Avenue, he liked simple things: the outdoors, life in camp—things of the mind, heh. I was with him in Athens in 1949 when we got word that the Soviets had tested a nuclear weapon. He was devastated. 'Nestor,' he told me with sad eyes, 'now we can end the world at the press of a button; either that or this war with the Communists will never end.' We went out and got drunk in the Plaka; it was the only time I really knew him to get so pissed. I had to take him home in a taxi."

"Do you suppose he was right—that it will never end?"

"The worst is that the young people make the same mistakes all over again."

As we began walking, the trail steepened; I better understood Nikos's concern. Nestor's shirt was plastered against his hairy back.

"Are you okay? Nikos was worried about you."

"He's a good son to worry. But I'm still pretty good at cheating death." He smiled at me, as if making a joke. "And cursed with the name given me by your father . . . that at the end of my life I must live up to such a name by becoming a bookworm with a bad heart and bum lungs. Not like my father," and he gestured with his staff to the bay and the sky and the hills. "Just this, every day, poor—dirt-poor and more of the same. I was happy in America. I was crazy to come back in 1940, but I wanted to see my father before he died, to find a wife. Eight years fighting—for what?—a socialist government that now throws kisses to the Communists. Better to have remembered a poor childhood tending my father's goats in the old country than a life as a rich guy in America—heh?"

"Listen, I try to stay out of discussions of Greek politics when I'm in Athens—get a Greek on the subject of NATO and Turkey and the bad vibes do loop de loops all night long—but at some point those wounds from the civil war need to be healed."

"That is what death does for us."

"Not for the living, not for the sons."

Nestor stopped and rested on his staff.

"Killing Communists was all I cared about—isn't that what Joanna told you?" Something in his tone suggested I, a guest in his home, had betrayed him: that I had spoken at length to Joanna; that Laura had rushed off to Joanna's hospital without breakfast.

"Killing Kaleyias, that did seem a lot on her mind."

"And she hasn't spoken to me in forty years, not since I got her released from a military prison."

"You invited her."

"I owed her at least that much. Shit, I hired her husband to design my home."

"What a terrible thing, about her son . . . my father's son."

"So she tells you."

"You don't believe her?"

"What am I supposed to believe in this life after everything I've seen?"

"The child, Giannis, Joanna said he looked like my father."

"Your father? There were three or four guards with them at all times in the mountains that winter. Young, strong men. John was near death. This was not a love nest in the Poconos. You're a smart boy; how can you trust what a woman tells you?"

"You did kill Kaleyias?"

"My only regret is that I didn't do it sooner, here in the Peloponnese. Somehow he escaped us in 1948, flapped his bat wings and disappeared. Do you know that he and his men executed an entire village that was loyal to the royalists: men, women, and children—more than a hundred—their bodies dumped down a well. Explain such a thing, my philosopher and fellow bookworm. His own people. We had him surrounded"—Nestor held up his thumb and forefinger, nearly touching—"but he slipped away and escaped north and disappeared into Albania with the rest of the Communist scum."

"Greece owes men like you a debt of gratitude."

Nestor rolled his eyes at my inept platitude. "At a price—just like the E-boat base. Worth shit, all those men who died, some like brothers to me, and what happened to your father."

"Do you regret it? Did my father?"

"A fool regrets what's done. Who can appreciate the world that never was because we stopped it from being? Just ask Nikos; he runs one hundred and eighty-five movie theaters in malls all over New England—people want entertainment, not the end of civilization. And that Joanna, I bet she went on and on about what a crazy, tough son of a bitch I was—heh. She won't talk to me for forty years, but she talks to you, son of her sugar daddy."

"Something of a shock to find out I have a half brother somewhere behind the Iron Curtain."

"Or not. But she—Jewish people are like that, you know—got her hospital from her rich American."

"Was she in love with him?"

"What do you think, a young Jewess?"

"Was he in love with her?"

"Are you crazy? A rich American guy who went to Princeton. He was ashamed of himself. In America, she'd be considered jailbait. Here, guys get killed by the father or the brother for less."

"So, when you contacted the American embassy in—what?—early 1948, asking if they could get my father back to Greece to help the American military mission to the government in the civil war, get him to join the CIA, Joanna wasn't . . . part of the equation?"

"I'd forgotten about her. When John asked, her uncle in Athens told us she'd been taken as a hostage by the Communists when they withdrew from Athens in December of 1944. Or she'd joined them—he wasn't very clear. When I got word of her capture in '49 by our forces, I told your father. She should be thanking me; she was an *andarte*, a Communist soldier; she was wearing their uniform when she was captured. Many were executed; some were kept in prison for years."

"I hear her hospital is quite something."

"The pride of Pylos. Everybody loves her, a fucking saint—that's what people say. While me . . . in Pylos, I still get looks, from fathers, brothers—who knows: relatives of guys dead in the civil war, or just back from fucking Hungary or some Commie cesspool."

His sudden turn to sarcasm was hard to measure. I watched his worry beads slipping through his stubby, powerful fingers. I was a little uncertain about where he was taking me with this conversation.

Then he laughed. "The dreams of an old man when he can manage to sleep." He offered me one of the two cigarettes secreted in his shirt pocket; I declined. "Too much talk at dinner, too much wine." He lighted up. "Doctor says no more booze, no cigarettes, but what the hell do doctors know about life; they only try to keep back death." He handed me his Zippo lighter. In the steel face his name had been beautifully incised: *Nestor*, and underneath, *1944*. "It was your father's. He gave it to me on the beach before he left. In the winter, in the mountains, he made it for me."

I weighed the Zippo in my palm, thinking of those long winter days and nights: the cold, the warmth of a young woman, stories told by the fire. My own youth now gone, I found it hard to imagine how I would have survived what my father went though. Perhaps I was still overromanticizing his predicament, or maybe his Homeric visions of a simple life really did get him through. I squeezed the Zippo tight in my palm and then handed it back.

"You probably think I'm a hard-ass," he said, "after all that talk last night. Did Joanna tell you I'm a hard man?"

"She had a tough time." Nestor paused on the path and eyed me over the top of his dark glasses.

"It is one thing to fight the Italians, and then the Germans . . . but to have to kill your own people is a soul-crushing business. I don't recommend it to anybody."

In this, the sudden tension of muscles at the cheek and jawline, I sensed a sadness that put me in mind of another old man, my great-grandfather, General Alden, walking among the graves of his men in the Winsted cemetery.

"Civil wars are always the worst," I said. "Just read Thucydides. Fratricidal wars like that between Athens and Sparta can be the most brutal and dispiriting. The great irony is that the ancient Greek fondness for competition and conflict among their own kind laid the groundwork for individual freedom and democracy—small farmers defending their rights." I pointed toward a strip of land on the near horizon. "Did my father ever mention anything about Navarino Bay and the island of Sphacteria—right out there, where the Athenians cornered a force of Spartans?"

Nestor pulled at his face, as if with vague relief that I'd moved us into a deeper past, as if the prevailing winds might still lead our conversation elsewhere.

"Ah, so the scholar son prefers to hear another version of his old man—heh?" Nestor laughed to himself. "I don't blame you; I'll never tell my sons about Kaleyias, or about the easy money in the twenties with Prohibition." Nestor gently tapped my shoulder. "And yes, I remember him with his binoculars looking out at Sphacteria—today we call it Sfaktiria—saying something about how the Athenians had a chance here"—Nestor made a chopping motion with his hands—"to cut the knot, the stalemate of a war they could not win."

My heart leapt at his words—so often the case when names come together in a place rich with associations. I pointed. "Yes, yes, see that, that spit of rock and sand, it looks like an island. If I'm not mistaken, it was a peninsula and an island back in the time of the Peloponnesian War and—right there, the Athenians managed to blockade a Spartan force. They captured the cream of the Spartan army and might have negotiated a favorable peace."

Nestor laughed again and took my arm as if to calm my enthusiasm. "When your voice rises like that, you remind me of him."

Then he motioned toward the bay with his walking stick. "There, too, the Venetian fleet had the Ottoman fleet cornered in Navarino Bay, at their mercy, except the Venetian admiral lost his nerve at the last minute and let the bastard Turk escape. They hung the cowardly admiral when he got back to Venice."

"Ah, there you go, all the books I saw in your palatial abode."

"Abode? Yes, yes, blame your father. Such a name. What do you think—a burden or a blessing?"

"Nestor, a great warrior and then a great king full of years and wisdom."

"Will reading enough books make it so?"

"But the wrong books can be dangerous."

"Spoken like a true scholar, I'll leave it to you guys to fight over the fine print, the footnotes." Again Nestor pointed ahead of us along the path to a wide plateau coming into view. "I saw your eyes hanging out last night when I was telling you about Epano Englianos."

"Talk about conjuring names, Karel Hollar, a romantic, if slightly discredited, figure in my field. Who managed to be right there when the University of Cincinnati team under Carl Andersen discovered Nestor's Palace and that horde of Linear B tablets. Karel Hollar, a British SIS agent no less, had a nose for the right place at the right time—and access to a convenient source of funding to expedite matters."

Nestor tossed his head, not quite sure which bait to take.

"The good citizens of Pylos love this place now. There are lots of tourists; it's a destination point for tour buses. The shops in town sell souvenirs. Better"—Nestor gestured in front of his face to indicate the presence of a mask—"an ancient palace and the stories of heroes and gods than memories of a civil war."

We halted again for a few minutes to catch our breath. I took the opportunity to stretch my back.

"Does it give you much pain?"

"Hey, modern miracle drugs."

"Elliot Goddard told me they gave you a Silver Star for heroism."

"So you two still stay in touch?" He shrugged; I shrugged. "A place, a battle, a river with a name difficult to pronounce—zero name recognition at cocktail parties—where I shouldn't have been."

"Be proud, my friend. So maybe you're not a fighter at heart—you're a scholar and romantic like your old man—but don't regret your fate. Like Achilles' mother, who wanted to hide him away from death and its sorrow, 'the hardness of his fate.'"

I slapped Nestor on the back. "Not bad old king, you know your *Iliad*, too."

"Your father told me he found it, the *Iliad*, depressing, all the killing. So sad, he told me, how Hector and Achilles are fated to be the death of each other in a useless war."

"To read the latest scholarship, the war with Troy probably took place over decades, Greeks killing Greeks, until they'd exhausted themselves with their raids, destroying one another's cities until they destroyed their civilization, as well. At least your civil war wasn't a useless war."

"Nor yours?" asked Nestor in a lowered voice filled with sober kindness.

"Our advisory team got caught in the North Vietnamese invasion of Hâu Nghĩa Province in '73. Our intelligence people missed the timing of the attack. We got hit by a whole division coming across the Vam Do Cong River. I was calling in B-52 air strikes on their staging areas and we still couldn't stop them from pouring out of their sanctuaries in Cambodia."

"I guess Communists are Communists—heh?"

"By the time I got to Vietnam, the Vietcong networks had been almost totally destroyed. The problem was, the North Vietnamese never got the message; they just kept sending more men and weapons down the Ho Chi Minh Trail and waited us out. When I was medevaced from Saigon in late '73, the South Vietnamese had stopped the North Vietnamese invasion during the dry season. We thought the South was on the verge of winning the damn war."

As we walked the last few hundred yards to the top of Epano Englianos, Navarino Bay and the lovely olive-clad hills spreading around us, I realized I'd drifted into a confession of sorts, something I had never shared with my peers, but which Nestor's evocation of my father made possible, even appropriate. He listened carefully and I could see in his nodding expression that my words were registering something in his mind.

"When your father was back as CIA station chief in Athens in '48, he would often join us up north on the battle lines with the Communists, north of the Kalamas River. With help from the Americans, the Communists were finished, but they never gave up—fanatics, crazy people. It does something to you, to see something so against human nature try to root itself on your native soil. And in the late summer and fall, the mountains in the north are so green and lush, the purple grapes thick on the vine, and the air clear and sweet. And yet here the Communists were fighting us with women and children. Bet Joanna didn't tell you about that? Once the Yugoslavs closed the border, they could only get resupplied from Albania. We had them almost cut off, and still they fought us, Greek against Greek, like your Trojan War. We could watch them from our observation posts, the women bringing the fighters food and ammunition—and some fighting. It made you sick. They were torturing and executing villagers until the end."

"At least you won. We got reeducation camps, thousands of drowned refugees, Pol Pot and the Khmer Rouge—"

"You're a smart guy, so where does it come from? I remember your father on one of his inspection tours of the front lines handing me the binoculars in our observation post, just shaking his head, disgusted. We became such philosophers—failed philosophers, he and I, in those days in the north, trying to puzzle it out—how this thing across the Kalamas River had come to be—Greeks enslaving Greeks. We never found a good answer."

As Nestor went on, I found my mind drifting from images of those northern mountain ramparts beyond the Kalamas River to the muddy meandering course of the Vam Co Dong River, to the words in General Alden's diary from his Harvard days, sitting on the Hannibal quay, staring across the Ohio River at a benighted landscape . . . all places where the lands of the free and unfree meet in disquieting proximity.

"Your father talked about the trouble with a utopia."

"A utopia?"

"The payment in death for a utopia, how the price keeps forever rising."

"He said that?"

"Something like that. Or, if it's a really good thought, maybe I should lay claim to it."

"Your claim is duly noted. Plato also had ideas along such lines—that's what I mean about books to avoid."

We reached the summit of Epano Englianos and found the archaeological site spread before us, surrounded by pleasant olive and ash trees. A steel shed had been built over the main excavations to protect them from the weather. The guard who had been walking far ahead had already scouted the area and now waited for us with bottles of water. We could see tourists ambling about the well-marked-out ruins. We were winded and sweaty and we sat on a rock outcropping in the shade of an olive tree, sipping water.

"Did your Communists in Vietnam steal children, too?"

"They would use children to carry messages and ammunition. Their indoctrination and discipline was frightening."

"They fought well, I'll bet, like our Communists."

"Suicidally well. The NVA troops wore tattoos like 'Born in the North to Die in the South,' or 'Go South and Attack the Americans.'"

"Do you think it is just the teaching of lies, or does it go deeper?"

"The prisoners we captured, they really believed we were exploiters and bandits and puppet masters, their brothers in the South our slaves."

"It always bothered me how the Greek Communists—how many had brothers in America—hated Americans, as if they saw only danger in what we were."

"The political cadres appealed to their pride; they told the NVA soldiers they were liberators, that the starving farmers would flock to their cause. They were always surprised when the prosperous farmers they found only wanted to be left alone and in peace."

"Lies become the perception, the reality."

"They do, just ask your pal Elliot—world's expert."

"So your Communists, the rank and file, were uneducated people: they didn't know any better?"

"When we had a prisoner of high value, an NVA officer, we often took him to Saigon and let him see the reality; they simply couldn't believe their eyes: the prosperity, the mountains of food in the stalls of the street vendors, the beautiful Vietnamese women in the shops, the cars and scooters. They soon became disillusioned and opened up to us about how completely they'd been duped and manipulated by their political cadres. The best way to get a captured prisoner to tell us about NVA staging areas in Cambodia was to take him to Saigon for a good time."

"Ah, but you see, this is the perplexing thing: Our Communists were not so stupid. My God, they were teachers and lawyers and, like Kaleyias, architects. Educated men. Nobody brainwashed them with such lies; they read them in books. Then spent their lives trying to make the impossible true, terrifying people into obedience. I saw it time and time again. Even at the end, dying like dogs, they blamed one another for their failures, believing the flaw was in the commandant up the line of command, not their crazy ideas. Do you suppose that is the sickness, to fall in love with a bad idea?"

"Be careful with all those books, Nestor, you never know—"

"Christ, even today they return as old men—like me—and still believe they were misunderstood gods. They wanted to be gods to their people; they craved respect but could only rule with terror. They make me sick. They weren't willing to work like everyone else because they thought their ideas put them above such things. They didn't want to work hard like ordinary people. They were gods, you see, and gods want men to sacrifice themselves for their false promises . . . envy, jealousy, hatred—always the same shit."

I took Nestor's arm and helped him to his feet.

"Mighty King Nestor, giver of justice, your palace awaits."

"A fucking old man, that's what. Once I walked these hills and didn't even work up a sweat."

"Hey, you don't think *I'm* sweating? Your security detail is sweating."

"He says the tourists are Germans." Nestor spat.

I looked over at the sprawling open-sided steel shed, pleased with the professional job to protect the excavations.

"They seem to be moving off; the tour guide is waving them to the bus. It will be yours again, for a while."

"What do you think, was the world of the ancient gods and heroes any better? Before there were Communists and Nazis?"

As I led Nestor to the cool shade provided by the shed, I could barely disguise my thrill in seeing the Pylos excavations. I knew everything about the work that had gone on since 1955, but to actually be there among the ruins of this Bronze Age palace rekindled the youthful emotions I had first known on Crete the summer before my senior year—the thing that set me on the path to my chosen career. I found myself blabbing away to Nestor, dragging this exhausted man around as I mapped out the ground plan in my mind and tried to recreate for him something of the splendor of the architecture and frescoes that had once adorned the palace.

"You're worse than your father when you get going like this. He and that Karel, that fucking Communist of a German, were like excited children around each other. I never heard so much conversation about nothing—I'm sorry. And there was nothing here back then, not like all this today."

"I think he was Czech or Austrian, and you're sure he was a Communist—right, not a British SIS agent like my father insisted?"

"The Austrians were the worst Nazis, more German than the Germans. And he was both, SIS and NKGB, a double agent. Those fucking English are all Communists—haven't you figured that much out by now? During the war in the north of Greece, the British armed ELAS to the teeth; they couldn't get them enough arms. Without the stupidity of the British, there would have been no civil war."

The tone of his voice, the casual denunciation of a longtime ally sent a chill down my spine, even in all that heat.

"You mean guys like that Kim Philby, who died in Moscow last year—now that you mention it, he was SIS, too."

"Those snakes, Maclean and Philby, sold us out. Albanian boys I knew and equipped and trained sent into Albania, hundreds, to die within hours—the butchers warned by Maclean and Philby were waiting for them. May those two soulless vipers rot in hell."

"Well, if there's a hell for traitors, they're *all* there—now."

"They lived to die as old men in their ritzy Moscow apartments."

"I read in the *Times*, alcoholism and heart disease."

"Not my Kaleyias . . . not that one."

The old heartsickness brought about by the mention of Kim Philby put a damper on my scholarly effusions. I was glad Laura was not along; I sensed that name was pure poison to her spirit.

"As a schoolboy, my father dreamed of finding this place. At the final hurdle, with the coming war nipping at their heels, he made a bad bet; he bet on Delos, while his best friend picked the winner, Cincinnati and Epano Englianos."

Nestor looked at me and nodded sadly.

I could tell he was exhausted, and angry at being tired and old. When I went to get some more water from the guard, we talked it over and he got on his walkie-talkie and arranged for a car to pick us up in the parking lot. Nestor never would have made it back on foot.

I handed him another bottle of water. "So, where were they when you found them that night?"

Nestor reached to one of the steel support columns of the shed, disconcerted as he jutted his jaw at the surrounding excavations. "So much has changed. Then there were only a couple of trenches, a few walls, and the moonlight." He shrugged and we walked over to one of the higher standing walls and peered down at the red dirt floor of what had been one of the many storerooms of the palace. Then he turned to the west and pointed out a fully grown ash tree. "I remember that tree on my left in the moonlight as I held my Tommy gun on that Communist Hollar."

"In 1939, Carl Andersen and his Cincinnati team found over six hundred Linear-B tablets in the storerooms right over there." I pointed to the excavated chambers about ten feet from where we stood. "So, this, where we are, would be the earliest excavations."

"Ah, the tablets, yes, they jabbered about those, what might be written there, new histories of the ancient world, more stories from Homer. Even in the moonlight, their eyes were like headlights. Like schoolboys making their figures in the dirt, strange figures and signs."

With the end of my staff, I drew a few symbols in the dirt, the Linear B for Pylos, as well as I remembered.

"Like that?"

"Like that."

"What a disappointment. It wasn't until 1952, when an Englishman,

Michael Ventris, managed to translate Linear B. He used the transcriptions of the Pylos tablets made by the Cincinnati team to pull off his coup, beating out my father and others to the prize. You see, having the critical mass of signs allowed for the decipherment; the more examples of potential syllable combinations increased the probabilities of discovering key words: the Greek names of Cretan cities like Knossos. The Pylos tablets made all the difference . . . except they turned out to be palace inventories for perfumed oil, cloth manufacture, and axels for chariots—stuff like that. Pretty prosaic—huh?"

Nestor laughed, clearly pleased at the irony.

"Hah, no good stories—tell me about it. You run a couple of dozen restaurants, you realize it comes down to inventory control and catching the waiters who are stealing from you. Your prosaic stuff—heh."

I was reminded of Virgil Dabney and his obsession with finding the buried library at Herculaneum, and his disappointment at what was found. His last letters to me before he died were filled with heartbreaking disappointment.

"But Nestor, that's what we do; we dream of finding buried books, or tablets, or papyri . . . stories from the past. We want to release a few souls from Hades to tell their tales. I think it is a fundamental human dream, to hope and wonder."

"Well, those two were sure pleased with themselves. They told me their tablets were special."

"Special?"

"Something like that. They seemed pretty damned sure they had something going."

"Okay."

Then, like a mourner at an interment, Nestor nodded sullenly and tossed a few pebbles into one of storerooms. "Some things are better taken to the grave—or left there."

"Oh, don't say that—it's what *I* do." And again I began pointing out the highlights. "I like to think about the sculpted sphinxes facing one another across the propylon, the frescoes of dancing women and leaping dolphins covering the walls of the throne room, and the huge circular hearth around which the sagacious Nestor told his tales. Once upon a time: an age of grace and refinement—perhaps a golden age."

"*Sagacious,* I like that. But will it help me die happy? I don't think so."

"Wasn't that the point—certainly in the *Iliad*—to be remembered for heroic deeds?"

"Like I said, your dad didn't go in for that *Iliad*. Neither do I. Better to die with no regrets."

We began walking a roundabout route in the general direction of the parking lot, savoring the views framed by the scattered groves of olive trees surrounding the once-upon-a-time citadel.

"Yes," I offered, seeking a better coda, "I suppose, like you were just saying: What's fated is fated."

"I could have just shot that Hollar and had done with it, no E-boat base, no Kaleyias—your father would have been okay. How many lives might have been saved?"

"Like Hollar told you, the reprisals would have been terrible."

"I wanted to please your father. That was my mistake, a smart-ass educated American—heh?"

"You could have taken another trail back from Kalamata; you could have had flankers or scouts or recon out ahead of you so you didn't walk into that ambush."

Nestor slowed and smiled broadly.

"That-a-boy, I like that: You defend your dad. That's good; what a fine son you are."

"Karel Hollar, our SIS man, our double agent—did you ever see him again?"

"Only in my bad dreams when I see the bullet I should have put in his educated brain."

"Joanna was telling us last night about the massacre in Pylos, how the Germans executed exactly one hundred citizens."

Nestor stopped and examined me from behind his sunglasses.

"Oh, they shot a few more in their homes, and some were burned to death. They may have been meticulous—but they were on the high side of one hundred. You can go count the names on the memorial next to your friend Joanna's hospital."

"Do you know how they came up with their list?"

"Look at who was killed: the royalists, professional people, landowners, the Jews . . . that was how Kaleyias liked to play the game, let others do his dirty business. You think there is such a difference between the Nazis and the Communists—just ask their victims."

"Joanna thought my father had recognized one of the German officers carrying out the reprisals."

"John never told me that."

"The name sounded like Hollar—that's what she thought: a German name beginning with H."

Nestor grunted and went over to a stooped olive tree and leaned his bulk against its trunk.

"Well, there it is. Hollar and Kaleyias—just like I told you." He pointed his arm like a rifle and convincingly demonstrated the recoil. "I should've done it—such an idiot."

"My father had blood on his hands."

Nestor waved me off.

"What the fuck is it with you? We all have blood on our fucking hands. You, too, by the sound of it. I hear those B-52 strikes in Vietnam really fucked up those North Vietnamese bastards. That's the way of war: We are men, not gods. Men die; gods do not. We *are* their entertainment." Nestor poked a finger in my chest. "Can't you hear them laughing?"

We fell silent for a moment as the ringing changes of the cicadas filled our ears.

"Do you know about my father's disappearance into East Germany?"

"Not the details, but I figured something went wrong, because that guy Elliot Goddard came here with a whole CIA team in 1955 to check things out."

"In the fall of 1953, he walked into East Berlin and was never seen alive again. According to Elliot Goddard, he was captured and held in a Prague prison for almost a year before he died."

Glancing beneath the brim of the Panama hat, I could detect something of relief or pleasure come into Nestor's face.

"Fucking good for John."

"Why would a top CIA officer do something like that?"

Nestor looked at me and a toothy smile formed.

"Unfinished business."

"What kind of business?"

"Maybe I was wrong, what I said about him last night. Maybe he wasn't as much of a bookworm as his son."

"You mean he went after Karel Hollar."

"Wasn't it you who told me Hollar, your SIS man, was killed in the war?"

"What I read—and you told me he was SIS—was that he died in a Soviet prisoner of war camp."

"Well, there you have your answer."

I turned back to the excavated site and pondered a moment. "You mentioned that Hollar had a Linear B tablet with him that night, two tablets?"

"Yes, one in each pocket of his sheepskin coat. He would take one out and carefully replace the other in his pocket."

"The six hundred or so tablets from the palace storerooms excavated in the summer of 1939 were carefully, meticulously inventoried, and placed for safekeeping in the vault of the Bank of Greece in Athens, where they remained throughout the war and for years after—untouched until the early fifties. None was missing."

"Clearly, some had gone missing—lousy Communists."

"A few . . . special ones, so it seems."

"What does it matter?"

"You know, my father's CIA buddies feared that my father might have defected."

"Of course they did—they're idiots. In early 1955, Elliot Goddard and a whole circus of clowns descended on Pylos to question Joanna. She suddenly had all this money in her pocket to build her hospital. Elliot made a big fucking stink—they were so indiscreet. They put her and her work in danger. They interviewed me, too, in New York—my God. Everyone knew the Americans were poking around for something."

"What did they want to know?"

"Your Elliot Goddard was convinced Joanna was a Communist."

"And what did you tell him?"

"She was captured in a uniform and she was armed."

"Well, *that* was fucking helpful of you."

"I'm just kidding. I told him she was a loyal woman."

"How the hell did they know about her—no, no, don't tell me."

That was the moment I realized that Elliot would have gone to my grandmother, and she would probably have allowed him access to the family trusts, where the CIA investigative unit would have discovered the payments to Joanna and the endowment for the hospital in Pylos. And again a thousand pieces of my childhood began shifting about: how much did my mother and grandmother know about Joanna—a lover, a mistress—and the child? Did my grandmother tell my mother, or was Suzanne enough trouble for one marriage?

"Hey, you okay?"

There hadn't been a word about Joanna or Giannis in the correspondence between my father and Suzanne . . . for obvious reasons: Once he knew she was a KGB agent, he couldn't risk her knowing.

"Did Elliot know about the boy, Giannis?"

"Are you kidding—your friend Joanna was only too delighted to spill the beans. She hoped those CIA whiz kids would get her son back. Goddard kept asking me, 'Could the Communists have been blackmailing John about the boy?'"

"Could they?"

"Would the Communists do that? Sure, and worse. Kaleyias had parents tortured and executed in front of their children—or their children . . . whatever it took to get them to confess. But the Soviets, the KKE, they like to pretend the kidnappings never happened."

My mind was swimming. Joanna, Hollar, Suzanne, and Bobby: There was enough circumstantial evidence of Communist associations to convince even a loyal son—or wife—of my father's defection!

"Jesus, all my father wanted was to be a scholar, a teacher."

"Maybe I underestimated him."

"What about Hollar? Did Elliot know about Hollar, too?"

"Not from me, and Kaleyias was in no position to blab. But the intelligence from Hollar on German troop strength in the Peloponnese was radioed in to Cairo by the British SOE radioman, to British SOE and SIS, and OSS. Your pal Hollar must be in the OSS files—heh—or no?" Nestor pushed himself back from the olive tree and surveyed the view of the surrounding countryside with what seemed like a sigh of regret. "Listen, this guy Goddard was no friend of your father's—just another fucking preppy playboy, if you ask me. Philby and Maclean fucked him over good, too. In October 1949, when we had finally finished off the Communists in the north of Greece, Goddard shows up and suddenly wants to get agents into Albania to overthrow the regime. The CIA had its own airfield, Polish pilots, who parachuted the poor bastards into the hands of the secret police. It was a sad joke. The Soviets knew all about these teams—Philby saw to that. The secret police shot them before they hit the ground. Those boys died on the beach before they knew what had hit them. Then Goddard came to us to see if we could establish escape routes for his boys over the mountains into Greece. Maybe one or two made it out alive. They never had a chance. Your dad was furious about those operations. I'd hear him and Goddard screaming at each other over the phone. 'A waste,' your dad called it, dropping those exile Albanians into the meat grinder. Your dad was so pissed, he requested to be reassigned to Washington—early."

"Philby and Maclean, according to Elliot, compromised all those missions, before they were exposed as Soviet agents in 1951."

"Doesn't matter. John accused Goddard of being careless with those boys' lives. No love lost there . . . seems to me, Philby and Maclean fucked up your dad's career good—but that Goddard was no fucking help."

"But my father did the right thing: He took care of Joanna before he left."

"Smart woman. She played him for all he was worth, and some."

"You really don't like her?"

"I believe that some women will do what it takes to survive—and I don't say I'm blaming her. You do what you have to do. But blaming me for Kaleyias . . . She tried to poison my friendship with your father, going on like that with him in Athens, with their little walks in the Agora. Made me sick to think about it. If she hadn't cozied up to that snake . . . and now she blames me."

"Would it have been better if you'd spared Kaleyias? In Vietnam, NVA prisoners were our best asset for gaining intelligence on their Cambodian marshaling areas."

Nestor smiled and spread his arms to the far horizon, as if in jocular imitation of his namesake.

"You mean, would I have been a better person? A humanitarian, a wise king? Praised by Joanna instead of scorned? Sure, I wish we'd gotten more information out of Kaleyias, we tried. But he was a dead man—his own people would have killed him; they had assassins on his trail. He was a liability for the Greek Communists after he organized the abduction of the children. A propaganda embarrassment that lost them the support of their socialist brothers."

"Was my father pleased?"

"I would not have bothered his delicate soul with the details of revenge. He was my means and I was his ends. Ours was a true friendship for hard times."

"Are you telling me that he was a man *incapable* of revenge?"

Nestor put his arm around my shoulder, whether to comfort or impart a confidence, I wasn't sure.

"Such a primitive emotion for an upstanding American. Better left to others, heh? He always liked to say of the *Iliad*, the wrath of Achilles—such a primitive emotion."

We began walking again, circling the perimeter of the great citadel of Pylos for the last time, where Nestor had come so often as a boy with his father's goats. As he talked, I realized that the confession he was about to make had as much to do with being near the end of his rope as it did about bidding farewell to me and the world of his youth.

"You see, we were up against it, on the Kalamas River, on the southernmost extent of the Iron Curtain—what would become the Iron Curtain. It was not a fixed line in the earth for us in Greece, but a thing alive and wanting to swallow us all. For two years, we fought over the foothills of those beautiful mountains beyond the Kalamas River. We had many rumors and then firsthand accounts from those who had escaped, but nothing prepared me for the spring of 1949, when we finally busted into that nest of vipers, to find villages emptied out, populations enslaved to support the guerillas, and the mass graves and torture cells, the bodies still fresh from the beatings and starvation. The buckets of gouged-out eyes. I was with the toughest commando outfit in Greece, veterans of the three years of fraternal struggle. What we saw turned us into madmen. We knew how to move fast and at night and so, this time, we caught Kaleyias before he could escape.

"Kaleyias was hiding in a tiny village in the Mourgana range, less than ten kilometers from the Albanian border. We surprised the few *andartes* protecting the village and killed them. He was asleep in bed, in his office on the upper floor of a mill, with his whore bitch—his comrade secretary. He thought he was safe just ten kilometers from the Albanian border. His things were packed for quick evacuation. He had four passports with different names and different countries: Soviet Union, Hungary, Yugoslavia, and Albania. It was four in the morning when my guys smashed down his door and spoiled his dreams forever. We dragged him and his woman screaming and bare-assed from their bed. We tied him in his chair, there at his desk with his typewriter—that typewriter had come all the way from Kalamata. On that typewriter he had typed the death sentences for hundreds. He was meticulous in recording the evidence to convict his victims of treachery, extracted from terrified informers and confirmed by torturing others. They had long lost the respect of the people; they ruled by fear alone. *Hey, pal, no more talk about architecture this morning, I'll bet—no proud words?* Kaleyias is begging for his life; he has already shit that chair. The woman is in another chair in the corner, weeping hysterically, trying to cover herself. Cold, too, her breath showing. I was pleased we had the woman as a witness to Greek justice.

"We interrogated Kaleyias for two hours and he refused to talk; he claimed he was a soldier and protected by the Geneva Convention. He had a beard then and his beautiful black hair showed much gray. So, I had his whore prepare a confession on the typewriter. I stared into Kaleyias's bloodshot eyes and dictated to her his responsibility for all the men—the friends I had lost, for the people he'd killed in Kalamata and Pylos, for all the men and women he'd tortured in the north, for the children he'd stolen from their families. 'Sign it and it will go easy with you,' I told him. But he would not sign; he spat on the paper.

"My machine gunner is a guy named Andreos, a butcher and shepherd before the war. Andreos knows what must be done, and he smiles with pleasure when he does the Lord's work . . . his brother and father, the Communist killed two years before in his village. Andreos understands the poetry of the knife. Kaleyias pleads as Andreos touches his face with his knife and assures him of his expertise in these matters and that he has nothing to fear. 'Just sign the paper; sign your confession.' He still refused to sign—imagine, just an admission of his sins—a piece of paper with words. How many confessions had he extracted over the years from his victims—all traitors to the cause? The men hold his knees open and Andreos cuts out his balls, two shiny pink marbles in his palm—'like the devil's dice,' Andreos says, shaking them and showing them to their former owner. Kaleyias is screaming. The woman is vomiting. And I am standing there, watching, waiting for my answer. I found myself fascinated, that I could find my own soul to be as black as this emasculated fiend's. His woman is covered with her puke, on the typewriter, too, but at least she finally became very quiet, as if hoping she had been forgotten.

"Andreos asks if he should take the eyes, too, like the Communists. I tell him no, Kaleyias must see everything.

"'Make your peace with your Maker, Kaleyias. Admit your sins—sign the fucking paper, and it will go fast.' Still he refuses. I nod to Andreos and he takes the butt of the knife and first smashes in his teeth and then slices the jaw muscles. Kaleyias screams and passes out. I throw water on his face to bring him back . . . for my answer. 'Whisper, Kaleyias, just whisper your confession for these witnesses—repent of your sins.' Like a puppet face with the strings cut, he nods wildly, his jaw flapping open like a garbage shoot. Andreas holds his head back and expertly feeds him his useless manhood through his broken teeth, one at a time, like Delmonico's finest oysters, making sure they go down. Andreos begs for the honor of the coup de grâce, to cut his throat. But no, I tell him, a quick pig's death is too good in his case. We must honor our comrade commissar. The woman has been very quiet, too quiet. So I ask her, 'Is this black devil your lover? Is he your Apollo? A god of the new order?' She denies everything. She says she hates him and only sleeps with him out of fear, to eat. I tell her if she does exactly what I say, we will let her live; we will see that she gets to the border to join the others in their flight to the Communist paradise. She swears that she hates him; she only types his orders. I tell her to go to the typewriter and type again for me. I tell her to type an epitaph for her lover, her *komindante:* 'I am not a man but a viper. I sow hatred and fear. I commit murder to further my tyranny. I kidnap and destroy children. I make women carry guns. I spread the devil's poison in my words. I am the destroyer of civilization. Everything I believe in is a lie.' I make her type this in capital letters and again until it is perfect. I make her hold up the testament before Kaleyias so he can read the thing. We even take a photograph as Kaleyias nods his head to acknowledge his confession. 'Read it to him again,' I tell her. And she reads it to him. And again he nods. You can smell his blood and fear and shit. She is crying and pissing down her leg. Then I tell Andreas to give her the knife. I tell her if she wants to save herself, she must cut his throat, that Andreas will instruct her. Andreas holds his head back and shows her where to cut. At first, she can't do it, she is trembling too hard, but then she manages, just a little cut, but not enough. He is screaming, his feet kicking against the ropes. 'Deeper,' says Andreas, 'you must cut deeper, bitch, or he will take hours to die.' Again she tries, but again she fails her lover.

"His eyes bulge as his throat fills with blood. 'Tell me, Kaleyias,' I plead, 'tell me what alien gods brought you to this lovely place in the mountains far from your home in sunny Kalamata, and here to die like a beast. What did you want with the glorious world to die like this, like an animal?' I stare into his gray eyes and realize he is struggling to speak, his lips foaming with blood. 'What, what,' I shout. Louder. 'What is he saying?' I ask the woman. 'Tell me what he is saying.' She bends her ear to his mouth, crying like a little child. 'What? What is it, woman?' She turns to me and blubbers, 'He says he only wanted to free the world.'

"'To free the world!' I scream. I go and fling open the windows to the dawn on the mountain peaks. 'Freedom, it is here, Kaleyias. Feel the sweet air of freedom that is coming now that you are departing from us. Feel the freedom of the living as your soul passes into hell. A new day for Greece, a new life for our country in celebration of your death.'

"We drank a toast to freedom as he gasped out his life like a dolphin in a fisherman's net. When he was dead, we poured kerosene over his body and burned it. The woman fled to Albania and then to Moscow. She told her story to all her comrades. Years later, someone told me that her comrades, in some stink-hole of a village in Hungary, became so sick of her story that they reported her to the authorities and her membership in the Party was taken away: an unreliable comrade, a crazy woman. After the Soviets invaded Hungary after the uprising in 1956, she was arrested and taken away to the gulag and never heard of again."

Nestor stopped for a moment and gazed back at the excavation site and the hills of olive trees in the valley below.

"Well . . ." I was reeling in the backwash of the story he had told with such compelling relish. "Clearly, Nestor, you are also a master of political theater."

"Eight months later, I was back in America, just another Greek-American restaurant owner—heh, worried about getting enough staff through immigration."

"Was it really about revenge?"

"Calibrated, as you say, for the occasion." Nestor touched the side of his eye. "But the Communists know that somewhere in Greece is their nemesis—you like that word, *nemesis*? If I live long enough, I'll be as smart as you and your dad. They know that somewhere there is someone more terrible than they who is willing to defend freedom. If your enemy does not fear you, you are lost." He looked me over and slapped my shoulder. "Americans want to be loved, but better to be feared and respected."

"We published Kaleyias's confessions in the Athens newspapers, along with the lists of his victims." Nestor continued to pause and look over his shoulder. "How long ago it seems now, even as his comrades are returning from the Soviet Union. The new socialist government has given them amnesty—pensions, even. The Communists tell the young people that none of these things happened, and the young believe because they prefer the idea of bringing down the rich. As Nikos says,

'Dad, don't you get it? They want your stuff, so sell up Greece and stay put in America.'"

"I hate to tell you: Your sons love you."

"You think . . . ," he laughed. "They sure want me to die back in the States—at least I wouldn't end up in Joanna's hospital. Before you arrived, I sent her copies of letters I have received over the years from the families of those Kaleyias murdered. I will show you the letters when we get back. They thank me for giving them peace. Others live in fear and hate of those who destroyed their loved ones. Every time they turn a corner of the street and see an old face, a tormentor, they wonder, Is it him . . . returned from Hungary?"

We began walking again. I sensed a reluctance in his steps just as a vast corner of Navarino Bay came again into view, as we began an easy descent toward the parking area. With the sun dipping toward the western horizon, spates of reflected light danced up the face of the cliff and spilled into the branches of the olives trees along our path. I kept my eyes on the bay, where some boats, small fishing rigs, had drifted into view. We could see the shadows of the boats on the sandy bottom, like opaque twins. The subtle transitions of color, crystal along the shallow shore, pinkish green farther out, and then pale blue and turquoise—were hypnotic. My eyes ached with the richness as they had long ago on Crete. Sometimes it almost felt as if the sole purpose of all that blue was to endlessly wash the shore and free it of stain, real or imagined.

"The list of children—Joanna was going on and on about a list of children."

Nestor grunted, as if I might have physically assaulted him.

"It was right there on Kaleyias's desk, next to his fucking type-writer. It killed me how they could sow such chaos and yet keep such meticulous records of their evil. That woman had typed it perfectly. The Greek intelligence service spent years working on that list, but impossible to match the names to her son. Kaleyias stole the boy's name, the child's patrimony. You see"—and he grabbed my shoulder to steady himself—"this was a man with four passports, four names. One of the surnames on one of the passports—I think it was the Soviet passport—matched a name on the list of children."

It was my turn to bridle. "Would that have been enough—for my father to do something . . . crazy?"

"Not unless Joanna made him crazy. The Greek government has

spent forty years trying to get those children returned. And still the parents wait—Joanna is not alone."

"Tell me about that photograph in your office, you and my father and a bunch of military men standing in the portico of a temple."

"Athens in June 1949. All the scum in the north cleaned out. It was the day your dad was decorated for his work with the OSS against the Germans and against the Communists in the civil war. They gave him every medal they had and even a few they made up for the occasion. All the big generals were there. And a couple of the guys at the table last night, who had been with me since the beginning against the Italians. It had to be a discreet ceremony, John being a CIA guy and every-thing. But we wanted to do it for him. And for some reason, he asked Joanna, or maybe she just showed. She wore a blue silk dress and held a green umbrella and waited in the shade of the temple behind us—like an invisible goddess—the only other person there besides the officials and the photographer. She was all alone there. I felt bad, and I think your father did, too, because they could not acknowledge each other . . . because it would have been dangerous for her missing son."

We stopped at the crest of the plateau at a sign—NESTOR'S PALACE—pointing the way for visitors along the well-worn path from the parking lot. Nestor tapped at the metal sign with his staff.

"As a boy, I came here all the time, with my father's goats, and it was nothing but a beautiful place to spend the day. Then I followed your father here one night in the middle of a war and found that I had a famous name, a name that prevented me from doing the smart thing— pull the trigger. Now I find myself here for maybe the last time, to find the name of a palace that people from around the world come to visit . . . when once upon a time it seemed to belong *only* to me."

A big white Mercedes sedan was waiting in the parking lot and the guard was holding the door open. Nestor paused a moment before climbing in.

"You asked me about the photograph. After that ceremony, John and I stood together as we told the others good-bye. He kept looking in the direction of the temple, where Joanna had been standing with the umbrella, except she had already gone. But he remained looking for the longest time. Then, when we were finally alone, he took my arm and asked a favor: to go to her uncle's house the next day and take her to the station and the train for Paris. Maybe he had his hopes . . . but the whole way to the station, not a fucking word; her lips were sealed against me."

And that was how a photograph I had once passed daily in the Winsted gym took on the immateriality of memory, and so began altering before my eyes each time I passed it again in later years. Gone are the paragons of youth. In the sweltering sun of the Agora, among a group of uniformed and irregular fighters on the steps of the Temple of Hephaestus, I find only vague shadows of those two warriors: an archaeologist both brave and foolhardy, romantic and naïve, who cut corners at will to risk all those he loved and who loved him, and a Greek restaurateur and bar-stool philosopher, who got overtaken by events and then stuck with the name of a sagacious king, only to find that the act of naming had led to a role he would later regret, not unlike the wandering Lear as he sought to shed memory of the bloody sacrifices that had kept his kingdom whole, as nightmares gnawed his life away. Names will do that as they shift and form and re-form and recast the lives to which they become attached . . . as do memory's tides, the swirling currents that send us back in search of a name and a place to call our own.

29 IT WAS ALWAYS SAD RETURNING TO SMOG-gy and dingy Athens in the fall, at the end of the summer digging season, especially when I had the semester off. Colleagues and friends had returned to the States, my Princeton students had departed, often with tearful good-byes, and there were always mail and administrative tasks to catch up on in my office at the American School of Classical Studies: journal articles to complete and a syllabus to flesh out for spring classes back at Princeton. And so the cycle of the years had sped by. . . .

Laura couldn't sit still. And she couldn't stop talking.

"She's a saint, really. To watch her at work in the children's ward, I felt like I'd wasted my life."

"Hardly . . . maybe a change of careers."

"I can't even manage to produce a child."

I turned and saw her wrinkle her nose as the industrial stink of Athens's outskirts began to inundate us.

"You know, it might have been nice if you'd stuck around for breakfast with Nestor's family yesterday."

"I know, but I just really wanted to see her again."

"Your mother's rival."

"Don't go there." She fumbled in her purse for a stick of gum, a substitute for the cigarettes she'd sworn off months before. "It's like, when I'm around her, life has a purpose."

"Why are you so jumpy?"

"She told me to get off the meds."

"Which ones pray tell?"

"Prozac, to start."

"I thought you were only anxious around me."

"She told me to get angry, that I need to be more aggressive, less frightened. She was so supportive."

Clearly, she was missing her shrink on West End Avenue. The shrink, so she liked to tell me, she could no longer afford; for whom, needless to say, I was no substitute in the therapy department.

"You . . . *more* aggressive?"

"So, what's with you? Ever since your walk with Nestor, you've been acting like the cat that swallowed the canary."

I was thinking: I had a story to tell and maybe the time had come to give Max a run for his money.

As I stood by the open door, trying to work out the kinks in my back, Laura unpacked the Land Rover. When she was done, she stood becalmed, surveying the length of Apollonos Street: a traveler in tight jeans and T-shirt, a duffel bag slung across her shoulder, a plastic bag of dirty laundry at her feet. I suppose it wasn't a particularly welcoming sight, that dusty, smelly, narrow street of shops, cluttered with garish lights, funneling the eye in the direction of the sheer walls of the Acropolis, where the blue-lit corner of the Parthenon rode the dimming sky. Then from somewhere, a guitar riff, the scream of feedback from a sound system being tested in a nearby disco. Her eyes lit up; she licked her lips and turned to me with an excited smile, as if she'd made her mind up about something.

"It's not exactly New York," I said.

She held up her bag of laundry. "I hope you've got a washing machine."

"Well, there's a laundromat, sort of, down the street there. You give your stuff to these old biddies and they wash it for you, for peanuts."

I gave the brass knocker, in the form of an upside-down ibis, a few sharp raps.

Waiting, I shrugged. "I leave my key when I'm away for an extended trip."

She stepped back apprehensively and took in this tall, gloomy building with its pseudo-Baroque entablatures streaked with soot and God knows what concoction of lethal particulates. Jagged rust stains with the appearance of claw marks clambered in the stucco beneath the metal grillwork of the windows facing the street. She gestured to the blue enamel sign: PENSIONE CLEO, BY THE DAY, WEEK, OR PERMANENT.

"Are you permanent?" she asked.

"As permanent as it gets around these parts." I reached to the knocker again. "Sacred bird of Egypt—the ibis. Just thought you'd like to know."

She smiled gamely and started as a metal shutter clattered to the pavement across the street. Her hair, in a ponytail held by a green rubber band, had an odd metallic sheen in the sodium glare of a nearby streetlamp. The air was heavy with the fumes of sulfur coal, car exhaust, heated grease, and perpetually overburdened sewer lines. At last, a cleaning woman with mop and pail in hand opened the door and we made our way up the winding stair to the second-floor landing and into the clutches of my landlady of almost twelve years.

"Aaaah . . . so there you are." A French-accented cackle and sixty-something Madame Cleo was upon us with a furious rustle of dull silk. "So, Mr. Alden, Mr. Alden," she repeated with sardonic delight— the old witch—seeing Laura come up behind me, "you have returned from the summer, and with a friend, I see, *très bon, très belle, ma chère fille.*"

"Laura, this is Madame Cleo. Madame, may I introduce Laura Williams, the famous ballerina from New York."

"A *danceuse!*" Her jade mascara flashed lustrously in a flurry of staccato blinks as she inhaled Laura, eyes traveling up and down her body at warp speed. Madame planted a wet kiss on each of Laura's cheeks and then gave me the same treatment, but with less enthusiasm. She went to a side table in the hallway and rummaged for my keys, her silk robes falling open, revealing a pink satin negligee beneath, her habitual dress unless she was going out, which she did less and less over the years.

"Your mail is on your desk, and the cleaning women spent six hours in there yesterday. The charge is on your account."

She let out another cackle of pleasure as she led us up the two flights of stairs to my apartment, something she'd never have bothered to do if she hadn't detected the possibility of romance in the air. We followed in the backwash of her cheap perfume.

"I have been so crowded this summer with young people, now that I am in the Frommer guide. Delightful students. You would approve, Professor Alden. They would like to meet you, my celebrated writer, but you are never here, so what am I to do?" She threw up her arms and then opened the doors to her tiny rooftop garden chockablock with trellises and her ratty pink and off-white roses. "Aaaah!" she exclaimed, breathing deeply. "My roses this summer are the best in a long time—you can smell them, yes?" She eyed Laura as I went to unlock my door. Madame rushed in behind me, ostensibly to make sure the cleaning lady had done her job, but probably to indulge fantasies of a love life that might transform my scholar's retreat into a love nest worthy of gossip with her Friday-night bridge group. For years she had been trying to hook me up with strangers, occasionally with some success. She gave the large desk in my library, piled with mail, a quick swipe with her elbow. Then she sailed into my bedroom and threw open the shutters, pronouncing her benedictions. "The best view in all the Plaka. And smell my roses, how *charming*." She took Laura's hand and led her to the window. "Do you like it?"

"Charming," Laura echoed, gazing out over the inland sea of terracotta rooftops to where they careened into the rock walls of the Acropolis.

With a wink and a toss of frizzy curls and the admonition: "Take care of my professor," Madame Cleo was gone.

Laura rolled her eyes and began an immediate inspection of my bookshelves and the odd bits of pottery fragments scattered around. After testing a comfortable old leather reading chair, she proceeded to the bedroom and plopped down on the bed, emitting a moan of pleasure as the mattress met with her approval.

"The mattress is imported, state-of-the-art Sealy Posturepedic. Check out the bathroom; I had a Jacuzzi put in. A small fortune, but worth every dime."

"The place is still a dump."

"Well, thanks . . . but it's *my* dump. I opted out of faculty housing at the American School."

"It's not much better than a student hostel."

"When was the last time you were in a student hostel?"

"I just thought—"

"You prefer the Four Seasons, the Ritz. I can get you a room at the Grand Bretagne if you like, a five-minute cab ride, and you can marinate in five-star luxury."

"This fits my budget just fine. I just . . . never quite imagined you in a place like this."

"How did you imagine me?"

"I dunno, big house on a hill, book-lined study, a garden—something really nice."

"I Tatti perhaps, the Bernard Berenson thing?"

She went and peeked in the bathroom and gave an appreciative nod. "Well, okay, this is certainly doable . . . a bidet no less, *charming*."

"I splurged on the Jacuzzi."

"Hey, I'm a believer."

"I make a point of living off a professor's salary."

"Hah, the famous Alden parsimony."

"My parsimonious grandmother bought all her clothes at the Junior League thrift shop."

"I always heard she was an icy-cold snob."

"To people she disapproved of."

She sat up on the bed and eyed me like a petulant adolescent.

"Listen, if you really want to know," she said, "my father—so to speak—managed to lose almost all his money, whether through bad investments or by giving it away to his left-wing causes; the accountants still haven't figured it out. My mother is broke. That's why she's shacked up with the colonel at his place in Sussex. I'm not even sure we can pay our share of the property taxes for Elysium this year—that's what the accountant said."

"You're kidding." I was genuinely amazed.

"So, Herr Professor, I've lived on my salary since I was twenty-two. Then Max had a pretty good income, for a while. Now, I'm getting disability and unemployment insurance. Pretty soon I'll be down to my savings, which won't even pay a month of taxes at Elysium."

"What about Max's books? They're on their gazillionth printing."

"You think he left me, the wicked muse who refused all his entreaties to marry, the royalties on his work? I was his celebrity rich girl, heir to millions. He left everything to a foundation that supports research on family history and the Holocaust." She got up abruptly and went to the window, as if drawn to the distant buzz of the Plaka and a vague disco beat. "Who got us on this depressing subject anyway?"

I lay down on the abandoned bed, joyful expectation washing over me at the thought of the Jacuzzi and a good night's sleep and a relatively happy back in the morning.

"How's your knee?" I asked. I knew it had been aching on the long drive.

"Okay. Joanna examined it. She suggested holding off from starting classes for a while longer." Laura came over and sat on the bed and pulled up the leg of her jeans. She eased off the spandex support and flung it onto a chair. "How about you?"

"I'm Jacuzzi-bound."

"Turn over. That's an order. I've been neglecting you, I know. I promised you a massage in Nafplio, but you kind of freaked me with that nightmare."

"Take enough painkillers, you sleep like a baby."

"I told her about your Demerol; she said it's totally addictive."

She began to massage my back, very gently at first, then harder. Then she had me pull up my shirt and unbuckle and loosen my jeans. She went to her bag and got some baby oil and began again, really kneading the muscles with slow, firm strokes, getting into the tissue to drain it of tension. I couldn't believe how strong her hands were, almost as strong as Maureen's, my therapy nurse at the San Diego VA hospital. I could smell the baby oil. Maureen had worn latex gloves. Sometimes I could feel Laura's chewed nails. Then she really got into it, like she'd scoop out my kidneys.

"That Madame Cleo is quite the cat."

"Claws and all."

"She your dating service?"

"I think she did it professionally once upon a time."

"Married?"

"At least four she admits to. She was King Farouk's mistress, so she tells it."

"Ah . . ." Her fingers slowed as they encountered the delicate lines of jagged scar tissue below my waist, to the left of my backbone. "What the fuck is this?"

"Shrapnel wounds."

I felt her fingers pause, linger over the runic web of ugly scar tissue, like a braille reader of my flesh. Then she began again, but more tentatively, as she seemed to explore every nook and cranny of my lower spine, taking a sounding or two along the way.

"You really *were* wounded."

I had to laugh. "That feels great."

"I feel bad that I never knew. . . . Neither did Max."

I smiled again to myself, seeing those endless articles in *People* magazine about the seventies celebrity couple.

"Perforated muscle tissue and a fractured spine."

"Joanna wanted to know everything about you, and I felt kinda awkward about how little I knew. She asked about your back; she spotted it right away."

"According to the doctor, I was lucky. Another inch and it

would have shattered my spine. Then I'd have been a quad in a wheel-chair."

I felt her shiver.

She slapped my ass. "Don't say shit like that."

Her fingers seemed to soften as they explored, as if they'd melted into my muscles, a strange and wonderful sensation—that and the baby oil and thoughts of Maureen, gentle and good Maureen. Then I realized I'd gotten painfully hard. I kept very still, hoping she wouldn't catch on, but in the darkness of my pillow, my senses seemed only further aroused, and I became intensely aware of her womanly presence, her breath, her perfume or deodorant mixed with the sweat of the long drive from Pylos . . . and the baby oil. Music echoed in the street outside the window. Her crafty fingers seemed to have a life of their own, slipping into me as if seeking an exposed valve, and slowly pinching it shut to open another.

Passages from my father's letters to Suzanne from occupied Germany spilled through my mind:

Six months now since I've seen you and sometimes I think I'll go crazy with the lack of your kisses and your strong arms and the smell of your body—how I crave the perfume of your sex after the terrible stench of decay in the bombed-out ruins of these nightmare cities. Your body is the only sanity left on earth for me. As I write you, it is strangely warm and the stars above the city are so bright, like points of shattered crystal; and this because there is barely any light in the city, or what is left of the city. Here and there in the streets there are wood fires, which people use to warm themselves and cook cabbage. The winter here will be cruel and hard and will find many unfortunate victims, especially the very young and old.

Even in the worst of the Blitz, London was never like this. I know Hiroshima and Nagasaki are beyond comprehension, but they can't have been much worse. In some places, the devastation is so complete that you cannot even picture what the city had been like before. The people speak of firestorms that literally sucked the oxygen out of entire blocks, suffocating and burning alive men, women, and children in the cellars where they hid.

At night, after interviewing countless Nazis suspects, shifty-eyed men with fake names and equally fake accounts of what they did in the war, and then filing useless reports, I often turn to the pages of

Homer's *Odyssey* for the comforts of a simpler age. I suppose the *Iliad*
would be more appropriate, given the pillaged cities, where the gods are
as often on the side of evil as good, as perverse and capricious as men
themselves. But even Homer fails me—as does Odysseus: a pillager of
cities. As does my memory of student days, when Germany seemed a
land of quiet scholarship, an orderly and industrious life—how many
foolish boyhood dreams are buried beneath this rubble. I've had my fill
of these devastated cities and all the lying faces. I want only you and my
home, my woods and lakes and you, and to drown myself in your sweet
cunt. If I never see this damned continent again, it will be too soon. I
love you with a thousand kisses. I yearn to devour you body and soul.
Keep writing; I live for your letters. Let me know how Bobby is doing.
How strange that you should now be bearing his cross—a bombardier
no less. Tell him from me he did a marvelously good job. The gods of
war are as perverse as they are cruel—only good fucking keeps them at
bay—the only truth that seems to stick.

Their halcyon years, when their only betrayal was of Bobby.

I must have fallen asleep, for when I woke, I was not sure where
I was. Something about a field hospital, struggling to regain consciousness and the clatter of surgical instruments in a metal dish . . .
and women's voices . . . and something about my father's letters . . . a
sweet cunt—a word . . . perhaps my vocabulary around women needed
upgrading.

I started at the sound of the bathroom door being flung open. I saw
Laura parading by the bed in bra and panties, a towel wrapped around
her wet hair.

"What you waiting for?" she said. "Jacuzzi's all yours."

She went to the window and breathed deeply of Madame Cleo's
roses, working her leg back and forth. I mentally winced at the six-
inch white scar tracing the contour of her knee. Nearing forty, she was
almost the same age as Suzanne when I'd been captivated by the mirror
image of mother and daughter sitting next to each other at the Founder's Day service in the Winsted chapel.

"Come on, sleepyhead, I'm starved. I left the Jacuzzi full of hot water
like you said, if you can stand my cooties."

I was a little embarrassed getting up with my pants unbuckled
and half my ass hanging out and an erection that wouldn't go away. I
found she had thoroughly moved herself into my apartment. The sink

was cluttered with her toothpaste and brush, contact lens rinse, various Clinique lotions, and, near the small open window, a discreetly hung pair of washed-out panties. As I climbed into the warm, soapy water of the Jacuzzi—at least the hot water hadn't run out—I spied her pearl-handled razor in the soap dish.

The sight of the razor conjured Suzanne's long legs at our swimming beach, and a forgotten comment by my mother to my grandmother as my swimming lesson was cut short: "Who the hell is she bothering to flaunt her legs for now? I wonder." As I luxuriated in the soapy warmth, like a helpless voyeur my imagination embraced the infamous scene in Max's second novel, when the protagonist seduces his new girlfriend by shaming her into letting him shave her pubic hair.

I discovered Laura sitting at my desk, still in her bra and panties and her head wrapped in a towel, pretending to read the latest *Newsweek*. I observed that my stack of mail had been disturbed. A number of postcards had been extracted and awkwardly slipped back in.

She looked up guiltily. "Oh, I was wondering if you had a converter for my hair dryer."

"No, but there's a hardware store on the corner where you can get one."

She tossed the *Newsweek* onto the pile of mail. "There's all this commotion about East Germans escaping through Hungary, mobbing the West German embassy in Budapest."

I noticed she'd gone through my bookshelves: Max's second novel, *Gardens of Saturn*, lay on the desk at her elbow.

"Well . . ." She stood, grabbed her hairbrush, and went to the window. She removed the towel from her damp hair and proceeded to comb it out. She kept her eyes turned resolutely toward the skyline and the Acropolis as she brushed. I began to get dressed, torn between desire for her scantily clad body and being pissed off at her snooping. The postcards were from ex-students and colleagues—before the days of cell phones and e-mails, the way we kept in touch from scattered digs over the summer season. Standing by the window, she made quite a show of combing out her hair, her muscled thighs merging into tight buttocks, her pliant back curving into the soft incline of her bony shoulders and long neck.

"I can tell you've slept with those women," she said, as if continuing a previous conversation.

"What women?"

"The ones who sent you the postcards."

"Do you always read people's mail?"

"I just happened to see them."

"You were reading my mail."

"You want to know how I can tell? Because I know how women talk when they've slept with a guy, when they kind of like him, when they want to stay in touch, when they figure they don't have much chance but they want to keep their hand in."

"You are so fucking pathetic. You're a worse snoop than Max."

She smiled defiantly. "I had to learn all his tricks to survive. But how pathetic, sleeping with your goddamn students—at your age."

"Fuck you."

"You wish."

She turned back to the window and pretended to ignore me. Beyond, on the purple-blue skyline, the Acropolis hovered like a threatening stony fist, to which she seemed oblivious or immune as she listened to something far off . . . music, a faint rhythmic tide, a beat growing louder as it infused the mosaic of the light-and-shadow-filled streets beyond. Memories, I figured, of a thousand and one nights in the New York disco scene of a decade before.

Then she glanced back at me, and I saw tears suddenly fill her eyes.

"You have his goddamn books."

"Books?"

"Max's novel—about me."

"So what?"

"Christ, the binding is broken and you've underlined the shit out of *Gardens of Saturn*."

"What do you want? Remember, *it's out there*."

"Do you know what it's like to have people read that stuff about me, how I taste, how my twat looks?"

She turned away and began furiously brushing again. Outside, a twanging syncopation echoed in the night; then sweetening, the sound seemed to float toward us, infused with the cloying scent of those damned roses—though to give the devil her due, they masked worse from the streets.

"I thought you'd be more upset about the description of the abortion in Venice." I'd wanted to ask about that since Delos.

"It was a miscarriage."

"Well . . . there you have it."

The last chapters of *Gardens of Saturn*, the ones set in Venice, draw on the scandalous history of the Williams family, especially fabled Palazzo Barberini on the Grand Canal, the summer abode of Laura's great-aunt, Isabella Williams, the famous art collector and builder of Boston's Palazzo Fenway.

I couldn't help smiling, thinking of our budding, if unlikely, alliance to break free of Max's fictional straitjacket, with Nestor's and Joanna's stories now in hand.

Beyond the window, an electric-guitared scream sluiced through the cooling evening air, and for a moment, hairbrush poised, she reminded me—as her mother had—of Saint-Gaudens's golden statue in the Met of Diana with bowstring drawn. The tendons in her neck stood out and her still-young body tensed as she relieved the weight on her bad knee by shifting to her other leg. Her breasts swelled as she breathed deeply.

I found myself consumed with a ravenous curiosity to find out just how much truth *Gardens of Saturn* contained. Like the scene in which the young dancer leaves the stage after her first triumphant performance as a principal dancer in Antony Tudor's *Lilac Garden*, bringing down the house, only to walk into the dressing room of her partner—a young *danceur noble* phenom from Denmark—her arms overflowing with bouquets of roses, only to discover him, tights around his knees, in the bathroom, kissing and fondling her mother's bare breasts.

> Returning in shock to her own dressing room, she sat catatonic before her mirror. She picked up her lipstick and swiped at her lips, distorting their contours. Then she carefully drew red target circles on her cheeks in imitation of a clown she remembered from a birthday party when she was six. Something was still lacking. She pulled down the maroon tulle top of her costume and examined her girlish breasts. She grabbed a cigarette, lit up, inhaled a lungful of smoke, and, as she slowly exhaled, pressed the burning point into her breast, just above the rigid nipple, searing the flesh without flinching. She repeated the process two more times, until she had three perfect red burn marks like tiny satellites orbiting the pale moon aureole of her right breast. So branding herself, she had altered her body irrevocably. Nobody could ever again compare her with her mother—or with her mother's dancing—with quite the same confidence.

I turned away when I realized that my erection showed in my jeans . . . and not a little aghast that my father's lustful thoughts in his letters to Suzanne might as well have been my own.

As if privy to my clandestine voyeurism, and calculating the best way to take me down a notch, she turned from the window, her hair long and lustrous, and said in the most casual of asides, "By the way, Joanna told me—not in so many words—your father was as much a virgin as she was."

The moment we were out of the apartment and walking down Apollonos Street, Laura was transformed. I figured she'd popped a couple of Prozacs—so much for cold turkey. When she took my arm, she became positively girlish, determined to regain her "old self—the real me out there, somewhere, someplace, over the rainbow, wherever." She swirled her white cotton skirt with its floral smocking, showing off her legs and her bare knees—the brace abandoned at the last moment as we left. She'd spent a good half hour on her makeup: her smallish mouth a pale ruby crease, long lashes accented with mascara, those high cheekbones shaped and toned to cover splotches of sunburn, and her hair done up in a tight chignon so that her natural elegance seemed to ride high and proud amidst the throngs of revelers who began to meet us in the streets. Then she took my hand and squeezed hard, like a cantering rider would the reins, as if to let me feel her quickening pulse, the delight she took in the music belching forth from every garishly lit disco and taverna we passed.

"Far-out!" she exclaimed, lifting her eyes to see the raw face of the Acropolis teetering overhead as we turned down another winding street. She took a deep breath of the heated air thick with charcoal smoke, grilling lamb, and less-than-virgin olive oil.

"I'm putting on pounds just breathing this shit."

I had hopes of a small, discreet restaurant off the main drag, but I sensed I might not get that far. The music seemed to float Laura down the street; her blue eyes glittered with star power. She attracted the attention of the angular young men who bracketed the doors of the seediest discos; taffy-complected and smoothly handsome, these gigolos cried out to her—as they did to even the dowdiest female tourists—with baited insolence and leering come-ons to sample, in their strong arms, the shadowy dance floors within. I was fascinated how faces in the crowd of pedestrians turned to her as we passed: ever the celebrity Max had cashed in on, which had sustained her for the twenty years of her youth, and still enough in the tank to sell out the house. Sidewalk venders sidled up to us with their trays of pistachio nuts, others dangling multiple yo-yos from spread fingers at Laura's sandaled feet. She yelped with pleasure. She laughed, sticking out her tongue at them like a two-year-old, waving them off, giving one the finger, jutting her ass at another. She loved it; they loved it. I was thrilled to be along for the ride, to feel something of that now-defunct pre-AIDS seventies disco era of careless hedonism, when she and Max were sideshow attractions at Studio 54.

Whole scenes out of Max's second novel flashed through my mind.

Out of the stream of jostling humanity, someone grabbed my arm and I was face-to-face with the one person I'd hoped to avoid.

"Hey, babe, you're back."

He hadn't changed a bit, not in a decade—not in a thousand years. Same marble-jawed face and jet black hair moussed into a pudding of rich light-catching curls. Adonis incarnate. We shook hands and embraced.

"Laura, Orestes—Orestes, Laura."

I could almost detect the crackle of electricity between them as she shook his long, graceful hand.

"Nice to meet you," she said very politely.

Orestes maintained eye contact, as if spellbound by the apparition before him. "Hey . . . so the professor here has finally got himself a *real* woman, I see." This was a compliment; Orestes was used to me with bejeaned, muddy-nailed archaeology students. Laura glanced at me, as if unsure how to take the remark.

"'A *real* woman'—I think I like the sound of that."

And so she began shamelessly flirting with Orestes.

Orestes laughed, smoothing a hand along Laura's shoulder, as if appraising the wares on offer. Then, grabbing my arm in a Greek pal-like embrace, he headed us toward his main hangout.

"Been missing this grave robber," he said to Laura, motioning for her to follow. "Place ain't the same without this guy around to give shit to. And Constantine's been lonely."

Constantine was Orestes' boss.

Orestes quickly led us upward toward the sheer rock face of the

Acropolis, all the while exchanging the usual insults with his confreres until we reached the entrance to the Taverna Sisyphos, aptly named for the steep climb required of its patrons.

In all the years I'd been coming to the Plaka, the joint hadn't changed: a tourist trap with a marketing formula down to a fine art. We negotiated our way among the crowded tables. Wire trellises overhead were woven with plastic vines and grapes—darkened with gritty dust—and enlivened with garish Christmas lights. The only redeeming feature of Taverna Sisyphus—even the food was third-rate—was the best bouzouki band in Athens—and Orestes, who performed three shows a night. His posse of matronly hangers-on was legion.

The irascible and highly opinionated Constantine, our gray-haired host, bar-stool philosopher and owner of Sisyphus, was already half-drunk and deeply engaged with his evening news. After an opening barrage of irony-edged non sequiturs aimed at me, he insisted on our joining his table and then sat back and returned to his paper and pipe, grunting out reflections on a fucked-up world, as was his wont, for the rest of the evening.

After making the rounds of his guests, Orestes joined us, pouring the wine, a sweet, thick white wine from his home island of Samos, which I could barely get down, but which he considered the finest wine in existence.

"It's guys like your boyfriend here," said Orestes, giving Laura his patented dark lothario-eyed grimace, "he and his pals at the American School of Classical Demolition"—(Orestes' idea of a joke)—"who wanna pull this place down so they can do more digging."

"And the Ministry of Culture . . . ," added Constantine from behind his paper, a damning finger held in the air. "Bastards."

"Dig?" asked Laura, nibbling the bait.

"Dig everything and everywhere," and Constantine glared at me. "They want to destroy my business. They want to ruin me."

"Ruined with ruins," I proclaimed. "Taverna Sisyphus is first on my list, if the health inspectors don't close you down first." I made a face as a waiter passed with a mountain of plates piled with the most wretched fried calamari.

"Over my broken bones," muttered Constantine, grabbing the wine bottle and pouring all around.

"One small step for civilization," I said. "One giant leap for a healthier gastrointestinal system."

"Look at him"—Constantine aimed the wine bottle at my heart—"the great scholar—what, no book with you tonight?" He smiled at Laura. "He always brings a book with him to dinner, just in case we bore him."

"I'm doubly honored, then . . . *better* than a book." Laura preened, already on her second glass, and stuck out her tongue at me.

"Look at this." Constantine pointed to his paper. "The fucking US of A is selling more fighters to the Turks, F-16s, they are called—the newest and best."

And so the evening went . . .

"How do you like the music?" asked Orestes, exasperated with the conversation, and squeezing Laura's arm.

The band was picking up the tempo. Diners were clapping, calling out Orestes' name.

"I love the music," Laura said, leaning into the hand that fondled her arm.

"Theodorakis," said Orestes, his tapering shoulders swishing, his plunging shirt showing a rippling chest. "*Agapi mou, amore mio,*" he sang out, and planted a kiss on Laura's cheek. "Do you like dancing?"

"Oh, I can take it or leave it."

Constantine grinned at me and rolled his eyes at Orestes. "You see here, all these East Germans are leaving—think of it, Orestes: more German women for you."

Orestes in a faux whisper to Laura: "Did Peter tell you I'm the best dancer in all the Plaka?"

"Baryshnikov of bouzouki," I said.

"Come and dance with me, baby; you'll see, it will be okay."

"Maybe later," she said hesitantly.

Orestes made a disparaging gesture in my direction. "Your bookworm professor can't dance worth shit."

"Orestes," said Constantine with a jerk of his chin toward the band and the empty dance floor. "Your services are wanted."

Orestes pushed back his chair and strode toward the dance floor, casually merging with the beat of the bouzouki band like a pimp with his street crew of whores. He seemed to go into a trance, his face tightening about his agate eyes, black silk shirt unbuttoned to his hairless navel and points south, where his tight white slacks left nothing to the imagination. The audience joined in clapping to the beat. He stamped the floor with his heel, slapping a thigh, leaping upward and back to slap the heel of his shoe again, then collapsing forward in ecstatic release, to swivel and grind his hips, groin imploring some invisible lover—a move sure to catch the eye of every woman in the joint. Soon he was glistening with honeyed sweat as he glided among the tables, twisting his torso in lubricious rapture as the women, whether matrons or virgins, seemed to rise as one to his allure, wide-eyed maenads shaking their dyed curls as they reached to touch his hands, his bulging thigh, yearning to fill their parched lips at the springhead of his wild youth.

The crowd applauded as Orestes sashayed back to our table and took Laura's hand and led her, unresisting, to the dance floor.

They stood side by side, holding hands, as he demonstrated the steps to her, accompanied by the band's slow buzzing syncopation. She looked shyly down at her sandaled feet, as if desperate for her clumsy appendages to follow his instructions. But then, wonder of wonders, those ugly prehensile calloused feet seemed to take on a life of their own, following his leads as if by magic, moving like an upstart Ginger Rogers to a perfunctory Astair. Her cheeks flushed and her eyes lit up with unconcealed pleasure. The tempo of the music brightened: a liquid energy further animating the handsome couple on the spotlit dance floor. Orestes was delighted and then a little rattled as she instantly caught on, adding steps, variations, then whole new combinations. She stayed with him like a shadow until banishing him to her own. Her hair flashed silken gold (clipped into a tight bun the moment Orestes had first left our table) above the long vee of tendons merging into the arabesques of her ears as she flashed her face from side to side. Her idolaters, first bemused at the switch of their affections, became very quiet as cutlery was abandoned. A slow but rapidly mounting clapping added urgency to the male catcalls and whistles.

I had never seen her dance professionally. I had read glowing reviews in the *International Herald Tribune* of performances in New York, London, Paris, and Venice. Aware of the breathless cavity that was the pit of my stomach, I realized I had joined the fan club.

Then with the guile of a pickpocket, she stole the limelight completely, trumping Orestes' impetuosity with a fluid languor and jagged disdain. She countered his broad implorements with delicate and comely gestures of endearment barbed with wicked laughter. His expansive movements became in her things of speed and staccato grace, subtle variations cast like loose change to her new fans, now flirting with balletic grace, now with steps nuanced and lithe, where his had been heavy and even awkward. Her long, sinuous legs flicked shoulder-high like switchblades, displaying her flowing line—and her white panties! As she stalked her onetime teacher, her impetuous breasts seemed to pummel his gleaming torso into submission.

Orestes, so used to running circles around his tourist clients, was a little crestfallen: tossed from Olympus to become an earthbound beggar, while she, goddesslike, was lifting in flight, her skirt a spinnaker catching an offshore breeze of frenzied acclaim from the women she now championed. Orestes shot sporting glances of dismay at his pals in the orchestra, and they returned comical hoots of amazement, piling on the tempo at the sandbagging of their suave confederate. The crowd was on its feet, yelling as if it were a boxing match. Even the most jaded waiters cheered, deserting their chores.

Orestes gamely tried to reassert himself with more difficult steps— he'd actually trained as a teenager with the Athens Ballet and was no slouch—looking intently into Laura's stormy eyes as if he might yet tame her. But she simply ignored his strutting macho to leave him rooted with her sweeping leg extensions, spinning, rippling arcs of sinew and muscle ending with a pyrotechnic display of pirouettes that left the crowd gasping with pleasure. The musicians were throwing all they had at the dancers, fingers ablur across their strings. Then a plate crashed, and another, precipitating a cascade of shattering crockery across the dance floor. Even Constantine gamely tossed a saucer.

She seemed to feed off her own motion, off the frenzy of the bouzouki players, frothy with sweat, like a frolicking filly alive to its own nature.

For a few glorious moments, the years fell away.

As the music reached a final crescendo, she leapt high, as if to catch the arc of her motion at its apogee, straight legs suspended in midair . . . a series of spinning turns, feet flickering at her calf, to finish in a blazing triple pirouette and a leap into Orestes' abashed arms.

The crowd stood, cheering, drawing in passersby from the street. More plates crashed. She bowed to her partner and the crowd and carefully picked her way past the shards to our table.

"Was I aggressive enough?" she asked, panting.

"And how."

"Ice," she whispered to me, keeping her stage smile perfectly in place. "Quick."

30 IT MUST HAVE BEEN WELL PAST TWO WHEN we left Sisyphus. A drunken Constantine had fallen asleep at his table, and Orestes had disappeared with two tall blond Australian matrons in tow. We were just a little tipsy. Laura took my arm. She was unsteady on her feet and walked with a faint limp.

"How's the knee?" I asked.

"What an idiot," she slapped her forehead. "The ice pack helped. I hope it kept the swelling down. If it hadn't been for all those damn plates, I'd have gotten through okay . . . but then, I didn't exactly do a warm-up, either."

I led her along back streets, a circuitous route that would get us back to my apartment by way of the ancient Agora. We walked in exhausted silence. At the bottom of a rutted cobblestone street, I watched as the familiar, if dreary, specter of the Agora came fully into view, a ruin-strewn landscape firmly locked away behind a stockade of spear-tipped wrought-iron fencing until morning, when the tourist tides would again have their way.

I felt her shiver.

"Why so glum?" she asked.

"I'm not glum."

"This is your world, your stage."

"Hardly sexy, or as alive as Orestes and *your* glamorous life."

Beyond the fence, the nearby Temple of Hephaestus took on a milky glow as the moon above the Acropolis slipped beneath a veil of mist. While in the distance, resurrected in the thirties with funds from the Alden trusts, as well as money from other foundations, the columned porticoes of the Stoa of Attolos glittered like ivory fretting against obsidian. Now serving as headquarters for the American School of Classical Studies, it included my office, restoration labs, and a museum. This was my workplace, my heritage, and a home of sorts, where my father had had an office until 1940, where he and Karel Hollar must have hatched their schemes, where he walked arm in arm with Joanna in the spring of 1949, where he was photographed with Nestor and other Greek generals at the Temple of Hephaestus, just to the right of the fence where we stood.

As one Princeton colleague in a jocular moment put it to me, "Well, Professor Alden, how many can say they have roots in a graveyard?"

Laura's hands tentatively reached to the wrought-iron bars of the fence, as if to ascertain their permeability.

"Oh, this has its glamour, too; I can see that now, like a moonlit stage set for some version of Balanchine's *Apollo*. Balanchine was the only real genius I've ever known."

"Not Max?"

This she ignored.

"I danced it with Kyra Nichols, Suzanne Farrell, and Peter Martins—and we were pretty damn good, let me tell you; even Mr. B. said so."

Well, there you go, the Hephaisteion is the best preserved of the Doric temples in mainland Greece, dedicated, no less, to both Hephaestus and your Athena—your alter ego, goddess of arts and dance, wisdom, and many other good things."

"Wouldn't it be nice if true? Do you suppose it was a better world, how the ancients filled their lives with gods and goddesses, nature's personifications—that they lived closer to some essential reality?"

"Closer to nature red in tooth and claw . . ."

"But don't you think it's worth it, to portray those essences of the human spirit so people might remember—feel connected . . . *something?*" She reached between the imprisoning bars and plucked a red poppy growing amidst the overgrown grass. She examined the flower and brought it to her nose and breathed of its immemorial scent.

"Poppies . . . poppies," she said in a rising incantation, as if in imitation of the Wicked Witch of the West.

I caressed her arm and touched the papery red between her fingers. "My wise Athena . . ."

"I think it's kinda like experiencing the universe from the inside, don't you? After all, we gave them their names in the first place—right? The gods and their starry messengers wouldn't exist without our having given them names. They need us as much as we need them, maybe more. And by embodying some approximation of their personifications—what dancers do—we make the world a little more alive, don't you think?"

The dreamy thinking of a Williams? Or just how much of Max had rubbed off?

"My wise Athena . . ."

"I've got to pee in the worst way."

On the way back, stopping at an all-night bar, we got some ice in a plastic bag. The moment I opened the door of my apartment, Laura disappeared into the bathroom with the ice. I got undressed, popped some old Darvon lying around for a change of pace, turned off the lights, and got into bed and lay on my back, blissing out. The windows were open wide and I could just make out the columned corner of the Parthenon, looking not a little like the prow of a ghost ship heading for rocky shoals. I was anxious—contemplating bumming one of her Prozacs, wanting her and not, as fearful of success as failure. My compass needle was spinning with all the alcohol and the Darvon kicking in. By the time she returned from the bathroom, I had drifted into an uneasy doze. She lay beside me in her bra and panties and carefully adjusted the plastic bag of ice to cover her knee. She was so natural and matter-of-fact about her ministrations that my apprehension began to ease. The room was still warm from the day, even with the slight breeze and the windows wide . . . and the smell of my landlady's roses like some cheap English country hotel. We lay there for a time, two battle-worn veterans in a trance, as if telepathy might do the trick, or some rogue wave of Dionysian release might move us on.

Then she spoke, as if she'd been undergoing a similar soul-searching.

"I'm terrified . . . I think."

"Why?" I thought she meant of having sex with me.

"What's been on your mind—right: Yeah, she was probably screwing Kim Philby, too, although she denies it."

I felt her bridle in disgust. And I knew there had to be more she wasn't telling me.

"Everything scares me now: the plug pulled on my career—without a paycheck. Half the guys I knew in ABT sick and dying, like some terrible plague because of something we did, or didn't do . . . all the sins of a selfish life."

"You've had a great career of making people happy; I saw it in their faces tonight. You lifted my spirits; you really did."

I heard her turn toward me.

"You *always* were a good person."

I cringed.

Her hand touched my arm. "Max believed in you, you know."

"Yeah, with friends like that . . ."

I turned on one elbow to look at her body, the ambient light from the street allowing me a lovely view. I squinted, focusing on her breasts, which were covered by thin lacy cups, the smooth planes of her midsection dipping at the belly button and merging into the line of her black panties.

As if she understood the purpose of my scrutiny, she put the bag of ice aside for a moment and flexed her swollen knee.

"Don't hate me; don't hate us. You must understand that Max was relentless; he was funny and charming, and he could spill you out and put you back together again, and for a little while, the world seemed like pure magic, like we could do no wrong."

"For quite a few years."

Her hand went to her mouth; I thought the knee pained her. She shivered.

"Does it hurt?"

"Anxious, that's all, sometimes it creeps up in little waves."

"Maybe just do half a Prozac?"

"I did. I did two—"

"Tell me what scares you and I'll try to make it go away."

"So sweet. Listen, you're the only one who can actually understand what he was like, what I was up against."

"Why did you leave him?"

"I didn't mean to bring this up—really."

Scenes from Max's novel flooded my mind: the demeaning affair with the greatest male dancer of his generation, the cocaine, and the gay guys instructing her on advanced fellatio techniques to please her demanding lover; not to mention the descriptions of sexual calisthenics that a dancer's body is capable of—the "love grip" from a near lifetime of holding a turnout. And the stuff they did in Venice!

And strangely, wondrously, my mind filling with those vivid

descriptions, I felt desire flood back into me, along with something of that long-ago fall at Winsted, dashing through space with the wind at my back, as I did in my dreams, and the smell of dried leaves and wood smoke and rotting apples.

But I no longer wanted young and innocent, not now, not anymore. I wanted the coke-fueled lover of Max's pages. I wanted revenge, to feel the fire.

As if reading my mind, she sighed and said, "It's almost creepy, you know; I feel like I've been here before."

"Yes . . ."

"Like we're just an echo."

I moved to her waiting face, her intent eyes, brushing my lips across the salty dampness of her brow, the scent of her shampoo and the fine strands of hair so incredibly soft against my cheek. I sensed her stiffen and then relax, the rhythmic caress of her breathing lips against my neck. And then a great calmness. Her lips found mine and her kisses were thankful and kind as she wet my parched lips with the tip of her tongue, as if to quench some long-standing thirst. I slipped a hand to her breast, my soul electric with the act of possession. She reached behind and slipped the bra free for me. The hardness of her nipples against my palm seemed a silent cry of return. Her kisses were more eager. I moved down to her breasts, kissing them, exploring. She gasped. I found and then kissed her pale scars, those tiny moons, one by one by one in what must have seemed to her a ritual motion, the lustrations of youth in the grass beneath the apple trees, still fumbling and unsure. Her hands pressed me there as if forever thankful, and I felt as if I'd given her beating heart space to roam.

I turned to the inside of her lower arm and kissed the tiny network of scars, and she sighed as if in forgiveness.

But after the tenderness came something else. A kind of passion, but more an act of triumphant will, to prove to her and her dead lover that I was no second stringer. By then, I knew my way around a woman. I luxuriated in the flat plane of her belly and below—easing her panties down—where she was beautifully groomed, with only a vestigial patch of soft downy hair . . . different from when she was seventeen, that pearl-handled razor having been put to magical use. And as her smooth long legs parted, I was careful, oh so careful, to avoid that tender knee. And oh the difference from the scholarly women I'd known, with their to-do lists and feminist agendas and gender-biased debunking of the classics. Her deeply muscled, pliant thighs and tensile, tough loins spread for my kisses . . . the power in that nexus of muscle and tendon, her small buttocks like soft fists of pleasure grinding against my palms and pressing upward into my mouth. Her thankful cries filled the room—once, twice, maybe three times.

I was triumphant in the dismissal of my invisible competitor.

She kept calling my name, as if unsure of herself, pleading for me to stop.

"Yes," I said finally.

She smiled faintly, as if she didn't quite recognize me, and pulled me upward, pulled my mouth to hers and began to soothingly lick the womanly wetness at my chin and lips, like a cat her newborn kitten. Then she very simply and forthrightly wrapped her arms about me, and then her thighs, taking my weight and moving her hips to find me. Her breathy whisper swam in my ear.

"She said he was very gentle."

"What?"

"Joanna. She said he was very gentle and loving with her . . . for you not to think it was anything bad."

"Why did you tell me she said he was a virgin?"

She laughed, as if it had been a big joke.

"Joanna said it was as if he were a virgin, like it was the first time for both of them. Forget it."

"What—"

She put a finger to my lips. "But I don't need gentle. Fuck me. I can't stand it anymore. I want you inside me."

I raised myself on to my elbows to see her face, her hair gathered on the pillow, her words at once exciting and wonderfully strange, as if coming from a vast distance. I saw in her eyes, blue and tightly focused, a frantic but concentrated soul. As her hips eagerly sought mine, her blue eyes glowed with hope, tenderness, kindness, and a kind of submission sweetly erotic yet estranging, demanding something that I was not yet ready to give. I wished to join her there in those blue pools of her eyes, in the sun-drenched woods and lakes of our childhood home . . . and yet crush them to oblivion.

I kissed her hard and long. "Your cunt is so sweet."

She laughed. "Then fuck me like you fucking mean it."

Oh my God . . . the letters.

As I maneuvered across her good leg to get at the drawer of my bedside table, my back gave a twinge of pain and I grunted.

She held my wrist.

"You don't have to bother."

I had the foil packet in my fingers and was tugging at the seam.

"Better safe than sorry."

"Just fuck me."

"You're not worried?"

"Worried—about you?" I thought she was mocking me, and I felt my erection begin to dissolve. She took the condom and threw it across the room. "I'm on the Pill."

"Oh . . ."

"I'm an old gal anyway."

She made a valiant attempt at a careless smile and we began again. Somehow the ground had shifted. She was lovely and encouraging and reached down to guide me into her. I hadn't felt a woman like that in such a long time, and I gasped with the sensation and the strength of her grip on me. I knew I had something to prove and tried a better angle, careful of her bad knee. Then I got a back spasm and a bolt of pain went up my spine and I held myself still for an instant, waiting for it to pass. She knew immediately and her hands went to the small of my back, rubbing there, encouraging, but there was, too, a hint of desperation in her voice. She squeezed me, an unbelievable feeling.

"You okay?" she asked.

"Just my back, all the driving."

"Okay then, ah . . ." She gently pushed me off and grabbed a pillow and folded it tight and maneuvered it beneath her pelvis, raising herself higher. "Try it like this, darling. That's right, on your knees—right, just watch out for my fucking goddamn knee."

That word, *darling*, was intoxicating in its exoticism, like a forties noir movie, something her mother might say. She pulled her legs back and her bad knee wide and out of harm's way. She was such a pro, and the elevation was perfect, not a stitch of stress on my back once my weight was on my knees. And she was so unbelievably sexy and I was so in love with her squeezing that I thought I'd lose my mind.

"Yes, yes, go for it—that's right, deep, nice and deep. Oh, I love it. I want to feel you come."

She was fingering herself with an ease and self-possession that was thrilling. And yet her words sounded a little tinny, more clinical than ecstatic. Somehow they broke the spell, as did those heartbreaking scenes from the Venice chapters of Max's novel, rising like specters in my mind: when the dancer, despairing and alone, finally goes to a local

Italian doctor for her abortion. The cheesy examination room, the stupid nurse and supercilious doctor shoving her feet into the stirrups . . .

Kim Philby.

And there I was, kneeling between her upraised legs like a great big
idiot, coming all over her stomach.

I rolled to the side, mortified at the incontinent mess I'd made of it.

I thought I heard her cry out in surprise or disappointment, or
maybe she'd brought herself to another orgasm.

I was reeling but crestfallen, as if I'd crashed and burned from a
great height. I stared up at the ceiling, and I thought I heard her sigh or
sniff back tears. Out the corner of my eye I was aware she hadn't moved
a muscle, but lay flat, with her knees raised, very much like a woman
in labor. Then I felt her move. Whatever she was doing, she was being
very careful, exacting and deliberate. I could just make out her sliding
an outstretched finger of her left hand along the skin of her belly. She
seemed to have sucked in her gut. She kept repeating this purposeful
bit of choreography, varying it slightly as she maneuvered that finger
over other areas of her torso, but ultimately directing it toward her
navel. I was spellbound.

Then, with seemingly practiced ease, she began dipping her finger
into what she had collected about her navel, then quickly shifted that
finger lower, between her legs, secreting it there and working the finger
in slowly, carefully feeding herself. I was transfixed. A few minutes later,
she took the pillow from beneath her head and added it to the one
underneath her pelvis, tilting herself still further. And then, reaching
for the ice pack, she draped it over her knee, swollen like a grapefruit.

Nothing she ever did surprised me after that.

I awoke early, feeling exiled from my own life, as if nothing quite fit
anymore. My apartment looked the same except for the female clothes
hung across the chairs. And Laura was fast asleep, curled up under the
sheet on the opposite side of my bed. The plastic bag of ice had left a
damp puddle on the floor. I got up quietly so as not to wake her and
gazed out the window at the pale glimmering light and eerily empty
and noiseless streets. I realized it was Sunday. I couldn't quite explain
what had changed, except the obvious. Something in the atmosphere,
as if her panic attacks were infectious. My hand was shaking, my head
spinning, my back actually okay. We had been drinking a lot.

For some reason, I found myself going over to my desk, where she'd left my copy of *Gardens of Saturn*, and returning it to the bookshelf, as if one could just *put* Max away. And as I did, I felt the pull of an even larger story and so began searching for other volumes as that moonlit scene of two men bent to a clay tablet, scratching symbols in the dirt, returned to me more vividly than ever. There was Karel Hollar's first major book from 1934, *The Search for Homer,* translated into a dozen languages, an international best-seller, and followed by more. There were his journal articles covering all his excavations, first in Crete and then the Peloponnese, some with my father's Princeton team, some with the German Archaeological Institute (DAI), and the last with the University of Cincinnati. The sudden onset of war in the fall of 1939 and his Wehrmacht call-up (he'd taken on his mother's Austrian citizenship) had prevented him from publishing anything about his partnership with Cincinnati's Carl Andersen, discover of Nestor's Palace and the six hundred Linear B tablets.

I began checking the indexes of a bunch of postwar journals, turning to the references and examining footnotes. There had been a flurry of mentions of Hollar's career in the early fifties, when Ventris had deciphered Linear B, mostly noting his participation in the 1939 excavations at Pylos and the discovery of the first tablets outside Crete—the critical mass of data that had made the decipherment possible. There were mentions of his early prophecies that Linear B would be found on the mainland and that a whole new chapter in Bronze Age history only awaited that event. After the fifties, his career, like my father's, faded from the literature. The footnotes all referenced the same story: an early wunderkind in the field of Greek Bronze Age archaeology— the "great white hope of the DAI," as one cutting British journal put it, "brilliance extinguished by allegiance to the Fatherland." As an Austrian citizen, he'd been called up by the Wehrmacht when Britain and France declared war in late 1939. "His engineering skills made him an asset to the German military, while serving in Poland, France, and the Soviet Union." His obscure death in a Soviet prisoner of war camp in February 1945 was termed "a loss to German archaeology, from which it will be a very long time recovering."

No mention he had ever served in occupied Greece.

It was late 1945 when my father got wind of Hollar's death while stationed in a defeated Germany, when he suddenly threw in the towel, grabbed his disability release, and left the OSS. After a long month in London over Christmas and New Year's with Suzanne, he took up his

Princeton professorship in February 1946. He spent barely two years at Princeton, during which time he'd dash up to Elysium for his outdoor assignations with Suzanne—the sheer happiness and joy in their love-making pouring in torrents from their love letters of those years. Until the spring of 1948, when Elliot, with or without Nestor's prompting, took a walk with him along the banks of Lake Carnegie and spilled the beans about Bobby and Suzanne. Then nearly two years as Athens CIA station chief without a single letter. And then a few months after his return to Washington in February 1950, he married my mother, with whom he spent three and a half years, while his tortured affair with Suzanne resumed sporadically—Laura interpreted her mother's epistolary pleas as those of "a woman desperate to get pregnant; I should know"—before he disappeared into East Berlin in October 1953 without a trace, cause, or explanation.

Seeing that Laura was still fast asleep—her mention of Kim Philby the night before sent an involuntary shiver down my spine—I got dressed and headed for the Agora and my office at the American School of Classical Studies.

The streets of the Plaka were deserted. A bell rang out with a harsh grating tolling. A miniature Greek Orthodox church squatted toadlike in a sunlit square. I stood frozen in place until the tolling stopped, surrounded again by a dull echoing silence. I had a sinking feeling I couldn't staunch, the kind you get just after liftoff in a Huey, when the nose dips, when one moment you think you're home free and the next you're headed straight for a fiery crash, only to be lifted skyward.

Where was the lift? I hadn't taken my Demerol or done my exercises, but my back felt okay. Nothing like a little fucking for what ails you. Even my hangover was fading. I was a little fixated about the thing she'd done with her finger. And I was thinking about the two Linear B tablets in the pockets of Karel Hollar's sheepskin coat.

I blinked in the harsh sunlight. There was an old dog in the shadow of a piss-stained doorway, scratching fleas. Nearby, down a cloacal alley, scrawny cats chewed on splintered bones, making the most obscene cracking sounds. Farther on, a stooped old woman in black swept the gutters with an immemorial cadence, pushing small piles of rubbish from the night before into bigger heaps. Her sun-stricken, leathery face lifted to mine without so much as a smile as I passed. What horrific memories of the civil war did she harbor in every swipe of her broom?

The guard at the entrance to the American School recognized me immediately, tipped his hat, and let me in. I'd forgotten my pass. My office was just the same as ever, with a huge stack of journals still in their manila envelopes in the middle of my desk, and an in-box full to overflowing. Friendly volumes and familiar periodicals lined the walls. All as it should be, a safe, scholarly life to be blithely resumed and slipped into my back pocket.

And then the stone unturned that had been staring me in the face all along. Across the street from my office was the Carl Andersen Library, the greatest research library for material on late antiquity, classical and pre-classical history in Europe. I found it nearly deserted on a Sunday morning, which suited me just fine. I went directly to the section containing all of Carl Andersen's papers and found the file drawer for the year 1939, labeled PYLOS in faded blue ink. Just the smell of those dusty and yellowed documents, touched with mildew, took me back to Epano Englianos and my debrief of Nestor. As I began to pick through the contents, not entirely sure what I was looking for, I felt, too, as if I were channeling something of the illicit thrill that Max must have felt as he surreptitiously combed the Winsted files for dirt on my father and family. Even as I kept assuring myself I wasn't interested in a demolition job.

It didn't take long before stray letters from Karel Hollar to Carl Andersen began turning up. Most were written in Hollar's beautiful, exacting hand, just like the letters from his student years I'd found squirreled away in the pages of my father's books. It was an artist's hand with an engineer's precision, reminding me of the schematic plans of the E-boats he'd drawn up, described to me by Nestor. The letters were all professional exchanges about technical matters in the field but were filled with breathless excitement about the implications of recent finds in the area of Pylos. Carl Andersen's Cincinnati team, with the approval of the Greek Department of Antiquities, had been feeling their way toward a likely site for Nestor's Palace since the twenties. Karel Hollar and my father had been concentrating elsewhere, exploring likely sites where they hoped more Linear B tablets might be discovered, the decipherment of which my father had been pursuing since at least 1931 at Winsted, all the while encouraged by Hollar, who was the first to admit he didn't have the patience for that sort of exacting scholarship. "Patience and money you have in abundance, my friend," Hollar had once written with his acerbic humor, "the marriage of heaven and hell."

By early 1938, Hollar had sniffed the air enough to sense that the Cincinnati team might be onto something; Carl Andersen had discovered a series of tholos tombs north of modern Pylos, near the coast, clearly tombs of wealthy aristocrats that would indicate a nearby palace or citadel, if the tholos tombs at Mycenae and Tiryns were any guide. But the looming citadels of Mycenae and Tiryns had also distracted my father and Karel: They were fixated on looking for similarly high and massive fortifications. Later that morning, when I got to my father's office files from 1938 to 1940, I found a letter from Karel Hollar from early 1938, first calling into question their misplaced logic: "The hell with walls, let's hire a team of local men and have them scour the countryside north of Pylos for artifacts, and more importantly, for signs of Mycenaean roads. . . . Surely, if we can discover the road networks in the area, they will lead us to the gates of the palace. Perhaps the walls were torn down by invaders or reused for building material in the Dark Ages." My father had paid for these teams and they had reported back their findings to Karel, who had immediately begun currying favor with Carl Andersen.

My dear Carl,

Just a note to let you know that we've had men out combing the hills along the coast between Coryphasion, Fillatra, and Hora for signs of Mycenaean roads, and the results have been very promising indeed. We have found survivals in many locations of raised stone-built fragments, some extremely well made and well preserved, often along the contour of a hill and employing minimal gradients that might well accommodate chariots and carts. There is a marvelously preserved stone bridge near Hora that leaves me breathless (photographs enclosed). One cannot but recall the passages from the *Odyssey* where Telemachus is driven in one of King Nestor's chariots at breakneck speed along the road to Sparta to visit King Menelaus "in lovely Lacedaimon." And yes, my dear Carl, when we plot the direction of these roads, they seem to converge on your tholos tombs and, more precisely, on the Epano Englianos Ridge just to the west of Hora.

By early 1939, Karel Hollar had sweet-talked his way onto the planned Cincinnati excavations on the Englianos Ridge—exclusive rights to which had been assigned to Carl Andersen by the Greek Department of Antiquities—scheduled for that summer's digging season. Andersen was already a veteran and had done pioneering work at Troy, but at that time the young Karel Hollar was the more famous of the two, with his popular books and articles, a wunderkind at the German Archaeological Institute, where he become something of a poster boy. The DAI was run by the German government, and by 1939 controlled by the Nazi P. It was no small feat that Hollar managed the coup of joining with Andersen's team, given the soured relations between the United States and Germany. I suspect Karel's friendship with my father made it possible. (My father had been made an honorary member of the DAI in 1934 and the fact that he failed to resign officially until the fall of 1939 was held against him by some at Princeton.) By any measure, Karel, "with his nose for the prize," and deep expertise in Greek Bronze Age archaeology proved to be a tremendous asset to Andersen's team, until a bizarre incident interceded. My father's office file included the letter he'd received on Delos from Karel Hollar telling of the discovery of the Linear B tablets and cryptically asking for funds to equip more workers. The telegrammed acknowledgment for the wire transfer from the Bank of Athens to Hollar's account was also in my father's file. Only when I finally got to Carl Andersen's daily diary of the excavations on the Englianos Ridge did the full implications of this transfer become apparent.

> Wednesday, June 22. Arrived back at Epano Englianos after six days of consultations with Greek antiquities chief—found to my horror that an extensive new series of trenches had been dug in an odd herringbone pattern to open up what turned out to be some adjoining chambers of the megaron. Karel Hollar, in all his Teutonic excitement, couldn't wait to show me around, pointing out the further layout of the palace and bits of frescoed wall that had been discovered that week. He was quite beside himself. Aghast, I asked him to explain how these trenches had come about, since our excavation crew had been explicitly instructed to go in the opposite direction—and had clearly done so. Oh, he told me, indicating his nose with his forefinger, "I hired some extra boys to expedite the digging here. It was so clear that this was the heart of the palace." "Heart, heart—what do you mean, heart?" I asked. "The heart, the beating heart," he exclaimed, "where Nestor would have related his tales of Troy and the wily Odysseus to the young Telechamus around the megaron!" I was so shattered at this intrusion on his part that I was left speechless. "Where are these extra diggers?" I asked. "Oh, I let them go once the work was done—they are no longer needed." I immediately went to my foreman and asked him what had happened. I was told that he'd assumed the order for the new diggers came from me. I asked if he knew the men—no, they were from Kyparissia; but they worked like the very devil; they worked night and day. At night? Yes, at night with

lamps; they were good and strong men; they barely broke for food and drink.

Over the following weeks, Carl Andersen's diary made little specific mention of this shocking disruption of scholarly protocol. He kept his outrage close to his chest, hoping to feel out more precise details from Karel Hollar. But Karel was his typical effusive scholarly self and had seemingly forgotten about the whole thing, keeping busy with the new finds and making "beautiful, absolutely splendid" hand copies of some of the Linear B tablets, "which are to be shipped off to Athens for safekeeping as soon as they are recorded." Rumors of war percolated into camp. Then, in August, the Molotov-Ribbentrop nonaggression pact was signed between Germany and the Soviet Union. Something Karel Hollar found "unsettling." "Karel has gone silent at meals, not a peep, as if a member of the family died. He absents himself from our camp more and more often these days—met by a car from the DAI no less! He's picked his side, one doesn't wonder." With Hollar's departure and the hurried work to pack up the site as war loomed, Carl Andersen went back to his foreman, pressing the man about the team of diggers that Karel had hired, concerned about irregularities, if anything was amiss—missing. But his foreman, whom he'd known for years and trusted, gave his assurances. "My foreman always has a smile on his face at the mention of Karel Hollar, and plenty of spending money in his pocket, as do many of his men."

There was nothing more in Carl Andersen's file about the incident of the trenches dug on the sly or Karel Hollar. The war overwhelmed everything; the Linear B tablets were deposited safely in the Bank of Greece in Athens; Karel Hollar "evaporated, without even a good-bye"; and Carl Andersen and almost every American and European archaeologist left Greece to return home for the duration of the war—a hiatus that would last for fifteen years. Carl Andersen settled back at the University of Cincinnati to begin the arduous process of publishing the contents of the unearthed Linear B tablets, and did not return to Athens and Pylos until 1955—by then, famous as the discover of Nestor's Palace, and even more so for the Linear B tablets, which had resulted in the decipherment of Linear B in 1952 by Michael Ventris, while Karel Hollar and my father were nearly forgotten.

My father was one of the very few Americans who remained in Greece after the fall of 1939. Over the years at Princeton, I had picked up scraps about this unsettling period between late 1939 and June of 1941, when America was not yet officially at war, when my father helped fund and drive an ambulance after the Italian invasion of northern Greece in the fall of 1940, when he made it out of occupied Greece by the "skin of his teeth" in the summer of 1941. It was talk of his efforts on behalf of Greek war relief during this period that seemed to trump his active years of scholarship in the minds of his Princeton colleagues: "Stayed behind and tried to keep the American School and its Greek staff and the collections safe from Italian bombers." Given what I'd heard, I was somewhat crestfallen when I closed the drawer on Carl Andersen and sought out my father's American School office files from 1934 to 1940.

His files provided meager pickings, at least to the story I'd come for. Amongst the masses of routine official correspondence with students, academic journals, Princeton faculty, and the Greek Department of Antiquities, I found only a few bits of scattered correspondence before 1939 from Karel Hollar, and that one letter from the summer 1939 to him on Delos concerning the discovery of the Linear B tablets and the funding for extra diggers, and the record of a wire transfer of ten thousand dollars—a lot of money in 1939—to Hollar's account. No follow-up, no further correspondence about what had transpired, as if the impending war and subsequent invasion by the Italians and Germans had simply wiped the slate clean. Or my father had carefully purged the files and overlooked the Delos letter and wire transfer.

Remaining in Athens after September of 1939 was foolhardy at best; remaining after the fall of France and the Italian attack in the fall of 1940 was reckless. My father and his colleagues, especially those who had returned to Princeton, expected the worst, feared the destruction of their work in the Agora and the descent of a new dark age should the fascists prevail. With the disastrous fall of France in the spring of 1940, few believed Greece could remain neutral or untouched. The files contained letters and telegrams from Princeton expressing these fears and concern for his safety and the fate of the American School. Both Princeton and the American legation in Athens advised him to leave. My father kept doggedly on. While setting up a Greek relief committee funded by his mother, the Alden trusts, and colleagues back in the States, he took care of the American School's physical plant and its Greek staff, even participating in small digs around Athens, "as if providing a veneer of normalcy might keep the wolf from the door," as one colleague put it. All the while, he worked into the night with the photos and copies of the new Pylos tablets—surely provided by Karel Hollar (Carl Andersen and the Cincinnati team would take years before officially publishing anything)—in his attempt to decipher Linear B. He worked with the Greek Department of Antiquities to keep up morale by giving lectures at the Athens Archaeological Society, presided over by the king, on the latest Linear B finds at Pylos.

Most of his file for 1940 was devoted to practical matters of physical upkeep of the American School's facilities and Greek war relief, including receipts for wire transfers of funds from Swiss banks to purchase and maintain badly needed supplies for the American School Committee's ambulance. After the Italian invasion in October 1940, he'd managed to find a GM chassis at an Athens factory and have a custom-built ambulance cab constructed to his specifications; it could carry four wounded lying down and four sitting, with supply storage inside and on the roof. He drove the ambulance throughout the fall, winter, and spring of 1940–1941, ferrying supplies north and wounded south along the treacherous mountainous roads of northern Greece near the Albanian border, and even to Koritsa, inside Albania, which the Greeks had taken in their counterattack. There were receipts for tens of thousands of dollars for medical supplies, bandages, woolen blankets, boots, socks, chocolate, coffee, and cigarettes, much of it imported through neutral Turkey, and repair bills for the ambulance, tires and more tires, engine parts from shops in Athens and Piraeus. The last item in the file was a creased road map of Greece from the thirties, folded almost to the point of falling apart at the seams, stained with motor grease, coffee, and what looked like blood, smelling awful when I held it to my nose, my hands trembling. It had been heavily marked up, dozens of towns along the northern frontiers with Albania and Yugoslavia circled, routs and alternate routs noted, inky scribbles—*snow, bridge out, captured, bombed, mined!!!* I was about to return the map to the file, when I unfolded the bottom half, containing most of the Peloponnese, looking pristine, as yet untouched by the Italian invasion or the later German occupation. Something caught my eye. Only one place, one town had been circled, not once or twice, but three times—and not Pylos, but a town north of Pylos along the west coast, Kyparissia: Kyparissia, where the digging crew hired by Karel Hollar had come from, the men who "worked like the very devil." Various routes from Athens to Kyparissia had been marked.

I stared at the name of the town for a long time and then put the map in my pocket and left.

Outside, amongst the ruins of the Agora, the early-morning sunlight, so harsh in the Plaka, had given way to a more gentle hue by afternoon, the litter of time's immemorial artifacts garlanded with wild poppies and perouka and kampanakia flowers—red, pink, and milky white brushed into the crevices of ancient walls as if to invest the ages with fall's early splendor. The stones of Periclean Athens composed themselves with a troubling familiarity as I walked, as they must have first intrigued my father when still a teenager, when the landscape of the classical past remained wonderfully solid and unavailing to a fate yet foretold.

The environs were pretty much as my father had left them in July of 1941, when he closed his office at the American School for the last time—the premises having been turned into an annex of the American legation by then—and took the plane to Rome provided by the skeleton staff of the legation to fly out the remaining Americans in Greece. And from Rome, he had endured a harrowing train trip to Lisbon, where there was an exchange for German detainees, and then taken the boat home. A few weeks after reaching New York—the crossing had taken nearly a month—he was in touch with Bill Donovan and the gestating ranks of the OSS. Two years later, he was dropped on the beach near Pylos.

When he returned again to Athens in 1948 at the height of a vicious civil war, the rehearsal for all the Cold War insurgencies to come, the Agora and the American School remained closed. As a CIA official and military adviser to the nationalist government, he had to tread carefully if he was not to tarnish his previous, and future, life as a scholar—the one Elliot Goddard had pried so deftly from his grip. Even as a respected philhellene, he had to watch himself, lest he find himself on the wrong side of history in a devastated nation ripped apart by occupation and party strife, and more than a little conflicted about America's new role as a protector of Greece's anti-Communist future. The American School would not reopen until 1955. During his time in Athens as station chief, his beloved Agora must have seemed as tantalizingly near and yet far as the lands of the unfree beyond the Kalamas River that he and Nestor had gazed upon with such perturbations of the soul. And yet even then, during these perilous days, he grabbed every spare moment in his race to be the first to decipher Linear B, perhaps sensing that others were nipping at his heels, that with the ongoing publication of the Pylos tablets by Andersen and his team in Cincinnati after 1945—someone, somewhere, would soon stumble on the key.

After the Peloponnese was completely cleared of Communists by late 1948, he returned again to Kyparissia, as he had in his ambulance in 1940 and 1941, and found nothing. He personally interrogated members of local Communist cadres, some of whom had worked with Hollar's special team on the Pylos excavation. They must have told him that the hidden tablets were long gone, gone with the retreating Germans.

And shortly thereafter, he found out the truth about Joanna, his Nausicaa . . . as if he and his reckless romanticism had plunged down yet another rabbit hole.

So, on that afternoon in the momentous fall of 1989, fifty years from the start of the war, I found my steps leading me toward the Temple of Hephaestus, where the medal ceremony for my father had been held in June of 1949. It made perfect sense since the Hephaisteion—named after Hephaestus, fabricator of the most fearsome and splendid weapons of war—was the best-preserved temple in the Agora, an iconic backdrop for these defenders of Western civilization, even as the final butcher's bill from the civil war was far from complete. I climbed the steps, took a deep breath—the fumes of sparse Sunday traffic sweetened with pine and oleander—and looked for my bearings: where the line of fighters and generals had stood beneath those wonderfully preserved fluted columns of the Doric order, where the photographer had been positioned, where, in the cool shadows of the white marble interior, Joanna, in her blue dress, had stood, waiting for her unacknowledged American lover, the man who had meant the death of her family and the loss of her child. Though she would never have put it that way. Once I had it all mapped out in my mind, exactly where he had stood, where he might have seen her out of the corner of his eye, where he'd gazed upon the Agora, I slumped down to the lichen-scarred floor, rested my back against a column, and closed my eyes. Joanna's description of him, his kindness and basic decency, his skills as a teacher, stirred something in me—enough to dismiss the more disconcerting facts—and I found myself missing him as I had as a child. As I had in the first years after he left, when his absence was absolutely real, before memories of his last hugs and kisses had dimmed: how he'd carried me in his arms above the lake as he kicked us out to the raft, with the stars shining like heavenly lamps. When his absence grew into an unaccountable space inside me.

I would defend him to the end.

But when I removed the battered road map of Greece from my pocket and again located the triple circle around Kyparissia, hoping maybe I'd only imagined it, I began to cry.

Fate is not one thing, but a legion of fuckups.

When I got back to my apartment, suddenly a little panicked at my long absence, I saw that Laura's things were still there, but she was gone. I went into the bathroom. The creams and lotions, the pearl-handled razor, the drying panties by the window, the smell of her spilled shampoo in the Jacuzzi—all were still there. Relief flooded through me. I wandered around my apartment in a childlike daze, breathing in the smells of my bookshelves, handling her clothes, and then, going to the window, I thought I heard voices rising above the knelling of a church bell. I breathed deeply, and again, the way Maureen had taught me, inhaling the perfume of Madame Cleo's roses.

I thought of Laura's hopeful blue eyes as they had been the night before.

Maybe that's all it takes to head us back to where we belong, that glimpse of home in the eyes of the beloved, a change in the wind or drop in air pressure that sharpens the surly, sullen bell as it summons us . . . before we have drifted beyond recall.

I walked to the hallway and the French doors leading out to Madame Cleo's private rooftop garden. I saw them through the glass, sitting there bent over the tea table, a late breakfast on a large silver tray between them. Madame Cleo was holding Laura's hand, whispering, chortling to herself, and then they were both laughing. Behind them, a thousand dilapidated roses on trellises rained down brown petals.

When I pushed open the door and walked out, they turned to me as one with delighted smiles.

"There you are, you naughty boy!" exclaimed Madame Cleo. "I've been chatting with your new friend, Professor Alden, and I thoroughly approve—thank God, not another dreary student."

PART THREE
PRAGUE

Exile is partly in our nature, partly our lot. As is choice and necessity. The choice was mine.

I once was a student of civilization but have since found myself increasingly an expert on its undoing.

—excerpts from John Alden's Pankrác Prison diary

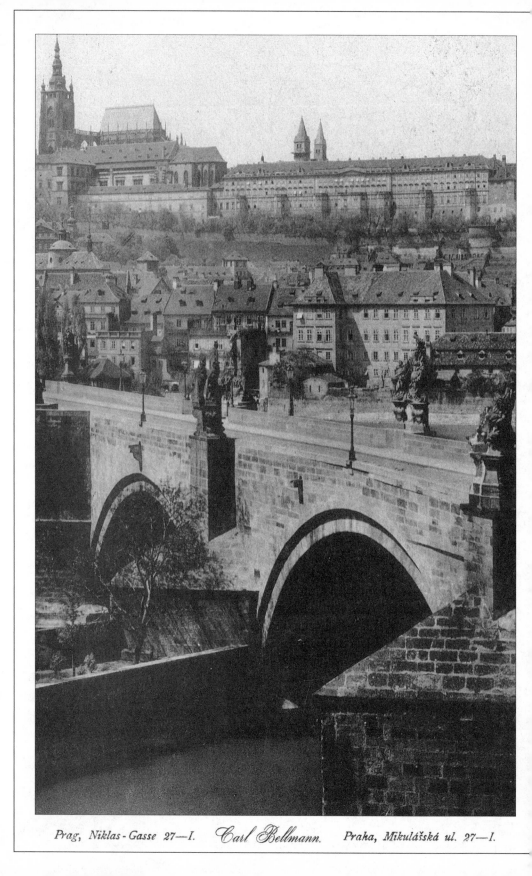

Prag, Niklas-Gasse 27—I.　　*Carl Bellmann.*　　Praha, Mikulášská ul. 27—I.

31 TRY AS I MIGHT TO PREPARE MYSELF, EVEN after a week of driving in its pursuit, I was still shocked at how those gentle rolling hills along the Austrian border gave way to an expanse of ripening grain, slashes of yellow-sepia against a darkening sky, then an abrupt line of scythed stubble, where, just beyond the scabrous crest of a small rise, a muddy strip of barbed-wire fencing congealed like the shadow of a rusty scar across the earth. Nothing prepares one: the observation towers barnacled with searchlights and binocular-gazing silhouettes, the Kalashnikov-toting guards in muddy boots—Alsatians leashed at their sides—patrolling an endless strip of garroting barbs . . . and trip wires and mines and machine-gun nests from the Baltic to the Black Sea.

When time is no more, the monstrosity of this inhuman artifact will still baffle the undying gods.

It had been seventeen years since my patrolling days along the Vam Co Dong River, and the closest I'd ever gotten to Churchill's Iron Curtain was a conference in Munich.

But seeing *is* believing . . . the thing my father and Nestor had trailed north of the Kalamas River, the thing that had perplexed and tempted and swallowed my father alive: the bolt-hole to which Kim Philby and the other Cambridge spies, Donald Maclean and Guy Burgess, had escaped.

In a sense, Laura and I had been on the hunt since childhood, certainly from the moment we drove north from Athens in my Land Rover, following my father's battered map from the ambulance. We tried, when feasible, to weave our way through the towns he'd circled, the routes he'd marked and traveled from Volos to Larisa to Florina to Ioannina and the border of Albania, and Koritsa, inside Albania where the map no longer allowed us to go. The roads were much better now, some spectacular, even as we tried to imagine the torturous mountain switchbacks covered in ice and snow, pocked from artillery fire and bomb strikes, where frozen soldiers marched, advanced and retreated, and died in the thousands, each an individual and terrible death to some mother or father, wife or son or daughter or brother. I often thought of an older Greek colleague's description, how when he'd opened the back of the ambulance when it arrived at the hospital in Koritsa, "the blood spilled out the gate like a red tidal surge."

We visited the towns Joanna had mentioned to us, where she had lived with her child, where she had worked as a nurse for the Communists—the glimpse of the blackened eye sockets in the torture cell preying on her mind—where she'd finally been captured by government forces. These places were so changed as to be unrecognizable, so beautiful and green and so overflowing with fall wildflowers that it simply took our breath away, belying all the harm and disaster that had once been visited on them. With the exception of some old pillboxes and concrete strongpoints in the mountains, and the barbed wire near the Albanian border, it would hard to believe anything bad had ever happened. After decades of digging up sites of battle and pillage, as I told Laura, it is always hard to believe in the horror that unfolded in those places. Or as Joanna told us, "The earth forgets and people the same if they are to survive." And we certainly weren't going to bring it up with any of the friendly people we met at the tavernas and small hotels where we stayed. So we followed the map for as long as it would lead us, skirting Albania and entering Yugoslavia, where the map ran out and we were on our own, but still on the trail for the inexplicable that had so perplexed my father and Nestor . . . for that invisible boundary: a river, a wall, a line of barbed wire that divides the free from the unfree.

For the classical mind, for a Mediterranean sensibility steeped in the logic of clear and rhythmic proportions, the Iron Curtain was an invocation to some inchoate, hyperborean barbarism. The Czech border, strung with its web of barbed wire, had the feel of a metastasized dogma, a Spanish Inquisition on steroids, invoking the self-inflicted wound of the *flagellanti* or a crown of bloody thorns from a Grünewald altarpiece. Or how Vlada put it to us, "terror first and last and foremost: how the fearful criminal mind thinks it can hold time at bay." The archaeologist and historian in me had to marvel, for walls are practically our stock-in-trade. As we drew closer and slowed in a long line of traffic backed up at the crossing, I groped for precedents: the Great Wall of China, or Hadrian's Wall, or even the cyclopean walls of Mycenae or Tiryns, which had so spooked me only weeks before, citadels to keep the barbarians at bay . . . but walls to keep entire captive populations from escaping? Even the slaveholding South had never contemplated, much less attempted, such a hideous thing. A shameful evil that put the lie to the lie of which it was the very essence.

And yet there it was.

I saw Laura stiffen in her seat as we crossed the grizzly strip of barbed wire and plowed earth on a two-lane culvert toward the Czech border post. The Austrian police had barely given a cursory glance at our passports. The panic attacks, banished since Athens, crept back on little prancing feet.

My hands were clammy on the wheel of the Land Rover as we halted behind the cars in front of us, each being thoroughly inspected by the Czech border police. Looking out a windshield streaked with raindrops, one couldn't but be impressed by the technical virtuosity of this Cold War artifact—the upgrade, I suppose, of two or three generation's expertise since the improvised laying of barbed wire at Mons, on what was to become the Western Front, and the first gulags of the twenties and concentration camps of the thirties and internment camps of the forties—reaching a kind of rare perfection before our eyes. Not that I hadn't laid my fair share of concertina wire, passing on my expertise to our Vietnamese militias, but the Iron Curtain was impressive by any stretch and seemingly an immutable fixture of forty years' standing: a continent-wide prison camp. As an archaeologist who'd excavated more than a few toppled walls in my time, I should have known better.

"What are they looking for?" Laura asked, staring anxiously through the windshield at the gray-uniformed guards searching the cars in front of us.

"Stuff to confiscate, like your Joni Mitchell cassettes—running-dog-degenerate-exploitive-capitalist-pig-love-and-peace-bourgeois-faux-hippie music."

"Oh, that."

"Serve you right for leading me on a wild-goose chase."

"Vlada promised me he knew something."

"Well, he once led me on a wild-goose chase, too . . . almost got us shot, arrested, and thrown out of Winsted—miracle that we didn't."

"You never told me that."

"Remind me when we've got more time."

"So, what do you think?"

She asked me that a lot.

"Well, these sons of bitches have certainly done themselves proud."

"I was trying to imagine what it was like crossing into East Berlin and knowing you might not be coming back . . . the courage to do that."

"To right a wrong, huh? Or maybe save the world?"

"Or maybe save one child."

"Ah, your romantic hero."

"What's with you? If anything, you've only gotten more cryptic since Athens."

"It's what you haven't told me that scares me.'"

"You calling me a liar?"

"Call it a sin of omission."

"I'm such an open book," she said with a rigid, straight face and perfect lawyerly aplomb. "Just turn my pages . . . with feeling."

"Listen, it's a whole lot better than being a defector or traitor—got to hand you *that* . . . let's hope."

"There, you see, even with all the Alden smarts and millions, I'm still your greatest asset."

With that facetious or half-hopeful remark, Laura reached behind and got her carrying case of cassettes. In Vienna, while we had cooled our heels waiting to get visas from the Czech embassy, she'd insisted on taking the Land Rover to an audio shop and having a very expensive Blaupunkt cassette stereo system installed, including four speakers, which had to be jerry-rigged as unobtrusively as possible in a vehicle that hadn't been designed for decibel-juiced joyriding. She pushed in her favorite, the Joni Mitchell *Blue* album tape, and turned up the volume, and stepped out onto the rainy pavement.

I wish I had a river I could skate away on . . .

A moment later, she was dancing with herself to the plaintive voice of Joni. I got out on the other side and, bemused or aghast—I wasn't sure which—watched her. Other drivers braved the drizzle for a better look, leaning on doors and sitting on the running boards of truck cabs, some amused, some a little spellbound—anything to break the boredom. Even the border police inspecting cars down the line stopped and turned their heads in our direction—just what we needed! And out there amidst the no-man's-land of mud and wire, a patrolling guard turned in slow motion to Joni's California siren song wafting across that sodden Styx to gaze upon a longhaired not so-young woman in jeans and sweatshirt dancing in circles with eyes half-closed, outstretched arms linked to invisible partners. The bemused guard patted the pricked-up ears of his Alsatian and offered a comical salute, like a Charon summoned to his duty.

I knew, of course, from Max's second novel that Joni Mitchell's *Blue* album was their signature leitmotif from the early seventies as their celebrity rocketed forth. They had an apartment on West End Avenue and Ninetieth and played Joni through the night while smoking dope and keeping a lookout for their dealer on the street. In the eighteen months I'd spent along the Vam Co Dong River, Joni's *Blue* album seemed to invoke a world I'd missed out on at the tail end of the anti-war movement, when most of the troops had left Vietnam, a time of introspection and yearning for a quieter spirituality after the uproar of the late sixties. I'd hear it in the Saigon bars, in the Cam Ranh Bay PX, along with James Taylor and Jackson Browne, and wonder how'd I'd gotten myself into the spot I'd gotten into, which Vlada and Max and Laura had had a lot to do with.

So, listening to Joni Mitchell along that divide of rusty barbed wire, stretched like airy incisions to the horizon, felt like a faltering tribute to an age of insouciant hopes that the world as we found it might be transformed by love and good sex—a hope I'd always had a hard time buying into.

When our turn came for inspection, I thought we would certainly have drawn extra scrutiny due to the antics of my shotgun-seat muse, but the border police halfheartedly checked our passports and visas, and then, with a cursory rummage through our bags, confiscated only our week-old copies of *Newsweek* and the *International Herald Tribune*, and sent us on our way. At my insistence, we'd stashed my father's and Suzanne's letters in a hotel safe in Vienna.

We had a visa for three days; when we finally made it back seven weeks later, the guards were gone, the fences down, and exuberant entrepreneurs were selling strands of barbed wire as souvenirs.

2303 P Street
Washington, D.C.
August 6, 1952

Dear Suzanne,

I know I missed you Saturday in New York. A crisis—another crisis; I just couldn't tear myself away from the office. I'm going stark raving crazy here on my tiny back patio with my lone scraggly, long-suffering gingko for company, and a few cicadas to keep me amused with their mating calls while I work the charts of Linear B.

New York is out-of-bounds for the foreseeable future.

I just had a call from Mary at Elysium. What the hell were you—or was it Charles Fairburn?—thinking, inviting her over for your daughter's birthday celebration and dinner? Are you mad! A slip of the tongue—anything—and the whole sorry mess could be out of the bag. Please, please, never do it or anything like that again; the idea of you two sitting at the same dinner table—that table!—with Bobby drives me to distraction. Mary went on and on about how you put your beautiful little girl in her arms, and how she now wants to go for a daughter herself.

I know how you're drawn to spit at fate by embracing it, but don't push your luck. McCarthy is on a rampage and the FBI is doing security clearances on every Tom, Dick, and Harry who ever dipped into *Das Kapital.*

Yes—to answer your last letter, of course some part of me still loves you—how can I not after all we've been through?—like a first breath, like memory of home and the wellspring of one's physical being. You are my nourishment, the soul of some malevolent and wild freedom from which I've been banished—never to return, to which I fear to even give a name. But the lying and uncertainty of this life just grinds one to dust. Longing for you—and hating myself for it—exhausts me. Living off the searing fumes of our furtive lovemaking hollows my heart. I see how you get charged up with risk, but it makes me only question everything. I mull over my stupid mistakes—things you can't even imagine. Philby is just the latest of my careless stupidities. I should've seen through him, just like I should have canceled the Albanian operations. I fear my judgment is faulty—and all we have in this awful job is faith that one's judgment has not been fatally compromised by all the cutting of corners. If one can't believe in one's integrity, much less the fundamental decency and integrity of one's country, how can one chance the lives and well-being of millions?

I can just see you laughing at me, the raw cynicism in your eyes burning in the moonlight—your higher morality. I can see you pulling off your clothes, touching your wet cunt, and holding out your fingers for me to suck. Why bother with saving a fallen civilization when I can fuck you to eternity? How can you exist so completely in the moment; it's a trick I yearn to steal from you, like fire from the gods. Time and age make triage seem the inevitable lot of our lives. The gods take away indiscriminately; they make one settle for half rations—they give us traitors like Philby to harrow our hearts and twist us into shadows of our former selves.

And don't think for a minute that just because Maclean and Burgess are gone to ground and Philby is under wraps in London, relentlessly—so MI5 assures—interrogated to confess, that you or I are out of danger. If Philby gives you up, I'm finished, as well. My office diary shows half a dozen lunches at the Met Club, and doubtless he picked my pockets of plenty of classified information. But it is one thing to be hoodwinked, another to be in bed with a KGB courier—even if you swear it wasn't for him. But no more meetings in New York. It will have to be Elysium—soon, weekend after next if I can get away.

Black clouds tumbled from an overwrought sky, scrubbing the greens of farm fields and low hills until smudged to a tarnished silver gray. Then torrential rains spattered the potholed road we were sharing with farmers' tractors and dilapidated diesel-spewing trucks. Explosive clods of mud from the tractor treads detonated on the windshield. Even the small farms along the route seemed eerily barren of life, except for the occasional herd of dirty cows or a wallowing pig. The rain was relentless, the potholes jawbreakers. I couldn't help thinking back to Karel Hollar's letters about searching for those Mycenaean roads, and Homer's ominous words as Telemachus sped toward Sparta: "And the roads of the world grew dark" I shivered as even the heater began to fail us. Only toward evening did the showers settle into a constant mist and the gray horizon yield up lurid rectilinear stockades of apartment blocks, their concrete facades pricked by patterns of urinous light. Then the narrow highway we'd followed all the way from the border turned into a modern six-lane boulevard with sleek aluminum streetlights fit for a German Autobahn. It was as if we'd suddenly been tipped onto a giant's concrete water slide, sluiced and rocketed into the medieval heart of Prague, city of spires and Kafka and cheap beer, so the guidebooks say, and a history of religious, ideological, and ethnic genocide going back to Jan Hus.

A real love nest.

"Tell me something: You said you wrote to Vlada about my father. Just how specific were you?"

"Roundabout, like Elliot told me."

"He advised you?"

"Sure. 'Don't use his name—just Peter's father and something to the effect he spent some unhappy months in Prague in 1954.'"

"Pleasantries, just in case the secret police read your letter?"

"Right."

"Did they?"

"Vlada didn't mention it. And he was equally general in his reply, a lot of personal stuff, with specifics tucked in between the lines. He and Max wrote each other quite a bit, you know, and the letters always got through."

"Did it look like his letter might have been opened?"

"Nope, but it wouldn't, right? You know about all that kinda shit, right?"

Blind leading the blind.

"We're thoroughly fucked is what I think."

My sense of apprehension only deepened as we found ourselves in a narrow, labyrinthine nightmare of one-way streets. I felt lost amidst a host of fearsome stony faces staring down from buildings and lintels, lips twisted in anguish, many with grotesque sneers, like slightly dyspeptic gods ready to bring down vengeance on intruders. Those damned creatures seemed to peer out from every dilapidated and dreary medieval and Baroque facade we passed. Of course, we'd failed to follow Vlada's instructions to make a reservation and every fleabag hotel was full. "You are ye-ew-en convention—no?" The city was booked up by a UN convention on Third World population growth, of all things. Laura had memorized a telephone number for Vlada. He'd given her precise instructions to take a room, call from a pay phone—he'd come to us. How do you put such precise and conspiratorial instructions in a convivial letter? I didn't ask.

After an hour of fruitless searching, Laura was soaked from her forays to hotel reception desks, and my back was one molten meltdown. Every cobblestone, every pothole added to my misery. Not a room to be had, and yet the city seemed deserted except for a steady flow of mostly East German two-cylinder Trabants packed with entire families, roaming the streets like lost souls—like us!

"Christ, you don't suppose they're looking for hotel rooms, too?" I glanced at Laura, who was torturing a strand of hair wrapped around a finger, as we passed yet another puffing Trabant filled with anxious faces. "Or the guy running the Xanax concession."

"I think they're looking for the West German embassy. That's what I heard at the last hotel; the receptionist asked in German if I wanted the West German embassy."

Then, out of the rising mist, a sign appeared in red letters: CEDOK TRAVEL AGENCY. The sign was illuminated by a lone wrought-iron lamp, a grotesque vinelike appendage of Belle Époque vintage—something out of a forties film noir.

"You stay put," I told Laura, needing to stretch.

I parked the Land Rover and she hunkered down in her seat, shivering, twisting that damp strand into knots.

Inside the Cedok office, I found an overweight matronly clerk, who curtly informed me that all the hotels in the city were full. Then she began to scold me for stupidity. "It is against regulations, yes, to come to Prague with no confirmed reservations . . . like stupid Germans from GDR!" Her heavily mascaraed eyes barely lifted from a ledger she was pawing through, as if mirroring the bowed figure of a Moorish slave holding up the lintel of the door through which I'd just passed. "Passport, visa, MasterCard—you have?" I handed them to her. She picked up a phone and made a call. Her face lighted up and then, after a brief conversation of exasperated grunts as she read my name and details into the receiver, she slammed down the phone. "One room," she snorted, "last room in all of Prague. Hotel Red Star—you will like very much." She smiled with something between pitiless irony and disdain as she noted the credit card details and, with an ink-stained digit raised, repeated her mantra. "Hotel Red Star . . . *and* with a river view."

2303 P Street, September 28, 1952

God yes, I'm disappointed about the news of Ventris getting the decipherment of Linear B, flabbergasted more like it. How could an architect with, it seems, from what Nigel Bennett told me, a genius for languages have pulled it off—that inspired leap that it was Greek and recognizing the place names for Knossos? I was sure it was Greek, too, since at least the thirties; that had been my working assumption. Of course, Alice Kober, who died two years ago, and whom I consulted with often at Princeton after the war, did so much of the preliminary work of identifying repeated syllables and their inflected endings. Without her charts and grids of the repeated syllable patterns, Ventris couldn't have pulled it off. I was so close—so close. If I hadn't been distracted for the last four years of madness, if only Elliott had left me be at Princeton, I would have broken the code two years ago—I'm sure of it. At least now we can translate the damn things, but so far it looks like pretty mundane stuff.

And please, no more resentment and jealously about Mary from you. And don't pretend you tried to like her with your little birthday get-together. Of course you don't—how could you. "My little golfer?" She is a stoic who takes her pleasure in small things. She gave up a lot to marry a near cripple like me—a champion tennis player before she switched to golf—yes, for me. She lives close to hearth and home. She does not want or need to cast her eyes wide and worry about the fate of civilization. Or, like you, plumb her soul for every glimmer of feeling and disappointment for your lost stardom—your lost goddamn cause! You are an artist—you live your inner life. But inner lives are not enough. I have a son and a country to defend. We can't just let ourselves get carried away forever, you and I. We've gotten so used to living close to the fire that we can no longer warm ourselves without a bonfire, and bonfires are for the young, who have the energy and the faith that the future belongs to them. All I see is the abyss of another dark age, if we don't first blow ourselves to kingdom come. How much longer do you think you can bend our sorry lives to the white heat of your desire?

We're both getting too old. Fucking's not enough.

What you can't seem to understand is that Mary and I are good for each another because we can get through the day at a snail's pace, and learn to live with less, to draw small pleasures from small things. Of course, you're a better lover—the world's champion—but idolatrous sex doesn't change the reality. Mary walks in the door and sees this tiny house as a kingdom of domestic bliss for her husband and child. She is happy to build a simple life in this world as it is—not in the constant friction of future doubt. Her future is in the creeping minutes of daily existence. Children need that; my son needs that, I need it. I need to remember that more than ever. I'd do anything to retreat back to Princeton and my scholarship—a whole new world has been opened up with the decipherment. She yearns to be a professor's wife and out of this rat race of infernal hubris that is Washington. I've promised her Princeton by the end of next year.

Love your daughter—let her be enough—and lay low.

Prepaid voucher in hand, I climbed back into the car and we ventured again into the miasma of one-way streets. I finally found the Vlatava River and, hugging the shore on a broad boulevard, headed north until our hotel hove into view. The Hotel Red Star turned out to be a converted nineteenth-century river steamer hovering in the fog off the edge of a waterfront parking lot. A closer inspection revealed a ghostly ship held fast to the shore by a series of steel beams welded to the hull and sunk into concrete pilings at bow and stern. Laura wrinkled her nose. The air was fetid with diesel and sulfur fumes—and worse: The river reeked like an open sewer. From somewhere, the telltale splash of a bilge pump. A rickety gangplank rose at a precipitous angle to the main deck. As I moved to the hotel entrance, the upper decks, as if I'd hit a trip wire, suddenly became illuminated in festoons of lightbulbs strung from the two funnels amidships to bow and stern. A large red star in neon lights blinked like a faulty heartbeat between the twin smokestacks, reminding me of smaller versions found on the lapels of North Vietnamese regulars, which our South Vietnamese militias avidly collected as good luck pieces.

"Fifty bucks a night for this stinking Dumpster," I said, bending from side to side, watching the hypnotic blinking.

Laura wiped at her damp hair. "Just as long as there's hot water and a shower."

A scuffling noise came from behind us. I turned and saw a small figure bent into the open tailgate of the Land Rover.

"Woaaa . . . there," I cried, rushing back to the car. This strange gnomelike creature was struggling with an armful of our bags.

"I will take bags—yes?" This seemed less a question than a command. The man was tiny, an overgrown midget with a birdlike face and heavy-lidded eyes; his hair, what there was of it, combed over a disproportionately large skull.

"No you don't," I said. "Put them down."

"I like to take bags to hotel."

"How'd you get into the back? It was locked."

Laura came up beside me and took my arm.

She said, "It was probably left unlocked at the border."

"I locked it again."

This elfin figure, his head turreting between us, pleaded once again. "I like to take bags."

"Drop them," I demanded.

He stepped back, clutching the bags more firmly.

Laura pointed. "He's wearing a uniform; he must be the porter."

I squinted in the poor light and could just make out an ill-fitting gray jacket with patched sleeves, matching trousers with faded red piping down the leg.

"Okay, okay." I waved disgustedly, and the man scurried off and started up the narrow gangplank, somehow maneuvering the bags through the constricted space and disappearing onto the deck above.

"What's with you?" she asked. "You've been uptight all day."

"Me? This whole thing stinks."

"Nobody twisted your arm."

She gathered up her cassettes and Walkman and headed up the gangplank.

The lobby, once upon a time a huge cabin on the main deck, was harshly lit with flickering fluorescent lamps reflecting off scuffed mustard-colored linoleum and a scattering of nearly opaque mirrors. A few sticks of threadbare Danish modern sulked in the corners.

"Mr. Alden," chimed out an attentive receptionist, "we have been expecting you. Passports and visas please."

The clerk, neatly shaved and groomed, inspected our documents with officious care, lingering on Laura's photo and then on her face, as if reminded of someone. I wondered if her celebrity life had even penetrated to this benighted backwater.

"We will keep the passports, and tomorrow we register them with the police. You are staying for three days—very good. The porter will show you to your room." The clerk flipped a key to the waiting porter the way an al fresco diner might toss a scrap of meat to a feral cat. The man scuttled off down a narrow and dingy corridor, looking not a little like a load of baggage on legs.

"The last room in Prague," I muttered to Laura.

We never saw another overnight guest at the Hotel Red Star.

Our room, a steerage-class cabin by any reckoning, was dirty, cramped, and dank-smelling: two tiny bunks, a single porthole rusted shut, a bathroom with a wooden floor, smelling of mildew. The porter dumped the bags and with manic hand movements proceeded to flutter around like an epileptic budgerigar, desperate to draw our attention to the amenities of the cabin, as if it were a suite at the Ritz. I held out a generous tip in hopes of getting rid of him, but the sight of the cash brought him to a dead halt. Had I insulted him? His fragile chin nodded thoughtfully; his eyes inspected our attentive faces. Then he retreated to the door, glanced out into the corridor with a conspiratorial furrowing of the brow, and pulled the door shut with a barely audible click.

"Would you be so kind to change money with me?" Suddenly, his English was near perfect. He bowed his head obsequiously. "If you have foreign currency, I can give you an exchange rate for Czech crowns that is substantially better than the official rate."

I gave Laura an incredulous look.

"We exchanged at the border," I countered, not a little taken a back at the educated tone.

"It's nothing." He sighed, as if disgusted at the mere thought. "The official exchange rate is a poor joke; in fact, it is scandalously absurd. I can give you a rate that cannot be bettered anywhere in Prague."

His beautiful voice, accompanied by his fiendish darting eyes, gave me the creeps.

"Beat it, okay—we have enough."

At this, he began a desperate pulling at something wedged deep in his pants pocket, finally working lose an enormous bankroll.

"I will give you the very best rate in all of Prague," he hissed, as if desperate to make a deal.

I went to the door and was about to open it to make clear our lack of interest, when Laura stepped forward and produced an Austrian thousand-shilling note from her jeans pocket.

"How about this?" she said, as if embarrassed to have discovered the crisp new bill on her person.

The porter, like a carnival performer repeating an old trick, snapped the shilling note from her fingers and, without so much as examining it, stuffed it into his pocket and proceeded to count out a huge pile of ratty Czech currency on the bureau, doing so with practiced theatricality until the pile spilled over.

"Please enjoy our fair city." The porter backpedaled from the cash, bowing and smiling, and in a matter of seconds slipped out the door.

"That was a mistake," I said.

"I felt sorry for him." Laura went and gathered up the notes. "Mad money. We'll have a blowout. We'll get drunk. You'll make mad love to me, like in the Plaka."

She batted her eyelashes, as she often did to make light of the endearments she offered.

"Do you want to call Vlada, or do you want me to?"

She headed for the shower. "He's *your* friend."

I sat on my sagging bed—another ominous sign—and contemplated the antique rotary phone on the bedside table. I hadn't seen a house phone in the lobby, and the hotel was a long, rainy walk from any pay phone I might or might not find nearby. I called the number Vlada had given Laura. There were a series of strange clicking sounds and abrupt dial tones, and I imagined an electronic signal passing through exchange after exchange and wandering down wires strung through those eerie, rain-swept medieval streets until some feeble electronic impulse found its way into an anonymous room and caused some similar piece of antique equipment to herald my belated arrival. Finally, a Slavic-sounding man's voice answered. I asked for Vlada Radec. There was a pause, as if my English had startled the person on the other end. Then in cautious but educated English the man asked for my number and the hotel where I was staying. Then I was told to hang up and wait for a return call. In ten minutes, the phone rang and the same voice as before gave instructions for me to go to the hotel parking lot in an hour and wait. The line went dead. I lowered the receiver and reached to the iron bulkhead at my shoulder and found the paint-chipped rivets sweaty and oozing rust.

2303 P Street, N.W.
September 3, 1953

Don't you dare call the office again, or the house—never! And no more letters—anything you do like that puts us in jeopardy. The FBI is tapping phones all over town. With the new administration, security has never been tighter. I'll write to you at Hermitage when and if I can. I'll try to get away in a week or so—all hell is breaking loose in East Germany.

Believe me, I'd do anything to get away. My office is a sweltering pigpen. Washington has been hellish all summer. I arrived at work this morning to find my secretary's luncheon sandwich suspended by a piece of string on a pipe in the ceiling. Ants, she tells me; it's the only way to preserve her lunch from attack. The office smells, too, damp in the summer, drafty in the winter; and from such digs we are supposed to take over the running of the world and keep the barbarians from the gates. Allen Dulles and his big bluff of a brother have me over all the time for consultations; they are desperate for a breakthrough in Eastern Europe—salivating over the uprisings in East Germany. Allen thinks because I played football for his beloved Princeton that I must be some kind of superman, when I'm just a glorified ditchdigger at heart.

Be careful to whom you speak and what you say. Elliot Goddard gave me a start the other day, back from Berlin for consultations with his new boss—as hard-charging as ever. Over lunch he brought up your wedding at Colonel Fairburn's "splendid faux-Tudor pile in lovely Sussex"—that perfectly glorious English spring day, where he met Margaret. He tends to wax nostalgic, but I think he did it just to feel me out, to see if we are still in touch. He's curious about Charles Fairburn, too, hanging about the British embassy here as much as he does; he says Angleton suspects Charles is with MI5 and that all his RAF business is just a cover.

And don't delude yourself; just because Bobby is out of circulation and a decorated veteran, it doesn't mean he's safe from further scrutiny or revelations by HUAC. Elliot assures me they have his name—and yours—and the political atmosphere in Washington is poisonous. The new administration is accusing Truman of having harbored Soviet spies and losing Eastern Europe—and China, and Korea—to the Communists. If it is ever revealed that Bobby passed on information about the Norden bombsight, you two could end up like the Rosenbergs. Don't fail to burn this letter. *DO NOT WRITE.* I'll find a way to get up soon, I promise. But I'm not going to compromise my job or my marriage—nor should you. If I were you, I'd tell Charles to keep his fucking distance from you and his goddaughter. No word on the Philby interrogations in London, or nothing MI5 will share. Allen threatened to end all liaisons on intelligence matters with London if they don't put Philby away for good. Better pray they don't break him; they won't settle for anything less than a complete confession. Why don't you ask your love-struck Charles how they're doing with Philby—if you dare! Just keep your head down.

We began our wait for Vlada standing by the hotel entrance at the bottom of the gangplank. Fog swelled up frothy and sulfurous yellow from the invisible river, where it began cascading into the parking lot like an insidious tide of ooze, sniffing at the tires of parked cars. A misting of rain seemed to have settled over the known world. I could sense that Laura was out of sorts. She started if I touched her. She didn't hold my hand the way she'd always done since Athens. It just floored me how blasé she could be about things of the body, as if everything came down to a roll of the biological dice: "If you don't get me banged up, I'll try for a third comeback—if any company will have me." Her insouciant devil-take-the-hindmost attitude, disconcertingly echoed in the love letters, left me exhausted with performance anxiety. Now, as we waited in the merging mist and fog, I sensed that even her capricious soul had been worn down by the baleful stare of Lady Luck and her many handmaidens peopling the facades of Prague.

A nonstop parade of cars began to arrive in the parking area. And not junky Czech Škodas, or the smoke-belching East German Trabants we'd seen earlier, but the most expensive and flashy German and Italian sports cars. Out of silver and red Mercedes, Porsches, and Ferraris emerged gorgeous, well-dressed young couples—cheekbones to kill. They looked like movie stars, cocky and laughing between drags on their Marlboros, huddling together as they dashed through the mist as if to avoid a gauntlet of paparazzi, when all they had to suffer were our bemused stares as they passed quickly up the gangplank. A few shot us airy looks of dismissal at our ratty clothes, as if questioning our very existence. The receptionist who had relieved us of our passports stood at the top of the gangplank with clipboard in hand and dutifully checked off names as he scrutinized faces.

Laura touched my arm.

"What's that all about?"

"Search me."

"Did you notice how they're dressed?"

"Pretty snappy, I guess."

"Like . . . the most recent Milanese and Paris fashions, expensive as all get-out."

Laura self-consciously swept a hand over the thighs of her tight jeans and fingered her NYCB Balanchine Festival navy blue sweatshirt. "I have nothing warm to wear," she said as she turned to yet another laughing and joking scrum of suits and tight dresses passing us without a glance. Petulant at such neglect, Laura shook her still-damp ponytail—lukewarm water and no adapter for her hair dryer—reflecting a crimson glow from the decks above, where the five-pointed red star continued its Mayday calls out of the enveloping fog. "Hear that?" She directed her gaze toward the upper deck. A vague and tantalizing aquamarine glow filtered from oblong windows on the poop deck, the flash of strobe lights . . . and then a slow, steady pounding, as if an antique steam engine had begun laboring in the bowels of the ship. My hearing, never great since Vietnam, barely discerned the disco beat. She shivered and grabbed my hand.

"The hell with this bullshit," she said. "Let's wait in the car."

As we walked to the Land Rover, two pairs of headlights eased into the parking lot, two huge Mercedes sedans slithering across our bow.

"Creepy weird—huh?" she said, climbing into the car and staring through the misted windshield.

She fumbled among her cassettes in the glove compartment and fed one into the new stereo system, in theory, according to the audio technician in Vienna, as good as the ones in those passing Mercedes. It was Crosby, Stills & Nash, the 1968 recording from our senior year—when Vlada had sung many of the same songs at the fall dance—like an anthem to our failed dreams, or, in Laura's mind, to mark the anniversary of when I'd first failed her: a causal chain of events that, unfolding by circuitous paths, had led us to this place. Sitting in the fog, cocooned in memories of a shared disaster, I realized she was trying to prepare me for something: how her underlying decency always confounded the telling of hard truths, until their inevitable unleashing did more harm than good. My heart lurched as it had on those jungle trails along the east bank of the Vam Co Dong River, when an unusual cast of light, a broken branch, a muddy sandal print got my head pounding like a steam cooker.

Had it really been her first dance with Max when the itch took hold (in his novel, it is the moment he falls in love with her)? But then she had danced with Vlada, too, before he had disappeared back to the library, where his books awaited him, and only a few weeks later, when his father died, he'd returned to Prague, becoming a specter in our lives. Or was it really as simple as my flunking Sex 101?

"I wanted to tell you something."

For lack of an erection . . .

"Do your worst," I replied.

"You know . . . Max and Vlada stayed in touch. Max even came to Prague for a PEN International Writers' Conference and tried to get him a visa for—"

"You've already told me this."

Teach your children well/ Their father's hell did slowly go by/ And feed them on your dreams/ The one they pick's/ the one you'll know by . . . .

Beyond the misted windshield, a point of orange light materialized near the edge of the parking lot. The spark, passing upward to the face of an indistinct figure leaning against a telephone pole, flared and was tossed to the ground. I flashed the headlights. The figure froze in place, watching. I opened my door, as Laura did hers. I was filled with the sensation of violating some hermetic seal, exposing our safe time capsule to the perils of blind contingency. There was the sound of footsteps on broken tarmac and the soft outline of a pale, longhaired man giving wide berth to the expensive cars that now bunkered the entrance to the hotel.

Vlada came toward me. He took my hand and we embraced. Tears of shame filled my eyes. The smell of damp permeated his workman's clothes, which gave off the scents of cigarette smoke, sweat, plaster, and concrete. A black beret was pulled down over his large brow. Lank dirty blond hair dripped onto the collar of his sweater. He patted my back, caught sight of Laura, and moved to her. They embraced and remained embracing for long seconds, lingering like that until the headlights from another Mercedes drove them apart.

I pulled the shotgun seat forward and Vlada slipped into the rear of the Land Rover. Laura turned down the music and Vlada laughed and made a show of playing a guitar, nodding his head and singing along for a few bars. We stared and laughed, as if nothing had changed. But even in the ambient light, he'd clearly aged—not in slack at the jaw, but in his hardened and weathered features, characteristic of grinding outdoor work, the dark bags under his darting, wary eyes. His wide Slavic cheekbones set off a nose that now looked slightly distorted, as if broken since last I'd seen him. Vlada flicked drops of water from his chapped and colorless lips, unable to preserve a fading smile. His ratty sweater and green canvas pants and work boots were caked with dried concrete.

"How did you find such a place?" he asked, short-circuiting our nostalgic interlude with a disgusted wave toward the river and the hotel.

"The Cedok Travel Agency," I said with a shrug. "I was told there were no other hotel rooms in Prague."

He made an obscene gesture and snorted.

"This place is only for apparatchiks, for their spoiled children, where they can keep them safe and happy. They have their disco here. This is no place for you."

"Disco?" echoed Laura.

We turned and stared toward that *Flying Dutchman* of a river steamer and the inflamed bee-stung glow on the topmost deck.

"Of course, a dancer must have her disco." Vlada laughed with a labored heartiness and bent forward to better see Laura's face. "Now I perfectly understand Max's novel about you." And he quoted, as if reciting directly from *Gardens of Saturn*: "'. . . that recklessly beautiful woman who gloried in breaking the hearts of her admirers—not with scorn, but by envy of her powers to transform a life onstage into an unattainable glory, as cold and efficient as a goddess on a high . . . which was often the case.'"

"Oh, my God, no . . ." Laura groaned.

"Here"—Vlada handed her a bulging envelope—"for the immortal muse. I believe this is what you wanted, Max's letters."

Not a word to me about those letters.

In the instant he handed her the envelope, I knew that she'd slept with Vlada. I knew with such absolutely certainty that I could barely turn the ignition; I knew she had walked away from me that night on the Circle and lost her virginity to him.

Once we were under way, all willpower drained from my body; I was an acolyte at his disposal, relieved to be directed through the winding, rain-swept streets, as I had on that fall night when we broke into Fort Devens. Each command filled me with bitter joy.

Our destination was a restaurant in the Staré Město, Prague's Old Town. Vlada was being exceedingly careful: choosing a circuitous route, constantly checking to see if we were being followed, then selecting a parking space behind a building, where the Land Rover could not easily be spotted from the street. We entered an inconspicuous door, over which a red neon carnation glowed faintly against a wall of sooty stucco, and then felt our way down a long, unlit staircase, and finally, passing through velvet curtains, we emerged into a vast subterranean nightclub. Cigarette smoke eddied in the carmine glow of small table lamps, where hushed couples bent in whispered alliances. A mirrored globe twisted over a tiny dance floor, sprinkling the lethargic dancers with shards of tarnished silver as they eddied in the back draft of a mournful Benny Goodman standard. A vision stirred from the depths of a Depression-era dance marathon.

Vlada steered us quickly to a back corner, passing huge Klimt-like murals of blond Nordic gods in horned helmets and gold chain mail, where, writhing in wan sensuality at their sandaled feet, a covey of flaxen-haired brides or slave mistresses stared longingly at their diffident masters.

After a brief argument with a waiter who vehemently objected to Vlada's preemptory table selection, money was exchanged, tempers cooled, and menus appeared.

"Socialist equality," hissed Vlada as he lighted up a cigarette and tossed his empty pack to the floor. He took the menu from my hand. "Don't worry; I'll do the ordering. When the Soviets have a bad harvest, all the best cuts of meat go east and we are left with pig guts."

Vlada gestured with little chopping motions, his calloused hands agitating the smoky air as he launched into an explanation of Czechoslovakia's spiritual malaise. The chilblained joints of his fingers were reddened and puffy, the nails broken, caked with patches of something impervious to vigorous scrubbing. I became acutely aware of the ricocheting glances exchanged with Laura. As hard as he tried to reestablish the male camaraderie of twenty years before at Winsted, he was clearly drawn to Laura, either in her role as muse to Max or as reminder of an unfinished romantic interlude—perhaps both. I kept wondering who was going to admit it to me first. He looked beyond exhaustion, every gesture a testy protest at some malevolent conspiracy preying on his mind. With the wine and our questions, his tone became increasingly confessional as he tried to justify his sudden departure before Christmas '68, more, I sensed, for Laura's sake than mine. How he'd never forgiven himself for not seeing his father again before he died of a heart attack. Then he was making excuses for his stubborn refusal to take up the invitation to a PEN International Writers' Conference in Paris that Max had wrangled for him five years before. A chance to escape.

"Would they have given me a visa? Sure." He grimaced and waved toward the sea of diners. "But without my subjects, where would I be?"

I realized that the table he'd picked, in the corner, in dense shadow—and seating himself between us—allowed him to watch the comings and goings in near anonymity.

"See, look at them"—he gestured to the phantom dancers under the diffident gaze of the Nordic princes on the muraled walls—"the tanks are gone from the streets for twenty years, but their spirits are crushed. They still groan in their sleep. They hear the treads of the tanks on the cobblestones, the cough of the motors and the rattle of machine guns. They have grown old on the fears of their childhood and youth: fear in their mothers' milk. They are slaves to the tales of war told them by the old men, first of the Jews destroyed, then the Sudeten Germans, the Trotskyite apostates—the endless list." He raised an admonishing finger, as if to correct himself, with a sardonic smile at Laura, who sat intently listening. "But nobody starves."

He kept returning to his father's last weeks, a sick man confined to his apartment, while Vlada had been "trapped" at Winsted. How all the liberal reforms of the Dubček era had been rolled back—his father's life's work "come to nothing." Vlada had gotten back just in time for the funeral. He'd been devastated that the police outnumbered the mourners. The privileged world of his childhood as the son of a government minister had evaporated, replaced by something sinister and alien.

"I tried to honor the work of my father when I was a student at Charles University. I was editor of a student literary magazine. Just essays and poetry and short stories. . . . After six months, I was arrested for antistate activity. Then I was no longer a student." He snapped his fingers. "I had no money. No job and no work permit. They told me I could teach school in the country, not academics, but football and gymnastics, at a place near Mladá Boleslav. You haven't heard of it, but it's far from here, a school for the sons and daughters of peasants. Then there were complaints from the parents about how I talked to my students, when we discussed the '68 Olympics and our gymnastics team. Again, no job. I came back to Prague and lived with friends. The police were always there, asking questions. My mother, my sister, and her husband were afraid to have me come to their apartment; they were warned they would lose their jobs if they tried to help me. In the last ten years, I have been allowed to work as a manual laborer on state construction projects. I carry the bricks and I dig. I pour the concrete for the socialist vision. Perhaps as you arrived in Prague you saw some of my masterpieces; they are everywhere, reaching to the sky outside the city."

Vlada smiled uneasily, as if concerned we might interpret his words as soliciting pity. He took a long swallow of wine, closed his jittery eyes, and then opened them wide, as if intent to collect his thoughts. For just an instant, I thought I detected the old spark I remembered from football days.

"My books are banned in Czechoslovakia. Even my father's early publications, his poetry and short stories from the war years, are prohibited. As I told Max, I owe it to him to stay. The old men would be delighted for me to take a visa and run away to Paris or London like Kundera—he, too, has urged me to leave. But this is my home"—he gave Laura a significant look—"as *your* Max liked to say—my material."

He reached to her arm and gave it a squeeze and then turned to me. "And then when Laura contacted me through my publisher in Vienna and told me about your father, that he had been imprisoned in Czechoslovakia—how interesting it wasn't you, Peter, who contacted me—I dismissed her story as crazy. Until"—he raised a finger and glanced around to make sure no one was in earshot, or perhaps the writer in him was intent on dramatizing his narrative hook for his listeners—"I spoke with an old friend of my father's . . . and I saw the fear in his sad eyes."

"So you really did find something?" My relief must have been obvious—that Laura hadn't concocted this reunion with her onetime lover on a bogus premise—for Vlada smiled and patted my arm.

"My father's friend, now an old man, was a member of the government back in the early 1960s—he had survived the war, the bloodbath after, the show trials of the fifties. He is a philosopher by training, in the ministry of education in '68, a reformer and confidant of Václav Havel, a man with deep roots in Czechoslovakia, who worked in the Resistance against the Germans in the war. He knew all about an American agent who was captured in the GDR, or perhaps here in Czechoslovakia, on the border with Hungary. He was held for a long time, maybe a year in Pankrác Prison. Not a beauty spa, I can tell you. My father was there for five months before he died; I have been arrested and held there three times. Three years ago, I was there for nine months."

"How do you know you can trust anything this guy told you?"

Vlada lifted his bloodshot eyes to me with a puzzled but amused gleam—my brittle tone as yet unaccounted for. He held up the outspread fingers of one hand.

"I can absolutely trust five people, including Havel, and he is one of them, one of us; he was one of the few at my father's bedside when he died, and at the funeral."

"What more could he tell you about the circumstances of his capture—and what happened to him?"

"A secret that even after so many years would mean his death. Even meeting with me, the younger generation, was taking a big risk." Vlada snapped his fingers. "Like this, and his pension is gone, his children's jobs are finished—or he, too, disappears into Pankrác." Vlada demonstrated with a gesture of putting an upward-pointing finger to the nape of his neck. "He told me in strict confidence that this was not a Czech matter, but a Soviet matter . . . and little Czechoslovakia better not complain to their bosses." He shot his crusted eyebrows for emphasis. "This man—I cannot give you his name, for it would endanger you and him if I told you—was still bitter about this incident; he called it an affront to our pride, our sovereignty—our socialist humanity. He gave me a document that might be of use to you." Vlada raised his hand in a gesture to halt himself, and then, with a merry-go-round motion of his finger, continued. "You cannot trust anybody. The old men have their eyes and ears everywhere. Our waiter has probably already reported us to the security police. I must be careful—not for me, you understand, but for the friend I have spoken to. He was a true friend of my father's and I don't want to endanger his last years; his health is failing."

Strangely, it was not his revelation about my father that most moved me, but the care he took in protecting his own—his solidarity with this older generation of reformers under Dubček who had paid such a harsh price after the Prague Spring of 1968. It was the loyalty of a son for his father, the very thing that had so captivated me at Winsted . . . even as his gaze drifted again and again to Laura, where her intently watching blue eyes took in his every word.

The surly waiter brought another bottle of wine and then lingered by the table. I saw Vlada's eyes roll with irritation as he fell silent, waiting for the waiter to leave.

"So," he said as the waiter finally moved off, "he's made the call and has been told to keep an eye on us." With this, Vlada reached under his sweater and pulled out a book, which he must have concealed in the waistband of his pants. He pushed his translation of *Gardens of Saturn* over to Laura.

The title was in Czech, with MAXWELL ROBERTS printed in small caps on the bottom edge of a pale blue cover of cheap cardboard. The jacket illustration showed a young ballerina dancing on a darkened stage in front of a huge family portrait in a gilded frame, a cruel caricature of a nineteenth-century robber baron.

"I translated it last year—anonymously, but the fee was quite good. The publisher was told to change the title to *A Flight from Infamy*. It passed the Party censors and has sold more copies in Czechoslovakia than all my combined sales in the United States and Europe. It is very popular among young women readers, I am told."

Laura tentatively reached for the book, as if it might be radioactive. She fanned the pages and examined the cover.

"The virus spreads."

"It's a fine book," said Vlada. "You will see in Max's letters that he asked me to do the translation." I noted the proprietary tone in his voice. "The publisher told the party apparatchiks that it was an indictment of capitalism by a famous American author. But it is nothing of the kind. I find it a sad and beautiful book, of dreamers who have failed to survive the new age, of a family and way of life on the edge of extinction."

"*Edge of extinction* . . ." Laura whistled mockingly, looking from me to Vlada. "Oh great, I guess that's me in spades." She shoved the book back toward Vlada. "I hope your translation . . . all the fucking lies . . . didn't infect your own writing."

"Of course it is a lie; every book is a lie. But beautiful lies, artistic lies that touch on the truth in us all."

"*Lies* are lies," she retorted, draining her third glass.

"What is important is that you believe in the fiction, the internal logic of its truth. The reader is free to choose to believe or not, to embrace the story or discard it. Fiction is our ultimate way of freedom."

"Not if you're exploiting other people's lives . . ." She shot me a burning look of solidarity. "Right?"

Vlada smiled, staring into her eyes, his voice lower, searching. "Art is not a religion or ideology that insists on belief or threatens damnation. Great art demands choice, the struggle of a critical mind. The best enlarges our freedom."

Laura met his stare with a compression of her brows. "You ask too much of art."

"But you are an artist, too. Is not your illusion"—and Vlada made motions like a puppet master with his fingers—"a beautiful lie? Max wrote about this so brilliantly; when you perform, the audience believes only in the illusion, not in a woman like themselves who bleeds and shits, but a goddess."

An uneasy silence fell across our table. The subject at hand, I sensed, echoed a thousand conversations Laura had had with Max, if not a few of our own. I felt thankful I was an historian on my Olympian perch, delivering judgments at a two-millennia remove.

Vlada bent toward us.

"When I was young, when I knew you at Winsted, I was proud of my father's philosophical and political writings. People still talk about them, but nobody, I think, really loves them. Even I have fallen out of love. Now what I love are his early works during the war, his poetry and short stories. That was how he survived. You see, my father was Jewish, but not truly Jewish. Do you know why? Because four hundred years ago, they were Protestant and converted to Judaism so they wouldn't have to become Catholic. Yes, it is so. Can you believe such a thing? They thought, Okay, maybe for ten years or twenty, until things are better. But things did not get better, and then they forgot why they had done what they had done . . . they forgot who they were, and so remained Jewish, even though they were not Jewish. And then in the eyes of the world, they were Jews. My father was taken to a concentration camp in 1943, a place called Terezin; he was sixteen and survived only because he pretended to be a child, a child who does not understand evil the way an adult understands. His wealthy parents died of the hardship and shock. He survived by hiding and telling himself stories.

"Terezin, you see, was liberated by the Soviets—why he first became a Communist; he knew from a young age the paranoia of the Soviet character. In the concentration camp, he became used to a life of the slave without power over one's fate, a place where people were put on trains to Auschwitz and never returned. So he told himself stories about a forest in a faraway place where children lived when their parents went away. In this place, the children were adopted by the trees. The trees took care of them and fed them and sheltered them. At night, the children went to sleep in the trees and became the branches of the trees, the leaves their hair. From behind the barbed wire of the camp, he could see some four or five large elms that had been left standing when the camp was built, and beyond the elms, mountains. For the rest of his life, a line of trees—like in a landscape painting, do you see?—with hills beyond represented the freedom of childhood. He loved trees; he loved mountains. When he died . . . my mother found him by the window of their apartment in his favorite chair. He was staring across the street to the park, where there were tall trees and, beyond this, beyond the river, the distance hills of Prague. In his adult life, except between 1945 and 1948, and for a few years before 1968, he was never truly free. Only in his early stories about the inner lives of children was he truly free . . . where he felt safe. Two years ago, I got all his short stories and poetry published in Vienna."

"And your own stories?" I asked, not a little spellbound by his ruminations. "I remember some very good ones you read me in the library at Winsted."

"A strange life for me. I grew up the son of an important government official, a nice apartment, the best schools like those kids you saw in the parking lot in their Mercedes. When I got back from Winsted after six months in your wonderful country, I found everything gone. Freedom, hope, my father—gone. And everybody was so afraid. They all told me I was an idiot. 'Why did you come back?' they asked. But I never saw the tanks and the people who died. For me, it is always an illusion," and he waved a hand theatrically, as would a conjurer. "I try to see like the others, but it is like a dream I have forgotten. My days in America, they burn in my mind. Here, all I know is the weight of fear from the war and later. I still can't believe it—isn't that crazy? Twenty years and I still feel as if I'm living in an imaginary world. I want to wake up, but I can't . . . surrounded by madmen."

"And you're not frightened?" Laura asked, clutching her glass.

"Sure, I can tell you this, I don't want to be arrested again. I was in solitary confinement three years ago for nine months. No books, no writing—nothing, alone. . . . That scares me, now—not like when I was young. That I could lose my mind to depression. For nine months, I wrote a novel in my head; I memorized every word. So yes, I try to be careful."

I found the note of caution in his voice distressing. Some part of me still longed for the fervor behind his once-fearless smile . . . climbing that fence at Fort Devens . . . even if it had led me to a jungle clearing and a crossing point along the Vam Co Dong River.

As if reading my mind, he went on: "A day doesn't pass when I don't think about a visa. When I don't think about my time in America. Some of my best friends have gone to Paris . . . and then you disappear; what is there to write about?" He smiled and opened his empty palms, calloused and reddened, his fingers nervously tapping the table.

"Milan Kundara seems to have managed it," said Laura, glancing down at Vlada's drumming fingers.

"He's brilliant; he brought his stories with him. But are there any more stories from Milan? We shall see."

"A present," Laura exclaimed with a burst of pent-up, inebriated energy. "A small quid pro quo." She pulled a couple of packs of Kent cigarettes out of her purse and, with a sheepish glance in my direction, handed them to Vlada. A gift from one addict to another. Although swearing she'd quit months before, in Vienna I'd occasionally detected a smoky aftertaste in her minty kisses.

Vlada's face lit up and he fondled one of the packs, lovingly breaking the cellophane seal.

"But aren't things changing?" I asked. "Certainly Gorbachev's economic reforms have made a difference? I was reading just the other day in the *Herald Tribune* about East Germans escaping through Hungary, lots of them. And we saw some East Germans driving around Prague as we came in tonight, looking for the West German embassy—what was that all about?"

Vlada lit up a Kent and flopped back in his seat, his body relaxing as he exhaled.

"It's all a Stasi trick. Czechoslovakia is a special case. We have been disappointed so many times by history that nobody believes anything anymore. Glasnost and perestroika are a joke for the Western media, to sew complacency. Things go on as before." Vlada tapped the pack of Kents and bent to kiss Laura's cheek. "A gift of the gods."

"Everything changes . . . *in the end*," said Laura, as if feeling no pain.

The waiter finally arrived with dinner and another bottle. Vlada kept looking at his watch and, between voracious mouthfuls, sparring more and more with Laura, who, I got the feeling, was trying to deflate his enthusiasm for Max, downplay her role as his muse, or, more likely, trying to feel her way back to some fleeting image of the exotic eighteen-year-old boy she'd lost her virginity to, who, so she told me later, lay crying in her arms after they made love.

"We don't have the luxury to play so lightly with our fate the way American writers do. You have never been an occupied country. The Catholics, the Nazis, and Soviets, then the Czech nationalists, and then the Communists all divide the world into enemies; they encourage one group to destroy the other: Protestants, Jews, Communists, Gypsies, and Sudeten Germans—or the rich, or their class enemies, until there is no morality left except survival by destroying others. It falls to the writer to remember who we once were, our common humanity, and where we came from. It is the nothingness of the lie that the Party upholds with terror, a kind of death mask for a former life. Our lot in this infernal machinery is to hold death's door open just wide enough that the light of day gives some hope. So we don't forget."

"Hey," said Laura, a little fed up with what she always called "existential writer mumbo-jumbo," "it doesn't mean you can't have a good time on the road to hell—right? Max sure enjoyed *his* ride, let me tell you, infernal machinery and all. Got him laid big-time: Those writers' conferences were his free pass to whoredom."

This outburst of pique quieted things for a moment as Vlada drew deeply on his cigarette, sighed, and nodded.

"I wish I could write stories like Max of the sweet problems of ordinary life. Instead, I must write the stories of lives that never were and the truth that lies buried behind the facade."

He made a gesture of a mask concealing something. But Laura was having none of it; she touched my arm and pointed, and as I looked to the dance floor, she grabbed a cigarette and lit up.

"Let me tell you something." She made a face at me and blew a stream of smoke away from our table. "When I'm onstage, when I'm really *on*, I bring them back to life—my audience. They live—if just for a few moments; they come alive to themselves." She leaned forward within inches of Vlada's face. "I make them fucking live—right here, in the here and now—not through any fucking death's door."

"Bravo." He clapped. And then with a look of biting sarcasm, he added, "You are just as I imagined you to be from his novel."

"Lucky you. Lucky, too, you didn't have to put up with his thousand and one groupies and hangers-on. Not to mention his mood swings and his morbid search for his Jewish roots—and now his fans blame me."

Vlada leaned into her halo of smoke as if to minutely examine his rival. "He was a conspirator, like all Jews who have had to survive by betrayal."

Laura took another gulp of her wine. "The worst was how much he hated everything about his background, his Red grandparents, his social-climbing father, when all he really longed for was to be an uncomplicated WASP like Peter."

"Me!"

"He fucking loved you—don't you get it? He always said he couldn't write without being in bed with his subject. That's why he could never finish his third novel about his own goddamn family."

Vlada laughed and signaled for the check.

"I must go. I have been up since five this morning, and the same tomorrow."

Laura pulled from her purse the stack of currency she'd exchanged with the porter at the hotel.

"Here, let me pay," she said. "I'm loaded." She threw the money on the table with a show of disgust.

"You exchanged so much?" asked Vlada.

"The porter at the hotel," I said, "was very insistent on changing money with us."

Vlada rolled his eyes.

"This is how they trap you. Now you have black-market currency in your possession. You are only allowed to exchange at the official rate, and this is recorded on your visa. If you have more, they can put you in jail or make you pay a fine. It is an old game. So, yes, thank you, pay for everything, get rid of your money . . . stay and dance."

The waiter arrived with the bill and Laura unloaded a fraction of the cash.

"We'll drive you home," I offered, seeing how totally beat he looked.

"No, you stay. Buy some Soviet Champagne and caviar . . . dance. Better I leave alone. We will meet in Wenceslas Square by the flagpole in front of the National Museum at three tomorrow, okay?" Vlada put a hand on my shoulder. "You will meet the friend of my father; perhaps he will have more details for your ears. But it is dangerous and you must come alone. Park outside the Old Town. Park on a side street, leave your car, and walk. Keep walking. Lose yourself. Take an hour or two. Lose yourself in our socialist paradise. Make sure no one is following you. Then you come to the flagpole, and when you see me, you continue walking, and I will follow. I will be wearing a hat. If I take the hat off, then walk toward your car. If I keep the hat on, forget it. Go to a café and I will contact you later at your hotel. And one more thing . . ." Vlada got a slip of paper out of his pocket and handed it to me, pointing out the key words. "Here is the name of a shop for chocolates in Wenceslas Square, and here the name of the selection and the price of the box. Buy only this one and bring it with you, and the receipt, when we meet." He smiled wearily, "a gift for an old friend."

With these cryptic instructions, Vlada turned to Laura, thanked her for the cigarettes, and, after giving her a chaste kiss, disappeared through a back entrance.

32

CIA INVESTIGATIVE REPORT, MAY 23, 1954: INTERVIEW WITH SUBJECT'S MOTHER

"Mrs. Alden, when he got the call from the duty officer on the morning he left your place here, did he seem surprised or particularly upset by the call?"

"You should really talk to my daughter-in-law, Mary, John's wife, about that, but nothing I could see. He seemed to have almost expected it. I know he always had to leave a number for the State Department so they could find him on a moment's notice. He seemed serene, in fact; he packed up his bag, got all his things in his room—the room he had at the very top of the house since he was a child—squared away, and then spent time down at the boathouse smoking before coming up to say good-bye to Mary and Peter in the kitchen."

"Did he say good-bye to you, as well?"

"Of course he did; he's my son. And it was Allen Dulles, not a duty officer."

"John was saying—how can I put it?—emotional good-byes . . . as if he might not be coming back for a while?"

"We always have long good-byes in this family, especially at Elsinore. We have our roots here—well, my husband's family. The place is in John's blood, as it is now in mine. My son was conceived here."

"In the few days he was here, when he drove up from Washington, did he seem under undue pressure—out of sorts with his family, his wife?"

"I understand you gentleman have been under a great deal of pressure, what with the war in Korea, and the Soviet Union exploding a nuclear bomb. John and I spoke about that quite a bit—certainly a discouraging situation. But you know better than I that John couldn't really talk about his work . . . if you take my meaning."

"Did he complain about that, not being able to talk to his family about his job?"

"I think so, I hope so anyway."

"Do you know, when John was here, did he spend time with his neighbor—there, across the lake, the Williamses' place—Hermitage? I believe he and Robert Williams were friends from school—Winsted, wasn't it, so I gather."

"Not that I know about. But it's a big place. People stumble upon one another all the time along the trails, at the bathing beach. My son was not really close to Bobby Williams, not since childhood."

"And his wife; what about Suzanne Williams?"

"She is only a very recent addition to our woods. A British war bride, who takes wonderful care of her injured husband. I suggest you go talk to her, or perhaps you already have."

"Suzanne Williams is a remarkably beautiful woman. I gather she had been a ballet star back in England before the war. I think she knew your son during the war, when she was a nurse at a rehabilitation hospital."

"Gentlemen, my son is happily married, and has a two-year-old son. Our life here, gentlemen, is very different from, well, that of your English country house set. . . . We have standards that we live by."

"So, did you notice anything at all unusual in the days before his departure?"

"I sensed he had much on his mind, but he was a man who always did, like his father, who was a wonderful surgeon and developed many innovative surgical techniques before he was killed in the Great War."

"So nothing out of the ordinary?"

"He promised to write and let me know how things were going."

"What things?"

"In Germany, I suppose. You know he spent quite a bit of time there as a student, studying at Leipzig with some of the greatest archaeologists of the day. My son . . . he was famous before the war as an archaeologist. A little hard to believe these days."

"And did he write—have you heard from him?"

"Not a word. But I'm sure he has been busy. Surely you must know what he's doing—you said you worked together?"

"Does the name Kim Philby ring a bell with you by any chance?"

"If you mean the British spy working for the Soviets who was in all the papers last year, the answer is yes: I read the papers."

"Did John ever mention Philby?"

"All the time, since the news came out. He was, of course,

crushed—*betrayed* was the world I think he used, by the damned British. He used a stronger word."

"Speaking of the British, did Philby ever come up in conversation—say with mention of Suzanne Williams or perhaps Donald Maclean?"

"No, why would they? And refresh my memory—Maclean, who?"

"Donald Maclean, another Soviet spy."

"What is wrong with our British cousins? Maybe it's the frightful conditions in their public schools, turns them against family and home—miracle they reproduce."

"Your son's marriage was okay, then?"

"If you're suggesting, as you have for quite some time now, an affair between my son and Suzanne, give it up. I'm here all the summer, my hearing is excellent, and nothing moves in this house without my knowing about it. Besides, he's my son and I know him inside and out. An affair would be beneath his dignity—and mine. He couldn't look me in the eye—or in the mirror."

"Well, I'm sure his wife will confirm everything you've said."

"Explain to me the problem—there is a problem? And don't beat about the bush; I run the board of trustees at Winsted, men well above your pay grade, and I will be sure to let them know if you're prevaricating about the truth or get your facts wrong. Do I make myself clear?"

"We have every hope there's no problem whatsoever, Mrs. Alden. He's just a little overdue from an assignment, and, as we suggested, if you would be so kind as not to mention this discussion to anyone, including your board. We'll be sure to let you know as soon as we hear something—or if you hear from him, of course, I'm sure you'll do the same."

"I'm sure Mary will be relieved. Can I pour you some more iced tea before you leave? You are welcome to stretch your legs and walk around the lake; I know it's a long way back to Washington."

CIA INVESTIGATIVE REPORT JUNE 3, 1954:
INTERVIEW WITH SUBJECT'S WIFE

"For Christ sake, just call me Mary—enough with the Mrs. Alden bullshit. Don't you have anything more you can tell me?"

"He is late on an assignment. We just want to make sure that nothing unusual happened before he left for Berlin in September."

"Late . . . unusual? What the hell does that mean?"

"If he was under undue stress or something unusual on the home front."

"Stress . . . he worked night and day; you people know that. I barely saw him at all last summer. And he tries desperately to keep up with the scholarship in his field. The night before he left to return to Washington, he couldn't even be bothered to sleep with his own wife. So go ask his fucking mistress what was bothering him. She and her obsequious British cousin, Charles Fairburn, were nosing around John from the moment he arrived—what was supposed to be our family vacation. And he never tells me anything—the whole damn family is like that. His mother is even worse."

"Would you mind if we look around his study?"

"Go ahead, be my guest. Search it from top to bottom—that's what you people do, isn't it? That and open other people's mail. But there are no love letters, if that's what you're after—I already checked. Just piles of journals and notebooks full of symbols and photographs of clay tablets. That was the scholar I thought I was marrying, but maybe that was just another fucking cover, too. He's been out of sorts ever since that guy in England deciphered Linear B two years ago."

"He ever talk to you about Kim Philby?"

"Kim, lovely, conniving, rotten Kim?"

"So you know about him?"

"You think I'm a fool? He was over here for dinner; he was at Joe Alsop's parties two blocks over; we saw him at British embassy receptions; he had us over to visit with Aileen and their kids—a happy, happy family. Jesus, Kim was even up at Elysium a few summers back, flirting with Suzanne, right in front of his wife and her husband, who didn't seem to give a shit. Hell of a marriage they had. Everybody in this goddamn town got taken in by Kim Philby, including John. I hope your supercilious British colleagues stick the little fucker in the deepest, darkest cesspool of a prison in England. There's no dungeon deep enough."

"How long did John know Suzanne Williams?"

"Ah, so we're back to that scheming floozy again. She nursed him after Greece in a rehab hospital in England somewhere. Listen, I don't begrudge him all that—it was the war, before we married. I'm an admiral's daughter; I grew up around military bases. I wasn't born yesterday—I know what goes on; I know how men—and women—are. John told me all about Suzanne when we married, that it was over and done—that he wasn't a saint. He couldn't lie to save his life—that's what tore him to pieces about the fucking CIA: the business of forever lying. He had this exalted image of himself, from his mother—her royal highness, his family—Winsted: Who the hell can live up to that? If anyone, I blame Suzanne. She plays on his vulnerabilities, his goddamn Alden integrity; she was always finding a way to insinuate herself into our life at Elysium, to let me know who's boss—she even invited me to her daughter's birthday party when my husband was stuck in Washington. If I was a man, I'd want her, too. I was ready to steal her daughter if I couldn't make one of my own. Christ, do you mind if I pour myself another drink?"

I left Laura sleeping and made my way to the deserted lounge on the upper deck, where I spent an hour on stretching exercises. The rain had stopped sometime that night, and I watched as the fog lifted from the river. From the pitted wood railings, I could see quite a ways upstream along a bend in the river. There was a park with stately rows of trees rising from the bank and continuing on into the low green hills, where, at a distance, the trees became transformed into geometries of rising and falling horizontal patterns, patches of fall color and threadbare stretches of dun and gray, with hints of more green beyond. Nearer at hand were trees with bright yellow leaves clinging against a windswept sky. It was really a charming view, with paddling ducks and a lone swan nudging the shore. I was reminded of Vlada's description of the night before, of his father's stories about the children who lived in the trees, how he'd passed away in his favorite chair staring out at the tree-clad hills. His tale seemed to live in my mind, as if I kind of knew his dad.

A little curious, I climbed to the topmost deck, just beneath the huge red star suspended between the stovepipe smokestacks. From the top railing, I could make out the spans of elegant stone bridges and distant spires downriver. Then, turning and peering through the dark windows of the apparatchiks' disco, as Vlada had called it, I was able to make out small tables stacked with upside-down chairs, leather banquettes off to the side, and a long rosewood bar with hundreds of bottles, high-end brand-name spirits of every description, sheltering beneath gilded mirrors of Art Nouveau vintage.

Laura was still in bed when I returned: a headache . . . not a good sign.

"Maybe it was all that wicked Soviet champagne we drank," she said.

"You drank."

"Did we get through most of the money?"

"You put a good dent in it."

"Then take the rest, buy me some flowers *and* some of those choco-lates—pretend you're still crazy about me. Vlada obviously didn't want me along today."

"You always draw a crowd."

"You're my kind of crowd."

She held out her hand and I took it.

"I'm sorry if I wasn't very nice."

"I don't think he sounded so great," I said. "He looked terrible."

"He's not the guy I remembered, not at all . . . but then, none of us is a spring chicken anymore—worst luck."

"Why didn't you tell me about Max's letters—and *Vlada?* Is that why you dragged me here?"

"Another sin of omission you can chalk up."

"Just don't fucking lie to me."

"I see you've been looking at them."

"I peeked this morning."

"I just want to make sure those insidious academic spinsters don't try to turn me into the next Ted Hughes."

"Max is hardly Sylvia Plath. If anyone, you're the victim."

She squeezed my hand and pulled the blanket higher.

"You're so loyal." She twined her fingers in mine. "You'll come back and save me . . . you won't abandon me?"

"So you did fuck him . . . and I bet he was great."

"You're fucking me now: that's all that matters."

I kissed her fingers, one by one by one.

I parked in what seemed an out-of-the-way corner of a small square. Vlada had instructed me to lose myself—how hard could that be? I ducked into shops selling the most god-awful ersatz goods. Failing to find anything that might cheer Laura—not that she deserved it—I fueled up on Turkish coffee in a café. Strangely, the aroma of the cof-fee reminded me of my grandmother dressed in her sensible traveling clothes, sipping her cappuccinos in cafés in Venice and Paris. In fact, ever since Laura had insinuated herself in my life, memories of my grandmother sprang forth at the oddest moments, as a protective Hera or wise counselor, reminding me to keep my wits about me.

Let the sites of the world set your mind on fire . . . but never forget who you are or where you come from.

That's what my grandmother told me as a kid on trips to Europe—the

Europe she really hated in her Yankee soul for killing her husband and son.

So, dutifully, I found myself exploring the cobblestone streets, examining the old stonework, the medieval and Renaissance carvings and relief work that had so disturbed me upon our arrival—translating the Latin inscriptions I stumbled upon. Always a hint of comfort in that— the lingua franca of Western civilization. A fine mist began sifting from the low clouds, not enough to drive one indoors, but enough that I felt like a damp sponge. The air was thick with sulfur fumes and an all-pervasive smell of untreated sewage. Very quickly, I'd had enough of the claustrophobic medieval streets and opted for a walk across the famous Charles Bridge. My grandmother would have insisted on visiting Saint Vitas Cathedral and Hradcany Castle on the far bank, relishing, no doubt, filling me in on the defenestration of Prague.

No sooner had I reached the bridge than I felt a surge of apprehension mixed with dark regret. Ahead, along either side of the bridge, were statues of martyred saints, as if one was forced to run a gauntlet of vigilant confessors, each avidly displaying ghoulish wounds and instruments of an excruciating death. Even as a young boy traveling with my grandmother, I'd been chilled by such religious imagery—or as my grandmother described them, "idols of cruel superstition and repression." A little odd coming from a Radcliffe-educated woman of great charm and sophistication who prided herself on her lack of prejudice. She had an engaging habit, when we visited museums and churches in Venice, Florence, and Paris, of carrying a perfumed Hermès scarf in her hand, which I was instructed to keep in sight at all times—lest I be snatched away. I was allowed to wander and inspect artifacts in a gallery or church on my own just as long as I kept the scarf in line of sight. But the moment she draped it across her shoulder, I had to return to her side, mostly because she had something of significance to impart. And listen I did, because she read the guidebooks to me from cover to cover, and there would be quizzes over lunch and dinner. That's how I earned my allowance. Paying attention was my grandmother's eleventh commandment.

Crossing the bridge, I noticed more of the East German Trabants of the evening before—I heard them before I saw them, like underpowered riding mowers. They were packed with craning faces pressed to the windshield. They all seemed to be heading in the same direction, as if drawn by some invisible force. I saw more than one policeman and well-dressed citizen of Prague spit at them as they passed and give them the finger. Lingering animosity from the war? An old peasant woman in black was headed in the same direction as the Trabants; she carried bundles of little baskets filled with tourist souvenirs and tiny GDR flags. I was reminded of the aged peasant grandmothers one would see in Vietnam, sometimes along village roads, more often on the streets of Saigon, selling matchbooks or cans of soda, or just begging from the GIs, their rotten teeth black with betel nut.

Encamped at the feet of a decapitated saint with head in hand, a longhaired artist with an emaciated face called out to me. He sat under a plastic tarp, hawking a selection of pen-and-ink sketches of Prague's beauty spots. He did the thing Vlada had done at dinner—waved a hand in front of his face as if there were a mask there, then pointed to me and slipped a finger across his throat in what I assumed was a humorous commentary on the company he was keeping. I gave him a handful of Czech crowns and moved on down the line of martyrs, reminders of horrors past, of religious strife and fanaticism, of pogroms and suicide and genocide and show trials and gulags and just about every "cursed idiocy"—my grandmother's phrase—under the sun . . . of which I'd had my fill along the Vam Co Dong River, when, as an American intelligence officer with the South Vietnamese militia, it became my gruesome duty to search for documents on the dismembered bodies of slain North Vietnamese regulars. Compared to the aftermath of a B-52 strike, the saints on the Charles Bridge had it easy.

Well, I never told Laura about that . . . or anybody else, either.

Walking the gauntlet on the Charles Bridge in the backwash of such morbid memorials to slaughters past, predating mine by hundreds of years, I came to Saint Lucy . . . how sad and distant the blind stare of this Saint Lucy, displaying her salver of bloody eyes. I shivered at memories of Nestor telling me about the buckets of eyes, the heaps of hacked-up body parts, discovered by government forces in the Athens torture centers abandoned by ELAS, and Joanna's description of the blinded prisoners in the holding cell, and, as the clouds closed in again and a spattering of rain drifted across the roadway of the bridge, I found I'd had it with Lucy and her martyred buddies, and so beat a retreat. Enough of Prague, enough of this whole fucking continent: My grandmother's instincts were spot-on.

As my grandmother put it to me, fanaticism in a good cause can be a good thing, but you'd better get the good part right. There was always a touch of embittered madness lurking below the surface of her wintry stare, which, finally, terrified my mother into total submission and escape to her Colony Club bridge games and gin and tonics. She refused to return to Elysium in the summers and excused herself from our last trips to Europe, when grandmother and I visited Venice and later the Argonne, where we laid a wreath at my grandfather's monument on what would have been their fifty-fifth wedding anniversary, something she did compulsively on every fifth anniversary. When I asked her about visiting the place where my father died, she gave me the most haunting and baffled look, telling me that she'd been informed that the road, the place of the accident on the Autobahn, had been built over for a new cloverleaf. It was the best she could come up with, and I never raised the question again, even in her last days, when I went to visit her at Lenox Hill Hospital, where I hung on her every word. Her cheeks were sunken and lined like old parchment, her silver gray hair kept perfectly combed by the nurse and hairdresser who regularly attended her. And her eyes . . . a kind of pale sea-blown blue with a soft radiance at the centers.

On one of the very last days before she died, I found her lying wide awake, her head propped up on white pillows, a ray of sunlight finding its way past the high rises on Lexington Avenue to gently illuminate her face, her skin so pale and near diaphanous as to blend with the flurry of silver gray hair at her brow—fading like an old photograph before my very eyes. Perhaps her hairdresser had come to her that morning. She smiled and told me, in a tone that suggested a fairy tale, "Oh, I've just been far, far away in a place you could never imagine, Peter." I thought of all the places she had loved: the spring gardens at the Mount, Edith Wharton's place nearby Elysium; a pink-awninged hotel overlooking Harrington Sound in Bermuda, where she'd spent many winters; the newly built Ahwahnee Hotel in Yosemite National Park, where she'd taken her thirteen-year-old son in 1927; and her honeymoon at Palazzo Barberini in Venice, where, decades later, we'd once spent a whole week at the Gritti, as she had with her son; and, of course, Elysium, the place where she invested her love most fully, for her lost husband and son . . . and me.

None of these places seemed to be on her mind as I entered her sunlit room. Of all things, she'd been remembering the death of her own grandmother just after the turn of the century, when she'd been a young girl visiting for the last time in the town of Littleton, near Concord. She was quite bemused by her own memories and told me as much. "Deathbed scenes," she said with a girlish giggle. "I get the ones I've read about mixed up with the ones I've borne witness to." She laughed, as if she were self-consciously playing the role of dying grandmother for my benefit, perhaps to make light of my fears. But something intrigued her about this particular memory of her childhood. She began going over it with me, like someone just awakened from a dream and trying to discern its strangeness. A glimpse behind the veil of time through her grandmother's eyes. Her grandmother, Sarah, who had been near ninety-two when she died, lived in the same house in which she'd been born; in fact, she had died in the very same bed in which she'd been conceived. "Imagine that . . . imagine that." She reached for my hand, as if needing to steady herself in the face of the echoed wonder of such a thing.

When my grandmother as an eleven-year-old had sat with her grandmother in her bedroom overlooking the back garden, with the smell of lilac and honeysuckle burdening the air, her grandmother kept speaking of something that had occurred in her own early childhood, a most distressing period of her life, it seemed, when she'd been laid low with some childhood ailment, probably diphtheria—I think Grandmother called it "the croup"—that had kept her in bed for weeks and then months. Missing Sunday services in the nearby Congregational church devastated her. It wasn't the sermons or the hymns she missed so much as seeing the whole town of Littleton turned out in its Sunday best. Between services, gossip was exchanged and the children played, and large luncheons were eaten. The town was one close family. This must have been 1815 or thereabouts. Week after week, Sunday after Sunday, she had to lie in her bed and endure those lonely hours. She was going crazy, the supernatural stillness of the house, a fly buzzing against her window, the ticking pendulum of a grandfather clock, while outside she could hear the sullen clang of the meetinghouse bell, the clopping of hooves and the jingle of carriage harnesses, the raised voices as the psalms were sung, the solemn cadences as the long prayers were read, and the monotone of the sermon . . . the ache of lost human companionship in the final hymn.

My grandmother had caught a fading glimpse of the last wave of Puritan spirituality, which even by her grandmother's middle age had

evaporated with the coming of the railroads and factories and the dis-
persal of New England families to the West, as the old agricultural
world faded. But this wasn't the story my grandmother wished to
impart to me, when for a moment she had become something of that
lonely and ailing girl stuck in a dying New England town, where the
past was still joined to the present, the living to the dead, a small-town
community that enjoyed a kind of spiritual freedom, through terribly
circumscribed. "Soul liberty," my grandmother whispered to me, raising a finger as if to test the wind. A liberty of spirit bound only to the
obligations to one's community and one's God. Shame and dishonor if
one should fail or shirk the common task.

No, this wasn't the story my grandmother wished to impart, but it
was, as usual, between the lines.

"For you see, Sarah—that was my grandmother's name—almost
died of loneliness over those many months. And in sheer desperation, against all orders, she crept downstairs to her father's library and
took two volumes of Gibbon's *Decline and Fall of the Roman Empire*.
To save herself from going mad, Sarah not only read them but, over
the following months, until well into the fall, when she recovered her
health, she completely memorized the two volumes. A prodigious feat.
They, the historical characters, became her friends, her community, her
trusted guides as she traveled through the Roman Empire and the wide
Mediterranean. She became enthralled with the sound of the names
. . . *Elagabalus, Numidicus, Commodus and Caracalla, Septimius Severus*
. . . and oh my, *Valerian*—how she loved the sound of their names.
She spouted their names and described their exploits as if they were
her boon companions, and she soon became the town eccentric. And
then in time, she became Littleton's star attraction on public occasions,
especially on the Fourth of July, when she'd recite Gibbon for hours
on the common under a bunting of red, white, and blue. And so she
became the town schoolteacher—beloved of her students, who named
their children Marcus and Zenobia and Quintilius—imagine the rib-
bing with names like that in a small town. Sarah married a minister in
nearby Groton—utterly bewitched by her he was—and their sons all
went to Harvard and onward and upward to become prominent men
of scholarship and business. You see, that's where it comes from . . . 'Let
the sites of the world set your mind on fire. . . .'"

And with my grandmother's voice ringing in my ears, I realized I'd come to Prague for her as well, if not to lay a memorial wreath for her son, at least to give a name to the place of his execution and a meaning to his story, knowing that the passing on of true and accurate stories meant a great deal to her, and so to me.

Even if the stories of her nocturnal swims across the lake to Hermitage, where she posed nude for Amaryllis Williams ... and more ... never passed her lips, or certainly not in my hearing.

33

IN RAINY WENCESLAS SQUARE, I SEARCHED my way through labyrinthine underground arcades enveloped in dingy tiles and full-length mirrors. After many wrong turns, I finally stumbled upon the famous Czech chocolatier, Orion. I bought the large sampler selection Vlada specified in his note. The gaudy Orion box, emblazoned with gold seals of international prizes won around the turn of the century, was shrink-wrapped in shiny cellophane and topped with a handsome red bow—as fancy as anything one might find in Vienna. I then proceeded to our rendezvous in the huge expanse of Wenceslas Square. As I approached the flagpole in front of the National Museum, I was surprised to find more people milling about than earlier in the morning, mostly kids in their early twenties in animated conversations with one another. Even with my tourist eye, I could spot vigilant uniformed police lurking in doorways or peering out the windows of unmarked police cars. Some-thing was in the wind. As I passed the flagpole at precisely three o'clock, I spotted Vlada, dressed in the same ratty sweater and black beret as the day before. He was standing amid a gang of young people gathered around a street singer playing a guitar. Catching my eye, he took off his hat and let me pass, then casually fell into step about a hundred feet behind me. At the Land Rover, he waited until I got in, then slipped into the back, ducked down, and told me to drive.

We drove to the outskirts of the city, to one of the nondescript apartment-building complexes I'd noticed as we drove in the previous night. I was deflated to find my friend, this larger-than-life figure and famous writer, warehoused in such a Corbusier-like rabbit warren. It was nightmarish, the sameness, the shabbiness. The deserted lobby smelled of damp and crumbling plaster and leaking sewage. Vlada banged open the unlocked metal door of his mailbox, bringing down a shower of plaster from the wall, briefly examined his mail, and then flung it into a trash can. He smelled of stale sweat and was again exhausted. We moved toward the stairs. A repeated slapping noise echoed from above, bringing a quick smile to his pinched and chapped lips. A soccer ball of black-and-white octagons careened into view, followed by two boys. With catlike quickness, Vlada was on the ball, snapping it up with a flick of his muddy boot, bouncing it between knee and instep in a jarring little dance that I remembered from Winsted days. Then as the grinning boys watched, he spiraled the ball from his knee, head flung back to bounce it on his pale forehead . . . once, twice, then twice more, and then on the fifth bounce, he snapped his head and torso forward to send the ball straight into the arms of one of the boys wearing the colors of the Czech national team. They cheered and ran out the door to a rainy playground across the street.

"Red, white, and blue," he puffed out, with an ironic twist of his lips.

Vlada, breathing hard, put his arm around my shoulder and hugged me.

"We were a great team once—yes?"

"We were . . ."

It was all there again, the feeling of the first kick, as he had come forward and I took the snap, a kind of sympathetic vibration that surged through me, culminating in the instant of impact as the football evaporated under my cradling finger, missilelike, sailing through the uprights.

Tears welled in my eyes.

We had been young and had owned that hundred yards of green earth. We had been like gods.

Vlada slapped my back and indicated the broken elevator and then the concrete stairs, all twelve flights, which he assaulted at a rapid clip, urging me on as he sprang upward floor after floor, as if the years had done nothing to diminish his physical prowess. I followed as best I could, slowing as my back began to pain me. He waited for me at the top of his landing with a withering stare, and barely a drop of sweat. I thought he looked pretty beat-up, but it was clear who had come through the two decades in better shape.

He waved me down a stark paint-peeling corridor hung with naked and broken lightbulbs. His tiny apartment was at the end, past a dozen doors, from which low voices murmured and children wailed . . . a whistling kettle, the smell of boiled cabbage and leaky toilets on the hall. His room, and it was just one room, could have been a hermit's cell. There was a mattress on a plywood frame in the corner with rumpled sheet and blanket. In the center of the room was a plastic table with two folding beach chairs, one with a cushion facing an ancient typewriter. A single hanging lamp from the ceiling above the table provided the only illumination. Against the wall, low bookshelves of stacked boards on concrete blocks were crammed to overflowing with dog-eared volumes. A guitar case leaned into a corner nearest the mattress. In another corner, next to the only electrical outlet, was a hot plate and a tiny refrigerator. I detected a few items of food—half a loaf of bread, a piece of salami—and some empty bottles, perhaps beer bottles, but I couldn't tell from the labels. The solitary uncurtained window gave a view of row upon row of similar concrete bunkers stretched into the rainy dusk.

As if to dispel any concern for his lack of upscale mobility, he moved with a jaunty shrug to switch on the hanging lamp over his worktable. The plastic shade was patterned with silhouettes of cowboy iconography: a lariat, a branding iron, cacti, split-rail fences, a Stetson hat, a coiled rattlesnake, and the words *Tucson, Arizona* in green along the bottom. A memento from that long-ago summer of travel before he arrived at Winsted.

After my penance before the saints of Charles Bridge, I felt the need to reassert some measure of the solidarity—how sorely neglected—that had been ours twenty years before. I dutifully pulled out the box of Orion chocolates from my shopping bag and placed it on his worktable, and then from my raincoat pocket, I produced a very expensive bottle of Russian vodka. Of the box of chocolates, he seemed to take no notice, but at the appearance of the vodka, a lovely smile eased up his chapped lips.

"Ha-ha," Vlada exulted, passing appreciative fingers over the bottle as if caressing the splendid curves of a beautiful woman. "My good friend, you come to my fair city, a tiny moon of Moscow, and out of all the shit"—he waved wildly—"you find the single thing for which the Soviets have a genius. Which makes you a genius. It must have been that fine American school you attended."

Vlada went over to his bookshelf by the window and found two white enamel cups. With what seemed unconscious habit, he pulled out his shirttail and carefully wiped the insides. He got the cap off the bottle and poured.

"To Moscow," I toasted.

"To vodka."

"To old friends."

"No, to your father—who brought you back to me. All day I was thinking, Why did he never talk about his father at Winsted? A freedom fighter—a patriot."

I sipped the vodka, feeling the burn. Surely I'd said something.

"I think because of all the uncertainty around his story . . . it put me in such an awkward position."

Vlada smiled enigmatically, a flicker in the mottled blue depths of his eyes.

We touched cups, drank, and refilled.

"I remember"—Vlada shot me a pensive look—"you said he was a football champion, and during the war he fought in Greece with the Resistance."

"Yes, remember the display case in the gym with his medals?"

"Of course . . . of course." His eyes probed mine, waiting.

"We didn't know about this, about Prague. I don't think even the CIA knew about it back then. He disappeared into East Berlin. We—his family, I mean—weren't supposed to even admit he was in the CIA."

"Doubt." He snorted with a disgusted wave.

"Doubt?"

"Doubt, uncertainty, rumors"—Vlada gave me a knowing look—"these are the cards the old men play endlessly."

He went to his bookshelf and paused to select some volumes, as if to begin a seminar on certainty or the lack thereof. He brought the pile to our table and from the pages of one volume extracted a folded paper and placed it ceremoniously before me. It was a crude photocopy of some kind of official Czech government letter dated 1955. The name of the sender on the bottom had been blacked out.

"This is a letter from a high Czech official to the Russian premier, complaining bitterly that Czechoslovak sovereignty had been violated by agents of the KGB, who had organized the imprisonment of an American CIA agent in Pankrác Prison, a man arrested in the GDR and then executed on Czech soil without trial or involvement by Czech authorities."

I examined the document. Except for the official letterhead and date, the typed text in Czech was indecipherable. "Executed?"

"As was the Czech minister—so I was told—who wrote this letter by a KGB team one week after he sent this official complaint to Moscow. Khrushchev's orders, a warning to others. Stalin had been dead two years, but Moscow, so it seems, was taking no chances. My father must have known, but never a word to me."

Vlada reached a finger to the back of my head and indicated where the shot would have been placed. Six months later, I would find out he was wrong about the means of execution; it was far worse.

My hands shook and I wiped tears. For the first time in my life, the raw cruelty of my father's death hit me: death by an executioner's bullet to the back of his head, just another of the hundreds of thousands of similar executions since the 1920s.

"A year later," said Vlada, "and the Hungarians were fighting in the streets of Budapest. Little Czechoslovakia learned to keep very quiet."

Then Vlada took the paper from my hand.

"The man I mentioned last night, he has the ministry copy of the original. He keeps it, he told me, as a guarantee against the judgment of history. His possession of this document, if it was discovered, could mean his death."

"Why would they execute him in cold blood? Surely he was worth something alive."

"I was told it was very unusual, even for that time. Stalin was dead. An American spy would be a valuable asset for propaganda or for exchange for Soviet spies."

"Unless he knew something—"

Vlada couldn't resist a knowing smile. "Doubt, uncertainty. . . ."

"My mother took it upon herself, without ceremony, to dump his ashes in Lake Carnegie in Princeton."

Vlada shrugged, struck a match, and touched the flame to the corner of the paper.

"What are you doing?" I reached to the flaming paper, which he laid on top of his tin-can ashtray.

"Laura rejected the copy I gave her last night."

"She did?"

From the pile of books, he took out his translation of *Gardens of Saturn*. He flipped open the front cover and tapped the end paper.

"A copy of this letter is underneath. Wait until you are over the border. But you must promise me that you will not make this public, not until you hear from me." Vlada pushed the burning ash of the paper into the tin can and waved to disperse the smoke. "I don't think our friend, this ex-minister—now an old and sick man—will live many more years, but his children, even today, would be under threat."

As I tried to take it all in, I noticed that he'd inscribed the copy to Laura, with a heartfelt dedication to the author.

"I'm sorry if she was a little out of sorts last night. She's been going through a rough time. Her father, Bobby Williams, committed suicide last year. What's left of her career is on hold because of a knee injury. And, while we were in Vienna, she heard that one of her colleagues had just died of AIDS—an insidious plague in her circle of dancers."

"And Max—she has no respect for the man who has immortalized her?"

"I think she'd rather have taken care of that on her own terms. That's why she wanted his letters, before they fell into unsympathetic hands."

Vlada seemed uncertain of his next words. "She's not . . . the same as I remember . . . only as I remember from Max's novel."

"Believe me, that's the last thing she needs to hear from *you*."

He sighed and looked away, possibly ashamed, and I knew that he knew I knew about them; while I was not a little disconcerted at my own ambivalence: if I was glad he held no candle for her, or saddened by the possible truth of his observation.

"Your hotel room will be searched." Vlada reached and closed the cover of Max's book. "Your car will be searched at the border. The secret police probably already know we have met, so"—he touched his temple with a judicious scissoring of his jaw, and flattened his palm to signify something put into motion—"the translation, along with Max's letters, will make sense to them: The reason for your visit—let's hope."

Again, I sensed a life on the edge: a thousand minute recalibrations endlessly repeated to survive. How often had I seen it in the darting eyes and the tone of misdirection when interrogating NVA prisoners.

"You'll be glad to know I managed to spend the last part of the cash on the vodka *and* the chocolates."

Again a weary, cynical smile as he glanced at the glittering cellophane and gold seals and exuberant red ribbon adorning the Orion chocolates. This prompted a deep yearning in me to recover something of the younger Vlada I'd known twenty years before. I extracted five or six packs of Kents out of the pockets of my raincoat and placed them on the table—as if this splendid offering on the altar of deathless youth might yet bridge the years. It turned out Laura had bought a whole carton of Kents in Vienna, and that morning I'd taken it upon myself to relieve her of every pack I found secreted in her bag.

Vlada thanked me and pensively began stacking and unstacking the packs. "Did you read Max's letters?"

"I took a peek this morning."

From an envelope wedged between the pages of a book in the pile at his elbow, he removed some clippings and showed them to me.

"You fascinated Max. He sent me these newspaper reviews and interviews about your books." He smiled at what must have been my barely concealed astonishment. "After all, you provided him with a central character in his first novel."

I glanced at the familiar clippings. "And my father."

"Yes, but the character of his friend from school days was much more successful. I recognized him."

"I don't."

"How could you?"

"Tell me something: Do you remember that night we broke—for lack of a better word—into the base at Fort Devens?"

His eyes lit up. "The helicopters, yes—"

"Anything else—something you said to me?"

Vlada shook his head.

"Do you know how crazy, how dangerous it was to do what we did?"

Vlada busied himself with getting out a cigarette, and I realized how overwrought my voice must have seemed.

"I *was* crazy. I was wounded in love," he said with a self-conscious theatrical flourish. "Believe me, I was capable of anything."

I watched and waited as he lit up and his jittery voice and gestures calmed.

"Your *affair* with Laura?"

He reacted to the accusatory tone in my voice by first looking away as he had before and taking another drag on his cigarette, possibly contemplating the specter of a coiled rattlesnake on the wall above the bed, and then, settling his pale china blue eyes on mine, he sighed loudly.

"Did she tell you that?"

"No, not a word."

"Then better it never happened."

"Clearly it did happen."

"Is that why you never wrote me? Why in twenty years you never came here to see me?"

The hurt in his voice surprised me.

"No, it's not, because . . . I only figured it out last night."

He got some ointment out of a tin in his pocket and rubbed it into his chapped lips, giving himself a few moments to get the thing clear in his mind; and as he did, I found my wish of minutes before granted, except it was not quite the same fearless exchange student who was returned to me.

In the late fall of 1968, he told me, as he waited for word on the release of his father, as his mother urged him to stay at Winsted until the political situation clarified, he received a last letter from his girlfriend of almost two years. They'd known each other since childhood. Natalie was her name. Her father had been a finance minister in Dubček's government, along with his father, who'd been minister of culture. Vlada and Natalie had grown up together in the same privileged party circles, same schools, access to the same foreign-currency stores—and visas to travel to the West. She was an Olympic gymnast; he a pro prospect for the Czech national soccer team. Besides sports, their adolescent love had been spurred by the Prague Spring during the heady reformist era of the mid-sixties, when Czechoslovakia edged toward a more humane and democratic system, creeping ever so slowly out of the shadow of Soviet domination. Vlada and Natalie's reformist vision further fueled their passion for each other. They had written to each other while Vlada traveled in the States the summer before he came to Winsted. Natalie remained in Prague right through the Soviet invasion, training for the Mexico City Olympic Games in October. Vlada had planned to fly to Mexico City to see her perform; that had been their master plan for over a year.

"In October, I got a letter from Natalie. Her father had signed a document supporting the Soviet invasion . . . and so had Natalie, although at first she did not admit it to me. If she didn't sign, they would not let her go to the Olympics; she would be finished. She'd been training since she was five years old. Gymnastics was her life. We argued like crazy. I spoke on the phone to her in Mexico City at the Olympic Village. She pleaded with me to understand. She said I didn't realize how bad things were in Prague; she said her father had no choice—she had no choice. 'You go to jail now, Vlada,' she kept telling me. 'You live a life of shit, in the gutter—worse.' And I realized that unless my father did the same, support the Soviet invasion and the new government, we could never be together. I could hear it in her voice. She said she still loved me . . . but, but, but. She made her decision for the chance of a medal and the good life—life, you see, at the Hotel Red Star."

The last time he spoke to Natalie, before she left Mexico City to return to Prague, it was right before the Winsted senior dance. Natalie had finished out of medal contention, but her teammate, Vera Caslavska, had achieved a record-setting sweep of the gold medals for Czechoslovakia. Then at the closing ceremonies, Vera denounced the Soviets and called for a return to the path of democratization for her country. That ended Vera's career.

"My pretty Natalie now had her chance. With the brave and wonderful Vera banned from further competition, Natalie was sure she'd be number one on the team in a year or two."

As Vlada told me this, I remembered him singing the night of our senior dance, how moved we'd all been by the sadness in his voice, the depth of sorrow in his eyes; the girls had all been swooning. Laura had asked about Vlada and I'd been proud to acknowledge him as my friend, as I explained the worsening situation with his father in Prague. I remembered them dancing, very slowly—a strikingly handsome couple.

"Why didn't you tell me about Natalie?"

"I was ashamed of myself, ashamed of her—she'd let us all down. She ended up caring only about herself."

"But you stuck it out."

"The worst was the temptation to follow in her footsteps."

"You had all those football scholarships."

"Yale, Harvard, and your Princeton . . ."

"You could have been a football hero *and* a dissident. You could have championed the cause of Czech independence and democracy from afar—a nice life."

Vlada eyed me intently, and I was surprised at the chord I'd struck.

"So, who's the bigger fool, I, who went back, or you, who went to Vietnam?" Vlada tapped a magazine clipping that had mentioned my service in Vietnam. "Who ended up the real hero in our sad comedy?"

"And you don't even remember what you told me that night at Fort Devens."

"Do you regret—whatever I told you?"

"I only regret what I didn't do."

"Don't you see, my friend, Laura was part of my temptation . . . and my shame."

"Surely not shame?"

"Why do you think I agreed to do the translation after Max died?" Vlada poured us another round of vodka and shrugged. "Until last night, when I realized who she really was."

"Don't be so hard on her."

"And you?"

"And what about me—if you don't mind my asking. Whose idea was it . . . to sleep together?"

"Do you hold it against me?"

"No. Only that I failed her and let it happen."

He seemed to find this amusing. He ground out his cigarette and went to open the single window. He glanced out at the night and the endless apartment blocks forming ungainly grids of vertical and horizontal squares of yellow light. Then he turned back and touched the corner of his eye.

"I told you how three years ago I was held in solitary confinement for nine months for activities against the state. I wrote it all in my head, the temptations of a dissident life in America: the life I might have led instead of this one. In that life, we played football together at Princeton and I married Laura. What do you think of that?"

He laughed and closed the window against the slanting rain.

"Well . . . sounds like a very romantic ending."

The story he repeated to himself over those nine months in solitary confinement began, of course, with his night with Laura. A night he described in halting terms that began with the most piquant innocence, then heartfelt candor before tumbling into out-of-control passion.

"We lost our minds."

Laura, so she told me later, would not disagree. She'd been upset and had blamed herself for either being too eager or not experienced enough to do whatever it was she'd failed to do to get me to perform. She'd gone back to the faculty home and realized that none of the other girls had returned. "That only added to my humiliation." She walked back to campus, so familiar—and not from all the Founder's Days she'd attended since she was fourteen, the year my grandmother died and Bobby maneuvered himself onto the board by giving up Anthony Blunt to Elliot Goddard. Winsted haunted her; the family name was everywhere, and yet she felt an outsider. She knew enough to know how her father was scorned by Winsted insiders, inklings of which she'd gotten from the love letters.

"My mind was twisted into knots of righteous anger and resentment over how we'd been treated: I wanted to love the place, but I hated all it stood for. I guess I got that from my mother, too," she'd tell me. She wandered into the Williams Chapel, given by her great-aunt, mistress of Palazzo Fenway. "The Saint-Gaudens memorial . . . such a spooky weird and wonderful thing." She found herself drawn to the ecstatic faces of the angels, parted lips and compressed eyebrows more of erotic release than mournful sadness. "Those faces, they always made me feel a little off balance, kinda kinky and ethereal all in one—which was why Max was so drawn to them." Walking around the Circle, stalking the thing she couldn't fathom, she caught glimpses of shadowy couples hurrying off into the darkness, notes of drunken laughter. "I was so horny, drunk, and angry—not necessarily in that order; it was either keep walking or throw up."

Then she noticed a light in a library window. The main reading room of the library with the Sargent portrait of General Alden was dark and deserted, so she continued on back into the stacks: there she stumbled upon Vlada, almost hidden behind his bunkers of books. She was stunned. "Why wasn't he off with the most beautiful woman at the dance? In the girls' room, that's all I heard: the good-looking Czech dude with that incredible voice. They'd have dumped their dates for Vlada in a heartbeat."

But he had no date. He was depressed, half-drunk from the spiked punch, and studying the *Norton Anthology of English Literature* I'd given him. He was cramming for the AP English exams scheduled the week before Christmas, toying, as he told me, with the idea of staying in America and grabbing one of those football scholarships. That way, he would snub Natalie, who had just returned to Prague from Mexico City, and he'd preserve the family honor as a dissident, albeit safely in exile in America. His mother had even written to him suggesting as much. There was no guarantee that his father would be released from prison anytime soon. That was the state of mind in which Laura found him.

"I was angry with myself for entertaining happy thoughts of life in America—how much I loved your country, and dancing with that beautiful girl."

And like a fantasy of his adopted country, that beautiful girl appeared out of the gloom of the stacks and into the halo of his desk lamp.

"An angel of light—I was reading Milton—remember? I felt so alive in her presence."

Their rage could've set the place on fire. Both were looking for love in service to a calling that neither could exactly define: that amorphous late-sixties infatuation with art and truth and freedom and peace and a better world . . . and the fucking contradictions be damned. Vlada, incredulous but canny enough not to ask a lot of questions, got a chair for Laura and they sat and talked for hours, each an exotic and delight-ful distraction to the other. Being near strangers only added to their easy candor. They ached to confess their hurt, to talk endlessly about themselves. They were on the rebound, even if they didn't quite know it. Laura was enthralled by Vlada's shattered hopes for democratization in his homeland; he for Laura's ambivalent love for ballet and fierce ambition to outdo her mother. "In this, how much she reminded me of Natalie—from little girls, they work like dogs. They hate it, they love it, until the discipline and training imprison them body and soul, and they cannot escape." Laura even looked like Natalie: the same long blond hair and thin, flexible limbs. By the end of the first hour, they were holding hands, rocking back and forth with fierce whispers, eyes locked on each other. By the second hour, they were embracing, exchanging tentative kisses, losing themselves, drowning in sympathy for the oth-er's plight, which seemed to mirror their own.

"A bubble," said Vlada, and molded the air over his worktable. I would have preferred a somewhat guiltier or at least contrite look on his face.

Vlada finally shrugged, tears in his eyes, unable to go on.

They had retreated to his tiny single room. He was an experienced lover. He and Natalie had been experimenting with sex for over two years. He knew what a woman needed. After Laura's years of frustrating rejection and asinine commentary from the gay boys she'd trained with in her ballet school, and then the disaster with me—well, she stumbled upon a world-class athlete, a Nordic god with a head of steam from over six months separation from his girlfriend. He took her places she never imagined—or not quite. As she put it to me once in a moment of candor. "With Vlada, don't embarrass me by asking for details. . . . Well, if you must know, it was like those letters between our parents came alive between my legs. Poor guy, he cried at the end, you know—like a baby, really; he didn't want me to leave, not that I wanted to either."

Vlada shook his head. "I didn't want the day to come—no, not ever. . . ."

Seeing this mile-long romantic streak in Vlada for the first time as I sat in his dreary apartment sipping vodka, I was confounded: How could I have been so blind at eighteen!

His one night with Laura only exacerbated the conflicted allegiances that tugged at him over his last weeks at Winsted. For a while, he thought himself madly in love with her. That her coming to him so unexpectedly at that precise moment must have been a sign. And no, he didn't feel guilty about me: She'd assured him that we were only friends from childhood, distant cousins.

"You never mentioned her—not once," he said, gazing at me. "Not a word."

Which was true. I'd been too galled by my failure. But I also realized why so many of my classmates had assumed my success: Laura had sneaked back to the faculty house at five in the morning, showered, and been picked up by her taxi at six for the train back to New York and rehearsals. Reports from the girls filled the airwaves at Sunday breakfast, attesting to my prowess.

Vlada didn't even have her telephone number or address. As she'd slipped out of his room before five in the morning, hurrying to make her taxi, she'd promised to write.

"The temptation to stay in America glittered in my mind, like the fantastic colors of the fall leaves in America, the Grand Canyon—the freedom, the music I loved—oh my God. I got calls from football coaches; they came and took me out to lunch—do you remember, the Princeton coach?"

I'd forgotten. The Princeton coach had come up to Winsted and taken us both out to dinner at the Bull Run. And, of course, Vlada had seen the Green Berets dining at nearby tables and heard the air traffic overhead in the parking lot.

"So tell me, explain it to me: What were we doing breaking into a U.S. military base and almost getting ourselves killed?" I asked him.

"I told you, I was going crazy. Nobody stopped the Soviet tanks— nobody. America and the world let the Soviets participate in the

Olympics—nobody did anything for my country." Vlada tapped at the springy keys of his typewriter, as if aghast how it had all come together in his young mind. "I wanted to see with my own eyes the power of America . . . that somewhere there was a power willing to defend our freedom. Otherwise, everything was lost."

"And that was enough to convince you to go back?"

"And the letter from my mother that my father had had a heart attack. And two weeks later the phone call that he had died, and this . . ." He slapped one of the books on the table.

"Did Laura write you?"

"She wrote me. And I didn't know what to write back, which life to choose. When I got the phone call from my mother about my father, I tossed everything in my bag and went to the airport. When I flew into Prague, they confiscated all my papers and my books. I got most of the books back, and my notebooks, but not my letters . . . from my mother, from Natalie, from Laura; they were gone."

"So she never heard from you?"

"Perhaps no explanation was possible." He reached out and squeezed my arm. "Do you blame me . . . for Vietnam?"

"I blame only myself."

"Listen, we must believe in what is passed down from our fathers; otherwise, you have a world like this. . . ." He slapped the table and made a despairing gesture to the four corners of his dingy room, where phantom images quivered to life on the walls as the light shade above our heads swung in an uneasy arc.

"'Passed down?'—*Passed down?*" I said. "My father abandoned his family."

"You really believe that? Even Laura, as we were leaving the library, stopped by the portrait of your grandfather—a sigh, a look, something."

"Great-grandfather—and he had nothing to do with her."

"You told me about him, remember? A general in the fight to free the slaves—you don't think such things are important?"

"Perhaps we should have played at Princeton." I smiled. "Except in that version, I got to marry Laura. We could have grown old as teachers in a fine school for boys and girls, coaching the kids—what do you think—teachers?—a better ending?"

"But is that not what this fight is about? I have lived with that dream, a kind of perfection in my mind: that by struggling with the deepest truths we—writers—can make it better in our lifetimes."

He nodded as if to encourage me. Or was it irony in the crinkle of his sleepless eyes for two childless men nearing their sell-by date?

"Change the world . . . hey . . . we've survived so far." I held up my cup, not sure if I was mocking my host or celebrating the return of that young exchange student.

He leaned toward me. "You were there, with the helicopters—so you must understand?"

"It was a different war by the time I got there—after a year of language training; at least for *us* it was different. The South Vietnamese were doing most of the dying, and in the end we let them down; we abandoned them."

Vlada tapped the endpaper of Max's novel. "Perhaps knowing this thing about your father will make it easier for you. It has come full circle." He made spiraling motions with his hands. "As with a great novel, there exists an inner coherence to our lives that is invisible, until we near the end, until there is some completion, and we can see with different eyes."

A long silence fell between us as he injected this new note into our conversation.

Vlada seemed to register my momentary bewilderment. He slapped the metal housing of the typewriter as if to signal a move on to other things. He got up and went to his makeshift bed, sat and pulled off his work boots. He wrinkled his nose in mock agony at the stink of his feet.

"I was pouring concrete foundations all morning. The rain always makes it difficult." He massaged his feet for a moment. "Sometimes the work is not so bad, when the weather is good, the air fresh. For you see, I work with some of the greatest poets and dramatists of my country. The talk is good. Some things they cannot take away from a man." He fixed me with a grimace, something between sarcasm and helplessness. Seeing those dull sapphire eyes gazing at me from the half shadows around his bed reminded me of how he had looked at his desk in the Winsted library, peering out from his stacks of books, when his only battle was with a petite gray-haired librarian.

"Clearly, you've become an expert on the workers' paradise."

He smiled at my feeble irony.

"Except when the construction materials never come. And sometimes the materials are so bad that you fear for the people who will one day live in what you have built."

I got up and went to the window, looking out to where building after building stood like bleak stockades, stockades within stockades. My mind drifted to thoughts of those mountain walls raised by Zeus around the island of the Phaeacians, the terrified villagers beyond the Kalamas River, the deep jungle bunkers beyond the Vam Co Dong River . . . the destitute lands on the far shore of the Ohio.

I turned at Vlada's sigh and saw him close his eyes for a few seconds, seeming to nod off; then his eyelids fluttered and he spoke softly, groping as a writer does for the right words.

"In my new novel, I have experimented with autobiography—in the same way Max's novels are partly based on his life."

I winced inwardly but bent forward with a curious smile.

"But that is their weakness, don't you think," I said, "if you're too close to your subject? If the subject is *you*—it becomes too subjective and lacks objectivity—and generates a false consciousness because you're so *self*-conscious about your actions. You end up playing to the camera in your head—like football: If you play to the crowd, you lose the purity of the practiced instinct and muscle memory."

He nodded thoughtfully—I hoped in agreement.

"I wrote about my childhood, my father, my time in America, my fantasy of another life and a woman and . . ." He leaned forward and rubbed his eyes. "You must write about your father, give him a story—you owe him as much."

"Yes, yes . . . maybe now I've got a good start along those lines."

"It is frustrating how time steals from our memories. What can we really know of another life? My father was a distant man, a silent man, like a monk. After his adolescent experience in the camps, he found it hard to be close to anyone, as if fearful they might disappear. He feared to love, I think. He had been weakened by the hardships of the camps—his heart, you see. He walked alone in the parks, in the woods on the hills above the city. I have always this picture in my mind from when I was a child—of him walking in the woods—but always from behind, the back of his coat, mud on the heels of his boots. My mother and my sister and I followed behind so as not to disturb him. My mother always told us that intellectuals cannot be disturbed."

"Scholars . . . are the worst." I caught sight of the guitar in the corner. "Do you still play?"

He shook his head and held up his dirty chilblained hands.

"It is not in me anymore." And he smiled gallantly and hummed as he mimed a guitar. "I feel it in my fingers, I feel it in my toes . . . Love is all around me—"

"But you were so good when you sang for us at the dance. Do you remember how warm it was? Do you remember the game and your winning touchdown?"

He watched me intently. I was unconsciously stretching.

"What is wrong with your back?"

"I was hit by shrapnel from a mortar round."

He winced. "Was it serious?"

"A year in a VA hospital."

"So"—a flash of anger flared in his eyes—"you paid a price?"

"I was lucky."

"Lucky?"

"We . . . football and crew."

Vlada's brows knit with concern, and I turned away.

"Tell me the truth, Peter: Did Laura lie when she told me that you were not in love with her?"

"Oh, how I wish it had been a lie. . . ."

A smile eased up his lips, as if the joke was really on the two of us.

"So"—and he made a show of washing his hands—"Max stole her love, as he did in his novel. And when we are all dead and gone, it *will* be—"

"And the truth be damned."

"I will miss him," Vlada said, "except life goes on with you . . . *and* her?"

"Women . . . ," I said, as if in echo of some universal male complaint. I went to the typewriter and tapped on the keys, much as Max had done on my father's typewriter many years before. "But guess what, I wrote my last two books on a computer. It makes it a breeze, really; you'll love it."

Vlada got off the bed and padded to his chair in his bare feet.

"A computer, a word processor—here, never. Anyway, I like to feel the making of the words. The security police are terrified of computers, technology—they would return us to before Gutenberg if they could. Without the BBC, VOA, Radio Free Europe, the darkness would be very dark indeed."

"Listen, if it's only a matter of money, the least I could do would be to get you a computer and printer. I saw them in the shops in Vienna—"

"Peter, the old men watch over us like jealous gods." His alarmed

red-veined eyes took me in, the blue seemingly drained to gray as he
sat back in his chair, his face half-shadowed in the penumbral boundary beyond the area of brightest illumination. The muffled wail of a
child echoed from the hallway and the sound of running water through
rusted pipes. He gestured toward his sturdy, if antique, typewriter. "It
is language they fear. These gods of the new order, *Homo sovieticus* . . .
as they like to think of themselves." He raised his eyebrows, as if seeking an analogy for his captive audience. "And like the jealous gods of
ancient days, they have always feared that man will steal—not fire, but
the power of speech; that mortals will turn the gift of language against
the gods to free themselves, to create a future, a magic circle where
their lies cannot find willing ears. Language is our lifeblood; it is what
allows us to survive, to change and renew and find our way forward. It
is the greatness of your tongue, the English language—that it adapts
and endures. For a Czech, it is very different prospect. Our language
was suppressed for centuries, by the Germans, the Hapsburgs, the
Catholics, the ruling nobility, and the Nazis . . . and now the apparatchiks. The language of the old men, Charon's minions, is a corruption
because it is forged from jealousy and hatred. The language of the artist
is born anew in each and every man and touches on the individual
truth of human experience, uncorrupted by fear, envy, and the thirst for
power. This essential truth lives eternally, but without language to give
it wings, it turns to dust, where the lies creep in to fill the void, whether
official lies or socialist lies or the lies of a bureaucracy that wants the
world to remain forever in thrall to its puppet theater. Marxism is just
another jealous god: first corrupting language, then every institution of
humanity, until freedom is banished, along with memory and hope."

As he leaned forward in his seat to refill his cup, I yearned more
than ever to regain the solidarity of years before, in those warm fall
days when we were the swiftest of the swift. Now, his wings clipped,
his matted and dirty hair showed flashes of tarnished silver as he bent
to light a cigarette, swirling the smoke behind him in deference to me.

"So," he continued, businesslike, "never speak ill of your country. You
play into their hands; they are masters of sowing doubt and distrust,
which they turn to the destruction of their enemies. Take pride in your
struggle to expunge the sins of your ancestors from your soul. Here,
sin is the sinew and bone of who we are; no one is immune: those who
have sold their souls and those who whistle past the graveyard. Their
souls are in a war against themselves, and the priests have long lost their

powers of absolution, as intercessors for the damned. Sin is the mute face you see everywhere in the streets. It comes in our mothers' milk."

I reached to his arm. "Listen, it's not that I haven't done my fair share of sinning."

"You killed your enemy, the North Vietnamese."

"Way more than my fair share."

A strange glimmer of light flashed in his eyes and he slammed the table so hard that my vodka sloshed and the lamp began its pendulum swing once more.

"You almost sound like you admire the North Vietnamese."

"Tenacious, driven, they survived everything we threw at them."

"They murdered; they imprisoned, tortured, and exiled; they took control of everything, until their captives starved. Our apparatchiks celebrated their victories in hopes of preserving their own. Now from Saigon to Hanoi, their sons and daughters take over the sweet Party jobs and perpetuate the system of oppression. And the Khmer Rouge . . . even for Max, it was an abomination."

Vlada pushed another bunch of newspaper cuttings my way. Articles about the International PEN conference of 1977, when Max had called for the intervention of the UN and the international community to prevent the Khmer Rouge genocide.

Tapping the table, Vlada shook his head in disgust. "Don't apologize—you have no need."

"I had many friends among the South Vietnamese; they trusted us, believed we'd stick by them."

Vlada squeezed my hand and then reached to his typewriter in what amounted to a loving caress, touching individual keys with his dirt-encrusted, broken-nailed fingers. I was instantly reminded of another lover's touch, as Max first spied my father's green Underwood at Elysium all those years before. And in the same moment . . . the clatter of typing—related in Nestor's sardonic telling—from the shade of a British Army tent in the hills above Kalamata.

Then he rose and padded over to his shelf and got out another book and placed it on the desk in front of me. It was my copy of the *Norton Anthology of English Literature*, a little worse for wear. "Your gift to me, do you remember?"

"Yes, I hoped it would keep you from going."

"But do you understand our role, how long it goes back, to Shakespeare and Milton—for you, Homer, of course." He flipped the pages, searching. "We provide the fiction that keeps the system functioning— the possibility of sin. Otherwise, our keepers lose interest in the game and become fat and careless. We make their jobs seem important— their endless reports on our activities. They point to us and see how few of us remain, how many publishers are shut down or publish only crap, and they count their successes while remaining vigilant. Time does not exist in a system that devours memory. Perhaps we have evolved a new law of nature: the end of evolution." Vlada gestured to the four walls. "I have become critical to the health of the ecosystem. The old men in their offices would destroy time, so that death will not rob them of their creation, so that their sons will follow them in lockstep to their graves. It was the dream of Marx—to abolish history, so his idea would become a timeless god. This is the dream of God, of the old men, a thing only fit to be dreamed in the grave. You see, I feed their bad dreams, and their satisfactions."

He laughed and pointed out the text from John Milton's *Paradise Lost*, heavily underlined and annotated with Charlie Springfield's commentary.

What though the field be lost?
All is not lost; the unconquerable will,
And study of revenge, immortal hate,
And courage never to submit or yield:
And what is else not to be overcome?
That glory never shall his wrath or might
Extort from me.

Those words, like a blood sacrifice, brought the shade of Charlie Springfield before me, standing tall and drunk in the chapel pulpit as he excoriated the Winsted faithful, who, for brief moment, ruled the Western world.

Tears flooded my eyes. "Oh, Vlada, if only you'd known Charlie Springfield . . ."

"But I do, in your notes, in Max's dedication of his first novel."

"Yes, that . . ."

"Listen to me: If Max had lived here and been a member in good standing of the writers' union, he would have written a wonderful novel about a dutiful son and patriotic father and how perfect a country they served."

"You mean . . ."

"Instead, he wrote an extravagant critique of the country that had given him everything, a country that saved his people in the war and kept the Communists behind their wall. A man like your father, a writer like Max, the bureaucracy cannot make such individuals; they must struggle up from the toils of their own conscience."

He laughed again uproariously, as if to make light of his summation before the jury, and so reached his cup to mine.

"Salut."

"Salut."

"I'd better not drink any more if I'm driving."

"Yes, they're very strict now about this." He glanced at this watch. "We must get going; our meeting is at nine in the Staré Město."

"And the chocolates, a gift?"

A touch of ironic indifference flickered across Vlada's face. He rose and went to the metal shelf by the tiny kitchen sink and got what looked like an antique wooden-handled chisel, its tip honed to a glinting edge. Then, with an oddly vacuous expression, he went across to his bed and bent to the mattress. He pulled it up and folded it back and began feeling under the padding the way an obstetrician might check for the position of the fetus. His fingers seemed to find what they were searching for. He steadied the turned mattress and then, with what seemed a precise and practiced motion, passed the chisel blade along a seam and parted the fabric without a snag. Putting the chisel aside, he reached into the incision with both hands and carefully maneuvered the thing out. He came over to the table and placed the shiny gold-sealed Orion box with the elaborate red bow next to its twin.

Under the hanging light in the dingy apartment, the boxes glowed like the holy of holies. We both stared as if spellbound, or perhaps slightly drunk. Then Vlada leaned back and spoke with an eerily staged smile, tinged with guilt perhaps or just pure exhaustion. He reached to the box that had been hidden in his mattress and plucked at the red bow as if to get the loops matching just right. "It is the work of my last three years. It is, as I told you, a novel about a life I never had: *Dreaming of the Grand Canyon*." He made a fist. "It is the best I have written. I have put everything I know into this book. It is dedicated to you and Max . . . and Laura. I have a publisher in Vienna who awaits the manuscript. His name and address are on the inside, with the manuscript."

He blew off a bit of lint from the cellophane.

"Peter, can you take this to Vienna for me?"

I don't think I even hesitated.

"Of course, of course I can."

He touched the gold award seals on the box of Orion chocolates from turn-of-the-century competitions in Belgium and Paris and Munich. He chuckled to himself and studied me a moment as if to assay my competence as an accomplice.

I now recognize the voice of temptation when I hear it. It is often framed in the call to pride and the hope of redemption, but it is still the voice of temptation, and it gets mostly young men into trouble, less those nearing middle age. But it was my last chance, perhaps the last chance of any in my generation to enlist ourselves on the side of the rebellious angels, or, as Vlada had so splendidly put it, in the struggle of memory against the powers of oblivion.

"Put this box in the bag with your receipt. Do not try to hide the bag or put it in one of your suitcases. Put the bag in the backseat of your car, with the maps and tourist guides, and the translation of Max's novel. When the guards at the border come to search your car, you must get out and leave the doors wide open and walk away and not watch them. Look into their eyes if they speak to you. Do not tell Laura about this; do not mention the document hidden under the frontispiece of the novel. Tell her it is a present for a friend. The guard will see if she is nervous, and she already seems very nervous."

"Sure, sure . . ."

"Tell me about her. I have spent twenty years remembering her, reading about her"—and he tapped the Orion box containing his manuscript—"wondering."

34 WHAT I DISCOVERED IN VLADA'S WORDS TO me is that history, especially one's own history (five weeks in Pankrác Prison), often feels like a series of rooms through which one is compelled to pass. Some are more like prison cells, constricted inner landscapes of the mind, while others, given to wide, spacious windows, offer more sanguine views of the parading landscape of our days. Vlada described his nine months in solitary confinement that way: rooms and mindscapes he painstakingly canvassed for his fantasy novel about his six months in America and an alternate life forgone. One passes through such rooms as dreams pass through us: furniture fading at the touch, artifacts a feathery weight in our palm, the varnish-darkened faces eluding our embrace, while we, often in free fall or sprinting in quicksand, seek to find a comforting lodgment. Max likened such rooms to his "memory points," moments of intense emotion set like the jeweled Pleiades in the darkened quiet of our minds: the crucial stepping-stones of life-enhancing moments that mark our path and so plot our place in the world. But such rooms, too, are contingent memories we share with others; and so, if we fail to embrace those other lives, throw the windows wide to the light—the life we shared—those memories will shrink and fade and avail us little: a life of barren ruins that will chill your bones with aged regrets. For we are those rooms, the landscapes through which we pass. That is why the clues are never where you expect to find them . . . until your eyes have adjusted to the prevailing light, until you've thrown the windows wide and listened deeply—oh, ever so deeply.

Even now I must stare fixedly out my window over the lake to catch the phantom of Vlada's rapt face against the rainy night, where he sat beside me as we drove back to the Staré Město, where one of the only five people in the world he trusted awaited us at an obscure working-class beer parlor—so he assured me. His hair was matted with the damp, his thrusting chin dangling a cigarette—a warrior's face, not unlike one of those supercilious Nordic gods that presided from the murals above the dance floor of the previous evening. How many such proud portrait faces have I glimpsed in darkened galleries, or in daguerreotypes of uniformed figures, mere flecks of silver nitrate on glass—those oh so steadfast abolitionists posed before Union pup tents . . . who saved a nation's soul, whose sacrifices, like their fragile images, are doomed to fail and fade like frost on a sunlit windowpane, lest we welcome them as our own.

It was Vlada's curse that first alerted me. At the farthest reach of our high beams we saw a car barricading the boulevard. A soldier with an AK-47 at the ready and a flashlight waving us down. More soldiers stood off to the side with capped heads bowed to the rain. Vlada's hand went to my knee, tight.

"Don't worry. Play the tourist. You speak only English. Don't answer if they question you in German."

I was braking gingerly. The front wheels skidded and caught and we slowed. The car across the road was a decrepit Škoda in camouflage green, a wreck, something that could be sacrificed to a speeding crash. There were more cars along the side of the road. Two large searchlights suddenly flared, screaming light in our eyes.

"Remember"—and I felt Vlada's hand again on my knee—"shake your head, tremble, act frightened and confused, like a lost child. Give them fear."

"They—who are 'they'?" I squinted into the harsh beams of light and could make out the lines of soldiers in pea green uniforms, their faces just hidden beneath the dripping visors. The vodka made me braver than was probably good for me. "Just as well it's not a DUI stop; I'd fail a Breathalyzer."

"Let me do the talking. If you must speak, look them in the face, in the eyes, and show them how confused and scared you are."

I was confused by Vlada's tone suggesting I play the buffoon. What had happened to the belligerent cynic of minutes before?

In the explosion of light around us, that line of security police looked like a slightly ridiculous chorus out of Aeschylus. Then another car came up behind us, its headlights adding to the drama unfolding on all sides.

A flashlight tapped my window and shone in my eyes.

The door was pulled open.

"Mr. Alden, you will please get out."

The toneless pronunciation of my name made me want to piss my pants. I panicked when I remembered I hadn't even had a chance to get my passport back from the clerk at the hotel.

Hands grabbed me and took over the task of hastening my exit from the Land Rover. I was aware of a few curses in Czech from Vlada before he, too, was manhandled out of the car. I was led off to the curb by a young soldier, just to the edge of the most intense illumination. Vlada was held by two soldiers next to the Land Rover, where an older man in a dark raincoat stood waiting. I wasn't sure if I was relieved or saddened not to be center stage with Vlada. As the man in the raincoat and hat began interrogating Vlada, the Land Rover was attacked by a team of men in civilian garb. Within moments, everything not screwed down was on the tarmac. Experienced hands searched every nook and cranny of my clothes and then some. I could smell humid bodies and cheap cologne. A rifle barrel bumped me in passing. My wallet and change and watch were removed. I felt strangely light-headed, as if I might float away if released, and I breathed deeply to try to rid my system of the vodka.

Vlada, a soldier on either side gripping an arm, had a look of utter exasperation on his face—a drill he knew only too well—as he confronted the man in the raincoat. The man wore a broad felt hat that dripped with rain. I could make out his flat nose and double chin and, when he raised his head slightly, the most impassive eyes I'd ever seen. Their conversation seemed well-rehearsed. Vlada chucked his head and rolled his eyes as if bored by the whole thing: been there, done that. Shoes jittered out the doors of the Land Rover, like something out of a comic routine, as the undersides of the seats were still being searched. And another pair of shoes stuck out from under the chassis, where someone had a flashlight flicking around. The man in the raincoat took off his hat for a moment and shook it, as if the rain dripping from the brim had been annoying him. He was nearly bald except for a strip of short gray hair that looked like the tonsure of a monk. The soldiers besides Vlada relaxed their grip, and he now began gesturing, pointing to the slick tarmac, and ticking off the imbecilities being perpetrated at his and my expense. The jowly face of the older man remained near blank of emotion, as if he, too, had been through this little charade once too often to really have his heart in it anymore. Better to get it the hell over with and out of the rain and home to his wife and a warm bath. To my untrained eyes, the fox terriers searching the car were absolutely convinced of something.

When they were done, the man in the raincoat snapped his fingers and pointed to the contents on the tarmac: maps, owner's manual, Kleenex, tour guides, cassettes, a hair band, a box of throat lozenges, breakdown kit, first-aid kit, some of Laura's discarded novels, Vlada's translation of *Gardens of Saturn*, the jack and spare tire, and a plastic bag with the box of chocolates. A soldier handed him the translation and he opened to the frontispiece and read the inscription, tapped the cover, smiled at Vlada, and slipped the book into his coat pocket. The soldier then handed him the bag. The weight, I thought, the weight of the box would give the game away. But the man didn't even bother to test for the weight; maybe he didn't have to. He got out the box of chocolates and slit the cellophane with a thumbnail and spilled out the typed contents. At least a dozen pages wafted to the tarmac while he stood for a moment absorbed in the manuscript. Vlada became very still, blond hair hanging straight down and dripping, shoulders losing their lift, his eyes seeming to fade, drawing inward, as if some life force was draining from his body. I thought to myself, Surely it can't be his only copy—the book he'd written in his mind during all those months in solitary. If there was anything offensive or dangerous or perhaps even beautiful on those pages, the man in the raincoat's fossilized expression gave nothing away. In fact, he looked profoundly bored and fed up, and after a few minutes' examination, he handed the thing off to the waiting soldier, who failed or didn't bother to pick up the pages on the road.

I wanted to protest the sloppiness of leaving the neglected pages soaking in the rain—perhaps gorgeous scenes of the Grand Canyon or the exhilaration of catching a well-thrown pass—and as I leaned forward—I discovered that there was no leaning forward. Hands restrained me and tightened their grip.

A flash of violence exploded, then instantly subsided with staccato grunts. I think Vlada had taken a swing at the man in the raincoat, or what would have been a swing if he hadn't been restrained by the two soldiers. Now they pinned his arms—hard, up behind him. A blunted cry tore from his throat. The man, the policeman, the security officer, the whatever functionary, had not even flinched—an actor onstage would have at least registered the mayhem directed at him—but simply shook his head in disgust, wearied at the judgment required of him by some immutable calculus. I tried to sort it out in my mind as Vlada had explained it to me, the pathology of oppression that held his countrymen in its grip, the death grip of the old on the young . . . a thing that shed the husk of theory as I saw the pain convulse Vlada's face.

The man in the raincoat took a step toward Vlada, shaking his head, wiping the rain drips from his lapels, a look of relief that he could now go home and get into that warm tub. And then, as if needing to at least go through the motions of his official role for the long-suffering rain-soaked soldiers who witnessed this scene, he raised an admonishing finger to Vlada, paternal, almost solicitous. The prisoner had become very quiet, pinned under the arms by the soldiers behind. They were young men with bad acne and high Slavic cheekbones, probably recently off the farm or from distant villages and only recently brought to the city to do security work. Strong, too, the way Vlada had been strong when I had first known him. The older man, the honcho, began to speak in low, measured tones, now stamping his feet in a delicate, almost comical two-step, his brown leather shoes soaked through. He was asking questions, repeating them, for the record—a font of reasonableness. Vlada just shook his head. The older man finally shrugged and turned his head to me and smiled like a gracious host would across a crowded room upon sighting a newly arrived guest. Vlada said something. The man turned back as if he hadn't quite heard. Vlada spoke again, in a voice deliberately low. The man bent forward, a cocked turtlehead stretched from the carapace of the raincoat.

I saw Vlada's head move like the strike of a snake, and a thick gobbet of spittle slid down the man's cheek. A spasmodic single reflex from the two young soldiers behind, two vicious upward jerks. At least one, if not two, audible cracks. A shriek. The man in the raincoat retreated a step and carefully, exactingly, wiped away the spittle from his cheek, flinging the unmentionable to the tarmac, rinsing his face with water off the lapel of his coat. This done, he gave a nod to a young soldier who carried a Kalashnikov. The soldiers behind, who had broken Vlada's arms, lowered him slightly, and as they did, he let out another shriek of agony. The soldier with the Kalashnikov adjusted his position and with the mechanical ease of a flywheel executed a blow into Vlada's midsection with the wooden butt, doubling him over, and then an upward blow into the side of the jaw, caving it in like a piece of rotted fruit. The soldiers dropped him facedown onto the wet cobblestones.

Something in my brain snapped. A sound escaped my lips, but a blue steel barrel thumped convincingly across my chest when I tried to move.

I began shivering in horror, as if the vodka had magically exited my system. I could only stare at the broken teeth and bloody drool from Vlada's flaccid lips, his shattered jaw hanging agape. The blood seemed to have a life of its own, branching out in tiny reddish rivulets between the cobblestones. I couldn't see his eyes . . . and I was desperate to see his eyes, desperate that the spark, which I loved, hadn't been—couldn't have been—extinguished.

The image of his sprawling body remains, like that of a rebel angel flung to earth from some unimaginable height.

When this scene of violence returns to me in dreams—which it does regularly, when I see the upward flash of that Kalashnikov butt and scream out to Vlada—something in me—a default setting of the historian's trade—tries to fathom the causal chain of civilization's DNA that could make such a thing possible. Had it begun with Plato's banning of Homer in his ideal society, or Romans burning Christians, or Christians burning heretics and Jews, or Catholics burning Protestants, or—as my great-grandfather General Alden would surly insist—the lynching and destruction of black slaves and freedmen? Ideological man—bred on fear, greed, and hate's mendacity—is the monster in our night. But this act of violence, like the insidious causal chain that killed my father—not a bullet through the brain, I would find out later—had its genesis in Lenin's embrace of terror to protect and spread the Bolshevik Revolution, elaborated and refined by his Cheka and Stalin's NKVD and KGB, and so made available wholesale to the fanatic anti-Semitism of the brown shirts, the SS and Einsatzgruppen, first in the gulags and then the concentration camps, the genocidal famines and killing fields, expertly refined methodologies of manipulative hatred, off-the-shelf ready-mades available to Mao and Ho Chi Minh and Pol Pot, Kim Jong-il and Castro, and all their tin-pot dictatorial epigoni in every far-flung hellhole of existence . . . only to flicker out on that wet cobblestone street in Prague. Or so I once liked to think. Until, sadly, it got revved up again in various ethnic and religious guises in Kosovo, and later in a thousand nameless terrorist massacres across the globe. The hardwired ideological killer in our DNA.

It gives me some comfort to think that the spasm of punishment I witnessed, that particular strain of violence—the young soldier didn't even grimace when he delivered the blow to Vlada's jaw—was a final malignant twitch in that particular dying ecosystem of human degradation locked behind the Iron Curtain, which expired with the fall of the Berlin Wall. A few days later in the streets of Prague, a bunch of protesters would be badly beaten by the security police, but the demonstrations that followed in Wenceslas Square in the coming weeks, as the Velvet Revolution unfolded, were, thankfully, largely peaceful.

Vlada was one of the last casualties . . . along with my cellmate.

This I knew, of course, only in retrospect. At the time, I was just terrified. I kept thinking about when Vlada had put his finger to the back of my head and touched the bullet's entry point. In 1971 and 1972, nothing had frightened me more than the thought of being made a prisoner of the North Vietnamese, for I knew exactly how they went about their business.

I was wedged between two soldiers in the backseat of a waiting vehicle. The soldiers were wet and smelled as if they'd been out on maneuvers for days. After the initial shock, I made a few feeble protests and uttered the necessary demands. I demanded to see a representative of the American embassy. No one paid me the slightest attention. In fact, I got the distinct impression that I was the last thing on anyone's mind. They were all exchanging uneasy glances and jittery words. The plainclothes policeman in the front seat, next to the driver, had steam rising off his jacket and had lighted up a cigarette, cracking his window to flick out the burgeoning ash. The windows were fogged, a smear of dingy habitation rushing by as we sped into the heart of the city. I was filled with a sinking feeling, as if we'd been spilled over the edge of a whirlpool and into oblivion: the suck of air past that cracked window, the g-force of hard turns through narrow streets, hurtling into the belly of that godforsaken city.

I wasn't even sure we'd make it. The suspension was shot and the tailpipe grated on potholes. Something dug into my side painfully. I finally reached around and found the open holster flap of the soldier beside me pressed into my hip. I felt the wooden grip of his pistol. The man was oblivious, wiping at his window as if preoccupied with the groups of figures filling the sidewalks; he looked worried by what he saw. I could have taken that pistol. I could have shot the motherfuckers. I did nothing, of course. I felt strangely neglected and in a concave of souls preoccupied with private anxieties. The guy in the front seat was wiping at his window, too, as if intent on examining the pedestrians, who seemed out in prodigious numbers compared to what I'd seen the day before. Through the fist-size peephole the soldier next to me had made in the fogged glass, I could make out the gnarled turrets and writhing Baroque facades with their stony faces, and a flaming window or two high up in an office building, but little else.

We came to a screeching halt at a barrier and checkpoint. The driver opened his window and got into an animated discussion with an armed guard, a discussion that everyone else around me craned their necks to hear. Although I couldn't understand a word, I got the distinct impression it had nothing to do with me, but with something more general and far more compelling. A moment later, the barrier was lifted and the clanking of a garage door sounded behind us and the car was engulfed by an enormous underground garage. I detected a release of tension all around. The precipitous drive was because of something going on in the streets of Prague, and it had all these guys worried.

And they were as right to be worried as they were eager to rid themselves of me.

I was marched through a concrete bunker of a parking lot, through a red door with a blinking red light, down one interminable passage after another lined with dingy offices, then down echoing metal staircases, then into another corridor of reinforced-concrete walls and massive jail doors. Here, under strips of fluorescent lights, the smell changed from musty paper and file folders to one of unkempt bodies, stale sweat, and open latrines.

Just when I thought there could be no more *down*, more steps appeared, and these of concrete, as if hewn out of solid bedrock. We descended to a final corridor; this one was hung with bare lightbulbs, and the roughhewn stonework appeared like something from a road cutting or mine face. Metal brackets in the ceiling carried the ductwork and utility cables, much of it patched with electric tape. The doors on these cells seemed even more massive than the ones before, or maybe it was the thick layers of chipping paint and overlapping metal plates and rivet points that had the look of archaic machinery. Cell numbers were stenciled under the judas holes and it was clear that the numbers had been changed many times since the nineteenth century, the specters of erased figures showing through the paint, as if the accounting system for the containment of human souls had to be constantly updated.

Finally, we stopped at what felt like an exhausted pithead. A massive door bore the number III stenciled in Roman numerals, or just possibly 111. A guard sat at a table reading a newspaper and seemed annoyed at being disturbed. He gave me a cursory frisking, removed my shoelaces and belt, handed me a grimy roll of toilet paper, and a seconds later the door of the cell closed behind me.

I surveyed my domain. A pair of facing cots with folded blankets. Pewter gray walls that had been scraped at and gouged and rubbed and carved into, so much so that my archaeologist's eye was galvanized for a second in an attempt to interpret the symbols and patterns that might be discerned. A gleaming white toilet bowl, strangely clean and even smelling of disinfectant, cleaner than the one on the Hotel Red Star. There was a ventilation duct near the ceiling by the door and a single hanging lightbulb, clear, not frosted, where a squiggle of filament did a lazy hula dance. I pictured again Vlada's smashed jaw, which made me concerned about Laura, which got me angry at her all over again for having gotten me into this mess and lying about Vlada. The vodka was wearing off and anger and fear rose in my throat like vying riptides.

I lay down and pulled the blanket over me and stared up at the lightbulb and the fragile filament that flickered and danced like some homunculus caught in a web . . . and then went out. Darkness as absolute as anything I'd ever known engulfed me. I pulled the thin blanket to my chin. To try to staunch my fear, I began an examination of the situation with all the clarity and logic I could muster.

But the more I did so, the more troubled I became. Strange how the police in the car had ignored me, but their anxious faces and relief at depositing me in Pankrác Prison did nothing to lessen the serious charges I knew would come: attempting to smuggle state documents, a dissident's manuscript—and they could throw currency violations in for good measure.

The 1955 ministerial letter to the Soviets, protesting the execution of my father—that really had me fucked: It could mean years, or worse.

I started shaking uncontrollably. I wanted to reach out and find Laura's hand and tell her it would be okay, to believe my own words. But when I reached out, all I found was the cold, dank walls scratched and incised with a cacophony of indecipherable symbols, each a cry of fear or despair.

The darkness in that chamber was like embalming fluid; it had texture and weight and even a smell, a mixture of human effluvium and disinfectant, which produced a certain surcease of inherent contradiction . . . the oddly comforting and even liberating possibility of brass-bottom reality, along the lines of death and taxes, or in Vlada's words: "Don't worry your mind about ultimate truths; when all contradictions are overcome, as Marx would have it, and we come to rest after our long journey—you, me, like our fathers, will all be dead or in a prison cell." His brave vodka-soaked insouciance and edgy irony, which had engendered such courage and even inspiration just an hour before, now seemed to mock me.

And worse, I felt like I deserved this fate: I'd been obsessed with such places most of my life, fascinated with walls and crypts, the gruesome pickings to be found in tombs and graves and burial chambers—the artifacts of ultimate captivity.

But what really got to me: I couldn't help thinking along the lines, how as a toddler led along the paths of Elysium by my grandmother, staring up where the tall white pines straddled the blue sky. . . . He was here, where I am now . . . waiting and wasting and wondering.

As if I were fated to follow his footsteps.

Crazy?

I think not. Some inbred instincts have an infernal logic all their own.

How to reconcile the glorious freedom of life and the mind-forged manacles of dark captivity in the same world? A question my father asked himself in his prison diary, a question Vlada's father wrote about in his short stories of his youth in a concentration camp, and Vlada in his Pankrác Prison novel, as Max failed to do in his unfinished novel about the destruction of his mother's Viennese family in Mauthausen. All services we tender to the memories of the dead as much as to the living: as the dead live through us, as we through them.

For who can fail to be moved by Achilles' sigh of parting gratitude from the dark captivity of Hades as Odysseus tells him of his son's triumphs . . . that something of his glorious flesh and blood still walked earth's sunny uplands. Or how, in turn, Odysseus gained the strength to see his own life through, sustained by the knowledge that his own son, Telemachus, and his ever-faithful wife, Penelope, had never forsaken him.

I only hope my father glimpsed such a vision with his last labored breath.

In the summer of 1943, in the lush orchard-covered hills of western Maryland, our OSS trainers liked to put us through our paces with

old school gusto and hazing. They were often British or Common-
wealth ex-military, with experience gained in the far-flung corners of
the empire. They had few scruples, few illusions. I remember one in
particular, a British ex-police chief out of Hong Kong, who taught
hand-to-hand combat, a kind of jujitsu street fighting, lethal stuff.
This chap looked like a gentle professor but was fully capable of killing
you in seconds with his bare hands. As a Princeton colleague put it
to me after our first week of training and his third bourbon, "this is
not just starting from scratch. We have to reinvent ourselves; we have
to become very different people, nasty sons of bitches, as nasty, if not
nastier, than our enemies. We're learning to sell our souls cheap." That
was a terrifying thought to me. In it I heard echoes of Thucydides as
he described the slow embitterment and hardening of the Athenians
as expectations of a short war and easy victory over Sparta turned into
a devastating drawn-out slog. I thought of the historian's lament that
war teaches only reliance on blind violence, how party ties replace those
of kin and country, when the wicked are perceived to be clever and the
good foolish, when the sensible is seen as weakness, when the circumspect are derided as do-nothings.

I feared in that moment, with still fresh memories of the Nazi occupation of Greece, that we had entered another dark age and could only
hope it would not last as long as the Peloponnesian War—God forbid the four hundred years of darkness that descended with the fall of
Mycenae and Pylos. Ten years later, my worst fears seem confirmed.

If such is the case, I am well quit of it.

—excerpt from John Alden's Pankrác Prison diary

35 IN THE DARK AND THE CHILL AND THE loneliness—throughout awful meals of tasteless dumplings, gritty spinach, boiled cabbage, and rice soup shoved through a slot in the door, I thought of what Vlada had told me about his nine months in solitary confinement, how he had used the time to compose a novel in his mind, sweeping up memories of his visit to America in 1968 and translating them into a narrative of what might have been, and I remembered the eager spark in his eyes as he touched the box of those prizewinning Orion chocolates. But the thought of even another day in confinement, much less nine months, or worse, was a crushing fear. First, I began to seek ways to keep my terror at bay by remembering better times in the Greek islands, or childhood scenes in the Berkshires, or even early years at Winsted. But then it was my time in Vietnam that came to dominate my thoughts. Somehow the sumptuous jungle greens, the saturating humidity, the smells of cordite, scooter exhaust, curried eel and barbecued duck, watery Vietnamese beer, and the vegetal decay of the Vam Co Dong River were a balm to my imagination, as if my imprisonment represented an opportunity to make sense of my time as an intelligence officer with the South Vietnamese militia in Hâu Nghĩa Province. I had gotten very close to my commanding officer, Theo Colson, and our master sergeant, Willie Gadsden, and our Vietnamese militiamen; many for whom I'd developed a deep affection, and the many more we'd betrayed and left behind. Over the days and weeks that followed, I found that releasing my repressed anger helped with the fear and lingering sadness, as if by constructing a forgiving narrative in my inner

mindscape, I might make sense of my pathetic little disaster, hoping all the while that my cell wouldn't turn out to be its final coda.

CIA INVESTIGATION, INTERIM REPORT, JUNE 2, 1954:
INTERVIEW WITH VIRGIL DABNEY,
SUBJECT'S ACADEMIC MENTOR, EX-CIA 1948–1950

"What was it, a year ago now, September? John said he was rushing back down to Washington—the Berlin blowup, I suppose—but wanted to stop by for a chat. His head was filled with Michael Ventris; he was the British architect who had deciphered the Linear B script, which promised unprecedented breakthroughs in Bronze Age archaeology. John and I sat in my study, relishing the possibilities. Our minds were abuzz—to think that the lost world of Homer might open its doors to us. I remember him patting my knee before he got up to leave and telling me if he had it to do all over again, he'd rather be a schoolteacher. I laughed and told him, 'Some must teach and some must do—and some a little of both, so that there's something left to teach about.' He liked that, I think. Is there some problem that no one's heard from him in almost a year? . . .

"Yes, I know all about Philby, or as much as I read in the papers: Hoover was onto him early in the game. Such a mournful tolling across England's green and pleasant land, to have bred such a creature in the bowels of Cambridge. John was deeply troubled by the traitor, to have been led on by a trusted ally no less. No doubt it's brought him under suspicion, but he's in good company there—all you boys are looking pretty bad right now. I consider myself lucky to have gotten out when I did, after Italy was saved from the Red hordes. Teaching the next generation to set the world aright will be no easy task. Our own Kim Philbys were legion in the thirties, and they still lurk in the highest offices in the land, homegrown scum nurtured in the bosom of our finest institutions. Alger Hiss was just the tip of the ice cube. As I'm sure you know, my brother's a top dog in the FBI—be careful, my friends: You have your work cut out for you."

I had been in solitary confinement for a little over two weeks when the change came, when the weight of the world—or was it memory?—shifted. A concrete chamber with the regular alternation of light and dark, where I couldn't get comfortable. Shooting pains in my back would yank me from sleep or thoughts of the faces of the North Vietnamese I'd interrogated, of the dead on the battlefield whose bodies I'd searched. When hot, my own stink was abhorrent; my panicky sweat burned. When freezing, I listened to the Morse code of my teeth chattering, hoping to detect a clue left unturned.

I was worried sick about Laura: Could she have been arrested, too? And Vlada?

Then, in the dark, I awoke to the smell of smoke. I panicked at the thought of fire, until I realized it was tobacco smoke. On the cot opposite, the faintest image of a face, a figure propped against the scarified wall, as if this stony personage had simply emerged from some shadowy corner of my cell, or, worse, from my dreams. The scantily bearded face had a diabolic mien, the red-tinged features picked out of the blackness by the steady glow of a lit pipe. The pipe was held in cupped hands. I was alarmed and yet relieved, for I'd been yearning for company, for my interrogation to begin, for someone to tell my side of things, to explain the holy terror I'd brought down on the heads of entire NVA divisions . . . as if such things might be mitigating factors in the scales of justice.

Then as the novelty of this spectral being began to wane and I came to my senses, my heart seemed to drain in a furious pumping to my lower extremities and I felt like I might faint. There was something familiar in the old face, as if I'd recently caught a glimpse—perhaps an iconic version—haunted, as I still was, by the fanatical faces along Charles Bridge.

"Who's there?"

The bearded man had the look of a Victorian scholar, and my mind inventoried a catalog of look-alikes, a Darwin or Freud, a Marx or Engels. Hopefully, someone who might cast a favorable light on my long-ago sins. In my panic, I pulled myself up higher against the wall of my bunk, raising my thin blanket to my neck as if to protect myself, until I realized the air was warm, almost stifling. I couldn't remember being so hot. And then I was assaulted by my own wretched smell. I reached to my whiskered chin as if to substantiate my overripe existence, that it had only been days and weeks and not the years of confinement I imagined in the mirrored figure on the cot opposite.

"What's going on?"

As if wishing to be responsive to my plea, my new cellmate raised the lit pipe to his lips and then held out the pipe toward me as he exhaled, bending forward as if to better examine my familiar features. I could see his fragile, thin-boned face; he looked eighty or older, someone who might have once been very handsome. On his pale cheek was a thin scar half-obscured by whiskers. His eyes were sunken but glinted with acute intelligence as he examined me.

"What the hell is going on?" I finally asked, trying to summon all the indignation I could muster. Why hadn't I heard something when the door opened? Normally, I woke the instant the food tray was shoved under the door.

"How remarkable, you really must be his son—stunning to think it."

The voice was educated, German-accented, not English and not American, but Middle-European, a kind of refined hybrid that might float out of the static of a shortwave broadcast from some obscure propaganda transmitter.

"Who are you? What's the story?"

"The story—ah, the story. Another chaser of stories. But *you* are the story, now, after the catastrophic event of a few days ago."

"Catastrophic event—what happened?"

"You don't know about the wall? How long have you been in here?"

"It must be about two weeks by now."

"Of course, when you missed our rendezvous. A blink of an eye. Five days ago, the Berlin Wall came down—kaput."

"Don't be ridiculous. Who are you?"

"It's no joke, young man—you can celebrate your father's vindication."

"How do you know my father?"

"We were colleagues, although, to be honest, he might have regarded me as his nemesis."

I realized, in that moment—probably the scar—who he was. Or more likely because of the author photo I had recently stared at in his 1934 book, *The Search for Homer*, in my Athens apartment. That was a very much younger version of the man who sat before me now, but he retained in the half-light a narrow-faced refinement of the bone structure, a certain grace of composition in the way the long taper of the nose and expressive lips and good teeth bespoke a rare intelligence. In retrospect, our meeting seems too fantastic to believe, that I'd simply made it all up to satisfy a craving, prompted by some heightened expectations on my part, going back to our meeting with Nestor, that Karel Hollar must've had something to do with my father's disappearance. With my head spinning, as if my mind by pure force of will had compelled the impossible, leavened, too, with the equally fantastic news about the Berlin Wall, a simmering anger took over and my fears fell away, to be replaced by my training as an army intelligence officer. In tandem with the cold-eyed instinct to disguise myself or, at the very least, assume whatever persona required to transform fantasy into reality or, as Max might put it, fiction.

"We all thought you had died in a Soviet prisoner of war camp," I told him.

"'We?'"

"My colleagues in the archaeology field: Karel Hollar was even more famous than my father in the late thirties: partnering with Carl Andersen to discover Nestor's Palace and the first Linear B tablets in mainland Greece. Surely you've read my books on Athenian history."

"I have indeed, and you do your father proud. While I, alas, was forced to change fields due to unforeseen circumstances. I practice a different kind of archaeology now," and he laughed, as if to make light of the remark, "of human souls in extremis . . . so it would seem."

There was something almost Viennese in his soft vowels, with a touch of prewar American slang, perhaps picked up from movies or books.

"It's sad you haven't kept up. Bronze Age archaeology has been on a roll recently, wonderful new finds at Pylos and on the island of Thirassia, whole towns and frescoes intact under the magma from Santorini."

There was a long pause, during which I could just make out his rapt breathing or perhaps—did I imagine it?—sighs of regret.

"Ah, but, you see, I've been summoned from a long retirement, from my little corner of purgatory, all because of you, it seems. You have them worried—a CIA agent out to revenge your father, so they told me. And yet, I'm confused. A friend, too, of the son of my dear colleague Janos Radec. And an archaeologist. How can you be all of these things? And yet you arrive on our doorstep—a CIA provocateur, just as the wall is down and our streets fill with protestors—hardly a coincidence in a believer's eyes. Either I am going mad or the world has gone mad—I'm not sure which it is."

"I believe I have a right to see a representative from the American embassy. That way, we could clear up any confusion about identities, much less matters of cause and effect."

"They don't know if you are an avenging angel or their savior, now that they've been abandoned by Moscow, not to mention the GDR. Surely you must be pleased with your father's long labors."

"I'm happy to give my father and his CIA colleagues all the credit, but as I told you, I'm an archaeologist, not a CIA agent. All I want to is to get out of here *and* find my girlfriend—they haven't arrested her, have they?"

"No idea."

"Is Vlada okay?"

"Do you not have a proposition, a deal perhaps—assurances?"

"I don't understand. Not to repeat myself, but I'm an archaeologist. I came to Prague to visit an old school friend."

"Don't insult their intelligence. You were trying to take out a very important document concerning the death of your father. I know, because I provided it to your friend Vlada. And they don't have my original, so that is something in our favor. Incompetent and brutal as they may be, I assume they now want a quid pro quo. No one in the present government was responsible for what happened to your father; neither was anyone in the Dubček government in my day. It was a KGB operation. Nevertheless, our present masters—for how long, I wonder—assume the CIA is interested in a deal for their cooperation, some details perhaps, some information useful to besmirch the Soviets. Why else would you be here? Can you give them a guarantee?"

"Guarantee?"

"Where will they go?"

"Go?"

"Kaput, dismissed, shrugged off, if they escape the wrath of their countrymen."

"I see, amnesty for forty years of crimes."

"Twenty, if you insist."

"But there *are* a few things—anomalies, crimes—that need explaining." I stared at the wizened face across from me, barely legible in the glow of his pipe, my mind grabbing up and discarding cards, new cards—yes, better cards, but already concerned how long I had and how best to play them. I reached back into my intelligence training to fish out the wildest surmise I could think of and see if it had any traction. "My father had a meeting with you in 1953. He walked through Checkpoint Charlie into East Berlin and . . . found you, his erstwhile friend and colleague alive and still kicking."

This produced a long silence and then darkness as his pipe went out. Then a match flared to life. Karel Hollar, or the man who had once been Karel Hollar, motioned to me, placing a finger to his lips and touching an ear with an upward glance to indicate we were being recorded.

"A former life," he said just above a whisper, "of which, though a necessity, I'm not proud."

I, too, lowered my voice, not a little amazed but wonderfully heartened that I'd reached down into the muck and ooze and actually snagged an artifact that might offer answers to my father's fate.

"What, some unfinished business about a horde of Linear B tablets that went missing at Pylos almost under the nose of Carl Andersen?"

I sensed him stiffen at this news, perhaps the very thing he never dreamed I nor anyone else could have known about. A most unhappy subject.

"One doesn't come on a collegial visit with a concealed gun. Nor does one do a lot of illegal traveling, presumably gathering intelligence during a very delicate moment in East-West relations."

"Nevertheless, I suspect that you were the primary objective of his journey."

"The indictment—and I believe this was formerly presented to your embassy—was that he assassinated a government minister of the GDR."

"Come on, that can't be true. They don't send a senior officer to do that kind of thing; even I know that much. He'd been station chief in Athens, for Christ's sake."

"Yet, he did it. I'm a witness to the fact."

At this, I thought I detected a smile that wavered between pain and irony.

"Well, talk about the pot calling the kettle black—look at you: a famed German archaeologist before the war—DIA role of honor, yet with strong Communist sympathies—then a Wehrmacht captain with expertise in explosives—and/or an agent with British SIS and intimate ties to ELAS—an unfortunate hiatus as a POW in a Soviet camp, and then . . . Vlada swears you were in the Dubček government."

At this, he drew deeply on his lit pipe and again motioned with a finger to his lips at my raised voice.

"I was the GDR minister of mines."

I shook my head. "So you weren't in Dubček's—"

"From 1950 to 1953, in the GDR."

I made a motion—trying to repress my incredulity—with my right hand, a little series of leaping gestures: of one thing following after another. And he silently nodded. And I realized that Nestor had him perfectly pegged: He had to have been NKVD/KGB from the get-go; he'd been Moscow's man in both the GDR and Czechoslovakia.

"Minister of mines, well, how appropriate for a digger of souls. You did your Ovid one better: a protean Lazarus twice over."

"I am a man of my age. And for those of us in the Party, the war and the Cold War were often a matter of survival by any means."

"Your Wehrmacht career in Greece as an engineer and demolitions expert hardly classifies as one of desperate survival."

"Of all things, I am most proud of the role I played in the liberation of Greece from the Nazis."

"Are you suggesting you were working for the Allies—*and* the Soviets?"

"Never, I was working for the Soviets; I was in constant contact, coordinating strategy."

In the intelligence business, it is known as the essential lie: when you know you've got your man between a rock and a hard place.

"For Stalin's takeover of Greece?"

"It was a common policy between the Allied powers and the Soviet Union to encourage the Greek Resistance forces to work together against the Nazis."

"You encouraged the Greek Communists to eliminate their royalist and republican rivals?"

"If I didn't know differently, I'd almost think—like father like son— you came to Prague to indict me."

"There is the matter of Kostas Kalayias. Does the name ring a bell?"

"A rather obscure Communist leader and a Greek patriot; you *are* well informed."

"I've worked and lived in Greece for sixteen years."

"A chip off the old block, as the British say."

"Americans say it, too, but your Cambridge connections are compelling, as well. Trouble is, your version of this story makes little sense. Why would a high-ranking CIA officer, forgoing diplomatic immunity, slip into East Berlin to carry out—was it an assassination attempt you're alleging? Not on you? When or if such a thing had official sanction, the hit would have been assigned to a local shooter, to a disaffected Ukrainian or ex-Nazi with a score to settle."

"That was the most unsettling feature of this affair. . . . Perhaps it wasn't official policy."

"You mean it was personal, against a colleague, a friend he'd known since student days? But what could have prompted such a thing?"

"Those were trying times, not unlike the present moment. We had worker strikes in Berlin and uprisings in Leipzig. Only Soviet tanks saved the situation. We hemorrhaged tens of thousands of citizens in those days; there was no wall to hold back the tide. And the Soviets were on our neck."

"So, you were lying just now, about the wall coming down."

"Rest assured, I've seen pictures on West German television, Austrian television—young people by the thousands sitting on the wall, smashing the concrete with sledgehammers. Berlin is one great drunken celebration."

"Do I detect gladness in your voice? You're a Communist and—or at least you were—a high-ranking official in the GDR. Surely you can't be pleased by such events."

"I haven't lived in the GDR for twenty-five years. As I told you, I am a permanent exile—thanks to your father."

"Well, if that's all true, maybe now you can return."

"I prefer to live out my days in Prague, if Havel and the others will have me. I never expected to live to see it."

"But, if true, it's the end of everything you believed in."

"We fought for freedom from oppression, not the imposition of a Stalinist tyranny."

"Perhaps you can travel again—where would you go if not the GDR?"

"Ah, that is easy; I'd return to Greece, to where the green hills meet the blue sea. A small cottage where I'd continue my studies."

"To sandy Pylos, where the citizens, long ago, sacrificed bulls to Poseidon on the sea-girt shore."

"How sweet can be one's memories of Homer, an age as innocent as it was brutal at the dawn of recorded time."

"Ah, of course, and I suppose that must have been the thing that drew you, as it did my father, back to Greece during the war? Neither one of you, it seems, could keep away: the Linear B tablets hidden in nearby Kyparissia."

This baited question produced a long silence.

"I had almost forgotten . . . so many years of nothing but politics. I only wish we'd had our time to drink in a beer cellar together, a much more convivial setting for a confessional mode, if that's what's meant to be."

"Confessions, I suppose, it does seem to be the season. But I must admit to an intense curiosity about those Linear B tablets."

"God has always enjoyed confession, to occupy his long, dreary winter afternoons by the fire in his comfortable chair—don't you

think? The kind of stories that will go down well with tea and brandy."
He gestured to what I assumed was the ventilation duct and microphone in the ceiling. "Besides, it keeps his priests endlessly busy. It
is when they lose interest in their work . . . that is when the trouble
begins."

"Tell me about the last time you saw my father, before he suddenly
showed up in 1953 intent on assassinating you?"

"I told you: That is in the official indictment. It was not precisely my
recollection."

"Well, you had me worried for a few minutes. An assassin, an awful
thing to contemplate—much less meeting with a ghost. Believe me,
I understand professional rivalries between old colleagues—even best
friends. Academics are the worst, you know. But if it wasn't for tea and
brandy and confession, then what?"

I heard him sigh contemplatively, and his breathing quickened.

"I hoped he still loved me."

"Loved?"

"The young scholars we were in Leipzig and Cambridge, Crete and
Mycenae and Athens, and Venice—even romantic Venice."

"In Venice?"

"Palazzo Barberini, such a splendid place. When we were young men
in the thirties, our passion for a lost world drove us nearly mad—truly."

"Partners and rivals until you snatched the stolen Linear B tablet
in—what, 1944, with the German retreat from Greece? Until Ventris
deciphered the script in 1952, when suddenly you needed help." I bent
forward into the near dark. "I would have gone fucking crazy if I'd
unearthed those tablets, if I had them to myself."

"Yes, you know, then, the feeling—"

"For lost stories, yes. How many did you have?"

"One hundred and three."

"Not in the storerooms with all the hundreds Carl Andersen
excavated?"

"In an anteroom of the throne room. They had been fired and had
once been stored in wooden boxes."

"Jesus, so not inventories, but palace—what—genealogies, diplomatic records, histories . . ."

"We thought they might be messages from the gods." He laughed
to himself and I heard him tap the wall, perhaps to empty the bowl of
his pipe or to draw my attention to the desperate script scraped and

scratched into the concrete. For an instant, I heard an echo of Max's words as his fingers had found another inscription: *the Libro d'Oro . . . the prison house of our desires.* "That the stones—such tablets might yet speak to us."

"Are you telling me there are one hundred and three Linear-B tablets—purposely fired in a kiln to preserve them—and—what?— remnants of wooden storage cases, unknown to scholarship?"

"Not precisely, thanks to your father's—what shall we call it?—*mission.*"

"In Berlin, you hadn't seen each other since the fall of 1943, under what had to have been extraordinary circumstances. You were sworn enemies."

"Yes, Pylos, the fall of 1943 . . . Allies in the antifascist cause, philhellenes of the deepest conviction—and yes, drawn by dreams of those tablets."

"Ah, on the windswept heights of Epano Englianos, the cypress, the olive trees, the chirp of the crickets at dusk—especially in moonlight, with the white sea glittering in a distant corner of the bay, almost magical to behold, and the undeciphered tablets to contemplate: the stories untold."

"You speak as if you had been with us there."

"Oh yes, in a manner of speaking, and quite recently. I was invited to a celebration in Pylos, a reunion of the Resistance fighters who fought with my father in the war. It was quite the Homeric occasion . . . old king Nestor with stories told around the barbecue pit of heroic and not so heroic days past, of attacks on E-boats in Kalamata, of ambushes and massacres, narrow escapes—stuff to rival the *Odyssey.* Except the interesting mix of OSS and SOE agents and one KGB or—I get them mixed up—NKVD agent possibly working for British SIS, as well. The acronyms are so damned confusing."

Again there was a pregnant pause and then the flick of another match as Karel Hollar relit his pipe, sending flaming shadows over the pocked walls of our cell, gray-green walls incised in the hand of those who had come before us, counting down or adding up the lost days of their lives. I saw his flame-lit eyes spark to attention, blinking as he examined my face, his expression something between bemused wonder and incredulity edged with fear.

"So, you prefer to play the part of Telemachus come in search of news of his father's long-delayed return—alas, forever." He watched the match burn down to his fingers and waved us back into darkness. "Well then, let me relate a tale to you both splendid and perplexing, a tale for our terrible age, of two dreamers who took different paths. Imagine, if you can, a large, splendid room with wide windows looking out over a gray and ruined city on a fall day some thirty-five years ago. A note was passed to me from my assistant, 'Mr. John Alden, Ph.D., will meet you at the entrance of the Neues Museum two this afternoon.' This note had been dictated to the guard at the entrance of the ministry—hardly a means of discretion."

"So he knew where to find you—your new career?"

"Minister of mines for the GDR. From thin air, a name from my past—a man I wasn't even certain was alive. I was stunned. We were dealing with one crisis after another. The Soviets had withdrawn their tanks to the outskirts of Leipzig, but each day another problem, another workers' union. I canceled all my meetings; I told my staff I had a bad cold and was going home to bed. I did not take my official car, but went alone. I walked to the Neues Museum, where John and I had spent time in our youthful days. The place was a bombed-out ruin, a sad reminder. I feared a ghost, a trick. . . . I was no longer that man."

"But how could he have known about your resurrection? Where to find you? You must have contacted him."

The pipe-lit face shook off the idea.

"He was in the business of knowing such things. I was a terrified ghost facing a tormentor."

"You mean he was a threat to reveal *your* past—but which one?"

There was a mild grunt out of the darkness, perhaps at the ease or perfunctory nature of such transformations in the upheaval of the postwar years. His voice rose in defiance, growing louder after our adopted tone of conspiratorial whisperings as he explained his convenient capture in Poland in late 1944 by the advancing Soviet forces. His two years in training with the NKVD in Moscow and émigré training centers in the Caucasus as he prepared for his role as a Moscow Communist, with a new background and identity, and a prominent position in the postwar GDR government, where he could keep an eye on things from the inside for the Soviets. As he would do again with the Dubček government on his home ground in the sixties. This much, I presume, he was happy to rehearse again for our listeners, as they were still making desperate calls to Moscow as the regime crumbled in the streets of Prague.

"Except for his cane, your father looked splendid and healthy, well dressed in a suit and carrying a heavily laden attaché case: a distinguished Princeton professor on a tourist visa—so he assured me—for a scholarly tour of the GDR."

"Surely not—"

"I took him at his word. What else could I do? You see, he presented me with the keys to the kingdom." Again an echoing knock on the wall of the cell, as if to assay the weight of the precious thing. "To open the door of the past. This was 1953, you understand. . . ."

My heart hiccupped in my chest as I realized what my father had to have had in his bag.

"No, he didn't—he brought you Michael Ventris's charts on the decipherment of Linear B?"

"Ah, so you *do* see . . . Everything: papers, journals, Ventris's charts—all carried in an attaché case. I believe he had met only days before with Ventris, Nigel Bennett, too, at Cambridge. Still early days, but these were earth-shattering discoveries, that Linear B was not a lost Minoan language, but early Greek. And in Leipzig, you see, were my Linear B tablets, and still unpublished."

"You mean 'our' Linear B tablets. If memory serves, '*I* paid for the extra diggers from Kyparissia."

Even given my flood of lustful anger, I was amazed at my bizarre deployment of the first-person singular, my proprietary tone, but I wanted him to know in no uncertain terms it was as good as the same.

"Hah, your scholarship, like your father's, is of the highest standard."

"Why you needed him, someone with the patience to do the drudge work."

"I envied him that; I was always too impulsive."

"He brought you the key to your lost stories."

"We stood for a long time, staring into each other's faces. What failures—oh what failures we were."

"Failures?"

"It had been our dream—first to find such a thing, then to decipher the tablets. But the war had come and everything after. And now this Michael Ventris, an architect, a linguist, had beaten us to the prize."

"But Ventris was an intuitive genius and it was the architect in him that allowed him to grasp the structure of the language. And to make the leap, to make the assumption that some of the triplet syllables on Sir Arthur Evans's Cretan tablets referred to the names of cities."

"Yes, it was genius . . . to throw out the dogma of Evans, who had always been convinced Linear B was a Minoan language."

"And Ventris's own conviction that it was Etruscan. What archaeologist or linguist hasn't rehearsed in his mind the discovery of those names, those Cretan cities: Amnisos and Knossos and Tulissos, Phaistos, and Luktos, in Greek—of all the scholarly leaps in the dark."

"And we had failed," Hollar repeated.

"But you had the trump cards and you were meeting again at the Neues Museum, a dead man and an ex-scholar—certainly you had more to share than failure? Nor can I believe in an assassination plot on a GDR minister. Surely nothing the CIA or the Brits would dream of: Berlin was a hair trigger for World War Three."

"You see—and I think you *do* see—we were confronted with our buried lives: what all the disasters of fate had not spoiled in us."

"Except you were still the GDR minister of mines under threat from your own people, and he was a top CIA officer, possibly with war crimes on his mind."

"It had always been part of our plan for after the war, if I managed to survive, which I thought unlikely."

"One hundred and three purloined tablets, which, if revealed, would end the professional careers of both of you, but virgin material—housed in boxes off the throne room, you mentioned—that might go beyond the mundane inventories in the storerooms. You could even make a scholarly case that the new tablets were a kind of control group, adding to the available inscriptions, a means to check the decipherment. Hell, you might even fake a discovery from somewhere else. Who had to know they were stolen from Pylos? My father had the money to do all of that . . . and the archaeologists were beginning to return to Greece in 1953. Anything was possible."

My breathless fantasizing caused a silence to fall, as if we were both exhausted, as if there had been a little too much slippage for comfort between lives past and present. I found myself both marveling and terrified at the ease with which I'd assumed the voice of a man I barely remembered.

And I silently scolded myself for not being more circumspect and professional in my interrogation.

Once upon a time in another life, as an army G-2 officer, I had prided myself on the subtlety I'd mastered in breaking down the lies and indoctrination instilled by the North Vietnamese political cadres.

I was good at my job, even as I sometimes trembled at how well the Party cadres had indoctrinated our prisoners with distortions and fears; the captured NVA officers were almost impossible to break. Our South Vietnamese allies relied on intimidation and torture; I preferred the personal touch, often taking prisoners into my quarters, where they were allowed to watch TV, both U.S. armed forces and South Vietnamese channels; and later we'd expose them to life in South Vietnam—a trip to bustling Saigon was often all it took for them to realize the lies they'd been told about the exploited slaves of Western imperialism in the South. Once an NVA prisoner realized he'd been hoodwinked, he became more willing to work with us and provide the critical intelligence on the troop concentrations and staging areas in Cambodia: the precious coordinates that allowed the B-52's to reap their deadly whirlwind.

Karel Hollar, I quickly realized, was facing a fine line between renunciation and confession. His caution was warranted. Even if the fall of the Berlin Wall were a fact, it didn't mean the imminent liberation of Czechoslovakia or the fall of its Communist government. That he was a Soviet spy and agent of influence going back to the war years might keep him alive if the present regime survived; if not, he could be convicted of treason by a new government for having sold out Dubček in '68. While revelations about war crimes in Greece could complicate any hopes he might have of relocating to the West.

As I listened to Karel Hollar's story, desperate for a clear picture of my father's intentions as he slipped past Checkpoint Charlie with a document-crammed attaché case, and a pistol, I had an uncanny feeling that he had stepped back for a play-action pass as he checked the defense across the line: He wanted to give Karel a chance to confess, as I did, to redeem himself, to recover the man he might have been, before their clandestine meeting was either discovered or ended in a disastrous confrontation. Or worse, an international incident or even a hot war, given the heightened tensions as the United States and Soviet Union went eyeball-to-eyeball over a teetering East Germany in the fall of 1953.

But I also knew with absolute certainty that my father—after seeing him through Nestor's eyes—had wanted to get his hands on those Linear B tablets—as I did . . . and perhaps one or two things more.

I have walked the route from the carnival attraction that is now Checkpoint Charlie to the rebuilt Neues Museum any number of times, as if the streets and buildings will allow me an insight into the tinderbox of impulses that vied in my father's mind on that cloudy morning, just weeks after my grandmother presented him with the evidence of a hideous crime committed by his grandfather, General Alden, and Suzanne threatened his marriage with the paternity of her daughter. I found that the rooms—memory's rooms, some with windows, some without—first described to me by Karel Hollar, were sound in construction but that the stage props and lighting shifted like a mirage. And little wonder: Every role he'd adopted put him in danger, depending. . . . Or as Elliot Goddard put it about ten days later, "Shakespeare would have been hard-pressed to create such a conflicted character, much less find him a happy exit."

"Oh, yes, I recognized your father immediately, from a block distant, a tall man standing alone in the street, wearing a gray raincoat and a most beautiful Savile Row suit. He was leaning on a cane as he gazed upon the blackened shell of the Neues Museum, as if contemplating a two-thousand-year-old ruin. Just seeing John there, lost in thought, I felt the monstrosity and waste of the years." Hollar went on and on about how in their youth the Neues Museum had housed a fabulous collection of ancient artifacts, including the famous bust of Queen Nefertiti—as it does again today. But in that fall of 1953, it was a forbidding derelict. Weeds grew out of the blasted brickwork pocked with shrapnel hits. Karel admitted to me his extreme trepidation as he approached my father along the deserted sidewalk—only feral cats, it seemed, inhabited that part of East Berlin—and how his apprehension almost got the better of him. "Yes, I had a pistol, too, concealed in my coat pocket. One could never be sure."

My father had simply turned to him and smiled, held out his hand, and continued a conversation that might have been left off only moments before, instead of the ten years since their frequent moonlight meetings on Epano Englianos in Pylos.

"'What do you think, Karel? I am reminded of Piranesi's *Temple of the Camenae*—right there, the exposed vaulting and shattered columns and the gloomy evocation of an irredeemable glory.'"

Karel shared this moment with me, chuckling, while I was riveted, seeing that Piranesi etching on the wall of Virgil Dabney's study, where my father had visited with his mentor on his way back to Washington a little more than two weeks before.

They shook hands and continued staring into each other's poker faces.

"'Do you mean will it ever be repaired? As a member of the government, I cannot say. Roosevelt and Churchill devastated this land—I salute you. We are struggling to feed and house the people and provide hope for a better future. As you know, we had no benefit of the Marshall Plan.'

"'Hope . . . well, now that Stalin is gone, maybe there's a chance we won't have a repeat of another age of iron, another Greek Dark Ages after the destruction of Mycenae and Pylos.'"

The reference to Stalin's death immediately cast an uncertain light over their subsequent conversations: Talk of a fresh start, in Hollar's Party circles, might bring charges of disloyalty and hasty execution. Ten years before, on the heights of Epano Englianos, Stalin was still a heroic figure in Karel's eyes. "No more," Karel said to me, sighing, "no more." Although he maintained that he didn't know my father was with the CIA, he was hardly a fool; he was suspicious and fretful. At the very least, my father knew Karel's prewar identity as a world-class archaeologist, much less his wartime role as a Wehrmacht captain, hardly the working-class origins on his résumé as the GDR minister of mines. The wartime SIS connection—that he was a double agent working for both British SIS and the Soviets—would have finished him. Karel assiduously maintained the fiction to me that he knew nothing about what had happened to my father in the Communist ambush ordered either by Kostas Kalayias or by his Soviet bosses. An acknowledgment of that would have connected him to the SS executions in Pylos, in which Joanna's family had died.

Nor, according to Hollar, did my father allude to any of that on their first day. Instead, after a minute of tentative reminiscences of better times in Greece, my father indicated his gimpy leg and waved Karel to sit at the base of the steps of the Neues Museum, where he opened his expensive black leather attaché case to reveal Ventris's journal article and charts and made a present of them to Karel. As he did so, according to Hollar, the Walther P38 was clearly visible in the case.

"The pistol and Ventris—what was I supposed to think? A test, I think; it was all part of his crazy plan."

Hollar used the word *crazy* to me a lot. My father also had a carton of Lucky Strikes in the attaché case, which he split with Karel, and they were soon intently smoking away on the steps as my father went through Ventris's research, of which Karel had caught wind in a BBC broadcast narrated by Ventris the year before, but without access to the technical details.

"Within minutes we had reverted to adolescents with stars in our eyes."

I, too, have sat on those steps trying to imagine this bizarre meeting, in the dingy gray of a fading fall afternoon in East Berlin, with American and Soviet tanks facing one another in the streets, while these two middle-aged scholars pored over the diagrams of ancient scripts that Michael Ventris had managed to decipher.

"You see, mine—our tablets were distinct: smaller and standardized, perfectly proportioned, scripted like calligraphy, fired with purple glazes, things of beauty in themselves, as a book hand-printed, and hand-sewn, on the highest-quality paper, with calfskin boards, might be admired—to preserve something . . . essential."

The aching possessiveness of Karel's description actually brought tears to my eyes, which, fortunately, the darkness concealed.

My father took him through the charts and photocopies of the tablets excavated by the Cincinnati team at Pylos in 1939, with which Hollar and my father had long familiarity. My father was now able to point out the possible place names and the lists of agricultural products, mundane but tantalizing, that brought to life the thriving manufacturing center that Nestor's Palace had once been. Dancing in their heads were the 103 tablets that Hollar's team of hastily hired diggers from Kyparissia had found in the anteroom of the throne room hidden in Leipzig.

"All in one place," exclaimed Hollar, "the length and breadth of a man, perfectly aligned in the red clay, as if they'd been housed in custom-made boxes! There were still minute fragments of wood, metal fasteners, probably held with leather straps."

"Jesus fucking Christ . . ."

"Beautiful things. We had them gathered up and stored in twenty minutes."

"And hidden in Kyparissia—where?"

"The basement of a house of a Communist Party leader, the man who organized the digging team."

"A comrade. Why weren't you able to get them out in 1939, before you got called back to Germany?"

"When the Hitler-Stalin pact was announced in August, the Greek government under Metaxas rounded up all the local Communists and put them in jail. They exiled this man to a penal island and confiscated his home and turned it into a police station. The tablets were buried in the basement."

"So you had to hightail it back to Germany."

"The NKVD insisted; they had a job for me in the Wehrmacht—so they ordered."

"So my father stayed behind in Athens. . . . You told him about the tablets, about Kyparissia?"

"Of course, about Kyparissia—"

"But not, you fucking liar, where they were specifically hidden?"

"A police station—they were safely buried in the basement."

"You didn't trust him. You knew if he'd gotten his hands on them, he'd have spirited them away to America while you were stuck doing Stalin's—your fucking ally's—dirty work."

"I warned them a hundred times of the German invasion in the spring of 1941, and they never listened—idiots."

"I can assure you he combed the area between Pylos and Kyparissia between the fall of 1939 and the spring of 1941, when the Germans invaded, searching, and he had a splendid ambulance to get around in between runs up north to the battle lines in Albania."

I recalled Nestor's words to me about how surprised he was when they climbed the path from the beach that first night, how my father was so well acquainted with the local topography . . . and yet he'd never done any field work in Pylos before the outbreak of war in 1939.

I was annoyed that I'd let my emotions get the better of me: I'd tipped off my subject to a piece of my father's biography that my father hadn't seen fit to broach, and that Hollar might well adjust his tale to accommodate that new bit of information.

And so he remained coy and cryptic about their meeting on Epano Englianos in the fall of 1943, as well he might. He was like the cat that had swallowed the golden canary. When the Germans took over from the Italian occupation force in the Peloponnese, when Italy surrendered to the Allies, his Wehrmacht unit took over the Italian headquarters in Kyparissia: the same police station where the tablets were buried.

"Brilliant. So you had complete access to your hoard, where you got the two tablets you had with you, in the pockets of your sheepskin coat, that night when Nestor could have shot you."

"So beautiful, so elegant, the script was that of a master."

"But you still needed my father; he was your best bet at getting them deciphered."

"We had been colleagues and competitors before the war, but always the same dream from childhood: evidence of Homer, to prove the truth of his tales . . . but this could reveal the original stories of Homer, or even new stories of Troy and Odysseus. We sat on the steps of the Neues Museum until the light had faded and we were in near darkness. I had totally lost track of time. My office would be concerned without a call from me; just that morning there had been rumors of more strikes in the coal mines. I suggested dinner in a nearby restaurant, where I could phone my office."

Going to a public place for a meal could have put them both in jeopardy, but Hollar came to the conclusion that it was better to keep the whole business out in the open, giving him more flexibility if things went south.

"Was he a Princeton professor with an American passport and visa, a CIA agent with a diplomatic passport and immunity, or something else? We left it alone. Nor did he ask me to explain myself: how I had to give up my wartime identity, or my two years training by NKVD and GRU to work undercover for the Communist GDR that was coming into being. The Soviets hated the Germans; even their Communist comrades they didn't trust. I was to be their eyes and ears on the inside. Even the Stasi was not to know. I knew I could be cutting my own throat, but I was always impulsive. I wanted to believe the best, and, frankly, our conversation was so wonderful that I surrendered to the moment. Your father, like you, was a very clever man: a mind impossible to read."

It was a tiny, discreet restaurant, Lutter & Wegner on Charlottenstrasse, according to the Stasi report, where Karel knew they could get a decent meal, where his Party rank allowed him access to the better wines. As they walked the dreary, dusk-shadowed, bomb-damaged streets to the restaurant, Hollar found himself ashamed of the wrecked Neues Museum and the ruins at every turning eight years after the war's end, as if the dismal scenes were a reflection on his life choices and Party loyalties. Over dinner and two or three bottles of white wine, their talk became more animated. My father began to press him on the subject of the Linear B tablets, which Hollar explained had been carefully recovered from the cellar in Kyparissia and transported to Leipzig, to the Museum of Antiquities, where he had long connections going back to his student days; they were secreted in the storage bins of the museum without identification of any kind, where they remained, the museum miraculously spared destruction by Allied bombing.

My father grabbed Karel's hand across the dinner table.

"So, they're still safe, all one hundred and three?"

"I don't know, but the building is undamaged."

"You haven't checked to see, just to visit, to view them?"

Karel smiled at my father's excitement, bemused, his throat tightening, as he gazed into his colleague's eager, shimmering eyes. Both men knew that the few translated tablets from the storerooms at Knossos and Pylos had so far yielded only inventories of agricultural goods for export. But these were different. Karel glanced across the restaurant and made a circular motion around his face as he turned back to my father.

"They might remember me there from before the war; it is too dangerous."

My father gripped Hollar's shoulder.

"You've grown a beard—that will help. Tomorrow, we'll drive there, to Leipzig, just you and I, and we'll take a look at those tablets—with this," and he tapped the attaché case on the floor. "Who knows what we might find: *our* tablets, my cipher key. We can put Ventris to the test on untouched material. What do you say, Karel?"

Karel was fascinated, or, as he put it, "drunk with wonder."

"Also, I was very frightened. I knew it was a game and not a game. We were rolling dice; we were playing with our lives, and maybe more lives than we wished to think about. Tensions were very high all over East Germany—especially in Leipzig, where in June and July of that year there had been worker strikes and uprisings. Without Soviet tanks . . ." There was a long hiatus and I could just make out his shallow breathing. "Perhaps I was hypnotized by his eyes—those eyes of John like lightning from heaven, glittering with stardust . . . crazy, crazy . . . when you looked into them, you might find yourself driven to embrace such a crazy desire."

That wasn't the first or last time I heard such expressions. In her love letters, Suzanne, too, had swooned over my father's eyes: "Your fanatical eyes, your splendid flame-lit eyes—my darling, it's been so long since I've seen you, and without your eyes to light the way along our moonlit path by the lake I don't know what I'll do."

I kept waiting for Karel to admit some shocking thing: Had he and my father been lovers in their student days, when they first met in Venice with their parents? Perhaps a teenage infatuation or dalliance that had strayed into physical affection or sexual experimenting? But if that had been the case, he spared me any such indignities, which would have added nothing. The way he portrayed it—the way this bizarre detour had begun to take shape on the steps of the Neues Museum: They were two unhappy men disillusioned with the paths along which deplorable fate had directed them; they were seeking a way out. But if Ventris's charts allowed them to decipher a lost work of Homer, or even some early or obscure historical event in Bronze Age Greece—a voice, a human story, a fragment of lost time—they would be world-famous; they might yet redeem themselves, and relieve themselves of the bitter disappointment that a nonspecialist like Ventris had cracked the code. In the darkness, as our voices fell after a heated moment of discussion, I wondered if it was my heart I heard pounding, or Hollar's.

"Hell, yes, you could just defect with the tablets and my father could discreetly relocate them and they could conveniently be rediscovered in a new dig."

My father spent the night in Karel's chilly but palatial flat on the Smetenastrasse, where they drank more wine and Karel showed him his private library of expensive German nineteenth-century editions of the classic Greek and Latin texts, many of them beautifully illustrated and extremely rare. These were things he'd bought discreetly, "for a few pfennigs," on the black market and from street vendors, careful not to betray his educated upper-class origins, his Viennese mother and Sudeten-Czech father. He'd learned to speak working-class dialect. He said that when they handled the leather-bound volumes and read the inscribed names of some of the greatest Jewish scholars and bibliophiles, "our hands shook with the knowledge of what had become of these people." As Karel showed my father around his many rooms, mostly bare of furniture or artworks or photos of any kind, they tried to banish evil thoughts—the splendid apartment confiscated from Jews, then confiscated from high-ranking Nazis by the occupying Soviets, and now given to high-ranking GDR Party members—fearing that precipitous candor might break the spell.

"I think your father was saddened by what he saw of my flat, of the empty history there, of families long gone, of my lovely view of the gardens in the square."

Waking in the morning, a little hung over but with a better grasp on reality and the dangers he faced, Karel decided to go through with the trip to Leipzig, but to do so right out in the open, brazenly, so that if something should go wrong, he could spin it to his advantage: how he had been drawing out this American provocateur to find out what game he was playing. He called his office and told them he was going to check on things in Leipzig and that he'd be gone for the day but would put in a call to the office as soon as he arrived. Hollar found my father up and about after spending the night sleeping on a comfortable Biedermeier sofa of beige satin that had somehow survived the early years of the Soviet occupation; he was standing by the elaborate etched French doors that opened onto a balcony and a view of a small park with linden trees. Hollar casually mentioned that the apartment had once belonged to a cousin of Kaiser Wilhelm II.

"Before the First World War, when Lenin got his chance."

"Look at the patterns of green in the linden trees, Karel, how from this height and in the morning light the thinning branches show the shiny underside of the heart-shaped leaves. Do you see how the lighter and darker green tones flicker like turquoise waves? How splendid. You're a lucky man to have such a view in a city of rubble. In 1945, when I was last here, I would never have expected to find you in such a grand place."

I often wonder if Karel, so distracted by his friend's poetic effusions, even registered that aside: the year that my father was hunting him after the Normandy landings. My father wouldn't have let it slip out. Karel placed a hand on his shoulder as he would an old rival's. "We only require some dryads now, I think, to remind us of our fidelity as old friends—yes. Perhaps I will have my official car and driver take us to Leipzig. What do you think of that—an official visit?"

"In style, then? That would certainly be in keeping with your exalted position."

Karel's voice echoed in that dingy cell, coming out of the darkness like a low moan.

"Of course, he was being what you would call sarcastic, for a man of his wealth and stature. I had visited him before the war at Princeton and in New York with his mother; I knew how a wealthy American lived—and how our side of things behind the Iron Curtain—as you called it—must have seemed to him. Even I had finally realized the horrors of Stalin. You see, those lovely sad lindens had spoken to him of his home, where he should have remained. He should have listened to the dryads and walked out of my apartment and two kilometers up the road to your Checkpoint Charlie and returned from where he had come. There was no *Berlin Wall* back then, nothing really. We were just beginning to crack down on illegal crossings, but I don't think he would have had a problem returning. They might have stopped him, arrested him . . . maybe, but probably no."

Riding in the backseat of Karel's official black ZIM sedan for the two-hour drive to Leipzig, the two conspirators began turning up their cards. My father kept his face to the window, taking in the passing scenery, marveling, so he told Karel, at how little of the countryside had changed since they were students, and yet how many of the damaged towns and cities remained unrepaired, unlike West Germany, where most of the war-damaged infrastructure had already been swept away and replaced by new factories and housing for the workers.

As Karel put it to me, "Yes, I knew it was like a beehive over there in West Germany but our Soviet comrades had raped and pillaged, taking entire factories for reparations. Of course, this also was included in the charges brought against him, that he had hijacked me at gunpoint to observe forbidden military installations."

The Stasi report noted all the military installations along the route. When I drove the same route a year later, it was clear that most of the installations weren't even visible from the road. According to Hollar's driver, his boss had been bragging about the success of the GDR recovery all the way to Leipzig, which Hollar may well have done to protect himself by preemptively filling the flapping ears of his driver.

The Museum of Antiquities was a repository for a small academic collection attached to Leipzig University, where my father had studied over two summers in the early thirties, after he and Karel first became friends in Venice. As they drew near, Karel began to panic. Would members of the curatorial staff—beard or no beard—recognize him from prewar days? It was drizzling as they drove through the battle-scarred cobblestone streets of Leipzig. Sullen faces turned to the black ZIM sedan. Soviet tanks had only recently retreated to the outskirts of the city, and Party honchos were hardly welcomed by the rebellious workers. "They were perfectly capable of hanging a Party official, just as those bastards had hung Jews and Poles during the war." As if insensible to caution, my father asked to be driven around the city and the university, indicating his gimpy leg. "Our old haunts, Karel, do you remember Café Grundmann on Mahlmannstrasse? We went there with my mother in 1931 for a meal fit for a king—do you remember how lovely it was, before Herr Hitler came along? My God, do those wrecked vehicles go back to the war?"

Hollar said such disingenuous remarks by my father caused him much anguish: Anything in the way of a reply, truthful or not, would be duly reported by the driver. Once they were out of the car, he could be more candid.

"Those burnt-out cars were hit by Soviet tanks only six weeks ago. And before Hitler, for most Germans, there was only hyperinflation and the First World War. I was lucky; I grew up in Prague, an oasis in those times." Karel walked with my limping father toward the Museum's entrance. "And, I don't want to disappoint you, but you should know that the Soviet army confiscated tens of thousands of artifacts from museums all over the GDR for reparations, perhaps our Linear B tablets also . . . or worse. I have heard tales of Soviet soldiers warming themselves with bonfires of paintings."

They exchanged horrified looks. Karel found himself perplexed again at how cautious he'd become, how even after many months Stalin's dead shadow hung over his every stillborn hope.

"Another life . . ." The darkness in our prison cell was filled with his choking smoke.

They found the small museum, miraculously, largely intact, with most of its collections still in place, though it was open to the public only two days a week and was looked after by caretakers, not professional curators—and none of the staff, to Karel's relief, remained from before the war. Karel decided it would be best to bluff his way to their goal. He'd had his driver pull the ZIM right up in front of the museum and marched in with my father. He assumed his role as a high Party official with full brio, introducing the famous American professor of archaeology from Princeton, who was interested in examining some Bronze Age tablets that had been deposited in the fall of 1944 by the deceased German archaeologist, Karel Hollar. It helped that my father spoke perfect German and impeccably acted the part assigned by Karel in their charade. The head caretaker told them he had no idea where the tablets might be; the museum records were in total disarray. But Karel knew, or thought he knew, because he had personally deposited the tablets while on leave from his unit. He'd placed them on a metal shelf in an obscure corner of the basement storage bins, but without labels of any kind, even going so far as to arrange them slightly haphazardly and out of order from their configuration when first unearthed, sprinkling them with dust to make it look as if they'd been there for ages. In effect, he'd hid them in plain sight. The difficulty was to get the stupid caretaker—"a Cretan of the lowest order"—to lead them to the right section of the storage area without catching on to the fact that he was being directed, and then let my father be the one to actually identify the things.

"I had to pretend to be a disinterested Party functionary, while your father discovered their exact whereabouts—exactly where I had placed them, but with plodding reverence and not the emotion of one coming upon Ali Baba's cave, yes?"

They got the caretaker to set up a long table and a light and chairs so that my father, "the world's greatest expert," could begin an examination of the tablets. Once left alone, the two began an eager inspection, using Ventris's tables and syllabic charts to guide them. Their first problem was reestablishing the order in which the tablets had been unearthed in Pylos. "I was a little uncertain how I had rearranged the tablets on the storage shelf; I had a system, but after nearly ten years, I wasn't sure anymore. Your father was furious with me because we both felt they had originally been stored in consecutive order, like chapters in a codex. He cursed my stupidity even as his hands trembled as he began to handle these wonders." Unlike many of the Linear B tablets on Crete that had crumbled because of damp and mishandling, these were rock-hard—and not because of the heat of the fire that had consumed Nestor's Palace around 1200 B.C., and so preserved the thousand or more clay tablets that Carl Andersen would eventually find. "These were like Delft tiles fired with a purple patina, like pages of ceramic tiles—like nothing we'd ever seen." Karel described how he had held the tablets up to his nose. "To breathe in the time stored there, the heat of three thousand summers, the chill of how many winters . . . a thousand lifetimes, the fragrance of ash from the fire that had destroyed the palace, the sea air of Epano Englianos. Such thoughts made the troubles of our moment in time seem of little importance."

It was tough going, arranging and rearranging the tablets on the table, each about the size of a small loaf of bread.

"Yes, they're numbered!" my father exclaimed after about two hours of examination.

That helped things, but nevertheless, the task confronting them was daunting under the best of conditions.

"Again and again, John was able to identify the names of animals—cows, boars, horses, goats, and sheep—and, of course, agricultural goods—wheat, barley, figs, olives, and perfumed oil, and so forth. Words that Ventris had identified in the Pylos tablets from the storage rooms: numbers and measurements for goods . . . the accounting for an agricultural society, for a king, a ruler, and all the ceremonial feasting that goes on in such a society. Interesting, perhaps, insightful, yes . . .

for collecting taxes, tribute, everything required for a rigorous authoritarian control of society. But many of the other words would take much more time to decipher, and we were in a hurry to find more than an accounting of ceremonies and celebrations; we wanted epic poetry or history or literature: the things passed down from the dawn of Mycenaean-Minoan civilization, the stories that had reached Homer. Once, as young men, it might have been enough—a good start—but for us, with our earlier careers long behind us, well, it made for a sinking gloom and apprehension."

Then, according to Hollar, my father got up from the worktable, hobbled around the storeroom to stretch his legs, and returned to examine a group of tablets that seemed to have a distinctive glazing and script more ornamental than the others.

"The group was of twelve tablets, every figure perfectly incised, the lines of script so elegant, straight and true.

"'There are more and various ideograms on these tablets.'" John pointed them out, noting the frequency, the patterns. "'Here *man*, here *woman*, *wine*, *amphora*, *red silk*, and this—what do you think, the syllable for a ship? A type of ship, maybe a merchant ship or a trader? Maybe three ships, warships or merchantmen. And this . . . do you suppose these syllables might be a word for the season, maybe spring or summer—an indication of time? And here, the signs . . . the sounds suggest the Greek for Poseidon—don't you think? Perhaps an archaic version. And here, and here . . . here—the name of a city perhaps, and again here. Surely these are the names of towns—my guess is Crete, or maybe—who knows.'" John began furiously recording the signs in a notebook, as if by getting a feel for their shape in his fingers, they might reveal themselves. "'Perhaps it's the record of a trading expedition . . . a spring or summer voyage, a captain, a warrior prince seeking . . . something.'" John's face was flushed and sweaty. "'Could it be a poem, a tale of loss or discovery, or finding a loved one? Oh, Karel, we need time . . . time. There is a labor of decades here—a career!'"

"How I wanted to embrace his romantic impetuosity—as if a lost part of myself—in that moment, for both our sakes."

And so it was in that moment, listening to Hollar's rasping voice, that I truly recognized something of my father in myself—realized, too, as painful as it was to admit, that he was as much a cutthroat seeker of stories as Max, and willing to go to lengths that would have left Max in breathless awe. I knew this to my horror, because it was then that

I realized the truth about the texts on the postcards sent by my father from East Germany in 1954 to my grandmother and Suzanne, and, as if would turn out, to my mother, as well.

"We were going crazy but also were disappointed as we recognized the limits, the time, the problems—how much there was to lose with one false step."

The two scholars finally began to tire and become testy at their labors. The caretaker wanted to close the museum, and so, reluctantly, they gathered up their notebooks, with plans to return the next day. "We ascended from the darkness of three thousand years to the greater dark of the moment." It was pitch-black when they left the museum; most of the streetlights were broken from the recent uprising. The driver of the ZIM was clearly uneasy; the big sedan had been attracting hateful looks from students and workers all afternoon as he stood guard. Karel directed the driver to a restaurant on the outskirts of town; there, in a better neighborhood, their presence would not draw as much attention. Hollar demanded a table in a corner, where they could speak without being overheard. Then he called his office, only to return to their table shaken. That morning, more labor strife had broken out in the coal-mining town of Heuersdorf, just south of Leipzig, less than a twenty-minute drive. Karel, carried away with the tablets, had failed to put in the promised call to his office; he found himself in trouble with the Party secretary, who had been unable to locate him all day. To cover his tracks, he made vague excuses about taking soundings of unrest in Leipzig and promised to go straight to Heuersdorf after dinner. A meeting in the town hall had been scheduled with the disaffected miners, the mine management, and the district Party secretary.

They drank beer, "to clear the dust of the millennia from our throats," and then followed up with a local white wine from Saale-Unstrut, a Silvaner vintage of which Hollar was quite proud. But even the good wine and the cozy confines of the restaurant couldn't allay their anxieties: "the grandest thing, so close, so far." An uneasy feeling came over Karel. He had a sense that their exciting discoveries, instead of reviving old bonds between them, had heightened feelings in my father that he'd been cheated, deceived—which he had: how Hollar's request for extra cash when my father had been on Delos had made no mention of going behind Carl Andersen's back and stealing artifacts—stealing, too, from the Greek government and people. It was then, as Hollar told it, that my father began toying with him, playing mind games that began to feel like a deadly charade.

"When I first found the Linear B tablets from the antechamber of the throne room, he didn't seem to mind."

The second bottle of wine fueled both exhilaration and brittle panic, and Karel's nervousness grew, along with his curiosity. He realized how strange some of my father's requests had been, further compromising the situation. How my father had casually gotten him to stop the ZIM at a clothing shop in a town on the way to Leipzig: How could he work with the dirty and dusty tablets in his suit? "He told me he'd neglected to bring a change of clothes. So he went into the store and bought some workingman's clothes, shirts, trousers, even a hiking pack and walking shoes." This, too, was detailed in the Stasi file: "The subject was apprehended in the traveling disguise he had purchased in Coswig (Anhalt)." But once they reached the museum in Leipzig, my father had been too preoccupied to bother to change. Hollar realized he was in a very tight spot: What to do with my father during his meeting in Heuersdorf? He thought he might have his driver drop him off at the Heuersdorf town hall, then drive my father back to Berlin and Checkpoint Charlie. He'd tell my father that the Stasi was onto him and that if he didn't go back immediately, he'd be arrested. "My God, a crisis in Heuersdorf, and I was sitting at a table with an American who might well be a CIA agent." He began to panic, and my father must have caught wind of the change, because he did a total about-face, or, as Karel explained it to me, "another trick to put me off guard and then throw me under the train."

"I need your help, Karel, I need to get a boy—my son, in fact—back to his mother."

Karel was stunned at this turn in the conversation; he had no idea what my father was talking about.

"Your son and wife . . . in America?"

"Surely you remember your comrade Kostas Kaleyias?"

"Well, yes."

My father brandished his cane.

"Then you understand what is at stake."

"You regret the E-boats—but it was your idea."

"What came after."

"It was out of my hands."

"You coordinated with ELAS, orders from Moscow—you can't wash your hands of it, none of us can."

"John, you must believe me, I was always in a perilous situation. The SS had their eyes on me, and then the Sicherheitsdienst got their claws into all our operations by late 1943—fanatics, breathing the stink of Hades, sniffing out disloyalty. Today, the Stasi have learned all their tricks."

"So you had to prove yourself a loyal Nazi?"

"Never a Nazi; I had not the acting skills to make such a thing possible. The same as you, I played the role for which I was appointed: a Wehrmacht demolitions expert with superb language skills and local knowledge."

"And the massacre in Pylos, the executions, over a hundred men, women, and children executed in cold blood? In the town where you spent so many glorious sunny hours at the tavernas in the summer of '39 with the Cincinnati team. And how many locals did Carl Andersen have working on your dig? How many of those men did you know personally? How many were mown down that day, or family members?"

"It was out of my hands, John, as it was yours. The price for the E-boats was high—we all understood that."

"For Kalamata—nobody there was touched, not a single reprisal."

"Are you questioning the price of a wounded American OSS officer?"

"Some paid a higher price than others. Of those executed in Pylos, not a single Communist supporter was on the butcher's list, not one. Almost without exception, the most important royalist and republican supporters were shot that day, the professional people—Jews: the mayor, the town doctor . . . *and* his wife *and* daughter."

"I told you: There was no stopping this thing. I could do nothing."

"But you had to have made up the list—how else could the Communists have escaped so completely!"

"Like you, an expert on the language and the people. I had no choice: It was one hundred citizens of Pylos whether or not I edited the names."

"Edited . . . crossed off or added, goddamn you?"

"Yes, I knew the Communist supporters. What would you have done? I had my loyalties, my responsibilities to save my people."

"And the town doctor!"

"Keep your voice down. You must not draw attention to us. My driver is seated over there; he probably reports to the Stasi—I have no doubt he already has."

"I was there, Karel; I was a witness. I saw you with the list, checking off the names with the SS officers. And the total was one hundred and six . . . wives who would not leave husbands, children who would not leave parents, babes in arms."

Did my father really put it in so many words? I have little doubt.

Over the almost ten days that Karel remained with me in the cell, he always insisted on his innocence, that there was nothing he could have done to change the fate of those citizens of Pylos executed by the SS. But clearly it weighed on him. On the other hand, he blamed my father for having compromised him ten years later, and in such a stealthy, underhanded way.

"Everything was a charade. He played on our professional friendship, on our youthful love for Homer to put me in a perilous position where I would have no choice but to do his bidding."

The light in our cell was glimmering when he told me this; I believe it was three days into his incarceration, and he was beginning to panic. His prescription medicine for high blood pressure had not been returned to him as promised. His high forehead was pasty and his tangled blond hair lay matted; the gunmetal blue of his sunken eyes was something pitiful to behold. I was struggling to maintain a patient and unemotional stance, as I had been trained to do with my NVA prisoners: Present the facts—slowly but steadily feed the prisoner more evidence to break down his allegiance, establish rapport, even friendship.

"It sounds to me like all he wanted was for you to help him locate Joanna's son, to get the boy returned to his mother. In a small way, it offered you a way out."

"Are you, too, now accusing me?" With this, he stood from his bunk and pounded on the door of the cell again, screaming at our jailors to get his prescription. It seems it had been left behind in the rush, when he'd been awakened by the Czech security police and brusquely manhandled out of his apartment in a rural town ten miles from Prague. "What," he asked, turning back to me, "because of your little bastard of a half brother? Don't you understand what a harmful policy it was for the Greek Communists to have done such a ridiculous thing? It lost them Greece; it stained the Soviet reputation in the Balkans for decades. And can you imagine if I had gone to my Soviet KGB handlers, even to my counterparts in Bulgaria or Hungary—or God knows where the child could have been—with such a mad request. One boy, one lost boy with no name who—yes, I think he told me he remembered lines from Wordsworth learned from his Greek mother. Aaaargh . . . the sheer imbecility of such a thing."

"Is it so far-fetched for a father to want the return of a child?"

"A child he had never seen. If you had only known the places I have been and the things I have seen after the war, you would know about the millions of fatherless children—a drop in the sea of lost lives."

"The boy's mother had saved my father's life, and because of you— and his bad judgment to trust you—your actions brought about the death of the woman's parents and sister."

"Were you there? There is no redemption for such deaths except to build a better, more just world on the ashes of the perished."

"You could have made a start with that lost child."

"You sound just like your father, always trying to press the responsibility for things onto others. Americans love to blame the ills of the world on us, when your own history is filled with hatreds and deceits and the murder of innocents. Your history is nothing to be proud of. You think your sins can be redeemed by preaching to us?"

Again, he went to the cell door with his empty cup and banged away, turning his face upward so that the tendons in his ragged throat stood out like taunt cables, gesturing toward the ventilation duct, where he assured me, "from long experience," the recording mike was housed, repeating his demands for his prescription and threatening he would refuse to continue with my interrogation otherwise.

"Yes, I'm supposed to be getting information from you, a quid pro quo—to save these sons of bitches, even if they are different idiots from the ones in '68 or '48. Perhaps, if I'd declared my Czech nationality as a boy instead of choosing my pathetic mother's Austrian passport, I might have been saved from such indignities."

"Why didn't you just defect? If, as you tell it, my father was recruiting you, why didn't you just leave? You could've loaded up those hundred and three tablets and talked your way into West Berlin."

"To return with him to the West? Wouldn't that have been a coup for him, to have me defect. He would have been a prince—a career maker for sure, instead of a dead man. And let me tell you, I had a few tales to tell, and I still do, about Stalin's murderers, about the Soviet military installations in the GDR, where they hid their nuclear weapons. You'd better hope I don't tell you, my boy; otherwise, they will never let you out of here." He leered at me and wiped the spittle from his lips. "You should be apologizing to me for what your father did—abandoning you! He tried to blackmail me; he used me as expertly as I—no better—manipulated the Wehrmacht, the SS, and, yes, the Soviets. The Greek boy may have been his excuse, once the charade with the Linear B tablets was played out, but I think defection was what he really had in mind. He used the term *war crimes* with me more than once: how, as a high-profile defector, I might have the slate wiped clean. A new name, a new identity, he promised . . . a small town in Greece, perhaps. But how could I? And with Stalin gone, we thought we had our best chance to begin again."

As they returned to Karel's official ZIM sedan, the driver was clearly agitated; he'd carefully observed them over dinner: the wine, the display of agitation as their voices rose to embittered shouts. "My driver had big ears." It was then that Karel made a decision he would come to regret. "Yes, I could have taken his offer; we could have returned to Berlin and the West—yes, even with the tablets. I was tempted to throw myself on his mercy, but he had hurt my pride—I, the discover of those hundred and three tablets that might change history, and GDR minister of mines, who had been caught neglecting his duty. So I thought, Well, let us make the short drive to Heuersdorf, a virtue out of a necessity, and I will show him how we run our country—a real workers' democracy. That way, he could at least see what a big shot I was in the Party. Perhaps I hoped for some respect—a big fish—that he might really see what a prize I would be for the West." Karel knew he was tempting fate. "I always believed in looking Fortuna in the eye and kicking her ass all the way to Hades and back again."

As they drove south through the darkened outskirts of Leipzig, my father continued to comment on the dismal landscape of dilapidated buildings, broken by only a few feeble electric lights. Then he dropped an almost casual observation that was "like an ice pick through my brain. Oh, how matter-of-fact John was.

"'You know, Karel, back in June, when the Soviets sent in the tanks, we had requests from your striking workers to supply them with arms . . . and we did nothing.'

"He said it loudly enough for the driver to hear—that was very foolish. Why he said it, I don't know. Perhaps to alert me that he, too, was a big fish, that I should take his offer seriously, that he could take care of me if I gave him what he wanted. Or, to make my positon more dangerous than it already was."

In the Stasi report, the driver is quoted as saying that the American agent "offered to provide arms of every description to traitors in the ranks of the workers."

When the ZIM pulled into the hamlet of Heuersdorf on October 12, 1953, two other official cars were parked in front of the medieval

town hall. Hollar told his driver to park down the street as inconspic-
uously as possible. The demonstrations of the morning had quieted
down. A few miners lingered in the streets, many belligerently drunk,
watched by security police who stood in darkened doorways, smoking.
It had started to drizzle. Hollar looked at his watch. The meeting with
the mayor, mine officials, miners' union representatives, and the district
Party secretary had been going on for twenty minutes, if things had
started on time.

"I told your father to wait in the car, not to get out for any reason. I
told him—and I'm sure I made a good show for him—that I'd return in
less than an hour, that I knew how to take care of these people. When
we parted, I thought he looked tired. We had had much wine to drink.
A long day. I told him we would be back in Berlin in a few hours. I
nodded my head and winked and made a sign to him to be careful not
to say anything to the driver. I think I left the impression that we could
do business together."

"Okay . . ."

"But he disappeared, anyway."

"What do you mean, 'he disappeared'? You mean you informed the
Stasi and they arrested him?"

"I wish it were so; we all might have been saved a lot of trouble."

That was the last Karel saw of my father until four months later,
when he, by then also a prisoner—officially, assassinated—was brought
into my father's cell in Pankrác Prison by the KGB to identify him as
the man who'd shot him. And here was the point where Hollar's story
got confused, where all the stories became confused, where even the
Stasi files don't match up with the various accounts I've turned up over
the years. Hollar told me he had gone into the old medieval town hall,
where the officials sat around a table before the disgruntled miners, who
occupied seats in the darkened hall. It turned out to be more of a con-
frontational meeting than Hollar had expected. The miners demanded
higher pay and shorter hours and better living conditions and threatened to sabotage the mines if the Stasi wasn't withdrawn immediately,
or if the Soviet military was brought in to break the strikes.

Heated arguments flew back and forth around the negotiating table.
Soon there were grumblings and threats from the inebriated miners
in the hall, who were listening to the proceedings. There were scuffles
and shoving matches between miners and Stasi—or perceived Stasi—
agents and informants. "Nobody trusted anybody in that room." The

Party secretary was angry and kept looking to Hollar to take care of the mess. He admitted to me that he'd been exhausted and off balance from the wine, his usually astute political skills blunted by conflicted emotions. Finally, he stood and raised his hands high in the air to calm the proceedings, calling for silence. That was when the shot rang out. A single shot, according to the Stasi report, "which shattered the shoulder of the minister of mines." Chaos ensued as everyone dropped to the floor or headed for the exits. The Stasi agents, now with their pistols drawn, only added to the confusion as to who was the shooter and where the shot had come from. It was minutes before any kind of order prevailed. The Party secretary and the wounded Hollar were hustled out by the security police and into the secretary's waiting ZIM, which sped out of town. According to the Stasi report, Hollar was taken to the nearest hospital, in Leipzig, where his wound was attended to and where he spent the next few days recovering.

Not once in the final days I spent with Hollar did he admit he'd been shot, or that anyone had been hit by the fired bullet. He called it a KGB trick. Perhaps he was concerned with my sensibilities, or he, even after all the years, just couldn't admit it to himself. He stuck to his story.

"At first, they assumed that a disgruntled miner or traitor had taken a shot at the Party secretary. Only later did the facts come out. When I got back to my car, I found that John was gone. As we drove around town—how far could a man who could barely walk have gone?—my driver tried to explain. He told me that after I went to the meeting, he had left the car for a smoke and one of his fellow Stasi men had called him over to chat. The driver told me they spoke about nothing, but I think not, because at the investigation the driver gave a complete report on all our movements and much of what was said. It turned out my driver spoke English, and so he would have understood even our conversations in English. The driver testified in the inquiry that your father got out of the car when he went for a smoke, standing under a tree nearby, speaking to one of his fellows. John pointed up the street to the town hall and said he was going to use the toilet; he took his attaché case and the package of clothes he had bought on the trip down. Later it was discovered that the fine suit he had worn crossing into East Berlin had been left in a trash bin next to the bathroom. The Walther pistol was found in the fields outside the town. One shot had been fired. The pistol had been wiped clean of fingerprints. Your father evaporated into thin air, until three months later, when he was arrested on the Czech-Hungarian border. The whole business was an embarrassment to the Stasi; the KGB was outraged, the new Soviet politburo paranoid and belligerent.

"Do you think my father feared your driver might turn him over to the Stasi?"

"I think he had a plan; I think it was all part of his plan—I was part of his plan."

"To do what?"

"He was eventually accused of assassinating the minister of mines. It was a useful way for the Soviets to remove me from the GDR government. Internally, for East German consumption, they blamed my murder on a disaffected miner: to keep the pot boiling on the clampdown. The KGB then used the accusation of murder to blackmail for better terms in the exchange of agents with your government."

"My father, you know, was an expert shot. He wouldn't have missed."

"He missed only by centimeters."

"One shot? Why not a second and third if that was required?"

"I prefer to think he just wanted to scare me, to let me know what had been possible. In the confusion caused by the shot, he escaped and fled. I had my driver circle the streets of Heuersdorf, hoping he might still be there. Then the possibility of what had happened overcame me. I told the driver to return to Berlin. I was terrified for my life. Perhaps I should have gone straight to the West. Two days later, I was arrested. My driver had told everything. Secretly, I was tried for treason in Moscow, but even the KGB was uncertain, and with Stalin gone, they went easy with me: ten years in the gulag, until my resurrection once more. If Stalin had been alive, I would have shared the fate of your father. Instead, I arrived back in my hometown of Prague in 1963, after a decade in a Soviet prison camp, a reformist Communist, son of a Czech nationalist, an intellectual, a professor of classics, ready to join the Dubček government of reformers in the ministry of education, to bring a human face to socialism, a new spring for all the fallen angels of the old regime.

"You said he was arrested on the Hungarian border with Czechoslovakia?"

"He was arrested with four passports, American, GDR, Czechoslovak, and Hungarian. He had a hundred thousand dollars in gold and currency. He had traveled by foot and bicycle, train and automobile, staying at small hotels and visiting museums and libraries. He told people he was on holiday, a traveling scholar on sabbatical. All this was presented at my interrogation and trial in Moscow. He was interrogated for almost a year—harshly, I am sure. I believe he stuck to his story that he was an American scholar on sabbatical from Princeton, but, of course, they knew who he was—what they had."

"Why wasn't he exchanged? It would have been a huge propaganda coup."

Hollar looked me firmly in the eye and shrugged, popping his ragged eyebrows, as if truly at a loss. For a while, I believed him, but only for a while. To give the devil his due, he didn't have all the facts—in the end, a useful fool.

"I was in Kolyma, in the Arctic Circle, where they sent you to die of the cold and exposure and exhaustion. I didn't even know your father's fate until my return. They may have believed he knew too much. I swore that I hadn't told him about the nuclear weapons hidden in the GDR; they couldn't be sure. He had attempted to assassinate a Party official and blame it on the workers. I think their hands were tied."

"That's ridiculous. The CIA offered three top Soviet agents, big fish, in exchange for one compromised intelligence officer. There's an unwritten rule, you know as well as I do: The KGB and CIA don't execute each other's officers."

"Why do you think in the sixties under Dubček I searched high and low for the answer? The document I gave to Vlada Radec was the only thing I found in the files, from a brave Czech nationalist who stupidly complained about a KGB execution in Prague. Like it never really happened: an invisible moment."

Hollar made a gesture to me of something going up in smoke.

"Maybe the KGB wouldn't have wanted it to come out: Pylos, war crimes by a Soviet agent?"

"You like that phrase, don't you?" He spat at me. "You think it gives you a certain righteous moral power."

"An ex-Wehrmacht captain working for the NKVD, who worked hand in glove with the SS to execute defenseless citizens, much less . . ."

Hollar laughed and waved me away.

"That is what saved me in my trial: They found it laudable that I'd saved loyal Communists; they who have slaughtered millions of their own people to save their own skins."

"It still wouldn't have looked good to the international community if the truth had come out."

"You forget; I was dead. I was a martyred GDR official, a convenient death. A very useful member of the Dubček government who kept his masters au courant. And even now, they trot me out one more time, like the old bears of my youth, the bears the Gypsies brought to our town to dance and entertain the children. The poor old bears had rings in their noses. I think the Gypsies treated them badly. I remember my mother saying that they seemed so unhappy."

"And what about the Linear B tablets in the Museum of Antiquities—how did that go over in your trial?"

A barely concealed smile and nodding look of disapproval, as if I was either a fool or an insolent child who needed disciplining.

"I told the truth; there was nothing to hide. Our professional relationship before the war was common knowledge in our circles."

"So . . ."

"Listen, forget your cover story and provide these idiots with something to amuse them; at least offer them some hope. Let them think America the great is disposed to save sinners like them. That way, you get out of here and maybe these Moscow sycophants will return my heart medicine."

He turned to the door again and began a weak bashing of his cup, calling out his demands; he was rapidly losing strength.

"Did my father ever mention he had a wife and a son back in America?"

"Crybaby—is that it? Poor father didn't love you enough? You know nothing about the cruelty of fathers. And let me tell you, he was no saint. Stupid, selfish bastard could've gotten thousands killed—millions."

"Fuck you."

I reached to a half-eaten plate of dumpling stew on the floor and rubbed my finger around in the greasy brown residue. Then in block letters I drew a name on our cell door: PHILBY

"Did that name ever crop up with your esteemed KGB colleagues at your trial, a Cambridge man, who was first secretary to the British Embassy in Washington in the early fifties, but, in reality, the MI6 liaison with the CIA? And come to think of it, a colleague of yours as well, another double agent."

Driving to Heuersdorf today from Leipzig is an even more depressing journey than it must have been for my father. Hundreds of villages in the area have since disappeared, mined out of existence for the brown lignite coal that was stripped from the earth to power East Germany's electric grid. Only a few residents of Heuersdorf now remain; the others were bought off by an American coal company and have relocated. The village is nearly deserted, surrounded by wheat fields and slurry pits that look like small lakes.

When I went to visit Heuersdorf about a year later for the first time, and examined the shell that had once been the medieval town hall, I carefully paced off the dimensions of the council room where the meeting between the government ministers and the miners took place. The lighting might have been poor, but even if my father had slipped into a seat at the very back of the room, he could not have been more than fifty feet from the table where the officials sat, and probably a lot closer if he had placed himself near one of the four side doors. At such a range, he could have put his shot precisely where he wanted it. And in putting that shot through Hollar's shoulder instead of through the heart of his quarry, he might have ended up saving his old colleague's life . . . while sending a message. The Stasi files made it clear that they considered the target of the assassination attempt to have been the minister of mines. Nor did Hollar bother to tell me, as was detailed in the Stasi files, that immediately following the shooting, my father, disguised as a common laborer, had slipped away and hiked cross-country to Leipzig, where, on the following morning, he had walked into the Museum of Antiquities and—according to the flummoxed custodian—resumed his work of the day before, when he'd been accompanied by a high Party official, only to disappear that afternoon with a dozen Linear B tablets. Or that is my surmise because the report only makes mention of the number—ninety-one: "archaic clay tiles with ancient writing"—left on the abandoned worktable.

36

WHILE I TOURED THOSE MANY SHAPE-shifting rooms with Karel Hollar as my cicerone, Laura was hardly wasting away in fretful silence. When I didn't return from my meeting with Vlada, she called the American embassy the next morning and the embassy filed a report with the local police. On the second day of my disappearance, she elaborated a bit with the Foreign Service officer in the consular section, mentioning that I'd been meeting with a known dissident—and, oh, by the way, Peter Alden's father was in the CIA and, well, there was something of a scandal around his death in the mid-1950s—just thought you'd like to know. That got the young officer's attention, although, like everyone else in the embassy, he was riveted by developments in East Germany that would culminate in the fall of the Berlin Wall a week later. The embassy, after inquiries, then got word from the police that I'd been arrested for currency violations—no mention of Vlada or the attempt to smuggle out a document or manuscript. So the embassy people told Laura to cool her heels, stay put, not to leave the hotel. They'd work on the problem, they said, but the timing was bad: "The whole Czech government is jittery as hell right now; there's a Richter scale nine headed their way." Then she called Elliot Goddard at his home overlooking the Potomac; he was glued to CNN. Then she did something incredibly stupid. The night before the fall of the Berlin Wall, she went to the apparatchiks' disco on the top deck of the hotel and managed to talk her way inside, and after too much to drink, she said some things she shouldn't have. Or as she eventually confessed to the Prague CIA station chief and the ambassador, "Well, I was frustrated; I didn't know what to do. But it was like

Nero was fiddling, and so I thought I'd blow on the flames." The next day the Berlin Wall came down, and a day later Elliot Goddard was on his way to Prague.

It was late afternoon when, from her deck chair on the stern of the river steamer, she saw Elliot arrive in a taxi. Aged seventy-five, standing by the open trunk of the taxi, where he paid the driver, he seemed a little shaky, a little older than during their spring meeting in Washington. But he carried his garment bag and small suitcase up the gangplank— no porter in sight—with the jaunty steps of a born sailor and planted a sturdy kiss on her cheek in the reception area, where she greeted him.

"Jesus, where is everybody?" He gave her the once-over, perhaps surprised at her sweatpants, the man's sweater—mine—that she wore, her hair in a ponytail and her face sans makeup.

"Since the Berlin Wall, nobody comes here—even the kids of the apparatchiks; it's a ghost ship without ghosts."

The young woman at the reception desk had been glued to the radio and simply handed him a key after he registered, not even bothering with his passport or visa. He stowed his things in a cabin and Laura led him up to her favorite spot on the back deck, overlooking the river, where they could comfortably talk.

He sat back bleary-eyed, jet-lagged, a shock of blond hair standing up from his broad brow, and gazed out at the river and wooded hills beyond, all bathed in the fading afternoon light.

"All the way in from the airport . . . there are people everywhere in the streets. The taxi driver said there's a general strike for two hours between four and six and demonstrations in Wenceslas Square—the people are out for blood, as he put it."

"You haven't lost your knack with cabbies."

"I gather some student protesters were beaten up by the security police the other day."

"And I'm stuck here."

"Just as well, for the time being. Did you see the pictures on television of the kids celebrating as they climbed over the Berlin Wall—astonishing, beyond my wildest dreams. I still think I'm dreaming—that I'm even here, now, with this."

"It's what you've spent your career working for, isn't it?"

"Do you suppose I could get something to drink? Even vodka would do."

Laura got out of her seat. "I'll check with reception, but the maids and cleaning ladies didn't show this morning. The receptionist got me breakfast. Careful of the railing"—she motioned to a section—"lean too hard and I think you'll go right into the drink. I wake up every night worried I'm sinking."

She returned with two glasses of vodka and orange juice and told him everything she knew.

"Vlada Radec? Oh, yeah, the exchange student—the kid, the field goal kicker. I tried to recruit him for Yale. I had the football coach come up to take him out to lunch."

"Now he's a famous dissident writer."

"I had no idea after our little get-together this spring that you'd try some stunt like this, much less that you'd enlist Peter."

"It's not a stunt. . . . Wouldn't you want to know what happened to your father?"

He turned a slightly more relaxed expression her way as a flush of emotion rose into his cheeks.

"How about thirty-five years of trying to explain, much less live down, that disaster." Elliot raised his eyebrows. "And how was Peter, by the way, before he got arrested by those goons? I haven't seen him since an unpleasant meeting at a VA hospital in San Diego in 1973."

"Living a simple life out of the limelight, licking his wounds."

"Ah, haven't we all. I've been specializing in lives in the shadows recently . . . one Edward de Vere."

"Oh, that."

"Doesn't matter—my own thing, as your generation likes to put it. Since I can't legally write a memoir and my career's in the Dumpster anyway, I'm finishing my magnum opus on Edward de Vere, the seventeenth earl of Oxford, the man who wrote the plays attributed to Shakespeare."

"Right, I remember; you did go on about him when you had me over for dinner."

"Ah, did I? Must be the jet lag. A discussion for another time and place. But all the way here . . . well, how one realizes the ease with which the historical record is distorted—things hidden or lost, how tenuous your own life and times seem, if you know what I mean." He made a gesture with his powerful hands of something malleable, even precious. "How impossible to know anything, much less about those close to you, with any kind of certainty."

"You mean, one day the wall is there, the next day . . . not."

"And what, in God's name, was keeping it there?"

"I thought the CIA was omnipotent. Weren't you geniuses supposed to know all the secrets?"

"That's what I'm trying to tell you, young lady: The young think *they* know it all. And yet *this* shows how much we don't. Take it from someone who spent two years tunneling into East Berlin to tap Soviet phone lines. Your kids and my grandchildren will think it was all a joke—what we spent our lives doing." He gestured to the river, where a small squadron of swans lingered on the near bank, beating against the current. The sky, a pewter blue mixed with strands of lemon-lilac, glittered softly in the small eddies and wavelets where the swans paddled. "It's like when I headed up the CIA investigation about the disappearance of Peter's father—*your* mother's lover: I could never get the characters to inhabit their roles. The same way the character of Hamlet doesn't fit until you realize who wrote the play."

"You think it's all just a fucking play?"

Elliot molded the space between them with his hands, his perfectly clipped nails polished to a nacreous glow by his favorite manicurist at the Metropolitan Club.

"The context, the air we breathe, the wind at our back, the current, the drift—the author who fills our sails."

She turned with a disgruntled pout, seeing his distant stare directed toward the white semaphores momentarily framed in a patch of sunlit water by the shore. The river smelled so awful that sometimes she feared for the swans as they swam, trying to remain abreast of the shoreline. If she and Elliot stood by the railing, the swans, she knew, would come. More and more, she found herself spellbound by this strangely fluid, untethered conversation, not so much because it echoed a thousand conversations with Max, but because she could never figure out if it was the personal or professional interlocutor she faced, or if they were one and the same. So she dug in her oar and pulled.

"Well, I've danced Juliet a hundred times, and it always feels like *I'm* the one telling the story. It's in the movement, you see, the expression, too, on my face—and yes, the Prokofiev, I suppose. But what people really want is you; that's what they're paying for. If you can't move them with *your* story, it falls flat."

"Fascinating—*your* interpretation of the story—who's playing it for whom and why." He drained his vodka and orange juice. "I do hope you've been discreet about all that I've told you. I'm still liable under my Agency contract for revealing top secret information. There are people in Congress who would still like to put me in jail, if they could."

"I should thank you. You see, we met with Nestor in Pylos. We found something out that you might be interested in: John Alden had a son by a Greek woman. She's a doctor now; she nursed him after he was wounded."

"Yes, I interviewed Joanna back in 1954—can it be that long ago?— about the kidnapped boy. It's all in my report on the investigation. He certainly hid it pretty well from all of us, including his wife and mother—*and* his lover. A blow to his pride, at the very least. As I wrote in my report, it clearly inflamed his anti-Communist fervor, if not enough to provoke World War Three."

"Surely you're exaggerating."

"Berlin was a trip wire for either side. I was Berlin station chief in '53. If we'd supplied arms to the workers during the uprising, there's no knowing."

"Are you saying he tried to supply them with arms?"

"A matter of expectations . . . if we told them we'd do A and so they did B—the Soviets accused him of doing just that; that's what they told us—but I never told you this, right?"

"So he wasn't just charged with spying?"

"For materially assisting in the overthrow of the GDR, *and* for the assassination of a top official—so they told us."

"That can't possibly be right."

"A split decision inside the Agency. I say no, because the worker insurrection had largely been suppressed by Soviet tanks that fall; no, because I don't think he had it in him."

"Because he wasn't crazy enough?"

"His better judgment . . . he wasn't *that* crazy."

"But determined enough that he went off and abandoned Peter, his wife—and my mother, as you never stop reminding me."

"Suzanne, the bewitching Suzanne, siren of sirens. You obviously have a high opinion of your mother's charms."

"Oh, it's been a thrilling ride. Someday I'll tell you how she seduced my partner on my debut at the Met."

"Sorry, dear, I've read all about it in that novel—what was the title?"

"Well, fuck you."

He laughed and turned to her, staring into her eyes, which were bathed in the reflected green off the river.

"What a stunning bride she was, your mother. I only wish she had had her claws into John more deeply than she did, but he, even as attractive to women as he was, never let that sort of thing get in his way."

Laura leaned forward, squinting, as if visualizing her words.

"You're awfully sure of yourself: He *never* got over my mother."

His eyes lit up, as if half in awe, half in embrace of his amour propre. "I admire your loyalty, but that's what every woman wants to believe— that they trump a man's ambition. Look at Kim Philby, three—no, four—wives and countless lovers left in the dust. Your mother too, perchance?"

She waved it off like a bad smell.

"Yeah—what about our ambition when it buries yours?"

Elliot's eyes lifted and glittered at the prospect of combat, and for a moment he gazed longingly into his empty glass.

"Ah, the motivation of the players, but a Lady Macbeth, I think not." He looked her up and down and ran his tongue over his lips as he longingly inspected his glass once more. "For a scholar, he was as much of an operator as anyone I've known—because no one suspected it of him. Like his OSS days in Greece. Greece, the Balkans were the Brits' backyard in 1943, close to their center of operations out of Cairo, long-standing intelligence contacts and all that. But old Wild Bill Donovan wanted the OSS to have a piece of Greece. And do you know why Donovan demanded a piece of the action? Because John cornered him in his New York law office as the OSS was being organized in early 1942 and volunteered for Greece, convinced the new head of OSS that America must have a stake in Greece, and not leave it solely to the Brits. Why? Because of all the Greek-Americans in our county—we somehow owed it to them. But that was a self-serving argument. John wanted the OSS in Greece because *he* wanted to go back there: his old stomping ground, I guess. The fucking war was one big inconvenience in his celebrated career as an archaeologist, and he had this romantic idea that he was some kind of Lawrence of the Hellenes. Believe me, all through our OSS training in the stinking rural sticks of Maryland in 1942, it was all he could talk about. He read Homer in the shithouse— sorry, but all the major fuckups in my career have been because of half-baked romantic numbskulls without an ounce of common sense."

"Ah, the human factor—"

"Don't start with the fucking Graham Greene, please."

"Did you know that he had a rendezvous—is that the right spy word?—in Pylos with his colleague, Karel Hollar?"

Elliot stiffened. "Karel, who?"

"Hollar, a friend and rival, an archaeologist before the war . . ." Laura smiled as she noticed the renewed intensity of his stare. "He was in the German army but Hollar was a British agent—what do you call it?"

"S-I-fucking-S," enunciated Elliot.

"Yes, SIS. He gave some information to John about German troops. Only he later turned up at an SS execution in Pylos. Peter thinks he may have been a double agent, working for the Soviets, as well."

Elliot grimaced and sat back, his lips pursed. "There's no mention in his OSS file about a meeting with a British SIS operative, or a KGB guy, either. But that doesn't exactly surprise me, given how badly those files were compromised by the Communists in the Balkan division of OSS. And I did a little housecleaning of his files myself when I finally got John away from Princeton. Maybe that guy—Nestor—mentioned it, but if he did, I've forgotten."

"You look worried—tell me what worries you?"

"Memories . . . or their lack; you don't want to know. It's always what you can't quite see." And he held up a finger as if testing for the wind direction.

"Like what?"

"Like a luncheon I had with Kim Philby, one of many, at the Metropolitan Club in the fall of 1950, just before I was posted to Berlin. Dapper, unflappable Kim was our poster boy for all the experience and cunning of our cousins in the business of secrets. He was the best of their best. He'd been a correspondent in Spain during the civil war; he'd developed new protocols for SIS from the ground up during the war. In the late forties, he'd practically written the rule book for the early CIA about how to execute covert operations. We'd learned our business at his knee. So I went to him—just months before Maclean and Burgess defected to Moscow, when Kim became suspected, too, as a KGB spy—for advice about how to handle Berlin. He couldn't have been more helpful sorting out all the players: disgruntled Communists, ex-Communists, Nazis and ex-Nazis, disaffected Soviets and Lithuanians, Belarusian and Ukrainian émigrés with axes to grind, unredeemed Jews—double agents all looking for revenge or to line their pockets—endless lists of willing suspects that even de Vere couldn't weave into a coherent plot. How do you run agents when you can't trust anybody, when even the border of the playing field is fluid? Philby was sympathetic and insightful and he offered me gold—what I thought was gold—fool's gold. He told me that SIS—MI6—had a man in the GDR government that they could trust to give us the lowdown on Soviet troop deployments and intentions in Eastern Europe, that his man could vet our agents—that if I passed the names of our agents on to him, their SIS man could give us the thumbs-up or -down. First I was impressed, grateful, then a tad suspicious of his certainty, since the Brits had hardly distinguished themselves since the war. They'd flopped as badly, if not worse, than we had. Their savoir faire was wilting at the jowls and would evaporate in the coming months with the exposure of Maclean and his defection with Burgess. When luck ran out on lucky Kim and he was banished to ignoble limbo in London and then later Beirut, until he fled in '63. I remember him staring out the window of the dining room at the traffic on Connecticut Avenue, telling me how much he was enjoying his Washington posting after depressing London; it was a wistful look, perhaps with the White House only three blocks distant."

Laura listened intently as Elliot expanded on that long-ago conversation.

"'How's your lovely Margaret?'"

"'Two girls so far and a third baby on the way.'"

"'Third time lucky for a boy?'"

"'A boy would be the nuts.'"

"'She was such a glowing maid of honor at Suzanne's wedding.'"

"'Oh . . . right, enough that I fell in love at first sight and married her—stole her away from Old Blighty.'"

"'Lucky man. We were all in love with Suzanne, of course. I dearly loved her brother, poor chap. Your friend—Alden—seems to have gotten over her—yes?'"

"'The women may save us yet. How's Aileen holding up in the Washington whirl?'"

"'Barely, nerves, you know. And I have an old friend staying with us, Guy Burgess, second secretary in the embassy. Guy drives her to tears.'"

"'I hear he's quite the livewire at diplomatic gatherings.'"

"'My God, the spell of that wedding—that Sussex spring . . .

Suzanne, well, John and I were just reminiscing about it the other day. Do Margaret and Suzanne still keep in touch?"

"'The occasional letter from the Berkshires or Beacon Hill. It can't be easy with Bobby Williams in a wheelchair."

"'Yes, so John was telling me. We were talking about his time in Greece—near thing, the civil war. The suffering of the children from starvation was terrible. By the way, the chap I was telling you about, our man in the GDR, was a big asset for us in Greece during the war— trustworthy fellow.'"

Laura was struck by the look of vulnerability that flickered across Elliot's features as he described that distant, fading conversation with Kim Philby. Now that Philby was dead, it was as if some restless part of himself had been left tilting with "that spirit-damned." To Laura's eyes, he appeared to be contemplating just how much he'd foolishly given away to the Soviets, and if there had been an overlooked slipup by Philby, a thing left unexploited in return.

Elliot rattled the ice cubes in his glass with alarm.

"If Philby's cover hadn't been blown"—he shook his head—"I might well have vetted the names of our agents with his man in the GDR."

"The one who'd been a *big asset* in Greece?" she asked, watching as a flicker of doubt passed across Elliot's pensive face. "Like I told you, his name was Karel Hollar."

He became very still, closing his eyes, as if trying to see the thing he'd missed.

"No one"—he grimaced—"likes to be had. For years, I fantacized about what I'd say to Kim Philby if I saw him on the streets of Moscow. Now it's too late."

"Was the attack on the E-boats in Kalamata a mistake?"

"John was always good with his mistakes: He knew how to make his own luck, cover his tracks. As I took care of his OSS file."

"I don't see how being caught in a Communist ambush and shot was very lucky."

"Communist ambush?"

"In Greece, in the mountains on the way back from Kalamata."

"His OSS files only mention a German bullet in the Kalamata raid."

"Well, you're the expert."

"So, going back to our little conversation of a few months back: Was Philby mentioned in the love letters?"

"Like I told you, only because he had come under suspicion."

"No one acting, well . . . jealous—aggrieved?"

Laura just stared off.

"No documents, official or otherwise, cables, communications—that sort of thing—in your mother's possession?"

Again, Laura did not respond.

Elliot sighed. When Laura mentioned this to me, she told me she was quite shaken by how much he didn't know—or had missed—by how he hardly bothered to try to cover it up anymore. She wondered about his health, if his sigh was one of relief or frustration.

"Listen, don't get me wrong: John was my friend. I loved the guy; and I loved his family. I visited him in the hospital after they got him out of Greece; he was lucky to walk again. But you never knew what John was weighing in his mind. Philby was much the same—fucking smart-ass, cynical Brit. Problem is, we just got left holding the bag: fixing the damn world they stuck us with, which can't be fixed, and so we got suckered into dreaming up grandiose ideas to justify having to be just as bad as the other sons of bitches. It's a rotten deal, and it's not like our own house is a democratic bed of roses; that's what John always complained about—having to balance it out. Some guys have to pump themselves up to keep at it, be superpatriots and ring the bell of freedom every morning before they fuck their wives and take a pee. I'd rather get the dirty job done as quickly as possible and go home. I'd rather be sailing on Buzzards Bay. And that's why Hamlet was so fucked-up, because he thought he was the author of his assassination plot, that he could patch up his stinking Denmark, but he couldn't even fix his own life, or not drive Ophelia crazy in the process, probably because he was mooning after his mother, Queen Elizabeth—the First, that is."

She frowned at him and shook her head dismissively. "You lost me on Buzzards Bay."

"Don't mind me—long day; jet lag, and the change of flights in Frankfurt was a pisser. And fucking Philby—fucking Brits. It's always about the upper crust, old Etonians and Trinity College and the barroom at White's, as if their little club is the only one that matters— that's why they let Philby escape: They couldn't believe one of their own betrayed them. Oh sure, we have our own club, I suppose, Winsted and Yale, Skull and Bones, and it helps if your family is in the *Social Register*, but that shit is only skin-deep—we're all new boys in our country.

Of course, there's Alger Hiss and all his Harvard crew of traitors." He shrugged. "But I always like to believe we're more about an idea, that the country stands for something, freedom and justice. And we're not in it to rule an empire, but to foster an empire of believers in a better way of life."

"Maybe you need another drink; you're sounding like my mother."

At this, he scowled and brought his face close to hers.

"Listen, I was more a fan of John than he was of himself. I revered his grandfather, the Civil War general and founder of Winsted, one of the few men of his generation who told the truth about the Civil War—that it was about ending slavery. My grandfather's generation wanted him to run for governor of New York; they would have put the man in the White House if they could have done it. Can you imagine growing up with a moral imperative like that weighing on your shoulders? It can't help but distort how you understand yourself: the burden of our all-too-human frailties. People never understand how deep such ambitions run in families—how could it not, as it's mother's milk. And if you'd known his mother—and I loved her: a flinty piece of New England scrimshaw—you'd understand. You should have seen the look of horror on his face when I told him at Princeton that Suzanne and Bobby were named as KGB agents in decrypted Soviet cable traffic. One moment he was content to be a tweedy prof in Tiger Town, the next he's on his way to being CIA station chief in Athens. Suzanne was the poisoned chalice to his noble image of himself."

"You really must hate my mother. Well"—and Laura looked at her watch—"not to worry: She just married Charles Fairburn at his home in Sussex. Needless to say, I've missed their wedding—second time, or is it third time lucky?"

Elliot lowered his face to his hands and shook his head.

"Jesus, I just realized Philby *had* been at Suzanne's wedding, but of course I didn't recognize him then, I didn't know him. But he sure as hell remembered who I was—a tip-off, stupid of me."

Laura rolled her eyes in exasperation.

"John never stopped loving her. Even after he found out he had a son by Joanna."

"Listen, young lady . . ."

"Do you have to keep calling me that? And I'm not so young anymore, worse luck."

"None of us are, but I want to keep you young, I want to keep my daughters young. I want my dear wife, Margaret, alive and young again."

"That's what children are about, I guess."

Something in her tone, her bleak gaze at the river, must have given her away.

Elliot reached a hand to hers.

"Don't get me wrong; I'm not saying he didn't do a great job in the Greek Civil War. He did a terrific job, even if he gave me hell about our Albanian operations, when it was Philby who compromised them. We were desperate to find a way to counter the Soviets. His career soared until he got mixed up in their web, the Kim Philby, Maclean, and Burgess disaster. Berlin saved me, got me out of Washington and the taint of Philby. I'm racking my brain to remember if Donald and Melinda Maclean were at Suzanne's wedding as well, if I got introduced by Charles Fairburn. I think I vaguely remember Philby now . . . I think. We were young; I had eyes only for Margaret *and* Suzanne."

"Anthony Blunt was there. I remember my mother talking about *Anthony*, the man who got Bobby his famous triumph at Wigmore Hall. As a kid, Bobby used to tell me about the program he played that night, how he played each piece, how the audience loved him."

"Really . . ." Elliot examined Laura with what she later described as a look of stricken despair. "Terrible, my memory is so faulty. How can it be we've become old men?"

"So, it's all Kim Philby's fault?"

"The thing that really rankled is that the Brits, MI6 and MI5, couldn't or wouldn't convict Philby; they couldn't break him with interrogations. They never got the goods on him. Like I said, too concerned about the damage to their self-image to pursue him tooth and claw. We couldn't be sure how much he'd sold us down the river. And worse still, we were pretty sure there were others in his Cambridge spy mafia. We could never trust the Brits again."

"Is that why you stuck by John after he disappeared, played down his relationship with Bobby Williams and my mother?"

At this, Elliot became still, his ruddy cheeks flexing, his voice softening.

"I investigated their asses."

"But Winsted remained untarnished. Think of it: the grandson of one of the founders a KGB agent, perhaps abetted by another. And you never missed a Founder's Day or trustees meeting, flying all the way from Saigon if need be to have one more shot at my mother."

"So, how about letting me see the letters?"

"When we get Peter out, you can ask him."

"Your instinct for loyalty is wholly admirable."

"Would disappearing into East Berlin, doing whatever John did, be some kind of gallant gesture to save his skin, his reputation?"

"Berlin—hardly: We'd had our chance. After Maclean and Burgess disappeared behind the Iron Curtain in 1951, and Philby smoldered under investigations and dishonor in London, we were encouraged by the new administration to figure out a way to free Eastern Europe. Berlin was a snake pit, a house of mirrors—nothing in the way of good intelligence about Soviet capability or intentions. Then in early '53, Stalin died, Beria grabbed the reins and withdrew all his resident KGB men for consultations in Moscow, and the shit hit the fan: Workers in East Berlin and Leipzig rose against the government, demanding better hours and pay. We did nothing; we backed off. The Dulles boys turned out to be pussies and fumed about the criticism that we did nothing. They sent John from Washington, anointed by his Princeton buddy Allen Dulles, our old OSS resident in Geneva, Eisenhower's man. John was Dulles's golden boy, the man who would shake things up and get us back on track after Philby. That September in Berlin, John was like Billy Sunday when he caught a whiff of hellfire. I never knew him so consumed, as if he was sure there was something we had missed, some chink in the Soviet armor that we could exploit. He read our GDR intelligence files and cable traffic day and night—I wondered if he ever slept—as if certain something was there. He made me feel like an incompetent, and, worse, that I lacked the chutzpah to do the necessary thing, as if it was I who had decided not to offer arms and support to the German workers. As if tapping Soviet telephone lines was blue-collar bullshit. Then he evaporated into thin air . . . and left us all to clean up the mess—our own Maclean-Burgess-Philby mess. As if to spite us. I still hear the whispers behind my back."

Laura had gone to get him another vodka and orange juice—heavy on the vodka; she knew when she was on a roll.

"How do you know that he didn't just flip out—go AWOL, as you put it? Maybe he was doing just what he wanted to do—needed to do."

Again, Elliot took his time, quenching his thirst, rolling the ice cubes.

"Sometimes, I get the feeling you're more a champion of John than his own son, much less your mother."

"What about the Czechs? What are we up against here and now?"

Elliot gestured downriver, toward the spires and domes of medieval Prague.

"The Czechs are a fucked-up people. After the war, they thought they were fervent Communists; they kicked out the Germans in the Sudetenland, idealized Stalin, until the Soviets swallowed them and they realized the horror they'd embraced. Then there were the show trials. They sacrificed their Party members to the revolution like their lives meant nothing, scripted the confessions, hung their friends and family in an orgy of self-sacrifice. Even with Stalin gone, they kept reading from the old script. That's the kind of thing we were dealing with in the early fifties—you don't think the sheer absurd horror of it kept us up at night? Talk about a fucked-up plot and demented characters."

She watched Elliot as he downed his screwdriver, jingling the ice cubes as if about to roll the dice for drinks at the Met Club.

"Vlada told us something pretty awful," she said. With her photographic memory for gesture and movement, she reached a finger to the back of Elliot's head and tapped a spot where his dirty blond hair curved in a cowlick. "Vlada said he had it from some former Czech official: John Alden was executed in Pankrác Prison."

Elliot had flinched at the touch of her finger, turning to look at her with a careful squint in the pale light from the river; he glanced around, as if by instinct, to check for anyone in earshot.

"'Fraid not, young lady." Elliot's counterpunch revived him and he faced her straight on. "His body was returned to us intact. A little worse for wear—a year in solitary can do that. His war wound had completely healed; his weight was on the low side, according to the pathologist's report, but they found no signs of drugs, poisons, what constituted foul play. The Soviets told us he'd had a heart attack, very sudden. Pathology was inconclusive on that score. The body was cremated and the ashes returned to his wife."

"But if it's true, does that change things?"

"As far as I know, the dead don't rise again. We thought we had a deal for his release, an exchange, three of their guys—I told you this back in Washington—for him. It was all set . . . and then it wasn't. They even apologized. One of the KGB officers, a guy I'd known for years, told me they were sorry—that they'd kind of gotten to like their American spy. I almost believed him."

"How do we get Peter the fuck out of here?"

"The Czech government is coming apart at the seams. But that doesn't mean bad things can't happen. If, as you said, the Soviet Union executed an American CIA officer in cold blood on Czech soil, that's not something the present government would want to get out. Neither would the Soviets, of course, but I'm not sure they've got much say in the matter any longer. That was not how the game was played, even in the darkest days of the Cold War." He flung his glass into the river. "If I ever get my hands on the . . ." Elliot glanced skyward and got it under control. "I'm clearly slipping; I should be flirting with a beautiful young woman like any old CIA guy worth his salt. Instead, I'm becoming a cliché of a tiresome old man, a Polonius or, perish the thought, a Falstaff." He cut himself off with a theatrical gesture, palm outstretched, as if to halt the river's flow. "My dear, you'd make your mother blush, and she was a real Mata Hari—the real deal."

"You might have told Peter the truth—me, too, for that matter."

"And which truth is it that we're speaking of?"

"That you got Bobby to betray his Cambridge recruiter, Anthony Blunt, to the CIA in exchange for a place on the Winsted board."

"Who told you that?"

For the first time that afternoon, Elliot seemed truly alarmed.

"You're fucking slipping, old man."

He smiled warmly, as if now relishing the sparring . . . to unburden himself to a woman again.

"It was your father's idea."

"For the Winsted board?"

"Bobby's soup to nuts. All I did was relay the name to MI5."

"You must have been over the moon."

"MI5 had suspected *Tony* for over a decade, ever since Maclean and Burgess defected to Moscow in 1951, but Bobby confirmed it. Blunt was the key to the whole rotten bunch—if too little, too late . . . of course, he would've been at their wedding."

"A betrayal that shocked—to her very soul—even my unshockable mother."

Laura eyed Elliot intently, wondering why he continued lying, when Suzanne had facilitated Bobby's exposure of Anthony Blunt by passing the information to Elliot.

"Pity, 'tis true . . . ," he said with the merest hint of a repressed smile, "she, well, wouldn't have tried to do something about it, do you think?"

"What, torture him with her infidelities for another twenty years?"

"Only two or three days after Philby died in Moscow, those bullets arrived at your place in the Berkshires. All it would have taken was one call to the appropriate contact at the Soviet embassy."

At this, abruptly, she stood and walked to the railing, where he followed.

Laura gave the railing a shake, testing its strength. "I'll leave that to you. What I remember: At all the Winsted events—how relentless you were . . . still trying to get the truth out of her."

She grasped the railing at arm's length—as if to mime the subject at hand—assuming first position and descending in a plié, while her free arm moved with fluid ease. She fixed a coquettish smile on her audience of one.

"For both our sakes," he replied, seemingly mesmerized by her graceful transformation, at how graciously she'd exposed his lie. "For the record, as you put it: to save herself. It was the least I could do for John, for Peter."

"And for your legacy," she said, turning to the river, pushing back strands of hair from her forehead. "Keeping Bobby—what? the Iago of your play."

"History's judgment can be harsh . . . for the children."

"*If* she was a courier for Melinda Maclean in New York or Philby. If she had something on Philby that would've stuck. If she had something to do with her sometime lover's disappearance in East Berlin."

"If she was Philby's lover, as well." He turned to her averted profile and gave it a good thirty seconds. "Well, I admire your loyalty to your mother *and* her taste in men."

"We need to stick up for our blood—if not that, the record, then what?"

"Loyalty in a woman, priceless."

"Her drinking over the last ten years . . . it almost killed her."

"I was sorry to hear about her hospitalization."

"Don't worry about her: Even if her brain's pickled, she's bounced back and is suing me for return of her personal property. And married now to millions."

"The letters . . ."

"And a few other odds and ends. What, with malice aforethought, she removed from Hermitage to Charles Fairburn's home so the stuff didn't burn up in the fire."

"Goodness, gracious, *Charles* . . . 'odds and ends'?"

"With my lawyers."

He brought his face nearer hers. "We *know* she was a courier for the secret documents Donald Maclean brought from Washington and left with his wife, Melinda, in New York."

"He accuses her of as much in the letters—and Philby."

Elliot popped his lips. "Ah, the perfidy of women and the careless ambitions of men . . . there seems no end to it."

She tapped his pugnacious nose. "Being her *loyal* daughter was no bed of roses."

"I've got three daughters, with two and a half messed-up marriages. And my rose, your mother's best friend and maid of honor, Margaret, died of ovarian cancer, still as beautiful on the day of her diagnosis as on the day I married her. That's when she began to hold it against me, all the years I was away, the years in Berlin, and Central America, and Vietnam."

She patted his hand. "Peter told me you are doing great things on the Winsted board with minority students."

She took his hand and kissed it.

"His name and my name remained connected in people's minds. I was head of the Berlin station. When they tried to hang me for the Bay of Pigs, the review board always went back to the Alden fiasco and started pointing fingers."

"So, do you still blame him—or only my mother?"

He cocked his head, as if detecting an odd tremor in her voice.

"When I sat for a month with my dying wife in Sibley hospital, I spent hour after hour wanting to rewrite the play: the one where I don't come out the embittered, regretful old man. Perhaps he was lucky to die in harness when he did. That way, he's managed to remain a golden-hued enigma to our once-glorious ambitions. Surely a theatrical artist like you must know her *Lear*: 'Love cools, friendship falls off, brothers divide . . . We have seen the best of our time: machinations, hollowness, treachery, and all ruinous disorders, follow us disquietly to our graves.'"

"You old Winsted boys? You all think you can fucking write your way into life."

"Don't be too harsh—you're beginning to sound like your brilliant mother. As a kid, I wanted to be like John's grandfather, the general. Sargent knew how to capture the spark of character in a man's eyes, you see. And that man in the portrait had blood on his hands and made good on it . . . all the bondsman's blood." Elliot shook his head and gazed at her with weary longing. "I go back to our place on Buzzards Bay, back to the old house where generations of my mother's people grew up. I putter around, repair the sash cords, recaulk the sailboats. And when I'm out on the water, slipping through the wind, I can't believe where I've been or what I've done. The men who died on that beach in Cuba, to whom I'd promised air cover—and the marines, if it came to that. How I could have strayed so far. I'm not particularly spiritually inclined, but the water and the wind and our old house on the shore, where the rocks lead down to the water, are my religion, and I am left to wonder at the folly of not embracing them more fully."

Elliot smiled grimly, slumping as he held on to the rail, but the thing rankled her mind.

"Would the KGB have come after Bobby at the end, like you said, just two days after Philby died in Moscow . . . because of Blunt?"

"That's a good reason to keep your mouth shut about Anthony Blunt; only a very few people know who—the *traitor* who dropped the dime on him. Memories are long in our business, even with dear fucking Tony dead these last six years."

"You must be pretty proud, how you pulled that off—then ditching Bobby five years later? Welshing on the deal."

Laura watched him intently as the bronze glow of sunset on the river deepened, flooding the deck, so that the filigree patterns in the wrought-iron railing cast writhing arabesques across the planking.

"The damage had already been done, and a soured reputation is irrecoverable. History and time will see to that . . . just ask my daughters and their cousins. Summers when they get together, they talk about all their vacations at our place on Buzzards Bay. Even after their mother died so horribly, they're like kids there again as if she never existed. Nobody talks about the old days in Berlin and Washington."

The sadness in his voice almost stopped her cold. They were watching as the swans edged closer.

"I'm sorry," she said. "I'm sorry we never met."

"You did, at Founder's Day in 1966. Suzanne and Margaret, her maid of honor, practically fell all over each other."

"Yes, I'd forgotten . . . that happy, happy wedding."

He regripped his hold on the railing, knuckles bulging, eyes squinting into the reflected light. "I can't help feeling there's a missing character in our little drama."

"Your deus ex machina, your hidden author."

"Maybe your—or is it Philby's?—SIS operative in Greece and Berlin will fill the bill."

"John Alden's rival and friend. I read his book on Homer in Athens. He died at the end of the war, in a Soviet POW camp."

"Ah, now that sounds promising." He bent and kissed her head. "You know your mother cut Margaret dead after we dropped Bobby from the board. Letters unanswered. Suzanne wouldn't even visit when she was dying in the hospital."

"My mother, and rightly so, never trusted you an inch."

"Our sorceress—men into swine."

"Old man, you're just jealous because you never got to fuck her."

"Your felicity of expression surpasses Suzanne's. Then again, I never had the pleasure of seeing her dance. But I had the better woman."

As the unrelenting hours passed, Karel Hollar began to weaken. He no longer banged on the cell door, demanding to be released, or at least to be given his blood pressure medication. He was afraid to raise his voice or get excited. He complained of headaches and a pounding in his chest. Then he began to get confused and tired easily. His voice was labored, as if he had difficulty breathing. I began taking his pulse, comparing it to mine, and even without a watch, I could tell it was dangerously raised. I began reporting his heart rate, sometimes shouting it out, occasionally banging on the door when our meals were passed through and there was no prescription. I watched in horror as he passed through stages of anger, pleading, despair, and quiet meditation, and finally resignation. I found myself blamed and forgiven and blamed again—what felt like a thousand times over—and then asked for forgiveness. I knew I should hate this man, that I should take some satisfaction in his hideous demise, but I felt only pity . . . and fear that he might drag me down with him. And worse, dismay that a crucial witness to my father's fate was disappearing before my eyes.

"For God's sake," Hollar urged me, lying back on his cot, "just tell them something to ease their minds. They love theory; they learned everything from the KGB—like dogs, they licked up theoretical vomit. Unlike your father, who was always full of counterfactual theories. He liked to dismiss Hegel and Marx as frauds because, as he told me, we live though our ancestors and they through us; bad ideas are always bad ideas, but blood endures. He told me how as a boy he was haunted by an ancestor . . . a military man, I believe."

"A general in the Union army; he fought to free the slaves in the South."

"Ah, you see, I do remember. So tell them a story about your revolution. Revolutions make them happy. And perhaps they will reward you."

"It was the Civil War . . . but a revolution, too, I guess."

"Your country was born in revolution, like the Soviet Union, a revolution that spawned the Cheka, and the gulag—what tales I could tell you—and the KGB, whose ring these idiots kiss with so much admiration, Czech Communists who failed to fight the Nazis, and then groveled at the boots of their Soviet handlers. Surely you rebelled as a youth of the sixties? Your country—and I have been a student of your history—takes pride in being the avatar of the future, the free and democratic future of the world. There is much to be admired in such a proposition. Don't forget, we once believed the same as you, when we— John and I—were young and passionate warriors against the fascists; we were going to change everything. I was dedicated to the destruction of the old. . . . It burned in my soul."

Hollar lapsed more and more into long silences as his breathing became labored, silences that blended with the lengthening periods of darkness. I could detect a low gurgle, a slight rattle of the cot across from me. Then his voice would begin again . . . as if from somewhere far away, as if our conversation had led him to an unexpected place in his mind.

"I thought of myself as an artist when very young. My mother only wished for her little boy to go to seminary to join the ancient empire of Christian believers. Ah, my friend, what a temptation, to embrace that ancient empire of belief. Such power delivered into your hands from the very lips of the Savior: 'I will give unto thee the keys of the kingdom of heaven; and whatsoever thou shalt bind on earth shall be bound in heaven, and whatsoever thou shalt loose on earth shall be loosed in heaven.' My mother trembled at the thought of her son claiming such a power from the lips of Saint Leo. As a little girl, my mother presented flowers to the emperor Franz Joseph; she touched the mantle of the ages. Can you tell me that you have never desired such a faith, for a doctrine that fills past, present, and future? The eternal moment, as Augustine described it. This is the gift of the father, which one embraces or overthrows . . . I think along the lines your father believed. Why do you never talk anymore about your father?"

The question weighed on me.

"I was only two when he left. But I think I remember him taking me swimming in the lake at night. He'd carry me in his hands above the water while he lay on his back, kicking with his feet, carrying me to the raft and safety. We'd lie there under the stars, the back of my head against his bare chest. I barely remember his voice, but sometimes when I stare up at the stars, I think I hear it . . . or the lapping of water . . . or something."

"Draco was the North Star for the Greeks; the stars and the earth and the rivers were everything."

"Athena threw him up there, the serpent, the dragon."

"Your father was a good friend. . . . I still dream of our days in Crete, the sound of the cicadas in the heat of the afternoon, the frogs at night—and yes, the stars. Even Athens back then along the river Ilissos—the flowers: hyacinths, anemones, cyclamen, asphodels, irises, larkspur, and, oh, so many others."

"Crete, yes, my first taste of the life, the oleander and myrtle, the pine and cedar and laurel . . . the perfume of the earth."

"Yes, that, too."

"Landscape and memory, the stuff of all our mythmaking. Like Philby, I suppose, the mythology—the myths that will surround him now."

"Oh many, many . . ."

"Did you ever meet Kim Philby? He and my father were practically colleagues in the early fifties in Washington."

"Not at Cambridge, not professionally, only later."

"When he was—what, retired, living in Moscow?"

"Yes, I visited twice, once for an official celebration, a medal ceremony, and once at his fine apartment in Moscow with his last wife, Rufina Ivanona."

"Three wives, wasn't it?"

"Four. I knew his first wife, Litzi, very well in the early years of the GDR. A wonderful and dedicated woman; she still lives, I believe. An Austrian Jew, her accent was the same as my mother's. Philby would have done well to stay with her; she was still in love with him. But his work came first, an ambition that blinded him to everything else."

"You didn't happen to mention my father to him?"

"Of course I did. John was the reason for my last visit."

"Surely not."

"The year before he died. The KGB was allowing more access than before for those of us in the same generation to pay our respects. The new men, the younger men, had forgotten about him and his heroic days."

"What did you want to know?"

"The same as you; why a top CIA official would have done such a crazy thing, and why his execution—why there had been no exchange."

"Did Philby have any theories?"

"He smiled as Rufina gave us tea and left us alone in his study, just the two of us with all his books, two old scholars—maybe two years ago now. He remembered your father well, their many lunches at splendid clubs in Washington."

"Where Philby extracted information."

"Philby respected his dedication, respected his valor in Greece against the Nazis, his stand for racial justice in your country."

"They spoke of such things?"

"You think Philby was an unfeeling monster and not dedicated to a more humane world? You think us so callous in our youthful ambitions to fight fascism?"

"He sold out everyone he loved or who loved him; his first three wives and his children, much less his country. How many deaths did he cause?"

"You know what he admired about your father? That he shared with him the secret of his lost son, the child of the Greek woman who was taken into Albania by the Greek Communists."

"He told Philby about that?"

"He was desperate to recover the boy, but it was a very delicate situation. I don't believe he even told his CIA colleagues."

"Because Philby . . . had connections—not to Moscow? Because he knew or suspected Philby was a KGB agent?"

"I remember Philby sitting back in his chair in his book-lined study when I asked him that very thing—he had thousands of books, a literary man spouting Turgenev, Tolstoy, and Dostoevsky as if they were intimates. He was one who examined a question from every angle, what it required to discover anything that was hidden from him. He had an instinct about how things would unfold. But your father's fate baffled even him.

"I asked him, 'Could it be that John Alden knew or suspected you were KGB and was seeking your intervention for the return of his child—as he did with me?'

"And he replied, 'Comrade, you knew him for many years before the war, and in Greece during the war, when you worked for our friends *and* the British. Would a man of such iron discipline have used the kidnapped child to investigate my connections to Moscow, much less tip me off that I might be under suspicion?'

"'Of course not. . . . He was not such a driven apologist for the West that he would have used his personal agonies for the benefit of the CIA. He was a moralist, a romantic, never an ideologue.'

"'That was my opinion also. He was one of the few Americans I liked. In another world, perhaps another life, we could have been comrades. I liked his wife as well, daughter of an admiral, very down-to-earth. He felt deeply about the failures of his country.'

"'So, like me, you could do nothing about the child?'

"'I offered him professional courtesies—so to say: if MI6 could help or if we ever turned up anything useful.'

"'When he mentioned the child to me in Leipzig, it so rattled me that I made stupid mistakes.'

"'Our Greek friends were fools of the first rank to engage in that kind of kidnapping. It lost them the support of the world. It lost us Greece and resulted in incalculable damage to our cause.'

"'I, too, explained that I could do nothing, that even inquiries would only endanger the child.'

"'Yes, but surely he must have understood as much when he crossed with such blatant disregard of all protocols into East Berlin. He must have been a very desperate man to try such a foolhardy thing.'

"'The romantic belief that good intentions will produce good outcomes.'

"'But tell me, how *did* John find you in '53, a dead man, a new name and new identity?'

"'A West German agent working for MI6 noticed me buying books of classical authors in Greek and Latin, rare books—the habits of the bourgeoisie, not a miner's son and champion of the working class.'

"'We all make mistakes; it's in our nature.'

"'But you, never.'

"'Oh yes, many. I was just incredibly lucky. My nervous anxiety about John Alden, how much he knew or suspected—if he had anything in the way of proof—weighed on me in the terrible years from '52 on, when I was first under extreme scrutiny, after I discovered the CIA had Maclean's alias in the decrypted communications from Moscow Center.'

"'The famous "Homer." It always made me smile, such an epic author. So, even you were concerned when he brought up the kidnapped boy?'

"'Nothing like the years in London after my recall from Washington. That was when the real nightmare began, interrogation after interrogation. I told thousands of lies and had to keep them all straight in my mind lest they trip me up. My mistake about you and Greece weighed heavily, as well.'

"'What mistake about me?'

"'In conversation with John's colleague, the "Bulldog," we called him in our cables, I alluded to an SIS agent we had in Berlin; this would have been in 1950. The chap was heading off as CIA station chief in Berlin and needed a little bucking up, a little scanning of the horizon concerning the world he was about to enter from experienced hands. And I mentioned you.'

"'Me, by name?'

"'No, of course not. Pour yourself another cup of tea—Prince of Wales, from Fortnum & Mason; they fly it in for me, you know. I told him we had an SIS agent in Berlin who might help the Americans, if they needed help vetting agents—an exchange. Moscow Center was desperately in need of information on our competitors in Berlin. And at some point, I let it slip that you—our phantom SIS chap—had been in Greece, too, and useful to us and the Americans.'

"'But even if your Bulldog had put it together, I had a new name and identity.'

"'Minister of mines—yes, you were safe enough, but it was a slip nevertheless. Maybe not as fatal as your penchant in reading matter. For the record, for almost twenty years I never allowed myself the purchase of a single book or periodical of a socialist bent—not one.'

"'Your self-discipline is an example that will last the ages.'

"'Nevertheless, it weighed on me for years, even now. Even if our friends had made sure John's OSS files—SIS, too—were scrubbed and there was no record of you, our SIS friend in Greece.'

"'Surely not even now?'

"'Loyalty, dear comrade, more precious than a king's ransom . . . the only thing that really matters.'

"'That and luck. . . . You are indeed the luckiest, to have survived them all.'

"'It is not a race, my friend . . . only how we are remembered for the actions we took.'

"'Was it bad luck, then, even with Stalin gone . . . to execute a high CIA official?'

"'I felt badly, truly. . . . In another life, we could have been bosom mates.'

The periods of complete blackness became longer as Karel Hollar weakened, as he took me back in his near-disembodied voice to his meeting with Philby, a supplicant to a KGB god, enthroned, in my mind's eye, in his splendid book-lined Moscow apartment, like the Cambridge don he might have been. Perhaps he thought that invocation of Philby's name might yet bring about Moscow's last-minute intervention, or at least his prescription.

"But how could Philby have slipped up about you back in 1950, resurrected as GDR minister of mines, an SIS agent from wartime Greece, if you weren't still working for the Brits as well—a double agent? For the British, or the Soviets?"

"Probably, Kim had it from London, from an MI6 colleague, that they had an agent of influence in the highest reaches of the GDR. Perhaps he was just bluffing."

"So, you were working for both British and Soviet intelligence, at least, claimed by both?"

"It was a long time ago. . . . Memories are merely shadows drifting across the landscape; at nightfall, they all disappear."

"Then you, still a double agent, must've known about Philby from KGB circles, that he was one of the Cambridge moles in British intelligence, in Western intelligence. So, in 1953, you were in a position to confirm Philby was a KGB mole, at the very moment he was being held, virtually under house arrest, in London by MI5"

"Did I tell you, you sound like your father sometimes when you get excited?"

"Who didn't shoot you when he could have."

"As you know, it is the most basic procedure not to be informed of other networks, in case you are caught and tortured. In 1953, the name Philby would have meant nothing to me."

"Old man, your lies are falling flat, like the Berlin wall. It must have been Philby who told my father about your new role in the GDR. How else would he have known?"

"You are playing with me like a cat with the mouse—you have the voice of a steady and experienced hand . . . you, who would lie to a dying man."

"I dabbled in army intelligence in Vietnam."

"Oh God . . . I've soiled myself."

"You'll be okay. Your pulse is only slightly raised, nothing to worry about."

Karel Hollar, or the man who had been Karel Hollar, grabbed my hand.

"It wasn't Philby . . . 'a king's ransom' . . . loyalty."

As his voice grew weaker, he seemed even more intent on confronting me on some obscure subject of his imagining. He kept returning to my father and their early days in Leipzig and Crete and even Venice—dazzling Venice—and occasionally of their times in Cambridge archaeology circles with Charles Fairburn, and the legendary Nigel Bennett, although he was clearly reticent on that subject. As he lay dying slowly in his own filth, my father's end seemed to fascinate him: what exactly it was the KGB wished for him to take to his grave.

"I'm pleased you followed in his footsteps."

"I did nothing of the fucking sort. Vietnam was Vietnam, and I took up classical archaeology—your stupid Homer has been done to death."

"Your father could be cruel, as well."

"Well, he checked out before I could properly have the pleasure."

"Ah, perhaps that is why you lack a rebellious spirit—without a father to truly hate, to curse. We artists are made in opposition. The curse and blessing, I think, of the artist. My father was a socialist. He hated priests almost as much as he hated the ancient and imperial pretensions of my mother and her family. My Viennese mother believed herself a queen among the swine of provincial Prague. My father was the most modern of men. He thought only of the future, my mother only of the past. Perhaps it was from her that I learned my love for the ancient world, a golden age of equality. My father was a great admirer of your country, too, of your President Wilson, who bestowed upon the Czech people their freedom and democracy. You see, your connection with us runs more deeply than you think. Perhaps it is so again; perhaps your country can ease the way for all our many sinners . . . how many now have passed through the gates of Pankrác Prison: the Gestapo tortured and executed thousands, the Communist Party thousands more of their own. When I press my ear to the wall, I can hear their cries."

"Was it true what you told me, that my father was arrested on the Czech border with Hungary?"

"About such an insignificant detail, why would I lie?"

"The Soviets claimed he was arrested in the GDR."

"The KGB would not want it known how long he had eluded them, or that he had crossed into Czechoslovakia. . . ." His voice became softer, lower. "We are never free—embrace your father's fate. My generation rallied to the most brilliant propositions, a new world built on our fathers' graves. We would make ourselves masters of our own destiny. History was in our grasp. If you never knew the intoxication of such a dream . . . well, I pity you."

"You and Philby, true blue to the end."

"Philby was only true to himself, his idea of himself, that his noble idea of himself might survive. He was his father's son, a rebel to the British establishment, a tired story."

"Yet, you admired his loyalty. You told me he quoted Somerset Maugham to you, that only a man's actions bear witness to his true nature."

"Oh, Philby was an old windbag by then, so in love with his idea of Russia from his Turgenev and Tolstoy, home to the true revolution, that he could overlook Stalin's terror, the famines and the gulag, the millions executed, including your father . . . and it didn't matter to him."

"I thought you said he was baffled by my father's execution?"

"As I told you, he was old, feeble, his heart was hurting him and he could not sleep; sometimes for days he did not sleep, so his wife, Rufina, told me. I was fascinated that a man of his character could be so blind to himself. I wanted to ask him about Stalin's terror, but the thought of upsetting our great hero was too much. I was desperate to know if he knew the truth about his early handlers, whom he claimed to have loved, who inspired him with the fire of the Bolshevik revolution. Three, maybe four were shot between 1937 and 1939. Reif, whom he admired like a child would a wise uncle, shot as a German and Polish spy; Maly Teodor Stepanovich, shot in 1938 as a German spy; Gorsky, shot as a Polish spy; Ozolin-Haskin, shot as a German spy. I asked Rufina if he knew, and she looked at me sadly and shook her head, finger to her lips."

"So, you'd been giving the matter some thought—your last visit with the master."

"Never once a word of criticism for the KGB—what does that tell you?"

"Absolute loyalty—"

"Only to his own self-image. For two years during the war, the KGB suspected him of being a traitor because he refused to provide them with the names of SIS agents in the Soviet Union."

"As you said, because there weren't any British agents. Clearly, Philby's doubts perplex you."

"Time . . . all any of us have, unlike your poor father."

"Until the files are opened and all is revealed."

"Who cares? We are all dead men."

"Better," I said, nearly overcome with the stench from Hollar's side of the cell, "that we never got involved with this stinking continent, at least not in its twentieth-century guise."

He actually laughed at this, a low, grinding chuckle as his teeth clattered with the cold. "My boy, my boy, but we had such need of one another. Without us . . . your father's life has no meaning. When we are gone, where will you go for salvation? How will you know yourself?"

"Enough, already . . . enough."

"Have your people made an arrangement with Gorbachev? He has been a most unsettling model of leadership, although it was he who graciously allowed me to visit Philby."

"Enough of your fucking Philby."

"It may surprise you that in '68 I tried to prevent the catastrophe; I told the Soviets to just give us a little room to grow and change, that little Czechoslovakia was no threat to our socialist brethren. Leave us be, I pleaded; we will be good boys and girls."

"Clearly, not persuasive enough."

"Why is it you never speak of your mother?"

"She's dead now, a long time."

"Sad, John never mentioned her."

"Leave her out of this."

"Allow me to tell you a story about my mother. I offer it as a parable, as a means of refining your capacity for confession . . . from one artist to another."

His voice was feeble yet lucid, as if he'd gone into a trance.

"It was nearly the last year of the war, when the last of the Jews were being rounded up in Prague. My mother was quite hysterical by then, according to the letters my father wrote to me on the Eastern Front when I was busy blowing up bridges and tunnels as the Wehrmacht retreated on all fronts. She hated provincial Prague, she hated Czechs only a little less than Slovaks, but most of all she hated Jews because they had taken all the jobs in Vienna and forced her father, a second-rate doctor, to move to Prague to establish his practice after the First World War. There she had married my father, who had made his career in politics, first as a Czech nationalist and then a national socialist. She betrayed her prejudices in every flick of her long nose. During the war, she had only one amusement, sitting in front of the large window with her knitting and waiting for the trucks and the soldiers to come and take away her enemies, the wealthy Jews living in her neighborhood. The servants ran the house and stayed out of her way. All day she would sit and knit, and at night she would pull the knitting apart—such was the shortage of wool—and begin again. When my father left in the morning, she would be asleep in her chair. When he came home from City Hall, she would be there, a smile on her face, like a child watching its playground enemies about to be punished by a favorite teacher. Rumors and more rumors.

"Every day she expected the trucks to come to our neighborhood for the rich Jews. She knew the roundups had already taken place in Vienna and Germany; the Sudetenland had long been cleared out. She had been well informed by old family friends whose children had taken the apartments of the Jews and stolen their businesses. Of course she would not admit to her passion, sometimes pulling the curtains closed but leaving them open just a crack so that the servants would not suspect. She knew that the richest of the Jews in our neighborhood had paid off the authorities, including my father, to be spared, to remain unmolested. My father controlled the lists of who were Jews and who Aryans. As she waited, my mother often sang to herself songs of her childhood, when first she had been filled with hatred at her confessor's knee, the tales told by the old priests of how the Jews had poisoned the wells and stolen Christian babies in the night for sacrifice at cannibal rites. She whispered names under her breath, the names of the rich Viennese Jews of her early girlhood who sat next to her in Mass, who had converted to Catholicism years before and pretended to be more Viennese than the Viennese. Such people she hated most of all . . . because she was one of them.

"Now my father, the model functionary, tried to pretend that nothing amiss was happening in the city, even though his office was pressed by the SS every day for the lists, even though reports of the roundups were common knowledge among officials. But he was—and he prided himself on this—a practical man, the perfect liberal nationalist bureaucrat

. . . Ecclesia abhorret a sanguine . . . Illud ab eo fit, cujus auctoritate fit.
You see, many of the Jews had been his friends, comrades in his early
days as a radical politician. But my mother's obsession and unconcealed
delight—she would tell her friends with secret whispers: 'Tonight will
be the night, surely they will come'—began to drive him to distraction.
He was playing a delicate game to his advantage, with the SS howling
for blood and the Russians and Americans coming closer day by day.
So he plotted his revenge upon my mother. At this time, reports of
the Allied bombing raids in Saxony were whispered among the prominent families, both Czech and Austrian. Terrible things, entire cities
engulfed in flaming storms that sucked away the oxygen, people dying
by the tens of thousands, entire districts turned to smoking rubble. My
mother had letters from cousins in Vienna and elsewhere to this effect.
When would it be Prague's turn? When the air raid sirens sang their
haunted cry in the distance, she would begin to tremble with fear and
fall to her knees to pray.

"So one night, after a troublesome day at the office, my father could
stand it no longer, and with his finger held up to the wind, he announced
to my mother at the dinner table that he had official confirmation that
the Americans would never bomb Prague, as they had bombed so many
other cities, including Vienna, as long as the richest Jews were allowed
to remain in our neighborhood. Their wealthy relatives in America
would see to this, the wealthy Jews who paid the American government to spare their cousins and their property in Prague. But—and
my father waved his ink-stained finger under her nose—when the last
Jew was removed from Prague, as they had been removed from all the
other bombed cities, including her beloved Vienna—on that day, the
arrangement with Washington would be kaput, and the bombers would
come and finish everyone off. As if signaled by my father, at that very
moment a convoy of German trucks rumbled through our neighborhood, and my mother stood up from the table and screamed. She ran
up the stairs to her window and threw back the curtains and watched
in terror as the trucks continued down our street without stopping. My
father was laughing so hard that he nearly choked on his cabbage soup.

"My father fell in love with his little game. He tormented her endlessly. 'No trucks tonight, Gretle?' She couldn't sleep; she woke sobbing
with fear. She sat by her window with her knitting, muttering to herself,
praying that no trucks would come, and vowing to the servants that if
they did, she would go out and explain to the SS the peril they would

put us in if they accomplished their worthy task. During the day, she abandoned her post and went to her old friends, the rich and influential Jews she had gotten along with so well before the war, before the Nazis came, and encouraged them not to fear the roundups and at all costs to remain in their homes. She pleaded with them and lied about their safety. She told them that her husband, the great minister, would protect them from the trucks and the soldiers—she had her husband's promise on this. The rich Jews, knowing only too well her perfidy, lost the last of their nerve and began to panic, some leaving immediately, others going into hiding in other parts of the city. They began to disappear in the dead of night. At which point, my mother stopped going to bed altogether and remained vigilant in her chair by the window, and if she so much as caught the shadow of a movement, she would run out into the cold in her robe and slippers in hopes of stopping whoever it was from leaving. Sometimes a policeman or soldier would deliver her home in hysterics. During the night, there came more and more sirens as more bombers passed overhead, headed for Vienna or Leipzig; the night would be alive with their motors, pitiless, like creatures from the harrowing of hell. My mother stopped eating; she grew thin; she had a bad cough. She pleaded with the richest Jews, imploring them to come and live in her house. At the sound of the sirens, she went to the basement, where we had a shelter, and she prayed at an altar of the Virgin Mary. She confessed her hatreds to Mary; she beseeched the mother of God to spare the Jews; she repented of the evil she had wished upon them. My father and the servants heard her wails from the basement. And then one night, the trucks came for the Jews in our neighborhood. My father had given up the final list; he did it purely in hopes of driving my mother mad.

"And yet, the SS found few Jews in our neighborhood. Because of my mother's pleas, most had already fled into hiding. So what do you think . . . were her prayers answered? Was her confession, the betrayal of her profoundest hatreds, enough to bring her consolation and save her soul in the eyes of her Maker? The night the SS came, she ran into the snow and pleaded with the SS, and when they wouldn't listen to her pleas, she cursed them and spat on them. The soldiers slapped her and threw her into the snow. She caught pneumonia and died a week later, wheezing her last breath in stark terror."

The darkness of our cell was punctuated by a chuckle and then a long sigh.

"If you go to our old street in Prague today, you will find a bronze marker on the wall of our home, with an inscription praising her bravery in standing up to the fascists. Even Jews who escaped have returned to lay flowers at the wall and her memorial. My mother has a memorial stone in Israel, at Yad Vashem. She was proclaimed a righteous person who helped save the Jews of Prague.

"So who do your think heard her prayers? Did Bomber Command hear an old woman's prayers? Did an angel touch the shoulder of the commander of your Eighth Air Force and whisper in his ear? It is a mystery. As it is a mystery why your young gods failed to come and replace our old gods. Just as you spared Prague with your bombs, Patton spared us his tanks . . . when his tanks would have been welcome, when American tanks in the streets of Prague would have changed everything. This is not an academic matter. Czechoslovakia, unlike Germany or Poland, had escaped the altar of sacrifice and so our sins have gone unpurged. The Viennese managed a miracle; no one even thinks they fought on the side of the Nazis, believing, wrongly, that they were a righteous people overwhelmed by their tyrannical neighbor. Well, I am half Austrian and I know an Austrian accent when I hear it . . . as was always so with the most vicious SS officers, the demons who organized the massacre in Pylos. Like Persephone, we have dwelled in the underworld all these years, to dream of a world that could never be. So, tell our jailers a fine story about American forgiveness, how you will bring us light and the blessing of democracy and freedom and so, like Persephone rising from the caverns of night, our benighted land will be born anew."

"Quiet down; you'll only exhaust yourself."

"You see, my American friend, my father expected to be liberated by the Americans, with tales he had to tell about how he had saved the Jews. He died here, too, you see . . . lynched from a lamppost. Why I could never go back to what I was before the war. Like you, I am a man without a father."

Hollar fell asleep for some time . . . hours, a day—I lost track of time. Then he would begin again.

"What was I saying about our revolution?"

"It doesn't matter, really. Just rest yourself."

"But even with the show trials, the purges, the confessions and executions, our little sins were, as Augustine knew only too well, the fuel of the infernal machinery of redemption, without which any faith is kaput. It does not take a metaphysician to understand the necessity of opposition, the false dichotomy that must be eternally overcome. Without such a faith provided to gallant men like your father, where would your country be? In what would you then believe? For a while more, perhaps, you will believe that your marvelous idea has triumphed, but you will find that you are like Lazarus, of whom it was said that he spent the rest of his days fearful of having to pass through death's gate once more. Perhaps your father is the lucky one . . . to have died only once in the vital flame of his faith—his sins unexpunged."

"Arrested on the Czech-Hungarian border—but why there?"

"Perhaps they lied, to give his conspiracy wider currency among their dominions, as a warning for vigilance."

"A faith, as you like to call it . . . so much so that he could just walk away from his family?"

"Ah, so you do blame him for abandoning you . . . yet you follow his trail. I am truly sorry for you. My father wanted me to be an engineer, but I was interested only in the past—like your father. I excelled in my studies, pretending one thing to do another. I betrayed my father from the age of sixteen. I reported on his activities. A man who will betray his father will do anything; he is as dangerous as he is wondrous in the eyes of his colleagues. Such rumors are endlessly useful. Such a sacrifice for the revolution offers a son the guise of sinner and redeemer both. One—how can I put it—becomes a most interesting character in the logic of the revolution. Unpredictability in our line of work is our greatest asset. So you see, I, too, have lived in the shadow of a martyred father, haunted by the uncertainty of those who admired him as a Czech nationalist and hated him as a collaborator and reactionary. Hanged in the streets of Prague by a mob of retreating German soldiers, or so it was said. My comrades' trembling eyes never leave me . . . because I am their worst fear . . . and sometimes their only hope: someone who has embraced both betrayal and loyalty as one and the same."

"Quiet down now; try to get some rest."

"You're not listening; I'm trying to save your life. You see, in time, everything changes. My mother and father became heroic figures and so prepared the way for my resurrection in the sixties as a dutiful son of Czechoslovakia, a Communist reformer, yes, but heir to a patriot and a savior of Jews."

"Okay, I got it: Perspective is everything."

"Did I tell you that my father met your grandmother?"

"Yes, yes, you're regaled me already a dozen times about Palazzo Barberini."

"Oh, for one more evening of music and the candlelight and the mirrored waters of the Grand Canal."

"Be quiet; you're only stressing your heart."

"Then tell me a story, confess."

"Shut up."

"Do not look on confession as a crime, betrayal as a sin, but as a release from purgatory, an expiation of the original sin that binds you to a father's memory. He would never wish you so burdened. The wine of confession will cause a revolution in your soul and you will look upon the world with new eyes. Believe me, the world will never be the same. Everything will feel different . . . and the saints on Charles Bridge will bless you, as they do all sinners."

"If you promise to shut up, I'll tell you a little story, at least as much of it as I can remember. The story he stole from you, perhaps the real reason—even the great Philby couldn't have guessed—that brought him to you on the steps of the Neues Museum."

"A story . . . from me?"

"Yes, tough luck about that: You got rolled; he published first."

And I began:

"'I, Lakedanos, merchant prince of sandy Pylos, do here tell the story of my travels in search. . . .'"

Ƃ

37 KAREL HOLLAR DIED APPROXIMATELY ELEV-
en days after the fall of the Berlin Wall and two days
before the Communist Party in Czechoslovakia collapsed. Two days more and he might have survived.
I knew he had died because it had gone very quiet and very dark, and
when I reached over in the darkness and found his hand, it was stone
cold and stiff. The stink has never left me. I screamed and cowered
on my bunk. I announced to everyone who could hear or bothered to
listen that he was dead and they should get him out. It didn't seem to
do any good, because no one came. In fact, it was so dark and silent
that I feared we, or I, had been abandoned, neglected, or, worse, forgotten in the midst of whatever momentous events were transpiring in
the upland world. Of course I couldn't be sure that anything momentous was happening, or that anything that Karel Hollar had told me
was true—except that withholding his blood pressure medication had
killed him. I thought of all the tombs and graves I had unearthed in
my career, how my breath would catch in my throat on sighting the
first bone or funerary artifact—no more. I continued to cower, to shake
with fear, calling out the news from my tomb every few minute until
my voice went hoarse.

I had seen a lot of death in Vietnam, especially in the aftermath
of air strikes, and some of it up close as I searched bodies, but this
had both a shattering intimacy and infinite distance. I might, in some
other life, have loved or hated this man, but losing his stories about my
father's time with him in Berlin and Leipzig disturbed me deeply. In
those horrible hours after his death, as the smell of shit and putrefaction
permeated my cell, I tried to force myself to commit everything he'd

told to me to memory, much as Vlada had done during his months in solitary. The experience did clarify for me a philosophical problem that seemed to have been bequeathed to me, even if the bequeathers never understood the bequeathing. It was the disturbing vision confronted by my great-grandfather, General Alden, as he sat on a dock overlooking the Ohio River; and by my father, who had inspected the Greek government outposts along the Kalamas River; and by my younger self as I glassed the muddy emerald green banks of the Vam Co Dong River with my binoculars; and by my first and last glimpse of the Iron Curtain along the Austrian-Czech border: these inscrutable meeting points of the free and unfree. As I cowered under my thin blanket, I felt the presence of that invisible border, dividing the land of the living from the land of the dead, in the narrow space between our two cots, as the river Styx did for Odysseus.

It turned out to be as simple as that.

I finally fell into an exhausted, obliterating sleep that lasted, in my best estimate, at least twenty-four hours. For when I awoke, there was a vague lingering yellow light through the half-open cell door, and the stark emptiness of the cot across from mine. Like anyone awakened from a dream, initially I had a hard time separating the dream from what had actually transpired. I hadn't eaten in days and I had a terrible thirst. My throat was sore and parched. I kept my eyes fixed on the half-open door, afraid I was still dreaming. There were hideous smells and I could see large fecal stains on the indented mattress and puddled blanket on the empty cot. My hunger and thirst were excruciating. When I first rose to my feet, I fell back in a faint, as if some invisible force of gravity was intent on keeping me from rising. Finally, I managed to steady myself and got to the half-open door. I tested the slab of cold metal, pushed it, and found it opened easily into the corridor. As I stepped into the corridor, I blinked and shielded my eyes, even though the milky illumination from the rows of lightbulbs barely reached to the corners of the passageway. I walked slowly, reaching out to the scarified, paint-chipped walls to steady myself. There was a table with two chairs. The table had recording equipment and notebooks and open newspapers, seemingly abandoned in haste. Pages had been torn from the notebook and the tape recorder had only an empty reel. I felt as if the evidence was evaporating before my eyes. My back was a knot and I was forced to stop and stretch, even though I was filled with an instinct to run like hell. It took me a long time to reach the first staircase, and as I did, I realized I smelled something awful, much worse than when returning from days in the bush in Vietnam. I mounted the staircase, thinking I might outdistance the smell, but it hung close. I reached tentatively to my chin, stunned at the two inches of beard.

Another two flights of stairs from the underground cells led me to offices along a vast corridor. I was exhausted from the climb and feared I'd faint again. There was sunlight from the office windows, and even with the drab gray-green of the walls, it seemed splendid, if not miraculous. I felt as if I were actually breathing in the sunlight. I stood for minutes at the threshold of huge office spaces, staring across the empty landscape of desks to the dingy sunlit windows and the streets beyond. Empty desks and chairs and miles of filing cabinets, many of them emptied of their contents, papers all over the floors. The desks had been swept clean of anything of a personal nature, except file folders, thousands of file folders lying all over the desks. I wandered through one office, touching the ocher-gray files and closing log books on the desks, noting recent photographs of crowds in the streets, and a few police mug shots . . . a distinct smell of developing chemicals and musty pages. There were typed lists with names checked off. I picked up a phone on one desk and held it to my ear. There was a crystal clear dial tone. I went over to the windows and found myself looking out on more office blocks, with hints of spires in the distance against a lemon sky. It was strangely beautiful.

An apple teetered on the edge of a nearby desk and I grabbed it and began devouring it, savoring the sweet juice. Then I heard distant music, a saxophone solo, of all things. A jazzy lilting riff of an old standard instantly recognizable: "My One and Only Love." I sang the words of the song to myself, remembering the Frank Sinatra version my mother had played endlessly during the years I was growing up. I gnawed the apple to the core and went in search of the saxophone player.

The narrow corridor expanded into a wider corridor with spacious offices on either side. Papers, documents, and more lists lay scattered everywhere, as if in the aftermath of a whirlwind, a desperate rush. More sunlight—a thing of wild extravagant luxuriousness—filled the windows. The saxophone music echoed like a plaintive voice, urging me on. Then the music stopped and began again. I turned down another corridor of plush offices with oak filing cabinets emptied out and large desks and leather chairs. And there, in what seemed the largest of the offices, stood a young bearded man playing a saxophone, so absorbed in his music that he did not notice my entrance. Brassy sunlight glinted on his instrument as it nodded in time, his long, dexterous fingers rising and falling to the pulse of the melody. His eyes were half-shut. His hair was long and curly and he wore a threadbare russet tweed jacket, something a college professor or writer might wear. For a minute, I just stood mesmerized, but then my legs grew shaky and I drifted over to a black leather sofa and sat down, closing my eyes for a moment as my mind filled with images of our New York apartment and discordant memories of my mother's smiling eyes. . . . *The very thought of you makes my heart sing/ like an April breeze on the wings of spring.* The words in my head made me feel the most abject longing I'd ever experienced.

Then the saxophone player noticed me and stopped, as if embarrassed but not necessarily surprised. He smiled gently, aware of my stink, and set the saxophone on the enormous desk behind him, which, too, was piled with folders.

"It's you," he said. "They told me you were sleeping and they feared waking you. I was going to get you in a few minutes, but the guard with the keys has disappeared. There is a car waiting to take you to your embassy. Things have been confused in the rush. The government only resigned yesterday. There is much to think about. I only hope you will forgive the confusion."

I shook my head like an idiot. I saw a crystal flask of water on the desk and pointed at it.

"Could I have some water?"

"Of course."

He poured water into a glass and handed it to me, and quickly stepped back. I drank greedily.

"The Berlin Wall . . . is it really down?"

"For nearly two weeks now it is kaput."

"And the Czech government—"

"Kaput. All the little rats have run to hide from the sun."

"And you . . ."

The man gave me a toothy smile. "Václav Havel asked me to take over the interior ministry"—he made a face like a bad smell, more than understandable—"until the elections. But there is no one here. Only two guards came to work this morning, and now I don't know where they have gone."

"There was a man in my cell, an old and sick man. He died a day ago, I think."

"I believe you were alone. We let the political prisoners out last night and this morning. The Party Central Committee resigned yesterday morning. We had no time to make preparations. So, I understand your confusion. I have been imprisoned in this place five times in eleven years. The quality of the StB, the secret police, has only declined since Charter 77; they can't even write a decent report—all their facts are muddled. Their official summonses for interrogation are filled with errors—my daughter could do it better."

He shook his head indignantly.

"So many files," I said.

"They were looking for something . . . the mess we must now face."

He poured me some more water.

"They didn't have time to burn the evidence of their crimes." He picked up a gray faded notebook of poor-quality paper, the kind of thing a schoolchild might be given for composition class in Eastern Europe. "I think the previous minister forgot this; it was on his desk." There had been a memo on an official letterhead appended, and he glanced at it. "They located this just two days ago, after weeks of searching." His eyebrows rose. "From a KGB archive . . . perhaps it was for you?"

He handed me the notebook and I fanned the pages of script in smeary lead, recognizing the handwriting of my father. I began to tremble. There was a faded white label on the cover with words typed in Russian.

"What does the label say?"

"'For the personal use of the accused.'"

"What does it mean?"

"For political prisoners, for intellectuals, for those condemned to long sentences or execution, the StB, the KGB provide a book to record whatever they wish—perhaps to gather information, perhaps to be passed on to the family. Sometimes we were allowed to write letters."

I glanced again at the pages, turning to the first passage and the familiar words in a familiar script. Tears came to my eyes.

"Thank you," I said. "Yes, it was for me."

"Until the last hour, the Party leaders were on the phone to Moscow and the KGB, pleading with the Soviets to save them."

I was taken by an embassy car directly to the American embassy on a wide boulevard full of bustling people. The moment I was through the front door, I was immediately shepherded by the CIA station chief, Paul Reinhardt, who seemed to know everything about my father's case. He walked me upstairs to the embassy doctor, who did a complete physical. He said my temperature was slightly raised and my lungs were congested. He gave me some antibiotics and lots of vitamin pills. I showered and shaved and was served a huge breakfast in the infirmary. With the coffee, I began to feel almost human. My bag from the hotel had been brought to the embassy, and I luxuriated in clean clothes. The CIA chief peppered me with questions, which I attempted to answer as best I could before our meeting with the ambassador. Everyone in the embassy was in a giddy state of shock and incredulity and not a little apprehension that some kind of backlash might occur at any moment. I was told that Laura and Elliot Goddard were already in with the ambassador.

"I'm still rubbing my eyes," said Paul Reinhardt, the CIA man. He was in his late forties, slightly balding, with a midwestern accent, an ex-marine, by the look of the Semper Fi tattoo on the inside of his wrist. He put his hand on my shoulder as we prepared to go to the ambassador's office. "This is all a little tricky, since what I've got on your father's case is classified—even trickier that the author of the CIA report on his disappearance is Elliot Goddard, and he's not an easy man to deal with."

I had to smile. "I'm not sure he ever was."

Reinhardt glanced at his watch and nodded thoughtfully.

"I'm not sure if your timing was good or bad. A year ago, two months ago, you could have been stuck for months, maybe years. The Czech secret police are incompetent and ruthless and unpredictable, a retarded version of the KGB. Two weeks ago, they viciously beat up a crowd of student protestors—and it ended up being the straw that broke the government's back. But you and your cousin need to get out of the country pronto, just in case these bastards try a comeback or do something stupid."

Reinhardt led me down a corridor, past a marine guard, and through a lavish reception area. The ambassador's secretary got up and waved us on to the large rosewood doors with brass handles. Laura and Elliot Goddard were seated in a semicircle before the ambassador's sprawling mahogany desk. They fell silent when I entered with Reinhardt. Laura looked up, and I could see a look of irritation on her face that dissolved into a gladness mixed with uncertainty. Elliot Goddard looked a little out of sorts, as well. He'd been gesturing to make a point and his voice echoed as the door opened. I went straight to Laura and we embraced. I held her tight, wanting to feel her through and through. She stepped back and there were tears in her eyes.

Then Elliot came up to me with an outstretched hand.

"Don't I get a hug, too?"

We embraced. It had been over fifteen years since I had last seen him at the VA hospital in San Diego.

He looked older. The flesh about his eyes and along his cheeks sagged, the cocky aggressiveness now softened. For some reason, when I saw him in the flesh, all the blame and anger drained out of me.

Then ambassador Jess Stevens introduced himself and warmly shook my hand. He was a lanky and somewhat laconic Texan, with a brilliant mane of white hair swept off a high brow, an oilman and political appointee, a courteous man with a lot of horse sense. A pal of the president. I could tell that he'd found his conversation with Elliot trying. We all took seats around his desk, where he presided, with the American flag draped to one side and a sunny view of steepled Prague through a window on the other. His desk was strewn with papers, which he continued to shift around and make check marks on as we talked. It was clear from the moment the conversation began that Elliot considered Reinhardt and Stevens rank amateurs; they, in turn, were indignant that he was even in Prague, much less sticking his nose in the business at hand.

"Just so you know," the ambassador said to me, "we worked the angles on your arrest as well as we could under the circumstances. As you might imagine, the previous government was mightily preoccupied over the last few weeks with saving its own hide. We weren't sure if they'd forgotten about you or if they might have been using you— holding up negotiations—for some other purpose, a bargaining chip maybe."

I took a deep breath, as if trying to describe a dream. My voice was hoarse.

"They seemed to know who I was . . . or, I should say, they knew about my father's imprisonment in Prague."

"Long memories," opined Elliot with a grunt.

Reinhardt shot Elliot an uneasy glance. "Nevertheless, thirty-five years and there was no one in the former government around back then—most got taken out in the purges after 1968. From the original

CIA report, the U.S. government assumed the imprisonment of John Alden was entirely a Soviet matter anyway, and that Czechoslovakia simply provided convenient cover for the KGB."

"I was shown a copy of a very official-looking 1955 document from a Czech minister," I said, "protesting the execution of my father on Czech soil by the KGB . . . something about a matter of sovereignty, I was told."

"Do you have the document?" Elliot asked, shooting forward in his seat.

"It was taken when Vlada and I were arrested. It was hidden under the endpaper of a book"—I glanced at Laura—"a translation of an American novel."

"Dynamite," said Elliot. "The execution—but they claimed he died of natural causes, a sudden heart attack—of an American CIA officer, especially a high-ranking one, would have amounted to—well, if not an act of war, it would have poisoned relations in such a way as to make any kind of business between governments almost impossible. Hell, in the same year, 1954, in Moscow, two American CIA agents were compromised, one in an affair with his landlady, a KGB agent, the other caught red-handed stealing secrets under the nose of the Kremlin. Both were arrested and exchanged within weeks. When we caught their people in Washington, they were expelled or exchanged; that's how we did business. Such a despicable act is unheard of. At the very least, they'd have been shown to be liars."

Reinhardt was clearly uncomfortable with the drift of the conversation.

"Mr. Goddard, I spoke on the phone this morning with Langley. You should not be in this room discussing top secret matters; in fact, you should not be in this country at all. You are a retired CIA officer. You have no official or diplomatic status. You put yourself and your country in jeopardy by coming here. Without diplomatic immunity, you could have been picked up and held and interrogated, and there would have been next to nothing we could do about it. You have broken all the procedures and rules, and you know it. My instructions are to get you a temporary diplomatic passport and put you on a flight for Frankfurt."

Elliot laughed.

"Mr. Reinhardt, young man, fuck Langley. The goddamn Berlin Wall has just fallen. We have just witnessed the Second Coming and you're worried about spilling the beans on one of the most painful CIA blunders in history. I think Mr. Alden here deserves better."

Reinhardt glared. "Rumor has it you're something of an expert on blunders."

Ambassador Stevens held up his hands, tips to the palm. "Gentleman, let's see if we can't find a discreet way to handle this without . . . breaking any rules. After all"—and he tapped the thick sheaf of papers on his desk—"I believe this is Mr. Goddard's report I've been reading."

"Two years of my life," said Elliot. "Two years *exhaustively* following up every lead around this case. Even if I did manage to leave a few rocks unturned."

"Your report remains classified," said Reinhardt, "and we remain sworn officials of the U.S. government and you are bound under the Official Secrets Act. As you know, your retirement from the CIA changed nothing. You are bound by your separation agreement, and these documents remain classified."

"Those documents will soon be fodder for freedom-of-information junkies, investigative journalists, and historians."

"Then let history judge. . . . You didn't exactly come up smelling like roses in the Church Senate hearings, much less do credit to the Agency."

"I'm surprised you boys are still in business, now that the bean counters run the place."

I cleared my throat. "For what it's worth, in Vietnam my security clearance was about as high as it gets."

Reinhardt looked at me knowingly; he'd mentioned he'd been a marine officer in the Central Highlands from 1969 to 1970.

Laura raised her hand like a timid schoolgirl.

"I've got a confession to make." We all turned to where she sat bolt upright in jeans and a robin's egg blue sweater, hair in a tight chignon, as businesslike a pose as she could muster under the circumstances. "I may have, sort of, clued them in. You see, after Peter was arrested, right before the Berlin Wall fell, I got a little stir-crazy and mad . . . call it, cabin fever. I mean, being stuck on that tin can was depressing. On the top deck of the hotel was a disco and bar, I guess for all the bright and beautiful kids of Prague."

"A select few," Reinhardt chimed in. "Hotel Red Star, a long-standing watering hole for all the sons and daughters of the apparatchiks. Dad's got to be on the central committee to make the list."

"That's right, because I tried. The bouncer wouldn't let me in. But then these two young guys arrived, Armani suits, Hermès ties, gorgeous, couldn't have been much more than twenty. Well, they decided to take up my case. They had a furious argument with the bouncer, who controlled the list of names. They actually backed the guy into the corner before he relented. The tallest of these guys—told me he was an Olympic skier—finally escorted me in. They spoke almost flawless English. The disco was beautifully appointed, with leather seats and rosewood tables and an incredible sound system, and all the latest hits were spun by the DJ. These guys ordered bottles of Veuve Clicquot like it was Poland Spring water—paying in U.S. dollars—and we began to party. They were quite fascinated with me, the exotic older woman, and once they found out I was from New York and a dancer, they seemed to lose their minds. They were desperate to impress me. Then their dates arrived and the sparks began to fly—the girls were not pleased. The conversation got a little sharp. The girls kept asking me what I was doing in Prague and how I got into *their* disco—the guys were just a little sheepish about the whole thing. The guys took turns asking me to dance. I was so glad just to be able to move after being cooped up for so long.

"As we danced, these kids each tried to put the moves on, telling me what big deals their fathers were, how they loved to party in Vienna, offering to take me around Prague the next day and show me a fantastic time. They were just kids, but the whole thing was getting on my nerves. I was a little drunk, and their dates were pissed off. One of the chicks accidentally on purpose spilled her champagne in my lap. As I wiped off my one and only good dress, I explained to the idiots that I couldn't leave their Red Star hotel. My cousin had been arrested by the police and I was pretty much under house arrest, I told them. The taller of the two guys, the wannabe Olympic skier, just laughed when I told about the arrest. He preened and exclaimed that such a thing was an insult to America—it shouldn't be allowed. He assured me he personally would take care of the situation. Dad, it seemed, was best pals with the minister of the interior. 'Your cousin will be out by lunch tomorrow; you have my word,' he proclaimed. Then his girlfriend called him a liar. They got into a furious argument. He began to tell us how stupid the Prague police were, how many times he'd been arrested for drunk driving. I was really plastered by then, and I guess I said some things in front of the pesky girlfriend, something along the lines of: 'Okay, big shot, you better get my cousin out, because his father was a big deal in the CIA, and if you don't get him released, the CIA is going to come in and overthrow your fucking government.'"

I moaned in disbelief and lowered my face to my hands. "You didn't."

"I was a little drunk."

Elliot, eyes round as Ping-Pong balls, almost speechless, was chortling under his breath.

"Overthrow the *Czech* government?" echoed Reinhardt.

"Whatever I said . . . but here's the amazing part: the next day, the Berlin Wall came down, and not a single person arrived at the disco that evening. The disco was padlocked and never opened again."

Elliot clapped his hands like a schoolboy after acing a final exam. "You're just a little spooky, my darling. All these days together and you never popped that one for daddy."

I glanced at Laura, who'd turned her head to the window, her tapering nose and expectant lips outlined in a halation of saffron yellow light, as if in disbelief of the story she'd just told.

I spent the next hour relating everything I could remember about what Karel Hollar had told me, realizing as I did so—reminded by Elliot—how his recollections of my father could have only been distorted by the circumstances of his sudden arrest. Exhausted as I was, my voice reduced to a croak, I took some pleasure in how mesmerized Elliot seemed, as he asked for clarifications, as Reinhardt furiously took notes between sputtered warnings to Elliot not to give out classified information. I wanted to get everything out before it got even more jumbled in my memory.

"We were told he was arrested in the GDR," Elliot said. "In fact, their whole complaint to us was that John had incited the workers in Leipzig and assassinated a top member of the government. We were surprised that he had been held in Prague; we assumed it was because they didn't consider the GDR safe and didn't want him held in the Soviet Union because of the different complexion it would put on the whole matter."

"Hollar told me he was arrested along the Czech-Hungarian border," I repeated, "but I don't really trust the accuracy of anything he said, given the pressure he was under."

"If he was escaping, the Czech-Hungarian border might have been a better bet," Elliot added. "And Prague in '53, '54 would have suited the KGB, since the Czechs were utterly under the sway of the Soviet

Union; the KGB practically ran the place. When the KGB ordered it, the Czechs saluted and executed their best friends, their fathers and sons—you can't imagine what fucked-up toadies they were. And when Maclean and Burges defected in 1951, they headed for Prague, and from there, Moscow."

I kept glancing at Laura, who was listening intently, a vague expression of guilty contrition on her face.

I said, "Hollar told me he saw a pistol in the attaché case and that my father didn't try to conceal it."

"He definitely checked out a pistol," Elliot replied. "He signed his name for it."

"Why would he have brought along a firearm," I asked, "if he didn't plan to use it?"

Elliot tapped his temple. "In case something went wrong with his plan."

"What plan?"

"That's what we've all wanted to know for the last thirty-five years . . . unless we take the Soviet claims at face value."

"That he assassinated the minister of mines?"

"An assassination *and* an incitement to an uprising by promising workers arms and other types of military assistance. That was the Soviet accusation."

"Well"—I cleared my throat—"the minister of mines was alive and kicking until a day or so ago."

"The worker uprising was pretty much over—we'd missed our chance to start World War Three in June and July," said Elliot with a pronounced tone of savoir faire.

I waited for him to go on and then followed up. "Somehow, even Hollar couldn't bring himself to accuse my father, *his old friend and colleague*, of attempting an assassination. But a shot *was* fired—so he told me."

Elliot smiled icily and shrugged. "The real pros will tell you that the intended victim died in total disbelief."

Ambassador Stevens piped up, reading where his finger marked the place in a document. "'The minister of mines was shot and taken to a hospital in Leipzig, where he died of his wounds two days later. Three days following, there was a state funeral in his home town of. . . .' I can't quite pronounce the German."

"Poor sod," said Elliot, "who got that duty."

I shook my throbbing head and rubbed my watery eyes. "And then there's the stuff Hollar told me about the Linear B tablets and the Museum of Antiquities in Leipzig—crazy shit?"

Elliot smiled again at my consternation, as if something were clarifying itself in his mind.

"His home office on P Street was full of that kind of stuff, journals, charts. . . . Perhaps it was a brilliant ploy. John was a genius in misdirection."

"You mean . . ."

"Your cell mate, your pal Hollar, had to be a liability for the Soviets—that's why they got rid of him. I would need to go back and check the intelligence history"—Elliot nodded at Reinhardt with a supercilious smirk—"but I was always surprised they didn't make more of a stink about the assassinated minister of mines; they could easily have blown it up into an international crisis. Instead, they used it to beat the Stasi over the head. During our negotiations to do a trade of agents, it was barely mentioned."

"Because of a security breach—meeting with my father—they tried Hollar in Moscow and sent him to the gulag for ten years."

Elliot pointed his forefinger at Reinhardt and pulled the trigger. "If it was considered a serious security breach or disloyalty, he would have been shot: Stalin or no Stalin."

"So . . ." I was casting around. "The SS massacre in Pylos?"

"Enough of an embarrassment in terms of the West"—Elliot rubbed his palms together as if warming to his subject—"if a high GDR official was found to have been part of an SS death squad. But certainly not enough of an embarrassment to have him shot if it had been in service to the KGB. Say what you like, the KGB protected their agents; in '54 and '55, we dug a tunnel into East Berlin to tap Soviet underground cables, and they knew all about it from a spy in SIS London, and they just let us go ahead and monitor Soviet communication for almost a year so as not to blow the cover of their agent. So your guy, Hollar, lucky man, got tucked away in Siberia for a few chilly years and then a nice new billet in the Dubček government—nice work if you can get it. Until you came along. . . ." Elliot looked at me and at Laura and smiled brightly. "Given the circumstances of the last few weeks, a lot of our unanswered questions may soon be forthcoming."

"Kim Philby," suggested Laura. "Elliot, you told me you had lunch with him and he offered to help you with Berlin, that British SIS had an agent in the GDR government."

"Did I tell you that?"

"Maybe it was the screwdrivers and jet lag."

"Well, I'm sober now." Elliot's features went lax with some realization. "But you're right; Philby did mention their man in Berlin, an SIS agent of influence . . . and that he'd been SIS in Greece. It was Philby's way to get me to spill the beans about our Berlin operations."

My head was aching, I had a fever, and I could barely focus on the conversation. "Hollar told me he was no longer an SIS operative in Berlin. But he was pretty ambiguous on that point. In fact, I think he was terrified I might get the wrong impression, much less expose his work as a double agent in Greece, when the Allies and Soviets were, in theory, partners."

Elliot cocked his head like a bird dog. "No longer a double agent, but how do you know for certain?" Elliot looked around the room and then back at me. "Philby knew: a double agent, for the KGB."

"The war against fascism was over: Hollar had a new name, a new country, a revolution to run."

"Doesn't mean a thing. I'm sure that Nigel Bennett, SIS, MI6, still had a piece of him—or thought they did."

"Nigel Bennett, the archaeologist?" I asked.

"During the war and the years after, Nigel was a top dog in British intelligence."

"Karel Hollar and my father worked for Nigel Bennett in Crete before the war. The man's a legend in the field. A Cambridge don."

"Well," said Elliot, much pleased with himself, "there you have it."

Laura sat up with a significant look at Elliot, and cast a stone in these murky waters: "You called it a mistake, that Philby told you that their SIS agent in Berlin had also been in Greece during the war."

"It *was* a stupid mistake; I could have gone back to our OSS files on Greece and cross-referenced the name. Not that it would've done any good."

"Hollar knew Philby," I said. "He was a little in awe of his reputation."

Elliot almost erupted from his seat. "Knew him, *then*, or later?"

"Later, so he assured me. Hollar said he even met with Philby in Moscow a few years ago, to discuss my father. Neither could figure out why he'd done what he did: illegally enter East Berlin without diplomatic cover or protection. Even the decision to execute him baffled Philby."

Elliot guffawed. "Kim, our Kim—then Hollar was fucking with your mind. He was playing you. Philby knew, he always knew, before he knew himself, before you even knew there was a question to be asked. He was the most unctuous, conniving son of a bitch who ever walked the planet. And brilliant, what can I say. You can't take anything Hollar told you at face value—nothing."

Given my rising fever, my confusion, Elliot was hardly a comfort.

"None of this is in your report," Ambassador Stevens said, motioning to the pages before him.

Elliot looked a little sheepish. "The only problem with the report, any report, is what's not in it . . . and time . . . the thing that betrays all our best hopes."

I was tired and woozy by this point and not in the mood for games of one-upmanship.

"You mean what you missed, such as Karel Hollar?"

Elliot looked at me sympathetically.

"What always worried me," he replied, "it's not just getting into the mind of your father—a difficult thing at best—but what might have been told him in confidence . . . assurances he might have been given by Dulles. Frankly, it worried me like hell."

Reinhardt looked up from his legal pad. "If it's not in your report, if it's speculation, I suggest we leave it be."

Laura got out of her chair, annoyance written all over her face. "You all act like John Alden was some kind of dummy. Whatever he did, he knew exactly what he was doing. He wasn't a fool on someone else's fool's errand."

Elliot clapped. "Thank you for your loyal insights. Your damn mother had him by—"

"What's this?" said Reinhardt.

The ambassador turned over some pages on his desk.

"What I mean to say," said Elliot, recovering his composure, "he was one of the finest football players I've ever played the game with. John played football like an actor for the thrill of an extemporaneous performance. That's what made him so dangerous as an opponent. You see, he was almost too good at being what others wanted him to be—his fallibility could be mystifying. It's a certain talent, you know. Those who have it are often unaware of it in themselves."

Laura rolled her eyes and glumly took her seat. I was trying to concentrate as my mind clouded, and I furtively clutched my father's prison diary, hoping no one would notice.

"Come again?" said Reinhardt.

"You see, he'd call a play in the huddle, and we'd set up on the line, and he'd take the snap, and then do something totally contrary to the called play. We'd be more surprised than our opponents—we'd run around like chickens with our heads chopped off. But in a tight game, at a crucial moment, he'd take a seemingly broken play and turn it to our advantage. You had to have speed and strength to do that, but also a kind of reckless, sneaky genius, using both friend and foe to pull the thing off. Our coach, Paul Oakes"—and Elliot winked at me—"hated when John did that—as if he was breaking faith—but marveled at the audacity he couldn't grasp. And John would never admit to changing the play; he'd say he forgot or bungled the thing. And it always left you thinking he knew something you didn't, when his real genius was turning a mistake to his advantage. Like I said, an actor who prefers to substitute his own lines—wing it."

We sat and just stared at Elliot.

"So," the ambassador said, looking from Reinhardt to Elliot, "would the KGB have gotten the reason—the *real* reason—for his mission out of him? Would they have interrogated him? Tortured him?"

"Once they went there," said Elliot, "there was probably no turning back. A year of solitary confinement will break even the best. And once you rough up an agent, they're damaged goods."

"You mean they couldn't give him back—alive?" the ambassador asked.

"We went to the mat on this, but it's tricky: You show too much eagerness, the bargaining gets harder. We offered to exchange three KGB guys for him; they hemmed and hawed, and we thought we had a deal, and then we didn't."

"They fucking shot him," I blurted. "I suppose you covered up that, as well."

Elliot actually took Laura's hand at my outburst and squeezed gently. "No, they didn't. His body was returned intact." He looked at me sympathetically. "As I told Laura, we ran a full pathology check: a little worse for wear, hadn't been eating well, but no signs of physical abuse or torture. What they put him through mentally, one can only guess. They said a heart attack. But no gunshot wound except the one from Greece. I got the distinct feeling when they turned him over that they were quite unhappy with the result—funny, but there it is."

"So, who requested the cremation?"

"Your dear mother . . . she wouldn't even view the body."

By this time, my head was spinning; the fever I would have for the next week was clouding my thinking. But after what had happened to Hollar, I wanted to extract what information I could, while I could, while I could remember.

"Do you believe what Hollar told me about the Linear B tablets?"

Elliot turned to me with a delicious smile, as if happy for the change of subject, his face brightening.

"Well, you're our expert, young man. And that's the most compelling part of your story. If I was going to turn someone, get them to work for us—a literary scholar, say, or an official with a passion for Shakespeare—I'd find the best Shakespeare scholar in the Agency to do the job. Sex, scholarship, stamp collecting, passion for whatever—always a man's weakness. You dangle the filet mignon and then play the line for all it's worth. However you parse it: still crazy—reckless and irresponsible—whatever he really had in mind."

"And the chances of getting Joanna's boy out?"

"With Hollar, not a chance in a million. That cockamamie business lost Greece for the Communists. No GDR minister or Party member would go near it if he valued his life."

There was something else I wanted to ask about Philby, something Hollar had told me about their Moscow meeting. But it simply slipped my mind.

I slumped back in my chair, and Laura came over and felt my forehead.

"He's got a fever."

"We'll get you some more Tylenol," Reinhardt said.

I reached for her hand and squinted at Elliot.

"What part of Hollar's story doesn't make sense to you?"

"Every last word. If he wasn't playing you, playing the Stasi and Soviets, playing the Czech police, playing for time, he may have been as mystified as we were. A man trying to save his skin will say anything." Elliot looked around at our faces as if to gather our reactions to this profundity, and getting nothing, he tried one better. "What I'd like to know is, who tipped off John about Hollar's new role as GDR honcho in the first place?"

We stared at his raised finger, and some vague sense of loyalty tinged with terror limbered up my brain just enough for me to feebly redirect the hanging question.

"That my father arrived on his doorstep with a crazy proposition?"

"You're the archaeologist; how crazy was it?"

"Back in '53, with Ventris's recent translation of Linear B, given their early rivalry—the competition—around the subject? Given what they had . . ."

I shrugged, for I had not exactly given out the whole story about how Karel Hollar had stolen the tablets from under the nose of Carl Andersen and the Greek government, and so fell silent. I had also withheld the facts that my father had financed Hollar's illegal digging in 1939, that he'd returned to Greece in 1940 to search for the purloined tablets, that in 1943, he and Karel had surreptitiously met at Nestor's Palace on the windy heights of Epano Englianos to discuss, among other things, the prospects of deciphering the tablets. Two men who treated the war as an inconvenience in pursuit of their youthful ambitions.

I saw Elliot carefully examine my face, as if touting up my sins of omission, and then turn to Laura with a knowing glance.

"Here it is," announced the ambassador, staring at a document. "In 1968, in the Dubček government, minister for higher education in the humanities: Conrad Anspacher. Seems he signed the document acquiescing to the Soviet invasion and retained his post for another ten years, until his retirement."

I stared, a little shell-shocked, at Jess Stevens's leonine mane of hair, waiting for more of his liquid West Texas drawl. "Anspacher . . . his mother's maiden name, a Viennese Jew from way back and a savior of her people and her son."

"What were we saying?" asked Elliot after a few moments of dead silence. "About those tablets . . ."

"Love and ambition . . . ," said Laura, my fellow conspirator, reaching out to squeeze my hand.

"As I said," offered Elliot, "we lack a playwright."

I murmured under my breath, "We have a partial text. . . ."

Laura cut me off with a hard squeeze of my hand: a warning.

"Oh, Elliot, let's not go there. Peter's had enough; he's not well."

"No, go on," I managed to say.

"The play and the cast of characters keep altering over time, but the mind of the playwright remains constant—if we can only read it."

Reinhardt scowled. "I'll leave you to it while I get the Tylenol."

Elliot continued for my benefit.

"Back in the fifties, the original cast of characters was pretty much in place. Now most are gone or gone missing or, like me, over-the-hill.

But the true history is yet to be written, which will make sense of the play—the mind of the playwright. The plot seems sketched in, but the motivation remains unclear. That, I daresay at this point, resides within you two. And, of course, dear Suzanne—how is she, by the way?"

I don't think I even thanked him for his forbearance and for pointing out the right path.

PART FOUR
VENICE

In the darkness of my cell, I find myself drawn again and again to Lucretius: that all we are and ever will be are atoms drifting in random currents, coming together and dispersing, loving and being born and dying again to the light.

—excerpt from John Alden's Pankrác Prison diary

Rio o Canale delle Maravegie

Dear Mrs. Taylor Venezia we have been having a fine time here in Venice. The gondola rides are the best of anything. It is pretty warm today but there is a breeze. Such music as we have in the evening. Gondoliers singing and sometimes from a lighted boat they will give almost a whole opera. It seems like a kind of play day and will do just for a vacation. I hope all at your house are well

Kindest regards E. E. S. Drinnell

3 8 IN LATE AUGUST OF 1932, WHEN I WAS
eighteen and recently graduated from Winsted, Karel
Hollar and I took a tramp steamer from Heraklion to
Venice to meet our parents. We had spent most of the
summer in Crete, working on a dig with Nigel Bennett and his Cambridge University team at Knossos. When we got to the Gritti around
two, we discovered my grandmother and Wilfred Hollar still at the
lunch table; his wife had gone to their room for a nap. They were so
deep in conversation, swirling their wineglasses, that they didn't notice
us until we dropped our bags and sat hungrily at their table. What a
change since my first outing in Venice with my grandmother back in
1928, before the Depression hit and Hitler loomed on the scene, when
I was a still an obedient child and she my long-widowed, intolerant
taskmaster. When Mussolini was all the rage among foreign tourists
in Italy, and now something of a comic character out of opera buffa
compared to the strutting monstrosity of the north.

Back in the halcyon days of the late twenties—or is childhood
always halcyon?—my mother was her usual stern cicerone. She refused
to include Greece on our itinerary: "Too far south, too hot, too pesti-
lential this time of year—besides, all that's left is already in your books,
or at the Metropolitan." And so we docked in Naples in early July and
wound our way north in a rented touring car with a driver, with stops at
Pompeii and Herculaneum ("I suppose we must satiate your groundhog
instincts"), Rome and Florence, and then Venice, which was really the
one place she had her sights set on for my education. This she accepted
as the motherly duty she owed to my martyred father. As she put it to
me, "Yes, I know you want classical ruins—you always seem to want
them—you're worse than your grandfather on that score, but Venice
will teach you how the classical tradition was transmitted to Europe

843

and America—what we all made of it, for better or worse. Perhaps you can learn something practical, like architecture or engineering—Lord only knows you'll never put your hand to doctoring; your father would be so pleased—or glass blowing!"

She laughed at her little joke as she nudged me toward a useful vocation along the lines of her famous surgeon husband. But she had her own reasons for taking me to Venice: a little romantic history that she was loath to divulge. She and my father had been invited there on their wedding trip by cousin Isabella Williams, spending two weeks in her splendid Palazzo Barberini. Try as she might, she could not quite cure herself of longing for the Barberini. Odd, I thought, even then, since she'd recently triumphed in a three-year battle to fire Amory Williams from the headmastership of Winsted School, so consolidating her position as president of the board of trustees. She became, as one wag of the board told me years later, "more an Alden than the Aldens." The Williams scandals from the twenties still hung over the school like a miasma as I started at Winsted that following fall.

In the summer of 1928, as we walked the *calles* and *campos* of Venice in the quarter nearest the Barberini (when I first met Karel Hollar), mother's demeanor would alter as she waxed on in an uncharacteristically passionate tone, slipping back to when she was a young woman—"newly minted," so she put it. This must have been the summer of 1910, when she and my father had met Sargent and James—"those detached expatriate aesthetes"—in a ringside seat "surrounded by griffins" overlooking the Salute. Her eyes teared up as she guided me past the land entrance of the Barberini, which I soon realized was cheek by jowl with where we were staying at the Gritti. It would be the same in the evening when we floated past the Gothic traceries of the Berberini in a gondola on the Grand Canal; she would point up to the candelabra-lit interior, where figures in evening dress laughed and smoked and flirted out on the balcony ramparts: "Sargent painted old Isabella there when she was still in heat . . . and the Tiepolos on the ceiling, a wonder! And James, so they say, wrote the *Aspern Papers* in a back bedroom." I was quite embarrassed by her effusions—especially after her steely triumphs at Winsted, which, irony of ironies, had made her persona non grata in the one spot her heart could not forget, for which the magnificent Gritti and her ascendant role as queen of New York society provided little solace. Somewhere behind her puritan facade she harbored a phantom respect for painters, something I noticed when in the presence of Titian's nudes, a subject one would imagine not to her liking, especially with her son in tow, but which she seemed to relish for their fleshly beauty and the genius who had immortalized them.

Her ambivalent fixation on the Barberini was, I quickly realized, akin to what she felt for painters, and, more particularly, Venice, seeing it not only as necessary for one's education but as a respite from civilization's pathologies, from money grubbing and war and untimely death. A place of artifice and wonder, the enduring—and love, forbidden and otherwise: things taken from her or lost, as I, too, am now lost.

Come hell or high water, she could never again bring herself to darken the door of that Aladdin's cave, even when sorely tempted.

In the darkness of my cell, I find my imagination wandering again and again to the Barberini in all its light-filled splendor, as I do Hermitage, rising in white-clapboard grace by Eden Lake as I would row past, a Chopin étude lifted skyward on boughs of white pine. Recalling for me the evening four years later, in 1932—the last time we would be in Venice together—when mother and I had an alfresco dinner with the Hollars at the Gritti, a pianist serenading the canalside diners. Wilfred Hollar could not have been more charming; my grandmother was like a girl of sixteen—I'd never seen her like that. When she and Wilfred weren't chatting up a storm—they talked mostly politics—her candlelit eyes would lift to the nearby balcony of the Barberini, where couples with champagne glasses stood gazing toward the Salute. After dinner, it turned out that Wilfred and his wife had been invited to, of all places, the Barberini by ancient Isabella Williams. He was, after all, an important man, the minister of culture in the new Czech government, debonair, amusing, speaking three or four languages, including impeccable British-accented English. Isabella's Barberini soirees for the fashionable artistic set were legendary. "Oh, but you must come, dear lady, and your son; they are chockablock in there and won't notice two extra. And I hear the great American artist Amaryllis Williams— you know, the one who was Picasso's mistress—is there, though on death's door, they say—poor thing, just released from a sanatorium in Bern." My mother perked up at that bit of news, but nevertheless, she made her excuses to Wilfred: "Forgive me, but I'm exhausted, such a long day; besides, I must really get back to my room and write a few letters." Karel Hollar insisted that I must join them. Well, I wasn't going to miss the chance—Amaryllis, who had shocked me as a child by swimming naked in Eden Lake—even after my painful break with her son Bobby Williams at the end of senior year. I even wondered if old Isabella would remember me; I had been just a kid the last time I saw her at Hermitage. And in truth, I had longed terribly to visit Palazzo Barberini four years before—in fact, all my childhood I had visions of it when visiting Hermitage, filled with sparkling Sargent watercolors, which I associated with the sound of Chopin: the music and art of a fairy-tale city by the sea. But of course, my mother was right in the end, as she was about most things: The taint of the Williamses traveled far and wide, even as far as Venice.

—excerpt from John Alden's Pankrác Prison diary

My head felt as if it were spinning slowly underwater as I first read these recollections of my father's written from the abyss of Pankrác Prison, in the very moment I was being spirited away to that lagoon city by another ersatz Williams, there to find myself enmeshed in the lives of yet another constellation of temperamental lovers past and present. Like my father, I, too, had been to Venice with my grandmother as a boy. And so my memories began to merge with his, when not trumped by scenes from *Gardens of Saturn* bubbling out of my fevered brain, with passages from Max's letters insinuating themselves for good measure. I was inundated by voices. How many exhausted lovers, like the harrowed Odysseus shipwrecked on peaceful Phaeacia, had found their way to the shores of that ageless city where the past is forever present? Lovers as much in thrall to art as to each other. Which now, I realized after reading my father's diary, included, of all people, a transmuted vision of my stoic grandmother (Hera into Aphrodite), not to mention revitalized memories of her nude figure as painted by Amaryllis Williams at Hermitage years before—Bobby Williams's revenge, which I now found myself embracing more and more. As the Greeks prayed to the river gods to help them conceive children, so Venice, married to the sea, seemed ever pregnant with desire, a place so saturated with water-reflected light and the sound of lapping waves—the embodied ache of longing—that when I hear the wind in the glittering pine boughs along the lake shore at Elysium, arms buoyed by aqueous reflections, I am still reminded of the Gesuati's and Redentore's bells echoing across La Giudecca, tolling the febrile hours as I lay recovering in our room above the Zattere, yearning to renew our lovemaking.

Perhaps my father put it best in his Pankrác diary, quoting Montaigne on Lucretius: "Our lives we borrow from each other; and men, like runners, pass along the torch of life. As the stories of our lives flow, now gently, now violently, according as the water is angry or calm." A thing suggested in Elliot's parting words to me after all our frustrated sifting of fact and fiction: why bedrock truth remains tantalizingly beyond the reach of abiding certainty, for the light of memory changes at each and every telling and turn in the path, our deepest desires reflected back to us in the windows of the rooms we dare to claim our own. A prospect both daunting and galvanizing, since perishable memory must be gathered in like a fall harvest lest it wither and irretrievably slip away upon the wind. Why I clutched my father's Pankrác diary to my chest like a child's rag doll all the way to Venice, shivering with sweaty despair as images of that evacuated tomb and open door materialized again and again in my mind, along with the interrogator's logbook with its hastily ripped-out pages and the empty reel on the tape deck.

And the touch of Karel Hollar's stone-cold hand.

As if to dramatize his own admonitions as he wished me luck, Elliot, sadly, died suddenly the following August of a massive stroke as he walked along the beach at his summer place on Buzzards Bay. His magnum opus on Edward de Vere remained unfinished (the manuscript was subsequently sent to me, as his daughters found it laughable). Elliot's bafflement and long-suffering loyalty convinced me that I should write a biography of my father, or, as it turned out, a novelistic memoir. It was a case of fighting fire with fire before Max's novels became the common wisdom, in a world where perception is accepted truth. I found myself, in the end, indulging both Max and Vlada, exploiting fictional devices when the scarcity of precise data failed to convince. As Elliot suggested, the play did indeed need a devoted playwright to allow, at least, the essential truth to shine through. Though much of the credit must go to Laura, who produced many of the key characters and crucial evidence. She became an essential character in her own right, if not Athena to my Telemachus—muse to both Max and me.

As she repeatedly pointed out to Elliot, all the real ambition was hers anyway, and her mother's—since life itself is the only true ambition and the womb its sole incubator.

And such was the ambition that commandeered my Land Rover, as Laura juggled driving, nursing, and a renewed determination to rid her system of every addictive substance legal or otherwise that she'd indulged in for over twenty years. She rattled on excitedly about all she'd seen of the demonstrations in Wenceslas Square. While I'd rotted away, she and Elliot had witnessed the Czech Velvet Revolution. On the afternoon of Elliot's arrival in Prague, in a final spasm of seven decades of violence, the Czech StB had brutally broken up a peaceful student demonstration and proved themselves more ruthless than their East German counterparts. The blood they spilled in the streets galvanized the populace, resulting in the downfall of the Communist government little more than ten days later, though not soon enough to save Karel Hollar. Throwing caution to the wind, Laura and Elliot had audaciously circulated among the protestors in Wenceslas Square, feeding on the exhilaration as the crowds grew larger day by day, providing the huge stage set for the bravery and acumen of Václav Havel to work his spell—"Ah, talk about a playwright who wrote history as he produced it," crowed Elliot. Havel played his hand with consummate steadiness to undermine the confidence of a moribund but still dangerous Communist regime. Elliot had cheered and sobbed like a baby, while Laura had celebrated by dancing in the streets, as if her little riffs to Joni Mitchell on the border had been an avatar of the liberation to come. She was so thrilled by the experience that she gave up cigarettes for good and threw all her antidepressants and sleeping pills into the river: "I worried I'd sent those swans to never-never land." The crowds of the unfree chanting for freedom made her brave again and gave her back her confidence—and ambition. As did Elliot's parting words to me as we stood by the Land Rover in front of the American embassy. He held my hand for the longest time and looked into my bleary eyes, his voice choking up. "I'm witness for John, okay, I'm witness for your dad: I was here and I saw these fine people regain their freedom— okay? You remember that now; you remember him. You owe him at least that much; we all do."

And even though I was burning up with fever, my ears ringing with confusion like a survivor creeping from a foxhole after the barrage has lifted, I tried desperately to remember while Laura drove like a madwoman. I rehearsed over and over in my mind what I'd been told by Karel Hollar so that I could write it down verbatim when we got to Venice. Laura was so pleased with herself, she could barely keep her eyes on the road, especially pleased that she'd missed her mother's wedding to Charles Fairburn: "Sorry, Mother, I'm stuck in the middle of a revolution." She had promised to be at the colonel's Sussex home for Christmas, if I, too, was invited. Once that deal was extracted over a phone line in the ambassador's office, we had a few weeks to ourselves in Venice to lick our wounds. Laura took charge of everything and I hung on to her bandwagon for dear life, convinced she was going to kill us, the way she was always fiddling with the radio dial at high speed in a search for a little good-time music.

"What do you want? The creeps stole all my tapes."

I have only the vaguest memories of people milling in the streets of small towns along the route, and the absence of lines at the border checkpoint—no guards whatsoever on the Czech side of the border, where the barbed wire had been cut and the observation towers abandoned. Vendors along the road were selling snippets of barbed wire as souvenirs, and we bought handfuls of the stuff. At the Austrian border, we showed freshly minted passports, courtesy of the American embassy, and we were gone, with a quick stop at the hotel in Vienna to pick up our copy of the love letters: love letters to Venice—how fucking appropriate.

Gone, too, seventy years of history in the blink of an eye.

Laura had her own reasons for wanting that intermission in Venice, partly a little revising of her own history there, partly another chance, perhaps a last chance, for us. She now had Max's letters from Vlada with which she hoped to put an end to speculation among Max's wannabe biographers that his final depression and suicidal overdose was due, in whole or in part, to her abandonment of him after "supposedly" aborting "his" child in Venice. And her knee was definitely on the mend given the enforced shipboard layoff. It was in her body language: ABT's coming spring season, her adoring, if fickle, fans, one more chance at a comeback. And Venice, where she had danced some of her greatest roles at La Fenice, where she was remembered as a star and not the subversive muse of America's seventies literary wunderkind. Even if it was in Venice where they'd hit rock bottom.

Venice, October 16, 1983

Dear Vlada—old buddy, old pal:

Thank you for your generous praise. Yes, I've been gratified by the continued success of *Gardens of Saturn*, but I wonder if it has been a Pyrrhic victory. It has devastated my relationship with Laura, what with all the material I took from her about her family and others. When you write fiction in semimemoir form, you realize how much of it is a self-absorbed playing out so as to gin up material. Looking back, now that we've escaped to Venice to save our necks, I'm a little horrified at what's become of us. That's partly how the drinking and the cocaine mess started—the whole Studio 54 thing, to see if self-consciousness could be banished. How the cocaine took on a life of its own. We've tried rehab, but I can't stand the insipid language all the therapy sessions are couched in, like I'm back in kindergarten. So we've headed for the hills—a lagoon in this case, with hopes of not ending up back in the same rut. I pride myself that I can write no matter how bad things are—seriously, I don't think it affects my writing, not really, not the great Amarone reds that are cheap as Coke. Well, maybe the energy level is a little affected. But Laura's dancing suffered. She kept having injuries and blanking out. Balanchine threatened to fire her, so she quit. Her fiendish mother twists her into guilty knots. She really hates being a vessel of clay in others' hands; she wants to get at her own life in her dancing, not someone else's idea of life. The company she's in—and the company she keeps—I fear, don't help her cause. And now so many of her colleagues are getting sick and dying; it's horrifying. I fear she's going to lose her mind.

How I envy your dedicated and simple life and the cause of artistic freedom you serve. Your subjects are so much more profound than mine. Your latest fantasy stories are wonderful. I thought in my first novel, *Like a Forgotten Angel,* I'd touched on some pretty important themes—at least the critics seemed to think so: the killing of hoary shibboleths about American exceptionalism. Now, I wonder. The novelist must, by the nature of the beast, be against something—there is no tension otherwise: the thing that needs overcoming, or otherwise it won't fly. So we've run away to Venice to clean up our act and for me to start work on my promised third novel, long overdue. I'm planning some trips to Vienna to get up material on my mother's family and all her Jewish relations who died in the Holocaust. I think it will be about ghosts and recalling the dead—something I can stand back from that's not really about me. It was a theme that served me so well in my first published stories when I was still at Winsted. How distant those days seem—as if we've traversed Andromeda and then some.

New York is a plague zone and Laura and I have, even in fathomless Venice, scraped bottom. Maybe we can rendezvous in Vienna? Would they give you a visa—just for a few days? Laura sends her love.

Max

We drove through the night toward storied Venice, stopping only to pee and for coffee breaks, when Laura diligently plied me with liquids and antibiotics, as my temperature soared, as we soared into the Alps on a near-empty Autobahn through pelting snow showers, slithering past Innsbruck and then onto Bolzano, slaloming on the sleety concrete as if about to rocket out into empty space. Never was I more thankful for four-wheel drive. Through my fevered daze, I caught glimpses of distant villages perched on invisible hillsides, the amber glow of frosted

Christmas windows in hasty retreat, rainbow-lit conifers that evaporated behind us as we dropped into snowcapped valleys. Sleep was my best escape. And when I dared to wake from the free fall, the signs were in Italian and my ears were popping. She'd found an armed forces radio station in Vicenza that played oldies but goodies after midnight to the patter of a black DJ, at which point her driving improved, or so it seemed in the steady parade of factory buildings around fair Verona whizzing by at eight-five miles an hour. The next thing I remembered was the tolling of bells, like calm, dignified voices in the chilly night, waking me from my distant stupor. Blinking, I saw the concrete deck of a huge parking garage shrouded in fog, out of which red letters blazed: CINZANO.

"What's that?" I mumbled.

"Cinzano" she replied with a most beautiful Italian intonation. "We're here. Can you walk? It's only about a hundred feet and a flight of steps."

I could smell the briny fog.

"Where are we?"

"Safe and sound—so there. Can you carry one bag? It's not heavy . . . Oh dear, you feel very hot."

"I'm okay."

She grabbed two bags and I followed her across the garage and down the stairs to a doorway and a Plexiglas shelter along a quay.

"There will be a vaporetto in five minutes. I know the pensione will have a room for us—I just know it."

If she'd suggested I try a cannonball into the canal, I would have asked how big a splash. I sat on the bench in the shelter and squinted to make out the silhouetted railway cars on a siding across the canal, and behind these, cranes reaching into the sullen gray like huge praying mantises. Spools of rubber cable were stacked along the far quayside. The water was an oily pea green in the light of the shelter, smelling of diesel fuel and the sea. Then a single light shone from under a distant bridge, followed by the purr of a motor as a sleek vaporetto nosed out of the fog.

I sat in the heated cabin while she flirted with the mustachioed captain in spiffy uniform and cap. She spoke perfect Italian, her hands assuming the rhythms of the language with a inborn grace, which had the effect of constantly bringing a smile to the captain's peering face above the wheel, at the same time distancing herself from me . . .

transforming her into the woman out of the pages of Max's *Gardens of Saturn*, which I realized I knew better than I cared to admit. I watched with addled eyes as she caressed the gold-braided sleeve of the captain and then slipped over to the railing, the swirling mist across the deck snatching her from view like a ghost dissolving into nothingness, only to appear again seconds later in her tight jeans and crimson parka with another ghost by the exit gate, a red-cheeked young man with stringy, damp hair who held a docking rope in his calloused hands, tattooed forearms bulging, conjuring for me all the young men she had known: Baryshnikov and the aging Nureyev, and all the once virile dancers who had partnered her from San Francisco to New York, from Venice to Saint Petersburg, many already dead and others dying slowly, often alone, withered and ulcerated and coughing their lungs out. And Vlada . . . (I'd left a check for twenty thousand dollars with Reinhardt, the Prague CIA chief, exacting a promise that he would do all in his power to find Vlada and get him to a medical facility in Vienna.) Who wouldn't want to escape to Venice and reclaim a healthy past while the going was good, while your body could still manage it? Though injury and disease may defeat us, it is memory of lustful youth that allows us to prevail, until that, too, is no more.

The vaporetto moved slowly, smoothly navigating a wide canal and treading a series of low bridges, then slipping into an even wider canal with quays stacked with shipping containers. Then the bow began to pitch as the vaporetto picked up speed and plunged forward like a jet letting loose for takeoff. Peering through the mist, I could make out the purple glow of streetlamps, the vague patterns of Gothic fenestration, and looming Palladian facades. I watched Laura as she broke off her flirting with the long-haired first mate and turned to scenes of the city precipitating from the fog, a look of aching wonder on her face as she began swaying on her sea legs, scheming, I hoped, to wipe the slate clean with her new lover in tow. Her eyes widened and her lips parted in smile after ecstatic smile of recognition, her body bending forward and outward as if to embrace a second chance.

Perhaps it was then that I truly fell in love with her smile and her laughing, flirtatious lusty aliveness, carapaced in battered sarcasm . . . and all the celebrity years that were never to be mine. Duplicity be damned.

The number 5 vaporetto took us nowhere near the Gritti or Palazzo Barberini, but steered us to a past, a port of call not my own. The night

I could keep my eyes open, I was surprised to find how critical my grandmother had been of her son, who had always been portrayed to me as an exemplary child who rarely put a foot wrong. Of her gimlet-eyed toughness, I realized I got a double dose, especially when I tended to bookishness. As my grandmother put it, "Stop indulging such an excess of intellectual and aesthetic masturbation"—an invective she used more than once to my face, humiliating me. No doubt—this was a warning, as the diary made clear, about my father's perceived foibles—lest I, too, be drawn to a life of sorry contradictions and thwarted resolution. On her deathbed, she tapped my head as I bent to kiss her and whispered, "Just be damned sure you do something useful with this; there's still so much left of your father's work to do . . . and my John, as well." And then she'd waved me away, as if annoyed at indulging in self-pity, or probably even angrier at herself for dying just as I turned fourteen, leaving me prey to the whimsy of my "mealy-mouthed" mother. Of course, she'd enlisted all her cohorts in a rearguard action: Elliot Goddard first and foremost, who immediately betrayed her trust by bringing the banished Bobby Williams back on the Winsted board. I suspect, too, she probably played on Charles Fairburn's guilt by never exposing him in her CIA interrogation, while insisting on his dutiful role as my godfather. She must've known something about his part in the Berlin fiasco as the MI5 officer who, by way of Nigel Bennett, tipped off my father about Karel Hollar's new role as GDR minister of mines; and, no doubt, she paid off and otherwise extorted her crew at Winsted to get me settled into a productive life. To be fair, only a few times did she ever suggest I think about Harvard Medical School. Maybe I got off easy.

Reading my father's Pankrác diary, I felt as if I'd been shortchanged: Unlike my father, who had benefited from three trips abroad on his mother's five-year anniversary pilgrimages to her husband's grave in the Argonne, I had the pleasure only once on the way to Paris after Venice in the summer of 1964. My mother liked to say that the strain of that last trip killed Grandmother, but she always said things like that if it might call into question "our Queen of Hearts'" judgment (this double entendre having as much to do with Grandmother's prowess at the Colony Club bridge tables as Alice's tormentor).

It was in Venice where I first experienced my grandmother's drill with her perfumed Hermès scarf, which, when not draped across her shoulders, she kept in one hand, fifty-year-old Baedeker in the other, so that when the odor of a fetid canal became too much, she would hold the scarf to her nose for a few seconds of relief. Touring Venice with me in 1964, she sought out—she checkmarked them in her Baedeker, which strangely reminded me later of the checkmarks in my father's diary!—the most disgusting, violent, and cruel imagery she could dredge up in the religious and civic art of this seafaring people. There was Titian's *The Martyrdom of Saint Lawrence* in the Gesuati, at least two dozen pincushioned Saint Sebastians, and Tintoretto's spectacular *Ecce Homo* and *The Crucifixion* in the Scuola Grande di San Rocco. "They've even got San Rocco's little finger in a reliquary in the treasury, if you care to gaze upon it." She took perverse joy in ferreting out the more gruesome mummified priests and saintly body parts stored in dusty reliquaries and displayed on altars and wall niches. I vividly remembered Grandmother pointing to a memorial on the wall of the Frari—with Titian's magnificent *Assumption of the Virgin* only steps away—which contained a stone urn preserving the flayed skin of an unfortunate Venetian admiral who had been caught by the Turks off Corfu. "Skinned alive—alive and kicking, no doubt," she emphasized in her pinched nasal tones, perfumed Hermès scarf waving back and forth as if to dispel the stink even after three hundred years.

I sometimes think Grandmother and Max would have gotten on like a house afire.

But I realized from my father's recollections, reminding me of Bobby Williams's little bombshell tour of Amaryllis's studio at Hermitage, that much of my education in Venice had been a ruse: My grandmother was revisiting her lost loves. When we came to Titian's *Danaë and the Shower of Gold* in the Academia (a counterpart to the one in Palazzo Fenway but forever associated in my mind, thanks to Max, with a very different setting), she stood spellbound, breathless, Hermès scarf and Baedeker ballasted in either hand as tears flowed. I remember her wiping at her eyes and turning to me at my approach. "Damned dust in these mausoleums," she said, erasing all emotion in her voice. "I mean . . . to think that a bewitching courtesan from the streets might be so immortalized for all eternity."

Which, indeed, she herself has been in Amaryllis's Fauvist nudes, now selling for hundreds of thousands, though too late for Bobby to cash in, nor carry out his threat to publish the name of his mother's model. (He'd consigned every last one of his mother's canvases to a Boston dealer the week before he burned down Hermitage.)

"If you ever feel in the need of a subscription to *Playboy* magazine," she said, giving her eyes one last dab with the Hermès scarf, "just let me know. I suppose fathers take care of that kind of thing these days."

As she had with her son, we, too, stayed at the Gritti, nearby the Barberini. I remember my grandmother, after her long afternoon naps, when I was restricted to the hotel with stacks of guidebooks and histories to while away the siesta hours, coming out for tea on the Grand Canal esplanade of the Gritti, where she took the same table at precisely 4:00 P.M. each day and where I awaited her and the *dolci* platter. It afforded her a waterside view of the nearby Barberini, a dramatic angle Sargent had relished to capture the sumptuous reflections off the water playing over the carved traceries of the balcony above. We would talk about many things and she would quiz me on that day's adventures into Europe's lurid past, but not once did she mention her days at the Barberini with her husband in 1910, nor her Czech lover of 1932—if my father's diary is to believed—nor my father's beguilement by the brilliant and handsome young Karel Hollar as they left her alone at the Gritti after dinner, arms thrown around each other's shoulders, to make their way to festivities at Palazzo Barberini with Karel's parents.

Bizarrely, on our last trip in 1964, she had been making furtive inquiries about the Barberini of Venetian real estate brokers. I remember one morning coming down to breakfast and finding her sitting with them, a couple of well-dressed Italians in clean-fitting business suits and dark glasses, going over ground plans and sheets of figures. It seemed the Barberini had fallen on hard times and was in bad repair and looking for a possible buyer. A *savior*, I believe was the word used by one of the Italians. I don't know if my grandmother was actually serious; she certainly had the money and the yen for real estate deals— if not quite on the order of her patron saint, General Alden—but it would have gone against all her deepest instincts about the pitfalls of the Old World. Besides, her heart was bothering her, her breathing was often labored, and she was almost eighty. But I remember her stare shifting as she raised her teacup, her light brown eyes following the play of dancing light on the watching griffins from the nearby balcony, which loomed proudly over the Grand Canal like figureheads on the prow of a Gothic ship, and saying to me with a farewell sigh, "Well, money isn't everything; it can only buy so much."

Twenty-five years later, often lying alone in my sickbed in our pensione, it was not the ghoulish saints paraded by my grandmother for my edification—joining, in my feverish dreams, those along the Charles

Bridge—nor even the more perplexing pages of my father's diary that struck to my heart, but passages from *Gardens of Saturn*, like a hypnotic siren song of a giddy, tempestuous life, and a lover who might yet steal her away again.

She pulled on her leotard, sweaters, leg warmers. Plugged her workout tape into her Walkman. Grasping hold of the antique bed board, just behind the cherrywood wave-leaping dolphins, she arranged herself between the two facing mirrors and began her barre exercises. What a fucking death struggle. After months of inactivity and now the suicide detox—"no twelve-step bullshit for us, babe"—changes in her body had to be thwarted. The numbing cold and early hour didn't help her atrophied muscles. Her uterus still ached.

How she recoiled when she stripped to her bra and panties and the mirrors revealed the new fat at her waist, even on her thighs—my God, real-live buttocks, too. Fat she'd never known, even in puberty. To her critical eye, it was anathema, abhorrent, diseased tissue good only for the surgeon's scalpel. Tears welled into her frightened eyes. But then, slowly, much of the old pliancy returned, some of the strength and quickness, and with it her confidence and sass and ambition, enough to confound even Mr. B, who had fired her with a one-sentence note left on her dressing room table.

And when her morning barre was complete, when the radiators sang, the cool light off La Giudecca laving purple tincture over the lace curtains, she would draw close to Saul to press her conqueror's foot on his neck, to exult in her lustral power to bestow and destroy life.

Fuck motherhood. Fuck you, Saul, and your cheating, irresponsible, excuse-ridden life.

Think of me as your avenging angel and your sorry carcass as dead as the disease cut from my womb.

She would straddle him and maneuver him inside, deep as anatomy allowed, where she could continue her workout with the same precision and determination as at her barre. Her Kegels contractions were as strong as a milkmaid's fist and she sang as she labored to her seventies disco tape . . . "Last dance, last chance, for love . . . 'Cause when I'm bad, I'm so, so bad." When the telltale tightness entered his eyes, she would rev up her clit with blurred finger strokes, bringing herself again and again as long as Saul lasted. And then as if to thwart him one last time, no matter how well he tried to disguise it, she pulled off at the last second and took his ejaculate in her mouth. "Bitter, bitter . . . sweet for my sweet—sugar for my honey . . . ," she sang and teased, smiling at him with her white-streaming lips, daring him a kiss, hovering there, bending, hovering, watching his eyes, tempting him . . . swallowing as they kissed, licking his lips clean like a cat her newborn kittens.

"No babies for you, boy, until you get fucking straight, until you finish the goddamn novel. Then we'll see—after the reviews are in—if you've still got what it takes."

What made it doubly perplexing, I lay in her previous lover's bed, was Laura's cool and distant kindness. She nursed me like Maureen had all those years before at the VA hospital in San Diego. She was gentle but firm. She brought me cold compresses, Tylenol and tea and fresh orange juice and Pellegrino, then food, fabulous pasta and mushroom risotto and the freshest salads I'd ever tasted, and then sips of Amarone to be savored: incentives of every kind to get better—like mother like daughter. She washed me, massaged my back, shaved me, combed my hair, tidied me up, and brought me newspapers and magazines. When my fever began to break, she teased me, tested me, stroked me to see if I could get hard. When she did her barre exercises, as if in perverse imitation of her literary double, between those two hideous mirrors at the crack of dawn, her body created a kind of energy field of pent-up carnal lust to edge me back to life, sometimes stripping herself bare to flaunt her firm, proud breasts bathed in flickering sea-reflected gleams of sunrise as the bells of the Gesuati and Redentore echoed in profusion across La Giudecca.

Once I was well, she insisted on straddling me like a high priestess channeling the celestial gods on a brand-new SONY sports-model Walkman—think Stravinsky, Satie, Mahler—dreaming of when she might someday choreograph herself. Even before my fever broke for good, those heaven-sent morning erections made all things possible. Her weight remained poised in her thighs, a floating, fluid tension, a weightless presence to spare my back. She gazed silent and imperiously down at me as she maneuvered herself. She seemed especially happy for me to take her breasts and stroke them. She fingered herself to her music without hint of self-consciousness. It was quite something to see a woman's pleasure so serenely indulged. Her sweat dripped into my mouth and eyes. As I came inside her, my spirits soared with thoughts that even in replay mode I might be reclaiming her from her phantom lover as I eased myself into her past, there to strangle any lingering memories of my rival.

Better a second fiddle than no fiddle at all.

I discovered there is something both unsettling and invigorating about vying with the souls of the dead through the eyes of the beloved; it has the quality of a dream in which you dare a second-story job at two in the morning, forcing the window and stealing in, only to find the place already ransacked and the occupant long fled.

It was not a little disconcerting how she just disappeared for a whole day—a dance class near La Fenice, visiting her old haunts, especially the Bellini Madonnas, reproductions of which had filled her childhood room at Hermitage. She would arrive back at the pensione at six with shopping bags, a new manicure, an enigmatic smile. Then we'd be off to dinner on the Zattere at an intimate quayside restaurant, followed by a walk under the stars to the tip of the Dogana and a stroll through the back streets to our pensione, and then to bed. She barely finished her one glass of Amarone at dinner, which meant I got to finish off the bottle. Her body was humming with pleasure in itself.

But I refused to settle for her body alone.

I became anxious during the day when she was gone, when I went through my father's Pankrác diary—note taking that felt like digging in shifting sands, and transcribing everything I could remember of my conversations with Karel Hollar. As I looked up from my papers and gazed out the French doors at the boat traffic on La Giudecca, I tried to take heart in how well I had managed to supplant my rival in bed. But I knew she wanted more from me, and our lost years were really not on offer, no matter how good a lover I proved.

I was being tested, and with only a few days left before we needed to leave for England and Christmas with Suzanne and Charles Fairburn, I began to panic. In search of ammunition, I dug out Max's letters to Vlada in the bottom of Laura's bag and discovered one written from Venice in the month before their widely publicized breakup.

> We're desperately trying to rewrite our lives. We've gone cold turkey on the coke and cigarettes—and booze, even wine. She's become quite the taskmaster, harder on herself, if that's possible, than on me. She's skeptical of everything I say. So, here is the strategy I've adopted: Ignore her at all times—be cruelly indifferent. Give her a space as wide as San Marco to do her own thing. Pretend to be my typically procrastinating self. Then get the writing done on the sly. I go to work in cafés, ramble about the city, especially the old Jewish quarter, which will be the inspiration for my next novel, my Vienna novel, even if I can't summon

the courage to go there. Walking, I find, clears my head. I've even taken to working in churches if I have to. And then when her curiosity gets the better of her and she begins to rattle my cage once more, I'll spring it on her. I'll simply hand her the longhand chapters of the new novel: part confession, partly a plea for forgiveness about our life together. Surely that will be enough to convince her I've turned the corner. Then I think she'll give me the stuff she got out of my mother about Vienna days of old before the Alzheimer's left her mute—then we're off to the races. Fingers crossed: I think she's pregnant, even if she won't admit it. I'm terrified but so, so, so pleased!! We are conceived in lust and die for its lack—don't you think?

Replacing the letters in the bottom of her bag, I discovered an unopened box of Tampax stuffed into a side pocket. My heart soared.

The sea breeze on the Zattere felt good. I breathed deeply of the brine-scented air, a hint of fuel oil from the four or five oil barges moored against the quay nearby. I felt a little like Lazarus blinking in the day-light, needing to get my Venetian sea legs, to make the city mine, to make it my father's and grandmother's, to get a history in this place, lest the history of others stifle my own. I walked toward the ungainly white hulk of the Gesuati church—marooned just down the quay off the number 5 vaporetto stop—whose bells had serenaded me through my week of fever: doleful voices that already seemed to fully inhabit passages from my father's Pankrác diary and *Gardens of Saturn*. In the trattoria on the corner of the Rio Terrà Foscarini, there were Christmas lights blinking. The smell of baking pizza was heavenly, until the bells of the Gesuati tolled the hour—sending wheeling flocks of pigeons skyward—and once more Max's siren song floated up to me.

Kristin stood bundled in scarves and sweaters and a white wool hat on the fog-bound Zattere after her morning workout; she stared across the uneasy waters of the Canale della Giudecca, where the buildings on the far shore, with their serried line of terra-cotta rooftops, anchored the Palladian calm of the Redentore. She dismissed the city now as she dismissed all her inadequate lovers: that pastiche of Gothic and Baroque facades merely a fissure in a pale wall of sea and sky, more an artist's conceit than brick-and-mortar reality, airy brushstrokes of a breakwater holding back the deluge. It had begun to annoy her how the city expected to brave the elements, as if it could forever scorn wind and tide and remain proudly aloof. It smacked of that male pride that had been the bane of her professional life. When *acqua alta* inundated the streets, she felt a near-orgasmic trembling up and down her spine. Something in her wished to wipe the slate clean and begin again. Even the grand tintinnabulation of the Gesuati—so disdainfully content behind its massive columns—left her with a willful indifference. She was glad that the sea would have its way with the city. In the end, the sea would prevail, with all pretensions drowned. She knew this in her bones and it pleased her to know it. She had so recently felt life pass through her, and it was no small consolation to find that her complicity was only one more shrug of inevitability in an unfeeling cosmos.

Worse, as I made my way toward the Rialto and the church of the Frari, I recalled a stinging passage out of Max's first novel, *Like a Forgotten Angel*.

> His romantic soul was trapped in obedience to a higher loyalty, a loyalty so jejune and hidebound that he could neither give it a name nor find reason enough to escape: for beauty, he had not the eyes to see; of love he felt little—and so little moved him.

The years of bitterness and bile and self-doubt contained in that one phrase, *of love he felt little*, seemed to weigh upon my every step.

So much so that when the soaring brick facade of the Frari finally appeared around a turning off a small bridge, I found myself headed for sanctuary.

The moment I entered the familiar and cavernous redbrick belly of the Frari, I remembered the droning, lecturing voice of my grandmother as she led me around with her well-worn Baedeker in hand. She seemed to have a presence as insubstantial as the pale sunlight filtered through the Gothic windows of smoky glass, as real as the scent of burning wax and incense, as terrible as the appearance of a classical urn placed in a niche high up in the brick wall. This was the tomb of the Venetian admiral who had been captured by the Turks off Corfu and skinned alive—*alive and kicking*. How she relished the gory details as she recited from the guidebook, believing, as the letters from her surgeon husband in France had urged her to do with her own son, that I would be inoculated against "romantic notions of glorious war in faraway places."

When all she really wanted was to set her eyes once more on Palazzo Barberini before she died. So much so that she had neglected, only a few steps away, to show me Bellini's *Madonna and Child* in the sacristy.

What gave me hope, even brought tears to my eyes . . . *of love he felt little* . . . was the inexplicable relief I felt in the presence of that glorious painting, which served Max as a central image—not, it should be noted, the sexy Titians and Tintorettos of his school days—for all that ailed his characters in *Gardens of Saturn*. An image of renewal and inevitable loss that returned me to a thousand conversations from our Winsted days.

> She often felt something akin to terror when confronted by the Madonna's tear-verging eyes, causing her to reach to her womb, where the pain of the curettage still lingered, where she felt most empty. Mother of God, Bride of Christ, Queen of Heaven, eternally pure, and so ascending bodily into heaven with the angels . . . a virgin queen pre- and post- and eternal partum. She felt only scorn for such male-icious madness, those ridiculous ejaculators who never gave birth to anything except shit. Only the deluded male mind could idealize some painless, bloodless grand uncunting for their little circumcised God. Of course, babies without sex—a little in vitro action perhaps, that wouldn't be such a bad thing, come to think of it. Imagine having an angel arrive on your doorstep: Oh, yeah, by the way, you're pregnant—yes, you—God's kid; I know it's a little far-fucking-fetched, but you'll be cool with it—a little squeeze play in the ninth inning—a breeze; just wait and see what a thumping great mover of heaven and earth he'll grow up to be. Not that you have any choice in the matter. And Mary, was it as good for you as it was for Him—whoops, sorry, just asking. I mean in the old days, you know, when grumpy old Zeus hit on Oh, please stay by me, Diana: The heavens really did rock and roll—talk about a shower of gold, a Vegas jackpot-o-rama! Lust, rape, abduction, and golden showers—talk about a money shot! Hi-ho, Silver! Away!

I felt a hand on my shoulder.

"What are you doing here . . . with that?"

I had stupidly bought a Penguin paperback of *Gardens* in a bookstore on the way to the Frari.

"I was looking for you."

"So, that's where you think you'll find me, in that crock of shit?"

"No . . . I was just trying—I don't know."

"If that's where you're looking, I can just catch a flight from Marco Polo Airport to London tonight and save us both a lot of trouble."

"A Penguin Modern Classic . . ." I shrugged and tossed the paperback across the floor of the sacristy.

"If you start mouthing off about any of that shit, we're finished."

"Max was my friend once, too, you know, and how many years with you—you think we can just excise him from our lives so surgically?"

"That, and the fact that you informed on Bobby Williams to Elliot, his leaks to *The New York Times* about the Winsted board."

"Oh, so that's it."

"You've got quite a reputation as an informer. Perhaps you missed your calling; perhaps you should have stuck it out as an intelligence officer after Vietnam."

"I'm afraid I'm not in the same class as you or Max, or your mother, *and* let's not forget Kim Philby—talk about a born conspirator. Not to mention all your lies about fucking Vlada and getting your mitts on Max's letters. What other lies or unpleasant oversights do you still have up your sleeve? You've been using me, probably just like you used Max."

With that volley, she rose without further ado from the pew beside me and headed for the hills. I followed, drifting in her wake at about twenty paces. I found myself vaguely amused at the whole ludicrous situation: how her amber woolen scarf draped across her shoulder was reminiscent of my grandmother's ever-present Hermès scarf. Talk about two conspirators on the trail of lovers past. For I realized in that moment, as the full implications of my father's Pankrác diary began rearranging my life as I'd known it, that my grandmother's last visit to Venice in 1964, only six months before her death, had been less about me than about her husband . . . and her lovers: the phantom, Wilfred Hollar, last seen, so described in the darkness of my Pankrác Prison cell, swinging from a Prague lamppost; and the nearly drowned Amaryllis saved by my father from the Grand Canal.

It is a sad truth: Our children may be our flesh and blood, our pride and joy, but our lovers are the shooting stars that spark our hidden lives into being.

I began following Laura in her light blue parka, tight corduroy jeans, and practical running shoes. She'd forgone her usual sporty incandescent yellow headphones, as if movement around the city required being attuned to more terrestrial voices. I indulged the sight of her at a remove:

walking purposely down the enormous nave of the Frari, honey glints in the outside French braid of her hair accentuating her cheekbones and high carriage. Once in the narrow streets, I let myself gradually catch up to her, reeling myself in as we passed Christmas-decorated shops. I could have been any random stranger in pursuit of a beautiful woman. When I finally drew even, she pretended to ignore me, even as she attracted glances from many we passed in the other direction, men, of course, but it was the women who tended to recognize her.

She stopped on a bridge for a moment, holding on to the railing as she pretended to watch passing traffic on the canal. "You have no idea what it's like to get letters from obscure academics," she said, "citing specific page numbers, asking for clarification on some innocuous incident, as if it might reveal my true perfidy—or what the fuck. The fan letters are the worst, in which I'm accused of being the death of him."

"He was desperately in love with you."

"Saul, you mean. Max was always careful to make his protagonist sympathetic." She snapped a glance at me with blue brimming eyes, the brittle hurt in her voice a near agony.

"When I go back to Princeton for classes," I offered, "the department secretary keeps all the fan letters in a box, along with the inquiries from biographers and writers of dissertations; I just throw them out."

"You, too—you never told me." I shrugged at the insignificance of the thing. "It's hideous how his writing seems to weave a spell and everything is accepted as gospel truth."

"Worse than that," I said, "I hear his voice—it suddenly just floats free from the page, and I even kind of miss him."

"Don't sentimentalize him. He was so in love with his creation that he didn't have space for anyone else." She said this with a halfhearted touch of irony and a vague smile. She descended the steps of the bridge and went to where a couple with a baby stroller was maneuvering a fir tree, pressing in some of the branches as they squeezed through a narrow door and up a staircase at a sharp right angle. Laura remained with the stroller a moment, cooing at the baby, until they returned and carefully carried the stroller up the stairs. They thanked her as she closed the door for them and she wished them Merry Christmas in her wonderful Italian: a beautiful display of the ease with which she moved between personas. She picked up a sprig of fir and held it to her nose and brought it to me like a peace offering. "Which is another way of saying that he was mostly in love with himself." She eyed me pointedly.

"Did I tell you, he couldn't bear to be around his mother—poor Hannah—when she was dying of Alzheimer's, or when my friends were sick, as if it might be catching. He was terrified of death even as he poisoned himself."

It seemed such a cruel thing to say, but what did I know? I hadn't been around. Their years together remained tantalizingly beyond my grasp.

"So why come back here to Venice, why torture yourself?"

"I was happy here"—her face darkened—"and yet I really wasn't. I just need to put it behind me"—she touched my collar—"for all our sakes."

She began walking slowly, as if gathering her thoughts. We were nearing the Rialto, passing street vendors selling the fine and not so fine wears of Italy's black-market economy.

"Just for the record, all I told Elliot was that Bobby had bragged at dinner about the *Times*' dumping on the Winsted board—and how your mother sarcastically suggested the op-ed pieces."

She twisted her mouth in dismissal. "Speaking of the devil, what do you think—should I get my murderous mother a Christmas present or a wedding present?"

"What would she like?" I asked, glad for a mundane topic.

"You think of something for Colonel Fairburn; she told me to treat him like my father, or else."

"Or else what?"

"The Fairburn fortune she just married. So, it's truth-or-consequences time: Which of her three lovers do I get to choose?"

She waved this off like a hideous stink as she examined a display of leather gloves.

"You see, the thing is, I had my greatest triumphs at La Fenice, performances that were both technically and artistically perfect. I remember them from second to second, and not because of the great reviews—which *were* great—or the Italian balletomanes, who are a little crazy. Those performances gave me a feeling of having touched something splendid, almost spiritual, transcendent. I felt so alive, I sometimes burst into tears of pure joy. And you see, the company put me up in the Gritti, right next door to Palazzo Barberini, where my great-aunt had hung out for decades. Growing up, *that* all seemed so remote and strangely sinister, to hear my mother talk about it, all the scandals that darkened what once had been so splendid."

She picked up a pair of black suede woman's gloves and began pulling one on. "In the end . . . well, it's like all people really ended up caring about were the bits and pieces of art, the paintings and pastels and etchings—which Bobby sold off to dealers piece by piece over the years to keep solvent—and the scholars and book dealers picking through the library at Hermitage, reading the inscriptions in the volumes to find whether Henry James had been staying at the Barberini when he wrote *The Aspern Papers*—or not." She inspected a pair of gloves and shook her head. "Books and art—huh? You see, for those three seasons when I danced at La Fenice, when I had a suite at the Gritti, when I walked past the Barberini every day, or took a gondola in the evening after my performance, when people stopped me for autographs with tears in their eyes . . . well, I felt as if I'd done something good; I'd danced the best I knew how and touched on something that might endure. That I'd made it up to the world—the mess with my family. Even as I got stuck with my own mess." She pulled off the glove and picked up another pair. "So when Max suggested we needed to save ourselves, get out of the rat race, on our own terms, Venice—and it was my idea—seemed the perfect spot. We'd both get clean. He'd get back to writing. I'd get back in shape. We'd find our way back to each other."

"Well, I guess it worked," I replied, "at least for one of you."

"Like I said, a disaster." She held up a gloved hand. "What do you think: My mother and I have the same size hand?"

"Perhaps a mailed gauntlet would be more appropriate."

I dared not ask if she really got pregnant or had an abortion or if she might possibly be to blame for any of it. Or if she'd told Max the same things she'd told me: "Listen, maybe I get pregnant; okay, that's great—okay. So, that's the deal: if I do, I wrap up the career and see how good a performance at motherhood I can manage."

She looked at me curiously, as if wondering why I didn't hit her with precisely those questions—she was steamed up enough to take anything I might throw at her.

"I think maybe she'd like these." And she reached to my throat as if to wring my neck, laughed, and turned to the vender and began negotiating a price, I suspected more to use her Italian than to haggle. "Now, maybe a silk tie for Charles, or some steel-plated underwear for when she kicks him in the balls."

Then we began walking briskly again, until she touched my shoulder and we stopped at a doorway with a very old lintel carved with acanthus leaves in which a songbird was perched. She reached to the carved bird and so did I, laying my hand over hers as if in a ritual blessing—or just to touch.

"I don't think Max was ever really happy," she said, tracing the carved acanthus leaves with her fingertips, "and it wasn't simply the depression. To keep himself going—to stay alive, as he put it—he had to keep stirring the pot in hopes that the next emotional crisis might offer a new insight, open up a narrative door—something! He thought he could resolve our problems by writing them out of existence. Worse than my therapist. It was as if I never changed out of costume, never removed my makeup—when everything was just another performance, a substitute for dealing with life."

"The carving is wonderful," I said. I looked at her averted face, thinking the braid in her hair was as beautiful as those acanthus leaves, wanting to take her hand.

"The Lombardi," she said, "a family of sculptors. They're not sure if this is by Pietro, the father, or one of the sons. They worked together for so many years that their hands are almost indistinguishable. Isn't that amazing, such a family of artists."

"'For beauty, he had not the eyes to see,'" I murmured.

She looked at me oddly.

"I'm starved."

Wheeling sharply like a hawk in a stiff breeze, she headed down a narrow *calle* that ended in an intimate *campo* presided over by the scabrous walls of an old church. There were children playing soccer. Toddlers pedaled tricycles under the watchful gazes of mothers on benches. The storefronts were festooned with blinking colored lights for Christmas. I saw her hesitate as she breathed deeply of the smell of a nearby bakery; her face gladdened at the familiar.

"When you're young, I guess, the race is all about maintaining airspeed." She walked briskly to the bakery window and stood inventorying the seductive display. "My gynecologist says that before trying drastic fertility treatments, I should just quit dancing, get off all poisons, eat, gain weight, relax, and not stress the system."

"Your knee sure seems better," I offered hopefully.

"It actually doesn't hurt in class, not very much."

I joined her at the window. We were like two little kids with our noses pressed to the glass.

"Well . . . you could marry me." The words just spilled out with the juicy saliva.

She laughed wildly and turned and went into the shop. I stood waiting, stunned at myself, chagrined at her reaction. She emerged with two large doughy and very sugary pastries in waxed paper, handing one to me as she began wolfing down the other. She smiled as she chewed.

"We'll get old and fat together—huh." She turned on her heel and began walking again, but more slowly, pensively looking around as if to gather in every flickering patch of sunlight or note of late-autumn color.

As I walked at her side, savoring each bite, I realized that she was following precisely the same route as described by Max in *Gardens of Saturn*—"her daily pilgrimage to her confessors: the Bellini Madonnas in the Frari, Madonna del Orto, and San Zacarria." I couldn't decide what was worse, that she'd really been reprising her fictional pilgrimage on a daily basis, or that this was a special edition for my benefit alone, as if I'd gone in search of her, only to be shanghaied for a little time travel, and a testing of the currents, the habitual haunts of the soul.

Crossing the Grand Canal near the train station, we walked through the working-class district of Cannaregio and on to the old Jewish quarter, the Ghetto Nuovo. The buildings here were unusually tall, foursquare, and functional.

She directed me to sit on a bench under a mimosa tree in the middle of the *campo*.

"The Council of Ten kept a close watch here." She said this the way a tour guide might. "There were restrictions on their movements, on their businesses. The gates of the ghetto were closed at nightfall. The Jews were tolerated—but only just, because they were useful for banking and trade."

I had a sinking feeling that not a few colloquies of a similar kind had taken place on the bench under that mimosa tree.

"Hannah was almost gone, except for all the family stories, which she whispered to me—her breath stank by then: how Uncle Alfred, the bassoonist in the Vienna Philharmonic, with the gimpy leg from frostbite in the trenches, hobbled to his seat during a rehearsal and told Bruno Walter he'd misread a passage in Mahler's Fifth . . . I've forgotten so much."

The mimosa tree was flooded with the waning afternoon light, and when she looked up, its delicate shadows veiled her face. From somewhere came the sound of piano practice.

"There was a boy living on the second floor over there—the one with the wrought-iron balcony—who had a piano lesson every afternoon at three. He was maybe ten or eleven, with raven hair and big soulful eyes. The lesson was very punctual. His teacher would arrive wearing the same floppy brown hat and he always carried a thin leather briefcase."

We could hear a Mozart piano sonata being played at top speed with thrilling technical virtuosity.

"And just there, behind us, is Shylock's penthouse."

I turned to where she pointed to see a tiny two-window annex to a larger building suspended above the campo on three supporting columns.

"Penthouse?"

"'There,' she recited, 'is the penthouse under which Lorenzo desired us make a stand.' The detailed description in *The Merchant of Venice* matches perfectly"—she hesitated, as if to the whispered echo of her own words—"*so* perfectly that the playwright had to have had an intimate knowledge of this place."

I groaned. "Not Edward de Vere?"

"Max's secret author, his daemon, he called him. De Vere spent months in Venice, and Max liked to say he felt closer to the author of the plays *here*—seated here beneath the mimosa—than anywhere else. Closer to his lost Viennese family." She blinked back tears and bowed her head to her lap. "He called me Port, short for Portia . . . when he was happy."

I could hear Max's voice in hers, and I wondered if she realized that all this nonsense had originally come by way of Elliot.

"No wonder you went a little crazy."

"There is something I need you to forgive me for," she said matter-of-factly.

"Somehow I doubt it."

"I sometimes used you against Max. When he did something really stupid, like when he started buying drugs on the sly from Italian dealers, I tried to shame him by pointing out what a dependable and responsible person you'd turned out to be."

"Oh, great."

"He loved you in his masochistic way, at least the character in his book did. He idealized us and Hermitage, as if we inhabited some magic circle that he wanted to be part of almost as much as he needed to reject everything we stood for. Contradiction was his modus operandi: the eternal outsider, the exile, peering in with wonderment. 'My wandering Jew thing,' he called it."

"It gives his narrative a certain tone of longing and loss—effective in its way."

"You know, you're a little sneaky in *your* way. You seem to run a pretty tight ship, pretend to be quiet and reserved, but you miss nothing and let on about nothing—unless I drag it out of you."

"I've never lied to you—can you say the same?"

"Really."

"I've led a boring life."

"Vietnam? You think I can't take it . . . what you did or didn't do?"

"Funny, I could swear I proposed to you back at the bakery."

"It's terrible, really, how this place, Venice, reminds you at every turning . . . how the years get by us . . . and love eludes us—nothing *really* ever changes."

She could be relentless when she'd made up her mind to something, as if the choreography was already there in her mind and only had to be teased out.

We kept walking, dropping in at little cafés for a glass of wine, until the glasses began to add up. The evening came quickly, the air fresh and bracing, the sky a shimmering shell of emergent stars. When we reached Madonna del Orto, the redbrick Gothic church in the working-class district of Cannaregio, she took my hand and led me into the candlelit interior. It was spare, intimate, so peaceful that it seemed a place apart even for Venice, pervaded by a simplicity and somber grace. She had me sit in the first side chapel and then went over and flicked on a light switch to illuminate a jewel-like Bellini *Madonna and Child*. She held my hand tight, as if we were stranded divers on a wreck, kicking for the surface, praying for currents to return us home.

"We're not leaving here until you tell me everything."

39 WHAT COULD I POSSIBLY TELL HER? THE Vietnam War for us was not the war that everyone thought they knew, the war of *The Deer Hunter* or *Platoon*, or on the CBS nightly news with Walter Cronkite, or the debacle in *The New York Times*. That war, the search-and-destroy war, the body-count war, the pre–Tet Offensive war of 1968, in which 500,000 American troops had fought the Vietcong and then the North Vietnamese to a standstill in far-flung jungle battles, was long over by 1972. Our war was a Vietnamese war: the South Vietnamese fending off the North Vietnamese army as they moved massive numbers of men and armaments down the Ho Chi Minh Trail to mount successive invasions through Cambodia and Laos. The Vietcong were a spent force in most of the country, certainly in Hậu Nghĩa Province, where I was based. The major cities, especially Saigon, were thriving and vibrant. You could drive freely almost anywhere—and we did. The few thousand Americans who remained were almost all advisers to the South Vietnamese regular army and the local militia forces; it was their show, not ours. Some of the Americans were drafted, but most were volunteers with long experience, many combat veterans, like Theo Colson and Willie Gadsden, who were in it to save the South from the Communists, and, truth be told, to make good on the sacrifice of so many of their comrades who had perished in the early years—so the deaths of their brothers would not have been in vain. That was the thing I tried to tell her—the thing I'd tried to explain to my students over the years about the tragedy of war: Soldiers fight to beat an enemy, to make good on commitments, but just as often they keep on fighting to save and honor their fallen comrades—and to give value to the

sacrifices already incurred. The sacrifices of the decade before weighed heavily on the minds of my two friends.

As Theo Colson put it to me a hundred times over our daily chess games, "If those men died in vain, then there is no hope for their survivors."

How could I explain such a terrible devil's bargain to my classmates, my students, my colleagues: how to explain the dead rats hung with masking tape on my door at Princeton with scrawled messages of hate; the blank, cold stares of women in my class and the embarrassed sorry shrugs of the men; and later the apprehension of my students when I explained the bloodcurdling business of hand-to-hand combat in hoplite formations; or my colleagues' obsequious disdain when I made a case for Athenian democratic imperialism—flaws and all.

As I tried to explain it to Laura, our war, the American advisers' war, wasn't the Vietnam War everyone remembers. Our war doesn't exist: we don't really exist. We were the rear guard. We almost had it won; the South Vietnamese almost had it won . . . until the United States withdrew its support: resupply, logistics, airpower. We sold the South Vietnamese down the river as we sold out the soul of a generation of America's best.

And all she could do was look at me with sympathetic incredulity.

"So, you've been trying to save him—your father—for all these years."

But she held my hand in the side chapel of Madonna del Orto, where the Christ Child struggles under his mother's sad, averted gaze—a painting that would be stolen four years later and remains unrecovered—and urged me to continue.

After the death of Colonel Thanh, ambushed in his jeep by an NVA assassination squad on the road to Tân Mỹ, Theo went into a depression that lasted all of a single day. Theo had a lot invested in Thanh and liked him personally: Thanh hadn't been corrupt, and he was a gifted and spirited leader's leader—and Theo greatly admired the colonel's no-nonsense aggressive tactics in the Duc Hue and Duc Hoa districts. Even after their defeat around Tân Mỹ, the North Vietnamese regulars kept up the pressure throughout June of 1972, continually infiltrating men and supplies across the Vam Co Dong River from Cambodia. Because the NVA occupied many South Vietnamese hamlets, our militias were forced to take them back at great cost to the villagers and their homes. Invariably, the hamlets would be flattened by an excessive use of artillery strikes or bombing by the South Vietnamese air force. This tactic grated mightily on Theo: "They gain back the ground but lose the hearts and minds of their countrymen—that won't do, that can't do. Better the militias stop the NVA on the border than have to mop them out of the hams later."

Major Colson, a fourth-generation army brat from Jackson, Mississippi, was a West Point graduate and on his third or maybe fourth tour of Vietnam. Theo headed up the American advisory team in Hâu Nghĩa Province; he had been in Vietnam since 1966, decorated with three Silver Stars in battles from the DMZ to the Delta, and he spoke Vietnamese perfectly, if with a slight southern drawl. He was one of the few American advisers at a high level whom the South Vietnamese respected; Theo did not condescend or berate or try to humiliate or buy loyalty with access to U.S. largesse; he inculcated a faith in a joint cause. He had fought in combined operations; he had survived eighteen months of night patrols with Vietnamese PFs in a hamlet of Quảng Ngãi Province, when they'd cleared out and then destroyed the VC infrastructure; he'd been wounded twice, sporting a huge scar across his shoulder, where he'd been ripped by a machine-gun bullet; and he had a baby with a Vietnamese girlfriend he was thinking of marrying. In the spring of 1972, with the onset of the North Vietnamese invasion of South Vietnam, Theo had one thing on his mind, to make good on the sacrifice of so many of his men, Vietnamese and American, who had fought under him in the early years. The success of Vietnamization was not simply a policy objective of the U.S. government; for Theo, it was a personal crusade he intended to honor.

Theo became convinced that only by making the NVA pay a heavy price nearer their Cambodian staging areas could the pressure on the fortified hamlets be relieved. He was also convinced that the militias needed to gain experience in offensive tactics, lest they become too enamored of remaining in a defensive crouch, and thus overly reliant on air support and artillery to beat off attacks by the enemy. The North Vietnamese had committed thirteen divisions to the invasion of the South in May of 1972, and in Theo's mind, the South couldn't afford to sit back and absorb the blows, but needed to take a more aggressive posture: "ARVN, even the militias, must take it to the bastards before the NVA bleeds them dry of initiative."

As a G-2 intelligence officer, it was, in theory, not my place to accompany a South Vietnamese unit into the field. Outside of basic training, I had zero experience in infantry tactics, although I did have some experience as a radio operator and map reader; much of my intelligence work debriefing captured NVA prisoners involved following up on intelligence and determining the coordinates for air strikes on the North Vietnamese staging areas in Cambodia, or uncovering caches of weapons hidden on our side of the border.

"It will be good chance for you," offered Theo, "some field experience in the bush. You wouldn't want to go home to Princeton without tall tales of derring-do and the hell of battle." He grinned at me and his eyebrows pressed into the crease above his battered, slightly flattened nose. "The militia radio operators need all the help they can get, and Willie can clue you in on anything you need to know—just stay out of the way with the maps and radioman and make sure you keep in touch with HQ."

Three platoons of South Vietnamese militia, about one hundred men, were flown into a clearing on the east bank of the Vam Co Dong River by a squadron of Hueys. How Theo got hold of those choppers, I will never know, because they were in very short supply, with the main thrust of the North Vietnamese invasion still engaged around An Loc and farther north in the Central Highlands and the DMZ. Then to my surprise, Theo Colson turned up in the lead chopper and remained behind with the troops in the LZ to give support to his green South Vietnamese counterpart, Colonel Lin. Lin was the replacement for the assassinated Colonel Thanh.

Even Sgt. Willie Gadsden was surprised; he turned to me and shrugged. "Good news, bad news: The gooks figure Theo is around means the Americans goin' to stick by them if Charlie begins to beat their ass—little do they know; but Lin loses face if they see Theo givin' orders. And Lin ain't no Thanh by a long shot." A year before, there had been two hundred American advisers in the district; by late 1972 we were down to forty—and the South Vietnamese were skittish about being abandoned. Theo's lack of subtlety—maybe the bad odds got to him—was surprising, since he'd been the ultimate diplomat with Colonel Thanh, for whom he'd prepared meticulously written memos, which I edited, suggesting improvements in training and counterinsurgency strategy, allowing Thanh to read and absorb his ideas at his leisure—and then make them his own. Thanh slowly but surely made improvements, much to the surprise of many American advisers, who considered the South Vietnamese militias hopeless cases when it came to taking on regular NVA units. "Winnin' the war against the VC was middle school playground; takin' care of these North Vietnamese bullies is Ivy League—West Point to you: our guys can't even understand their lingo." So for Lin to arrive in the field, cheek by jowl with his American counterpart, raised issues of his competence and might inflame underlying resentments toward the Americans, a thing that always ran right below the surface of our relations with our allies.

Theo was struggling with a delicate balancing act: He wanted to build up the South Vietnamese pride but found himself intervening to make damn sure the best leaders were in place. "We've got to help them build a nation and let them do it on their time, not our time; we've got to stop insisting on getting it done the right way—our way; we've got to resist the urge to take over, because it's their damn country and they're going to face the consequences once we're gone." Theo's genius was to gently mention a problem, give his counterpart a chance to think about it and absorb the idea, and with any luck, the solution would end up a South Vietnamese one and the initiative theirs.

Such issues of protocol were, thankfully, above my pay grade. But I found myself developing a great affection for the Vietnamese, who really just wanted to be left in peace, and a growing stake in their success at defending themselves.

I remember being struck by the absolute silence of that LZ—one hundred sweating men and equipment—once the drone of the returning Hueys died away. Only the buzz of mosquitoes disturbed the tall elephant grass studded with termite mounds, and off to the west, below a gentle rise of high ground, the muddy yellow curve of the Vam Co Dong River nestled in a flat landscape of late-afternoon green. Our intelligence, the latest captured maps and prisoner interrogations, pointed to a crossing point for NVA troops a few hundred yards downriver from where we were inserted, a fordable stretch of river only about two feet deep. I watched Theo in the distance quietly encouraging Colonel Lin to get his men positioned, dug in, and concealed on a slight scrubby rise above the river, where they could interdict a night crossing along that stretch of the river, even a large force. We had excellent intelligence that three or four companies of NVA regulars would be crossing out of Cambodia that night, reinforcements for NVA attacks already under way. Our intelligence was wrong; it turned out to be of battalion strength. Theo had been sobered by the intelligence: "The gooks are getting more and more brazen about their troop movements; they're smelling blood. They think their dry-season plan is panning out—let's hope they get more careless. I feast on careless." Willie pointed out to me what he called "field marks," imprints of tire-tread sandals in the mud along the river, spilled grains of rice and matted grass and bamboo arrows pointing south and east along the infiltration route out of Cambodia toward the South Vietnamese district capital of Bao Trai. I was so nervous, I kept fingering the safety on my M16, until Willie slapped my shoulder and told me to cut it out.

"Sittin' Pretty, you got nothin' to worry about—not yet. As long as we stayin' this side of the river so that the gooks come to us. Not like the old days, man, when we went huntin' the Vietcong all over this patch of green-cursed creation." But the normally cocky Willie looked uneasy; he kept glancing over the LZ, ashimmer with late-day heat, mentally mapping the clearing and watching to see if the Vietnamese militia set up their CP in the best spot. He eyed Theo, too, a tad skeptically, where he stood towering over Lin near a copse of palm trees and bamboo. Theo in his best avuncular manner was trying to put some steel into a worried Lin. "Theo should not be out here. His can-do bullshit gonna get that Vietnamese colonel pissed off; his men not goin' to know whose orders they gettin'. Then they get rattled if Theo isn't around. These gookers pretty good at defendin' their homes and villages—but out here in the bush, I don't know, man—wasn't my idea."

At Willie's urging, I established an observation post on the highest point of the southwest corner of the LZ, where a bunch of trees had either been blown down in a monsoon or had taken a direct hit from an artillery strike: amazing how fast the jungle absorbed evidence of mayhem. The shattered trunks offered concealment and a sweeping view of the Vam Co Dong, while, in the near distance, the purple-blue jungle that was Cambodia radiated a pinkish halo above the tree line. Knowing only too well what was concealed there, I found it an ominous landscape, alive and sweltering beneath the red sun: Cambodia, where I had never set foot, but of which I had heard a thousand stories from deserters and prisoners—a jungle haven of triple-tiered canopy hiding bunkers, field hospitals, supply depots, and hundreds of thousands of men and thousands of tons of equipment painstakingly transported down the Ho Chi Minh trail. I saw a lethal green monster beneath that splotch of red controlled by insanely indoctrinated and disciplined political cadres. They wanted us dead and gone and South Vietnam for themselves.

If you'd let yourself dream for a minute—as I did more than once while sitting in that first side chapel of the Madonna del Orto—such apprehensions might have seemed ridiculous, given the peaceful scene bobbing in my binoculars, where the Vam Co Dong simmered between banks of jade and cinnamon-gold, a sinuous curve of tinted russet mauve, a magical highway to a distant sea. But sadly, a border dividing the lands of the free and unfree. And it was our job to keep that invisible border just where it was.

Willie and I bivouacked behind the OP, using the upturned roots of the felled trees to hang our maps, canteens, flak jackets, and weapons. I went over my map coordinates again and again to make sure of our position, so I could quickly direct air support, practicing with my Vietnamese radioman so that when the moment came, there'd be no fuckups. "No artillery support—no, none at all," lamented Willie, "and the militia mortar teams are only used to firing from fixed emplacements." Willie told me how in the late sixties the brown-water navy had swept up and down the Vam Co Dong River in their fiberglass patrol boats, trying to interdict the Vietcong being supplied out of Cambodia. Now the navy and the Vietcong were mostly gone, and the North Vietnamese regulars, hardened after a harrowing two-month march down the Ho Chi Minh Trail, were intent on turning the Vam Co Dong River into just another river, removing its gentle banks from the acrimony of an international boundary. As I learned during interrogations, the NVA soldiers spoke with high-pitched northern accents and were felled in droves by the unaccustomed heat and malaria. They were as much strangers to the Vam Co Dong River as Willie and I were.

I got settled in for the night, resting my binoculars on the highest of the rotten palm trunks, while the militias dug in and camouflaged their positions on the wooded rise above the river; encouraged by Willie, they set a little barbed wire on their exposed flanks and put out the claymores where they'd do the most damage. As the sun settled deep behind the jungle, the curving arc of the river simmered like a seam of molten lava from an invisible but very active volcano, a fluid black and burnished crimson as darkness fell. In the dark, in the jungle, setting an ambush at some obscure map coordinate, it is easy to talk yourself into feeling either very safe or utterly exposed, as if by being on no one's map but the one in your hand, the thing that wants to kill you might get forgetful and overlook you for an easier target. A nonexistent place tucked into your private imagination can be of great comfort.

Suddenly, Theo was at our side, beaming and bright.

"Beautiful, isn't it?" he said.

"Fucking, kraits around here, come out at night, man," said Willy, who was deathly afraid of snakes.

Willy saw snakes in his dreams; Theo had nightmares of inexorable droves of black rubber-sandaled feet snaking like thousand-footed centipedes down the jungle trails. Theo had been obsessed with interdicting and closing down the Ho Chi Minh Trail since the Tet Offensive of 1968. Chess game after chess game, I would hear some variation on the theme as he made his penultimate move: "There, check . . . if we don't put a stopper in it, well, it's just a matter of time before the numbers prevail. Grant knew he had the numbers, and the time. Trouble is, we got till the next damn election; the gooks got eternity—or they think they do." Theo stood against the near dark of evening and removed his helmet, standing tall and erect, like some nocturnal bronze statue of his flesh-and-blood self. He was relaxed, smiling, skin aglow above his red-white-and-blue Confederate flag bandanna, which he wore around his neck in the field to annoy Willie. Even caked with mud and sweat, he looked every inch the commander who knew exactly how he was going to win this war, except the means were slipping from his grasp. He could no longer allow himself the luxury of breathing down the neck of Colonel Lin, who was apprehensively lying in wait for the NVA three hundred yards distant on the rise above the river crossing.

"The serpent you need to worry about is the Marxist-Leninist variety about to slither itself across the Vam Co Dong any minute now."

"I don't get it," said Willie. "Why would some gook get himself killed for a bunch of old honky white guys in Europe who been dead for a hundred years?"

Theo laughed, his nut brown eyes alight with pleasure. "Willie, if those sons of bitches were my great-grandfathers, they'd be whipping your ass on a plantation and telling you how lucky you are to be a slave in our communal household. If they were Sittin' Pretty's [Theo, a West Point running back, used this nickname because he didn't have a high opinion of Princeton football, where I was slated to play when I got out of the army] great-grandfather, they'd be telling you to get a job in a northern factory, where you'd be a disenchanted proletariat, a wage slave, and ripe for the revolution sure to liberate your ass for all kingdom come."

Willie smiled. "Well, Major Colson, I thought all your great-grandfathers were dead Confederate generals, so I don't see how they'd be giving my people any kind of orders at all."

"Oh, as good Christian gentlemen, they'd find a way to keep you people in place, or their sons would."

"Well, sir, they sure managed it for almost a hundred years, until the freedom riders came along and got President Kennedy to kick your lily-white southern assholes out of Selma and Montgomery."

"Amen, to that, brother," and Theo saluted his sergeant. "Otherwise, how was I to get all you fine colored boys into my outfit to fight this white man's war? It would be a shame for you, Willie, to be still working on my great-grandfather's plantation—or that Texaco garage, for that matter—and not fighting with your Vietnamese brothers, even knowing how much you prefer pickin' cotton."

"That why I'm staying in this white man's army, just so when I make major, I can kick me around some rednecks and show how tough us black boys can be."

"That why I keep promoting you, Willie. Trouble is, Nixon keeps withdrawing our troops because he knows too well what you have in store for all my fellow rednecks. You scare Tricky Dick to death, Willie. He wants to make the world free from communism and your kind keep scaring off his best recruits. Without old Dixie, there would be no American army."

"Fore long, we blacks going to take over this white man's army and join up with the Black Panthers and then we'll run the whole country. First we'll kick Ho Chi Minh's teeth in, then we kick Nixon's in—you just watch."

"Fine by me, Willie, just as long as you get these militias to fight, get 'em tough as you black boys so they don't get their ass whooped as soon as we're out of here. I'm depending on you to build up the confidence of these people—tonight's a good start, but it's tomorrow I'm worried about."

Theo and Willie went on like that—sometimes for hours. They'd been together for almost five years. Willie had saved Theo's life, and Theo had once done the same for Willie. I never heard so many insults fly between friends before or since.

Telling my tale in the chapel of Madonna del Orto at the remove of seventeen years, I remember wondering if Theo was who he was, or the man I wished him to be, or the soldier I wished myself to be and knew I never would be. Every male in my family over the last four generations had failed at being a professional soldier, unlike the true warrior, who learns to live with the risk of loss as the price of victory. The instinct, the fear and pride and need to live up to my father, or atone for his betrayal, drew me to Theo's flag. Such youthful effusions might fade as quickly as they'd appeared when fortune refused to rule in your favor, but for a moment or a night longer, my still-young life yearned for his certainty—the young part about to go up in smoke, before the tides of memory would take over again, just as the currents in the Vam Co Dong would flow seaward no matter whose boundary it became, whether between the free and unfree, or the unfree and the unfree: something all the map coordinates under the sun radioed into the air gods could not change.

Theo chuckled at some private joke and reached for his canteen, splashing water on his sunburned lean face, turning suddenly to catch my lost stare, which he seemed to recognize.

"Yeah, Pete, I had the same reaction: What's stopping them from crossing the river upstream and either evading us or outflanking us?" He called Willie over. "Why don't you sidle over to a couple of Colonel Lin's deputies and suggest they set up some LPs upriver and down, just in case the NVA have out scouts or try to sneak by us."

Willie rolled his eyes. "Colonel, they don't know about LPs; they don't have the radios or the trainin'—they be spooked enough as it is. We ain't the Hundred and First Airborne anymore, sir."

"Willie, how come you're still a sergeant, with such brilliant insights?"

"'Cause you haven't promoted me quick enough."

"Well, tonight you can consider yourself a commissioned first lieutenant. I put it in last week and your first bar is in the mail."

"No shit."

"That is, if we stop the NVA crossing. If we fail or you get kilt, you don't get to pass Go. So sidle over yonder to Lin's second in command and suggest—you go with him, Sittin' Pretty, to make sure he gets it—they keep the first platoon's left flank tight at a sixty-degree angle to the trail coming off the crossing point. See that they got their machine guns set up so the fields of fire intersect fifty yards in from the riverbank."

"They don't want to hear that from a black man—or an American officer or General Abrams hisself—we don't matter."

"Sure they do; it might save their lives. And while you're at it, suggest they move the mortar teams farther back to the east side of the clearing, where they can lay down fire along the ridges of the rise, between us and the river—just in case the NVA get that far."

Willie Gadsden, brother of Jerry, who had been my fullback for two championship seasons, did as he was ordered, even though he didn't like it one bit, but the fine tuning, indeed, might have been enough to save our lives. We made the rounds of the South Vietnamese militia and I translated with a confident can-do smile, holding out my flashlight to spell it out on the map.

"This is a bad idea," Willy said later, as we settled back in at the OP.

"The Vietnamese seem okay with it."

"If it was ARVN, it would be one thing—our boys don't like bein' away from home, don't know what they're fightin' for out here."

"Like us."

"Like you and Theo—I'm just along for the ride, stamp my tickets."

"Hey, an officer."

"Listen, Lin would bring his wife with him if Theo let him. NVA hit him hard, it will be dee-dee all the way home, and you and me better get out the way."

"You and Theo are thicker than thieves."

"We been though deep shit, lost too many good kids. When Sergeant Kittle got killed after Tet Offensive—like his daddy died. That man had seen it all. That Kittler saved all our asses."

"I feel like I missed out never knowing him."

"You missed nothin'—you wouldn't have lasted two seconds in the bush, way it was. Life too cushy where you come from."

"Doesn't mean we can't fight. My great-grandfather—"

"You done told me about the general. Now Theo, he got four of 'em goin' way back, and look how fucked-up that boy is."

"Looks like you're stuck."

"His folks and my folks go back a long way. It's complicated."

"Like Jerry and me."

"Sports, the military—band of brothers bullshit. When you're dead, you're dead."

"I miss Jerry, you know."

"He momma's favorite—hell of a lot more ambitious than me. He thought because he got brains and could run like Jessie Owens, he could beat the white man at his own game. And look where it got him."

"Into Yale on a full scholarship and all the white pussy he could handle."

"He never should have come home. People in my neighborhood don't like anybody thinks they better. Uppity niggers die young—from their own kind as much from honky rednecks. You go north, you better stay there."

"Like you and the army."

"It's a fuckin' life, man. You gotta like structure. Once I make general, ain't nobody gonna say we can't play by the rules and run America."

"Why not the first black president?"

"Listen, I'll settle for sendin' my sons to that school of yours, and you make damned sure they get Jerry's Yale scholarship, too—that's why I'm tryin' to keep you alive and get you home in one piece."

"Theo will want your sons to go to West Point."

"Fuck Theo. He really believes in this shit; he really believes Americans are God's anointed. He prays for us, you know it—every mornin', every night, as if God gonna help him stop the NVA comin' down the Ho Chi Minh Trail. Well, those motherfuckers don't believe in God, so God ain't concerned what they think, or not. Anyway, this man's army gonna be sunk after this war; no self-respectin' white boy gonna join up. So that way, the brothers get to run it; then we really kick ass. Those Black Panthers, that Eldridge Cleaver—got shit for brains. We army brothers take a page out of Lenin: You got to take the bitches over from the inside."

"I don't think you believe a word of what you're saying."

"Ninety percent be true. The Yale scholarship for sure."

"The winters are milder in Princeton."

"So you always say."

"I wish I could believe like Theo, love his men the way he does—it would be easier, especially for a lifer like you."

"No you don't. His people owned slaves; they fought to own slaves—long time ago maybe, but he got to somehow believe it's still all part of God's plan, that by makin' America the hero of the world, people will forget about what his people did. Nobody gonna forget."

"Still, it would be a whole lot easier."

"Tell me about it tomorrow, or a year from now. Who's gonna sleep better when this all goes to hell? You get your ass home, play some good football, and wait for my boys down the line—teach them about what a great education can do to make life sweet again."

Willie pointed off to the west, toward Cambodia, where a series of stabbing white flashes lit up the horizon, the air vibrating like the universe was farting in its sleep.

"Well, looks like we gettin a little help—yessiree: those B-52's be the only American God I believe in, makin' the gooks pay for their sins. Too bad Grant didn't have some of those babies, woulda whumped Theo's great-grandpappy's people somethin' awful."

I was shaken awake at around 3:00 A.M. Theo whispered in my face; I could smell the Choo Choo Cherry drink mix—his favorite, on his breath.

"The NVA are late."

It was inky black except for a half-moon nudging the tree line of the perimeter. I was relieved at the news until I realized I was covered with mosquito bites.

"Sir, maybe they aren't coming. Maybe the intelligence is wrong—maybe the B-52's fucked them up good."

"They're coming. We're just early. Stop scratching, or you'll drive yourself crazy, and it's worse when they get infected."

"Do you think our militia can really stop them?"

"That's what we're here to find out. Pretty soon it will be their country to defend and maybe they can stop bitching. 'What will Nixon do, Dai Uy? Why the M16 have only twenty bullets and the AK-47 have thirty, Dai Uy? Why the NVA have rockets and the USA don't give us rockets, Dai Uy?'"

I laughed at his near perfect imitation of Colonel Lin, or a dozen other of the South Vietnamese militia.

"They're all terrified we'll run out on them."

"And they should be: The American people don't have the stomach for casualties."

"Then . . . what'll you do?"

"I pray to the Lord for miracles morning, noon, and night."

"After the miracles."

"Get a Ph.D. in mechanical engineering at Virginia Tech and teach at West Point."

"Like your dad, the general."

"He was a drill instructor, football coach; he fought two wars and never built anything."

"He's got you and—what, is it two or three daughters?"

"Army brats, PX rats, grown up on every army base between Korea and Sicily."

"Better than being an only child."

"Same thing, he don't give a fuck about the girls, and they know it. Two of them married hippies just to fuck him." Theo looked over at the Vietnamese radio operator snoozing against the side of the palm log. "How are you two communicating—he savvy your Vietnamese okay?"

"Just fine—speaks French, too. He's half Chinese."

"When the shit hits the fan, it's important he's got rapport with the South Viet air. Our gooker air force just loves to flatten everything in sight. You must constantly repeat and get them to repeat back to you the precise physical geography or coordinates—repeat and confirm the target. Make sure they're packing the right ordnance. Make sure they're seeing what's on your map."

"Yes, sir."

Theo cocked his head.

"You think it's a fucking game?"

"No, sir, I just enjoy seeing you holding hands with Colonel Lin. It's just I had you figured more for a lifer in the mold of a Patton, or even a George C. Marshall, an expert in military strategy, what the Greeks called *techne*, or art, except the Greeks didn't draw much of a distinction between the practical arts and the fine arts."

"Ah, there's the Princeton man talking. You, *rich boy*, say *lifer* like it has a kind of bad smell attached."

"No disrespect intended, sir."

"Nice you have choices. Lot of guys in my father's generation, it was all they had, the army, like Sergeant Kittle." Theo glanced away a moment, the moonlight illuminating the pinched eyebrows and accordion folds in his broad forehead. He sighed. "But I'll take it—your art of war—huh. Better than God's hell on earth."

"Is there a difference?"

He pointed toward the Vam Co Dong: "The land of the unfree and the land of the free—that's how the Kittler put it to me once."

"Simple, I guess. . . ."

"The smart soldier knows he's only got one good war in him, if his luck holds. And one's plenty for this life if you're God-fearing enough to be numbered among the righteous . . . *and* on the winning side. When my twenty years are up, I want to build bridges all over the world, beautiful and strong spans of steel and concrete that glitter in the sunlight."

"I'll settle for teaching, maybe history, ancient history, as far as I can get from all this."

"Well, by this time tomorrow . . . maybe we'll all be a little closer."

I still remember Theo's voice and the squint of his eyes over hundreds of chess games and the endless stories he told me of their early days in Vietnam in the coastal hamlets, when they chased off the VC with night patrols and ambushes, in scores of firefights at three in the morning in the pitch-black; when he and Willie and their Vietnamese PFs ambushed any VC who dared to infiltrate and intimidate or indoctrinate their villagers, or extract taxes in rice and assassinate their opponents; when Theo and Willie hunted and fought and killed their stealthy enemy less by sight and more by a sense of movement or even smell. How many hundreds of nights had they lain out in the monsoon cold and the summer swelter, up to their eyebrows in damp and putrid decay, with the mosquitoes feasting—a slap could mean discovery and death—to take back and secure village after village, until they could drink rice wine with the farmers and fishermen to celebrate the defeat of the VC. Theo and Willie came to admire the simple lives of the Vietnamese peasants, as if their determination to endure under adversity reminded them of their own people of generations past. With the failure of the Tet Offensive in 1968, the VC were eliminated as a serious threat and the emphasis shifted to defending the western borders of South Vietnam from NVA infiltration from Cambodia and Laos. I hung on Theo's every word, seeking to know the secrets of such a competent warrior. Did he ever doubt his cause? Did anything really scare him?

Theo nodded as he moved his queen in for the kill.

He told me about a pitch-black, moonless night when the VC had walked into the sites of his ambush team lying in wait. Theo had placed three shots in the chest of the shadow figure on point. Then a scream in English, and Theo screamed in turn for his team to hold their fire. It was a Charlie Company patrol that had gotten lost and strayed into their sector.

"The lieutenant, the point man I had shot, rose from the muddy trail and started cussing me out, 'You fuckin' blew me away; you just killed me, you motherfucker.' I switched on a flashlight and we inspected the stock of his M16, neatly stitched with three bullets holes. I hauled off and busted the idiot in the jaw and we returned to our base."

For a week, Theo was so overcome with depression, he could barely move off of his cot. Not the wounds, not the enemy he killed, not the villagers executed and tortured by the VC, but an incident of friendly fire in which a miracle saved a brother officer's life.

Why I fell in love with Theo, I cannot say. We barely spoke the same language. There was a manliness about him to be sure, an unself-consciousness of his power over others that could be simply mesmerizing. Women loved him, treated him like a lustrous god, even though he lacked flamboyance of any kind, or eagerness to please, and he never cared for or sought their solicitations. He had the naturalness of an animal, a purebred, that led its life by instinct to do the thing that God had set it upon the earth to do. I suppose Theo was a natural-born warrior. In my early years, with what I heard from Elliot and others, Theo seemed a lot like my father, or the man I hoped to be. It was enough to be his friend.

The NVA were late. They did, in fact, get caught up in arc-light strikes on their Cambodian staging areas and ended up crossing at dawn. A bad idea, but they hadn't met any resistance this near the border in years. It was a brazen thing to do, but these were disciplined soldiers with orders. They thought they were on the march to final victory and Saigon; the NVA were off by only three years. These NVA replacements were being rushed in to reinforce attacks that were already under way in other parts of the district. Colonel Lin followed Theo's aggressive tactics to the tee; he had his troops hold their fire in the dawn mists along the Vam Co Dong River until two companies, maybe three hundred NVA, were across or crossing. Then the South Vietnamese opened up with everything they had. Theo wanted to trap as many on the east bank of the river as possible. But this resulted in so many NVA being stranded on our side of the river that they had no option but to fight. Fleeing back across the knee-deep river would be suicide. They might have thought it was only a small ambush, or they were overly cocky, or they simply had orders that were not countermanded. The NVA on the west shore dug in to support their cut-off comrades, and within minutes our South Vietnamese militia had a full-scale battle on its hands. Mortar rounds began dropping—at first, indiscriminately. We were outnumbered three or four to one but were in a good defensive position. Theo did his best to let Colonel Lin handle the situation, but he couldn't resist creeping forward to reconnoiter, sending Willie in to make suggestions. I was told in no uncertain terms to stay fixed on the OP with my radioman and get the South Vietnamese air force ready for support. Fifteen minutes into the battle, the NVA were penetrating our perimeter on the high ground above the river.

I watched through my binoculars in panic and horror as the initial slaughter unfolded along the banks of the Vam Co Dong. The green-and-khaki-clad NVA were chopped to pieces by concentrated machine-gun, rifle, and mortar fire, the river in the misty light of dawn boiling and geysering and foaming pinkish green. Then the thickets of undergrowth and bamboo along our perimeter on the rise above the river began hemorrhaging khaki uniforms in ones and twos, the NVA often firing their AK-47's wildly from their hips—a wasteful thing, it struck me, since their ammo had to be carried so painfully far. Militia riflemen stationed around the clearing picked them off pretty easily. But then the mortar rounds from across the river began to get the range of our LZ. The rush of explosions and whipsaws of shrapnel through the tall grass began in earnest. My ears ringing, my mouth full of dirt, I realized my teeth were chattering and I had wet my pants. I felt naked without Willie around but tried to remain calm for the Vietnamese radioman, who cowered next to our makeshift bunker of logs. The elephant grass in the clearing began vomiting geysers of smoke and fire and occasionally bodies in a spray of red. The roar of machine guns was deafening, and my radioman was struggling to hear over his headphones. Bullets whipped by overhead, making wicked thwacks in the branches of the palms nearby, raining leaves and splinters down on our heads. Soon the perimeter was shaking with automatic-weapons fire, as if some furious wounded organism was lashing out at anything that breathed.

Theo came dashing back to me from lower down along the hillside, his hands covered in blood from helping drag out the wounded. "We're going to need air," he said, then translated for the radioman. "We need napalm, all they've got, and some five-hundred-pound fragmentation bombs. Get them up here now, and guide them in along the river from the south. I need napalm on the crossing point west of the river and five-hundred-pounders on the east bank—the militia has almost been pushed off the hillside; they're dug in on the perimeter of the LZ." Then he was off again. I was working with the radioman, translating, giving him the coordinates for the South Vietnamese air, which gave me some qualms, as they were neither as accurate nor as dependable as our guys.

Bullets began slamming into the trunks where we huddled, now coming in waist-high through the grass, singing as they zipped past our elbows. Vietnamese of every stripe were swarming on the edge of the clearing—thank God our guys were fighting. I was so proud, and relieved; none of them had been in a firefight like this. There were casualties, screams, and no dedicated corpsmen, not like in an American outfit. I had never been in heavy combat, never in combat of any kind. I'd been sniped at while working over bodies after a battle and I'd seen the terrible results of artillery and air, but never the thick of it. I was terrified and strangely fascinated and determined not to make a mistake. Our Vietnamese were doing a pretty good job killing their countrymen.

We loved those militias; we hoped they were saving us from a lifetime's regrets.

I saw Theo and Willie conferring out in the center of the LZ, as if it were a Sunday afternoon stroll in the park, Theo pointing out gaps in our defenses while preparing fallback positions behind two M60's that would cover the western half of the clearing once the South Vietnamese had withdrawn from the slopes of the rise. That was where I figured Theo was going to put the five-hundred-pound bombs: on the hillside between us and the river. The stubborn withdrawal of the militia had the effect of shifting the NVA attack more and more to our flanks. A new command post was set up next to our OP. The South Vietnamese began dragging some of their wounded into the shade and cover provided by the grove of trees at our back. I was frantically working with the radioman to get the air on the way to us, but the controller had been saying fifteen minutes for the last hour. There was fog on the air base.

Then a lull. The NVA had obviously been hurt; they weren't rushing our positions anymore like madmen; they were crawling and crouching and coming in small groups. And they were tossing grenades, concealing themselves in the high grass. A few of the wounded behind me in the shade were screaming for water, or their mothers. For a while there was relative calm, then, vaguely in the distance, these hollow jarring sounds, and Willie was waving like crazy and yelling, "Tubin'—tubin'—tubin'." Explosions ripped and erupted in the clearing. "Fuck," said Willie, "they've got a mortar team across the river, on our side."

My heart was beating so fast I couldn't get myself calmed down. The mortar rounds seemed to be landing closer and closer to the OP, now the CP.

The air support was delayed by fog farther east, but the fog had lifted off the river, and the crossing point through my binoculars now seemed deserted of activity. But as I shifted my gaze downriver about five hundred yards, just beyond a gentle bend, I caught movement: three or four squads of NVA testing the shallows, as if about to attempt a crossing. It was deep there—we'd checked it out—four or five feet, not good for fording with weapons, but the NVA looked as if they were going to give it a try. If they got across in numbers, they could outflank our position or come in behind us and cut us off. I shouted for Theo, but in the melee I couldn't see him, or Willie. I panicked. I felt personally threatened because I seemed to be the only person to see the second crossing. I yelled to some of the South Vietnamese officers, but they either didn't hear me or were too preoccupied. Even my radioman wasn't going to break off from the net for a look. More mortars came crashing around us. It occurred to me with sudden lucidity that they were trying to keep us pinned down, distracted . . . to screen the new crossing to the south.

My fear and frustration crystallized into something like blind aggression. I grabbed the radioman, pulled him to the observation post, and pointed out the NVA downriver. I told him to inform Willie or Theo as soon as he saw them, or his Colonel Lin, or any of his officers, that we needed to counter the flanking movement pronto. I repeated myself to make sure he understood. His brown eyes darted to my mine and away; he was even more scared than I was, because he knew what the NVA would do to him if he was captured. Seeing his panic, I felt a senseless rage at the insanity of it all. I grabbed my M16, stopped by the dead and wounded to pick up as many extra ammo clips as I could stuff into my pockets and the webbing of my flak jacket, and ran. The mortar rounds felt like hellfire nipping at my heels across the backside of the clearing—a hell I wasn't sure if I was escaping or embracing. I dashed into the thick elephant grass and scrub on our southern flank, tripping and running downhill toward the river. The sounds of battle faded once I was over the ridge and nearer the river. The curve in the river, I realized, cut off view of the battle above—except for our OP, probably no one else had seen the new crossing to the south. The NVA troops in their pith helmets were spread out into the shallows on the far shore, feeling their way into the deeper water like a human tide out of the dark jungle behind. It was two hundred yards to cross and the water was soon up to their waists, their arms raised, gripping their AK-47's. I got as close as could without breaking cover and flopped down behind a rotten log, where I could steady my M16. Wisps of fog played over the river, dispersed by the rising sun at my back. The Vam Co Dong River was bathed in a glassy, hovering yellowish gray-green sheen beyond the sites of my M16, out of which khaki torsos closed with slow, creeping steps. The sun was directly in their eyes, doubly so with the glare off the surface, and as I took aim, I detected the curved visors dipping across shadowy faces.

I had been target shooting since I was eight; in basic, I had won a badge for expert marksman, the best shot in my outfit. I had the slow-moving targets in my sights, outlined in the sunlight, and methodically began picking them off, placing the shots in the upper chest and, for the targets in the deeper water, in the head. It usually took one shot per figure, except when I hit an AK-47. The impact staggered them, the AK-47's splashing as the figure slumped backward and begin to float away. I began with the closest, nearest the middle of the river, and worked backward toward the far shore. Troops waiting on the shore opened up with their AK-47's on automatic, peppering the scrub in my vicinity, but the sun was in their eyes and I doubted that could even detect my muzzle flash through the glare. The AK-47 is much less accurate than the M16 at distance, and I knew that once they began firing, even the steady snap of my rounds would be hard to discern.

I was surprised they kept on coming, but I shouldn't have been, because one of the things I knew about the NVA was that when an order was given, they executed, to a man. What I remember, even if I didn't register it in the moment: Their comrades refused to be distracted by the bodies that began floating away downstream, or even to pull them ashore, so intent were they to get across that river. I have no idea how long this went on, presumably about ten to twelve minutes, because you figure about eight seconds between rounds, and I think I went through six or seven ammo clips. When I fired my last round and discovered that I had no more clips on me, I panicked, as if I'd suddenly come to—woken from a good dream of supreme competency, only to find myself alone in a bad dream, stark naked and alone. I'd slipped into the zone of a cold-blooded killer and just as easily slipped back into my terrified human self. Fortunately, the few remaining standing figures in the river had their backs to me by then and were retreating into the shallows. And the NVA firing from the far shore seemed to have used up their ammo, too.

"Jesus fuckin' Christ . . . what the fuck are you doin' here?"

It was Willie with a squad of South Vietnamese militia and a M60 machine-gun team. They immediately began blasting away at the far shore as the last of the bodies began a slow descent of the Vam Co Dong River.

"Shit, man, what honky motherfucker taught you to shoot like that?" He grabbed my arm. "But you in even worse shit back at OP; Theo wants your scalp. You left the radioman—you got the friggin' maps for air support?"

I had taken the maps with me; I had abandoned the radioman and left him without a map to call in the coordinates for the air support. Willie and I ran up the rise through the brush as fast as we could, back toward the din of battle in the clearing above the river. Willie was out in front of me, crashing through the underbrush, as if he knew exactly where he was going, as if to make a path, as his brother Jerry had carved his way through tacklers on an end around. The clearing was a mass of confusion even though the mortar rounds had slackened. Bullets clipped the grass at shoulder height. I saw Theo across the clearing by the CP, huddled with the radioman and Colonel Lin. There was blood on Theo's shirt where a bullet had grazed his shoulder. My heart was careening inside my chest, less from the scramble we'd made up the hill than for having fucked up something so basic as keeping the map reader and the radioman together. As I drew nearer, I could see the concentration on Theo's face as he explained the communications to the panicked radioman. I was also aware of the sound of aircraft circling, preparing their runs over the battlefield.

The moment Theo spotted me and Willie running toward his position, his face lit up with animal rage.

"You stupid spoiled brat—where have you been? Don't tell me. Give me the map, just give me the fucking map."

I pulled the map out of my pocket and went to the radioman.

Willie tried to intercede on my behalf.

"Shut up, Willie." Theo turned to me and the radioman, screaming above the din in Vietnamese, telling the radioman to call off the strikes until he had the precise coordinates. "Call it off, call it off."

The radioman spoke into his handset, repeating the order again and again, but got no reply. We could hear the aircraft making the turn for a run. Without the map coordinates, Theo had been talking them in by eye but—and rightly—he was concerned that something might be lost in translation. The South Vietnamese air jockeys were careless as shit and clearly intent on their run and dropping the ordnance precisely where they thought they'd been told . . . or where it was easiest, or where they thought it would do a world of good.

Theo kept yelling, glancing up at the skies. "Cancel, cancel—fuck . . ."

He ran out toward the center of the clearing as the Vietnamese air force's Skyraiders came in for their first pass—to drop their bombs on the rise nearest the river, from which most of the militia had now been withdrawn. I ran out toward Theo, desperate to help, and to redeem myself. The first A-1 Skyraider dropped its ordnance right where it had been directed, west of the perimeter along the rise, but the second plane went for the more obvious target. I was standing fifty feet from Theo when I heard Willie scream out my name. I turned, catching a glimpse of Willie squatting next to the radioman and waving me back. That was the last thing I remember seeing of that day; the world as I knew it disappeared in a rush of heated air and metal. The second Skyraider had dropped its five-hundred-pound bomb right in the middle of the fucking clearing.

As they say in the movies, the next thing I knew, I was lying on my stomach on something soft. I was cool, almost cold. I couldn't imagine such coolness was possible. There was no grass, no noise, no smoke, no stink of cordite . . . peace, unearthly peace. I could smell disinfectant. I wanted to open my eyes, but I was afraid to find out I was dead. I realized how beautifully silent everything was, and if I opened my eyes, all the terrible din might return. A murmur of voices. The clink of metal on metal. Then I knew I was in an operating theater. And I knew it was my back they were working on. I couldn't feel anything, though, which was the second scariest thing once I knew I wasn't dead. I didn't know how much of me was left.

Someone rubbed my face with a damp cloth and I opened my eyes. I saw a woman's hand in a blue rubber glove and the bulge of an engagement ring and the tie string of a green surgical gown.

"How bad?" I murmured.

She bent to my face and smiled reassuringly.

"Welcome back, soldier." She called to the doctor.

I saw another rubber-gloved hand smeared in blood and then a southern voice, reminding me instantly of Theo, or what Theo might have sounded like had he gone into medicine, like my grandfather.

"Son, you gonna be okay. You got a lot of metal in your back, queer stuff, too. Not all of it shrapnel. Plenty of souvenirs. The good news: It cut you up good but missed the backbone. You've lost muscle tissue, and there's some damage to the kidney, but nothing that shouldn't rehabilitate with time." He squeezed my shoulder. I felt the squeeze and was happy for the sensation. "You relax now, hear. Think about home and your best gal, 'cause that's where you're headed real soon now. You hear, son? Real soon."

It seemed like the happiest moment in my not so young life.

I was under heavy sedation and painkillers for at least a week. They wanted to make sure there was no nerve damage and so didn't fly me out sooner to the Philippines and the Subic Bay military hospital, where further operations awaited me. On the day before I left Vietnam, Willie Gadsden came to see me in the hospital in Saigon. He was a sight to see in his dress khakis, as if he were on his way to a funeral. Not even a Band-Aid. His Afro had a kinky sheen and he looked solemn, concerned, even though he tried to be anything but. He never admitted to saving my life, but he probably had; he'd hauled me out of the clearing and packed my back with bandages and gotten me medevaced out with the first of the South Vietnamese wounded.

"How you doin', man?" he asked.

It was the first day I felt half-human. They had lowered the dose of painkillers. My back ached and the dressings itched, but at least I had a back to ache and I could twitch my toes. I was lying on my side, looking at Willie where he sat fiddling with a piece of paper in his lap; there was a window behind him that showed a blue sky.

"I'm still in the world, Willie. How's Theo? How did our guys do?"

"They did good, Sittin' Pretty. The NVA dee-deed after the air started to hit them big-time; the napalm on the west bank, they didn't like one little bit."

I was still having trouble rewinding my brain to where it had left off by that grove of trees and the log OP.

"Did I really leave my post?"

"You did what you had to do—you did good."

"Vietnamese killing Vietnamese—that's what we need to get the hell out of here, right?"

I looked at his handsome black face and shining oatmeal brown eyes and quick smile, which reminded me of the Jerry I had loved until he began to hate everything Winsted stood for.

"You said it."

"We stopped them from getting across the river."

"So it seems, at least for now."

"Did my radioman do okay?"

"Your gook did fine. The gook in the Skyraider with the five-hundred-pound bomb . . . I'm going to have his ass."

There were tears in Willie's eyes.

"Well . . . the nurses are something else."

"Theo was my main man."

The expression of horror on Willie's face as he shook his head dropped me into an abyss. I couldn't even turn away.

Willie took my hand and squeezed it. The nurse told me I'd been bleeding like a stuck pig from the deep puncture wounds but that someone had done a bang-up job with the compression bandages in the field.

"They've begun an inquiry," Willie told me.

"An inquiry?"

"I told them you were a hero. I told them you should get every medal they got."

"Christ, Willie, I don't even remember half of it. I was panicked; I was terrified."

"Your training kicked in, man, your instincts. You just tell 'em what happened, Pete. Don't leave anything out."

"I left the radioman and I had the maps."

"That's what the South Vietnamese colonel, Lin, been saying—blames you for the five-hundred-pound bomb. But I was there; I know."

The inquiry would meander around for a few more weeks but was quickly dropped in the euphoria of the South Vietnamese victory, when they defeated the North's invasion in that summer of 1972. The North Vietnamese signed the Paris Peace Accords the following year, and we thought we were home free.

Willie and I chatted together for a long time. He wasn't going to re-up for another tour as an American adviser. "I'd like to see Germany, Italy maybe—even Korea, if it has to be."

Before Willie left and I started to nod off, he left a telegram on my bedside table.

It informed me that my mother had been killed in a car accident. She had fallen asleep and crashed her Mercedes into the abutment of a bridge on the Taconic Parkway at two in the morning. Unlike my father's cover story, hers was the real thing. The coroner's report noted her high blood-alcohol levels and a triple dose of Valium to boot. How she even got the car out of the garage in New York was anybody's guess. She hadn't been headed anywhere, as far as anyone could tell. It was the route we took to the Berkshires, but she hadn't been to Elysium in years. She hadn't even brought her pocketbook. There were no skid marks, no attempt to turn the car back onto the highway, which was also consistent with someone falling asleep at the wheel. That afternoon, a telegram from the Defense Department had been delivered to the apartment. When she returned from her bridge game at the Colony, the doorman handed it to her. The telegram said I was missing in action.

I spent a month at Subic Bay for more operations and procedures. Twice, I got kidney infections that almost killed me. The family lawyer called and asked if I wanted to sue the Defense Department over the stupid telegram. Because I'd gone through a clearing center for South Vietnamese wounded, my paperwork got delayed. They might have confused me with Theo, since his father got a telegram saying he'd been wounded.

I told the lawyer not to bother.

By the end of my time at Subic, I had accumulated quite the collection of shell splinters extracted from my back. I kept them in a plastic Tupperware bowl with a baby blue cover. There was one piece, longer and shinier and more sinister than the others, with a curved edge like a broken clamshell; it began to intrigue me. It did not look like a bomb splinter. When I got back to the States, I gave it to an army weapons specialist to examine. A week later, the report came back. It was a piece of an American combat helmet. Theo had taken the full impact of the blast.

Often they gave you a choice of rehabilitation hospitals, so you could be close to home and family. I picked San Diego for the weather and because it was as far away as you could get stateside. If Maureen had been twenty years younger and not married, I would have married her, if she'd have had me. She spoiled me for anything but hand jobs.

When I got to Princeton, nothing was how I had imagined it. I was three years older than the others in my class and I had been places people thought they knew but didn't: they thought I had been there, but I hadn't. The faculty considered me an exotic. I was pitied by some, shunned by others as bearing bad karma, and reviled by a few who were disappointed they no longer had a war to protest. Some people were unbelievably kind. I got angry and then depressed in my sophomore year, in the months around the fall of Saigon. In the suite next door, they cheered the fall of Saigon. I sometimes couldn't get out of bed. I had a dozen names among the Vietnamese I knew and loved: I even went to the chapel and prayed they'd gotten away and hadn't been executed or imprisoned. Maybe one or two of my prayers were answered over the years when a letter found me, but not many. I didn't talk to anyone about it, for fear of getting into a fight. Everybody seemed so relieved that the nightmare of Vietnam was over and life could return to normal. The biggest thing at Princeton that year was a new fad called "streaking": singletons, and ten or twenty and sometimes more students, both men and women, ran through classrooms and across campus buck naked, indulging a crazy freedom their parents had never dreamed of.

I learned to become invisible. I explored map coordinates as distant and obscure as I could find them, a past as deep as it was silent on the subject of victory and defeat . . . where the story line of heartache had long played itself out.

Until Laura came along and brought an updated map.

It is a strange thing how the river of memory carries you along. I cannot think back on the Vam Co Dong River without seeing the sad face of Bellini's Madonna, or hearing the tolling of the Gesuati and Redentore, or breathing in the scent of brine and incense, or without the sensation of waves buoying us up, or the squeeze of Laura's hand as we floated past Palazzo Barberini on a Venetian evening filled with voices heralding the end of the Cold War—the end of our fathers' world. It was truly the Christmas season, one in which the deadly romance of war faded into the enduring romance of the past, shorn of misery and defeat, as time's gentle lapping urged us both onward and back in a gliding lullaby.

40 KAREL SPECULATED ENDLESSLY, DIS-
dainful of the guidebooks we employed, disparaging
their accuracy about the dating and provenance of artifacts. "You see, Dummkopf? They just repeat the old
myths and lies handed down from one generation to the next, without
checking the facts or analyzing the stylistic evolution. Every human
artifact evolves—why we are bound to murder our fathers, according to
Freud." Even at twenty, he had an exacting eye, photographic memory,
and a remarkable mind—encyclopedic in scope, with detailed knowledge of stylistic variations I could only dream of fully grasping. When
we came upon some exotic carving embedded in San Marco, he would
rattle off a dozen examples of similar kind that he had seen in various
museum collections or catalogs, and on the basis of stylistic affinity,
he'd make a determination as to date and origin. He actually scribbled his revisions into my mother's Baedeker guide—mother was much
impressed. I hung on his every word. He set a scholarly standard I felt I
could never hope to attain. All he lacked was patience, patience for the
tough slog—attention to details—to decipher Linear B. He knew it; I
knew it. It locked us in.

—excerpt from John Alden's Pankrác Prison diary

Exhausted with walking—my back, her knee—we opted for a gondola,
like any two lovers nearing middle age might do, in funds enough to
afford it.

"We can't leave Venice without doing something goofy, like . . . a
kiss beneath the Bridge of Sighs."

She said this in a hopeful humor, yet leery, too, since this, as we both
knew, was a running gag in the last chapters of *Gardens*.

So we huddled together on the padded seats, and the young gondolier gave us a thin blanket to spread across our knees. We agreed to a price and a circuitous route that would allow us to double back along the Grand Canal and so make two passes by Palazzo Barberini, doubling down on our exhausted emotional capital—without either one of us having set foot in the place. The gondolier swung us out into the foggy stillness of the Bacino and we were launched. It was the oddest sensation for me, not having had the pleasure since my trip with my grandmother a quarter century before, to be nearly prone on my back, this time next to my lover, while someone else did the rowing— my rowing days having ended on that godforsaken clearing above the Vam Co Dong River. The accumulated ballast we shifted in tandem brought to mind Matthew Arnold's old chestnut, "The Future," echoes of which, I would discover in the following months, had found their way into *Essays and Prayers* by virtue of polymath Pearce Breckenridge: "Vainly did we fable and dream of that past, though lost to us as the world before our birth, yet alive as the intuited names and places which had first set us adrift upon the river of Time . . . those murmurs and scents of the infinite sea." Max would laugh at such a gerrymandering of a stogy literary source, but then, he never found out about Pearce Breckenridge. What intrigues me are Arnold's insights absent any knowledge of genetics or neuroscience, although he should have been tipped off by Darwin. And I still have to knock it into my distracted students' heads that it is not the Lockean immediacy of experience that best fits us out for the journey, but the voices of our progenitors as they whisper to our inner ear.

I remember beams of amber light seeping from behind the cracked blinds drawn over the Gothic windows of the Barberini, spilling in flashing triplicate upon the waves, as if signaling us to a safer port. The Istrian stone facade and quatrefoil windows—spandrels crowned with circular disks of colored marble carved with beasts of the apostles—was just as Singer Sargent had it in his watercolors—the very same *Roman copies of Hellenistic originals* that had almost caused my father and Karel to tip over as Karel stood in the gondola for a better look. While the Barberini returned me to the side of my grandmother as she droned on about its history, cagily excising the brief interlude when Isabella Williams had owned it, much less the two weeks she'd spent there with her husband on their honeymoon. My father's Pankrác diary had revealed her deep ambivalence about her life of squandered love, as it had his.

While to me, she had only seemed to care about the Barberini's "dreadful state . . . a real mess, they tell me; the foundations are rotten and waterlogged" when it had been the place where she had been most in love, and the scene of another, if brief, love affair, and her son's love-hate relationship with Karel Hollar.

Karel smoked, but my mother forbade me. As soon as our gondola was under way down the Grand Canal, Karel shared his cigarette with me. Mother and Wilfred, his so very handsome father (his wife had returned to Vienna for a wedding), hired their own gondola, which lingered so far astern that we lost sight of it for an entire hour! As we passed the Barberini, Karel pointed out the porphyry columns on the water entrance, convinced they were from a Greek temple in Smyrna. But it was the pair of sculpted griffins, vaguely lionlike, with one raised front paw and curlicue of a tail, perched on the balcony railings that threw him into paroxysms of scholarly effusiveness. "Surely they were liberated from the temple of Apollo on Delos—one remains in the museum there, but it must have originally come from Alexandria by way of Antioch. How else to explain the mongrel mixture of late Hellenistic and Assyrian influences?" As we hovered in the reflected lights of the Barberini, I could just make out the sound of a piano from the flame-lit interior, a Chopin nocturne—so familiar that I was quite taken out of myself. "Oh," says Karel "that must be Robert Williams, the nephew of the old lady who owns the palazzo." The week before, when I had first visited the Barberini with Karel's parents, Bobby and his mother, Amaryllis, were not there, delayed for medical reasons, so we were told.

Ancient Isabella, draped in silks and satins and dripping jewelry, held court amidst a crowd of European and American intellectuals—in such a stupor that she didn't even recognize me. When I got back to the Gritti and reported in to Mother, she listened intently to all I had to tell, especially about how Wilfred Hollar had held forth on the floor of the piano nobile about how little Czechoslovakia, "the child of your Woodrow Wilson," so he put it to Isabella, was determined to stand up to Herr Hitler and so champion the antifascist cause in every way possible. And yet Mother still resisted my entreaties to join us at the next soiree scheduled for the following week.

"There are just some things you would find hard to understand at this point in your life—trust me, we are not welcome there with those people. I hear the old witch surrounds herself with sycophant Jews and

their nouveau hangers-on." Only when I tried to convince her otherwise, when I told her about Wilfred's brave comments to resist both
Stalin and Hitler, did she come around, if just a bit, and she finally
revealed how she and my father had spent two weeks at the Barberini
in the summer of 1910. At first hesitatingly and then with more candor,
lying in her bed in the Gritti, she described how she'd been dazzled by
the splendid drawing rooms of the Barberini, the frescoes and tessel-
lated floors, and how the honeymoon couple had spent a wonderful
evening with Singer Sargent, a distant cousin of the Williamses, on
the balcony of the Barberini discussing international affairs, the state
of Europe and America, artistic controversies at the Paris Salon. "Your
father dazzled Sargent with descriptions of his many advances in
heart surgery at Harvard Medical School. Sargent, with his Beaux-
Arts training in anatomy, hung on his every word." It seems Sargent
talked about his longing to return to America—Boston would be his
choice—wondering out loud to the young couple visiting Venice for
the first time if he'd spent too much time in Europe—"too many damn
days painting frivolous portraits of British toffs; perhaps if I'd been a
landscape painter back in New York, I might have more respect among
my countrymen." My father, it seems, was very taken by their conversation. According to my mother, he was a very fine draftsman and was
known in medical circles for his extraordinary illustrations of surgical
techniques in the professional journals. Relating these memories to me,
my mother had suddenly laughed as gaily as a newlywed, wiping at
her tears. "What if your father had decided to become an artist and
Mr. Sargent had returned to America to paint his own country? Then
Europe would not have wasted them both."

As we drifted past the Barberini on our first run down the Grand
Canal, I shivered at the thought of my father writing those words in
his Pankrác cell, surely a despairing nod at his own *wasted* life.

I gripped Laura's hand tighter and she turned to me. I felt her examining my profile, lingering pensively. What did she see now that she
had heard about Vietnam? A callous cold-blooded killer, a warmonger,
a fool?

"Funny," she said, "but of all our fucked lives, you, the practical, diligent one, turned out to be the real romantic."

We were passed by other gondolas floating out of the mist,
disturbed only by the slow churn of a No. 1 vaporetto and by the
distant sounds of newscasts from television sets, the excited reporters

giving freedom's updates from various cities in Eastern Europe. Then silence.

I was reluctant to ask Laura if she harbored any feelings of loss or even nostalgia for the Barberini's storied past during Isabella Williams's tenure—for fear of bringing up the palazzo's many cameo appearances in *Gardens*. The sound of the lapping water and the stars overhead reminded me of that night at Elysium when Max had gotten us invited to Hermitage, when I had my first good look at the Sargent watercolors of Venice, and the shock of Amaryllis's nudes of my grandmother—and Suzanne's unmatronly embrace—when Max and I hung out on the boathouse dock by the lake, wondering which of those millions of stars to make our own.

Around a bend, the shadowy outline of Palazzo Pisani appeared ahead, where Max had spent a summer helping with his mother's master class. Aka Chef Boyardee, he had sent me erotic missives as he came under the spell of Venice past, especially the golden years, when Isabella and Bernard Berenson held sway at the Barberini, collecting old masters for Palazzo Fenway in a time of relative peace before the First World War turned the world into a quagmire of death and destruction . . . as if only now, in the passing moments—the splash of our gondolier's oar, water sprinkled on the steaming embers—was the stinking thing finally burning itself out.

"So what do you think," she asked, "did Max write himself into our lives, or we into his?"

She said this only partly tongue in cheek: Some part of her always believed she had been in control, if not of the outcome exactly, then certainly of the scenes along the way, where she reigned like an erotic goddess: "Do you suppose teenage boys will seek me out in the good bits, the sexy bits . . . when I'm a dried-up fossil, and beat off to my pages?"

"Once upon a time, in a golden age of peace, when the likes of Whistler and James and Sargent ruled the roost, to be remembered with the immortals."

"But Max *was* of his time."

"And us in the dust."

"Speak for yourself, old man."

She squeezed my hand as if to say, *Well, we, the living, don't you think, still have some benefits.* I thought of the aching, ecstatic beauty of her face when she climaxed on top of me in the mornings, and so found myself well pleased with our gondolier, the way he indulged the glide between strokes, as if to encourage the currents to have their way, as Max had that night on the boathouse dock when he'd cast his broken staff into the lake and shattered our looking-glass stars . . . and any last hopes, after the shooting of Charlie Springfield, and the slow fuses lit around the dinner table at Hermitage, that life might just let us get on with it.

I could feel Laura looking up at those same stars, surely trying to anticipate the meeting with her mother and her godfather—her new stepfather, now putative father, which the Pankrác diary threw, if anything, into even graver doubt. Worse, between the love letters and now the diary, there was enough evidence asserting Philby's claim over my father's that the best we could manage were the feints of a snake charmer.

"I think I'd almost prefer just to take my mother's word for it," she finally said to me. As usual, she could read my mind before I could. "For the sake of *us*, if you know what I mean."

"Mum's the word," I offered, attempting to get us off the hook on that most delicate subject. "Besides, I've got a few bones of my own to pick with Charles if that meeting in Cambridge with Ventris and Nigel Bennett really happened."

"What meeting?"

"My father wrote about it in his diary."

"That Linear B stuff is way over my head."

"My father spent two days in England before flying on to Berlin. Ventris and Bennett were the two greatest experts in the field—Ventris had just made the breakthrough in the decipherment of Linear B, after generations of failure. Why would my father have included a description of that meeting in the diary? Was it for us, his family, or for the Soviets, to throw them off the track, or something else?"

"Maybe it was to protect Hollar, to substantiate their meeting in East Berlin."

"Just old colleagues getting together to discuss the latest news in the field."

"Something like that. Your Karel Hollar comes off pretty well in the diary."

"A supercilious young man dedicated to the Communist cause, who, if Nestor was right, worked for British SIS, as well as the KGB. But a double agent for whom? Or more to the point: Who brought them together in East Berlin? How did my father know Hollar was alive, much less his circumstances?"

"Charles Fairburn?" she asked.

"Charles had to have been part of it; he and Nigel Bennett were always close. As a kid, for my birthday, Charles always gave me signed copies of Bennett's books on Minoan civilization."

"Would your father have made up stuff, in the diary, to save himself?"

"Wouldn't you?"

She let out an uneasy laugh, as if we'd been over this before, which we had. She gestured extravagantly to the walls of a palazzo we were passing, "Once there were frescoes on the walls by Palma Vecchio and Titian. Gone, too. Isn't it all so sad?"

"Sad," I echoed, sensing that this non sequitur, begotten of the mists, had been part of a conversation—a life not mine.

She continued along the same line: "I sometimes feel as if I've been living inside a cocoon of half-truths and lies so long that I can no longer tell the difference." I was hopeful she was speaking of her mother, her family—that near-moribund clan. "Christ, it was scary, freaky how well Max got on with my parents by indulging all their subterfuges as his own. Like cats, they licked up after one another." I felt her shiver, as if the thought brought on a rising tide of anxieties. "The most amazing thing about my mother is how guileless she is, how unconscious she is of her secret deceptions. And there's no margin for guilt in her because she's always managed it so effortlessly—bending the world to her wishes; she's so dazzling, so convinced of the righteousness of her cause—if *people* could only see it through *her* eyes. She believes in herself absolutely: a true believer. It's what made her such a great dancer, the fearlessness that comes from a total absence of doubt. Much less guilt for the roadkill left in her wake."

I graciously held back my catty rejoinder, because it no longer mattered.

"If you believe the papers, the *Times*' obituary, that's how people felt about Kim Philby, too, after everything—not a shred of self-doubt—world-class."

"Listen, she was my Circe, too . . . swans into swine."

On that score, Max must be given the last word.

And like ingrained muscle memory, she felt again the tug of her mother's hand, the creak of the old rickety stairs to the entrance of the ballet studio, the firm, exacting motion of her mother's fingers as she wrapped and rewrapped the shiny pink ribbons around her ankles, a discreet knot tucked beneath the top loop. It was like a ritual blessing, a laying on of hands. There, repeated endlessly in the mirror, in every studio from Lincoln Center to the Mariinsky: mother goddess and graven image—upper back arched and elegant, blond hair in a tight chignon so that every feature and emotion showed to telling effect, feet formed in glowing arches, as if to stamp herself indelibly onto her daughter's soul. "You must understand, dearest, the steps come from the grandest tradition in Europe: Petipa and Pavlova, the Kirov and Bolshoi and Vaganova Academy, and Diaghilev, Nijinsky, and, oh, the Ballets Russes—an art of purest grace and revolutionary ardor that connects us with the distilled genius of Russian civilization. Let me show you again, and this time, dear, get it fucking right. And don't worry about the other girls; they don't have the talent you do. Talent trumps all. They'll be happier, anyway, as waitresses and adornments for rich bankers." She knew her mother was capable of murder, if not of the body, certainly the soul.

The gondola turned in an easy arc and glided into a side canal. Dark stone walls teetered above us, as if we'd slipped into a narrow grave with just a crack of starlight.

She sighed. "I was wondering if my mother will try to charm the pants off you, or scare you off . . . or worse."

Her hand gripped mine. Shadows hid her face. Then her voice echoed like an offstage voice in an opera.

"Do you ever worry about *being* the person you were . . . *meant* to be?"

"Like in Plato, in the *Meno*."

"How's that?"

"In Plato's *Meno*, true knowledge—or knowledge—of yourself, you see—was understood as remembering ideas from a previous existence."

"I knew"—she laughed—"I could count on you."

"Dependable me."

"So, then it does matter . . . if she admits the truth."

"Not as long as we have each other."

We drifted in silence.

"That's why Max wanted to return to Venice, that it might save us. Like he always said, because it never changes, you can find some part of you that never changes—the better part, that which age and bad choices can't fuck up. He hated getting older, you know, like he always said: 'But my narrator is a young man; he can't age. He'll lose his edge if he gets old.'"

Hearing her perfect imitation of Max's voice was so uncanny, I had to laugh.

"So he wrote a novel, about you, about Venice, about himself as an ageless young lover."

I hoped I wasn't being a gracious loser.

The gondola swung into a series of tight turns, as if sucked by a riptide, through a maze of tiny canals. Gesticulating, low-voiced, Piranessian figures hurried over bridges and disappeared. It was like drifting on wings of antique silence. Then around a final turn, the ornate arch of the Bridge of Sighs appeared at the end of a high passage of rusticated stonework, a palace and prison on either side.

She said with sympathy, "Thank you for doing this for me."

"Aye-aye, captain."

The great ivory span loomed before us. Somewhere down the piazza, music played.

"Shall we do this thing?" she said, turning her luminous face to mine, a moment later engulfed in shadow.

I felt her lips on mine and I put my arms around her. Somehow it felt more like a stage kiss, as if her heart wasn't really in it. Who could blame her for being preoccupied: a repeat performance with a new leading man and Lady Macbeth lurking in the wings.

"My home Port," I whispered in her ear, half in jest. She stiffened and fell silent.

I felt the gondolier lean into his oar and we surged forward and into the clear moonlit night, gliding, surrounded by the murmurs and scents of the infinite sea.

My mother's gondola, which she was sharing with Karel's father, never reappeared that evening. Karel and I were left parentless at the gondola landing by the Gritti. I was in near panic but Karel offered an insouciant smile—"My father, the great liberal chameleon!"—put his arm around my shoulder, and led me to Palazzo Barberini, where a party was in full swing.

Old Isabella, tottering on her last legs, sniffed the air upon our entrance and retired without even shaking my hand (I believe she was dead within the year). Bobby's mother, Amaryllis, was indeed there, just released from a Bern sanatorium. I was shocked by her ravaged features, as I hadn't seen her in almost a decade. Once considered the most radical American painter in Parisian artistic circles—rumored mistress of half a dozen artists, she was so drunk that she could barely stand up as we were making the rounds of the guests. Then she confused me with my father—they'd first met at Palazzo Barberini in 1910, when Amaryllis was studying in Paris—as if she didn't even remember he'd been killed in the war. Her raven black hair had streaks of gray and was in disarray; her eyes were dull and dark-ringed, her face waxy pale and slack at the jaw—hardly the ravishing beauty of my early childhood, when she had been the life of Hermitage, hosting party after party, summer after summer, when her artist friends from New York came up to perform, to dance, to pose and paint, and drink the night away. Amaryllis's aggressive, boisterous incoherence was a terrific embarrassment, especially for Bobby, who sat at the piano, playing show tunes while we were introduced to the gathering. The guests were all Europeans of a fast arty set in various states of inebriation. Someone put a record on the Victrola of Louis "Satchmo" Armstrong, and the crowd began dancing, releasing Bobby from his piano duties.

Bobby and I shook hands, as if nothing had happened our sixth-form year at Winsted, but he moved quickly to rejoin his friends from Cambridge. Karel and I stationed ourselves in a corner of the piano nobile to watch this cavorting crowd beneath the twinkling chandeliers of Murano glass, the walls soaring with frescoes filled with rather plump angels and roly-poly cherubs. I noticed Bobby hanging around a tall, gangly Englishmen at least five years older, face of a mortician, an art historian from Cambridge, someone had told me, who was introduced to me only as Anthony, as if the first name alone was all that was required. This Anthony seemed more intent on the pictures than on the dancing, and on Bobby rather than on the gorgeous females circling like cats in heat, all in various states of dishabille. Among the dancers was the most beautiful woman I had ever laid eyes on, tall and graceful, with long reddish blond hair and flashing blue eyes, who drew the gaze of every man in the vicinity. "Suzanne Portman," Karel told me as he handed me champagne. "They say she will be the next Pavlova." Many years later in the hospital ward in Guilford, we would meet again. It was days before we remembered where we'd first laid eyes on each other. Not until our first kiss, when she finally came up for air:

"The Barberini . . ." "The dancer," I replied, and again I found her lips. I have never forgotten how she looked that evening, a beacon of light even in star-encrusted Venice. I had been too shy to ask her to dance.

Later, Karel and I, now joined by a sheepish Bobby, clutching glasses of bubbly, escaped the crowd on the dance floor and went out onto the balcony. Karel and Bobby soon became quite chummy but shared little except enthusiasm for Stalin's Five-Year Plan. I was worried about what had happened to my mother, inspecting every passing gondola in hopes she might turn up. But soon, after Karel plied me with a second or third glass of champagne, we got into a rapt conversation about the well-traveled griffins that bracketed the balustrade of the balcony. We speculated on the griffins while fingering the worn carving, the mane and nubby wings, as if they were domestic pugs purring at our indulgence. I was at the height of my fervor for Homer's *Odyssey*, as was Karel, after a summer with Nigel Bennett's team at Knossos, when we turned up yet more Linear B tablets; unfired, they were friable as autumn leaves and left us mad with curiosity about what tales they might tell, as did stray bits of *spolia* discovered in far-flung corners of Venice. For two weeks, we had been like terriers sniffing the air for prey.

As we stood at the balcony railing, Karel put his arm around my shoulder and launched into more shoptalk, as if to further exclude Bobby. I remember how he pointed toward the Salute, or beyond the Salute to the wide Adriatic—southward, to Greece and the islands from which we'd just sailed, telling me in a slurred voice how our future lay there. "Homer, the world of Homer and the Greek Bronze Age, which the great Schliemann revealed to the world, beckons us! Think of the stories yet to be told of the golden age of heroes, when Crete and Mycenae and Pylos were at their height. Crete—perhaps the kingdom of Atlantis, the blessed isles—maybe Homer's Phaeacia, where ideas of justice and equality were first born to human civilization. As Marx had it, 'From each according to his ability, to each according to his needs.' Imagine, my American friend, the fame, the crown of laurels to the man who reveals that lost world of our common humanity."

With a raised glass to mine, Karel, sensing something of the family history between us, gave my cousin Bobby a significant look, as if to signal that our senior partnership was the only one that really mattered. And so we three young men toasted the future, as Karel continued to laugh off my anxious scrutiny of the passing gondolas.

Our glassed tipped skyward, we watched as Amaryllis Williams stumbled through the French doors, Gaulois in one hand, whiskey in the other, and fell all over Bobby, slobbering kisses on her son.

"What do you think of that splendid Singer Sargent portrait of Isabella in the Grande Salle, boys? Such shitty bourgeois garbage should be dumped, don't you think? Only Picasso and Matisse matter now." And she turned to me as she clung to Bobby for balance. "And where's that witch of Winsted mother of yours? I've finally remembered whose viperous offspring you are. I wonder, Did she misplace her broomstick, or just hide it up her ass?"

Bobby turned red and tried to quiet her down, but to no avail.

"Your mother was quite the swimmer in her day, sneaking over to Hermitage to pose for me. But it wasn't enough—never enough; maybe that was my problem, if the carping critics are right: didn't have the balls, not like a man who can sire true art." Amaryllis came over to me and tried to kiss me, humping my leg, slobbering on my face as she ground out her cigarette on my shoulder. Her breath stank. "So what if I couldn't fuck her like a stallion and sire a specimen like you—a real man, a real son."

She threw her glass into the Grand Canal and gestured wildly, as if to that distant chorus of admirers or critics, as if to make her case; and as she did, she stumbled forward, pushed me away, and sent herself tumbling backward, over the balustrade. She sank like a rock and was a deadweight when I managed to latch onto a leg near the muddy bottom. Then she grabbed me with a death grip around my neck, as if to keep me under.

PART FIVE
ENGLAND

So tangled in the nets of love they lie,
Till man dissolves in that excess of joy.

—*Lucretius*, De Rerum Natura,
Book Four, translated by John Dryden

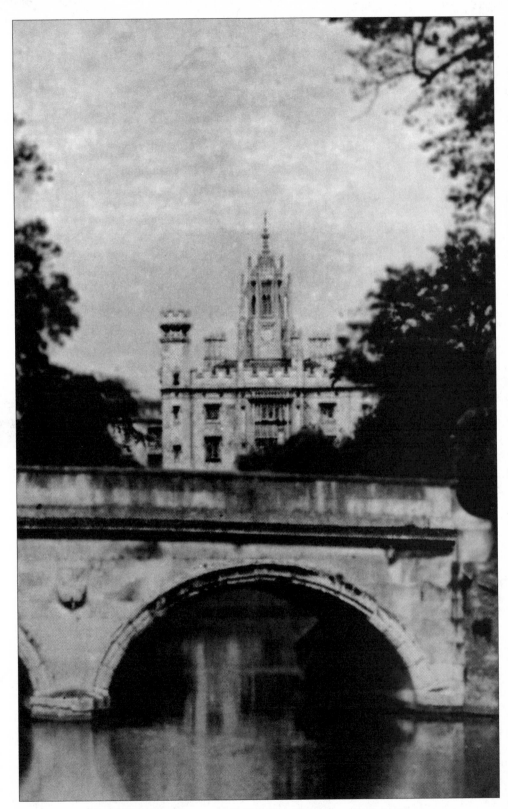

St. John's College and Trinity Bridge, Cambridge

41

WHEN I RETURNED—SOAKED, SCARED shitless, and still a little drunk—late that night to the Gritti, I knocked on my mother's door, but there was no answer. I went to my room, shivering and cold, and threw up in the toilet, then fell into bed. I barely slept, terrified at how Amaryllis had almost managed to drown me with herself, and that something awful had happened to my mother. I awoke from a nightmare to furious knocking on my door. My mother was standing there in her traveling clothes, distraught, and her eyes streaming with tears. She told me to pack and that we were taking the Paris train in one hour. She knew nothing about Amaryllis, who was in the hospital. All the way to Paris, she cried and refused to tell me anything. Nor did I want to further upset her by relating what had happened at the Barberini. Never in my life, before or since, had I witnessed my normally imperturbable mother in such a state. I was desperately worried about her, still in shock myself, and felt very much alone and helpless to aid her. Arriving in Paris, she hired a car and we drove to the American World War I Meuse-Argonne cemetery. Again, not a word. She was shaking, in such a distracted state that she was barely able to light her cigarettes. When we got to the cemetery, she told me to wait in the car. She ran off in the direction of the memorial chapel, where her husband's name was included with the missing. I followed carefully at a distance until I came in sight of her kneeling by the memorial wall of names; she was crying her eyes out, wailing like a madwoman, as if all the years of repressed grief had been released.

The experience was so traumatizing that for many years I was fearful of anything having to do with sex, which to my impressionable young

mind was a danger to body and soul, such unsated appetites the cause
of life's worst betrayals.

—excerpt from John Alden's Pankrác Prison diary

As we drove across Europe during those brilliant late December days
of 1989, as one historical era slipped away to be replaced by another
yet unknown, we felt like children headed back to childhood's rooms.
Prospects of parents, living or dead, tend to do that, as the rooms we
remember from childhood grow fewer in number but loom larger in
imagination. But it also may have had to do with the fact that we were
driving the very same route I'd driven with my grandmother in August
1964 from Venice to the American World War I Meuse-Argonne
cemetery. My father's recollections of his mother's disastrous affair in
Venice—and his saving of Amaryllis from a spectacular drowning in
the Grand Canal—and their dash to the cemetery cast a transfiguring
light over everything.

In 1964, Grandmother had hired a car and an Italian driver who
smoked these miniature cigars, *sigaro Toscano*, the kind Clint Eastwood
smoked in his early spaghetti Westerns. He chatted away like Marcello
Mastroianni about how Italian labor unions were ruining the country,
as Grandmother and I sat together in the backseat. On doctor's orders,
she'd given up cigarettes years before, but sucking in the driver's smoke
seemed to make her giddy with desire, and she, neglecting her grandson, flirted shamelessly with this animated Marcello as we made our
way across Italy and into France, then through the wine country of
Burgundy and, northeast of Paris, to the American cemetery, where
her husband's name was carved on a marble wall of the missing. Her
husband's body had been atomized. She had to have known it was her
last visit.

Twenty-five years later, entering that vast cemetery where fourteen
thousand white crosses—corralled between tree-lined enclosures—
march silently in place on immaculate fields of green . . . well, it just
seemed to kick the bottom out of us. Laura was crying before I was;
even as I was still busy reliving my first experience there with my
grandmother only six months before her death late that fall of '64.
Everything was exactly the same except some of the trees lining the
enclosures had filled out and were a bit taller. But as we walked along
the lines of white crosses and then made our way to the chapel and covered loggias where the names of the missing were carved, I realized that

things were not exactly the same: We were alone—no flags or flowers recently placed on the graves. Twenty-five years before, in August of 1964, fifty years after the start of World War I—with Americans just beginning to die in numbers in Vietnam, my grandmother and I encountered a smattering of careworn elderly ladies and hobbling veterans, wives and comrades of the fallen, the kind of total strangers that my eagle-eyed grandmother had fallen upon like the oldest of old friends. I remembered one eighty-year-old widow from a town in Iowa, who'd managed to stuff herself into a fashionable silk chartreuse dress from the twenties, hurtling down the path between the enclosures and practically colliding with my grandmother in a tearful embrace. After standing together for ten minutes, holding hands and futilely exchanging names, these total strangers parted forever.

"That dress—really!" was all grandmother could say by way of making sense of her unbridled display in front of her gawking grandson.

As Laura and I wandered the fields of crosses, a realization loomed up from the changing geometries of angled white on green: most of these men's widows, like my grandmother, would now be long dead. And how many of their scanty brew of sons and daughters would still be alive? Who would be left who had actually known and loved these young men under their lonely white crosses? Such questions seemed to make the immensity of the disaster—the absolute chaos of the trenches—the rattle of Maschinengewehr 08's and shriek of shells—tucked into such a peaceful ordering of stark symbols all the more chilling to contemplate. For an instant, I was returned to another shrine of civic remembrance, the Parthenon, where I'd recently taken Laura, where the Athenians, too, had tried to heal their terror of violent chaos by imposing monumental order. I shivered, feeling some irrevocable shift in my sensibilities. I wanted to tell myself that maybe it was a good thing that such a sea of human grief had seeped dry, as it had on the Acropolis. *Wailing like a madwoman* . . . as the widows of Athens during the Panathenaea, summoned by Praxithea, wife of King Erechtheus, had sounded the shrill cry of the *ololugmata* to invoke Athena's protection of the city. Perhaps it was only the holiday season, and the living preoccupied with sorting the last remnants of World War I carnage, and perhaps with spring the last of the widows in their wheelchairs, on their walkers . . . for one last rendezvous with the beloved.

We wiped our tears, and our breath dispersed in the chilly afternoon as more clouds rolled in from the west.

We found my grandfather's name among the more than nine hundred names of the missing in the huge marble panel under a walkway of Romanesque columns beside the cemetery chapel. Silently, we stood holding hands. My grandfather had not really been missing; they knew exactly where he had been standing at an operating table when the five-hundred-pound shell made a direct hit: a red mist, nothing left to label. Then, as if spurred by some sudden need, Laura gripped my hand tighter and reached up to the carved letters. Something in her reaching fingers and perfectly manicured nails, the ragged crimson sleeve of her sweater, and the silver Navajo rings of lapis lazuli spoke to our solidarity, as had Max's hand when he reached up to my father's memorial in the ambulatory of the Winsted chapel: *By Their Fruits Ye Shall Know Them*.

Seeing the woman I loved fingering the carved name of a man she'd never known on a chilly December day under a leaden French sky, letters in stone like symbols on a clay tablet, yearning to speak, to tell the story of a lost life, of a life cut short, and only one of so many thousands of lives of men who might have done wonderful and brilliant things, and even saved the world from the twentieth century, I realized that my story, our story, had been set in motion by the black hole of my grandfather's unfinished life. His unfulfilled aspirations filled his letters from France to his anxious young wife and father, the general, who had made him swear never to join the army, who thought the war in Europe would prove a disaster for civilization because he remembered what concentrated rifle fire had done to his men at Antietam, and knew how much better the British Maxim machine guns—spitting five hundred rounds a minute—had managed it: mowing down more than 25,000 mounted Sudanese cavalry at Omdurman on September 2, 1898. But his son, the brilliant Harvard Medical School surgeon, had enlisted in the army medical corps. "The only thing that gets me through the slaughterhouse of my days, and the suffering these imbecilic and callous generals on all sides have inflicted on our boys, is the hope of saving lives hour after bloody hour, day by excruciating day, and developing radical new surgical techniques that might well save millions more once I can get them into the medical journals and textbooks and put into common practice. I experiment like a madman with the devil's own spawn," he wrote.

He never did so, as Theo Colson never got to make good on the sacrifices of all his boys, nor Nestor to make sense of the sheer barbaric cruelty inflicted by their own kind on his countrymen, nor my father to make amends for what was unamendable. As General Alden realized only too well when he visited the graves of his men in the Winsted cemetery: justice left undone. As do I when I touch Theo's name carved in black marble on the Washington mall.

Walking the lines of white crosses on our return to the Land Rover, I was more in awe than ever of my grandmother's unyielding resolution to give meaning to her loss, sacrificing love to sink millions into her many worthy causes. A better cause, I fear, than fugitive words in a prison diary, or hoarded lies in love letters, or tantalizing symbols on a clay tablet, or the deceptions that fill even the finest fiction. Unlike her son, she left no diaries, no explanations or rationales for her life, just good works (and thousands of glowing letters from students and patients her foundations helped). So unlike my father, who seemed to struggle at every turning to make sense of the obsessions that consumed him. But love will do that. Love is relentless in justification of itself.

Life is full of baffling moments, some so baffling that we are tempted to draw wrong conclusions just to settle our minds. And worse, seeing those moments—the intervention of the capricious gods in our lives—as providing a causal chain of events that directs our destiny. Or as Lucretius wrote about human motivation: The goal of life is the enhancement of pleasure and the avoidance of pain—the hope of love that guides us. The first improbable moment came in Pylos, on the hilltop of Epano Englianos, when, as an OSS officer with the Greek Resistance, I left camp late one night and walked the few miles to the site of the 1939 excavations of Nestor's Palace. Under a blazing moon, I found, seated on an uncovered palace wall, a tall Wehrmacht captain totally engrossed (I could have walked up behind him and put a bullet through his head with my pistol, as I might have been tempted to do, given the circumstances) in examining a clay tablet cradled in his hands. But those hands were so full of love that instead I laughed hysterically as I put my arms around my old friend and hugged him to my chest. How many Americans can say, at least after 1941, that the first German they met on the continent of Europe was greeted with an embrace? Of course, my friend will complain that he was not really German, a touch of Austrian perhaps but really Jewish, or possibly a bit of a Bohemian Czech, but a Communist through and through and so above such petty issues of ethnic origins and nationality. Or perhaps scholars should have no nationality: we seekers after ultimate enduring truths, circumspect to a fault, though viciously territorial. But what could I say to my friend: He had the goods, the goods for which I had paid so dearly, the goods I had searched for from Pylos to Kyparissia, to no avail. And he needed me as much as I needed him, and so a perfect misalliance was formed.

Certainly more baffling, if less improbable, than that lovers' reunion on Epano Englianos—the laws of war and unintended consequences being what they are—was the invitation that arrived only days after my return to active service at OSS in London. This was in the late spring of '44, less than a week before the Normandy landings. Actually, two invitations to the same wedding, one from the bride and one from the groom. Suzanne Portman and Bobby Williams, my lover and my erstwhile childhood friend, had independently and without consulting the other—so Suzanne stubbornly maintained—decided at the eleventh hour to invite me to their wedding. Bobby, whom I had not seen since many years before, when I dragged his mother out of the Grand Canal and gave her artificial respiration, wanted me to be his best man. Having given up his career as a concert pianist, he was now a flyboy champion of American democracy—and all man, so he was quick to assure me. While Suzanne, the woman whose arms I had left barely weeks before at the rehabilitation hospital in Guilford, just to make sure there was no misunderstanding, scribbled in the margin of her engraved invitation, "This changes nothing, my love!" My bafflement was complete!

Heading for Hillders, Colonel Fairburn's fifty-three room mansion—forty-six rooms closed and only intermittently visited since the war—we were retreating into the world of our parents at the very moment of its demise. We napped on the rough crossing of the Channel and then managed a scary drive on foggy and icy motorways, clinging for dear life to the left-hand lane all the way from Dover to Midhurst. The whole thing had the feel of a half-run race, only to find yourself stranded in no-man's-land with no finish line in sight. It was the last time in our lives we felt like children: our own past in a bleary limbo, our own failures inundated by the failures of those who bore us, and a hazy future still up for grabs. Or perhaps it was the creeping realization, though long suspected, and confirmed moments after the wheels of my Land Rover sounded on the white gravel drive of Colonel Fairburn's vast Tudor mansion in the South Downs, that the role of our godfather and his lover in this little drama we thought of as our own, in effect, had been an extemporaneous affair all along. They had simply winged it, managed an unfolding disaster of deceit and deception by an elaborate sideshow, while the main attraction, the England of their childhood and youth, was put into mothballs until their return. And for good reason: Suzanne would probably have been arrested because of her ties to Kim Philby. With Bobby's suicide, the burning of Hermitage, and the exhaustion of the Williamses' fortune—"and when she gave up on my career," Laura would note—the habitual certitudes of a rural, "country," as the English would say, life once again sounded its virtues. What our remaining role in their torturous past might entail was the subject on offer. But the sadness of it all still leaves me aghast, for if we were treated like children, or at least remembered as the children we once were, it was because children, too, had once been a part of that vast mothballed country house and were no more.

"Well, better late than never."

Charles Fairburn, shouting his greeting, stood in front of the lamp-lit medieval portico, then strode full of purpose to the passenger door to embrace his wayward daughter. Holding Laura at arm's length, he set the ground rules. "Suzanne has been through one hell of an upset, a terrible year. The accusations in the trial laid her very low; hopes about you are what kept her going. You must give her a chance; you owe her that much. Give her a chance to explain herself. She needs you now, more than she's ever needed anyone, including me."

I hadn't seen Charles in years and most of our desultory correspondence had been perfunctory: a kind note about a book review, a birthday card, and his foreword to my *History of Athens in the Age of Pericles*. Suzanne had been his mistress for well over thirty years, and, if Laura was to be believed, he was just one of the legion of lovers who had replaced my father. But now they were married and the recent trials and impending old age had brought them solidly to roost. Charles was well preserved: slower, but still wiry and agile, and, even in his seventies, he retained a winning elegance, displayed in spades that Christmas Eve, dressed as he was in his hunter's red dinner jacket with wide black satin lapels and a sprig of holly berries, a touch of the twenties, of family traditions not quite forgone, when his family had been a big deal in British political and industrial circles. His thin ginger moustache crinkled with a hint of chagrin as we shook hands. His hair, more silver-gray than reddish blond, was brushed back in discreet waves to dangle in curlicues on the satin collar of his jacket.

"You'll need to give her a few minutes alone with her mother—hate to say it, but you're a bit of a distraction right now."

Those words were hardly a jolt, not because of their perfect aptness, but because it was borne in upon me, with Elliot's theatrical analogies bubbling in my head, that I had no idea if Charles had been Suzanne's enabler all these years, her bad conscience, or MI5's watchdog. His guilty role was what I'd come for, especially as it might pertain to his mentor—and my father's—at Cambridge, Nigel Bennett. Suzanne's, too, it went without saying; a thing of labyrinthine betrayal.

I was glad of the momentary neglect to go along with my well-broken-in second-fiddle status. I was just as happy to retreat to the wings and make out what I could of the moonlit frosted lawns spread to distant tree lines, while, closer to hand, magnificent stands of rho-dodendrons glittered in amorphous blurs of olive iridescence. Though I had to smile at the transformation Laura underwent; her head suddenly drooping, she looked tired and defeated, something like a disoriented child awakened suddenly at the end of a long drive. The dancer's high carriage had been deflated to an adolescent slouch in anticipation of the worst. Then, after a few more prompts from Charles, with a snap of her head and an audible grunt, she pulled herself to full height and strode forward to get the thing done.

So, while Charles and Laura went ahead, I hung back in the lighted hallway, poking my head into drawing rooms and galleries with dust-sheet-draped furniture and portraits of Victorian vintage displaying stern but astute faces where they glimmered opaquely on the dam-ask and paneled walls. What did truly distract me was a grouping of gold-matted watercolors and drawings of the Parthenon. I couldn't believe what I was seeing. It was one of the most famous groups of archaeological drawings by an English artist of the eighteenth cen-tury. Executed in 1763, the drawings showed the Parthenon still largely intact, converted to a mosque, before being blown up years later, in 1786, when a Venetian artillery shell touched off a Turkish powder magazine stored inside. I'd seen vague and dated black-and-white reproductions of these works, but the originals had been missing for a century. Scholars at Princeton had been searching for them since before the war because of the details they offered of the sculptural friezes, especially those on the east depicting Erechtheus and his daughters, before they suffered damage in the explosion. These watercolors and drawings were both precious artworks and critical documents, which

Charles had clearly been unwilling to share with the profession, either because of scholarly parsimony or because he didn't want to admit the family's wealth of artifacts. Touching the glass of one framed watercolor of the friezes, Erechtheus with his wife and three daughters, I found it to be filthy dirty, my finger tip uncovering a splendidly preserved snapshot of recovered time that fairly took my breath away.

And yet, after the Meuse-Argonne cemetery, it made me infinitely sad: The thing I had once loved had lost all savor . . . and I couldn't quite understand why.

As if in a daze, I could hear raised and querulous women's voices from a brightly lit room down the hall, but the discovery of those lost watercolors had taken me down a notch, the realization how both Charles and I had retreated from the distant Mycenaean Bronze Age to the post–Dark Ages uplands of the classical world, which the Parthenon had always exemplified, with its ideas of moderation, proportion, restraint, and avoidance of excess, summed up in the ideal of *sophrosyne*: discretion, temperance, self-control. It was as if we had both instinctively withdrawn ourselves from the field of Greek Bronze Age studies on the fault line of recorded history, which had so inspired my father. Something that was confirmed as I peeked into other darkened rooms, where I caught glimpses of more splendid classical artifacts, things of museum quality, examples of red- and black-figure pottery in cabinets and fragments of Athenian and Corinthian tomb sculpture. I passed bookshelves full of Victorian archaeological journals and engineering quarterlies from various royal societies. Hushing my cat-burglar footsteps were tattered Persian carpets worn smooth from use. And there was the all-pervasive smell of beeswax; armies of cleaners must have been brought in to spruce the place up for the return of master and mistress.

And yet it all added to my disillusionment: that the ordered uplands, like all uplands, as the Proplaia on the Acropolis had been built upon cyclopean walls of a dark Mycenaean past, might obscure the foundations of the old, but the same dark powers of chaos are rarely supplanted and will take their toll again and again and again.

Finally, Charles came to break my brooding spell and extracted me from his treasure trove and ushered me forward: "Into the melee, young man. Looks like you've—and don't mention Bobby's suicide, please—put the cat among the pigeons."

I, naturally, at least since Winsted days, suspected that Charles's diffidence toward me over the years had been due to my father's being a rival for the love of the colonel's life. But I was wrong and Laura spot-on about her mother's guileless expertise at misdirection: He had no idea—well, almost no idea. And so the issue of Laura's paternity hung like fire between us: four Kabuki dancers circling the question as mother and daughter maneuvered for advantage. With the Pankrác diary, the love letters, and Elliot's revelations, Laura and I could have easily ruined what little was left of their lives. Even without the bomb-shell Laura still held back from me. All it would have taken would have been a deft query about Kim Philby or the nature of "Firebird's" relationship with Melinda Maclean in New York after the war; leave my father out of it. About the love letters, Charles had not an inkling.

"Don't you dare . . . don't *you* dare."

These stinging rebukes of Suzanne's met us as we entered the vast living room, where mother and daughter had taken advantage of their few moments of privacy to get at brass tacks. Suzanne was standing with her back to the fireplace with a glass of champagne, imperiously eyeing her daughter. The instant we appeared, Suzanne lapsed into silence. Charles waved me forward and removed himself from the line of fire to get me a glass of bubbly. Suzanne bristled, the pleats of her white wool skirt seeming to vibrate and her older woman's blue eyes widening and becoming tense with something akin to a controlled burn. Then a change came over her—a nanosecond, but it was there, because Laura saw it, too, and knew it when she saw it, swiveling to meet my eyes as I approached her mother: *Keep your head down and wits about you.*

But Suzanne had already released the jib and was off on a new tack.

"Peter, I hear you've been unwell—but better. Come and kiss me and tell me about all your misadventures."

As I strode forward, no spring chicken and a little crooked from two days of nonstop driving, something in me wanted to deny the aged woman by the fire, as if a transfusion of forgiveness from the healthy-looking daughter at her elbow might yet save her. I realized how enamored I'd become of the ageless diva mother in Max's *Gardens*. Suzanne's gray-blue eyes dilated at my approach, and every angle in her face tensed; the jawline in particular firmed as it rose toward me to present her fine English nose and rose-blushed cheeks, as if testing the new direction of the wind. She ignored my hand and embraced me, a reserved and matronly embrace, holding me for seconds and whispering in my ear below the crackle of the fire, "Don't you dare mention anything about your father and me—nothing!" She smiled sweetly. She might have bitten my ear off. If I had found her an older version of her daughter, she must have found me at about the same age my father had been on their final confrontation at Elysium, when he had abandoned my mother's bed to meet her by the lake beneath the white pine in the old pasture. But if she was struggling with the ghost of her lost lover, she camouflaged it beautifully with a stream of small talk that banished such threatening subject matter. I saw Laura roll her eyes as she endured her mother's meticulous rewriting of the story of their lives, Suzanne developing a narrative line that would leave her and Charles—the seemingly clueless Charles—a happily married pair at the end of their expatriate lives. The foundation myth of that tale was a happy childhood at Hillders: a retreat for illustrious military and industrial families that had served England well since the early days of Queen Victoria.

Suzanne, as if recognizing the difficult editing job ahead, retreated to the sofa for a breather and relieved herself of her stunning ruby red high-heeled pumps. She rubbed her feet and placed herself on the front edge of the cushion in case she needed to spring into action again.

"We've been glued to the television for weeks since the wedding," Charles said as he moved to add a couple of logs to the fire. "One really can't believe the Berlin Wall is finished."

"Thank God you're safe," added Suzanne.

"We want to hear about all your adventures and how you managed it," Charles declared. "Do you think Romania might be next? Will Gorbachev last—or will the whole damn house of cards just come tumbling in?"

I noticed his nonchalant glance at Suzanne on the sofa: Was he softening her up for the coup de grâce?

Before the fire, voluptuous bronze andirons of rearing centaurs embracing nude maidens, freshly polished, glittered in the renewed blaze like a set piece from *The Rape of the Sabine Women*. Laura moved a step back from the heat while her mother gazed with new fixity from the sofa, flickering orange highlights spreading across her sunken cheeks, detonating in sharp glimmers of sapphire in her eyes. Her hair was brassy and short and hung in a limp fringe. On closer inspection, she did not look well. Something in me cried out against the depredations of aging.

"Yes, yes . . . ," Suzanne added in an unsteady voice, an almost kindly nod in my direction. "Momentous, like the invasion of Normandy—don't you think, Charles? When the fate of the world hung in the balance, when all our lives hung suspended in anticipation of the final blow to fascism." She turned to her daughter. "When Bobby and I were married here just days before the balloon went up—right here at Hillders."

Charles immediately came to attention, as if this sudden concession to their official history had not been part of the game plan. "Yes indeed, a grand occasion . . . perfect weather for the ceremony in the garden."

"Oh yes, the sunshine and the roses, almost as if the war were just a bad dream . . . or perhaps the herald of a better dawn."

The colonel glanced back from the flames as if from a happy vision. "An oasis of fond hopes in the midst of war." He smiled adoringly at Laura, as if he grasped the gist of Suzanne's strategy for a shift in allegiance. "You should have seen your mother as a bride back then, a Titania, queen of the May. We collected everybody's ration coupons and scrounged up wine and champagne and a wedding cake like no one had seen for years." Charles patted his wife's shoulder. "And she looked as beautiful at *our* wedding here in the Midhurst town hall a month ago."

"Thank you, my dear, but don't overstate the case. It's enough we still care to share the same bed."

Laura flashed a look at my silent face, as if to say, *Are we really going to let them get away with this bullshit?*

"Why, just the other day up in London," Charles said, " I ran into a chap, an old colleague—hadn't seen him in thirty years—and the first thing out of the fellow was a remark about the wedding. 'Horrible spring weather in '44, but for that one day, kept me going for years.' That's how he put it."

Suzanne, attuned to her daughter's irritation and the pitfalls of the subject at hand, nodded to me as she carefully lit a backfire to aid the defense. "Peter, your father was best man, of course, since he and my first husband were childhood friends—founding Winsted families and all that. He arrived with a cane, remember, Charles? He needed a cane to get around. And you were showing him the rhododendrons—how many varieties are there?"

"Eighty-three," said Charles as he refilled her glass.

She reached to her new husband's arm in a gesture of almost child-like excitement. "Oh, I can't wait for bloom time in the spring."

I saw Laura flinch at the note of happiness in her mother's voice, as if to say, *No you don't, Mother; it's my turn.*

Time had now given Laura the advantage. Seeing Suzanne, I realized how much healthier Laura looked than when she'd first arrived on Delos, and not a little like the way I remembered Suzanne sitting in the chapel on the morning of our confirmation, a scene preserved with exquisite verisimilitude in the pages of *Like a Forgotten Angel.* Laura was biding her time, standing straight and tall, an imperious sparkle in her blue eyes. Even in jeans and a sweatshirt, her natural elegance came to the fore, her long nose, like her mother's, emphasizing the crease in her brow, a crease that tightened and became elongated as she pensively planned her next moves. Unconsciously, she flexed her right knee. Again and again I saw her mother's eyes flicker in the direction of the knee: the trainer evaluating her filly.

As Laura put it to me as went up to our separate rooms to change for dinner, "She's gauging if there is one last race—one last season—in me before I'm put out to pasture."

And so our little minuet was played out. And to give Charles due credit, he beautifully stage-managed that Christmas Eve with gracious aplomb. I found myself almost captivated by his old-school love for both women: master of ceremonies in his magnificent home and dutiful husband and father. How often over the candlelit table did he speak our names with such sibilant affection, in such welcoming tones that one felt almost as if one had always belonged there. This was what Suzanne was bent on preserving, the illusion of a life that should've been. Over a Christmas Eve roast and incredible Bordeaux reds, he kept the conversation rolling, much of it a monologue on his part as he related the history of Hillders, most of it through the eyes of the teenager and young scholar he'd been before the war, as if he were intent on rerooting himself as much as his new wife and daughter.

He told us about his great-grandfather, who had founded a successful glass-making factory in the Midlands; his grandfather had expanded the business to specialty glasses for industrial and domestic use, setting up more factories in Czechoslovakia and France, the same grandfather who had purchased Hillders from the original family in 1870. Charles's father had been trained as an engineer but loved gardening and airplanes; it was he who had collected and planted the rhododendrons from all over the world, flying the plants back in his own private biplane right after World War I. Between the wars, his father had gone into politics as a Liberal member of parliament, vowing never to allow a repeat of the Great War, which had taken so many of his boyhood friends.

In the forest of candlelight from six fully loaded silver candelabra massed along the long dinner table, the colonel pointed out the family portraits on the paneled walls, including two uncles who had been killed in World War I. "Poor sods. So all the loot from all the factories went to my father, but he felt like he had his brothers' blood on his hands for the rest of his reckless life." Again and again, he gravitated to his own youth at Hillders, relating stories of the dinner guests, Lloyd George, for one, who, when he wasn't flirting with the women at the table and deep in his cups, would go on and on about the inexorable horrors of the Great War, how he'd failed to dismiss the politically entrenched Douglas Haig, and how he and the socialists and Labour Party were committed to preventing another European war.

"My father died in a flying accident in 1937, testing the new Spitfires in an ice storm. The prospect of another war devastated him. He was already a heavy drinker by then . . . when it happened," Charles said.

As to the halcyon prewar days at Hillders, he and Suzanne vied for stories of idyllic childhoods, as if to sink foundation after foundation into the wooded hilltop on the South Downs, and tuck their late marriage under a firm tent pole: a last triumph over the adversity that had denied them the obvious choice of each other as mates, which their fumbling confusion as lovesick adolescents had thwarted in the first place.

"Oh my yes, do you remember, Charles, when I'd show up with Nanny and Johnny and Margaret for the summer from dreary, awful London, when Ninette de Valois—now Dame Ninette de Valois— would allow me time off from ballet school? How we played amongst the rhododendrons and lost ourselves for what seemed days in the woods and hills. And your father would fly us to the Isle of Wight for a picnic lunch and home for dinner with the other cousins."

Charles had tears in eyes, as did his bride, as they raised their glasses to toast their new life.

"To those, family and friends, no longer with us." Suzanne and Charles stared at each other for a long moment, and I felt a world passing through their eyes. "And"—Charles turned his toast to us—"the continuity of the season and hopes for better days yet to come."

It was as if Bobby and my father and the years of woe had been officially banished.

With that, we retired to the living room, where a large Scotch pine was standing, ready to be decorated. The lights were already strung, while underneath were stacked twenty or so ratty cardboard boxes with dividers containing the glass ornaments. Charles eased himself down on stiff knees, a little unsteady from all the wine, and began opening the boxes. Something of his initial enthusiasm seemed to wane as he wrestled with recalcitrant strings and knotted ribbons, uncovering the most exquisite Christmas balls I'd ever set eyes on, each hived in its little compartment of yellowed cotton wool. There were glass angels and winged horses and bearded saints, magnificent creations of the glassblower's art, many going back to before the turn of the century, all products of the family glass factories in prewar Czechoslovakia, near Brunn, he told us. He handed us the ornaments to hang, carefully picking a few gems from each box and going on to the next, or silently pondering the contents, only to hand the box to Suzanne, commenting occasionally on certain ornaments, noting the workmanship. Some had names and dates engraved or painted on the glass. More than once I saw him take out an ornament and examine the name and replace it in the box.

These crumbling cardboard boxes and their contents were the age-less metaphors for their new narrative, the editing of which required scrutiny and tact. Therein lay preserved the half-remembered lives of people who had grown up in that house, who had walked the grounds, who had planted and enjoyed the gardens, who had slept and made love and dreamed within its walls and were no more. Their lives, or memo-ries of their lives, had to be sorted, some to be displayed gladly, others reluctantly, and some not at all.

This once-happy ritual seemed to exhaust them, and Charles and Suzanne were soon off to bed, supporting each other, as would any other long-married couple, up the broad, winding staircase. And like good children, we said good night and headed for our own rooms, less out of propriety, so it struck me, than out of a feeling that lying in each other's arms like languorous conspirators, we might goad ourselves into battles better not fought. "She's aged," Laura whispered to me, as if stricken by the very thought and the implication for her own mortality.

In my room, I quickly went to bed, where my mind filled with my father's descriptions of Suzanne's and Bobby's wedding as recorded in his prison diary. I was exhausted but could barely fall asleep, half-expecting Laura to come to me, as she said she might, "if the coast is clear." As her mother had gone to my father on her wedding night. When I did fall asleep, when I dreamed, it was of those crosses in the Meuse-Argonne cemetery and the watercolors of the Parthenon in the gold-matted frames in the downstairs hallway, as if there was no separating tombs and sacred places and the voices that call out from within, even as their widows and orphans are winnowed on the wind.

I was not simply baffled; I was stricken. The woman I was madly in love with, without so much as a word during our many weeks of furtive trysts, had presented me with a wedding invitation—a phantom invitation, if her beautiful blue script was to be believed, but an invitation, nevertheless, to witness her marriage to someone I'd come to detest. What the hell to make of such a thing? A coincidence? Was she inviting me, dropping me, or crying out for help? There was no telephone number and only a Sussex address, "Hillders," and an RSVP to one Cecily Fairburn. Could it be the wife of Charles Fairburn, a colleague from Cambridge and Crete? I wondered. Careening between heartache and curiosity, I made my way down to Hillders by train from Waterloo to Midhurst. The day was enchanting. I took a taxi to save my strength. My heart cried out at the sunken roads dappled with spring sunshine and shadowed by ancient oaks, and the hillsides of ferns and tall pines—reminders of my boyhood at Elysium—and views to the south of the purple Downs. And as the taxi wove up the steep drive, rhododendrons—a kingdom of plundered rhododendrons—a rainbow of blossoms wherever one looked. The war and bombed-out London—banished.

I was early, just in case it was all a terrible mistake and I could retreat, as if I'd never come. Standing in the driveway, surveying nature's most lavish splendor, I noticed a couple by a distant gazebo in fevered conversation. I hobbled my way toward them with my overnight bag in hand, cane in the other, the scent of rhododendrons and roses burdening the air. I recognized Suzanne before she did me, and then Charles Fairburn, indeed my colleague from Cambridge days with Nigel Bennett. I had never seen her out of her nurse's uniform. She wore a simple summer dress, her hair twisted up tight with combs, her features intent on conversation. Suddenly, like some startled woodland animal, she turned toward me—quivering and pale, clearly overwrought. I knew she recognized me, but she gave no sign as she spoke to her attentive confidant. On greeting me, she pretended I was a total stranger;

a discreet flex of her brows was all it took for me to accept the role assigned me. Charles warmly gripped my hand: "Ah, our savior!" he exclaimed, not entirely in jest. "You are just in time to save us all—we're very much in need of the services of a best man. Consider yourself enlisted." I knew Charles was with Bomber Command, and a flier since I'd known him. "Alas now grounded to my desk," he told me. He looked no worse for wear from his thirty-five missions over Germany.

Suzanne's face bore frown lines of repressed panic, but I detected a hint of gleefulness as well, and could tell she was actually pleased with herself—having thrown fate to the winds by inviting me, she was girding herself to let the thing play itself out. She shook my arm and gave it a quick viselike squeeze. I managed to throw out bland generalities until getting more of the lay of the land, unable to take my eyes off Suzanne in her sleek dress of yellow and beige silk, like an apparition from the fashion pages of years before—and even more alluring absent her nurse's uniform and the stink of the hospital wards and linen rooms where we'd hidden during our lovemaking.

Charles Fairburn, resplendent in a white suit, his red hair brilliant in the sunshine, quickly put me at ease with banter about digs past and the wedding crisis of the moment: The groom was dead drunk. Suzanne blessed me for coming to save the day—a flicker of a passionate glance as she headed for her bedroom, where her bridesmaids awaited her. I felt as if I'd been pushed onstage from the wings without costume or script, and yet, with Suzanne's eyes imprinted in my mind, I found a kind of desperate pleasure in grabbing whatever extemporaneous role was on offer. A minute later and Charles turned up with Bobby in the back garden, where the ceremony was to take place. What a change, finding him in his blue Eighth Air Force uniform, in ruddy good health and far from the hysterical, bawling son of Amaryllis who had stood watching as I managed to drag his stinking mother up the marble steps of the water entrance of the Barberini.

The moment he opened his mouth, I knew some things hadn't changed: I could smell the whiskey on his breath. He was not falling-down drunk, but Dutch-courage drunk. He grabbed my hand and then my elbow and let me know, humorously but convincingly, that he needed help to make it through the day. "That's why I invited you—a best man to stand beside me and hold my feet to the fire. I've reformed, Scout's honor; after the Nazi-Soviet nonaggression pact, I realized my utter stupidity. I was young and impressionable and taken in by Party hacks. I've changed; I'm an airman now, John, and we need something to come home to—a good woman—isn't that the point of it all? A good woman and home and children—freedom—isn't that what this

fight against the fascists is about? But Christ, after the frigid cold, and
the German 88's, and the Messerschmitts—Christ, you can't imagine
what I've gotten myself into." Bobby's face went ashen and filled with
foreboding, as if his very words had put him back 35,000 feet over Germany. I actually was sorry for him instead of feeling the jealous outrage
I had every right to, seeing that he was indeed marrying the woman I
loved. But it took only a few minutes to figure out that whatever it was
between him and Suzanne, it wasn't exactly love . . . but some sneaking
malevolence.

Anxious Bobby—delicate, sensitive, and furtive Bobby—had a
three-day furlough from hell over Germany to get hitched. His nerves,
never strong in the first place, were shot to pieces. I walked him around
the grounds and kept him from the booze, probing for the essentials
of the charade that was about to take place. Seems, according to his
garbled story, he'd met Suzanne on the train to London (a cover story
they'd concocted); Bobby laughed as he bent to smell a rhododendron
blossom, going on and on about how he'd wooed her with song, trapped
her with pity, dangled the Williamses' cash and artistic savoir faire—the
machismo Bobby of his pitiful dreams. His insouciance about Suzanne,
so perfectly in character, made me shiver with horror—as if every
instinct cried out for me to save Suzanne from such a cad. "Ah, but you
see, I've enlisted you and Elliot, and your football coach, Old Ironsides,
all my biggest fans at Winsted, to see me through, to make me the man
you people always wanted me to be. The Winsted way: freedom, justice,
love, and honor. Well, I give you love, abiding love. I want you gridiron
heroes to be witness to your creation—my transfiguration." He let out
a sodden laugh and I saw sudden fear in his eyes as he gripped my arm.
"I'm scared out of my mind, John. Our losses are terrible. I know I won't
make it, I know . . . but at least I'll have married."

Oh, the malevolent pleasure I took in that plea.

Paul Oakes came over and embraced me in his Third Army chaplin's
uniform. His fervent eyes and stentorian voice steadied us all that afternoon. He wanted to know all about Greece and my leg and regaled us
with tales of Patton in North Africa and Italy, the general then licking
his wounds in obscurity, prior to what would be the outbreak from the
Normandy beachhead a month later. As ever, Paul was a bulwark, and
between us we managed to get Bobby through.

Surrounded now by clammy prison walls, I cannot get the dazzling
picture of that glorious spring afternoon out of my mind. I yearn for
the smells of that rose-embowered ceremony, with the yew hedges as
backdrop, and all the splendid pastel colors of the women's dresses and
feathered hats. Suzanne resplendent as she strode to where Paul Oakes

waited. Charles had to give her away, since her father had died just months before and her brother, Francis, at Tobruk in '42. Charles's darling son and daughter were joint ring bearers, and his wife, the always laughing, if headstrong, Cecily, led the contingent of bridesmaids. And all the handsome cousins were attired in black-and-gray tails—those not yet posted to far-flung battlefields. I had Bobby somewhat sobered up with coffee but was prepared to catch him should he stumble, since Elliot, weeks away from seeing action behind German lines in Brittany, had eyes only for a certain beaming, giggling redheaded bridesmaid: "the fair Margaret." I watched Suzanne, hoping against hope she'd fumble the ball on the one-yard line, tears flowing down her cheeks, going through the motions like a victim to the guillotine. Bobby was literally wobbling on his knees, a dumbstruck little boy in a Christmas pageant. The masquerade was complete. I had to prompt Bobby twice on the words to his wedding vows. Suzanne kissed Bobby with a chaste and harmless kiss, which produced a sardonic laugh on Bobby's part— and the deed was done. Paul blessed them and sent them on their way.

The gathered faithful in their dress uniforms and festive gay dresses were doing their best to forget the war and buy into this fairy tale . . . the blue sky and the flowers and the banquet to come very much out of a fairy tale after years of war. Looking back, it seems so unreal, the five of us in a semicircle around Paul Oakes: Charles, happily married but with a boyhood crush on Suzanne; Bobby, still madly in love with Elliot, his boyhood crush at Winsted; me, with my battered body yearning for the sexual favors of the most powerful and seductive woman I had ever encountered—forever seductive of my better judgment; and Elliot, ever-driven and ever-practical Elliot, utterly entranced by his future wife—if not lifelong obsession—fair Margaret. And where was Suzanne in all this? I ask myself a thousand times, and so must finally take Elliot's warning at face value: "only following orders from her Soviet handlers"—so he told me years later on the banks of Lake Carnegie—so she and Bobby could more easily milk that crowd of notables on the cusp of D-day and pass on the latest technical details about the Norden bombsight.

I ransack my feeble brain to see the faces at the reception—distracted, too, by Charles's collections, trying to remember who else was there besides Philby, who danced with Suzanne for what seemed hours—since I couldn't. In Washington, he always acted as if we'd known each other in another life, as if we'd shared a family secret. I do remember Donald and Melinda Maclean; Melinda and Suzanne talked endlessly about the latest American movies. And there was a tall gangly Brit, a pompous rag doll, I didn't recognize at first, who hung all over Bobby, poking his nose into the artwork, another in that Cambridge circle; then I remembered the noted scholar "Anthony," who had visited Palazzo Barberini with Bobby, "hunting down pictures in every piss-stinking cranny and crevice of Venice."

Clearly, I was thwarted by an idiot's allegiance to decorum and a scholarly parsing of the tea leaves. What if I had just busted it up and pulled down the curtain, as Suzanne never ceased to ask; taken up arms against a sea of troubles—Elliot's mocking advice? What if I had just spirited her away and saved the day, like in the movies? What if we had married and I had taken my disability leave, with Suzanne's body to return to and not the torments of horribly botched operations and all the futile justifications of saving the world? A trade of her futile illusions for mine, absent the Williams family's curse. So might we have been left in peace, I as a Princeton professor of archaeology on the cusp of deciphering Linear B, she to resume her career on the New York ballet stage. An apartment in Manhattan, a house in Princeton, just a peaceful island life worshipping at Calypso's altar while pursuing the lost stories of the Mycenaean past, which—faithless, faithless sinner that I am—was and remains my one and only true ambition.

The next morning when I woke and went to my bedroom window of leaded glass, frosted with lemony halations as the sunlight began to burn through the fog, I saw footprints in the hoarfrost of the lawn, two pairs of footprints leading to a vast panoply of rhododendron groves. And there, where the trail of footprints ended, two women stood in Wellingtons and long green loden coats; they bent back and forth toward each other in sometimes pensive, sometimes animated conversation. The loden coat, an early Christmas present for Laura from her mother, was perfect for damp and chilly English winters. Laura had failed to come to me in the night, as I had failed to go to her. For the last time, she was trying to play the dutiful daughter to her mother. As she put it to me later, "I was going to let her hang herself, I was going to give her all the rope she needed, until I realized she could walk on air, as well."

1301 P Street

June 9, 1952

Don't you get it? It's one thing if you lied to me about your past when we first met, even if you continued lying until you were found out, but it is quite another that you continued to lie after renouncing that past to me, after you promised on everything sacred that you loved me and you'd given it up. Tell me the truth about 1948, when I was in Athens; did you continue to go to New York and meet Melinda Maclean? Did you continue to be a courier for Donald Maclean—after everything? With Maclean and Burgess now fled, presumably gone to ground in Moscow, and Philby under investigation in London, it will all come out, including your role in this debacle. And what do you know about Philby? How far back do you two go—at least to your wedding? Did you act as a courier for him, as well—even after I returned from Athens? Did it go beyond that? Mary and I were witness to a least one of your get-togethers at Hermitage—cooing—cooing like two lovesick doves. Was that to throw her off the scent? I have no right to reproach you on that score except to believe that you must have conclusive proof of his KGB spying. The damage—the lives lost—Philby and Maclean have done is beyond reckoning. I want you to think very hard about this and tell me the truth next weekend when I will be up at Elysium. Then you should consider going to the FBI and making a full confession. You can claim to be an unwitting dupe, a fellow traveler, that you always thought it was general information for the Popular Front or the Comintern. Otherwise, all our lives, much less my reputation and career, may be finished, or worse. The conviction of Alger Hiss and this awful war in Korea have changed everything.

I want the truth; I want a firm answer.

John

"You think I'm really such a monster? You think I did it all just for myself, for you to be the dancer I knew you could be?"

"I don't care anymore, Mother. I have to stop caring."

"You fed Max all those lies about me, the stage mother from hell."

Laura laughed in disbelief. "You fed him plenty yourself—you forget how for years you two were thick as thieves. Besides, he saved you; he enthroned you in literary history as an oversexed, ambitious ballet mother instead of the KGB agent you really are."

"You've become a cruel, cruel woman."

"Come on, Mother, you encouraged all Max's worst habits. You fed him disinformation about your glorious and romantic days dancing for the king. You're safe now; your fucked-up dreams are finished, so drop it."

"There are plenty of old men in this godforsaken country who would still like to send me to prison. Believe me, Charles has a half a firm of solicitors keeping them at bay."

"What did Elliot call you, 'the real Mata Hari for our times'?"

"A lousy dancer, and she wasn't even a spy, condemned by the same stupid men who used her." Suzanne shook her head with exasperation. "How can you understand if you've never been there? You like to pretend the ambition was mine, when it was really yours. I was just desperate to claw back some of the lost years and find some good after the terrible sacrifices we endured."

"Tell me what it was like to work for Soviet intelligence?"

"Is that what Elliot told you, that man who has tried to poison my life?"

"By telling the truth?"

"Truth, he seduced my friend, my childhood confidante, and got God knows how much out of her about my private affairs."

"Well, at least they were a love match, with three children, and he stood by her to the day she died of cancer."

"Oh, the ever-loyal Elliot."

"Till the day she died, and you, her childhood confidante, never even bothered to visit her in the hospital."

Suzanne tried to smile bravely and then wiped away a tear. "They told me nothing had to change. Unlike my father, they wanted me to remain dancing, to entertain the troops, you see, something to remind them of what they were fighting for. But the fascists, and my father, had other ideas."

"You never take responsibility for what you did—never, *never*, as long as I've known you."

Suzanne brought her face forward, as if needing to confront her daughter, a pensive half smile quivering on her chapped lips as her frozen breath drifted off. She motioned skyward, as if in half salute to a pair of contrails out of Gatwick, like skate marks on fresh ice.

"You live a secondhand life, a bubble of celebrity—you were never *there*."

"Was Kim Philby part of that glorious world of art and artists, the Cambridge crowd of aesthetes—the Apostles, right? Your brother, who was killed, was part of that, too? Tell me the fucking truth before I go crazy. Were you still lovers when John Alden was stationed in Washington after Athens?"

"It was a fall like this, sunny and crisp and clear. I remember the exact moment, walking along the Thames Embankment, a little tired from rehearsals. Then I realized there was a soft, constant noise, so low and distant that I hadn't even recognized it. I looked down the river, to the east, and discovered way up in that flawless china blue September sky these tiny pinpricks of silver light, glinting ever so brightly, little airplanes flying in perfect formation, like toys on display in a shop window. Oh, such a lovely parade of silver airplanes sailing across our blue sky. There was something quite compelling about them, enough that I stopped by the railing and just stared. People had been talking about them for months. I remember thinking, So, those are the little German bombers everyone has been afraid of and nothing has ever happened. Even after they removed all the pictures from the National Gallery.

"It was like whispers, when they first fell, very precise thumps. Then puffs of white began to curl up from the distant skyline, the thin strands beginning to find one another, until a bulging mushroom cloud had formed. I was completely rooted, fascinated. Nearby streets began to fill with sirens and fire engines, the noise sucked east in a fury. I felt this impulse to do something—but what? I couldn't tear myself away from the scene, as if I were at some grand theater of the wide world, some vast Turner deluge at the Tate, and taken out of myself. Especially when that cloud of white began to blacken around the edges, and then, as the afternoon dimmed, turning an ugly red, like a great ugly sore in the sky. It was so compelling, so peculiar, almost as if there were two sunsets on the Thames, one in the east and one in the west, the one in the east growing like an inflamed tumor, and then as evening came on, staining the river with an oily bloodred sheen, as if the wounded city had begun to hemorrhage. I could smell the burning by then. It was the beginning, you see, when the smell of burning never left the city. During all the years of the blackout, it was the way London smelled—it *was* the city. To me, the Nazis always had a smell to them: it was that of burnt things . . . of burnt young men and cities . . . and my husband.

"When I finally made it home to Cadogan Gardens, I found my father impatiently waiting for me—not that he was worried for my safety. His war-office staff car, with engine running, was waiting at the front door. He was at his desk in his study, dashing off telegram after telegram. He looked up at me with a face filled with exuberance now that his war had finally come to our doorstep. No more of our little conversations, my dear, no more sweet hints and encouragements. *The war has come for you, too, my dear.* He took me roughly by the arm and bought his lips to my face: 'For once and for all, I hope this puts a stop to your childish enthusiasms for your Red pals: Those German bombers are allied with the Soviet Union, fueled from Soviet oil fields, and right now they are killing our people.' With that, he marched me straight to his staff car and drove me directly to Saint Michael's Hospital, where he'd insisted I train two days a week over the previous six months. The first victims of the bombing in the East End were being received. My father turned me over to the head nurse, an old friend from their days together at a field hospital on the Somme. Millicent was the most terrible bitch I have ever known, but she knew how to save lives. She started me with the injured children and later with the burn victims."

Suzanne turned back to her daughter and made a theatrical curtsy, as if to an audience at curtain call.

"That's when it began," she went on, "for five weary years. And then all the years taking care of—well, I suppose you're thrilled to finally know Bobby's not your father. I guess that's the point of all this."

"You used him, Mother, just like you used everybody else. Was it to get information on that bombsight, or get to America, or just to get your hands on their money?"

Her mother snorted in disbelief.

"I thought I raised you to be smarter than that. I gave you fine books to read; even Max wouldn't have come up with such tired scenarios. What happened to that grand imagination you once had, that fire and spirit that allowed you to dance rings around all those vapid girls in New York? You've become such a hard woman, and without insight— are you really *off* the medications?"

"It's been weeks."

"Thank God for small miracles."

"So now you're using moneybags Charles."

"Using him—I'm trying to save him."

"Just like Daddy—Bobby—fuck sake, what else do I call him?"

"Men . . . so disappointing, and then they turn out to be such weaklings. Oh, they strut and sound off, but when the chips are down, they blame us and then look to us to pick up the pieces."

"Did it come down to that in the end, blackmailing your lover John Alden, keeping him near enough the roost to prevent him from exposing you?" Laura shook her head. "Should I be thanking you or hating you? What am I to think? Do I get any say in who my father turns out to be?"

Suzanne laughed.

"Oh, such a plea might rattle down the ages; should we ever be granted such choices."

"You *will* tell me?"

"I got you here, didn't I?"

"And got yourself off from the grand jury. How did you convince them that it wasn't you and Charles who ordered the bullets for Bobby's pistol, that oh so convenient Federal Express delivery?"

"Don't demean yourself further; you'll only embarrass yourself."

"The gun store in Dayton, the owner said a man on the phone with a slightly foreign accent put in a phone order for the ammunition to be shipped to Hermitage, paid in cash and delivered by Federal Express. Just wondering how you two managed it."

"Your capacity for fantasy is remarkable, onstage and off."

"The day after Kim Philby's death in Moscow made it to the front page of *The New York Times*. Taking your secret life to his grave. What, a call to a comrade at the Soviet embassy to relieve you of a burdensome cripple and traitor to the cause?"

"Dear, you hallucinate."

"And Mother, it wasn't your father who forced you into nursing; that was probably Philby, too—perfect for scrounging information from wounded soldiers; perfect, too, for a courier of secrets into and out of London."

"Is that Elliot talking, filling your head with garbage?"

"Mother, your memory is going. I've got the letters—I've got Philby's goddamn autobiography signed and inscribed to you. *And* the documents. *And* the photo—Christ!—the photo of me as a little girl."

They began walking again along well-laid-out paths that Suzanne had walked thousands of times as a child. "You think I never loved Bobby? You, my dear, only knew the shadow of the man I once knew." The familiar surroundings, as Laura remembered it later, seemed to give her mother strength and allowed her to spin her lies with growing conviction. "I met Bobby on a train. I had a few days' leave from the rehabilitation hospital in Guilford and I was returning to London. I was at rock bottom. I was depressed. I had gained weight and hadn't even taken a ballet class in two years. Bobby was sitting across from me in his smart American uniform, looking out the window of the carriage at those awful drab blocks of South London before Waterloo station. Many of the blocks had been bombed to dust in the Blitz. You could see entire buildings standing open to the sky, rooms stacked one upon the next, as if the side of a doll's house had been opened. All those lives . . . The roadways were filthy with gritty plaster and mud. I remember Bobby's face reflected upon that wasteland in the window. He was nice-looking, perhaps not handsome in a classic way, and his jaw was a trifle short. But unlike so many of the Americans who had trooped into our midst, he was quiet and reserved, and I thought, looking at his luminous face in the window, sad, as I was sad, at the sheer waste of it all. Some of us had hoped for big changes before the war, that the world might be put to rights, and now that, too, seemed a near disaster. The Americans were throwing their dollars around as if they owned the world."

"You've gone up on your lines again, Mother. Remember, the Germans invaded the Soviet Union and we were all on the same side again—well, sort of. And you met him at a party thrown by an intelligence officer of the Soviet embassy."

"Did I tell you that?"

"Christ, I thought you were supposed to be off the booze; you can't even keep your lies straight."

"They were our allies, then; they had most of the burden of the war on their shoulders."

"For crying out loud, Mother, the Berlin Wall is down—it's finished; everything you lied for is finished. Can't you ever stop? It's a lost cause. Just like now, I'm one more of your lost causes."

"But you look splendid. I haven't seen you looking so well in years. I can get you back with ABT. The régisseurs are old friends."

"Did you tell them about my knee?"

"They know about the knee; they're more concerned about the cocaine."

"I told you, I'm clean. I haven't touched a cigarette in three weeks."

"They're planning a revival of Tudor's *The Leaves Are Fading*. It's not difficult, not the Rose Adagio, more acting than pyrotechnics. It needs a mature woman who can get at the layered emotions."

"Mother, you forget, I premiered it with Gelsey Kirkland in 1975."

"Like yesterday, yes, yes . . . of course."

They came to a point on the hilltop that offered a view of the South Downs scudding in misty hummocks of tan and olive toward the invisible Channel.

"Mother, let's talk about my father, not what's left of my career. Tell me the truth, I don't care about the spying—Peter does, but I don't— just tell me about my father and you; that's all I really care about. Just as long as it's not Kim Philby; that, I couldn't take."

"I was an idealist, and a virgin to boot. I know that doesn't fit in with your agenda, or, God knows, Max's in his filthy novel—the stage mother from central casting. I had a glorious life as a girl and then in ballet, a world filled with the most fit and beautiful and strong bodies, people full of love and passion to change the world. Then the tiny silver airplanes arrived and I found myself stuck in a place filled with an inexhaustible supply of mutilated young men. Shall I draw on a cliché that even you might understand? Bobby was my Ashley Wilkes, John my Rhett Butler. And Bobby and I did take a train together, except it was coming back from a meeting with our handler in Brighton."

"Oh Mother, that sounds intriguing—you're getting it all mixed up with *Brief Encounter,* or is it *Waterloo Bridge,* another one of your fantasies? If you go on like this, you'll make me sick. Just stick with Cambridge, for God's sake."

"All I wanted was to escape the deathly stench of the hospital. Bobby was educated, polished, from money . . . and he knew London almost as well as I did from the years before the war, when he'd played recitals in town. Now he was a bombardier on a B-17—a concert pianist! I suppose no more ridiculous than a ballerina being a nurse. The war was like that, you see. But underneath we tried to hold on to our essential humanity; otherwise, we'd have been lost. That was the real trick; that's what we loved in each other—that secret life in the anti-fascist cause."

"Mother, you met Bobby Williams in the early thirties in Venice, at Palazzo Barberini, or was it before, at Cambridge? Anthony Blunt was there in Venice; he probably introduced you. And Bobby was gay— surely you knew, of all people in our business."

"You know I took him home to Cadogan Gardens after our handler insisted that we marry. Only Maggie, our ancient housekeeper, was at home. My father had died of a heart attack six months before, literally working himself to death over preparations for the invasion of France. Mother was off on one of her Catholic relief efforts in Birmingham. Francis, my brother, had died at Tobruk. Father had been so bloody proud of Francis. Our family had certainly done our bit. I had Maggie make Bobby some tea while I went up stairs to bathe and change. I scrubbed myself raw with scalding water to get out that hospital stink. I wanted to be fresh and beautiful and drown myself in a good time. I had trouble finding an old dress that would still fit, but I managed to squeeze myself into something. And as I was leaving my room and heading for the stairs, I heard piano music from downstairs in the parlor. It was Chopin, played with such delicacy and poise that I was utterly taken out of myself. I couldn't move. Francis had played the same piece. He had been good, not like Bobby, but good enough. I revered him, my older brother Francis. He laughed at all the troubles in the world as if they were nothing. In the summers down here at Hillders, he was the leader of our gang, taking us for long hikes to the Devil's Punch Bowl, or into town for a beer at the local pub. And he played that Chopin in the living room on those long evenings at the height of summer, when light seems never to fade and the smells of the gardens overrun the place. Oh, those times when we were young . . . I cried so hard, I had to go back to my room to redo my makeup.

"When I finally came down, I found Bobby still playing, absorbed, distant, but the moment he saw me, he smiled and breezed into a rendition of Cole Porter's 'You're the Top.' He sang it wonderfully. I was laughing so hard, I feared I'd break into more tears. What a joy it was to feel like a woman again, not a nurse or mother comforter to my burnt and disfigured boys, but to be beautiful for a man who was whole and, like me, wanted to build a better world out of the rubble. And then, of course, he knew half of Francis's set at Cambridge—an American no less. We knew all the same people; we'd even met in Venice at his aunt's palazzo over ten years before. You can't understand the thrill of that feeling, to meet someone again you hardly knew and suddenly realize you are connected in the most deep and secret ways. Of course, this was before Bobby had flown his first missions. I had Maggie prepare a picnic lunch and we went across the street to Cadogan Gardens and nestled in the grass under some California lilacs and drank wine and ate sandwiches and talked the afternoon through. We talked of our lives, I of my ballet career, he of his years as a concert pianist. Of course, we had to be extremely careful around the people we knew at Cambridge; we had to be careful about that. It was so odd, as if we were prisoners out on furlough, stranded in this captive life. We talked . . . well, we talked politics, too. We were very committed back then; it was the lifeblood of our artistic circles. We cared about ideas; we cared about our fellow men. We had hopes for the future even in those dark days."

"Mother, enough." Laura clapped, her gloved hands a quiet thudding.

"Your extemporaneous lying leaves me breathless. . . . Did you ever actually fuck him? Did he ever really believe he was my father?"

"What's made you so cruel?"

"Having been fucked over by the wrong guys—or not at all."

"And so crass."

"Pot calling the kettle black. Tell me the truth; you don't need to pretend about Bobby anymore. Who *is* my father? And don't say Charles. I just know it's not Charles, even if you obviously did manage him as part of your ménage à trois—or is it quatre? Or have you just lost count?"

"What's between you and Peter? Are you sleeping together?"

"Is there a reason I shouldn't be?"

"Like my father said of me as a little girl, if I didn't have things my way, I'd tear the house down brick by brick and then put it back together the way it suited me."

"Oh, there's a comforting thought—with Hermitage gone."

"There was never a step or combination I couldn't do better than any dancer alive. Margot Fonteyn admitted it to me more than once; so did Ashton and Tudor."

"Mother, face it, there just weren't that many great dancers around in your day—now New York is packed with pyrotechnical bunheads."

Suzanne pulled herself to full height and pointed toward the luminous horizon of receding hills.

"I think I was three or four, standing here with my mother one summer's day. There were these distant sounds, like rolling thunder, except the sky was perfectly clear. My mother held my hand tight and whispered, 'Daddy's out there, darling, and we're going to keep him safe.' She got me down on my knees and we prayed. It was the Somme, I think, or Passchendaele—I forget. Our prayers were answered, you see; her faith was unshakable. And I thought I could save Bobby, I really did."

"By making him a man, getting him to fuck you?"

"His life—his soul, you little idiot. When he began his hops, he was undone, unnerved. Nothing really prepared them for the antiaircraft fire, the fighters, the subzero cold. On his second mission, his side gunner, a man he *liked* very much, was shot in the stomach and bled to death in Bobby's lap, his guts spilling out. Try to understand—"

"Enough."

"Two months before the wedding, I was assigned a new patient, an American OSS officer just evacuated from Greece."

"Yes, a bullet wound in the thigh, which hadn't healed properly and required an operation and lots of therapy."

"I wasn't sure he'd make it through the wedding."

"So you fucked your husband's best man on your wedding night."

"How can you say that to me, you bitch!"

"It's in the letters, mother, among other things. . . ."

"My memory must be going, too. . . . Oh, so who's the blackmailer now? You could just show them to Charles and destroy us. Is that the plan—a little revenge before you abandon me for good?"

"The letters mention an early miscarriage with John—can I call him John, for now?"

Suzanne waved her daughter off, sniffing back a sudden burst of tears.

"Five weeks after the wedding, Bobby's plane was shot down on a raid over an oil refinery in Germany. Another pilot had seen two parachutes emerge from the disintegrating aircraft. I held out little hope. Frankly, I'd thought him a hopeless case before that. His nerves were shot. I was surprised they even allowed him to fly. I'd told him to try for a medical discharge."

"But there was still useful data to be passed on about the bombsight."

"Then, when I'd given him up, two months later the Red Cross got word to me that Bobby was safe in a POW camp near Leipzig. He was out of the war. I was ecstatic."

"Mother, I've read your letters a dozen times. You—even you—were racked with guilt. Both of you were."

"You are such a wicked child. I should have burnt them, like John told me to do."

"Well, you didn't. You didn't because you figured—what? You might need them someday to establish paternity? A little insurance . . . Alden money? Or did you, like that stupid, self-serving Philby memoir I found with your things, want to make sure that history got your role right, the Mata Hari who passed along Donald Maclean's gleanings of atom bomb secrets to the Soviets?"

"You horrible stupid girl."

"Or worse, to use those documents for blackmail, against John Alden, or Kim Philby . . . or was it to save yourself if the FBI got too close?"

Suzanne turned a cold eye on her daughter.

"To save you."

Laura reached a gloved hand to her face, pressing her fingers to her forehead, as if finally overcome by it all.

"Tell me the truth about my father and I'll burn the fucking letters and the documents and just let Max's novel stand as the record for your deceitful life."

Suzanne took Laura's arm and headed her back to the house and the Christmas festivities.

"They brought him back to Southampton late in the spring. We'd been married exactly a year. John had been away for months in the most godforsaken parts of Germany. Not a word that anything was amiss about Bobby, other than that he'd been ill. The confusion of those days was indescribable. I took the train from Victoria with the most enormous bouquet of lilacs I could carry. All the way down, I clutched those flowers in my lap, bathing my senses in their fragrance. The disembarkation center was a sprawl of confusion, with nobody knowing where anything was. I had never seen so many Americans in one place in my life. I had to ask directions five or six times before I found the right building. It was one of those queer temporary wartime buildings, a recovery center for men just released from the POW camps. As I walked up the steps, clutching those stupid flowers, I was filled with sudden terror. It must have been the smells—smells I knew only too well. Even with my nose buried in flowers. It was my nightmare of hell. I vomited into my bouquet.

"It turned out that Bobby had been moved from the POW camp and relocated to a makeshift hospital on the outskirts of Leipzig, run by the Sisters of Mercy. He and the other prisoners—Poles, Russians, and English—everyone in the hospital had been caught in one of those final horrific raids. The basement shelter had collapsed. His legs had been crushed and he suffered internal injuries and third-degree burns to his face and hands. The care he had received from the Germans had been competent, but they didn't have the critical supplies of proper bandages, morphine, much less antibiotics. That he even survived was a miracle. The pain he endured for weeks without morphine—you don't want me to tell you. The man who played Chopin for me at Cadogan Gardens was gone—obliterated."

"But you had your lovers to tide you over."

"Is that what Max taught you—to look for the worst in people? My father and brother were gone, and my mother was a fanatical Catholic. You don't know what loneliness is."

"Are you looking for pity?"

"No. I think you're even worse than Max. He, at least, had artistic reasons for making it up; you do it out of petty spite and bitchery. Has your life really been such a disappointment—with all the chances I provided you—everything that was stolen from me?"

"For God's sake, just tell me the truth—tell me John Alden is my father . . . and you weren't fucking Kim Philby, too. You weren't, were you, Mother, acting as a courier for Kim Philby in 1951 during the Maclean-Burgess fiasco, before he was recalled to London as a suspected spy?"

Suzanne waved off her daughter's entreaty.

"You selfish brat; you only see life as being about sex and secrets. I was raised a proper Catholic by my insanely devoted mother; I was a trained nurse. So, Bobby became my cross to bear—I owed him that, don't you think? We truly believed in making the world a better place. So, I had to at least try to save him; otherwise, our beliefs meant nothing, and that nothing was our godforsaken abyss. And you, dearest, were my *true* salvation. Only when you came along could I finally give up my vows. Only with you in my arms did I join the living and begin a life again, for the two of us."

"Mother, please, spare me. You've been watching too many old movies during your recovery. Was it during the assignations in New York, the Plaza or the Carlyle, certainly not Hermitage, with Bobby around? I was kind of hoping it might have been out at Pine Meadow, down by the shore. I almost feel like I could know him there—that I could feel him there . . . inside me. Just that much would be nice to know."

"You keep talking about the truth, but is it *my* truth or yours, or just a convenient truth? Be careful what you wish for."

"Yes?"

"I loved your father to the bottom of my soul. Isn't that enough?"

42 I CANNOT GET THE DAY OF THE WED-
ding out of my mind. Room after splendid room lights
up in my brain during the long hours of darkness. And
my little bedroom, where the trap snapped shut. My
life hijacked, my woeful judgment yet again played a fool. After the
very trying festivities of the wedding celebration, after I had feasted
my eyes on my host's library and the famous Smithson watercolors of
the Parthenon, I retired, emotionally drained, to my bedroom down a
long corridor in the west wing. Hillders was packed and my last-mo-
ment inclusion meant digs far from the epicenter, which suited me fine.
Nevertheless, it was a small and charming bedroom with chintz and
lace curtains and soft pastel-colored fabrics, a little sweet, a little cloying for my taste—very country English. There were Victorian prints in
gold-matted frames of smiling fishing trips to Scotland, show horses in
mid-leap, a phantom Giselle with her dreaming prince, frothy young
things playing hide-and-seek and the like. And a shelf of books on
botany, which I thought to read myself to sleep with. I settled into bed
with a volume on English wildflowers, having thrown the windows
wide to the fragrant and warm night, where a full moon, bloated to a
milky canary yellow, hovered in the far tree line, sending luminous forest shadows in feints and rushes across the wide lawns. I couldn't sleep
for the strangeness of the day and my thigh ached terribly after my
standing around all afternoon at the reception. And Paul Oakes, who
had to rush back to base, admonishing me like a figment of my mother,
to stand guard on my mortal soul. I tossed and turned. In my haste to
pack, I'd forgotten my aspirin.

The door opened and shut before I was fully aware of the sound.
Suzanne was standing there in a red robe, hair spread wide to her imperious shoulders, her hungry face set with an intent feline rapture, her

skin a striking alabaster in the moonlight, now in full flood above the
trees. Her eyes burned, blinking rapidly, as if to adjust to the room. She
brought a finger to her lips and instantly began a quick inspection, like
a chambermaid, to make sure everything was as it should be. She even
straightened a print on the wall. Then she came to me and disrobed. She
had completely shaved her pubic area and she laughed when I reached
out my hand. "Sugar and spice and everything nice—and still a nice
little girl, don't you think? You see, this was my room, where I spent all
my summers as a girl. Isn't it lovely—and the smells, oh the scents of
wisteria." She plucked the book from my hand and immediately bent
to my thigh and began kissing the many scars, and then licking me
there, nibbling and licking, licking and biting, and then massaging my
thigh, my legs, maneuvering herself to where I could stroke her long
and strong and so incredibly muscled thighs, and so fill myself, glutton
that I'd become, of her womanly essence. If I'd lost my heart, my soul
in the hospital, it was then I must have completely lost my mind. It
was only later that she—my white angel of mercy—admitted to having
drugged Bobby with a sedative that knocked him out cold for ten hours
straight. And so her recruitment proceeded apace.

After all the dancing, I was not a little relieved it was me and not
Kim Philby.

—excerpt from John Alden's Pankrác Prison diary

Seeing Laura and her mother disappear across the lawn and into the
surrounding woods, I felt less than second fiddle: I felt as if I'd evaporated from sight, merged with the specter of the man who had arrived
at Suzanne's wedding forty-five years before, abandoned by one lover,
leaned on and lied to and betrayed by the erstwhile companion of his
youthful years at Elysium, only to be sexually consumed by his bride on
their wedding night. And worse, I felt overwhelmed by the difficulty
of weaving together these disparate events into a coherent story that I
could embrace as my own. I could feel around the edges of my father's
life: the odyssey of guilt and revenge and lust—and certainly his intoxicating ambition to get his hands on the Linear B tablets—that I could
understand . . . and how these conflicting desires began to slowly isolate
him to the point where his various lives became sealed rooms known
only to himself. For the first time, I could feel their dimensions, almost
touch the furnishings and artifacts, and even enter a few as my own, but
I could not figure out how he managed to move so effortlessly between
them, nor what critical mass of combustible desire had prompted him

to the extreme recklessness of walking through Checkpoint Charlie and putting all in jeopardy. There was motive, of course—half a dozen whirling through my mind—but the essential galvanizing force of will was missing, as it was missing in me: the lethal thing that would have caused him to risk not just his life and family but even a world war.

Nevertheless, my confidence as my father's son was growing: I could guilelessly assume whatever role was required as I explored the colonel's—and his new wife's—many-roomed mansion, perhaps just another of its many ghosts, but one, given my professional expertise as grave robber and onetime intelligence officer, fully prepared to ransack its secrets. But I knew to be careful, as if one wrong word, one misplaced step and the whole delicate edifice of memory might collapse and bury the truth with it.

After dressing, I immediately went down to the hallway, where the Smithson watercolors and drawings of the Parthenon were hung, now bathed in the wan glow of morning light through distant windows. For incandescent minutes, everything else fell away, and something of my old sense of wonder returned, even as it had for my father on the day of Suzanne's wedding. Inspecting these exquisite works depicting the friezes and pediments of the Parthenon, miraculously still intact, I felt as if I were reading back into time, as if the Parthenon were really just a book of foundation stories for the Athenians, as for us—as the stained-glass windows were for the worshippers in Gothic cathedrals during the Middle Ages—telling the tales of Erechtheus and the sacrifice of his daughters, the epic struggles against the Giants and Titans, Theseus against the Amazons, and the triumph of Athena in her contest with Poseidon, and, of course, scenes from the Trojan War, which marked the end of the Bronze Age and the descent of the Dark Ages—that terrifying abyss in my father's imagination, as it must have been for the Athenians, the black hole separating mythical and historic time. As I stared at those watercolors, as if into the past itself, my father's terror of a new dark age circa 1953 became viscerally apparent to me, and I knew with sudden certainty that fear, apocalyptic and personal, had been packed in the attaché case he carried past the Iron Curtain to meet his nemesis, his mind perhaps eased by hopes of revealing that mythic past, the golden age of his boyhood dreams.

Tears filled my eyes at the sheer waste of all the ravished years. For a moment longer, I lingered in the library, marveling at the rare and beautiful volumes on archaeology and ancient history, some nearly two centuries old, only to find they stopped abruptly circa 1939. Charles Fairburn had once been a big deal in Bronze Age archaeology circles, not quite on a par with my father and Karel Hollar, but no slouch. And it was suddenly blindingly clear to me how he'd closed this door sometime after the war, moved to America to teach the classics at a range of fine New England universities and prep schools, almost entirely forgoing field work, while pursuing his passion for restoring vintage motorcars, test-piloting for the RAF, and working undercover for MI5, British counterintelligence. All to be near the woman he loved. He'd walked away from one life for another, stranded on Calypso's—or was it Circe's—shores, godfather to two children and a life that had all the hallmarks of convenient window-dressing.

But I had to clear my mind of all the static; I had to immerse myself in the life of the love letters and diary, where my father awaited my call across the river Styx, his words, his voice, the undead past, alive still in others, my guide. For the moment, all that mattered was Charles Fairburn's part in my father's unscheduled stopover in Cambridge on the way from Washington to Berlin in the fall of 1953, where he met his old mentor, Nigel Bennett, in the company of Michael Ventris, the man who had astonished the world in 1952 with the decipherment of Linear B.

This scene in Bennett's Cambridge study had been recorded in some detail in my father's Pankrác Prison diary. The realization struck me more powerfully than ever: that whatever he left in or edited out—such as the scene with Karel Hollar on Epano Englianos absent mention of SIS—had been done with precision and forethought. I was surprised that he'd included mention of Kim Philby at Suzanne's wedding, even if only in passing, without casting aspersions as to his possible links to the KGB, with the issue still hanging fire in London in 1954. Did he somehow believe that mentioning Philby in the diary might help his chances of release?

As I made my way through Charles Fairburn's many treasure rooms filled with the accumulated flotsam of generations, I couldn't escape the disconcerting feeling—how often I had felt the same at Elysium—that nothing is really lost . . . and all is lost, except the stories that linger, so that we, in their telling, might yet keep something of the dead alive.

I finally tracked down the colonel in his rose garden. It seemed so out of character to find him kneeling in the mud on a ratty bit of cardboard, tending his winter-shorn roses in their symmetrical beds.

I'd never known him to show a jot of interest in gardening—cars and aircraft, the classics and snooping had always been his thing—much less dressed in a patched Barbour coat and ratty sweater and mud-caked trousers. But then I realized that I had only known him in exile, a sojourner in the New World, and never on his native ground. And without that, you never really know anybody.

And a new wife, who, if the books on botany in her childhood room were any guide, was a lover of gardens almost as much as men.

"Merry Christmas, young man."

I looked behind, as if to make light of the young man being addressed.

"Merry . . . but I don't know about the young."

"You do look a tad crooked."

"I skipped my exercises this morning, and it's chilly out here," and I buttoned up the Burberry coat I'd borrowed from a peg on the mud-room wall. "My masseuse missed her appointment, which didn't help."

"Ah, yes," said Charles with a flicker of proprietary alarm in his eyes as he gazed up from where he knelt in the dirt and straw mulch. "I'm afraid Suzanne kidnapped Laura first thing—mother and daughter, a relationship, I have on good authority, you and I can well do without."

Even as my godfather sought to establish a hardy air of male camaraderie, I could sense his deep affection for the two women in question—a grab at happiness that I was not going to spoil if I could help it. And a pretense that had its uses.

So we spoke of many things and kicked around the intervening years, during which we'd barely been in touch except for the occasional conference in Princeton or Athens. I couldn't resist mentioning the Parthenon watercolors, and something in my voice clearly betrayed my dismay.

"Yes, John, too, was rather smitten with the damn things."

"Well, it might have been useful to let someone know you have them, at least have them photographed, available to scholars."

"My father snatched them from some faltering earl in the twenties, for a pittance, no doubt. I haven't been back here except for brief visits, sometimes many years between. Somehow, the thought of giving them up, letting them out, so to speak, even having scholars come by . . ." He shook his head. "Rather a closed chapter, you see, for which I can only blame myself. But amends are due. Shall I place them in your hands—you decide what's best for them? A museum or library perhaps?

"I know some young scholars, women in particular, who would love to see Erechtheus and his sacrificed daughters as the centerpiece of Athenian mythology: a career maker."

"And yourself?"

"I'm struggling. . . . The weeks in a prison cell messed with my head and then some."

"Ah yes, the war . . . it changes a man, though few will admit it."

"It occurred to me just now that we both seem to have drifted away from the field of Bronze Age Greece to the more salutary precincts of classical archaeology, while, come to think of it, this is first time I've seen you digging up anything."

"Digging, a young man's trade. But Suzanne is partial to roses, you see."

"Did you encourage that in me on purpose: a different field from my father's?"

"I think we were all a little down in the mouth after Ventris cracked the thing, and all we turned out to have was a bunch of palace inventories—interesting but hardly earth-shattering."

"Yes, it might have been a very different story if some history or epic literature had turned up, something pre-Homeric from the dawn of the Greek experience."

"Indeed. And you know, for all Homer's sparkling elegance, his heroes, in the end, are all in it for personal glory and renown, so that their names might outlive those of their fellows. And well, for those of us who have fought together—and the crew of a Lancaster is about as tight a band of brothers as it gets—the shared sacrifice for your fellows and your country is the only way that putting your life on the line makes sense. Say what you will for our greatly flawed Athenian: he fought and died beside his brothers, his fellow citizen hoplites, to save them and his city. The common good, if you will, trumps self-interest."

"So I tell my students, or variations on that democratic theme: balancing the individual's responsibility to the community, and the community's upholding the rights and freedoms of the individual."

"I feel badly that I didn't do more for you as a boy. I promised John I'd keep an eye on you if anything happened . . . in my role as godfather, needless to say."

"I know my grandmother appreciated all that you did."

"Rock of Gibraltar."

"Did he seem—the godfather thing, I mean—concerned about something happening?"

"In his line of work, well, one hardly knows. After the war, we all felt we were on borrowed time."

"I guess what I'm getting at is whether he expressed such concerns around the time he disappeared, late September '53."

"Not in so many words. I was visiting at Elysium with Suzanne, you see . . . always awkward with Bobby hanging about in his wheelchair. John found out from Suzanne that I was up and invited me to his house. He was in a bit of a state."

As I watched Charles glance off toward the distant tree line, his breath rising from his mustached upper lip, I had an image of my anxious father on our boat dock chain-smoking Luckies.

"Something was bothering him?"

"East Germany was blowing up, and he'd been ordered to Berlin to fix the bloody mess."

"You mean he didn't want to go?"

"Not if he could bloody well help it, but orders are orders. He put his arm around me and jokingly offered to exchange lives—being a lowly professor at Princeton, he told me, was all he had ever really wanted."

"Well"—I sucked in a lungful of that cool early-morning air in hopes of clarity—"1953 . . . only that spring excavations had been renewed at Pylos and more Linear B tablets discovered, and Michael Ventris had just decrypted Linear B the year before—didn't you set up a meeting for him with Nigel Bennett and Michael Ventris before Berlin?"

Charles gave me a slightly querulous look as I dropped this nugget from my father's diary, as if he'd caught me poking through his lovely library, perhaps mishandling the rare books. But he was quick to make the necessary adjustments, almost as flawless a pivot as Suzanne's had been the previous evening.

"That's right, and he was all in a tizzy about it; he couldn't stop talking up the subject—wanted me to put him in touch with Ventris and Bennett. Bennett was a mentor to John, of course, from Cambridge days and OSS, but Ventris was a retiring type and hard to get hold of. I knew him socially—his wife was a friend of Cecily—and so with a few overseas calls, I was able to set them up at Cambridge."

"Why, if Berlin was burning, would he want a meeting about Linear B with Ventris and Bennett?"

"Oh, it's worse than that: He behaved very badly; it left a bad taste in my mouth after I heard about it. I fear it somewhat soured my feelings toward you over all the years—not your fault, of course, but I was reminded—"

"What did he do?"

"He stole one of Ventris's charts on the decipherment. You can ask Bennett about it if you like, but I believe he asked to borrow it for a few hours to have it photographed—something like that—and instead absconded with the thing to London and was off to Berlin. Before the days of copying machines, a chart like that was hard to reproduce. I believe it took Ventris weeks to reconstitute it—he never forgave me or Nigel for sending that *crazy and deceitful*—those are the words he used—American his way. As I say, it left a bit of a stink."

Even though I had promised the ambassador and the CIA man in Prague that I would keep any new details about my father's disappearance in confidence until cleared by the Agency, Charles's acknowledgment of the meeting with Bennett and Ventris only whetted my appetite. So I began to let on about the Berlin connection with Karel Hollar, and, as much as Charles tried to finesse it, I got the distinct impression I wasn't telling him anything he didn't already know: that Hollar hadn't died in a Soviet POW camp.

"Hollar was a free spirit"—Charles maintained his equanimity as he pruned his roses, producing a rather feeble whistle to register his astonishment—"brilliant as he was crafty—doesn't surprise me; but actually stealing the things from under Carl Andersen's and the Greek government's nose . . ." He paused and glanced up, trying to keep his game face in check. "The throne room, you say—fancy that. Don't suppose they're still there, do you, in Leipzig?"

I had to laugh, and he laughed with me. I made no mention that my father had paid for the extra diggers and had been in cahoots. I left the blame squarely on Karel Hollar's shoulders. Dead men tell no tales.

"Oh," and, I sighed, "one can understand the temptation—know how it is, on-site, when the season is closing down and the Meltemi is rising, maybe just a few more spadesful . . . and the something you've dreamt about all your life might be there waiting for you, as you brush the last bit of dirt away."

"For most of us, it never pans out."

"Perhaps you gave up on it too soon. Didn't you miss it . . . the cicadas, the crocking frogs at night, lying out under the stars—never knowing what tomorrow might reveal?"

"Somehow, it just wasn't in me anymore. I grew fond of teaching college kids their Latin and Greek, schoolboys, too. Not that I didn't stay abreast of developments."

"Funny, though, how my father got wind of Karel Hollar's reincarnation as GDR minister of mines, much less that he had those one hundred and three Linear B tablets at his disposal, precisely at the moment the crisis in East Germany was at its height in 1953?"

As I watched him kneeling there, squirming, I thought I detected the merest crack of light showing under at least one of the doors of those rooms long locked to me.

"Yes, the next spadeful"—and Charles held up his dirty trowel for my inspection—"to be numbered with Evans and Schliemann." I watched his muddy-gloved fingers pause in their work, hesitate, then shove the trowel home. "Tell you what: As soon as I finish up here, I'll put in a call to Nigel Bennett in Cambridge. You might want to get to him sooner rather than later; I hear he's on his last legs."

And so a critical key was generously put in my hand: The colonel had been the go-between but not the instigator.

"You taught at Deerfield and Exeter—why never at Winsted?" I asked. "It would have been such a natural for you."

"Your father offered me a position on a silver platter after the war. As you Americans like to say, a done deal."

"And why not?"

"With me and Suzanne . . . making a cuckold of the scion of the Williams clan, a war hero by then . . . I felt bad enough as it was."

"How far back, if you don't mind my asking, were you and Suzanne . . . a pair?"

"Oh, I should've married her before the war when I was at Cambridge with her brother Francis, but I doubt she would have had me: an engineer, a scholar in ancient languages—*and* we were first cousins. I was like an older brother. Once she became a star with Sadler's Wells— oh my, if you'd seen her dance back then—she ran in a very fast set, White Russians, Red Russians, Bloomsbury and Cambridge socialists, aesthetes all . . . people I—and my father—thoroughly disliked."

"I guess Bobby fit the playbill."

"I couldn't stand the man when he was at Cambridge, nor his Red pals. No denying his talent as a pianist. But frankly, we were a conceited bunch during the war—the way we treated your people. Not that you brash Yanks didn't always try to rub our faces in *our* inadequacies."

"The *English*-speaking people."

"I suppose it is the language that truly unites us. Oh, we have history and family ties and even affections and affinities—the special relationship. But in the end, it is Shakespeare and Wordsworth and Kipling and the like, an atmosphere of the mind, which promotes good habits and loyalty to what we stand for."

"Loyalty," I murmured, reminded of something Karel Hollar had pronounced out of the darkness of our cell. "I was thinking something along those lines while looking at your art collection and library just now. As you say, the stories we tell to remind us who we are."

"Watching on the telly as the Berlin Wall was being pulled down, the crowds in the street—it's as if their language of lies just gave way like a dam weakened by constant undermining. All that misuse of language, the unreality of it—don't you think? The adulteration of words and meaningless verbal constructs, the perversion and twisting of ideas, the underlying illogic of things. I do believe that's been at the root of the disasters of this century."

I followed his backward glance to the lawns and the line of trees, their bare branches glistening and sparking as the pale winter sunlight melted the frost. I thought about Vlada in a hospital room somewhere in Czechoslovakia and his precious volumes on the ramshackle shelves of his tiny room, and my father's library in his boyhood room above the pine tops, and Charlie Springfield . . . and Max.

"Don't you think," he went on, "it's as if everyone suddenly got sick and tired of the bloody charade, as if the old untruths spouted ad nauseum couldn't summon the mental energy to keep it all going? As you say, the stories, the myths stop holding water and all that's left is a wasteland."

"'The corruption of language' was how a friend of mine put it recently."

"That's why I always insisted on precision of language, why we still need Greek and Latin in our schools to keep us honest. When the boys and girls complained that I allowed little scope for interpretation and whimsy, I told them, 'If your translation, if your reasoning were the motor of an airplane, would you be happy to cross the Atlantic in that aircraft? The last thing a pilot does is to check his engines to make sure the mechanics have done their job, and then reads off his checklist to his copilot, in case his mind wandered.'"

I laughed, thinking of the all the conversations I'd had over the years with my own students.

He went on. "Then I often found myself feeling a bit ill at ease: my British savoir faire trying to prick your native idealism."

"Did you have to do that often for my father . . . prick his idealism?"

"I often felt John was more of an artist than a scholar and not really cut out for soldiering—but then, how many of us were?"

"What, too much of a romantic?"

"You've got to be bloody-minded. Like your poor boys at the start in North Africa, after Kasserine Pass . . . until they got their noses bloodied, until they learned to be killers like the Germans. Bobby, of course, had no business being part of a bomber crew. I'd have never allowed such a callow fellow in my squadron; he'd have been out on his ear."

"Another artist . . ."

"A backstage homosexual. That's how Suzanne explains it . . . that their marriage was never consummated. Certainly not after the poor sod returned from Germany. And then, year after bloody year, what I had to put up with from him: all his invective against your father and grandmother, and the Winsted board, absolutely endless. It drove Suzanne wild. Just the squeal of his wheelchair . . . You see, she never oiled the damn wheels, so we'd know when he was about."

This note of irritation caused him to look at his watch, perhaps in anticipation of a Christmas celebration around the tree and the return of the two women. But the gesture recalled for me his gaze out the window of the Bull Run during our Sunday lunch—what seemed a lifetime ago. Had he been preoccupied with those C-130's, or was he simply longing to be back in his mistress's arms, to be with his daughter . . . wondering why he was wasting time on me? While I, foolishly, only had eyes for those Green Berets.

He shook his head. "I always felt the car wreck on the Autobahn was such a hopelessly bad story, ignominious for a man like that."

"I think we all did. . . ."

As he began working on a new row of roses, I saw his chest expand and his pruning gain a ruthless ferocity, as if our candid conversation had expanded the beachhead of his usually soft-spoken equanimity.

"I had to give her away, you see"—and he indicated the place with a jut of his jaw—"my first love to a drunken American queer. I should've bloody well put my foot down."

To that counterfactual *what if,* I felt like saying, *Well, if I'd only fucked the girl you think is your daughter on a wonderful late-fall evening under the apple trees, we might have married a long time ago and I'd have stayed the fuck out of Vietnam—little guidance you offered me on that score.* Or I might have mentioned how my great-grandfather spent the rest of his life chaffing at McClellan's failure to follow up his men's sacrifice at Antietam with an attack on Lee's defeated Army of Virginia, which might have saved the country two more years of war and hundreds of thousands more lives. And how he'd been aghast and heartbroken at Grant's failure to enforce Reconstruction in the South, and thereby ensure another century of servitude and terror.

I should have told him about the Vietnam cluster fuck, but I checked the instinct to self-pity in hopes of shedding a bit more light where I needed it.

"The hinge of fate," I said. "The Athenian expedition against Syracuse. The delay of Operation Barbarossa because of Serbian resistance."

Charles didn't miss a beat.

"The failure of the Luftwaffe to go after the radar sites and Spitfire airfields—they were days from winning the war."

"And Normandy, a near thing . . . if Hitler had released the panzers in time."

With that, Charles stood and went to a basketful of bulbs on the path, next to an empty bed of dirt. He grimaced, and I could hear his old knees creak with the cold and arthritis as he knelt once again and pointed with the trowel.

"They were married, just days before Normandy, right in front of that yew hedge, remarkable yew, fixture there as long as anyone can remember. Such a splendid occasion, and such a complete waste. And I've never believed a word about why Bobby invited your father at the last moment—or Elliot Goddard, for that matter. John had no idea why he was here; he got out of the cab blinking like a mole in the sunlight. Suzanne was equally surprised—said Bobby probably wanted to show off to his old pals. Truth is, he was desperate to have someone hold his hand, to get him through it, at which point he proceeded to be a total cad about the whole thing. Forgive me; I probably blame your father for that, too."

That note of confession along with his nervousness about what was transpiring between mother and daughter unleashed a tale as vivid as it was misconstrued.

"Don't get me wrong; I was really very fond of your father. We were all struggling with a noose around our necks—the war, I mean. I remember that day as a hopeful time. John and I were chatting in the library about all the exciting excavations that would take place once the damn war was over. And yes, Pylos was high on his list, with the new cache of Linear B tablets discovered by Carl Andersen tucked away in the bowels of the Bank of Greece. All he could talk about was continuing his work deciphering the things, damn sight easier with all the new material at hand. The way we figured it, one way or another, Karel Hollar was out of the running: No way the Greeks would ever allow him or any other variety of Hun back to dig up their national treasures. I could see it your father's eyes: the damage done in Greece."

He slumped for an instant, his breath showing in quick bursts, and then he caught a second wind and was off.

"Feels like yesterday sometimes, the way the daylight was lingering in the sky beyond the library bay windows, the most serene pinks and purples bathing the cirrus layers in the highest reaches, like some painter had brushed it on for the occasion. The men were inside drinking; the women were off in the garden, rounding up the children and trying to get them fed and off to bed. The evening was filled with children's cries and laughter as they hid in their forts in the rhododendrons. We were a convivial bunch, most of us in uniform; most of us had known one another from school days and Cambridge; all of us had endured four years of war . . . and the losses. Francis, our dear Francis—Suzanne's older brother—light of our childhood gatherings, was gone: Tobruck.

"We were on the brink of winning the damn thing. The invasion was about to go off; half the people in that room were in on the planning, as was I. Anxious, yes, but given the long road endured . . . the end was finally in sight. And Bobby had begun the evening playing the piano—by Jove, he was good, too. For a few moments, one could detect what Suzanne saw in him. John and I were standing by the door, after our long chat in the library—and, yes, admiring the Smithson watercolors of the Parthenon, and I tried to be sporting and thanked him for getting Bobby to the altar, so to speak, considering how sodden drunk he'd been that morning. I noticed that Bobby's champagne glass on the piano remained full and untouched. John did not seem to share my benevolence, as if Bobby's performance at the piano was an act he'd seen once too often. John was putting a brave face on it, I think, trying to be charitable about Bobby: an old school chum, a Yank among Brits. Of course, I had no idea then about the bad blood between the families.

"Then an odd change took place. Bobby began to huddle with one group of men after another, full of bonhomie and a bottle of champagne in hand, refilling everyone's glasses. He was asking a lot of

claim that we'll have Germany wrapped up in time for Christmas.' Bobby was almost in tears by then, desperately looking to John for salvation. Oh, I was being bloody awful, no doubt about it. . . . I shall never forgive myself, a guest in my home—the husband of the girl I'd loved since thirteen. And the worst of it: I was done with flying; I had no more ops to face. And still I went on, some stupid bragging remark to the effect that our RAF boys knew a thing or two about winning the war: burn down the Kraut cities, bring them to their knees—no more repeats of the 1918 armistice.

"I think even John had had enough of it by then. I felt him pull me away. Bobby just ran off to Suzanne in the garden. Only then did I realize what a damper I'd put on things. At the top of my lungs, I called out: 'Women, where are the women? . . . Gentlemen, the night has only just begun.' With that, I had John accompany me to the cellar, where we scrounged up some more bottles of champagne. We arrived back with armfuls of the stuff and I got myself filthy drunk, my best drunk of the whole bloody war."

When Charles's agitated voice suddenly became quiet, I felt as I'd been jolted awake; I could barely believe where I was amidst the winter-shorn rose bushes: how that soft, luxurious spring day had been replaced by a December morning's chill. Charles might have been exorcizing a few private demons, but I found myself privy to an operation by Soviet military intelligence to gather information on Allied D-day landings. Those two wedding invitations to my father had all been part of the plan. Along with attendees Kim Philby, Donald and Melinda Maclean, and Anthony Blunt, who must have been aghast at Bobby's fumbling indiscretions. And Charles, the long-suffering, love-struck Charles, was still clueless—or so I thought for a few seconds more.

"Where are they?" He tossed the trowel into the basket with the remaining bulbs. "Laura's all she has left—and me, I suppose." He extended his hand and I helped him up. "Laura's her only flesh and blood . . . and mine." He gave me a querulous look, as if I might dare a contradiction.

I smiled gamely. In truth, there was nothing more I would've liked than for his every word to be spot-on, except there were the letters and the diary.

"Was Kim Philby there, at the wedding, dancing with the bride . . . gathering information on D-day? Moscow Center must have been hot under the collar to know in June of 1944."

He'd been wiping his hands on his pants, and they slowed and became still as he looked up at me with a squinty expression of being had.

"The fiend's dead now, may he rot in hell, like that whole rat bag of traitors."

His tone had given him away, and he knew it.

"And Donald and Melinda Maclean, and, dare I make an educated guess, Anthony Blunt, touring the pictures with his star American recruit from Cambridge days."

This produced a sheepish grin and a knowing nod. "You're bloody good, you know—ring-around-the-rosy. So how much do you know?"

"I know that Karel Hollar was working for SIS in Greece during the war, while working for the KGB, or whatever it was back then."

"NKVD . . . or GRU, their military intelligence."

"So, he was a double agent, and was he *still* a double agent in his new guise as the minister of mines in Berlin—and for which side, exactly?"

"I'm only a part-timer—in case you haven't figured that out, too," and he put his finger to his lips and turned anxiously in the direction where he expected to see the two women at any moment—and the outcome of a conversation a hell of a lot more important to him than the one we were having. "A not so fleet-footed Hermes. You'll have to ask Nigel—he ran MI5 in those days, and I'm afraid he's been slipping of late."

"Laura is an extraordinary woman," I said, my rush of magnanimity wishing him all his famished heart desired. "You two should be proud."

"You can't imagine what it's been like for all these years to watch my daughter from afar . . . the ups and downs, curtain calls at Lincoln Center and the drugs that almost killed her, that miserable Max Roberts, who made a shambles of her life—and those despicable novels. And I could do damn all. Without Suzanne's say-so, I was powerless to help."

"I will help."

"Can you? She does look better."

"If being head over heels in love means anything."

He rested his hand on my shoulder, about as close to a hug as the English get.

"Lord knows, she needs a steady man like you."

"Steady, well . . ."

He smiled, squinting at my face. "Like father like son—a man I felt I could never get to the bottom of."

"I seem to have joined that club some time ago."

"Then, we're a team—mum's the word."

The colonel seemed to chuckle at this and gave my shoulder a shake, as he had sometimes done when I was young, as if reaching for that bottom.

"Let's go in. Plenty of champagne to take off the chill. It's Christmas, after all. Then I'll make the call to Nigel in Cambridge—good chance for me to wish him Merry Christmas."

43

I HAVE DISCOVERED AFTER SIX MONTHS in solitary confinement, without so much as a glimpse of the sky, that my mind—body and soul—craves release into the out-of-doors. I dream of the sun and clouds and blue skies and the places I have known and loved. I find I can only summon the energy to write of places in sunlight, outdoors in the Berkshires, on the playing field or rowing on the river. And always the blue seas and skies of Greece, of Crete and Delos, chirp of crickets and smells of laurel and oleander, the humpbacked olive trees on Epano Englianos. So with Suzanne, it seems I only really knew her in the outdoors—where we made a virtue out of a necessity, given our joint infidelities. After the hospital and our one night at Hilldes—after she was a married woman—it seemed to all come down to the garden in Cadogan Square. Later, it would be Elysium (the hotel rooms in New York blur into dark abstractions). For three months in the late spring and summer of 1944, before I left for France and Germany, Cadogan Square was our oasis in drab, bomb-scarred London. She would come up from Guilford, I from the OSS London office, and I'd let myself into the gardens with a key she provided. Often it was in the late afternoon, or evening, sometimes night. Often, too, I had to wait long hours there for her, or she for me, schedules and transportation always being problematic. I would lie back on the rectangular lawn, surrounded on all sides by a magnificent array of rhododendrons and lilacs, horse chestnuts and plane trees, and stare up at the pale sky framed by the profusion of tan gables and odd-shaped chimneys of the Dutch Revival town houses that populated the square like so many oversized fairy cottages from a child's storybook. Even at the height of the Blitz, flowers grew in profusion, so Suzanne assured me, a note of sanity in the terrifying gloom—their floral scents an antidote to the stink of burning that burdened the air of the city. I remember lying in Suzanne's arms at night, listening to the sinister buzz of V-I's pass overhead in the weeks after the Normandy invasion; the drone of their engines would suddenly cut out, and we'd wait the interminable silent seconds—the distant and not so distant reverberations erupting from the earth at our backs like earthquakes on a planet not ours. I was going back to the killing, and she had always just come from the wounded—the burn cases her specialty—so we banished death in our wine-sodden lovemaking.

The children of Cadogan Square were long gone, sent away to distant countryside villages, like Charles Fairburn's children, and a few off to America; even Winsted had three or four "British cousins" in its ranks during the war years. Suzanne's house on the square was overseen by a fierce old Scottish housekeeper and very proper butler, and there was always the chance that Bobby or her mother might turn up without notice. So Suzanne preferred to arrive at home, change out of her uniform into a loose summer dress, no underwear, and have the housekeeper prepare a picnic with wine, sandwiches, and a thick plaid blanket. Once it was dark, and with all the surrounding houses under strict blackout precautions, Cadogan Gardens was ours. Suzanne would sometimes take whole blossoms of the California lilac that grew in profusion and rub them all over her body to rid herself of the stink of the hospital. She became pregnant. The baby would have been a boy, "my Cadogan Gardens boy," she called him. He was conceived there but died from a miscarriage while I was following in Patton's wake through France. Suzanne never got over it. It happened after Bobby was shot down over Leipzig—of all places—and Suzanne regarded it as God's punishment—less for her infidelities than for hoping Bobby never made it out of his flaming bomber. I still see her face raised to the searchlight-illuminated sky and the silhouettes of a fairy-tale city as she desperately tried to hold back her screams of agonized release, as if for the son we would never have.

—excerpt from John Alden's Pankrác Prison diary

On the way from Midhurst to Cambridge, I had to change trains between Waterloo and Paddington, and so had the cab drop me off at Cadogan Square for an hour. The enormous town house at the north end of the square that had belonged to Suzanne's family, a confection of gables and polychrome brickwork, turrets and terra-cotta chimneys, had long since been divided into multiple luxury flats, mostly given over to international bankers and Saudi playboys. The curbs were lined with flashy Mercedes and BMWs. As the old gardener who let me into the gated park put it, "Guv'nor, makes you wonder who won the war."

Suzanne's California lilacs were still there, so the gardener assured me as I surveyed the forlorn bushes. The children have long since returned, and the bomb-damaged blocks nearby had been rebuilt with modern flats; the Scottish church at the end of Pont Street stood on what had been a block of rubble when Suzanne and my father had indulged in their assignations nearby. Young boys and girls from nearby Hill House School, dressed in their tan knickerbockers and mustard-colored jumpers and marching in lines two by two, regularly passed the gardens on their way to Hyde Park, little suspecting the mayhem of the gods that had once descended from the sky. As I walked the brick paths of the garden, I found myself gazing up at the oblong of winter sky bordered by a confection of leaded glass and softly blinking Christmas lights, and, as I did, seeing a woman's orgasmic features poised against that London sky, as I had Laura's face against the gray clouds through the French doors of our room above La Giudecca, and something, too, of that angelic release in the face of the figure in the Saint-Gaudens memorial.

I was both relieved and anxious about what had seemed like a reconciliation between mother and daughter after their long walk. A modus vivendi between conspirators? They didn't say much around the Christmas tree as the presents were handed out, but I had a distinct feeling that a deal had been struck. And when Suzanne opened her present from Laura, a pair of leather gloves from Venice, she fairly flew into her daughter's arms with thanks. It was almost touching.

How was it that every time I was around Suzanne, I felt as though there was a conspiracy afoot?

I think any memoirist—is that the right word for something scribbled into a child's lined notebook?—is tempted to note the most influential men, or women, in his life. Too many, at this juncture, for me to safely list. But I might mention two, or rather, a brief meeting between two of them, one the greatest humanist intellects I ever knew, the other possessing the greatest intuitive insights into the nature of language, or should I say the architecture of human narrative? Nigel Bennett, my teacher and mentor, I had known since the thirties; we had collaborated on a number of journal articles on Bronze Age Greece. What set Nigel apart for me was how, behind all his blinding insights, there lay a brooding abyss of sadness for the horrors he had witnessed in the trenches, when he'd seen many of the finest men of his generation butchered: the experience—of love extirpated by high explosives and machine-gun fire—like an atmosphere of the mind, informed his every utterance. This labyrinth of degradation was the thing from which he sought to extricate his fellow man.

So unlike the prickly, introverted Michael Ventris, an amateur linguist, a professional architect, of whom the world knew nothing until his extraordinary cracking of Linear B a little more than a year ago. What made the meeting of these two so spectacular was the fusion before my dazzled eyes of Nigel's unparalleled mastery of the facts and fancy of history, literature, and mythology, and Ventris's grasp of the inner dynamics of a lost language, which only a man of perseverance, logic, and meticulous methodology—much less the fortitude to take great risks—could have pulled off. Realizing how Ventris had done it by throwing out the received wisdom—that Linear B was unrelated to Greek—made me realize that only risk takers could change the world. I had tried and failed; I had struggled doggedly for years but had failed to make the final leap—to give up everything for the prize. To watch these two men go at it in Nigel's book-lined Cambridge study was to witness two of the finest intellectual talents of the age begin to merge and pull in tandem in hopes of revealing the lost civilization of Homer's stories. Nigel, like his mentor, Arthur Evans, pined for Minoan Crete, believing it the source of our common humanity, the golden age, perhaps Plato's Atlantis—as echoed in Homer's land of the Phaeacians. Ventris cared only for facts and analysis. I prided myself on holding my own, and contributing a few telling insights, but the main show was not Nigel and Ventris, but in the darkness somewhere east of Berlin. I walked away from that Cambridge meeting floating on air, my head spinning at the possibilities that awaited.

—excerpt from John Alden's Pankrác Prison diary

Later, as I walked the empty streets from the Cambridge train station to Corpus Christi College, I found the near silence oppressive, an echo of the quietude and distance I had detected in Laura at the Midhurst station when she dropped me off. She seemed jumpy when I touched her, as if something of her mother's prickliness had rubbed off. And I was not a little apprehensive about meeting the "ancient" and "legendary" Nigel Bennett, as Charles had described his Cambridge mentor. Before I'd read about my father's meeting with Ventris and Bennett in his Pankrác diary, I vaguely knew my father had studied with Bennett, an acolyte of Sir Arthur Evans and world authority on Minoan archaeology and ancient languages, but I had no idea Bennett had been the team leader behind the cracking of the German Enigma ciphers during the war, heading up the code breakers at Bletchley Park. After the war, Bennett had run MI5, British counterintelligence, before returning to his role as a master of Corpus Christi College in the early sixties.

Nor, for obvious reasons, could my father have mentioned those dangerous facts in his prison diary. But that he had included mention of this meeting at all spurred me on, torn between the fantasy and the hope, that my father had wanted *me* to know this man. And even the alacrity with which Charles Fairburn had put me in touch with Bennett, I now recognized as a kind of confession.

As my shoes crunched on the damp gravel of the quad, which framed that eerily immaculate rectangle of frosty green, reflecting milky glimmers in the ranks upon ranks of medieval leaded-glass windows—so reminiscent of Princeton's collegiate Gothic—I couldn't help wondering if this white-tower existence was really the scholarly life my father had so pined for. Or was it only in that moment during his clandestine stopover in Cambridge, which had totally escaped Elliot Goddard and the CIA investigators, when he realized the genius of Ventris and the window thrown wide onto the past, that he had opted for that reckless mission? His steps, my steps, and the thousands upon thousands of like-minded footsteps, if the cupped stone stairs were to be believed, spoke of a pilgrimage site and a far-seeing oracle. The master's oak door was scored with rust stains and absorbed my tentative knocks like a feather pillow. Then a young woman with disheveled auburn hair and rheumy eyes let me in. She was wearing the rattiest gray cardigan I'd ever seen and carried an open paperback of *Middlemarch*. Clearly, I had interrupted her read.

"Thank God you could come on such short notice; the idea he might have no visitors on Christmas Day—besides me, who doesn't count—was making me very sad. He's simply outlived everybody. Now, if you haven't seen him recently, you should know he's a trifle forgetful and quite deaf—especially when he doesn't care to hear what you're telling him." Her spiel was rattled off by rote. "Hearing aid gives him a headache, he says, but he got quite agitated when I mentioned your name—something about a chart." She waved me around a corner toward a study crammed with more books in one space than I'd ever encountered, with the possible exception of Virgil Dabney's study. "If you lean forward and speak directly to his face, he can hear quite well—actually, I'm convinced he can read lips, although he'd never admit it.

He's just as happy to do all the talking anyway. A nod or shake of your head is often sufficient." By then, we were through the doorway of Nigel Bennett's study and were confronted with a minefield to be negotiated if those precious stacks of books interleafed with file cards were not to be toppled. The wan sunlight of late afternoon, shadowed by black clouds, filtered in by way of a bay window overlooking the quad. A smell of burning coal was pervasive. At first, I couldn't spot the fireplace, which was screened by two massive armchairs with scrolling armrests. Glancing at the mantel, where a vigorously ticking Victorian clock chimed the hour, I could make out framed photos of khaki-clad soldiers bracketing the clock, along with a scattering of artifacts.

"The *master*"—and I noted the supercilious irony in her tone—"woke up with a bit of a cough this morning, a cold, perhaps, coming on, so there's no saying how long he's going to last—normally, it depends on how well his guests amuse." Her accent suggested she was from the north of England, working-class but well educated, and I assumed she was a grad student putting in her hours as factotum. "But after Colonel Fairburn's telephone call this morning, he's been quite uppity. He's been talking a blue streak about you, Mr. Alden; he's been going on a fair dance." She gave me a crooked-toothed, exasperated smile and weaved her way to the chair on the right. There she knelt like a supplicant to announce my arrival with slow, deliberate syllables. An arm appeared from around the back of the chair and waved me forward. I negotiated the roundabout route blazed moments before by Miriam—whose name I got later—and shook hands with this "extravagant genius of his generation," as the *Times* obituary would state two weeks later, "spy master's spy master . . . who had elaborated on Michael Ventris's pioneering triumph in the translation of Linear B." His hand was cold, limp, and liver-spotted, and his eyes bore into mine—eyes greatly magnified behind the thick lenses of his oversized tortoiseshell reading glasses. Gray eyes, truly gray, grayer than the grayest English winter day—and seeing right to the pithy core of his subject.

"John, you haven't changed a farthing."

"It's Peter. I'm his son, Peter."

"Sit down, man—no ceremony, please."

Twice I tried to release his hand, and twice it gripped tighter as he scrutinized my face, his kidney-colored lips pressed inward with concentration. His glasses were so large, like demitasse saucers—they might have passed as clown glasses at the circus—that they made it

hard to fully register his broad yet delicately boned features. His wide
brow constituted an expanse of wrinkled flesh, a snowfield of flesh at
winter's end, furrowed by wind and rain. His thin white hair flew about
as if perpetually windblown.

"Peter," I repeated, saying my name loudly at Miriam's prompting;
at this, she just smiled as she left me.

Nigel Bennett was one of the oldest-looking men I'd ever encountered. He was like an emblem of oldness, his skin so fine and luminous,
like bone china, so delicate, in fact, that it seemed to emanate an inner
light.

"Sit, sit . . . good, good, wondering when you'd turn up again. I hope
you damn well returned that chart to Ventris—apoplectic he was."

He laughed heartily, and I obeyed and swung myself into the
neighboring chair, which I soon realized had been strategically placed
to afford the master full scrutiny of his guests at close range. I bent
forward, my mind going blank as I was overcome with conflicting sensations: Was my leg being pulled—some inside joke?

"But you had what you needed, I suppose," he continued. "Did Hollar come through on his end? Everyone seemed well pleased with our
catch." A raspy wheeze hissed from his lavender-gray lips, like some
archaic engine laboring to gather momentum.

"Karel Hollar, who"—I paused again, fearing to disclose my father's
role in the stealing of the Linear B tablets—"seemed to have come
upon an unknown cache of Linear B tablets at Pylos?"

"Hollar's tablets—from the throne room, wasn't it?" An open book
slipped unnoticed from his lap to the floor and a tweedy leather-patched
arm rose in some agitation, conducting soundless violins for seconds,
only to lose momentum and drop to his side.

"Miriam," he whined, and then went into a fit of coughing, "get us
some nice tea and biscuits like a good girl, the chocolate ones in the
blue wrapper—honey biscuits—and the Darjeeling. Sustenance for our
embattled American brother. I've a terrific appetite on my hands, if my
memory serves me."

A shout in the affirmative came from a nearby room.

Nigel Bennett adjusted his reading glasses and craned toward me.
"Hollar was always a sneaking blaggard, but to hold those hundred
and three tablets back for his private use was inexcusable." His sagging
limbo eyes watched me intently; I felt stripped naked. I licked my lips
in desperation to find a promising point in which to slip the blade of

my shovel. "What—cat got your tongue, you great lout of an American—trailing clouds of glory, is it? Expect the nations and peoples of the world to fall into your welcoming lap like manna from above."

I tried a confident smile, confronted with what I took to be a favored mode of joshing from a legendary god of our profession, while the hands on the mantelpiece clock spun wildly. A little panicked, I twirled my mental dial, desperate for the right frequency. I knew this was my only chance, convinced that the possibly foolhardy mention in my father's prison diary of his meeting with Bennett and Ventris in September 1953 had been for me, his posterity. Bennett's name, like Philby's, had been circled twice and checkmarked.

"I believe Sir Arthur Evans sequestered his Linear B from Knossos for many years, for *his* exclusive use."

"Don't mention those two names in the same breath. Hollar—he did have them?"

"Oh, he had them all right, all one hundred and three tablets, right where he said he did."

"So the exchange for the names came off without a hitch?"

"The names . . . the names." I felt some vague paternal injunction to keep my wits about me. "Yes, he knew the names, but without proof, purloined documents . . ."

"Where'd he hide the tablets—were they safe?"

"Leipzig—the Museum of Antiquities in Leipzig."

"You mean the good ole red, white, and blue didn't bomb it flat? Or the Soviets didn't make off with them?"

"Oh, I think your RAF boys weighed in plenty on Leipzig. And no, they're safe. The Soviets would have had no idea what they were. Ingots of bullion would have been a different matter."

"Safe—good, good."

"Beautiful things, like the finest porcelain, handcrafted to last for eternity."

"Really . . . so, not like Evans's, from Knossos"—a stricken look came into his gray eyes—"crumbled to the touch, and your heart would sink to your toes." He peered hard at me, as if there were something he couldn't quite yet discern in my face. "And the names?"

"Names . . . on the tablets?"

"You found names written on the tablets?"

"Well, yes, a prince of Pylos, Lakedanos, and a Phaeacian princess, Philowona—as well as I could translate it."

"Not Nausicaa, our lovely burner of ships?"

"Perhaps an earlier archaic version, perhaps Cretan in origins. With the Berlin Wall down, maybe we can go back and do some more work on Hollar's tablets."

"Berlin Wall—Kennedy's folly. Kennedy—heh, there's a foolish cad—get railroaded by Khrushchev like that. Then, without that wall, where would we be? Stabilized a very tricky situation. Wouldn't want you Yanks getting us into another fight for which there could be no winners on this side of the pond."

"What Frost said, something about walls making good neighbors."

"And I've uncovered—as I know you have—a few in my day. But did Hollar really let you see his little cache, his insurance—before he got out?"

I stared into those antediluvian gray eyes, paddling hard to stay afloat.

"I think he wanted to make sure the charts were the real thing— that they worked—before he gave up the names."

"Well, he would—full of Hun precision. Did you really get your hands on the tablets; did you get to work with them?"

Bennett leaned within inches of my face. I gave him a reckless smile: the smile of an inveterate risk taker.

"Some were just inventories," I said, "like the others from Pylos and Knossos, but there were a few tablets that seemed different, the symbols and syntax more complex, pointing to a narrative of a kind, a sailing voyage, perhaps a voyage to Crete, or even the island of the Phaeacians—"

"Good God, and fair Nausicaa?"

"Well, I'm still struggling with the translation—the code is damnably difficult and the syntax impossible. But definitely Knossos and the names of other cities and a seafarer or wayfarer. I've roughed out a translation."

"Oh, you ambitious thing, and how unlike Hollar to show you the damn things, unless he thought he might need you—that's how he always was, insisting on the holographs of the charts."

"I know Ventris wasn't pleased."

"Won't speak to any of us again—gone off in a pique."

"But Nigel, we had no choice—right? That was the deal you negotiated," I said. "And Hollar wanted to make damn sure they were the genuine article before he'd give us the names."

"So, it must have been the tablets, then, which kept him from defecting sooner. He insisted he could finish with the tablets in a month, maybe six weeks, and then he'd be out—come home to us, as he put it."

"Those Leipzig tablets were a lifetime's work. But a defector—yes, that makes sense: a famous man who had deciphered the Linear B tablets he'd discovered—and, of course, he could just make something up about where he found them. Numbered among the immortals, like Evans and Schliemann. That's what he wanted since childhood . . . even if I did have a bone or two to pick with him."

I saw his face break into a smile of almost childlike grace at the Christmas present I was about to offer, his iron gray eyes filling as he turned to a more oblique angle, drawn to the warmth of the coal fire, perhaps distracted by something else that just arrived over the antenna.

"A bone or two—heh . . ."

"Yes, I took care of it my own way."

"You wicked boy."

As I stared into Bennett's ancient face touched with flame, I sensed a closed door swinging open to the light.

"You see," I said, "I slipped a bunch of his tablets into my backpack when he wasn't looking, the most propitious of the lot, with certain telltale hallmarks. It's why it took me so long to get back to you. I will make a holograph"—I laughed, almost more amazed than the doddering Nigel Bennett—"a copy of my translation of those tablets for you tomorrow and put it in the mail first thing, for old times' sake."

"Could you—even before you publish!"

"It's the least I could do for all you've done for me."

"You were always my prince, my prince from Princeton, my favorite American cousin. And you know, such stories don't come easily to a generation of diggers like us. Especially those of us who learned our trade at a tender age, at the end of such a tender age." I saw his great eyes fill with tears and shift their focus to the silver-framed photos on the mantel. "Off to Ypres for a little sport, we thought." His hands came together almost prayerfully, his fat fingertips rubbing just barely. "Bit of a chill today. Put a shovel of coal on the hob, there's a good man."

I moved from my seat to the fireplace, kneeling by a sack of glossy coal and a small hand shovel. Gingerly, I dug out a few chunks and spread them evenly upon the grate over the glowing but chalky remnants, the orange sparks that leaped stirring half-remembered images of other rooms hovering on the edge of recollection. As I stood, the objects on the mantelpiece fully caught my eye. There were faded sepia-gray photos of young soldiers in waders, knee-deep in flooded trenches, peering over battlements of earth and barbed wire. One of the photos, a studio portrait, I realized, was of the Great War poet Rupert Brooke, dressed not as a soldier, but in a shirt open at the throat . . . a beautiful young man with soulful eyes who had yet to know the trenches. Arranged around that mahogany clock of Victorian vintage were archaic artifacts: a tiny white marble figurine of Cycladic origin with exaggerated hips and breasts and a well-defined genital cleft (exquisite and worth hundreds of thousands in the antiquities market), a clay oil lamp common on Crete, a bronze Mycenaean spear point with a mottled green patina, and various potshards from Knossos of leaping dolphins and octopi and a large fragment of red-figure ware displaying heroes and gods in various acts of butchery and buggery. I picked up the Cycladic figurine and rubbed my thumb down the cool marble to the smooth cleft, feeling an immensity of blue spread before me . . . and my father's hand reaching in the moonlight toward his lover. And a little prayer to Demeter to keep me in play.

Nigel Bennett's voice startled me.

"We owe you much, helping to get those traitors out of Hollar. You were the only man who could do it—I was always convinced of that. He insisted, the dirty bugger."

I returned to my chair and bent forward as his voice trailed off and he coughed into a large handkerchief. His old eyes were now fixed on the fire, as if fascinated to watch the new coals catch, their edges glowing, absorbing the heat and giving off new . . . the energy of a million-years-older sun.

"Oh, I suppose their names were the easy part . . . but evidence that will hold up in court is always the hard part, if you can't catch them in a lie and get them for perjury."

"All Cambridge men, too, though not Corpus Christi, the gods be praised. If they'd turned out to be my boys, I might have lost all hope."

"Of course, Maclean and Burgess had already fled to Moscow. Kim Philby was being interrogated by your men at MI5 . . . why couldn't you break him, get a confession out of him? He'd been at it for almost two decades. You'd think someone in his past would have come forward and at least confirmed his Communist connections."

At mention of the name Philby, I saw Nigel Bennett's demeanor alter, his eyes flickering with an active light, and I knew he was seeing his nemesis once more, perhaps from behind the two-way mirror of the interrogation room.

"The cool aplomb of the man under fire, one had to admire it. He sloughed off our best people with the cunning ease of a Houdini; we didn't have the straitjacket to hold him. Both Skardon and Dick White set their traps, and I don't think Philby slipped up once. The man could utter a thousand lies, a thousand variations on the truth, and never forget . . . impressive that."

It came to me in that instant, from the accounts I'd read in the papers when Philby had died in Moscow the year before, that Nigel Bennett had been dismissed as head of MI5 in 1963 because of Philby's defection to Moscow from Beirut. Not only had MI6 returned Philby to the payroll and stationed him in Beirut but when they confronted him with new proof of his spying, he'd actually agreed to confess, only to slip away from under their noses and board a Russian ship arranged by his KGB handler in Beirut. A week later, he was safely ensconced in Moscow, proclaimed a hero of the Soviet Union. Talk about a fuckup to end all fuckups. It had ended Bennett's career and pretty much ruined his reputation. A reputation that today stands even lower: Most historians agree that Nigel Bennett connived with MI6 to let Philby escape on purpose to avoid the embarrassment of a trial. Either that or MI6 made Bennett the fall guy for their own elitist ineptitude.

"Of course, Hollar must have known Philby, between Cambridge days and NKVD networks. And even if Philby didn't run Hollar in occupied Greece as an SIS agent, he would have had access to his intelligence, which he could've then passed on to his NKVD handlers in London. Jesus—a double agent working for the Soviets and the British, except he was only working for the Soviets, and Moscow Center could double-check his intel and his loyalty against what they got through Philby—talk about a deer in the headlights: Hollar couldn't put a toe wrong without calling down the wrath of the gods."

"That's why we sent you, to get him out, our star witness, a KGB defector to expose Philby and put him away for good."

In 1953, after Maclean and Burgess escaped to Moscow in 1951, Philby under virtual house arrest in London, and Anthony Blunt lying low at the Courtauld Institute, Hollar would have been able to reestablish contact with his MI5 handlers without fear of his potential defection being revealed by a Soviet mole inside British intelligence.

"I'm only sorry I got so delayed; there were complications. Hollar was just a tad conflicted in his loyalties, or, more to the point, terrified his link to SIS, MI6, and MI5 would be the death of him.

"Our deep sleeper, biding his time. . . . His loyalty, John, was always to us"—and Bennett swept his arm around his book-lined study—"to me, and to this and what we are about . . . to you as well, of course. With Philby under wraps and incommunicado with Moscow Center, Hollar should have been quite safe to plan his exit."

I was stunned at this old man's assurance—Karel Hollar's loyalty to him personally—that the scholarly world and its values encompassed in his mind's eye remained so sacrosanct, at the last, inviolate, even for a man like Hollar—a man like my father. Or was the problem in the parsing of those scholarly ideals?

"I think part of my difficulty was that Philby still had a piece of him. You see, Hollar knew Philby was being interrogated by MI5, that any moment they could break him and Philby might give up every Soviet agent he'd ever known—or that he might escape, as he eventually did. . . . No wonder Hollar wanted out."

"Philby was out of circulation; we had him watched night and day. He couldn't get within fifty feet of his handlers without us knowing—and he knew that, knew that if he was spotted, it would have been game, set, and match."

My heart fell at his continued assurance.

"Except there was still Anthony Blunt outstanding—if Philby, had somehow gotten to Blunt, or Blunt to him . . ."

Something in his eyes extinguished and his head nodded, as if he was overcome with extreme exhaustion, or was it that I had questioned his professional competency?

As if reading my mind with absolute precision, he said, "Philby wouldn't have dared meet, or try to meet with Blunt; it would have meant the conviction of both for treason. Odd thing is how both went down to ghosts out of their past in 1963, nemesis one and two biting them in their Red arses."

My brain lit up like a Christmas tree and I momentarily lost my thread: Who was to ask the next question?

"A coincidence . . . or just time, allowing the rats to exit the sinking, stinking ship? It was an American who dropped the dime on Blunt, if my memory serves. But tell me about who confirmed Philby's spying."

Bennett's head drooped farther, his eyes closing as if he was nodding off, his brain shutting down in face of the hard facts of how completely British security had been compromised.

"Oh!" I exclaimed in a lighter tone of voice, watching as his eyes shuddered back to life. "Nice of Charles to put us in touch."

"Yes, yes, good of Charles . . . poor man, always a little paranoid that there were more Cambridge traitors in our midst."

"Well, Charles should know; Suzanne Portman was his cousin, and the man she married, Bobby Williams, was another of Anthony Blunt's recruits at Trinity College."

"And you, John, our bulwark, our most trusted sleeper—keeping a close eye on Suzanne must have been jolly good sport."

I took a couple of deep breaths, all I could do to keep calm.

"Loyalty to you, Nigel, to this . . . Hollar and I . . . and Charles"— and I waved my hand as this ancient digger had done a minute before, very much needing the reassurance—"to everything that we are and stand for—scholars."

"Of course, you and Hollar, our pocket aces in the hole, as you Yanks like to call it. Pity about Hollar getting delayed. He was looking forward to full defector status and that cushy villa in Greece. But you know better than any of us that he was a man of divided loyalties who could never trust anyone . . . except what he turned up from the silent earth, things that spoke ambition to his name."

"But surely Suzanne Portman, who married my American cousin, must have given you some concern in the early going about Philby; at the very least, she could have testified that he'd recruited her. Why else have Charles and I keep an eye on her all these years?"

"Our 'Firebird.'"

"Firebird?"

"In the Soviet decrypts your boys brilliantly managed, that was her alias."

"Of course, I'd forgotten."

"Our darling Mata Hari was quite the seductress, like her namesake. Outside of Suzanne's obvious charms, she was too caught up in her own career to bother with more than passing on her father's files before the war and doing the occasional courier job. I thought once she'd married herself off to that rich American and flown the coop to the land of the free and brave, she'd give it up. Wasn't it you who just told me that—'harmless', I think you said—or was it Charles?"

It was in that moment that I began to wonder if the whole point of the game had been to keep Suzanne on ice, keep her quiet . . . and let the Philby embarrassment to the British establishment just fade away. And if MI5 had picked my father precisely because, for both public and private reasons, he might very well have wanted to shoot Karel Hollar, a witness against Philby.

"Charles should know—he just married harmless Suzanne."

"Well, that was quick work, poor man. Widow one day, married again the next. What happened to the American flier? And Charles is a careful man. Hold on . . . Miriam, where's the tea, damn it—and didn't I get an invitation to a wedding recently?" He tilted his face pensively. "Hillders, wasn't it, beautiful spring day, bride as glorious as Gloriana in her prime—perhaps more Titania, queen of the fairies in that fairy garden—fair Albion, the very fairy tale we were fighting for."

Yes, I thought, as Elliot might have it: "we few, we happy few, we band of brothers" . . . "this scepter'd isle . . . this other Eden" . . .

"I was best man."

"And didn't she know it! Always the crowd pleaser that woman, a Titania relentless in pursuit of her man."

"My Calypso . . . but perfectly harmless."

"Better bet than Hollar, if you don't mind me saying so."

I flinched, and from somewhere, an unknown, unacknowledged anger flared.

"Lucky Hollar . . . almost as lucky as Philby. If he'd gone back on our deal, I would have had to shoot the son of a bitch—maybe I should have, considering the ambush of our men and the massacre in Pylos."

"But Philby was worth the candle . . . after all the damage he did to us in Albania, much less you in Korea."

"Yes, I try to forget about the Albanians who died. It ruins one's sleep. But then, better part of valor and all that—for all concerned, better such a mess not see the light of day."

Bennett started up, as if waking from that very sleep. "But what did delay you after they executed Hollar? I remember something about a delay—did something delay you? The tablets you just mentioned, of course. We were all so concerned about your delayed return."

"Time . . . I'm afraid Hollar took his time, but in the end, I think he came clean, in his way, navigating to the very end down a very narrow trail of conflicting loyalties."

"Not to mention your fears about Eisenhower, that hair trigger John Foster Dulles—not to mention harebrained Allen, and his wildly faulty judgment. No wonder you were so paranoid about another dark ages, not that I wasn't in on its inception: four years on the Western Front."

"Well, just as well you had at least one Yank in harness, keep an eye on things in Washington."

"Without real Americans like you keeping us up to scratch, who knows what troubles those Dulles boys might have gotten us into."

"It was the least I could do to thank you for Greece, for Pylos."

"How is Allen, by the way?"

"Last I heard, he was doddering around, still chasing women."

"You always were a quick learner. You had me worried in the early going. . . ." His voice fell off, as if he'd, too, lost the thread, as if he were distracted by the spreading flames in the coal fire. "An imperial power must at root be as ruthless as its best first sergeants—and even more brutal when it's absolutely necessary. An uncongenial thing for a democratic people; you lack, don't you see, the aristocratic hauteur of a ruling class. We worried if you had the belly to rule others. Takes a velvet glove, co-opting the elites—and an iron fist when required to keep the little people in line."

"Not unlike the Athenians, I suppose, pushing around their erstwhile allies in the Delian League until they brought down their own ruin against Sparta."

I found myself transfused with rare energy, my brain, for a few minutes yet, abuzz with the world of my father's secret life, which resonated with my own secret failures in Vietnam: in life as in love. But I could also sense the slow ebbing away of that world, crumbling as the Berlin Wall had crumbled weeks before, as life drained from Bennett's noble face—as the spirits of the dead had finally fled Odysseus's gaze to Erebian gloom—his chin beginning a kind of mechanical nodding, entering a hypnotic trance, even as the coal fire flared, reflecting steaks of ruby red in his glassy eyes.

Something of my grandmother's steadfast and loyal voice steadied mine in defense of the man I never knew and the country I yet loved.

"Well, at least you can't blame us for blowing up the world—even if your Cambridge traitors did their jolly good best to pass every atomic secret we possessed to our competitors. Eisenhower and the Dulles brothers just managed to keep a lid on the worst, until Kennedy almost got us blown to kingdom come."

His old eyes became fixed on the fire as there emerged another sound, a low-level roar that I realized was torrents of winter rain. I turned to the bay window, where sheets of rain blotted the milky green quad. He shifted himself closer to the warmth of the fire and again gathered the thread.

"The rain would drive you mad. And the mud, of course. But what I remember was the sound of their feet, as if American feet had a distinctive sound. It was a damp, vibrating pounding coming off the muddy road that stretched across the low black hills, where the dawn fogs rolled like phantom waves. No one marched like that anymore. They were trying to impress us. Bolt upright, too, sniffing the morning air like the queen's horse guards on parade in Hyde Park. Hard to know whether to laugh or cry, those of us who hadn't been out on the wires all night. Why should one hate their fresh-scrubbed faces? Especially since we knew what awaited them down the line. A few miles and a few days would change them forever, and they would lose those smiles and become like us . . . or worse.

"One of my sergeants shouted disgustedly, 'Goin' to tidy it all up fer us, gov'ner?' We saw them smile and give us the thumbs-up. 'Come with me, then,' shouted my master sergeant. 'Give you Yanks a guided tour, if you like—you'll see, it'll be just the thing.' The man spat in the mud as their ranks swung past our position. 'Who the 'ell do they think they are? Bloody tourists—that's what.' I remember the look on their faces as they saw our support trenches and barbed wire for the first time . . . as if they'd been transported back to some barbaric age of iron, or just the merest eccentricity of a doddering civilization. Off they marched for their little snatch at glory . . . a matter of months and it all just fell into your laps."

Miriam finally arrived with a large tray of tea and chocolate biscuits. She gave me a knowing look and a wink for good measure as she poured our tea and handed Nigel Bennett his cup. In my mind, I kept seeing those endless white crosses on green.

"Are you cold?" she asked. "Want me to bring you your wrap?"

"No, no, dear." He shook her off and rattled his cup and saucer in doing so. "That won't be necessary. We've got our tea now and Johnny has put some more coals on the fire. Run along like a good girl and leave us to it."

She handed me my cup and a biscuit and made a hasty retreat, weaving her way through the stacks of books. Nigel's cup again shook as he carefully fitted it to his lips, savoring the sweetness.

"Elusive thing, the human soul, when you try to remember those you have lost, their faces, I mean. Like those chunks of coal you just popped in . . . black and impervious to speculation, then something touches off a spark, a stray memory—call it love, a bit of heat that finds its own, loyal to its own, illuminating that vital and unique life, its fuliginous center glowing—for seconds transparent, its essence finally exposed, but so dazzling that its essential mystery—that life of the soul, don't you think?—remains obscure . . . that white star in the sky sur-rounded by the infinite night of ourselves . . . and like all things, headed for dusty oblivion."

I handed him the plate of chocolate biscuits.

"Nigel, you missed your calling. . . . You should have been a poet, a teller of tales—not a digger, but the magnificent teacher you are. . . . Perhaps we all have."

Nigel Bennett quickly grew tired and suggested dinner at his favorite restaurant after his nap. "The Eagle—Watson and Crick, talk about code breakers, downed their pints there." This meant my staying the night at the Royal Cambridge Hotel, recommended by Miriam. The rain was miserable and travel a mess, and so I readily accepted, even though Nigel seemed pretty worn-out. By the time I'd showered at the hotel, Miriam called my room to say that she thought Nigel was too weak, and, in fact, she'd just put him to bed. "I feared he had a cold coming on." She suggested I visit in the morning, when she hoped he might be better. I tried calling Hillders to let Laura know I was staying over, but the line was always busy. The hotel receptionist said there were ice storms in the south and telephone lines were down. After a restless night in my beautifully appointed, antiseptically clean room, waking to the rain and to dreams of shadowy rooms I couldn't recognize, I called after breakfast and got a flustered Miriam, who was hoping I might be the doctor returning her call. Nigel was worse, she told me; he had a temperature and his mind was wandering. "That Alzheimer's is a tricky devil, but he seems quite delirious." I spent an anxious couple of hours wandering the Fitzwilliam Museum and then called again. The doctor had been by and was concerned it was pneumonia; if he wasn't better by the end of the day, they'd put him in the hospital. I stopped by and sat by Nigel's bed for a few minutes. His lethargic, dull eyes, shorn of glasses, were open and staring into space—the gray reflecting the white of the ceiling—his head composed on a fluffed pillow in his spartan bedroom. His breathing was labored. I don't think he recognized me, and he didn't respond to my voice. I said good-bye and pressed his cool hand on the blanket, feeling a terrible sense of loss, of time nipping at my heels, as caretakers of memory, one after the other, slipped away, closing doors as they went.

I spent an hour before my train walking around chilly Cambridge, lingering in the immaculate quad of Trinity College, as if that panoply of humanist endeavor and scholarly remove might yield some essential insight into the traitorous instincts that had produced the likes of Kim Philby and his spawn, a man I never knew or wanted to know but who terrified and fascinated me in equal measure, that such talent and beguiling brilliance could be turned from the values of Western civilization and embrace with steely-eyed commitment a boundlessly malignant evil. Something, I knew, had preoccupied my father—enough that he'd carelessly or purposely, named Philby in his Pankrác diary—who had felt the hot breath of his unctuous evil; as Elliot would have put it, "lilies that fester" . . . A specter, too, I realized, lingering like an unhealed wound, preying on Laura's mind even though she dared not breathe a word of those fears to me.

From these hallowed halls of academe, not a little reminiscent of the Anglican Gothic of the Winsted chapel, had come a band of traitors, young men who came to believe, against all the evidence—certainly by the time of the Nazi-Soviet nonaggression pact and Stalin's terror—that they were enlisting their country on the side of the angels in Moscow. And between the atom bomb secrets passed on by Donald Maclean, the Allied strategy passed on verbatim by Guy Burgess and Anthony Blunt, revealing Eisenhower's and Truman's reluctance to drive on to Berlin and Prague, and Philby's revelation of the decryption of Soviet ciphers by the NSC, thus leaving the United States blind to the invasion of South Korea, they nearly managed it: the fondest desires of their romantic youth, a decadent West under the boot of the Soviet Union. But then we had plenty of traitors on our side who'd managed as much, if not worse. As Virgil had always told me: "Alger Hiss . . . tip of the ice cube."

Even with the recent fall of the Berlin Wall, I realized it had been a near-run thing, and I felt as never before the agonies of doubt and deception that had warped my father's scholarly equanimity and that of his once-proud family—my grandmother's "European diseases" echoing like a dreary refrain over scenes of barbed wire–encrusted earth, or reflected in the hazy light of a sluggish river on its way to the sea, those fiendish yet permeable boundaries that separate the free from the unfree, and the deceitful brilliance that could justify the enslavement of millions.

A dark age that might have trumped all dark ages.

And I thought again of all those white crosses in the Meuse-Argonne cemetery, and all their millions of comrades, and how, if they'd lived, what a better world they'd have bequeathed to their children, and their children's children.

When I exited the Midhurst station late that afternoon—I still hadn't been able to get a call through—I was stunned to see through the mists that swirled in the small parking area next to the High Street my blue left-hand drive Land Rover: our time machine, our home, our chariot of escape. For a brief, wonderful moment, I thought Laura was there waiting to pick me up, but I found it empty, the doors unlocked, and the key on the seat. I looked around, went back into the station, checked the platforms, with the expectation she'd left the Land Rover for the warmth of the waiting room. She was nowhere to be found. The seven-minute drive through sunken, winding roads and up the steep drive of Hillders brought a change from damp mists to a couple of inches of wet snow that had transformed the house and grounds into a canvas of white. I opened the heavy front door, burdened on either side by ropy wisteria vines, and was immediately aware of distant voices arguing. I walked slowly and deliberately down the central hallway, feeling, more than ever, the interloper in those rooms and now a sneak, too, as I strained to make out the conversation.

"How could she—how could she just run off like that, after everything I've done for her?" Then the colonel: "You always bargain with her, scold her, fawn over her; no wonder she acts like she's sixteen. And I'm regarded as a nonentity even in my *own* home, by my *own* daughter?"

As I entered the living room, the fire ablaze, the two contestants fell silent where they stood by the mantel. Then Suzanne made a rush for the door and, as she passed me, flung this in my face: "I suppose we have you to thank for all this."

All I could get out of the colonel was that mother and daughter had had a huge fight over dinner the previous evening, during the ice storm, and first thing that morning, Laura had taken all her things and fled in my Land Rover and disappeared.

"Did she say anything about me?" I asked him. "Did she leave a note?"

"Her room is empty—not a word to any of us."

"Where did she go?"

"Your guess as good as mine. New York, her apartment. Suzanne is fit to be tied; she was sure they had an understanding."

"What kind of understanding?"

Charles just shook his head, looked at his watch, and moved to the door. "I'll go up to Suzanne and see what I can do. Dinner is in an hour. If I can lure her down to the table, I suggest you two should try to talk things through. I will absent myself after the first course. Quite frankly, I suspect you've now ended up *being* the problem. I had no idea."

For the next hour, dismayed, hurt, I wandered from room to room, inventorying the books and collections, the fabulous watercolors and prints, trying to find distractions, but without Laura, I felt a numbing sense of panic: doors shutting like heart valves being clamped off one by one by one. A sentence out of Max's *Gardens of Saturn*, ostensibly about the dancer's mother, but apt for the heroine herself, kept running though my mind: *She was the supernova in their galaxy, the sole source of light and energy in their outrushing star life. Run if you dare, people, sprint for the exits if you can, but beware: There is no light to shadow your steps in the outer darkness.*

Dinner was an ordeal. Three at a table designed to seat thirty, as if all the guests had fled from the plague. Charles saw to it that the wine flowed, an accelerant to the flames of his new bride's alcoholism. We drank a '59 Pomerol—six bottles that required careful dusting just to access the corks—that deserved to be savored like the nectar of gods but which we guzzled like Bowery winos. Charles kept us afloat on tales of Lloyd George's mistresses and Stanley Baldwin's boorishness in the face of Hitler's and Stalin's evil leers. Every candle was lit, a bonfire of wax, so that the family portraits glittered on the paneled walls like jurors out of a Rembrantesque gloom. And then quite abruptly, the colonel got up, excused himself, and told us like a stern paterfamilias not to leave the table until we had "resolved whatever needs resolving. Obviously, I'm just a pawn in your mess."

Suzanne laughed wildly as if she'd snapped to out of the ether, as she raised her glass to salute the departed.

"Peter can play Hamlet to my debauched Gertrude perhaps," she called after him, "now that my beloved Claudius has exited the scene."

I was tempted to ask her, in a jovial aside, if she'd been privy to Elliot's theories on Edward de Vere, the seventeenth earl of Oxford, but I had sense enough to know that mention of his name would not help my cause. In the soft candlelight, she looked a lot better than when I'd seen her so overwrought in the living room. The lines on her face weren't nearly so visible, the years disguised behind her elaborate makeup—nothing overdone, but it had been carefully and expertly applied by the new mistress of the house, the stage performer to the end. And compared to the faces in the portraits on the panel walls, she was still a cracking beauty. After the part I'd so easily assumed with Nigel Bennett, I was tempted to resume my role (not as a special friend to MI5) in order to find what my father had so loved in her . . . if it was, too, to be found in her daughter, who had just walked out of my life.

"I want you to know, Peter, I don't blame you, don't hate you; in fact, I want to commend you for saving my daughter. I really mean that. I've not seen her look as well in years. Almost like the daughter I remember when she first auditioned for ABT, what, almost exactly twenty years ago, the little bitch."

Suzanne began carefully pouring the Pomerol, concentrating to keep her hand steady.

"Her dedication and discipline are almost scary," I offered.

Suzanne lowered the bottle and delicately wiped the dust from her fingers with her napkin, dust that the colonel had missed when he'd opened the fourth bottle. Then she shoved it across the table to me.

"To be as good as she: It's a calling, and very few are chosen." She sipped the wine and sighed. "Ripe, a touch of mocha and hints of something I can't quite put my finger on. All my Cambridge cousins knew their stupid wine."

I took a sip. "Perhaps it needs to breathe."

"I've told her, if she's smart and careful, she may have three or four seasons left. Pick and choose the parts, go to your strengths, cover your weaknesses—where the younger girls can't harm you. Fonteyn danced into her fifties."

"I'm looking forward to seeing her dance."

She looked at me sharply and took a deep breath.

"Distractions are what got her into trouble before."

"You mean Max?"

"She could have been the greatest dancer of her generation, right up there with Suzanne Farrell—how I loved her having my name—and Laura has a more beautiful line, much better feet, and something of the same spiritual quality. If only she hadn't wasted herself on that boy." Her voice was slurry, her lips pressed tight between sips of wine. "Talent like that is a gift, yes, from me, from who knows where. Good God, if you'd seen her as a little girl—when this wine was still young—she would walk into ballet class and take her place at the barre, and everything stopped. All the chattering little things just fell silent. She had that kind of presence, that kind of effect among her own kind." She shook her head. "I've been at the Met when she had entire audiences in tears, for Macmillan's Juliet." She raised her long, delicate hand and closed her fingers. "Like that . . . thousands of people stirred to the bottom of their souls."

"I hope I'll have the chance."

"Problem is, your generation has no idea what real sacrifice is about." She raised her glass toward me to encourage me to refill mine, which I did. Her full lips formed a sarcastic pout; wet with wine, they had a peculiar liquid quality in the harder angles of her cheeks and chin. "Weddings were, well, sacrosanct in our day—new beginnings and all that, jolly good hopes for the future."

I wanted to scream with frustration, to let loose with a barrage of invective, as my father had in a few letters, but something my grandmother had repeated to me held me back: "When a person is unhappy you must be firm but kind."

"Listen, Prague was really my fault, not hers. I want you to know how much I care about her, admire her; she's made everything possible . . . to find out what really happened to my father."

By the alarm that flared in her eyes, I knew I had a bargaining chip. What I didn't know was how much Laura had already told her, much less gotten out of her.

"Oh, well, yes, she mentioned something along those lines."

"There's a side of her," I said, "perhaps you've missed: a remarkable mind and moral passion. . . . She inspires me."

"Oh, so now she's *your* muse, is she?" She laughed and pulled herself up in her chair, shoulders set so the décolletage of her lavender silk evening dress fully set off her neck and the rising curve of her breasts. She patted her head as if to make sure her chignon was firmly in place—ready for business. "Problem is, she always had bad luck with men. It seems to run in the family . . . up to now."

Behind her in the dull flickering light, we had an audience of soldiers, inventors, and statesmen—all safely behind varnish, spectral figures into whose line she had now managed to fully graft herself, and her daughter—the whole nine yards: Pomerol, candelabra by the dozen, and rooms in which to secrete regrets for eternity.

"Really, I thought she and Max hit it off pretty well. And no small thing," I added, taking a page from Vlada, "to have her early life immortalized in the pages of one of the best-selling novels of our generation—you, too, in walk-ons around the edges."

"That is hardly the kind of immortality—or did you say immorality?—she should have been seeking."

"Well, it seems you've relieved her of the incubus of the Williamses—that's certainly a fresh start at life."

"Incubus, an interesting word for my dead husband and his pathetic brood, but perhaps more apt than any I could have come up with. Chip off the old block, I see: Your father couldn't stand Bobby *and* he was always correcting me, adding to my vocabulary. I never went to college, after all, unlike my brother, Francis, and my brilliant Cambridge cousins; I was just a glamorous dancer—not much better than a chorus girl in many eyes, trying to make a mark on the world."

"Then you should be proud of Laura—a voracious reader, and I never have to correct her on anything. But maybe she has Max to thank . . . a genius with words. Keeping up with him can't have been a cakewalk."

She stared at me boldly, brazenly as her tone grew angry.

"I don't subscribe to the theory that pain is good because it deepens the artistic range. When you've seen the real thing, when you've tended burn victims as I did for five long years, and tried to console their wives and mothers . . . there is nothing noble to be got there. But don't get me wrong; I liked Max, in a way; he was not an entirely frivolous artist, but he shied away from the seriousness of life, preferring sly humor to profundity, or bettering the human lot. I may dislike his novel for the unflattering light it casts on my daughter, but it's not to say it's inaccurate in many of its details; it's just . . ." She seemed to halt before some looming crevasse. "I love my daughter, Peter, but I also know who comes first—her cruelties to me and Max were many."

"You prefer socialist realism, then—all good things all the time?"

"Don't get clever with me, young man."

I found her eyes beginning to settle on me with a furious intensity, as if she needed to fully read my face, her long nose and oval nostrils lifting ever so slightly, savoring the powerful scent of burning wax. I felt a hard stirring in my crotch. The candles fluttered and I shivered. Perhaps a cold draft from the banks of windows at the far end of the dining room, or from the huge empty fireplace decorated with Delft tiles, which could not be used, so Charles told us, until the chimney had been repointed.

"I find it hard to believe she would just up and leave without telling me—something," I stammered.

Oh, the icy smile that hint of vulnerability produced. "Perhaps she'd just had enough—wouldn't be the first time."

"Are you warning me off her?"

"Max blamed her for his troubles; she blames herself for what happened."

"Once upon a time, I took care of him, too."

At this, she snorted dismissively.

"I gather you've read your father's letters to me, and mine to him; Laura's cruelty—and crudity—knows no bounds. So, you *know* how your father put me through hell."

"So, like father like son . . ."

"Look at it as if I'm saving your life, at least a heartache as great as mine. . . . I was absolutely faithful, in my way."

"Is that why she left so abruptly, to save me?"

She laughed again, her glass and lips all atremble.

"You're almost exactly the same age as your father was when he left me on September 7, 1953, or was it September 8? You see, it must have been well past midnight—past your bedtime—if not dawn, when he left my bed."

"And his daughter? His wife and son . . . And I believe you fucked in the great outdoors, at Pine Meadow by Eden Lake."

I kept my eyes trained on her face as I drained my glass and poured another, then pushed the bottle back across the table. Her eyes widened with a combustible mixture of alarm and ecstasy as she reached with barely intact aplomb for the bottle.

"Did she tell you how she stole my personal and private letters?"

"You had them hidden."

"Charles pleaded with her to come and see me at the Spaulding Rehab Hospital. She took the train from New York, popped her head around the door of my room for a quick word with Charles, grabbed a taxi to his house in Brookline, ransacked it until she found my things, and was on the next train back to New York."

"There were things she needed to know."

She rolled her eyes.

"I've tried for a reconciliation, and I had a miserable wedding day without Laura here—not that she wouldn't have managed to spoil it anyway, and for *her* father." She smiled enigmatically, her expression more sorrowful than pensive. "I've had two miserable wedding days— and John certainly managed to royally spoil the first." She glared at me, tendons in her long neck straining out as if to snap. "You'll make it a bloody tradition."

"You bloody well invited him."

"Did I?"

"'This changes nothing, my love!' Scribbled in your hand on the invitation."

I saw her waver, wine sloshing, as she grabbed a linen napkin to wipe her hand. The score of candle flames, a tiny conflagration, merged in the brittle blue of her eyes, two points of light drowned in tears.

"Oh my God . . . I wanted him to come and save me, to blow it all up and take me away from everything, from the burn ward, from the war—where I could be myself again."

"Where you could recruit him, or at least get out of him what you needed for your Soviet handlers."

"Oh . . ." She cupped her lips with her palm as if terrified. "Is that why my daughter called me a liar—a *fucking* liar, I who rescued her from a manic-depressive and paranoid homosexual and his degenerate family. Who warned her off Max a dozen times." She reached to a fiercely dripping candle and let the molten wax stream in smoky rivulets down her fingers, oblivious to the burning. "Can you imagine my surprise when John arrived and it turned out not only that he *knew* Bobby but that Bobby had invited him, as well, to be his best man?"

"That's bullshit. You two had to have dreamed it all up in some scheme to milk him and the other guests for intelligence on the D-day landings. Why else would you have invited Kim Philby, the Macleans, *and* Anthony Blunt?"

She froze at the sound of those names, watching the whitening wax harden on her fingers. Just the hint of a smile indicated that perhaps she recognized a worthy opponent.

"My Cambridge crowd. All friends of our dead Francis, my brother. We toasted him a dozen times if we toasted him once."

"It wasn't Kim Philby, was it, who recruited you, Firebird? Or did he seduce you first and then recruit you, or was it all the same thing in your Cambridge crowd?"

At the mention of Philby, she seemed to stiffen as if in the face of a hard wind, her eyes watering as she picked at the wax coating her hand.

"The others, yes, that was Bobby's idea, to compromise all the people he hated and who hated him. But not John—if only it were so. Bobby was in love with John. He pretended it was Elliot Goddard, but it was always John."

"Pure coincidence, then, of all the Americans in England—*all the lousy gin joints*—during the war, that you were—what, lovers of both, or all three?"

"No, just your father."

"You realize the statistical improbabilities of what you're telling me?"

"That's just how John put it—this is truly a nightmare—you're just like him."

"Beyond baffling." I drained my glass and motioned for the bottle. "So you admit it . . . you and Bobby were working for Soviet intelligence?"

"Actually, I first saw John years before in Venice, a glimpse, a smile, at Palazzo Barberini."

"When he had to dive into the Grand Canal after Amaryllis Williams to save her from drowning."

"Terrible thing . . . At night, he'd tell me about it sometimes, how she had a stranglehold on him in the muck at the bottom—pitch-black—how she almost managed to drown both of them. Can you imagine for a young man . . ."

"An artist, a Circe, a sorceress, a seducer of souls; and you, eighteen, your glory days, when you danced for the king, before Philby got his mucky claws into you, as well. Was it as early as Cambridge, or later, in London, when you were a star? Or later still?"

She wiped at her lips.

"Why is it I feel an echo? . . . Well, we were small fry. I did mostly courier work, and Bobby was too much of a coward and an idiot to be terribly useful—as desperately as he wanted to be. But I could never get John to believe me: that it had nothing *whatsoever* to do with him, that I would never do anything to compromise or endanger him—that

I loved him too much for that. But after Elliot Goddard snitched on us, long after we'd been active, John read back into the past as if it had all been part of a grand conspiracy. He never really trusted me again and it just ate away at our love. It is one thing to lose love, to have it dim or be thrown over, but to have love smothered by distrust is an agony beyond bearing."

"You confessed as much to him at Elysium sometime in the spring of 1947, before he went to Athens as CIA station chief, when he first broke it off with you. But in late 1947 and 1948, you were still meeting with Melinda Maclean in New York; you were still a courier for the KGB."

"You and your father—he had no goddamn proof. Neither did the FBI or McCarthy or the CIA or anybody else. Without proof, it didn't happen."

"You were toxic to his career—in the early fifties: a CIA officer with a lover who was a Soviet fucking spy!"

"Havoc, sheer havoc. It twisted him into knots no matter what I did. I renounced the one thing that had meant so much to me. I swore on my life to him. I even offered to betray other agents to him—to prove my fidelity to our love."

Hearing that, I lowered my glass. Desperate to keep my wits about me, I found myself staring straight into her eyes as I began a mental ransacking of room after room after room—terrified of the lust rising inside me.

"You offered Philby—Maclean had fled to Moscow by then?"

"I told him I'd give them all up for him, if he'd marry me."

"On your last night together, in the field by Eden Lake, under the great pine, the last of the first-growth white pine, the only one that remains in all of Elysium. You watched the dawn, the shadow of that huge tree 'reaching out to Eden Lake like the hand of God.'"

Was it a hint of relief or horror on her face as I played back to her my father's words in his Pankrác diary?

"Please, you're terrifying me."

I knew then Laura had made no mention of the Pankrác diary; like me, she was using it as a check to her mother's lies.

"And it wasn't just that Bobby was in the house; you had Charles up, of all people: Charles, who arrived for a meeting with my father to let him know that a person of great interest to British intelligence had offered a deal to defect, a high East German official, sick and exasperated by the Soviet repression of German workers—and a revolution gone sour—who was in possession of certain names, among other things, who was willing to defect and stand witness against Kim Philby, who was under interrogation in London."

This all came clear in my head in the very seconds I spoke the words, as if the words weren't even mine.

"Charles?"

The look of dismay on her face, whether real or feigned, worried me, that I'd let down my side of the bargain with Charles Fairburn. A room she hadn't entered.

"Surely you knew he was keeping an eye on my father, a freelancer with MI5 . . . to keep an eye on the American cousins."

I could see the upper curve of her breasts actually deflate as her diaphragm lost buoyancy. Something she hadn't known, or, more probably, something she'd feared or sensed: My father, too, was freelancing for MI5. I might have added, "keeping an eye on you," but I left that pin unpulled if it might save her marriage to Charles. She eyed me with the expression of a guilty child caught red-handed, then a moment later, raised a mock toast, only to make a slightly mystified inspection of the rubied liquid in her glass, as if the taste had gone off, or, like an alchemist, hoping to find some precious precipitant. She nodded her head in the recognition that we had, after all, arrived at the same place, and her gaze lengthened to encompass the windows at my back.

"There is an old saying that all is revealed on the marriage night, *tout comprendre c'est tout pardoner* . . . not just the past, mind you, but the future, as well. You see, when John arrived unexpectedly at the wedding, I had dear Cecily put him in one of the few unoccupied rooms, the room I always slept in as a child when I was down at Hillders for holidays. A magical room with pictures of dancers, and windows overlooking the gardens. On a spring night after a long winter, that room would be infused with scents of the countryside, of roses and freshly mown grass, and of wisteria and lilac once they were fully in bloom . . . like an aphrodisiac to a young woman." She held a cork in the candle flame, watching the flame lick and burn, wafting the smoke back and forth as if holding a miniature incense burner. "From that room, I schemed as a little girl to be the next Pavlova and take to my bed the greatest lovers in the land—the power to bend them to my will. When I met John in the rehabilitation hospital in Guilford, I was not a virgin—far from it. I had been seduced by very experienced men when I was fifteen and sixteen. I had been adored by skilled lovers. And I knew my capacity for joy and was never shy to have my fill. When I fell in love with John, with his beautiful hurt body, I found him to be a virgin—so he professed—unused to the ways of a woman's body. But he took to my instruction like a champion. I brought him alive; we feasted, and fasted, and feasted again. Having his child became my way of saving him, saving us. . . . Perhaps you find this hard to understand."

"No, not in the least."

"There was no artifice, no ambition." She shrugged helplessly. "I just loved him with all my heart. But we lost our first child."

I found myself wanting to reach a hand across the table and take hers, but I steeled myself.

"So when you found out he was going back to Berlin, perhaps on a dangerous mission, perhaps a mission that would end in the conviction of Kim Philby, you offered—what?—to confess all you knew to MI5 and MI6, to give up Philby?"

"He didn't have the guts to marry me—if he really loved me."

"The end of his marriage, his career, his reputation—even Princeton . . . a hard bargain."

"And a daughter . . ."

"When was the last time you saw Kim Philby, or slept with him—not in Washington in the spring of 1951, when he came under suspicion along with Maclean, when he desperately needed to get word to Maclean in London to warn him of his imminent arrest by MI5 on espionage charges?"

"We never met in Washington; I swore that to John—suicide to dare such a thing in the nest of the FBI."

"In his letters, he mentioned lunches with Philby where Kim all but bragged about fucking you."

"That was Kim's way to get under the skin of the competition, to get at their vulnerabilities. Kim was married and had children. You must believe me. Without that trust, there is nothing."

"You invited Philby to Hermitage the summer of '51, along with my parents—just to make sure they—my father—got the message."

"Fiddlesticks. Aileen and their children were there, as well. I'd barely gotten the stitches out after Laura."

"*Kim* . . . this is what you do, your specialty—sneaking around, so to speak."

"It was to make John jealous—his one weakness. Kim and I had known each other since Francis's Cambridge days."

"You lied about everything else, so why would you give up Philby, the lodestone of your Popular Front aspirations, your youthful flame of antifascism, the just cause of your glory days at Cambridge?"

An imperious, if sad, smile curled her lips.

"John didn't love your mother. I'm sorry, but it's the truth. You must know that."

"You had that, too, for purposes of blackmail."

"Why would I stoop to blackmail, as you call it, about something as inconsequential as their marriage of convenience? John could be a real bastard at times. He could be steelier than his mother. Seems to run in your family, that bloody puritan streak of yours."

"Refusing your offer and taking on that mission and never returning to you?"

"I offered him the crown jewels; he would have gone down in history. A love that triumphed over the evils of communism."

"Like Elliot Goddard getting Bobby to expose Anthony Blunt—or was that your idea, as well?"

"You can't imagine what I would have been giving up for your father—the danger, too. Moscow Center was expert at eliminating traitors, or potential traitors, or the completely innocent, if necessary, to protect their people. During the Alger Hiss trial, witnesses dropped like flies or simply disappeared. If you've never felt the anxiety of such terror, the sting of such guilt, of shame for disloyalty to your comrades, you can never know."

"Well, all it took was a call to the Soviet embassy to take care of your previous husband."

"Don't act like a bastard; you don't have it in you."

"If not Washington, when—when was the last time you saw Philby?"

"I never betrayed your father. . . . I never stopped loving him."

I stared into the trembling glassy blue of her eyes, searching for that sympathetic spark, the moral courage, as I'd known it in her daughter, to do the right thing. If there was anything left to believe or if she was just a pro's pro down to her prehensile toes.

Tears filled her eyes.

"Kim Philby, or my father?"

"I sought him out in London in the summer of 1954. John had been gone for ten months, just a silly postcard. I was terrified he was dead or imprisoned. I couldn't contact anybody for information. His mother, his wife . . . What could I do? All our networks had been compromised by the FBI and shut down by Moscow. I was willing to do anything to save him."

"There's no way you could have gotten to Philby. MI5 was investigating him, interrogating him. They must have had him under constant surveillance. For you to have gone to him, a known KGB operative, would have meant his ruin. He wouldn't have let you get within a mile of him."

"I saw him in a pub near the Ruislip tube stop. He spent half the day making sure he wasn't tailed, as did I. We even laughed at how badly MI5 handled the most basic tradecraft. But you're right: He was already a ruined man, drinking too much, his wife, Aileen, going slowly mad, close to a nervous breakdown, and out of touch with his friends—so alone. He hadn't been in direct touch with Moscow Center since 1951."

"No Soviet agent would dare go near him under those circumstances."

"All I wanted was to get help, find out . . . if he might put in a good word for John—get him back to me."

"You can't have been that stupid. Who could he have gone to, anyway? Besides, if the KGB knew that my father had conclusive evidence against Philby, they'd never have let him go."

At this, she broke into tears, nodding, wringing her wax-covered hands like a bad parody of Lady Macbeth. We sat in silence for many minutes.

"Say what you will," she finally choked out, "loyalty was the currency of the realm." And she looked at me through mascara-running eyes. "This is hard for me. . . . You remind me of him in so many ways. I feel like you're his avenging spirit."

At that, I had to wipe my own tears.

"If anything of what you say is true"—and Elliot's Cheshire cat grin swam up to me out of the penumbral darkness of hovering portraits: how history is always struggling to rewrite itself in the mind of the playwright—"why would you have had a signed copy of Kim Philby's autobiography in your possession? Correct me if I'm wrong: 'For Suzanne, A love never betrayed. And you, my darling, the best of all. Kim.'"

"Laura stole that, too—would steal my very soul if she could. Which," Suzanne said, sighing and swiping at her streaming eyes, "she does every time she dances."

"Such an endearment!"

"Kim was at heart an ironist; how else to stare into the abyss of his lies—the show trials, the executions and gulags—and never flinch."

"You can't have ventured to Moscow to get it, because they would never have let you near him. So he must have had the KGB deliver it to you personally, or was it a Federal Express gift of memory from an old man sitting in his book-lined study sipping Prince of Wales tea—a last hurrah for the road. Or a hint from your old handlers to finish off Bobby to save yourself."

She looked straight through me until a shiver of cold or fear brought her back to where we sat across from each other.

"I imagine he did the same for every woman he'd known."

"Even for the one, so I heard yesterday from the horse's mouth, who arrived out of the blue in London in 1962 and visited an old Cambridge friend, a Rothschild scion no less, a bosom friend and colleague of Philby in SIS, and told him in quite exquisite detail how she had been recruited by Philby in the spring of 1938, when Stalin's terror had taken its toll on London's NKVD handlers . . . how badly he, so alone and needy, was desperate for someone to help out in the shortage."

"Charles mentioned you'd been to visit that pathetic old man."

"What really fascinates me is the timing, and it perplexed that pathetic old man, as well, since it 'eventuated,' as he put it, in his demotion to master of Corpus Christi College after Philby's clandestine escape from Beirut. But more to the point, from an entirely different source later that year, Anthony Blunt had been revealed as a spy by an American who had been recruited by him at Cambridge in 1937. Irony or coincidence . . . you and Bobby were both trying for a clean break from your past?"

Suzanne smiled easily, as if her self-confidence was returning now that all our cards were on the table.

"You silly child. Fucking Nigel and his imperialist minions"—she held her finger to lips as her voice dropped to a near whisper—"only wanted their self-satisfied incompetence to fade away."

"Philby?"

"Everything in good time: That is how I've led my life." She smiled so sweetly through her tears that I was tempted to utter an endearment. "You see, there was a recklessness in your father that defied all logic. I was reckless only within what I could control. A dancer has to be that way. Otherwise, the risks are too great. When you've performed the Rose Adagio before the king of England at Covent Garden, the shifting about of a few papers is child's play."

"Did he tell you about the risks he took in Greece, the massacre in Pylos—what he witnessed?"

"He didn't need to, because his body told me all I needed to know. A dancer knows. But he recognized the temptation in himself as a weakness to which he was drawn. It was an addiction, tempting fate—call it what you will—that he developed as a young man to befuddle and challenge his best friend, if not his lover, Bobby, my late husband."

It was then I realized that my father had never told her about Joanna and their child. How many rooms—with everything—they kept off-limits to each other.

"You're avoiding the subject at hand."

"I should tell you about the story about the rattlesnake they found as boys at Elysium."

"Let's go back to risks, cost-benefit analysis, probabilities—it's all the rage in academia these days."

She gestured across the table with her open palm.

"In 1962, when Laura was ten going on eighteen, I stopped coaching her full-time and put her in classes with other girls. It was something of a revelation, for the first time standing back from my creation and observing at a distance how she outshone the other girls . . . how she looked, how she ran rings around them—risking falls and humiliation at every turn to be better than the rest. That's when I knew . . . when I took my revenge."

"When you dropped a note to Elliot Goddard that Bobby might well be susceptible to a trade: *Anthony* for a place on the Winsted board."

She smiled as she realized there were still depths I could not quite fathom.

"You do your father proud, that bloody puritan streak that never rests until you've had your chance to hammer in the last coffin nail, as well. But flexibility of mind, well . . . I was out to revenge the death of your father."

It went right over my head, so much so that I found myself listening passively to a few more slurred tales of my father's cruelties to Bobby Williams in their youth, trying to parse the edits as she creepily pulled lines of congealed wax from her hand like strips of flesh—ever the performer.

"I loved his strength, that he'd survived, that he learned his way around my body like the finest athlete—all the right instincts in a man."

I pulled the final cork and reached across the table to fill her glass. She held it out to me, drunk as she was, her hand steady and firm; her fingers were streaked with angry red, her eyes daring me on.

"You're such a darling and so handsome . . . *my* darling." She held her full glass high, anticipating the filling of mine, and mine reaching hers as I offered a toast.

"The fall of the Iron Curtain, and America, and second acts," I proclaimed.

"Oh yes, that is the price you wish to extract, is it? With the Berlin Wall down and all in ruins, we must seem like fools to you and your kind. But giving them the bomb, you see, we saved the world from destruction; even John understood that in the end, the balance of terror, the Iron Curtain . . . all that stood between us and doom. And John and I held fast to one conviction: We never betrayed each other. Loyalty, you see, is everything. I owe him that much." She shot me a searing look. "Do you understand, that what is *his* should shine forth . . . a light unto others?"

I knew she meant Laura, and without me.

"I only want to set the record straight."

She laughed hysterically.

"You're a historian: I forgot. And my record, what will the history books say about us?"

"How about I leave it *all* to Max."

"So gallant . . . *mon amour.*"

She struggled to her feet and fell back in her chair. I made a move to go around the table to help her.

"No, stay where you are, darling, lest mother *seduce* you. Unless you're tempted to know what only your father knew. Charles will take care of everything: MI5 and MI6 prefer to keep all their dismal failures swept under the rug. And just so you know, forewarned is forearmed. Max protected her in that trashy novel; all the really naughty bits he put on me, adding to my villainous character, far worse than any conniving Queen Gertrude. It was my brilliant diva daughter who seduced—her partner but my lover—in her dressing room the night of her first triumph at the Met. And she didn't even fancy him, but she sure showed me who was boss."

I let her leave it at that for Charles's sake; I let it go, the lie, the truth my father never revealed to her, that in turn for being allowed the mission to Pylos in 1943 by British intelligence (probably with the blessing of Nigel Bennett), he must have agreed to secretly help MI5 around the edges, which would come to include his love affair with Suzanne. Lying to and spying on each other may have been their ultimate aphrodisiac. A double agent's stock-in-trade.

Even as she had the last word as she headed for her bedroom.

"He was coming home . . . back to me."

44

ALL I WANTED TO DO WAS SLEEP, SLEEP LIKE I'd never slept before. The '59 Pomerol—thirty years in the making—proved the best painkiller I'd come across in quite some time.

When I woke, it was early afternoon, the pale winter sunlight in the western sky filling my bedroom. An orgy of prismatic azures and rosy reds danced in the antique windowpanes . . . of the blue Aegean, of a young girl in a red bathing suit swallowed in emerald ripples, the honey-eyed highlights in her hair as she walked the beach on Delos, her lashes wet and long, her sea-stained eyes like a still-young and intrepid Nausicaa. I was aware of a warm throbbing in my loins and a vague yearning, as if I'd been flying in my dreams, or running, more likely, since I often dreamed of days on the football field, or rowing on the river, returning to first things, when I had been young and strong . . . returnings echoed in the poignant final pages of my father's Pankrác diary . . . and a young woman's bedroom, where the scents of the countryside whispered tender felicities to a feral child and her equally feral lover, to which she forever sought return. *To know what only your father knew,* as Odysseus and Penelope had certain secret signs, erotic signatures, known only to husband and wife.

Her longing voice filled my dreams, as well.

Perhaps it was simply the impulse to pleasure of which I dreamed: our longing to inhabit one another's rooms in the way we desire to merge with the beloved's body, to mingle our dreams with theirs and so render those dreams less perishable. As my father wrote in his diary, quoting Dryden's Lucretius,

"*So, tangled in the Nets of Love they lie/ Till man dissolves in that excess of joy.*"

But as my dreamscape fell away, something began to rankle from my conversation with Suzanne, something about a trip to London in 1962 and meeting with an old MI6 colleague of Philby's, the year before Bobby had exposed Blunt in 1963, the year—January '63—Philby escaped from Beirut and defected: the final unraveling of the Cambridge spy ring. Nigel Bennett had told me about Suzanne's surprise foray to London in a kind of regretful tone, a mere afterthought as I took my parting, almost as if the side of him that once wished to condemn her now offered her absolution: about a key, that she, "like a good girl," had handed over, which precipitated the blunder or cover-up in Beirut and Philby's escape to Moscow, the fiasco that ended Nigel's career, as he'd always feared it would.

"Revenge," she'd called it, but on whom? I found myself briskly brushing away at the dirt over this promising find at the bottom of a decades-old trench, trying but failing to bring the outlines of the thing into view.

More distant voices broke the spell of my querulous hangover and called me to my bedroom window.

They were there just where I knew they would be. They were standing in the winter garden. He was inspecting his pruned roses, getting the last of the bulbs into the earth. She stood to the side on the moss green gravel path. The snow had melted to a piebald white. I saw their breath pop and froth from their moving lips in curt volleys. He wore the same green Barbour jacket with the leather-patched elbows that I remembered from days before. She wore a heavy gray overcoat, not the elegant loden green of Christmas Day, and pea green Wellingtons and a baby blue wool hat—nothing of the fashionable svelte beauty I remembered from that first Founder's Day at Winsted in 1965, when, I suddenly realized, she and Bobby had been well embarked on a new start, a chance to reinvent themselves after betraying both Blunt and Philby two years before. Now she was a woman of a certain age trying the conjurer's trick one last time. I didn't need to hear their argument. They are just holding on, I thought, until spring, when the earth will lighten their load with new color, when the rhododendrons will run riot and there will be roses and lilacs, the wisteria escaping like Jack's bean stalk to embrace their childhood rooms in the clouds. Spring was where they might yet find new currents to tide them over from all the dark years. She repeatedly brought her new leather gloves to her face, touching at her eyes, pushing back a strand of hair flickering at the edge of her wool hat, perhaps inhaling the rich scent of leather. She kept her shoulders high and proud, her back straight . . . against all odds.

I put a palm to the windowpane, to the refracted light within the antique glass, surprised to find it still cold. I wanted to be the wrecking crew to their secrets, and I didn't; I wanted to plead my case, and I didn't. I recognized in my reflection the face that could only be a sad reminder to them: a face that could never really hope to inhabit the rooms and landscapes they had known, any more than they could his. For those memories were gone where they were going. Then I saw the woman turn from the man: a moment of irresolution or anger. She took a step away and stopped, her lower lip drawn hard inward (my heart leapt in recognition of that look), paused, staring hard at something far off, and then turned back from those lovely snow-mottled lawns and the latticework of rhododendrons, and the hardy yew hedge just below my window, where I watched like a ghost. Then she just opened her arms and went to him and embraced him and kissed him. It was not a kiss of passion, but of kindness and compassion and perhaps resignation. She brushed his face with her gloved fingertips, speaking softly, as if comforting a child. Then she turned with a shy wave and proceeded on her walk out over the thawing lawns to the woods beyond.

My grandmother's words came back to me: *firm but kind.* I had not mentioned to Suzanne anything about Joanna or the missing boy— one lost boy was enough. I had not insisted on the truth about Laura. Nor that my father had moonlighted for MI5 along with Charles: one hoping she'd give up Philby, the other that she'd keep her mouth shut, which she did, biding her time until she knew the only truth that really mattered to her. The whole truth and nothing but the truth might have spelled disaster for all our spring hopes. And the hug in the garden below relieved me greatly, that I had not blown Charles Fairburn's cover, because, clearly, his ties to MI5 had allowed her to come home and keep the tabloids at bay. I was happy for them; I wished them Godspeed.

I dressed and limbered up and waited for my head to clear. When I went into the hall, I was still a little dazed, still wandering, waiting for the thing to come to me about Suzanne's 1962 trip to London to meet with Philby's erstwhile Rothschild friend—something to guide my next steps. Down the hall was a patch of stray sunlight from an open door. I could hear workmen in the other wing re-pointing the bricks. I moved toward the patch of light and the open door, where a broom and mop were propped next to a pink wicker trash basket. On a small landing of steps going to the top floor, probably servants' quarters, was a large portrait, seemingly out of place from the legions of portraits downstairs. It was a modern painting in bold brushstrokes of a dashing man in his late twenties wearing a British World War I flying uniform, leather helmet, and goggles astride a high alabaster brow. A bristling mustache rode above his clenched lips. He stood in a fearless pose, leaning against the propeller of a biplane. I read the brass plaque at the bottom of the painting. *Captain Edwin Striker Fairburn, Royal Flying Corps, VC, MC, 1890–1937.* I recalled stories about the colonel's father told me as a boy and elaborated on around the Christmas Eve dinner table. An ace with twenty-plus victims, incredible escapes from burning aircraft, surviving two or three crash landings, one behind enemy lines, which required making his way through no-man's-land at night, where he avoided being shot by his own side by singing at the top of his voice a London dance hall number while German machine guns spat rounds over his head. The stuff of boys' adventure magazines. Later an MP in Lloyd George's government, only to die while test-flying a new Spitfire in an ice storm.

And I thought I had a tough act to follow.

I walked to the open door, listened, and went in. A small, intimate bedroom, full of charming English country furnishings. A smell of cleansers and wax. The maid must have just finished cleaning, having abandoned her broom and mop in the hall. I stood in the doorway, gazing at the bay windows and the single bed and the prints on the wall of jumping horses and fishermen and one, in pride of place, of Pavlova with her dreaming Albrecht in *Giselle.* The winged ballerina stood on point, poised in flight from her inconstant lover. I smiled and adjusted the frame on the wall. Suzanne had put her daughter in her own childhood room. "A little creepy," Laura had whispered to me on Christmas Eve as we went down to dinner. And there on a side book-shelf were the volumes on botany that my father had noted in his diary, and I wondered which one Suzanne had plucked from his hand as she came to his bed. The one thing they deeply, absolutely shared: the love of nature and the outdoors. As I went out, I glanced down at the pink wicker basket by the mop and broom, and there, nestled in the bottom like ejected cartridges, lay two white cardboard tubes. I stared at them for quite some time as tears filled my eyes, grieving for our lovemaking in Venice in a room overlooking the Giudecca Canal . . . that it had come to that: two cardboard Tampax tubes in a wastebasket.

I wandered on to give my tears time to dry. I tried another door farther along the passageway. The room was dark, blinds and curtains drawn, dusty and untouched. I could just make out a dollhouse in one corner and cardboard boxes overflowing with wooden toys spilling from a large walk-in closet. By the window seat were shelves crammed with children's books. Light glittered like a blade at the parting of the curtain. I drew back the curtains and raised the blinds to release the luxuriant winter sunshine into the room. The cushions on the window seat were of red velvet and soft. Goose down spilled from a tear when I pressed my hand on the fabric, and motes of dust fountained the beams of sunlight. As my eyes adjusted, I noticed a broken-down rocking horse in the far corner, a chipped and peeling stallion with a silver saddle and reins of aquamarine. I went over and stroked its moth-eaten mane, fondling its stiff leathery ears to the lullaby of a nodding creak. The motion produced a rising sensation in me, like a serious toke hitting your brain, and somewhere inside that giddy sensation a memory of an early birthday party at Elysium, my third or fourth, when the colonel—when he had acted something of the part of a surrogate father—had given me a similar rocking horse, which I had ridden to destruction within a matter of months. I had taken him—Trigger, I'd named him—outside and ridden him over the lawns, over rocks and branches, until I managed to shatter a rocker. Left out in the rain, Trigger soon rotted and then got thrown away.

The rocking horse made a sharp squeak, and I turned like a guilty brat toward the door. To the left of the open door, a mobile was suspended from the ceiling: a small squadron of biplanes made out of balsa wood: handmade, lovingly detailed with painted British and German insignias. They drifted in the soft, luxuriant light, undulant as a swirl of dust beams. I was entranced by the Daedalian ingenuity of the things hanging on their threads of angel hair: a precision and patience I'd never possessed as a child. I reached to them, delighted in their weightless minuet . . . so fragile. And then something about those tiny airplanes patrolling the abandoned nursery drained the blood from my head.

I trembled with inchoate fear as I went directly to the red velvet window seat and got out a book from the shelf by the floor. The binding was cracked and the pages yellowed and brittle. *Tales of Hans Christian*

Andersen, and under the title, written in a flowing blue feminine script: *To our darling children, Peter and Laura, from Mummy and Daddy, Christmas 1938.*

By the time I got downstairs to the back garden, one of those typical English rain showers was passing over and the colonel was nowhere to be found. I spent a few minutes with the watercolors and drawings of the Parthenon frieze, vaguely mulling over the scholarly coup to be had by their rediscovery and publishing, a coup, too, for the Princeton Art Museum, and a fabulous Ph.D. dissertation for one of my grad students, a brilliant woman who was intent on a reinterpretation of the friezes with the sacrifice of Erechtheus's daughter as key to the sculptural program. I examined again the beautiful detailing in the critical panel of the frieze showing an older man and woman, presumably Erechtheus and his wife, Praxithia—if my grad student was right—and three young women or girls, one being offered a piece of clothing, which, in the detailing of the watercolor, certainly looked to be her burial shroud. A slam dunk . . . a young woman's willing sacrifice to save the city of Athens.

It was then that the housekeeper found me and suggested I try the carriage house where, she said, "the Colonel keeps himself on rainy days." I made a dash through the rain showers down the drive to a large Edwardian carriage house of polychrome brick with five arched entrances. Inside were five, maybe six antique automobiles in various states of disrepair. Lying higgledy-piggledy were piles of discarded parts. I found the Colonel on his back beneath a thirties Jag roadster. The jacks holding up the car looked flimsy to my eye, but I assumed, as I always had, that he knew exactly what he was doing.

"Won't be a minute," he shouted.

I made a quick inspection of the old tires and tool chests, frayed fan belts and numerous brightly labeled boxes of recently arrived spare parts. My inadequacies about such things weighed heavy. It was barely warmer than it was outside. My breath showed. An ancient space heater, its coiled electric filaments aglow, gave off a pathetic flow of heat. I couldn't help thinking, *A bit of gasoline, an oily rag, and the place goes up like a Molotov cocktail.*

Charles emerged from under the chassis, clutching parts of the transmission in his hand. His face was smeared with oil.

"Quite something, isn't she?" He chuckled, caressing the rusted bonnet, and got himself a rag to dab at his face. The happiness in his voice, now that he was in his element, almost brought tears to my eyes. The roses, I realized, were a duty for his lover; this, his abiding passion, along with the classics. "What's so wonderful about these old girls is that everyone is an individual. They were handmade and hand-assembled. You can still feel the individual workmanship, the craft and pride that went into these machines. And they respond so eagerly to your personal touch. . . ." He smiled shyly, embarrassed. "When men took real pleasure in machines, before utter standardization took over. Soon it will all be done by robots."

"But maybe . . . we'll be safer."

"Safer for sure, and they'll be more dependable—the standardization of all our lives. And soon there will be pilotless aircraft. They'll fly themselves with computers. And the fighters and bombers . . . operators will remain safely on the ground, pushing buttons, watching the destruction from a safe distance. Fortunately, I won't be part of it." He put a hand on my shoulder. "By the way, I got a call first thing this morning for you." My heart surged with the hope that Laura had called. "A chap from the American embassy in Prague. I thought you needed the sleep. He left his number. They located that friend of yours in a military hospital near Bratislava."

"Vlada. Did he say if he was okay?"

"Recovering, slowly."

"That's great. I've told them I'll pay all expenses to get him to the best hospital in Vienna."

"Good of you to do that."

I felt giddy with relief, as if infused with something of Vlada's resolution: to absolutely see this thing through.

"The least I could do . . ."

"You recovered from last night?"

"What, the '59 Pomerol? Wouldn't have missed it for the world."

"Suzanne seemed better this afternoon, cathartic, I suppose."

"Tough, having your daughter just leave like that."

"Oh, it's not the first time. I don't know what it is, but they can't seem to stand being around each other. I hoped to be a referee. . . . Sometimes I think women are more competitive than men."

"And hard for Laura, the shock of finding out that you are her father."

"I always hoped, from afar, to mediate their relationship, that I might put things in perspective."

"I imagine she just needs time for it to sink in."

"Time? I've been waiting . . . well, for a bloody long time."

He was looking at me with an affectionate intensity I'd never felt in all the years of my childhood.

"I was just upstairs in the nursery and I was paging through a Hans Christian Andersen book. . . ."

"I was wondering when you'd figure that one out." He was trying to be matter-of-fact. "Kept waiting for the right moment to mention it: when you were old enough, when you got back from Vietnam—that really threw me, by the way, when you went off like that." He shrugged. "Time gets away when you put things off. And yes, you and Laura were named after my—and Cecily's—children."

"I don't know what to say."

"It was your father's idea. Suzanne's, too, of course; she came to it pretty much on her own, bless her." He shook his greasy face with a look of bemusement, as if the matter had withdrawn to such a distance in his mind as to become an unnoticed fixture. He went to a pile of tires and sat and motioned me to a nearby crate of Jaguar parts.

"It was my son, Peter. You see, we'd kept him cooped up down here practically the whole war, out of harm's way. All he saw was the news-papers, listened to the radio, and heard the adults in passing. I kept rigidly silent about what I did. The children were never even short of the best food. War was an abstraction. Peter was champing at the bit to go up to London, which retained an aura of the marvelous from his earliest childhood. Laura, my first Laura, I don't think cared much one way or another. She had her horses. All she really cared about were the horses. And that bothered Cecily. She feared Laura would be spoiled by such a sheltered childhood; she'd become a snobbish country girl, out of touch with the suffering of others. Then in the fall of 1944, Cecily's mother moved back into London from their Hampshire farm. She'd had enough, too, stuck down in the country. Everyone consid-ered it pretty safe by then. London hadn't been bombed lately and the V-1 attacks had almost ceased as the allies pushed deep into France. Cecily decided to go to her mother's home on Duke Street and take the children, just for a long weekend. She wanted them to see the bomb damage; she wanted them to know the hardship that the country was experiencing and so not grow up a privileged and spoiled lot. Fifty minutes by train to Waterloo. It seemed a good thing to do.

"It was a day not unlike this one. Crisp and bracing, a near-perfect late-autumn day. I had been weeks without a break at High Wycombe with Bomber Harris, my direct CO, who was always badgering me about the latest damage reports brought back by Mosquito reconnaissance. Even then, he was still browned off that Eisenhower had been given overall command of Allied operations. And worse, that summer and fall the RAF had been forced to abandon the German cities to concentrate on supply lines, rail facilities, and petrol-processing plants. Old Harris still wanted one more go at the cities—Thunderclap, what we would call it, still only a gleam in his eye. By then I was fed up with him and his cronies; I was fed up with the whole stinking business. If it hadn't been for my father, I would never have gotten into flying in the first place. I did love it, though, and experienced pilots were a scarce commodity in the early days. Once bitten—that's the thing." He shook his head with painful chagrin. "I had a three-day leave and the plan was to spend it in London with my family. It was to be splendid. We were going to reclaim our prewar life, summers in Crete—you know what I mean. And it was such a nice day when I arrived at Paddington that instead of taking a taxi directly to my mother-in-law's house, I decided to walk it.

"London seemed peaceful enough, basking in the warm December sunshine. The stink of war and burning was still about. And the bustling faces I met in the street were tired and haggard, but then, it had been a long haul for all of us. The city was reviving, I felt, no longer cringing at the slightest wail of a siren. One anticipated the end of the war, the tastes and smells of peacetime, all the foods and flowers that had disappeared from the shops with the onset of war. Even the bombed-out buildings I passed . . . I remember thinking how like medieval ruins they seemed, pink rosebay and yellow Oxford ragwort growing in the cracks of the broken masonry. If one hadn't known better, one might have thought they were relics of some dark age long past.

"And just like that, a sudden shattering explosion. Immensely powerful, rattling every window along Baker Street. The air itself vibrated. The thing seemed close by and far off in the same instant. Then a moment later, this obscene noise like the clattering wail of an express train bursting from the mouth of a tunnel—then a second explosion, more muffled and compressed. I dropped to my knees, thinking I should go to a shelter before the next bomb dropped—that's what I thought it was. Then nothing, absolute silence. So I kept going. I was glad, because I was less than a mile from the house on Duke Street and I expected to see the bomb damage around the next corner, or perhaps the next. But there was nothing. Just stunned faces, queer faces of incomprehension and fear and relief, like mine. I kept walking, assuring myself the war was almost over and it was ridiculous to be concerned. There had been nothing, no buzz bombs, no high-flying aircraft. A gas explosion was more like it, or a UXB that had been set off by a crew—poor lads, I thought, if that's what it was.

"Then there were fire engines. Black smoke drifting from the south with a kind of pink-brown haze to it, something you might see in a tropical sunset. And then . . . I was walking at quite a clip by then, I began to smell the burning wood and blasted masonry, that awful acrid stench of high explosives, and underneath, the sweet, rather nauseous odor of escaping gas. I began to come upon people who were wandering around dazed, some disheveled, their hair burned, faces blackened, as I neared Wigmore Street. That's when I panicked. I ran. As soon as I turned on Duke Street, the terrible clutter of a bomb site appeared. Fire trucks and hoses and air raid wardens milling around like chickens after a henhouse raid by a badger. Yet they seemed to have things under control. They knew their business. I actually smiled, relieved, when I saw the blackened and smoldering wreckage; part of Selfridges had been hit. My mother-in-law's house was appreciably beyond, almost a block. Ah, well, I thought, Peter will get his little taste now; that will satisfy his curiosity about what his pa did in the war. I continued past the medical personnel on the scene, who were attending the wounded on stretchers; they looked like ghosts, faces masked with white plaster dust and streaked with blood. A scene out of the Blitz of years before.

"I began to take my bearings, looking for a way around the mess to the next block. The wardens had cordoned off the site. I felt almost cocky with relief to be a bystander. So I ducked under the rope barrier and went up to a warden who was talking with a policeman. The man's face was quite black with soot and smoke. 'How do I get down Duke Street to the next blocks?' I asked. The warden turned on me with some annoyance, his white eyes blinking at me out of his blackened face. It was as if I'd said the silliest thing in the world. Maybe I seemed strange to him, being so calm about it all. His red lips turned up in a kind of sneer, perhaps at my RAF uniform. 'You don't want to go there, gov'ner,' he spat out; 'that's where the bloody thing hit.' For a very long moment, all I could do was stare at that blackened face. At some point I must have pulled out my identification, and he passed me though with a grunt and a rude remark, which I missed. I picked my way past the burned-out facade of Selfridges dripping with water until I came to what remained of the street beyond.

"There was nothing left, only a deep blast crater. Nothing had escaped the initial explosion, hardly a foundation. It was as if a giant mailed fist had come down and pulverized the place and then scooped the bits away. The explosion had been very clean in its way, surgically so, shearing away every sign of habitation. Very Teutonic, I liked to tell myself. Even the usual smell of a bomb site dissipated quickly. No human remains near the point of impact, just a blink of extinction. There were these military chaps, intelligence people, who were going about with tape measures, of all things, taking notes, probing the debris with iron rods, measuring and photographing. They were very methodical. As an archaeologist, I knew all about such a methodical trade: We prided ourselves on our thoroughness and accuracy when opening up the innards of an ancient site. They were so intent, those chaps, as if they might actually find something useful in the nightmarish depths of that crater. I couldn't really fathom the thing until I happened upon a doll's broken arm and realized my family was gone. I just dropped down in the rubble and sat there. Hours later, a kind policeman came along and helped me up.

"Of course, we had known about the V-2 rockets. Details had been hushed up from the general public for fear of causing undue alarm. No one had any idea how bad it might be. For me, it was like a vision of some future, where our lunacy, begun on the battlefields of the Western Front, found its ultimate expression. You see, I think human beings begin to mistake themselves for gods when they become capable of mass killings at a distance, relieved of the odium of bloodstained hands.

"For a time, I tried to console myself that their end had been quick and painless, their utterly unique individual souls evaporated in a flash of heat. They never had to creep into shelters, hearing death loom above them in the wail of sirens, the whistle of bombs. They had been kept safe from all that . . . and then they were gone. They were some of the very last civilian casualties. And, I must tell you, if there is one thing I truly appreciated in your father, it was his capacity to pity me, not for my family so much, though he did that, but for my contribution to the disaster. I read all his OSS bomb-damage reports in '46 before I left for America. You see, I managed to drown my grief—or was it revenge?—in constant work. The gods of war had allowed me a special providence. I was part of the decision-making team near the end of the war to go after the last of the German cities: Dresden, Darmstadt, Leipzig. Bomber Command's last stab at glory and the final apotheosis of our area-bombing strategy. The truth is, I relished every minute, every detail as I reviewed the reconnaissance photos. Perhaps you better understand now the situation Suzanne and I found ourselves in . . . with Bobby."

Staring into another blackened face trying with great dignity and resolve to repress the hatred he felt for himself during this moment of confession, I glimpsed another of the rooms that had been closed off to me: they had all wanted Bobby gone; they all shared that guilt, the shameful hatred that trapped them in an unacknowledged conspiracy of silence.

And then I remembered something Elliot had told me as an aside in Prague, when Laura was out of earshot, something my father had told him in Berlin after a few too many drinks: "When I make love to her, you know, it's like I'm murdering him and loving her even more."

I shuddered and wondered again about the telephone call, the man with the foreign accent on the phone to the gun store in Ohio, who purchased the ammunition for Bobby's Colt pistol. Just a day after Philby's death had been reported on the front page of *The New York Times*, when Philby's memoir had been sent to Suzanne or put into her hands, probably with a note, when Suzanne, as she testified at the inquest, was in the Spaulding Rehabilitation Hospital, incapacitated with cirrhosis of the liver and nervous exhaustion.

That was a room I'd lost interest in entering.

"It seems Nigel Bennett was aware of your loss, your dilemma, as well, getting you a posting to the States."

"Nigel? I was meaning to ask you how that went." The edge of concern in his voice was palpable.

"He's not well; in fact, you might want to call Miriam, his housekeeper. He had a bad cold when I left yesterday, maybe pneumonia. But before that, he was going on at quite a clip about my father and Karel Hollar. A little disjointed with the Alzheimer's but quite lucid and uninhibited about the past, if you know what I mean."

"Pity, a great mind like his; he was a god to us, all of us with youthful aspirations in the field."

"What I hadn't fully grasped in Prague, that Hollar, it seems, *was* willing to defect and he was ready to give up a lot more if the deal was right, a deal that included the Ventris charts and my father—a villa in Greece."

Charles looked intently into my eyes, as if concerned at the inadequate disguise of his grease-covered face.

"He would trust no one else."

"His old friend and colleague—how did you put it, 'youthful aspirations'?"

"Nigel was a spellbinder. He was able to make one see how even . . . well . . . how almost anything might seem totally aboveboard in terms of the larger scheme of things."

"Saving Western civilization."

I hadn't meant it to sound facetious.

"Nigel knew about Suzanne's leftist connections, her Party affiliations during her brother's Cambridge days. She doesn't know . . . well, everything, you understand."

"So Nigel asked you to keep an eye on her?"

"I was convenient—when help might be needed on our side of things."

"And then you fell in love: a virtue out of a necessity."

"I mourned Cecily and the children for years. I was inconsolable; I blamed myself—that the gods had asked me for their sacrifice."

I reached a hand to his shoulder. "As Erechtheus was asked to sacrifice his daughter to spare Athens."

"Suzanne and I talked about Cecily and the children endlessly in the early years when we moved to America. Perhaps you only see one side to her; she can be ever so sweet and loving—loyal to a fault."

"And she had her own cross to bear."

"You must understand even returning here is a risk." He gazed hard into my eyes. "Long memories. If the London tabloids ever got hold of her name, there'd be no end to it. It's all I can do to call in every favor to keep MI5 off her back."

"Because you failed to keep her mouth shut about Philby?"

By the alarm that flashed across his face, I realized why Suzanne had practically begged the night before as we parted not to mention Philby or Blunt or anything about my father to Charles. They lived in sealed-off rooms: things never discussed, left forever unsaid.

I broke the silence as best I could.

"You were saying the other day about how you came to feel more comfortable in the field of classical studies, and you got me thinking that there is indeed something uplifting, particularly in Periclean Athens, that fusion of the real and ideal in art as well as life, the sense of discovery in fleshing out the ideal patterns that underlie the hubbub of immediate experience—not in its shadowy transcendence—like a breath of fresh air in the Attic sunshine."

"Oh, I think it's more a desire for order if anything, the human mind's capacity for symbolic abstraction, that we might shape the world to our own vision—whether a Parthenon or a beautiful car. An engineer understands the lovely tension between what the mind knows and what the eye sees—the fascination that makes the thing seem vibrant and alive. One can never quite exhaust its appeal."

"But, you know, I think my father's love for the past, for the lost Mycenaean world of Homer, had more to do with the origins of all that, a mythic but very real golden age, before men had to build walls to defend themselves, a millennium of peace when gods and heroes were—I don't know, at one with nature, with a better human nature, when the rivers and mountains were named for the gods, sacred spots invoking in their very names an abiding sense of place and ultimate belonging."

"Your Elysium." He laughed. "Before all our damned machines."

"Of course, it's all ridiculous—as you said, to be numbered among the immortals, pirates and raiders of cities, a world as red in tooth and claw as any other. But to touch the taproot, to plumb the wellspring . . ."

"And Pericles had no use for the citizen who took no part in civic affairs, worse than useless. It's what made Washington after the war such a heady place."

"You were down in Washington—saving the world—a lot in the late forties and early fifties."

"Convenient access to old friends and new while doing RAF procurement."

"How did my father react when you, an old friend, a sometime MI5 operative, met him at Elysium in September of 1953—September seventh to be precise—when you told him that not only was Hollar alive but that he was the East German minister for mines, *and* he wanted to defect, with certain strings attached?"

Charles looked at me with a kind of amused bereavement.

"Good Lord, was that little spiel just now your way of slipping in the blade—and just the way your father would do it. Could have been him, the way you led me down the garden path and crowned me with my own shovel the moment my back was turned."

I bent closer and nodded slowly. The overhead bulb, a spare and antique thing itself, dramatized his features, emphasizing the crisp lines in his aging face, the sunken cheeks I hadn't really noticed before, the slackening along the jaw, but which, for a moment, reminded me of the dashing young flier in the upstairs passageway.

"I'm just trying to picture it in my mind. Was it on the back porch overlooking the lake, down by the boathouse? You two had to have been very discreet."

"It was in the early afternoon on the back veranda. You and your grandmother were down for a nap and your mother was in the kitchen helping prepare dinner."

"What did he do when you told him?"

"He poured us both a very stiff drink."

"Was he hesitant, concerned, surprised?"

"I remember his face lifting to the tall pines that grow there along the lake, like a hunter catching the scent."

"Of course, you both had a thing about Philby, as well, the competition, so to speak."

"One's enemy gives life its savor, its raison d'être. My albatross was always Bobby. Toward the end, he was totally paranoid, as Suzanne testified before the grand jury. He saw assassins everywhere, hiding in the woods . . . every creak of the floor. Some nights, he insisted that his attendant wheel him into the fallout shelter and lock the door—spend the night underground. Then he was forever suspicious of the attendants—firing them left and right. A bloody nightmare for Suzanne, until she finally cracked, too."

I knew then it was Charles who'd made the call to the Soviet embassy that had resulted in the purchase and shipping of bullets for Bobby's gun. But that was the least of it.

"'Like a hunter catching the scent,' you said. Was that the point, that he was the perfect patsy, the perfect shooter to take out Hollar and protect all your fucking reputations?"

"Balderdash."

"You didn't threaten him, did you, to expose him as a double agent for the Brits? Fucking hell—that's treason!"

"You're way over the top, young man."

"Nigel made it crystal clear you *and* my father were the MI5 watchdogs on Suzanne. . . . Was it to get her to give up Philby or to keep her silent? Looks like you failed on both counts."

Gamely, Charles motioned to the nearby Jaguar. "They don't make women like her anymore. I'm a lucky man."

I left it at that, a minimal-damage assessment and plenty of rooms locked solid, but I had enough of what I'd come for, and I wasn't going to spoil my chance to get my dirty hands on the watercolors of the Parthenon frieze.

Elsinore, September 7, 1953
Meet me in Pine Meadow tonight at eleven. I have just had a very trying meeting with Charles. I'm back to Washington in the morning and then probably off to Berlin on Agency matters. Charles confided in me many things, staggering me not once, but twice: He informed me in the most offhand way that Laura was his child. He obviously has reason to believe this is true. Eleven—sharp!

PART SIX
ELYSIUM

*Our woods and lake were both home and my first place of
exile. The woods and lake, like my books, were my constant
companions, and I found myself compelled to give them
names, or learn their names: the wildflowers and trees,
the woodland creatures and their favorite haunts, as if
by bestowing names—especially to birdsongs—I might
discover added dimensions to the places I loved, as the gods
did for the early Greeks. That sylvan landscape peopled
with nymphs and dyads, I suppose, was the first book—the
book of the gods. I cannot remember reading children's
books, only the books in my grandfather's library, the
naturalist philosophers like Emerson and Thoreau, but
mostly histories of the classical world, Plutarch, Herodotus,
and Thucydides, then Homer later, and then Civil War
memoirs. My mother did not believe in children's books. In
my child's mind, there was Greece and Rome, and then the
American Civil War . . . and the abiding earth.*

    —excerpt from John Alden's Pankrác Prison diary

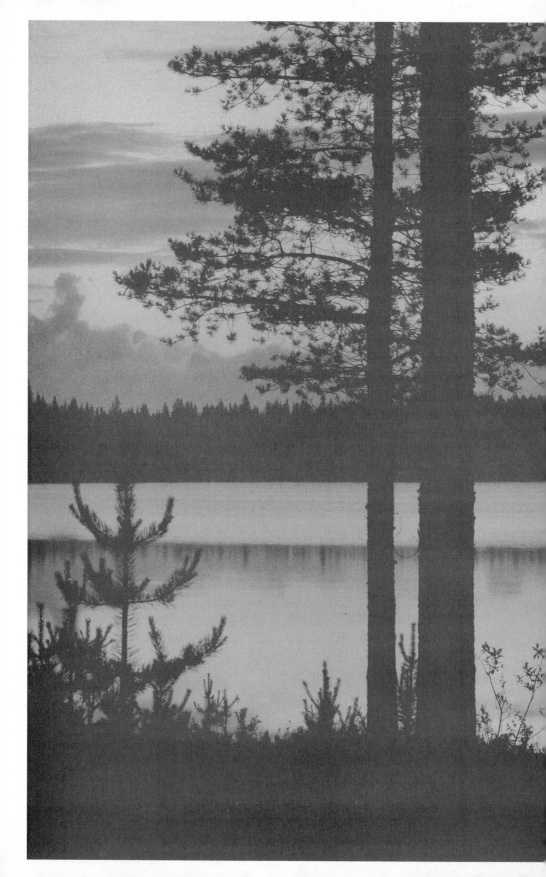

45 SITTING HERE AT MY FATHER'S BOYHOOD desk, where he dreamed of the lost world of Homer's *Odyssey* while staring out over Eden Lake, I still marvel at my final conversations with Suzanne and Charles, Karel Hollar and Elliot Goddard, Nestor and Joanna, and the miracle of Nigel Bennett—my dramatis personae, all of whom allowed me to breathe the air of those long-darkened rooms of my father's life. As a historian accustomed to sifting the pathetic residue of thousands of years for a glimpse into the past, I am humbled by the synergies that the human bond affords in portraying the paradoxes that rule our lives. It is why we pine for five minutes to speak with a Pericles or Socrates, why we dig and fight like starved hyenas for shards of mute pottery . . . in hopes of echoes of such a conversation.

My interrogations were designed not so much to snatch the corroborating detail, or to reveal the self-serving lies, but to breathe the atmosphere of mind that my subjects shared with my father. Sharing what the Greeks called *pneuma*, or the animating spirit of a moment, is what allows one the glittering prize: the dynamic of the living, breathing human consciousness that we in this digital age neglect at our peril. An Internet link alone, as I tell my students, will not cut it. I believe my father was trying to share something akin in his Pankrác diary: offering up the animating spirit of his soul without doing irremediable damage to those he loved, or to his country—needless to say, he omitted any mention of his connection with MI5 and MI6, the CIA, or OSS. Just enough to allow the telling of *his* story as he wanted it told. So yes, Max, a kind of fiction.

A performance not unlike what I glimpsed in Suzanne's marine blue eyes, as morning after dreary English winter morning she entered the rehabilitation hospital in Guilford to find her lover working like an "inspired Achilles to regain his powers," to rebuild the strength of his damaged leg . . . a scene that floored me, recalling, as it did, Laura's equally determined workouts in our room in Venice.

On my flight to New York to find Laura, who, I realized, to my growing chagrin, embodied so much of my father's grit and gambler's instinct, I found myself increasingly drawn to my early images of him, seeming to gain substance and heart-wrenching nuance in every iteration. The very earliest, gotten from my mother and grandmother, where he stands on the boathouse dock chain-smoking Lucky Strikes the morning he left for Washington, Cambridge, and Berlin, took on tantalizing new dimensions. Just the day before, Charles Fairburn, on behalf of British counterintelligence, MI5, had told him not only that Karel Hollar was alive but that he was a high-ranking East German official who wished to defect if all his demands were met—specifically, my father delivering to him Ventris's holographic charts on the decipherment of Linear B and some ironclad assurances as to his future in the West as a KGB defector and ex-MI5 double agent: A defection that would spell Kim Philby's doom.

It is one thing to find that your coconspirator and competitor from early youth, the man you had set out to kill in the last days of the war, or at least bring to justice, was alive after being confirmed dead, quite another to find your nemesis has summoned you to his resurrection. Adding to my father's consternation must have been Charles Fairburn's seemingly innocent remark that Laura was *his* love child. Who could blame Charles for staking out a claim to the love of his first cousin *and* his daughter—even if some part of him must have suspected Suzanne's veracity—much less trying to hasten his possible rival's acceptance of a dangerous mission: A mission that might well eliminate both of his rivals. Suzanne's ambiguous fidelity, in September of 1953, at least to the truth of paternity, may have been ironclad: she really wasn't sure.

Looking out the window of my flight to JFK, I saw a tortured soul standing on that boathouse dock, devastated about his infidelities in the eyes of both his mother and wife, tempted by Suzanne's offer to give up Philby if he'd divorce, presented with the possibility of revenge—or justice, as I'm sure he'd have called it: justice for Karel Hollar (and the kind of justice spelled out in an envelope of documents recently put into his hands by my grandmother); and, yes, there's no denying it: hungering for a glimpse of those 103 Linear B tablets.

Charles and MI5 had him by the balls; they probably didn't need, as Charles insisted, to threaten or blackmail him about his off-the-books job for British counterintelligence, for his relationship with Suzanne and Bobby had already compromised him plenty. Not to mention that Nigel Bennett must have suspected my father had something to do with Hollar's pilfered Linear B tablets. The sly, all-knowing head of MI5 probably figured my father would either succeed in getting Hollar to defect and nail Philby for good or he'd kill Hollar (and probably be captured and executed himself), and thus save the British intelligence establishment the humiliation of having to try Philby for treason. Brilliant, really: using the cousins on the sly to do the dirty work and repair the breach between the free world's premier intelligence services. The CIA and FBI were baying for Philby's blood. Either way, Nigel would come out smelling like roses.

At thirty thousand feet, finally grasping the full extent of my father's betrayals (including that of his scholarly profession) and the Hobson's choice he faced, I had a full-blown panic attack, causing me to retreat to the WC to throw up and splash water on my face.

As if fate hadn't dealt him enough bad cards, there was, too, the heartache of Joanna's boy. When I got my hands on the financial records of the family trusts after landing in New York, I realized this had been an agonizing preoccupation. Between the end of the Greek Civil War in 1949 and his disappearance in late 1953, my father had spent well over one million dollars trying to get information about the lost boy; he had instructed the family law firm of Brandt & Harrison to bribe Greek Communists and ex-Communists for news or leads. The firm had hired a number of the Greek military officials and ex-Resistance fighters—some of the very men standing with my father in the photograph in the Agora—to discreetly make inquiries, to dispense bribes. Such a dangerous business could just as easily have resulted in more harm than good. By 1953, the inquiry had produced only a few vague clues as to the boy's whereabouts—Hungary was the most promising—but nothing actionable, as far as Brandt & Harrison were concerned. Surely this must have been another factor in my father's decision to go after Karel Hollar, as Hollar admitted to me in our Pankrác prison cell.

But motivation for the successful playwright, as Elliot would have it, is both essential and often an abysmal cliché. For the essence of motivation must be deep and abiding and not just the inflamed desire of the moment. My father had plenty of reasons, but alternatives as well, some better than others. He could have gone to Elliot Goddard, or even Allen Dulles, told everything he knew, and simply resigned on the spot and taken up his professorship at Princeton. Instead, he opted for the mission dangled by MI5. My grandmother, perhaps unwittingly, became his enabler. That million dollars, a lot of money back in the early fifties, was controlled by her as head of the family trusts. She had to have known about the kidnapped boy. Why else would my grandmother have placed the story of Pearce Breckenridge in my father's hands only days before his departure from Elysium for the last time—as a warning or encouragement? His silence about his kidnapped son in his Pankrác diary is telling, a sympathetic take that even the KGB might have viewed as a mitigating factor. That wretched room he shared only with Joanna, Nestor, and his mother—and with Hollar and, disastrously, Kim Philby.

Sometime in the forty-eight hours before he left, my grandmother handed her distraught son an envelope full of newspaper clippings from the *Natchez Weekly Democrat* and nearly thirty Pinkerton Agency reports. The documents—marked up and underlined in my father's hand—detail a series of horrific events from the mid-1870s in Natchez, Mississippi, and the agonizing choices of conscience faced by General Alden concerning the fate of Pearce Breckenridge: choices uncannily like those my father faced in September 1953. That yellowed manila envelope with its equally yellowing newspaper clippings and documents had been left on the desk in his room, placed by his Underwood typewriter and tucked under a cigar box containing the skin of a monstrous eastern Diamondback—a calculated juxtaposition from one archaeologist to another that I only now fully understand. But as a young boy coming upon these clues for the first time, the rolled-up snake skin only fascinated and diverted me. The contents of the manila envelope seemed irrelevant and so I'd stuck it away in the bookshelf, where it remained in plain view for over twenty-five years, where Max and I had even given it a cursory inspection, where I finally stumbled upon it again the winter of my return. As Elliot always liked to remind me, the mind of God's playwright is a thing of marvelous feints and infinite fancy; but moldering therein, surely, lay a tale, the restless, unconquerable spirit of the enduring past, *my father's* abolitionist past, that claimed its own and cried out for justice.

And one more thing that I knew—just knew: Laura had been keeping something from me. A name, a place, a town that made all the difference.

Landing in New York City just before New Year's Eve, what I discovered while searching for Laura surprised me. As a kid who'd grown up on the Upper East Side, who hadn't lived in the city for years, the New York I found belonged to Laura and Max. The early chapters of *Gardens of Saturn* are filled with Laura and Max's thinly disguised life on the Upper West Side and the quirky denizens of the literary and ballet worlds. When I reached Laura's apartment on Sixty-eighth Street and Columbus Avenue, the brownstone neighborhood, the diners and bookstores, the Korean grocer on the corner were all eerily familiar. But my vague literary nostalgia was quickly crushed when her landlady told me Laura had given up the lease on her apartment back in August, when she'd flown to Greece. It was a lovely old brownstone, where she had lived for over ten years in a modern duplex on the top floors. "Expensive but worth every cent," her ex-landlady assured me. The lean middle-aged woman in jeans and a heavy sweater clearly didn't share my dismay: "Well, dancers, they have a few good years and then an injury comes along and soon they're having a hard time paying the rent; she wouldn't be the first."

The forwarding address for her mail was her agent. So I walked in the cold to an office on Broadway and Fifty-third Street and checked in with *the* Harold Goldberg of Goldberg Associates, a paunchy older man wearing a huge seasonally correct red-and-green bow tie with little dollar-sign characters jumping up and down with raised flutes of bubbly. He couldn't have been more cagey and noncommittal. "Dancers from the Kirov and Bolshoi are now going to be a dime a dozen. You don't think the Soviet Union is next?" He pointed to a signed black-and-white publicity shot of Laura from the early seventies and rambled on in an irritated tone, telling me that a client who couldn't even bother to stay in touch was a client who couldn't be marketed. "I have no idea where the hell she is. City Ballet will never have her back anyway. She's burned more than one bridge in that snake pit, and I'm not interested in getting my hand bitten trying." I found him amazingly indiscreet.

Then I checked with the offices of the American Ballet Theater, and the people there took curious, even polite, interest in my inquiries, once they gauged that I'd had recent contact with their star of the seventies.

The company was performing at the Kennedy Center in Washington, and the business manager, back in town to catch up on paperwork, let me know, with a kind of sweet regret that Laura hadn't even "guested" for the company since 1987 in a new production of *Cinderella*. "Give her our best if you catch up with her," said Florence, a dark-haired older woman in a velvet chinoise jacket with velvet brocade trim, "*and*"— she eyed me tellingly over her reading glasses—"no hard feelings from Misha." I didn't even want to know what that was all about. With the help of some dancers hanging around the waiting area, I later managed to run down her orthopedist, physical therapist, and Pilates instructor, all of whom had had no word from her since August.

It was as if she'd simply evaporated into the mists of time: the ballet machine's constant churning out of young bodies for old.

Doggedly, I continued to ramble along the windy cold streets of the Upper West Side, which seemed to be sprouting new restaurants and brand-name retailers on every block, visiting all the places mentioned in *Gardens*: the diner on Broadway and Seventy-ninth Street where they'd had dinner on their first date after her performance as the Snow Queen in *The Nutcracker*; the Riverside Drive and Ninety-sixth Street prewar apartment building where Max's mother had had her teaching studio, where they'd first made love (at least in the novel—Laura had assured me it was the Watergate Hotel in Washington), and where Laura spent two years in the early eighties tending Hannah off and on in her first stages of Alzheimer's, before she was moved to an assisted living facility.

As I stared at the icy Hudson River from the ramparts of Riverside Drive, with the forbidding gray Palisades of New Jersey in the distance, I remembered Laura's sad recollections of how Hannah had slipped away into the Vienna of her youth, and then into nothing, and how Max, time and time again, would promise to stop by and see his mother, and never did. And then there were the apartments of her colleagues and dance partners who were felled by the terrible onslaught of AIDS, when nobody knew what to make of the insidious plague. As I walked back down Broadway toward Amsterdam Avenue, eyeing the brownstones where many of those victims had their homes, I thought of her struggles to write postcards from Greece, wondering what to say: "Should I write how beautiful it is, or just tell him I miss him and to be sure to get better? Bullshit—whatever." And how she'd stood on the dock at Nafplio in the glittering light from that bay with its brightly painted fishing boats while one of the great danseurs nobles of his generation died a hideous death at the end of an overseas telephone line. The glittering disco hedonism of Max's novel had turned into a plague zone. I only hoped she'd told her mother something about all that, what she did for her friends . . . that *her* sacrifices and *her* pain were no small thing.

Saul reached across with his napkin and wiped the drop of catsup off her chin. Kristin laughed and apologized for making a pig of herself; she was always ravenous after a performance. "A Snow Queen pig," he quipped. They speculated on a proper menu for a Snow Queen: icicles and Popsicles of course, baked Alaska . . . artic-chokes, perhaps freeze-dried penguin feet. They vied to keep their chatter as frivolous as possible, which had the soothing effect of making them refugees from their real desires. Nervously, they glanced up at the tinsel-decorated TV over the empty counter stools as the eleven o'clock news blared: one moment, three inches of snow forecast; the next, grainy grays and greens of battle footage in the Central Highlands of Vietnam, where jungle-fatigued figures fired weapons into a distant tree line as helicopters evacuated the wounded.

Snow and fire . . . how was it possible?

Saul led her the few blocks to the Riverside Drive apartment of his mother, who was conveniently out of town for the New Year's Eve festivities in Vienna. The smell of antique Persian rugs and heavily waxed Biedermeier furniture engulfed her like a spinster aunt's wet kiss. The steam heat wafted smells of crumbling sheet music and spilled wine and . . . could it be Channel No. 5? She breathed deeply . . . something else? Cabbage soup, Saul told her, and the stale strudel his mother served all her students. On the Bösendorfer grand were lined up dozens of family photographs in tarnished silver frames. The pantheon, he explained, extinct before he was born. "Most played in the Vienna Philharmonic—you don't want to know what happened to them." The walls of peeling wallpaper were chockablock with paintings of quaint Tyrolean villages interspersed with nineteenth-century prints of Liszt, Brahms, Chopin . . . the usual suspects. Kristin was not unused to such overstuffed nests of Eastern European nostalgia. Her Russian ballet teachers lived in such places, but this hummed—was it the steam radiators?—with active artistry, a hothouse shrine to which world-class pianists made daily obeisance.

Shadows of genius blown down the wind.

"So you never had, well, thoughts of playing the piano?"

He made a face of long suffering.

"I've dabbled."

"Dabble for me," she said with a laugh, drawing closer, a latent instinct to charm and flirt rising into her eyes—Saul really wasn't her sort, no, not at all. Yet something of her mother's imperious physical prowess spurred her to it. The realization caused her to bridle, and she offered to go make tea while he played.

Saul was revolted at the thought: not his bag—seduction by piano. He could no longer trust himself to operate on the level of cliché, now that the writing life demanded his all.

He sat at the keyboard—how to play like a shy virgin?—and went right to the Chopin Nocturne in E-flat Major, knowing he could keep it quiet, knowing he could cast a spell, knowing his unpracticed technique would not betray him nor irritate him enough to spoil what little pleasure he still derived from the music. He wondered if his brain had really become so rewired for literary expression—not to mention cocaine—that his love of music had been proportionately diminished.

Saul segued into his own somewhat jazzy version of the Mozart Sonata in E-flat and left the final note ringing as he came to her on the ratty sofa.

"You lied. You're unbelievably good."

"It's not what I do."

"You still lied."

"You were pretty incredible tonight yourself. Not that I know anything about ballet."

"The point is . . . like you, you're supposed to think . . . it just happens."

Saul could not take his eyes off her. And it wasn't just her unadorned beauty stripped of all stage makeup, nor the afterimage of that lonely sweat-streaming face on the huge stage of the New York State Theater, arms overflowing with pink and white roses; it was the blue glinting eyes of an ambition sharpened to cut your heart out. His mind fluttered in its canary cage. How they'd learn to lie to each other about that: the synergy of raw ambition. Now he yearned to bring his face close, to breathe in the scent of her ambition as his own, to lick and taste it off her lips and cunt, to examine her pores and orifices the way he liked to dissect a paragraph in *Ulysses*. Even if she should fight him for every inch of beachhead. Even if she'd want her pound of flesh in return—so be it. Nothing worth having was easily won.

He brought his face closer, tasting her tea-stained lips before they were his to taste.

He knew from that initial kiss that he wanted first dibs on her fame, to steal her teeming limelight of a thousand clapping hands. The fame of a writer was a more lonely and insidious venture, lacking the big-time glamour. But together! They would ride the tigers of fame in tandem. And then there'd be the whole exotic tribe of her dance world, clamoring to touch the skirts of her fleeting youth. What material to be had there! If her mother was a beast, as she called her, then she was a mini-beast, a fire-breathing beast, a cuttlefish bone in his cage to keep his beak forever sharpened.

"You'll go easy with me?" she asked.

"I'm not as . . . well, worldly as I seem."

"Do you always lie?"

"Prove me wrong."

"Just go easy. I want to remember—really."

They slipped out of their clothes and began kissing again. He loved the feel of her muscled legs and the fluid arch of her back, the hardness of her buttocks . . . a marvel beyond marvels. Such a Ferrari of flesh and bone required a lover of prodigious technique and skill, but he was not going to be made a liar. Their hands shuttled back and forth, back and forth. She went limp against his neck, like a little possum playing dead, knowing her heart wasn't in it. He maneuvered and kissed her, at first barely touching her lips with his, and then more deeply. Would she bite? For a moment, he was terrified at her lack of response. Then her lips began to move in imitation, her tongue jousting with his when he slid it between her lips.

She drew back and examined his soft flesh quite clinically.

"Are you okay?"

"It's just you're so beautiful."

"Liar."

"Really."

"Do you want me to do something?"

"Just be yourself."

"It's too bad you can't play the piano and . . . how ridiculous."

"Shall I put something on the stereo?"

"That would be nice. And, well . . . while you're at it: The mirror there on the wall, why not take it down and lean it there by the piano."

"Really?"

"Why not? I like to see. . . . I want to remember."

And so he did. And so she watched herself lose her virginity.

I made my way back down Broadway toward Lincoln Center, stopping at the Shakespeare & Co. bookstore at Eighty-first Street, where I found Max's *Gardens of Saturn* proudly on display at the front of the checkout counter under a small sign that said UPPER WEST SIDE

NOVELS. The woman behind the cash register smiled at my inquiry and noted, proudly, "Seven or eight copies a day, and mostly to tourists; they want to know which diner on Seventy-ninth Street."

New York City Ballet's winter season was in full swing. It had been years since Laura had danced with the company, and after what I'd heard from her agent, I figured I wouldn't be doing her any favors by making inquiries. As I neared Lincoln Plaza, I began to notice dancers everywhere I looked. Droves of young women, same long legs and small buttocks pulled up tight into carved denim, backbones like schooner masts over a narrow deck of hips, hair pulled back in torturous chignons, duffel bags slung over shoulders, feet slightly turned out, and bowlegged. All that I had thought inimitable about Laura was, I discovered with some dismay, ubiquitous in that neck of the woods. *And* they *were* younger . . . so, so young. I still thought of Laura as young, but these legions of teenage women, some prepubescent, by the look of them, vying for the limelight—talk about replacement parts—was enough to make you cry.

All Laura's agonies about age and injuries suddenly felt like the deepest of bruises.

At Fifty-seventh Street and Broadway, I spotted the Melissa Hayden Ballet Studio, and recognized the name as the place where Laura had taken classes for many years. A rickety elevator to the fifth floor opened on a reception area littered with prone bodies, pick-up sticks of limbs, men's and women's; they were stretching, their faces florid and sweating, draped in earphones, eyes inward-focused, towels draped around their necks. So young and strong and flexible. I wanted to rob them blind. The place reeked of cheap perfume and cheaper cologne. An exotic cult I'd laughably stumbled upon. The air was humid with exertion and flowing with physical desire, not quite sexual, but akin. I carefully picked my way past the sprawl of delicious youth.

"Laura Williams?" The woman receptionist, maybe eighteen or nineteen, repeated the name between staccato chews on her gum. She gave me the once-over, as if I were some kind of clueless antediluvian who had emerged blinking from my cave. "Long, long time—never see her."

"I thought she went to school here?"

Her heavily mascaraed eyes twisted up at me in a goofy look of disbelief. She put aside the toe shoe on which she had been sewing a ribbon.

"You mean took classes, and that was probably before I was even born. She was a principal—right, a star; those guys got their own private coaches. Know what I mean?" She paused to punch a card for a woman who was hurrying over to the open door of the studio. "Like she's retired or something. Wasn't she injured? She was the best when I was a kid." She worked her gum from one cheek to the other and pointed across the room to a beat-up poster by the window, under which a radiator hissed.

The ABT poster was at least ten years old, a spring season at the Met in the seventies: a young Laura Williams, backlit, poised on toe in an arched arabesque, every line and curve of her fit and sculpted body showing to perfection. A tiara glittered on her brow; sequins in her tutu gave off a starry sheen. My gorge rose in my throat: once the iconic image of the company and American ballet . . . gone with the wind.

On my way out, I stopped by the door of the studio as a piano began playing. Glancing in the mirror at the front of the studio, I could see the rows of dancers at their barre. They responded as one to the music, filling the air with their perfectly articulated movement, rank upon rank of perfectly arched feet and shapely legs. In the swish of feet, I was momentarily returned to our room in Venice, to the counterpoint of the waves in the canal below, where I had watched Laura perform similar ablutions to the goddess Terpsichore. The dancers in the studio seemed impossibly young; most were teenagers with bad complexions. At such altars and others across the city, youth and vigor and talent were celebrated, an art of quicksilver pliancy made to look effortless. I yearned for an hour, a day of their strong backs and ease of motion. Instead, I felt a fraud and voyeur, and with it a terrible sadness I couldn't quite articulate.

This had been her meteoric life for twenty years, as short and fabulous and risky as it gets—on which I'd feasted at a remove in *Gardens* and occasionally indulged in *People* magazine—now going down in flames. As Suzanne had intimated, candelabra aflame in her piercing stare: the apotheosis of her father. I realized suddenly all she'd lost when I had first seen her on Delos, shorn of career and family and lover on the path to the summit of Mount Kynthos. She'd given me her all, rolled the dice, humiliated herself . . . and what had I managed in return? I hadn't even managed to get her pregnant. But perhaps that was just as well. Talk about a broken-down old machine. What a terrible chance she'd taken with me. How could she have been so desperate—so brave? I felt she'd trusted me with love and I'd let her down . . . again.

I took the train to Princeton to check on my condo and to talk to the department about the fall semester, when I would be back in the saddle teaching Classical Archaeology 101 and a graduate seminar on the Parthenon friezes (hopefully, Charles willing, with the Smithson watercolors in hand or with detailed photographs of them). Then I bought a four-wheel-drive Jeep Cherokee and loaded it up with essential books and my computer and headed north. I hadn't visited Elysium in winter for decades, not since the early days with my grandmother, before her arthritis made winter in the Berkshires untenable. When I got on the Taconic Parkway, the old feelings of heading home came over me, as I suppose they had for my father when he'd driven up from Princeton in the first years after the war, headed for his assignations with Suzanne—before Elliot tipped him off about the intercepts of Soviet cable traffic; before the longer drive from Washington upon his return from Greece in 1950; before the years of his marriage, when he drove up with his wife and infant son to see his mother, and lover. But their voices did not accompany me; in the shotgun seat was another, and his manic enthusiasm threatened to become mine. Though the Cherokee was handling pretty well on the icy parkway, time and again I found myself navigating my first car, my Chevy Impala, to Elysium with Max at my elbow in the days after Charlie Springfield's death. As so often the case, just as he'd always predicted in his life and novels, his memorable company trumped all—especially that bittersweet last week of our friendship at Elysium, when Laura had first come between us. I found my love for the groping empty oaks and the whitening hills—even after everything—buoyed by his crazy love . . . sha la la la la la la la la la la dee dah . . . an ever-present counterpoint to the growing pressure in my ears and the sensations of long-ago childhood.

Soon I was slipping between fieldstone-walled meadows of white, cushioned on silent unploughed roads. It was snowing. Ahead was an abandoned gatehouse with most of the signage stolen by local vandals down from Pittsfield. The burning of Hermitage and the subsequent grand jury investigation had gotten plenty of publicity in the local press and so had drawn curiosity seekers to our scandal-ridden woods. The caretaker said he'd given up replacing the signs for Elysium. "The kids just steal them again. Better now, anyway, that the little buggers can't find their way to Hermitage." Snow-laden hemlocks made their tentative oblations as I passed the gates, as if they knew I'd never been a fan of winter; it was the wasteland that separated my football and crew seasons, the cold that now only added to the painful stiffness in my back. But I was glad—glad of winter's numbing whiteness and of the stark simplicity of the scenes I passed, rather than the outrage of summer colors and smells and the irrecoverable longings, often voiced in Max's words, therein. Winter was a way of letting go of him, perhaps of Laura, as well, of moving on. Or so I hoped.

I briefly checked on the burned-out hulk of Hermitage and found more of it remaining than I had expected from Laura's description. The roof was gone, but a few of the white clapboard walls and the wide verandas remained. Huge tarpaulins had been stretched over the roof areas to try to preserve some of the interior woodwork, but it looked as if the rain and snow had done their worst. So I was happy to leave and retrace my tire tracks in the rising snow until back on our side of Eden Lake.

The lake lay stretched in space like a taunt safety net tucked beneath the gray of the fading afternoon sky, there held aloft by tent poles of the tallest white pines. The mightiest along the dirt road to our house, clothed in somber white plumage, seemed resigned to hibernation and the withholding of their glory for another long season of introspection. As did Elsinore, rising from white lawns in sprawling fieldstone walls and gables and copula and leaded-glass windows shawled in green shutters. The caretaker had failed to close the window shutters, but I was glad of the windows' glassy stare, relieving what had always been a forbidding mass of Romanesque stonework. Parking behind the house, I found a powder of snow had already collected on the front porch over-looking the lake—my grandmother's favored westward perch during her summer Inness hours—like blowing sands beginning to cover a desert tomb. I had thought New York was cold, but this was the real thing, and it was only getting colder as the wind sluiced from the north and blew spumes of snow down the lake. I was not wearing clothing for such cold but found myself diligently inspecting for damage, as my grandmother would have expected the man of the house to do. Or was I just imitating my snooping doppelganger of years before? The story of a dying clan now even more the case that the Williamses had been extirpated from our woods, like the Puritans of old a casualty of change and social Darwinism that no longer had much use for our kind. As sole survivor, I cleared a spy hole in the frosted pane of the living room window and peered inward, as if needful of a last look, before replacing the mystery of memory with the newly minted shape of the thing itself:

inviolate for a moment more. Because I knew even as I slipped in the door key, those rooms would begin shifting themselves, animated by recently gathered memories, whose voices already churned within me, clamoring to accompany me as I turned the handle to what awaited.

The seal of vanishing childhood broken, the scent of pine and varnished rosewood paneling greeted me, distilled with damp plaster and the sour stink of moldy carpets, held in timeless suspension at exactly forty-two degrees. I remembered writing the check for the new furnace and thermostat while seated at my desk in my apartment at Madame Cleo's, inhaling the scent of roses and charbroiled olive oil. On the front hall walls, sheathed in dust—had the housekeeper simply been cashing my checks and doing nothing?—were framed antique photos of Minoan pottery with the fluid intricate patterns I had so loved as a child. My father had bought the prized color photographs from a museum shop in Germany in 1930, the summer when he'd first spent time with Karel Hollar as a student in Leipzig. I had to smile to myself: The sensation, the dizzy multiplying dimensions of those faded photos, the cartwheeling tentacles of the octopi and the blue leaping dolphins and nubile flying fish were so firmly fixed in my imagination as belonging on those walls—of animated sea creatures seemingly born and nurtured there on a wall by the front door—that when I first stumbled upon the original pots in a museum in Athens, I was stunned, unable for minutes to acknowledge their separate reality from their mere shadow approximations as I had known them growing up. They belonged, I felt, on that wall by the front door, where I passed them coming and going, objects, in my impressionable boyish mind, speaking not just of the peculiar beauty inherent in artifacts of the Minoan past but of some symbiotic correlation between the world of art and the splendors of the natural world. They were a window not just into the golden age of a lost civilization but a symbol of the past's eternal present to the delight of the beholder's eye! And yes, the school to the Athenians and the Parthenon, and everything that made us fully human planted on home ground.

I lingered for a moment more, examining a framed photograph hanging higher than the rest of a fresco from Knossos, a detail showing a blue monkey sniffing a stylized lily. As a kid, it had been too high to really view; now it struck me as wildly fabulous and magical. And somehow . . . hopeful.

I moved on to the living room and turned up the thermostat. From the basement, a satisfying distant shudder, and in a few minutes warm air was percolating upward, lifting gossamer sails of abandoned webs from the heating grates in the floor. I stood very still, grounding myself in the sensations of returning and all the rising associations, obscure vortexes of my mind suddenly alive to every quivering voice. Swaddled in the warm updrafts of new and surviving memory, I surveyed the immense bluestone fireplace, the ceiling rising in half-timbered arches to the lunette windows and Tiffany skylights, where decorous patterns of swirling plant and animal life, in colors azure and turquoise, vied with the steel gray of a winter sky . . . comforting promises of the spring to come. While my distracted gaze began sifting for my true purpose, I contemplated the thing I had really come for. To simply let the past bury its own, my father's slightly tarnished but fading reputation, or to shine a harsh light? Like him, I could have simply shifted my oars and resigned myself to the calming comfort of the wake.

Pondering these always perplexing issues of family loyalty, I reviewed some of the portraits and the daguerreotypes of rigidly posed patriarchs, thankful that my grandmother had banished most to the Boston Historical Society. On a side table was a photograph of my great-grandfather in his last years, his hair and flowing moustache gone as white as the snow piled on the windowsill, his eyes retaining something of their youthful power and intensity—eyes that had watched the slaughter of his Massachusetts volunteers in the Cornfield at Antietam. He was an old man in the silver-framed photo, resting in a wicker easy chair on the back porch, where he surveyed the sunset over Eden Lake, when my grandmother had first known him: What disappointments were harbored there in those gray eyes beneath such extravagant silver-gray eyebrows? Did he, at the very last, inventory his regrets, still chide himself for not having put some backbone into General McClellan? If he had not been shot, if he had not been too woozy from loss of blood, he might have better made the case for chasing old Bobby Lee into the Potomac and sinking him there. But then he might never have come upon Pearce Breckenridge and the slave who would become Pearce Breckenridge. I picked up the photo and turned it to the back and saw that it had been dated 1916, two years before his death from influenza and from shock at the news of his surgeon son's death. I stared at the face in the photo and heard myself say, "Thank God you didn't know as yet." And as I said those words, I knew in every bone of my body that although the loss of this man's son in the Argonne had left an unfillable gap in our family, it was not this loss alone that had come down to my father at a particularly vulnerable moment in his life . . . standing on the boathouse dock when that great blue heron swept the skyline.

What the fuck, Hawkman, open your goddamn eyes.

Fuck you, Max. The general pleaded with Grant, and later Cleveland and his pal Teddy Roosevelt to do something: to stop the killing and lynch-ings—the darkness of a hundred years that had descended on the South.

I stood stock-still (oh the painful origins of that expression), shocked at my echoing voice, trying to resist the bastard as I breathed in the smells of that eerily clamorous room, of antique furniture and thread-bare rugs (my grandmother would never throw out anything if it still retained usefulness) and the metallic distemper of the bronze cook-ing utensils hanging near the fireplace, artifacts of pre-Colonial days, which had been antique even in my great-grandfather's time. I went to the bookshelves in the alcove, reveling in the eternal comfort and loyalty of books that never shortchange your friendship. I found myself taking down precisely the volumes to which Max had been drawn, to befriend them as he had and smell their sweet mildewed pages and the beeswax rubbed deep into the morocco bindings—timeless narcotic for all that ails the weary time traveler.

Outside, it was snowing hard over the fading lake; the great pines were almost invisible, alarmingly so. I had stopped and bought a little food, but not enough if I really got snowed in—three or four feet on two miles of unplowed roads, a challenge even for a jeep Cherokee. I could hear the wind in the disappearing pines and behind that . . . pure silence.

"You stupid fucking antiquarian dogsbody—get to it, kemosabe: a gold mine of material."

As if to counter my ghostwriter's echoing admonitions, another spectral voice intervened and I heard my grandmother's reprimand in her quick, excited cadences as she instructed and cajoled. The job of the senior male in the family upon returning to Elsinore was to wind the clocks. Three clocks, to be exact. The Eli Terry & Sons on the bluestone mantel. The Ithaca No. 9 with barometer on the cabinet by the window. And in the niche, once inhabited by a gas lamp, the steel-encased E. N. Welch Eclipse Regulator, a Sherman tank of a clock that looked to withstand anything but a sledgehammer blow. Each had its own pecu-liar key and winding procedure. My task completed, I was filled with the satisfaction that comes only by way of praise from a demanding parent. The sensation, the longing for approval and its satisfaction, was so powerful, brittle and keen, that it momentarily drained me of energy. My back cried out for rest, and so I settled on the sofa and closed my eyes.

I listened for the clocks, each pronouncing its rarified mechanical cadences like glancing heartbeats—"like archaic time bombs," Max had written—lacking a dominant rhythm or guideposts beyond the occluded present. If only I could concentrate hard enough, I kept on assuring myself, the spaces of time and memory might yet yield a way forward.

The heat was distilling new smells . . . a dog, wet with lake water. Trudy, my father's golden retriever . . . *Trudy, Trudy, Trudy* she had been called, in imitation of Cary Grant. Trudy had cuddled with me on that sofa when I was a child, had accompanied me on walks, often rushing for the door at the sound of approaching car tires. She had been three and a half when my father left, bought when my parents married. In one of his last letters to Suzanne, he made mention of having to carefully lock Trudy up when they met at night in Pine Meadow by Eden Lake; it seemed the dog had escaped the house on previous occasions and had followed my father to their rendezvous site. "Even with your temptation to indulge a ménage à trois," so my father had written, "Trudy would be scandalized." A touch of acid humor, I suspect, since they were both cheating on their spouses, if not Charles Fairburn, if his claims of paternity were to be believed. But thoughts of that letter suddenly clarified something in my mind: As a boy when I walked Trudy, she would suddenly go off on her own, and I would follow, and she would go to the lakeside meadow and sniff around the base of the gargantuan old pine that grew there, running around in tight little arcs, sniffing and pawing and whining at the pine-needled ground, pitiful little staccato whines that troubled me: a bear or bobcat or raccoon? For Trudy, they were still there; he was still there. Even years later, when I was walking Trudy along a trail, she'd spot Suzanne coming in the opposite direction and her tail would wag and she'd nuzzle Suzanne and look up into her face with the most imploring brown eyes: lover's eyes meeting lover's eyes.

That old sofa, like a magic carpet, seemed to spin many such scenes through my head. There was one story that came to mind, and I still think of it as slightly unreal because Max stole it and deployed a version of it in *Like a Forgotten Angel*. It was about me at four or five. I'd been playing on the carpet and my mother had been reading one of her naval histories on the sofa and my grandmother had walked in, preoccupied, and seeing my face suddenly, she'd turned to my mother and exclaimed, "My goodness, he looks just like John at that age!" My mother had broken into tears, and my grandmother, instantly in control of the situation, had pulled her away and out the door, where she'd severely scolded my mother for breaking down in front of me. "You'll unman that boy yet." That was the expression Max had used in the novel, but for the life of me I couldn't remember if that was really the expression she'd used, if that was what I'd repeated to Max, or if he'd simply invented it. But it was now how I remembered it.

Thoughts of my mother's tears reminded me of how she had stood by the window overlooking the lake the last time I ever saw her. I'd been in my uniform after basic training, saying good-bye, standing by the mantelpiece after having wound the clocks. She hadn't been to Elysium in probably ten years. I had agreed to meet her on neutral ground, at least not at the apartment in New York. She had offered me money—money to go AWOL, to Canada, to Europe, to do whatever I wanted for as long as I wanted. She'd fund it all. I told her she was overreacting: Princeton had admitted me with or without a Winsted diploma; I told her I was only going to language training in San Diego, and then intelligence school, at least for a year. It wasn't like I was actually *going* to Vietnam, and more American troops were coming home every day. I just needed to feel part of something bigger and better than myself. I told her I didn't want any family money. I told her my grandmother would never have acted the way she did—never. I told her she had to stop drinking. But nothing I said seemed to sink in, and finally, exasperated, I just left without kissing her good-bye, or even giving her a last hug. I never wrote her, not once.

I had no excuse. . . . Nor did my father: not a single mention of me or my mother in his Pankrác diary.

Get over it, Hawkman. It's all great material. If you're going to be a writer, you gotta be snooping your own doorstep: the mother lode, baby—how sweet it is.

I sat up as if awakened by a jackhammer, suddenly furious at myself, how that son of a bitch had lied about so much, besmirching me and my father and family in his damned novels.

I left the living room and went down the long hall, past the Inness gallery and on to the document room, so called by my grandmother.

I hadn't been in there since going through copies of the *Mid-Week Pictorial* with Max all those many years before, as we titillated our adolescent minds with the ghastly horror of the Western Front. I found the key in the same drawer of the highboy where it had resided in my grandmother's day and opened the door.

I turned on the light and stared around at the well-ordered shelves full of leather-bound photograph albums, scrapbooks of newspaper clippings, ledgers, folders of architectural renderings for General Alden's buildings and railway terminals, and on the topmost shelves, where the light barely reached, file box after file box, all neatly labeled in my grandmother's inimitable block letters, containing over a hundred years of business records, correspondence, and memorabilia. Only with the help of a stepladder, like a tottering second-story man, could I get my greedy paws on those whispering voices exiled to the back shelves: all the correspondence year by year between General Alden and Samuel Williams, from the Civil War to the building of Winsted School, and all the years through the turn of the century, when they had run Winsted jointly, and right on through the twenties and thirties, when Grandmother had led a coup against headmaster Amory Williams and then become president of the Winsted board. I checked a few of the file boxes and was stunned to see how meticulously Grandmother had organized everything. Sitting for hours on the back porch, she had done her thing in the years after the war, read every scrap and then precisely squirreled it all away in neatly labeled and annotated folders in chronological order. Nothing had gotten past her. She was clearly prepared for the truth to be known . . . sooner or later.

My father was the truth's first casualty.

"Fuck you, Max," I said aloud.

Filled with a terrible angry energy, I picked up the first two file boxes of General Alden's Civil War correspondence and his years out west as an engineer building railroads, and marched them up all fifty-three steps to my father's boyhood room at the very pinnacle of the house. My breath steamed from my lips and congealed on the leaded-glass window that looked out on the whiteness. And then I fetched my computer and monitor and all the rest of the file boxes, as my back protested every one of those fucking fifty-three steps. Crazy: a tiny room, freezing cold, no heating, and removed from not only the document room but the bathroom, phone, and kitchen. A form of madness, both homage and hatred directed at Max and the two boys we'd once been, when Max had caught wind of his heart's desire and swept all before him.

Amidst the golden green of the pine boughs, with views of the clouds scudding above the lake, he'd vowed—or threatened—to create a fictional universe: "To save us from ourselves—what do you think, Hawkman?—an anchor to our mortality before we, too, go up in smoke."

I immediately called the family law firm of Brandt & Harrison and reiterated my marching orders of days before in New York: They were to file a Freedom of Information Act request for anything and everything in the CIA files on my father, and to buy, bully, steal, and bribe—whatever it took—to get their hands on East German Stasi files, Czech secret police files, and, hopefully, KGB files on the inter-rogation and execution of my father, an execution that went against all protocols and belied the commonsense solution of an exchange of agents. Two lawyers were tasked to reopen the investigation into the whereabouts of Joanna's lost son, put on hold after my father disap-peared, which, with the end of the Cold War and the return to Greece of many Communists long banished behind the Iron Curtain, might yet prove promising.

My rash relocation to that remote aerie did later require the help of electricians and extensive rewiring to accommodate my computer, a Xerox machine, a printer, and, critically, an electric space heater to keep my fingers mobile and my back flexible enough so that I could climb all those fucking stairs. I got the phone company to run up a phone and fax line so I could badger the lawyers at will. I carefully placed my father's Pankrác diary and his and Suzanne's love letters within easy reach in a file cabinet, which quickly began filling with gleanings from my overpaid eager beavers at Brandt & Harrison. There, amidst all my father's books, journals, typescripts, artifacts, photo albums—and, there by the door, the framed postcard from Leipzig's Museum of Antiqui-ties, where I knew the story would ultimately lead, I began.

As I made my way though the file boxes of General Alden's cor-respondence, I found myself immediately vying with Max—*Like a Forgotten Angel*—for advantage. I was building my case contra Max, but try as I might, I couldn't quite escape the gravitational field of his nov-els—or the queasy feeling that he was there reading over my shoulder. I knew exactly what he'd have been looking for: Had General Alden used the largesse provided by U.S. government subsidies for the railroad right-of-ways out west to build his first small fortune? Had he and the railroad men cheated the Indians out of their land and killed off the buffalo to line their pockets? Had they exploited and ill-treated Chinese coolie labor in their furious race to build through the Rockies and the Sierra Nevada? Had he driven sharp deals in his first forays into New York real estate, turning over properties at a fast clip because of insider information about infrastructure projects that would make the land more valuable?

Yes, Max . . . probably so. The circumstantial evidence is certainly there, although no one—you'd say they were all in cahoots—ever accused him of such things. In fact, his career and success were based on his unusual probity in such matters. But as I made my way though the files, the contentious Max ever at my elbow, my alter ego grew silent as the real story—a story that Max not only missed but couldn't have dreamed up in a thousand years—came into view. This was the tragedy of Pearce Breckenridge. Pearce Breckenridge's story, our story, the country's story, all turned out to be about the heavy price of freedom won and then lost and how as those losses multiplied they poisoned the nation's soul.

In a less exalted vein, as we used to say in the intelligence business, I began to take countermeasures . . . and put distance between me and the snoop on my tail.

I was only a few days into the first file box of General Alden's papers from the Civil War when I first came upon the name of Pearce Breckenridge, when the general described in a letter to his first wife the circumstances of finding Pearce's body and his slave Jason among the Confederate wounded in the paddock by the surgical station at Antietam. I was riveted by Alden's outlandish decision to send the body of Pearce, their friend from student days at Harvard, back to Cambridge and the Brattle Street home of his first cousin, the Reverend Samuel Williams. Nothing of this had made it into the histories of Antietam or the memoirs of General Alden's comrades, and there were many. As the story unfolded through Alden's correspondence and eventually the Pinkerton reports from the 1870s, as I glanced up at the snow-encrusted pine boughs against the white of Eden Lake, the name Pearce Breckenridge kept nagging, ringing a bell whose tones faded before I could make them out. Then, about a week into my research (as the first gleanings of Brandt & Harrison were trickling in from East Germany), at the point where Alden and Williams bowed to Pearce Breckenridge's rash demands, I remembered.

I remembered Max standing in front of the Williams Memorial in the Winsted chapel, perplexed, the thing gnawing at his imagination without resolution. He had reached to the bronze intaglio letters in the memorial inscription to Samuel Williams's dead son, picking out those in maroon where they formed a jagged vertical row.

"You see the pattern they make . . . it spells out 'Eternal love and peace—Pearce Breckenridge.' I can't figure it out, Hawkman. Who is Pearce Breckenridge?"

$\times$

46 I HAVE TRIED TO IMAGINE WHAT SAMUEL Williams's reaction might have been upon opening his door on a quiet Cambridge evening in September 1862 and finding a Union officer, reeking and blood-stained from battle—the outcome of which was still largely unknown in Boston—standing exhausted in his front portico, while by the gate in the flickering lamplight, slumped next to a horse cart and coffin, was a tall man of noble countenance, a bloody bandage around his head, and his face bringing back a thousand memories of carefree days long gone. "My God, John, I mistook him for Pearce when first I laid eyes on him, and my heart soared, only to plummet like a stone—and yet the beauteous soul that yet shone in those raven eyes! It was as if an angel had touched my shoulder, whispered in my ear. But what? I keep asking myself. But what?"

If Samuel mistook him, Jason was quick to put him to rights, yanking open the nailed lid of the coffin where the spoiling remains of Pearce stared up at him clothed in his once-splendid officer's uniform of gray with brass buttons and yellow piping at the collar, "his distorted features a puffy gray-green turning black around the eyes and sunken cheeks." The delicate Samuel was sick on the sidewalk.

"When this spectral Pearce closed the coffin, he tried to offer me comfort, saying my name almost as if he knew me, not in a Negro dialect, but with the precise musical tones that might have sprung from the lips of our great friend."

The Union officer's telegram from Hagerstown had failed to arrive, and Alden's letter accompanying the body did little to lessen the shock.

Cousin, you may imagine my dismay when I came upon this man near the field hospital, lying in the grass with a mortal wound, and finding out his name from his devoted slave and manservant. I could hardly believe him to be the dashing Pearce Breckenridge, our classmate and your bosom friend. The disjunction of that Stygian scene and Pearce's bloody countenance with memories of halcyon times and places—Pearce's rhetorical splendor burning in my mind's eye—was enough to make me crazy with grief. I had seen the enemy butchered by the thousand but they were abstractions without names and faces. As you might expect, I was much overwrought with the battle at hand and our damned awful leadership. The slave, Jason, would simply not leave the body of his master, so I determined to give both over to your keeping. I remember well your fondness for Pearce, your Wordsworthian colloquies, much less your gentle testing and baiting each other over abolitionist matters. How often you two brought me to tears of frustration. How often I stormed out the door, vowing never to return. Can you now still love such a man—after everything? So here is your chance for redemption, my poet, my philosopher theologian cousin. Take Pearce's manservant and turn him into a philosopher king for his people. Or better still, make him a Moses for his people and let him lead them to the Promised Land, before it is too damned late for any of us, if anything good remains to us after this war has had its evil way.

Samuel Williams, spiritual light to a generation, whose *Essays and Prayers* lived on into our days at Winsted like a phantom missal from a blinkered era, managed to cover his tracks remarkably well. Much of his correspondence about Jason must have been conveniently lost or destroyed—possibly by Bobby Williams when Hermitage burned; not a scintilla is to be found in the Winsted archives. An official biography of Samuel Williams, written in 1905, makes only passing reference to a "scion of the South," one Pearce Breckenridge, equally famed for his soaring scholarship and rousing good times in Samuel's Harvard class of 1855, a period when Samuel had dallied with poetry and studied painting with William Morris Hunt. The slave Jason Breckenridge receives only sketchy footnotes, the author referencing rumors that the youthful Samuel Williams had been involved in the Underground Railway, funding and hiding escaped slaves as they made their way to Canada. There is another vague reference that in late 1862 a onetime slave was taken into Samuel Williams's household for a few months before joining the Fifty-fourth Massachusetts Volunteer Infantry

Regiment under Robert Gould Shaw, the first black regiment recruited in the Civil War.

When I checked the enlistment register of the Fifty-fourth Regiment, I found the name Jason Breckenridge listed as one of the very first recruits in March 1863, but he was withdrawn after a "rigid and thorough" medical exam revealed nearsightedness that made him ill-equipped as a rifleman. At no point is any connection drawn between Pearce and Jason Breckenridge. The biographer, who wrote from the perspective of the turn of the century, when Winsted's early reputation was at its height, focuses almost exclusively on Samuel Williams's spiritual evolution, his early falling away from the Congregational Church, and his attraction to abolitionist circles surrounding Henry Lee Higginson, encouraged by his cousin Gen. John Alden. The Civil War years and the postwar years of Reconstruction receive scant attention—odd, given that the Williamses had been one of Boston's most vociferous abolitionist families. Instead, the biography focuses on Samuel Williams's disillusion with the war's terrible toll among his classmates and their families, leading to his infatuation with Emerson and the Transcendentalists, and then his growing attachment to all things British—a sentimental literary culture spared the horrors of 600,000 dead on nearby farmers' fields. In short order, Samuel converted to the Episcopal Church, while his torturous theological self-examination resulted in his most famous work, the *Essays and Prayers* of 1885, this the inspiration for the founding of Winsted School with his cousin. The Winston school motto is emblazoned on the frontispiece of *Essays and Prayers*: Freedom, Justice, Love and Honor.

No one reading Samuel's biography, or the official school history, for that matter, could have suspected that the founding of Winsted had everything to do with the Civil War and the sad fate of Pearce Breckenridge, and the even more terrible end of his slave Jason, who became Pearce Breckenridge.

As I made my way through the files my grandmother had so carefully organized, my mind played little tricks as familiar names invoked other names, as quirky disconnects sparked associations surrounding my father's disappearance. There was something profoundly strange yet utterly captivating about the whole affair of Pearce Breckenridge. Why had General Alden written as if condemning Samuel Williams for "loving Pearce, after everything"? Samuel wrote back, "How could he, the most gracious and wise soul in our class, have found his way into the ranks of the rebel taskmasters?" I can only imagine what Alden must have thought of such naïveté in his "dreamy-eyed cousin." Strange, too, that it was Alden, of the two cousins, who had visited his classmate Pearce in 1855 at his Natchez, Mississippi, plantation, who had met his family, and Jackson Breckenridge, his "beastly father, who liberally employs the bondsman's lash to get his last cent in sweat out of his Negro slaves."

This part of General Alden's story had been told to me as a child by my grandmother: how on the way back to Boston from Natchez, utterly disillusioned at all he had witnessed, he'd sat on the steamboat quay along the Ohio River, staring across the muddy waters at the Kentucky shore, "that benighted land of the unfree," where he'd come to the realization that such an "unnatural" division of his country could not stand.

For all his abolitionist fervor, Samuel, in some hidden part of himself, refused to acknowledge such a reality, nor its violent implications—at least as embodied in Pearce Breckenridge. Instead, Samuel wrote in endless detail of the torments and unpleasant complications that greeted his efforts to find "brother" Pearce a proper burial place, "where I might walk at my leisure and pay my respects to my beloved Pearce." There was no discussion in the letters about an interim burial arrangement until the war's end, or when circumstances might allow Pearce's body to be returned to his family in Mississippi. Come what might, Samuel was intent on keeping Pearce close by. In this, both men conspired: Not once in the wartime letters was there any suggestion of even informing Pearce's family of the circumstances of their son's death at Antietam, much less seeking to return his body to home ground.

The weirdness of this haunted me, in the way that the name of my grandfather on the wall of the missing in the Meuse-Argonne Cemetery haunts me, as the return of my father's body by the Soviets, his cremation by the CIA, and the subsequent and surreptitious scattering of his ashes on Lake Carnegie in Princeton by my mother, absent his son or mother, haunts me.

This was the thing for which my grandmother never forgave my mother. As my father's Pankrác diary makes more than clear, Pine Meadow was where he would have wished his final resting place to be.

So I was not entirely surprised, later that year, when I walked the Mount Auburn Cemetery in Cambridge and found in a shady corner under an enormous elm a prominent headstone of gray Vermont granite with Pearce Breckenridge's name and the anomalous dates 1834–1875 and the following inscription:

Grant this boy, my son, may be like me, first in glory . . . strong and brave like me . . . and one day let them say, "He is a better man than his father!"

It required prodigious digging in the archives to locate that headstone. How many would know Hector's parting words to his beloved son, much less the many faces of this Pearce Breckenridge, slave owner, Confederate officer—"scion of the South," Harvard graduate, and man of peace and preacher of racial harmony, of freedom, justice, love, and honor, who in death would enjoy an anonymity as deep as time itself?

The epigraph was General Alden's doing, for he had known Pearce's father only too well.

The surviving correspondence from Williams to Alden in the years following the delivery of Jason Breckenridge and his master to Cambridge is scanty. These were, after all, Alden's "wilderness years" in the family mythology, when he went out west to build railroads and make his fortune. Some of Samuel Williams's letters may never have been received and others mislaid. The best I could piece together from my grandmother's meticulous archive was that Samuel Williams first took Jason into his household as his ward. Then at some point, the name Jason slipped away in Samuel's letters, to be replaced by Pearce, almost as if the slave name had been an unfortunate misunderstanding. Who was responsible for this? Initially, I assumed an overwrought—"don't let your delicate constitution betray you, Cousin Williams"—and sentimental Samuel had taken it into his quixotic mind to redress history, but the more I found out about Jason, the more I suspect that he might well have been a fellow conspirator.

As Samuel Williams wrote to General Alden:

He reminds me more of Pearce each day, and indeed, dear cousin, as surely you must have suspected, they share the same blood. Not only do they share the same father but the ladies' maid that is his mother was herself the offspring of Pearce's grandfather and another mulatto household servant. Jason is not shocked in revealing such things to me, but acts like it is a commonplace where he comes from, as is the torpid humidity in the Mississippi Delta. Jason even takes a certain— how can I put it delicately?—plantation owner's pride in this fact—his dignity is only enhanced far beyond the common run of slaves. He has admitted to me more than once his jealousy over his master's years with us at Cambridge, and still treasures Pearce's letters written him from Harvard, full of wonders and friendships and the splendors of civilized discourse. Jason has all the sensibilities of our brother Pearce; in truth, they are very like twin brothers. I cannot help but feel as if God has directed him to my lonely door.

"Lonely door." Another haunting phrase, considering Samuel had married Lisa Bartlett in 1856—the year after his graduation from Harvard, when Pearce headed back to Mississippi. Lisa Bartlett was heiress to a huge Lowell cotton mill fortune that lay the foundation for the rise of the Williams family to social and economic prominence in the Boston of the 1870s.

Samuel Williams personally tutored Jason until he was ready to enter Harvard, at which point he was enrolled as Pearce Breckenridge from Cambridge, as if his master and half brother, graduate of the class of 1855, had never existed. "Dear Cousin, Pearce makes fantastic strides in his education. He is fully as talented as our beloved Pearce, in every respect; he is a light to our household. He writes like a god and his piano playing is the envy of Brattle Street." With at least two generations of white blood in his veins from the same family line, Pearce seems to have passed as white among unsuspecting New Englanders. In 1868, Pearce Breckenridge got his Harvard diploma in divinity. His Harvard record makes no reference to his race, only encomiums to a brilliant scholar of Latin and Greek who graduated summa cum laude. Classmates noted his shining gray-green eyes and splendid voice for song and Transcendentalist oratory; they noted that he was a master of the sonatas of Beethoven and Mozart, and devotee of Emerson, sage of Concord. During this time, his voice must have transitioned from the long, mellifluous southern vowels of his upbringing to the shorter, more staccato rhythms of the Boston Brahmin. From 1862 to his graduation in 1868, Pearce lived in the Williamses' large house on Brattle Street, which Lisa's mill-owner father had bought for the young couple in 1858. Pearce—I am tempted to refer to him as Pearce the Second, but shall refrain—first occupied a room in the servants' quarters on the top floor, but at some point, he was given a large corner bedroom on the second floor with a view of the gardens behind the house. "Better, I think, for his studies," Samuel wrote. Between 1865 and 1868, the three Williams children were born in quick succession, two boys and one girl. Born after the couple had been married nine years, the eldest was Samuel, the Harvard golden boy and classics scholar who took his own life in 1891; he was the Williams after whom the Winsted chapel was named, and to whom the Saint-Gaudens memorial was dedicated, including the bronze inscription where Pearce Breckenridge's name is encoded. The second son, the hapless Amory, who married late and disastrously to a highly strung and incredibly talented painter, succeeded his father as the second headmaster of Winsted, until fired by the board under my grandmother in 1925. The daughter, Isabella, that fiery raven-haired beauty who captivated Boston society for over forty years, married into a New York shipping fortune equal to her mother's, and went on to build Palazzo Fenway to house her collection of old masters. For three decades, she entertained the greatest writers and artist of the age and summered at Palazzo Barberini on the Grand Canal.

Just another circle of ripples in Pearce Breckenridge's invisible legacy.

After his graduation from Harvard, Pearce traveled to England for two years to study theology at Oxford University, then returned to Cambridge, where he was ordained an Episcopal priest and so began his remarkable and short-lived run as one of the most charismatic figures in Radical Republican Unionist politics and Episcopalian circles in Boston, as if something of Samuel Williams's high-flown Yankee Transcendentalism had begotten a mysterious twin, charismatic, cultivated, the hybrid General Alden had called for: a Moses for the black race.

What I found most extraordinary in the correspondence between Alden and Williams was how much was left unsaid, as if they communicated to each other in a kind of cryptic code, reading each other's minds, often at distances a continent wide, their letters full of sublimated guilt and frustration. Even though they had known each other since childhood as first cousins, they had not been close until Harvard days, when friendship with Pearce Breckenridge and the festering wound of slavery joined them in an uneasy alliance. Alden was an outdoorsman, a doer, an engineer, with a no-nonsense and opinionated personality, very much a public man. Williams was bookish and scholarly, a literary man, a friend of Emerson, a tortured moralist who shed and picked up allegiances the way some men change clothes. He had a Congregationalist upbringing, was a Unitarian at Harvard, but by 1870 joined the Episcopal Church in tandem with his protégé Pearce Breckenridge, who, if anything, was considered even more brilliant in the few accounts of his Cambridge days that I turned up. For Alden, slavery was a straightforward issue of law and principle—a monstrous cancer in a republic of free men: The Civil War had been a fight for freedom, for free labor. Williams saw the question in theological terms, as a matter of sin and free will. Both railed against the hypocrisy in their circles of mill owners, State Street bankers, and those involved in shipping interests, men who had turned a blind eye to the outrage of slavery for reasons of profit. But it was Alden, even as a Harvard student in 1855, who had ventured to visit Pearce Breckenridge at his plantation, Hermitage, in Natchez, Mississippi, where he both witnessed his "crimes against man and God and pled for him to join us in a peaceful resolution of the crisis that confronts this nation." In all his eighty years, Samuel Williams never set foot in the South. He was convinced that his money and his "brother Pearce" could do the job of reconciliation for him, a prospect that Samuel brooded over in his letters to his cousin in far-off Nevada.

> How could Pearce have been silent all those years at Harvard about his black shadow, his half brother waiting for his return to Mississippi? The business quite turns one inside out. Did Pearce recognize the wicked-ness in his bosom? Or was he truly oblivious? He was such a fine and principled man. How often the lofty thoughts expressed by him moved my younger self to tears. My God, one doesn't know whether to cry out to the Lord in bitterness and despair at the evil of Pearce's world, which he hid from us so well, or to see in his cruel death—and, dare I say, resurrection under such extraordinary circumstance—a crack of light in the darkness and hopes to make amends, now that this terrible war is at an end. I believe a better Pearce is risen up from the ashes, one to inspire his people and turn the bondsman away from the abyss of their sins.

General Alden was astonished at the changed Pearce he found on a visit to his wife in 1867 and on two subsequent visits before her untimely death in 1870.

> My Lord, what have you wrought? What has this Pearce of yours wrought? Where is the slave who clung to the body of his master like a spirit damned? Who is this man who spouts the Gospel as easily as Wordsworth and interweaves the two like streams of uplift from the same source? Who champions the Negro's right to vote and to government land grants for the oppressed and education for all, as if this should be a God-given right to Americans. Indeed, he is a Pearce transformed, a Pearce with a conscience, who espouses life, liberty, and

property like the canniest radical Unionist one moment, only to weave in the necessity of a subjective passion to fully grasp the glories of nature in the next. Sometimes I see him, in the pursuit of our better angels, as following in the footsteps of our glorious martyred Lincoln. What necromancy have you conjured: a spirit blessed or goblin damned? Beware, dear cousin, that you tread lightly lest that name Pearce Breckenridge come back to haunt us all.

I assume that was in reference to the unreturned body of Pearce Breckenridge lying in Mount Auburn Cemetery, which Jason alone could have testified to. And the grave of Jason's half brother that Samuel hoped might anchor the ex-slave in the bosom of his growing family.

In letters to his wife and to Samuel from such places as Truckee, Winnemucca, Battle Mountain, and Elko along the route of the Central Pacific Railroad, General Alden followed Pearce's progress, "this Lazarus at the open tomb," with a combination of fascination and foreboding, as he did political events after the war, with the passage of the Fourteenth Amendment substantiating hopes that the black population of the South might yet find its way to equality and the guaranteed rights of citizenship, which the growth of Black Codes and growing violence in the guise of the Klansmen threatened to overturn. Alden knew personally many of the Union army men who tried to make congressionally imposed Reconstruction a reality in the South. Many of his letters are filled with frustrating asides, critiques of President Johnson's failure to enforce voting rights and "thus the enforcements of the rights of the black laborer to the fruits of his labor, to land and liberty and education for his children. What did our people fight and die for if not for this basic right to free labor and the uplift of the people out of abject servitude and darkness? We New Englanders can provide the South with capital and workshops, with energy, intelligence, and enterprise. When the world sees what wonders of engineering we are providing the nation in the Sierra Nevada, the tunnels and trestles and vast bridges that will unite the East and West, the work of creating a better South will seem child's play in comparison." (Reading such thoughts in General Alden's letters, I was reminded not a little of America's anti-Communist crusade in war-torn Europe and the Marshall Plan.) Alden's frustration with the "spoiled fruits of our sacrifice" only grew with time. Even Grant's election in 1868 and the completion of the transcontinental railroad a year later could not alleviate his dark moods. "This creeping amnesia about what our fight was all about astonishes me—all the sweet sentiment about soldiers' common sacrifice that forgoes the moral differences over which we fought, all disregarding the causes and consequences of the fight. This was a death struggle between right and wrong—nothing less."

General Alden was oppressed by the faltering of Reconstruction and the growing violence and intimidation of blacks and Republicans in the South. More unsettling was the change in mood, even among old line abolitionists and radical Republican Unionists to forgive and forget. "They long to heal at any price—a monstrosity of forgetting and insult to the glorious memory of the brave men who died." Samuel Williams did not seem to share Alden's agony over such matters; he was welcoming children into his happy home, pushing his protégé Pearce to establish himself as "a light unto the world" among his Cambridge congregation of Radical Republicans; and urging Alden to visit his wife, "who wastes in longing for your return to Boston."

There is an odd silence in the Alden correspondence about the general's first wife, Elizabeth, daughter of a Harvard professor. They married just before the war, and between the lines of his letters one could detect a fragile personality, perhaps a manic-depressive, which Alden's infrequent visits, his near abandonment of her for years at a time couldn't have helped. In mid-February 1870, Elizabeth died suddenly of pneumonia. Alden made it back only in early April for a memorial service for his wife, buried six weeks prior. I could find little in the way of deep grief over her loss; he seemed a hard man, a builder, a driver of other men for hard-won goals. It was then that he met Pearce again after Pearce's return from Oxford. "My Lord, how eloquent, how fiery his brown eyes, the erudition of a scholar mixed with that of a seeker. He has read everything on recent developments in the South and makes a wonderful case for the liberation of his people, for their rights to land and education, and yet insists on hiding his color, his parentage? Why the pretense when the pretense does his cause no benefit and will result only in more trouble should it be discovered?"

Alden's unease about Pearce Breckenridge's pretense became clear to me when I got two interns in Brandt & Harrison's Washington office to dig through the National Archives for the general's Union army discharge. McClellan had indeed dismissed him for insubordination and disloyalty, for complaining to the newspapers about the lost opportunities at Antietam, but there was also the matter of his having used his authority to cause the "dereliction of duty" by one of his officers for "the unauthorized return of a soldier's body to the dead man's family." The name of the dead man was not recorded, but Alden must have known there was enough evidence to connect him to what amounted to the stealing of Pearce Breckenridge's body, not to mention failing to inform the deceased's family. By the late 1860s, Jackson Breckenridge, father to both Pearce and Jason, had recovered much of his Natchez plantation and would not have taken such a hideous sacrilege lightly. Alden's relocation to New York in 1872 in the wake of his wife's untimely death seemed, in retrospect, less about a savvy business opportunity, investing his considerable fortune in burgeoning Manhattan real estate, and more like a man escaping one life for another. While the lovesick Samuel Williams seemed to have embraced Pearce as something more than an alter ego, "like one of your own family," as Alden delicately put it: Pearce had both cousins over a barrel if the truth should come out, especially his relationship to Lisa Williams and her three children. As much as Alden railed in his Republican circles about the work undone and the failures of Reconstruction to "seal our sacrifices with the betterment of the black man's lot in this life," Pearce's growing aspirations remained a scandalous threat.

Going through the Alden papers, time and time again I detected echoes of my father's experience—if not his quixotic love-hate relationship with Bobby Williams—how after being wounded in Greece he, too, had been drawn back into the battle against dark forces, first in Germany with the OSS against the Nazis and then, reluctantly, with the CIA against the Communists. Even the imposition of the Iron Curtain and the subjugation of the captive nations of Eastern Europe had uncanny echoes in the South after 1870 as Reconstruction was undone state by state and black servitude reinstalled by a regime of terror and intimidation under the Ku Klux Klan, and then directly imposed through force of law by state governments. The divide of the free and unfree had been reimposed upon the land. Both men had watched in horror at the imposition of a new age of darkness.

The embrace of the brilliant, if mercurial, Pearce, first by Samuel and then John Alden, reminded me, too, of my father's inveiglement by Karel Hollar. While, between the lines, Pearce's intimate, if unspoken, ties to the distaff side of the Williams family sent a frisson of incredulous wonder up and down my spine. All prelude to an act of retributive justice (*lex talionis*, in Latin): the avatar of revenge that set the stage for my father's act of reckless vengeance as he passed through Checkpoint Charlie.

General Alden's new life in New York was rudely interrupted by a letter from his cousin Samuel in the spring of 1872. "Pearce wants to go south, and not just south, but home to Natchez, Mississippi, straight back into the clutches of his father, as he crazily calls him—beyond abomination, beyond horror. I have tried reason, but the most fervent and heartfelt pleading will not change his mind. He is greatly distressed at the latest news out of the South and seems at times unbalanced with grief and anger. After all I have done for him, how can he now threaten to leave—and Lisa?"

My one great frustration in all my researches was the lack of a photo of Pearce Breckenridge alone, either master or onetime slave. If the Williamses ever possessed such a photo, I suspect it went up in smoke with Hermitage. All I could find was a photo of the Harvard Choir from 1868, in which Pearce stands in the back in half shadow; he is tall, the tallest in the group, and his skin color seems no different from that of the other choristers; his hair is dark and parted to the side and shines dimly, as if held in place by prodigious use of hair tonic: the nose is strong and tapering, the lips wide and expressive, the eyes by all accounts a deep chocolate brown, which often ignited with dazzling hazel highlights when he preached or smiled his broad, endearing smile. He was known to become fiery and agitated when the subject of Negro suffrage was broached.

General Alden invited Pearce to his office in New York to discuss the situation. "You would have thought he owned you and me, cousin, by the way he marched in and placed his demands on the table: a big man, an impressive specimen, how like our dear departed friend to so inveigle his sponsors, only to put in the bayonet. How well I remember a trip to New Orleans—did I fail to trouble your darling ideals with this?—during my visit to the family plantation with the young Pearce, when our taking in the sites turned out to be a visit to the finest whorehouse in the city—whores of every complexion, I might add." That discussion, one of many at Alden's downtown office and brownstone home, was recorded in letters to and from Samuel as their plan was negotiated. Alden found himself quite taken with "your Reverend Pearce," whom he described as a white man's version of Frederick

Douglass, "if anything, even more pushy—not such a bad thing, given what we are up against." Pearce wanted to preach to the South; he wanted to establish an Episcopal church in his home parish of Natchez.

"All I want, Mr. Alden, is a chance to raise up my people, let them see the light from the hilltops and give them hope."

"Hope is one thing, Pearce; the weight of white oppression is another. I have many friends in the Union army who served in the occupation, who labored in the government's Freedmen's Bureau to build a foundation for a free labor society, setting up black schools and churches. Their good work is being undone everywhere."

"I have faith in President Grant; he will not let us down."

"That is more faith than I have, and Grant is a friend. Grant has his own problems: The country has lost its nerve to suppress these annual autumnal outbreaks of unrest in the South. Soon there will be no hope for federal intervention."

"Mississippi is different. The Republicans are still in government there; the laws protecting the rights of my people are enshrined in legislation."

"Here today, my friend . . . gone tomorrow, if the big planters have their way. Even Pearce, your dear half brother, was terrified of his father, was he not?"

"He shamed my brother into the army—called him half a man."

"A poet, a truth seeker, what makes you think you are any better . . . for war, for it may come to another war, or not."

"I have my name—Breckenridge—a distinguished name in Natchez parish."

General Alden eyed him, thinking he was surely mad.

"I know your father, your once-upon-a-time master. I met him before the war—do you remember my visit in July of '55—where were you?—a man I feared even then to trifle with."

"I was sent away on a cotton-selling trip to Baton Rouge. I was an embarrassment to a northern visitor."

"Well, the name will hardly save you in Natchez."

"He has no legal hold over me now, neither body nor soul."

"Did he ever acknowledge his paternity to you personally, legally?"

"Of course not; such things were never said and less acted upon."

"But you know?"

"My mother told me—everything. She was a very beautiful quadroon, a striking beauty from New Orleans with French blood in her veins, and when alone in the house, she would touch the works of art, the fine silver and family portraits and point to me and whisper the name."

"Breckenridge?"

"Breckenridge."

"Is your mother still there?"

"She was sold in 1859 . . . once her age began to show. She disappeared one day without a trace. They wouldn't even tell me who had bought her."

In his letter to Samuel Williams, General Alden described what occurred in the aftermath of his conversation with Pearce.

Dear cousin, an edge of anger then sparked in his intense eyes and I thought to be very careful. It was clear he longed to return to the land of his birth, his heritage, and who could blame him? And I, in turn, found myself intrigued, and after all the terrible reports from the South, after all the failures of good men to ameliorate that hideous society, I was tempted to put some kind of plan into motion, to dig in my oar one final time to see if the situation was yet retrievable: a success that could be a light to others. But how to make it possible for this romantic dreamer of yours to realize his throne without bringing all crashing down? The Gospel and all the good intentions under heaven would not be enough. I told him to return to Boston and his Cambridge congregation; I told him to keep an eye out for some good men, black men, who might make fine schoolteachers, or had experience in practical things, engineers and mechanics, farmers. I would scout the way. "Land and property," I told him, "is your only protection—and that of scant defense. But the name Breckenridge you cannot use: That is my unalterable condition. A lamb in wolf's clothing is still a lamb." To this he agreed and we shook hands and embraced—oh, dear cousin, that I might feel again the dreams of youth. For I, too, have a small debt to settle.

I retraced my student steps of nearly twenty years before, neglecting my usual mode of travel by taking the train only as far as Pittsburgh and then traveling by barge and paddleboat down the Ohio to the Mississippi and on to Natchez. Even seven years after the end of the war, devastation and degradation are everywhere in Natchez. I found a town full of skulking thieves and one-legged hangers-on. The Negro walks the street with head still bowed, fearful to look the white man in the eye. Cotton has only just begun to recover but is nothing like its former glory. Many plantations have fallen into disrepair or abandonment,

but not Hermitage. After touring the area in horse and buggy, checking the dikes, talking to every stranger I could engage, I found my
way once again to the splendid Hermitage, with its processional line
of grand oaks, its splendid two-story portico of white Doric columns
greeting the visitor like a vision of Greece, along with a strange central cupola with balcony and a single octagon window, a cyclopean
eye—so it struck me—to watch over recalcitrant slaves. The place had
clearly gone through difficult times; many of the outbuildings and the
old slave quarters were in bad repair, and the place deserted of blacks
compared to my memory. But the old tyrant Jackson Breckenridge—
remarried with three young children—still reigned, if under straitened
circumstances.

As soon as I made myself known to an ancient black footman who
answered the door, I was shown into the "Masta's" fine study at the back
of the house, overlooking the English garden. He still played the role of
the cavalier gentlemen to the hilt, dressing in a fine jacket and breeches
that would be twenty years out-of-date anywhere above the Mason-
Dixon Line. We shook hands and I struggled to hide my dismay at
the resemblance to a Pearce grown old and weary and spiteful of life.
These Breckenridges all share the same hard-edged nose and delicate
chin and even a bit of the gunmetal-blue eyes, though in our Pearce
there is a kind of soft glamour, more a chestnut hue, and hint of exotic
sensuality from his quadroon mother. And I was not a little jolted
when I noticed the portrait on the wall of the planter's beloved son,
the gallant officer lost at Antietam. Jackson remembered me from my
visit of almost twenty years before—"the glory days"—so I made the
reason for my visit quickly known, saying that I, friend and classmate
of Pearce, had witnessed his final moments among the Confederate
wounded at Antietam, and so I wished to pay my respects to him and
his wife and let them know that Pearce's final thoughts as he expired
were of them. I gave the old tyrant that much and no more, feeling
that perhaps Pearce would have, at least, wanted me to do as much.
He gripped my hand as if he were playing Patroclus to my stubborn
Achilles and almost embraced me, but not, seeing I was a still a Yankee
invader and cause of all his present hardship. But he eagerly invited me
to sit, and we talked long into the afternoon about his glorious son. A
dozen times he thanked me for confirming Pearce's place and time of
death, much of which had been reported by Pearce's comrades. Fortunately, the removal of his body had gone undetected by those people,
and the old buzzard assumed his son slept with his comrades in a common Maryland grave. How he went on about the valorous Pearce. "If
only his poor dead mother could have had the news from me as well, a

brave soldier defending southern rights and the honor of his home and people." It was enough to make me sick, this old slave driver, his face scarred with smallpox, his white hair cascading to his shoulders as he went on in similar vacuous tones about the hardship of the war's aftermath, still blaming the blacks, uncaring and unrepentant. Not once did he ask me about Pearce's manservant, Jason—not once—he who had stuck by his son to the end—and verily, beyond.

"My Pearce, I never understood why he wanted to go north to that abolitionist nest of yours, Harvard College. There was much of his mother in him, my queen of Charlottesville, a Virginia lady who spoiled him and indulged him with books of every kind. Life here never as grand and cultivated as in Virginia, so she always let me know."

"Pearce was a fine poet, full of magnificent thoughts that more than once brought us to tears," I replied.

"Tears, really . . . well, he fought gallantly in the end; that is what matters. That his name will be remembered among those who defended their homes and way of life."

"A way of life that has undergone some alterations since the last time I was here."

"Do you congratulate yourself, Mr. Alden?"

"Slavery was an abomination, sir."

"Easy for a northerner to pontificate. Slavery was a necessity for the planter. Without the control of labor, the business cannot be done at a profit." He bent forward toward me surrounded by his family portraits and his garish bits of French silver, and continued. "You see, General Alden—and it is *General* if reports I have read of Sharpsburg are accurate—the black man won't work as before; they either refuse to work on the plantation—and won't allow their children nor their wives to do so—or they ask for wages that we can no longer afford until the market recovers. Most only want their own land, which they cannot pay for and we will not give them. The land is ours, our birthright. They are scattered all over now as sharecroppers; that seems to be the only arrangement that will suit them. Many seem to have money and they spend it in the local stores. But they are not like us, General. Even if allowed the suffrage and odds and ends of education, they cannot be depended upon to share our way of life. And the cotton business requires the predictability of enforced labor—there is no other way."

"Mr. Breckenridge, I beg to differ with you, sir. The Negro only wants to better himself, like any other American citizen. They require a grubstake, ownership of land, a stake in the business of prosperity, a prospect of bettering their position and educating their children for a better life. Give a man a stake and the chance at a better life and he will do wonders for you and himself. The trick, dear sir, is that you must faithfully align your interests with his. I believe you have a Republican governor and administration and even blacks in positions of responsibility—something to build with."

The old viper bristled at this report.

"Mr. Alden, General, you were a friend of my son and now a benefactor of news to my broken heart, but you do not understand the coloreds as we have for generations. They are limited by mind and culture. They can be trained, yes, but rarely do they show initiative on their own, nor the constancy of our race. Just to get them to show up for a job on time can ruin one's disposition."

"Then you must change that culture. I will make a friendly wager with you, Mr. Breckenridge. I am an engineer by training and a man of business; I have employed Negroes, Irish, Chinese, and Yankees to build railroads through the most forbidding of natural obstacles. I know how to get men to do my bidding. I am also a Christian and a supporter of an Episcopal missionary society out of Boston. Here is my wager. I will bet you that I can bring in a few skilled blacks from up north, educators and mechanics, and, yes, a fine minister I admire— successful people with the work ethic you seem to find lacking in this neighborhood. I will build you a fine school and they will educate your people, practically and morally, to benefit the community as a whole. To underline my seriousness, I will buy from you, or anyone else, for top dollar, lands that require draining or are underutilized. I notice that many of your dikes need repairing—that, too, is something I know a thing or two about. I will wager you, sir, that with the support of fine upstanding citizens like yourself, with my capital, human and financial, we can turn things around in this part of Natchez. If I lose my bet, I will sell you back your land for what I paid for it. Knowing your son Pearce, I think it is a wager with the Yankee devil that he would be the first to embrace. And so you understand the spirit of my offer, my bona fides, I will make one more pledge to you: I will also build at my own expense a fine Episcopal church and name it after your son Pearce Breckenridge. Come what may, the church and his beloved name shall endure."

47 OVER THAT LONG WINTER, AS I MADE MY
way through the meticulously arranged files that
my grandmother had assembled and which she had
annotated in her precise hand to clarify dates and
identify writers, I realized how completely she had mastered the details
of this slow-motion train wreck, and how she, as I, had been rooting
for a good outcome against all the odds, if not mesmerized by General's
Alden's guile, subterfuge, and sheer audacity in the face of what I can
only describe today as a terrorist regime. I discovered something I had
not suspected, that my great-grandfather, a practical man of business, a
world-class engineer who knew how to calculate the odds, was, at heart,
a wily gambler. Calculating, yes, but also a man drawn to risk, to the
inside straight—precisely like his grandson, my father. He got his deal
with Jackson Breckenridge, whom he had shrewdly detected needed
the money, needed to raise capital, who figured he had nothing to lose
. . . and would gain a chapel built to his son's memory.

But the phantom narrative that had me by the throat were the
uncanny parallels between General Alden's dealings with the ex-slave
who became Pearce Breckenridge, who became William Percy Emerson, and my father's with his fellow archaeologist Karel Hollar:
ex-Wehrmacht officer, ex-minister of mines in the GDR, ex-minister
in the Dubček government. A duo of shape-shifters erased from history. Not to mention how General Alden and my father had disguised
themselves, as had the garrulous Odysseus with his tall tales, to infiltrate the land of the unfree, spurred by good intentions and hopes as
glorious as they were doomed, only, in the end, to exact an exquisitely
calculated revenge as Odysseus had blinded the one-eyed Polyphemus.

I know, Max, my historical parallels are not as edgy as your stirring metaphors, but history does repeat itself—if you look hard enough . . . into yourself.

General Alden didn't waste any time. Jackson Breckenridge introduced him to his new young wife and three adorable children, and his daughter from his first marriage, Pearce's sister, who embraced him like a lost brother. She had lost her husband in the war. They drank that night to the spirit of enterprise and better relations between North and South. The next day, he went out in his horse and buggy and toured the countryside north and east of Natchez. He talked to everybody, white and black alike, and got a feel for the land and the people and the possibilities. On his fourth day, he found an old abandoned farm on a hilly rise not too distant from a gentle bend of the Mississippi. He was drawn to the apple orchard in particular, which reminded him of his New England boyhood north of Boston. "The best parcel of real estate in twenty miles, lovely to the eye and gentle to the disposition and out of danger come flooding season. With some pruning, the apple orchard should bring a good crop in a year or two," he wrote. He found himself a local lawyer of Republican bent and negotiated a price in hard cash with a strapped owner. He didn't try to drive a hard bargain; he wanted sellers to come to him, and they did. The lawyer helped him assemble parcels of land that connected with the old farm, until he had a tract of almost two thousand acres of various types of soil, some for cotton planting, some for subsistence agriculture, some for raising livestock. He invested in existing plantations, including Hermitage, buying marginal parcels in some spreads, providing for capital improvements to upgrade others. The master plan seems to have come to him in a moment of whimsy. "I was planning for the promised school and church on the hill when I thought, If a church, why not an academy, too? An institution where the boys can come and stay and become part of a community to uplift their minds and bodies. Isn't that what our ambitious Pearce wants—to preach and educate? Well, now we shall give him his chance."

As with Winsted a decade later, Alden personally drew up all the plans for the buildings. There was to be one large schoolhouse, which would contain classrooms and a dormitory for the boys. "I thought, What better way to educate these poor Negro children than keep them in a safe and invigorating environment for weeks at a time, develop proper habits, let our talented Pearce inspire them like a father, an exemplar of all they might aspire to." He envisaged a kind of utopian citadel in a land of burning hate. Originally, Alden proposed a stone church, but when the depression hit the country the following year, he resigned himself to a simple but elegant clapboard design with a tall steeple and sturdy bell. The old farmhouse and outbuildings and barn on the property were to be renovated for homes for the teaching faculty. Within a matter of weeks, all was on the drawing board, contractors hired, and construction moved ahead with good Republican men to see his vision succeed. "I was eager to show these people what a railroad man can do, to set a shining example of New England get-up-and-go: a shining city on a hill." Within a year, the new Concord Academy and what became the school chapel were finished, the name having been selected by Pearce Breckenridge to evoke the town outside Cambridge where his mentor Emerson resided. An homage that also produced his nom de guerre as headmaster and chaplain, William Percy Emerson, Esquire, Harvard and Oxford, Doctor of Divinity.

As I made my way through the invoices for everything from cut stone and lumber to Latin and Greek and English primers, blackboards and chalk, and busts of great statesmen and thinkers—Lincoln, Washington, Socrates, Pericles, and so on—I was amazed at the prodigal expense and the sheer logistics and planning to build such an institution in a distant and alien land, and, as it proved to be, an increasingly hostile and dangerous place. Pearce Breckenridge had done his part; he had recruited six or seven black teachers on a one-year contract to teach Mississippi children, along with skilled black carpenters, mechanics, and farmers with extensive expertise. Pearce had to have been a charismatic figure to get such people to venture to the Deep South, and the Alden paychecks up front didn't hurt, either. In the spring of 1873, they arrived at Concord Academy on a rolling bluff overlooking the Mississippi and prepared to open their doors that fall, tuition-free. The paint was barely dry, and their timing could not have been worse. The country had been hit by a panic and depression in 1873; railroads were failing and cotton prices were falling. Behind the scenes, southern Democrats were scheming to overthrow the federal government's imposition of Reconstruction. Within a year, with the election of 1874, which resulted in widespread Republican losses, the deadly pogrom was under way in Mississippi and across the South to violently reimpose white supremacy and black servitude.

When William Percy Emerson boarded a steamboat in Pittsburgh and headed south down the Ohio to Natchez, he did so in complete secrecy: He was a new man, a black man, a supremely educated and cultivated teacher—a spiritual divine. Pearce Breckenridge took an extended leave from his Cambridge congregation, supposedly to return to England to raise money for Episcopal ministries to Africa, and again disappeared from history, as had Karel Hollar circa 1945. Somewhere on the train trip between Boston and Pittsburgh, the transformation had taken place. Samuel's wife, Lisa Williams, and her three children, who forever remembered their dashing Pearce filling their Brattle Street home with piano music and song, were, as far as I could make out, never told what happened. Joining Pearce as he got on the steamboat was a onetime Union army sergeant from General Alden's Fifteenth Massachusetts Volunteers, an Irishman from Back Bay, Boston, on leave from the Pinkerton agency, Sean Malloy. Sean was an imposing broad-shoul-dered man with pale skin and reddish hair—"fearless Sean Malloy," Alden called him—who carried a Colt pistol and hunting knife under his jacket, along with ten thousand dollars in gold. Sean was Pearce's personal bodyguard, alter ego, and General Alden's insurance on his venture. Sean reported directly to Alden, who then passed the reports on to Samuel. These reports, along with Pearce's letters, carefully annotated by my grandmother, constitute almost everything we know about what happened, along with the Pinkerton investigation in the aftermath. By 1873, with the sullen resentments and blazing hatreds of southerners burning through county after county, Alden thought it best that he keep a very low profile in the life of Concord Academy; he advised both Pearce and Sean Malloy to try to build bridges to Missis-sippi Democrats instead of relying exclusively on Republican allies as Alden had done the year before.

As I stared out at the bleak winter landscape, I found myself longing to speak to the elusive Pearce Breckenridge, to fathom his heart and mind as he traveled south on the Mississippi River—he who had been raised in a fine plantation home as a manservant for his half brother and yet whipped within an inch of his life if he dared step out of line; who, as the Army of the Potomac moved north into Maryland, had been mistreated like any field slave in the baggage train, hauling artil-lery pieces and ammunition boxes and digging and filling latrines, the kind of labor he'd never known back in Natchez. For close to ten years, he had passed as a Harvard-educated white man in Boston and

England, respected, even revered, most certainly loved. In the home of his mentor Samuel Williams, he had assumed yet another role: The love he invested there one can only marvel at, if not comprehend. What can have passed through his heart as he said good-bye to Lisa Williams and the three children? What can have been going through his mind as he stepped off the riverboat at the landing, Natchez-Under-the-Hill, and stared up at the city he'd known since childhood, to which he was officially a first-time visitor and new headmaster and rector of Concord Academy?

Oh Max, such a tale . . . but how to enter such a mind?

"It was a strange and remarkable thing to see," wrote Sean Malloy; "all the way down the Mississippi, our righteous reverend was the toast of the first-class cabin, while I was disregarded. As our man descended the gangway to the Natchez landing, I watched the waiting white faces examine him from stem to stern in his suit and clerical collar, a Bible clasped to his chest, his gold watch chain shining, and they all knew what I had never seen in all my weeks in your employ; they saw him as a black man and knew him as they knew the devil, and if we hadn't had our transport waiting, he would have been hard-pressed to get a ride up the hill into town, even as he turned the heads of every woman in the vicinity. In Mr. Emerson's company, I find myself suddenly a prince among beggars."

Two large, expensive leather trunks accompanied the odd pair, holding all Pearce's books and clothes, with more supplies for the school soon to follow. All was loaded into the waiting Concord Academy "omnibus" with the school's name prominently painted on the side in blue and gold letters. Waiting at the new school buildings north of the city along Cemetery Road was the first contingent of fifty black boys of all ages who had been recruited as possible candidates for Concord Academy. Two members of the teaching staff were already on hand to greet the new headmaster when he rode up the hill past the orchards and barns to the schoolhouse and newly constructed chapel named, as General Alden had pledged, after Pearce Breckenridge.

Malloy described the scene:

> He sat straight and tall in his seat, as fine and splendid an example of a Negro gentleman—although I would never have guessed—as had ever been seen in these parts. He tipped his hat to the gathered ranks of Negro children, all with round, expectant eyes in their scrubbed faces,

standing rigid as little flagpoles. None knew what to make of this exotic come into their midst, much less that he might be one of them. You might have thought they were witnessing the Second Coming, the boys were so quiet. Then one of the boys at the front of the line saluted, like a cadet at attention, and instantly all the others followed suit. As soon as our omnibus passed, they began screaming and jumping for joy. What a strange scene it was to behold. And so we gathered in the foot soldiers of our future Gilead.

Strange and a little disconcerting that when Pearce addressed the children, few could understand his peculiar New England vowels and long words. And so as days turned into weeks, his New England diction reverted back to the honeyed and more languorous rhythms of the South of his upbringing, or as Sean Malloy put it, "A change came over our black stallion as do the seasons. Within weeks, he was speaking like a plantation owner's son, and that's not a trifle unsettling, given that there are already far too many of such nasty sods around, just looking to stir up trouble. As one said to me the other day while I waited at the boat landing for a freight delivery, 'Why you all wasting your time? An educated nigger won't work. And this time, there won't be any federal gunboats coming down the river to save their black hides.'"

By the fall of 1873, Pearce's school was up and running, with sixty students, ages thirteen to sixteen. Many had been tutored over that first summer in the basics of English and reading. Pearce ran a disciplined school. "I believe in strict rules, strict habits, and proper English diction and syntax. I will not hear of concession to regional speech. The Queen's English is the Queen's English. How will they deport themselves in this life and be standard-bearers for their race if they cannot hold their own with the educated citizens of the world? Some cannot take it and go back to their parents and complain, but things sort themselves out. The ones who want to learn, who yearn to lift themselves up, return to us, or are replaced by others, who take to our dream. It is a natural winnowing process, which I'm sure you and Samuel well understand, of which Mr. Darwin would approve."

The boys could take the omnibus to and from school or could stay in the dormitory, where they were fed, bathed, and clothed. A simple uniform of white shirt and dark trousers and a blue-and-gold cap was introduced. The colorful caps, ordered from a London haberdasher, mimicking the fashion of Eaton and Rugby headgear, began to be seen far afield from the school, a status symbol of the proud Concord boys. Sean Malloy thought the caps silly and provocative and worried that it made the boys too conspicuous to the school's detractors. Not Pearce: "I assure you, a uniform is a symbol of solidarity and pride, loyalty to an institution and its goals, something these people badly need—a goal larger than themselves." Shoes were provided for those whose parents could not afford them, as were all books and school supplies. According to Sean Malloy, word quickly got around in the black community about this exotic New England mulatto, the fiery, charismatic Reverend Emerson, who taught with a passion, preached like an angel, played the piano like the devil, and was ready to use the cane whenever one of his boys disappointed. "Some of the Negroes call him a Yankee half-breed, but many are just as pleased to turn over their sons in hopes some of his wealth will rub off on their kind."

With the countrywide depression taking root, cotton prices faltering, and the white Democrats pressing Republican holdouts in Mississippi's government, the black community of Natchez found Concord Academy a sanctuary of support, where their children could be fed and educated and promised chances to further their education in the North on full "Episcopalian scholarships." But there was some grumbling, and much of it from the black community, about what the children were being taught. As both Pearce and Sean Malloy noted, the Negro boys who tended to stick it out came from parents who had been raised in plantation homes as cooks and servants, not field hands; they tended to be lighter-skinned and aspired to hold on to their role as relatively privileged folk and leaders in the black community. "They remind me of myself, it is true," explained Pearce. "But I do not pick them—we are open to all—they pick themselves."

Pearce had been greatly influenced by the Transcendentalists, not just Emerson but educational reformers like Bronson Alcott and others who stressed the development of the inner spirit and the subjective imagination of the child. "I encourage the boys to read on their own, to go to our growing library and choose books for themselves and find their own way. I can light a fire, I can give them the tools, but they must learn to seek for themselves, to allow the spark of their curiosity to light their way." Pearce's teachers were like-minded and encouraged the boys to explore ideas while they worked doing their chores on the school farm, which, within a year, was self-sustaining and providing much of the food for Concord Academy. As Sean Malloy noted, "The teachers are teaching more than highfalutin airy extravaganzas. They talk to the boys like good radical New England Republicans, telling them about Negro equality and voting rights and how the black man is as good as the white, if not better. They tell the boys about the heroics of black Union troops and the glorious days ahead for the race. As you can imagine, such notions don't go down well with certain parties in the white community. When I sometimes take charge of the school omnibus to deliver boys thither and yon, or pick up the mail and freight in Natchez, I get looks from white folks that remind me of times in the war that I'd just as soon forget. The atmosphere down here has been getting heated up and poisonous as the Republican Party has been getting more beat up in Washington."

By the fall of 1874, as the Republicans lost heavily throughout the country, heartening white Mississippians who interpreted the result as a repudiation of Reconstruction, the older boys of Concord Academy, with a little over a year of education under their belts, were beginning to cause a stir in both the black and white communities. Among blacks, wrote Sean Malloy, they were seen as uppity and too proud for their britches. "Their New England ways and big words and even bigger ideas do not go down well with the traditional black churches." A black pastor complained to Malloy that one of Concord's seventeen-years-olds had engaged him in a conversation about a Mr. Charles Darwin, who said all men were descended from monkeys. "The old Negro minister told me his people were having enough trouble down here without bringing animals into it."

Sean also sent along in his weekly reports a short editorial from the *Natchez Weekly Democrat:*

It has come to our attention that a group of older boys from the recently established Concord Academy, a school for Negro boys out Cemetery Road, have been causing an unhealthy stir in certain circles for their high-handed talk and proud manners. They do not wait their place in stores or at the depot, nor show deference to their white betters. More than a few times they have been found arguing over matters for which there is no argument. Education is one thing, as the Reverend William P. Emerson should understand, even for a New England Negro, but teaching boys to act in ways unacceptable to their community, filling them with ideas contrary to the norms of our society and its traditions is to ask for severe judgment. The Reverend Emerson's sermons have also stirred up ideas uncongenial to our community. Although he may think of himself as following in the footsteps of his namesake, Mr. Ralph Waldo Emerson—no friend of the South—such New England rhapsodies fall on deaf ears in these parts. Such preachings should not come from the pulpit of a church dedicated to a scion of the South, a noble son and martyr of one of the finest families in our great state.

Pearce's sermons—"performances," as Sean Malloy called them—got a lot of people rattled, and they just kept coming. "His sermons are so rapturously abstract and romantic in lineaments that his hearers are hard-pressed to explain exactly what he has preached to them—except they felt better for it and enjoyed themselves immensely, thank you very much." What kept the white community wrong-footed was that the Concord Episcopal Church, as it became known, was open to all comers on Sundays, white and black alike. The singing by schoolboy choir members, dressed in blue-and-gold robes, led and accompanied on the piano by "our Reverend Pearce (WPE)," became the high point of the week for many in the surrounding area. The service was conducted with high-church solemnity and grace unlike anything, certainly in the black churches, but also in the Presbyterian and Baptist congregations, and so appealed to a kind of vestigial snobbism and pride in some Natchez plantation families, who considered themselves an aristocratic breed apart, begat of cavalier Englishmen of old. Pearce, dressed in the purple-and-white regalia of the Episcopal ministry, gave the sermon, played the organ and conducted the choir, and led the congregation in the stately hymns he had come to love in his two years at Oxford. As Sean Malloy put it, "The whole thing is, if you don't mind me saying it, more English than the damned English. If I cannot make heads nor tails out of what our Mr. Pearce spouts, I doubt the Negro can, and just as well. Same for the whites—our bedazzler just weaves his spell and the hosannas ring out."

My Dear Samuel, All I preach is Christ's Gospel as you preached it to me, as we studied at Harvard and Oxford. In Christ, there is no North or South, no Negro or white—all are brothers in the Holy Spirit and God's redeeming grace. I am particularly drawn to the mystical union of the Trinity, Father, Son, and Holy Ghost. I preach Mr. Emerson, too, that we are all God's creatures and partakers in His glory and the natural wonders that bespeak His sojourning hand. One and all seek uplift, and I give it to them.

Such ringing sentiments, ten years later, would make a name for Samuel Williams in progressive educational circles in New England.

Pearce's popularity and renown began feeding on itself. Even Sean Malloy was surprised to report that the Sunday congregation was almost evenly split between black and white, "And they sit all mixed up and careless of it—so enchanted are his listeners—and the women, well, they seem fit to be tied. More than two or three leave the service with tears in their eyes. Our Mr. Pearce is quite the Moses—it's the Red Sea that worries me, 'cause this is no Promised Land."

Sean Malloy took some trouble to copy out bits of Pearce's sermons for General Alden, which he must have seen in draft or fair copy. Alden was clearly concerned lest Pearce overstep his bounds: Emerson and Wordsworth were one thing, but Darwin might be pushing his luck.

As I read these excerpts from Pearce's sermons, I felt, yet again, faint echoes.

All human consciousness is grounded in the experience of nature. Every tree and rock and light-reflecting stream dreams in us as we dream on it. Our spiritual inheritance lies all about us and, too, in one another . . . all God's children—we are all reflectors of nature's glory. Standing at the pinnacle of creation, inheritors of her bounty, as Mr. Darwin has written: "There is a grandeur in this view of things." Nature wears all the colors of the spirit, and the symbols of the spirit—the apple tree, the thunderhead, the unyielding boulder in that field yonder— surround us with glory if we learn to open our blinkered eyes to them and read their dreaming minds. There is God's design in every blade of grass and green-shaped oak leaf. Be like a painter to your soul and keep your eyes wide . . . and so let your soul float free on the river of life, the river of Time. My friends, when you leave our tiny chapel of Concord this morning and turn your gaze to the mighty Mississippi, remember that the river of life and the river of Time are one and the same, and all men and women travel on its bosom and drink of its sustaining waters, the knowledge of past, present, and future hopes sustaining all equally. I leave you with our school motto: Freedom, Justice, Love, and Honor . . . for all peoples who make up this glorious creation beneath the river of stars. Amen.

Sean Malloy dutifully reported on the reaction to these sermons:

Our right reverend is big on the autonomous soul, so he keeps reminding his congregation. You should see all these round-eyed faces—black and white—bending forward in awe and rapture, and I'll be damned if any of them knew what the hell your man WPE was going on about. But they nodded to one another as if they did, figuring, I am sure, it had to be good for the soul. As long as your darling boy keeps himself to such things, I think we are safe.

A tingling incredulity took root as I made my way through the letters and reports, confirmed finally in a note in my grandmother's hand amended to a report where Malloy had quoted verbatim a section of one of Pearce's Sunday sermons: "Pearce obviously sent full copies of his sermons to Samuel Williams! See *Essays and Prayers* published 1885!!!" Those exclamation marks said it all. I had been wondering, as I tried to conjure a picture of that white clapboard chapel, and the dark-haired, agate-eyed Pearce leaning forward from the pulpit to engage his congregation, why his words—even the few sentences quoted in the reports—brought a face to mind: echoes of another fiery Southern preacher who made a liberal mix of sources in his sermons extolling the civil rights movement of the sixties and questioning the Vietnam War. Charlie Springfield, too, had drawn on parts of *Essays and Prayers* to anchor his sermons in Winsted's invisible legacy.

By the spring of 1875, with the depression still taking a heavy toll on the country, things were white-hot in Mississippi and throughout the South as Democrats were emboldened by party gains in the U.S. Congress to begin striking back at Republican organizations, all to the end of intimidating black voters and preventing them from casting ballots. Black political meetings were broken up. Democratic rifle clubs of mounted white vigilantes began parading through Negro areas, beating up and assassinating prominent blacks. Reading Malloy's reports of these violent events was like reading William Shirer's descriptions in *The Rise and Fall of the Third Reich* of the intimidation by the Nazi brownshirts in the early thirties, or the Bolshevik Cheka secret police in the Soviet Union of the early 1920s, or Stalin's purges in the thirties, or Mao's political cadres hunting down the educated bourgeoisie during the Cultural Revolution.

These nasty buggers, many ex-Confederate officers—and they don't even bother to disguise themselves—like to hunt their prey at night, knock down a door, murder a black man in his bed in front of his family. I have heard reports from some of our older boys that fifty miles east of here they shoot down blacks "just the same as birds." They go after schoolteachers and church leaders, people of a Republican political persuasion. More and more boys flock to us, choosing to remain here in the dormitories, where they feel safe. So far, Concord Academy seems an oasis from the troubles in the vicinity. At your suggestion, I have recommended to Mr. Pearce to shy away from mentioning the violence, but it is on everyone's mind. I'm not sure he can be satisfied with the mysteries of the Trinity and the autonomous soul for long. Violence and fear have become the currency of the realm in these sorry parts.

By 1875, that was not all that worried General Alden from the "safety of his New York City office," as he put it to his cousin Samuel, "watching all our work hanging over the precipice." Both men had weathered the depression of the early 1870s relatively well; Alden had cashed out his railroad shares early and had been using the cash to pick up cheap New York properties in the downturn; the mills in Lowell that had come directly to his wife were still producing. "The country always seems to need cloth," he wrote. The two cousins funded Concord Academy to the hilt, anything that was requested, from books to building materials and extra cows to provide milk for the growing classes of boys.

It was Jackson Breckenridge who really began to worry General Alden. Their correspondence was regular and businesslike and it was clear that Alden's capital and the lands sold to him with a guaranteed buyback price kept Hermitage Plantation afloat through hard times. Slowly but surely cotton prices are "coming back to life," wrote Jackson, "and the new lands, those drained and those refurbished, should bring bumper crops."

The content of one letter was what caused worry.

I must tell you, Mr. Alden, though I resisted for almost two years, my wife and daughter finally convinced me to attend a Sunday service at your Reverend Emerson's church, dedicated to my beloved son Pearce. I was reluctant to go, as you might well imagine, since the whole business has a bad smell about it, even as you write to me in hopes that the venture might make for a healing balm between our two sections. Raising the Negro up is the last thing on people's minds in these parts, when we can't even get them to sign labor contracts on the plantations. Once, these Negroes of ours were happy with their lot; now all we get is slackness and complaining—but those days are now coming swiftly to a close. I think you will find the productivity of the new fields by this time next year will be a marvel as Mississippi and Natchez and Hermitage rise again.

But I diverge from the point at hand. The church you had built is very fine and the bronze dedication plaque fitting and generous to the memory of my son, though perhaps overdone in terms of his accomplishments as poet and pianist, which my daughter noted with some enthusiasm—that troubles me. Nor is there mention of his prowess on the field of battle, appropriate, one would think, given the circumstances of his death. But I am not unthankful for your efforts. If my daughter and my wife are pleased, I will leave it at that. On the subject of your Reverend Emerson, I am quite baffled. Where did you find him? He is quite the prophet, a conjurer of visions, his voice like honey in its evocation of the earth, even as I have a difficult time following his arguments. His Episcopal rituals, unlike our Presbyterian ones, are long on beautiful ceremony; his blue-and-gold-robed choir of Negro boys, a sight of harmony. You said he was a Massachusetts black, and yet he sounds to me like someone born and raised in the South, but educated, of course. as he seems to be, at your Harvard—Oxford, too, according to my widowed daughter, who takes great interest in all he has to say. So much so that she now fills our parlor with the likes of Mr. Ralph Waldo Emerson, Henry Thoreau, and Herbert Spencer, and returns to the piano that once Pearce played, to the delight of his dear-departed mother. Your William Percy Emerson is a most compelling preacher and a fine figure of his race, Mr. Alden. Like a spiritualist, he manifests ghosts to the mind's eye. His piano playing stirs the hearts of white and black alike, but I fear for our serenity, that with the end of the North's armed intervention in our affairs now at hand, your people may yet seek other means of subterfuge.

Sean Malloy was getting downright jittery.

As I reported to you last week, the Breckenridge family now arrives at Sunday service in force. The old patriarch strides in like a circling hawk, while his blond daughter in her best Sunday attire scouts the seating so as to put the family among the greatest density of whites, planters mostly in all their royalty, along with a few local white businessmen of the hounded Republican sort. The three young children of the Breckenridge clan with their sweet young mother follow quickly to take their place, surrounding their father like a cavalry screen, while the blacks eye them and they eyeball the blacks as all wait with baited breath for

Mr. Pearce, bowed to his fistfuls of notes, contemplating his sermon, to rise and bring the congregation to life like a disturbed beehive. The daughter now regularly delays after the service is done to waylay the good reverend by the door, to hang on his arm with dreamy-eyed conversations about the sermon and books she has recently devoured. Dare I say it, but our horse has another rider, another convert, and the old man ain't well pleased. He left in a huff yesterday, herding his family into the Hermitage phaeton and heading off in a gallop, leaving the daughter to find her way home with another family.

Not to add to your worries, Mr. Alden, nor mine, but Mr. Pearce has been making very discreet inquiries among members of the black congregation and a few of the parents of his boys; he has been making inquiries after a certain woman, a house slave who used to be part of the Breckenridge plantation, who was sold off before the war. I have warned Mr. Pearce that any such talk or queries connecting him with that previous life is putting him in grave danger, especially at this time, with so much hatred and vindictiveness in the air. He just puts me off and tells me to mind my own business. When I remind him that he is my business, he dismisses me. He has taken to riding out at all hours of the day and night without a word to the staff. He lives high on his dignity. I believe he has come to firmly believe in all he preaches and thinks, that it will save him and prove him invulnerable to the world beyond Concord Academy, which remains a model of life, as it should be, and an oasis among the thorn bushes. The boys worship him, as do the teachers, and the Sunday services are more packed than ever . . . and I am more worried than ever.

In the fall of 1875, with state and local elected offices up for grabs, the simmering violence of the spring and summer turned into a torrent of intimidation and murder. Unlike the Ku Klux Klan, whose members masked themselves, the vigilantes who shot and lynched their opponents did it in broad daylight and undisguised. President Grant had refused the request of Mississippi's Republican governor for armed federal intervention that summer. As the fear of federal intervention faded, the Democratic killers—liberators of the white man, extolling the "Redemption" of Mississippi—drove freedmen from their homes and threatened any who tried to vote. Ballot boxes were destroyed or stuffed with Democratic ballots. The black lieutenant governor was impeached, and the Republican governor, threatened with the same, resigned and fled the state, for fear of assassination. A second revolution had taken place and blacks throughout Mississippi returned to a condition of serfdom, "an era of second slavery," as the fleeing governor put it.

Alden had personally gone to President Grant's summer home on the Jersey shore and pleaded with his old friend, to whom he had provided financial support throughout his election campaigns, to intervene in Mississippi. Grant had told him that the country was simply worn-out and sick to death of the whole business. During that fall, Alden and Pearce exchanged sharply worded letters, Alden begging his protégé for caution, encouraging him to cozy up to the Democrats if need be and "give no cause for anger or resentment of any kind. . . . You are in a pit of vipers and must keep very still, as if you are not even there." Pearce was no fool. If anything, his sermons became more esoteric and obscurely Transcendentalist than ever, his siren song, as Sean Malloy put it, "too captivating for words, of which he may have dropped a few too many." Pearce sought to allay the general's concerns. "Have no fear, my dear friend Alden, I bring only calm upon the waters. I preach to the high and low and weave their souls into a more universal tapestry, where they understand themselves as more alike than not. The school thrives, the students grow in stature of mind and body, and the farms produce more and better crops—a bumper crop of apples this fall. We are as a light from heaven upon these gentle hills."

As the violence spread throughout the region, the Reverend Emerson spoke about beauty and the soul's journey to paradise. He told stories of the great literary lights he had met on Cambridge Common: Lowell in his slouched hat; Agassiz, the great naturalist; and Charles Eliot Norton, a Harvard professor and a contributor to *The Atlantic Monthly*, copies of which were circulated among his boys. He read the poetry of Whittier to his students before bedtime. And the library continued to grow as more books arrived every day. I combed through the invoices by the hundred for works by Longfellow, Paine, Gibbon, and Franklin, and multi-volume editions of Emerson's essays, which the boys were encouraged to take home and read to their often-illiterate parents. Everyone was anticipating the spring, when the first class of Concord boys would graduate, all with guaranteed scholarships to northern colleges, the five best to Harvard.

Sean Malloy knew it was bad news when three days after Christmas a telegram from General Alden arrived for him at six in the morning at his aging mother's home in Boston's Back Bay. "Hurry back with all speed. Have arranged four Pinkertons to meet you at train station in New York. Fear the worst." On the day after Christmas, Alden had received a terse telegram from the Reverend Emerson: "Have Malloy return immediately—help urgently needed." When Alden telegraphed back for more details, he received a reply from the Natchez telegraph office the following day: "Delivery Impossible." All the way to Natchez by train with four fully armed Pinkertons, Malloy berated himself. His mother had been ailing; it would be her last Christmas. After the fall elections, the tension and violence had seemed to die down with the complete victory of the Democrats and the overthrow of the last vestiges of Reconstruction. Mississippi had been redeemed from the carpetbaggers, scalawags, and uppity niggers. Things had been quiet, maybe too quiet, but quiet enough that Alden had given Malloy permission to return to Boston for a week to visit his mother.

Malloy knew enough not to arrive in Natchez with four armed Pinkerton men. They got off the train at Jackson under assumed names and supplied themselves with a buggy and horses and rifles. Using back roads, they made their way to the northern outskirts of Natchez, following Cemetery Road as it wound its way west toward the high bluffs overlooking the Mississippi.

Malloy reported in detail what they then found:

I knew it was going to be bad when we were within two miles of Concord Academy; the smell of burning was on the cool afternoon air, and not a stir of breeze, the odor like a presence in the deserted landscape. And it was deserted, not a soul, not even in the outlying Negro shacks, as if God had shaken everything loose and sent it tumbling away. When we got to the bottom of the rise near the gate, it was clear that everything had been burned, and what couldn't be burned, had been pulled down in some violent manner. The buildings—schoolhouse and dormitories, church, barns and stables and equipment sheds—all burned with some deliberation, given the number of empty kerosene cans left behind. Scattered around the devastation like a strange fall of blackened snow were thousands of pages from burned-up books from the library and schoolrooms.

I was strangely relieved at first; I thought, Well, at least they were all just run off. Even the burned barns and chicken roosts were empty of animals. But the worst yet awaited us. There was a sweet sickly stink above the smell of burned wood, the source of which we could not at first discover, as we inspected the warm rubble burned down to the foundations, a trickle of white smoke still rising in some places. We figured it had been five days, sometime right after Christmas, when true fiends from hell might wreak their worst on the unsuspecting. Then one of the Pinkertons pointed down the hill to the blackened remains of the apple orchard, marveling that it, too, had been put to the flame— and he had seen some expert burning when he rode with Sherman. "I never seen it done so well," he said. "Johnny Reb musta learned an extra trick or two since Sherman plowed Georgia clean." I, having so much more at stake in this terrible Golgotha, could not summon the admiring distance of my colleagues. They pointed out the hundreds of horses' hooves that had cut up the mud and grass and exchanged estimates among them, settling on at least thirty riders or more. I kept staring at the burned orchard and then realized, to my horror, that the smell of cooked flesh was coming from that place. As we approached the orchard of thirty-six blackened trees, six lines abreast, I noticed a strangeness about them, a broadness at the base and a thickness to the trunks, as if hideous carbuncles had attached themselves. When the carbuncles took on form and substance, I fell to my knees in piteous despair and had to be helped back to my feet by my comrades.

Thirty-six men and boys had been chained to the trunks of the trees. Pyres of wood had been set around the base of each tree and doused with kerosene. From the very few survivors who were willing to talk to us, we were told that the others, all boys, ages thirteen to sixteen, were herded down to the orchard to witness "the lighting of the Christmas trees," as one of the white men described it, white men, I should hasten to add, who did not disguise themselves in any way. As close as we can figure it, there were about forty black boys who were forced to watch the immolations and then allowed to scatter to the winds to give their reports to the Negro community. The pyres were lit one at a time so that those next in line could properly appreciate what awaited them. The wailing and screams of those being consumed and those to be consumed by the flames must have been something indescribable, for none of the boys we turned up could get the words out through their sobbing, only hints from their parents. Each victim, so we were told, was soaked in water just before his pyre was lit, so that his clothes would not catch fire with alacrity and so hasten the end of his agony. Some scorched tree trunks showed the scars from chains twisted deep into the wood. The bodies were burned beyond recognition and had been scavenged by animals. We numbered the bodies and trees and recorded whatever scraps of clothing or personal effects were discovered. I was able to identify Mr. Pearce's body by his watch and gold chain (enclosed herein), which had slipped into the ashes of the pyre.

He was certainly the tallest of the victims. All the witnesses' accounts agree on one point: Pearce was the last to be burned alive and was witness to the destruction of his teachers and eldest students. Besides the empty kerosene cans and a few abandoned saws that had been used to cut the lumber for the pyres, there were some forty bottles of expensive Kentucky bourbon and even imported Scottish whiskey. Witnesses spoke of speeches and celebrating throughout the night of living hell, toasts to a Mississippi redeemed and revenge for brave comrades lost in the war for southern rights.

We had great difficulty burying the bodies. There were five of us in a hostile land, and not a moment when we didn't fear our own lives were in danger. No one in the vicinity would sell us shovels for any price. We had to go halfway back to Jackson to find a general store that would sell us the shovels and food and drink to nourish ourselves. Then followed three days of digging and burying thirty-six bodies. I have often wondered if there had been more trees in that orchard, if they would have burned more. We collected every scrap of possible evidence from the site of the massacre and anything of a personal nature that might have belonged to the executed. On the third day, there began a steady rain, which extinguished the last of the smoking embers. That rain, like a million tears shed, made our final day's work all the more awful, as the roads turned to mud, as the Mississippi River turned gray and misty, as it got colder, as that sickly smell of burned flesh got into our very skin.

But it was the silence that I found most disturbing. Silence everywhere we went. The Negroes retreated at our approach and hid in their homes, and only with our most fervent entreaties, and often with bribes of gold dollars, would they speak to us and tell us what they knew. It was as if that rain brought a pall of dark, fearful silence over the land. And among the whites we encountered, the silence was even worse, full of half smiles and looks of triumphant glee. Not a face turned away in shame or remorse. All wanted to share with us their shameful glory. Although we could not get any positive identifications out of the boys who had borne witness to those crucified with fire, they knew the faces of the murderers, pillars of the white community known to all: "very big men" was all they would say. We felt lucky to get out of that place alive—what had been an Eden on a hill above the Mississippi—a place resplendent in my mind's eye, now translated into a mass grave, as if the name of the road that passes it by had been a premonition all along that we had failed to heed. Only when our train reached New Jersey did we feel safe, and only when I was in a New York hotel and could properly bathe did I begin to free myself from the stink. I am finished with the South, Mr. Alden, truly and forever finished. It is a land of darkness and terror, and should we have the war to do over again, I would vote to let the bastards go their own way, I would want no part of it. Killing those people was never enough.

That was the last of Sean Malloy's reports from Concord Academy and Natchez.

The name Pearce Breckenridge disappeared from all the correspondence, as if it had never been. So abruptly, so brutally, so unfinished a story that I sat at my father's desk with my grandmother's files and picked through them like a madman, my anxiety and devastation growing. I felt like screaming out to my grandmother, "What happened? What did General Alden do? Did he go to President Grant? Did he plead for federal troops to be sent in to get justice for the victims? Did he go to Republicans in Congress and demand an investigation?" I was overcome with a grief and anger I couldn't fully fathom. Even Max, that cackling voice in the back of my head, fell silent with dismay.

In disgust, I went downstairs, grabbed a coat, and tried to walk it off. I went down to the boathouse and stared over the white expanse of the frozen lake and the dark fringe of winter-shorn woodlands that hemmed in the gray sky above, trying to see it through General Alden's eyes—my father's eyes. Was this the story of an unpunished massacre that my grandmother had told her son about before he left for Washington and Berlin—a stain on the family honor? I walked out on the lake, feeling the weight and solidity of the ice beneath my feet, as if there really was a rock-bottom reality in this life that I was just too damned congenitally blind to see. And so I began to walk the perimeter of Eden Lake, hoping that this unaccustomed vantage point might reveal the missing thing. Halfway around the lake, I spied through the white pine along the shore the remains of Hermitage, a sad and silent derelict, with just portions of its wide piazza showing in horizontal lines of white where the carved log railings balanced inches of fresh snow. I shied away from the sudden pleasure I took in its destruction.

"Why in God's name . . . Hermitage?"

I turned in exasperation as yet another Williams folly clarified, as if someone had tapped my shoulder, seeing our boathouse and the vague contours of fieldstone walls through the trees across the lake. Snow was falling, and more was forecast. For an incandescent moment, I remembered that moonlit night on the piazza of Hermitage, when Suzanne had embraced me, when I had caught sight of our place across the lake and felt the strangeness of it, the untold sadness. And keeping my eye on the boathouse, I beelined back, letting the boathouse and Elsinore, the homestead named after General Alden's beloved second wife, whom he married in 1881 with such fanfare in New York society circles (touted by *The New York Herald* as the perfect governor's wife), take shape before my gaze, bound and braided by white and held tight in the snowy embrace of the lakeshore: hope, faith, and love to survive all life's foolhardy disasters.

Back at my father's desk with a cup of strong coffee and a couple more file boxes lugged up the stairs from the document room, I began again to search for some trace of Pearce Breckenridge, hurrying through the correspondence from the late 1870s and into the 1880s, when Samuel Williams and General Alden built Elysium and Winsted.

Nothing but painful allusive scraps from Samuel and two curt responses from General Alden.

May 14, 1876
Leave it to God's eyes to know, leave it to His justice. . . . Samuel.

May 23, 1876
The only justice is human justice; there is no other in this life or any other life. A life without justice is no life at all. . . . John.

December 23, 1881
My dearest cousin,
It seems every Christmas brings back old buried memories. Sometimes Lisa breaks into bitter tears and will remain silent for days, retreating to her room and books. Amory mopes around our home and asks uncomfortable questions about Uncle P. Sam dallies endlessly at the piano in the parlor, saying he will be a pianist as good as U.P., while his inspired repertoire puts all into a melancholy, subdued mood. Whenever Sam plays, Isabella prances around like a fairy nymph and calls out his name from the coal cellar to the attic. He haunts us, dear cousin; he is part of us.

September 22, 1883
I know the name disturbs you, dear cousin. But John, all in the family are enthusiastic, even if they only see "Hermitage" as bit of a romantic conceit, or a Russian winter palace, as Mr. Stanford White describes it—a royal retreat from busy Cambridge. In truth, and I know it is the same with Lisa, I can't help remembering how P. talked so often of his

days growing up in that place, longing for its splendid rooms filled with French silver and Dutch old masters and distinguished family portraits, where he learned to play the piano with his master—taught by his mother! Did you know, did he ever mention that his mother taught the half brothers to play? Can you imagine the thing? Of course, between us, it was his mother—how beautiful when he described her—I believe, for whom he longed, whose face he saw . . . cleaning and polishing those splendid rooms.

September 26, 1883
You stupid imbecile—you were never there . . .

48

AS I BEGAN TO GET INTO THE DOCUMENTS from the era of building Elysium and Winsted, there was a gentle lifting in the tone of Alden's and Williams's language, a kind of desperate clinging to each other, though they were very different men, almost as if a fresh breeze had filled their sails. As the South descended into a deepening hell of racial hatred, culminating in the decades of macabre lynching of blacks around the turn of the century, an atmosphere of retreat, sentimentality, and reconciliation to the injustices of the world at large seemed to settle over the construction of Winsted. Then as my disgust reached a point of complete frustration, I looked up from the endless files of architectural renderings for Winsted's schoolhouse and dormitories and Olmstead's layout for the landscaping and spied a manila envelope that had been shoved into the bookshelf long ago. I stared at it for minutes, frozen in my seat, my eyes straying to the wall by the door where the framed postcard of Leipzig's famous Museum of Antiquities hung, beckoning for answers, as well.

I lunged for the envelope, almost swooning when I saw again my grandmother's hand and the words underlined twice: Handle with Extreme Care! What I had once interpreted as a warning about the physical condition of the documents. I carefully spread its contents of newspaper clippings, Pinkerton reports, and one last letter from Jackson Breckenridge on my desk. The articles from the *Natchez Weekly Democrat* were so yellowed and friable as to be nearly unreadable. Hands shaking with caution, I managed to transfer the delicate clippings, fragile as last year's dragonfly wings, to the glass window of my new Xerox machine and make copies, playing with the light/dark adjustments—my heart nearly stopped—until I held a smudgy inky version that was just readable. More than once, raising the cover over the glass, I found the newsprint dissolved into fragments.

Natchez, Hermitage Plantation, March 16, 1876.

Mr. Alden, Enclosed please find a check for $51,000 for the repurchase of all lands sold to you since 1873 at full purchase price, per our agreement. This concludes all business transactions and so ends any and all connection between us whatsoever.

Jackson Breckenridge, Esquire

Dear Mr. Alden:

We have now sent three investigative teams to Natchez in an attempt to ascertain the facts around the killings that took place at Concord Academy sometime on December 27th or December 28th of last year. At your direction, we sent our most experienced men, men who have encountered difficult and dangerous situations in mining towns and hellholes throughout the West—but nothing like this. In all my years of experience, and I include my service in the Union army in the war's aftermath, I have never encountered such a conspiracy of silence. State and local officials are virulent and triumphant Democrats; there is not a black ally to be found. The general populace refuses cooperation of any kind. Not only are our agents' efforts sabotaged at every turning; their very lives are constantly threatened. No white man will admit to knowledge of the massacre or even the existence of the school and adjacent farms. They grin and explain that only a cemetery is to be found along Cemetery Road. The code of silence among whites is self-reinforced. My men discreetly offered payment for information, and even at exorbitant rates there were no takers. Among the blacks, even when meetings are arranged in total secrecy and anonymity, even when gold dollars are offered, their fears of retribution are so extreme as to make the most tentative testimony suspect. Negroes fear that any information they provide, which might subsequently be acted upon, will only bring more hellfire their way. Fear and hate prevail everywhere. As an amateur historian, I can think of nothing of its like. Perhaps the Spanish Inquisition at its height.

As to your specific requests for information, we have only the most tentative details, which do not rise much beyond rumor and hearsay. Your man was much beloved by the Negro population and even by elements of the white community, at least in the early days of the enterprise. The revolution in government in 1875 that destroyed the work of Reconstruction root and branch left no room for a free black man who speaks his mind. I suspect it was just a matter of time before your man's experiment in freedom and the "equality of the autonomous soul," as one brave black boy of seventeen put it to one of our men, was doomed to destruction. Specifically, we did receive corroboration from blacks that your man visited the plantation house at Hermitage on at least two occasions, specifically to meet with the widowed daughter, Miss Emily. Whether these were purely social calls or something else cannot be verified. We do have reports that he sought information about his mother, a house slave named Isabella, who was sold off suddenly in the years before the war. He posted queries in local newspapers throughout the South, offering rewards for information, requesting reply to the Boston address of your cousin, Mr. Williams. He also made inquiries about her of local blacks who were slaves at Hermitage in days gone by. One can only speculate that such indiscretions, given the degradation of relations between the races, may have made his enterprise in harmony and uplift vulnerable to the worst pathological killers in the community. Such creatures now rule the roost. They believe they have won the war.

Beyond these bare bones, I fear there is no more to be gotten at this time—perhaps not in our lifetimes.

Natchez Weekly Democrat
Natchez, Mississippi, January 5, 1877
Responsibility for the arson murders at Hermitage Plantation last week, on the night of December 27, are now thought to be the work of a white man, or possibly two white men, according to the sheriff of Natchez County. Three days before Christmas, two northerners arrived at the Jackson train station dressed in business attire. The train conductor said they were salesmen for a pipe-fitting company. One of the alleged assassins was tall, bearded, with prominent eyebrows and a tapering chin. He spoke like an educated New Englander and walked with a slight limp. The other man was shorter, stocky, with reddish hair, and spoke like an Irishman. The conductor who helped with the baggage said the men carried two long and heavy cases—samples for pumping equipment. The two were convivial, engaging the conductor with talk about their business out of Baltimore. The conductor thought it a little unusual, given the season, to be making sales calls. The men hired a buckboard and two horses at a Jackson livery, then proceeded to a dry goods store, where they bought lanterns and kerosene and other supplies; they gave out the same story in both places as they had with

the conductor. Five days later the buckboard and horses were left at the Simpson railroad depot, where the same two men were observed boarding a train north.

The sheriff described the arson and assassination of the Breckenridge family as having been carried out with military precision. Knowledge of the plantation and the layout of the house are clearly indicated. The Negro servants were mostly gone to their homes for Christmas, and two dogs had been poisoned. The rope to an alarm bell had been cut. The fires, set with liberal amounts of kerosene, were so placed as to make sure the rear portion of the structure burned first and burned fast, including both back entrances, thereby ensuring that those escaping the conflagration would do so by the front entrance, under the white columns of the portico. The buckboard had been placed some three hundred feet from the entrance to Hermitage, in the cover of the lane of Dutch elms that form the processional approach to the property. The sheriff's assumption was that the marksman—and he would have had to be professional sharpshooter—was lying prone in the buckboard with the tailgate down and so would have had a clear line of fire to the entrance. Two Winchesters, Model 1876, known as the Centennial Model, with .45–.75-caliber cartridges were found in the abandoned buckboard under blankets at the depot in Simpson.

The old nigger manservant of Jackson Breckenridge, awakened by the smoke where he had a cot in the kitchen, ran to alert the rest of the family, who had eaten well that evening and drunk much wine, according to the old Negro. He described the flames as having engulfed the entire back of the house in a storm of heat and smoke by the time he awoke everyone. The family members ran for the front entrance in their nightclothes as the conflagration grew; they emerged from the front door, only to behold another extraordinary sight. There, gathered on the gravel carriage driveway, were thirty-six lit lanterns set upon the open pages of thirty-six Bibles, in six rows. This strange sight cannot have had much chance to sink in, for the shooting commenced within seconds of each member emerging from the front door. According to the old Negro, Mrs. Gloria Breckenridge, accompanied by her three children, was the first to be shot; she was shot straight through the heart. Then her older boy, Robert, was shot in the chest and daughter, Elizabeth, the same. Only the youngest son was spared, either by happenstance or deliberation.

As the children were felled by single bullets, Jackson Breckenridge, old and somewhat frail, emerged from the jaws of hellfire with a drawer of documents clutched to his chest and so beheld the spectacle of his wife and two children lying sprawled in their nightclothes on the broad flagstones of the portico. The youngest son stood fixed in place, crying out in perplexed alarm. The old nigger explained that with the roar of the fire and creaking of timbers, no shots could be discerned, while the bright shining lanterns in the carriageway prevented a view of the drive beyond. Mr. Jackson Breckenridge, according to the old nigger, first assumed they had been injured from the flames. This misapprehension was clarified moments later when his eldest daughter emerged from the doorway, carrying a picture saved from the parlor; she screamed as she beheld the ghastly scene, and was instantly felled herself by a shot to her heart. Only then did Breckenridge grasp the enormity of the moment and the nature of the deadly animus directed his way. According to the old nigger, he held up a hand and screamed, "No . . . no . . ." as he moved to his dead daughter by his first marriage, only to be hit by a bullet in the stomach, so that he staggered and dropped the drawer of documents. He was then killed instantly with a shot to his head.

Only the eight-year-old boy, Pearce Breckenridge II, was spared the massacre. The old nigger grabbed the boy as he saw his master shot through the brains and whisked him away from the Stygian scene of mayhem and desecration. The two were found still hiding in a nearby copse the following morning as the community descended on the inferno in utter disbelief. Hundreds came from thither and yon, like pilgrims to the smoking ruins of this most gracious and grand building in the Greek style, consumed by the flames, along with all its heirlooms of great historical importance. The blackened bodies of this illustrious family, two of whose sons were sacrificed in the War of Secession, were laid out for all to witness. The crowd murmured about the thirty-six open Bibles, beautiful and expensive leather-bound King James Versions, upon which the lanterns had been placed. Many were greatly disturbed by the meaning of the lanterns, which still flickered in the dawn, and the presence of the Scriptures, unsure of the intent and what should be taken away from the thing. Many spent hours peering down at the open pages of the Old Testament, not daring to shift the smoking lanterns to better make out the drift of what was written therein . . . if some obscure prophecy of the Breckenridges' doom.

Most settled on this passage from Deuteronomy, and it was soon on the lips of all Natchez: "The secret things belong unto the Lord our God . . . I have set before you life and death, blessing and cursing: therefore choose life, that both thou and thy seed may live."

By nightfall, all the Bibles had been removed by the onlookers as souvenirs of this most wicked deed.

The remarkable thing about the remaining articles from the *Nat-chez Weekly Democrat* was how scrupulously any connection between the Hermitage killings and the massacre at Concord Academy was repressed. Silence on the subject, as per the Pinkerton report, was iron-clad. Suspicion was repeatedly directed at the two Yankee assassins and possible northern "business interests" of Jackson Breckenridge, evidence of which was destroyed in the fire. Even the funeral for the slain family members drew "only a small attendance of mourners," as if the extermination of all but one of a prominent local family had left the city traumatized and only wishing to forget as quickly as possible. The one poignant note was the mention of the surviving eight-year-old son, Pearce Breckenridge II, standing at the grave site as five coffins were lowered into the earth, "grasping the hand of an old nigger man and a distant uncle from Baton Rouge." A ghostly check mark had been placed in the margin and my grandmother's annotation: "See SW and JA letters of March 1883."

Dear Alden: PB II's studies are fine, a bright boy, but his attitude is atrocious. He waltzes around like a little southern prince, sassing faculty and sixth formers whenever he is corrected. He is outright rude to the black kitchen staff. The other boys detest him and make his life miserable. No matter how much Eliza and I talk to him, share our home, and coach him in New England manners, he remains stubborn and unrepentant. He will not last; he cannot last.

Dear Samuel: I know you will do your best. It is a hard case. The uncle in Baton Rouge was a cavalry officer with Jeb Stuart and is now a perpetrator of all that is worst in the southern mind, a man full of the most wretched excuses for battles lost and hatred for the freedmen. I had to bribe him every inch of the way with scholarships and tales of my devotion to his nephew's lost half brother. The thing is truly a lost cause. If you can get no improvements out of the boy, let him go; let him return to that sinkhole of lapsed memory and bitter hatred. And we will—finally—have done with the thing.

Which he did, and so the name Pearce Breckenridge disappeared utterly from history.

There was one final piece of evidence in the manila envelope, and this my grandmother had sealed in a small plastic bag with masking tape. When I opened it, there was a distinct and unpleasant smell.

Holding the partially melted gold pocket watch and chain in my hand, I found it tacky to the touch. The hands were melted into the dial at 3:35, presumably A.M. The once ivory-colored face was a murky phlegmlike green. Bringing it close to my nose, I detected a metallic and rancid odor. The cover still swung open on its tiny hinge, revealing the inscription: *Pearce Breckenridge, Harvard Class of 1855.*

Beyond exhaustion, with a glimmer of dawn coming over the lake, I went downstairs and made for the gun room, unlocked the door, and found them exactly where I knew them to be. There were two Winchesters, Model 1876, the so-called Centennial Model, in celebration of the American Centennial in 1876, and the first in the Winchester line of lever-action repeating rifles to accommodate full-powered center-fire rifle cartridges. They were durable and powerful hunting rifles, fully capable of bringing down a buffalo or grisly with a single shot. Sean Malloy had remarked more than once in his letters on General Alden's expert marksmanship: "best in the Berkshires, if not east of the Mississippi." Malloy had been caretaker of the Elysium lands from 1880 to 1913, when he died of a heart attack at the fiftieth anniversary Gettysburg Reunion of the Blue and Gray. His son, Tom Malloy, would take over as caretaker in 1919. The Winchesters were bought in the spring of 1876 and engraved with General Alden's name. My grandmother had even located the invoices from the Winchester Company in New Haven, Connecticut: two engraved Models 1876, two without engraving. I'd shot them as a boy at the rifle range. Even though untouched for thirty years, they were well oiled and the action was smooth and clean. I loaded one, and without even putting on coat or gloves, headed down through the deep snow to the boathouse. I stood on the dock and levered off precisely six rounds at a pine across the frozen lake, feeling to my soul the kick of the rifle against my shoulder and the resounding echoes that came crashing back through the woods as from eternity itself. In the kick, and the snicker of the lever, and the sounds and smell of the shots, I saw those desperate escaping figures bracketed by tall white columns and outlined against the flames, lit, too, by thirty-six lanterns, as if on a stage set. I saw, too, another figure, the minister of mines rising to quell a boisterous meeting hall, falling back across his chair, as scores of khaki-clad NVA had fallen back into the waters of the Vam Co Dong River. More troubling, in recollection, was the purity of the instinct, the split-second calculation that is no calculation, when the hunter delivers his verdict upon the prey, the bullet as visceral a part of his being as the thought, or its lack. An instinct, as every true hunter knows, embedded deeper than nerve and fiber, deeper than genes, deeper than the deepest muck at the bottom of the deepest sea. A thing acknowledged in my grandmother's nasal tones, the moment I'd got off the shots, her scornful words for the dangerous and foolhardy act I'd just committed ringing in my ears above the dying echoes. I screamed at the top of my lungs and, like Max had his staff on that spring night of years before, flung the Winchester as far out over the lake as I could, where it disappeared in three feet of snow and ice.

As a teacher of history, I could only nod at Santayana's hoary aphorism: "Those who cannot remember the past are condemned to repeat it." It is now translated into Polish and convoluted English in a sign that greets all visitors to Auschwitz.

I found my way to bed and my first dreamless sleep in quite some time.

Later that year, in June, I made a trip to Natchez to see what that "sinkhole of lapsed memory" might yet have to offer. Indeed, the slate had been neatly scrubbed clean. The ruins of Hermitage and the Breckenridge plantation are part of a National Historical Park run by the Department of the Interior. There is a photograph of the Greek Revival plantation house on the Park Service historical signage, and some of the outbuildings and slave quarters are preserved as tourist attractions. The line of elms leading up to the front entrance remains, but it frames only a grassy mound where the house once stood. There is mention in the historical signage of a terrible fire and the "mysterious deaths" of the owners but nothing more in the way of detail or historical context. The incident seems lost even to local historians and academics. This may have to do with the burning of the *Natchez Weekly Democrat* building in 1920, when a fire consumed the archive; subsequently, the newspaper went defunct during the Depression.

The site of Concord Academy was a little harder to locate along Cemetery Road, which meanders for miles along the banks of the Mississippi north of Natchez. You take Martin Luther King Boulevard north to Country Club Road to where it intersects with Cemetery Road. Much of the area, once dotted with small farms in Civil War days, has gone back to hardwoods; large tracts along the banks of the

Mississippi have been bought up by land preservation trusts. It took me two days of nosing around to find what looked like an abandoned logging road off Cemetery that wound its way west up to a bluff overlooking the river. There was a clearing full of young saplings and a few taller oaks and acacias. Walking through the high saw grass—watching out for timber rattlers and copperheads, which, so I was warned, were everywhere—I stumbled on the foundations of old buildings long since grown over and covered in brush. The archaeologist in me longed to pick over the bits of board and stone, rusted nails, glass bottles, and a fragment of a teacup that were easily visible, but the distinct sound of a rattle from a nearby rocky crevice dissuaded me from doing more. It was hot and humid and so I walked to the crest of the bluff, which provided a scenic view of the Mississippi as it wound its way south toward the Gulf. I was put in mind of the lines spoken by Charlie Springfield so many years before in the chapel—his eyes burning beneath that bouncing forelock, just weeks before he was shot, when he quoted from Samuel Williams's *Essays and Prayers*, pausing only to add his laconic epigraph.

In the great river of souls flowing through our lives comes the terrible knowledge of the lands of justice and injustice, of the free and unfree, of our brothers in bondage both black and white, for servitude is an unnatural condition of the soul. All God's children are sojourners along the river's joyous banks and partake of its cool waters to slake their thirst for knowledge of good and evil; all are bound on the river of Time, as one to another, and with all who have come before and will henceforth come . . . joining as one in praise of the creation, which allows all God's creatures to partake in its everlasting glory and eternal life.

"Boys . . . we are how the universe knows itself."

As I turned from that magnificent muddy flow, I saw down the bluff through the tall grass and thistle and creepers a broad crowned tree of medium height bent almost to the ground. I struggled through the saw grass and brush down to the last of the apple trees that had somehow survived the burning. It had budded and leafed but, lacking others with which to cross-pollinate, had forgone the production of fruit. I walked in widening circles around the lone tree and was able to locate a few of the stumps, trying to re-create the layout of the six lines of six in the orchard. I returned to the living tree and circled its trunk again, but this time in tighter and tighter arcs, a little spooked, a little terrified of stirring up a copperhead, until I found a half-buried flat stone into which the number 36 had been crudely scraped. According to Sean Malloy's numbering, they had started with the sixteen-year-old boys and burned the teachers and Pearce Breckenridge last. Ever the cool, consummate professional I pretended to be, I replaced that stone in the consecrated earth exactly as I had found it, leaving everything undisturbed.

By then, standing in that defunct orchard, I had read Elliot Goddard's preliminary 1954 CIA report on my father's disappearance, which included the interviews with the Winsted teachers whom my father had visited on the way back to Washington in late September 1953. Paul Oakes's memory of the year before, when they'd walked the Circle for the last time, leapt to mind:

It seemed he was in a bit of a rush to get back down to Washington and so I walked him to his car that we might extend our chat. We had gone through much together during the war, and his agitation was nothing new to me—what with his great responsibilities. As we rounded the Circle, I noticed his eyes swivel again and again as we talked to the apple trees that grow there—you can see them, just there through my window. Stately old fellows full of grace and character. Suddenly, he stopped, frozen in mid-sentence, and grabbed my arm, exclaiming, "Paul, the apple trees—the apple trees! First thing General Alden laid eyes on, the thing that decided him on this spot." John stood fixed, gazing for almost a minute, lost in wonder, and then turned to me. "Paul, next time we meet, remind me to tell you the story . . . all the story." That was the last I ever heard from him.

Only days earlier, before he left for Cambridge and Berlin, my father had read the same Pinkerton reports organized for him by his mother that I had now read.

I returned to the Natchez Historical Society for a last round after two futile earlier visits. A volunteer I hadn't met before was there, an older lady, who kindly asked if she could help. I mentioned the name Breckenridge. She shook her head, paused, and then nodded. "Well, there's the portrait in the storage room; I think the name is Breckenridge." She took me down to a vast storage area of dusty castoffs and donations to the society, and we rambled around until she finally located a portrait in an oval gilded frame in a bin in the back. In the fluorescent lighting, I could just make out a face of someone in a Confederate officer's uniform. We walked the portrait to the front, where there was better lighting. The plaque at the bottom read: *Pearce Tebbetts Breckenridge, Second Mississippi Cavalry, 1834–1862.* The face was indeed dashing, with intelligent eyes under an extravagant flurry of brows that flowed in an upward taper; the forehead had a scholarly fullness in contrast to narrow, almost fragile cheekbones and a long, delicate nose. Even the firm chin and hinted dimple could not turn him into a military man for me.

"What a dashing fellow," said the old woman, a spit-wet finger easing away the dust covering the gold braids in the Confederate uniform, then moving to the hairline.

I couldn't stop starring at the face, the refinement in the nose and cheekbones—framing the lamp-lit eyes . . . reminding me not a little of a young Bobby Williams seated at the piano in the silver-framed publicity photos on the Steinway; and of his father, Amory, in the snapshot I'd seen, posed between Amaryllis and my grandmother on the veranda of Hermitage in the twenties; and the fulminating sparks—dollops of saffron-orange pigment—in the eyes of the famous Singer Sargent canvas of Bobby's aunt, Isabella Williams, posed on the balcony of Palazzo Barberini, now hanging proudly in the forecourt of Palazzo Fenway.

"Pearce Breckenridge was killed at Antietam—Sharpsburg, I believe you call it down here," I said.

She pointed to a ragged round hole in the officer's uniform in the portrait. "It looks like the picture suffered in the War Between the States, although there was almost no fighting around Natchez, the Lord be praised. A minié ball, I expect."

I, too, touched the hole and together we gently turned the portrait around to view the rear and the ragged area where the bullet had exited, where the wood of the frame and stretcher and the bottom corner of the canvas were stained with blood.

"That, my dear lady, is a forty-five caliber slug from a Winchester rifle that only came into use in 1876, during the nation's centennial."

Before flying back to Albany and Elysium, I drove up to Jackson, Mississippi, along the Natchez Trace Parkway through Fayette, Port Gibson, and Cayuga, retracing the route taken by General Alden and Sean Malloy to Hermitage from the Jackson railway station. Willie Gadsden owned a Ford dealership in Clinton, a suburb of Jackson, just off I-20, and I had called ahead to suggest a visit. We had stayed in touch off and on for twenty years, but this was the first time we'd had a chance to get together. He welcomed me to his small ranch house and introduced me to his wife and two boys, ages nine and eleven.

"Twenty years in the army and I made it to major—maybe not general, but not bad for a black boy from the streets of Jackson. And twenty years is plenty, what with my army pension, besides, Mr. Ford . . . he's been waitin' for me."

After visiting with his family and checking out his Ford dealership, we made the visit to Greenwood Cemetery north of Jackson. Some six confederate generals and two hundred soldiers from the Civil War are buried there, but Willie didn't seem to give them a moment's thought as we passed through to the graves of dead from World War I, World War II, the Korean War, and finally those from Vietnam. There, in a peaceful corner shaded by mature oaks and willows, he led me to Theo's grave.

LIEUTENANT THEODORE COLSON, 1948–1972.
A SON OF THE SOUTH AND A LEADER OF SOLDIERS,
WHO DIED WHILE SAVING THE LIVES OF HIS MEN
IN THE BATTLE OF THE VAM CO DONG RIVER.

"Well, he saved my life," I said.

"Saved mine, too, but then I saved his ass at least twice by my reckonin'."

"Battle of the Vam Co Dong River—sounds good, I guess."

"If you were his pappy, that's how you'd write it, too."

"They didn't bury him in Arlington National Cemetery?"

"He wanted to stay down here with all his family. His daddy, granddaddy, and the general who rode with that bastard Stonewall Jackson are over yonder. He wanted to be with own men."

"A real mess all that, all those terrible years, of the Civil War and after."

"I thought you was talkin' about Vietnam."

"That, too, I suppose."

"Yep," and he waved toward the lines of willows under which the Confederates rested, "but they all dead now, and the devils they stirred up losin' ground, too. One way or the other, without them sons of bitches, I wouldn't have my Ford dealership, or my family. Now I'm as free as a bird. Grab any car on the lot and take off for the hills, until it's time for dinner."

"So," I said, waiting as he summoned another smile.

"So, I guess we gotta play it for the long run."

"Stick around for the long run."

"Even with that back of yours—believe me, when I got to you, I thought you was dead and gone, much less you'd ever be walkin' again."

"Lucky, I guess."

"Lucky you knew how to shoot, or there'd have been no luck to go around."

"Well, least I haven't put on as much weight as you."

"A man's got to put bread on the table so his children can get along in this life. And I haven't forgotten your promise, either, about that fancy school that Jerry went to. I've got two Yale boys back home, great football players, even if they're not as fast as Jerry."

"Nobody was that fast."

"You right about that. Jerry was the fastest, but I was the one learned to keep my head down."

"About Yale, I don't know, but I can help you with Winsted. Players, huh . . . how good?"

49 THERE ARE ONLY A FEW PAGES LEFT UN-
filled in my notebook—is it mine? I have no idea if I
am only allowed one or even if this will ever see the
light of day. I tire easily. The long hours of darkness
are draining me like an interminable winter. Maybe it's time to try to
explain about my mother, at least to myself. She is my light, my soul's
connection to the living past. For me, now, she lives in the sunlight, on
the back porch of Elsinore, walking the trails, winding the clocks in the
living room bathed in lilac sunbeams. It is hard for me to reconcile the
person the world knows: famous philanthropist for medical research
and president of the Winsted board of trustees, and the mother I
knew—or barely knew—from childhood.

My mother was wildly in love with my father. His lost brilliance
and promise shone in her tearstained eyes in all my earliest memories
of her. She wanted me to be a doctor, and I always knew that my being
a doctor would make her happy. But it wasn't to be. Once as a child
when I asked her what being in love was like, she looked at me across
the table and dipped a finger in her wine and held it in the candle
flame until steam rose. "Like that." I often wondered if she'd have loved
me more if I'd been a doctor. She wasn't an uncaring mother, but one
struggling, so it seems to me now, to make sense of what was taken
from her. I have heard it rumored that in the years after my father was
killed in the Argonne she led a fast and frivolous life, drank like a fish
and partied like a flapper in heat. I never saw any of this. By the time I
was older, my mother had become the person she was always reputed
to be, and no one dared to whisper about her early days, at least not
in my hearing. Once my best friend, a third cousin, did, and what he
told me so shocked me and hurt me that I began to hate him with an
underhanded irrational hatred. It was his way of justifying himself and

manipulating me. He told me that in the early twenties my mother had an affair with, of all people, his mother, an artist with a fiery reputation who seemed hell-bent on destroying all she touched. I was told my mother used to pose nude for her. According to my cousin, she would go down to our boathouse at three in the morning, strip naked, and swim across the lake and go to Amaryllis's studio by a back door and pose on the daybed. She would then swim back before dawn. She was a champion swimmer as a girl. And just as well, because Amaryllis would have drowned her as she almost did me, throwing herself off the balcony at Palazzo Barberini in one of her more spectacular suicide attempts. I had to dive in after her and search for her in the pitch-black at the muddy bottom of the canal. The instant I found her—I was groping blindly and nearly out of breath—she grabbed me with both arms around my neck and pulled me down with her. The furious force of her hold was absolutely terrifying—have I already mentioned this?—I can't remember. I had to pummel her with my fists and knee her in the stomach to break free and get to the surface. She died a few years later at a Swiss sanatorium.

I was lonely as a child. My mother saw to it that the nannies and, later, the tutors filled my days with useful activities, but I was lonely. The woods and the lake and books were my companions. Perhaps I was angry with myself for never being the son she wanted, or as good as my father—or for never becoming a doctor. I do not blame her for her aloofness; she is absolutely magnificent in her way. Once she'd put my father's death behind her, she took over the board of trustees at Winsted with a vengeance, determined that the school should emerge from its "Victorian quiescence," as she termed it, and start making a difference in the world. She insisted on more scholarship boys, especially from the South and the West, so that the student body would be more representative of the nation. She insisted on the admittance of Jewish boys and the first black student in 1932, at the end of my senior year. She rarely missed a football game or crew race and made a point that I write her in detail about my life. We got to know each other better during those years than before or since. She was heartbroken when I chose Princeton over Harvard. It was the only time she shouted at me: "Cambridge is your roots and Princeton is practically a southern college." I hated to do it, but I knew her dream was for me to go to Harvard Medical School, and if I had gone to Harvard, the pressure to follow in my father's footsteps would have only gotten worse. When I went to Princeton, our relationship returned to a chilly distance as her dedication to medical philanthropy and antilynching legislation only intensified, even as the Depression constricted her means.

During the war years and after, we kept a respectful distance. I heard from others that her anxiety about me consumed her: if fate would claim another Alden in a foreign war. She pulled strings in 1944 to get me relocated to a rehabilitation hospital in New York, when the best specialists were in England. She was pleased with my marriage and our son, and once the die was cast, she became my mother confessor and confidante. Recently, we have been closer than at any time since Winsted. She has steeped herself in the family's past, making it something palpable and very human, instead of an amorphous mythology housed in vague symbols. Age has given her a commanding strength of character informed by her passionate convictions. In the hours of darkness that engulf me, I ask her indulgence, ask for her strength. I think of her always on the back veranda at Elsinore, bathed in reflected light off the lake as she organizes the family archives. She told me it began as a lark, to finally "see what I'd gotten myself into, marrying your father . . . what skeletons rattled around in which closets." Well, she certainly turned up a roomful. I would come up from the boathouse after rowing myself dry and find her on the veranda with the family papers spread about, intent, immersed in another world, exclaiming to herself between sips of iced tea, "Oh my, oh my—oh my!"

That is how I will remember her, reaching into the past, fortified by reflected glory as much as loss, as she turned to me with a spark of inextinguishable spirit in her wise eyes—my fair Hera, her love a final bulwark against the madness of the unfeeling and careless gods, keeping the ever-threatening darkness at bay for one day more, one more hour.

—excerpt from John Alden's Pankrác Prison diary

Rereading the last pages of the diary late that winter of 1990, I was more convinced than ever that my father, as he passed thorough Checkpoint Charlie, carried the full burden of Pearce Breckenridge with him, along with a Walther pistol, Ventris's charts, and $100,000 in cash and gold that had not been provided by Nigel Bennett and MI5, nor the CIA. I knew because I had a team of forensic accountants wade into the financials from those years, where they discovered the withdrawal of $100,000 from the family trusts, rather hurriedly it turned out, in late September of 1953, and neatly covered it up by some quick real estate transactions. Hidden as a capital loss, it was the tax deduction that gave it away, so I was gleefully told by Brandt & Harrison. Something else Elliot's CIA investigators failed to turn up.

After the initial exhilaration of finding the material on Pearce Breckenridge, my frustrations returned as the winter stretched on interminably. I was lonely, as if my father's loneliness as a child had taken me over. I had banished Max to mute stupefaction. Not a word from Laura, even though I'd checked in with her agent and ABT a dozen times. I kept calling the lawyers in New York, pressing them for results, concerned that the crucial Stasi files in East Germany might be destroyed, or lost, or taken over by the Soviet Union, and that anything more on my father would disappear for good. The same with the Czech secret police. According to the Brandt & Harrison team, they were "spreading money like drunken bandits" among fired East German ministers and ex-Stasi agents to gain access to the files. They even claimed to have a retired KGB man in their sights, who was negotiating for a huge sum to tell what he knew. I told them to pay him. The CIA was trying to be "helpful" with the report on my father's disappearance, but the review process that required the redaction of sensitive material was still weeks away from completion. The search for Joanna's son continued apace, I was assured: "Our guy in Athens has bribed half the Greek Communist Party. The kid would be in his forties now, you know, if he's still alive . . . and he may not want to be found."

With some trepidation, I also told the Brandt & Harrison team to start making discreet inquiries with the Museum of Antiquities in Leipzig to check on the whereabouts of a group of a hundred or so Linear B tablets, deposited there in 1944 by a famous Austrian archaeologist, Karel Hollar, suggesting in my wording that the tablets might be considered war loot and so needed to be returned to Greece.

I found myself going back to the pages of Max's novel, where the brilliant and sensitive Samuel Williams II stands on the bridge, drinking himself into a stupor before jumping or falling into the Charles. A man who had played the piano obsessively in his youth. Did he know or suspect, liquoring himself up, that an ex-slave, a mulatto of incandescent talent and righteous fervor, the charismatic firebrand that had once lit up the Williamses' home on Brattle Street, was his father? And the dithering, feckless Amory? And Isabella, who as a girl ran around the house calling out Pearce's name, who even in old age spoke that name in her sleep, dreaming of her lost childhood as the waves lapped beneath her windows in Palazzo Barberini? What of those fading embers or recollections, if not genes or talents, had flowed into Bobby Williams on currents at once distorted, etiolated, and utterly mysterious? As do parts of *Essays and Prayers* to us to this day.

How does one detect the traces of such ghosts in the rooms that have shaped our lives?

How many times did I look up from my computer keyboard to the snowbound world beyond my window and plead with the silent Max for inspiration: . . . when it's *your* family? For Max, too, had finally stumbled when confronted with telling the truth about the destruction of his mother's Viennese family in the Holocaust.

And that is how I found myself increasingly drawn out into the melting snow of late March and down to the boathouse dock, where my father had stood smoking his Luckies, where my grandmother, or the beautiful young woman she had been in the 1920s, had slipped naked into the water to swim to the arms of her lover, the artist Amaryllis. No wonder she had felt forever banished from Hermitage and Palazzo Barberini, as she banished her youth in the guise of Winsted's steely-eyed Athena. I took to standing on the dock just to let the coldness fill my lungs, as if to tempt myself to accept the uncharacteristic rashness that might free me. I was testing myself against the hated cold to see who would give way first. I liked to think it was my father's gambler's instinct, inherited from General Alden, and my grandmother's get-up-and-go. And my way of compensation for my utter lack of imagination in Max's eyes. Then, as if each day's snowmelt conspired to hasten my folly, I could just make out the shape of the Winchester way out on the ice. How far I'd heaved it! I longed to go get it: a beautiful antique, worth probably twenty thousand dollars to a gun collector, given the fact that General Alden's name was engraved on the barrel. But, even more, I liked to look at the Winchester there on the ice, as if reminding me of the things I couldn't quite grasp: General Alden staring across his desk into the demanding face of Jason Breckenridge, who had become Pearce Breckenridge, who would become William P. Emerson . . . and then no more; my grandmother swimming toward the far shore and Hermitage and the lover who would immortalize her body but not her soul; my father at Checkpoint Charlie, staring in the direction of the bombed-out hulk of the Neues Museum in East Berlin and the call to justice in the added weight of the Walther pistol in his briefcase—and the self-justification that awaited him there.

There were late afternoons when it got almost impossible to return to the house and face my frustrations—worse, my lack of talent, as my body lost feeling, yearning to embrace those steadfast pines around the lakeshore yet standing guard over our better angels. I felt as if I were drawing close to knowing all I would ever know in the way of facts and figures but lacked the animating spirit to turn a coherent theme. *Of love he felt little.* I suddenly remembered that night staring out the window of the library, where a lone figure tramped across the four feet of snow on the Circle and entered the chapel. Like a predator in ambush, was I biding my time for the chance . . . for revenge? Had I not suspected the truth for weeks, if not months?

And I was reminded of something Elliot had said to me in Prague, almost in despair at his own words: "In your father's position—risking it all—Christ, World War Three, perhaps thousands of agents' lives if they broke him with torture . . . He dragged his entire history—our history—with him into that miserable hellhole."

I would never have risked it, never have headed to Natchez. . . . Such moral fervor had been bred out of me.

And I was so far from being the masterful playwright Elliot required in both art and life. I was no Edward de Vere, nor Hamlet's alter ego, privy to the music of the spheres . . . "to the river of stars that rule our lives," as Max had written in *Like a Forgotten Angel.*

I lacked Max's talent to re-create life out of life, even after the shooting of Charlie Springfield, even as Max broke his Prospero's wand and threw it into the lake, even with his depression and all the drugs that finally killed him.

That icebound Winchester began to prey on my mind.

The sunlight of early April glinted off the blue steel barrel; it would be only a matter of days before it went to the bottom. I resisted the temptation to get it, both longing for and fearing that talismanic object. The ice melted to slushy gruel in the sunlit hours and froze again in blue welts at night. As the contours of the land began to show, scrubbed and kneaded to bare bones, so the Winchester stood out, a gleaming, tantalizing rod of silver encased in ice. I almost feared to lose the emptiness of winter, like the emptiness of time, the comfort of a stilling wake. The gun became an object of wonder to goad my fate, to tempt it into being—to risk it. The thing consumed me, even as I sat marooned at my desk, trying to read the mind of my father, as I stood on the dock where he stood, as he crossed through the Iron Curtain to a rendezvous on the steps of the Neues Museum with the man—friend and coconspirator and war criminal—whom he planned to kill or bring to justice.

Or was it just to get his hands on those Linear B tablets? Or free his son? Revenge, love, desire—even loyalty . . . what a witch's brew.

Across the lake, visible through the bare trees, the ruins of Hermitage began to show, yet another trail of treachery gone cold.

A sunny, blustery day the second week of April brought a blood orange glow to the ice around quitting time. I knew it was now or never. Standing on the boathouse dock, I felt a raw wind blowing from the northeast, defying the signs of spring, the upper branches of the white pines groaning, shifting their shoulders and bowed backs against the bronze sky. The cold felt good in my tangled hair and bearded cheeks. I stepped down onto the ice, watching as the pearly pockets of trapped air expanded in welcoming sighs of near relief. Beyond the shadowed shore, the sky glittered in the ice like a dome of golden mosaics. Beyond the horizon stockade, a rose window hovered.

I stamped my foot like a petulant child and smiled at my inveterate caution, remembering my grandmother telling me how when she had been a young wife with her new husband, General Alden made them wait on skating days until Sean Malloy had hobbled down to the frozen lake and driven in an iron spike to test the thickness. I smiled, keeping my eye trained on the gleaming Winchester, which lay just beyond the shadow line in a pool of intense crimson light. A few more steps and I reached that great rose window of light, welcoming like a sorceress's embrace. I was aware of the slap of my boots in the melt but careless of its warning. The ice was alive, like some diaphanous and plangent breast, inveigling, beckoning, a promise of love eternal. The ripples in my wake were returned in plenitude by the wind: the whispering currents, the river of Time, released once more by my daring. I took the last careful steps on the slick, watery ice and carefully reached down to the Winchester, lying there like a broken staff, as if I were back to that starlit night of last boyhood and only reaching into the sky to reset our course.

The ice hit me smack in the face. For the longest instant, I was aware only of the soft emerald buoying descent. Then came the stab of cold like a bayonet thrust in the belly. Every nerve in my body detonated. I was at the surface, flailing, screaming, coughing. Wicked fragments of black ice bobbed everywhere. My true hatred of the cold again reigned supreme. I tried for the ice edge only feet away, but as I swam and reached, there was no edge, just more floating ice. The solid world sank or shattered at the touch of my fast-numbing fingers. The cold in my lungs had such a grip that I was struggling just to breathe. I kept trying for the next edge and then the next. My clothes weighed me down like chains. I began to panic as the ice swam in my veins like some vengeful spirit clamping off feeling to my extremities as it went. I screamed for help and then realized it was useless. The boathouse and safety were so close, less than thirty feet. The ice began breaking off in slabs. I pushed chunks aside with my elbows, cursing like a banshee, trying to summon some unholy untapped anger to keep myself going. Anger and cool animal cunning, that was what Theo Colson always told us to rely on to get us out of a tight spot. Another and then another ice outcropping folded under my weight. I spat out water and ice, coughing for air as my diaphragm began to seize up. I was shivering uncontrollably. I shook my head and yelled to keep conscious.

Another outcropping in shadow, more solid than the rest. I beseeched it to hold as I eased my upper chest forward onto the ice. It broke away beneath me and I spat more water. The next held as I eased myself farther forward. I wormed and squirmed, getting the ice under my chest and belly, twisting forward and spreading my limbs and my weight until my knees were on ice. I yearned to rest and wait for my strength to return, but knew that it would mean my death. The wind was blowing and the sun was gone, the lakeshore in near darkness. I could feel the cold having its way, beating through me, breaking one bulkhead after another.

I screamed and turned my hips and flipped over. On my back, I was able to get traction with the rubber soles of my boots. I pushed off and shoved and eased myself back from the jagged edge of black water. When I thought I was far enough, I flipped myself again, and on hands and knees I crawled toward the boathouse. Blood was filling my eyes, dripping on the ice. I staggered up, falling and stumbling until I was able to reach the dock and collapse. I curled myself up and didn't move and decided to let myself freeze right there and have done with the whole sorry mess. That shocked me, that I would even be tempted by such a fate. I hauled myself up and stumbled up the path to the house. I couldn't even grasp the handle to open the door, my purple fists just raw and frozen stumps. I flailed at the handle and somehow got it to function, and then I was inside. It was as if I entered a tropical forest, the heat was so intense on my frozen skin. I crawled to the bathroom and into the tub and managed to turn on the hot water.

I slept for days; I was never sure for how long. I think I was delirious for much of the time when I was awake, somewhere between fever and chills; I felt in limbo between one life and the next, a bodily interregnum where nothing ruled but sleep and the compelling warmth of my bed.

What I remember is waking to sunlight through the windows of my childhood room. That light was spellbinding, broken into triangles and lozenges by the leaded glass, tints of amber and citron and amethyst-blue and, beyond, where the pines waved in the sun, a lush welcoming green. The light was redolent of the earth and dust and mildew, all the familiar smells of my summer home. It was the light I remembered seeing when I was a small child and my mother would get me up. When she would cook me breakfast. Her specialty was blueberry pancakes with hazelnuts crushed in maple syrup. I remembered her voice as I'd known it as a child, and it seemed to be a happy voice, and I found myself crying at the memory. My tears were happy tears, even as I resigned myself to the fact that my father had barely managed a single word about my mother or me in his Pankrác diary.

I forgave her, forgave her for my grandmother, forgave her for spreading his ashes on Lake Carnegie . . . all alone . . . at night . . . without his family.

It was during those days of recovery that I went for the first time to the bedroom at the back of the house that my mother had used in the years after my father's death, when she abandoned the grand master bedroom overlooking the lake they had shared in the days of their marriage, before she stopped coming up to Elysium altogether after my grandmother's death. When I got back from Vietnam and rehab, I sold the apartment in New York and gave away most of her stuff to charity. Some of her books and photographs I had shipped up to Elsinore and then arranged them on the shelves of her "widow's retreat," as my grandmother snidely referred to my mother's compact bedroom with its intimate woodside view, where my mother tucked herself in with her naval histories. And there I found myself pondering their wedding photographs, taken during the reception at the Chevy Chase Club in the spring of 1950, where they had met, where they had played golf when my father returned to Washington at the end of his stint as CIA Athens station chief during the Greek Civil War.

My parents stand together with the wedding party on the fairway of the ninth hole, an expanse of lush green framed by a copse of spruce and pine. My auburn-haired mother is dressed in a cream-colored gown stitched with rows of pearls, her veil pulled back to reveal her smiling face. She is at once petite and tensile-tough, as one might expect of a woman from a military family, a family used to its men going off to war for long stretches. She holds tight to my father's hand. In her other hand, she grips a two-wood, a humorous attribute, as she explained it to me once, since so much of their "courting" had been done on the fairways, when she gave up tennis to "traipse the links with your father." For a champion tennis player, golf was a cinch, as she always liked to tell me with a shrug. My father stands at a slight stoop beside her, also holding a club, perhaps favoring his bad leg, looking out at the photographer with keen approval, his prominent brows set tight with something of an air of relief mixed with regret at his reduced mobility, handsome and stalwart as ever.

Staring at that photograph now, I realized that all the wedding guests were dead.

Elliot Goddard is there with his English wife, Suzanne's brides-maid, who is wearing a hat that looks like a cornucopia overflowing with fruit. The president's adviser, who was then a lowly undersecretary of state, stands at Elliot's side, his keen intelligence burning in his eyes; he who would spend his declining years trying to explain his role in the escalation of the Vietnam War. Among the party is Allen Dulles, who, three years year later, would become head of the CIA under Eisen-hower; his reputation would plummet in the decades after his death, when it was realized what a careless and slapdash operation he'd run. The Alsop brothers, journalists Joe and Stewart, are there, presumably garnering tidbits of insider gossip and news to fortify their anti-Com-munist opinion column, "Matter of Fact." There are five or six CIA officers, whom I knew only in passing from their attendance at Found-er's Day events; as history records, they would have a few spectacular successes and not a few unmitigated disasters. Virgil Dabney stands amidst this contingent of intelligence officers, looking younger, even dapper in his ill-fitting suit, perhaps a little uneasy in the company of such polished gentlemen of the eastern establishment. Surely Virgil took pride in having taught them their classics, and in saving the mon-uments of Western civilization during the war, and later saving Italy from the Communists in his role distributing unvouchered CIA funds to pro-Western, pro-democratic groups in the critical elections of 1948. Next to Virgil, standing with his arms around two of "his boys," smiling and serene, is Paul Oakes in his minister's garb; marriage ceremonies, as he once told me, were the "best part of the job." All would remember the wedding as a happy occasion, and the cool crisp weather and the "fabulously blooming dogwoods" in that long-ago Washington spring. Gin and tonics and mint juleps flowed easily and the conversation was animated and good-spirited as, for a few hours, the weighty task of saving the world was put aside.

All gone and, with the fall of the Berlin Wall, the crusade, too, that changed them and their country.

Only weeks after the wedding, the North Koreans invaded South Korea. Because Kim Philby and an American KGB spy in army intelligence had alerted Moscow to the American and British decrypts of Soviet cable traffic, the Soviets changed their codes and the United States was blinded to the Soviet T-34 tanks and supplies flowing south, and the buildup of the North Korean People's Army along the thirty-eighth parallel, intelligence that might have allowed Truman to ward off an imminent attack by threatening Stalin with immediate retaliation.

How relieved I was not to find Kim Philby in that photo, much less Suzanne or Bobby, as if for a time, a halcyon honeymoon had allowed my parents a season of untainted joy that had infused my conception.

Contemplating the wedding photographs, I pulled out one of my mother's favorite books, the first volume of Samuel Eliot Morison's *History of United States Naval Operations in World War II*, in which her father figured glowingly. Inside, I found a folded note from my father written two months before their wedding.

Dearest Mary: So much fun to have had lunch with you at Chevy Chase on Sunday after your championship match. I could not take my eyes off you on the court. I was inspired by how beautifully you moved, your speed, agility, strength—dare I say, I am just a little in love with your gorgeous legs, and envious, too. Your serve is a thing of art, and when you're at full throttle out there and with the color up in your cheeks and your eyes bright, you remind me of a Diana on the hunt. I feel I must take every opportunity to enfold you in my arms, since I'll never be able to catch you on the fly. Your mortal lover, John.

As I read that stray and so earnest endearment from a crumbled past, I broke down in tears, as I had with Laura in a side chapel of the Madonna del Orto. How long—weeks, months?—after their wedding

before Suzanne was again in ascendancy? If it hadn't been for Elysium
. . . No, their letters are littered with mention of assignations in New
York. And yet, I still clung to the hope that my father would have stuck
with my mother had he been exchanged for those KGB agents.

With that discovery, I began to make a systematic search of all my
mother's books I'd saved from P Street and the New York apartment.
Like my father, she'd had the habit of squirreling away correspondence
in books she was reading. Twenty minutes later, opening her favorite
Hornblower novel, *Ship of the Line*, two postcards fell out, both of the
Museum of Antiquities in Leipzig, addressed to my mother at their P
Street home, the first with the same text as the one sent to Suzanne,
the second different from both Suzanne's and the card sent from East
Germany in late 1953 to my grandmother. I sprinted up the stairs to
my office and took down the framed postcard from the wall by the door
and compared them with the copy of Suzanne's postcard. All four were
sent from different small villages along the East German border with
Czechoslovakia. And with the third card, the missing one, the middle
portion, I now had a complete text of the twelve Linear B tablets my
father had taken from the Museum of Antiquities after shooting Karel
Hollar. And not just the complete text but also proof that he'd hedged
his bets, probably sending nine postcards in total, three sets to three
women, in hopes that a complete set would get through.

With this knowledge came the realization of how meticulously he
had planned everything.

For the longest time, I just stared at the blizzard of note cards that
covered every inch of the desk and spilled onto the floor, like a disease,
an alien presence from a previous life.

"You fucking pedantic historian," I muttered.

Casting my eye around the cluttered room with its collections of
flora and fauna, the Indian artifacts from the Navajo excavations I'd
brought back from Arizona when I was sixteen and merged with my
father's collections, I again spotted the cigar box. I smiled in recognition. Nesting on a bed of yellowed cotton was the coiled skin of an
eastern diamondback rattlesnake. I carefully unrolled it, and the ends
drooped over either side of the desk. Seven feet and some! Thirteen
rattles. How had this creature found its way into the Berkshires, so far
from its range in the southern lowlands, where these creatures thrive?
Nobody had ever heard of such a thing. Even the timber rattler had
only a scattering of dens in the Berkshires. I remembered seeing the

wedge-shaped head once in a jar of formaldehyde; my mother had probably gotten ahold of it and thrown it out.

I stared in wonder. And as I did, Suzanne's words across the dinner table at Hillders returned to me as if spoken only minutes before.

"He was unmerciful to Bobby. My pathetic husband lying drunk in my arms on what was supposed to be our wedding night, still trying to grapple with John's spiteful bullying as a child, pushing him, punishing him for being physically weak and cowardly, as if dropping bombs on women and children in Germany wasn't enough penance.

"It was summer vacation, August, I believe, before Winsted started again, and they were hiking around Eden Lake and through some of the old forest at the very farthest point of the property. 'Unexplored,' was how Bobby put it, as if the word had a special resonance for John: the unexplored, the unstoried that always fascinated him. I heard Bobby's breath catch time and again as he described it to me, the rattlesnake in the path. And not just any old timber rattlesnake, which they knew well enough to avoid, but an eastern diamondback, like nothing they'd ever seen in those parts. Six feet, maybe seven! The depth of a grave, John had joked. Bobby immediately moved off the path to avoid the creature. John went right for it, fascinated, mesmerized, according to Bobby. 'It shouldn't be here,' John kept saying, shaking his head. 'We're too far north; this old fellow, this mighty worm is way out of its range.' By then, the snake was rearing back and threatening, its rattle buzzing.

"'Isn't he beautiful,' John went on. 'Come and look at him, Bobby.' Bobby drew closer; he described the snake as having shimmering diamond markings in tan and black, and tiny slanted yellow-orange eyes: a single death-dealing taut muscle. John moved even closer. Bobby shouted at him to get back. Then John got down on one knee, mesmerized. 'He shouldn't be here,' John kept muttering, shaking his head. Bobby was terrified. They were miles from help. The viper's forked tongue flickered. Bobby pleaded for John to get away. He was so terrified, he peed in his pants. Bobby was shaking in my arms as he told me this. John was in a trance, laughing off Bobby's pathetic entreaties. 'How many have died, Bobby,' he said, 'before their time, before they were able to carry out what they might have achieved—fate or folly? What if Alexander had not succumbed to poison when he did?' That, said Bobby, was the kind of romantic nonsense he had to put up with from John when they were boys. John was testing him, testing the damn serpent, tempting fate; he kept thrusting his outstretched hand closer, the beast's head jabbing and withdrawing, and jabbing again, the rattle like a hive of angry bees.

"Then John asked Bobby for his handkerchief, demanded it. Bobby came around from behind and held it out to him. Never taking his eye off the rattlesnake, John took the handkerchief and tied it around his forearm, using his teeth to tie the knot—a tourniquet of a kind, I suppose. With that, he returned to harassing the beast, using his outstretched hand the way an Indian charmer uses his pipe to distract the cobra, holding a stick at the ready in his other. 'I'll catch him.' His face was rapt, beaded with sweat, one hand stretched forward, the other, his right, poised with the stick. He moved forward on his haunches, readying himself. When the snake struck, it grazed the back of John's hand. John slapped it down, pinning it right behind the head with the stick. He stood in triumph, holding up the entire writhing length of the beast, yelling—'a bloodcurdling war whoop,' was how Bobby put it to me—his face ecstatic, like some Perseus with the reptilian curls of Medusa in his clutches. John yelled at Bobby to get the hunting knife from his belt; he was having enough to do to handle the seven-footer in his grasp. Bobby couldn't bring himself to go any closer. 'Get the knife,' John yelled. Bobby somehow summoned the courage and got the knife. 'You do it,' John commanded. 'Cut its head off.' Bobby just shook his head. In exasperation, John finally grabbed the knife, pinned the head to the ground with his foot, and cut it off. Bobby watched in horror as the body continued to twist and curl and finally went still. By then, John had discovered the puncture marks on the back of his left hand, which was swelling. He held it out to Bobby. 'Cut it, cut through the fang marks,' he told Bobby. 'Cut it and then suck out the poison. You might be saving my life; then you can tell everyone at school how you saved my life—you can be the hero.' Bobby was paralyzed. 'Do it,' shouted John. 'You always say how much you love me, so—do it, save my life.' Bobby tried to cut, but as the blood oozed, he fainted dead away. When he came to, John had lanced the bite and bandaged his hand. The knotted handkerchief had prevented the venom from spreading farther up his arm. He then skinned the snake and put the head in his shirt pocket. He didn't say another word to Bobby. They hiked back home in silence. By the time they got back to the house, John's hand was badly swollen and his breathing was shallow. The caretaker drove him to the hospital in Pittsfield, where he got proper medical attention. He was in the hospital for three days . . . almost died."

The light through the window, that weary afternoon sunlight moving through millions of miles of space, filtered through the ionosphere and stratosphere, and then passing through the highest boughs of the white pines, and finally refracted in the swirled panes of leaded glass, caused a dull lucent patina of umber and black to emanate from the scales where I'd stretched the skin over the desk. The patterns of the markings were very beautiful and seemed to take on a luminous density as other colors, richer colors, appeared from beneath, like pigment under faded varnish. The thing seemed to speak of fable and dream, an enigma deepened in the telling, a palimpsest of time so overwritten as to distort memory: the serpent in our garden that leads men to temptation, to abandon home ground for cruel and bloody wars in faraway lands, to enslave his own brothers and so himself. I ran my finger lovingly over the pattern of light and dark scales to feel the reticulated pulse to my core, the graven message of that inexplicable mix of good and evil that perversely attaches to our every desire. I picked up the length of skin and brought it to my lips, like a priest making a blessing, and then carefully tacked the length to the top of the window casing.

My father had left this talisman for me on his desk, a reminder to his son of the lure of pride and revenge, and the treacherous path ahead. And so I appended these words on the back of a note card and pinned it beneath the skin: *Et in Arcadia ego.*

In the first week of May, along with the first trickle of translations from the Stasi files obtained with hard cash bribes by Brandt & Harrison's representatives in Berlin, a Federal Express envelope arrived from the American Ballet Theater with a single ticket to a gala performance at the Met the following week.

I was thrilled to hear from Laura, even if indirectly, after all this time! Going to her performance in New York would also give me a chance to den the Brandt & Harrison team and review ongoing strategies.

Laura was dancing the lead in a revival of Antony Tudor's—the choreographer, an old friend of Suzanne's, had died two years before—*The Leaves Are Fading,* to a Dvorak string quartet. My seat was in the second row, and I soon realized I was seated with members of the company who were not performing. There were handsome and athletic young men and women on either side of me, along with regisseurs and ballet masters; all were bubbling with insider gossip and catty asides to one another.

When the curtain opened on the ballet, a hush of anticipation filled the house. Even the company people around me fell silent and behaved themselves; the two women on my right looked at each other and held up crossed fingers. My stomach knotted. The moment she appeared onstage, a ripple of applause could be heard over the music, heads steadied, and the balletomanes and ballet groupies gasped. It had been over two years since her last performance. I would not have recognized her immediately if I hadn't known. She wore a one-piece unitard of autumnal hues that clung to every line and sinew of her body like a second skin. I was shocked by how thin and fragile she seemed . . . more beautiful for the fragility. Her expression of loss and pain and wonder barely changed as she danced, as if she embodied a remote loneliness, a sky spirit unused to the eyes of onlookers. To my untrained eye, her technical mastery seemed flawless as she filled that enormous space with her presence, riding the wave of sound as if to someplace outside the temporal realm. She soared in her partner's arms, free as a wind-blown leaf. Her colleagues next to me let out little sighs of relief and wonder. She seemed alive in ways I could never know, at least not since my days on the football field and river, if then.

I was taken back to that long-ago beautiful fall afternoon when she'd held my arm and said to me, ". . . you like to move." Yes, I thought, yes, I did. If only I'd known how precious a gift. And I could see why Max would have fallen in love with her—why anyone would. How his novel is filled with love and awe at her gifts; how his words flow with her and buoy her in scene after scene. Seeing her dance onstage for the first time, I felt as if I finally shared in that love and the power of his words, feeling released to love her even more. In each step, in the joy and sorrow of every movement and the fluid counterpoint of her lyrical arms and arched feet and flowing torso, she arrested the moment of love incarnate, suspended in the timeless stream of sound, only to let it flow onward in the memories of those who beheld it. She seemed age-less as she moved, less in how she shaped the space through which she moved than in how her powers grew as they filled the stage with a vital force. Even the jaded young dancers in my row were leaning forward as if to drink in that power and gather it to themselves, steeping their youthful ambitions in the fading glory of hers.

It was the first and last time I ever saw her dance professionally.

I stood trembling and clapping, tears in my eyes. Those around me cheered. "She got through it," said one dancer. "She survived magnificently," said another. "What fucking courage." Her face was radiant at the curtain calls, asheen with sweat. Relief and joy and a kind of aching sadness flickered in her blue eyes, in her genuflections of gratitude. The audience refused to let her retreat from the proscenium, calling her back time and again. She held three overflowing bouquets, handing flowers to her handsome young partner and then the conductor. This was followed by avalanche after avalanche of flowers flung toward the stage. She bowed and bowed under the onslaught of bravas and flowers, looking so small and exposed and alone. I could count every tendon in her neck and back. Her chest was heaving with emotion. It seemed to me she clutched those roses for dear life.

When I went to the stage door at the end of the evening, I was told she was long gone to a private gala party. She'd returned to the celebrity life enshrined in Max's novel, disappointing other fans at the stage door, who clutched copies of *Gardens of Saturn* for her to sign.

50

THE STASI REPORTS OBTAINED BY BRANDT & Harrison were a mixed bag, and confusing, because the East German Ministry for State Security was in many respects an arm of the Soviet KGB, certainly in 1953, a loyal and dependable apex predator. As Karel Hollar had been a loyal and dependable agent for the Soviets since sometime in the thirties. He was Moscow's man in the GDR, with ambiguous ties in his past to British intelligence and Nigel Bennett during the war years in Greece when England and the Soviets were reluctant allies. Hollar's story to me in Prague—that he was identified by a West German agent working for the British because of his esoteric tastes in classical texts— holds up, and explains his sudden change of heart and offer to defect to the West: MI6 and MI5 had the goods on him, as he had the goods on Philby. Which also explains why my father was held in Prague and not in East Germany, where delicate issues surrounding Karel Hollar's true identity needed to be finessed and then liquidated by the Soviets. The ever-protean Karel somehow convinced his Soviet handlers that his bona fides rated at least a stay in the gulag, avoiding the executioner's bullet while being put on ice for yet another role a decade later in the Dubček government.

When the Stasi headquarters in East Berlin was stormed by angry crowds in January 1990, many files were shredded or spirited away, so what Brandt & Harrison managed to buy—in one case, I would find out years later, outbidding British and American intelligence services—may well be incomplete. Much of what Hollar told me in our prison cell was broadly accurate, but many details were left out or slightly altered, the most glaring that he had been surprised by my father's sudden appearance. In truth, he had specified to British intelligence, MI6, and then Nigel Bennett, who ran MI5 counterintelligence and was handling the Philby case, that the conditions for his defection required that my father contact him in East Berlin and bring Ventris's charts on the decipherment of Linear B. Nowhere was there any mention that Hollar requested a $100,000 in cash and gold. It would have been useless to him in the East and would only have endangered his plans to defect, much less cross into West Berlin carrying so much cash. Only later, once he was in the West, when he'd testified conclusively about Philby and every secret he'd ever been privy to over nearly twenty years as a double agent for the Soviets and the British, would he have received such a payment, much less that dream villa by the sea in Greece.

But more persuasively, like my father, middle-aged and disillusioned, he wanted a shot at immortality: the authorship and first translation of the stolen Linear B tablets from Pylos. He summoned the only man who could make it possible, a dark angel who might be fatal to both their dreams.

That is why my father did not tell Elliot Goddard or his CIA colleagues about "a freelance mission for the Brits," as a dumbfounded Elliot called it in a tone of disbelief when I discussed it with him over the phone that spring. Nigel Bennett probably asked my father to make the contact with Hollar as a personal favor, to avoid further embarrassment about the Cambridge moles who had deeply compromised both British and American intelligence in 1953, to the point where the Americans lost all trust in their British cousins. "Christ, we were barely speaking," said Elliot. The British were profoundly chagrined by the defection in 1951 of Maclean and Burgess, and even more so that they didn't have conclusive evidence against Philby, who by 1953 had been interrogated for over two years by MI5 to no avail. Not a single person in the British establishment, among scores who must have known or been involved in Philby's Communist activities, ever came forward to tip the balance of suspicion against him—that is, not until 1962. American intelligence was aghast and furious. With the bloodbath of the Korean War just unfolding, the hydrogen bomb on the horizon, CIA director Bedell Smith warned British intelligence that if they did not convict Philby and root out his colleagues, American intelligence would refuse to share sensitive information with their British counterparts in the future.

My father had no choice about keeping Elliot and Dulles in the dark: If British intelligence let it out about Pylos and Hollar in 1943, about the massacre of non-Communists in the town, how my father had been keeping an eye on Suzanne and Bobby for MI5 probably since at least 1944, his career, both in the CIA and at Princeton, would have been finished.

To this day, British intelligence files about the bungling of the Philby case, much less the screwup with Karel Hollar, remain under lock and key, as does Suzanne's London intervention in 1954 and again in 1962.

Suzanne's role was something I was desperate to clear up that spring with Elliot Goddard when I phoned him at his Buzzards Bay home.

"She told me she'd flown to London in 1954 to confront Philby about my father's disappearance, to see if he might intervene with the Soviets."

"Suzanne wouldn't have been such a damn fool. Besides, she wouldn't have been able to get within a hundred yards of him without being spotted by the MI5 security detail that monitored him night and day—or so they assured us."

"Why would she have made up such a thing if she hadn't done it?"

"Because she's a washed-up alcoholic making up stories to salve her conscience."

"She said the MI5 tradecraft was pitiful."

There was a long pregnant pause on the line.

"She should know; back then, she was as good as she was beautiful."

"So maybe she really did get to him; she even gave me the name of a tube stop and a pub, which stupidly I failed to write down." I didn't mention I was falling-down drunk at the dinner table.

"She also knew all the rules and the risks, as did Philby. Even returning to England, she could have been arrested. Coming within a mile of Philby—she a known KGB courier—would have blown the game for him. He would never have allowed it or condoned it. A conviction for treason could have meant a death sentence and a disaster for the cause."

"If you'd seen her eyes, her face . . . I think I believe her. And Philby wouldn't have been the first . . . if she'd told him her daughter was his."

"By golly . . ."

"Which she isn't."

"All right . . . let's hope not, let's hope not . . ."

"Because, if she did see him, if he got word back to Moscow . . ."

"It might explain . . ."

"Christ, if you'd seen her face."

I heard a loud sigh.

"'*On Helen's cheek all art of beauty set, And you in Grecian tires are painted new*'—do you know the sonnet?"

"Let's not go there."

"We see only the shadow of the real, like the flickering dappled hulls of the sailboats skimming the bay beyond my living room window."

"Tell me something: How did Bobby get in touch with you back in '63? Was it his idea or yours that he give up Anthony Blunt in exchange for a place on the Winsted board?"

"He knew your grandmother was ailing, that she wouldn't last."

"So you proposed it?"

"Suzanne called my wife, her bridesmaid, my Margaret."

"Suzanne proposed it?"

"On Bobby's behalf, she made the contact, and then I went to see him at Hermitage."

"You must've been beside yourself."

"I figured it was a small price to pay, and I'd keep him bottled up on the board—fat chance."

"So she knew all about it."

"Husband and wife, same team—same coach, broken game plan."

"Nigel Bennett told me she flew to London again in 1962. She said it was after one of Laura's first performances—or maybe it was a class or something. It seems she met with an old friend of hers and Philby's going back to Cambridge days, a Rothschild connection, some guy who had actually worked with Philby during the war and after for MI6. She told me that's when she dropped the dime on Philby, when she got her revenge."

Another long pause, I almost thought I could hear the calls of seagulls over the line.

"Poor Nigel, what a legend, what a beautiful mind."

"Well?"

"I'll be damned . . . good for her."

"You didn't know?"

"You'd think Nigel and MI5 would have shared that after we gave them Anthony Blunt."

"So it wasn't Blunt who gave away Philby in 1962?"

"It took years to bring Blunt around, and by then, Philby was long gone to Moscow."

"So she really did it, then . . . once she knew."

"What?"

"She ratted on Philby in '62 and then got Bobby to do the same to Blunt—using you—the following year."

"Wow, a twofer—what a ballsy broad. How the fucking Brits let the bastard escape them in Beirut beggars belief. I'd have had armed guards around him at all times. Unless they wanted him to flee to Moscow to avoid trying him for treason." There was another pregnant pause. "Unless she warned him."

Now it was my turn to fall silent as I stared out the window at where the spring buds were beginning to obscure the ruins of Hermitage across the lake, pondering the thing I couldn't quite grasp.

"Tell me something: You said it was my mother's wish to have my father's body cremated—right?"

"It was your mother's request. We offered to return the body after the pathologist was done, but that's the way she wanted it."

"The ashes?"

"The ashes."

"And there was no sign of torture or abuse or mistreatment?"

"Nothing that would have caused his death. Solitary confinement . . . loneliness—you've had a taste. You tell me."

"And your pathologist?"

"Best in the business. As I told you in Prague, the deal for an exchange had been agreed to. We were giving up three of their very best. Again, my counterpart, Dimitri—known him for years—who handled their side of things, seemed genuinely disturbed by what he described as 'an unfortunate outcome,' as if . . . well, almost as if he'd gotten to like John."

"I think his mind was pretty good right to the end."

"How do you know that? You're not holding out on me now?"

"When you last saw him in Berlin, how was his leg? How was he getting around?"

"Just fine, all that traipsing around the Chevy Chase links. He didn't even bother with a cane anymore."

"And the war wound, you're sure about the OSS files: no mention of a Communist ambush or an SS massacre of citizens in Pylos, or a British double agent working for Moscow?"

"Again, OSS Balkan branch was chockablock with Soviet agents and fellow travelers. Anything that might have cast a poor light on Moscow was probably expunged from his files . . . easy, if you catch my drift."

"How's spring treating you?"

"About as well as might be expected. Water too damn cold as yet for my old bones."

"Yeah, stay away from cold water—you have no idea."

"Come on, you scheming son of a gun, give your uncle Elliot some candy to chew on in his dotage—I can't fucking take it with me, you know."

I think my father thought it might go quickly. And the last thing he wanted to do was to get the CIA involved in a British operation—given the existing enmity, especially while his long-standing affair with Suzanne remained a looming pitfall, no matter how much Elliot stuck by him or scrubbed his files. And only MI6 and MI5 had the proof he needed that placed Karel Hollar in Pylos during the massacre by the SS. On that score, he bided his time, as his grandfather, General Alden, had. But if he had succeeded in pulling off Hollar's defection, those SIS-MI6 files from 1943–1944 would have been critical for his conviction on war crimes.

And he wanted freedom for his kidnapped son.

And he wanted the stolen Linear B files all to himself.

As I combed through the fragmented Stasi files, with the equally frag-mented bits and pieces from the Pinkerton reports and newspaper clippings on the crimes surrounding the case of Pearce Breckenridge at my elbow, I became convinced that my father's journey through Check-point Charlie, as it had been for General Alden taking a southbound train as far as Jackson, Mississippi, was, in the end, a very personal matter.

The real wild card, the one truly incalculable factor in my father's plan, were the 103 Linear B tablets. And I still hear Elliot's cackle over the long-distance phone line from his summer home on Buzzards Bay as I hinted about those tablets without mentioning they had been stolen. "Ah, the lure of the honey pot: power, love, revenge, to be numbered with the immortals—an unknown author, how delicious!" Only a translation would prove their worth. Where Hollar miscalculated was summoning the one man he thought was a trusted friend, or at least a safe coconspirator, necessary for the decoding of the tablets, who might yet hasten the crown of laurels both men sought. But the one man, perhaps the sole witness, who might identify him and want to bring him to justice for those murdered in Pylos, including the grandparents and aunt of my father's son with Joanna.

And so I stepped into my father's shoes, tempted to see though his eyes and feel what he felt as he passed through Checkpoint Charlie and walked through the desolate streets of East Berlin to the Neues Museum. I am convinced he thought he could pull the thing off in a day or two and be back in the Western sector—with or without Hollar—dead or alive—before the CIA Berlin station even missed him. But the $100,000 in cash and gold complicates that picture. The plan, plan A, must have been for a perusal of Ventris's charts and a quick excursion to Leipzig—perhaps he thought Hollar had the tablets with him in Berlin—and the Linear B tablets before a return to Berlin and Hollar's defection. That would explain why he wore a fine Savile Row suit and didn't bring a change of clothes, unless he had an alternate plan, a plan B if Hollar proved difficult, or if it turned out to be a trap . . . or if Hollar couldn't or wouldn't help him with the kidnapped boy. I also feel sure that, like his grandfather General Alden, my father was hardwired with a gambler's instinct—confirmed by Elliot's experience with him on the gridiron, especially when faced with bad odds and bad choices, an impetuous talent he'd conspicuously displayed on that hillside above Kalamata, and a romantic faith that the gods would bless his righteous cause. His "damned puritanical—one of the elect—streak," according to Suzanne, led him to believe that good works and good intentions—success—"makes you one of the anointed." I had felt similar things in my days on the football field and perhaps along the banks of the Vam Co Dong River before the Skyraiders brought the curtain down, before I knew of the fate of Pearce Breckenridge, when any lingering romantic notions that good deeds made for good outcomes were extinguished.

Neither British nor American intelligence knew about my father's obsession with getting back his son by Joanna. Neither did Hollar until their testy dinner in Leipzig. But Kim Philby knew, because, at least in the story I want to tell, it is the only way my father could have known if the boy was dead or alive, much less where he might be found.

Hollar's driver was, indeed, a Stasi informer, something Hollar knew only too well from being a KGB agent—he counted on this to cover his ass. His clandestine meeting with my father on the steps of the Neues Museum, their dinner at Lutter & Wegner on Charlottenstrasse, and their night together at Hollar's splendid, if run-down, East

Berlin apartment on Smetenastrasse were only uncovered long after the fact by the Stasi. Hollar flat out lied about how my father, out or the blue, had left a note at his office to arrange that first meeting. The arrangement had always been to meet at the Neues Museum. After close editing, the one part of Hollar's story that remains unshakable is how these erstwhile friends longed to return to a life of scholarship and discovery, that primal desire that had so inflamed their adolescent longings, and the perverse roles they had otherwise adopted, which so grated on their essential nature. Contrary to what Hollar told his interrogators, when he described the American agent on their first meeting as "unbalanced, crazy, more than a little agitated, his hand wet with anxiety," the driver reported differently. "I picked up the American professor, who walked slowly with the aid of a cane, and the minister at his apartment on Smetenastrasse for their journey to Leipzig. The American, though well dressed, seemed in a holiday mood, smiling like a curious tourist. Both men carried bags, the American a large attaché case, the minister two compact travel suitcases." I assumed the large bags were to smuggle out the Linear B tablets. The detail of the cane is significant, which is why I had brought it up with Elliot: By 1953, my father had long dispensed with a cane and walked briskly with my mother on the golf course at the Chevy Chase Club.

I often dream about that drive southwest from Berlin to Leipzig, which I have now driven a number of times, as these two old friends and competitors neared their goal of possibly revealing a hidden chapter of Homer's *Iliad* or *Odyssey*, or even the urtext of Homer's tales. I see them in the plush backseat of the minister's official ZIM, feeling each other out as they had the previous day, tapping into the glittering prospect that had once stirred their youthful dreams of glory. I can see my father trying to stay cool, maintain a professional skepticism as he evaluated the intentions of the man he'd stalked through France and Germany in the last year of the war, an audacious gambler in his own right, who as a Soviet double agent had outwitted the Sicherheitsdienst and Gestapo for five harrowing years, only to arrange his death in a Soviet POW camp and resurrection, with the help of the KGB, as a GDR minister. Not a man to be taken at face value. I'm certain it was not love that prompted Hollar to enlist my father's help in deciphering the 103 Linear B tablets; in Greece, he'd been willing to give up his coconspirator to the Communist Resistance on word from Moscow Center, leaving him alone in possession of the stolen tablets.

Something that surely must have made my father wary, if not a little paranoid. He had to have been concerned if it was a trap, as the attack on Kalamata had ultimately been a trap. But then, he had insurance: confirmation of Hollar's connection to SIS-MI6 and Pylos, enough to execute him in Moscow and hang him in London for war crimes.

Time was short for both men if they were to complete their business and get out alive. East Berlin before the Berlin Wall was porous; Hollar and my father could have walked from Karel's apartment on Smetenastrasse (I often wonder if Karel picked that address in silent homage to the preeminent Czech composer) and passed into the Western sector with a little bluffing at any of the various checkpoints. Traveling to Leipzig, epicenter of the recent worker uprisings, was a very different matter, a huge risk for a final snatch at glory. Hollar may have wanted to make sure the charts were genuine, and more to the point, he couldn't do it without my father's help. It had been almost fifteen years since he'd worked with Linear B, and my father was the brains of their team. If my father was really as cool and calm as the Stasi driver described, it must have been because of the dinner the day before and the night at the apartment, which Hollar had described to me in nostalgic detail, when both men carefully evaluated each other and the risks. I believe they came up with a kind of mutual suicide pact that locked them into a plan that neither could betray without bringing about their downfall.

Contrary to what Hollar told me, that it had all been my father's crazy idea, the Stasi files reveal that Hollar had a week's vacation scheduled: "Due to the recent stress and long hours at his post in the Ministry of Mines, the minister had previously requested from the General Secretary a week of leave to recover his health." Over one hundred undeciphered Linear B tablets would have taken a team of the best scholars on the planet the better part of a year to decipher. Hollar was going to give it a week, and my father was essential. He must have figured that in a week they'd at least know if the stolen tablets from the anteroom of the megaron were promising, and, if so, then they might attempt to smuggle them out of East Berlin. My palms still sweat when I see these two gamblers refining their scheme over dinner and at Hollar's apartment, how they simply talked themselves into it, as if some vagrant gust of romantic fancy from their days on Crete or gliding down the canals of Venice as carefree young men caught their sails and sped them down the Autobahn to Leipzig.

Real life, Max, is never mapped out to plan as in a novel, but happens in the process of a million neural adjustments, an unscripted muddle, as emotion time and again trumps reason. Or, as you would say, desire: the desire of desire.

"The minister and the American professor seemed excited about the prospects of indulging their antiquarian passions," reported the driver. "They argued and bickered in the backseat of my ZIM like smarty-pants schoolboys. I believe it had to do with the language of the ancient Greeks or something of the sort—all the way to Leipzig. It was truly Greek to me. Yes, the minister did brag occasionally about the great accomplishments of the government in bettering the life of the people, but no better than a tour guide."

So, the minister of mines—how appropriate a title for a digger of souls—had a problem: how to square the unexpected arrival of the American scholar and his medical leave. "I believe the minister had scheduled the car for his vacation at least a week ahead, if I remember, to spend time at his old university, to relax his mind in antiquarian pursuits. I knew how hard he'd been working—I felt for the poor fellow. Why, even on vacation, he was required to keep in touch by telephone and keep me close at hand in case of emergency. Given his proletarian upbringing, I suppose I should have found this university connection odd, how he sometimes slipped into an uppity lingo, but at the time it all got by me."

The driver, examined carefully by his Stasi interrogator with his KGB counterpart looking over his shoulder, confirmed that a stop had been made along the route for the American to purchase some work-man's clothing in case the storerooms of the museum should prove filthy, as indeed they did. Twice during that first day in the bowels of the museum Hollar had invited the driver down to their work area to order in beer and sandwiches. "Those two could barely spare me a glance or a good word. They were intent on the table, where there were many clay tablets with strange markings. They had papers everywhere and were intently filling notebooks with their findings, like gnomes in a cave by lamplight. Their hands were filthy, their faces, too. The place smelled of old things. Dust everywhere. My mother would have died of shock."

In late April of 1990, at a cost of thirty thousand dollars, Brandt & Harrison's man in Berlin bribed an ex-Stasi official to produce the file of Hollar's interrogations by both the Stasi and the KGB. These were conducted in a Stasi prison in Berlin, while he was still recovering from the gunshot wound in his shoulder. This proved to be a fascinating document because the Stasi interrogator was digging like a fox terrier, while the aloof and slightly cynical KGB operative, who knew all about his colleague's prewar incarnation as an archaeologist, Wehrmacht officer, and Soviet spy, was trying not to blow his agent of influence's cover, yet he was clearly skeptical about how Hollar was going about squaring the circle. The Stasi man couldn't understand how a poor boy from a working-class mining background could have known anything about Greek antiquities, much less have once been friends with an American professor—"if the fugitive assassin proves to be your American professor."

"I'm a self-made man, an intellectual; that is how I was drawn to Marxist-Leninism in the first place," Hollar told his interrogators. "I knew enough of ancient history that when the American professor came to me with his proposition to let him study the tablets, I could manage an intelligent conversation. I suspected he might have had other motives. Men of his class, the intelligentsia of America and England, were often engaged in the spy services, as they had been in the war against fascism. So my plan for this Professor Alden was to engage him in conversation about his colleagues, to see what the great minds in the field of code decryption were doing in the West. It seems these Linear B tablets he was intent on seeing had been deposited at the Museum of Antiquities before the war. I thought it might present an opportunity to recruit him; I thought if I dangled the Linear B tablets before his eyes, trading on the accolades that would come to him for their translation, I might, at least, get some useful intelligence. I knew that our Soviet brothers has been concerned for years that their wartime codes might have been deciphered by American intelligence. I was presented with an opportunity—simple as that—and I took it. My plan was going very well—very well indeed—until those imbecilic miners went on strike yet again."

That's when both their plans went awry. The driver, who was checking with the Hollar's office every two hours during this crisis period, was told about the miners' strike called that morning in the town of Heuersdorf. He was informed that the workers were demanding better hours and wages and threatening to blow up the mines if the Soviet military or Stasi was brought in, and that an important meeting had been scheduled that night with the miners' representatives in the local town hall.

"The minister was clearly angry when I informed him. 'How dare those spoiled bastards disturb me on my vacation? Haven't they wasted enough of our time as it is?' The minister ordered me to call the office to say that he would attend the meeting in the Heuersdorf town hall. I observed the minister making an exasperated face to the American as they returned to their work with the tablets."

I clearly remember Hollar's agitation in our jail cell when he told me of the sudden complications of the Heuersdorf strike. When I had recovered in Venice, I made detailed notes of everything Hollar had told me: how he was tempted right then and there to drive back to Berlin and defect, as he told me my father had urged him to do. The driver saw it differently, describing my father and Hollar as fully engaged—"spell-bound"—in their work of translation: "Soviet T-34s couldn't drag them away." Hollar could have left my father at the hotel room he'd reserved for a week, gone to the strikers' meeting, and returned later. The driver confirmed that Hollar had booked a room at a local hotel (something the Stasi interrogator came back to again and again)—the week set aside to work with the tablets; he also distinctly remembered the raised voices of the minister and the American at dinner. "They spoke about Greece—Pylos, I believe that was the name—repeated a number of times; they became quite agitated. I was concerned they might come to blows and prepared myself to intervene if necessary."

Hollar had admitted to me that it was at the small restaurant on the outskirts of Leipzig, the Thuringer Hof, in the Stasi report, where my father had confronted him with his war crimes and the abduction of the Greek boy by Kostas Kaleyias. Perhaps the Heuersdorf strike broke the spell of the tablets, or an excess of local wine with dinner, or their exhaustion or mutual suspicion, prompting my father to put his cards on the table to move the planned defection along. Hollar told me the initial work on the tablets had proved disheartening, but I think that was a lie; it was the exact opposite. Just before he died, when I pressed him once more about the tablets, he mumbled something about the names that had caught my father's eye: "Names of towns, islands, gods—we were on to something."

Perhaps it was true, what Hollar said about the kidnapping: that there was nothing he could do about the boy without giving the game away. "John tried to bribe me; he said he had enough money to allow me the good life in Greece, to finance my own expeditions, if only I would help him with the boy. He had the name of a town, somewhere in Hungary—the name escapes me. 'Gold,' he said, 'gold to bribe the Hungarians.'" Whatever the precise truth, by the end of dinner, the two colleagues no longer trusted each other. And there was no way Hollar was going to leave my father behind in Leipzig . . . not for a minute, certainly not for an evening in the hotel room he'd reserved for his week off. They were locked in a deadly standoff.

"The minister took me aside," the driver reported, "as if his holiday mood had totally changed, and told me in no uncertain terms that when he joined the meeting of strikers and Party bigwigs in Heuersdorf, the American was to remain in the car, and I was authorized to use force to keep him there. 'If he tries to leave, shoot him.' I was stunned by what he told me."

"Why did I tell the driver to shoot Alden if he tried to leave the car?" Hollar asked rhetorically in his interrogation. "I realized his intention all along was to get me to defect. He was a dangerous man. I would finish the meeting in Heuersdorf and drive him back to Berlin and either have him arrested or escort him to the Western zone. On that point, I hadn't quite made up my mind. Yes, I realized I had blundered in the first place—to trust him in any way, even as I tried to get something useful out of him . . . it would not look good for me under any circumstances. Perhaps that was Alden's plan all along, to maneuver me into an untenable position, discredit me, and then blackmail me. I was exhausted by the months of strikes; my judgment was faulty."

What fascinates me most about Hollar's lies and distortions, even thirty-five years later, after the fall of the Berlin Wall and years in the gulag, was his inability to admit to me—and possibly himself—that my father was the one who shot him during the Heuersdorf meeting. For me, it is *the* most significant detail. And it probably saved Hollar's life.

The Stasi driver noted another critical detail: "The cane was left in the back, shoved under the front seat—when I found that later, I knew things were in a bad way."

The driver was grilled about how as a professional (an ex-Gestapo man, the KGB agent blurted out at one point) he had managed to let the American elude him, especially since he'd been expressly told to keep an eye on him.

"He was dozing in the back. I stepped out to take a piss, to smoke, and a colleague, the driver for the Party secretary, came over to chat. I was less than two meters from the ZIM. I told him about the minister's strange guest and our day in Leipzig. We were distracted by the miners in the streets of Heuersdorf; they were a brutish bunch. I don't understand it: I would have heard the car door open; I would have seen something. When I got back in the ZIM, he was gone, and his case with him. I thought he had gone to use the toilet—the way he walked with the cane, he couldn't have gone far. I asked the other drivers and Stasi men, but no one had seen him. I went to the Town Hall to tell the minister, but the meeting was under way; voices were raised in the hall, people shouting."

"Did you think to check the toilets?"

"I was supposed to stay with the ZIM. Who knew what those miners might try to do."

Hollar was almost an hour into the testy shouting match between the Party bosses and the representatives of the miners' union when a tall figure in a cap rose from the packed seats nearest the side door of the hall, raised his pistol, and shot the minister of mines in the right shoulder. The Stasi investigation turned up a dozen descriptions: tall, a miner's cap covering his head, mustache and small beard, some said a goatee, a single shot from the pistol in the outstretched hand, a cold, unflinching, steady aim . . . a yellow flame in the dim lighting of the hall. Hollar had been standing at the table, gesturing in an appeal to reasonableness among the parties, when the bullet hit his shoulder, spinning him around so that he fell backward over his chair to the floor. In the chaos, the shooter disappeared.

"What did you think when you were shot?" Hollar was asked.

"What the hell was I supposed to think? I was shot. One of those pigs had shot me; I wasn't the first. We'd all been in danger for months— those stinking ex-Nazis still hadn't killed enough people in the war."

"What did you think when it turned out to be the American?"

"I still don't believe it was him. Have you found him—did he confess as much? If he had wanted to kill me, he could have done it at any time in Berlin, or, God knows, in that putrid storeroom in the museum, and easily escaped."

"Did you check to see if he had a gun?"

"Why would I have checked for such a thing? It was the miners who worried me, greedy bastards."

Hollar had told me otherwise: He had spotted the gun in my father's attaché case.

Even when presented with evidence to the contrary, Hollar continued to believe that it was a disaffected miner who had tried to kill him.

I don't think he was being disingenuous with his interrogators. In this, his romantic streak might have been more deeply ingrained than my father's . . . but of course he knew nothing about Pearce Breckenridge.

The Stasi reports that Brandt & Harrison initially recovered, those from the weeks my father remained at large, proved the most revealing. Bits and pieces more were recovered over the years, but they lack the raw data of the first batch and tend more to speculation on motivation. I believe I now have a pretty clear picture, probably as clear as we will ever have, unless the KGB files in Moscow, covering my father's interrogations at Pankrác Prison, come to light. Though I doubt he would have told them anything they didn't already know.

I feel—and this is a matter of belief, not faith or logic or invention—that my father took a page out of his grandfather's plan to go after the perpetrators of the massacre of Pearce Breckenridge and his teachers and students. Like General Alden when he sent in three teams of Pinkertons to see if justice might be had in Natchez, he hoped to bring Karel Hollar to justice by enabling his defection—a defection that would also bring to justice another killer: Kim Philby, yet another of Suzanne's lovers. But he was also prepared, failing that, to take matters into his own hands and do the necessary thing: to risk everything. Something that was said over that dinner in Leipzig must have convinced him either that Hollar wouldn't defect or that his defense of his actions in Pylos might well stand up in a trial in the West for war crimes. Perhaps he was disillusioned by Hollar's lack of forthrightness about the kidnapped boy, something I'm sure my father blamed on Hollar as well. Or just maybe what they had discovered about the Linear B tablets had shifted some dynamic variable in their relationship—a lust deeper than time: They no longer trusted each other. Then with the sudden crisis in Heuersdorf, my father was faced with putting plan B into motion: the misdirection, play-action pass that was his forte.

The cane had been a subterfuge from the get-go. He pretended sleep and then slipped out of the ZIM with his briefcase and new clothes. He went into the Heuersdorf town hall and changed in a toilet stall into the workmen's clothes he had purchased earlier on the way from Berlin, then carefully packed his Savile Row suit in his bag. He disguised himself further with a false mustache and beard or goatee, which he must have brought with him, in case he needed to escape. He then slipped into the hall, where close to fifty miners sat monitoring their union representatives negotiating with the Party bosses. By all accounts, the minister of mines was in the thick of the arguments, trying to placate the miners but not give more than was warranted "in the austerity of the times." Even the Stasi reports praised Hollar's handling of the situation. Was my father impressed, as Hollar had represented to me in our Pankrác cell, faced with the prospect of what a bigshot defector the West might have had? No matter, the thing was in motion. My father, seated near a side door to the hall, stood, aimed his Walther pistol, and pulled the trigger. I have no doubt he could have killed Hollar. I've been in the run-down remnants of that town hall—swallow droppings where the seats once were—and the distance from the side door to the proscenium where the negotiations took place around a long table was less than thirty feet.

My father didn't kill Hollar—had it been a split-second decision, his whole life, his family history framed in his mind's eye?—because some part of him remembered that General Alden had spared the one son of Jackson Breckenridge; because killing Hollar would have turned Hollar into a martyr, or worse, sparked a third world war (a CIA assassination of a high Party official, even providing a pistol to a disaffected miner, could have been catastrophic, given the hair-trigger relations between Washington and Moscow); because he wanted Hollar to know he could have killed him but didn't; and because shooting him in the shoulder, making it seem like he was a target of assassination, might save his life—not from the gulag, but at least from a summary execution in Lubyanka prison. Perhaps, it even had something to do with his mother's affair with Hollar's father, that "liberal chameleon," which had sparked such an outpouring of grief for her lost husband in Venice and the American Meuse-Argonne Cemetery. I believe, as deeply as I believe anything, that my father wanted Hollar to live in purgatory— stuck in the toils of the Communist meat grinder he'd championed since their youth—with the knowledge of his crimes, and the denial of that final crown of laurels that a translation of the stolen Linear B tablets might have bestowed. I believe this profoundly because that is precisely what happened. There was no cushy defection and Greek villa and exoneration for his war crimes. Only years in the gulag and another round of disillusionment as the Prague Spring was crushed by Soviet tanks in 1968.

Shooting Hollar, wounding him, also bought him the time, the head start he needed.

Or as I prefer to view it: sparing Hollar for my final coup de grâce:

making sure my father got the credit for translating those Linear B tablets from the throne room of Nestor's Palace.

Oh Max, I know . . . how could any man have all this compacted into a single thought in the split second of execution? Believe me, Max, it's possible. All the spadework over all the years, and Pearce Brecken-ridge, and his mother's grief, and Joanna's, too . . . So when the moment came with pistol in hand, the prepared mind became the future's avatar. The Green Beret and the gifted athlete understand these things, how training and muscle memory take over.

Or would you prefer it be a matter of conscience, Max—how you would have written it? If my father had killed his coconspirator and made off with the Linear B tablets, how self-serving would that act have seemed?

Ah, but what about Philby? Isn't that what you want to know, Max? How would you, the world-famous novelist, deal with such a con-spiracy against man and nature? What about Hollar's defection and confirmation of Philby as the lodestone of that infamous Cambridge spy ring—wasn't that the whole point of the mission in the first place? I think Philby, too, had been part of the disagreement and mistrust that developed over dinner in Leipzig. Because my father did have the name of a small town in Hungary where his Greek son had been set-tled with a Hungarian family. As Hollar had told me, in early 1951, my father had mentioned the kidnapped boy to Kim Philby over lunch at the Metropolitan Club, seeking thoughts from this master of British intelligence about how he might go about finding the child and getting him back for Joanna. What Hollar didn't know was that Philby had followed up on this conversation to Moscow Center with a suggestion that John Alden might be ripe for the picking as a double agent: The kidnapped boy might be the perfect bargaining chip for intelligence of the highest importance. "John Alden is an up-and-coming golden boy of the CIA; his work in Greece during the civil war there received the highest accolades. As a friend, his value to us would be incalculable," Philby informed Moscow Center in a message carried from Washing-ton to the Soviet consulate in New York by his lover, Suzanne Williams.

Suzanne, as I was soon to learn from her daughter, had kept a copy of Moscow Center's reply to Philby's overture. Precisely at the time when Donald Maclean was detected in the decrypts of Soviet cable traffic, when Philby, too, had come under suspicion and was in turn recalled to London as an alleged spy, but not before he had provided my father with the name of a small town in Hungary. This name was part of a longer communication from Moscow Center warning Philby that Maclean was in imminent danger and needed to flee England and defect to Moscow. It turned out to be the very last communication that Philby received in Washington from the KGB out of the New York consulate. The courier, again, was Suzanne Williams.

Of course, Suzanne made no mention of this to me, since she always denied her role as KGB courier; but it is one of the cruelest ironies of this sorry affair: She carried the crucial intelligence detail—meaningless to her at the time—or that she hadn't even bothered to read, according to her daughter—that fortified my father's resolve to take up the Hollar mission.

I believe this to be true because of what my father did next.

In the confusion of the shooting, my father managed to slip out of the hall and away from Heuersdorf and headed north cross-country back to Leipzig. The Stasi found the Walther pistol in a field outside the Heuersdorf: one shot fired, no fingerprints. The Walther could easily have been discarded in a pond, where it probably wouldn't have been found. Discovery of the pistol probably kept the Stasi searching among the dissident miners in the immediate area for a crucial extra day or two. I often imagine my father resting or sleeping in a field under the stars on the outskirts of Leipzig. If he'd gone straight to Berlin, there was a good chance he could have slipped back into the Western sector unnoticed and undetected. The alert on the day following was for a tall miner with a mustache and goatee. By the time—around 10:30 the next morning, according to the caretaker—my father arrived at the Museum of Antiquities, he was showered and shaved and wearing his Savile Row suit, and ready to begin again where he'd left off the day before with the Linear B tablets in the basement. He'd used the hotel room in Leipzig—to shower and change (a fact that didn't help Hollar's cause in the Stasi investigation)—Hollar had reserved for his vacation. The minister, my father explained to the caretaker, had been caught up in the crisis with the striking miners and would be delayed. My father spent the entire day working with the tablets, not breaking for lunch or refreshment of any kind. He was counting on the wounded Hollar not to hastily blab about the museum, which would indeed prove the most difficult thing for the minister of mines to justify during the Stasi investigation, and presumably to the KGB when he was later tried in Moscow. The driver was upbraided often during the interrogation for delaying so long in bringing to the attention of the authorities what had happened at the museum. The driver, too, was certain it was a miner who had shot his boss, until two days later, when he found the cane jammed under the front seat.

When the Stasi finally arrived at the Museum of Antiquities, three days after the shooting, my father was long gone. A dozen Linear B tablets were missing, a fact only brought to light weeks later, when my father was still at large and Hollar in prison with a bandaged shoulder, about to be extradited to Moscow by the KGB. An odd position, given he'd been officially pronounced "assassinated" by a foreign provocateur in the East German press. A dead man testifying, trying to save himself. But since the Stasi was still firmly under the thumb of the KGB, anything was possible.

"Minister, you have repeatedly stated that there were one hundred and three tablets. We have now counted them three times. The figure is ninety-one."

"The figure is one hundred and three."

"You are mistaken or lying."

"That thieving American bastard . . ."

"When we find him, providing he hasn't managed to slip back into the West, you will be able to compare figures."

The last part of my father's tale, his weeks on the lam in East Germany and Czechoslovakia before he was arrested trying to cross into Hungary, remains a thing of myth and conjecture. It seems safe to speculate that by the time he was done at the museum, selecting the most promising Linear B tablets with the critical hallmark, he figured that the Stasi had probably gotten a detailed description of him out of Hollar and his driver, and that escape back through Berlin would be next to impossible. The Stasi, long after his arrest on the Czech-Hungarian border, turned up an old lady in the town of Oderwitz—near the Czech border with the GDR—who rented out a room in her farmhouse to itinerant workers on the sugar beet farms in the area. My father, dressed in the dowdy suit of a "Prussian scholar," as the old woman described him, rented a room there for over two months. She described him in the Stasi report as "an educated man with the most impeccable pronunciation." He was finishing up a book on ancient Greece and needed the peace and quiet of the countryside to concentrate. She described how he had spread his papers all over the table in his room and was filling notebook after notebook with scribbles and signs, the likes of which she'd never seen. "When I brought him his meals and his coffee, he explained that it was ancient writings from the days of the Greeks; I was very impressed and pleased to have a man of such intellect staying with me."The Stasi were very intent on the missing twelve tablets when they questioned the old woman. "Oh yes, they were always right there on his worktable by the window, in full view; he told me it was Greek writing and very, very old . . . older than any Greek history we knew, old as time itself. I thought that was truly astonishing."

When the time came for him to leave, my father thanked the old woman for her gentle hospitality, paid his bill, and headed off down the farm road in the direction of the Czech border—"Yes, yes, his backpack was full; he must have taken those things with him"—but not before posting nine postcards in total to his wife and mother and Suzanne from the small town of Oderwitz and eight other nearby towns, at which point he slipped across the Czech border. Ten days later, he was caught by a Czech border patrol as he was trying to cross into Hungary, near the small Hungarian village of Beloyannis. He carried a leather backpack in which were found food, drink, a German edition of Homer's *Odyssey* in Greek, and $100,000 in currency and gold. His notebooks, the twelve tablets, and Ventris's charts were never recovered. As the Stasi speculated, and as any number of CIA veterans of those days have confirmed to me, the border between Hungary and Austria was the preferred escape route out of Eastern Europe. The Hungarians were notoriously lax in patrolling their border with the West, an attitude writ large in the Hungarian uprising of two years later, in 1956, much less the events leading up to the fall of the Berlin Wall, when the Hungarians began dismantling the country's fortified border with Austria in the late spring of 1989. My father might well have been headed home, home to his wife and son, and lover, headed for that porous crossing point between the lands of the free and unfree, with a stop for some unfinished business in the Hungarian town of Beloyannis, but for the Czech border guards along that part of the border near Beloyannis, who had long been on the lookout. That much, the KGB knew from Kim Philby.

And yet, as spring turned to summer in 1990, something of my father's story still eluded me, something inside me, some buried feeling that remained tantalizingly out of reach and kept me stymied.

Until my fair Athena reappeared, once again, to release me.

51

IT WAS THE FOURTH OF JULY, AN APPROPRI-
ate date to end one's independence. I had been out
for an afternoon walk and, upon my return, found her
note on the door.

"Maiden (worst luck) in distress—Hermitage!"

I could see recent tire tracks on our dirt and gravel road. I took the
Jeep Cherokee around Eden Lake to the Williams place and found a
loaded Volvo station wagon with the driver's door open. I hadn't been
by Hermitage since my arrival in January; if anything, it looked worse,
and the smell of burning, mildew, and rot was everywhere. I climbed the
wooden stairs to the remnants of the wide veranda and circled around
the burned-out husk of Stanford White's masterpiece until I found
her sitting on a swing seat toward the rear. She had cut her hair to just
above her shoulders. As I slowly approached, shocked at the loss of that
silky long blond hair, she didn't look up or acknowledge me, but kept
looking out past the broken railing to the overgrown English gardens
and the pines and the lake beyond, across which our boathouse nestled
on the far shore. Not until I was steps away did the fiberglass cast on
her right leg come into view; it went from her ankle to just above the
knee and the cuff of her khaki shorts. Aluminum crutches lay beside
her. I saw her quickly flick away tears with a fingertip. I just sat down
next to her in the long swing seat and said nothing, restraining myself
from the embrace I desperately wanted to give her.

"Looks like I'm going to need a new gig." She gestured not at
her cast or the crutches, but at the yellow sports-model Walkman
clipped to her shorts, the earphones nestled into the collar of her pink
polo shirt.

"Are you all right?" I reached a hand to the seams of yellowy hardness that immobilized her knee.

"Of course I'm all right. I'm as all right as the Williamses and Hermitage. I suppose you heard from our lawyers?"

"I heard."

"Nonpayment of taxes, nonpayment of joint upkeep on the property. So, it's all yours now."

"That doesn't matter."

"Of course it matters; money always matters—only people with money pretend it doesn't."

"I don't care . . . then."

"I used to think I was something—not sure quite what—coming from all of this. Now it's gone and I find out I was never really part of it anyway."

"You grew up here, the land, Elysium."

"It's not the same."

"Is that what your mother told you?"

"A-a-ah, mum's the word; we're not supposed to talk about it. She even got me to sign an agreement from her lawyer to keep me quiet, although, now that I'm done"—she tapped the cast—"maybe our deal is no longer valid."

"Deal?"

"The Met revival of her old flame's masterpiece . . . 'and, oh, by the way, if you play your cards right, young lady, you'll be a very, very rich woman someday.'"

"Seriously, are you okay? Is it your knee?"

"A new knee, with metal pins to prove it, and promises I'll be able to walk again. I got through every scheduled performance except the next to last, when they had to carry me off the stage in San Francisco. They actually paid me for all fifteen performances; so, after my agent's cut, I've got exactly fifty-three thousand dollars and few odd cents to my name. I believe in laying out a full bill of particulars before the buyer commits to anything. I haven't touched a cigarette since Venice, or anything else—except for the painkillers in the hospital . . . and a few glasses of wine. The cast comes off in four weeks. I'm only thirty-nine; I'm still producing eggs each month, though that doesn't seem to be a guarantee of much, 'fraid to say. So, what do you think?"

I had turned to her stubborn profile, still mourning the loss of her long tresses. Now I tried to gage her tone in the flex of her eyebrows, the animated tilt of her head, and the play of honey highlights as she swept lose the strands of hair from behind her ear.

"You were so wonderful at the Met. You moved me . . . really, like nothing I've ever known."

"Don't hyperventilate; you're supposed to be dependable and not extravagant in your praise."

"Sorry, but you brought tears to my eyes, you were so damn good—so beautiful. I think I fell in love with you all over again, even if I got ditched."

"That's nice of you." She placed her hand on my knee, and I laid my hand over hers. "I'm glad you saw it. But it's not my life anymore. I guess it now belongs to Max . . . like Hermitage and so much else." She looked at me with a questioning squint, then a facetious twist of her lips. "I'm winnowing out my choices, triaging the bodies."

I glanced behind us at the ruins of Hermitage, remembering the bucolic dancing dyads of Thomas Dewing over the mantelpiece, the watercolors and pastels of Venice by Sargent and Whistler that Bobby had sold off one by one over the years, until none was left—along with every last one of Amaryllis's canvases, so that he was down to the silver and the Ming blue-and-white porcelain and the Steinway grand, which also went eventually. So when Bobby set the fires and shot himself, the place was, even then, only a shadow of what I remembered . . . what Max had described so lovingly in *Gardens of Saturn*.

"Yeah, but I've been dealing with Max," I said.

"Well, does your offer still stand?"

Her hand turned under mine and her fingers intertwined with mine.

"What's that?"

"The one you made in Venice while we stood drooling at the bakery window."

"Oh, that one."

"At least now you really know what you're getting into, the bottom line—the bikini line." She rapped her knuckles on the cast with her free hand and a weak smile quivered on her lips as she turned to look at me full on for the first time. The blue expectancy in her eyes was like an electric jolt in my chest.

"Do I? Do you?"

"We can always pretend, just make it up as we go along."

"Take a page out of Max, huh, and just reinvent ourselves?"

She fitted herself into my arms and gave me a long, tender kiss.

"Then, since you're asking, the answer is *yes*. Especially since I've got nowhere else to go. I mean, I do, but I'm not interested in walking the streets of New York as an unemployed has-been."

I helped her up, giddy with impromptu joy, and handed her the crutches. She was already getting around on them as if they were added appendages, inconvenient but serviceable. We circled the veranda, careful of our steps, avoiding the broken and burned sections that were caving into the foundations. It had already been scavenged by kids from Pittsfield, who had left a scattering of beer cans in the rubble and spray-painted slogans—*Yo-ho-ho the wicked rich are dead* was one—or by architectural preservationists who wanted a memento of one of McKim, Mead & White's greatest country cottages. For me, the loss of the library was the real tragedy, with its signed first editions of James, Emerson, Thoreau, and Whitman, and John La Farge's sketches for the Winsted chapel windows, and Saint-Gaudens's studies for the Williams Memorial. I had no doubt that there were family letters, documents, and photographs that would have cast light on the strange life and disappearance of Pearce Breckenridge; and I couldn't help thinking how Bobby Williams, during his last years, left alone with his caretakers for months at a time, must have made his way through some of those letters and documents, possibly letters from General Alden, and come to many of the same conclusions that I had about Pearce Breckenridge. To this day, I never cease wondering what was going through Bobby's mind when he sent his caretaker on an errand to Pittsfield and began setting those fires: the hidden author to his soul's deepest yearnings.

We were about to leave, when Laura pointed down into the blackened timbers amid the fieldstone foundation walls, where wildflowers and ferns had begun to grow in earnest in the rubble.

"What's that?" she asked. "Can you get it?"

I eased myself off the veranda and carefully slid down a thick beam into the mess of the cellar, where a recent rainstorm had washed a glittering round object free of the ash and dirt. It was a Venetian paperweight, resplendent with colorful flowers and barely worse for wear. I rubbed it clean on my jeans and clambered back up with my prize.

"Well," she said, and tossed the paperweight in her hand so that it sparkled in the afternoon light, spinning like a roulette wheel, "travel light, travel light." She stuck it in her shorts, sighed, and went to flip off the Walkman radio, pausing as she detected a sound beyond my hearing. She put on the earphones for a moment and then placed them on my ears, as I had done that first day on Delos by the excavations. It was WGBH out of Boston, a Tanglewood concert by Malcolm Frager, playing a selection of Chopin nocturnes. I listened for a moment, my eyes tearing up, as did hers.

Before we drove our cars to Elsinore, we walked over to the fallout shelter and paused before the concrete ramp and stairs that led down fifteen feet to a huge steel door, which was standing ajar, emitting the musty smell of damp and decay and God knows what dead critters that had gone in there to eat the survival rations, or had simply starved after a long winter.

"He hid out down there in his last years," she said with a shiver, turning away.

"What do you suppose he was so scared of?"

"Was it the end of the world . . . or a KGB hit man?"

"He was right to be worried, even if he didn't quite make it to the end of their world. All it would have taken would have been a phone call."

"So I made a pact with the devil."

She gave it all a pitiless shrug, as I suppose I did, as well. But for a split second, I remembered that awful vision I'd had on the Circle all those years before, when I saw that wall of flame and superheated air engulfing everything we knew and loved, turning it to cinder and ash. And a moment later, Charles Fairburn appeared in my mind, black wingtips covered in wet grass, his hands exploring the ventilation cowlings of the Winsted gym, our blast bunker with its ten-foot concrete walls . . . built to save the boys. Charles, who, with that phone call to the Soviet embassy, had most likely put to rest Bobby's worst nightmares.

"Coming." She had turned back to me and must have seen something in my face . . . her little sin of omission.

I helped Laura unload some of her stuff from the back of the Volvo. "Everything I own is here," she said with a facetious shrug, gazing up at the house; "do you think it'll all fit?" I was walking on air, hovering between joy and sadness, pinching myself as I was overcome with the profound mystery of the life that surrounds us, and runs through us, and had, somehow, now brought us together. We barely spoke, as if afraid it might be an illusion that could be snatched away at any moment. I was embarrassed that she'd never been inside Elsinore, and it seemed a cosmic cruelty that it had been so, that her life had been such a crazy exile. She walked through the rooms as if in a daze, as if waking into some great forgiving heart of her long-lost self, as if memories or the ghosts of memories were rising around her. The violet-and-emerald light from the Tiffany skylights played over her face, as it had when Max first came up that spring so, so long ago. She ran her fingers over the gold-stamped titles of the morocco-bound volumes in the library, as Max's protagonist had in *Like a Forgotten Angel*; and when we got to the gallery of Innesses, she kept looking at me and then back at the landscapes, as if incredulous at such loveliness, and her eyes filled with tears of ineffable melancholy at those figures in the gloaming fields of Montclair, watching for husbands and sons and brothers who had never returned from southern battlefields. "Oh, Max . . . Max talked about these as if describing another country, somewhere over the rainbow." She insisted on hobbling up the fifty-three steps to my father's room, counting the stairs just as Max once had, as had his protagonist in *Like a Forgotten Angel*, where the sight of the desk, the computer screen replacing the typewriter, and the view over the lake to where Hermitage lay in ruins caused her to catch her breath in wonder. She sat in the desk chair, breathing hard from her climb, and just shook her head in astonishment.

"This is you; this is Max. This *is* the dream in the novel of how a certain room with a certain view would allow the writer to fathom the secrets of the known universe. Or was it the unknown universe? He talked about this place; he wrote about this place. I almost feel I've been here . . . like it's in my bones," and she gestured to the window and the pine boughs and the lake beyond, ". . . as if you've been spying on me."

"I have, worse than Max in all his wildest dreams. But without you doing the spadework, I'd never have found my way back here."

"But I feel that part of me belongs here, too . . . somehow."

"Elysium," I reminded her again, and I think I said it hopefully.

Her words were less a plea and more a joyous release from servitude. She wandered around the room in a happy, girlish daze as I pointed out everything to her, all the most recent reports from Brandt & Harrison out of East Germany, and, more recently, Greece, and even the redacted CIA report that had finally arrived. I told her about Pearce Breckenridge, and her eyes widened further, like those of a child being told a strange and even terrifying fairy tale: too fantastic to be true, too real not to be. More than once, her hand went to her face, as if examining her features for some flaw, some telltale sign; then her hand dropped to her side, in resignation or relief, I could not decide. And as they had for me, those rooms of memory began to shift for her, filling with unheard voices. I took down the framed postcard from the wall, the nineteenth-century photo of the glass vitrines containing the collections of the Museum of Antiquities in Leipzig, one of the nine postcards my father had posted home like messages in bottles cast into the sea.

"It's important that you remember the details of this: the postcard my grandmother framed, the two sent to my mother, stashed in her copy of a Hornblower novel, and, of course, the one you found among your mother's letters and things."

"Why me? Why does it matter?"

"You're witness that I didn't just make it all up—like Max made it all up."

I walked her to the map of East Germany pinned to the wall and pointed out Oderwitz and the eight other villages within a ten-mile radius, where he'd mailed the nine postcards. "He mailed them within days of one another from nine different villages. The Stasi files mention five intercepted postcards. He used my grandmother's, my mother's, and Suzanne's maiden names so as not to draw attention."

"So, only four of the postcards got though?"

"Amazing those got through with a U.S. address. A rash thing to send them. Seeing the postmarks, the Stasi or, more likely, the KGB figured out where he'd been hiding out in Oderwitz, and that he'd probably escaped across the Czech border."

"Why would he risk it?"

"To make sure his translation of the twelve Linear B tablets survived, to be numbered with the immortal archaeological—maybe literary—discoveries of all time."

"His three muses: mother, wife, and mistress—pretty pathetic . . . sorry."

"Who loved him—Joanna, too, who might cherish his more romantic dreams."

"How about to punish his nemesis."

"That, too, I suppose—justice or justification of a kind for stealing the tablets. I like to think he never quite knew what Karel Hollar was up to, even as he funded the damn thing . . . voices from the silent earth."

"What do you really think . . ."

"Me, I'd probably have done the same thing."

"No, I mean the text, the translation."

"A voyage . . . a homecoming . . . the groom arriving for his betrothed, to tell a story, to dream a dream?"

"A return to the beloved . . . a golden age."

"Maybe the ur-text, from which Homer got some part of his story."

Laura smiled with just a hint of chagrin. "Nausicaa . . . such an older guy's thing."

She turned to the window and the lowering sun and waved.

"Andiamo," she cried, "before the light is gone . . . before you or I change our minds."

Her pace along the root-strewn Eden Lake path, even with the crutches, was fast and agile. I was terrified that she'd fall as she swung herself along the overgrown and treacherous trail, hurtling around tree falls and exposed roots as if they were nothing. Gradually, her impetuosity eased, as if the woods were taking her over, like a map to her soul. Her pace slowed, a half smile on her lips as scenes of childhood met her around every turn. "A time before Mother was Mother, before the ballet thing came between us." When they had gathered flowers, gone mushrooming, and skinny-dipping in the lake, lying naked in the sunny meadow grass. "She was like a feral animal, you know, really . . . ever searching for its even wilder mate." She bared her teeth at me, as Max had in imitation of Bert Lahr's Cowardly Lion—"courage"—and continued. Laura could identify every wildflower, every tree, and the most indistinct birdcalls; she could even detect the difference between the wood thrush and the hermit thrush, far better than I could. When she spotted the flash of a scarlet tanager, she let out a shriek of joy that made me jump.

And with it came a realization sobering and sad and infinitely wonderful, that my father's love of the woods had come through Suzanne to her, in the years immediately after the war, before he returned to Greece, when they had roamed the woods as lovers will, when he had introduced her to his home ground, shared all the secrets of his childhood—their halcyon days, before Elliot ruined them at Princeton, which Suzanne, in turn, had shared with her daughter. Her dual loyalty, her duty, Suzanne had intimated to me at Hillders: a child with wings to do justice to her father, *a child who should shine forth . . . a light unto others*. When, by 1962, she was sure.

So I swallowed my hurt pride and embraced Laura's sweaty body and kissed her deeply, as if to drink of that dryadic love from her veins.

Of course, I knew where she was leading me, where she always believed—in the worst way—her life had come into being. She could barely restrain herself, hurrying along the path as the fading sunlight burnished the lake surface in spates of canary yellow and bronzy green, reflecting along the path in jagged tree-shadowed pools of emerald and gold. The russet carpet of needles laid down by the white pine perfumed the air and led us onward as my grandmother's Inness hour approached. I marveled at the new muscles in Laura's arms and shoulders, hardly the stuff of a fey Giselle. She had gained weight, good weight, no longer the fragile dancer taking those curtain calls, but a cunning creature of the woods, as would become even clearer to me on the following day.

Even in his eighties, Lew Boyd was a powerful and striking fellow with perpetually windblown white hair and huge calloused hands, who, as a young man back from service with the Army of the Potomac, loved nothing better than felling trees and pulling stumps with his team of oxen. It was said he could out-cuss the devil to get his ox team moving. When as a boy I knew Lew in the twenties, his stump-pulling days were long over and he spent his time keeping up his small farm and helping out Tom Malloy in caretaking for the Elysium syndicate. Tom Malloy was the son of the previous caretaker, Sean Malloy, who had died before my time. Tom's life had been saved by my father in France in 1918, with a line of fine embroidery across his chest to prove it. Never much for hard work, Tom was a superb hunter and fly fisherman, leaving the arduous tasks to Lew. (My mother recently admitted to me that Tom's job was a "lifetime sinecure," a legacy from General Alden, based on a promise to Tom's father, Sean Malloy, for what she described as "loyal services rendered.") Not something that I, nor Tom, nor even Lew, who had been around Elysium forever, had the slightest inkling about.

Lew Boyd, the last of the original settlers of the land that became Elysium, was a man of very few words. So I always kept an ear cocked when I tagged along on his rounds for those precious few utterances, which had the wonderful effect of populating the lonely woods for me. I find, even now, that I am haunted by Lew's stories, by the vast unknown of him and his lost country, of which he was the last of the breed.

"When a youngster like you, I used to see this Indian fellow with a government-issue blanket over his shoulders and a worn pair of gentleman's breeches. A face like dented tin. Barefoot, he was, and missing toes from frostbite. He'd show once or twice a week, looking for a handout or an odd job. He was the last Indian in this part of the Berkshires. One day, he never showed again. Either gone off like the rest or froze to death after too much to drink."

By the lake, there was an old pasture we referred to as "Pine Meadow," which had once belonged to an early settler in our woods. Lew would walk there with his scythe and mow it three or four times a summer. My grandfather had left a single great white pine to grow there, and Lew mowed the long grass and any small white pine sapling that might dare stick up its head. He took great care to mow around any boulders and hackberry bushes, leaving a fringe of grass stalks to set them off. Toward end of day, I would often see him walk Pine Meadow from the uphill end to the lower by the lake, shoring up a stone wall here or there, admiring the natural artifacts, of which he was the sole curator. In high summer, when his pasture was a rich velvety green, his boulders and bushes cast peculiar lilac shadows, like translucent pools of earth and sky, all overseen by the huge white pine. Once at the end of an afternoon of mowing, Lew stopped, wiped his brow, and stared out over the lake and the mantle of low hills covered in second-growth forest of mostly white pine. A breeze blew his scant white hair and a puzzled look came into his blue eyes. "My neighborhood has lost all its inhabitants," he said, as if struck with wonder at his own observation. "Once there were farms as far as the eye could see." He gestured broadly for my benefit. "Your age, I was never beyond earshot of the sound of an ax, or the dainty music of a cow's bell."

Imagine, a cow's bell at Elysium. I believe Lew's ashes were scattered at Pine Meadow, as I have asked mine to be.

　　　　　　　　　—excerpt from John Alden's Pankrác Prison diary

The sun dipped over the pine-serried horizon until the trail ahead of us was bathed in the most gorgeous translucent liquid light, turquoise greens in the ferns and laurel like throbbing vortexes in the understory of pine and hemlock and sweet birch, as this woodland world gave way to the old pasture we called Pine Meadow along the shoreline, where a heroic and gnarled first-growth white pine still presided over creation, spared by the first settlers and then by my great-grandfather and Lew Boyd.

I followed her into the long grass of the meadow, past the tumbled fieldstone walls of the first settlers, past the stands of mullein and purple thistle and Queen Anne's lace just bowing onto the summer stage, to where that massive giant of a first-growth pine with its titan's girth and sprawling arms overshadowed us, so unlike its tall, leggy progeny in the close-knit woods all around. This antediluvian had feasted in the sunlight of the abandoned pasture for hundreds of years, left in peace by the original settlers, who had preserved it as a reminder of all that had once been, now the oldest resident in our woods. Pine Meadow had been a place of refuge for children and adults, a site for picnics, a secluded spot for lovers' moonlit assignations, as it had been for my father and Suzanne. My father had loved nothing better than the excuse to walk Trudy, his golden retriever, there. In dry weather, the scent of pine and sweet fern in the meadow was enough to make you swoon.

Leaning against the great pine, we still had time as we watched the swollen mass of the red sun, like a warning flag above the distant treetops, impale itself and flounder; and then, in the far distance, a gash of searing pink opened on the underbelly of a line of white clouds, spilling out over the wounded surface of the lake. The sloping meadow was quite steep in places, and I was about to ask Laura if she wanted help to get to the water's edge, when she took matters in her own hand. She just dropped the crutches, lay down and crossed her arms across her chest, and rolled herself down the grassy incline, trailing shrieks and giggles. I found her lying at the water's edge, covered in grass and nettles and pine needles, laughing hysterically into the sky. I knew I'd glimpsed a moment out of her childhood with her mother—was everything so easily forgiven? And imagined how my father and Suzanne, in tight embrace, had rolled down that hillside, as perhaps he had once done with Bobby Williams when they were boys.

"Was that smart with your cast?"

"Don't be a scold or such a fraidy cat."

We sat for a few minutes more, watching over the lake as the day surrendered to dusk, as that wedge of pink cloud thinned and faded and flickered out as it had on Delos almost a year before. The dusk blew a purple haze over our world. A simulacrum of the thoughtless, careless numbing of childhood, before there is a past worth fathoming and the future encompasses only the next mealtime. Before the river of Time was even a trickle. A pale, bloated moon nudged the titan pine on the slope behind us, a huge eye waiting in the wings for the night to birth its full glory. Then, as if a signal had been given, a great blue heron took off from a marshy area across the lake and winged low and steady, accompanied by its watery twin. Swallows dashed and darted and faded as bats spelled their ranks against the incipient stars. Down the lake, on the edge of the far northern sky, Draco slithered into view above the trees, long ago cast into the outer darkness by Athena, where she fixed this monstrous serpent at the very pole of heaven.

I was startled, as if by the voice of the goddess's mortal self.

"I'm going for a swim."

She had shed her shirt and bra and was struggling with the sneaker on her left foot.

"You're crazy! You can't go in with that cast. It's heavy; you can't get the inner liner wet."

"Oh fuck, you're right—you're so damned practical. Are you always going to be so practical?"

"Better safe than sorry."

"I want a swim in the worst way—and I've got to pee."

I couldn't take my eyes off Laura, her skin so white and glowing in the blur of the gray-green grass—the white of an angel's wing against the luminous water of the lake—or was I just confusing her with someone else's character in a novel?

"Okay, you go—swim for me, young man—swim and return to me and tell me of your roving adventures and all that you've found—go."

"Swim, in the dark?"

"Christ sake, and it's so fucking awkward peeing with this cast."

"Okay, okay . . ."

"I'll be he-e-e-re . . . waiting."

I stripped off my clothes and walked into the warm embrace of the moonlit lake. I hated the mucky bottom and quickly dived for deeper water, out of range of the snappers. I swam far out and turned on my back to look at the moon behind the titan pine, where its groping shadow reached across the meadow to the shore. The pain in my back eased as the water buoyed me up, as it had my father when he'd swum with his two-year-old son out to the float, holding me up to the star-laden sky. I drifted, arms and legs spread wide, staring up as even more stars sifted free, feeling the silent currents of the lake, poured from hidden springs, wash away the months of anxious waiting and watching and searching. And in that lustral sensation, something more. The fear of night's waters was replaced by a deep sensual gratification, as if it had always been second nature, as if my grandmother had told me as much herself—about her secret nocturnal swims across the lake to her assignations with her lover Amaryllis, who not only brought her alive sexually but set down her hot-blooded eroticism and beauty on canvas after canvas, keeping her forever young and beautiful in the eyes of collectors and art lovers. That promise of love, of eternity, soon brought me gliding back to shore like the shipwrecked stranger of lore.

She was waiting for me up the hill, as if sheltering at the feet of a titan. She was out of her clothes, lying on her back moon-bathing, and I saw her open her eyes, as if I'd suddenly awakened her from a nap or a dream.

"Oh, there you are. I've been waiting for you." And she placed a musky-tasting finger in my mouth for me to lick.

I bent down in the tall grass to kiss her, but she would not have it. Instead, she began to lick me and rub herself against me and smell me and lick me some more, nuzzling my hair and pressing her lips and tongue into my flesh as if starved, desperate to taste the lake.

"Kiss me now," she finally whispered. "My Odysseus, my Telemachus, my Albrecht—do you mind if I include him, them, in our story, for a little while longer?—my shipwrecked stranger . . . whoever you are, I'm all yours."

"My Nausicaa."

"Hey, that's as good a name as any. Wasn't she once a great ballerina?"

She was wonderfully warm against my chilled lake-damp skin. Moving into her as the forest titan's shadowed arms embraced us was like giving in to the purest gravity, like a hidden wave moving across a hidden sea. Sometimes when I paused, when she pressed me upward to give herself room and to adjust her cast, I could see the stars reflected in her eyes, or perhaps it was the moonlight flickering between the branches above us, shining in her lustral eyes. She had her hand down between us, her fingers moving where we were connected to keep pace, moving to urge me on as she was urging herself. It was like merging into a dream with the wind at your back, like kites rising off that hillside and soaring into the moonlight.

And so we sank our claim to that sacred place, to that abandoned hillside pasture and the past's presiding presence, sharing our secrets with those who had come before and were no more and so became one with the cradling silence of all who venture out on the river of Time.

Later, a little exhausted as we stared up into the vastness of space, she leaned over and kissed my lips and gently spread a drop of semen on my cheek.

"For luck, what do you think—pretend luck, do we still need it?"

"Not now, not here—we're safe now."

"Out here, I feel like I've been fucked by all creation—how safe is that?"

She laughed, and like a little girl performing her favorite trick, she grabbed me and told me to hold on to her tightly, and we rolled our way down the hillside, chortling like wicked children. There, at the shoreline, where the grass grew longest, where bunches of blue flags leaned out as if to lap the water with their thirsty tongues, she slipped her left leg into the shallows and tapped out ripples to the distant horizon . . . a naiad transformed by love, goddess Athena or mortal Nausicaa . . .

"Are we really, safe," she asked?

"Never, not without all the answers—or at least the most important ones."

"Always the scholar—well, I have something for you back at the house."

"Yes?"

"Certainty, of a kind. But that can wait, at least until tomorrow. And then, maybe, we'll have to come up with our own answers . . . our pretend stories to see us through."

And yet her face was full of uncertainty.

The next morning, after breakfast, after I'd helped her unload most of her stuff from her Volvo, we climbed the stairs to my workroom, where she handed me a book and a packet of documents.

"I stole these—what, almost two years ago now—with the love letters. They were in my mother's closet in the colonel's home when she was lying close to death at the Spaulding Rehabilitation Hospital."

I kept glancing to her concerned, quivering, guilty face as I began to go through them.

"You're telling me this—showing me this—now?"

"I'm not proud, Peter. Frankly, I'm aghast."

I fingered the signed copy of Kim Philby's autobiography published in the West two years before, which she'd told me about along with the inscription. Among the documents was a photostat from a 1947 top secret report that disclosed developments of an American superbomb, a hydrogen weapon, revealing that the Americans had abandoned the electromagnetic method of separating the isotopes of uranium 238 because of inconsistencies, opting for a diffusion method. The page included a sketch of the hydrogen bomb's mechanism and estimates that the Americans planned to produce fifty bombs a year. The official letterhead of the U.S. Atomic Energy Commission was proof positive that the document could only have come from Donald Maclean at the British embassy in Washington. The second document was a cable message from Moscow Center to the Soviet consulate in New York—meant for Kim Philby, the first secretary at the British embassy in Washington—in which the Hungarian town of Beloyannis appeared, along with the warning about Maclean's imminent arrest in London. I pointed to the critical passage.

> . . . Very pleased to have this information about Achilles [John Alden]. The child, we believe, is with the Greek Communist resettlement in Beloyannis, Hungary. Perhaps tempt Achilles with this information; tell him it comes from MI6 sources, and then carefully explore to see how eager he might be to get the boy returned to his mother. . . .

"You," I screamed, "had this—this—the name of the Hungarian town the whole damn time?"

"I didn't know what it meant until—"

"Joanna, when she told us what happened to Giannis?"

"Maybe, maybe then. I don't know; I wasn't exactly thinking straight."

"This confirms precisely what Karel Hollar told me in Prague, that my father had gone to Philby, unsuspecting, for help finding out what happened to Joanna's son."

"So, thank me," she pleaded.

"Thank you—Jesus. Do you know what an actual communication from Moscow Center to an agent like Philby means?"

"My mother had him by the balls."

"This"—and I shook the document in front of her nose— "would convict for treason in any court of law here or in England."

She took my hand for a moment to calm me.

I went through what remained. There was a used Pan Am ticket from New York to London, dated October 7, 1954, along with a London Underground ticket from the Ruislip tube station dated October, 8, 4:34 P.M., and a stained cork coaster from a nearby pub, the St. George's on Victoria Road. There was also a wine-stained BOAC roundtrip air ticket from June of 1962, Boston to London.

"That's it?" I asked. I examined the coaster and held it up to my nose; the smell of whiskey was still distinct.

"I sent the originals of the letters, and these documents, back to her at Hillders; that's in the agreement our lawyers worked out."

"'Agreement?'"

"You get to see these and then I put them in the hands of lawyers for safekeeping."

"Until?"

"Both of us agree not to publish anything about any of this until after her death—the colonel's, too. I play the dutiful daughter on all special occasions."

"What do you get out of it?"

She shook her head violently and caught her breath, closing her eyes a moment to inhale deeply.

"I get to fucking pretend—that's what—like we said. *I get you*, I guess, *and* your father . . . all spelled out in an affidavit in the possession of both our lawyers to be released after their deaths."

"Wouldn't a blood test be easier?"

"No blood tests. . . . Let's just keep a smidgen of doubt . . . to pretend."

"If she's so bloody sure—do you believe her or not?"

She reached out. "Kiss me, and not a pretend kiss."

I kissed her and held her, thinking I could let it go.

"Well," I said, looking over the documents again. "Her insurance against . . . Fuck, these would stand up in court as concrete damning proof beyond a reasonable doubt. Enough to have convicted Maclean and Burgess, Blunt and Philby, put them all away. The government prosecutors of Alger Hiss didn't have evidence half as good."

"'The end of the world, as she called it.'" She took my hand. "I just needed time; we needed time."

I was pretty steamed up, feeling not a little betrayed that she'd withheld this from me over all the months we'd been together. Sandbagged, more like it. Just like her mother, she'd kept something back, something in reserve . . . just in case. But she was right: We'd needed the time, the ambiguity.

"Retribution, I wonder." I nodded. "Even now, with the wall down?"

I could see something in her face, a hesitancy, a question that burned in the blue of her eyes. And, as if needing to further scrutinize something in her soul, I opened the Philby memoir to read the inscription, which she'd first recited to me in Nafplio. "For Suzanne, a love never betrayed. And you, my darling, the best of all. But six in one life? I think not! Kim."

A faded color snapshot with a deckle edge tumbled from between the pages. It was of a little girl staring up with wide eyes. I held it up to the light and handed it to her.

"Cute kid. Is it you?"

"It is. I suppose she gave it to him at the St. George's pub in 1954, and he returned it thirty years later with the book."

I checked the inscription again and looked at her. "'But six in one life? I think not!' You never mentioned that part?"

She shrugged. "Well, he would, wouldn't he? I think when she got the memoir, after he died—that's what got her drinking again, putting her in detox at Spaulding."

I tried to contain my exasperation.

"What? He had four wives and five children. . . . That meeting in 1954 . . ." I picked up the Ruislip tube ticket and the coaster from the St. George's pub, assessing their almost intangible weight. "An excuse for a meeting that could have meant Philby's execution for treason if they'd been discovered." I shot her a pained glance, recalling Elliot's words to me over the phone just weeks before. "So, she really pulled it off, got past the MI5 watchdogs who had him under surveillance twenty-four/seven."

"She told me she hated Philby with a hatred that would fill an ocean, but she tends to hyperbole when she's been drinking."

"Perhaps not in 1954, when she—used you—pleaded for his help to get my father out. But by 1962—when she'd decided who the father really was, what Philby had done—she probably meant every word of it."

I walked to the open window, took a couple of deep breaths, and then went over to my wall map.

"Beloyannis, Beloyannis . . . there," and I pointed to the name of the Hungarian town mentioned in the cable from Moscow Center on the large map of East Germany, Czechoslovakia, and Hungary tacked to the paneling. And as I touched the map, it all came clear in my mind.

I took another deep breath. "Did she know—did she realize who Achilles was, the significance?"

Laura nodded thoughtfully and grimaced. "I don't think so. It never came up, anything about Hungary or Joanna's child. She's intellectually flabby—really; it's all emotion with her: first impressions, instinct, and impetuous passion. Such details—anything not about herself—bored her."

"And you never mentioned Joanna or the child?"

"Not a whisper."

"But surely Philby would have told her . . . or not."

"What did you say about him? The consummate professional—operating on a need-to-know basis, never mixing business with pleasure, never giving more information than was required by the moment."

"She was just the courier"—I fingered the message from Moscow Center—"the go-between, the cutout, and yet . . . she carried the message that would lead to the death of her lover." I eyed Laura, shaking my head, wondering which one of us needed more convincing about the tragedy of the thing. "Damn it, you should've told me about these, the inscription, the photo, I could have been more exacting in getting the truth out of Karel Hollar. And your mother."

"Clearly, you've missed your true calling."

"Fuck you."

"I didn't know how you'd react, what you might do. Like you said, dynamite . . . in the wrong hands."

"You didn't know whether to trust me. So what's different now?"

"I love you. I trust you. I need you. And I'll pretend anything to keep you."

She came to me and placed her head on my chest. We embraced and kissed and I held her in my arms and looked into her teary eyes.

"And the colonel's money?"

"My insurance in case you dump me."

"Tell him you don't need it."

"You tell him."

"Well, he's got something I want, as well."

"Enough to be dutiful children."

I returned to the map on the wall and pointed.

"You see . . . the place along the Czech border where he was captured is only a few miles north of Beloyannis, where many of the Greek Communist refugees and the kidnapped children were relocated."

"It would have been suicidal," she protested. "Don't you think?"

"I suspect that plan A also included an offer to Hollar, a deal: If Hollar got the boy out, or helped him get the boy out, the defection would go ahead and my father would forget about the charges of war crimes. Besides, Philby was the real prize. He may have been a gambler, but he wasn't a fool. . . . I think he felt he owed at least that much to Joanna."

"Well, I guess *you* should know."

"Got any better ideas?"

"Three years before, he'd spent eighteen months in Athens helping destroy the Greek Communists. Hardly a man to be welcomed in such a place."

"He had a hundred thousand dollars in cash and gold; he spoke Greek like a Greek and German like a German, and the Hungarians were lousy Communists . . . And he'd just translated the most important document in ancient archaeology since the Rosetta stone. Maybe he thought he was on a roll."

"Until the Czech guards on the Hungarian border . . ."

"They must have been waiting for him." I sighed, grimacing, as I held up the message from Moscow Center containing the name Beloyannis. "Or, at the very least, they must have been alerted by his real nemesis."

"Yes, probably . . . yes . . . something like that." As if it had almost become a habit, she reached to her nose, her lips, and then quickly pulled her hand away.

I handed her the BOAC ticket to London from June 1962 and forced a smile. "Until she discovered who you really were."

"Yes . . . 1962 was a good year for me. It all came together."

"I'll give my lawyers the name of the Hungarian town, Beloyannis. Maybe it's just the thing, the breakthrough they've been looking for."

"And if he'd made it out of Hungary, made it back?" She looked fiercely into my eyes. "Who would he have chosen?"

I took the measure of her intent stare, realizing for the first time just how much my answer to that question meant to her.

"You're relentless, you know, just like your mother."

"Just one thing: Never, never call me Port again."

And that's when it came to me: It was all about choices, about loyalty. To do what he did, my father had to have made a choice and decided where his ultimate loyalty lay. And with that question from Laura's lips, the answer came to me, if not in that second, certainly in the days and weeks that followed, all of it building on Suzanne's daughter's absolute determination, her guilt, her love, her grit as she struggled to regain her mobility and establish herself in an alien home and build a life with the man she'd chosen against all the odds, and even nature itself. Just dealing with her feisty independent streak, not a little overwhelming at times—the frisson of her wild swings of emotion—I discovered in myself a kind of dynamic empathy for all the people I had cared for and those I had not. As their lives and times—everything I'd been tracking through the details of letters and diaries, the data points in crumbling documents, and the snatches of remembered conversations passed on to me—began to take shape, a pattern emerged. Brandt & Harrison's final intelligence reports provided an armature for the whole. It allowed me to make the final leap of imagination, and the dry facts to take wing. I began to feel the inner workings of my father's mind as if it were mine. I could feel him yielding, finally, to the woman he loved and hated, and to the ambitions of youth and his talent for subterfuge—that "fire and motion of the soul," noted by Virgil Dabney . . . and his grandfather's call to justice, which led him to risk all.

And that is how, as summer waned, as our days at Elysium unfolded together, as I typed away at my computer, as Laura got her cast removed and began to teach herself to walk again, as we made frantic love again and again and again in the torpid evenings at Pine Meadow, I discovered the answer to what had happened between my father and Suzanne on their last night together at Elysium, the twenty-seventh of September, 1953, at Pine Meadow. I yielded the field to Max by re-creating what must have been, had to have been for everything else to have made sense, dipping my oar into the river of Time, thereby allowing their lovers' shadows to gain form and substance and so move on.

"What did Charles mean that Laura is his daughter?"

"Oh, darling, it's nothing; he's been in love with me since I was thirteen."

"A man doesn't say something like that unless he's fucked the woman in question and she's made paternity claims on him."

"Don't be ridiculous. Charles and I are more like brother and sister; we're first cousins, for Christ's sake."

"Why would he tell me such a thing if it were not possible and you'd led him to believe as much?"

"He's delusional; he's still not over losing Cecily and the children. He blames himself, poor man. I feel desperately sorry for him."

"You're lying again."

"I've never lied to you."

"You just did."

"Oh, all right, it was just once, when I was already pregnant and you were being your fiendishly elusive self. I thought it would be good for him, give him something to live for, a little hope perhaps."

"Your lying insurance."

"That way, he wouldn't always be wondering whose it was. Bobby, too—surely you can understand the usefulness of such a white lie."

"From a den of conspirators, a lie as insignificant as a fart on the breeze."

"Please, Laura's going to be a most beautiful, most wonderful woman."

"You probably lied to me about Philby, too. Goddamn him. You probably fucked him, as well. Laura's not his daughter, is she? My God—the way you flaunted your daughter to him that night at Hermitage. I couldn't take that."

"Now you're being absolutely ridiculous."

"When I got back from Greece, you were a bitch in heat. If it wasn't here, it was in New York. Always wanting to meet in New York, always on the same days of the month—even after I married Mary."

"I only wanted you, forever."

"You were a courier, first for Maclean, then for him. It's Philby's child; admit it."

"Don't demean yourself with such idiocies."

"Kim had to have been forewarned about Maclean. Did Moscow warn him, through you? Or did Philby warn Moscow about the decrypted Soviet cables that pointed to Maclean? Damn you."

"Moscow be damned, and Kim—you know how brilliant he is: the fox never to be run to ground."

"Sounds like you're not a little in love with our dear Kim."

"He was close with my brother. I ran in his antifascist circles. . . . We believed . . . in a new world—a better world. We faced the terror of discovery and dishonor together. Surely you can understand that much."

"I saw you with him that evening on the piazza at Hermitage."

"A performance entirely for your benefit. Don't you understand? You're the only man I've ever truly loved, fool that I am."

"Then give him up, testify that he recruited you. If you give them Kim, they'll forget about everything else and leave you be—Bobby, too."

"I can't do that—you know I can't."

"They can be discreet about your testimony, and if necessary, the FBI can protect you. Confession, if not pleading the Fifth, is now all the rage in your Red circles."

"They'd hunt me down to the ends of the earth. What do you think happened to all those witnesses in the Alger Hiss trial? Harry Dexter White poisoned, Duggan pushed out a sixteenth-floor window, and that poor man at the Justice Department, falling six stories."

"Do you know that? Or are you just posturing?"

"It would be the end of me, without you. And Laura *is* yours."

"So prove it. Give up Philby."

"Oh, how fine you'll look to your pals, how safe and sound. Won't Elliot be pleased, and fucking Nigel."

"And Charles."

"*And* Charles."

"You're a liar—all you people live and breathe lies like the fumes of Hades."

"Nine million Soviet soldiers died fighting the fascists."

"A drop in the bucket compared to Stalin's hecatombs. And now they've got the bomb, too."

"All your fancy words."

"And my mother's little bombshell."

"Bombshell?"

"Oh, nothing. Ancient family history she's dredged up about my grandfather. Talk about lies and deceit . . . a terrible crime of revenge. There seems—the world turned upside down—no end to it."

"Isn't that what you're asking of me . . . revenge?"

"Justice, so I'd like to believe."

"Kiss me."

"I'm exhausted."

"So prove you love me."

"How many times does it take?"

"Not that . . ."

"Not what?"

"Divorce Mary and marry me and make your daughter legitimate."

"So, you really did fuck Charles just to throw him off the scent. . . ."

"A kindness. Surely you can understand that. If I need him, to keep fucking MI5 close."

"Or would Bobby prefer Kim for his progeny?"

"Look at you . . . you're already hard. Cowards don't get hard like this. . . . Divorce her and make us whole."

"You're a fucking liar."

"Your cock never lies."

"Enough, I've got to get back. It's late, a long drive tomorrow."

"Stay, stay. . . . Divorce her and I will give up Kim on our wedding day. To the FBI, to Nigel and MI5, to Charles—to all the fucking fascist bastards you can name."

"Liar."

"I swear, on my daughter's life. And I've got what it takes to put him away, all of them, for good, forever."

"You don't have . . . You kept something—documents?"

"Fuck me now to seal our pact. Fuck me here, and here—everywhere, deep as the ocean, vast as the sky . . . like we did in the old days in Cadogan Gardens, under the searchlights, under the buzz bombs. Let the immortal stars be our blood oath and have done with this fucking terrible world."

The moment I finished writing the above, I knew it was the truth, had to be the truth: the truth of the desire that rules our lives, as Max always maintained in his fictions. I knew in my bones that if my father had managed to escape from Hungary, as he'd planned, he'd have divorced my mother and married Suzanne. Holding her to her promise—*and* she had the evidence. And so he'd have revenged himself on Philby (the man who'd caused the death of hundreds of Albanian saboteurs dropped into Albania in the late forties by the CIA). In 1954, at the very least—with the secret documents in Suzanne's possession—Philby would have been put away in prison for the rest of his life, instead of living out his life, first in Beirut, and then for twenty-five years as the revered doyen of Soviet intelligence in his Moscow flat.

The truth of my fictional account of their final assignation in Pine Meadow, much less her final meeting with Philby at the St. George's pub in 1954, has held up over time, confirmed some years later in a memoir by Yuri Modin, Kim Philby's and Anthony Blunt's London handler:

> In October of 1954 Anthony Blunt contacted me for an important meeting in London. He'd spoken with Kim Philby, a pass-by one minute conversation at a Courtauld Institute lecture. Philby warned him of an American agent being held by the East Germans, a man who knew him and possibly had conclusive evidence of his work with the KGB. I passed this warning to Moscow Center.
>
> —Yuri Modin, *My Cambridge Network: Burgess, Maclean, Philby, Blunt, and Cairncross* (Transaction Press, 1993)

A slipup in judgment that Suzanne took care of in her own way eight years later, in 1962.

Would Suzanne have given up Philby in 1954—if my father had been traded for those three KGB agents—when she still wasn't sure who her daughter's father was? When she'd tempted her comrade of over fifteen years to a dangerous clandestine meeting to plead for help, with a photo, she'd claimed, of his daughter, as a pledge of good faith?

Absolutely, because her life was a lie. And Philby knew her as well as anyone, and knew precisely what she was capable of.

Although Laura, being Laura, penciled into the margin of my manuscript where her mother pledges to give up Philby in return for my father divorcing his wife: "If he'd agreed to her terms, if he believed she'd do it, then going after Hollar was really about Joanna's son and the Linear B tablets—and the prosecution for war crimes in Pylos."

Either way, he was going to hold MI5's feet to the fire, and see Philby convicted.

Laura never followed up with her mother on any of this, feeling that the truth would only hasten her precipitous decline: that the man she'd loved—with or without her promise of betrayal—had, nevertheless, risked his life—their life—for another woman's son . . . and a bunch of stone tablets.

Suzanne died in 1994 of cirrhosis of the liver, still believing she'd been forever loyal to my father, to his daughter, even if her plea for my father's release to Kim Philby at the St. George's pub in June of 1954 had resulted in his execution. As she had hoarsely whispered in my ear as we parted at Hillders: "My one misstep, my one slipup . . . will you forgive me, darling—please?"

What, in retrospect, seems insanity, an impossible mission, I now know my father believed he could pull off: get his son out of Hungary, the Linear B tablets and Hollar out of the GDR, where he could testify against Philby (with or without MI5's blessing) in exchange for a plea bargain on reduced charges for war crimes in Pylos. This ending allows my father to claim the crown of laurels, finding and translating the most important document in Bronze Age archaeology—a story that predates Homer and even rivals his epic authorship—and so, at last, return in triumph to the arms of his lover in Pine Meadow. After all, he'd led a charmed life, one in which his talent and desires had trumped all adversity. The sorceress's vision conjured by his beloved, an incandescence of love and sex and ambition mixed . . . a fire quenchless and insatiable. I wish for an alternate ending, that he was on his way back to me and my mother and grandmother at Elysium, but it was not to be. Instead, he left us with his own alternate ending.

52

WE NEVER DID TELL SUZANNE THE TRUTH about my father's end. Need to know. The information was delivered to us by Federal Express in late summer at Elysium. Brandt & Harrison's hot lead from a Soviet defector, Dimitri—yes, Elliot's Dimitri—finally came through in August. Dimitri was an old-school NKVD man who had a bad conscience and needed money, pronto, to get out while the going was good and start a new life in the West.

In late November 1954, after all the arrangements had been completed for an exchange of my father for three-top level KGB agents, a special team was sent from Moscow to Prague to take care of the logistics. Dimitri had been part of the KGB interrogation team in Prague at Pankrác Prison. He said they had interrogated my father intensely but not brutally. They knew exactly who he was, and John Alden hid nothing from them except, of course, secrets that might compromise other CIA assets or agents or his country. He told them he had been interested in working with the Linear B tablets stolen from Greece during the war, and that his onetime colleague Karel Hollar had double-crossed him and so he'd shot him in revenge. He made it clear that he'd hoped to recover the Greek child for his mother. He pleaded that his actions were primarily motivated by private matters. Dimitri said they actually believed him for the most part. Dimitri had read my father's Pankrác diary, and it generally fitted the facts as he stated them under interrogation and what they already knew.

"He was a big CIA fish; he was worth a lot. For propaganda, very much and, yes, to get some of our best boys back. They were comrades of mine. Stalin was dead; things were much more relaxed. We were ready to make the exchange, when something suddenly changed."

The special team that arrived from Moscow was headed by Dr. Grigory Moiseevich Mairanovsky, a colonel in the NKVD Medical Corps.

"This doctor, if he can be dignified as such a man, was Stalin's favorite executioner, for all his special cases. When I saw Mairanovsky come in the door, I lost all heart."

Mairanovsky, according to Dimitri, had huge bushy eyebrows, ears that stuck out, and reptilian eyes; he was a professor of pathophysiology, with a specialty in toxic poisons, which were administered to his many victims in his Lubyanka laboratory. He pioneered the Soviet use of traceless poisons as a means of execution.

"We told our CIA man that he was being exchanged, that he was going home in time for Christmas, back to the West. The relief on his face made me feel terrible. But first he needed to be checked by medical personnel so that there would be no question of our having tortured him. So we led him into the prison medical facility, where the doctors would give him a checkup before his exchange in Berlin. Mairanovsky waited for him there with a pleasant smile, 'Stalin's Mengele,' we called him. He asked the prisoner to lie on the examination table, where he checked his heart and pulse, his eyes and throat. Then he gave the prisoner an injection. He said it was vitamins; he said prison food was always deficient in vitamins."

At that point, Dimitri and the other NKVD men were asked to leave the room.

My father was injected with curare, a poison, a brackish resin extracted from tropical plants of the genus *Strychnos*. South American Indians still use curare as a way of poisoning their prey and paralyzing them. The poison has the effect of constricting every muscle in the body, including the heart. It takes only minutes for all nerve impulses from the brain and spinal cord to the muscles to cease functioning.

Mairanovsky carefully cataloged in a KGB handbook the symptoms as death takes hold:

Loss of voice and strength, muscular weakness, prostration, labored breathing, cyanosis and death with symptoms of suffocation while retaining complete consciousness. Death was excruciating, but the subject was deprived of the ability to shout or move while retaining complete awareness. Death of the "patient" ensued within ten to fifteen minutes after a sufficient dosage. In all autopsy reports, no traces of the poison whatsoever have been found.

His body was turned over to U.S. officials in West Berlin two days later. The autopsy and pathologist's report revealed nothing.

Laura and I read this report on the back porch at Elsinore, overlooking the lake. For minutes, we couldn't get a word out. Finally, we broke down in tears and held each other. For days, we found it hard to sleep, or eat, or make love. It was as if something in us had died. I was haunted by the phrase "retaining complete consciousness." Sitting at my computer, I became obsessed with what had passed through my father's mind in those final ten or fifteen minutes, when he thought he was returning home, and then . . . not. In my imagination, I see him lying there on an examination table in a dingy room with a single lightbulb, staring up at the flickering light in the concrete ceiling, remembering the women he loved, the children he'd left behind, the meadow by the lake, where, perhaps, he'd been happiest . . . and the scent of tall pines . . . and sex.

Of course, I told nothing of this to Joanna a few months later when we met in Budapest. I pretended something quite different. Laura and I told her what we knew, that we had evidence from documents that John had intended to locate her son, their son, in Hungary, pay a ransom for his release, and so return Gianni to her.

Brandt & Harrison had finally turned up the crucial information about Joanna's kidnapped son. It had taken scores of interviews and bribes and the crucial nugget of information, the name of a Hungarian town which Laura had provided. My team at the firm believed they had it narrowed down to a few Greek exile communities north of Budapest; now they focused on the village called Beloyannis, named after a martyred Communist leader. Months before, they had traced a number of orphaned Greek boys from the area of northern Greece where Joanna had been trapped by the civil war to Beloyannis; those without families had been placed with new families, and many had moved on to other Greek exile communities throughout Eastern Europe and the Soviet Union. By 1990, most of the kidnapped children were in their forties; many had learned Hungarian and married Hungarians and had been largely assimilated. With this information and the whittling down of names and some hard sifting of government identity documents with the eager assistance of Hungarian authorities who were only too happy for the U.S. dollars liberally dispensed, Brandt & Harrison rounded up a dozen possible matches for Joanna. I was not eager to put her through the heartache and frustration, but she was game to try, although she was quite fatalistic about the possibilities. "The time is late," she told us, "so much time has passed. . . ."

Laura and I had flown to Budapest in early November of 1990, a year after the fall of the Berlin Wall. We met Joanna at the splendid Budapest Hilton on the Danube, which looked as if the Cold War had never happened. After eating like royalty in Budapest for nickels and dimes, we drove to the town of Beloyannis the following morning, where the Brandt & Harrison team had brought together a number of possible candidates. Joanna interviewed six or seven that first day, and it was so awkward and surreal that everyone despaired. Many of the men no longer spoke Greek, or spoke it haltingly, and their memories were so vague about their childhoods in Greece and the traumas they'd experienced during the civil war that they either couldn't remember critical details about their parents and the villages they'd been taken from or they'd managed to forget the most nightmarish parts.

But when we returned the next day for the second round of interviews, Joanna immediately spotted a dark-haired man sitting in the corner of the office of the local school, where we were set up. She went right over and sat next to him and introduced herself. His name was Kostas, which made us all bristle. He was soft-spoken, shy, and had lustrous dark eyes. Joanna turned to me more than once as they awkwardly conversed. I looked at Laura and she at me, as if we recognized the similarity of the faces. Kostas spoke almost no Greek and only vaguely remembered his mother as a tall woman whom he'd seen only occasionally. All he really remembered was being herded around with other children, being scared all the time, always cold and hungry. Kostas had a Hungarian wife and son and worked as a mechanic in a suburb of Budapest. All he ever knew or had been told about his background was that he was named after a Greek Communist patriot, but he could no longer even remember who had first told him this. After the Hungarian uprising against the Soviets in 1956, and the Magyars' inherent dislike of anything to do with communism, many of the old-line Greek Communist exiles had fallen away from the cause and slipped back into Greece, or been assimilated into Hungarian society. This had been the case with Kostas. Joanna was clearly distressed and frustrated, and poor Kostas seemed uneasy in his role as lost son.

We were about to go on to the other candidates, who were patiently waiting in the office, when Laura bent to Joanna and whispered something in her ear. Joanna smiled and nodded with a distant, somewhat dubious expression on her long, angular face.

She looked directly into Kostas's eyes.

"'Like angels stopped upon the wing by sound of harmony from Heaven's remotest spheres . . .'"

Kosta's ebony brown eyes flashed with recognition and his face became alert. He bent closer to Joanna, as if he hadn't quite heard what she'd said. "What," he asked in broken Greek, "what did you say?"

She repeated the lines of Wordsworth, stopping halfway and, with an expectant smile playing on her sensuous lips, bending to Kostas as if to prompt a child.

"'. . . by sound of harmony from Heaven's remotest spheres . . .'" It was as if he were recalling a dream, his accent utterly unlike anything he'd said up to that moment.

We were hearing a ghost. Laura and I grabbed hands like terrified children. Joanna's eyes welled with tears and she reached out her arms, and Kostas, as if in a hypnotic trance, simply gave himself to his mother's embrace.

Later, I embraced Kostas, and Laura did too, our tears dispersing the heartache of a terrible century, finally on the mend.

I told my half brother that his father had died trying to reach him and obtain his release back to his mother. I spent hours filling him in on his father's life. I assured him that in his last hours, dying of an infected wound in a Prague prison, his lost son and—here, I took Joanna's hand in mine—the mother of his love child had been on his mind. I'm sure that had been the case, even if he could not have written as much in his Pankrác diary. I offered Kostas funds to relocate to Greece if he and his family so desired, along with housing and financing to start a garage business, if that appealed. We also invited them both to visit us in America, at Elysium.

Joanna laughed and Kostas smiled at the thought of America.

"Tall trees," said Joanna. "Tall trees against the sky."

"Yes," I replied. "White pines . . . the smell of the needles in the summer heat is like the ambrosia of the gods."

Laura and I then took the train to Prague, a Prague transformed, to spend a few days with Vlada. The specialists in Vienna had done wonders for his jaw and teeth, although he was still plagued by headaches and memory loss as he struggled to recover his health. We were moved by his optimism and confidence that everything would now be possible. And when I told him something of my weeks in Pankrác Prison, and the stories told me by Karel Hollar, his face became rapt with attention. I felt sure that, presented with such rich material, he was bound to steal it for his own work. I encouraged him to return to America, to spend time with us, which he would, in years to come.

The manuscript of his novel was never recovered. Saddest of all, he found himself unable to re-create his "American" novel, which he had committed to memory while in solitary confinement. In later years, he wrote and phoned me, asking me for details about our time at Winsted together, and what I remembered of the stories he had told me about his travels that summer of 1968. Sometimes when I got off the phone, I had tears in my eyes. I still have bad dreams: images of the stock of a Kalashnikov like a piston pump into the side of his jaw. Nor was he able to adjust entirely to the new freedoms in post-Velvet Revolution Czechoslovakia. A promising political career was short-circuited when conflicting reports emerged from his secret police files, implicating him as an informer on his fellow dissidents. He told me it was all disinformation planted by his first great love, Natalie, the Olympic gymnast, whom he had abandoned while at Winsted when she turned against the Dubček government. Vlada is now a professor at Charles University, as was his father, teaching American literature. Max's books figure large in his teaching curriculum, and his connection to Max has made him a minor celebrity in Czech academic circles. "My young students love his books, but my early stories they find incomprehensible," he told me.

Later, his sad ironies prompted me to tell my students to hold defeat as close as victory. If it hadn't been for that Alden scholarship and Vlada, I would never have gone to Vietnam; I would never have gone to Prague and come across Karel Hollar, nor gained access to that holograph copy of my father's Pankrác diary, of which no other copy has been found in Czech files or in Soviet KGB files, although the Soviet-era intelligence archives were precipitously closed to Western scholars after the heady days of Boris Yeltzin in 1994, and so a translation, presumably into Russian, along with records of his interrogation in Pankrác Prison, may still await future scholars.

"And you can forget about the Brits, MI5 or MI6; they've got those files sealed for at least fifty years." So I was told by Charles Fairburn before he died.

I was sad not to have Kosta's story or Vlada's to share with Elliot Goddard, who had died in late August. But at least he'd had most of the story, although the importance of the Linear B tablets perplexed him, and the satisfaction of knowing that the reputation of his friend, which he'd loyally upheld for all those years, had remained sound, even as I redacted mention of how the tablets had been stolen in the first place, not to mention any details about his freelancing with MI5. But, of course, Elliot should have understood about the tablets, a man who, like Max, carried the flag of the seventeenth earl of Oxford, as made clear in his last words to me at our wedding in the Winsted chapel earlier that August: "Ah, you see, you *are* my Edward de Vere, the true author of our play—of that I never had the slightest doubt."

Nor did I share with him the details about my father's final hours . . . not something he needed to unpack for his final journey.

And so we were faced with the rest of our lives: a defunct ballerina and a classicist/archaeologist who had suddenly and, shockingly, to my colleagues, become obsessed with Bronze Age Greece, and more particularly with some obscure text from a series of lost Linear B tablets. We spent a couple of years at Princeton, where Laura taught dance and began to work as a choreographer. But our lives began to go downhill. As a pregnancy failed to materialize, and the fertility treatments failed to take hold, she started to have doubts about herself, and, most of all, about us. She took what she saw as her failure hard. She had nightmares about her abortion in Venice. And soon we were in joint therapy, which I obstinately resisted. Suzanne's miserable death from alcoholism didn't help. At the end, her memory had deteriorated badly and Charles was beside himself at his inability to prevent her from drinking herself to death. It didn't help that we felt compelled, more than ever, to acknowledge Charles as Laura's father—at once a kind of odd comfort and a mind fuck, both disastrous to our equilibrium as a couple.

I had my own preoccupations. I was determined to publish my father's translation of the stolen Linear B tablets from Pylos. But every time I submitted yet another revised version of my paradigm-shaking article to a journal, I was asked to rewrite or provide better documentation to substantiate my claims. The fact is, I didn't want to admit the truth of what my father had done in helping Karel Hollar steal the tablets in the first place. Everything I wrote contained some degree of subterfuge, or carefully crafted obfuscation for how the throne room tablets had disappeared, along with my father's lost notes about the translation. My editors complained about my resort to "fictional methods" to substantiate my claims of authenticity. My colleagues complained about my lack of focus, and my grad students felt that I wasn't really interested in their work anymore. All of which was true.

I gave up my apartment in Athens. I took a leave of absence from Princeton.

And I continued to be haunted by thoughts of my father's final ten or fifteen minutes, and where he had traveled in his mind, imagining for myself the life he yearned for as his heart began to seize up and his breathing became labored. I tried not to think about the pain. I chose not to believe in the pain. I imagined him thinking back to his youth, to Elysium, of course, to Pine Meadow, where he'd made love to Suzanne, but also to Winsted and the Circle and the apple trees, where his thoughts along with my own merged most fully and happily, which finally led me back to a Winsted quite transformed.

Life at Winsted is bittersweet. Here, two or perhaps three invisible authors hold sway over my days.

I am reminded of Pearce Breckenridge when I watch the Frisbees fly past the chapel and the apple trees on the Circle (the Winsted boys and girls lying out in the spring sunshine, listening to their iTunes: the Beatles and Stones and Crosby, Stills & Nash, and other "classics of the sixties"). Because this ex-slave, scholar, teacher, and preacher—his prophetic voice echoing along the banks of the Naushon between the splash of fervid oars, as it does in the hearts and legacies of the men and women who loved him—inhabits our lives in ways that I am still discovering, and not only in *Essays and Prayers*, where his hopes for reconciliation and diversity are expressed most wonderfully. His story not only guided my father on his last mission but his call for justice and love inspired his and my grandmother's—and Winsted's—commitment to civil rights, as well.

And so it is that when I enter the chapel and hear an echo of Charlie Springfield's Carolina drawl booming down the nave as he launched imprecations against our false presumptions to make war in Vietnam, glaring down at the congregation from the pulpit, flipping through *Essays and Prayers* for an appropriate passage, and then placing his hand over his patriotic heart as he sought to catch the eyes of the youngest boys gathered below, encouraging them to listen to the whispers of their soul's desire, I think of Pearce Breckenridge and all the other invisible bearers of his flame.

He is only one of the invisibles that channel the river of Time; the others can be visited on any Memorial Day if you know where to seek them.

Such stories, their stories, our stories, the lost stories, are legion, even as they flutter from our windblown fingertips.

Prompting me to scramble to get them down as I knew them: Paul Oakes behind his desk, blowing smoke rings as he stared out longingly at the playing fields from which he'd been exiled; Virgil Dabney gesturing through the pall of smoke and BO in his study, muttering "Ah-da-dum," as if in immemorial solidarity with the gesticulating figures in his Piranesi prints; and, of course, Max, always Max, a fugitive presence ever in flight around the Circle at all hours of day or night . . . slowly stealing away, as he stealthily steals our stories, and so transforms them into us.

Of course, all the Winsted girls in Laura's dorm have read Max's novels; she is famous in their eyes. They adore her for her ballet celebrity and tales of her coke-crazed nights at Studio 54. They come up to her and hug her and yearn for something of those wild seventies to rub off, while she tries to advise and guide them past all the poor choices they invariably make. She remains forever young, her star power undiminished, while I am left to toil in the shadow of Max's WASP protagonist.

The boys in my Latin and Greek and ancient history sections see me as the stodgy old man of Winsted, son of a man who was a fervid anti-Communist, probably not much better than Joe McCarthy, and a committed Cold Warrior in a war that never need to have happened and so never needed to be fought, a man with extravagant views on American exceptionalism that only led the country to bad times and bad places, where we had no business being and nobody wanted us to be in the first place. Most wonder how I survived the legacy of such a man. We never talk about Vietnam—never.

Nor does it help my cause that the English Department includes both of Max's novels in the syllabus, as if Winsted doesn't have enough trouble explaining away the fictions that have become common wisdom, as Princeton forever festers in the shadow of Fitzgerald's *This Side of Paradise*. It's fiction with a capital *F*; those times are long past and the sixties were tough on everybody. So says the Admissions Office, which, irony of ironies, is inundated with applications from all the kids who want to go the famous prep school featured in *Like a Forgotten Angel*. Max would surely get a chuckle out of that.

As teachers, entrusted with the values of the young, we prefer to think we are all about personal integrity, leadership, and fine scholarship, trying to find the good in people and passing that good on. And the motto still stands: Freedom, Justice, Love, and Honor.

Sometimes I wonder if the word *Loyalty* shouldn't be somewhere in the mix.

And even though Winsted is almost as diverse as the country, it doesn't get our boys and girls into the Ivies the way it once did, but then, we've given them a better education than they'd get at most colleges anyway.

Fortunately, Max's antihero in *Like a Forgotten Angel* was a supremely good football player, which gives my coaching some credibility. And some stories survive against all the odds in the blood and muscle and genes. Even if only Willie Gadsden's boys know that I was in Vietnam with their father. They are not as fast as Jerry, but if anything, they are stronger and less prone to injury and wiser in the ways of the world; Willie saw to that. One of his sons is my senior quarterback and the other is a wide receiver, and that combination has won us two championship seasons. To watch his son Willie throw the ball is to watch time stand still, and to see his son Jerry catch it on the run at full tilt with one outstretched hand, which he's done for winning touchdowns, is to believe Christ walked on water. Laura and our twin adopted daughters, San Mai and Hué Tran, enjoy attending the games and watching the Gadsden boys work their magic—magic that may yet go Princeton's way.

All those who saw my father play are pretty much gone now, or too old to come to games, much less stand around on the chilly sidelines and shoot the breeze. No one remembers my father or invokes his name outside of unthinking references to the Alden gym or the scholarship funds set up by my grandmother. The Alden name is pretty much interchangeable in most minds, a generic marker of some vaguely illustrious, near-mythological past when the school was founded after the Civil War. School tours for prospective students always pause at the Sargent portrait of General Alden in the library, but the fame and skill of the artist overshadows that of his subject. Every now and then, I will see a boy pause at the display case in the gym to gaze at my father's medals and the ancient photograph of a ragged band of Greek Resistance fighters posed on the steps of a temple in the Athenian Agora. How could anyone believe such a story, much less its aftermath, when World War II seems as distant as the Civil War to the kids . . . and Vietnam is mostly good for the stirring protest songs it engendered, along with iconic films like *Apocalypse Now*, which the English Department insists on showing when the third formers read Conrad's *Heart of Darkness*.

Even Max would be aghast.

But we have given the devil his rightful due. Not only did I manage to get our most famous author reinstated on the graduate rolls, along with the others expelled in our class; Laura and I chose the inscription for his memorial in the chapel, the final lines of his novel, which inspired the title:

> She seemed to him to wait there upon the muted shore like a forgotten angel, wings folded pensively across her back, seeking in her stellar soul the lost whispers of heaven, the recollections of ancient memory forever born anew in night's glittering array: those distant cries of playing children echoing down the ages.

When we reach to the lettering, we think of him and, of course, back to our fruitless lovemaking in Pine Meadow: Max who saw to the root of us, lies and all . . . besotted by love.

But for me, Laura and the girls, and my students, the best part of Winsted is our annual summer break in Crete and the archaeological excavations I fund and head. Observing my students, I am returned to my passionate embrace of that Cretan summer before my senior year. It is a place where I feel my father's love of his work like no other. For three all too short months, we spend our days digging, searching, turning up scintillating bits of the past. Under vivid blue skies, with the smells of oleander, lemon, and brine on the breeze, I hold my breath, hoping against hope that more tablets may be found, even a fragment that will substantiate my father's translation. Just one, one voice, one similar story, would do the trick.

I find there is no escaping that final story in his hand, that final author who never leaves my thoughts and dreams, as he must never have my father's as he lay there in Pankrák Prison on the examination table, staring up at the flickering light as the minutes fled his grasp, until his romantic heart gave out.

In October 1953, the Soviets confiscated the remaining tablets from the Museum of Antiquities; they were then deposited for further evaluation in the vast KGB warehouse in Yaroslavi, northeast of Moscow, where they were misplaced, like so many lost souls in the vast constellation of gulags. The twelve tablets my father took with him have never been recovered. He told Dimitri and the KGB that he'd simply tossed them into the river Elbe where it crosses the border of East Germany into Czechoslovakia—a "disappointment," in his words. I suspect he stashed them somewhere with his notebooks and Ventris's charts. He needed to travel light.

We always plan a stopover in Leipzig on our way home from our summers in Crete, where we make our way to the farmhouse in Oderwitz, just to spend a few days poking around. My father had set up his worktable by the window of his rented room, with a view of farm fields beyond. The old lady who owned the house is long dead, but her grandson runs the farm, and when I first visited, he was happy to show me the room that the family rented out in the desperate years after the end of the war. The window frames a handsome five-hundred-year-old oak in a nearby field, gigantic, gnarled, and craggy—a famous personality in the locality, where in the summer the cows will congregate to enjoy its shade. One huge serpentine branch of the oak, low to the ground, actually dips and reaches into the earth and then reemerges as a fully leafed bough, as if scooping up its young; as if mocking me, tempting me, as do the cow bells. Our girls love to climb on that tree, the tree that kept my father company as he translated the twelve tablets from the throne room of Nestor's Palace. It was a partial copy of this tale of travel and marvelous wonders that I placed in the shaking hands of Nigel Bennett on his sickbed, and which he still clutched, so I was told, in his hand as he died in the hospital of pneumonia two days after my visit.

This partially told story I shared, too, with another old man, this one in a dark prison cell, giving him a glimpse, as I think my father would have wanted, in his dying hours of the glory and fame denied him at the last.

I have sat in that room in the farmhouse in Oderwitz and started out at the oak where our girls scrambled and played, wondering at the strangeness of it all: two beautiful Vietnamese faces cavorting on that huge branch in a land freed from the grip of tyranny, two exiles free and lovely and alive, who barely remember the land of the unfree they escaped as infants, when their parents drowned in the crossing to Thailand. What stories will they tell one day? What past will they seek to explore?

The tale—my father's tale—I have tried to share with the world was a missive out of the deepest past; about a voyage and a betrothal, about a groom arriving to find his intended—but with conditions: to tell the beloved stories of his roving days, of battles won and perilous escapes, perhaps a glimpse of a golden age of peace and prosperity before the fall of Knossos, Mycenae, and Pylos, before the chaos of the Dark Ages obscured all from view.

Told on tablets, buried again somewhere along the border of lands now free, this story about the return of a lover to his beloved that must, in some variation, have been going through my father's mind as the seconds ticked down . . . a tale of the vast blue of the sea and sky, and the blessed isles.

They call me Lakedanos, merchant prince of Pylos, a rich man, but richer yet in tales of travel and the wonders I have seen, the currency of love that roving the wide world brings the well-traveled heart. I sailed, goods laden, to windblown Delos, where the fairest palm trees grow, where, at the temple of Apollo, the finest dancers perform to the song of the flute players. Stocked with more goods stowed deep in our fine black ships, we rowed for the peaceful shores of Scheria. Seventeen days we struggled with Notus, god of the south wind, and with heavy seas and crushing waves, until our men were exhausted. We sacrificed to Poseidon and prayed to the deathless gods to speed our journey, until Borealis heeded our pleas with a following wind and sped us on to the rocky shores where the Phaeacians dwell, most peaceful and generous of all peoples, whose graceful ships speed travelers over the white scudding seas. We hailed the high circling walls of their splendid harbor and slipped into a safe anchorage at last. There, at the white altars of Poseidon's sacred temple, we gave sacrifice for our safe arrival, only the best parts of goats and sheep; we spared nothing for the earthquake god, father of the Riverrun Sea. And so the men unpacked our trading goods in the marketplace, the best wooden axels and sturdy spoked wheels, olive oil and spiced wine, perfumed ointments of rose and iris, fleeces and ox hides, and red cloaks spun by the most nimble artisans among the Achaeans.

How the tall and fair Phaeacians in their fine silk robes welcomed us and our trading goods, probing us for news from afar. As I broke away for the palace, I could hear from every oaken doorway the sound of singing and flutes and the laughter of playing children. No war or sorrow had yet sown bitterness and fear among these fine people, a land surely blessed by the deathless gods. All along the way, strangers offered food and wine if only I would stop and tell them of happenings in lands far from their own. But I was in a hurry to reach the golden gates of the palace, where Philowona, Mistress of Wild Beasts, awaited my promised return. The walls of the palace I found sheathed in hangings of bronze and gold, blazing out like the sun itself from a cloudless sky. When the gates opened upon the call of heralds, I was led through the reception rooms, their walls resplendent with paintings of leaping bulls and flying dolphins, fair dancers and acrobats and all the abundant wonders of this prosperous kingdom by the sea. Passing through rooms numberless, I reached the sheltered gardens at the center of the palace, where my beloved awaited me.

Everywhere I found groves of trees sacred to the gods: olive and lemon, apple and fig and oleander. The fragrance was ambrosial, fit for the Olympians. I passed fountains and streams flowing from deep springs, forever cooling and watering my goddess's hidden garden. In a grove of hyacinth and freshly budded crocuses, the dark-eyed princess, Philowona, awaited, gesturing to me from her carved chair of sandalwood inlaid with ivory and silver, with bronze griffins for armrests, laughing as I approached. She stood resplendent in her flounced skirt of Tyrian purple wool, her breasts high and round and inviting to the touch of her many admirers. She then placed her hands on her hips, as if she might begin to dance, head thrown back, lips parted as in a swoon, and her braid of dark hair whipping from side to side, her hoop earrings of gold glittering. Again she laughed and scooped up handfuls of crocus petals, white and yellow and blue, which she sprinkled on my bowed head. Then she gestured to the chair next to hers that I might sit and entertain her desires. I presented her with a box of favorite scents: cumin, coriander, fennel, sesame, and sage. She only smiled and rang a tiny silver bell. Her serving women appeared, lovely every one, and giggled, as did their mistress; they led a troop of blue monkeys, who served us wine in golden goblets with ivory handles, along with delicacies of every kind, fruits from her garden orchards, apples and pears and pomegranates. I laughed along with the women as they watched the blue monkeys attended to our every need until led away again by the serving women. "What do you think now, Lakedanos, of your gifts? I trained them myself, gotten from lands far south of Egypt by our intrepid traders. Can you match such things of wonder?" I took her hand in mine. "I bring you things of far greater worth," I told her, enchanted by her smile and girlish voice, matched only in sweetness by the birds that flitted the day away in her gardens. "I come with stories that will fill your dreams, and love to fill your nights, and children to run free in your garden—or mine." She laughed her girlish laugh, like the song of the lark at rosy-fingered dawn, and turned her glowing almond eyes to me, hers lips parted with panting expectation.

And so I began my tale. . . .

And so I rest my case. A golden age . . . a better place and time.

Unless, of course, sitting at his worktable in Oderwitz, staring out at that gargantuan oak where my girls now play, my father had found, to his dismay, only bureaucratic palace inventories, and so, in desperation, simply made it all up, a fiction out of thin air, and headed for the hills. But I think not; that wasn't like him. He was headed home, at least in his mind, with his last labored breaths, dreaming of those tall pines against the lucent rose of sunset, and of a story out of the deepest past, out of the bluest blue, a message of love and hope for his beloved, and his sons, his glorious sons and daughter . . . and granddaughters.

ACKNOWLEDGMENTS

AS ALWAYS, WITH LOVE TO MY WIFE, PATRICIA, WHO early on placed her hand firmly in mine for this crazy literary journey, and our two sons, Carter and Christopher, who survived that journey to find their own crazy path, and so inspire us onward every day.

For Charles Sheerin, a great teacher, preacher, and humanitarian, who filled our school days with literary lightning, passionate reading, and the love that allowed us to laugh at life's absurdities and, most importantly, our own. Charlie, your life made the world a better place, and your sweet laughter echoes endlessly on the river of Time.

The journey proceeds, and friends, new and old, continue to come and lend a helping hand. My profound thanks to my editor—one of the very greatest editors of our generation—Allen Peacock, who early on blew the breath of life into my sails and kept our frail craft steady and moving forward, when most had long given up on epic length in the modern novel. Allen's uncanny eye for the good, bad, and indifferent made for the necessary pruning, while embracing the good stuff. Allen, you're still the best.

And what can I say about the legendary Carol Edwards, copy editor to so many great writers and publishers. Carol found the flaws and got them corrected and reinforced our confidence in the integrity of the whole. And she caught the one fatal flaw in any novel of length, and so helped to bring our time traveler home, truly home . . . where it needed to be. For that crucial insight alone, you have my profoundest gratitude.

Our proofreader, Patricia Fogarty, diligently captured all our slipups with great skill and patience.

And for Marc Estrin, my editor at Fomite Press, I have only the greatest respect, not just because he believed in *Time's Betrayal* from the get-go, but because he unstintingly put his heart and soul into making it even better, pointing out many things that only another fine writer and editor, polymath and musician, might catch. And thanks, too, to Donna Bister, production manager at Fomite Press, for all her support and help shepherding our project forward.

To my agent, Mitchell Waters, at Curtis Brown, thanks for believing in *Time's Betrayal* . . . from the first few pages, ten minutes after first receiving the manuscript, through all the ups and downs of the submission process. Your confidence in the book got us through—and yes, I think, hope, our novel would make your client, the late, great Louis Auchincloss, proud, if not a little amused.

And the design and production team headed by Drew Stevens—my hats off to you, sir! What a marvelous feel for the elegant font and grace notes to make the book sing in the reader's eye and ear. And what a steady, competent, and always reassuring voice getting us through the production process with style and humor.

Penguin's Jason Booher provided us with a stellar cover, combining design brilliance with a deep sensitivity to the narrative, and so producing cover art that is as close to a mirror of the story within as can be imagined. Jason, we and all your colleagues stand in awe.

The publicity team headed up by David Ratner and Emi Battaglia is simply as good as it gets: a strong right arm getting *Time's Betrayal* launched, and hopefully loved.

And now to a few of the invisibles who inspired some of the players in *Time's Betrayal*. Their names are known to only a few, their lives and legends and foibles to even fewer—lives that hopefully echo down the river of Time in these pages: Charles Sheerin, Paul Abry, Norris Getty, Richard Irons, and others who shall remain nameless. Gentlemen, your lives made all the difference to those many young men who benefited from your pastoral care and inspiration. And to that generation of greats I'd like to add my thanks to "coach" Jake Congleton, and Charlie Alexander and Jonathan Choate, who shepherded my own boys in the classics and math, and their successors: Nishad Das, Hoyt Taylor, and David Prockop in math and science, John Tulp in classics, and, most especially, Ted Goodrich, teacher of English, who has galvanized the younger generation so brilliantly, inspiring so many in the love of great books. And last but not least, a legendary teacher of the classics and famed archaeologist, who, though never quite inhabiting a character herein, inspired so many of the pages of *Time's Betrayal*: the inimitable Hugh Sackett.

DAVID ADAMS CLEVELAND is a novelist and art historian. In August 2014, his second novel, *Love's Attraction*, became the top-selling hardback fiction title for Barnes & Noble in New England. Fictionalcities.co.uk included *Love's Attraction* on its list of the best novels of 2013. His first novel, *With a Gemlike Flame*, drew wide praise for its evocation of Venice and the hunt for a lost masterpiece by Raphael. His most recent art history book, *A History of American Tonalism*, won the Silver Medal in Art History in the Book of the Year Awards, 2010, and Outstanding Academic Title, 2011, from the American Library Association; it was the best-selling American art history book in 2011 and 2012. For years, David was a regular reviewer for *ArtNews*, and he has written articles for *The Magazine Antiques* and *American Art Review*. Early in his career he was a dance writer for *Dance Magazine* and *Ballet News*, and he danced with the Washington Ballet, where he met his wife, Patricia. For close to a decade, he was the Arts Editor for Voice of America. He and his wife live in New York, where he works as an art adviser with his son, Carter Cleveland, founder of Artsy.net, the new website making all the world's art accessible to anyone with an Internet connection.